DEATH'S
MISTRESS

TERRY GOODKIND

DEATH'S MISTRESS

SISTER OF DARKNESS

The Nicci Chronicles, Volume 1

TOR

A TOM DOHERTY ASSOCIATES BOOK
NEW YORK

DEATH'S MISTRESS

Copyright © 2017 by Terry Goodkind

All rights reserved.

A Tor Book
Published by Tom Doherty Associates
175 Fifth Avenue
New York, NY 10010

www.tor-forge.com

Tor® is a registered trademark of Macmillan Publishing Group, LLC.

The Library of Congress Cataloging-in-Publication Data is available upon request.

ISBN 978-0-7653-8821-6 (hardcover)
ISBN 978-0-7653-9578-8 (international, sold outside the U.S., subject to rights availability)
ISBN 978-0-7653-9412-5 (signed edition)
ISBN 978-0-7653-8822-3 (e-book)

Our books may be purchased in bulk for promotional, educational, or business use. Please contact your local bookseller or the Macmillan Corporate and Premium Sales Department at 1-800-221-7945, extension 5442, or by e-mail at MacmillanSpecialMarkets@macmillan.com.

First U.S. Edition: January 2017

First International Edition: January 2017

Printed in the United States of America

0 9 8 7 6 5 4 3 2 1

DEATH'S MISTRESS

CHAPTER 1

Another skull crunched under Nicci's boot, but she kept trudging forward nevertheless. In the thick forest, she could not avoid all the bones underfoot or the clawlike branches that dangled near her head. The way would have been treacherous even in full daylight, but in the deep night of the Dark Lands, the trail was nearly impossible.

Nicci never bothered to acknowledge the impossible, though, when she had a task to complete.

Piles of moss-covered human remains cluttered the shadowy forest. Yellowing bones stood out in the gloom, illuminated by moonlight that seeped through the leafy vine-strangled boughs overhead. When she climbed over a rotted oak trunk that had collapsed across the path, her heel crushed the old shell of another skull, scattering ivory teeth from a gaping jaw—as if these long-dead victims wanted to bite her, like the cannibalistic half people who had recently swarmed out of the Dark Lands.

Nicci had no fear of skulls. They were just empty remnants, and she had created plenty of skeletons herself. She paused to inspect a mound of bones stacked against a lichen-covered oak. A warning? A signpost? Or just a decoration?

The witch woman Red had an odd sense of humor. Nicci couldn't understand why Nathan was so insistent on seeing her, and he refused to reveal his intentions.

Crashing through tangled willows ahead, Nathan Rahl called back to her. "There's a big meadow up here, Sorceress. We'll make better time across the clearing."

Nicci did not hurry to catch up to the wizard. Nathan's impatience often led him to make rash decisions. She pointed out coolly, "We would make better time if we didn't travel through the thickest forest in the dark of night." Her long blond hair fell past her shoulders, and she felt perspiration on her neck, despite the cool night air. She brushed a few stray pine needles and the ragged lace of a torn spiderweb from her black travel dress.

Pausing at the edge of the wide meadow, the wizard raised an eyebrow. His long white hair seemed too bright in the shadows. "Judging by all the skeletons, we must be close to our destination. I am eager to get there. Aren't you?"

"This is your destination, not mine," she said. "I accompany you by choice—for Richard." The two had trudged through the trackless forest for days.

"Indeed? I thought you were supposed to watch over me."

"Yes, I'm sure that's what you thought. Perhaps I just wanted to keep you out of trouble."

He arched his eyebrows. "I suppose you've succeeded so far."

"That remains to be seen. We haven't found the witch woman yet."

Nathan Rahl, wizard and prophet, had a lean and muscular frame, azure eyes, and handsome features. Although the two men were separated by many generations, Nathan's face, strong features, and hawklike glare still reminded Nicci of Richard Rahl—Lord Rahl, leader of the much-expanded D'Haran Empire, and now leader of the known world.

Under an open vest, Nathan's ruffled white shirt was much too frilly to serve as a rugged travel garment, but he didn't seem to mind. He swirled a dark blue cape over his shoulders. The wizard wore tight but supple black pants and stylish leather boots with a flared top flap and dyed red laces for a flash of color.

As Nicci joined him, he put a hand on the pommel of the ornate sword at his hip and gazed across the starlit clearing. "Yes, traveling through the night is tedious, but at least we keep covering distance.

I spent so many centuries in one place, locked in the Palace of the Prophets. Indulge me for being a little restless."

"I will indulge you, Wizard." She had agreed to take him to the witch woman, but after that she had not decided how best she would serve Richard and the D'Haran Empire. "For now." Nicci was also restless, but she was a woman who liked to have a clear, firm goal.

He smiled at her brusque tone. "And they say prophecy is gone from the world! Richard predicted you might find my company frustrating as we traveled together."

"I believe he used the word 'obnoxious.'"

"I'm quite sure he didn't say it aloud." They crossed the dew-scattered meadow, following a faint trail that led to the trees on the other side. "Nevertheless, I am pleased to have such a powerful sorceress protecting me. It befits my position as the roving ambassador for D'Hara. With my skills as a wizard and a prophet, we'll be nearly invincible."

"You are no longer a prophet," Nicci reminded him. "No one is."

"Just because a man loses his fishing pole doesn't mean he ceases to be a fisherman. And if my gift of prophecy is taken away, I will still muddle along. I can draw upon my vast experience."

"Then perhaps I should let you find the witch woman yourself."

"No, for that I need your help. You've met Red before." He gestured ahead. "I think she likes you."

"I've met Red, yes, and I survived." Nicci paused to regard a knee-high pyramid of rounded skulls, a sharp contrast to the peaceful starlit meadow. "But I am the exception, not the rule. The witch woman likes no one."

Nathan was not deterred, nor had she expected him to be. "Then I will work my charms. So long as you help me find her."

Stopping under the open sky, Nicci looked up into the great expanse of night, and what she saw there frightened her more than any moldering skeletons. The panoply of stars, twinkling lights strewn across the void, were all *wrong*. The familiar constellations she had known for nearly two centuries were now rearranged with the star shift Richard had caused.

When Nicci was a little girl, her father had taken her out into the night and used his outstretched finger to draw pictures across the sky, telling stories of the imaginary characters up there. Only two weeks ago, those eternal patterns had changed; the *universe* had changed, in a dramatic reconfiguring of magic. And when Lord Rahl realigned the stars, prophecy itself was ripped from the world of the living and sent back through the veil to the underworld. That cataclysm had changed the universe in unknown ways, with consequences yet to be seen or understood.

Nicci was still a sorceress, and Nathan remained a wizard, but all the intricately bound lines of his gift of prophecy had unraveled within him. An entire part of his being had now been simply stripped away.

Rather than worrying about the loss of his ability, though, Nathan seemed oddly enthusiastic about this unexpected new opportunity. He had always considered prophecy to be bothersome. Imprisoned in the Palace of the Prophets for a thousand years, considered a danger to the world, he had been denied the opportunity to lead his own life. Now with prophecy gone and the undead Emperor Sulachan sent back to the underworld, Nathan felt more free than ever before.

He was delighted when Richard Rahl sent him off as a roving ambassador for the newly expanded D'Haran Empire, to see if he could help the people in the Dark Lands—a thinly disguised pretext for Nathan to go wherever he liked while still ostensibly achieving something useful. The wizard had been eager to see lands unknown. (And the way Nathan said the words made it sound like the name of an actual country, "Lands Unknown.")

Knowing his intent, Nicci couldn't possibly let the wizard go off alone. That would have been dangerous to Nathan and possibly dangerous to the world. While the battered D'Haran army returned from the bloody battles, and the dead were still being tallied and mourned, Nicci had accepted an important mission of her own. A mission for Richard.

Everyone from Westland to the Midlands, from D'Hara to the Dark Lands, and even far south into the Old World, needed to know that Lord Rahl was the new ruler of a free world. Richard had decreed that he would no longer tolerate tyranny, slavery, or injustice. Each land would remain independent, so long as the people followed a set of commonly agreed-upon rules and behaviors.

But much of the world didn't even know they had been liberated, and there would surely be petty warlords or tyrants who refused to accept the new tenets of freedom. Richard needed to know the extent of his empire, so much of which remained unexplored, and that was a service Nicci could provide, gathering information as she traveled with Nathan.

Nicci believed in her mission wholeheartedly. This was the dawn of a golden age. In the Old World, what remained of the Imperial Order in the aftermath of Emperor Jagang and his predecessors was now a mixed bag of local leaders, some of them fair-minded and enlightened, others abusive and selfish. If any local leader caused trouble, Nicci would deal with the problem. Though she knew Richard would back her up with his full military might, she did not intend to bother the whole D'Haran army, unless it became absolutely necessary.

Nicci would make certain that it did not become necessary.

On a more personal level, although she loved Richard with a depth she had never felt for anyone else, Nicci knew that he belonged with Kahlan, and she would always feel out of place close to them. She didn't *belong* there.

By going off with Nathan to Lands Unknown, she could serve Richard, but also have a new freedom. She could have her own life.

I 've heard what the witch woman can do." Nathan strode along with far too much cheer in the brightening morning. He tossed his blue cape over his shoulder with a flourish. "I need to ask something of her, and I have no reason to believe she won't grant it. We're practically colleagues, in a certain sense."

They maneuvered through a dense grove of spindly birch saplings, pushing aside the white-barked trees as they followed the mounds of crumbling bones. Nathan sniffed the air. "Are you certain this is the way?"

"Red will be found if she wants to be found." Nicci glanced down at the staring empty eye sockets filled with moss. "Many people regret finding her."

"Ah, yes—be careful what you wish for." He chuckled. "That should have been another one of the Wizard's Rules."

"Up on her mountain pass, Red left the ground strewn with thousands and thousands of bones and skulls from a great army of the half people she slaughtered single-handedly." Nicci looked from side to side. "But some of these remnants are much older. She has been killing for a long time, and for her own reasons."

Nathan was undeterred. "I shall endeavor not to give her a reason to kill us."

The granite boulders around them grew more prominent, shaded under lush maples and domineering oaks. A tingle crept along the back of her neck, and Nicci looked up to see a muscular catlike thing regarding them from the top of a large, rounded outcropping. The strange creature had green eyes and darkly spotted fur. Seeing them, it let out a sound that was partly purr, partly growl.

Nathan leaned against a birch, unafraid. "Now, what is that animal? I've never seen a species like that before."

"You lived most of your life locked in a tower, Wizard. The world has many species you haven't seen."

"But I had plenty of time to peruse books of natural history."

Nicci had recognized the animal at first glance. "The Mother Confessor named him Hunter. He is Red's companion." The catlike thing's pointed ears pricked up.

Nathan brightened. "That must mean we are close."

Without seeming to hurry, Hunter jumped down from the boulder and trotted off through the birches, guiding Nicci and Nathan along. "He has led me to the witch woman before," Nicci said. "We should follow."

"And of course we shall," Nathan said.

They moved at a fast pace, following the creature through the slatted birch forest and tangled underbrush. Hunter paused every so often to glance over his shoulder, making sure they were still there.

Finally, Nicci and Nathan emerged above a serene, hidden hollow. The outstretched boughs of a gigantic lichen-covered oak spread over the entire glen like an enormous roof. The bitter smell of smoke rose from an ill-tended cook fire that burned in a ring of stones not far from a fieldstone cottage constructed against the side of the opposite slope.

As if waiting for them, a thin woman sat primly on a stone bench in front of the cottage, watching them with piercing sky-blue eyes. She wore a clinging gray dress, and her hair was a mass of tangled red locks.

Black-painted lips made her smile ominous instead of welcoming. The crow perched on her shoulder looked more curious about the visitors than the witch woman did.

Knowing full well how dangerous Red could be, Nicci met the other woman's gaze without speaking. Even though he had seen the countless skulls, Nathan ignored the danger and strode forward with a hand raised in greeting. "You must be the witch woman. I am Nathan Rahl—Nathan the prophet."

"*Wizard*, not prophet," Red corrected. "Everything is changed now." Her black lips smiled again, without warmth. "You are Nathan Rahl, ancestor of Richard Rahl. I have been called a seer and an oracle, but I have had enough visions to last me for quite some time. I foresaw that you would come to me."

The spotted catlike creature sat beside her, blinking his green eyes as he faced the visitors. Still seated on her stone bench, Red fastened her gaze on Nicci. "And Nicci the Sorceress. I'm pleased to see you again."

"You have never been pleased to see me," Nicci said. Part of her wanted to summon her magic, release a flow of destruction, both Additive and Subtractive Magic, anything that might be necessary to blast the witch woman into ashes. "In fact, you commanded the Mother Confessor to kill me."

Red laughed. "Because I foresaw that you would kill Richard." She must have seen the dark edge of Nicci's anger, but she showed no glimmer of fear. "Surely you can understand. I had only the best of intentions. It was nothing personal."

"And I did kill Richard, just as you predicted," Nicci said, recalling how that decision had nearly torn her apart. "Stopped his heart so he could travel to the underworld and save Kahlan."

"See? So it all worked out for the best, then. And I did help you to bring him back." The crow on Red's shoulder bobbed forward, as if nodding. The witch woman hardened her gaze. "Now, why have you come here?"

Nathan stood straight and tall. "We've been searching for days. I have a request to make."

Widening her black smile, Red indicated the countless skulls around her in the glen. "I receive many requests. I look forward to hearing yours."

CHAPTER 2

Without asking permission, Nathan adjusted his cape and took a seat beside the witch woman on the stone bench. He let out an exaggerated sigh. "I am a thousand years old, and sometimes I feel the age in my bones."

Nicci looked at the wizard, not hiding her skepticism. She had traveled with him for many days and many miles, and he had seemed completely healthy and spry. She doubted such an obvious ploy for sympathy would work with Red.

The crow took wing from the witch woman's bony shoulder and flapped up to settle on one of the lower branches of the enormous oak. The bird scolded Nathan from above.

Red shifted her legs and turned toward him. "A thousand years? You must have stories to tell."

"I do indeed, and that is part of the reason I'm here. Since the Palace of the Prophets was destroyed, the antiaging spell has failed, so now I grow old as all mortals do." He looked at Nicci with a twinkle in his eye. "The sorceress is aging too, although she certainly doesn't show it."

"'Aging' is another word for 'living,' old man," Red said with a sharp chuckle. "And I presume you'd like to go on living."

"I've just begun to live." The wizard leaned back on the stone bench as if he were relaxing in a park. "Now . . . for my request. I have heard of a thing that witch women can do, and I'd be curious if you might do me the honor?"

Nicci also listened attentively, just as intrigued, since the wizard had refused to tell her his plans, despite the lengthy and arduous journey here from the People's Palace.

Red tossed her thick braids, making them wriggle like restless snakes on her head. "Witch women have numerous skills, some wonderful, some dangerous. It depends on which ability interests you."

He laced his fingers together over one knee. "The Sisters of the Light possessed journey books, spell-bonded journals in which they could record their travels and also send messages over great distances. But a *life book* . . . ah, now that is something different. Have you heard of it?"

Red's intense pale eyes showed her interest. "I've heard of many things." She paused for just a moment. "And, yes, that is one of the things I know."

Nathan continued, as if he still needed to explain to the witch woman, or maybe it was for Nicci's benefit. "A life book chronicles the journey of a person's life, all the accomplishments and experiences." He leaned closer to her, adjusting his vest with a tug. Overhead in the tree, the crow cawed.

"I would like to have a life book for myself, since I am starting a new phase of my existence, a new set of adventures." He rubbed an imaginary stain from the sleeve of his ruffled shirt, and he looked back at her. "Can you work your storyteller magic?"

Nicci stood apart from them, watching. Once the wizard got an idea in his head, he was very insistent. She had led Nathan through the untracked wilds to find the skull-cluttered lair of the witch woman—all because he wanted to ask Red for a *book*? Nicci said with dry humor, "You lived in a tower for most of your life, Wizard. You think the sum of your experiences would fill an entire book?"

Hunter squatted in the dry oak leaves strewn all around. The feline creature snuffled the ground, nudging fallen acorns, equally unimpressed with Nathan's request.

The wizard sniffed. "Given enough time, the interesting events of even a tedious life can fill a book." Nathan turned back to Red. "I've always been a storyteller myself, and I wrote many popular tales. You may have heard of *The Adventures of Bonnie Day*? Or *The Ballad of General Utros*? Grand epics, and relevant to the human condition."

Nicci made an acerbic observation. "You were born a prophet, Nathan Rahl. Some would say that your very profession was to make up stories."

Nathan gave a dismissive gesture. "Yes, some would say that—and these days, with the great changes in the universe, I'm afraid telling stories is all a prophet can do."

Red pursed her black lips as she considered. "The stories of your life might make a book, Nathan Rahl—and, yes, I do have the magic to extract it. I know a spell that can preserve everything you've already done in a single volume, and that will be the end of its own story."

"Volume one," Nathan said with delight. "And I am ready to start a new journey with my sidekick Nicci."

Nicci bristled. "I am no one's sidekick, Wizard. I am your companion, perhaps, but more accurately, your guardian and protector."

Red said, "Each person is the main character of his own story. That may be how Nathan views you, Nicci—as part of *his* tale."

"Then he would be wrong." She refused to soften the edge of her tension. "Is this life book meant to be a biography? Or a work of fiction?"

Even Nathan chuckled at that.

The crow left its branch, swooped around the clearing, and settled on another bough, as if to get a better view.

The witch woman rose from the bench. "Your proposal interests me, Nathan Rahl. There is much you need to do—whether or not you know it yet." When she cast a glance at Nicci, her ropy red locks swung like braided pendulums. "And I know much of your life as well, Nicci. Your past would constitute an epic. Since I am working the storyteller magic, would you like a life book of your own? It would be my pleasure." Red had an unsettling hunger behind her sky-blue eyes. "And I also know there is an importance to you as well."

Nicci thought of the catastrophes she had survived, the dark deeds she had done, the changes she had undergone, the damage and the triumphs she had left in her wake. She was important? Other than a handful of witnesses and victims along the way, the only one who knew that story was Nicci herself. She gave the witch woman a cold, hard look. "No, thank you."

After a brief hesitation, the witch woman brushed her hands together dismissively and turned with a smile to the wizard. "So, a single life book for Nathan Rahl, then." She left the bench and headed toward her cottage. "First, I will need supplies. There are preparations to make." Red pushed aside the discolored leather hide that hung across the doorway and ducked inside.

Lowering her voice, Nicci turned toward Nathan. "What are you about, Wizard?"

He just gave her a smile and a shrug.

Red emerged with a small ivory bowl: the rounded top of a human cranium. She set it on the stone bench next to Nathan and reached out to him. "Give me your hand."

Happy that she had agreed to his request, he extended his hand, palm up. Red took hold of his fingers, stroking one after another in a strangely erotic gesture. She traced the lines on his palm. "These are your life lines, your spirit lines, and your story lines. They mark the primary events in your life, like the rings of a tree." She turned his hand over, studying the veins on the back. "These blood vessels trace the map of your life throughout your body."

When she stroked his veins, Nathan smiled, as if she were flirting with him.

"Yes, this is exactly what I need." Red snatched a knife from a cleverly hidden pocket in her gray dress and drew the razor-sharp blade across the back of his hand.

Nathan yelped, more in disbelief than in pain, as blood gushed out. "What are you doing, woman?"

"You asked for a life book." She clutched his hand, turning it over so that the red blood could run into the skull bowl. "What did you think we would use for ink?"

As she squeezed his fingers, trying to milk the flow, Nathan was flustered. "I don't believe I thought that far ahead."

"A person's life book must be written in ink made from the ashes of his blood."

"Of course it does," Nathan said, as if he had known all along.

Nicci rolled her eyes.

The blood flowed steadily from the deep gash. Hunter sniffed the air, as if drawn by the scent of it.

When the skull bowl was a third full of dark red liquid, Nathan said, "Surely that's enough by now?"

"We'd better make certain," Red answered. "As you said, you've had a very long life."

Finally satisfied, the witch woman released Nathan's hand and took the bowl over to her smoky cook fire. With a blackened femur, she prodded the coals, nudging them aside to create a sheltered hollow in the ashes. She settled the bone bowl into them, so the blood could cook.

Nathan poked at his cut hand, then released enough magic to heal the wound, careful not to let the blood stain his fine travel clothes.

Before long, the blood in the skull bowl began to bubble and smoke. It darkened, then turned black, boiling down to a tarry residue.

The light slipping through the crowded branches overhead grew more slanted in the late afternoon. High above, birds settled among the branches of the expansive oak for the night. The crow scolded them for their trespass, but the birds remained.

Red ducked back into her cottage, where she rummaged around before returning with a leather-bound tome that bore no title on the cover or spine. "I happen to have an empty life book among my possessions. You are fortunate, Nathan Rahl."

"Indeed, I am."

Red squatted next to the cook fire and used two long bones to gingerly remove the skull bowl. The blood ink inside the inverted cranium was even darker than the soot charred on the outer surface.

Nathan watched with great interest as she set the smoking bowl on the stone bench. She opened the life book to the first page, which was blank, the ivory color of freshly boiled bone. "And now to write your story, Nathan Rahl."

She called the crow down from the tree, and the big black bird landed on her shoulder again. It used its sharp black beak to stroke her red braids in a sign of affection. The witch woman absently caressed the bird, then seized its neck. Before the bird could squawk or flail, she snapped its neck and caught its body as it fell. The dying crow's wings extended, as if to take flight one last time. Its head lolled to one side.

Red rested the dead bird on the bench next to the skull bowl. With nimble fingers, she combed through its tail and wing feathers, finally selecting a long one, which she plucked loose. She held it up for inspection. "Yes, a fine quill. Shall we begin?"

After Nathan nodded, the witch woman trimmed the end with her dagger, dipped the pointed shaft into the black ink, and touched it to the blank paper of the waiting first page.

CHAPTER 3

The life book wrote itself.

Red sat on the stone bench, hands on her knees, not noticing that she left a smear of dark soot on her gray dress. As she worked her spell, a guiding magic suspended the crow-feather quill upright, and then it moved of its own accord, inscribing the story of Nathan Rahl.

Bending closer, the wizard looked on with boyish delight, resting an elbow on his knee. Nicci stepped up to watch the words spill out across the first page, line after line, and then move on to the next page. Each time the ink ran dry, the feather paused above the book, and Red plucked it out of the air, dipped it into the bowl of burned blood, and placed it back on the page. The flow of words resumed.

"I recall how many times I wrote and rewrote *The Adventures of Bonnie Day* until I was satisfied with the prose," Nathan said, shaking his head as he marveled. "This is far easier."

The story flowed, page after page, chronicling Nathan's long life as a dangerous prophet, how he'd been imprisoned by the Sisters of the Light, first to train, then to control him . . . how for years they monitored his every utterance of prophecy, terrified of the turmoil that could arise from false interpretations. And prophecies were nearly always misinterpreted, warnings often misconstrued. Merely trying to avoid a dire fate usually precipitated that exact fate.

"People never seem to learn the lesson," Nathan muttered as he read. "Richard was right to disregard prophecy for so long."

Nicci agreed. "I am not sorry that prophecy is gone from the world."

The words flew past faster than anyone could read them, and the life book's pages turned of their own accord. Nicci scanned back and forth, catching some snippets of Nathan's life, stories she already knew. On the road, he had spent much time telling her about himself, whether or not she asked.

He leaned closer as a new section began. "Oh, this is a good part."

In his loneliness in the palace, the Sisters had occasionally taken pity on Nathan, hiring women from the finer brothels in Tanimura to comfort him. According to the tale as written in the life book, Nathan enjoyed the conversation of an ordinary woman with ordinary dreams and desires. Nathan had once whispered a terrible prophecy in the ear of a gullible whore—and the horrified young woman had run screaming from the Palace of the Prophets. Once out in the city, she repeated the prophecy to others, and the repercussions spread and spread, eventually triggering a bloody civil war . . . all due to Nathan's reckless pillow talk to a woman he would never see again.

The Sisters had punished Nathan for that, curtailing his limited freedoms, even after he revealed that the supposed "mistake" had accomplished his intent of killing a young boy child destined to become a ruthless tyrant, a tyrant who would have slaughtered countless innocents.

"A relatively minor civil war was a small enough price to prevent that outcome," Nathan remarked as he skimmed the black-blood words scrolling out.

When the quill ran dry again, Red dipped it into the skull bowl, stirred the burned blood, and set the feather tip on the page, where it continued to scratch and scrawl.

Nathan's story went on and on—rambling, in Nicci's opinion—and the feather pen wrote word after word. Of course, most of his adventures had occurred only after he managed to escape from the palace: his brief romance with Clarissa and its tragic end, his work with Richard Rahl to overthrow the Imperial Order and Emperor Jagang, his battles to stop the evil Hannis Arc and the undead Emperor Sulachan.

Faster than Nicci expected, the entire volume filled up. When the

black blood finally reached the last page in the book, the tale ended
with the all-too-recent account of Nicci and Nathan trudging through
moss-covered skulls to find the witch woman in the Dark Lands. All
of the charred-blood ink in the skull bowl was used up, and the lifeless
feather dropped and drifted to the ground.

Nathan was obviously impressed with his own story. "Thank you,
Red." When he closed the cover, he was delighted to see that his name
had appeared on the leather front and on the spine. "I shall carry the
life book with me and read it off and on. I'm certain others would
like to read it as well. Scholarly libraries will want copies."

The witch woman shook her head. "That will not be possible, Nathan
Rahl." She took the tome from him. "I agreed to create a life book for
you, but I never said you could keep it. The volume stays with me. That
is my price."

Nathan sputtered. "But that wasn't what I thought . . . that isn't the
purpose—"

"You did not ask the price beforehand, Wizard," Nicci said. "After
living a thousand years, you should be wiser than that."

Red ducked back into her cottage, leaving the volume on the bench,
as if daring Nathan to take it and escape. He did not. She emerged
with a smaller, thinner leather-bound book, which was also blank.
"I will take your life story, but I give you something that's worth far
more. A new life book filled with potential, rather than stale old words."
She offered it to Nathan. "I have your past, your old story, but with this
book, I give you the rest of your life. Live it the way you would want it
to be written."

Nathan ran a fingertip over the smooth leather cover, disappointed.
"Thank you, I suppose." He held the book in his hands.

"I happen to know that you, and the sorceress, are both vital to the
future." The witch woman stepped uncomfortably close to Nicci and
dropped her voice. "Are you certain you don't want a life book of your
own? There may be things you need to learn."

"I am certain, witch woman. My past is my story to keep, and my
future will be written by me, in my own way, not through the control
or influence of you or anyone else."

"I just wanted to make the offer." She turned away with a hint of secret amusement in her eyes, followed by a shadow of unexpected concern. "You may still be required to do things, Sorceress, whether or not you want to hear about them."

Nathan opened his new life book and was surprised to find it wasn't entirely blank. "There are words written on the first page. 'Kol Adair.'" Perplexed, he looked up at Red. "I don't recognize the term. Is it a name? A place?"

"It's what you will need." Red bent over her cooking fire and used the blackened femur to stir the coals and reawaken the flames. "You must find Kol Adair in the Old World, Nathan Rahl." She flashed a glance at Nicci. "Both of you."

"We have our own mission," Nicci said. "Here in the Dark Lands."

"Oh? And what mission is that? To wander aimlessly because you are too much in love with Richard Rahl to stay at his side? That is a pointless quest. A coward's quest."

Nicci felt the heat in her cheeks. "That's not it at all."

Nathan came to her defense. "After our last great battles, I wanted to come back here, to see if I could help the people."

Red sniffed. "Another pointless quest. There are always people who need help, no matter where you go. In the Dark Lands? In the Old World? What is the purpose? Would you rather not save the world and save yourselves?"

Nicci turned her anger into annoyance. "You babble nonsense, witch woman."

"Nonsense, is it? Turn the page, Nathan Rahl. Read your new life book."

Curious, the wizard did as she suggested. Nicci leaned close, seeing other words written there on the second page.

Future and Fate depend on both the journey and the destination.

Kol Adair lies far to the south in the Old World. From there, the Wizard will behold what he needs to make himself whole again. And the Sorceress must save the world.

Nicci said, "I have helped save the world enough times already."

But Nathan was more perplexed. "This is a game for you, witch woman. You planted this joke for us. Why would I need to be made whole again? Am I missing something?" He touched his arm, which seemed remarkably intact.

"That is not for me to say," Red said. "You see what's written, a path established long ago."

"And prophecy is gone," Nicci said. "Ancient predictions mean nothing."

"Truly?" asked the witch woman. "Even pronouncements made when prophecy was as strong as the wind and the sun?" While Nathan flexed his fingers, as if searching for missing digits, Red brushed back her tangled locks of hair. "You of all people should know that it is unwise for others to interpret a prophecy."

Nicci tightened the laces on her traveling boots and adjusted her black dress. She could not keep the skepticism out of her voice. "As I said, there is no more prophecy, witch woman. How can you know where we need to go?"

Red's black lips formed a mysterious smile. "Sometimes I still know things. Or maybe it is a revelation I foresaw long before the stars changed overhead. But I do know that if you care about Lord Rahl and his D'Haran Empire, you will heed this warning and this summons. *Kol Adair.* You both need to make your way there, whether for the journey or the destination. If you don't, then all that Richard Rahl has worked for may well be forfeit." She shrugged, suddenly seeming aloof. "Do as you wish."

Nathan slipped the new life book into a leather pouch at his side and closed the flap. "As Lord Rahl's roving ambassador, my assignment is to travel to places that might not know about the changes in the world." He looked up at the darkening sky through the canopy of the ancient oak. "But the exact route is at our discretion. We could go to the Old World just as well as to the Dark Lands."

Nicci was not so convinced. "And you are going to take her babblings seriously, Wizard?"

Nathan stroked back his long white hair. "Frankly, I've had enough of the Dark Lands and all this gloom. The Old World has more sunshine."

Nicci considered, realizing she had followed him, but with no real goal otherwise. She just wanted to serve Richard and strengthen his new, solid empire, to help bring about his longed-for golden age. "I have my own orders from Lord Rahl to explore his new empire and send reports back of the things we find. At Kol Adair, or elsewhere."

"And save the world," Red added.

She did not believe Red's prediction—how was she supposed to save the world by traveling to, or seeing, a place she'd never heard of?—but the wizard had a valid point.

The Old World, once part of the Imperial Order, was now under the rule of D'Hara. Even those distant people would want to hear of their freedom, to know that Lord Rahl would insist on self-determination and standards of respect. She had to see what was out there, and take care of problems she saw, so that Richard need not be bothered. "Yes, I will go with you."

Nathan adjusted his cape and shouldered his pack, just as eager to depart as he had been to find the witch woman in the first place, but Nicci hesitated. "Before we go south to the Old World, we need to tell Lord Rahl where we're going. We have no way to communicate with him." She didn't want Richard or Kahlan to worry about the two of them if they disappeared for a time.

"We could find a way to send a message when we reach Tanimura," Nathan said. "Or some other town along the way."

Red surprised them. "I will take care of it."

She picked up the crow's limp carcass and cradled the bird in her hands, extending its flopping wings. She adjusted its lolling head, straightened its broken neck, then closed her eyes in concentration.

After a moment, the crow squirmed and fluffed its feathers. Red set the reanimated bird back on the stone bench, where it tottered drunkenly. The neck remained angled in the wrong direction, and its eyes held no glint of life at all, but it moved, like a marionette. The crow stretched its wings, as if fighting the remnants of death, then folded them back against its sides.

"Tear a strip of paper from a page of your life book, Nathan Rahl," she said, handing him the black quill. "There should be enough ink left for you to write a note for Lord Rahl."

Nathan did so, scratching out a quick summary on a thin curl of paper. When he was finished, Red rolled it tightly and bound the strip to the crow's stiff leg. "My bird has sufficient animation to reach the People's Palace. Lord Rahl will know where you are going."

She tossed the awkward crow up into the air. Nicci watched the dead bird plummet back to the ground, but at the last moment it extended its wings, stiffly flapped them, rose up beyond the enormous oak, and flew into the dusk.

Hunter's ears perked up, and the catlike creature sniffed the air before bounding off into the forest to dart among the shadows of the tall trees. Out beyond Red's sheltered hollow, Nicci saw a flash of fur, something as large as a horse prowling through the thickets. Hunter happily bounded after it, frolicking through the underbrush, and disappeared along with the large predatory shape in the deeper gloom.

Red looked up. "Hunter's mother often joins us for dinner." Her mouth formed an odd smile. "Would you like to stay?"

Nicci took note of the strewn bones and skulls and decided not to take further risks. "We should go."

"Thank you, witch woman," Nathan said as they headed into the thickening night. Even alone in the wild, dark forest, Nicci guessed they would be safer than if they chose to stay at Red's cottage.

Nathan strode along, paying no attention to the skulls. "It will be a grand adventure. Once we leave the Dark Lands, we can head south to Tanimura. At Grafan Harbor, we're sure to find a ship sailing south. We will find Kol Adair, and that's just a start."

Richard had told her to go to the boundaries of the D'Haran Empire, and she decided that the far south was a perfectly viable option. "I suppose the rest of the world will be sufficient for our purposes."

After Red watched the two disappear into the forest, Hunter trotted in and squatted by the cook fire. Moments later, his shaggy mother padded in, as big as a bear and bristling with cinnamon fur.

The much smaller son nuzzled her, wanting to play, but Hunter's mother thrust a huge head forward to Red, who dutifully scratched the silky fur behind the creature's ears, scrubbing with the nails on both of her hands. Hunter's mother made a sound that was somewhere between a growl and a purr; then she slumped heavily among the fallen leaves in the clearing.

Red picked up Nathan's hefty life book. Yes, even a quiet and tedious life could add up to significant events in a thousand years. She knew the real chronicle was just beginning for Nathan, and the real mission in store for both of them. Even though Nicci refused to let Red create such a book for her, the witch woman had been an oracle. She knew that the life of the sorceress, both past and future, would fill many volumes as well.

And the Sorceress must save the world.

Carrying Nathan's tome, Red pushed aside the hanging leather flap over the opening and ducked inside her cottage. The low dwelling was lit with the orange glow of guttering candles settled in skull pots. The front room was small and cramped, but at the back wall against the hillside, she pushed aside another door hanging.

She entered the main part of her dwelling, a large complex of wide passageways and grottoes burrowed into the hillside itself. Red stood before shelves and shelves that were filled with numerous volumes similar to the one she held now. She had collected so many life books over the years, over the centuries, that she had lost track.

But oddly, and chillingly, every single one of the books had ended with the strange and previously incomprehensible words:

Future and Fate depend on both the journey and the destination.

Kol Adair lies far to the south in the Old World. From there, the Wizard will behold what he needs to make himself whole again. And the Sorceress must save the world.

The same words in every book. Hundreds of them. Thousands of them. Each one with the same warning.

Red slid the story of Nathan Rahl into an empty slot on the shelf next to another volume. Countless life books, nearly one for each of those skulls buried under the moss. . . .

CHAPTER 4

With their new destination in mind, though somewhat skeptical of the importance Red had assigned to it, the two traveled for weeks through the Dark Lands before reaching the more populated areas of D'Hara. Heading south, they found well-traveled roads and villages, including inns where they could eat home-cooked meals instead of foraging for game or wild fruit, and they could sleep in actual beds instead of bedding down on the forest floor. As a woods guide, Richard Rahl had reveled in finding his own trails in the forest, but Nicci much preferred civilization, and Nathan certainly did not object to comforts.

Along the way, the two gathered news and disseminated their own tales about Lord Rahl's victory over Emperor Sulachan. Most people in the south of D'Hara knew little about the political changes that had occurred, but everyone had seen the stars convulse and shift in the sky, and they listened to the travelers with both wonder and dismay.

In the warm, crowded common rooms of inn after inn, Nathan spread his hands and explained in a deep, confident voice, "Truth be told, the end of prophecy means that you can live your own lives and make your own decisions. I was once a prophet myself, and I speak from experience—such powers were far more trouble than they were worth. Good riddance!"

Many local oracles and self-proclaimed seers, however, were less enthusiastic about the changes. Those with a genuine gift had already noticed the sudden lack of ability, and those who continued to sell their predictions were surely cheating gullible customers. Such "prophets" were incensed to hear themselves denounced as frauds and charlatans.

But chastising frauds was not the mission Nicci had adopted, nor did she consider it "saving the world." She moved ahead with her next goal in sight. She would go to the Old World, scout the new lands Lord Rahl now ruled, and help Nathan find the mysterious Kol Adair, whatever it was. Tanimura would be their starting point. The great port city was one of the northernmost bastions of the Old World, a place where the main overland trade routes converged.

As the two neared the coast, the air took on a fresh, salty bite. Traffic increased on the wide road through the coastal hills. Creaking mule-drawn carts passed them, as well as wealthy noblemen or merchants riding well-groomed horses with expensive tack. Farmers guided wagons laden with vegetables or sacks of grain, heading to the markets in the port city.

While walking along in the warm sun, the wizard held up his end of the conversation—more than his end, in fact, but Nicci saved her energy for the hike. When they reached the top of a hill, the view unfolded before them.

The old, sprawling city of Tanimura had been built on a long peninsula that extended into the sparkling blue expanse of the ocean. To the west, before spilling into the sea, the Kern River had excavated a broad valley. Croplands and villages dotted the countryside, interspersed with patches of dark forest. Nicci's focus, though, was on the whitewashed buildings of the extensive city.

The wizard stopped to rest, shading his eyes. "A splendid view. Think of all the possibilities Tanimura offers." He plucked at his threadbare sleeves, his frayed cuffs, his open vest. "Including fresh clothes."

Nicci said in a quiet voice, "It's been years since I was here." She narrowed her blue eyes, scanning the city, noting what she remembered and what had changed.

The wizard gave a noncommittal grunt. "Once I escaped the palace, I thought I would never come back . . . yet here we are."

Down the sweep of shore, Grafan Harbor was bustling with large cargo or military ships that sported creamy white sails, as well as fishing dhows with triangular sails. Nicci's lips quirked in a small, hard smile. "I see they've managed to rebuild the docks."

In the harbor here, she and her fellow Sisters of the Dark had destroyed the *Lady Sefa,* the ship that had held them hostage. Emperor Jagang had granted the women their revenge on Captain Blake and his vile crew, even encouraged it, and Nicci and her companions were not kind to the sailors who had raped and abused them. The Sisters had found a turnabout pleasure, peeling off the soft flesh of the men, strip by strip. Then, unleashing the full force of Subtractive Magic, they had destroyed the *Lady Sefa,* lifting the entire vessel out of the water, snapping the masts like twigs, crashing the huge ship down onto the Grafan docks, and then wreaking havoc upon the whole harbor, as if the other ships were no more than the toys of a malicious child.

Although that had been one of her darkest times, Nicci still smiled at the memory.

Nathan also stared down toward the crowded city, lost in his own memories. He lowered his voice to a conspiratorial whisper. "We both left such a mark on Tanimura, dear Sorceress, they might not welcome us back."

His gaze was drawn toward the southern end of the peninsula and a large island just off the coast. Halsband Island had once been connected to the mainland by a prominent stone bridge that allowed visitors, merchants, scholars, and Sisters of the Light to pass directly to the Palace of the Prophets. The mammoth edifice had stood for millennia, a place where gifted males were imprisoned and taught. The palace had been shielded in numerous ways, woven with a spell that prevented its inhabitants from aging . . . but Nathan had triggered a light web, bringing down the entire imposing palace so that its magical archives could not fall into Jagang's hands.

Halsband Island looked like a wasteland now, the palace vaporized. From what Nicci could tell, even after six years no hardy souls had returned to claim the devastated land for their own.

The wizard wore a bittersweet expression, but forced a smile. "I spent a thousand years there. What could be a better start to a new life than to erase all signs of the past?" He pushed aside his dark blue cape and patted the leather pouch at his side that held the new life book and its ominous pronouncement. "It's time for a new adventure, before we get too old. You and I are not used to aging at the same rate as everyone else. Tanimura awaits."

Nicci set off down the road to the city. As they walked down the hill, an oxcart rolled past, driven by an old farmer wearing a straw hat. The man stared at the road ahead as if it were the most interesting thing in the world. His cart was loaded with round green melons.

When Nathan asked for a ride, the old farmer gave them a casual gesture. The two sat in the back of the wagon among the piled round melons. Nicci picked up one. "It looks like a severed head." The ox plodded along, not caring whether the road went uphill or downhill.

Jostled by the slow, uneven cart, Nicci watched the approaching city. She remembered the tree-lined boulevards, the tall whitewashed buildings, the tile roofs. Banners flew from high poles, scarlet pennants of the city of Tanimura and larger flags of the D'Haran Empire.

She and Richard had stopped here for a time on their way to Altur'Rang, when she had forced him to play the role of her husband, hoping to convince him to believe in the Order. She had been so passionate, determined, ruthless, and so naive. He had learned how to cut stone here in Tanimura. . . .

Nicci's brow furrowed at the troubling memory. "We will not stay long, Wizard. We'll get supplies for a long journey and find a ship sailing south to the Old World. I'm sure you're anxious to find your Kol Adair."

"And you must save the world, of course." Nathan winced as the oxcart rolled over a large rock in the road, and one large melon rolled over the edge, but he deftly caught it and set it back on the precarious pile. "But why in such a hurry? Dear spirits, we traveled weeks to get to Tanimura. If that prophecy was written down a hundred years ago, there can't possibly be any rush."

"Whether or not the witch woman is correct, Lord Rahl asked us to explore the fringes of his empire and to spread the terms of his rule. Everyone here already knows who he is. Our real work lies elsewhere."

"Indeed it does," Nathan admitted with a sigh. "And I'm curious to find this place called Kol Adair that Red thinks I need to see."

He looked at his shirt, then tried to brush away a grease stain from a rabbit they'd eaten in camp, and a spot of gravy that signified the much better food that an innkeeper had prepared for them the following night. "Before we can go on, though, my first order of business will be to acquire a new traveling wardrobe. Without a doubt, Tanimura has many tailors and garment shops to choose from. I believe I can find what I need."

Nicci's black traveling dress was still in good shape, and she had a spare in her pack. "You worry about clothes altogether too much."

He looked down his nose at her. "I spent a thousand years wearing frumpy robes in the Palace of the Prophets. Now that I am out in the world at last, I am entitled to indulge myself."

Nicci knew she wouldn't change his mind. "I'll make my way down to the harbor and make inquiries with the dockmaster. I can learn which ships are ready to depart and where they are bound."

More carts joined them on the road, and they passed stables on the outskirts of the city, livestock yards where pigs and cattle wandered about, unconcerned with their fates. Charcoal kilns stood like tall beehives, letting a whisper of sweet smoke into the air. Across a meeting square, shirtless carpenters were building a tall tower that so far consisted only of support beams.

The listless cart driver did not speak a word to them, merely drove his ox along. As the city buildings clustered together, the crowds increased, as did the noise. People shouted to one another, merchants hawked their wares, washerwomen hung dripping clothes from lines strung between buildings.

Not far away they saw a large market crowded with rickety wooden stalls featuring good-luck trinkets, bolts of patterned fabric, wooden carvings, fire-glazed clay pots, and bunches of red and orange flowers. The old farmer flicked the ox with a switch to turn the animal toward the market, and Nicci and Nathan slid off the cart, ready to venture into the heart of the city. The wizard called out his thanks, but the old farmer didn't respond.

As he stood to get his bearings, Nathan adjusted the ornate sword in its scabbard, checked the life book, straightened his pack, and self-consciously brushed down the front of his shirt. "I may be a while. Once I secure the services of an adequate tailor, I'll have him make more appropriate attire for me. Capes, shirts, vests, new boots. Yes, yes, if I am to be Lord Rahl's ambassador, I must look the part."

CHAPTER 5

The ancient city of Tanimura was full of wonders, distractions, and dangers for the unwary. Nicci felt right at home.

She was all business as she made her way into the thick of the city, her mind set on finding a southbound ship and a captain familiar with the port cities in the Old World. From what the witch woman had described, Kol Adair might be far out in the sparsely populated fringe lands, not marked on common maps. But they would find it.

During her years serving Emperor Jagang, when she had been called Death's Mistress, Nicci had brought many outlying towns under the rule of the Imperial Order. Although Jagang had been intent on conquering the New World, he had little interest in the less populated areas far to the south of his own empire. He had once told her the land did not hold enough subjects or enough wealth to be worth his time.

Despite the distance, Nicci was convinced that those far-flung people also needed to know about Lord Rahl. She would be proud to tell them of their new life without tyrants and oppression, and she relished the challenge. She would do it for Richard.

Future and Fate depend on both the journey and the destination.

As she headed down toward the harbor, the streets were steep and winding. The crowded buildings were stacked haphazardly, two- and three-story structures that filled any spare patch of ground, buildings erected on top of buildings. Some homes and shops were tilted as if trying to keep their balance on the hillsides. Gutters lined the streets, filled with a brownish slurry of rainwater mixed with emptied chamber pots.

Broad-hipped women gathered and gossiped around a well, pulling up buckets of fresh water, which they handed to glum-looking teenagers to carry away. Scruffy barking dogs ran down the streets in pursuit of loose chickens.

Nicci passed through a fabric dyers' district, where the air was filled with a rich and complicated tapestry of sharp, sour odors. Cloth merchants hung bolts of dripping fabric—indigo, saffron yellow, or stark black—which flapped in the sea breezes as they dried. In the thread makers' district, boys ran down the street pulling long colorful strands, twisting bobbins to tighten the threads.

The tanning district reeked as leather workers cured and processed hides. Taking advantage of the foul smells, enterprising children ran about offering to sell passersby fistfuls of mint leaves as nosegays. A little girl with black hair in pigtails ran up to Nicci, waving the mint leaves. "Only a copper. It'll make every breath smell fresh."

Nicci shook her head. "The smell of death doesn't bother me."

The skinny girl could not hide her disappointment. She was dressed in rags, and her face was covered with dust and grime. She looked as if she hadn't had a good bath, or a good meal, in some time. Noting her industriousness, Nicci gave her the copper anyway, and the girl ran off laughing.

The markets were loud, colorful storms of people, vendors hawking shellfish or live octopus from buckets of murky salt water. Butchers sold slabs of exotic imported meats—ostrich, musk ox, zebra, even a greasy gray steak supposedly from a long-tailed gar—spread out on planks for display, although many of the meats drew more flies than customers. Smoked fish dangled by their tails across wooden racks like succulent battle trophies.

Food vendors sold skewers of spiced meat sizzling over charcoal fires. Bakers offered loaves of knotted brown bread. Two women stirred a steaming cauldron and ladled out bowls of what they called "kraken chowder," a milky stew with thready seaweed, bobbing onions, and rings of tender suckers that had been sliced from some large tentacle.

Nicci walked at a brisk pace, uninterested in the distractions. Jugglers performed in the streets, gamblers placed bets on a game of shells and cups. A musician sat on an overturned pot eliciting caterwauling sounds from a flexible stringed instrument.

In the spice merchants' district, men in long green robes haggled over the price of cumin, turmeric, cardamom. A toothless old woman squatted on a curb as she sorted lumpy roots of mandrake and ginger. When an errant breeze whispered along the street, the spice merchants rushed to cover their powder-filled baskets. One man bent over a clay bowl of red pepper, and the breeze feathered some of it into his face, making him cough and retreat, flailing his hands.

Tanimura was a crowded, vibrant city. Every person here was concerned with everyday living, but few of them considered the larger work of building and maintaining the D'Haran Empire. These people weren't soldiers. They had lived for years under the Imperial Order. They had survived the turmoil of the long, bloody war, and now they might not even realize how fundamentally their existence had changed. If Lord Rahl's rule endured, these people might never need to concern themselves much about it.

As she worked her way into the older, more crowded district just above the harbor, the streets grew tighter and more tangled. The buildings were tall and dingy, and every street degenerated into an alley. More than once, she found herself at a dead end of brick walls and garbage, forcing her to retrace her steps.

Nicci turned down a wider alley between leaning three-story buildings with cracked and stained walls. The buildings closed into shadows redolent of stagnant water, rats, and refuse. She pressed forward, supposing the passageway would open into a broader thoroughfare, but instead it turned along oddly skewed corners, and the passage narrowed.

Ahead, she heard a frightened shout and the sounds of a scuffle—curses, gruff laughter, the smack of a fist striking flesh, then the more muffled sound of boots kicking. She was already running toward the sounds when an outcry of pain joined what sounded like a little boy's mocking laughter.

"That's all the money I have!" It was a young man's voice.

Nicci rounded the corner to come upon three muscular men and a wiry boy, all bunched around a young man of perhaps twenty years. It took her only an instant to gauge the tableau, identify the predators, the victim. The young man cornered by these thugs didn't look like a Tanimuran. He had long ginger hair and pale skin covered with freckles; his hazel eyes were wide with fear.

He swung at his attackers, but the three larger men pummeled him with their fists. It was like a game to them, and they seemed in no hurry. The boy, no more than ten years old, pranced from one foot to the other, clutching a small sack of coins in his hand, obviously stolen from the victim.

One of the thugs, a heavyset man with short but extraordinarily muscular arms, planted a solid kick on the meat of the victim's thigh. The red-haired young man went down, sliding against the slimy, stained wall. Even as he fell, he kept his arms up in an attempt to fend them off.

Nicci said, "Stop what you're doing." It wasn't a shout, but hard enough to draw their attention like an unexpected slap.

The three men spun to look at her in surprise. The curly-haired boy's eyes went as wide and bright as coins, and he bolted down the winding alley, disappearing as quickly as a cockroach revealed by the light. Nicci ignored the child and faced the three men, the real threat.

The thugs turned toward her, ready for a fight, but when they saw only an attractive blonde in a black dress, their expressions changed. One let out a guffaw. They spread out so they could come at her from different directions.

The squat heavyset man called after the boy, who had disappeared down the alleys. "There's no need to run, you little bastard. It's just a woman."

"Let him run, Jerr—we'll find him later," said a second man. He was swarthy with a round face and bloodshot eyes that probably resulted from long familiarity with alcohol, rather than lack of sleep.

"We don't want the little brat to see what we're going to do with her anyway," said the third man, with greasy brown hair tied back in a ponytail. "He's too young for that kind of education."

The ginger-haired victim tried to get up. He was bleeding from his nose, and his shirt was torn. "They stole my money!"

The man with bloodshot eyes smacked him hard across the face. The young man's head hit the alley wall hard.

Although she felt coldness rise within her, Nicci didn't move toward them. "Perhaps you didn't hear me. I told you to stop."

"We're just getting started," said Jerr, the leader. In unison, the three men drew their knives. Apparently, beating the young man wasn't enough entertainment, and they had something else in mind for Nicci. Such men usually did.

Leering, they came toward her. The man with the ponytail slid around to cut off her retreat—but she had no intention of retreating. They obviously expected her to run in fear, but that was not something Nicci did.

"Nice black dress," said Jerr, holding up his knife. "But we'd rather see you without it. Makes things easier."

The young redhead tried to scramble to his feet, pressing a hand to his bruised thigh. "You leave her alone!"

The man with bloodshot eyes snarled at him. "How many teeth do you want to lose before this day is out?"

Nicci regarded the three of them with an icy gaze. "It has been several weeks since I had occasion to kill a man." She looked from one to the next. "Now I have three in one day."

The thugs were startled by her boldness, and the heavyset Jerr laughed. "How do you expect to do that? You don't even have a weapon."

Nicci stood with her hands loose at her sides, her fingers curled. "I am the weapon." From within, she summoned her magic. She had countless ways to kill these men.

The redhead finally managed to stand, and he foolishly lurched toward them, calling out to Nicci. "I won't let them hurt you!" He dove at the legs of the man with the ponytail, knocking him to the ground.

Bloodshot Eyes raised his knife and advanced toward Nicci, waving the point back and forth in the air in front of her, as if she was supposed to be intimidated. Jerr called out, "Cut her, Henty, but don't hurt her too bad—not yet. I don't want her blood all over me when I get between her legs."

Nicci could have unleashed wizard's fire and incinerated the three of them in an instant, but she might also kill the young man, as well as start a fire that could rage through the old town. That was unnecessary. She had other means.

Nicci created a wall of air that slammed into Henty, and he looked as if he had blindly smashed into an invisible tree. As he stood momentarily stunned, Nicci used the magic to fling him up and back fifteen feet above the ground. She was not gentle—she had no reason to be.

Bloodshot Eyes slammed into the high wall, and the impact crushed his head like one of the dark melons in the farmer's oxcart. A splash of red painted a broad round splatter on the already stained wall; then the body traced a long uneven smear as it slid two stories down to the ground.

Unable to believe what he had just seen, Jerr also came at Nicci with a knife. She used her powers to crush his larynx so he couldn't scream; then she pulped the bones in his neck for good measure. The leader's eyes bulged, bursting with a sudden web of red hemorrhages, and his head flopped to one side. When his knees gave out, he sprawled forward.

Ponytail kicked his way free of the scrappy redhead, who had tackled him, and slashed his knife across the empty air, trying to cut the young man, who ducked out of the way. Then, the last thug turned to snarl at Nicci.

She stopped his heart, and he dropped to the ground like a felled bull.

The young redhead looked around the carnage. "We're saved!" His face had gone pale, which made his freckles even more prominent. He gaped at the three dead men lying in the garbage in the alley. "You killed them! Sweet Sea Mother, you—you *killed* them. You didn't have to do that."

"Maybe not," Nicci said, "but that was the most convenient solution. They made the decision for me. Those men would have preyed on others, robbed others—and eventually they would have been caught. I was saving time and effort for the magistrate and the hangman."

The distraught redhead couldn't decide what to do. His lip was bloody, his face puffy and bruised. "It's just—they took my money, but I doubt they were going to kill me."

Nicci ran her gaze up and down his lanky form. The young man wore a loose homespun shirt dyed brown and sturdy canvas pants of the kind worn by sailors. He didn't have any weapons she could see, not even a knife at his side. "You don't *think* they were going to kill you? That is not a gamble I'd choose to make."

He swallowed hard, and she was struck by how innocent and foolish he seemed. If even the bruises and the loss of his money purse had not taught him the necessary lesson, then Nicci would not waste further time on him. "If you keep walking these alleys, unarmed and unaware, you will soon have another opportunity to learn whether or not the thieves around here intend to kill you." She turned to walk away. "Don't count on me being here to help next time."

The young man hurried after her. "Thank you! Sorry I didn't say that soon enough—*thank you*. I was raised to show gratitude to those who do good things for me. I appreciate it. My name is Bannon . . . Bannon—" He paused as if embarrassed. "Bannon Farmer. I'm from Chiriya Island. This is my first time in Tanimura."

Nicci kept walking. "I guessed that much, and it may be your last time in Tanimura if you don't stop being such a fool."

Bannon followed, still talking. "I used to be a cabbage farmer, but I wanted to see the world, so I signed aboard a sailing ship. This is my first time in port—and I came to buy a sword of my own." He frowned, and patted his hips again, as if he somehow thought he had only imagined the robbery. "They took my money. That boy—"

Nicci showed neither surprise nor sympathy. "He bolted off. You'll never find him. That child is lucky he ran, though—I would have disliked killing a little boy, even if he was a thief."

Bannon's shoulders slumped. "I was looking for a swordsmith. Those men seemed nice, and they told me to follow them, led me down here." He shook his head. "I guess I should have been more suspicious." He brightened. "But you were there. You saved me. Are you a sorceress? I've never seen anything like that. Thank you for rescuing me."

She turned to face him. "And shame on you for *needing* to be rescued. You should possess more common sense than to let yourself become a victim. I have no mercy for thugs and thieves, but there would be no thieves if there weren't fools like you to prey upon."

Bannon's face turned a bright red. "I'm sorry. I'll know better next time." He wiped at the blood coming from his lip and nose, then smeared it on his pants. "But if I had my own sword I could've defended myself."

He leaned against the alley wall and struggled to pull off his left boot. "Maybe I have enough coins left, though." When he upended the boot, several coins rained out, two silvers and five coppers. He held them in his palm. "I learned this trick from my father. He taught me never to keep all your money in one place, in case you get robbed." He looked forlornly down at the coins in his hand. "It isn't enough to buy much of a sword. I had hoped for a fine blade with a golden hilt and pommel, intricate workings. The coins might be enough, though. Just enough . . ."

"A sword doesn't have to be pretty to be effective at killing," Nicci said.

"I suppose it doesn't," Bannon replied as he replaced the coins in his boot, and stomped his foot back into place. He looked back down the alley at the bodies of the three thugs. "You didn't need a sword at all."

"No, I don't," Nicci said. "But what I do need is a ship sailing south." She began to walk back out of the alley. "I was on my way to the harbor."

"A ship?" Bannon hurried after her, still trying to adjust his boot. "I'm from a ship—the *Wavewalker*, a three-masted carrack out of Serrimundi. Captain Eli is due to set sail again as soon as his cargo is loaded. Probably with the outgoing tide tonight. He'd take passengers. I could put in a good word for you."

"I can find him myself," Nicci said, then softened her voice, realizing that the young man was just trying to help. "Thank you for the recommendation."

Bannon beamed. "It's the least I could do. You saved me. The *Wavewalker* is a good ship. It'll serve your needs."

"I will ask," Nicci said.

The young man brushed himself off. "And I'm going to buy my own sword so I won't be helpless next time I get in trouble." With an inappropriate display of conscience, he stared at the dead thugs in the alley shadows. "But what shall we do about them?"

Nicci didn't bother to look back over her shoulder. "The rats will find them soon enough."

CHAPTER 6

After the sorceress went on her way, Bannon wiped blood from his lip and felt the bruise. He tried to fashion a smile, which only made the pain worse, but he smiled anyway. He had to smile, or his fragile world would fall apart.

His canvas trousers were scuffed and stained, but they were durable work pants, a farmer's garment made to last, and they had served him well aboard the ship. His homespun shirt was now torn in two places, but he would have time to mend it once the *Wavewalker* set sail. There would be quiet listless days adrift on the water as they voyaged south, and Bannon was handy enough with a needle and thread. He could make it right again.

Someday, he would have a pretty wife to make new clothes and do the mending, as his mother had done on Chiriya Island. They would have spunky, bright-eyed children—five of them, he decided. He and his wife would laugh together . . . unlike his mother, who had not laughed often. It would be different with him, because *he* would be different from his father, so very different.

The young man shuddered, took a breath, and forced his mind back to the bright and colorful picture he liked to hold in his mind. Yes. A warm cottage, a loving family, a life well lived . . .

He habitually brushed himself off again, and the smile felt real this time. He pretended he didn't even notice the bruises on his face and leg. It would be all right. It had to be.

He walked out into the bright and open city streets. The sky was clear and blue, and the salt air smelled fresh, blowing in from the harbor. Tanimura was a city of marvels, just as he had dreamed it would be.

During his voyage from Chiriya Island, he had asked the other sailors to tell him stories about Tanimura. The things they had described seemed impossible, but Bannon's dreams were not impossible, and so he believed them—or at least gave them the benefit of the doubt.

As soon as the *Wavewalker* had come into port and tied up to the pier, Bannon had bounded down the gangplank, enthusiastic to find the city—at least *something* in his life—to be the way he wanted it to be. The rest of the crew took their pay and headed for the dockside taverns, where they would eat food that wasn't fish, pickled cabbage, or salt-preserved meat, and they would drink themselves into a stupor. Or they would pay the price asked by the . . . special ladies who were willing to spread their legs for any man. Such women did not exist in the bucolic villages on Chiriya—or if they did, Bannon had never seen them (not that he had ever looked).

When he was deep in drink, Bannon's father had often called his mother a whore, usually before he beat her, but the *Wavewalker* sailors seemed delighted by the prospect of whores, and they didn't seem interested at all in beating such women, so Bannon didn't understand the comparison.

He gritted his teeth and concentrated on the sunshine and the fresh air.

Absently, he pulled back his long ginger hair to keep it out of his way. The other sailors could have their alehouses and their lusty women. Since this was his first time here, Bannon wanted to get drunk on the sights of Tanimura, on the wonder of it all. He had always imagined that the world would be like this.

This was the way the world was *supposed to be.*

The white tile-roofed buildings were tall, with flower boxes under the open windows. Colorful laundry hung on ropes strung from window to window. Laughing children ran through the streets chasing a ball that they kicked and threw while running, a game that seemed to have no set rules. A mop-headed boy bumped into him, then rebounded and ran off. Bannon felt his trousers, his pocket—the boy had brushed against him there, possibly in an attempt to pick his pocket, but Bannon had no more coins for the would-be thief, since he'd already been robbed. The last of his money was safely tucked in the bottom of his boot, and he hoped it would be enough to buy a reasonable sword.

He took two breaths, closed his eyes, opened them again. He made the smile come back and deliberately chose to believe that the street urchin had just bumped into him, that he wasn't a feral pickpocket trying to take advantage of a distracted stranger.

Searching for a swordsmith, Bannon emerged into a main square that overlooked the sparkling blue water and crowded sailing ships. A heavy woman pushed a cart filled with clams, cockles, and gutted fish. She seemed unenthusiastic about her wares. Older fishermen with swollen, arthritic knuckles worked at knotting and reknotting torn fishing nets; their hands somehow remained nimble through the pain. Gulls flew overhead, wheeling in aimless circles, or shrieked and fought over whatever scraps they had found to eat.

Bannon came upon a tanner's shop where a round-faced man with a fringe of dark hair wore a leather apron. The tanner scraped and trimmed cured skins while his matronly wife knelt at a wide washtub, shoving her hands into bright green dye, immersing leather pieces.

"Excuse me," Bannon said, "could you recommend a good sword maker? One with fair prices?"

The woman looked up at him. "Wanting to join Lord Rahl's army, are you? The wars are over. It's a new time of peace." She ran her eyes up and down his lanky form. "I don't know how desperate they are for fighters anymore."

"No, I don't want to join the army," Bannon said. "I'm a sailor aboard the *Wavewalker*, but I'm told that every good man should have a good blade—and I'm a good man."

"Are you now?" said the leatherworker with a good-natured snort. "Then maybe you should try Mandon Smith. He has blades of all types, and I've never heard a complaint."

"Where would I find him? I'm new to the city."

The leatherworker raised his eyebrows in amusement. "Are you now? I wouldn't have guessed."

The tanner's wife lifted her hands out of the dye basin. They were bright green up near the elbows, but her hands and wrists were a darker color, permanently stained from her daily work. "Down two streets, after you smell a pickler's shop, you'll find a candle maker."

The leatherworker interrupted, "Don't buy candles there. He's a cheat—uses mostly lard instead of beeswax, so the candles melt in no time."

"I'll remember that," Bannon said. "But I'm not looking to buy candles."

The woman continued, "Pass the dry fountain, and you'll find the sword maker's shop. Mandon Smith. Fine blades. He works hard, gives a fair price, but don't insult him by asking for a discount."

"I—I won't." Bannon lifted his chin. "I'll be fair, if he is."

He left the tanners and went off. He found the pickler's shop with no difficulty. The tang of vinegar stung his eyes and nose, but when he saw large clay jars with salted fermenting cabbage, his stomach felt suddenly queasy, and unbidden bile came up in his throat. It reminded him too much of the stink of his old home, of the cabbage fields on Chiriya, of the bottomless prison pit that would have been his life back there. Cabbages, and cabbages, and cabbages . . .

The young man walked on, shaking his head to clear away the smell. He passed the disreputable candle maker without a second glance, then marveled at an elaborate fresco painted on the long wall of a public building. It depicted some dramatic historical event, but Bannon did not know his history.

He found the dry fountain, which was adorned with the statue of some beautiful sea nymph. Tanimura was so full of marvels, he almost didn't want to leave here, even after being robbed and nearly murdered. Was that any worse than what he had left behind?

He had fled his home in desperation, but he also wanted to see the world, sail the oceans, go from one port city to another. It wouldn't be right to remain in the first place he saw. But he was certainly impressed with that beautiful and frighteningly powerful sorceress, who was unlike anyone he had ever met on Chiriya. . . .

After spotting the sword maker's shop at the end of the street, he sat on the edge of the dry fountain, pulled off his left boot, and up-ended it so that the coins fell into his palm; two silvers and five coppers. That was all. He had a blister from the coins in his shoe, but he was glad he had taken the precaution. He'd learned that lesson from his father.

Never put all your money in one place.

Bannon swallowed hard and walked up to the sword maker. *Fine blades.* Self-consciously, he touched his empty pockets again. "I need to buy a sword, sir."

Mandon Smith was a dark-skinned man with a polished bald head and a bushy black beard. "I would imagine that to be the case, young man, since you've come to a sword maker's shop. I have blades of all kinds. Long swords, short swords, curved blades, straight blades, full guards, open hilts—all the finest steel. I don't sell poor quality." He gestured to show an array of swords, so many types on display that Bannon didn't know how to assess them. "What type of sword were you looking for?"

Bannon looked away, wiped at the bruise on his face. "I'm afraid you might not be able to provide the type of sword I need."

Mandon palmed his bushy beard, but the hairs promptly sprang back out into its full brush. "I can make any kind of sword, young man."

Bannon brightened. "Then, the sword I require is . . . an *affordable* one."

The swordsmith was startled by the answer. His face darkened in a frown before he burst out laughing. "A difficult request indeed! Precisely how affordable did you mean?"

Bannon held out all of his remaining coins. Mandon let out a long, discouraged sigh. "Quite a challenge." His lips quirked in a smile. "It wouldn't be right to let a man go without a blade, however. Tanimura has some dangerous streets."

Bannon swallowed. "I discovered that already."

Mandon led him inside the shop. "Let's see what we can find." The smith began sorting flat blank strips of metal that had not yet been fashioned and forged. He rummaged through half-finished long swords, broken blades, ornate daggers, serrated hunting knives, even a short flat knife that looked incapable of anything more dangerous than cutting cheese or spreading butter.

The smith stopped to ponder one clunky-looking blade as long as Bannon's arm. It had a straight, unornamented cross guard, a small round pommel. The grip was wrapped in leather strips, with no fancy carving, wire workings, or inlaid jewels. The blade looked discolored, as if it hadn't been forged as perfectly as the other blades. It had no fuller groove, no engraving. It was just a simple, sturdy sword.

Mandon hefted it, held the grip in his right hand, tossed it to the left. He moved his wrist, felt the weight of it, watched it flow through the air. "Try this one."

Bannon caught the sword, fearing he would drop it with an embarrassing clatter to the floor of the shop, but his hand seemed to go right to the hilt. His fingers wrapped around the grip, and the leather helped him hold on. "It feels solid at least. Sturdy."

"Aye, that it is. And the blade is sharp. It'll hold an edge."

"I had imagined something a little more—" Bannon frowned, searching for words that would not insult the swordsmith. "A little more elegant."

"Have you counted the number of coins you've got to spend?"

"I have," Bannon said, letting his shoulders fall. "And I understand."

Mandon clapped him on the back, a blow that was much harder than he expected. "Get your priorities straight, young man. When a victim is staring at a blade that has just plunged through his chest, the last thing on his mind is criticism about the lack of ornamentation on your hilt."

"I suppose not."

Mandon looked down at the plain blade and mused, "This sword was made by one of my most talented apprentices, a young man named

Harold. I tasked him with making a good and serviceable sword. It took him four tries, but I knew his potential, and I was willing to invest four sword blanks on him."

The smith tapped his fingernail on the solid blade, eliciting a clear metallic clink. "Harold made this sword to prove to me it was time he became a journeyman." He smiled wistfully, brushing his spiky black beard with one hand. "And he did. Three years after that, Harold was such a good craftsman that he created a fantastically elaborate, perfect sword—his masterpiece. So I named him a master." He squared his shoulders and leaned back with a wry sigh. "Now, he's one of my biggest competitors in Tanimura."

Bannon looked at the sword with greater appreciation now.

Mandon continued, "That just makes my point—it may not look like much, but this is a very well crafted sword, and it will serve the needs of the right person—unless your needs are to impress some pretty girl?"

Bannon felt a flush come to his cheeks. "I'll have to do that some other way, sir. This sword will be for my own protection." He lifted the blade, tried it in both hands, swung it in a slow, graceful arc. Oddly, it felt good—perhaps because otherwise he had had no sword at all.

"It'll do that," said the swordsmith.

Bannon squared his shoulders, nodding absently. "A man never knows when he might need to protect himself or his companions."

The dark edges of the world infringed upon his vision. Marvelous Tanimura seemed to have more shadows than before, more slinking, dark things in corners, rather than bright sunlit colors. Hesitating, he held out the coins, everything that the thieves hadn't taken from him. "You're sure this is enough money?"

The swordsmith removed the coins, one at a time, the two silvers then four of the coppers, closing Bannon's fingers on the last one. "I would never take a man's last coin." He gestured with his bald head. "Let's go outside. I have a practice block in back."

Mandon took him behind the smithy to a small yard with barrels of scum-covered water for cooling his blades, a grinding wheel and whetstones for sharpening the edges. An upright, battered pine log as tall as a man had been mounted and braced in the center of a dirt clearing strewn with straw. Fragrant piles of fresh pale wood chips lay around it on the ground.

Mandon pointed to the scarred upright log. "That is your opponent—defend yourself. Imagine it is one of the soldiers of the Imperial Order. Hah, why not imagine it's Emperor Jagang himself?"

"I already have enough enemies in my imagination," Bannon muttered. "We don't need to add to them."

He stepped up to the practice block and swung the sword, bracing for the smack of impact when the blade hit the pine wood. The vibrations reverberated up to his elbow.

The swordsmith was not impressed. "Are you trying to cut down a sunflower, my boy? *Swing!*"

Bannon swung again, harder this time, resulting in a louder thunk. A dry chunk of bark fell off the practice block.

"Defend yourself!" yelled Mandon.

He swung harder with a grunt from the effort, and this time the impact thrummed through his wrist, jarred his forearm, his elbow, all the way to his shoulder. "I'll defend myself," he whispered. "*I won't be helpless.*"

But he hadn't always been able to defend himself, or his mother.

Bannon struck again, imagining that the blade was cutting not into wood, but through flesh and hard bone. He hacked again.

He remembered coming home barely an hour after sunset one night on the island. He had been working as a hand in the Chiriya cabbage fields, like all the other young men his age. He had to work for wages rather than working his family's own land, because his father had lost their holdings long before. It wasn't even dinnertime yet, but his father was already out of the house, surely halfway drunk by now in the tavern. Getting drunk was about the only thing at which his father showed any efficiency.

At least that meant their cottage would be quiet, granting Bannon and his mother an uneasy peace. From his fieldwork in the past week, Bannon had earned a few more coins, paid that day—it was the height of the cabbage harvest, and the wages were better than usual.

He had already saved enough money to buy his own passage off of

Chiriya Island. He could have left a month ago, and he remembered how he had longed to be gone from this place, staring at the infrequent trading ships as they sailed away from port. Such vessels stopped in the islands only once every month or two, since the islanders had little to trade and not much money to buy imported goods. Even though it would be some time before he had another chance, Bannon had made up his mind that he wouldn't go—*couldn't* go—until he could take his mother with him. They would both sail away and find a perfect world, a peaceful new home like all those lands he had heard of—Tanimura, the People's Palace, the Midlands. Even the wild uncivilized places of the New World had to be better than his misery on Chiriya.

Bannon had walked into the house clenching the silver coin he had earned that day, sure that it would finally be enough to buy passage for himself and his mother. They could run away together the next time a ship docked in port. In order to be sure, he intended to count the carefully saved coins he had hidden in the bottom of the dirt-filled flowerpot on his windowsill. The pot held only the shriveled remnants of a cliff anemone that he had planted and nurtured, and then watched die.

Upon stepping into his cottage, though, Bannon had immediately smelled burned food, along with the coppery tang of blood. He stopped, on guard. Standing at the hearth, his mother turned from the pot she was stirring, trying to force a smile, but her lips and the side of her face looked like a slab of raw liver. Her pretense that everything was fine failed miserably.

He stared at her, feeling sick. "I should have been here to stop him."

"You could not have done anything." His mother's voice sounded hoarse and ragged, no doubt from screaming and then sobbing. "I didn't tell him where you hid it—I wouldn't tell him." She began to weep again, shaking her head. She slumped to the inlaid fieldstones on the hearth. "I wouldn't tell him . . . but he knew anyway. He ransacked your room until he found the coins."

Feeling an acid sickness in his stomach, Bannon ran to his room and saw his meager keepsakes scattered on the floor, the straw stuffing of his pallet torn out, the quilt his mother had sewn wadded against the wall—and the flowerpot with the cliff anemone upended, the dirt poured all over his bedding.

The coins were gone.

"No!" he cried. That money should have been a new hope, a fresh life for them both. Bannon had worked hard in the fields and saved a year to get enough for them to leave Chiriya and get far away from that man.

His father had not just stolen the coins, he had robbed Bannon and his mother of their future. "No!" he shouted again into the silent cottage as his mother wept on the hearth.

And *that* was how his father had taught Bannon never to keep all of his coins in one place, because then someone could take everything. It didn't matter how good the hiding place was, thieves like his father could be smart, thieves could be brutal—or both. But when thieves found at least *some* money, then Bannon could make a convincing plea that it was all he had, and they might not think to look elsewhere. . . .

"By the good spirits, my boy!" The swordsmith's voice cut through his dark haze of memories. "You're going to break my testing block, break that sword—and break your arm while you're at it."

Bannon blinked and saw what he had done. In an unconscious frenzy, he had chopped great gouges into the pine log, spraying splinters in all directions. His hands were sweaty, but they squeezed the leather-wrapped grip in a stranglehold. The discolored blade thrummed in the air, but the sword was undamaged, the edge not notched.

His shoulders ached, his hands were sore, his wrists throbbed. "I think . . ." he said, then swallowed hard. "I think I've tested it enough. You're right, sir. It seems to be a good blade."

He reached into his pocket and pulled out the last copper coin. "One more thing from you, sir. Would a copper be enough for you to sharpen the sword again?" He looked at the mangled practice block and suppressed a shiver. "I think it might have lost some of its edge."

Mandon looked long and hard at him, then accepted the copper coin. "I'll put an edge on it that should last a long time, provided you take care of the blade."

"I will," Bannon promised.

The swordsmith used the grinding stone to resharpen the sword, throwing off a flurry of sparks. Bannon watched but didn't see, as his thoughts wandered through a quagmire of memories. Before long, he would have to get back to the *Wavewalker* so he could be there when they sailed out on the evening tide. The rest of the crew would be hungover and miserable, and just as penniless as he was. Bannon would fit right in.

He fashioned a smile again and touched his bruised lip, then ignored the soreness as he imagined everything he could do to the thugs if they ever bothered him again. Now he was prepared. He dipped briefly into his fantasy—no, his *belief*—in a satisfying life, a happy family, kind friends. That world had to exist somewhere. Throughout his childhood on Chiriya, during all the times his father had shouted and struck, Bannon Farmer had built up that picture in his mind, and he desperately clung to it.

By the time he had reconstructed the rosy image of how things should be, Mandon had finished sharpening his blade and handed the weapon back to him. "I give you this sword with my fervent wish that you never need to use it."

When Bannon smiled, this time he did feel the sting in his lip. "That is my hope, too. Always my hope." But he doubted that would happen.

Bidding Mandon farewell, he left the shop and made his way down to the docks and the waiting *Wavewalker*.

CHAPTER 7

Nicci reached the docks in Grafan Harbor after making her way from the darkly cluttered buildings to a more spacious district of merchants' warehouses and administrative offices. The harbormaster's hall was a busy place, with the windows and doors thrown wide open to let in the breezes. Clerks in high-collared jackets bustled along the docks with their papers and quills, interviewing ships' quartermasters to inventory and tax the exotic and ordinary cargo.

Dockside inns and taverns were adorned with garish signs and unappealing names. The Snout and Maggot was unusually busy, filled with people who conversed in shouts instead of normal voices. In front of the tavern, a pudgy boy offered burned meat pies to sailors who lounged on the steps or leaned against the outside wall.

Servicing the steady flow of lonely men in port, rickety-looking brothels were crowded so closely against one another that the patrons of one establishment could hear the lusty activities in the adjoining brothel. Wildly imaginative murals painted on their exterior walls advertised improbable images of the services their women or boys performed. As Nicci considered the murals, she doubted many sailors could manage the intricate, overly flexible positions. She bit her lower lip, where once a golden ring had marked her as Jagang's property. From her unwelcome experience in the soldiers' tents, she knew that while most men believed they had great prowess as lovers, they were usually just brutes who finished quickly and without finesse.

She walked past moneylender stalls, extravagant ones that financed whole sailing expeditions, or smaller and more usurious moneylenders who preyed upon desperate sailors. A forlorn-looking man was locked in a pillory in front of one moneylender's shack. Slumped and scowling in the restraints, he had been pelted with rotted fruit, and he sneered back as passersby jeered at him.

Nicci knew how Tanimura worked. Some supposedly compassionate captain would pay the man's obligation and take him aboard a ship as part of the indentured crew, but such "rescued" men were bound to such impossibly high interest rates that they were practically slaves. Although Nicci despised slavery, she also had little sympathy for any fool who would create such a situation for himself.

Walking along the waterfront, she assessed the ships tied up at the docks, keeping her eyes open for one named *Wavewalker*, which Bannon Farmer had suggested. Those vessels with large cargo holds were clearly trading ships, while narrower-beamed hulls and streamlined construction signified fast patrol ships or warships.

Groups of hairy, muscular men offered their services as porters like human oxen hauling cargo to where shouting merchants held auctions. Laborers pulled thick hemp ropes through squeaking pulleys to raise crates and pallets off the decks.

At one smoke- and grease-stained cargo vessel, the sailors struggled with a block and tackle to lift the severed tentacle of a huge sea creature. The leathery gray skin was covered with slime and adorned with suckers. The heaving workers swung the flopping appendage over the side, and it landed with a thud and a splat onto the dock. Butchers swept in, using saws and cleavers to chop the tentacle meat into smaller steaks, while young apprentices ran up and down the docks calling out, "Fresh kraken meat! Fresh kraken meat for sale!" The smell was so foul and fishy, Nicci couldn't imagine anyone willingly eating the stuff.

She was startled to hear Nathan's voice call to her. "There you are, Sorceress. I am ready to help you find us a ship to carry us on our grand expedition to the Old World."

When Nicci turned to look at the wizard, she nearly laughed at his appearance. Upon leaving the People's Palace, Nathan had worn fine traveling clothes, but during their journey through the Dark Lands and then down to Tanimura, his garments had grown bedraggled, the fabric faded, the cloth frayed around the cuffs, the hem of his cape tattered. Now he sported new brown leather trousers and a white linen shirt with fresh starched ruffles down the front, voluminous sleeves, and wide folded cuffs, each fastened with a golden link. He wore an open embroidered vest, a fine forest-green cape. He also carried a bound satchel, which no doubt held other shirts—probably another few impractical white ones that would become stained and dingy in no time at all—as well as vests, trousers, maybe even a second cape, as if he needed one.

Nathan seemed to interpret her expression as admiration. "Hmm, I may have to reassess my opinion of Tanimura. It is a marvelous city after all, despite my past unpleasantness here. An entire district devoted to nothing but tailors! Shirt makers, jacket makers, trouser makers, cloak makers. The selection is extraordinary!" He lowered his voice to a husky whisper. "Would you believe I found two alleys devoted to highly creative smallclothes for women?" He cocked an eyebrow, and Nicci knew he did it just to annoy her. "I could take you there, Sorceress."

"I think not," she said. "My black dress and my other travel garments are quite adequate, and I am traveling in service of Richard." She had no interest in obtaining lacy smallclothes to entice some unknown man. Nicci had never needed lace, if that was what she'd been after.

Nathan continued with his unflappable exuberance. "And cobblers specializing in all types of boots." He tapped the toe of his new black boot on the dock boards, adjusting the fit. "Belt makers, button carvers, bucklesmiths—did you know that was a profession? Bucklesmiths!"

Nicci could imagine him walking among the shops, fascinated by so many choices, like a child overwhelmed by a sweet shop. "I am surprised you made up your mind so quickly."

"Indeed! After I first escaped from the Palace of the Prophets, Clarissa and I went to a tailor outside of Tanimura, and he took some time to complete the job to my satisfaction. Very meticulous." A wistful flicker of memory crossed his face. "But here in the city, with such extraordinary selection, I merely needed to name the clothes I wanted, and some tailor would find the items, exactly in my size." He made a quick, satisfied sound in his throat, hefting his packs. "I bought several outfits."

He looked along the docks, scanned the numerous ships tied up in the harbor. "So, I am ready to depart. Have you found us passage?"

Nicci thought of the young man in the alley. "I'm looking for a ship called the *Wavewalker*, a three-masted carrack due to depart tonight, sailing south. It may be what we need."

"Follow me," Nathan said. "The *Wavewalker* is this way."

She didn't ask how the wizard could know such a thing or how long he had been exploring the harbor without her. Together, they walked along the pier and found the *Wavewalker* tied up to the third dock from the end. The ship's figurehead showed the face of a beautiful woman with curly tresses that flowed back, transforming into ocean waves— the Sea Mother, a superstition from the southern coastal towns of the Old World.

The last carts and barrels of supplies were being loaded on board the *Wavewalker* for departure with the outgoing tide that night. Sailors carried cages of chickens onto the deck, and the potbellied ship's cook led a forlorn-looking milk cow by a rope up the boarding ramp.

Sailors gathered at the rails, watching the activity on the docks, many of them looking miserable from hangovers or bruised from brawls. No doubt they had spent or lost all their money and had returned early to the ship, having no place else to go.

Nicci and Nathan walked up the ramp, carrying their packs. The wizard waved at an older man in a gray captain's jacket, who rose from a wooden stool on the deck. The captain looked perfectly comfortable on board, liking his own ship better than the amenities in Tanimura. From the corner of his mouth, he removed a long-stemmed pipe from which wafted a curl of greenish-blue smoke, pungent with the smell of dream weed.

"Are you Captain Eli?" Nicci asked.

The man raised his bushy eyebrows and bowed, meeting them as they came aboard. "Eli Corwin, ma'am. How is it that you're familiar with who I am?"

"One of your sailors recommended that we speak to you about booking passage south to the Old World. We wish to depart soon."

Captain Eli removed his flat, gray cap. He had thick, wiry black hair shot through with silver strands. A dark boundary of beard outlined his jaw, but the rest of his face was clean shaven. "If departing tonight is soon enough, then this is your ship. The *Wavewalker* is a cargo vessel, but we have room for a few passengers, provided the fee is adequate."

"We have more than a fee." When Nathan puffed his chest with pride, his fancy new shirt swelled, as if the ruffles were flowers blooming. From the leather bag at his side, he removed a document and extended it to the captain. "This is a writ from Lord Rahl, master of D'Hara, appointing me his roving ambassador. The protection and status also covers my traveling companion."

Captain Eli skimmed the writ so quickly that Nicci knew he wasn't actually reading the words. He did not seem impressed. "This writ and the price of a passage will be enough to pay for your passage."

Nicci felt heat rise to her cheeks. "Lord Rahl's writ should guarantee us free passage."

"Maybe it should." The captain put the cap back on his head and inserted the pipe between his lips. He inhaled a long slow breath, then exhaled. "But such documents could be forged. There are many tricksters out to cheat an honest captain." He sucked again on his pipe. "Surely a powerful man like Lord Rahl, master of D'Hara, has a treasury large enough not to begrudge me the price of your passage."

He gestured toward the adjacent ship, where men in exotic silk pantaloons unloaded crates of spiny fruit. "For most of the captains here, a letter from a ruler they've never heard of will gain you nothing. For me, I'll try to be fair."

The cow let out a low moan as the cook tried to wrestle it down a ramp to a lower deck.

"Informing the world about Lord Rahl's rule is part of our mission," Nicci said. She still placed little credence in the other quest that the witch woman claimed was so important.

Captain Eli returned to his seat on the stool. "And you are welcome to tell every member of my crew about your Lord Rahl's wonderful new empire—so long as you pay for your cabins."

Nicci stiffened, preparing to demand that the captain acquiesce, but Nathan stepped forward. "That seems eminently reasonable, Captain. You're a businessman, and we can be fair." He plucked open the bindings of a small pouch in his palm and dumped gold pieces into the captain's outstretched hand.

Surprised, the man looked at the coins, warred with his decision, and then handed two gold pieces back to Nathan. "This is enough, thank you."

When the captain secured the coins in his own purse, Nathan whispered to Nicci, "We can always make more. Why not keep everyone happy?"

Rather than carrying huge sacks of coins from the D'Haran treasury, Nathan used his magic to transmute common metals into gold, so they never worried about having whatever money they needed. The wild people in the Dark Lands had no use for currency, but here in the civilized towns of D'Hara, Nathan found it useful to carry a fair amount of gold.

"For that price," the wizard added, "my companion and I will each receive a private stateroom."

The captain chuckled good-naturedly. "A stateroom? I see you've never been aboard the *Wavewalker*. In fact, I wonder if you've ever been aboard a ship at all? Yes, I can find a cabin for each of you. Some highborn nobles might consider them closets, but each room has a door and a bunk. After a week or two on the waves, you'll think of them as fine accommodations."

As long as she got to her destination, Nicci didn't care about spacious rooms or padded furniture. "That will be acceptable."

Some of the crewmen lounged on the deck, assessing the new passengers as if they were some strange fish they had drawn up in a net. Since the ship was due to depart soon, a stream of sailors continued to return, some staggering with hangovers, some carrying possessions they had purchased in port. They glanced at Nathan with a curious expression, no doubt wondering about his remarkable clothes and his fine sword, but their eyes lingered on Nicci, drawn to her long blond hair and the black dress that accentuated her curves. Nicci saw no sign of the young man she had rescued in the alley.

Dismissing the scrutiny of the sailors, the captain directed the two guests to their cabins. As she crossed the deck, Nicci noticed five shirt-less men whose broad chests sported a waving line of tattooed circles. All five had dusky skin and mud-brown hair pulled back and tied like the tail of a warhorse. Although most of the crewmen turned their gazes away from Nicci's stare, these haughty shirtless men stared at her with undisguised hunger.

Seeing their lascivious grins, Nathan stepped in front of Nicci. "Make way! Don't you know this is Death's Mistress?" The shirtless men grudgingly backed off.

Their cabins in the stern of the ship proved to be just as small and unimpressive as Captain Eli had led them to expect. Nicci could tell that Nathan was disappointed in the accommodations, and she said, "Even a small cabin is better than lying on the forest floor in the cold rain and fog of the Dark Lands."

"You are ever the optimist, Sorceress," he said. "I concur."

For now, as the sun set over the delta of the Kern River and the tide began to go out, they went back up on deck to watch the preparations for departure.

Captain Eli shouted orders as his crew climbed the masts and crawled out on yardarms to unfurl sails. Others slipped thick hawsers from dock posts and loosed the ropes from stanchions on the pier. Hour bells rang from towers along the harbor.

She still had not seen Bannon Farmer aboard, and she feared the young redhead had blundered into another group of cutthroats in an alley and had suffered the fate she expected him to.

Just as the sailors prepared to lift the *Wavewalker*'s boarding ramp, though, a young man with long ginger hair bounded down the dock. "Wait for me, I'm coming! Wait! *Wavewalker*, wait!" Nicci noticed that he was now carrying a sword, which bounced and slapped against his thigh as he ran.

Bannon raced along as merchants and dockworkers scattered out of the way. He bumped into a reeling, drunken sailor who couldn't seem to remember where his own ship was, but Bannon spun past him and ran up the boarding ramp. His fellow sailors laughed, and a few exchanged coins. "I told you he'd be too foolish to jump ship when he had the chance."

Captain Eli gave Bannon a scolding look. "Some of our crew were betting you'd be a one-voyage sailor, Mr. Farmer. Next time don't be late."

"I wasn't late, sir." Bannon panted hard, swiping his loose hair out of his eyes. His cheeks were flushed with the effort. "I'm just in time."

When Bannon noticed Nicci, his face brightened, and the broad grin only emphasized the growing bruise on his smashed lips. "You're here! You came. Welcome aboard the *Wavewalker*."

"It seems we will be passengers. This ship is going where we need to travel." She took a breath, then added, "Thank you for the recommendation."

He held up his plain, unadorned sword. "See, I found a blade. Just like I said."

The other sailors joked. One said, "Some might call that a sword— I'd call it a grass cutter." Another said, "Who do you intend to impress with that ugly thing? A blind woman? Or maybe a farmer who needs to chop down tall weeds."

They all guffawed.

Bannon frowned at his clunky sword, then re-formed his expression into a cheery grin. "A sword doesn't have to be pretty to be effective at killing," he said, repeating Nicci's earlier words. "It's a sturdy sword." He held it up. "In fact, that's what I will name it. Sturdy!"

Captain Eli cut him off. "Enough showing off your sword, Mr. Farmer. Right now, I need your hands and your muscles on the rigging ropes. I want to be clear of the ships in the harbor and out in the open water before night falls."

Standing beside her at the starboard rail, Nathan mused, "Well, we are on our way, Sorceress. To Kol Adair, wherever it is." He gave her a wry grin. "I think I'm already starting to feel whole again."

CHAPTER 8

The sea was calm and dark, and the full moon rose like a bright torch as the *Wavewalker* glided out of Grafan Harbor. The three-masted carrack cruised past the chain of islands that strung out past Halsband Island, which now held only the pulverized rubble of the Palace of the Prophets.

After they had left the glowing lights of Tanimura, the night sky became a deep velvet black. Nicci stood on deck and looked up, trying to find new patterns among the bright stars that had shifted in the universe.

The canvas sails strained tight, creamy white as the full moon shone on them. The ropes glistened with a thin film of night dew. The carved figurehead of the Sea Mother stared forward with wooden eyes, as if watching out for hazards ahead.

Bannon came up to her near the bow, smiling shyly. "I'm glad you decided to come with us aboard the *Wavewalker.*"

"And I am glad that you survived Tanimura." Nicci couldn't tell whether he had learned any wariness or common sense from his time in the city. "It has been a day full of surprises."

He still proudly clung to his new blade. "You were right about the sword, that it needs to be serviceable, not pretty. And sturdy. It needs to be sturdy." He held the weapon as if it had become his most prized possession, turning it back and forth as he watched the moonlight play along the discolored blade. He swept it sideways in a practice stroke. "I can't wait for a chance to use it."

"Do not be so eager for that, but be ready if need be."

"I will. Do you have a sword of your own?"

"I don't need one," Nicci said.

His expression fell as he was suddenly reminded of what she had done to the thugs in the alley. "No, I doubt you would. I saw you hurl that man and smash his head against the wall. It cracked open like a rotten pumpkin! And that other man . . . you turned his neck to jelly! I don't even know what you did to the third one." Bannon shook his head. His eyes were wide. "I was trying to fight him for you, but he just . . . died."

"That is what happens when you stop a person's heart."

"Sweet Sea Mother," Bannon whispered. He brushed his hair back. "You saved my life, no doubt about that, and you were right—I was too innocent. I should never have blundered into a situation like that. I expect the world to be a nice place, but it's darker than I think."

"It is," Nicci said.

"It's darker than I want it to be."

Nicci wondered if the young man had stolen some of the captain's dream weed. "Better to see the dangers in the world and be ready when someone inevitably turns on you. It is a far preferable surprise to find that a person is kinder than you think, than to discover he is secretly a traitor."

Troubled expressions circled the young man's face like eddy currents. "I suppose you're right, and I want to thank you again. I owe you." He fumbled in the pockets of his canvas trousers. "I brought you something. To show my gratitude."

Nicci frowned at him. "That is not necessary. I saved your life because I was in the right place, and because I despise those who prey on the weak." She had no intention of letting this young man fawn over her. "I do not want your gifts."

He withdrew a tiny fold of soft cloth that he held in the palm of his hand. "But you have to take it."

"It is not necessary," Nicci repeated, in a harder voice this time.

"*I* think it's necessary." Bannon sounded more determined. He set his sword aside awkwardly, squatted against the side wall of the ship, and opened the cloth to reveal a pearl the size of a grieving woman's tear.

"I do not want your gifts," Nicci reiterated.

Bannon refused to listen. "On Chiriya Island I was taught manners and gratitude. My parents wanted me to be polite to everyone and to meet my obligations. You were there when I needed you. You saved me, and you punished those evil men. My father said that if I was to be an upstanding man, I had to show gratitude. It doesn't matter whether you expect anything in return. I am required to give it to you."

His breathing quickened as he extended the pearl. It seemed to be made of silver and ice. "This is a wishpearl, an advance on my wages. The captain says we'll have plenty before the end of the voyage, but I wanted it now." He nodded intently. "Right now it's very rare, and I want to give it to you."

A sailor on watch strolled past. "Rare?" His voice had a mocking tone. "That's just a leftover. We unloaded two chests full of them in Tanimura—it's how Captain Eli paid for his whole voyage. Soon enough, we'll fill more chests on our way down south."

Bannon whirled to face the eavesdropping sailor, clenching his hand tight over the wishpearl. "I was having a private conversation."

"This is a ship, cabbage farmer! Think again if you expect privacy anywhere on board."

Defensive, Bannon picked up his sword. "It's worth something now, and it's the last wishpearl. I want to give it to the sorceress, and if you don't treat her well, she'll crush your windpipe and stop your heart. I've seen it with my own eyes."

The sailor laughed again and strolled off.

Though Nicci did not want the offering, she understood the complexities of obligations. She had indeed saved him, although she had not set out to do so. "If you've learned your lesson and taught yourself not to become a victim, Bannon Farmer, then that is demonstration enough of your gratitude."

"Not enough for me," Bannon insisted, and extended the wishpearl again. "Just take it. Throw it overboard if you like, but *I* will have done what was right. I fulfilled what *I* needed to do."

The pearl felt slippery and cold in her fingertips. She rolled it back and forth on her palm with a fingertip. "If I accept this pearl, what does it obligate me to do for you? What are you expecting?"

Bannon flushed, deeply embarrassed. "Why, nothing! I would never ask . . . that isn't what I was thinking!"

She hardened her voice. "As long as you're clear on that."

"It's a wishpearl. Don't you know what a wishpearl is?"

"I do not. Is there some significance other than being a pretty bauble?" Seeing that she had hurt him, Nicci grudgingly softened her voice. "It is a beautiful pearl. I don't know that I've ever seen a finer one."

"It's a *wishpearl,*" he repeated. "You should make a wish. It might be just a legend, but I've heard that wishpearls are concentrated dreams and you can unleash one if you wish on it."

"Who would believe such a thing?" Nicci asked.

"Many people. That's why the *Wavewalker* makes such a profit on each voyage. Captain Eli knows the location of a long line of special reefs. He harvests wishpearls and sells them in the port cities—at least that's what the other sailors said." He lowered his voice and ducked his chin. "This is still just my first voyage, you know."

Nicci held the wishpearl, thought of where they were going, of the mission the witch woman had given to Nathan. No doubt it would be a long journey. She looked down at the icy silver sphere under the moonlight and said, "Very well, then I wish this voyage will help us get to Kol Adair." She closed her fingers around the pearl and slipped it into a small pocket in her black dress.

CHAPTER 9

The *Wavewalker* headed south across open water, beyond sight of the coastline. Having spent so much time sitting alone in the Palace of the Prophets, Nathan was accustomed to sedentary days, but at least now he was out in the fresh air, inhaling brisk breezes.

In the distance, Tanimura was only a memory—a thousand years of memories, as far as he was concerned. Time to make new memories. Red possessed the life book of his past, but he had a new volume for a whole new set of adventures. Now, without the gift of prophecy, every twist and turn of the future was a surprise to him. Exactly as it should be.

The captain and his crew knew how to guide the ship even when the winds did not blow in a favorable direction. The well-practiced sailors understood the intricate puzzle of how the rigging and the sails worked together, furling and unfurling canvas to catch any wisp of wind. It was like magic to Nathan, even though there was no magic beyond a well-seasoned familiarity with the mysteries of the sea.

Most of the crew had been with Captain Eli on numerous voyages, and each sailor had a job to do—except for the five shirtless, tattooed men who lay about and did nothing. Watching their lazy behavior and attitude, Nathan lost respect for them, and not simply because they leered so much at Nicci. They displayed no interest in participating as members of the crew. He supposed the arrogant men must have their purpose, or the captain wouldn't tolerate them on board. For now, though, they were primarily useless.

Bannon Farmer was the newest sailor on the *Wavewalker* and thus received the least-pleasant chores, dumping out slops, pumping the bilge, scrubbing the deck with a bucket of salt water and a stiff hand brush. But he performed the drudgery with a strange cheer.

Nathan watched the young man climb the ratlines and stand on the high platform to serve as a lookout, or crawl out on a yardarm to loose a sail. Once Bannon finished his chores, he would sit next to the wizard in the lazy afternoons, asking questions. "Have you really lived a thousand years? What fascinating things you must have done!"

Nathan patted the life book at his side. "I am more interested in what I have yet to do." He gave the thin redhead an encouraging smile. "But I'll be happy to tell you some of my stories, if you will tell me yours."

Bannon's shoulders slumped. "I don't have any stories to tell. Nothing's ever happened to me." Looking away, he rubbed the discolored bruises on his face. "Why do you think I ran away from Chiriya? I had a perfect life there, loving parents, a warm home. But it was too quiet and calm for a man like me." When he forced a smile, he winced from the scab on his still-healing split lip.

"I planted the cabbage fields in spring, weeded the cabbage fields all summer, harvested the cabbage in fall, and helped my mother make pickled cabbage for winter. There was no chance to have an adventure." He lifted his chin. "My father was very sad to see me go, because he was so proud of me. Maybe someday I'll return as a wealthy and famous adventurer."

"Maybe." Nathan detected something odd in the young man's words.

Bannon brought out his own sword as he sat on deck next to Nathan. Its steel wasn't perfect, but the edge was sharp enough. "I still think Sturdy will serve me well."

Since the young man seemed to expect sage advice, Nathan decided to give it. "A blade can only serve its wielder if he knows how to use it. You serve the sword just as the sword serves you." He withdrew his own blade from its scabbard to admire the fine workings on the grip, the inlaid gold, the gleam of the expensive steel. He had always felt that it made him look bold and gallant, a man to be reckoned with, a warrior as well as a wizard. Standing, he held the blade in front of him, watching the play of sunlight along its edge. He gave the young man a hard look. "Do you know how to use your sword, my boy?"

"I know how to swing a blade," Bannon said.

"We're not cutting cabbages. What if you were fighting against a bloodthirsty warrior from the Imperial Order? Or worse, one of the flesh-eating half men from the Dark Lands?"

Bannon paled. "I'm sure I could take down at least five of them before they killed me."

"Only five? So I would have to deal with the thousands that remained?" Nathan flexed his arms and bent his knees in his supple new travel pants. "Why don't we practice? I could use a good training partner. I'll teach you a few moves, so that if you ever find yourself facing a savage enemy horde, you could maybe kill fifteen of them before they took you down."

Bannon grinned. "I'd like that." A troubled expression crossed his face. "Well, I don't mean I'd like being killed, but I would like to make a brave accounting of myself if I were ever in a great battle."

"Those fighting at your side would like you to make a brave accounting as well, my boy." Nathan stroked his chin with his left hand. "I may be a thousand years old, but I'm relatively new at being an adventurer. A sword looks so . . . dashing, don't you think?" He held up the point.

"Your sword is fine, sir," Bannon admitted. "But will a fine sword and a dashing appearance frighten away a horde of monsters?"

"I suppose not," Nathan said. "Maybe we both could use the practice." He wrapped his hands around the hilt and tried different stances. "Shall we learn together, Bannon Farmer?"

Grinning, the young man lifted his sword and stepped back to crouch into a fighting stance, or at least the best imitation of a fighting stance he could manage.

When Nathan swung, Bannon slashed sideways to meet the blade, but Nathan had to adjust the sweep of his arc to insure that their swords met with a clang. Then he struck backward, hitting the young man's blade as it came up in defense. In a flurry of attack, Bannon swung and chopped, flailing from side to side.

The wizard scolded, "Are you a woodsman trying to clear a forest?"

"I'm trying to slay a thousand enemy soldiers!"

"An admirable goal. Now let's try a combination of strokes and jabs and deflections."

Bannon responded with another wild combination of slashes and counterslashes, which the wizard easily met, although he was by no means a master swordsman himself. In any confrontation, Nathan would always rely on magic as his first line of attack rather than a sword, but to teach the cocky young man a lesson, he worked his way through Bannon's defenses and smacked him on the bottom with the flat of his blade.

Stung, Bannon yelped, his face flushing so crimson that even his freckles vanished. "You'll pay for that, Wizard!"

"Take my payment on credit," Nathan said with a proud smirk. "It may be quite some time before you can make me fulfill the debt."

Some of the other sailors observed, amused by the swordplay. They howled with laughter. "Look at the cabbage farmer!" snorted Karl, a muscular veteran of many voyages, who considered it his duty to make sure Bannon was well initiated.

"Indeed, look at him," Nathan called back. "Soon enough you'll be afraid of him."

Attacking again, Bannon released a bottled-up anger that startled Nathan, even frightened him. Ducking and defending himself, the wizard chided, "Show *control* as well as enthusiasm, my boy. Now then, let's do it slowly. Watch me. Match my strokes."

The two practiced for an hour in the hot sun, sweating with exertion. After Nathan had led him through several fluid but basic exercises, Bannon began to grow more confident with his weapon. He was bright-eyed and grinning as they picked up speed. The ring of blades brought out most of the crew to watch.

Finally panting with exhaustion, Nathan raised his hand to signal a halt. "Dear spirits, you've had as much instruction as you can handle for one day. I'd better give you time to absorb what you've learned." He tried to control his heavy breathing so Bannon would not notice how winded he was.

The young man's hair was damp with perspiration, but the sea breezes blew it in all directions. He showed no sign of being ready to give up.

Nathan continued, "Maybe it's time for me to tell stories and teach you a bit about history. A good swordsman is also an *intelligent* swordsman."

Bannon kept his sword up. "But how will a story from history teach me to be better with my blade?"

Nathan smiled back at him. "I could tell you the tale of a poorly skilled swordsman who had his head chopped off. Would that be a good enough object lesson?"

Bannon wiped his brow and sat on a mound of coiled rope. "Very well then, let's hear the tale."

Nicci spent the day at the ship's stern in Captain Eli's large chart room on the piloting deck. The captain had opened up twin windows at the rear to let in fresh breezes. The view of the ocean behind them showed a curl of foamy wake as the *Wavewalker* sailed along. The line of stirred water reminded Nicci of the broad imperial roads that Jagang had built across the Old World, but while Jagang's roads would endure for a long time, this watery path faded as soon as the ship passed.

"I would like to study your charts and maps," she told the captain. "As an emissary for Lord Rahl, I must see the far reaches of the Old World, where the Imperial Order conquered. That is all part of D'Hara now."

Captain Eli toyed with his long-stemmed pipe, tapping its bowl on the hard wood of a map table. "Many captains keep their routes confidential, since the swiftest passage means money for a trader. I once knew the currents and the reefs and the shoreline so very well." He sucked on the end of his pipe, musing to himself, but he didn't light it inside the chart room, lest a stray ash catch the maps on fire. "But I suppose it doesn't matter anymore."

"I am not your competition, Captain," Nicci said. "I have no interest in a map of the ocean. I want to know the coastline and the landscape inland. My companion and I are searching for a place called Kol Adair."

"Never heard of it. Must be far inland, and any place away from shore doesn't have much meaning for my life." He scratched the side of his face. "But I did not mean you were my competition. I meant that the current maps don't matter because all is changed, you see. Everything's different now.

"In the last two months the currents have shifted. The wind patterns that I knew so well have now changed direction, as if the seasons are all mixed up." He let out a long groan. "And the stars at night are in the wrong places. How am I supposed to navigate? My astrolabes and sextants are useless. My constellation maps don't show the same stars. Sweet Sea Mother, I don't even know if the compass points true north anymore. I am making my way by instinct."

Nicci knew full well what had happened. "It is a new world, Captain. Prophecy is entirely gone. Magic has changed in ways that we haven't begun to fathom." Then she turned her bright blue gaze toward his, and drew a breath of the damp air as a breeze rippled the papers on the chart table. "But someone has to be the first to make new star charts, the first to map out the changed currents, and the first to discover the best places to drop anchor. You can be one of those firsts, Captain."

"That would be a wonderful thing . . . if I fancied myself an explorer." The captain scratched his trim of a beard around his jaw. "But my ambition has always been to serve as a successful cargo captain going from port to port. I have families to support, many children. I see little enough of them as it is, and I want to be able to arrive on time."

"Families?" she asked. "More than one?"

"Of course." Captain Eli ran his fingers over his dark hair, tucking a silver-shot lock behind his ear. "I have a wife and two daughters in Tanimura, a younger wife and three sons at Larrikan Shores, and a very beautiful one in Serrimundi, the daughter of the harborlord."

"Do they know about your other families?" Nicci asked. "Is this an unusual arrangement among sea captains?"

"I take care of each one in turn, wherever I go. Every wife has a fine house. Each of my sons or daughters is comfortable, with food, shelter, and an education. Most sailors and captains would simply visit the brothels at every port city, and I know of many a captain who caught a loathsome disease and gave it to his wife when he came home." Captain Eli stared out at the endless sea behind the stern. "No, that's not for me. I have chosen my wives, and I am faithful to them. I am an honorable man."

Considering the countless women Emperor Jagang had taken, including her, and how he had thrown Nicci and others into the tents to be raped again and again by his soldiers, she did not judge Captain Eli Corwin. She had never felt any inclination to be a man's wife, or one of his wives, except for the time she had forced Richard Rahl to pretend to be her husband. Nicci had imagined a perfect domestic existence, sure that she could convince him to adopt the philosophy of the Imperial Order. That had been not only a lie, but a bitter lie, and Richard had hated her for it.

Unconsciously, Nicci rubbed her lower lip, still imagining the long-healed scar there from Jagang's gold ring. Nicci had never realized that her sick dream of forcing Richard to be her husband was a delusion as foolish as Bannon Farmer's imagined perfect world.

Fortunately, she was a different person now. After living secretly as a Sister of the Dark for so many years, then being enslaved by Jagang, broken, then rebuilt—but rebuilt *wrong*, until she was finally fixed by Richard—she understood everything better now. Nicci owed Richard more than she could ever repay. And he had given her a mission.

"Let me see your charts nevertheless," she said, driving away the memories. "The more I know about the Old World, the more I know for Lord Rahl's sake."

Captain Eli spread the maps out before her on the table, sorting the broad papers until he found one that showed the coastline far south of Tanimura. "These are our major stops. Lefton Harbor, Kherimus,

Andaliyo, Larrikan Shores, even Serrimundi—we have a special agreement with the harborlord there, thanks to my wife." He smiled wistfully at the thought of her.

Nicci ran her fingers to the edge of the map, seeing no sign of Kol Adair. "And what is farther south? These charts are incomplete."

"No one goes farther south, no reason to go there. That's the Phantom Coast. Barely settled, even though the imperial roads stretch far into that land." Captain Eli sucked on his unlit pipe again, set it aside, and wiped his lips. "Who knows what the old emperors had in mind when they built those roads?"

Nicci frowned at the cities marked on the maps. "I need to make sure that everyone in the Old World knows about the end of war, the defeat of Emperor Jagang. We'll ask for your help as well, Captain. Even after we depart your ship, I will give you something in writing which you can take to these ports and help spread the message about Lord Rahl. All lands must be brought under one rule, even though each will keep its own culture and separate governance—so long as the people do not break the basic rules as determined by all."

"A fine sentiment," the captain said, rolling up the maps, "if everyone felt the same way. But I doubt you will get them to agree."

"That is the core of our quest. We'll have to make them feel the same way," Nicci said, and added a small, confident smile. "I can be very persuasive. And if I'm not sufficient, then there's a large D'Haran army to help make the point."

She and the captain left the chart room, stepping out onto the high deck from which they could watch the sailors doing their daily chores. The five shirtless men lounged about, disdaining the work and the crew. They turned their arrogant gazes toward Nicci, and one called up to her, "Come to play with us? We've got time."

"You can waste your own time until we reach the reefs," said Captain Eli. "But I don't think the lady wants to play with you."

Nicci said in a hard voice, "I doubt they'd enjoy how I might play with them."

The shirtless layabouts responded with leering laughter, which annoyed Nicci. She turned to the captain. "Why don't they work for their passage? They are worthless men."

"They are wishpearl divers. They've been with me for three voyages—extremely profitable voyages." He nodded to them all. "Sol, Elgin, Rom, Pell, and Buna. They might be lazy louts now, but they will earn ten times their keep in one day, once we reach the reefs."

CHAPTER 10

Seagulls wheeled overhead, following the *Wavewalker* under sunny skies. Fascinated, Nathan joined the sailors crowding the ship's rails, excitedly pointing down at the strange drifting infestation that surrounded them on the open seas.

Hundreds of thousands of jellyfish floated on the surface like soap bubbles, each one as large as an ox's head, throbbing like jellied brain tissue. The mindless translucent creatures posed no threat that Nathan could see as the *Wavewalker* cruised along and nudged them aside. Some of the jellyfish splattered against the hull boards and left a glutinous film, but the rest simply bobbed out of the way.

Captain Eli stood on deck, cautious. "Steady onward. If it was a sea serpent or a kraken, I'd be worried, but those jellyfish are just a nuisance."

Bannon stared in wonder. He turned to his mentor, flushed. "I never saw the likes of these on Chiriya, but other kinds of jellyfish would drift close to shore in the quiet coves . . . where a boy and his friend might go swimming. They sting!" He let out a wistful sigh, dreaming of home. "Ian and I had our own special lagoon where there were tide pools. The water was just right for wading, but we didn't see the jellyfish. We both got terribly stung once. My leg swelled up like a week-old pig carcass, and Ian was even worse. We could barely walk home. My father was angry because I couldn't work in the cabbage fields for days afterward."

The young man's expression darkened, and then, like clouds parting, he smiled again. "We all had a good laugh about it." He blew air between his lips. "And those jellyfish were only the size of my fist." He leaned far out over the side to get a better look. "I'll bet a sting from one of those things would kill you—probably five times over!"

"Being killed once would be sufficient." Nathan liked the young man. Bannon Farmer seemed earnest and determined, perhaps a bit too innocent—but Nathan didn't mind innocence. The wizard had written his own tales for young boys like Bannon, *The Adventures of Bonnie Day* and countless other stories carried far and wide on the mouths and lute strings of minstrels. Right now, Nathan saw no reason not to take the young man under his wing.

Out in the open air, Nicci stood aloof, away from the sailors. Her thick blond hair blew in the breezes, and her blue eyes pierced the distance. The tight-fitting black dress embraced her breasts and accentuated her curves. Cinched tight at the waist, the flowing skirt angled down to her right knee. On board, she'd decided to forgo her black travel leggings and high boots. She looked beautiful in the way a pristine work of art was beautiful, to be admired and appreciated, but definitely not to be touched.

Bannon occasionally looked at her with the wrong kind of sparkle in his eyes. Not lust, but infatuation. Nathan would have to watch that, lest it become a problem later on. The young man had no idea what he would be getting into.

Now, Bannon lowered his voice to an odd whisper as he asked Nathan, "Is it true she was really called Death's Mistress?"

Nathan smiled. "Dear boy, our Nicci was one of the most feared women in Jagang's Imperial Order. She has the blood of thousands on her hands."

"Thousands?" Bannon swallowed.

The wizard waved his hand. "More like tens of thousands, maybe even hundreds of thousands." He nodded. "Yes. I would suppose that's more accurate. Hundreds of thousands."

Although Nicci stood presumably out of earshot, Nathan saw her lips quirk in a thin smile. He continued in a stage whisper, "She was also a Sister of the Dark, served the Keeper for years before she served

Jagang the dream walker." He glanced around, noting that some of the other sailors were listening as well, and they muttered uneasily. While Bannon seemed in awe of Nicci's past, the others were fearful and superstitious.

Nathan didn't mind. Fear generated respect. "But that was before Nicci joined Lord Rahl, saw the light, became one of the staunchest fighters for freedom. Did I tell you she stopped Richard's heart and sent him to the underworld?"

"She—she killed him?"

"Only for a time. She sent him to the Keeper so he could rescue the spirit of his beloved Kahlan. But that's another story." He clapped the young man on the shoulder. "And on a long voyage, we'll have plenty of time for tales. No need to tell them all now."

The young man muttered in disappointment. "I've had a boring life, growing up as a farmboy on a sleepy island. No stories worth telling."

"You got stung by a jellyfish once," Nathan pointed out. "You must have other tales."

The young man leaned back and pondered. Below in the water, the crowded jellyfish bumped against one another with muffled slurping sounds.

"Well, it might just have been my imagination," Bannon said. "A person's thoughts tend to run wild when drifting alone in a small boat in the fog."

Nathan laughed. "Dear spirits, boy! Imagination is a critical part of a story. Tell your tale."

Bannon pursed his lips. "Have you ever heard of the selka? A race that lives beneath the sea and watches the activities of people above? They observe our boats and ships from below, which are like wooden clouds floating high in their sky."

"The selka?" Nathan frowned, drawing thumb and forefinger from his lips to his chin. "Sea people . . . ah yes. If memory serves—and my memory is as sharp as a finely honed dagger—the selka were created to be fighters in the ancient wizard wars. Humans altered by magic into another form, like the mriswith, or even the sliph. The selka were made to be an undersea army that could rise up and attack enemy ships." He narrowed his eyes. "But they're either extinct, or just legends."

"I never heard that part of the story before," Bannon said. "We just told tales about them on Chiriya. Sometimes the selka grant wishes."

Nathan chuckled. "If I had a copper coin for every story about a mythical creature that grants wishes, I'd have so many coins that I could buy whatever I liked and have no need for wishes."

"I . . . I don't know about that either," Bannon muttered. "It was just a story they told in the village. And there are times when you just want something to believe in."

Nathan nodded solemnly, sorry he had teased the young man. "I've felt the same way myself."

Bannon stared out to sea, seeming not to notice the jellyfish anymore. He lowered his voice to a whisper. "Just as there are times when an unhappy person needs to run away. I was foolish and young . . . too young to know that I was foolish."

Perhaps too young for that still, Nathan thought, but kept his words to himself.

"I set off in a little fishing boat all alone, meaning to leave Chiriya forever. I didn't have any friends on the island."

"What about Ian? The one who was also stung by a jellyfish."

"This was later. Ian was gone." Bannon frowned. "I set off at dusk as the tide went out, and I knew the full moon would light my way throughout the night. I hoped to see the selka, but in my heart, I suspected they were just stories. I'd been told so many things that turned out to be untrue." He looked sickened, but with obvious effort he restored his expression to a happy grin. "There's always a chance, though. I rowed into the darkness as the stars came out overhead, and I kept rowing until my arms felt as if they would fall off. After that, I just drifted in the open water. For about an hour I could see the dark line of Chiriya Island, with the lights of hearth fires and lamps from the shoreline villages high above the beaches. Then they vanished into the distance, and I kept on rowing."

"Where did you think you were going?" Nathan asked. "Just heading out into the open sea?"

Bannon shrugged. "I knew the Old World was out there, a continent filled with cities like Tanimura, Kherimus, Andaliyo—a whole continent! I figured if I simply went far enough, I was bound to bump into shore sooner or later." He glanced away in embarrassment. "Growing up on an island did not give me a good grasp of large distances. I drifted all night, and when dawn came I saw only water—water in all directions. Like this." He gestured over the side of *Wavewalker*.

"I didn't have a compass or nearly enough supplies. I drifted on the open sea all day long under the baking sun, and I began to grow deeply worried. The heat of the day burned and blistered my skin, but the next night seemed colder than ever. And by the third day, I ran out of water and most of my food. I felt like such a fool. I saw no sign of land, had no idea which direction the Old World lay, or even how to find Chiriya again.

"I cried like a heartbroken child, and I'm not ashamed to admit it. I stood up in the wobbly fishing boat and shouted into the distance, hoping someone would hear. That made me feel even more foolish than crying.

"That night the moon was still bright, but a thick blanket of fog settled in—although it wasn't a blanket, it was cold and clammy. I shivered, more miserable than ever. I couldn't see anything around me—not that there was anything to see. The moon was just a gauzy glow overhead."

His voice became a whisper. "On a foggy, silent night you can hear sounds from far away, and distances deceive you. I heard splashes that I thought were sharks, then it sounded like swimming . . . an eerie voice. I called out again for help. In my imagination I thought it might be the selka come to rescue me, but common sense told me it was just a distant whale, or even a sea serpent. I shouted and shouted, but I heard no answer. Maybe my voice startled whatever it was, and I listened to the silence, nothing but the lapping waves and another distant splash, something that might have been laughter, a giggle . . . but that couldn't be true.

"I was so distraught, anxious, exhausted—not to mention hungry and thirsty—that I eventually collapsed during the darkest part of the night and fell into a deep sleep."

Nathan smiled to encourage the young man. "You have the makings of a storyteller, my boy. You've got me intrigued. How did you ever get out of it?"

"I don't know," Bannon said. "I honestly don't know."

Nathan frowned. "Then you have to work on a better ending for your story."

"Oh, there's a good ending, sir. I woke up the next morning, and instead of the silence of the endless waves, I heard the rush of water against a shore, surf riding up on the shingle. I realized that my boat wasn't rocking anymore. I stood up and nearly fell out. I had washed up on the shore of an island, a place I recognized! This was Chiriya, the same cove where Ian and I used to swim."

"How did you get back there?"

The young man shrugged. "Sweet Sea Mother, I told you—I don't know. Sometime during the night when I was unconscious from exhaustion, something had taken me back to our island, brought me safely to shore."

"Are you sure the currents didn't just circle you around to your starting point? In the fog, how would you ever know?" Nathan looked down his nose. "You're not saying it was the selka who rescued you?"

Bannon seemed embarrassed. "I'm saying that I found myself safely back on shore, where I had started from, and I don't know how. In all the vast ocean and all the islands in the sea, I had come back to the very place I called my home, the cove where I'd started from." He paused for a long moment, then looked at the wizard and smiled in wonder. "And in the soft dirt of the shore, beside my boat—which had been dragged much farther up out of the water than even a high tide would have left it—I saw a footprint."

"What kind of footprint?"

"It looked human . . . almost. But the toes were webbed, like a sea creature's. I saw the faint impression of what looked like a fin's edge and sharp points like claws, instead of human toenails."

Nathan chuckled. "A fine story that is! And you said nothing had ever happened to you."

"I suppose. . . ." Bannon did not sound convinced.

The jellyfish swarm showed no sign of abating. Egged on by his crewmates, the broad-shouldered Karl picked up a barb-tipped harpoon and tied a rope through the metal eye on the tail end of the shaft. As the others cheered and hooted, the veteran sailor leaned over the side and tossed the harpoon down to pop one of the jellyfish like a large ripe blister. The iron point pierced the membrane, bursting the gelatinous creature into a smoking puddle. As the residue drifted out among the other jellyfish, its companions scooted away from the remains like fleeing robber bugs.

With guffaws of laughter, the other sailors ran to get more harpoons, but when Karl pulled the harpoon back up by the rope, he grunted in amazement. "Look! Look at this." The sharpened iron tip was smoking, and it began to droop as acid pitted and ate away the metal.

The other sailors stopped, poised to throw their harpoons as part of the game to pop the jellyfish. Curious, Karl extended a callused finger, but before he could touch the smoking iron tip, Nathan barked a warning. "Leave that alone, or you might lose a hand as well as a harpoon tip."

Captain Eli scolded them all. "I told you to leave those jellyfish be! The sea has enough dangers for us. We don't need to make any more."

With a clatter, the other sailors lowered their harpoons, then sheepishly stowed them away.

CHAPTER 11

The *Wavewalker* sailed south for a full week. Captain Eli by-passed the larger coastal cities in the Old World, and Nicci was concerned about the changed currents, altered wind patterns, and unreliable stars in the night sky. "Are we lost?" she asked, standing next to the captain at the bow one afternoon.

"Lady Sorceress, I know exactly where I'm sailing." He wiped the thin end of his pipe between thumb and forefinger, then inserted it back into his mouth. "We are heading straight for the reefs."

Overhearing, Nathan stepped up to them. "That sounds ominous."

Pushed along by a steady sea wind, the *Wavewalker* moved at a fast clip. The captain gazed ahead. "Not if you know where you're going."

"And how can you be sure? You claimed the charts and currents were no longer accurate," Nicci said.

"They aren't, but I'm a captain, and the salt water of the sea runs through my veins. I can feel it in my senses. But before I can trade in Serrimundi or Lefton Harbor, I need to take on my most valuable cargo. Tomorrow morning, you'll see what I mean."

Captain Eli was right.

Taking his shift on the lookout platform high on the mainmast, Bannon called out, "A line of foam due south, Captain! Looks like rough water."

The captain leaned closer to the carved figurehead of the Sea Mother, shading his eyes. "That'll be the reefs."

Nicci watched the shirtless wishpearl divers rouse themselves, as if awakening from a long sleep. "Our services are required," said the one named Sol, who seemed to be their leader.

Elgin stretched lazily. "I'll get the ropes and the weights."

The other three, Pell, Buna, and, Rom, began breathing deeply, inhaling, exhaling, stretching their shoulders, loosening their arms. Given the size of their chests, and their commensurate lungs, Nicci guessed these divers might be able to stay underwater for some time.

Buna narrowed his eyes at Nicci. "After a good day's haul of wishpearls, maybe we'll all get to have our wish with the lady."

With a huff, Nathan took insult at the comment, but Nicci answered calmly, "If I get *my* wish, you won't be physically capable of thinking such thoughts ever again."

Even without charts, Captain Eli guided the *Wavewalker* through the choppy water, dodging dark barriers of exposed reefs, but the ship had room to maneuver in the deep channels. The crewmen tied up the sails, rolling the canvas against the yardarms and lashing it tight. When the ship slowly drifted into position, they dropped anchor in a calm sheltered area, while the waves continued to break and foam along the outer lines of submerged coral.

Once the ship was safely anchored, the eager sailors watched the five wishpearl divers make their preparations. Sol barked orders to his comrades. "We go down two at a time. I dive first with Elgin, second will be Rom and Pell. After they come up, I'll be rested enough to go down with Buna." He flexed his arms back to display his broad pectorals marked with a chain of tattooed circles.

The divers opened a clay pot of grease, which they smeared over their skin. The grease would keep them warm as they went deep into the intricate coves and crannies of the reef. The grease also made them slide through the water, according to Rom, who smeared an extra layer across his chest.

Although the five divers had similar lines of circular tattoos, some sported more circles than others. Nicci learned that the tattoos were a tally of how many chests of wishpearls each diver had collected. Sol had been down so many times, he had started a second line on the right side of his chest. They each wore a braided belt from which dangled long, curved hooks to hang iron weights on, as well as a mesh sack for harvesting shells while they were underwater.

As the first divers, Sol and Elgin each tied one end of a long hemp rope to the belt around his waist and secured the other end to the foremast. Then they climbed up onto the rail, poised on callused bare feet. They fastened iron weights to the hooks on their belts, which would drag them down to the bottom so they wouldn't waste time or breath stroking down to their destination. Once deep among the reefs, they could easily unhook and discard the weights before swimming back up.

As the two divers stood balanced in the sunlight, they inhaled, exhaled, then sucked in another great breath, expanding their chests and filling their lungs. With unspoken synchronization, the pair dove over the side and vanished with barely a ripple. The rope reeled out as they sank.

Captain Eli scratched the line of beard on his jaw. He seemed very calm and satisfied. "We might stay here at anchor a day or two. Depends on how long it takes to fill up our cargo chest."

"A chest holds a lot of wishpearls," Nathan observed.

"Yes, it does." The captain took off his cap and wiped his hair, then settled it back in place.

After some minutes had passed, Bannon looked over the side, watching for the two divers to return. He glanced at Rom and Pell, who were fixing belts to their waists, attaching iron weights to the hooks, and securing their mesh sacks as they prepared to make their own dive as soon as the first pair surfaced.

Bannon asked the two men, "Do you think I could be a wishpearl diver someday?"

Rom looked at him as if he were an insect. "No."

The young man's expression fell, but he continued to peer over the side. "Here they come!"

The divers burst to the surface. Gasping, they shook their heads, flinging water from their long, clumpy hair. It had been nearly ten minutes, and Nicci was amazed the men were able to stay underwater for that long. Their lung capacity was as great as their arrogance.

Each man grabbed one of the dangling ropes and scampered up the hull boards. After they swung themselves over the rail to stand dripping on the deck, Sol and Elgin emptied their sacks, spilling out dozens of lumpy gray shells, which were eerily shaped like hands folded in prayer.

"Sweet Sea Mother, that's lovely," said Captain Eli as the crew rushed forward. "Absolutely lovely."

The *Wavewalker*'s crew set to work with stubby flat knives to split open the wet shells, tear out the rubbery flesh, and pluck out icy-silver pearls.

Next, Rom and Pell dove overboard while their comrades rested. Sol spread his lips in a grin for Nicci. "If you offer me a proper reward, I'll give you your very own wishpearl."

Nicci simply said, "I already have one. Bannon gave it to me." Sol responded only with an annoyed grunt.

By the time Rom and Pell swam back to the surface with an equally successful harvest, the next two divers were ready. For hours, the bare-chested men went down and came up again, over and over, as the crew shucked the shells and removed the pearls.

Curious, Nathan picked up one of the split-open shells discarded on the deck. "Remarkable. They look like human hands cradling the pearls."

"Hands folded to make a wish," Bannon said.

To Nicci, the crudely formed fingers appeared to be holding tight to the treasure hidden inside.

"These reefs are lush with shells," said Buna after his third dive. "There's enough treasure for a hundred trips."

"And we'll keep coming back," Captain Eli promised.

Because the *Wavewalker*'s crew took some of their pay in wish-pearls, they pressed the divers to descend over and over again. Nicci was just glad to see the arrogant layabouts actually working.

But at the end of the day, with the sun setting in a blaze of orange and golden fire, the five divers were weary. Although Sol, Elgin, and

Rom did not seem inclined to do extra work, Pell and Buna agreed to make one last dive. The two tied ropes around their waists, attached iron weights to the hooks, and jumped overboard.

The sailors sat around on deck, chatting, shucking wishpearl shells, and piling the discards against the side wall. Pell and Buna stayed down for a long period—longer than any other previous dive that day. Nathan paced the deck, wearing an increasingly concerned look. The captain also looked worried.

Finally, Sol frowned, went to the rail, and leaned over to peer into the darkening water. "Pull on the ropes—haul them back up." He clasped one of the wet hemp cables and strained, while an eager Bannon took the other rope tied to the second diver.

Bannon's rope went taut in his hands, then suddenly yanked downward, tightening, burning through his fingers. He cried out and let go as the cable smacked against the *Wavewalker*'s hull. Something dragged it down from below.

"No swimmer could possibly pull that hard!" Sol said, straining against the rope.

The second rope creaked as an unseen force deep below dragged back. Rom and Elgin rushed to help haul on the ropes to bring their comrades back up. The strange grip tugged back with such strength that the whole ship began to tilt.

They all strained together, shouting, heaving. "Pull them up!" Sol yelled again.

Suddenly, both ropes snapped and hung loose in the water, like drifting seaweed. Working hand over hand, the men furiously pulled the ropes until the frayed end of the first one came free. "Why would they cut their own ropes?" Elgin demanded.

Bannon stared at the torn, stubby end. "That's *frayed*, not cut."

Nicci immediately understood the significance. "Something tore the rope apart."

As the would-be rescuers hauled up the second loose rope, Rom climbed on the rail, ready to dive overboard to rescue his comrades, but before he could jump, the end of the second rope came dripping out of the water, still tied to the woven belt that had been ripped free from the wishpearl diver. Tangled in the belt were flaccid, wet loops of torn intestine and three connected vertebrae, as if an attacker had simply ripped the belt entirely through the diver's spine and abdomen.

The sailors howled in fear, backing away.

"But how—?" Rom staggered backward, falling onto the deck. "We didn't see anything down there."

"Something killed Pell and Buna," Sol said. "What could have caused this? What attacked them?"

Elgin glared over at Nicci. "Maybe Death's Mistress summoned a monster."

The three surviving divers stared at the sorceress in horror and fear, which quickly turned to obvious hatred.

Bannon whispered to Nicci in amazement, "Did you really do that? Just like you killed the thieves in the alley?"

She quietly chided him for his foolish statement, but after having seen the potential violence in the wishpearl divers, she was glad that they feared her.

CHAPTER 12

The crew stared from the dissipating bloom of blood in the water to the shreds of flopping intestines that dangled from the loop of woven belt. Captain Eli shouted for the sailors to set the sails and weigh anchor as clouds gathered in the dusk. Although the *Wavewalker* was in warm latitudes, far to the south of Tanimura, the wind seemed to carry a chill of death.

Nimble sailors scrambled out on the yardarms to untie the ropes, while others pulled on the halyards and stretched the canvas. The ship moved away from the reefs, slinking like a whipped dog, while the navigator pushed hard on the rudder and the lookouts guided the course to keep from scraping the dangerous rocks.

The captain called in a hoarse voice, "We've already lost two men today. I do not wish to lose more."

Catching the wind, the ship retreated from the angry line of reefs and reached open water again. As full night fell, clouds obscured the stars, which mattered little since the captain could not navigate by the unfamiliar night sky anyway. He simply wanted to put distance between their ship and the reefs.

Although the crew was superstitious about deadly sea monsters, Nicci simply assumed that some shark or other aquatic predator had attacked Pell and Buna in the reefs. Nevertheless, she remained alert for danger. An ominous mood surrounded the crew like a cold and suffocating mist. After several hours, the blame the three surly wishpearl divers cast on Nicci took hold like an infection among the jittery sailors, and they all looked at her with fear. She did nothing to dispel their concerns. At least they left her alone.

The *Wavewalker* sailed for three more days, and the weather worsened, like an overripe fruit slowly spoiling. Troubled, the captain emerged from his chart room to stare at the clotted gray skies and the uneasy froth-capped waves. He spoke to Nicci as if she were his confidante. "With a full chest of wishpearls harvested, this voyage has been very profitable, despite the cost in blood. Every captain knows he might lose a crewman or two, though I doubt those divers will ever sail with me again."

Nicci gave the man a pragmatic look. "You'll find others. Where are they trained? One of the coastal cities? An island?"

"Serrimundi. Wishpearl divers are revered among their people."

"I noticed the arrogance."

"It won't be easy to replace them." The captain sighed. "Those three will talk once we get back to a port city."

"Then invest your new fortune wisely," Nicci said. "Those pearls in your hold may be the last you ever harvest." The single pearl Bannon had given her was tucked away in a fold pocket of her black dress.

When the watch changed, a lookout climbed down from the high platform, and another scrambled up the ratlines to take his place. Nathan joined Nicci and the captain on the deck as the windblown, deeply tanned lookout approached. "The clouds look angry, Captain. You can smell a storm on the wind."

Captain Eli nodded. "We may have to batten down for a rough night."

"Are there more reefs to worry about ahead?" Nathan asked. "Will we run aground? It would be much harder to find Kol Adair if we're stranded out on a reef somewhere."

"Yes, I'm sure it would be quite inconvenient all around." The captain sucked on his unlit pipe and pressed a hand on his cap to keep the wind from snatching it away. "We are in open water. No reefs that I know of." The sailor nodded and went back to his duties.

When the other man was gone, Nicci lowered her voice. "You said that your charts were no longer accurate and you weren't exactly sure where we were."

Captain Eli's expression was distant. "True, but I don't think reefs appear out of nowhere."

As the blustery wind increased, the anxious crew performed only the most important chores. The potbellied cook came up with a bucket of frothy milk, fresh from the cow kept tied below. "She doesn't like the rocking of the waves," he said. "Next time the milk may be curdled when it comes out of her teats."

"Then we'll have fresh cheese." Captain Eli took a ladle of the proffered milk.

Nicci declined, but the wizard was happy to taste it. He smacked his lips after he drank. The cook offered milk to the surly wishpearl divers, but they scowled at the bucket, focusing their glares on Nicci.

"She might have poisoned it," said Rom.

Hearing this, Nicci decided to drink from the ladle after all.

As the wind whistled through the rigging and the hours dragged on, Nathan suggested that he and Bannon practice their swordplay on deck. The clang of steel rang out in a flurry as the two pranced back and forth, dodging coiled ropes and open rain barrels that had been set out to collect fresh water in anticipation of the imminent storm.

Bannon had gotten noticeably better as a swordsman. He had a reckless energy that served to counteract his gracelessness, and Sturdy lived up to its name, receiving and deflecting blow after blow from Nathan's much finer blade. For a while, the performance distracted the uneasy crewmen from their gloom.

By the time the young man and the wizard were both exhausted, the afternoon clouds were so thick with the oncoming storm that Nicci couldn't even see the sunset on the open water. Instead, she merely watched the daylight die.

"Will you show me some magic?" Bannon suggested to Nathan, climbing up on a crate that was too high to serve as a comfortable chair.

"Why would I show you magic?" Nathan asked.

"Because you're a wizard, aren't you? Wizards do magic tricks."

"Wizards *use* magic. Performing monkeys do tricks." Nathan raised his thick eyebrows. "Ask the sorceress. Maybe she'll perform a trick for you."

Bannon glanced over at Nicci, swallowed hard, then turned back. "I've already seen her magic. I know what she can do."

"You know *some* of what I can do," said Nicci.

The carrack rocked back and forth in the rough seas, rising on the swells, then dropping into the troughs. Though most of the *Wavewalker*'s crew had iron stomachs, some sailors bent over the rail and retched into the open ocean. The masts creaked and groaned; the sails rippled and flapped.

Captain Eli stood with hands on hips and his woolen jacket secured with silver buttons across his chest. "Trim the sails! The wind is getting stronger, and we don't need any torn canvas."

Above, the lookout had strapped himself to the mast to keep from being flung overboard when the ship lurched.

With an exaggerated sigh, Nathan acceded to Bannon's request for a demonstration of magic, even though the young man had not continued to pester him. "All right, watch this, my boy." The wizard knelt down, smoothed the ruffles of his fine travel shirt, and briskly rubbed his palms together as if to warm them up. "This is just a small hand light, a flame we could use to ignite a fire or illuminate our way."

"I use sulfur matches, or flint and steel," Bannon said.

"Then you have magic of your own. You don't need to see mine."

"No, I want to see it!" He leaned closer, his eyes bright. "Make fire. Show me."

Nathan cupped his hands to form a bowl. His brow wrinkled, and he stared into the air, concentrating until a glimmer of light appeared. The wisp of flame curled up and wavered, but when a gust of wind whipped across the deck, the hand fire flickered, then went out. Nathan could not sustain it.

The wizard looked completely baffled. Nicci had seen him create blazing balls of fire before with barely a glance, not to mention far more horrific wizard's fire that caused great destruction. As if incensed, he concentrated again, then scowled when only a tiny thread of fire appeared, which was again extinguished by the breezes.

"Is it supposed to be that difficult?" Bannon asked.

"I'm not feeling at all well, my boy," he said, in an obvious, awkward excuse. "Magic requires concentration, and my mind is troubled. Besides, there's too much wind for a proper demonstration."

Bannon looked disappointed. "I wasn't aware that wizards could use magic only under ideal conditions. You told me I had to be ready to fight with my sword, no matter my mood."

"What do you know of wizards?" Nathan snapped. "Your sulfur matches couldn't light a fire in a situation like this either."

Stung, Bannon conceded.

In a more apologetic voice, Nathan said, "It isn't you, my boy. My Han seems to be . . . troubled. I'm not entirely sure what to do about it."

"Your Han?"

"It is what we call the force of magic, the force of life within us, particularly within a wizard. The Han manifests differently in different people. My Han was intertwined with prophecy as well as the ability to use magic, but now that's all untangled. I'm certain I'll get it sorted out."

"Are you sure you're not just seasick?" Bannon asked, with a teasing lilt in his voice.

"Maybe that's exactly it," Nathan said.

Disturbed by what she had seen, Nicci wondered what might be bothering the wizard. Nathan had lost his gift of prophecy with the shift in the world, but his core magic should have remained unaffected. Still, a fire spell was supposed to be quite simple.

"I'm retiring to my cabin." Nathan turned away, trying to keep his dignity and balance on the rocking deck. "If I am hungry, I may go to the galley for supper when it's ready."

Nicci decided to take shelter in her own cabin as well. She didn't want to distract the superstitious sailors by staying out in the worsening weather.

Despite the sorceress's cold beauty, Sol had known that she was evil and dangerous from the moment he first saw her. His companions noticed only Nicci's shapely figure, her long blond hair, and a face even more attractive than carvings of the Sea Mother.

When stuck alone on a ship, long at sea, sailors tended to lower their standards of beauty, but there was no denying that this Death's Mistress was more beautiful than the most expensive whore in the cleanest brothel in Serrimundi. And Nicci was right here for the taking. Whenever the woman flaunted herself on deck, her black dress clung to her curves and rippled around her in the breezes, tightening against her full breasts. Sol imagined the breasts would be soft and pliable, just waiting to be squeezed. He tried to picture her nipples, wondering whether they were dark or pale pink, whether she would gasp if he pinched them.

The other two divers wanted to lay claim to her, but Sol was their leader, and he would have to be first. Their two comrades were dead, and the survivors deserved something. The sorceress owed them all a few rounds of gasping, squirming pleasure. In fact, she owed them the lives of their murdered friends, Pell and Buna. She had somehow used her magic to summon underwater monsters to kill them. Nicci had taunted the divers for days, rebuffed their attentions, insulted them—and now two of his comrades were dead. It was her fault.

Back home in Serrimundi, Sol and his fellow wishpearl divers were treated as heroes. From the time he was a young boy, his parents had taught him to dive deep, and then they had sold him to a mentor for a portion of Sol's pearl harvest over the next five years. The mentor had trained him—and such training consisted of him trying to drown young Sol over and over, tying heavy weights to his ankles, sinking him to the bottom of a deep lagoon and counting out minutes. The mentor did not pull any of the apprentice divers back into blessed air until he decided they had been down there long enough. Over a third of the trainees came up dead, their lungs filled with water, their eyes bulging, their mouths open and slack.

Sol himself had drowned once, but he had coughed up the water and come back to life. That was when he knew he *would* be a wishpearl diver. He could have any Serrimundi woman he wanted, and he usually did. His lovers all expected wishpearls as gifts, which he freely gave. Sol could always find more.

Out in the southern reefs, the supply of folded-hand shells seemed inexhaustible, but Captain Corwin paid him in more than wishpearls. It was a lucrative arrangement, giving Sol and his companions power and status whenever they returned to port.

But Pell and Buna would not be coming back home. Because of Nicci. The aloof sorceress thought that she was untouchable, that she would not be held to account for killing his friends, but the Sea Mother demanded justice, and Sol knew how to deliver it.

After he whispered his plan to Elgin and Rom, the three met on deck where the sailors had piled discarded wishpearl shells. Most had already been thrown overboard, but these last few remained, unnoticed after the disaster and the rapid escape from the reefs.

Now, the divers used their knives to pry loose the inedible and worthless meat inside, but Sol knew more about these particular shells. A gland inside the flesh of the shellfish contained a toxin—a poison potent enough to incapacitate even a sorceress.

The three men worked quickly to gather the extract, because the cook would soon be preparing supper.

Bannon had first watch in the thickening night, and he was nervous. On Chiriya he had seen many terrible storms roar across the ocean, hurricane-force winds that whipped the flat island and tore the roofs off of houses. Fishing boats in the coves had to be tied securely or dragged to safety up on the shore.

He had never been through a storm at sea, but he could smell danger in the air. Sharp bursts of breezes tried to rip the breath from his lungs. He didn't like the look of the clouds or the feel of the winds.

The off-duty sailors had gone belowdecks to play games in the lantern-lit gloom. Some men swung in their hammocks, trying to sleep as the *Wavewalker* lurched from side to side; others puked into buckets, which they emptied out the open ports.

Bannon was startled when three shapes loomed up beside him on the deck, lean men who stood shirtless even in the blowing wind and pelting droplets of cold rain. Sol, the leader of the wishpearl divers, held a pot covered with a wooden lid. "The cook is finished serving supper."

Though he was queasy from the rocking deck, Bannon's mouth watered. He hadn't eaten all day. "Is that for me?"

Rom scowled at him. "No, you'll get your own meal when your watch is over. But the cook wanted to make sure the sorceress ate."

Bannon frowned. "He's never done that before."

"We've never had a storm like this before," Elgin said. "Best for the two passengers to stay in their cabins. If the fools walk around in the rain and wind, they might fall overboard, and the captain wants to be sure they pay him a bonus when we get into port."

Bannon nodded. That made sense.

"We already delivered a meal to the wizard, but the sorceress . . ." Sol looked away, as if in shame. "She knows we've been unkind to her, insulted her." He thrust the pot into Bannon's hands. "Better if you deliver dinner personally."

Rom nodded. "Yes, it would be awkward if the three of us did it."

"Awkward," Elgin agreed.

Bannon was skeptical. He'd never seen the wishpearl divers run errands for the cook before. But most of the sailors were belowdecks, after all. And the divers rarely did any work, so he was glad to see them cooperate. Maybe the deaths of their comrades had given them a change of heart.

Besides, Bannon was glad for the opportunity to bring Nicci her dinner. "I'll take it," he said.

CHAPTER 13

As the ship rocked in the sway of the increasing storm, Nicci looked at the pot Bannon had delivered to her cabin. She lifted the wooden lid and sniffed.

"It's fish chowder," Bannon said, happy to be of service. He caught himself against the door of her cabin as the ship lurched, but his smile didn't fade. "The cook wanted to make sure you ate."

"I will eat." Nicci had not intended to venture out into the wind-lashed night to make her way to the galley. The young man was so eager, so solicitous; if she did not accept the food, she knew he would only continue to pester her. "Thank you."

"I'm on watch. I have to get back to my duties." Bannon obviously wanted to chat with her, hoping she would ask him to stay for a few more moments.

"Yes, you have to get back to your duties." Nicci took the pot in a swirl of savory, fishy aromas, and when the young man awkwardly retreated, she closed the flimsy cabin door.

Her room had plank bulkheads, a washbasin, a narrow shuttered porthole, and a tiny shelf. A hard narrow bunk with a woolen blanket served as her bed, and a small oil lamp illuminated her quarters with a flickering flame.

Sitting on the bunk, Nicci lifted the pot's lid and used a splintered wooden spoon to stir the milky broth. Chunks of fish floated amid wilted herbs, gnarled tubers, and pieces of onion. She ate. The taste was sour, flavored with unfamiliar spices.

When serving Emperor Jagang, Nicci had traveled the Old World, eaten many strange cuisines, and sampled flavors that only a starving woman could enjoy. This stew was one of those, possibly because the milk had curdled in the broth. But she needed the nourishment. This was food, nothing more.

The hull creaked and shifted as the ship felt the pressure of the waves and the building wind. Finished with her meal, she turned the key in her oil lamp to retract the wick and extinguish the flame. In her cramped cabin she had only the darkness and the sounds of a struggling ship for company.

She lay back on her narrow bunk, trying to sleep, feeling her insides churn much like the waves outside. Before long, she wrapped the blanket around herself, shivering. The shivers became more violent. Her muscles clenched, her head began to pound.

Within an hour she knew that the chowder was poisoned. Not just spoiled, but containing some deadly substance. She should have known. She should have been more wary. Others had tried to kill her before, many others.

But she found it incomprehensible that *Bannon* would poison her. No, she couldn't believe it. The simple, eager young man was not a schemer, not a traitor. She had trusted the food because *he* had delivered it.

But he could have been duped himself.

Nicci curled up, panting hard, trying to squeeze out the fire in her gut. Sweat blossomed on her skin, and her shivers became so severe they were like convulsions. Her insides roiled as if someone had plunged a barbed spear into her stomach and twirled it, twisting her intestines until she feared they might be torn out, like what remained of the wishpearl diver.

Barely able to see or think, she slid off her bunk and swayed on weak legs. Her knees nearly buckled, but she clutched the joined planks of the bulkhead. Her head spun. She retched, as if some invisible hand had reached down her throat and was trying to pull out her insides.

Slumping against the wall of her cabin, Nicci was so unsteady that she barely noticed the *Wavewalker* shuddering in the heavy seas. Her vision blurred, but the cabin was so dark she couldn't see anyway. Her muscles felt like wet rags.

Nicci needed to find help—needed to get to Nathan. She could think of no one else. Maybe the wizard would be able to purge the poison, heal any damage. But she couldn't find the door. Her entire cabin was spinning.

She retched again—this time vomiting all over the floor—but the poison had already set in. She tried to call upon enough of her own magic to strengthen herself, at least to get out of this trap, but she was too dizzy. Her thoughts spun like a wheel edged with jagged razors.

She had to get out, had to find her way onto the deck, where she hoped the fresh, cold air would revive her.

She felt along the walls of her cabin, forced herself to focus, knowing she would find the door if she just kept moving. How could she be lost in such a cramped space? She encountered the small shelf and held on to it, placing so much weight on it that the nails ripped loose from the planks and came crashing down. She collapsed, and crawled across the deck, her hand slipping in the wet pool of her vomit. When she found her bunk again, Nicci was able to pull herself to her feet. Finding the wall, she worked her way around the cabin, one agonizing step at a time.

The deck kept heaving, but she needed to find the way out. She knew it was here . . . somewhere close.

Her cabin door burst open as someone pushed it inward. Nicci reeled back and barely caught her balance as she saw three men crowded in the doorway. She knew that Bannon was on watch, Nathan was in his cabin, and the rest of the *Wavewalker*'s crew were huddled belowdecks, hiding from the storm.

Nicci was here all alone.

The three wishpearl divers faced her. Rom carried a small lamp turned down low, so they could make their way along the corridor. They were still shirtless, and the unsteady lamplight cast dark shadows that chiseled their muscles. Their loose trousers had been cinched tight around their waists—and in her distorted vision, Nicci saw that Sol was aroused, his manhood poking against the fabric like a short, hard harpoon.

She retreated a step deeper into her cabin. Her knees wobbled, and her weak helplessness made Sol burst out in laughter. The other two divers joined him in their husky chuckles. "The sorceress appears to be under the weather," said Elgin, then snickered at his own joke.

"She'll be under *me* in a minute," said Sol. He pushed his way into the cabin with the other two close behind him. "You'll be too sick to fight or use your evil magic, bitch, and after we're done with you, you'll be too sore and exhausted to move."

"Go," Nicci managed, and forced herself to add, "last chance."

"I get the first chance," said Sol. "These two can take their turns afterward."

With a careless gesture, he knocked Nicci backward onto her bunk. The muscular man stood over her, slammed her shoulders down against the wadded blanket, and fumbled with her breasts. She pushed at his hands, tried to claw them. Even though she was sick and unable to find her magic, Nicci's nails were sufficient weapons, and she ripped deep gouges in his forearm. Sol slapped her hard across the face, and her head slammed against the pallet. Nicci reeled, but the physical blow was no worse than what the poison was doing inside her.

Sol managed to yank down the front of her dress to expose her breasts. "Bring the lamp, Rom. I want to see these."

The three men leered down, laughing. Sol said, "Pink nipples, just like I thought! It's good to see for myself after dreaming about them for days." He put a paw over her left breast, crushing down, squeezing hard.

Nicci fought against the poison, delved deep into her mind, and struggled to find her strength. She had been raped before, not just by Jagang, but countless times by his soldiers when he had forced her to serve in their tents, to be a toy as punishment . . . as training. The powerful emperor had been able to force her—but these worthless men were not dream walkers. They were not emperors. They were disgusting.

Anger made Nicci's blood burn. Whatever it was, the poison was just a chemical, and her magic was more potent than that. She was a

Sister of the Dark. She possessed the abilities she had stolen from wizards she had killed. She could summon a ball of wizard's fire and incinerate all three of these men, but that might also engulf the *Wavewalker* in fire.

No, she had to fight them in a different way, a direct way. A more personal way.

Grunting, Sol fumbled with the string on his trousers, loosening the fabric at his waist. He pulled his pants loose to expose his meaty shaft.

"For all your bluster," Nicci managed to say, "I expected something larger."

Elgin and Rom cackled. Sol slapped her again, then grabbed her thighs, pushing her legs apart.

It had happened so many times before. She had been powerless. She had been forced to endure.

But Nicci didn't have to endure now. Even weak, even poisoned, she was stronger than these scum. She was better than they were. She felt flickers of fire within her hands, not much more than the little flame Nathan had summoned on the windy deck. But it was enough.

She clapped her burning hands against Sol's naked shoulders, searing his skin. He howled and lurched back. Nicci released more magic into the fire in her palms, but it flickered and weakened.

The wishpearl divers backed away in fear. "She still has her magic."

"Not enough of it," Sol growled and came back at her.

Normally, calling fire was not difficult, but she had seen Nathan struggle with his powers, too. Still, she knew even more straightforward spells. She could move the air, stir currents, create breezes. Now, she summoned air in the confined cabin, not just as wind, but as a *fist*.

The invisible blow shoved Sol away from her, and he was so startled that his erection drooped. The other two men were still stiff, bulges poking prominently against the fabric of their pants, though the arousal probably stemmed as much from the promise of violence as from the anticipation of physical pleasure.

Sol recovered himself. "Bitch, you'll lie back and—"

Nicci ignored the poison, ignored the dizziness, ignored the sickness raging through her. She called on the air again, focused it, pushed it, forming a weapon.

The storm outside blew with greater fury, and winds lashed against the *Wavewalker*. Sizzling, splattering rain came down so loud outside that no one could hear her struggles inside the cabin. But if she made these men scream loudly enough, someone would hear.

Nicci manipulated the air, shaping it like a hand . . . and then a fist. She used it to clutch the testicles between Sol's legs.

He cried out in sudden alarm.

Nicci created two more hands of air that seized the sacs of the other two wishpearl divers. They cried out, flailing their hands against the invisible grip.

"I warned you." She rose up from the pallet, not caring that her breasts were still exposed, and she glared at the three with her blue eyes. "I warned you—now choose. Do you want them torn off, or just crushed?"

His face a mask of red fury, Sol lunged toward her. Nicci manipulated the air to tighten her hold around his scrotum, and then twisted as if she were wrenching off the lid of a jar. She contracted her air fist with sudden force—but not so swiftly that she couldn't feel each of his testicles squeeze until it popped like a rotten grape. Sol let out a high wail that could not begin to express his pain.

Giving the men no chance to beg, because she had no interest in mercy, Nicci crushed the testicles of the other two, leaving them moaning, whimpering, and unable to manage much of a scream as they fell to the floor of her cabin.

"I think you would rather I killed you." Nicci pulled the front of her dress back up to cover herself. "I can always change my mind and come back." Standing straight on her wobbly legs, she glared down at the writhing men. "Even poisoned, I'm better than you."

She didn't have time to clean up the garbage, though, before the main attack struck the ship.

CHAPTER 14

The air-breathing thieves drifted overhead in their great ship, vulnerable at the boundary between the water-home and the sky. The dark hulk cut across the waves high above, aloof but not unreachable. The interface was choppy and stirred, indicating a turbulent storm on the surface. The fragile creatures up there would be fighting for their lives against the wind and rain, but down here, the water was calm and warm—peaceful. A true home.

The selka were not the ones who had declared war.

The stirring currents carried the faintest echoes from the raging storm. The selka queen could taste the difference in the delicate flavors of salt as water flowed through the fine gill slits at her neck. Though the selka were far from the reef labyrinth where they kept their precious treasure, the queen could still taste the bitter, alien taint of humans in the water.

She swam faster than a shark, stroking along with webbed hands, her beautiful smooth skin sliding through the water. Behind the queen, like a school of predator fish swimming in formation, came her selka army. Enraged, they swooped through the currents with their fin-sharp bodies and claws that could mangle a kraken. The selka queen had proven herself in undersea battle many times, gutting a hammerhead with her hands, spilling its entrails in clouds of murky blood. As a people, the selka remembered the days of great human wars from thousands of years ago . . . when their race had been created. Those were times of legend, times of enslavement.

Selka history told of how human wizards had tortured and modified unwilling subjects, turning vulnerable swimmers into lethal aquatic
weapons to fight in their wars. Back then, the selka had been terrors of
the sea, sinking entire enemy navies.

But that had been long ago, and the air-breathing wizard masters
had forgotten about the selka. Their discarded warriors—former humans,
now changed and improved—had withdrawn into the deep cold waters,
building homes in the reefs and on the seabeds. The selka were a free
people now, frolicking, mating, exploring. They had their own civilization, unknown to the air breathers, undisturbed and at peace.

Until the humans intruded, until the thieves wrecked the reef laby-
rinths, took away those things most precious to the selka, losses that
could never be recovered. All those dreams . . .

The selka had killed and devoured two of the thieves that swam
down to take the wishpearls. They had seized those divers, holding
them down. The queen knew that the weak air breathers would drown
soon enough, expended air boiling out of their exhausted lungs, but
such a quiet death was not a sufficient price for them to pay. With her
long claws the queen had torn open the throat of the first diver, watching red blood gush out in an explosion of bubbles.

The second diver had struggled to escape from the selka soldiers,
but he was weak, unable to squirm away. As her people closed in to
drink the flowing blood from the first victim's gaping neck wound, the
selka queen saw the wide-eyed terror of the second victim, watched his
last breath of air gasp out in terrified astonishment. Before the light
could dim from his eyes, she tore open his throat as well and let her
people feed.

It was a beginning—and it was not enough.

From the shape of the ship's hull overhead and the lingering taste
that its barnacled wood left in the water, the selka queen knew this was
the same vessel that had robbed the reef labyrinth several times. She
knew it would come back, and therefore they must stop it. Perhaps if
they killed the entire crew and sank the wooden ship, this one battle
would be enough. The humans might be wise enough to stay away.

Perhaps . . . perhaps not. And then it would be all-out war.

Her people were hungry for blood. Human blood had a sharper, brighter taste than fish, and tonight the selka would feed well.

She arced upward, stroking toward the vessel that hung overhead. All told, more than a hundred of her people swarmed up to the hull and grasped the slimy wood with their clawed hands. Kicking and stroking, they emerged into the hostile air and scaled the side of the ship.

As she stepped over them, Nicci ignored the three moaning, emasculated men on the floorboards wallowing in her vomit just inside her cabin. She still felt weak from the poison, but she took satisfaction from the fact that she had permanently disarmed the would-be rapists. She left them entirely behind.

The *Wavewalker* shuddered in the throes of the storm, and Nicci stumbled against the wall of the narrow corridor as she tried to make her way to Nathan's cabin. She wondered if the old wizard had heard the men's screams, but the howling storm and the lashing wind were so loud she could barely think. Her skull pounded. Suddenly, Nicci doubled over, retching onto the deck. She hoped the wizard could help her, draw out the poison and spill it into the open air.

When she reached his cabin, though, Nicci found the door ajar. He had gone out on deck into the whipping wind and the spray of waves. When she emerged outside, cold raindrops slapped her face, but the frigid shock braced her. The wind flung her hair in all directions. She sucked in a breath and shouted Nathan's name.

She saw him clinging to a ratline at the base of the mizzenmast. His long white hair hung like wet ropes down past his shoulders. He had wrapped himself in an oilskin cloak, but the storm blew so hard that he was surely drenched. His face was drawn, his expression queasy, and Nicci wondered if the wizard had been poisoned as well. More likely, Nathan was just seasick. He wore his sword at his side, as if to battle the rain.

Nicci stepped onto the wave-washed deck, as if drawing energy from the storm to drive away the lingering effects of the poison. Her black dress was soaked, but she kept her balance. She made her way along by grabbing a ratline to hold herself steady as the ship plunged into the trough of a wave and then rose up again in a sickening lurch.

When Nathan saw her, his face split in a broad grin. "You look ill, Sorceress. The storm is not to your liking?"

"Poison is not to my liking," she shouted back into the howling noise. "But I'll recover. Unfortunately, Captain Eli will have to find new wishpearl divers." She said nothing more.

Nathan gave a small nod as he drew his own conclusions. "I'm sure you took care of them as was necessary."

Whitecaps foamed over the bow, spilling like a slop bucket across the deck. Several supply barrels broke loose from their ropes, rolled down the deck, smashed into the side wall, and bounced up and overboard to be lost in the waves.

Nathan caught himself on a rope and held on, then let out a disconcerting laugh as he straightened. "A good storm and a surly crew make for a fine adventure, don't you think?"

Nicci tried to quell the pain that echoed through her skull, the knotting in her stomach. "I'm not doing this for adventure, but for Lord Rahl and his empire."

"I thought you were supposed to save the world."

"That is what the witch woman thinks." She hunched as another spasm twisted her gut. "I will let Richard save the world in his own way."

The watch lookout had lashed himself to the platform for safety, but he maintained his post to scan for rocks, reefs, or an unexpected coastline. The swaying of the ship made his high perch like the end of an inverted pendulum, and he held on for dear life.

The storm clouds knotted tighter over the night sky, like a strangler's garrote. Flashes of lightning illuminated the sea and the rigging with jagged slices of liquid silver.

When Nicci heard a familiar shout, she shielded her eyes from the rain to see a drenched Bannon descending from the yardarm on the mainmast. He carried his sword, as if he might find enemies in the sky. It was an impractical choice, but the young man took the blade wherever he went. Nathan watched his young protégé with a measure of pride and incredulity.

Halfway down the mast, Bannon stared out at the roiling sea and yelled something unintelligible. He pointed frantically.

When another large wave crashed against the ship, the *Wavewalker* tilted at an extreme angle. Water rolled across the deck, sweeping away ropes, crates, and broken debris. One young sailor was caught unawares and slipped from his anchor point on the rail. He tumbled and rolled, scrabbling with his hands until he caught a precarious perch, holding on.

Nicci tried to gather her control of the air and wind, just enough to catch the hapless sailor, to save him. Then she spotted what had struck such a look of terror on Bannon's face from his high perch.

Just as the clinging sailor lost his grip and was about to fly over the edge in the curling wash of water, a *creature* climbed over the rail and caught him, a humanlike figure with clawed, webbed hands. The panicked young sailor grabbed for anything, any hope of rescue, and the thing snagged him. The pale-skinned creature grabbed the sailor's striped shirt and seized his wet brown hair with the other hand.

For a moment it seemed as if the slimy thing had saved him—but then it opened a mouth full of sharp, triangular teeth and bit down on the side of the seaman's head, taking away half of his face and the top of his skull. As the sailor screamed and struggled, the monster tore open his throat, then cast the body onto the deck, discarding its victim in a wash of blood and seawater.

Nicci knew instinctively what they were. "Selka," she whispered. "They must be selka."

Sailors on deck shouted an alarm as a dozen more slick figures scrambled from the depths, climbing the *Wavewalker*'s hull to swarm the decks.

CHAPTER 15

The invading creatures were sleek and smooth, with muscles rippling beneath their gray-green skin. Nicci remembered Nathan's story that the selka had been human once, tortured and reshaped into a race of aquatic warriors. These things, though, looked as if they had forgotten their humanity long ago.

They opened their slit mouths wide, gasping in the rain-lashed air, to reveal rows of triangular fangs. A filmy membrane covered their large eyes, and pupil slits widened to encompass the few hardy sailors on duty. A serrated fin ran from the hairless head down the spine, and frills of swimming fins adorned their forearms and legs.

The *Wavewalker* was vulnerable, caught in the fierce storm. The sailors could barely survive the weather's fury, and now deadly sea people swarmed aboard. Shouting for help, crewmen scrambled across the deck to find harpoons and boat hooks for weapons.

Three selka skittered forward like the flash of fish in a brook. The veteran sailor Karl grabbed a harpoon and swung the wooden shaft with a grunt to defend himself, but he had inadvertently seized the harpoon whose point was eaten away by jellyfish acid, rendering the weapon little more than a club. Karl fought nevertheless. He smashed the face of one selka, flattening its smooth head. Its gill slits flapped, oozing blood.

The other two creatures were upon Karl. The big seaman punched and struggled, but one selka held him down while the second ripped open his chest, splitting the sternum and peeling his ribs apart. Together, the selka dug into the gaping wound and yanked out his slippery organs as Karl shrieked into the raging winds.

Nicci stood her ground by the door to the stern deck, still trying to drive back her disorientation as she searched for magic inside her, any kind of spell that would let her fight. The poison had debilitated her, and she had just exerted herself to defeat Sol and his vile companions. She was in no shape to attack.

Nevertheless, she clutched at shreds of power inside her, trying to summon a fireball, but the winds tore around her. A cold, wet back-wash dashed into her face, disrupting her concentration. Flinging salt water out of her eyes, she used her anger to bring focus, and fire blossomed in her right hand. Finally. She felt a rush of relief.

A male selka prowled toward her, its slitted eyes focused on her. The creature lunged just as Nicci hurled the fireball, which splattered against its slimy chest. The flames burned and bubbled its skin, and the selka hooted a strange resonant cry that echoed through flapping gill slits in its neck. Mortally wounded, the selka staggered away and collapsed on the deck.

Bannon managed to swing himself down from the ratlines, holding his sword. He looked terrified, but ready to fight. When he tried to make his way over to the wizard and the sorceress, Nathan spotted him. His voice was hard, grim. "Remember what I taught you, my boy!"

Dozens more selka swarmed over the side of the ship and fell upon the sailors. Two burly men stood side by side, jabbing and slashing with the serrated iron spear points of harpoons. They sliced open slime-covered hides, wounding three attackers—but fifteen more fell upon them. The men kept stabbing with their harpoons until clawed hands tore the weapons out of their grasp; then the selka turned the weapons upon the sailors in a feeding and killing frenzy.

Bannon tottered forward on the rocking deck, trying to keep his balance while he swung his lackluster sword against the monsters. Sturdy's edge was sharp, and he took off the arm of one attacker, then swung backward to chop the neck of another, nearly cutting off its head.

A selka rushed toward Bannon from behind, webbed hands outstretched, but Nicci summoned another fireball and hurled it at the creature's head. The flames struck home, and its flesh steamed and exploded. Shrieking, the thing dove overboard, ignoring its victim.

Bannon whirled, blinking in astonishment, and shouted an unintelligible thanks to Nicci.

As the sailors kept yelling for reinforcements, some of the off-duty crew threw open a deck hatch and emerged from below. Seeing the swarming creatures, the crew shouted to rouse the sailors in the lower decks. Rallied at last, the men grabbed whatever weapons they could find and boiled up out of the hatch to defend the ship.

But when the disoriented seamen climbed into the open storm, hissing selka converged on the hatch. The next sailor up was a tall, thin man who had been adept at patching sails. As soon as he popped his head up into the air, a selka slipped claws beneath his chin, hooked into his jawbone, and lifted him like a fish on a line. The man dangled by his head, and his arms and legs jittered spasmodically as the monsters gutted him, letting his blood spill down onto the other sailors trying to climb up. The selka discarded the body and then poured down the ladder, invading the lower decks where the crew members were trapped—and slaughtered.

Four attackers stalked forward as rain slashed down and salt water scoured the deck. Nicci stood firm, defiant, despite the roiling dizziness inside her. She felt the rage within, and reminded herself that she had been a Sister of the Dark, that she had stolen magic from many wizards. Even weakened by the poison, she was more powerful than any foe these creatures had ever seen.

The wind howled, and she pulled energy from it, reshaped it, brought the storm closer. As the selka attacked her and Nathan, she pushed back, throwing a battering ram of air. The blow knocked six creatures up over the ship's rail, high into the air, and flung them far out to sea.

Striding forward, Nathan raised both hands, trying to summon a blast of his own magic. She could tell by his stance and his intent expression that he must be calling on a powerful spell. As ten more aquatic attackers climbed aboard the *Wavewalker,* Nathan gestured to fling a magical bombardment at them—and his face filled with a perplexed expression when nothing happened. He waved his hands again to no effect, and the selka surged toward him, undeterred.

"Nathan!" Nicci shouted.

The old wizard kept trying to summon magic, but failed. He seemed too confused to be afraid.

Just in time, Bannon leaped next to him, swinging his sword to hack into the nearest selka. As that one collapsed, he stabbed a second one, offering a dark grin to the wizard. "I'll save you if you need it."

Nathan looked at his empty hand in confusion. "I'm not supposed to need it."

Nicci wondered if the wizard had also been poisoned. She trembled dizzily. Her last spell had left her spent, but Nicci could not afford to be spent—there were still too many attackers.

A blond sailor picked up an empty barrel and threw it at a selka. The creature grappled with him just as a large wave smashed into the deck, sweeping both overboard. The sailor went under, and Nicci never saw him resurface in the churning cauldron of waves.

Captain Eli burst out of his stateroom, screaming commands to his men. "Selka!" he cried, as if he had encountered them before. "Damn you, leave my ship alone!" He had brought his cutlass and a long rod that he used for clouting unruly sailors. With a weapon in each hand, he marched forward to meet the attackers.

Identifying the captain, the selka closed in on him, but he stood his ground on the wet deck. As the creatures came forward, the captain struck sideways with his long rod and slashed wildly with his sword in the other hand.

The cutlass lopped off a webbed hand at the wrist, and he hacked and clubbed, driving the selka back, but more closed in around him. His rod flattened slimy faces, broke sharp teeth, but selka hands snatched at him. Finally, one seized the club and tore it from his grasp.

Outnumbered, the captain kept fighting with his cutlass, slicing and chopping the attackers, but one of the selka took up the club he had lost and used the hard rod to strike Captain Eli's wrist, shattering his forearm. He gasped in pain, no longer able to hold his sword, and the curved blade clattered to the deck.

Unable to fight, the captain retreated into the chart room, nursing his broken arm. He barricaded the door, but the selka made short work of it, splintering the wood before flooding into the chamber. Captain Eli's screams were quickly followed by the sounds of shattered glass from the stern windows. Hurled out into the night, the man's body floundered into the roiling wake of the ship. The sea creatures dove after him to have their feast before he could drown.

As the storm surged and Nathan struggled unsuccessfully to call on his gift, Nicci used every trick she knew, summoning a tangled combination of Additive and Subtractive Magic to draw bolts of black lightning. The first blast lashed one selka through the heart, leaving a smoking crater.

Beside her, Nathan looked bleak. "The magic . . . I can't find my magic! It's gone." He raised his hand again to work a spell, curling his fingers. His azure eyes filled with fury, but with no result. "It's gone!"

Nicci had no time to understand what was wrong with him. Desperate, she managed to call up a deadly gout of wizard's fire. When the crackling ball boiled in her hand, she released it. The wizard's fire swelled like a comet in the air and engulfed four selka that had cornered a lone sailor. The sailor's screams changed, then ended abruptly along with their hissing, writhing shrieks as the deadly incineration erased them all.

But the uncontrolled wizard's fire kept sizzling across the deck, charring a stack of barrels, and setting the deck and hull boards on fire. The magical incendiary kept burning, but the pounding rain and waves eventually doused the relentless fire.

Nicci sagged, not sure how much more energy she possessed, though she needed to keep fighting, because the selka kept coming.

Three weak and wretched men staggered out of the doorway from the cabins in the stern deck. The shirtless wishpearl divers walked with agonized scissorlike steps, blinded and disoriented. Sol, Elgin, and Rom could barely move, and they certainly couldn't fight.

But the men were not entirely useless. At least they provided a moment's diversion for the attacking selka.

When two sea creatures closed around the divers, Sol's eyes were filled with pain and blood. He reached out, as if he didn't realize that the selka was not one of his shipmates. The aquatic creature wrapped a webbed hand around his throat, slamming him against the wall as it grabbed his lower abdomen with its other hand. A hooked claw dug deep into Sol's pubic bone and slowly curled upward to slice through the man's groin all the way up to the base of his throat, like the knife of a fisherman gutting his catch. Sol's entrails spilled out like wet, tangled ropes. As he collapsed, the selka passed him into the arms of another creature, who pulled him open wider, then dug pointed teeth into Sol's chest cavity and began to eat his heart.

More creatures grabbed a gibbering Elgin, who slapped uselessly with his bare hands as the monsters ripped him open as well and tossed him aside for the other creatures to devour.

The third diver, Rom, turned and tried to flee, but the selka grabbed him from behind and sliced open his back, prying loose his entire spine with a few ribs still attached. After uprooting the vertebrae from his body, the creatures dropped the jellylike bag of skin and meat to the deck.

Giving up on trying to fight with magic, Nathan tore his ornate sword from its scabbard and held it up, defying the sea people. Standing shoulder-to-shoulder with Bannon, the two men attacked the monstrous creatures. With a fixed and brutal expression, Bannon swung Sturdy like a woodcutter hacking his way through a thicket.

For his own part, the wizard embraced his new role of swordsman. He threw off his rain slicker for freedom of movement and swung his blade in a graceful arc, catching one of the monsters under the chin and cutting its throat all the way back to the neck bone. He spun with a downsweep that cleaved through the shoulder and the chest of another.

While Nicci recovered from unleashing her wizard's fire, two selka closed in on her. She summoned enough energy to shove them aside with a barricade of air, but she couldn't call sufficient force to knock them overboard. Within moments, the selka came back, angrier now, and she faced them, ready to do whatever she had to do.

A panicked sailor scrambled up the ratlines, trying to climb to escape. He reached the yardarm on the mainmast, then pulled himself to the dubious safety of the lookout platform. When the attacking selka saw him unprotected up there, they swarmed up the ropes, closing in, and the man had nowhere to run.

With a loud and startling crack, a natural bolt of lightning struck the topyard, shivering the entire mast into splinters, and throwing the sailor from the platform. His smoking body was already limp as it crashed into the water out of sight.

The blast also scattered the climbing selka. Falling, one grabbed on to the furled mainsail, pulling on the unrolled canvas and slicing the fabric with its claws. With a groan, the smoking, splintered mast toppled forward, crashing into the rigging and snapping the *Wavewalker*'s foremast as well.

When Nathan gaped in dismay at the disaster, one of the creatures sprang on him from behind, grabbing his back and tearing his fine new shirt. Bannon ran his sword sideways through the selka's ribs, skewering it. He used all of his strength to tear the dying creature from the wizard, stomped on its slimy chest, and yanked his sword back out.

"Thank you, my boy," Nathan said in disbelief.

"You taught me well," Bannon said.

Nicci dredged deep for another scrap of energy to create a second ball of wizard's fire, but she knew it wouldn't be enough.

Bannon's expression fell as he looked toward the bow. "Sweet Sea Mother, they keep coming!"

CHAPTER 16

Storm waves slid across the deck, but even that wasn't enough to wash away the blood of the slaughtered sailors. The attacking selka devoured their victims, fighting over hearts and livers, gnawing through arms and legs.

Nicci summoned another branch of blue-black lightning that lashed the selka like a cat-o'-nine tails. The stench of roasting meat and coppery blood was mixed with a powerful odor of burnt, salty slime.

After releasing her lightning, though, Nicci reeled, barely able to keep her balance as she continued to fight off nausea and the hammering pain in her head. When she staggered back to recover her strength, Nathan defended her against more oncoming creatures. Although the wizard's magic had been rendered impotent, his sword remained deadly.

Wild and reckless, Bannon stabbed and slashed, but forgot to protect his flank. A selka dove in and raked a long cut down Bannon's left thigh, although before the creature could do more damage, Nathan leaped in and decapitated the thing. The selka's face stared up as it rolled, the thick-lipped mouth reflexively opening and closing to show its pointed teeth. Nathan kicked the severed head over the side of the boat as if it were a ball in a game of Ja'La.

When Nicci sensed a change come over the attackers, she looked toward the bow as one creature more magnificent than the others climbed over the rail. The selka was obviously female, and a flush of leopardlike spots swirled along her slick greenish body. The other selka turned to regard their queen with reverence.

Even with the howling wind, crashing waves, and creaking timbers, a hush settled over the *Wavewalker*. The selka queen stood at the bow, her back turned to the carved wooden figurehead of the beautiful Sea Mother. The queen spoke in an eerie, warbling voice, as if she had not spoken words in the air—or words in the normal language of humankind—in her entire life. "Thieves must die. Your blood cannot pay for the damage you've caused."

Nathan shouted, "We have stolen nothing."

Bannon's eyes went wide, as if he suddenly understood the answer. And then Nicci knew as well. "The wishpearls," she said.

The selka queen said, "Wishpearls are the seeds of our dreams. Teardrops of our essence, our greatest treasure. The selka are no longer part of your race, no longer part of your world. We have come to take our dreams back. Our pearls."

The dead bodies of sailors on deck far outnumbered sailors who remained alive. The ship itself was nearly destroyed, its mainmast toppled, the foremast smashed, and fires smoldered in the wreckage of sails and snapped yardarms. Vicious selka swarmed below, ransacking the lower decks and the cargo hold. More screams accompanied a clash of swords and clubs, until the last sailors defending the lower decks were also killed.

Through the large open hatch, Nicci could hear the desperate lowing of the milk cow rise to a crescendo then fall silent. Before long, three selka returned to the deck, carrying large hunks of raw, bloody meat to offer their queen.

As the female creature glared at Nicci, Bannon, and Nathan crowded together in mutual defense, two burly selka climbed back to the open deck. They hefted a wooden chest that they had found behind locked doors in the cargo hold, and now they dropped it with a crash in front of the regal creature. The queen's eye slits widened as her followers tore off the lid with such force that they ripped the hinges entirely off and splintered the wooden sides.

The chest was full of wishpearls harvested only days before.

Staring down at the treasure, the inhuman queen scooped the pearls in her webbed hands and held them up as if they were the raindrops of miracles. She raised her alien face to let out a hissing cry. "The seeds of our dreams!"

The queen cast the pearls back into the water, returning them to the sea. She picked up more wishpearls and gently, lovingly, scattered them into the raging ocean, as if she were planting a crop. She continued until she had emptied the entire chest.

As if hearing an unspoken command, the selka redoubled their attack and threw themselves upon the last desperate sailors aboard the *Wavewalker*.

Bannon and Nathan crouched on either side of Nicci, holding their swords and ready to fight to the death. As the attackers came toward them, Nicci opened herself to her magic, called upon everything she had learned, and stolen, from other wizards. Even though she had little left within her, she nevertheless managed to summon more wizard's fire, a desperate act. A small blazing sphere appeared in her hands, which she augmented with normal fire, then an even brighter halo of illusion. To the selka, it appeared as if she held a sun in her hands.

The crackling globe of wizard's fire hung ready, but Nicci kept it as her last defense. Once she used it, she doubted she would have any flicker of magic left with which to attack. But Nicci didn't need magic. She had taken a knife from one of the fallen sailors, and she would keep fighting.

The selka queen strode forward to face them. The rest of her warriors snarled and gurgled. Nicci lifted her wizard's fire into the standoff. "With this, I can kill most of you, including the queen. Would you like to taste my fire?"

The female creature was terrifying and magnificent. As the sea people pressed closer, several seemed curious about Bannon, their gill slits flickering. The queen fixed her slitted eyes on the young man. "We know you," she finally said. "We saved you. Once. Why did you come back?"

"We didn't mean any harm." He blinked at her, covered with blood. Claw marks and gashes marked his skin and face, and his sword dripped with blood and slime from the selka he had killed. He said in a whisper of dismay, "I thought the selka were magical. I called on you to save me when I was younger. But now I see you're just monsters."

A flush suffused the leopard spots on the female creature, and the frills of her bodily fins extended. "*We* are the monsters?"

From below, a loud cracking sound rumbled through the deck, a sickening, destructive blow to the hull. The selka were breaking the ship. Storm lightning shattered the sky again.

The queen turned to Nicci, who refused to flinch. Her crackling ball of fire reflected off of the slick greenish skin of the creatures. Even with all the selka they had killed, more than sixty remained to face them.

All the other sailors aboard had been murdered, and even if she used her ball of wizard's fire, Nicci knew she would kill some, but not enough, of the creatures. Then she remembered.

Nicci fished in the fabric of her dress, found the hidden pocket, and withdrew the wishpearl Bannon had given her just after their departure from Tanimura. It felt cold in her fingertips. One last wishpearl, probably the last aboard the ship. *The seeds of our dreams.*

She held it up in the fingers of her free hand, and the selka queen hissed. The other creatures reacted, simmering, ready to lunge forward even with the threatening ball of magical fire Nicci held.

While the selka watched her intently, Nicci threw the wishpearl as far out to sea as she could, and the storm-churned waves quickly swallowed it. "Let the fish have my wishes," she said. "I make my own life."

The selka queen watched her with respect and finally announced, "Maybe *you* are not thieves." She turned to the remaining creatures in her army. "We are finished."

The blood-spattered selka grabbed some of the remaining human corpses and dragged them overboard into the raging sea. Others took the bodies of the slain selka with them.

At the splintered side wall of the ship, the selka queen faced Nicci for a long moment, staring at the threat of the wizard's fire, before she turned and dove overboard in a perfectly graceful arc. The rest of her people joined her, abandoning the *Wavewalker*.

They left Nicci, Bannon, and Nathan alone as the storm finished the destruction that the selka had begun.

CHAPTER 17

The *Wavewalker* had been mortally wounded. Two of her masts were broken, and the torn sails whipped about like spectral streamers. The battle with the selka had smashed the vessel's bow, torn the ropes and the rigging. The deck boards were splintered, and an even greater slaughter had taken place in the lower decks. The smell of blood and offal wafted up from the open hatches.

Nicci and her companions stood together, the only survivors on the ship, tense and waiting for some renewed attack from the undersea creatures. Unable to maintain the flow of magic, she finally let the manifested sphere of wizard's fire dissipate in her hand. She hoped they were safe from further attack, even though the selka queen had made no promises. As the fireball faded, she heaved a deep breath and clung to the tattered remnant of a ratline to keep her balance.

As the *Wavewalker* rode up on the high crest of a wave and crashed down again, they were all thrown to their knees.

"Sorry I couldn't help you during the battle, Sorceress." Nathan sounded both baffled and afraid. He looked at his hands. "I could not find the magic inside me. I tried to summon spells I've used all my life, even simple ones. I couldn't do them."

"It was the heat of the battle. You couldn't concentrate," Bannon said. "But your sword proved deadly enough. You saved me."

"Oh, more than once, I expect." Nathan forced an unlikely smile. "But you saved me as well. We made a decent accounting of ourselves." His shoulders rose and fell, and he turned to Nicci again. "Try as I might, I couldn't touch my Han." He reached up, ran his fingers gingerly along his neck. "Is there an iron collar I can't see? An invisible Rada'Han placed on me to prevent me from using my powers?"

Nicci knew full well how the Sisters in the Palace of the Prophets had controlled their gifted male students through the use of an iron collar, which blocked them from using the force of life. Nathan had worn such a collar for much of his life as a captive prophet, and Richard had been forced to wear one when he was taken for training by the Sisters.

"I'm not aware of any outside force neutralizing your gift, Wizard," Nicci said as they stood back up. "But you were losing your magic earlier, even before the selka arrived. You couldn't even summon a flame as a trick to show Bannon."

Nathan hung his head. "Dear spirits, I knew I'd lost my gift of prophecy, but now I have lost my magic as well? I don't even feel whole anymore."

Rain continued to pelt them, and the wind was so heavy the droplets felt like thick pellets of ice. Another broken yardarm splintered, cracked, and crashed to the deck after a loud gust of wind wrenched it loose. The waves smashed the prow, sending a violent shudder through the entire ship, and Nicci barely kept her feet by clinging tighter to the ropes.

"If we make it through this night, I will be happy to consider further explanations," she said.

Bannon struggled to make his way closer to them. Water ran down his face, and Nicci couldn't tell whether he was crying. "What do we do now?"

Nicci found a grim strength in her answer. "We survive. That is up to us."

The deck had begun to tilt alarmingly, and the *Wavewalker* rode much lower in the water. "We should search belowdecks," Bannon said. "There might be other survivors."

"Yes, my boy, we'd better check." Nathan gave Nicci a knowing glance. They both understood there would be no survivors.

Nicci remembered hearing the sea creatures smashing about,

battering the hull boards. "We also need to see what damage the selka did. I think they intended to wreck the ship even after they killed us all."

They climbed down through the open hatches. The confined spaces reeked of blood and entrails, a gagging stench like a butcher shop filled with chamber pots. They found the cow's head and scraps of its hide that the selka had peeled away and left like discarded drapes against the bulkheads.

The selka had left the ravaged bodies of dead sailors down in the crew decks, hammocks torn loose from the bulkheads and support beams. One young sailor hung by the back of his skull from a hammock hook.

A thundering sound of rushing water down in the cargo hold was even more ominous. When they lifted the hatches and stared down into the lower hold, Nicci managed to create a small hand light to illuminate the inky shadows. Part of the hull had been smashed and splintered from the outside, the cracked boards pressed inward. Swimming beneath the vessel, the selka must have attacked the wooden planks until they opened a jagged hole. Water roared in now, unstoppable, filling the hold.

"The *Wavewalker* is going to sink," Nathan said. "It's only a matter of hours."

"We can seal the hatches," Nicci said. "Confine the flooding to the bottom hold. That might buy us half a day."

"Can't we patch the hull?" Bannon asked. "I could hold my breath, swim down there, and do some work."

Seawater gushed in, already half filling the lower hold. Nicci understood that the force of the flow would shatter any repairs as quickly as they were put in place.

"If I had my magic," Nathan said, "I could restore the planks, grow more wood in place."

"Let me try," Nicci said. It was Additive Magic, using the wood itself, building upon what already existed. She reached into herself, but her every fiber trembled, wrung dry. She had already used so much magic in the battle, and the insidious poison still hadn't worn off.

Nevertheless, the ship was sinking, and she had no time to lose.

Nicci squeezed her eyes shut, focused her thoughts, summoned all the magic she could find. With her gift, she sensed the shattered hull planks, found the ragged edges, and used magic to draw more wood, making it grow. She pulled the smashed hole together like a scab over a wound, but the ocean continued to push its way in, and her newly formed wood broke apart, leaving her to start all over again.

Nathan grasped her shoulder as if to force strength into her, but she could draw nothing from him. Instead, she thought of her anger, thought of the murderous selka, thought of Sol, Elgin, and Rom and what they had done to her—what they had done to the entire crew of the *Wavewalker*. The repercussions went far beyond their attempted rape, because if those fools hadn't poisoned her, Nicci would have been at her peak strength as a sorceress, and the selka would never have defeated them.

In the flash of her disgust and fury she found another tiny spark, pulled more magic, and made the planks grow again, closing up, until she forcibly sealed the hole that the selka had smashed through the hull. When the water finally stopped pouring in, she shuddered. "It's fixed, but still fragile."

Bannon sighed with delight. "Now that we're not sinking anymore, we have time to find scraps of wood! I'll dive down and shore up the patch. We can make it solid."

For the next hour the young man threw himself into the task, holding his breath like a wishpearl diver and plunging down into the flooded hold. Remnants of cargo and crew floated all around: crates, heavy casks, bolts of sailcloth, and several bodies. But Bannon eventually succeeded in reinforcing the patch of magically repaired wood.

Outside, the storm continued with full force, and when they finally climbed back to the open, tilted deck, they looked in dismay at the torn rigging, the broken masts, the charred spots where wizard's fire had burned the prow.

At the stern, the chart room was a shambles. The navigator's wheel had been knocked off its pedestal. The currents and winds pushed the wreck onward, unguided. They had no captain, no charts, no way to steer. Though the night had already seemed endless, the darkness remained thick, strangled with clouds.

Standing at the bow, shielding his eyes, Bannon pointed ahead. "Look at the water there. That foamy line?" Then he yelled in alarm. "It's reefs! More reefs!"

With added fury, the storm shoved the helpless ship forward, and Nicci saw that they were being inevitably pushed toward the fanged rocks and the churning spray.

"Brace yourselves!" Nathan shouted.

Nicci tried to manipulate the wind, the waves, but the ship was an ungainly, doomed hulk. The sea had an implacable grip. The winds were ugly and capricious.

With a terrible grinding roar the ship drove up on the reefs. Dark rocks broke the keel and gouged open the lower hull. The deck boards splintered and scattered apart. The mizzenmast toppled into the water.

As the night thickened through flickers of lightning, Nicci thought she saw the dark silhouette of a distant coastline. Impossible and un-reachable, the land provided only the mocking hope of safety. But only for a moment.

Angry seawater rushed aboard as the great ship broke apart and sank.

CHAPTER 18

Having wrought sufficient havoc, the storm dissipated and fled. The scattered clouds moved on like camp followers after a victorious army. Waves rolled and washed up on the rock-studded sand.

Nicci awoke to the shrieks of gulls fighting over some prized piece of carrion. Her entire body felt battered. Her muscles and bones ached from within, and her stomach still roiled, mostly from seawater she had swallowed in her struggle to swim ashore in the wind-blasted night. She brushed gritty sand from her face and bent over to retch repeatedly, but produced no more than a thimbleful of sour-tasting bile. She rolled onto her back and looked up into the searing sky, trying to get her bearings in her spinning mind and memories.

She heard the waves rumbling and booming as they crashed against the shore, slamming into the headlands, but here on the long crescent of a sandy beach, she seemed safe. She propped herself up on an elbow to reassess her situation, one step at a time. First, her own body. She felt no broken bones, only some bruises and abrasions from being thrown overboard and hurled by waves onto the shore.

Nicci inhaled again, exhaled, forced a calm on the queasiness inside her. Her heart was beating, her blood pumping. Air filled her lungs. She was restored now and could once again touch the tapestry of magic that was a familiar part of her entire life. She had been so weak after the wishpearl divers poisoned her, and Nicci did not like to feel weak.

The flood of memories crashed in like a riptide—the storm, the selka attack, the shipwreck. . . .

She climbed to her feet and stood swaying, but steadied herself. She was alive, and she was alone.

The gulls shrieked and cawed, challenging one another. A flurry of black-and-white wings settled around several corpses washed up on the shore, broken sailors from the *Wavewalker*. Birds fought over the bodies, pecking at the flesh, squabbling over choice morsels, although there was feast enough to gorge a hundred gulls. One seized a loose eyeball and plucked it out, held it by the optic nerve, and flew away while four other birds stormed after it with accusing screams.

At first Nicci thought one of the bodies might be Bannon's, but she saw that the dead man had long blond hair. Just one of the sailors she did not know. Since these dead men were beyond her help or her interest, she turned to scan down the strand for any survivors.

The beach was strewn with wreckage deposited by the storm: splintered hull planks, smashed kegs, a spar that had been strangled by ropes and tattered sailcloth. Larger barrels lay tossed along the sand, some halfway buried by the outgoing tide, like dice tossed by giants in a capricious game of chance.

She waited motionless, like a statue, just trying to regain her mental balance. So much for their quest to find Kol Adair. She was cast on this desolate shore, with no idea where she was. She had never believed the witch woman had any secret knowledge. Nicci stood there bedraggled and bruised, lost, and she did not feel ready to save the world in any fashion, not for Richard Rahl, not for herself.

Even with the crashing waves, the whistling wind, and the shrieking gulls, Nicci felt overcome by oppressive silence. She was alone.

Then a voice called to her. "Sorceress! Nicci!"

She spun to see Bannon Farmer coming toward her. He looked waterlogged, his ginger hair clumpy and tangled, his face bruised. His left cheek had been smashed and discolored, and a long cut ran across his forehead, but his grin overshadowed those details. He bounded around a large curved section of broken hull that had piled up against a rock outcropping.

"Sweet Sea Mother! I didn't think I'd find anyone else alive." His homespun shirt was drying in the hot sun, leaving a sparkle of crusted salt on the fabric. "I woke up with sand in my mouth and no one around. I'd been caught in some tide pools about fifty feet from shore. I called out, but no one answered." The young man lifted his arm to display his lackluster sword. "I somehow kept my grip on Sturdy, though."

Nicci ran her eyes over his body, checking to make sure he hadn't been wounded more severely than he realized. On the battlefield, she had often witnessed how shock and fear could deceive a man about how hurt he really was. Bannon seemed intact and resilient.

She asked, "Have you found Nathan?"

A look of alarm crossed his face. "No, you're the first person I've seen." He squared his shoulders. "But I just started looking. I'm sure Nathan's alive, though. He is a great wizard, after all."

Nicci frowned, knowing that Nathan had been unable to use magic during the selka attack. With concern for the old wizard, she made her way down the beach, shaking off any lingering aches and dizziness. "Where did you search? Have you gone this way?"

"I came from back there." Bannon pointed. "That's where I washed up. But most of the *Wavewalker* wreckage is scattered down here. Maybe the currents brought Nathan in this direction."

The sunlight was so bright on the sand that it hurt Nicci's eyes. She squinted, shaded her brow so she could look down the coastline, which curved out into an elbow of headlands that drew fierce waves like a magnet. Whitecaps battered the rocks, and the explosive boom could be heard even a mile away. If Nathan's body had been thrown into that cauldron, he would have been smashed into a pulp.

With surprising energy Bannon ranged ahead, calling the wizard's name. Nicci half expected that they would find his smashed corpse sprawled on the sand under another busy cluster of seagulls.

Halfway to the loudest crashing waves, they saw yards of sailcloth draped like a burial shroud on the beach, amid the remnants of splintered crates. Bannon spotted a tumbled pile of barrels, rope, and more wadded canvas. Nicci caught up with the young man just as he lifted a ragged swatch of sailcloth and cried out, "Here he is!"

Bannon grasped the shoulders of Nathan's ruffled shirt. The old man lay facedown, draped over a broken barrel. His long white hair hung in tangles around his face. When she saw him there unmoving, Nicci's immediate impression was that he was dead, drowned and cast aside.

Bannon rolled him off the barrel and laid the man flat on his back on the sand. Nathan's skin was a pale gray; his eyelids didn't even flicker. Bannon bent over him, listened for a breath, touched the older man's cheeks, peeled open his eyes. With an urgent, determined look, he rolled the wizard over, wrapped his forearms around Nathan's waist from behind, and put his fists right up against the abdomen. He pulled hard with a short, sharp jerk, forcing Nathan to convulse. Bannon clenched his arms again with enough power that Nicci thought he might snap the wizard's spine. Instead, a fountain of seawater spewed from Nathan's mouth. He convulsed again and then coughed.

His hands feebly swatted at Bannon, but the young man showed surprising strength. He laid him on his back in the sand again and began pumping his long legs, pushing Nathan's knees up against his chest as hard as he could. Nathan coughed and expelled more water from the side of his mouth before finally gaining enough strength to push Bannon away.

"Enough, my boy! I've survived as much as I'm going to." He looked miserable and shook his head, then ran his fingers through his hair.

Nicci looked curiously at the young man. "He was drowned. Where did you learn that?"

"On Chiriya we knew how to rescue drowned fishermen. Often it doesn't work, but if there is still a spark of life and we can get the water out of his lungs, the Sea Mother sometimes lets a man breathe again."

"I'm not just a man," Nathan said in a rattling voice. "I'm a wizard." He bent over and vomited copious amounts of seawater.

"Clearly the Sea Mother showed you mercy," Nicci said.

As he sat up, still wobbly, Nathan put a hand to his right temple, where a long deep gash in his forehead still bled. "I'm pleased to find myself alive again. A good way to start the day." He touched the gash again and winced. He closed his eyes, obviously concentrating, and his expression fell. When he looked up at Nicci, his face was forlorn. "Alas, the gift still eludes me. Might I humbly request that you heal me, Sorceress? Remove at least one inconvenience." He gave her a sudden worried look. "Or is your power gone as well? You were having difficulty during the battle—"

"I am fine," she said. "Those were aftereffects of the wishpearl divers' poison. Fortunately, I am recovering better than those men are."

Bannon turned to her with a strange expression. "The divers poisoned you?" He wiped sand out of his reddened eye.

Nicci gauged his expression carefully. "Yes, in the pot of chowder you delivered." She could tell by the look on his face that he hadn't known, which gave her a sense of relief. "That was why I felt so weak I could barely fight the selka. I was racked by poison."

His expression turned to dismay. "In the food I brought? *I* poisoned you? I didn't know! I didn't mean to! Sweet Sea Mother, I am so sorry, I—"

In a similar circumstance, Nicci knew that Jagang would have murdered the young man, slowly and painfully, for such an error. There were times when Death's Mistress would have killed him as well, but she was different now. Richard had changed her. Seeing Bannon's abject misery, his open honesty, she was reminded again of why she had not suspected the meal he'd brought.

Nodding slowly to herself, she said, "That is why they used you, Bannon Farmer. I would never think you capable of treachery or of trying to harm me in any way."

"I'm not! I would never poison you."

"You see, your very innocence was a weapon that others turned against me. They duped you." She hardened her voice. "Don't let it happen again." As he stammered and offered far too many apologies, Nicci flexed her fingers, felt the magic, felt *strong* again. "It no longer matters. I have recovered." She laid her hand on Nathan's temple and easily summoned what she needed to knit the torn flesh of his wound.

He let out a sigh of relief. "Thank you. It was not dire, but it was an annoyance."

She turned to Bannon, looked at his battered form. "And now you."

The young man took a step away, uneasy about her magic, or maybe not convinced that she had actually forgiven him. "There's no need, Sorceress. They are but minor injuries. I will recover by myself in time." He touched the slash on his thigh.

But Nicci, needing to reassure herself that she had full control over her powers again, reached out to grasp his arm. "I insist." She let the power flow, and his bruises vanished, his cuts healed. The flicker of fear vanished from his face. "That's wonderful! I feel like I could fight the selka all over again." He gripped his sword.

"Let's hope we don't have to do that, my boy," said Nathan.

Nicci brushed sand off her black dress and tied her hair back out of her eyes. "I want you both intact. We have work to do." She looked up and down the coast. "We need to learn where we are."

CHAPTER 19

After he accepted his disheveled appearance, Nathan insisted on searching the wreckage to locate his sword, as well as any other items they might find useful for their survival. After all the misfortunes they had suffered, he had little hope of retrieving his precious weapon, but by a stroke of good luck he did find his ornate blade. The sword was wedged between a splintered wine cask and a crate that had held brightly dyed fabrics for market, which were now waterlogged and ruined.

The wizard pulled the blade free and raised it into the sunlight with a sigh of satisfaction. "That's much better!" He winked at Bannon. "Now you and I, my boy, can defend our sorceress against any attackers."

"The gulls and crabs are surely trembling in fear." Nicci rolled her eyes and got down to serious business. "Before we set off, we should salvage any supplies we can find. There's no telling how far we are from civilization, or how long it will take us to get back to the D'Haran Empire." Even after their ordeals, she continued to think of what she needed to do for Richard and his vision for the future.

Along with several other mangled corpses of *Wavewalker* sailors, they found an intact keg of drinking water, from which they drank their fill, then a crate of salted meat. Nathan was discouraged to have lost all the new shirts, vests, and cloaks he had purchased in Tanimura, but he did discover a sailor's trunk that contained a fresh shirt that fit Bannon, a tortoiseshell comb, and a packet of waterlogged letters, the ink now running and smeared. The few decipherable words indicated they were notes from a lost sweetheart who would now never get a response from her beloved.

"Take only what we can use." Nicci pulled out a long fighting knife the nameless sailor had kept in the bottom of his trunk. She fastened the sheath to her waist. The bout with the insidious poison had left her weak and incapacitated, but it had taught her a lesson. Even if she couldn't use her magic, Nicci would not let herself be unarmed. Never again.

Using scraps of sailcloth, they fashioned makeshift packs to carry the salvaged supplies. Just after the sun reached its zenith, the three set off down the expansive beach.

Around them, the headlands rose up in sheer sandy ledges dotted with tufts of pampas grass and fleshy saltweed. They worked their way up to the point, from which they paused to look out into the sparkling sea. Nicci saw no other sails, no approaching ships, not even the line of angry water that marked the reefs that had destroyed the *Wavewalker.*

"We must have been blown far south," Nicci said, scanning back the way they had come. From Captain Eli's maps, she thought they might be somewhere down on the Phantom Coast.

In such an empty land devoid of any human markings, an artificial structure stood out like a shout. Bannon spotted it first with his sharp eyesight, pointing ahead across the windswept uplands to a promontory half a mile away on which stood a monolith of rocks, obviously built by people and just as obviously placed there so it could be seen from afar.

Squinting, Nathan said, "Without any frame of reference, it's difficult to tell how large the structure is."

Nicci set off. "We have to go see. It might give us our bearings, or point the way to some nearby town or military outpost."

Above the beach, the bleak, grassy emptiness played tricks on them, and the promontory with its stone tower was much closer than it had seemed. As they approached, Bannon sounded disappointed. "It's just a pile of rocks."

"A marker. A cairn—it's to signal a waypoint," Nathan said.

The marker was a tower of neatly piled rocks, with the largest boulders around the base stacked and wedged to form a solid foundation on which a thin, tall pyramid had been erected. The apex of the cairn was only a head taller than Nathan. Thick scrub grasses grew around its base, and orange and green lichen mottled the rough black surfaces of the mounded rocks. The rocks did not look like any others in the vicinity.

"Someone went to great difficulty to build this," Nicci said. "It has obviously been here a long time."

The wizard shaded his eyes and stared out into the sparkling ocean. "It might be for passing sailors. A point to mark on their maps. Or a signal tower . . . not that we could signal them anyway." He sighed. "There isn't enough brush to build a decent bonfire."

Nicci turned to him with a thin smile. "A ball of wizard's fire hurled into the air might draw some attention."

Bannon circled the cairn, looking for any clues. He squatted down, brushing aside the lichen and moss. "Oh! Words are carved on these bottom stones," he said, revealing chiseled letters. "It's a message."

Nicci and Nathan came around to see the first stone, and Nicci froze. The incised letters read, *To Kol Adair.*

"Well." Nathan rocked back, sounding pleased. "I suppose that is the waypoint we were looking for."

Nicci's chill deepened as she saw the rough, weathered words carved into the next stone. *From there, the Wizard will behold what he needs to make himself whole again.*

The words on the third stone made her throat go dry. *And the Sorceress must save the world.*

Nathan looked at her in astonishment. He lifted his hand, flexing his fingers. "Made whole again? Do you think it means I will be able to touch my Han again? Use magic? Red knew! She *knew.*"

Nicci frowned, feeling a knot in her stomach. "Much as I hate to admit it, this lends credence to what the witch woman wrote."

Bannon was confused. "What? What is it? A prophecy?" He looked from one to the other.

"Prophecy no longer exists," Nicci said, but her insistence did not sound convincing. Maybe if this prediction was old enough, burned into the fabric of the world before all the rules themselves changed . . .

"I thought we were shipwrecked and lost," Nathan said with a tone of wonder in his voice. "Ironically, this debacle may have put us exactly where we were supposed to go."

"I prefer to choose my own direction," Nicci said, but she could not argue with the evidence of her own eyes. She did not need a prophecy to help save the world or to aid Richard Rahl in any way possible. And if she had to journey toward a mysterious place called Kol Adair, then she would do it, as would Nathan.

The wizard pursed his lips as he regarded the stones. "Only a fool tries to resist a clear prophecy. In doing so, the person usually brings about the same fate, but in a far worse fashion."

Nicci set off, leaving the cairn behind. "We go to Kol Adair, wherever it is," she said.

After the tall stone cairn dwindled in the distance, Nicci heard a loud crack and rumbling clatter in the windblown silence behind them. They all spun in time to watch the spire of piled stones shifting and collapsing. The tallest rocks crumbled from the pinnacle, the center buckled, and the whole structure collapsed into a mound of rocks. The cairn had served its purpose.

L eaving the high point, they descended the headlands, and came upon the bones of a monster. A long skeleton sprawled among the rocks and weeds just above the high-tide line. Its head was the size of a wagon, a triangular skull with daggerlike fangs and cavernous eye sockets. Its vertebrae draped along the rocks and down into the sand like a rope of bones as long as ten horses in a row. Innumerable curved ribs formed a long and broken tunnel that tapered to a point at the creature's tail.

"It's not a dragon," Nathan observed.

"Dragons are mostly extinct," Nicci said.

Bannon crossed his arms over his chest. "Sea serpent, but just a small one. We often saw them swimming past the Chiriya shore during mating season, when the kelp blooms."

Looking at the long skeleton, Nicci surmised that the creature had died out at sea, and the tides had cast its body up on shore, where gulls and other scavengers picked it clean. Only a few iron-hard scraps of meat remained on the curved bones. "If that is a small sea serpent, I'm glad the *Wavewalker* did not encounter one."

They walked along the beach until the tide came in with late afternoon. The sun lowered in a ruddy ball toward the expanse of water. The three trudged on, finding no path, no villages, no docks, nor even old campfire circles that would indicate a human presence. This land seemed wild, unsettled, unexplored.

Bannon bounded off ahead, heading toward another large cliff that blocked their way, pushing out into the sea. "Hurry, the tide is coming in, and it'll block our way. I'd rather walk along the beach than climb those cliffs."

They were sloshing in ankle-deep water by the time they rounded the point, climbing over seaweed-covered rocks. "This way," Bannon said. "Be careful of your footing."

But when they came around the corner into a cove, the young man froze in place. He reached out to catch his balance on a tall rock.

Nicci saw what had caught his attention. Another wrecked ship had been smashed like a toy high up on the rocks. Little was left beyond a few ribs, some hull planks, and the long keel. Time and weather had reduced it to skeletal remains.

Nathan paused to catch his breath. "Now, that is interesting. What sort of ship is it?"

The wreck's curved prow was adorned by a ferocious carved serpent head—a sea serpent like the bones they had seen, Nicci realized. The hull planks were rough-hewn and lapped one over the top of the other, rather than being sealed edge-to-edge as those of the more sophisticated *Wavewalker* had been. Several of the ship's intact ribs curved up, draped with moss and seaweed. The rest of the hull had fallen apart.

Nicci turned to Bannon, who looked as if he had seen an evil spirit. "Is the design familiar to you?"

Too quickly, he shook his head. Nathan pressed, "Why are you shuddering, my boy?"

"I'm just cold and tired." He cleared his throat and trudged up on the rocks. "It'll be dark soon. We should keep going and find a place to make camp."

Nicci looked around, made her decision. "This is a good enough spot. The cove is sheltered, and that wreck is above the high-tide line. It'll provide shelter."

"And ready firewood," Nathan said.

Bannon sounded uncertain. "But maybe if we kept going, we could find a village."

"Nonsense. This is much better than sleeping out in the windy headlands." Nathan picked his way closer to the ominous serpent ship. "It'll all look better with a nice roaring fire." He began to gather shattered fragments of the planks for kindling.

Nicci found a sheltered area in the curve of the ruined hull. "The sand is soft here. We can build a fire ring out of rocks."

Bannon sounded defeated. "I'll go find us dinner. There'll be crabs, shellfish, maybe some mussels in the tide pools."

He trotted off into the deepening twilight, while Nathan gathered scraps of wood and prepared a fire, but he had to rely on Nicci's magic to ignite it. Soon, they had a large crackling blaze.

After smoothing the sand for a decent cushion, the wizard situated himself on the ground. Nicci dragged up a wave-polished log to use as a makeshift seat. Nathan propped his elbows on his knees and gazed into the cheerful bonfire, looking miserable. "I do not believe I've ever felt so weary and lost, even if I know we're on our way to Kol Adair."

"We've endured a lot of hardship, Wizard. This is just more of it." She poked a stick into the flames.

"I'm lost because my magic failed us when I needed it most. I've had the gift all my life. I wasted so many centuries locked in that dreadful palace, receiving prophecies and forced to write them down so that everyone could misinterpret them." He snorted. "The Sisters had the best of intentions, but their results left much to be desired."

He shifted his position, but could not seem to find a comfortable spot to sit. "They considered me dangerous! Prophecy was integral to me, woven through my flesh and bone and blood, and when Richard sent the omen machine back to the underworld, he unraveled that part of me."

"Richard did what was necessary," Nicci said.

"No doubt about that, Sorceress, and I'm not complaining." He fumbled around in his makeshift pack to withdraw the tortoiseshell comb he had claimed from the unnamed sailor's trunk. He began to wrestle with the tangles, grimacing as his unkempt hair fought against his efforts. "The world is a better place without that damnable prophecy."

He held up his hand, concentrated, even squeezed his eyes shut, but nothing happened. "But now I'm losing the rest of my magic. I haven't been able to use my gift properly since before the storm, before the selka. I have tried, but . . . nothing. How can that be, Sorceress?"

"Are you asking if magic itself is going away, as did prophecy? I don't see the correlation. My gift functions properly." Then, as an afterthought, she added, "So long as I haven't been poisoned."

"But I was a prophet *and* a wizard." He looked at her with a flare in his azure eyes. "If the gift of prophecy unraveled within me, what if it was connected to the rest of my gift? You can't pluck one loose strand from a complex tapestry without unraveling other parts. Could it have disrupted my entire Han? Maybe by yanking out prophecy, Richard loosened other strands of interconnected magic." He pushed his hands out toward the blaze, visibly straining. "What if I can't create a light web ever again? Or manipulate water? Or make fire? Will I have to resort to doing card tricks, like a traveling charlatan? How can I be made whole again?"

"I don't have answers for you, Wizard," Nicci said.

He looked stung. "Maybe you won't be able to call me that anymore."

Interrupting them, Bannon returned with an armload of misshapen oysters and mussels, which he dumped in the sand at the edge of the fire. "There were crabs too, about the size of my hands," the young man said. "I couldn't carry them all, and the crabs tried to run away. I can go catch some later."

Nathan used a stick to push the shells into the coals, and the moisture hissed and spat as it steamed away. The mussels yawned open, gasping as they died. Bannon used a stick to fish them back out of the flames, rolling them onto the sand. "They cook quickly."

Nicci and Nathan each picked up one of the hot shellfish, juggling them in their fingertips until they could pry the shells wide enough to get at the meat inside. After they devoured the entire haul, Bannon took a flaming brand from the fire and ventured into the darkness again. Before long, he returned with crabs, which they also roasted.

Squatting down on the smooth log near Nicci, Bannon laid his sword on his lap and ran his finger gently along the blade's edge. He kept glancing around, deeply uneasy.

At last having the chance to think and plan, Nicci gazed at the skeletal remnants of the wrecked serpent ship, then looked up into the sky to view the altered constellations. "Tomorrow, we decide where to go."

Paying little attention to their discussion, Bannon tossed the empty shells against the wooden ribs of the derelict ship.

Nathan opened the leather satchel at his side, glad he still had his life book. It had mostly dried, and the blank pages suffered little enough damage. Using a lead stylus he had procured in Tanimura, he began to sketch the coastline on one of the blank pages.

"I have no cartographic instruments, but I do have a good eye." He added the rocky points, the crescent-shaped beach, the site of the tall stone cairn, and now the sheltered cove that held the wreck of the serpent ship. "It's difficult to make an accurate map if you don't know where you're starting, but I'll do my best. After all, I am the roving ambassador, and Richard will want a map when we come home again." He worked his hands, concentrated, looked down at the pages, then sighed in disappointment. "A map-making spell could do a much better job, but this will serve."

Nicci said, "At least that book provides blank paper. It is not entirely useless."

Nathan sat up straight as a thought occurred to him. He looked at Nicci and extended a finger. "The witch woman wasn't useless. She knew we had to be here. *You* had to be here."

"Yes, to save the world, to save Richard's empire. I'm sure it will all become clear enough . . . once we find someone to ask."

Bannon looked up at them. "So if we find a place called Kol Adair, you'll get your magic back? And the sorceress will save the world."

"Yes!" Nathan said, then frowned. "Possibly. Or maybe it's just a foolish, vague prediction that has no merit at all."

Nicci added, "No one can be certain of anything a witch woman says. And prophecy no longer exists."

"Do we have another choice? We're here anyway. You and I came to explore the Old World. That quest seemed pointless before, but it is more important now."

"Then we will go to Kol Adair," Nicci said as she went to stand at the edge of their firelight, "as soon as we have any idea where to find it."

CHAPTER 20

Bannon did not sleep well, despite the shelter of the cove and the familiar lullaby of the surf. Restless, he fought against swirling thoughts of all that had happened in the past few days, and fears of what might lie ahead.

Since he was awake, he volunteered to keep watch, brooding through the darkest hours of the night. He jumped at every sound in the darkness, fearing that burly, ruthless men would stride up the beach to seize him, to gag and bind him. But it was just his imagination . . . his memories.

While the beautiful sorceress slept on the sand not far from Nathan, Bannon called upon peace, reshaped the world the way he *wanted* it to be, and fashioned a contented smile for himself. The wizard looked unsettling as he lay near the waning fire, sound asleep but with his eyes open. Near dawn, though, his eyelids fluttered closed.

The young man roused his companions as morning light edged the high headlands. He was amazed at how instantly Nicci came awake without yawning or stretching. She rose to her feet, her blue eyes bright and alert, her expression clear as she absorbed her surroundings in a flash. She brushed sand off her black dress, and despite all the ordeals, didn't look at all rumpled; that in itself seemed like sorcery to Bannon.

He'd been infatuated with pretty girls on Chiriya, but Nicci was unlike any woman he had ever met. She was more beautiful and intelligent than the young island women, but it was more than that. She seemed fascinating, but also dangerous. Bannon flushed with embarrassment when she caught him staring at her—and she stared right back, but with an expression that carried little warmth.

They set off into the wilderness together. After leaving the small cove behind, Bannon let out a silent sigh of relief to be away from the wreck of the ominous Norukai ship. . . .

"The beach gets rockier farther on," Nicci said, scanning south along the shore. "We'd better travel inland."

The wizard agreed. "That is where we'd likely encounter some settlement, since we haven't seen any docks or boats on this section of the coast."

"I'll find a way for us to climb up," Bannon volunteered. Scouting ahead at his own pace, he picked a feasible route, zigzagging up the crumbling sandstone cliffs. The other two followed him, hand over foot, and together they reached the open, windy flats above the surf.

The breeze was sharp and chilly, and thin clouds scudded across the sky. The tall pampas grass and low vegetation rippled as if some invisible stampede charged across the flatland. Dark green cypress trees hunched against the constant gale, their tufted branches pointed in the direction of the prevailing winds.

Nathan and Nicci discussed their plans, but the rustling breezes snatched their words from Bannon's hearing as he scouted ahead. He was reluctant—or perhaps not brave enough—to make small talk with the beautiful sorceress. He wanted to hear where Nicci had grown up, if she'd had a perfect life, a peaceful upbringing, loving parents. Bannon didn't need to know—didn't want to know, actually. He just *made it so* in his own mind.

When Nathan startled a black-winged tern from a matted clump of grass, the old wizard bent down. "Ah, look, a nest—and better yet, three eggs." He cradled them in his palms. "This can supplement our breakfast."

Bannon came back, feeling his stomach growl. "Eggs? Are we going to make a new cook fire?" They had only been traveling for an hour.

Nicci took the eggs from Nathan's hands. "No need to stop. Let me." She wrapped her fingers around them, and Bannon saw tendrils of steam rise up. Within moments she handed him one of the eggs, and the shell was so hot that he had to juggle it in his hands. "We can eat as we walk," Nicci said. "We have a long distance to cover—even if we don't know where we're going."

Nathan finished his breakfast and tossed the crumbled eggshell to the ground. He dry-washed his hands and rubbed them on his pants.

From the outstretched headlands they could see the coastline snaking southward for miles. The hills inland were covered with dark pines and silver-leaved eucalyptus with peeling bark.

The three maintained a steady pace, and the wizard called to Bannon, "If you see any more signposts pointing the way to Kol Adair, my boy, be sure you let us know."

Bannon cheerfully agreed, then realized Nathan was just teasing him. But was it such an unlikely possibility?

He ranged ahead, foraging, and wound his way through the bent cypress trees, then explored the stands of pine and the spicy-smelling eucalyptus. Seeing no sign of human habitation, the young man wondered if they were the first human beings to set foot on this untamed land. It felt wonderful, and it felt terrifying at the same time.

Chiriya Island had been settled for countless generations. The people grew their cabbages and set out in their fishing boats, and the only excitement was the occasional trading ship that tied up in the small harbor. He had long pretended that his younger years were perfect, with every neighbor waving a hearty hello, everyone chipping in to help one another, the weather always sunny, food on the table, a fire in the hearth on even the coldest winter nights.

He had left that place . . . a place that never really existed.

He was robbed in the dark alleys of Tanimura. He fought bloodthirsty selka and saw his shipmates slaughtered, certain that he, too, would die that night. But he had survived the *Wavewalker* being shipwrecked on an unknown shore. He had left Chiriya for this, had left his father's hard fists and drunken shouts, had left the blood. And the kittens . . .

Bannon winced at the memories. He brushed aside tall, brittle blades of pampas grass, walked around a hummock, and ducked into a rustling tangle of cypress that offered shelter from the wind. Even with the fearful ordeals, this was better than Chiriya. Far better.

Exploring by himself, he entered the forest. He heard the chuckle of a creek flowing through the pines to a beautiful round pool with a smooth sandy bottom. He saw the silvery flashes of small fish darting around, evading his shadow. Bannon knelt in the weeds and flowers on the edge of the pond and scooped handfuls of the cold, clear water, drinking his fill. Fresh water!

He studied the darting fish, but they were much too small to bother with. A handful would barely make a meal, even if he could catch them. The water, though, was pure and delicious. He filled his waterskin and ducked out of the pines and eucalyptus into the brisk wind again.

Now that he had shaken his darker memories, Bannon felt light-footed as he continued to explore. Yes, he had suffered terrible hard-ships, but he would make the best of his situation. He reminded himself that he had left Chiriya intending to seek adventure—and he had found exactly that. A small, shadowed part of him acknowledged that he had fled his island in shock and denial at what had happened . . . but he drove those thoughts away again, blinking his eyes and looking at the bright world. He drew another clean breath.

"I am not running away—I am exploring!" he said aloud with enough force to convince himself. He was in an unknown land with a great wizard as his mentor, a man who taught him history and swordplay. And there was the mysterious and beautiful sorceress Nicci, who intruded more and more into his thoughts. He could not help but be attracted to her.

As he roamed the grassy headlands, he headed back toward the cliff edge to watch the white waves roll in. He wondered who Nicci was, what drove her. Did she think about him, too? Bannon pondered what he could do to make her notice him, to consider him a worthwhile traveling companion, instead of just a coincidental one.

Bannon peered over the verge and watched rooster tails of spray leap into the air. A flash of color caught his attention, wedged into the mossy sandstone just down the cliff, and he knelt to see a clump of unusual flowers growing within arm's reach. The blossoms were vibrant, the deepest and most intense violet he had ever seen, shot through with veins of crimson and a central splash of yellow stamens. They had thick fleshy stems and swordlike green leaves.

The beautiful flowers gave him an idea, a perfect idea. Beautiful flowers for a beautiful woman!

Bannon stretched out, extending his arm over the edge to reach the blossoms. He picked four of them—a bouquet. It was a small gesture, but perhaps Nicci would be grateful. Perhaps she would notice him.

He bounded back through the grasses, searching for his companions, and he was panting hard by the time he caught up with them. The breezes blew his ginger hair wildly around his head as he hurried up to Nicci.

When he extended the flowers, all his suave words were snatched from his mouth as if the wind had stolen them. He could only manage to blurt, "I found these for you."

She frowned with a glimmer of annoyance, but when she looked at the flowers, her expression filled with interest. She narrowed her blue eyes and reached out to take one of the flowers from his bouquet, leaving him with the other three. She showed extreme care as she touched the stem with just her fingertips.

Bannon waited for her to smile with delight or nod in warm appreciation. He couldn't remember whether he had ever seen her respond with a genuine smile.

"Where did you find these?" she demanded.

"Over by the cliff." He pointed. "Growing in a cranny in the rock."

"Such flowers are rare. I could have made use of them many times." She looked over at Nathan.

The wizard's eyes were wide with recognition. "Do you know what those are, Bannon Farmer?"

"Pretty flowers?"

"*Deathrise* flowers," Nicci said, studying the one in her hand.

Bannon looked at the rest of his bouquet, confused.

"Deathrise flowers," she repeated. "One of the most dangerous plants in existence. They are extremely hard to find, and valuable. Assassins would pay a king's ransom for these four. But this is far more than we could ever use." She held up the stem in her hand. "One will be more than sufficient."

"What—what do you mean?" Looking down at the violet-and-crimson flowers, he felt his skin crawl.

"Do you expect to kill an entire city, my boy?" Nathan asked. "Or maybe just a village?"

Bannon blinked, still trying to grasp what they were telling him. "You mean they're . . . poison?"

Nicci's face smoothed in a fascinated smile as she rolled the thick stem in her fingers, careful not to touch the broken end. "The deathrise flower has many uses. From the petals one can concoct an ink so lethal that any victim who reads a message written with such ink will die a painful, lingering death. Consuming even one seed causes a horrible agony that has been described as swallowing mouthfuls of glass shards, then regurgitating them, and swallowing them all over again."

Bannon's stomach twisted into a knot. "I—I didn't mean . . ."

Nicci continued, "Tinctures, extracts, and potions can be made from all parts of the deathrise flower. Emperor Jagang had his alchemists and apothecaries test the various mixtures on his prisoners of war." She raised her eyebrows. "About five thousand died in those preliminary experiments. The camps for the test subjects became known as the Places of Screaming. Emperor Jagang pitched his tent nearby so he could drift off to sleep listening to that music."

Bannon felt sick. He stood trembling, looked down at the other three deathrise flowers in his hand, afraid to move his fingers.

"Even touching the juice to your skin will cause rashes and boils to break out." Nicci looked at the single flower she had kept, obviously impressed although not in the way Bannon had wanted. "I thank you very much. One never knows when such measures might be required." She wrapped the flower carefully in a scrap of cloth and tucked it into her pack. "I am pleased with how you think."

Embarrassment—and the fear that his hands and arms were about to burst into leper's sores or swollen boils—rendered him speechless. He turned and bolted headlong into the wind, running toward the pine trees, intent on reaching the pond and the stream again. When he reached the weeds of the shore he flung the deathrise flowers as far as he could out into the water, then dropped to his knees, plunged his hands into the pond, and dug his fingers into the sand. He scrubbed and scrubbed his palms, his fingers, the backs of his hands, his wrists, all the way up his arms. He frantically tried to remember any place he had touched with the deathrise flower. He filled his cupped palms, and was about to splash water in his face, but he didn't dare go near his mouth or eyes.

Even when his hands looked clean, he plunged them into the sand again, scrubbing and scrubbing. He scoured his skin a third time and a fourth, until even his fingertips were raw, his palms pink, his knuckles sore. Finally, he stepped away, breathing hard, still afraid that the poison had gotten inside him.

He swallowed. What more could he do? He would find no antidote here . . . if an antidote even existed.

Heart pounding, pulse racing, he struggled to regain his composure. Finally, he left the pond and ran to catch up with Nicci and Nathan.

At dusk, four dwarf deer crept out of the eucalyptus forest where they had rested in the tangled shadows throughout the day. They ventured forth, their delicate hooves stepping on twigs while they worked their way along a faint game trail.

Though there were few large predators here on the coastal headlands, the deer possessed natural caution on their journey to the freshwater pond where they drank each night at sunset. The deer approached the shore, uncertain and skittish. They took several steps, then paused, their ears flickering to detect any threat, then moved forward again. One hung back as a sentinel while the other three stepped to the pond's edge.

The deer sensed something amiss. The water was smooth and clear as always, but they noticed, without comprehension, the glimmering silver shapes that drifted on the surface of the pond. Hundreds of the small fish that had darted like small mirror flashes in the last sunlight now floated belly-up like a stain on the water.

The deer struggled to understand what had changed. Frozen like statues in the forest, they waited for long minutes, but nothing approached, nothing attacked. Finally, one of the deer dipped into the water and drank. The next two joined her, drinking their fill. When it was his turn, the sentinel buck also drank, and the twilight shadows deepened around them. . . .

By the next morning numerous fish still drifted on the surface, though some of the bodies had begun to sink. On the shore, four dwarf deer also lay dead.

CHAPTER 21

They camped in the shelter of thick cypress. During the night, the maddening, mournful breezes died down, which allowed a thick fog to settle in. The cold wet swaths made the three miserable while they huddled near a small fire, adding more moist twigs in an attempt to keep the blaze going. Nicci used her magic to maintain the fire, but the flames gave out too little heat.

Nicci had never been overly concerned with her personal comfort, so long as she could function. Now that they'd been shipwrecked on the unknown coast, despite the unexpected rock cairn reaffirming their destination of Kol Adair, she could not guess how many miles they might need to walk before they found a settlement in this wild coastal wasteland.

Despite the solitude, Nicci reminded herself that this land, bleak and untamed as it was, was now part of the D'Haran Empire. Nicci was doing what she had promised Lord Rahl, and she would, in fact, walk from one end of the world to the other for him, if that proved necessary. But neither she nor Nathan could continue their quest until they actually found a village or city.

Finally, morning brightened the murk, and Nicci stopped wasting effort to keep the useless fire going. "We should get moving. That will generate heat."

Nathan used the tortoiseshell comb to untangle his long white hair. "I don't know if even running will keep us warm enough." He looked in disappointment at his moist and rumpled shirt. "I never realized how many ways I relied on my gift. A little internal magic could always keep me warm on a blustery, miserable day like this."

Nicci shouldered her makeshift pack. "We won't be any colder than we are now, and at least we'll cover distance."

Bannon squinted into the fog. "But can we see where we're going?"

"We'll see when we get there," Nicci said.

Nathan tucked away his life book in the leather pouch and fastened the flap. "I doubt I can add much detail to my map today."

They headed out. Guided by the rush and boom of the ocean off to their right, they walked far enough from the edge to stay safe. "I'm not so much worried about falling off a cliff, as I am of reaching the edge of the world," Bannon said, panting. "Then we would just fall forever."

Nathan lifted his bushy eyebrows. "You believe we'll find the actual edge of the world, my boy?"

"I've seen maps that cut off. . . ."

"If we find the edge of the world, then we will know that we've come to the boundaries of Lord Rahl's empire." Nicci did not waste time or effort worrying about such things. "Then we will turn and explore in a different direction."

"I hope we find Kol Adair before then," Nathan said.

Ever since offering her the deathrise flowers, the young man had seemed subdued. Before she rebuffed him, Nicci had noted the bright gleam in his eyes, recognizing that he was probably smitten with her—and those feelings were woefully misplaced. His imagination was already too active.

Nathan had a certain fondness for the young man. Despite the thousand-year difference in their ages, the two had much in common, since even the old wizard had a flash of naiveté about him.

The fog thinned for an hour as they continued, but the chill deepened. Bannon shivered. "Maybe we should go inland to the thicker forest, where at least the trees will shelter us."

Nicci shook her head and kept going. She walked in a straight, determined line, defeating the distance as if it were an enemy. "If we follow the coastline, we'll be more likely to discover a river outlet or a port. And we can see farther ahead, once the fog clears."

Nathan kept his eyes to the ground, preoccupied with finding berry bushes, wild onions, or bird's nests and breakfast eggs. Bannon ranged ahead like a dutiful scout.

The wind went quiet again and the fog closed in, so that Nicci didn't see the young man until he was right beside her. He looked sheepish, smiling for the first time since the debacle of offering her deathrise flowers. This time, Bannon held a handful of orange lilies on long stalks. "I found these for you, Sorceress. I hope you like them better than those poison blossoms."

Nicci regarded him coolly. "But I valued the deathrise flower. I told you in great detail about all its uses."

"These are pretty flowers, though," Bannon said, extending them toward her. "Grass lilies. They used to grow all over Chiriya. They won't last long after they've been picked, but I wanted you to have them." When Nicci did not reach out to accept them, his expression faltered. "Are they not to your liking?"

She recognized that Bannon Farmer was competent enough, and he had proven his mettle in fighting the selka. She would let him accompany her for as long as she considered him useful, or at least not a hindrance. She could imagine far worse company, but she had to nip his infatuation in the bud.

She realized that her response to his clumsy offering yesterday had not been a sufficient rebuff. She had to set him straight, or she would have to kill him sooner or later.

Nicci recalled all the times she'd been abused, forced to spend weeks with Jagang's soldiers as a plaything for their sadistic enjoyment, as well as the times when Jagang had taken her himself, sometimes beating her bloody. With her twisted experience of so-called love, she had convinced herself she was in love with Richard Rahl. Back then, she had been a Sister of the Dark, corrupted by her service to the Keeper as well as her brutal enslavement by the emperor. Her attempt to express that misguided love for Richard—forcing him to live a false life with her as man and wife—had only made Richard resent her more.

Nicci had eventually learned her lesson. She herself had killed Jagang, and now she served Richard wholeheartedly, in her own way.

She knew that she did love Richard, that he was the only man she *could* love . . . but it was a different kind of love now. He had Kahlan, and he would never be satisfied with Nicci, not in that way, no matter how much he respected and valued her. Because of her iron-hard devotion, Nicci had made up her mind to conquer the Old World for Richard Rahl—single-handedly if necessary.

She had no time or patience for a young mooncalf who thought she was pretty.

Bannon beamed when Nicci reached toward the flowers, but instead of accepting them, she wrapped her grip around his wrist. Clenching tight, she released a warning flow of magic that sent a sharp tingle into his flesh like a hailstorm of steel needles.

His hazel eyes widened, and his mouth gaped open in shock. Before the young man could say anything, Nicci spoke through gritted teeth. "I am only letting you stay with us because Nathan likes you, and because you may be useful in helping us get where we need to go. But know this"—she lowered her voice to a growl—"I am not some fawning village girl looking for a stolen kiss."

His fingers spasmed and he let the lilies fall to the ground. Nicci didn't even glance at them. She maintained her tight grip on his arm.

"I'm—I'm sorry, Sorceress!"

She had to drive the point home, so that the problem did not occur again. She didn't soften her voice at all. "We face serious problems. We are lost, and we must find out where we are in order to continue our mission. If you ever get in my way, I will skin you alive without a second thought."

He gawked at her with just the proper amount of terror and dismay, which would resolve itself into appropriate respect soon enough. She would not need to worry about this nonsense from him again.

She let go of his wrist, and Bannon flexed his hand, flapping it as if to fling away the pain. He stammered, "But—but . . . I only—"

She had no wish to be part of his starry-eyed view of the world or his nostalgia for a peaceful island home. "I've heard the stories you tell yourself. I am not part of your perfect boyhood. Do you understand me, child?" She used the last word intentionally.

His fearful expression suddenly darkened, as if she had torn the scab off a still-festering wound. "It wasn't perfect. It was never perfect." Looking ashamed, he turned away to find Nathan standing there with a concerned and compassionate look on his face.

Nicci didn't interfere as the wizard put a comforting hand on Bannon's shoulder. "Best you understand the way of things, my boy. Remember, she was called Death's Mistress."

Bannon walked away, his expression downcast. Heading off into the thickening mist, he said, "No. I will never forget that."

The fog melted around him.

CHAPTER 22

After they traveled for three more days, the headlands shifted to forested hills and fertile grasslands. Bannon nervously kept his distance from Nicci and spent even more time with the wizard. Though she spoke no more of the incident, Nicci was inwardly relieved that he had learned his lesson.

She heard Nathan telling the young man tidbits of history or ruminating about his time locked in the Palace of the Prophets. Some of the legends sounded absurd to Nicci, as did events in the wizard's own life, but Bannon had no filter to determine what might or might not be true. He lapped up each of Nathan's tales like a cat facing a bowl of cream. At least it kept the two occupied as they trudged along, which Nathan did his best to document on the rudimentary map in his life book.

On the fifth day, they came upon a path that was too wide and well traveled to be a game trail. Ahead, they saw stumps where trees had been cut down.

Bannon cried out, "That means people have been here!"

The trail soon widened into a footpath, then an actual road. Coming over a rise, they could see the hills spilling down to a neat, rounded bay into which a narrow river drained. A large village of wooden homes, shops, and warehouses had sprung up on both sides of the river. A high wooden bridge joined the two banks. Piers thrust into the water, providing docks for small boats in the bay. A point of rocky land swooped around the far end of the harbor, punctuated with a lookout tower.

The hills held terraced gardens and pastures where sheep and cattle grazed. Down by the docks, people were unloading a catch from the fishing boats. Stretched nets hung on frameworks drying in the sun. High on the beach, five overturned boats were being repaired by shipwrights.

"I was beginning to think we'd have to walk around the entire world," Nathan said.

Nicci nodded. "We'll find out where we are, and choose our next course. We can inform them of Lord Rahl's rule, and maybe someone here can tell us where to find Kol Adair."

"I assume you are anxious to save the world, Sorceress," Nathan said. "As anxious as I am to be made whole again."

Nicci's mouth formed a hard, straight line. "I will reserve judgment on just how seriously to take the witch woman's words."

Nathan frowned down at his shirt, disappointed by the now limp and ruined ruffles of the garment he had purchased in Tanimura less than two weeks earlier. "At the very least, a town that size should have a tailor who can replace my clothes. I hate to feel so . . . scruffy."

Considering how barren the lands had been in their journey from the north, Nicci wondered how often these people saw strangers. When she noticed other roads leading upriver, as well as the fishing boats and the substantial harbor, she realized that they must have contact with other settled areas—just not from the wilderness up the Phantom Coast.

On the outskirts of town, the road took them past a cemetery on the hillside, where grave markers covered the slopes. Names had been chiseled into the low stone markers, while other graves were marked only by wooden posts with names carved into the wood. These flimsier posts were arranged much too closely to mark individual burial sites. Seeing the wooden posts and stone markers, Bannon seemed very disturbed.

Nathan ran his fingers down the weathered wood, where the name was all but unreadable. "I assume the two types of markers indicate a class system? The wealthy can afford fine stone markers and a spacious grave, while those less fortunate are simply marked with a post?"

"Maybe there are no bodies at all because there were no bodies to bury," Nicci said. "Fishermen lost at sea, for instance."

Bannon looked gray. "I think they are memorials for people who are not dead, but are gone."

Nathan's brow furrowed. "Gone? What do you mean by that, my boy?"

"Maybe they were . . . taken." The young man swallowed hard.

Nicci turned to give him a hard look. "Taken by whom?"

His voice came out in a whisper. "Slavers, possibly."

The idea troubled Nicci, and she led the way at a faster, more determined pace. Slavers had no place in Lord Rahl's new rule, and Nicci looked forward to putting the matter to rest. One way or another.

When they reached the outskirts of the town, children playing in the dirt streets noticed the three travelers coming from the unexpected direction and called excitedly for their parents. Stout women worked at their washing, while two older couples sat together mending fishing nets that were stretched across wooden benches. Men and women working in the vegetable patches and farm fields looked up to see the strangers.

Nathan shook trail dust and sand from his pants and shirt, frowning at himself. "I don't make a very formidable presence as the roving ambassador for D'Hara." He tapped the sword in its scabbard at his hip. "But at least my fine blade shows me to be a man of some note."

Bannon put his hand on the leather-wrapped hilt of his own sword, but couldn't seem to think of what to say.

Nicci cautioned them both. "We won't be drawing our swords unless there's a need. We come bearing word that the Old World is now at peace. They will be glad to hear it."

A middle-aged woman with brown hair tied in a thick braid raised a hand in welcome. A ten-year-old boy at her side stared at the newcomers as if they were monsters from the sea. "They came from the north!" he said, pointing vigorously. "There's nothing up to the north."

"Welcome to Renda Bay," said the woman. "You look as if you've had a long journey."

"We were shipwrecked," Nicci said.

"We've been walking for days," Bannon interjected. "We're glad we found your village."

"Renda Bay?" Nathan said. "I'll mark it on my map."

As more people gathered, Nicci assessed the modest homes, wooden common buildings, gardens and flowerbeds. The children did not look shabby, gaunt, or desperate. Much of the activity in the town had to do with cleaning fish in large troughs at wooden tables down by the docks. Iron racks loaded with fish filets hung over smoky kelp fires. Rows of broad basins were lined along the beach under the sun, filled with seawater that would slowly evaporate to leave a residue of valuable salt.

The villagers peppered them with questions. Nathan and Bannon told disjointed parts of their story, and the noise of conversation swelled around them. Nicci interrupted, "Call a gathering, and we will address everyone at once, so we don't have to repeat ourselves."

They met the town leader, a man named Holden, who was in his late thirties, with rich brown hair marked by a distinctive frosting of white at the temples. They learned that until recently he had owned his own fishing boat before he devoted his days to local administration.

Holden led them to the town square, where many eager people had already gathered to hear the strangers' tale. Nicci let Nathan speak, because the wizard was quite comfortable with the sound of his own voice. "I am Nathan Rahl, currently the representative of Lord Richard Rahl of the D'Haran Empire, the man who defeated Emperor Jagang." He looked at them, as if expecting cheers. "You may have been wondering why you are no longer under the crushing boot heel of the Imperial Order?"

The villagers' expressions did not show terror or even awareness. Holden said, "We've heard of Jagang, but it's been three decades or more since we saw troops or any representative from the Imperial Order."

Bannon interjected, "We were on a ship that sailed south from Tanimura—the *Wavewalker* under Captain Eli Corwin—but we were attacked by selka. Hundreds of them, maybe thousands! They killed our crew, and our ship ran aground on the reefs. Only the three of us survived. You're the first people we've seen since."

Many listeners stared at them in horror and fascination, while others frowned with clear skepticism, as if they expected castaways to embellish their stories.

Nicci interrupted, "The important news we bring you is that Lord Rahl has overthrown the evil tyrants, and that you are all free. You need not fear oppression, slavery, or tyranny. As he consolidates his empire, Lord Rahl is gathering emissaries so that all may decide a common set of laws to which everyone must agree. This will be a golden age for human history." She crossed her arms over her chest. "And you are part of it."

Nathan brightened as he looked out at the villagers. "You must have maps. You must know the area. Choose several of your best people to travel north, make your way up to the New World, the heart of D'Hara and the People's Palace, so you can join Lord Rahl. He'll provide the protection and support your village needs. Now is a very important time for the building of the new empire."

Holden had a habit of nodding sincerely, demonstrating that he listened to people when they expressed their concerns, but he didn't appear convinced. "That is heartening news, and I am proud to hear what your Lord Rahl has accomplished." He gestured to the gathered audience. "Our people here trade with villages upriver and larger cities to the south, but we have barely heard of D'Hara or Tanimura. It's grand for you to say that we are free of tyranny and slavery . . . but has everyone who would threaten us also heard this news?"

"They will," Nicci said.

He spread his hands, sounding perfectly reasonable. "Your Lord Rahl is too far away to have any real effect in our lives. How could any D'Haran help us from the other side of the world? We are on our own here . . . against whatever might prey on us."

"He will be able to protect you," Nicci said. She knew well enough not to underestimate Richard.

Holden gave them a conciliatory smile and did not argue further. "Still, it is good to know, and you are welcome in Renda Bay. We will help you as we can, since you seem to have lost everything."

"We could use a good meal," Nathan said. "And new clothes." He pulled up his frayed sleeve. "Do you have a tailor? I require several new outfits."

"We would also appreciate supplies and provisions," Nicci said, "before we continue our journey. We are looking for a place called Kol Adair."

The people didn't immediately show any sign of recognition, but they offered to help in any way possible. As conversation buzzed in the square, Holden declared, "We'll have a welcoming dinner tonight. Because of the season, our boats just brought in a fine catch of redfins. We can roast enough for a banquet."

Nathan smiled. "We appreciate your hospitality, and we would dearly enjoy a good meal. Now, from whom might I request a new shirt?"

That night, the villagers set up long plank tables in an open festival area just above the docks in the harbor. A warm, cheery glow came from the windows of the village dwellings, and tall torches surrounded the gathering. Candle pots flickered along the wooden bridge that crossed the narrow river.

As dusk descended, people came for the welcome feast. Fat redfin fish, seasoned with sea salt and pungent herbs, roasted over coals in fire pits. The meal was accompanied with tubers boiled in large cauldrons, and a salad made of bitter flowers.

Nicci found the redfin to be a dark, meaty fish with a strong flavor. Bannon had a second helping as he talked with his companions at the long table. To their great fascination, he described the many dishes that could be made with cabbage.

Nathan had obtained a new shirt, a gray homespun tunic that laced up the front. The old wizard found the color unflattering, but he agreed that it was far superior to the remnants of his once fine clothes. "Thank you so much, my dear Jann," he said to a short, dark-haired woman with plain features but pretty eyes. She was one of the town's seamstresses who spun her own cloth and made garments for her family and others.

"My last tailors in Tanimura had numerous patterns and styles to choose from, countless grades of fabric, endless cuts." Nathan heaved a sigh. "But they weren't nearly as pretty or as kind as you."

Jann giggled. "You should thank my husband. That shirt was supposed to be for Phillip." A broad-shouldered older man sat next to her. Nearly as tall as Nathan, he had tightly curled dark hair and a rugged face. When Nathan asked him about the scar across his nose, he explained that a fishhook had once cut him down to the cartilage when a line had snapped.

"I have plenty of shirts, and you obviously need that one more than I," said Phillip. "And now I can boast that the ambassador for Lord Rahl wears clothes made by my wife." His big callused hand clasped Jann's much more delicate hand. He savored another bite of redfin. "It's good to feast on fish I didn't have to bring in myself. Those days are over for me."

Jann explained, "Phillip is a successful fisherman, but he prefers to be a boat builder. We've just set up a new dry dock, and he'll be repairing fishing vessels and building a new one to sell."

Phillip smiled proudly. "A new one that I plan to name the *Lady Jann.*"

"That is sure to increase the asking price," said Nathan.

Town leader Holden stood up in the middle of the meal, and the dinner chatter died down. "We welcome our visitors from far-off lands. We give what we can and hope that the Sea Mother remembers our kindness to strangers."

While the villagers cheered and toasted, Nicci heard some of the villagers muttering, as if they thought the Sea Mother had let them down many times in the past. She realized that Renda Bay had no armed guards, no strong military presence, no defenses whatsoever. Nicci knew that if one relied on ethereal deities to solve problems, then those problems usually remained unsolved.

Suddenly, several villagers stood up from the plank tables, gesturing toward the dark harbor. A bright warning fire sprang from the watchtower on the southern point of the breakwater. Someone threw a torch into a pile of dry wood, which swelled into a blazing beacon. When Holden saw the fire, his face fell into an expression of dread.

Looking out into the harbor, Nicci could see the ominous silhouettes of four large, dark ships that closed in on the bay with unnatural speed.

Holden looked at Nicci with a sick expression. "Where is your Lord Rahl's protection now?"

Nicci straightened. "I'm here."

CHAPTER 23

Villagers bolted in panic from the outside festival area. Some ran to their homes to seize knives, clubs, bows, and anything else they could use as a weapon. Nathan and Bannon both drew their swords and stood together next to the plank feasting tables, although the young man's expression was far different from what Nicci had seen on his face when he fought the selka. This time, he looked disgusted as well as terrified.

The massive dark ships slid forward swiftly even though the night was without breezes. Each vessel had one mast with a single broad sail dyed a deep blue, so as to be invisible at night.

Nicci heard splashing sounds and the gruff shouts of men. Peering intensely into the night, she enhanced her vision with an obscure distance spell, which let her see that the four invading ships were propelled by long lines of oars. The oars cut into the water like axe blades and swept back to push the vessel forward, then lifted into the air dripping moonlight, and stabbed the water again.

Bannon's voice cracked. "Norukai slavers!"

"Norukai slavers," Holden echoed, then added his own shout. "Prepare to defend yourselves! It's another raid."

"What is it, my boy?" Nathan asked. "Who are they?"

"Nightmares."

The slaver ships came in fast, crushing a small fishing boat as they ground up against the Renda Bay piers. A chorus of guttural, challenging shouts came from the longboats. With a chill, Nicci saw that each of the four curved prows sported the monstrous carving of a sea serpent, and she recognized the design from the crumbling wreck they had found in the sheltered cove on their first night ashore.

The four raider ships careened like rampaging bulls into the harbor. Bright orange streaks soared into the sky from the longboat decks, arced downward, and scattered upon the village, striking streets, rooftops, and unfortunate townspeople. Several fire arrows stuck into the lapped roofs of the houses and set the buildings on fire.

Water crews raced with buckets to stop the conflagration from spreading, while the rest of the defenders converged toward the docks, carrying whatever weapons they had. But even at a glance, Nicci could see that the villagers could never drive off such an aggressive raid. By her guess, the four Norukai ships held nearly three hundred warriors. She turned to Nathan. "It is up to us to fight them."

He raised his sword. "My thoughts exactly, Sorceress."

Releasing magic, Nicci ignited a bright fireball in her hand and tossed it into the air, where it expanded, growing more diffuse until it exploded high overhead like a wash of chain lightning. The glow illuminated the big serpent ships and the raiders boiling off the decks. The nearest two vessels crashed against the piers and fastened with iron hooks and heavy planks, while the raiders from the outer two vessels dropped smaller boats into the water and rowed toward the shore.

Jann and her husband Phillip accompanied Nathan as they braced themselves for the attack. Jann cried, "Spirits save us!"

"*I* will save you," Nicci said.

The wizard turned to the retired fisherman. "Are your people at war with the Norukai? Why do they attack Renda Bay?"

"We are prey to them," said Phillip, his face haggard. "Normally, they dart in with a single boat, snatch five to ten victims, and flee into the night. But this . . . this is a full invasion."

"Then we arrived just in time," Nicci said.

Norukai warriors thundered across the docks, rushing to the village, while others jumped out of landing boats and sloshed up from the shallow water to shore, carrying clubs, ropes, and nets.

The sorcerous illumination dissipated overhead, but Nicci's magic swelled. She stretched her mind in one direction, tapping into Additive Magic and the energy there, while she also drew upon Subtractive Magic. Combining both, she conjured jagged lashes of black lightning, which she whipped against the first three invaders who reached the end of the docks. Her lightning ripped their broad chests into smoking wreckage, and the burly men collapsed into a heap of bones.

Despite this unexpected attack, the slavers showed no hint of fear or even caution. They charged forward, sneering at her lightning, arrogant in their invincibility. A team of four left their landing boats and waded to the beach.

Nicci killed the next wave of them as well.

The Norukai were squat men with disproportionately broad shoulders, shaved heads, and bare arms, and they wore vests of scaled armor made of some reptile skin. Most horrific, their cheeks had been slit from the corners of their lips back to the hinge of the jaw, then sewn up again, as if to widen their mouths like a snake's. Now, as they roared their fearsome battle call, their jaws opened wide, as if they were vipers about to strike. Only a few Norukai carried swords or spears, while the rest obviously expected to subdue and capture their victims, not to kill. They meant to harvest the people of Renda Bay.

A second rain of flaming arrows launched from the deck of a Norukai ship, pelting the village. By now several healthy fires were spreading among the wooden buildings, and when Nicci saw a blaze jump from one rooftop to the next, she flung out her hand and summoned her control of air and wind. Her directed blast swept the flames away, and as she pulled it back, she sucked away all the oxygen and extinguished the fire.

Nathan looked at her and groaned. "I can no longer help you in that way," he said, gripping his sword. "But I will do my part, even without magic." He ran beside Bannon, both of them holding their blades high as the muscular slavers charged ashore. As he prepared to fight, the young man had a strange look in his eyes—though not of fear. He seemed obsessed.

The villagers of Renda Bay had their own swords and spears, but did not seem skilled in their use. Holden shouted orders and ran bravely to meet the surge of attackers, although he had no tactical plan.

Nicci watched the fourth raider ship grind up against another dock, splintering wood as the invaders shouted. She did not intend to let them make it to shore. No longer crippled by poison, her command of magic was at its peak strength, and she could do more than summon wind or lightning.

She called forth a large roiling ball of wizard's fire, a molten sphere that she hurled at the prow of the ship just as the Norukai lashed up against the damaged pier. The magical blaze incinerated the carved serpent figurehead and billowed back over the bow. Flames spilled across the deck and ignited fifteen of the armored slavers. They shrieked as the skin boiled off their bones, and their ugly, slitted mouths yawned open in a scream so wide their jaws cracked.

Wizard's fire could not be easily extinguished, and it burned the ship's deck boards, set the tall mast on fire, and ignited the midnight-blue sail, which roared up in flickering orange curtains. When she had used weaker balls of wizard's fire during the selka attack on the *Wavewalker,* the storm and the washing waves had mitigated the fire, but here at the Renda Bay docks, the magical flames burrowed through the raider deck and ate through the hull.

Many Norukai leaped overboard, some with skin on fire. The ship went up like a blazing beacon. The death wails of the burning enemy satisfied Nicci. Although she had changed since then, those screams reminded her of when she had burned Commander Kardeef alive, roasting him on a spit in front of the people of a newly conquered village, just to prove how ruthless she could be.

By now, hundreds of Norukai had made their way into town. Raising their clubs and nets, they met the villagers who fought back with any weapon at hand. The hideous warriors showed no fear, and they were far more skilled with their cudgels and nets than the villagers were with their seldom-used weapons.

The slavers threw weighted nets on a group of three men who harried them with pikes and swords. Entangled, the men stumbled and thrashed, trying to throw off the strands, but the Norukai swarmed over them and clubbed them until they were stunned. It seemed to be a well-coordinated operation. Once the three men were beaten senseless, the Norukai bound and trussed them like wild animals. They picked up the fresh captives, one at each man's feet, one at each man's arms, and hauled them back aboard the nearest raiding ship.

Flaming arrows continued to soar through the air like shooting stars. Nicci tried to extinguish them one by one before they could fall upon new fuel, and she struggled to take care of other fires as well, but she could not keep up. There were hundreds of flashpoints. The Norukai seemed intent on destroying the whole town, strictly to cause chaos so they could snatch more victims. The slavers moved like professional hunters rather than a well-ordered army, ranging free and looking for targets. They swarmed into the town.

Nathan told himself that a blade could be as deadly as an attack of magic, so long as it was wielded by a skilled swordsman. His new shirt was loose, comfortable, and clean . . . for the moment. He charged into the front ranks of the burly Norukai, sweeping his sword sideways.

Beside him, Jann and Phillip recklessly joined the fray. Phillip carried a long hooked pike that he had used as a fisherman. He threw it like a harpoon and skewered one of the slavers through the sternum. Even though the hideously scarred man was dead with his heart punctured, he clawed at the shaft before he fell still.

Though she was small, Phillip's wife was nimble. Jann darted among the attackers with a long butcher knife, hacking at the arms of one slaver, slicing open the side of another. Blood ran down his exposed ribs.

Nathan swung his sword with both hands, using all his strength, and his blade went right across the wide-open mouth of one of the grotesque Norukai, slicing off the top of his head. Next to him, Bannon became a whirlwind, not even watching where he hacked and cleaved. Even the slavers backed away from the young man's mad, uncontrolled attack.

But the Norukai were not deterred for long. They let out a hissing growl as if it were a strange war cry, and a new group of invaders pushed forward, carrying long spears. Each weapon was tipped with the ivory tusk of some unknown animal, carved into serrated edges. As the front ranks of slavers swept in, holding thick clubs, the spear throwers took their stances and identified the centers of resistance.

Town leader Holden stood on top of one of the plank tables in the festival square and shouted to rally his people. "Stand up to them! Do not let them take our wives and children! Don't let—"

One of the spear throwers cocked back his arm and flung the shaft with a mighty heave. The weapon whistled through the air and buried itself in Holden's abdomen. The blood-smeared tusk sprouted from his back.

At the front lines, Nathan slashed with his sword, first to the left and then to the right, chopping off arms and stabbing through rib cages. He looked up just in time to see a spear hurtling toward him. He felt a ripple inside, a twinge that he thought might be a spark of magic. He reached into himself, trying to grasp it to deflect the spear. A simple, instinctive spell. Time seemed to move so slowly . . . but the flicker of magic vanished, snuffed out. The magic abandoned him again, and he was helpless.

Bannon grabbed his arm and yanked him sideways, and the spear whistled past. "Watch yourself, Nathan. I need you alive to help me kill more of these animals."

The vitriol in his voice shocked Nathan. Something seemed to have been triggered inside him. The young man's eyes were wild, his lips drawn back, and his normally cheerful smile had now become a death's-head grimace. Blood flecks were more prominent than the freckles on his face.

Bannon leaped forward, paying no attention to the clubs and nets and blades of the slavers. His ginger hair flew wild, and he howled wordlessly as he hacked through the neck of one squat man, then cleaved the shoulder of another. "Animals!" he shrieked.

A vicious slash from Sturdy opened the guts of another attacker, who sneered down at his snakelike entrails and reached out to grab Bannon's sword hand. But the young man tore himself away and spun to chop off the slaver's arm, and in an unthinking malicious retaliation, he cut off the other arm, so that both stumps spouted blood onto the man's exposed entrails.

"You'll get yourself killed, my boy," Nathan cautioned. He ran after Bannon, trying to keep up as the Norukai closed in on this unexpectedly wild attacker.

One of the enemy spear throwers hurled his weapon at the young man, but Nathan swept his sword just in time to strike the wooden shaft with a loud clack, knocking it aside. The ivory-tipped spear flew at an angle, ricocheted, and buried itself between the shoulder blades of another advancing Norukai.

Closing around the seamstress Jann, the slavers threw a net over her. She tugged at the strands, driven to the ground. She used her bloody knife to cut herself free, peeling the net away, but two muscular Norukai stooped over her and raised their clubs to beat her senseless.

Nathan came up behind them and stabbed one slaver in the back. When his partner turned to glare at Nathan, Jann freed her arm and plunged the butcher knife deep into the slaver's calf. Roaring, he reached down to grab at the knife, and Nathan sliced off his head with one clean blow. The old wizard quickly pulled away the remaining strands of the net, freeing Jann. The small woman crawled out, exhausted and shaking.

Her husband strode up, covered with blood and filled with gratitude. "You saved her. Thank you, Wizard," Phillip said. He reached out for his wife—just as one of the falling fire arrows struck him in the back of the neck. The steel arrow point, still covered with gobs of flaming pitch, sprouted from the hollow of his throat. Phillip reached up and grasped the arrow as if annoyed that it had distracted him from his reunion. Jann screamed, and Phillip turned to her, his eyes wet and longing, then collapsed, dead.

Bannon howled at the sky, slashing with his sword at the falling rain of fire arrows. He threw himself upon two more Norukai with such fury that they staggered back, and Nathan was forced to help him, leaving Jann to sob over her fallen husband.

* * *

Blazes had begun to spread through the town. Nicci extinguished as many fires as she could, but that was a losing battle for now. She realized that if she could not drive away these attackers, it wouldn't matter if Renda Bay burned.

The villagers made a good accounting of themselves, though by now at least thirty had been beaten into unconsciousness, trussed, and dragged to the first raider ship. Dozens of Norukai swarmed back aboard, stomping on the decks. Loud drumbeats rumbled through the hold, and the oars lifted and lowered as the galley slaves were forced to back the ship away from the dock.

Nicci summoned more black lightning and brought it down, killing six Norukai who thought themselves safe aboard the retreating ship. She didn't think she could stop the vessel from escaping, so instead she devoted her efforts to the remaining raiders on the shore.

Well over a hundred slavers still attacked. They had seen Nicci and her powers, and a few seemed to have decided that the beautiful, powerful sorceress would be a worthy slave. They were fools.

One monster-jawed slaver swung a mace tipped with a ball and chain, while two others held up their nets, closing in on Nicci from either side. They must have thought she would be an easy target.

She didn't have time for this. She stretched out her hand, pointing from one slaver to the next, and the third, in quick succession, stopping their hearts cold. They fell dead in a tangle of their own nets.

She panted, catching her breath, flexing her fingers. She had enough strength to summon another blast of wizard's fire. She could ignite the retreating slaver ship, but that would kill everyone aboard, including the new captives. Would they prefer that fate? That was not for her to decide. No, she would fight the Norukai here.

Nicci called up wizard's fire and, instead of concentrating it in a ball, flung a fan of deadly magical flames at the line of advancing slavers, spattering at least thirty of them. The relentless inferno did not sputter out. Even a glob of wizard's fire no larger than her thumbnail would burn and keep burning until it burrowed its way through its victim.

Writhing and screaming, the Norukai fell like trees in a forest blaze. Even though she felt depleted from expending so much magic, Nicci called normal fire and sent it through the air until it struck the sails and masts of two more ships, setting the dyed fabric on fire. Soon, the raider vessels were engulfed in flame.

Nathan and Bannon had each killed fifteen or twenty slavers themselves. They continued to attack with their swords, as did hundreds of shouting, angry villagers. The Norukai spear throwers hurled the last of their shafts into the crowd, indiscriminately choosing targets.

With the last of her strength, Nicci sent out a wall of wind, a solid battering ram of air that knocked the burly Norukai backward. With the angry armed villagers storming toward them, the slavers at last retreated.

As the Norukai frantically tried to extinguish the burning sails on their ruined ships, the attackers piled onto the last vessel with shouts and curses. Accompanied by threatening drumbeats, the slaves at the oars began to push the serpent craft back, tearing the ships free of the piers, leaving wreckage behind.

Nicci took out her knife and saw she had more work to do. She didn't need magic to kill the stragglers left behind when their raiding ships retreated. She and the villagers still had a long night ahead of them.

CHAPTER 24

Even as the Norukai ships limped away into the night, the pain and terror of their raid lingered in Renda Bay. The villagers pulled together to put out the fires, tend to the wounded, and count the dead—and missing.

Nathan looked down at his gore-spattered sword. His new homespun shirt—which Jann had made for her husband—was now torn and soaked with blood. The wizard found himself staring at the fabric, picking at the sticky, crusty mess. Magic was so much *cleaner* than this! When he realized he was focusing on such a trivial thing, he knew he was feeling the effects of shock.

He checked over his hands and arms, ran fingers across his scalp to see if he had been injured without realizing it. In the heat of battle a fighter could suffer grievous wounds and never notice until he dropped dead from blood loss. Thankfully, Nathan found only minor cuts, scratches, and a bump behind his right ear. He didn't even remember being struck there.

"I appear to be intact enough," he muttered to himself. He looked around at the flurry of people, some standing stunned and helpless while others ran about frantically trying to help. He realized with an ache in his heart that, even though he had briefly felt a twinge of his gift during the heat of the battle, he had no magic now and was unable to heal even his small wounds.

Bannon Farmer looked lost and drained, like a rag wrung out and left to dry. He was covered with blood, clumps of uprooted hair, gray smears of brain tissue, even bone fragments caught in the material of his shirt. During the battle, he had fought as if possessed by a war spirit; Nathan had never seen anything like it. Now, though, Bannon just looked like a broken boy.

But Nathan had to worry more about the injured and the dying. Without powerfully gifted healers, the people of Renda Bay needed to tend their wounded by traditional means. They had only a few trained doctors to care for maladies or injuries, such as when the fishhook had cut poor Phillip's nose and left a long scar.

Nathan swallowed hard, remembering the man. Jann knelt next to her husband's body sprawled on the ground in the festival square, the extinguished fire arrow still protruding through his throat. He had died with a look of surprise on his face; at least the man had suffered no pain. Jann wept, her head bowed, her shoulders hitching up and down.

Moving from person to person, Nathan helped the healers bandage knife wounds and wrap cloth around cracked skulls. The victims moaned or cried out in pain as doctors used needle and thread to bind the worst gashes. When the night breeze blew in his face, the smell of blood and smoke overpowered the salty iodine smell of the bay. So much damage . . .

Fortunately, Nicci had unleashed her full powers, and Nathan knew how formidable the sorceress was. But he was a formidable wizard himself—or at least he had been. If he had possessed his gift tonight, if he could have woven spells just as destructive as Nicci's, most of these casualties wouldn't exist. The raiders would have been driven back before they could set foot ashore. These villagers who lay wounded and dead would still be alive, tending crops, fixing nets, or setting sail into the bay for the next day's catch.

He had failed. Magic had failed him—and in his own turn, he had failed the people of Renda Bay. Nathan Rahl had failed *himself.*

If only he could have thrown wizard's fire at the Norukai vessels, incinerated the sails, kept the raiders from disembarking! He could have used a binding spell to stop them from advancing, or even unleashed a sleep web to fell them all like stalks of harvested wheat, and then the people of Renda Bay could have tied up the slavers, seized their ships, freed the captives chained to the oars below like animals in pens. . . .

Nathan clenched his fists, gritted his teeth, and shouted, "I am a wizard!" Even if prophecy was gone from the world, he could not lose everything. He refused to believe that with the unraveling of prophecy, his other skills had disappeared as well, no matter what the witch woman had cryptically predicted. No, he did still have magic. He knew it. It was part of him. He was gifted!

As anger swirled within him, Nathan felt an unexpected sizzle along his forearms, tracking back into his chest, as if some arcane lightning had shot through his bloodstream. Yes, he knew that spark!

The magic might have gone dormant inside him, but Nathan dredged it out, pulled it kicking and struggling like one of these captives being hauled to a slaver ship. "I am a wizard, and I am in control of my magic!" he said to himself. He could use it to help these people now.

He saw two matronly healers beside a man who made low gurgling sounds. Still feeling the rejuvenating tingle inside his fingers, inside his body, Nathan hurried over to them. He could help.

The victim lay on his back with a broken Norukai spear shaft through his chest. Although the jagged ivory point had missed his heart, it had ripped through his lung. Blood streamed out of his blue lips, and he kept coughing. He spasmed, and the two distraught tenders could do nothing for him.

When Nathan approached, the women shook their heads. The victim's face contorted with silent pain. His eyes were round and glassy. He coughed again, and a pink foam of blood covered his lips.

"We can only wait for the Sea Mother to take him," said one of the women. Her face was streaked with blood and tears.

Nathan looked down at the broken shaft of wood, which kept the dying man propped upright. "We must remove the spear," he said.

The other woman shook her head. "If you do that, he will die. Let the man have peace and dignity."

"And if you leave the spear *in,* he will die." His azure eyes became steely. "There might be a chance. He is beyond your skills, but I have magic—let me try." The two women stared at Nathan, and he encouraged them to leave. "You go tend to someone you might save."

They nodded, gently touched the dying man, and hurried off to the other injured townspeople.

When the pair of healers had gone, Nathan grasped the slick, bloody spear. As gently as he could, though there was no gentle way to deal with such an insult to the man's body, he pulled the wooden shaft out. The man let out a gasping scream. Fresh blood gushed from his mouth, and a bright flow ran out of the ragged hole in his chest. As the man writhed, the wound in his lung made a loud sucking, gasping sound. He would be dead in minutes.

Nathan summoned the magic within him, grasped for the tingle, the touch of his Han, and increased it to a surge, a flow of energy. Additive Magic. He had done this many times before—so many times. It was child's play for one with the gift, and he knew he could control it.

He pressed his hands against the open wound, pushed his palms down on the streaming blood. He could feel the healing force, and he let the magic flow through him. With his restored gift, he sought out the ripped blood vessels, the torn tissue inside the lung, the brutal hole the spear shaft had tunneled through his chest and back. He could reattach strands of muscle fibers, cement the splintered fragments of bone. He would fix this! He would knit it all together, make this man whole again . . . *whole*, as the witch woman Red had said Nathan needed to be. Whole again! The gift wasn't gone from him. The magic was still his to control, even if he hadn't yet found Kol Adair.

Nathan gritted his teeth and concentrated harder, *forced* this man to heal. The magic writhed like a serpent trying to escape, but Nathan made his demands. He could heal. He was in control. He was strong again!

But in a malicious twist, the healing magic fought back, recoiled, and did exactly the opposite of what he wanted. Instead of sealing the bleeding wound, the magic ricocheted and rebounded, becoming a monster that destroyed rather than repaired.

Magic flowed out of Nathan as he pressed down with his hands to stop the blood. The vengeful backlash erupted—ripping the spear wound into a huge gash, splintering the man's ribs, and turning him inside out. His heart and lungs spilled out in a horrific explosion of blood and tissue. The man didn't even have time to scream, but lay back arching his neck, then collapsed.

Nathan stared in revulsion and disbelief down at his blood-drenched hands. He had felt the magic. He had tried to heal the poor victim . . . but instead of just dying peacefully, the man had been split open like an overripe fruit. Nathan had done that! The victim would have died anyway, but not like this!

Nathan staggered back, opening and closing his mouth, but he had no words. He thought he had lost his magic, but this was worse than merely being impotent. The gift had turned against him. If his ability did come back to him, what if he couldn't control it?

He stared in dismay at the appalling, mangled corpse, sure that a crowd would gather to accuse him of a terrible crime. He wondered if even on her worst days as Death's Mistress, Nicci had done such an awful thing.

When he looked up, he met Bannon's glassy gaze. The young man seemed so filled with horror at the events of the night that this new instance had very little effect on him.

Bile rose in the wizard's throat, and he turned away, his shoulders slumped. He didn't want Nicci to see this either, though perhaps she could help him understand what had happened. How could his gift have turned so violently against him? For now, even if he sensed magic returning to him, he didn't dare use it. He might cause an even worse disaster.

Another astonishing realization came to him. What if he had decided to hurl a ball of wizard's fire at one of the Norukai ships during the battle, and it recoiled on him instead? If the furious white-hot flames had struck back, they could have wiped out half the town of Renda Bay.

Nathan groaned deep in his throat and lurched away from the people who were busy bandaging and tending the injured, splinting broken bones, propping up wounded heads on rolled cloths. He felt ashamed and afraid.

He was dangerous.

Instead, he picked up a bucket and joined the firefighting crews to help extinguish the last blazes that still spread through the town. In that, at least, he could cause little damage.

CHAPTER 25

The fires in Renda Bay burned until morning, and afterward smoke continued to curl into the gray sky, staining the dawn. Houses and boat sheds still smoldered, some charred all the way to blackened mismatched skeletons. A group of fishermen had salvaged six boats from the ruined docks, while throughout the town numb-looking people assessed the damage, talking in subdued voices.

Nicci reflected on the previous day's easy activity, the relaxed conversations among neighbors, the quaint town activities, the small but busy market square—a way of life now struck down by swords, fire, and blood from the raid.

Seemingly in a stupor, Bannon sat recovering on a splintered wooden bench next to an overturned gutting trough. Silver fish scales spangled the wood of the trough like miniature coins in the morning light. He gripped Sturdy's leather-wrapped hilt with both hands, as if drawing on its strength. His shirt was torn and stained with soot and blood.

As she stepped up to him, Nicci noted at least five deep cuts on his arms, across his back, on his shoulder. The young cabbage farmer looked engrossed in thought, refighting his battles. He had aged greatly.

Though Nicci was exhausted from expending so much magic during the battle and treating the grievously wounded afterward, she found enough strength to heal Bannon's cuts and wounds. He didn't even seem aware of them.

Nathan came up to them with haunted eyes, his long white hair and his borrowed shirt matted with clumps of gore. Dried blood caked his hands.

When Bannon looked up at his mentor, his face showed little recognition. The wizard said in a soft voice, "You fought like an unbelievable warrior last night, as if someone worked a rampaging spell on you—but I know that was no spell."

The young man's face was drawn and pale. "Slavers were attacking the village. I had to fight. What else could I do?"

"You did well enough," Nicci acknowledged. "You fought even harder than you did against the selka."

"These were *slavers*," he said, as if that were explanation enough. With an obvious effort, Bannon struggled to compose himself and even managed a false, horrid-looking smile. "It's what I was supposed to do. I hated the thought of all of these people being hurt . . . and enslaved. They . . . they had a very nice life here in Renda Bay, and I didn't want it ruined."

Nicci glanced at Nathan, who wore a skeptical frown. Neither of them believed Bannon's explanation. Nicci said, "That is an acceptable answer, but it's not the complete one. Tell me the truth."

His expression filled with alarm. "I—I can't. It's a secret."

She knew it was time to be stern, to push him in a way that would make him respond. His wounds were far deeper than the obvious ones, and they might become either tough scars or dangerously unstable fractures. Her assessment of him had changed in the past week, and she suspected there was more than the naive, careless country boy. She needed to find out.

Grasping Bannon's shirt, she pulled him to his feet and pressed her face close to his so she could capture his attention with her searing blue eyes. "I don't want your secrets for the sake of titillation, Bannon Farmer. I ask because I need to know the answer. You travel as my companion, and therefore your actions might affect my own mission. Are you unreliable? Are you a hazard to me and what I must accomplish for Lord Rahl?" She softened her voice. "Or are you just a brave, but reckless fighter?"

Swaying, Bannon looked at the sorceress and then at Nathan with a beseeching expression. He tore his gaze away to stare out at the burned wreck of the nearest Norukai vessel, which was half sunk in the calm bay. Nicci suddenly remembered how oddly the young man had also behaved when they camped near the much older hulk of a wrecked serpent ship.

"You've seen those ships before," she whispered. "You know about the Norukai."

Finally, he said, "It's because of *Ian* . . . my friend Ian. The slavers . . ." He sucked in a long, deep breath. His hazel eyes were bloodshot from the fires and smoke, as well as his own convulsive weeping. His eyes held much deeper secrets, a clear and colorful childhood memory being stripped away to reveal the raw bones of truth.

Hauling out his words like a man surrendering precious keepsakes to a moneylender, Bannon told his tale. "Ian and I were boyhood friends on Chiriya Island. We would run down to the shore or race each other across the windswept grasses. One time, we walked all the way around the island—it took us a full day. That was our whole world.

"As boys, we pulled weeds in the fields and helped harvest the cabbage heads, but we also had time to ourselves. Ian and I had a special cove on the far side of the island, where we would explore the tide pools. Most of the time we just played. We were best friends, both the same age, thirteen summers old that year . . . the last year."

His voice grew raspy and hard. "One morning, Ian and I got up early because we knew it was a low tide. We went to our special cove, climbing down the sandstone cliffs, finding footholds like only boys can. We had empty sacks stuffed in our belts because we knew we would bring home a good haul of shellfish and crabs for the dinner pot. Mostly we enjoyed the peace of each other's company, instead of being back in our own homes . . . which weren't very peaceful." His voice turned sour.

Nicci said, "You always described your island home as idyllic and perfect, but dull."

He turned his bleak, empty eyes toward her. "Nothing is perfect, Sorceress. Shouldn't you be telling *me* that?" He shook his head and stared out at the still-smoldering Norukai ship.

"That day Ian and I were preoccupied with the tide pools, watching hermit crabs scuttle among the sea anemones, the little fish that had been trapped there until the next high tide. We didn't see the slavers' boat coming around the point. The six Norukai spotted us, rowed in, then splashed onto shore. Before Ian and I knew it, we were surrounded.

"They were burly, muscular men with shaved heads and those awful scarred and sewed mouths. They had nets, and ropes, and clubs. They were hunters . . . and we were just prey." He blinked. "I remembered when hunting parties from my village would march across the grassy pastures in the headlands with nets, banging pots to chase down goats and round them up for the winter slaughter. The Norukai were just like that. They came after me and Ian.

"We both screamed and ran. Ian was ahead of me. I made it to the base of the cliffs and started to climb before the first two slavers caught up to me. I was just out of their reach, but my foot slipped, and I fell. The men grabbed me, swung me around, and dropped me to the rocky beach. It knocked the wind out of me, and I couldn't make a sound. But Ian was yelling from halfway up the beach. He had almost gotten away." Bannon sniffled. "He could have gotten away.

"I fought back, but there were two of them, and the Norukai were strong. They tried to pull my arms together so they could lash my wrists. Another slaver grabbed my feet. I couldn't get away, couldn't even scream. Even when I caught my breath, my voice was hoarse. I thrashed and kicked.

"Just when they were wrapping a rope around my wrists, I heard an even louder shout. Ian had turned and come back, yelling at the slavers. They threw a net at him, but it missed. He just shrugged them off and came running toward me. In the struggle he snatched up one of the Norukai cudgels and bounded across the rocky beach, leaping over tide pools. He came to save me.

"Ian swung the club. I heard a skull crack—it was one of the men trying to tie me. Blood gushed from his eye and nose. Grunting, the other man grabbed at Ian, but my friend smashed him in the teeth, turning his lips to pulp. Ian yelled for me to run, and I tore my wrist away, sprang to my feet, and raced toward the sandstone cliff. I ran as I never had before. Tugging the ropes from my wrists, I made it there and began scrambling up, climbing for my very life.

"Ian shouted again, but I didn't turn back. I couldn't! I found the first foothold and pulled myself higher. My fingers were bloody, my nails torn." Bannon was breathing hard as he told his story. Perspiration sparkled on his forehead. "I pulled myself up, found a foothold, climbed, and then turned back to see the slavers closing in on my friend. Two of them threw a net again. The men he had clubbed now pounded him with their fists. They crowded around him and he couldn't get away. He screamed."

Bannon's voice hitched with a sob. "Ian had come back to save me. He risked his life to stop those men from tying me up. He made it so I could get away! But when they captured him, I froze. I could only watch as they wrapped the net around Ian and beat him again, kicking him over and over. When he cried out in pain, they laughed. I could see blood running from a gash in his face—and I didn't do a thing. They bound his wrists and ankles with rope—and I just watched.

"It should have been me under that net. He had helped me—*and I just watched!*"

Bannon released his grip and let Sturdy fall with a clatter to the ground. He pressed his palms against his eyes, as if to hide. "I was halfway up the cliff when the slavers came for me again, and I panicked. When I reached the higher ground, I looked back down at the beach. The Norukai were dragging my friend toward the longboat. He still struggled, but I knew he was lost. *Lost!* I caught a last glimpse of Ian's face, full of despair. He knew he would never get away . . . and he knew I wasn't coming back to rescue him. Even at that great distance, his eyes met mine. I had abandoned him.

"I wanted to shout that I was sorry. I wanted to promise that I would come for him, but I had no voice. I was out of breath." He turned away. "It would have been a lie anyway.

"Ian stared at me with a look of shock and confusion, as if he couldn't believe I would betray him. I saw hatred behind those eyes just before the slavers threw him into the longboat.

"And I just ran." Bannon shook his head, sniffling. "I left my friend behind. I didn't help him. He came back to save me, and I . . . I just saved myself. I ran away." His voice hitched and he sobbed again. "Sweet Sea Mother, he fought to save me, and I abandoned him."

The young man looked down at the blood on his shirt, at the cuts on his arms. He touched a deep wound on his neck and winced in surprise, but he clearly didn't remember how he had gotten it. The tears in his eyes had not washed away the stinging, painful memory.

"That's why I fought so hard against the slavers here in Renda Bay, why I hate them so much. I was a coward when the Norukai took Ian. I didn't fight then, but I have a sword now, and I will fight to my last breath." He snatched up Sturdy from where it had fallen on the ground and inspected it, satisfied that the edge still looked sharp. "I can't rescue Ian. I'll never see him again . . . but I can kill slavers whenever I see them."

CHAPTER 26

After a full day of picking up the pieces, the grieving survivors of Renda Bay were exhausted. With Holden dead, a man named Thaddeus accepted the position of town leader. Thaddeus was a beefy, square-faced fisherman with a long, frizzy beard. He was well liked among the villagers, but he looked completely out of his element.

Nicci had been watching the people throughout the day. She had always hated slavery, and it was her mission to stop tyranny and oppression in the name of Lord Rahl, as well as for her own soul. In a way, this was how she could help save the world for Richard, but she doubted this was what the witch woman's prophecy had meant.

Nathan and Bannon had washed the grime from their hands and faces, but their hair was still tangled, and their clothes were still covered with blood that had long since dried.

Together, the villagers made a solemn procession out to the hillside graveyard, with mules and shaggy oxen drawing a line of carts to carry the dead. The people, already weary, sore, and heartsick, spread out to mark burial sites for the thirty-nine villagers who had died in the battle. The townspeople carried spades and shovels but seemed daunted by the task of digging all those graves.

"We must also erect twenty-two wooden posts," Thaddeus said in a wobbly voice, "to remember the good people taken by the raiders."

"Carve the names into the stone and make your wooden markers," Nicci said. "I can use my gift to assist with the other work." She re-

leased a flow of magic to scoop aside the grasses and dirt on the hillside
to fashion a perfect grave. It was easy enough once she went through
the process. She made an identical grave adjacent to the first, and then
a third. She had many more to go.

The villagers watched, too tired to be amazed, too frightened to
express their gratitude. When she finished the thirty-ninth grave, Nicci
stepped back, feeling weary. "I sincerely hope you will not need more
anytime soon."

With little ceremony and acknowledging that they would all
grieve later, in their own time, the people of Renda Bay buried their
dead. The men and women spoke the names aloud as they took each
body from the cart and interred the victims, a mixed range of farmers, a carpenter, a jovial brewer, two young boys killed in a fire after
the house in which they had taken refuge burned to the ground, and
town leader Holden, who had given up his life on the sea to lead
Renda Bay.

The seamstress Jann spoke her husband's name and wept, bowing
her head over the grave as Phillip's body was laid to rest and covered
with dirt. "He just wanted to build boats," she said. "After the accident
with the fishhook, he prefered to stay on land. He thought it would be
safer." Her shoulders shuddered. "Safer."

Nathan stood next to the small woman, his gaze somber, his head
lowered. Awkwardly, the seamstress held out a folded gray garment for
him. "This is another of Phillip's shirts, Nathan. You fought with us,
you saved me, and—" Her voice broke with a quick choking sound. She
sniffled, and her lips trembled. "And your first new shirt was ruined.
Phillip would want you to have this."

"I would be honored." The wizard pressed the clean linen against
his chest.

Although they had fought alongside the people of Renda Bay, Nicci
did not feel she had finished her mission here. After they had filled in
the graves and woodcarvers had cut names into the fresh-cut posts,
Nicci addressed the villagers before they left the graveyard.

"This is why you need Lord Rahl," she said. "His goal is to stop
such violence and bloodshed, to crush slavers so that all people can live

their lives in freedom. Yes, he is far away, but the D'Haran army will not tolerate such lawlessness and oppression. It may take time, but the world will change—the world has already changed. You must have noticed the stars."

The villagers muttered, listening to her with a different attitude after their ordeal.

She continued in a stronger voice. "But you have to be responsible for yourselves as well. When you've picked up the pieces here, send an envoy on the long journey north to the People's Palace. In D'Hara, swear your loyalty to Lord Rahl and tell him what happened here. Tell him about all the lands of the old empire that need him. He will not let you down."

Nathan said, "Before you send envoys, we will write a message for him, as well as a summary of what we have seen. If someone could deliver that, we would be most grateful."

Thaddeus swallowed hard. "Even though they were defeated last night, the Norukai will return. How soon can your Lord Rahl send his army?"

Nicci wasn't finished. "You cannot simply wait for help. All people are responsible for their own lives, their own destinies. You must improve your own defenses, and you will need more than a bonfire and a lookout tower. The slavers believe you are weak, and that is why they prey on you. The best way to insure your peace is through *strength*. Maybe last night was a lesson for them. We were here to help this time, but you would not need to be rescued if you weren't victims in the first place."

"You can learn how to defend yourselves," Bannon said, looking away. "I did."

"But how?" Thaddeus said. "Erect walls along the shore? String a barrier chain across the harbor? How are we to raise an army? Where do we get weapons? We are just a fishing village."

Nathan suggested, "In addition to your bonfire and lookout platform, build guard towers on either side of the harbor, and be ready to launch a rain of fire arrows down on any raiders who come. Keep several longboats at the ready to go out and sink them before they enter the harbor. The raider vessels will be flaming wrecks before they ever get to shore."

Nicci said in a hard voice, "The Norukai are slavers, not conquerors. You have an advantage, because they want to capture you alive, otherwise you are no good to them. Other attackers may just slaughter you all."

"I would be happy to kill them," Jann growled.

Nicci approved. "Let nothing hold you back. Arm your people so they can fight better."

"Keep boat hooks and pikes ready on the docks," Bannon said. "Even if the slavers get through, your people could fight them off as they try to disembark."

"Make them think twice before they come back here again," Nicci said. As she watched determination grow like a slow-burning fire among them, she felt gratified. "When your wounds become scars and you've rebuilt your homes, do not forget what happened here, or it will happen again."

The next day, Nicci, Nathan, and Bannon went to the small building that served as Renda Bay's town hall. The interior smelled of smoke. Three of the glass windows were shattered, and the roof was partially charred, but teams of villagers had extinguished the fire before it caused severe damage.

The beefy town leader's posture seemed hunched with duty. "I'll need workers to help rebuild this hall, but it may take time. Our first priority is to strengthen our defenses, as you said." Thaddeus looked at them with a hopeful expression. "Would you stay with us, defend us? We've seen how powerful your magic is, Sorceress. And the wizard could try to use his magic, too."

Nathan looked as if he might be sick. "No . . . that could be dangerous."

Nicci bit her lower lip. "I have a larger purpose to serve for Lord

Rahl, and now we must move on. The storm blew the *Wavewalker* far off course, and we need to look at maps and determine where we are."

"We need to find a place called Kol Adair," Nathan said. He patted the life book in his leather pouch. "We were told that something important awaits us there."

"We do have some maps," said Thaddeus, distracted and troubled. "They're in here somewhere." He rummaged in Holden's cabinets, shifting aside old documents that listed the names of registered fishing boats, a ledger for taxes, charts of land ownership. Finally, he found an old and sketchy map that showed the Phantom Coast, the southern part of the Old World marked with a spiderweb of clear, straight lines that joined the open lands.

"These are imperial roads that Emperor Jagang constructed to move his armies, but he spent little time this far south. All I know is that the port cities of Serrimundi and Kherimus are up here somewhere." He gestured vaguely off the top of the map. "And Tanimura is farther north. I've heard rumors of the New World, but I know nothing about it."

While Nicci studied the map, Nathan took out his life book and quickly sketched in some details on his own map, correcting some of his crude estimates of the terrain they had seen.

"Kol Adair . . ." Thaddeus sat heavily in the chair behind Holden's old desk. His brow furrowed as he looked at the charts, but they seemed unfamiliar to him. He scratched his frizzy beard. "I've barely been beyond Renda Bay, myself. Even in my fishing boat, I never sailed out of sight of the coast.

"I've heard stories of distant lands, though. I believe Kol Adair is well inland, beyond the foothills and over a mountain range, across a vast fertile valley, and then more mountains. The place you seek lies somewhere in those mountains . . . according to the stories."

He ran his hand along the easternmost part of the map as if he could draw topography on the scarred desk. "No distant travelers have come through here in such a long time." He pointed to the middle of the map. "But we know of other settlements upriver, ports, mining towns, farming villages." He shuddered visibly. "And in the other direction there are islands out at sea, rugged windswept rocks where the Norukai live." He bit off his words, then said with hollow calmness, "I would not suggest you go there."

"We won't," Nathan said. "We are looking for Kol Adair."

Nicci asked, "Can you supply us with provisions, packs, garments, tools for our journey? We lost almost everything in the shipwreck."

"Renda Bay owes you far more than we can ever repay," said Thaddeus.

"If you send your emissaries up to D'Hara bearing our message to Lord Rahl, that will be all the payment I require."

After resting one more day and helping the villagers collect the ragged debris of their lives, the three set out again. They all wore clean clothes. Bannon's sword, now sharpened and oiled, hung at his side in its plain scabbard. Nathan's ornate sword had also been cleaned, polished, and sharpened.

Bannon seemed troubled as they set off on the road. "Can we make a slight detour to the graveyard? There's something I want to do."

"We already paid our respects to the fallen, my boy," Nathan said.

"It's more than that," Bannon said.

Nicci saw how the young man had changed after his experience here. He no longer seemed so cheerful and naive . . . or maybe his cheeriness had always been an act. She said, "I do not wish to delay for long."

"Thank you," the young man said.

They followed the curve of the hill until they reached the line of new graves, the fresh-packed earth that held thirty-nine resting bodies. Bannon went straight to the part of the burial ground crowded with wooden posts. Twenty-two new ones had been pounded into the ground, each etched with the name of a villager taken by the slavers.

Bannon clenched his fists as he walked among the posts until he chose one—a clean, bright post of freshly sanded wood. On one side, a villager had carved the name *MERRIAM*.

Bannon dropped to his knees on the opposite side of the post. He pulled out his sword and held it awkwardly, using the point to gouge three letters into the fresh wood. Tears sparkled in his eyes as he looked at the name.

IAN.

Nathan gave him a solemn nod.

Bannon stood again, and placed the sword back in its sheath. "Now I'm ready to go."

CHAPTER 27

They followed the river inland from the town of Renda Bay, looking forward to "Lands Unknown"—the farms, logging towns, and mining settlements that Thaddeus had described for them. Someone along the way would know more about Kol Adair and give them guidance.

Occasional flatboats drifted by on the river as farmers or merchants brought goods down to Renda Bay. The flatboat pilots used poles to guide the loaded vessels downstream. Some of them would wave in greeting, while others just stared at the strangers walking the river path.

After the ordeal with the shipwreck, Nicci felt as if they had been given a fresh start. Her long black traveling dress was cleaned and mended; Nathan wore the homespun shirt from Phillip, and Bannon also had a new set of clothes.

As they went farther up the river valley, Bannon seemed to recover his pleasant fantasy of life again, but now Nicci realized that his smile and his optimism were just a veneer. She saw through it now. At least he no longer tried to flirt with her; she had frightened that foolish attraction out of him.

But the young man wasn't entirely daunted. He approached her, striking up a conversation. "Sorceress, it occurred to me that like prophecy, wishes sometimes come about in unexpected ways. And your wish did come true."

She narrowed her blue eyes. "What wish?"

"The wishpearl I gave you on the *Wavewalker*. Remember?"

"I threw it overboard to appease the selka queen," Nicci said.

"Think of the chain of events. After you made the wish, we sailed south, the selka attacked, and that storm wrecked the ship, but we found the stone marker, which confirmed the witch woman's prophecy. Then we made our way to Renda Bay, where we fought the slavers, and the town leader told us what he knew about Kol Adair. See, that was your wish—that it would help us get to Kol Adair." He spread his hands. "It's obvious."

"Your logic is as straightforward as a drunkard walking down an icy hill in a windstorm," she said. "I make my own wishes come true, and I make my own luck. No selka magic bent the events of the world around my desires just to put us here at this exact place. We would have found our way in any case."

"Wishes are dangerous, like prophecy," Nathan interjected, walking close beside them. "They often lead to unexpected results."

"Then I will be careful not to make any more frivolous wishes," Nicci said. "I am the one who determines my own life."

They continued inland for days and found several settlements, large and small. While Nathan and Nicci gathered any information they could, they explained about the D'Haran Empire and about Richard's new rule. The isolated villagers listened to the news, but such obscure and distant politics had little bearing on their daily lives. Nathan marked the names of the villages on his hand-drawn map, and they moved on.

Once, when he introduced himself as the wizard Nathan Rahl, the villagers asked for a demonstration of his powers, and he faltered in embarrassment. "Well, magic is a special thing, my friends, not to be used for mere games and showmanship."

When Nicci heard this, she flashed him a skeptical expression. When Nathan had possessed his powers, he did indeed use them for just that, whenever he considered it useful. Now, however, he had to pretend that such demonstrations were beneath him. When the village children learned that Nicci was a sorceress, they pestered her instead, although one glance from her made them quickly reconsider their requests.

Bannon offered to do tricks with his sword, but they were not interested.

As they left that village, Nathan quietly vowed, "I won't mention my magic again . . . not until I am made whole again after Kol Adair. For now I don't even dare make the attempt."

"You should still try," Nicci said as they continued along the forested road. "Can you feel your Han at all? You may have lost your gift, but you could regain it."

"Or I might cause a terrible disaster." Nathan's expression turned grayish. "I didn't tell you what happened in Renda Bay when I . . . I tried to heal a man."

They walked along a good path up into foothills, as the main river branched and they took the north fork. "I saw you helping some of the injured," Nicci said.

"You didn't see everything." Nathan waved at a fly in front of his face. "Bannon saw me . . . but we have not discussed it since."

The young man blinked. "I saw so much that night, I think my eyes were filled with blood and I couldn't absorb it all. I don't remember . . . I don't remember much at all."

"One of the Norukai spears had pierced the man's chest, and he was dying," Nathan said. "Even the healer women knew he couldn't be saved. But I felt a hint of my magic. I was desperate, and I wanted to prove myself. I had seen you save the town with your gift, Sorceress, and I knew how much I could have helped. I was furious and I grasped at any small spark of magic. I felt something and tried to use it."

He paused on the path, seemingly out of breath, although the route was quite level. He wiped sweat from the side of his neck. The weight of his tale seemed so great a burden that he couldn't walk and speak at the same time. "I wanted to heal him . . . but much has changed inside me. Dear spirits, I don't understand my gift anymore. I thought I touched my Han, and I released what small amount of power I could find. It should have been Additive Magic. I should have been able to knit the man's tissues together, repair his lungs, stop the bleeding." Nathan's azure eyes glistened with tears.

Nicci and Bannon both paused beside him.

"I tried to heal him . . ." Nathan's voice cracked. "But my magic did the opposite. It ricocheted, and instead of sealing his wounds and stopping the bleeding, my spell . . . *tore him apart.* It ripped that poor man asunder, when I was only trying to save him."

Bannon looked at the wizard, aghast. "I think I remember now. I was staring right at it, but . . . I didn't see, or I didn't trust what I was seeing."

Nicci tried to understand what he was saying. "You felt the magic come back to you, but it did the opposite of what you intended?"

"I don't know if it was exactly the opposite . . . it was uncontrolled. A wild thing. My Han seemed almost vengeful, fighting against whatever I wanted. That poor man . . ." He looked up at her. "Consider, Sorceress—if I had unleashed that kind of magic in a fight against the Norukai, I might well have annihilated all of Renda Bay. I could have killed you and Bannon."

"Can you feel the gift inside you now?" Nicci asked.

Nathan hesitated. "Maybe . . . I'm not certain. As I'm sure you understand, I'm afraid to try. How can I take the risk? I don't even want to practice. What if I try to create a simple hand light—and instead I unleash a huge forest fire? Those village children who asked to see a little trick . . . I could have killed them all. Magic that I can't control is worse than no magic at all."

Nicci said, "That depends upon the circumstances. If we are being pursued by an army of monster warriors, even an uncontrolled forest fire might prove useful."

As usual, Bannon tried to inspire them with his cheer. "Obviously, our best solution is to find Kol Adair as soon as we can. Then we will have our wizard back."

"Yes, my boy," Nathan said. "A perfectly simple solution." He set off down the road at a brisk pace.

Three days later, while passing through wooded hills with few signs of habitation, they came upon a wide imperial road that cut straight through the uneven terrain, then down into a broad valley. The road headed northward like a straight spear that Jagang had hurled toward the New World.

From the crest of the hill they looked down at the abandoned thoroughfare, which had been carved by great armies, but not in recent years. The road looked weathered and overgrown.

Nathan turned to Nicci. "When you were Death's Mistress, did any of your expeditions come this far south?"

She shook her head. "Jagang did not consider this wilderness to be worth the effort, although from his ancient maps, we knew there were once great cities and trading centers beyond the Phantom Coast."

"This road may have been a built by another emperor." Nathan smiled. "The history of the Old World is full of them. Have you heard of Emperor Kurgan? The warlord they called Iron Fang?"

They descended to the wide, empty road. Nicci raised an eyebrow. "I remember some of the history I learned in the Palace of the Prophets, but I'm not familiar with his name. Was this Iron Fang a ruler of any significance?"

"I spent a thousand years reading history, dear Sorceress, and countless rulers have laid claim to historical significance, but Emperor Kurgan might well have been the most infamous ruler since the time of the wizard wars. At least according to his chroniclers. I'm surprised you didn't know of him."

"Jagang preferred that I help him make history, not ruminate about it," Nicci said. She had certainly made history when she killed Jagang herself, without fanfare, without spectacle, exactly as Richard had asked.

"We have a long walk ahead of us, so plenty of time for the tale." Nathan strolled ahead, following the great empty road, which took them in the general direction they wished to go. "Fifteen centuries ago, Emperor Kurgan conquered much of the Old World and the vast lands to the south." He quirked a smile at Bannon as the young man walked on the weed-overgrown paving stones. "Not long ago at all, only five hundred years before I was born."

"Only five hundred years?" Bannon seemed unable to grasp that span of time.

"Kurgan was brutal and ruthless, but he earned the name Iron Fang mostly because of his affectation. He had his left canine tooth replaced." Nathan opened his mouth and tapped the corresponding tooth with a fingertip. "Replaced it with a long iron point. I have no doubt that it made him look fearsome, although I can't imagine how it was possible for him to eat with the thing in his mouth." He snorted. "And he had to replace it regularly, due to rust."

"Doesn't sound very terrifying to me," Nicci said.

"Oh, he was fearsome and powerful enough. Iron Fang's relentless armies overwhelmed land after land, conscripting all available young fighters, which increased his army . . . and thereby helped him conquer more lands and conscript more fighters. It was an unstoppable flood.

"But, as I'm afraid dear Richard is now beginning to realize, *conquering* territory is one thing, while *administering* it is quite another. Kurgan's downfall was that he actually believed the praise heaped upon him by the minstrels and criers, when as far as I can tell, Iron Fang's true genius was his main military commander, General Utros."

"Even an emperor needs excellent military commanders to conquer and hold so many lands," Nicci said.

Nathan waxed poetic. "General Utros was the strategist who led Kurgan's armies to victory after victory. Utros seized all the territory of the Old World in the name of Emperor Kurgan." Walking along the easy path of the ancient imperial road, he kept glancing to the foothills in the east, in the supposed direction of Kol Adair. "And once Utros was gone, Iron Fang simply could not function without his general."

"What happened to Utros?" Bannon asked. "Was he defeated or killed?"

"Oddly enough, that is not entirely certain, but I have my ideas. The story is far more complicated than a list of military campaigns. You see, Emperor Kurgan had married a beautiful queen from one of the largest lands he seized. Her name was Majel. Some say she was a sorceress, because her beauty was indeed bewitching." He gave Nicci a wry smile. "Perhaps like our own sorceress."

She frowned at him.

He continued his story. "Majel's beauty was so entrancing that General Utros was put under its spell. She found him to be a handsome man, not to mention brave and powerful—certainly he was a mate superior to Iron Fang himself, who might not have been as awe-inspiring as his propaganda would suggest." He gave a dismissive wave of his hand. "Or maybe there was nothing magic about it at all. It could just be that Empress Majel and General Utros fell in love. It's clear to me, and to many historical scholars, that Utros intended to conquer the world, then overthrow Kurgan and take Majel for his own."

"What happened then?" Bannon asked.

Nathan stopped at a shoulder-high pinnacle of weathered rock that had been erected at the side of the road, as a mile marker, although the carved letters had long since worn away. He removed his life book, opened to his map, and glanced at the foothills, trying to orient himself. None of the foundation rocks gave any hint about the chilling prophecy or Kol Adair, though. Nicci was almost relieved. . . .

"Utros took the bulk of the imperial army, nine hundred thousand of Kurgan's best soldiers, on a campaign to conquer the powerful city of Ildakar. And he simply vanished—along with the entire army.

"It's generally believed that they deserted, all nine hundred thousand of them. Maybe they even joined the forces of Ildakar. Suddenly finding himself without his army, Emperor Kurgan was weak and utterly lost. Then he discovered evidence of Empress Majel's affair with Utros, and in his rage at this betrayal, Kurgan stripped her naked and chained her spread-eagled in the center of the city square. He forced his people to watch as he used an obsidian dagger to peel away her beautiful face in narrow ribbons of flesh, leaving her eyeballs intact so she could watch as he skinned the rest of her body, strip by strip. He finally gouged out her eyes and made sure she was still alive before upending urns of ravenous, flesh-eating beetles onto the raw, bloody meat that remained of her body."

Bannon looked queasy. Nicci gave a grim nod, imagining that Jagang could well have done something similar. "Emperors tend to be . . . excessive," she said.

The wizard continued, "Iron Fang did that to strike terror into the hearts of his people, but he only appalled them, for they had loved Empress Majel. His people were so disgusted and outraged that they rose up and overthrew Emperor Kurgan. He had no army to defend him and only a handful of imperial guards, many of whom were just as outraged at the crime they had witnessed. The people killed Kurgan and dragged his body through the streets until all the flesh was ripped off his bones. They hung his corpse by the ankles from a high tower of the palace until jackdaws picked the skeleton clean."

"That is what should happen to tyrants," Nicci said. "Jagang himself was buried unmarked in a mass grave."

Nathan strolled onward, smiling. "And, of course, the citizens chose another emperor, who was just as ruthless, just as oppressive. Some people simply don't learn."

CHAPTER 28

The foothills rose up from the river valley to form a mountain range, and according to the information they had been told, beyond those mountains would be a broad, fertile valley with another line of even higher mountains beyond. And then they would find Kol Adair.

Nathan thought the journey would be quite a challenge. He corrected himself: quite an *adventure*. During his sedentary centuries in the Palace of the Prophets, he had waited for exactly this, although he had not foreseen losing his gift along the way.

Leaving the rigidly straight imperial road, which headed north, the three travelers wound their way into hills covered with aspens. The forest was eerily beautiful, with tall, smooth trunks of green-gray bark and rippling leaves that whispered and rustled in the breeze. They walked on a carpet of mellow, sweet-smelling fallen leaves.

By late afternoon, Nathan found an open spot near a creek and suggested they set up camp. Bannon went off to hunt rabbits for their supper, but came back with only some swollen crabapples and an armful of cattails, whose pulp, he said, could be cooked up into a filling, if bland, mash. They added smoked fish from their packs, given to them by the people of Renda Bay. Later, Nicci drifted off to sleep while Nathan recounted more obscure and barbaric tales from history. At least Bannon was interested.

The next day they continued into the rolling hills, following a path that was wide enough for a horse, although they had not seen a village in days. Nathan consulted his notes. "There should be another town up ahead. Lockridge, according to the map." He frowned as he looked from side to side, still trying to get his bearings. "At least, as best I can tell. We should easily reach it by nightfall."

"I'm happy just to travel with you as my companions," Bannon said, "for as long as you'll let me."

Nathan wondered how many days, months, or even years it would take them to find Kol Adair, but once they reached that mysterious place—whether it was a mountain, or a city, or some magical wellspring—he would become whole again. In the meantime, he felt empty and unsettled. Although he was perfectly competent without his gift, a decent swordsman and a true adventurer, the magic was part of him, and he did not like the idea that his own Han was a restless, rebellious force.

Alas, the farther they got from Renda Bay, the less reliable Thaddeus's sketchy map proved to be. "I'm sure the townspeople ahead will be able to help us out," Nathan said aloud.

When they reached an elbow in the ridge and walked out onto a cleared outcropping that sported only a single gnarled bristlecone among the rocks, Nathan paused to take a look around him, taking advantage of the exposed view to get his bearings.

Bannon pointed to a higher ridge several miles away, a large granite peak that stood above the other hills like a citadel. "There's a kind of tower over there. What do you suppose that is?"

"Another cairn?" Nicci asked.

"No, no. This is much larger. A great tower, I think."

Nathan shaded his brow. The midmorning sun was in his eyes, blocking details, but he could make out a stone watchtower topped with partially crumbled crenellations. "Yes, yes, you're right, my boy. But I see no movement, no people." He squinted harder. "It looks empty."

"That would be a good place to erect a watchtower," Nicci said. "A sentinel outpost."

Nathan turned in a slow circle, looking at the ridges, the trees, the unfolding landscape. "Yes, that's the highest point all around. From there, a person could see for quite some distance." He began to grow excited as an idea occurred to him. "I could get over there and come back to the main road in a few hours. Getting a perspective on the land ahead would definitely be worth the detour."

Nicci shrugged. "If you feel it is necessary, Wizard, I will accompany you."

Nathan felt strangely defensive as he turned to her. Since he had lost his gift, she clearly felt she needed to be his protector, his minder. "It is not necessary for us all to go on such a side trip. With or without magic, Nathan Rahl is not a child who needs a nanny." He sniffed. "Leave it to me. I'll make my way over there, get the lay of the land, and update my map while you two keep following the path. Once you reach that town ahead, I trust you to find lodgings and make arrangements for a meal. I'll certainly be hungry by the time I rejoin you."

Bannon beamed as he stepped up. "I'll come along with you, Nathan. You might need Sturdy and me to protect against any dangers. Besides, I'll keep you company. You can tell me more stories."

Nathan knew that the young man was earnest—in fact, Bannon was probably intimidated by the thought of being left alone with Nicci— but Nathan wanted to do this by himself. Ever since losing his grasp on magic, and now afraid even to try lest he trigger some unknown disaster, he had felt a need to prove his own worth.

"As tempting as that is, my boy, I don't need your help." He realized his voice was unintentionally sharp, and he softened his tone. "I'll be fine, I tell you. Let me go alone. I'll follow that ridge—see, it looks easy enough." He let out a disarming chuckle. "Dear spirits, if I can't find the highest point all around, then I'm useless! There's no need for you both to go so many miles out of your way."

Nicci saw his determination and accepted it. "That is your decision, Wizard."

"Just make sure you two don't need *my* help while I'm gone," Nathan added with a hint of sarcasm, and he nudged Bannon's shoulder. "Go with the sorceress. What if she needs the protection of your sword? Don't abandon her."

Nicci grimaced at the suggestion, while Bannon nodded with grave dedication to his new assignment.

Without further farewell, the wizard strode off into the slatted lines of aspens, following the crest of the ridge and marking the distance to the sentinel tower. He hurried out of sight because he didn't want Nicci or Bannon to change their minds and insist on joining him. "I am still a wizard, damn the spirits!" he muttered. The Han was still within him, even though it now felt less like a loyal pet and more like a rabid dog chained to a post. But at least he had his sword and his fighting skills, and he had a thousand years of knowledge to draw upon. He could handle a simple scouting expedition by himself.

The line of the undulating hills guided him down a slope following a drainage, then up around to another high point. He caught a glimpse of the tower, which still seemed miles away, but he didn't let himself grow discouraged. He would achieve his goal, find the tower, and learn what he could. This was all unexplored territory, and he was the first roving D'Haran ambassador to behold it, in the name of Lord Richard Rahl.

His legs ached as he bushwhacked over the rough terrain. He paused to marvel at a series of arcane symbols he found carved into the bark of a large fallen aspen—ancient and unreadable letter scars that had swelled and blurred with age as the tree grew. The symbols were not in any language he knew, not High D'Haran, not any of the old spell languages from the scrolls and books he had studied in Tanimura. The markings reminded him that he was indeed in a place far from his knowledge. . . .

When he was miles away from his companions, all alone in the wilderness and supposedly safe, Nathan let himself fully consider how his circumstances had changed since he and Nicci had left their lives back in D'Hara. Yes, he was certainly in fine shape for a man his age: well muscled, physically fit, active, nimble. And very good with his sword, even if he did say so himself. But his magic had gone astray, and that bothered him in ways he could not articulate—and Nathan Rahl considered himself a very articulate man.

He could never forget the horror of the backlash when he had tried to heal the wounded man in Renda Bay, how the magic had dodged and twisted when he tried to use it. He was afraid of what other consequences he might endure. Whenever he had tried to reach for it, struggling for some touch, some grasp, he had felt only a hint, an echo . . . then a *sting*. He didn't want to be around his friends in case some monstrous backlash might occur. But he needed to learn more about his condition.

Now, he decided to take his chance. Out here in the forest, walking along the wooded ridges, far from anyone else, Nathan decided to experiment.

Considering his options, he decided not to dabble with any fire spell, because it could so easily erupt into a great conflagration that he wouldn't be able to extinguish. Like Nicci, though, he had easily been able to manipulate air, nudge breezes, and twist the wind. Maybe he could try that.

Nathan looked around himself at the forest of dizzyingly similar aspen trunks, all the rounded leaves knit together in a crown. Winds rippled through the branches overhead.

What did he have to lose? He reached inside himself, searched for his Han, tried to pull just enough that he could create a puff of air, a bit of wind, to stir the twigs and leaves. A gentle little twirl . . .

At first nothing happened, but he strained harder, reached deeper, released his Han, *pushed* it, to create just an outflowing breeze, a gentle gust.

The leaves did stir, and suddenly the air sucked toward him. The wind swirled and twisted, wound up as a cyclone. Nathan had intended only to nudge, but the air whooshed around him in a roar and rushed upward, like a hurricane blow.

He struggled, grabbed at nothing with his hands, tried to pull it in, reining back his power—but the wind only increased as the magic fought against him. Branches overhead snapped. A thick aspen bough broke in half and came crashing to the forest floor not far from him. Leaves were torn asunder, thrown apart like green confetti in the air. The storm kept building, pushing branches, thrashing like a furious seizure.

"Stop! Dear spirits, stop!" Nathan tried to center his Han, reaching for some inner valve to turn it off, to calm himself, and finally the wind died down, the storm abated, and he was left standing there, panting hard.

His white hair was tangled, whipped around his head. Nathan steadied himself against a sturdy aspen trunk. That was not at all what he had intended! And it was an even more ominous hint of the dangerous consequences he might face if he tried to use his magic. Most of the time he couldn't find the gift at all, but when he did try to work a spell, he had no idea what might actually happen.

Certainly not what he wanted to happen.

He was glad that Nicci and Bannon hadn't seen this. He couldn't be responsible for what might occur if he blundered again. His throat was dry, and he gradually caught his breath. "Quite extraordinary," he said, "but not something I would like to do again. Not until I understand this more."

An hour later, another high clearing showed him that he had covered half the distance to the watchtower, and he picked up his pace. It was already past noon, and he wanted to see the view, take his notes, and make his way back to the main trail—and a comfortable village, he hoped—before nightfall.

And, no, he would not dabble with magic again.

The sentinel tower sat on top of a rocky bluff dotted with stubby bristlecones that grew among large talus boulders. The nearer side of the outcropping was a sheer, impassable cliff, so Nathan worked his way around to the bluff's more accommodating side, where he discovered a worn path wide enough for three men to walk abreast . . . or for warhorses to gallop up the slope.

The breezes increased as Nathan broke out of the forest and climbed into the open area around the base of the watchtower. The stone structure was far more imposing than he had first thought, rising high into the open sky. The looming tower was octagonal, its flat sides constructed of enormous quarried blocks. Such a mammoth project would have required either an inexhaustible supply of labor or powerful magic to cut and assemble the blocks like this.

He stopped to catch his breath as he looked across the open terrain. From this high citadel, sentinels would have been able to keep watch for miles in all directions. He wondered if this place had perhaps been built by Emperor Kurgan during the Midwar, and he imagined General Utros himself climbing to this summit from which he could survey the lands he had just conquered.

Nathan heard only an oppressive silence that pressed down around him. He craned his neck to get a view of the top of the single structure, he saw large lookout windows, some of them with the glass intact, while others were shattered. Several of the crenellations had fallen, and large blocks lay strewn around the base like enormous toys.

Nathan called, "Hello, is anyone there?" Any watchers would have seen him approach for the last hour, and a lone man would have been completely vulnerable as he ascended the wide path to the summit. If someone meant to attack him, they had certainly had ample opportunity. He wanted at least to begin the conversation under the auspices of friendship. "Hello?" he called again, but heard only the muttering whispers of wind in and out of the broken windows. Not even birds had taken up residence there.

Despite his uneasiness, Nathan felt the reassuring presence of his sword. He would not try to use magic again, but he reminded himself that he wasn't helpless if he encountered some threat. He stepped up to the broken tower entrance, where a massive wooden door had fallen off its hinges and lay collapsed just inside the main entry. He braced himself, inhaling deeply. He had promised his companions that he could do this, and he could hardly walk all this way and then be afraid to climb up to see the view.

"I come in peace!" he shouted at the top of his voice, then muttered to himself, "At least until you make me change my mind."

He stepped over the fallen door and passed under the archway to see another set of doors, iron bars, a portcullis—all of which had been torn asunder and *destroyed*. The iron bars were uprooted from where they had been seated in the blocks, twisted as if by some supreme force.

Inside the main chamber, wide stone stairs ascended the side wall, running in an octagonal spiral up the interior faces. Five ancient skeletons in long-rotted armor lay broken on the central floor, as if they had fallen off the stairs from a great height.

Though he couldn't find his Han, didn't dare try to summon it, he could sense a power inside this watchtower, a throbbing energy as if this structure had been bombarded by the magic of an attacking sorcerer . . . or maybe it had been saturated with magic by the defenders who tried to save it.

Nathan climbed the stairs and found himself out of breath. Though he was a fit man with travel-conditioned muscles, he was still a thousand years old.

The whistling breezes grew louder as he reached the pinnacle of the watchtower, a wide, empty lookout chamber with an iron-reinforced wooden floor. The ancient planks were petrified. Although parts of the outer walls had broken, the damage did not seem to be due to age. In fact, instead of merely crumbling and falling downward, as would have been caused by gravity, the missing stone blocks had been *flung* far from the base of the tower . . . as if blasted outward.

Every wall of the octagonal lookout chamber had an expansive window, which would allow sentinels to watch in all directions. Each such window had been filled with a broad pane of deep red glass. Three of the eight windows had been shattered by time or brute force, and now shards of broken glass protruded from the window frames like crimson daggers. The other five windows were miraculously intact despite their obvious age, which led Nathan to guess that the glass had been enhanced by magic somehow. The wind whispered more loudly, whisking through the broken windows.

Standing in the middle of the open platform, he turned slowly as he tried to determine what had happened here. Sprawled on the iron-hard floor were more skeletons, all clad in ancient armor. Dark stains on the stone wall blocks marked a varnish of blackened blood, and long white grooves seemed to be scratches, as if desperate fingernails had gouged the quarried stone itself.

Nathan walked across the wooden boards, and one plank gave an alarming crack, as if it was about to give way. He instinctively lurched back, and his boot came down on the femur of one of the fallen warriors. Stumbling, he lost his balance, fell into the wall, and reached out to grab for balance.

His hand caught on the open sill of a lookout window where broken red glass protruded. He hissed in pain and pulled back, looking at the deep gash in his palm. Blood oozed out, and he grimaced.

Looking at the blood, he muttered, "It would be such a simple task to heal myself if I had magic." He was embarrassed by his clumsiness even though he was alone. Now he would have to bind the gash and wait until Nicci could take care of the wound.

Just then he realized that the sound of the wind had taken on an odd character. The tower itself thrummed with a deep vibration. A bright, scarlet light increased inside the observation room, throbbing from the splash of blood Nathan had left behind.

The five intact red panes began to glow.

CHAPTER 29

Continuing down the path, Nicci moved through the forest, and Bannon hurried after her. "Don't worry, Sorceress, I can keep up. A woman traveling alone on an empty trail might attract trouble, but if any dangerous men see me and my sword, they will think twice before they harass you."

She turned her cool gaze on him. "You've seen what I can do. Do you doubt my ability to take care of any problem that might arise?"

"Oh, *I* know about your powers, Sorceress—but others may not. Just having me here with a sharp blade"—he patted his sword—"is sure to prevent problems. The best way out of a difficult situation is to make sure it doesn't arise in the first place." He lowered his voice. "You taught me that yourself, after you rescued me from the robbers in Tanimura."

"Yes, I did." Nicci gave him a small nod of acknowledgment. "Don't make me rescue you again."

"I won't, I promise."

"Don't make promises, because circumstances have a way of making you regret them. Did you promise your friend Ian that you would always stay by his side? That you wouldn't abandon him in times of danger?"

Bannon swallowed hard, but he kept walking beside her. "I had no choice. I couldn't do anything about that."

"I did not accuse you, nor did I say you had a choice. I just point out that if you had made such a promise, it was one you could not have kept."

He pondered in silence for a dozen steps. "You know that my child-hood wasn't as perfect as I wish it had been. That doesn't mean I can't hope for better." He moved aside an aspen branch that dangled across the path. Nicci ducked and kept moving. "And what about you, Sorceress? Did you have a terrible childhood? Someone must have hurt you badly to give you such a hard edge. Your father?"

Nicci stopped in the track. Bannon took several more steps before he realized she had paused behind him. He turned.

"No, my father didn't hurt me. In fact, he was rather kind. His business was making armor, and he was quite well known. He taught me the constellations. I grew up in a village that was nice enough, I suppose, before the Imperial Order came." Nicci looked up, finally admitting aloud what she had known for a long time. "It was my mother who made my childhood a nightmare. She scarred me with lessons that she called the truth, made me think that my hardworking father was the evil one, that his beliefs were oppressive to all people. And the Imperial Order reinforced those beliefs."

She strode ahead at a faster pace, not caring whether Bannon kept up with her. "She made me live in terrible, dirty places. Again and again I was infested with lice, but it was all for my own good, she said. It was to build my character, to make me understand." Nicci sneered. "I loathe my mother for it now, but it took me a century and a half to realize it."

"A century and a half?" Bannon asked. "But that's not possible. You, you're—"

She turned to look at him. "I am over one hundred and eighty years old."

"You're immortal, then?" he asked, wide-eyed.

"I age normally now, but I still have a long life ahead of me, and I intend to accomplish much."

"As do I," Bannon said. "I'll accompany you and do my best to help you and Wizard Nathan achieve your purpose. I can prove myself."

She barely gave him a glance. "You may stay with us, so long as you don't become a nuisance."

"I won't become a nuisance. I promise." He realized what he had said and bit back his words. "I mean, I don't *promise,* but I will do my best not to be a nuisance anymore."

"And will you know when you become a nuisance?"

He nodded. "Absolutely. There is no doubt."

Nicci was surprised at his confidence. "How will you know?"

"Because you will tell me in no uncertain terms." His face was so serious she couldn't help but believe him.

Though the wide path implied that it had once been well traveled, the downed aspens and oaks hadn't been cleared after several winters, and she and Bannon frequently had to climb over or step around. If there was a village ahead, its people did not often come this way. She had seen no footprints, no sign of other travelers, and she decided they would probably end up camping again in the forest.

The young man broke the silence again. "Do you think anyone has the perfect life I imagine? Do you believe there is an idyllic place like that?"

"We would have to make it for ourselves," Nicci said. "If the people create an oppressive culture, if they allow tyrannical rulers, then they get what they deserve."

"But shouldn't there be a peaceful land where people can just be happy?"

"It is naive to entertain a fantasy like that." Nicci pursed her lips. "But Lord Rahl is trying to build a world where people live in freedom. If they wish to make an idyllic place, they will have the chance to do so. That is what I hope for."

The path widened into a road, and the forest thinned into an open park, an expansive area where they could see homesteads with a patchwork of crops across the cleared land. The farmhouses were built from logs and capped with shake-shingle roofs.

Bannon said, "Those must be outlying farms for the village we're looking for. See how the trees have been cut down, the land cleared? All those fences made from fieldstones?"

"I see no one about, though," Nicci said.

Although the road remained a prominent track, it was overgrown with grass, showing no recent hoofprints or wheel marks. They passed stone walls that had fallen into disrepair; weeds and grass protruded from the cracks. Even the fields were wild and overgrown. The area seemed entirely abandoned.

Nicci grew more wary as the silence deepened. On one farm, a field of tall sunflowers drooped, their large heads sunbursts of yellow petals around a central brown circle. Bannon pointed out, "Those fields went to seed over several growing seasons. Notice how disorganized they are." He shook his head. "No cabbage farmer would be so unruly." He stepped up to the nearest sunflower, ran his hands along its hairy stalk. "These were planted in rows several years ago, but they grew up and went unharvested. The new ones are scattered everywhere. Birds spread them out, and next year after those go to seed, the pattern disappears even further." He glanced around. "And look at the vegetable garden. It's entirely untended."

Nicci felt uneasy. "This homestead has been abandoned. They're all abandoned."

"But why? The land looks fertile. See these crops? The soil is dark and rich."

Hearing an odd sound, she spun, ready to release her magic in case she had to attack, but it was only the bleat of a goat. Two gray and white animals came forward, attracted by their conversation.

Bannon grinned. "Look at you!" The goats came forward, and each one let him pat it on the side of the neck. "You look like you're eating well." He frowned at Nicci in puzzlement. "If goats run loose, they'll ransack the vegetable garden. My mother would never let goats come close to our house."

They walked up to a log cottage, where the shake roof had fallen into disrepair. An overturned cart with a sprung wheel was covered with weeds. "No one lives here," Nicci said. "That much is apparent."

They went around to the side of the farmhouse, where they came upon two unexpected ornamental statues, a life-size man and woman dressed as farmers. The expressions on their stone faces showed abject misery. The man's lips were drawn back in anguish, his face turned to the sky, his marble eyes staring. His mouth was wide open in a word-less wail of grief. The woman was hunched, her hands to her face as if weeping, or maybe clawing out her eyes in despair.

Bannon looked deeply unsettled, and Nicci could not help but re-call the stone carvings Emperor Jagang and Brother Narev had com-missioned in Altur'Rang, making sculptors depict the corruption and pain of humanity, rather than its majesty. Jagang and Narev had wanted all statues to reflect the most horrific expressions, just like what Nicci saw now. Was this some other follower of Narev's teachings?

When she had lived with Richard in Altur'Rang, he worked as a stone carver and ultimately sculpted a breathtaking representation of the human spirit, a statue he called Truth. That was when Nicci had experienced a fundamental epiphany. She had *changed*.

That had been the end of her life as Death's Mistress, as a Sister of the Dark.

But whoever had carved these statues had apparently not received the same epiphany.

"We should find another farmhouse," said Bannon. "I don't like those statues. Who would want something like at their home?"

Nicci glanced at him. "Obviously someone who does not share your vision of an idyllic world."

CHAPTER 30

The wind whistling around the sentinel tower took on a deeper tone, like a lost moan. The intact panes of crimson glass in the observation windows shimmered, pulsed, *awakened*.

Nathan held up his sliced hand, cupping the drops of blood in his palm. "Dear spirits," he muttered. As the upper observation platform of the watchtower throbbed with a deep angry light, he stared at the glowing red-glass panes with more fascination than fear. Though he couldn't use his gift, he still felt the restless magic inside him, twitching, uncontrollable. His innate, uncertain Han felt attuned to what was happening.

A memory tickled the back of his mind, and he smiled with recognition. "Bloodglass! Yes, I have heard of bloodglass."

The temperature around him increased, as if the glass reflected some distant volcanic fire, but this magic was heated by blood. Curious, the wizard went to one of the intact panes as the thrumming grew louder, more powerful.

Bloodglass was a wizard's tool in war. Glass bound with blood, tempered and shaped with the spilled blood of sacrifices, so that the panes themselves were connected to bloodshed. In the most violent wars, the seers of military commanders could gaze through panes of bloodglass to monitor the progress of their armies—the battles, victories, massacres. Bloodglass did not reveal an actual landscape, but rather the patterns of pain and death, which allowed warlords to map the topography of their slaughter.

Nathan stood close to the nearest window and peered through the glowing crimson glass. From the top of this watchtower, he had expected to see for great distances—the old imperial roads, the mountain ranges, maybe even the vast fertile valley that lay between here and Kol Adair.

Instead, he viewed the inexorable march of memory armies, hundreds of thousands of fighters who wielded swords and shields, sweeping like locusts across the land. The bloodglass was so perfectly transparent that he could look through time as well as distance at a panorama magnified by the impurity of blood in the crystal.

The Old World was vast and ancient, allowing him to gaze across the sweep of invasions and pitched battles, a succession of armies, of emperors, of countless generations of bloodshed. Barbarians struck villages, killing men who tried to defend their homes and families, raping the women, beheading the children. After the wild and undisciplined warriors came another type of predator: organized machinelike armies that moved in perfect formation and killed without passion but with relentless precision.

Nathan followed the octagonal wall of the tower and peered through a second bloodglass window. This one blazed even brighter, and the armies in the image seemed closer. The glass vibrated, and the whole massive tower structure thrummed as if awakened . . . as if afraid.

Nathan spun upon hearing a sound—a rattle of hollow bones. He looked at the dismembered skeletons scattered on the iron-hard wood of the platform. Had they moved? The light filling the watchtower seemed uncertain, a thicker crimson. Outside, the afternoon sun dipped lower, but this murderous magical light was entirely independent of it. Nervously, he rested his hand on the hilt of his sword—his slick bloody hand. He lifted his palm to look at the scarlet drops that ran down his wrist.

He whirled again at a louder clatter of bones, but saw nothing. Surely, the skeletons had moved. He hurried to look through two more of the intact crimson panes, and saw another army approaching. This one seemed more ominous than the others, more real.

The warriors had pointed steel helmets, scaled armor, and shields emblazoned with a stylized flame. Nathan remembered that flame . . . the symbol of Emperor Kurgan's army. Through the sorcerous magnification, he discerned a fearsome warlord at the vanguard, and Nathan realized that he might be seeing General Utros himself, suffused through blood and time.

The wind howled louder around the broken walls, as if an invisible storm swept across the top of the bluff. Carried along with the breezes came the shouts of soldiers, the clatter of steel, and the pounding thud of marching boots. The red light grew more intense, as if it shone through a fine mist of blood.

Nathan drew his sword now, clamping his fingers hard around the ornate hilt, but his blood made the grip slippery. He turned slowly, but saw no movement from the scattered bones. He hurried over to look through another of the windows and saw the army of General Utros marching toward the high citadel, an inexorable flood of armed men converging on the watchtower. Somehow, the magic had brought them back: these ruthless soldiers seemed absolutely real. They stormed up the wide stone paths, approaching the tower from three sides. He stared at the bristling, relentless force closing in.

Another clatter tore Nathan's attention away from the bloodglass. Whirling, he did see the bones of the long-forgotten defenders twitching, shuddering, reassembling. Bathed in red light from the eerie windows, the skeletons rose up as if they were marionettes.

The wizard raised his sword to fight them, but these were only a few clumsy threats. He was much more worried about the hordes of ghost soldiers pressing toward the tower. He could hear them below, a surging crowd of swords, armor, and muscles. A gruff voice—Utros?—shouted in an accented language that Nathan somehow understood, "Take the tower. Kill them all!"

Surrounded by suffocating red light, Nathan braced himself to fight the skeletons. A thunder of pounding feet came up the tower stairs. He struggled to find the magic within him, ready to release his recalcitrant gift, whether or not it caused a disaster. He was all alone here. Even if a backlash from using magic caused terrible damage and leveled this entire watchtower, at least he wouldn't hurt Nicci or young Bannon. He might, however, destroy these spectral soldiers.

One of the reanimated soldiers clattered toward him, bony hands outstretched as if the skeleton thought Nathan himself was an invader. The wizard swung his sword and sliced through the neck vertebrae. The skull toppled off and rolled across the wooden floor, its jaws still clacking. The fleshless hands and arms flailed, clawing at him. He smashed them, splintering the wickerwork of bones. Then he spun to dismember another skeleton, this one wearing tatters of armor. He kicked out with a boot to knock apart the loose bones of a third rattling opponent.

Then the greater threat arrived. Armored spectral warriors with flame-emblazoned shields and wide swords pushed through the door to the tower chamber, two abreast. They shimmered in the deep red light.

Nathan backed toward a wall, hoping to find some protection with his back to the stone blocks. He had no place to hide.

A flood of long-dead soldiers flowed through the door, as if they meant to take over the sentinel tower and simply drown anyone there with their sheer numbers.

The wizard faced them, mustering all his strength. "Come at me, then!" He slashed his blade across the air, surrendering the hope that he could find the ragged thread of magic within him again. The flow of Han wouldn't come to him now. He would have to make do with his sword.

Oddly, he wished Bannon were here. He and the young man could have slain dozens before they fell. "I'll just have to do it myself!" His straight white hair flew as he hurled himself at the ancient attackers.

Crimson light from the bloodglass throbbed around him, and he felt as if he were in a trance. He swung his sword at one of the ancient warriors, bracing himself for the hard impact against scaled armor, flesh, bone. But his sword passed through, and the enemy collapsed. Nathan didn't slow, but slashed at another, cleaving through misty armor.

He felt a sharp pain in his ankle. One of the clawed skeleton hands had grasped his boot like a vise. With a vicious kick, he flung it aside, then ducked as another ancient warrior charged at him. He realized he was yelling. He could barely see through the thick, almost palpable light around him.

Nathan lost track of his movements. He was in a wild fighting fury. Something about the magic of the bloodglass, the violence and the slaughter that permeated the history of this place, possessed him. He had no choice but to fight, to kill as many of these enemies as possible before his own blood stained the floorboards, before his own body lay here among the ancient dead, until he slowly became a skeleton just like them.

He charged across the platform, seeing enemies that were no more than crimson shadows, and he heard a shattering of glass like a crystalline scream. He whirled and attacked and slashed, but he couldn't see the result. He struck and shattered, struck and shattered. His blood and his sword seemed to know what to do.

The hard clang and sharp shock of his steel against stone jarred him enough to dissipate the red glare around his vision. His trance was broken. The enemy was gone.

Exhausted, Nathan heaved great breaths. His arms trembled. The blood from his cut hand ran down the hilt and onto the blade—but that was the only blood he saw. When he blinked, the air cleared to reveal bright yellow sunlight again and open air. The bloodglass was gone.

In his fury, Nathan had shattered the remaining panes. The red windows no longer looked out onto visions of slaughter and murder, only onto an open landscape in the slanted afternoon light. The spectral army and the remnants from centuries-old wars had faded, and the spell from the bloodglass was destroyed.

He had been fighting against illusions. The skeletons lay broken and strewn about, and he couldn't say if they had actually been reanimated, or if he had just been doing battle with his own nightmares.

He stood for a long time, catching his breath, shaking with weariness. Then he forced a smile. "That was an adventure. Quite exciting."

With his wounded hand he wiped sweat from his forehead, not caring that it left a smear of blood across his face.

He was alone in the tower, and the wind whispering through the broken glass sounded like the distant scream of ghosts.

CHAPTER 31

Leaving the abandoned and disturbing farmstead, Nicci and Bannon continued down the weed-overgrown road past houses and farms. The lonely goats followed them for a time, but eventually gave up and wandered off into a wild cornfield that was more tempting than the prospect of Bannon scratching their ears.

Most of the dwellings they found were empty, and some also displayed more unsettling, anguished statues in the yards. Why would the people feel a need to own such decorations of misery? Nicci led the way toward the main town, growing more tense, fearing what she would find ahead. Though the land seemed fertile and the weather hospitable, these homes had clearly been vacant for years. "It makes no sense. Where did everyone go?"

Nicci paused in front of a large home with unruly flowerbeds, a scraggly garden patch, and drooping apple trees with half-rotted fruit ravaged by birds. Two more statues stood there: a boy and girl no more than nine years old, both on their knees, expressions full of despair, weeping stone tears.

While Bannon stared at the unsettling figures, Nicci was angry that some mad sculptor would revel in displaying such pain, and that these villagers had willingly displayed them. Nicci had felt no deep emotions when Emperor Jagang commissioned such sculptures, because she knew what a ruthless, twisted man he was. Only Nicci, with her heart of black ice, had been his match.

But this isolated village, far from the reach of the Imperial Order, had for some reason decided to depict a very similar misery. Nicci found it deeply disturbing.

They came upon a stream flowing down the wooded hillside, where a miller's waterwheel caught the current and turned. Water sluiced over the paddles to rotate a grinding stone, but after years without maintenance, the wheel wobbled off center and made a loud scraping sound. Some of the wooden planks in the walls of the mill had fallen in.

She and Bannon reached the town itself, a hundred homes around a main square and marketplace. Most dwellings had been built for single families, but others were two stories tall, constructed with wood from the hillsides and stones from a nearby quarry. The entire town was simply deserted.

The open square held a stone fountain, now dry; a smithy fallen into disrepair, its forge long cold; a silent and empty inn and tavern. There were also a warehouse, several merchant offices, an eating establishment, a livery, and barns filled with old hay, but no horses. Around the square, wooden tables and kiosks showed the remnants of what must have been a thriving market. Shriveled husks and rotted cores showed what remained of the produce at farmers' stalls. Feral chickens scuttled through the town square.

Although peripheral details sank into Nicci's consciousness, her attention was fixated on the numerous statues in the square. Countless stone figures stood in the market, in the doorways, by the vegetable stalls, by the water well.

Bannon looked sick. Each of the sculptures wore the same look of horror and anguish, smooth marble eyes open wide in appalled disbelief, or clenched shut in furious denial, stone lips drawn back in sobs.

Bannon shook his head. "Sweet Sea Mother, why would someone do that? I always try to imagine a nice world. Who would want to imagine this? Why would someone do this to a town?"

A deep voice rang out. "Because they were guilty."

They whirled to see a bald man emerging from a dark wooden building that looked like the home of an important person. Tall and thin, with an unnaturally elongated skull, he strode down the street. A gold circlet rested on his head just above the brow. The stranger's long black robes flowed as he walked. The sleeves belled out at the cuffs, and a thick gold chain served as a belt around his waist. His piercing eyes were the palest blue Nicci had ever seen, as clear as water in a mountain stream. His face was so grim, he made even the Keeper look cheerful.

Bannon instinctively drew his sword to defend them, but Nicci took a step forward. "Guilty of what? And who are you?"

The gaunt man stopped before them, drawing himself even taller. He seemed satisfied to be surrounded by numerous statues of misery. "Each was guilty of his own crimes, her own indiscretions. It would take far too long for me to name them all."

Nicci faced the man's implacable, pale stare. "I asked your name. Are you the only one left here? Where did the others go?"

"I am the Adjudicator," he said in a deep baritone voice. "I have brought justice to this town of Lockridge and to many towns."

"We're just travelers," Bannon said. "We're looking for food and a place to sleep, maybe to get some supplies."

Nicci focused her concentration on the strange man. "You are a wizard." She could sense the gift within him, the magic he contained.

"I am the Adjudicator," he repeated. "I bear the gift and the responsibility. I have the tools and the power to bring justice." He looked at them sternly, his water-pale eyes raking over Nicci's form and then Bannon's, as if he were dissecting them and looking for corruption within.

"Who appointed you?" Nicci asked.

"*Justice* appointed me," he said, as if Nicci were the most foolish person he had ever met. "Many years ago I was just a magistrate, and I roved the districts by common consent, for the people required an impartial law. I would go from town to town, where they presented the accused to me, and I served as judge. I would hear the laws they had broken, I would look at the accused, and I would determine the truth of what they had done, as well as the punishment for their crimes."

He pressed a long-fingered hand to the center of his chest, which was covered by the black robes. "That was my gift. I could know the truth of what someone said. Through magic I determined whether they were innocent or guilty, and then I decreed the appropriate sentence, which the town leaders imposed. That was our common agreement. That was our law."

"Like a Confessor," Nicci said. "A male Confessor."

The strange man gave her a blank stare. "I know nothing of Confessors. I am the Adjudicator."

"But where are all the people?" Bannon asked. "If you passed sentence and the villagers agreed to it, where are they? Why did they all leave this town?"

"They did not leave," said the grim wizard. "But my calling changed, became stronger. *I* became stronger. The amulet, by which I determined truth and innocence, became a part of me, and I grew much more powerful."

The Adjudicator pulled open the folds of the black robe to expose his bare chest and an amulet: a golden triangular plate carved with ornate loops, arcane symbols, and spell-forms surrounding a deep red garnet. The amulet hung by a thin golden chain around his neck.

But the amulet was no longer just an ornament—the golden triangle had *fused* to his flesh. The skin of his chest had bubbled and scarred around it, as if someone had pressed hot metal hard into skin like pliable candle wax and let the flesh harden around it. Parts of the chain had cut into the Adjudicator's collarbone and the tendons of his neck, becoming permanently bonded there. The central garnet glowed with a deep simmering fire of magic.

Bannon gasped. "What happened to you?"

"I became the Adjudicator." His stony, accusing stare turned toward the young man. "For years, the crimes I judged were mostly small— assaults, thievery, arson, adultery. Sometimes there were murders or rapes, but it was here in Lockridge . . ." He looked up, and his water-blue gaze skated past them, over their heads, as if he was calling upon the spirits. "It was here that I changed.

"There was a mother, Reva, who had three fine daughters, the oldest eight years old, the youngest only three. The mother was lovely in her own way, as were the little girls, but her husband desired another woman. Ellis was his name. He cheated on his wife, and when Reva learned of the affair, she became convinced that it was her fault—that she paid too much attention to their three daughters and not enough to her husband. Reva was desperate to regain his love." He made a disgusted sound. "She was mad.

"So, Reva smothered her three daughters in their sleep, to make sure that they would no longer come between her and Ellis. She thought he would love her more. When he came home that night, after his furtive passions with his mistress, Reva proudly showed him what she had done. She opened her arms and told him that her time and her heart now belonged only to him again.

"When Ellis saw their three dead daughters, he took a hatchet from the firewood pile and killed his wife, chopping her sixteen times."

The Adjudicator's expression didn't change as he told his story. "And when I came to judge Ellis, I touched the center of his forehead. We all thought we knew what had happened. I called upon the power in my amulet, and I learned the full story. I learned his thoughts and his black, poisoned heart. I already knew the horrors of his wife's crimes, but then I discovered what this man had done. Yes, he had killed his wife after she had killed his daughters. There was no question as to the murder Ellis had committed, but some even sympathized with him.

"Not I. I found within Ellis a most poisonous guilt, because he had not truly killed Reva out of horror that she had murdered their girls, as we all expected. No, I saw in Ellis's heart that he was actually pleased to have the nuisance of his family gone, and he used it as an excuse to be rid of his unwanted wife as well as his children. He thought he would get away with it.

"As that guilt flooded into me, those crimes charged the amulet. The magic grew stronger, and I unleashed it with wild abandon. I was angry and sickened. I made Ellis *feel* the guilt. I made him experience that moment of the greatest, most intense, horror. It rose to the front of his mind, and I froze it there. I turned him to stone in that instant as he experienced the most intense, most painful guilt of his life, reliving that appalling moment."

The Adjudicator let out a long sigh. "And releasing that magic freed me." The wizard touched the scar where the amulet had fused to the flesh of his chest. "I became not just a magistrate, not merely one who uncovered the truth of the accused. I became the Adjudicator." His voice grew deeper and much more ominous. "I have to protect these lands. That is my charge. I am to find anyone who is guilty. I cannot allow travelers to pass over the mountains into the fertile valley beyond. I must stop the spread of guilt."

Bannon swallowed audibly and took a step backward, holding up his sword.

Nicci didn't move, though she remained poised to fight. "And you judged all of these people as well?"

"All of them." The Adjudicator turned his chilling, watery gaze on her. "Only those without guilt can be allowed to proceed." He narrowed his eyes. "And what is your guilt, Sorceress?"

Nicci was defiant. "My guilt is none of your business."

For the first time she saw the Adjudicator's thin, pale lips twitch, in what might have been the distant shadow of a smile. "Ah, but it is." The garnet in his amulet glowed.

She reacted by reaching inside herself, ready to release the coiling magic, but she suddenly found that she couldn't. Her feet were frozen in place. Her legs were locked. Her arms refused to bend.

Bannon gasped. "What's . . . happening?"

"I am the Adjudicator." He took a step closer. The fused amulet throbbed in his chest. "The punishment I have decreed for all criminals is that they must experience their moment of greatest guilt. Continually. I will petrify you at that exquisite point, so that you face that worst moment for as long as time shall last."

Nicci's legs felt cold, leaden. She couldn't turn her head, but from the corner of her eye she saw her arm, her black dress, everything becoming white. Becoming stone.

"You have nothing to fear, if you are blameless," said the man. "You will be judged, and I am fair. I am the Adjudicator."

He stepped toward them, and Nicci tried to find a way to fight, to summon her magic, but her vision dimmed. A buzzing roar built in her mind, as if her head were filled with thousands of swarming bees.

Though she could barely see him, she heard the grim wizard's words. "Alas, in all these lands, I have yet to find someone without guilt."

CHAPTER 32

As the Adjudicator's magic closed around her like a clenching fist, Nicci struggled, but her body wouldn't move and her brain felt as if it had fossilized from the core outward. She could hardly think. She was trapped.

The dark wizard must have sensed her own powerful gift, because he struck in a way that she could not resist, with a spell she had never previously encountered. Her flesh tightened, hardened, and crystallized her body. Time itself seemed to stop. The warm tones of her skin turned to cold gray-white marble. She felt her lungs crush, her bones grow impossibly heavy.

Vision dimmed as her eyes petrified. Her blue irises crackled, hardened . . . and with the last hint of vision she saw young Bannon with his long red hair and his pale, freckled face. His expression had often been so innocent, so cheerful and unscarred by reality, that it set Nicci on edge. Now, though, his face filled with despair and misery. His mouth dropped open, his lips curled back, and even though her own ears roared with the sound of encroaching silence, she thought she heard him say ". . . kittens . . ." before he became completely fossilized, the sculpture of a man buried under an avalanche of unbearable grief and guilt.

When Nicci's vision faded, all she was able to see were the nightmarish remnants of her own past actions. Her memories rose up, as if they, too, were preserved in perfectly carved stone. Horrific, tense memories.

* * *

Shaken from his encounter with the spectral army that manifested through the bloodglass, Nathan left the watchtower. Alone and wary, he made his way through the darkening, sinister forest as the sun fell below the line of hills.

He hadn't expected his side trip to take so long, but the experience had been valuable for what he had seen and learned, in a historical sense if nothing else. These lands of the Old World were soaked with the blood of centuries of warfare, petty warlords turning against one another after the great barrier was erected to seal off the New World during the ancient wizard wars. Reading history was one thing; experiencing it was quite another.

He picked his way through the increasing shadows, heading back in the direction of the faint road they had been following, but Nathan feared he would walk right past the trail in the deepening twilight.

Much as he would have liked to join Nicci and Bannon in a town, hoping for a fine inn and hot food, he decided to make camp where he was. He was eager to tell his companions about the sentinel tower, and just as eager to sample the local ale. Instead, he would have to spend the night alone in the forest. "Not all parts of an adventure have to be charming and enjoyable," he said aloud.

He found a quiet clearing under a large elm tree, where he could use his pack as a pillow. As he sat under the branches and the night grew darker and colder, he pondered his lack of magic and what had happened when he had tried to practice en route to the tower. Right now, looking at the pile of dry sticks he had assembled, he could not help but think how it would have been so simple to make a cheery campfire, if he had magic to light the spark. He had never been good at using flint and steel. He didn't have the patience or the skill; when had Nathan Rahl ever needed it, if he could simply twitch a finger and light a fire?

Resigned, he ate cold pack food and wrapped himself in his brown cape from Renda Bay for warmth, then bedded down to a restless, uncomfortable sleep. The homespun linen shirt that had belonged to Phillip also kept him warm.

He set off at first light, bushwhacking through low saplings and shrubbery, heading instinctively in the right direction, and when he finally encountered the main path, he felt a sudden flush of satisfaction. Now that he was back on the road again, he could catch up with Nicci and Bannon. According to the map, a sizable town—Lockridge—should be only a few miles ahead.

It was late morning before he saw the first abandoned farmstead. He drank from the well, sure no one would complain, and chased off two pesky goats who were hungry for attention. The hideous ornamental statues seemed bizarre and out of place, but Nathan had seen many odd and inexplicable things before. People often had questionable tastes in art, and these sculptures were indeed questionable.

The road took him past other farms and dwellings, all of them just as silent, all populated with anguished statues. Maybe some petty local prince fancied himself a sculptor and required each of his subjects to own his hideous work.

By noon, Nathan reached the town, a typical mountain village with all the expected shops and houses, a marketplace, a square, a livery, an inn, a blacksmith, a potter, a woodworker—but it was populated with hundreds more statues, stone people depicted at a moment of horrific nightmares.

Nathan cautiously walked ahead, scratching the side of his face, stepping carefully in his high leather boots, afraid he might awaken the eerie sculptures. He felt like an intruder here. Under normal circumstances, he should have been able to sense sorcery or danger, and he dug deep within himself, found the writhing, sleeping magic there, the frayed tangles that remained after his gift of prophecy had been uprooted. But his Han was restless and uncooperative, and he didn't dare use it. He knew better.

At another time, he might have raised his voice and shouted out, but the hush was too ominous, even more so than at the ancient watchtower. The palpable horror and despair in the faces of these sculptures made his skin crawl. He saw people of all sorts: tradesmen, farmers, washerwomen, children.

In the Lockridge town square two fresh statues looked whiter and cleaner than the others, new creations made by the mad sculptor. The appalled expression made the young man's face unrecognizable at first, but then Nathan knew. Bannon!

Next to him stood the beautiful sorceress, whose curves and fine dress would have been a work of art for any imaginative sculptor. Nicci's face showed less misery than the faces of the other statues, but her expression still carried clear pain, as if her guilt and regrets had been smashed into numerous sharp shards, then imperfectly reassembled again.

A deep chill shuddered through Nathan, as he slowly turned around. Some terrible magic was at work here, and even though he could think of no spell that would have caused this, he was certain these were not mere sculptures of his friends, but Nicci and Bannon themselves, transformed somehow.

A powerful baritone voice cut through the crystalline silence of the town. "Are you an innocent man? Or have you come to be judged like the others?"

A tall black-robed man came striding toward him, his elongated bald head crowned with a gold circlet. The robes were open at his chest to display bubbling scars and waxy skin fused around a golden amulet.

On guard, Nathan replied, "I have lived a thousand years. It's hard to hold on to innocence and purity for all that time."

"A righteous man could do it."

"I haven't been overburdened with guilt, either." Nathan was certain this grim wizard had created the statue spell, trapping or petrifying these victims—including Nicci and Bannon. "I am a traveler, an emissary from the D'Haran Empire. The roving ambassador, in fact."

"And I am the Adjudicator." The man stepped forward, and the deep red garnet on his fused amulet began to glow.

At another time, Nathan would have released his magic to attack, but he had no gift that would help him. His hand darted down to grab the hilt of his sword, but his arm moved slowly, lethargically. He realized his feet were rooted in place. Nathan guessed what was happening.

The Adjudicator closed in, his water-blue eyes fixed on him. "Only the innocent shall pass onward, and I will find your guilt, old man. I will find all of it."

Nicci was frozen inside a petrified gallery of her life, the accusatory moments of her actions. She had no choice but to face the terrible things she had done, the darkness of her life . . . Death's Mistress . . . servant of the Keeper. That psychological weight was far greater than tons of rock.

She had tortured and killed many as a necessary part of her service to Jagang. She had aided the Imperial Order, falsely believing that she served all humanity by enforcing equality, helping the poor and the infirm, redistributing the wealth of greedy manipulators. She felt no guilt for that.

From a long time ago, she regretted that she had missed her father's funeral, but the Sisters had not allowed her to leave the Palace of the Prophets. Her father, an ambitious armorer, a good manager (she realized now), a man whose work had been appreciated by his customers until the Order ruined him. Nicci had been part of that downfall, as a dedicated young girl, brainwashed by her mother. She had become a believer, a wholehearted follower.

When one believed and followed something that was wrong, must there be guilt?

Kept inside the Palace of the Prophets for so many years, Nicci had also missed the death of her overbearing mother. She had attended that funeral, however, although she felt no guilt over the loss of the abusive woman. In order to obtain a fine black dress for the ceremony, Nicci had surrendered her body to the groping, lecherous embraces of a loathsome tailor, but it was the price she had agreed to pay. She had done what was necessary. That held no guilt. And she had preferred to wear a black dress ever since.

As those preserved dark memories rose inside her mind, she felt a need to atone for abducting Richard from his beloved Kahlan, forcing him to go away with her in a sham partnership to Altur'Rang. That had been a terrible thing, even if Nicci had been doing it to convince Richard of the correctness of her beliefs. During that time, she had fallen in love with him, but it was a twisted and broken emotion that even Nicci didn't understand.

The worst thing she had done, perhaps, was when Richard had rebuffed her advances, refused to make love to her, and so she had thrown herself upon another man in the city, letting him treat her roughly, slap her and rape her—though it hadn't been rape, because she herself had insisted on it. And all the while she knew that because of the maternity spell that linked them, *Kahlan* would experience every physical sensation that Nicci felt . . . and Kahlan would believe in her heart that Richard had been unfaithful to her, that *he* was the one taking his pleasure on Nicci's body, wild with lust.

How that must have hurt Kahlan . . . and Nicci had taken great joy in it.

Yes, for that she felt guilt.

But Nicci had already made her peace with it. Kahlan and Richard had forgiven her. That embittered, evil person might have been who she was a long time ago—Death's Mistress—but Nicci was different now. She did not wallow in her past and was not haunted by the ghosts of her deeds. She had served Richard, had fought for him, had helped overthrow the Imperial Order. She had commanded Jagang to *die*. She had served Richard with relentless dedication and killed countless numbers of bloodthirsty half people from the Dark Lands. She had done whatever Richard asked, had even stopped his heart to send him into the underworld so he could save Kahlan.

She had given him everything except for her guilt. Nicci did not hold on to guilt. Even when she had committed those crimes, she had felt nothing.

And now in this new journey of her life, she served an even greater purpose—not just the man Richard Rahl, whom she loved, but the *dream* of Richard Rahl—and in that service there could be no guilt.

Nicci was a sorceress. She had the power of the wizards she had killed. She had all the spells the Sisters had taught her. She had a strength in her soul that went beyond any imagined calling of this deluded Adjudicator.

The magic was hers to control, and the punishment was not his to mete out.

Her body might have turned to stone, trapping her thoughts in a suffocating purgatory, but Nicci's emotions had been like stone before, and she had a heart of black ice. It was her protection. She called upon that now, releasing any spark of magic she could summon, finding her flicker of determination and her refusal to accept the sentence this grim wizard imposed upon her.

As her fury grew, the magic kindled within her. She was not some clumsy, murderous villager, she was not a petty thief. She was a sorceress. She was *Death's Mistress*.

Inside and around her Nicci felt the stone begin to crack. . . .

The Adjudicator's long face was sallow and dour, as if all humor had been leached away. He showed no pleasure as he explained Nathan's punishment and worked the spell to trap him. "They are all guilty," he said, "every person. I have so much work to do . . ."

Nathan strained, struggling to move his petrified arm. "No, you won't." His hand had nearly reached the sword, but even if he touched the hilt, it would do no good. The stone spell surrounded him and was rapidly fossilizing his tissues, stopping time inside his body. Nathan could not fight, could not flee, could barely even move. His only recourse would have been to use magic, to lash out with a retaliatory spell. But if he couldn't light so much as a campfire, he certainly couldn't fight such a powerful wizard.

Even if he summoned his wayward magic, though, Nathan knew he couldn't control it. He could not forget trying to heal the wounded man in Renda Bay, ripping him asunder with what should have been healing magic. Nathan had only tried to help him. . . .

Maybe *that* was the moment of great guilt the Adjudicator would force him to endure for as long as stone lasted.

He heard the grinding crackle as the spell petrified even his leather pouch, along with his travel garments, and the life book. He could not breathe.

Nathan felt the magic squirming within him, ducking away like a snake slithering into a thicket. What did it matter if he unleashed it now and the spell backfired? What greater harm could it cause than the harm he was already facing? Even Nicci had been trapped in stone, and Bannon, poor Bannon, was already paralyzed in endless anguish.

Nathan had nothing to lose. No matter what unexpected backlash his magic might trigger, if he could release it and strike back, even in some awkward way, at least that would be something.

His lungs crushed down as the stone weight of guilt squeezed him, suffocated him, but he managed to gasp out some words. "I am Nathan . . . Nathan the prophet." He caught one more fractional breath, one more gasp of words. "Nathan the *wizard*!"

The magic crawled out of him like a fanged eel startled from a dark underwater alcove. Nathan released it, not knowing what it would do . . . not caring. It lashed out, uncontrolled.

He heard and felt a white-hot sizzle building within his body. For a moment he was sure that his own form would explode, that his skull would erupt with uncontained power.

In front of him, the statue of Nicci seemed to be changing, softening, with countless eggshell cracks all over the white stone that had captured her perfection. Nathan didn't think he was doing it. His own magic was here . . . boiling out—and spraying like scalding oil on the Adjudicator.

The grim wizard recoiled, staggering backward. "What are you doing?" He raised a hand and clapped the other to his amulet. "No!"

The petrification spell that the Adjudicator had wrapped around Nathan like a smothering cloak now slipped off of him, ricocheted and combined with Nathan's wild magic. Reacting, backfiring.

The dour man straightened, then convulsed in horror. His lantern jaw dropped open, and his expression fell into abject despair. His water-blue eyes began to turn white, and his robe stiffened, changing to stone. "I am the Adjudicator!" he cried. "I am the judge. I see the guilt . . ."

With a crackling, shattering sound, Nicci fought her way out of her own fossilization, somehow using her powers. Nathan's vision became sharper as he felt the intrusive stone drain out of his body like sand through an hourglass. His flesh softened, his blood pumped again.

Nathan's unchecked magic likewise thrashed and curled and whipped. The Adjudicator writhed and screamed as he gradually froze in place, even his robe turning to marble.

"You. Are. *Guilty!*" Nathan said to the transforming Adjudicator when he could breathe again. "Your crime is that you judged all these people."

Stone engulfed the Adjudicator, crackling up through his skin, stiffening the lids around his wide-open eyes. "No!" It wasn't a denial, but a horror, a realization. "What have I done?" His voice became scratchier, rougher as his throat hardened and his chest solidified so that he couldn't breathe. "All those people!" The stone locked his face in an expression of immeasurable regret and shame, his mouth open as he uttered one last, incomplete "No!" He became the newest statue in the town of Lockridge.

Staring at the stone figure, Nathan felt his rampant magic dissipate. Just like that, it was no longer available to his touch. He sucked in a deep breath and felt life flow through him again.

CHAPTER 33

When the Adjudicator himself turned to stone, his spell shattered and dissipated throughout the town.

No longer petrified, Nicci slowly straightened and let out a long breath, half expecting to see an exhalation of dust from her lungs. Her blond hair and the skin of her neck became supple again, the fabric of her black dress flowed. She lifted her arms, looked at her hands.

Through her own determination, she had broken the fossilization spell that ran throughout herself, but Nathan had defeated the farther-reaching stranglehold of the twisted Adjudicator. Now, the old wizard flexed his arms and stamped his legs to restore his circulation. He shook his head, bewildered.

Nearby, the statue of Bannon, his expression locked in guilty despair, slowly suffused with color. His pink skin, rusty freckles, and ginger hair were restored. Instead of being amazed to find himself alive again, though, Bannon dropped to his knees in the town square and let out a keening wail. His shoulders shook, and he bowed his head, sobbing.

Nathan tried to comfort the distraught young man, patting him on the shoulder, although he did not speak. Stepping close to Bannon, Nicci softened her voice. "We are safe now. Whatever you experienced was your past. It is who you *were*, not who you are. You need have no guilt about who you are." She guessed that he continued to suffer over losing his friend Ian to the slavers.

But, why had he uttered the word "kittens" as he turned to stone?

In the streets and square around them, a low crackle slowly grew to a rumble accompanied by a stirring of breezes that sounded like astonished whispers. Nicci turned around and saw the villagers trapped in stone by the Adjudicator's brutal justice: one by one, they began to move.

As the gathered, tortured sculptures were restored to flesh, they remained overwhelmed by the nightmarish memories they had endured for so long. Then the sobbing and wailing began, rising to a cacophony of the damned. These people were too caught up in their own ordeal to look around and realize they had been released from the terrible spell.

Bannon finally climbed back to his feet, his eyes red and puffy, his face streaked with tears. "We're safe now," he said, as if he could comfort the villagers. "It'll be all right."

Some of the people of Lockridge heard him, but most were too stunned to understand. Husbands and wives found each other and embraced, clinging in desperate hugs. Wailing children ran to their parents to be swept into the warm comfort of a stable family again.

The disoriented villagers finally became aware of the three strangers among them. One man introduced himself as Lockridge mayor Raymond Barre. "I speak for the people of this town." He looked from Nicci, to Nathan, to Bannon. "Are you the ones who saved us?"

"We are," Nathan said. "We were just travelers looking for directions and a warm meal."

With growing anger, the townspeople noticed the grotesque, horror-struck statue of the Adjudicator. Nicci indicated the stone figure of the corrupted man. "A civilization must have laws, but there cannot be justice when a man with no conscience metes out sentences without compassion or mercy."

Bannon said, "If each one of us carries that guilt, then we are living our sentences every day. How can I ever forget . . . ?"

"None of us will forget," said Mayor Barre. "And none of us will forget you, strangers. You saved us."

Other townspeople came forward. An innkeeper wore an apron

stained from a meal he had served an unknown number of years before. Farmers and grocers stared at the ramshackle appearance of the village, at their broken-down vendor stalls, the remnants of rotted fruits and vegetables, the dilapidated shutters around the windows of the inn, the collapsed roof on the livery, the hay in the barn turned gray with age.

"How long has it been?" asked a woman whose dark brown hair had fallen out of its unruly bun. She wiped her hands on her skirts. "Last I remember, it was spring. Now it seems to be summer."

"But summer of which year?" asked the blacksmith. He gestured toward the hinges on the nearby door of a dilapidated barn. "Look at the rust."

Nathan told them the year, by D'Haran reckoning, but these villagers so far south in the wilderness of the Old World still followed the calendar of an ancient emperor, so the date meant nothing to them. They didn't even remember Jagang or the march of the Imperial Order.

Although he was as overwhelmed as the rest of his people, Mayor Barre called everyone into the town square, where Nicci and Nathan helped explain what had happened. Each victim remembered his or her own experience with the Adjudicator, and most recalled earlier times when the traveling magistrate had come to judge their petty criminals and impose reasonable sentences—before the magic had engulfed him, before the amulet and his gift had turned him into a monster.

One mother holding the hands of a small son and daughter walked up to the petrified statue of the evil man. She stood silent for a moment, her expression roiling with hate, before she spat on the white marble. Others came up and did the same.

Then the innkeeper suggested they use the blacksmith's steel hammers and chisels to smash the Adjudicator's statue into fragments of stone. Nicci gave them a solemn nod. "I will not stop you from doing so."

It was like a grim, furious mob as the Lockridge villagers battered and smashed the hated statue until the Adjudicator was nothing but rock shards and crumbling dust. When all that remained was a pile of rubble, the people were drained, though not satisfied.

Mayor Barre said, "We must go back to our homes and rebuild our lives. Clean up our houses, tend our gardens. Find all of that man's other victims and explain what happened."

Nathan said, "Magic has changed, and the world has changed. Even the night sky is shifted. After night falls, you will discover that the constellations are different from those you remember. We don't yet know all the ways the world has been altered."

Nicci also spoke up. "In the D'Haran Empire, Lord Rahl has defeated the emperors who oppressed both the Old World and the New. We came here to see his new territory and to tell you all that the world can be free and at peace. We found this town, we freed you, we destroyed the Adjudicator." She looked down at the unrecognizable rubble, saw a smooth curved chunk that might have been an ear. "This man is exactly the sort of monster that Lord Rahl stands against." She squared her shoulders. "And we did stand against him."

As the people muttered, absorbing the knowledge, Nathan kept shaking his head, troubled. He said to Nicci, "I studied magic for many centuries, and I recall stories of how the ancient wizards of Ildakar had a way of turning human beings into stone. Some of them even called themselves *sculptors*. They did not merely use convicted criminals, but also warriors defeated in their great game arena. Such statues were used for decoration."

He drew his thumb and forefinger down his smooth chin. "This kind of magic did more than transmute flesh into marble, like an alchemical reaction. No, this spell was another form of magic that allowed the slowing and stopping of time, petrifying flesh as if thousands of centuries had passed. I need to consider this further."

For the rest of that day, Nicci and her companions learned that there were many other towns in the mountains connected by a network of roads, and many of those villages had been served by the same traveling magistrate. Nicci feared that the Adjudicator had petrified other people as well, but with the spell now broken those populations would also be reviving.

Perhaps this entire part of the Old World had just reawakened. . . .

"Saving the world, just as the witch woman predicted, Sorceress," Nathan mused.

"You had as much to do with that as I did," she said.

He merely shrugged. "A good deed is still a good deed, wherever the credit lies. I left the People's Palace to go help people, and I am happy to do so."

Nicci could not disagree.

The unsettled townspeople drifted apart to explore their abandoned homes and find their lives again. Nicci, Nathan, and Bannon joined the innkeeper and his wife for a meal of thin oat porridge made from a small sack of grain that had remarkably not gone bad.

Bannon remained extremely distraught, though, and he struggled in vain to find his contentment and peace again. He was short-tempered, skittish, brooding, and finally when they were alone in one of the inn's dusty side rooms, Nicci asked him, "I can tell you are still suffering from the ordeal. What did you see when you were trapped in stone? The spell is broken now."

"I'll be fine," Bannon said in a husky voice.

She pressed him, though. "The expression of guilt on your face looked worse than when you told us about Ian and the slavers."

"Yes, it was worse."

Nicci waited for him, encouraging him with her silence until he blurted out, "It was the kittens! I remember a man from my island. He drowned a sack of kittens." Bannon looked away from her before continuing. "I tried to stop him, but he threw the kittens into a stream, and they drowned. I wanted to save them but I couldn't. They mewed and cried out."

Nicci thought of all the terrible things she'd endured, the guilt that she had lifted and cast away, the blood she had shed, the lives she had destroyed. "That is the greatest guilt you feel?" She didn't believe him. A greater halo of pain than what had happened with Ian?

His hazel eyes flashed with anger as he spun to her. "Who are you now, the Adjudicator? It's not up to *you* to measure my guilt! You don't know how much it broke my heart, how bad I felt." He stalked away to find one of the unoccupied rooms where he could bed down for the night. "Leave me alone. I never want to think about it again." He closed the door against her continuing questions.

Nicci looked at his retreating form, trying to measure the truth of what he had said, but there was something wrong about Bannon's eyes, about his expression. He was hiding the real answer, but she decided not to press him for now, although she would need to know sooner or later.

Everyone here in Lockridge had been through their own ordeal. Weary, she went to find her own bed. She hoped that they would all have a quiet sleep, untroubled by nightmares.

CHAPTER 34

After leaving the Lockridge villagers to pick up the pieces of their lives, Nicci, Nathan, and Bannon followed the dwindling old road deeper into the mountains. Though preoccupied with helping his people, Mayor Barre had confirmed for them that Kol Adair did indeed lie over the mountains and beyond a great valley. The ordeal with the Adjudicator had made Nathan even more determined to restore himself by any means necessary.

What had once been a wide thoroughfare traveled by commercial caravans was overgrown from disuse. Dark pines and thick oaks encroached with the slow intent of erasing the blemishes left by mankind.

Bannon was remarkably withdrawn, showing little interest in their journey. His usual eager conversation and positive outlook had vanished, still festering from what the Adjudicator had made him see and suffer. Nicci had faced the consequences of her dark past, and she had overcome that guilt long ago, but the young man had far less experience in turning raw, bleeding wounds into hard scars.

Nathan tried to cheer the young man up. "We're making good time. Would you like to stop for a while, my boy? Spar a little with our swords?"

Bannon gave an unusually unenthusiastic reply. "No thank you. I've had enough real swordplay with the selka and the Norukai slavers."

"That's true, my boy," he said with forced cheer, "but in a practice sparring session you can let yourself have fun."

Nicci stepped around a moss-covered boulder in the trail, then looked over her shoulder. "Maybe he thinks the actual killing is fun, Wizard."

Bannon looked stung. "I did what I had to do. People need to be protected. You might not get there in time, but when you do, you have to do your best."

They reached a fast-flowing stream that bubbled over slick rocks. Nicci gathered her skirts and splashed across the shallow water, not worried about getting her boots wet. Nathan, though, picked his way downstream, where he found a fallen log to use as a bridge. He carefully balanced his way across and arrived on the other side, then turned to face Bannon, who crossed the log with barely a glance at his feet.

Nicci kept watching the young man, growing more troubled at his worsening inner pain. A companion so haunted, so preoccupied and listless, might be a liability if they encountered some threat, and she could not allow that.

She faced Bannon as he stepped off the log onto the soft mosses of the bank. "We need to address this, Bannon Farmer. A boil must be lanced before it festers. I know you're not telling the truth—at least not the whole truth."

Bannon was immediately wary, and a flash of fear crossed his face as he drew back. "The truth about what?"

"What did the Adjudicator show you? What guilt has been eating away inside you?"

"I already told you." Bannon stepped away, looking as if he wanted to run. He turned pale. "I couldn't stop a man from drowning a sack of kittens. Sweet Sea Mother, I know that may sound childish to you, but it's not your place to judge how my guilt affects me!"

"I am not your judge," Nicci said, "nor do I want to be. But I need to understand."

Stepping up to them on the stream bank, Nathan interrupted. "You would not have us believe that the Adjudicator considers the loss of kittens to be more damning than losing your friend to slavers?" He gave a wistful smile, trying to be compassionate. "Although, truth be told, I do like kittens. The Sisters in the Palace of the Prophets let me have a kitten once—oh, four hundred years ago. I raised it and loved it, but the cat wandered away, happily hunting mice and rats in the palace, I suppose. It's an enormous place. That was centuries ago. . . ." His voice degenerated into a wistful sigh. "The cat must be dead by now. I haven't thought about it in a long time."

Nicci tried to soften her stern voice, with only marginal success. "You are our companion, Bannon. Are you a criminal? I do not intend to punish you, but I need to know. You are a handicap to our mission and safety in the state you are in."

He lashed out. "I'm not a criminal!" He strode away, following the stream and trying to avoid them. Nicci went after him, but Nathan put a hand on her shoulder and shook his head slightly.

She called after the young man. "Whatever it is, I would not judge you. I could spend months describing the people I've hurt. I once roasted one of my own generals alive in the middle of a village, just to show the villagers how ruthless I could be."

Bannon turned to stare at her, looking both surprised and sickened.

She crossed her arms over her chest. "You failed to prevent someone else from killing a sack of kittens. That may be true. But I don't believe the Adjudicator would condemn you forever because of that."

Bannon splashed cool water on his face, then left the stream and began climbing uphill through a patch of meadow lilies. "It's a long story," he sighed, without looking at her.

From behind, Nathan said, "Maybe it can wait until camp tonight, after we find some food."

As Bannon moved through the brush, he startled a pair of grouse. The two plump birds clucked and waddled quickly for a few steps before they exploded into flight.

Nicci made an offhand gesture with her hand and released her magic. With barely a thought, she stopped the hearts of the two grouse, which dropped to the ground, dead. "There, now we have dinner, and this is as good a place to camp as any. Fresh water from the stream, wood for our fire—and time for a story."

Bannon looked defeated. Without a word he began to gather dead branches, while Nathan dressed the birds and Nicci used her magic to ignite the fire. While the meal cooked, Nicci watched Bannon's expression as he dredged through his memories like a miner shoveling loads of rock, sifting through the rubble and trying to decide what to keep.

At last, after he had picked part of the grouse carcass clean and wandered back to the stream to wash himself, Bannon returned. He lifted his chin and swallowed hard. Nicci could see he was ready.

"On Chiriya Island," he began, and his voice cracked. He drew a deep breath, "Back home . . . I didn't just run away because my life was too quiet and dull. It wasn't a perfect life."

"It rarely ever is, my boy," Nathan said.

Nicci was more definitive. "It *never* is."

"My parents weren't as I've described them. Well, my mother was. I loved her, and she loved me, but my father . . . my father was—" His eyes darted back and forth as if searching for the right word and then daring to use it. "He was *vile*. He was reprehensible." Bannon caught himself as if he feared the spirits might strike him down as he paced back and forth. Then that odd look came to his face again, as if he were trying to paint over the memories in his mind.

"My mother had a cat, a female tabby she loved very much. The cat would sleep on the hearth near a warm fire, but she preferred to curl up on my mother's lap." Bannon's eyes narrowed. "My father was a drunken lout, a brutal man. If he had a miserable life, it was his own fault, and he made our lives miserable because he wanted us to bear the blame. He would beat me, sometimes with a stick, but usually with just his hands. I think he enjoyed the idea of hitting.

"I was always his second choice, though. I could outrun him, and my father never wanted to make much effort, so he hit my mother instead. He would corner her in our house. He would strike her whenever he lost a gambling game down at the tavern, or he would strike her when he ran out of money and couldn't buy enough drink, or he would strike her because he didn't like the food she cooked, or because she didn't cook enough of it.

"He made my mother scream and then he punished her for screaming and for screaming so loudly that the neighbors might hear—although they had all known how he abused her for many years. But he liked it when she screamed too, and if she didn't make enough sounds of pain, he would beat her some more. So she had to walk that narrow path of terror and hurt, just so she could survive—so we could both survive."

Bannon lowered his head. "When I was young, I was too small to stand up to him. And when I grew older, when I might have defended myself against him, I simply couldn't because that man had trained me to be terrified of him." He sat so heavily on a fallen tree trunk that he seemed to collapse.

"The cat was my mother's special treasure, her refuge. She would stroke the cat on her lap as she wept quietly when my father was gone. The cat seemed to absorb her pain and her sorrow. Somehow that restored her in a way that no one else could. It wasn't magic," Bannon said, "but it was its own kind of healing."

Nathan finished eating his grouse and tossed the bones aside, then leaned forward, listening intently. Nicci hadn't moved. She watched the young man's expressions, his fidgeting movements, and she absorbed every word.

"The cat had a litter of five kittens, all mewling and helpless, all so cute. But the mama cat died giving birth. My mother and I found the kittens in a corner the next morning, trying to suckle on the cat's cold, stiff carcass, trying to get warmth from their mama's fur. They were so plaintive when they mewed." He squeezed his fists together, and his gaze was directed deep into his memories. "When my mother picked up the dead tabby, she looked as if something had broken inside her."

"How old were you then, my boy?"

Bannon looked up at the old wizard, as if trying to formulate an answer to the question. "That was less than a year ago."

Nicci was surprised.

"I wanted to save the kittens, for my mother's sake. They were all so tiny, with the softest fur—and needle-sharp claws. They squirmed when I held them. We had to give them milk from a thimble to take care of them. My mother and I both drew comfort from those kittens . . . but

we didn't have a chance to name them—not a single one—before my
father found them.

"One night, he came home in a rage. I have no idea what had an-
gered him. The reasons never really mattered anyway—my mother and
I didn't need to know, but in some dark corner of his alcohol-soured
mind we were to blame. He knew how to hurt us—oh, he knew how
to hurt us.

"My father stormed into the house, grabbed a sack full of onions
hanging on the wall. He dumped the onions across the floor. Even
though we tried to keep him away from the kittens, my father grabbed
them and stuffed them into the empty sack one at a time. They mewed
and mewed, crying out for help, but we couldn't help. He wouldn't let
us." Bannon's face darkened, but he didn't look at his listeners.

"I tried to hit my father, but he backhanded me. My mother begged
him, but he just wanted the kittens. He knew that would be a far more
painful blow to her than his fist. 'Their mother's dead,' he growled,
'and I won't have you wasting any more milk.'" As he spoke, Bannon
made a disgusted sound. "The idea of 'wasting' a few thimbles of milk
was such an absurd comment that I could find no answer for it. And
then he slammed open the door and stormed out into the night.

"My mother wailed and sobbed. I wanted to run after him and fight
him, but I stayed to comfort her instead. She wrapped her arms around
me and we rocked back and forth. She sobbed into my shoulder. My
father had taken away the last thing my mother loved, the last memory
of her beloved cat." He swallowed hard.

"But I decided to do something, right away. I knew where he was
going. There was a deep stream nearby, and he would throw the sack
there. The kittens would drown, wet and cold and helpless—unless
I saved them.

"No matter what I did, I knew I'd get a beating, but I had suffered
beatings before, and I had never had a chance to save something I
loved, to save something my mother loved. So I ran out into the night,
following my father. I wanted to chase after him, shouting and cursing,
to call him a lout and a monster. But I was smart enough to remain
silent. I didn't dare let him know I was coming.

"The cloudy night was dark, but he was drunk enough that he didn't notice anything else around him. He wouldn't dream that I might stand up to him. I had never done it before.

"He reached the streamside, and I saw the sack squirm and sway in his grip. He didn't gloat, didn't even seem to think about what he was doing. Without any apparent remorse, he simply tossed the knotted onion sack into the swift water. He had weighted it with rocks, and after bobbing a few times as it flowed along in the current, the sack dunked beneath the water. I thought sure I could hear the kittens crying. Sweet Sea Mother . . ." His voice hitched.

"I did not have much time. The kittens would drown in a minute or two. I didn't dare let my father catch me, and if I went too close he would reach out and grab me with those awful hands. He would seize my shirt or my arm, and he would slap me until I collapsed. He might even break a bone or two—and worse, he would prevent me from saving the kittens! I hid in the dark for an agonized minute. My heart was pounding.

"He didn't even pause to savor his murderous handiwork. He stood at the streamside for a dozen breaths, then lurched away into the night, back in the direction he had come.

"I bounded as fast as I could run along the stream, stumbling and tripping on the rocks and low willows. I followed the cold current and tried to see in the dim moonlight, searching for any sign of the bobbing sack. I scrabbled along the banks of the stream, splashing and stumbling, but I had to hurry.

"After the spring rains, the water ran high, and the current was swifter than I remembered it. I couldn't see how far the kittens had drifted, but up ahead around a curve in the stream, I spotted just a flash of the onion sack bobbing up before it sank down again. I tripped on the mossy rocks and slick mud, and I fell into the water, but I didn't care. I splashed deeper, wading along, sweeping my hands back and forth ahead of me as I tried to grab the sack. I caught weeds, cut myself on a tangled branch, but the sack had drifted along, still under the water. I couldn't hear the kittens anymore, and I knew it was too long, but I kept trying. I sloshed forward and dove ahead until finally I caught the sack, wrapped my fingers around the folds of rough cloth. I had it!

"Laughing and crying, I yanked it out of the water and held it up, dripping. It was waterlogged and heavy. Rivulets of stream water ran out of it, but I stumbled to the shore and sprawled up on the bank. With my numb, bleeding fingers I couldn't pull open the wet knot closing the sack. I tore at it with my fingernails, and finally I ripped the fabric. More water gushed out, and I dumped the kittens out onto the streamside.

"I remember saying 'No, no, no!' over and over again. Those poor, fragile kittens flopped out, slick and wet, like fish from a net. And they weren't moving. Not a one of them.

"I picked them up, pressed gently on them, blew on their tiny faces, trying to get them to respond. Their perfect little tongues lolled out. I couldn't stop imagining them mewing for help, trying to breathe, dragged under the cold water. They were so young and hadn't even known their own mama, so I knew they had been crying out for me and my mother. And we hadn't saved them—we hadn't saved them!"

Bannon hunched his shoulders and sobbed. "I ran as fast as I could. I tried to get the sack from the water—I really tried! But all the kittens were dead, all five of them."

Nathan listened with a compassionate frown. He stroked his chin as he sat on his rock next to the campfire. "You tried your best. There was nothing else you could have done. You can't carry that guilt around with you forever. It'll kill you."

As Bannon wept, Nicci watched him intently. In a low voice, she said, "That's not what he feels guilty about."

The old wizard was surprised, but Bannon looked up at Nicci with remarkably *old* eyes. "No," he said in a hoarse voice. "Not that at all."

He laced his fingers together, then unraveled them again as he found the courage to go on. "I found a soft spot under a willow near the stream, and I dug out a hole with my bare hands. I buried the kittens and placed the wet sack on top of them, like a blanket that might keep them warm in the cold night. I piled rocks on top of the grave, so that I could show my mother where I had buried them, but I never wanted my father to find out where they were or what I had done.

"I stayed there for a long time, just crying, and then I made my way home. I knew I could never hide my tears or my wet clothes from my father. He would probably beat me for it, or maybe just look at me with smug satisfaction. At the time, with the kittens all dead, I didn't think he could hurt me any more and I was tired of running." The young man gulped. "But I came home to find something far worse."

Nicci felt her shoulder muscles tense, and she braced herself. Bannon spoke in a bleak voice, as if he no longer had any emotion in the memory. "After he drowned the kittens and came back to our cottage, my mother was ready for him. She'd had *enough*. After all the pain and suffering and fear he had inflicted on her, the murder of those poor innocent kittens was the last straw for her. When he staggered through the door, my mother was waiting.

"I saw the scene afterward, and I guessed what happened. As soon as he entered the house, she held a loose oak axe handle like a warrior's mace. She attacked my father, struck him in the head, screaming at him. She nearly succeeded, but it was only a glancing blow, enough to draw blood, perhaps crack his skull—and certainly enough to make his anger erupt.

"In a futile effort, she tried to hurt him, maybe even kill him. But my father snatched the oak handle from her hands, tore it right out of her grip, whirled around—" Bannon swallowed. "And he beat her to death with it." He squeezed his eyes shut.

"By the time I came home from burying the kittens, she was already dead. He had smashed her face so that I couldn't recognize her, couldn't even see the usual parts of a face at all. Her left eye had been pulped, and broken shards of skull protruded upward, exposing brain. Her mouth was just a ragged hole, and teeth lay scattered around, some of them pounded into the soft meat of her face, like decorations. . . ."

His voice grew softer, shakier. "My father came for me with the bloody, splintered axe handle, but I had nothing to defend myself with, not even a sword. I threw myself on him nevertheless, howling.

I . . . I don't even remember it. I hit him, clawed at him, pounded at his chest.

"This time the neighbors had heard my mother's screams, worse than ever before, and they rushed in only moments after I arrived. They saved me, or else my father would have killed me, too. I was screaming, trying to fight, trying to hurt him. But they pulled me away and subdued him. By that time, most of the fight had gone out of my father. Blood covered his face, his clothes, and his hands. Some from the gash on his scalp where my mother had struck him, but most of the blood belonged to her.

"Someone had raised the alarm, and one goodwife sent her little boy running to town to get the magistrate." Bannon sucked in a succession of breaths and kneaded his fingers as he stared like a lost soul into the small campfire before he could continue. Overhead, a night bird cried out and took flight from one of the pine trees.

"I couldn't save the sack of kittens. I couldn't prevent my father from drowning them, but I ran after him, nevertheless. I waded into the stream and tried to catch them before it was too late. But I always knew it would be too late, and when they were dead I wasted precious time burying them and crying over them . . . when I could have been there to save my mother."

He looked up at his listeners, and the empty pain in his hazel eyes struck a deep chill even in Nicci's heart.

"If I had stayed with my mother, maybe I could have protected her. If I hadn't gone chasing after the kittens, I would have been there. I would have stood up to him. I would have saved her. She and I would have faced him together. The two of us could have driven him off somehow. After that night, my father never would have hurt me again. Or her.

"But I went to save the kittens instead. I left my mother behind to face that monster all by herself."

Bannon stood up again, brushed off his pants. He spoke as if he were merely delivering a scout's report. "I stayed at Chiriya long enough to see my father hanged for murder. By then, I had a few coins, and out of sympathy other villagers gave me money to live on. I could have had a little cottage, started a family, worked the cabbage fields. But the house smelled too much like blood and nightmares, and Chiriya held nothing for me.

"So I signed aboard the next ship that came into our little harbor— the *Wavewalker*. I left my home, never intending to go back. What I wanted was to find a better place. I wanted a life the way I imagined it."

Nathan said, "So you've been changing your memories, covering up the darkness with fantasies of how you thought your life should be."

"With lies," Nicci said.

"Yes, they're lies," Bannon said. "The real truth is . . . poison. I was just trying to make everything better. Was that wrong?"

Nicci was sure now that Bannon Farmer had a good heart. In his mind, and in the way he described his old lie to others, the young man was struggling to make the world into a place it would never be.

When the wizard placed a reassuring hand on his shoulder, Bannon flinched as if in a sudden flashback of his father striking him. Nathan didn't remove his hand, but tightened his grip, like an anchor. "You're with us now, my boy."

Nodding, Bannon smeared the back of his hand across his face, wiping away the tears. He straightened his shoulders and responded with a weak smile. "I agree. That's good enough."

Even Nicci rewarded him with an appreciative nod. "You may have more steel in you than I thought."

CHAPTER 35

Rain and gloom set in for the next four days as they traveled higher into the mountains. The mornings were filled with fog, the days saturated with drizzle, and the nights accompanied by a full downpour. Low-hanging clouds and dense dripping trees kept them from seeing far into the distance, and they could not gauge the high and rugged mountains ahead of them. Eventually, Nicci knew they would find the high point and look down into the lush valley that lay between them and Kol Adair.

Nicci walked along wrapped in a gray woolen cloak the Lockridge innkeeper had given her, which was drenched and heavy. Bannon and Nathan were just as miserable, and the sodden gloom weighed on them as heavily as the young man's reticence.

On the fifth night out of Lockridge, the downpour increased and the temperature dropped to a bone-penetrating wet cold. Nicci was pleased to find a thick wayward pine, a pyramid-shaped tree with dense, drooping boughs. For those travelers who knew how to identify them, wayward pines formed a solid, reliable shelter in the forest. Richard had shown her how to find and use them.

Nicci shook the long-needled branches to disperse the collected beads of rainwater, then lifted the bough aside to reveal a dark and cozy hollow within. "We'll sleep here."

The wizard found a comfortable spot inside under the low overhanging branches. "Now, if you could just find some roasted mutton and a tankard of ale, Sorceress, we'd have a fine night."

Bannon sat with his knees pulled up against his chest, still withdrawn.

"Be satisfied with what I've already provided," Nicci said. She did use her magic to light a small fire inside the shelter, and the crisp greenwood smoke curled up into the slanted boughs and away from them. Because they were soaked and cold, Nicci also released more magic to dry the moisture in their clothes, so that for the first time in days they actually felt warm and comfortable.

"I can tolerate unpleasant conditions," she explained, "but not when I don't have to. We need our strength and a good rest. There's no telling how far we have yet to go."

"The journey itself is part of our goal," Nathan said. "After we find Kol Adair and I am whole again with my magic, we have the rest of the Old World to explore."

"Let us get a good rest for tonight," she said, "and explore the whole world tomorrow."

They warmed water over the fire and made a fortifying soup with barley, dried meat, and spices. Afterward, they collected enough rainwater in a pot outside the wayward pine that they could make hot tea.

Bannon rolled up in his now-dry cloak and pretended to go to sleep, and Nathan looked at him with concern. "Adventures rarely turn out the way one expects," he said in a low voice to Nicci, but Bannon surely heard as well—as the wizard no doubt intended.

The next day as they continued through the drizzle, splashing in puddles and slipping in the trail mud, Nathan exuberantly drew his sword and rounded on Bannon. "You walk like a sluggard, my boy. And with your eyes so downcast, a dragon could be upon you before you even noticed." He held up his sword and stepped in front of the young man, blocking his way. "Defend yourself, or you're useless to us."

Though Bannon was startled, the wizard swung his sword, but without malice, and he did so slowly enough that the confused young man had a chance to duck. "Stop, Nathan! What are you doing?"

"Waking you up." The wizard swung again, more earnestly this time.

Bannon leaped out of the way. He fumbled Sturdy from its scabbard. "I don't want to fight you."

"Such a pity," Nathan said, coming after him. "When bloodthirsty enemies come for me, I always let them know whether I'm in the mood for fighting. It makes all the difference." He swung again, and Bannon lifted his sword to meet the blow with a loud clang. Sparrows in the branches overhead were startled into flight, swooping away to find a drier, more peaceful bough.

Nicci knew exactly what Nathan was doing, although she also understood the young man's lethargy. After Bannon had been forced to face the fact that his nostalgic life was nothing more than a foolish fantasy, he was like a ship cast adrift with no rudder or sails. Nicci had spent years building shields around her mind and heart, but Bannon was still so young.

Nathan cried out in happy surprise as his opponent counterattacked, whistling his blade through the air. The solid ringing of steel against steel echoed through the waterlogged forest. "That's better, my boy! I want to know that you can handle yourself if we're set upon by monsters again."

They crashed through the underbrush as Nathan chased him. Bannon wheeled to defend himself and press an attack, sending the wizard into full retreat; then, in a furious volley of blows, they brought each other to a standstill. His face animated now, Bannon pressed forward, pushing Nathan, who slipped in the slimy mud of the trail. The wizard tumbled flat on his back, and then Bannon also lost his balance and sprawled beside his mentor. The two men picked themselves up, panting, and laughing. Both were covered in mud.

Nicci watched them, her arms crossed, the woolen traveling cloak pulled around her. Meeting Nathan's eyes, she gave him a nod of acknowledgment.

The wizard reached out to take the young man's hand, and pulled him up beside him. "Dear spirits, that didn't stop the rain, but it may have lifted your gloom."

"I'm sorry," Bannon muttered. "When I wanted to leave Chiriya Island, I think . . . I may have been running away. But now, I realize that isn't the point at all." He lifted his chin, which was smeared with mud. The rain kept coming down, fat droplets falling from the dense branches above in a constant cold shower. "I want to go with you. This is the journey I've always dreamed about."

"Good," Nathan said. "Then, let's keep exploring."

Nicci set off in the lead. "If we go far enough, we may even walk out of this rain."

The higher they climbed, the colder the nights got, but finally the rain ceased. The downpour had lasted long enough to wash the mud from their clothes.

Two days later, the skies cleared of clouds, opening to a fresh blue, and Nicci picked up the pace, rejuvenated by the sunshine. By now, the path had become all but indistinguishable from a game trail, and they had seen no one since leaving Lockridge. Nicci could understand why Emperor Jagang had not bothered to send his armies down to these isolated lands, where there were few people to conquer.

Occasionally, they came upon ruins of large stone buildings that had fallen into disrepair, overgrown by the forest and reclaimed by time.

"This land must have thrived thousands of years ago," Nathan said. "After the great barrier was erected at the end of the wizard wars, Sulachan and his successors were forced to push south instead, since they could no longer reach the New World. There were cities and roads, trading posts, mining towns, great leaders and internal wars. In fact, Emperor Kurgan devoted most of his conquest to the southern part of the Old World."

"That is why we've heard little of him in our history," Nicci said. "He was unimportant."

"He was important enough to these people," the wizard said.

"I don't see any people," Bannon said.

"Use your imagination. They were here."

They stopped at a mossy, overgrown building foundation. Squares laid out on the ground marked what must have been a large fortress, but now only crumbling remnants outlined the rubble. "The world tends to pass you by when you live your life in a tower." He kept talking while Nicci and Bannon followed him away from the ruins. "Did I tell you about the time I foolishly tried to escape from the palace? I was young, with little concept of how impregnable my prison was."

Nicci frowned. "The Sisters never mentioned to me that you had tried to escape."

"I was only a century old, just a boy, really. I was brash and willing to take chances . . . and I was also impossibly bored. Yes, I had the freedom to roam through the high tower rooms, to look at the wonderful books in the library, but such diversions can only distract a young man for so long before he begins to dream. I didn't want to be their pet prophet, so I laid my plans for months. Yes, they had placed an iron collar around my neck, and with the Rada'Han they could control me and my magic." His lips quirked in a smile, and he tossed his straight white hair behind him. "So I had to be resourceful and not just use a spell or two to get away.

"When I kept telling the Sisters I was cold, they brought me more blankets, and I used just a tiny bit of the gift to unravel the fibers, which I reassembled into a rope, a long rope, thread after thread. It was strong enough to hold my weight.

"I spent a week being cheerful and attentive to my studies so as to lull the Sisters into a sense of complacency, and then one moonless night I made my way to one of the highest rooms. I barricaded the door after claiming that I meant to study spell books throughout the night. I was a curious young man and wanted to build my powers as a wizard, even though I knew they would never free me." He unconsciously rubbed at his neck, as if he still felt the iron collar there. "Because a prophet is too dangerous, you see."

He looked at Bannon to make sure the young man was listening. "I opened the high window and fastened my rope securely to an anchor. I was precluded from using a levitation spell, so I had to resort to more traditional means. When I lowered myself over the sill and looked down, I felt as if the drop went all the way to the underworld." He regarded Bannon, cocking an eyebrow. "When one lives inside stone-walled rooms, it's difficult to get a sense of the vastness of the sky or the long drop to the ground below. But I was resolved. I wrapped the rope around my waist and began to lower myself down the wall."

Nicci was skeptical of the story. "The Palace of the Prophets is guarded by wards and shields. No one could just climb through a window and escape."

He lifted a finger. "And why do you think the Sisters added all those protective spells? Back then, the women assumed the shields blocking the lower doors would be sufficient. They never thought I would be foolish enough to climb out the highest tower." He cleared his throat. "The important part is that I was dangling by a rope from the tower wall—very brave, I might add. But I had miscalculated. When I was still nearly a hundred feet from the base of the tower, the rope ran out. I was just hanging there!"

He paused for suspense, and looked at Bannon. "I did know how to use Additive Magic, so I made the strands of the rope grow. I should have guessed that the Sisters would detect this through the Rada'Han, but what could I do? I certainly couldn't climb all the way back up. I extended the rope one foot at a time and eased myself down, but it took a great deal of energy. I was so exhausted I could barely hold on to the rope by the time I reached the ground."

He let out a long, wistful sigh. "By then, the Sisters had discovered what I was doing, and they captured me as soon as my feet touched the paving tiles."

"Even if you did make it away from the Palace of the Prophets and over the bridge into Tanimura, your Rada'Han would have prevented you from escaping. The Sisters could have rounded you up at any time," Nicci said. "I find your story questionable."

"My story is entertaining, and it also has a point." He turned to face Bannon. "Sometimes you must be daring to accomplish a great thing, but no matter how daring you are, your deeds will be diminished if you forget to plan properly."

They toiled higher along a steep switchbacked path. The trees thinned, leading up to a high point ahead.

Nathan stretched his arms. "After that, the Sisters kept me bottled up so tightly that I could never again plan a serious escape. Therefore, I amused myself by writing other adventures and secretly distributing them throughout the land. They became quite popular, enjoyed by many."

They were out of breath as they finally reached the summit of the ridge and crossed over to take in a sprawling, breathtaking view.

When asking about the way to Kol Adair, they had repeatedly been told about a vast fertile valley filled with green forests, croplands, and villages. But this sight was not at all what they expected.

As the three surveyed the landscape, Nicci saw only brown desolation to the horizon. This was no verdant valley, but a dry and cracked crater, bounded to the north by a high plateau. The heavily forested foothills spilled down to a pale, fuzzy boundary of death. Dust devils skirled across the dry basin. White expanses of sparkling salt indicated where lakes had dried up, leaving only poisoned soil. The terrible desolation spread outward from a central point, countless miles away.

And the dead zone was clearly growing.

Nathan drew a deep disappointed breath. "I will have to update my map."

CHAPTER 36

With all the vegetation dead, the old road ahead became more plain, and they walked down the rocky trail toward the wide desolate valley. When Nicci inhaled, the air carried a burnt, powdery smell with a hint of rot, as if vapors stirred up by thermal currents wafted into the foothills.

They paused at a rocky switchback to look across the great basin. Nicci could discern straight lines etched across the barren lands, man-made paths that were now covered with blown dust. She could also see what had been small villages, larger towns, possibly even the ruins of a city.

Nicci said, "This was a well-traveled and inhabited area, but something sucked it all dry."

"There are still habitable areas on the fringe of the desolation," Nathan said, pointing to the transition zone where the green of vegetation faded into the cracked brown of death. He shaded his eyes and looked into the hazy distance, beyond the valley. "That blowing dust impairs visibility, but you can see the towering mountains off in the distance far to the east." He pointed. "Kol Adair may be somewhere up on one of those mountain passes."

"But how can we cross that desolation?" Bannon asked.

Nicci scanned the landscape. "We should go around, skirt the valley to the north, stick to the greener areas in the foothills."

"In fact, I suggest we visit one of those villages," Nathan suggested. "I'd like to learn what happened down there, if that was once a great fertile valley." He screwed up his face in a distasteful expression. "It does not appear natural."

Nicci bit her lower lip. "Agreed. Lord Rahl will need to know."

"And the world may need saving, Sorceress," Nathan said, without any obvious hint of humor. She did not respond.

As the path descended, they worked their way into the badlands, where rocks towered like monoliths, reddish sandstone eroded by wind and water. The vegetation transitioned from tall pines to gnarled scrub oak, mesquite, and spiky yucca that had survived as the terrain grew less hospitable.

In the heat of the day, Nicci packed away her traveling cloak. Her black dress was comfortable, but the rocks underfoot were hard through the soles of her boots. Bannon's face quickly became sunburned.

Their road took the path of least resistance, following the curves of the slickrock bluffs and winding into rocky arroyos. Pebbles pattered down from above, and they saw skittering movement—lizards darting from sunny rocks into shadowy crevices.

Nicci listened to the silence punctuated by stray breezes and the rustle of twigs. She narrowed her eyes, sensing movement from something larger than a lizard. She and Nathan were instantly alert, while Bannon kept plodding, distracted by the scenery. Then he also stopped. "What is it? Are we being stalked?" He drew his sword.

"I don't know," Nicci said. "I heard something." She remained motionless, extending her senses, trying to pick up on some unseen threat.

They waited in tense silence. Nathan frowned. "Actually, I don't hear anything."

Suddenly, they heard a burst of bright and refreshing laughter, the high voice of a child. All three looked at the rocks overhead, the smooth bluffs marred with occasional blind ledges. A young girl stood up from a hiding place above. Small-statured and elfin, she looked about eleven years old.

"Been watching you for a long time." She placed her hands on her hips and giggled again. "I wondered how long it would take for you to notice. I was going to surprise you!"

She looked like a waif dressed in rags. She had an unruly mop of dusty brown hair that was styled more in tangles than curls. Her honey-brown eyes twinkled as she regarded them. She had caramel-colored skin and a triangular face with a narrow chin and high cheekbones. Her arms were wiry, her legs spindly beneath an uneven skirt made of patchwork cloth. Four large lizards dangled by their tails from a rope tied around her waist; the lizard heads were smashed and bloody.

"Wait for me," she called. "I'm coming down."

"Who are you?" Nicci said.

"And why have you been spying on us?" Nathan demanded.

Like a lizard herself, the girl scrambled down the rock wall, finding hand- and footholds that were all but invisible, but she displayed no fear of falling. Her feet were covered with moccasins made of rope, fabric, and scraps of leather. She dropped the last five feet, landing in a resilient crouch on the rocks in front of them. The lizard carcasses at her hip flopped back and forth.

"I am spying on you because you're strangers—and because you're interesting." She looked up. "My name is Thistle."

"Thistle?" Bannon asked. "That's an odd name. Is it because you're prickly?"

"Or maybe I'm just hard to get rid of—like a weed. I'm from the village of Verdun Springs. Is that where you're going? I can take you there."

"We're not sure where we're going," Nicci said. "Are you all alone here?"

"Me and the lizards," said Thistle. "And there aren't as many lizards now because I've had a good hunt today." She squatted next to them and opened a pouch on her other hip. "I don't often see people. I'm usually the only one who goes out exploring. Everyone else in Verdun Springs works all day just to survive."

She tugged open the pouch's drawstring and pulled out strips of dried, grayish meat. "These are yesterday's lizards. Do you want some? They dried all afternoon, so the meat will be just right." She put a strip into her mouth, seized it with her front teeth, and tore it into shreds. As she chewed and swallowed, she kept holding out her other hand to extend the offering of meat.

Bannon, Nicci, and Nathan each took a small portion of dried lizard. Bannon looked at it skeptically, but the wizard munched away without hesitation. "My uncle Marcus and aunt Luna taught me about hospitality," said Thistle. "They say we should be kind to strangers because maybe they can help us."

"We might be able to help," Nicci said, thinking about her broader quest. "First we need to learn what happened here. How far is your village?"

"Not far. I've only been out two days, and I have enough supplies for a week. Marcus and Luna won't be expecting me back home yet." Thistle's grin widened. "They'll be surprised when I bring visitors. You sure you can help us? Can you stop the Scar from growing?" She gave them a frank assessment, then sniffed. "I don't think you're strong enough."

"The Scar?" Bannon asked.

"She must mean the desolation," Nathan said. "The whole valley ahead."

"We call it the Scar, because that's what it looks like," Thistle said. "I've heard stories of how beautiful the valley used to be when I was just a baby. Farmlands and orchards and forests—they even had flower gardens. Can you imagine?" She snorted. "Flower gardens! Wasting water, fertilizer, and good soil just to grow flowers!"

Nicci felt sad for the girl, and her innocent comment was a poignant indication of what sort of life the people in her village must be enduring as the devastation expanded.

She continued to chatter. "If you can save us, if you can break the Lifedrinker's spell and bring the fertile lands back, how I would love to see it! All my life I've dreamed of making the land beautiful again." She sprang to her feet, ready to go. She trotted off, calling over her shoulder, "Do you really think you can destroy the Lifedrinker?"

"Who is the Lifedrinker?" Nathan asked.

Nicci cautioned, "We did not promise we could do anything."

When the girl shook her head, the tangled brown curls bobbed about like weeds. "Everyone knows about the Lifedrinker! The evil wizard at the heart of the Scar who sucks the life out of the world to feed his own emptiness." She lowered her voice. "That's what my uncle Marcus says. I don't really know anything more."

"Won't your uncle be worried about you alone in the wilderness for days?" Nicci asked.

"I can take care of myself." Thistle set off with a pert stride, skipping over the stones. Without slowing, she bent to snatch rocks in her right hand and kept moving down the wash, knowing that they would follow. "I've raised myself since my parents died when I was just a little girl. Uncle Marcus and Aunt Luna took care of me, but they didn't have any extra food or water, so I have to feed myself most of the time, and I try to bring in enough to help them."

Thistle jerked her head to the left, focused on a flash of movement she had spotted. Quicker than even Nicci could see, the girl hurled the rocks. They clacked, clattered, and struck their target, and she bounded ahead and squatted down to retrieve a small lizard she had just killed. Thistle held it up, pursing her lips. "Almost too tiny to be worth the effort." Nevertheless, she tucked it among the other carcasses at her waist. "Aunt Luna says never to waste food. Food is hard enough to come by these days."

The energetic girl led them along at a pace that Nicci had trouble matching. Nathan and Bannon started to slow down as they trudged over the rough rocks. Thistle scampered along, overjoyed to have company. "You're very pretty," she said to Nicci. "What is your home like? Where do you come from?"

"I am from far to the north," Nicci said. "In the New World."

"This is the only world I know. Are there trees where you live? And water? Flowers?"

"Yes. And cities . . . and even flower gardens."

Thistle frowned. "Flower gardens? Why would you leave such a nice place to come here?"

"We didn't know we were coming here. We're on a long journey."

"I'm glad you came," Thistle said. "You can fight the Lifedrinker. You'll find a way to restore the valley and the whole world."

Nicci felt a chill as she recalled Red's words. "Maybe that's why we're here."

"We will do exactly that, child," Nathan said, "if it's within our power."

They worked their way along the widening arroyo and around the bluffs to where the last line of trees had died and the creeks had long since dried up. Thistle gestured proudly ahead. "This is my village."

Nicci, Nathan, and Bannon stopped to look. They were not impressed.

Verdun Springs had obviously been a much larger town once, thriving at the intersection of imperial roads, forest paths, and commercial routes that led into the fertile farmland and trading villages deep in the valley. But the cluster of low mud-brick buildings had retracted into a squalid settlement, as if the population had dried up as well as the landscape.

Dust skirled along the streets. Rocks had been dumped in piles next to a building. A cart with a broken wheel—and no horse to draw it—leaned against the rubble mound. Countless empty buildings were covered with dust, some of them falling apart.

Nicci counted no more than twenty people toiling under the harsh sunlight. They wore frayed clothes and floppy hats woven from dry grass. Several men were working around the town's well. One man lowered himself by a rope down into the stone-walled shaft. "Keep digging! If we go deep enough, we're sure to find clear water again." Others tugged on a second rope attached to a pulley, drawing up a bucket that held only mud and dirt.

To announce their arrival, Thistle let out a loud, shrill whistle. The man at the well looked up, and the other haggard people stopped to stare. Thistle called out, "This is my uncle Marcus—I told you about him. Uncle, this woman is a sorceress, and the old man is a wizard, but he doesn't have any magic."

"I still have my magic," Nathan corrected. "It's just not accessible at the moment."

"The other one is named Bannon," Thistle continued. "I don't know what he can do." The young man frowned in annoyance.

Marcus was a skinny man with dark brown hair going to gray and a bristly beard. His shirt was splattered with mud from helping at the well; he wore a faded, scuffed leather vest. "I welcome you to Verdun Springs, strangers, but I have little hospitality to offer. None of us does."

"I brought lizards!" Thistle said.

"Why, then we can have a feast." Marcus smiled. "You always bring more than your share, Thistle. Our family will eat well tonight—and so will our guests."

Aunt Luna also introduced herself, a dark-skinned woman in a drab skirt with a scarf of rags tied around her head. Though faded now, the scarf had once been bright red. In front of her home Luna had been tending large clay planters, turning rich, dark dirt fertilized with human night soil. Each planter held a splash of green vegetables. Luna wiped her hands on her skirts and tousled the girl's mop of hair. "We may even find some vegetables that are ready. Better to eat them as soon as they're ripe than let the Lifedrinker have them."

Thistle sniffed. "As long as the vegetables are in the pots, the Lifedrinker can't touch them. He can't reach through the planters."

"Maybe he just doesn't try hard enough," said her aunt, adjusting the drab red head scarf.

The villagers muttered. The Lifedrinker's name seemed to fill them with dread.

"We're glad you could come," said Marcus, leading them down the main street. "If you visited any of the other towns nearby, you'd find them all empty. Verdun Springs is all that remains. The rest of the people went away, or just . . . disappeared. We don't know." He wiped dust from his forehead.

"Why didn't you pack up and leave?" Nathan asked, gesturing around at the desolation of the village, the drying well, the dusty streets. "Surely you could find a better place to live than this."

"Someday this will be a lush valley again, as it was a decade ago. We know how beautiful it can be," Luna said, and the few villagers next to her nodded.

Thistle beamed. "I can only imagine it."

Luna said, "I've urged my husband to pack up and go into the mountains. We hear there may be other towns up and over the ridge, even an ocean if you walk far enough west." She heaved a great sigh. "An ocean! I can't remember so much water. At the time when Thistle was born, there was a lake in the valley, before the Scar spread that far."

"We won't leave." Marcus brushed dried mud from his leather vest. "We will eke out our existence day by day." He squared his shoulders and added with great pride, "We are hardy people."

"Hardy?" Nicci raised her eyebrows, thinking that "foolhardy" was a better description.

CHAPTER 37

When night fell, Nicci and her companions sat around a fire pit outside of Marcus and Luna's home, which was built from mud bricks. The house was spacious and cool, with a large central room, wooden beams across the open, airy ceiling, and small high windows below a clay tile roof. The large home reflected a more prosperous time.

Sitting outside in the warm dusk as they prepared for the evening meal, Nathan and Bannon told the adults the story of their journeys, and Nicci explained about Lord Rahl's new golden age, though it was clear that neither Marcus nor Luna took hope.

"We can barely find enough water to survive," said Marcus, "and our food is rapidly dwindling. As I told you, the other towns that once filled this valley twenty years ago are silent and dead." He pressed his hands together, hunched his shoulders, and looked at Nicci. "I am glad to hear of the overthrow of tyrants, but can your Lord Rahl come to our aid? The Scar keeps growing."

Nicci narrowed her eyes. "We are here. Now. But we need to know more about the Lifedrinker."

Worry lines seamed Nathan's face. "I am not convinced how much assistance I can offer, Sorceress—at least until we get to Kol Adair."

Thistle sat cross-legged in the dust next to Nicci as she cleaned the fresh lizards for dinner. "Kol Adair? That's far away." The girl used her little bloody knife to skin another of the lizards, inserted a stick through the body cavity, and handed it to Bannon, so he could roast it over the low cook fire in the pit. Somewhat queasy, the young man lowered the carcass over the coals, and soon the flesh began to bubble and sizzle.

Bannon wiped a hand across his mouth while turning the stick over the cook fire so the lizard didn't burn. "How fast is the Scar growing?"

"In twenty years, the entire valley died away, and the devastation continues to spread," Luna said. "We are one of the last villages on the outskirts."

"The Scar grows faster as the Lifedrinker becomes more powerful . . . and his appetite is insatiable," Marcus added. "I remember when the heart of the valley started dying, just before Luna and I were married. But we'll stay here. We've lasted this long."

The night was silent, but the breezes carried an ashy breath with bitter chemical taint. At the scattered mud-brick houses or larger quarried-stone structures around the town, quiet villagers ate their own meals outside, keeping apart from one another. Verdun Springs had fallen into a sullen hush, as if caused by the mention of the Lifedrinker's name.

Luna looked sad. "Verdun Springs used to have a population of a thousand, and now fewer than a dozen families remain."

"We are the strongest twenty," Marcus insisted. It was clear they had had this argument before.

Bannon said, "There are forests and farmlands on the other side of the mountains, plenty of places for you to settle and be happy."

"It would only delay our fate," said Marcus, with a stubborn frown. "The Scar is spreading, and sooner or later the Lifedrinker will swallow the world."

Nicci hardened her voice. "Unless someone stops him."

Thistle retained a thread of optimism. "I want to stay until the land grows fertile and beautiful again—the way it was before my parents died. I remember it . . . just a little."

"You were too young," said Marcus.

The spunky girl finished cleaning the smallest lizard, which she cooked for herself. She licked the blood off her fingers and left a smear of red on the side of her mouth. Nicci reached forward to wipe off the stain. "Your face is covered with dust."

"We don't have much opportunity to wash," Marcus explained.

Giggling, Thistle licked her fingers and smeared saliva over some of the dust, which did little to clean her face.

The travelers had supplemented the meal by offering dried fruits and leftover smoked fish from their pack. The smoked redfin from Renda Bay was quite a novelty to the young girl, who frowned at the taste and announced that she preferred her fresh lizards.

Nicci got back to business. "Who is the Lifedrinker? And how can he be defeated? Does he have weaknesses?" Maybe this was indeed the reason why they had been driven here. She remembered the witch woman's words: *And the Sorceress must save the world.*

Marcus ground his heel in the dust. "We don't know the full story. We're just simple villagers affected by that ever-growing stain. But we know he was a wizard from Cliffwall, and something went terribly wrong." He nibbled on the last shreds of meat on the roast lizard, picking specks of flesh from the bones, and then he crunched the bones, appreciating every morsel. "That's where you'll find the means to destroy him—if it can even be done."

"And what is Cliffwall?" Nathan asked.

"A great archive of magical lore. We thought it was a place of legend for centuries," Luna said.

Thistle piped up. "It's real—I've seen it!"

"You haven't wandered that far, child," chided Marcus.

"I have! It was four days' walk up into the plateau, but I made it."

"It was hidden since the time of the ancient wizard wars," Luna said, "but it reappeared fifty years ago."

The wizard raised his eyebrows and looked over at Nicci. "A great archive? It sounds like a place we should investigate, regardless. We may find something to help my . . . condition, even before we reach Kol Adair." He stroked his chin. "As well as the background on the Lifedrinker, of course."

Thistle's honey-brown eyes sparkled. "I can take you there. I've seen it with my own eyes!"

"Now, girl . . ." Marcus gave her a scolding look.

"It is said that someone broke Cliffwall's camouflage spell decades ago," Luna said. "The location is still secret, but the hidden people who guarded the place invited a few outside scholars from the towns in the valley. That hasn't happened in a long time, not since the Scar started to spread and consume all the towns and farms."

The lonely breeze picked up, carrying more dust in the wind. Nicci heard the cry of a hunting night bird and something stirring in the empty houses. Unexpectedly, she saw shadows moving in the dark alleys between the abandoned stone structures. She sat up straighter, suddenly alert, trying to penetrate the darkness with her gaze.

She also sensed magic in the air—not the usual pervasive vibration that she could always touch. Since arriving in Verdun Springs, she had felt an odd and unsettling note that seeped out of the Scar, but now it suddenly swelled, like the flush of heat just after an oven door was opened. Tense, she rose to her feet and tossed the cooking stick and the last scraps of her roast lizard aside. She stepped away from the fire pit and out into the wide, dry street.

Before Marcus or Luna could ask her what was wrong, the night filled with screams.

CHAPTER 38

Things moved in the night beyond the quiet rustling dust. The terrified cries came from one of the few inhabited houses on the outskirts of the village, where an old man and his wife had been brooding outside by their small fire.

Nicci was already running, her black dress just a deeper shadow in the darkness. Another scream. She bounded toward the old couple's cook fire, saw many silhouettes as the gray-haired man and woman struggled against figures that closed around them.

The attackers looked gaunt and skeletal, lit by the orange flickers of the small fire. Without thinking, Bannon sprinted along beside her, drawing Sturdy from its scabbard. Ahead, Nicci saw that the attackers were the desiccated remnants of humans, their skin sucked dry of all moisture and baked brown like dried meat.

Running hard, Thistle caught up with Bannon and Nicci. "Dust people! They've never come into town before."

Three shriveled reanimated corpses closed around the old couple, who fought back with helpless terror. They had no weapons, but Nicci did. The sorceress swept out a hand and released her magic. A hammer blow of wind knocked one of the dust people into the air as if he were no more than chaff. When he struck the brick side of the house, his body broke apart, crumbling like twigs and straw.

The old woman battered at her attacker, raking the dried flesh with her nails, but the mummified figure wrapped its arms around her. Immediately, the dry ground beneath their feet *changed*, becoming no more substantial than foamy water. The desiccated thing pulled the old woman down, dragging her into the pit of dust until they vanished underground.

Seeing his wife disappear, the old man fought even more frantically. A strong blow from his hand knocked the mummified creature's skull loose, but even headless, the thing grappled with him. The ground turned to soup beneath the old man's feet, and he sank in up to his knees. He gave a despairing wail, reaching out for something to hold on to.

Nicci struck out with her magic again, the blow of concentrated air so sharp and forceful that it shattered the old man's undead attacker.

But four more hideous dust people boiled up out of the ground, emerging from the soft dirt like striking vipers, and together they grabbed the old man and dragged him under. His screams were drowned in sand and dust.

Nicci and Bannon arrived too late. The ground had smoothed over, the attackers gone and leaving only ripples of dry dust.

Bannon crouched with his sword upraised, alert for a continued attack as he turned from side to side in search of other enemies. Nicci grabbed his shirt and pulled him back from where the ground had become dry quicksand.

Then, from additional houses around the dying town, shouts echoed through the night—more people being attacked.

Nathan finally reached them, holding his sword as well. "What are the attackers? Have you seen them?"

"Dust people," Thistle said. "The Lifedrinker swallows up people wherever he can, and then makes them into his puppets."

Nicci stood close to the girl. "Stay safe."

"Where is safe?" she asked, and Nicci had no answer for her.

Darkness filled the streets of Verdun Springs, and the cook fires and lamps in the stone houses shed far too little light for certainty, but the ground stirred. The wind picked up, carrying a choking fog of dust into the town.

Nicci cautiously led her group back toward the center of town. "Stay with me."

The normally placid dirt streets squirmed, stirred, and gave birth to more horrors. Skeletal hands rose up from the dirt, showing long clawed nails and gray-brown skin that had hardened around the knuckles. The dry ground became as fluid as water, and dust people swam to the surface to hunt the last hardy survivors.

Grasping mummified hands surged around Nathan's feet, reaching for his dark boots. One latched on, but he swept down with his sword to sever the arm bones before kicking the clutching hand loose.

Bannon ran forward, using Sturdy to chop one of the reanimated corpses through the rib cage, scattering vertebrae, but the cadaverous creatures came on like an army of horrific puppets, boiling up from the ground.

Nicci blasted them with magic, knocking two creatures away from Thistle before she grabbed the girl's arm.

Bannon slashed apart another reanimated attacker, then cleaved one more down the middle with his backstroke. As he lunged toward a third, though, the dirt street turned into powdery soup beneath his feet, and he stumbled. He let out a terrified yelp as he started to sink, but the wizard was there to catch his wrist and wrench him back out of the dust trap.

In the center of town, a raised dais of bricks and tile stood empty, a stage on which minstrels might have performed at one time, or where town leaders gave speeches. "Go to the stone platform!" Nicci cried.

Still holding Bannon's arm, Nathan staggered and lost his balance as the ground shifted again. They both stumbled, but struggled ahead in the direction of the stone platform. Nicci used her magic to push them, lifting them up enough that they could escape the slurry of dust. Once on stable ground again, the men scrambled toward the raised dais, a safe island.

From the terrified screams that rang out around the town, Nicci realized that dust people were attacking other families, destroying other homes. She had to get her companions to safety before she could try to protect anyone else.

Bounding ahead on skinny legs, Thistle gasped as the dirt street collapsed beneath her feet. She plunged in up to her waist, flailing, but

Nicci grabbed her. With a great heave, she pulled the girl out and away from the grasping hands of more dust people. Nicci tossed Thistle closer to the stone platform, and the scrawny girl rolled, sprang to her feet, and ran the rest of the way there.

Extending her hand, palm out, Nicci turned in a half circle, using magic to knock the desiccated attackers back, and finally joined her companions on the dais. The tiles were stable beneath their feet, but mummified corpses kept coming for them.

Bannon and Nathan stationed themselves on opposite corners of the platform, their swords held high, and they hacked apart any of the dust people who approached. When the dry, shambling monsters closed in, Nicci thought of the brittle dead wood the villagers had collected for their cook fires. Everything here in the Scar was dry as a tinderbox, hard, dense . . . flammable.

She released a flow of magic to increase the temperature inside the attackers, igniting a spark. Gouts of hot orange fire burned from their chests, but even on fire, the scarecrowish cadavers lurched forward. The smell of burning sinew and bone filled the air, and greasy black smoke rose up from each staggering form.

Nathan and Bannon kept hacking with their swords. A defiant Thistle had pulled out her skinning knife.

Most of the screams in the outlying buildings had fallen ominously silent, but nearby shouts sounded like familiar voices. Thistle cried out, "That's Uncle Marcus and Aunt Luna. I have to get home!"

From a distance, Nicci could see the girl's protectors trying to fight off a combined onslaught from the dust people. Thistle tried to bolt toward them, but Nicci grabbed her shoulder. "You can't run. The streets will swallow you up."

"I have to. We've got to save them!"

Nicci did indeed have to save Thistle's aunt and uncle—or at least try.

"We can fight our way through," Bannon said, lopping off the head of a dried attacker with his sword. It bounced on the ground and rolled like a hollow gourd.

"We'll never make it," Nathan said. "In three steps, the ground would suck us down."

From their questionable sanctuary, they watched Marcus smash one of the dust people with a rock from the fire pit. Luna's red scarf drooped as she thrashed at the attackers, one wooden cooking skewer in each hand. The woman jabbed a hardened stick straight through the empty eye socket of the closest monster, but even with the shaft through its skull, the thing kept coming.

In a flash of planning, Nicci envisioned how best to run from the stone platform all the way to Thistle's home. "I need to make a safe path." The open dirt streets were deadly, unless she could change the substance of the ground itself, prevent the dust from becoming a possible conduit. She directed a flow of magic into the dirt and sand, using Additive Magic to coalesce and create, to fuse the grains together. The loose dust cemented into a narrow walkway, as if she had just frozen part of a stream. "Run! They might still break through, but it should stop them for now and give us the time we need. *Run!*"

The others did not question her. Together, they leaped from the safety of the raised platform. Nicci sprinted ahead, feeling the vitrified sand crunch beneath her boots. She could feel the vibrations as frustrated dust people moved under the ground, trying to break through the barrier with bony claws. The hard surface needed to last for only a few seconds, just long enough for them to run.

They finally reached Thistle's home. Her aunt and uncle were scratched and bloody, wounded by the claws of the dust people they had fended off. Luna's faded red head scarf had been knocked askew, and she pushed it back out of her eyes. Nicci loosed another flow of power to ignite the two nearest attackers as she shouted to the other woman, "Take Thistle and get inside!"

Marcus and Luna staggered to the doorway. The floor of their home was made of clay tile; Nicci hoped it would grant enough safety against an attack from below.

The house offered very few defenses, but this was their last shelter. Freed from the grasping hands of the undead creatures, Marcus and Luna retreated deeper inside.

Bannon and Nathan hacked apart two more dust people at the threshold, before they all crowded through the door. Behind them, the pathway of fused sand cracked, then shattered apart, and the dust people emerged from underground, pushing aside the hard slabs.

Marcus and Luna huddled in a corner of the home, holding each other. Luna sobbed, while Marcus opened and closed his mouth as if trying to think of something defiant to say. When the two saw that Thistle was all right, they cried out with relief and gestured for her to come over.

Nathan slammed the wooden door and threw the crossbar into place, but it was a flimsy barricade. Soon enough, the mummified creatures were pounding on it, scratching with their claws. The joined planks began to crack and splinter.

Nicci surveyed the home, studying its possible defenses. Bannon and the old wizard stood back-to-back with their swords ready as the thudding continued against the door. It would only be moments before the dust people surged inside.

Thistle's eyes were wild, but determined as she stood next to Nicci. "Are we safe?"

Luna reached out her arms. "Come here, girl. We'll be safe together."

Before Thistle could start to where her aunt and uncle huddled, the hard clay tiles in the corner dissolved into a soup, and the floor opened up like a trapdoor into a hunter's pit. Luna and Marcus screamed as skeletal hands grabbed them by the legs and hauled them under.

Nicci rushed to help them, but at that moment, the barricaded door shattered, and an army of dust people boiled inside. Nathan and Bannon stood to block them, sweeping their swords from side to side. Both were grimly silent as they fought with all their strength.

Nicci felt tiles shift beneath her boots as the foundation gave way. Glancing up, looking for any way out, she spotted the iron-hard wooden crossbeams that extended across the ceiling of the mud-brick structure. The beams led to an upper window that was open to the night and the roof. It was their only way out.

"Thistle, I'm going to throw you up there. Grab the beam and work your way over to the window." She snatched up the scrawny girl. Without arguing, Thistle reached out her hands, and Nicci tossed her high enough that she could grab the crossbeam and nimbly swing her thin legs over it. Once she caught her balance, Thistle scooted along the beam toward the high open window.

Nicci turned to the two men. "Bannon, Nathan, we've got to get up there."

"You're going to throw me up there too, Sorceress?" Nathan asked, then swung back to cleave the dried skull of another attacker. "Do you think I can fly?"

"Not flying, but with magic, I will control the air and change your weight. I can move you."

Without further ado, she released her power and yanked Nathan up high enough to grasp the crossbeam; then she did the same for Bannon. Not expecting it, the young man flailed and nearly dropped his sword, but managed to grab on to the beam without losing Sturdy.

Thistle had scooted her way to the window. The two men, balanced on the crossbeams overhead, reached down, and Nicci jumped, stretching out her hands as ten of the staggering monsters lurched into the dwelling. Bannon and Nathan deftly caught her and swung her up.

Dust people filled the confined home, reaching up toward the open ceiling, but they could not get to their four potential victims overhead.

At the open window, Thistle looked back and stared at the empty corner that had just swallowed her aunt and uncle. Tears streamed down her narrow face, carving tracks through the dust there.

"Climb out onto the roof," Nicci said. "We should be safe up there." Just then, the base of the home's mud-brick walls shifted and started to crumble, as if the hardened structure were beginning to dissolve back into dust. "Quickly!"

Thistle scampered through the window and swung herself onto the tiled roof, while Bannon and Nathan followed with as much urgency. Sliding along the wooden crossbeam behind them, Nicci looked down to see more dust people rising from the broken floor. The walls shivered with rapidly spreading cracks.

She realized that even the rooftop would not be a place of safety.

The group sat gasping for breath out in the open night air and heard the hollow hiss of an army of dust people plodding through the streets of Verdun Springs.

Thistle's entire home began to collapse beneath them. One wall sank down, destabilizing the roof, and loose clay tiles clattered like broken teeth to the ground. Bannon tried to keep his balance, but slipped and scrabbled as tiles broke under him. He was able to snag a wooden anchor beam, and Nathan grabbed the back of his shirt and hauled him back up to temporary safety.

Nicci stood at the roof's apex, searching for any possible escape. The orphan girl ran to the other end of the roof and pointed to an adjacent stone structure, a square, flat-roofed shop building made of quarried blocks rather than mud bricks. "Over here! This looks safer!"

The gap between the buildings was six feet wide. But with desperation, and a possible nudge of magic, the four ran across the crumbling tile roof, jumped, and all landed on the flat, open roof of the stone building.

Behind them, Thistle's home collapsed, the brick walls crumbling, the roof sagging inward. The girl watched in dismay.

Standing on the roof of the much sturdier building, Bannon stomped with his boot. "At least this roof is solid beneath our feet, made of old wood, reinforced. And these stone-block walls won't collapse so easily."

Nathan pointed out an opening in the roof, which led down into the main shop below. "But those creatures could follow us, climb onto the roof."

Pursuing them, the dust people tore open the unlocked door below and burst into the abandoned shop. They made their inexorable way upward, climbing the stairs to the open roof.

"We are still trapped." Nicci scanned toward the edge of town, the rocky bluffs and canyons on the outskirts of Verdun Springs. "If we can get out there away from town, in among the bluffs, the dust people won't be able to attack from underground. Maybe we can defend ourselves in the stone outcroppings."

"It's much too far," Bannon said from the edge of the rooftop, swallowing hard.

"And those things are much too close," Nathan added.

"They are slow-moving . . . unless they ambush us," Nicci said.

With gasping, scratching sounds, two dust people clambered to the top of the stairs and emerged onto the shop roof, climbing through the trapdoor. With a swift kick, Nicci knocked both stick figures back down the steps, but more cadavers surged up the interior stairs.

Nicci looked around into the night and realized that the rest of the town had fallen silent. There were no more screams.

"Are we the only ones left?" Thistle whispered.

Nicci did not give any excuses. "Yes. But we will get out of here."

They watched in dismay as two recently inhabited brick buildings also sagged and collapsed as the Lifedrinker's magic turned the brick structures into dust.

Angry, Nicci focused on the rugged bluffs outside of town—a place of sanctuary where the solid ground would protect them. Better than here.

"Be ready," she said. "I'm going to fuse the dust like I did before. I'll make another path for us to run on, and it won't last long. And the other dust people will come after us as swiftly as they can. We just have to be faster." She turned to the young girl. "Can you do it?"

"Of course I can," Thistle said. "Say when."

Nicci gauged the most direct path to the bluffs outside of town. She gestured. "That way. Don't look back. Don't stop for anything—just run. I'll make the ground hard, but we still have to jump off the roof."

"I would make a comment about my old bones," Nathan said, "but now isn't the time."

Bannon pointed down. "I'm more worried about *those* old bones."

Nicci unleashed her magic and marked a path. With Additive Magic she created a solid structure, melding the sand and dust into flat, hard islands. Stepping-stones, since she did not have enough strength left to solidify the whole area. This would be enough. She made one appear, then another.

"Go!" she shouted. "I'll make the rest along the way."

Without hesitation, Thistle leaped off the roof and landed in the soft dirt. Before the dust people could respond, she sprang onto the nearest hardened stepping-stone, then jumped to the next, running ahead. Nicci dropped after her, following close behind so she could reach out and keep creating the path as fast as the girl could run.

Nathan and Bannon tumbled down after them. By now, some of the dust people realized what their intended victims were doing, and the sticklike mummies streamed around the remaining town structures. Two dry cadavers rose up to the left of Thistle, dodging the hardened sand. Seeing this, Nicci reacted with an angry snarl and thrust with a blast of air, which smashed the dust people to splinters of bone and dried flesh.

But more came.

Nicci and the girl ran toward the rock outcroppings, with Bannon and Nathan close behind. They fled the abandoned town. When they finally reached the hard rocks, Thistle scrambled up the outcropping, finding hand- and footholds as she climbed higher away from the dust people. The other three followed her, crawling up the pocked bluff walls until they reached the relative safety of a solid outcropping.

Thistle didn't want to stop. "I know a way, follow me. If we go deeper into the canyons, they'll never find us."

Together, they fled into the night. Climbing higher into the rocks, Nicci glanced over her shoulder in time to see the last of the brick buildings collapse into dust. Then even the stone buildings began to shift as the ground underneath melted away and swallowed them. Soon enough, all sign of Verdun Springs had vanished forever.

CHAPTER 39

Even terrified and in shock, Thistle knew her way through the dark wilderness. Moving solely on adrenaline, she guided them by starlight along smooth slickrock ledges farther into the canyons, far from the reach of the dust people. They were all too exhausted and shaken to engage in conversation. The girl was obviously struggling to absorb what she had just been through, but she survived with a furious lightning-bolt determination that Nicci admired.

Finally, the companions reached the top of the bluffs, high above any threat from the Lifedrinker's minions, and Thistle squatted on a flat rock under the stars. Her thin legs and knobby knees stuck up in the air; her shoulders slumped. She rested her hands on her patchwork skirt and just stared into the empty distance.

Nicci stood beside her. "I believe we are safe now. Thank you."

Thistle began trembling, and Nicci didn't know how to comfort her.

Fortunately, the wizard came up and bent down next to her. "I am terribly sorry, child. That was your home, your aunt and uncle. . . ."

"They took care of me," Thistle said in a quavering voice. "But I spent most of my time alone. I was fine—and I will be fine." She looked up with fiery determination, but when her honey-brown eyes met Nicci's, they filled with tears. Her lips quivered and her shoulders began to shake. "Uncle Marcus and Aunt Luna always said I was too much responsibility for them to handle. Too prickly." She sniffled, and Nicci could see her iron-hard strength. "I will be fine."

"I know you will," Nicci said. "Truly I do."

A moment later, the girl broke down into sobs, rubbing her eyes. Bannon awkwardly put an arm around her shoulders, like a big brother. She turned, embraced him, and cried into his chest. The young man blinked, not sure what to do in the storm of grief. Reflexively, he held her in return.

"We will rest here," Nicci announced, looking around at their high ground. "This place is defensible. We can move on in the morning."

"Nowhere is safe," Thistle said in a harder voice. She shook herself. "Except with you. We'll all be safe together."

Nicci took first watch while the others tried to sleep. They had lost their packs and traveling supplies during their frantic flight, but they made do. Nicci had her magic to assist them, but she suspected that Thistle's survival abilities would be essential to their mission, even if they headed away from the spreading desolation.

Bannon and Nathan stretched out on the open rock, trying to rest. Exhausted, the old wizard slept soundly, and his eyes fell half closed, so Nicci could see only the whites between his lids. She was used to the fact that wizards slept with their eyes open, an eerie habit that un-settled those unaccustomed to seeing it. Now, though, she was more disturbed to realize that Nathan Rahl's eyes were mostly *closed*. Per-haps it was another indication of how much of his magic he had lost since the world had changed. He was no longer whole. How had Red known what lay in store for them?

Nicci sat in silence, staring up at the stars, still trying to understand the new patterns, but she could find no message there. She listened with suspicion to every rustle of underbrush and clatter of loose pebbles in the night, but the sounds were merely caused by scurrying rodents.

At last she had time to think. She pondered the D'Haran Empire, the sprawling Old World, this mostly unknown continent that Lord Rahl needed her to explore. How was she to save the world? The very idea seemed laughable. Right now, her most immediate concern was the Lifedrinker, whatever he was. His Scar was spreading, encompass-ing a greater and greater swath of land. And he had already attacked them with his dust people.

That was the Lifedrinker's first mistake, Nicci thought. It was personal now.

She needed to know more about the evil wizard, what his goal was, how and why he had sucked dry those other townspeople from the valley and turned them into his reanimated servants. Was it just his appetite? Stealing more souls, absorbing their energy? The Lifedrinker's dark magic, whatever it was, had spread like a potent poison more deadly than thousands of deathrise flowers, like the one she still kept with her, wrapped in her dress pocket.

She knew they needed to find the place called Cliffwall.

Having seen the people of Verdun Springs dragged beneath the dusty ground, including Thistle's aunt and uncle, Nicci felt a powerful resolve. She had a deep hatred for oppression, for the destruction or enslavement of good people. The Lifedrinker was the epitome of tyranny, and Nicci considered it part of her mission for Richard to put an end to the threat. Prophecy or not, that was what she knew she had to do.

The orphan girl woke before dawn, instantly alert. Thistle looked around, saw Nicci, and scuttled over to be next to her. The two sat in silence for a long moment before the girl spoke. "I can lead us to Cliffwall—I know I can. There, you'll meet the scholars and learn the information you need to destroy the Lifedrinker. I hate him! And I will take you there."

"I believe you," Nicci said. "And you will prove it to us soon enough. Nathan and I are both scholars of magic. If the answer is there, we will find it." She narrowed her blue eyes and looked down at the lost little girl. "Regardless of what is in the library, I swear to you, we will find a way to rid the world of the man who did this."

Thistle gave a solemn nod. Unshed tears welled in her large eyes. "And after that, can I stay with you? I . . . don't have anyone else." When her voice cracked at the end, the girl covered it with a loud clearing of her throat. She looked away, as if ashamed of her desperation.

Nicci could not imagine bringing this child, however talented she might be, along on their difficult journey to Kol Adair. But Thistle had already been broken so badly in one night that the sorceress simply answered with, "We shall see," rather than dashing her hopes.

They were ready to move as soon as dawn broke. Thistle shook Bannon and Nathan by the shoulders to wake them. "It might take several days to get to Cliffwall, and the canyonlands up in the plateau can be a maze, but if you follow me"—she gave them a forced smile— "I'll keep you safe and on track."

Bannon tied back his loose hair. "But we don't have any water or food. We don't have our packs."

The girl placed her fists on her raggedy skirt and lifted her chin. "I'll find what we need." She sprang off and led them along the top of the bluff, then into even higher canyonlands away from the once-fertile valley that was now the Scar. The seemingly endless expanse of slickrock rippled with upthrust fins of red rock formations, like the backbones of some mythical monster.

The landscape was scored with a dizzyingly complex labyrinth of cracks and canyons, deep gorges that spilled into oblivion with no exits that Nicci could see. The muted reds and tans were interspersed with dark green splashes of piñon pines, mesquite scrub, even tall cacti. Down in the sheltered canyons, a fuzz of pale green mixed with spiky black branches showed where thick tamarisks clogged the channels. This was a healthy desert with natural vegetation; the spreading stain of the Lifedrinker had not extended this far . . . but Nicci suspected that would change before long.

Nathan shaded his eyes and looked out across the desert highlands. "It is beautiful, I'll grant you that." He placed a hand on the leather pouch that still held his life book, one of the few things he had managed to keep with him. "But I despair at the thought of mapping it. How can we not get lost?"

Thistle said, "I already told you, I'll be your guide. I can show you where Cliffwall has been hidden for thousands of years. I've explored it all. I know where I'm going."

"You explored all of this?" Bannon sounded skeptical.

She huffed. "I *am* eleven summers old."

"I see no reason to doubt her." Nicci followed as the girl set off, prancing from rock to rock, scrambling up steep slopes while Bannon and Nathan worked hard to keep up.

Thistle guided them along the fingers of canyon rims, then back around again to a deeper cut. As they rested, the orphan girl stayed near Nicci, and gazed back at the barren emptiness of the Scar, many miles behind them. Thistle gave a long wistful sigh, her face a mask of sadness. "I heard people talk about how beautiful this land was once, with forests, rivers, crops. Like a paradise, the perfect place to live. When my aunt and uncle talked about it, they would begin to cry, saying how much it had changed in just my lifetime. It sounded so wonderful." She sniffled. "That's why Uncle Marcus and Aunt Luna insisted on staying here. They said our valley would come back . . . someday." She looked at Nicci. "You're going to bring it back, Nicci, and I'll help you. I will! Together we'll fight. We'll bring all the life back to this valley."

The girl showed such adamant hope that Nicci did not wish to disappoint her. "Perhaps we will."

Toward the end of a long day of traveling, Thistle led them to the lip of a wide canyon and found an impossible trail that took them painstakingly down toward the bottom. "There'll be water here and a place to camp."

Indeed, Thistle knew exactly where to find an excellent shelter under an overhang, where they built a campfire of brittle tamarisk and mesquite wood that burned hot with fragrant smoke. A seep of water provided all they needed to drink and to wash.

As twilight closed in, the girl darted off into the winding canyon and returned a short while later with four lizards for them to eat. They roasted the reptiles whole, and Nicci crunched the crispy scaled skin, bones and all.

Thistle led them onward for three days, climbing higher into the plateau through desert scrub, mesquite, sagebrush, creosote bush, and

spiky yucca. They entered the uplands well above Verdun Springs, circling around the foothills that enclosed the vast valley and up into the
high plateau.

Eventually, as if the ground swelled as it gained altitude, the land
split into more deep canyons. Confident in where she was going, the
girl wound them through the maze until Nicci, Nathan, and Bannon
had no idea where they were or how they could ever retrace their steps.
Even so, Nicci placed her faith in the girl.

As they traveled through one bright morning where the canyons
widened and the rock walls broke into towering hoodoos that stood
like eerie and misshapen sentinels, Nicci asked, "How old were you
when your parents died?"

"I was very little," Thistle said. "Back then, there were still many
people in Verdun Springs. The Scar hadn't spread to our town yet, but
the Lifedrinker was dangerous even if he was far away. I remember my
mother's face . . . she was very beautiful. When I think of her, I think
of green trees, wide fields, running water, and pretty flowers . . . a
flower garden." She laughed at the absurd idea of wasting garden
space on mere flowers.

"As the Scar absorbed the valley, my parents would try to scavenge
any crops they could still harvest. One time, they made an expedition
to an almond orchard, because even if the trees were dead, there were
still dried nuts to gather. My mother and father never came back. . . ."
Thistle walked in silence for a long moment, leading the group around
looming hoodoos. "The Scar might look dead, but some creatures are
connected to the Lifedrinker, and he doesn't just kill them. He changes
them, uses them."

"Like the dust people?" Nicci asked.

Thistle nodded. "But not just people. Also spiders, centipedes—and
lice, terrible monstrous lice."

Nicci felt a twist inside of her. "I hate lice."

"Lice drink life as well," Bannon said. "No wonder the wizard likes
them."

"What killed your mother and father?" Nathan asked.

"Scorpions—big scorpions had infested the almond trees, and when my parents came to harvest the nuts, the scorpions fell upon them, stung them. When Uncle Marcus and two other villagers went to look for them days later, they found my parents' bodies, their faces all swollen from the stings . . . but even though they were dead, the Life-drinker made them into dust people too. My parents attacked Uncle Marcus."

Her words tapered off, and Thistle didn't need to continue the story of what the villagers must have done to get away. "After that, I stayed with my aunt and uncle. They said they would take care of me, that they would watch over me." Her voice was bleak. "Now they're gone. Verdun Springs is gone." She swallowed hard. "My world is gone."

"And you are with us, child," said Nathan. "We'll make the best of it."

Bannon pushed ahead. "Yes, we will—if we ever get to Cliffwall."

Looking up at Nicci for reassurance, the orphan girl nodded. "We'll be there by tomorrow."

The next morning Thistle led them along the floor of a canyon whose rocky bottom looked as if it had suffered flash floods during storms, but not for some time. The sky closed in as the canyon walls rose higher and drew together, looking sheer and impenetrable.

The wizard frowned, trying to gain his bearings as the shadows lengthened. "Are you certain this isn't a dead end, child?"

"This is the way." Thistle trotted ahead.

The canyon narrowed, and Nicci felt uneasy and vulnerable, realizing this would be a perfect place for an ambush.

"It closes up," Bannon said. "Look ahead—it's a dead end."

"No," the girl insisted. "Follow me."

She led them up to where the rock walls formed the end of a box canyon, leaving only what looked like a narrow crack of two mismatched slickrock cliffs. Thistle turned to the travelers, then rotated sideways and shimmied into the crack.

She vanished.

Nicci stepped forward to see that the crack was a cleverly hidden passageway that led through a narrow elbow in the blind wall. After inching her way along through the claustrophobic passage, Nicci saw light ahead.

The girl squirmed out and stepped into a widening canyon. Nicci joined her, and Bannon and Nathan emerged behind them. Nicci caught her breath.

They all drank in the view of Cliffwall.

CHAPTER 40

Past the bottleneck of the closed-in stone passageway, the hidden network of canyons on the other side of the towering barricade wall was a whole world cut off from the rest of the landscape. Steep-walled finger canyons spread out like outstretched hands cutting through the high plateau. Nicci and her companions absorbed the view. This place was a hidden, locked-away network of secret, sheltered canyons.

The main canyon through the cracked plateau was broad and fertile, cut by the sinuous silver ribbon of a stream that collected drips from numerous overflowing springs. Sheep grazed on the lush green grasses, and fenced fields were bursting with tall stalks of wheat and corn. Vegetable gardens crowded with squash and beans had been laid out in confined ledge niches that pocked the cliffs. Orchards grew along the streamside, many of the trees in blossom. Wooden hutches held beehives that added a faint hum to the air. Hundreds of people worked the fields, tended the flocks, climbed the canyon walls on wooden ladders. It was a thriving, prosperous society.

All along the cliffs that enclosed the canyons, large overhangs and alcoves created natural sheltered caves in which buildings had been constructed, clay brick and adobe buildings. Some of the natural grottoes held only two or three dwellings, while larger overhangs held a veritable city of adobe towers connected with walkways.

The opposite side of the canyon held a singularly enormous cave grotto, a yawning alcove that held imposing stone buildings with blocky façades. The architecture had an air of ancient majesty. Nicci realized this must be the legendary wizards' archive, only recently revealed.

Cliffwall was like a fortress in its huge, defensible alcove, stone-block structures five and ten stories high, massive square walls with defenses. A narrow, winding path chiseled into the cliff was augmented with knotted ropes and short ladders to grant access from the canyon floor to the yawning grotto above.

Once through the bottleneck into the canyon, Nathan tilted his head back and stared in awe, his mouth agape. "It reminds me of the Palace of the Prophets. Ah, I do miss the library there."

Bannon displayed the same wide-eyed wonder Nicci had seen on his face when he was in the city of Tanimura. "Was the Palace of the Prophets really that big?" he asked.

Nathan chuckled. "Size is a relative thing, my boy. The cliffs and the overhang definitely make this look imposing, but the palace was at least ten times the size."

"Ten times?" Bannon said. "Sweet Sea Mother, that can't be possible!"

"No need for comparisons," Nicci said. "Cliffwall is impressive enough, and it has the advantage of being *intact*. Perhaps we'll find what we need to know about the Lifedrinker."

In the bright daylight, some of the local people had spotted the visitors emerging through the hidden entrance to the canyon. Two boys working a vegetable plot halfway up a cliff whistled an alarm. The shrill sound echoed and ricocheted, amplified by the angled canyon walls. Others converged, responding to the alarm.

While Nicci might have preferred to reconnoiter the canyon structures to assess the Cliffwall defenses and any possible threat, Thistle shouted and waved at the people coming closer. "Hello! We are strangers from the outside. We need to look into your archive."

More alarm whistles echoed from the alcove settlements, and in the towering fortress of the Cliffwall archive, dozens of people bustled to the windows and doors. Nicci couldn't hold Thistle back as she boldly strode forward into the canyon, confident they would all be welcome here.

A group of Cliffwall dwellers hurried toward the four travelers. Thistle put her hands on the hips of her ragged dress and raised her voice. "We are here to defeat the Lifedrinker! I brought you a sorceress, a brave swordsman, and an old wizard."

"I don't appear that old," Nathan said, salvaging his pride. "And I am a prophet as well as a wizard . . . although at present I am unable to use either of those faculties." He tapped his head. "Still, the knowledge is here."

"They are here to find out how to stop the Scar," Thistle proclaimed.

Nathan looked up at the people drawing closer. "Hello! We understand you have an archive of knowledge? Ancient records that might prove useful in dealing with this terrible enemy that plagues the land?"

Nicci added in a harder voice, "Information that will give us the tools and weapons to defeat him? We need it."

One middle-aged farmer wore a brown tunic flecked with grass ends and chaff from cutting wheat. "You would have to see Simon for that. He's Cliffwall's senior scholar-archivist." He indicated the towering fortress alcove up the side of the cliff, where more than a dozen people were working their way in single file down the narrow pathway to come meet them.

"And Victoria. They need to see Victoria," added a woman whose tight bun of pale hair was tied in a gray scarf. She had wide hips, stubby callused fingers, and biceps that were larger than Nathan's and Bannon's combined. "She's the one who decides what knowledge the memmers preserve."

The farmer brushed at the fragments of wheat, then placed a stalk between his teeth. "Now, now, it all depends on the type of information they need."

"We haven't seen strangers and outside scholars for years, not since the Scar wiped out the valley," said a red-faced shepherd who came puffing up, catching the end of the conversation.

"The scholars have needed new blood," said the hefty woman. "No one here has found a way to stop the Lifedrinker. We need help."

"Cliffwall was hidden behind a camouflage shroud for thousands of years," said the redhead. "And even though the spell is gone, the spirits of our ancestors would torment us if we simply handed over that knowledge to any bedraggled visitor who asks! We are very careful about how many outside scholars we allow here."

"We're here to help," Nicci said.

"And we're not all that bedraggled," Nathan said.

"I'm not a stranger," Thistle insisted. "I watched you a year ago, and you never noticed. I'm the only survivor from Verdun Springs."

"Never heard of it," said the shepherd.

"That's because you've been locked in these canyons forever," Thistle said. "The rest of the world has gone on while you stayed hidden here. Everything is dying, and you don't even know it."

Nicci put a hand on the girl's shoulder to calm her. "We have come here to help. If I have the right information, maybe I can find a way to stop your enemy."

"And bring back the green valley," Thistle insisted. "They can do it."

They all turned as the group of robed scholars hurried toward them from the towering fortress archive. The people began to talk at once. "Simon, these people came from the outside."

"This girl led them. She says she's from a place called Verdun Springs."

"One is a sorceress and the other is a wizard."

"And a prophet."

"Victoria, look, that one's a sorceress!"

"They want to study our information, look into our archives . . ."

"We've needed some fresh scholars."

Nicci tried to sort the overlapping chatter as a man stepped forward, obviously in charge. "I am Simon, the senior scholar-archivist of Cliffwall. I supervise the cataloging of the knowledge preserved here by the wisdom of the ancients."

Nathan raised his eyebrows. "Senior scholar-archivist? You seem rather young for the job."

Simon appeared to be in his mid-thirties, with thick brown hair that stuck out in unruly spikes, since he apparently didn't have the inclination to care for it. His chin and cheeks were covered with a wispy corn silk of beard. "I'm old enough to do my job. And I started young, brought here twenty years ago as a prodigy from one of the valley towns."

"The camouflage shroud broke down only fifty years ago," said a matronly woman who took her place next to him—Victoria, Nicci presumed. She was in her sixties, with gray-brown hair tied back into a braid that she wound in a coil around her head. Her face was smooth, showing only the beginnings of crow's-feet around her eyes, and her rounded cheeks were flushed a healthy pink. Her warm voice sounded to Nicci like the voice of a kindly grandmother from a children's tale, but with a hard edge.

"We've been the guardians of Cliffwall since the old wizard wars, but we have only recently opened the archives to outsiders again. Simon's scholars have completed barely half of the cataloging work. But my memmers can perhaps explain what you need to know, directly from our memories—once you convince us of your need."

CHAPTER 41

Simon, Victoria, and the other intense scholars led the visitors to the fortress archive up the sheer cliff. As they toiled up the narrow path that zigzagged along the rock wall, Nicci could see the size of the towering buildings constructed inside the cave alcove, and she grew more impressed with the ancient library. The great stone façades of the Cliffwall buildings towered higher than she had at first guessed.

"This is imposing," she said, trying to imagine how such a mammoth city could have been built in such an isolated place. "Maybe the Palace of the Prophets was only *five times* larger."

Thistle scampered ahead up the precarious path, never missing a step or a handhold. Impatient, she stopped partway and turned. "Come on, Nicci. Don't you want to see the library?"

As Nathan climbed the rock face, he admired the huge buildings, the tower faces, the windows and arches, and the imposing primary doors, twice as high as a man. "Look at the massive stone blocks in those walls. The only way such a fortress could have been erected—especially in this isolated canyon—is through magic."

"Powerful magic," Nicci agreed. "In a time before so much magic was purged from the Old World."

The wizard paused on the steep cliff path, resting a hand against the smooth rock at his left. He nodded. "Indeed, it must have been quite an undertaking."

After clambering to the overhang of the great alcove, Thistle waited for them in front of the imposing stone buildings. "Sweet Sea Mother," Bannon whispered. "I've never seen anything like it."

The matronly Victoria looked at him, a troubled expression crossing her apple-cheeked face. "Your Sea Mother had nothing to do with it, young man. She is far away and did not aid in the effort. This was accomplished through human labor, and it cost the lives and energy of many gifted wizards."

Simon turned to look at the buildings with clear reverence. "The most powerful wizards in the world came here in secret back at the time of the ancient wizard wars. It took them years to construct and hide this place, under the greatest cloak of secrecy, but their gamble paid off. Emperor Sulachan and his purging armies never discovered the wealth of knowledge those wizards placed here. The camouflage shroud remained in place for centuries, hiding Cliffwall completely from any prying eyes. Only the villagers here in the canyons even remembered it existed."

"Until fifty years ago," Victoria said, with obvious pride in her voice. "And now the preserved knowledge is available to all again."

Nicci turned to look across the canyon as afternoon shadows closed in. Some of the shepherds slept in tents near their flocks in the canyon-floor pastures. In the numerous alcoves studding the opposite cliffs, she saw other dwellings lit by cook fires and lamps, but the imposing Cliffwall complex shone brighter as the gifted scholars used magic to illuminate the library archive.

"And we are studying, and practicing, as quickly as we can." Simon sounded enthusiastic.

The farthest structure at the right side of the alcove caught Nicci's eye. A large tower was damaged, melted as if the stone had become candle wax. The slickrock overhang had folded in, reminding her of a drooping eyelid. The windows were sealed over like an ice sculpture that had thawed, slumped, then frozen in a fresh cold snap.

Before Nicci could ask about the damage, though, scholars opened the towering doors and Simon led them through the main stone gate into the front tower. "This is only the outer fortress, but there's much more to Cliffwall than what you see here. An entire complex of tunnels runs through the heart of the plateau all the way to the cliffs on the other side."

Inside the main library building, the ceilings were high and vaulted, the thick walls made of quarried stone. Their footsteps echoed along the blue-tiled floor of the entry portico, and bright lights glowed from perpetual lamps evenly spaced along the walls, burning with magic. The stone halls were lined with wooden shelves crowded with mismatched volumes, an odd assortment of leather spines or rolled scrolls, even hardened clay tablets with indented symbols that Nicci didn't recognize.

Nathan hungrily ran his gaze along the shelves. "I can't wait to start reading."

Simon chuckled. "These? Just minor overflow volumes that scholars took out because they looked interesting. The main vaults of knowledge are deeper inside the mesa—and much more extensive. All manner of knowledge is preserved here."

Three lovely young acolytes came up to join Victoria, sweet-faced and eager, none of them older than twenty. The matronly woman nodded at them with a gentle smile. "Thank you for joining us, my dears. We can use your help and attention." She introduced them to the visitors. "These are my most dedicated acolytes Audrey, Laurel, and Sage."

The three women wore white shifts, sashed tight around their waists with a fabric belt, and each girl was strikingly beautiful in her own way. Audrey had high cheekbones, full lips, and rich, dark hair, almost a blue-black. Laurel had strawberry-blond hair that hung loose, except for a decorative braid on the side; her eyes were green, her lips were thin, and her white teeth glinted in a ready smile. Sage's deep reddish-brown hair was thick and shining, and her breasts were the most generous of the three.

Nicci and Nathan gave them a polite acknowledgment, but Bannon made a deep bow, his face flushed with embarrassment when the girls fawned over him, paying more attention to the young man than to the others.

Victoria clucked at them. "These strangers must be tired and hungry, so let us eat while we hear more of their story. Go, prepare extra plates. Everyone will be gathering for the midday meal." The older woman smiled. "We have roast antelope and fresh corn, along with honeyed fruits and pine nuts for dessert."

Nicci was startled to realize how hungry she was. "That would be appreciated."

The wizard grinned. "And far better than munching on roasted lizards." When Thistle shot him an annoyed glare, he raised a conciliatory hand. "Not that we didn't appreciate the food, child. I just meant I was up for a bit of variety."

The dining hall held long plank tables covered with flaxen cloths. Men and women of all ages had gathered for the midday meal. Some were engaged in low conversation, exchanging new revelations they had found in forgotten scrolls. Many seemed too preoccupied even to notice the strangers; they wolfed down their meat and vegetables, then went back to their books without waiting for dessert.

After they took seats on the long benches, Simon served himself a hunk of savory meat, then passed the platter to Nicci and Nathan. As he filled his plate, Nathan said, "Please tell us more about Cliffwall, how it was constructed, and what it was for."

Simon accepted his tale-spinning duties as part of his role as scholar-archivist. "Three thousand years ago, at the beginning of the great war, wizards were hunted and killed in the Old World, and all magic was considered suspect. Emperor Sulachan sent teams to scour the land and destroy any magic he could not acquire for himself. He and his predecessors wanted no one else to have the powerful knowledge that had been assembled over generations.

"But the wizards did not surrender so easily, and they spread word from city to city, archive to archive. The emperor's armies were far superior in number, and the wizards knew that when they eventually lost, their vital knowledge would be destroyed. So the greatest gifted scholars gathered all books of magic and prophecy and slipped them out of known libraries, hiding any volumes that could not be copied in time."

Thistle sat propped up on the bench, paying little attention to the conversation. She used her fingers to take a second helping of antelope meat and corn. It was obvious she hadn't eaten a meal like this in some time, perhaps in her entire life.

Simon shifted his gaze from Nathan to Nicci. "The renegade wizards found this place in the maze of canyons up on the plateau, where no one could ever track them down. For years as Sulachan continued his conquests, the desperate wizards smuggled contraband books, scrolls, tablets, and magical artifacts to the new hiding place. They built Cliffwall to hold that knowledge, and many of them gave their lives to protect it, dying under horrible torture without revealing the location of this canyon.

"When every last book and lexicon had been stored inside the warren of chambers and shelves, the wizards knew they couldn't rely even on the isolation of these canyons to keep this knowledge safe. They needed something more powerful."

"More permanent," Victoria added.

Simon's eyes gleamed. "And so, the wizards conjured an impenetrable shield, an undetectable camouflage shroud that walled off the cave grotto. This entire cliffside was *hidden*. No one could see anything but a smooth, natural cliff face."

Victoria didn't seem to like how he was telling the story. "The shroud was more than a hiding spell, but also a physical barrier. No one could find or enter it. Cliffwall was meant to be sealed away—permanently, until those who would eradicate magic were themselves eradicated."

Nicci glanced at Nathan. "Like Baraccus hid the Temple of the Winds, whisking away the most vital magical lore by sending the whole temple to the underworld, where no one could have access to it."

"And that is how so much knowledge was preserved in a time of great turmoil," Simon finished. "Without Cliffwall and the camouflage shroud, everything would have been lost in Sulachan's purges. Instead, it remained intact here for thousands of years."

"Not everything," Victoria said in a crisp voice. "We had our alternative."

Reluctantly conceding, Simon let the matronly woman pick up the story while he chose an ear of roasted corn from a platter. He began to eat noisily.

"The physical documents were sealed in the archives," Victoria explained, "but the ancient wizards had a second plan to guarantee that the knowledge wouldn't be lost. They insured that someone would always remember. Someone special." She had a twinkle in her grandmotherly eyes.

"Among the people who lived quietly here in the canyons, serving as the guardians of Cliffwall, the wizards chose a few who were gifted with special memory abilities, perfect retention. *Memmers*, magically enhanced with a perfect-recall spell, who could memorize and retain all the words of countless documents."

"For what purpose?" Nathan asked.

"Why, to remember, of course," Victoria said. "Before the camouflage shroud was imposed and sealed everything away, the memmers studied the works in the archive, committing every word to memory." A rich undertone of pride suffused her voice. "We *are* the walking manifestation of the archives. For all the years when the archive was sealed, we remembered. Only we retained the knowledge."

Nicci was reminded of how Richard had memorized the entire *Book of Counted Shadows,* line by line, page by page, back when he was just a woods guide in Westland. George Cipher had made him learn the entire book, backward and forward, burning every page after Richard had learned it, so that the evil Darken Rahl could not have access to what it contained. Even though that book had ultimately been a flawed copy, Richard had used that knowledge to defeat both Darken Rahl and Emperor Jagang.

But *The Book of Counted Shadows* was just one book. Each of these memmers had committed hundreds of volumes to memory. Nicci could not comprehend the incredible scope of the memmers' task.

Victoria tapped her fingers on the tabletop. "I am one of the memmers, as are all my acolytes." On cue, Audrey, Laurel, and Sage came into the dining hall carrying bowls of honeyed fruit. The three young women made a point of offering the dessert first to an embarrassed Bannon; then they spread the plates and bowls around so that all could partake of the fruits.

Nathan chose a glistening peach slice, which he savored, then licked the honey from his fingers. He looked at Victoria, his forehead furrowed. "You each committed thousands upon thousands of volumes to your memory? I find that amazing—though somewhat hard to believe, I'm afraid."

Victoria's expression puckered. "No, one person could not hold all that knowledge, even with memory-enhancement spells and our gift. So the wizards divided the task among our ancestors. Each of the original memmers took specific volumes to study. All told, with enough memmers, our predecessors preserved most of the archive, but the books are scattered among many different minds, and those memmers taught the next generation and the next, dispersing all the books further, depending on how many memmer acolytes were available." She tapped the side of her head. "Nevertheless, the knowledge is there."

Nicci had no interest in the sweet fruit and passed the bowl to Thistle, who began to paw through the dessert with her fingers. "So you have taught and recited all these volumes for thousands of years? Losing nothing? Without a mistake?"

Simon said, "An expert memmer drills and practices with several acolytes, teaching them line after line, so that their students remember every word of every spell. In this way, the memmers kept the knowledge alive for centuries, even though the books themselves were locked away behind the permanent barrier. The camouflage shroud kept us all safe."

He paused to drink from a goblet of spring water, then wiped his mouth. He heaved a sigh. "Unfortunately, every wizard who was powerful enough to remove the shroud also died in the ancient wars, and no one could access the knowledge hidden here. It was lost forever, the impenetrable camouflage sealed in place. No one could break through the shroud."

Victoria interrupted him. "Until *I* figured out how to dissolve it, thus opening the archives again for study. Fifty years ago." She chose three fat strawberries and ate them quickly, then wiped her fingers and lips on a cloth napkin. "I was just a young woman at the time, barely seventeen."

Simon looked at the scholars up and down the plank tables, many of whom were buried in books, focusing on the words while they ate.

"Yes, and that changed everything. After guarding the hidden archive for millennia, the canyon dwellers suddenly had access to the vast treasure trove of information. But what were they to do about it? They were simple villagers with quiet untroubled ways. They had known little of the outside world for all this time. And even the memmers—they could recite the words they had memorized, but they didn't necessarily understand what they were saying. Some tomes were in languages no one could understand."

"We understood enough." Victoria picked up the story with an edge in her voice. "But we did recognize we needed help. The canyon dwellers occasionally traded with the towns in the great valley, although we were considered primitive and strange. The wizard wars were long over, and as far as we could tell, the Old World was at peace.

"So, when the camouflage shroud came down, we decided to bring in experts from outside. The best and most studious scholars from the valley, those who showed an aptitude for the gift. We were cautious. We invited only the exceptional ones, and then we guided them here through the maze of canyons, up from the valley and into the plateau."

"All told, this archive now supports a hundred dedicated scholars," Simon interrupted her. "I was one of those who came here long afterward, a gifted scholar—gifted in both senses of the word—summoned when I was young and eager, so that I could devote my life to relearning all the lost knowledge. I was quite skilled at reading and interpreting, and I learned many languages. I was so talented, in fact, that I rose to prominence here." His smile of wonder turned into a troubled frown. "I came twenty years ago, just after the Lifedrinker escaped."

Victoria's mood darkened, too. "For years now we have had no more new scholars. The towns in the valley are gone, swallowed by the growing Scar." Her voice became bleak. "We are all that remains. The Lifedrinker's devastation has not reached us yet, but it is only a matter of time, a few years at most."

Simon nodded somberly. "Our main work in the archive is simply to understand what we have. So much knowledge, but in such disarray! Even after half a century, two-thirds of the books remain to be organized and cataloged."

"All of my memmers recall separate pieces," Victoria said. "We have tried to exchange information so that we can at least refer one another. It is a vast puzzle."

Simon's voice took on a sarcastic edge. "Yes, and what the memmers say they remember cannot always be verified with printed documentation." He picked up a honeyed orange slice and sucked on it. "Thankfully, we can study all of the scrolls and tomes, and specialized memmers are no longer necessary. Entire teams of scholars have been reading tome after tome, studying and translating in order to relearn all that knowledge . . . and make use of it. We will become great wizards someday, but it takes time. We are all self-taught, and some of us have a greater gift than others. We are searching to find a spell powerful enough to fight the Lifedrinker." He swallowed hard and looked away. "If we dared to do so."

"Self-taught wizards?" Nicci was skeptical. "The Sisters of the Light spent years training gifted young men to use their Han, to understand their gift, and now you are attempting to train yourselves? Using old and possibly mistranslated books?"

Nathan's brows drew together in a show of his own concern. "I'm afraid I also have to worry that the memmers must have garbled some lines, misremembered certain words from generation to generation. Such trivial errors might not amount to anything of significance in a legend or a story, but in a powerful spell the consequences could be dire."

While Victoria took quick offense, and Simon mumbled excuses, Nicci suddenly recalled the damaged, half-melted tower in the Cliffwall alcove, and she drew her own conclusions. "You have already made mistakes, haven't you? Dangerous ones."

Simon and Victoria both looked embarrassed. The scholar-archivist admitted, "There was a certain . . . mishap. One of our ambitious students had an accident, an experiment went wrong, and the main library vault holding our prophecy books was forever damaged. We lost much." He swallowed hard. "We don't go there anymore. The walls are collapsed and hardened over."

"The memmers still recall some of those volumes that were lost," Victoria said. "We will do our best to reproduce them."

Nathan exchanged an expression of concern with Nicci, then spoke to the scholars. "I suggest you exercise a great deal of caution. Some things are too dangerous to be dabbled with. Your one 'accident' destroyed a building or two. What if another error causes even greater harm?"

Simon looked away as he stood up from the table. "I'm afraid you are correct. Another one of our scholars already made such a grave mistake and turned himself into the Lifedrinker. Now the whole world may have to bear the consequences."

CHAPTER 42

After the meal, Simon led the companions deeper into Cliffwall through the back of the stone-block buildings and into the warren of excavated tunnels that penetrated the vast plateau. The wide halls were lit with so many magically burning lamps that Nicci hoped this was the extent of their dabbling. Small light spells were one thing, but unleashing larger, uncontrolled magic was far more dangerous.

The main fortress buildings that filled the cave grotto were enormous, but the archive vaults were even more impressive. The spacious, vaulted chambers had walls lined with shelves crammed with books. In room after room, students sat in reading chairs or hunched over tables next to the bright glow of oil lamps. Bins filled with scrolls stood at the end of each long table. Ladders extended to the highest shelves to make hard-to-reach volumes more accessible. An intensity hung in the air, a hush as so many people devoted their full energies to relearning knowledge lost to history.

"Places like this were called central sites," Nathan said, "large caches of books hidden under graveyards, in the catacombs beneath the Palace of the Prophets, or in ancient Caska." He looked around, curious. "This appears to be more extensive than anything I have previously seen."

"And you are only seeing the smallest fraction here," Simon answered. "Remember, these archives have only been open for fifty years, and the wealth of information is daunting, tens of thousands of precious volumes." He spread his hands. "Even after decades, we are still trying to catalog what knowledge we have. That is the first important step. We don't even know what's here."

Victoria added, "When the ancient wizards compiled this archive, they were in a rush and under threat of extermination. They desperately needed to preserve as much knowledge as possible before Sulachan could destroy it. Caravans bearing magical tomes and scrolls came into the hidden canyons to unload, and riders arrived overland with packs of stolen books, half-scorched manuscripts rescued from libraries and universities that were burned by the emperor's hunters. As time ran out, books of all kinds were piled up and sealed away with little attempt at organization."

Victoria brushed a stray wisp of gray-brown hair from her forehead. "The memmers were assigned volumes by level of importance, rather than specific categories. Therefore, certain memmers might know about weather magic and prophecy, along with dire warnings about Subtractive Magic. Another memmer might preserve knowledge of how to manipulate earth, clay, and stone, as well as how to control lightning, and maybe change the currents in the sea, although we are far from the ocean."

"That is quite a jumble," Nathan said. "How does one locate any specific knowledge?"

Simon shrugged. "By searching. That is the life of a scholar. All knowledge is useful."

Nicci's response was harsher. "Some knowledge is more useful than others. Right now we need to know about the Lifedrinker. The Scar continues to grow, and he must be stopped."

Simon wore a troubled expression. "Let me tell you—or better yet, I'll show you, so you can understand."

He led them through passageways like wormholes, deeper into the heart of the huge plateau, and eventually up a winding slope until they reached the opposite side of the mesa. A natural rock window opened out from the cliffs of the plateau's sheer drop-off, which spilled down to hills and the sprawling valley. They stood together at the opening and looked out upon the sickening extent of the Scar, far away.

It was late afternoon, and the sun set in a glowering red blur at the horizon. Nicci could see the spreading desolation that rippled outward from a distant central point. "All of this used to be beautiful," Simon explained with a sigh. "A green, bucolic paradise. Until the Lifedrinker destroyed it."

Nicci frowned, more determined than ever. "Before we can fight him, we need to know who the Lifedrinker is, where he gets his power. Where did he come from?"

Simon sighed. "He was one of Cliffwall's most ambitious scholars. His name was Roland."

Bannon stared out at the desolation. "One of your own people did that?"

"Not intentionally," Victoria said, as if defending the man. "It was an accident. I was a scholar, married, in my middle years. Roland had been studying the archives for a long time. He was one of the first outsiders invited in after I brought down the camouflage shroud."

"Roland was revered among us," Simon interjected with a sigh. "I wanted to be like him—everyone did. He was Cliffwall's first scholar-archivist. But even the greatest scholars suffer human frailties." He shook his head. "Roland was not an old man, but he fell ill with a wasting disease, a terrible sickness that weakened him, made him grow gaunt. Tumors grew inside him like snakes. And the sickness was beyond the skill of our best healers."

Victoria picked up the story. "Roland lived his life in terrible pain, weakening, and he knew he would die before long. We could all see it. His eyes were hollow, his cheeks sunken, his hands trembled. He had such a great mind, and we were all dismayed that we would lose him. There seemed to be nothing we could do.

"But Roland did not accept his weakness. He did not surrender. He was afraid to die, in fact, and he vowed to save himself, at any cost. Roland said he had too much work to do here." Victoria swallowed hard.

"He asked questions, trying to find someone with the knowledge that he sought. He studied scrolls and books, searching desperately for what he needed in order to draw energy that would let him fight the wasting disease. So, he found a spell, a dangerous spell that would allow him to absorb life energy and keep himself alive. One of my memmers recalled it, at least partially, and that gave him a clue for his search of the uncataloged archives. He knew it was unwise, but he told no one. Knowing he would die soon, he worked the life-energy spell without hesitation, even though he didn't really understand what he was doing. He bound it to himself so that he could borrow bits of life from the world and rejuvenate his ailing body."

Victoria pressed her lips together until all the color drained out of them. "And it worked. Roland had been so weak and skeletal, clearly on the edge of death . . . but he grew strong again. The spell worked wonders. It brought back the flush of health. I remember seeing him." Her expression grew more troubled. "But then Roland didn't know how to stop. He couldn't control it."

Simon cut her off. "I recall those days of growing fear—I had just come here as a student. Roland felt guilty, horrified at what was happening to him—and at what he was doing to others. He kept draining more and more of the life around him, whether or not he wanted to. We tried to help him. His friends rushed to his side, offering their assistance, promising that they would help him solve the problem—but anyone who touched him *died*. Roland stole their lives and incorporated them into his own. We all began to weaken."

"He killed my husband," Victoria said. "To protect us, to save us, Roland fled Cliffwall. Unable to control the magic he himself had unleashed, he ran far from the archives and out into the valley wilderness, away from the towns . . . although not far enough. He hoped to live out his days there and harm no one else. But the Lifedrinker spell continued, unstoppable, never satisfied. Roland was like a sponge, absorbing life from the forest, from the grasslands. His very existence killed trees, drained rivers dry. And the desolation around where he had gone to ground spread wider and wider in an ever-expanding scar. He wiped out croplands. He erased entire towns." She straightened and brushed a hand across her eyes. "Roland didn't mean it."

Nicci thought of Thistle's family, of Verdun Springs, how they had clung to their hardscrabble existence, and then died. "His intentions don't matter. Think of all the damage that man has done. He must be stopped, otherwise his bottomless pit of magic will swallow the world."

Simon added, "For years our Cliffwall scholars have been scouring the books, trying any mitigation spell they could find. But no one could even get close to what was needed."

As the night deepened out in the dead valley, Nathan stared out at the Scar, watching the shadows move. "I wouldn't expect you to know how to stop such a powerful enemy. All of you are untrained wizards. You have read books, but you were never *trained* by a wizard, and you have never proved your abilities. Ah, I wish the Prelate Verna were here to help you. Wizardry untested cannot be trusted."

"You tried your best," Nicci said. "Now we will do our own research. If this archive is as vast as you say, it must hold the key, a counterspell. We simply need to find it."

"We would do anything to help you save us," Simon said. "But after the . . . accidents, we are afraid to try extreme measures of our own."

"That is wise," Nathan said. "But something must be done."

"That's why we are here," Nicci said, then finally admitted, "to save the world."

The orphan girl added with deep longing in her voice, "I want to see the valley the way it's supposed to be. I want to see the fertile land, the green fields, the tall forests."

Nicci looked at Thistle. "You will."

CHAPTER 43

Though Nicci wanted to begin her research in how to combat the Lifedrinker, she knew they were all exhausted from their long journey. Deep night had set in outside.

"Let us show you to your rooms," Victoria said. "You must rest." She glanced down at Thistle. "The girl needs her sleep."

"I'm still awake. I'll help." She looked at Nicci, determined. "And tomorrow I can study alongside you."

"Are you able to read?" Nicci asked.

"I know my letters, and I can read a lot of words. I will be much better after you teach me. I learn fast."

Nathan gave a good-natured chuckle. "Dear girl, I appreciate someone so willing to learn, but that is quite an ambitious goal. Some of these languages and alphabets are unknown even to me."

Nicci fixed her gaze on Thistle's dust-smeared skin, her bright and intelligent eyes. "When the Sisters trained me in the Palace of the Prophets, I spent more than forty-five years as an acolyte learning the basics."

The girl looked amazed. "I don't want to wait forty-five years!"

"No one does, but you're an intelligent girl. Since you learn quickly, it might take only forty years." Thistle did not at first realize Nicci was teasing her. Then Nicci continued in a more serious tone, "We need to defeat the Lifedrinker long before that, or there won't be any world left."

Victoria shooed them along. "Rest now, time for a fresh start tomorrow. We have separate quarters for each of you. They are austere, but spacious. We will let you unpack and rest."

"Not much to unpack, since we lost almost everything when the dust people attacked," Bannon said. "We've been living with little more than the clothes on our backs."

With a warm smile, Victoria promised, "We will provide clean clothing from the Cliffwall stores, and we will launder and mend your own garments."

The matronly woman showed them to private chambers deep within the plateau, where the temperature was cool and the air dry. Beeswax candles burned inside small hollows in the stone walls, adding a warm yellow glow and a faint sweet scent. Each room's furnishings consisted of a reading desk, an open floor with a sheepskin to cover the stone, a chamber pot, an urn of water, a washbasin, and a narrow pallet for sleeping. In each room, fresh, loose scholars' clothes had been laid out for them.

Victoria offered the spunky orphan girl a place of her own, but Thistle followed Nicci into her chamber. She bounced up and down on the pallet's straw-filled bedding. "This is soft, but it may be prickly. I'd rather sleep on the floor. You can have the pallet. That sheepskin looks warm enough for me. I'll stay close if you need me."

Even though the girl seemed perfectly satisfied with the arrangement, Nicci asked, "Why don't you want your own room? You can sleep as long as you like."

Thistle blinked her honey-brown eyes at Nicci. "I should stay nearby. What if you need protection?"

"I do not need protection. I am a sorceress."

But the girl sat cross-legged on the sheepskin and responded with a bright grin. "It never hurts to have an extra set of eyes. I will keep you safe."

Although she would not admit it, Thistle obviously did not wish to be alone. "Very well, you can guard me if you like," Nicci said, remembering all the girl had been through. "But if you are to be effective in protecting me, I'll need you rested as well."

After they had changed into the borrowed clothes, one of the Cliff-wall stewards arrived at their door to gather the bundled-up garments to be laundered and mended. The waifish girl's rags needed a great deal of repair, as did Nicci's black traveling dress. After handing over the old clothes, Nicci sorted through the scanty possessions she had managed to save from Verdun Springs.

Eager to help, Thistle laid out the items on the writing desk—the long sharp knife, some rope, near-empty packets of food. Although exhausted, the young girl kept up a chatter. "I never had any brothers and sisters. Do you have a family?" Her elfin face was filled with questions. "Did you ever have a daughter of your own?"

Nicci arranged the bedding on her pallet, keeping her face turned away so that she could ponder the proper answer. A daughter of her own? Someone, perhaps, like Thistle? The idea had not occurred to her, not for a long time at least. She touched her lower lip, where she had once worn a gold ring.

"No, I never had a daughter." It should have been a simple answer, and Nicci was puzzled as to why she had hesitated. "That was never meant to be part of my life."

After all those times Jagang had sentenced her to serve as a whore, or when he himself had forced himself upon her, Nicci surely had the opportunity to become pregnant, but thanks to her skills as a sorceress, she had never needed to worry about a child. She had always prevented herself from conceiving. Early on, Nicci had learned how not to feel anything—no passion, no love of any kind.

The girl examined the items Nicci had removed from the pockets of her old travel dress, her belt, and her side pouch. She unrolled a cloth-wrapped packet among the paraphernalia. "Oh, a flower!" Thistle said, looking at the violet-and-crimson petals. "You carried a flower all this way?"

Nicci instantly swept up the cloth packet, whisking the dried blossom away from the startled girl. "Don't touch that!" Her pulse raced.

Thistle flinched. "I'm sorry! I didn't mean to do anything wrong. I . . ." She cleared her throat. "It must be very special to you. Is it a pretty keeepsake from a suitor?"

Nicci narrowed her blue eyes, amused by the idea. Bannon had indeed offered the flower as a romantic gesture—a notion she had thoroughly quashed. "No, not that at all. The deathrise flower is deadly poison—one of the most potent toxins ever found, very dangerous." She wrapped it carefully in the cloth again, then placed it in the highest alcove above her sleeping pallet. "It would lead to a long and horrible death. Maybe the most horrible death ever known."

Thistle looked relieved. "So you're protecting me! And I'll be safe, too. Because we protect each other." The girl rearranged the sheepskin on the empty space on the stone floor, ready to curl up and go to sleep.

Nicci blew out one of the candles, but before she could extinguish the other, Thistle asked, "If that poison is so deadly, couldn't you use it to kill the Lifedrinker?"

"No, I don't think it is potent enough for that."

Thistle nodded, then wrapped the sheepskin around her and lay down on the hard stone floor, which she insisted was perfectly comfortable. "Then we'll have to find a different way."

Nicci used magic to snuff out the candle on the opposite wall, plunging the room into darkness.

Though he was anxious to study Cliffwall's wondrous books and scrolls, Nathan slept for many hours that first night. He felt safe, warm, and comfortable for the first time in a long while.

After waking refreshed, he hurried to the dining hall, where he scrounged a few scraps of breakfast, since most of the scholars had eaten much earlier and hurried to work. His borrowed scholar's robe was comfortable, though a bit drab and not at all fashionable. He supposed it would do until his more acceptable clothes came back from the washing and mending teams. For now, he would scour the library in hopes of finding how to stop the Lifedrinker's voracious, out-of-control spell that sucked away all life.

In the first of the library chambers, he considered a wall of fat leather-bound volumes. So many of them! Scrolls lay unfurled on tables as intent scholars discussed the possible meanings of obscure lines;

other readers hunched over open tomes, writing notes with chalk on flat slates.

When he looked at the dizzying number of shelved books in front of him and the other walls with an equal number of shelves—and knowing there were numerous rooms identical to this—the scope of Cliffwall's knowledge felt as intimidating as it was exhilarating.

In the Palace of the Prophets, books had been Nathan's quiet companions for a thousand years, his source of information about the outside world. Recently, Richard Rahl had also granted him access to all of the books in the People's Palace of D'Hara, but most of those works had dealt with prophecy, and so were no longer relevant. Now the world's future might depend on what he read here.

And there was so much more than the witch woman's cryptic line in his life book.

Being surrounded by these works made him feel as if he had come home again—even if it was a huge home and a cluttered mess. "Dear spirits, how can I find any information here, except by accident?" He paced in front of the shelves, pondering, while acolyte archivists rolled scrolls or replaced volumes in their proper spots.

Victoria approached him, accompanied by her three lovely acolytes. "My memmers and I are here to be of assistance, Wizard Nathan. Simon's catalog system is confusing to most, and he is the only one who knows where the volumes are. But I have committed many of these works to memory, and my lovely acolytes each hold more than a hundred volumes in their own minds. I can also bring you Gloria, Franklin, Peretta, and ten more well-trained memmers. You could sit back while we recite our knowledge to you."

Nathan found it amazing that these young women—or any of the memmers—were able to commit thousands of pages of dense and precise magical lore to memory, even if they did not organize or, perhaps, understand the words they could recite.

Audrey, Laurel, and Sage looked at him with such intensity that he felt a warm flush come to his cheeks. He gave Victoria a polite, gentlemanly smile. "I am impressed with your skill, madam, and I would certainly welcome the company of such beautiful ladies, but I'm afraid they would distract me. I've spent years reading books with my own eyes, and that's the way I should search for the information."

Victoria's grandmotherly face wrinkled with disappointment. "Generations of memmers have well-respected skills. We possess the information you need. If you tell us what you are searching for, we can quote the relevant passages for you, if we remember." She waved a hand dismissively. "These books are just the static preservation of words. We would bring those words alive for you. We could tell you everything we know."

The woman's determination made him uncomfortable, and he wanted to get to work in his own way. "It doesn't seem pragmatic, I'm afraid. I can't study so much magical lore if it is locked inside your heads, and I don't have the time to listen to your people speak aloud one book at a time." He traced his fingers along curious symbols on the spine of one black volume. "Some of these tomes are written in languages I don't recognize, but I am fluent in numerous others. I can read quite quickly."

"But not all the books are available to you," Victoria said. "You saw the archive tower that melted in the . . . accident. All those books were wiped out."

"Your memmers can recall the volumes that were lost there?" Nathan asked.

The three young acolytes nodded. Victoria lifted her chin with a measure of pride. "Many of them. We don't exactly know what was lost. For the most part, they were works of prophecy, but many were miscategorized."

Nathan let out a sigh of relief. "Prophecy? Well, then, with the star shift, prophecy is gone and any such volumes would contain little of practical value. Prophecy is of no use to us—and certainly of little interest in our quest to stop the Lifedrinker."

But he did not so easily dismiss the prediction Red had made. *And the Sorceress must save the world.*

Victoria could not hide her indignation at his attitude. "If that is what you truly wish, we will leave you to your studies, then. My memmers are always here to assist. We can recall many things that Simon and his scholars have not yet bothered to read."

Nathan gave the woman his sweetest smile. "I thank you. Everyone at Cliffwall has been so generous. If the knowledge is locked away here, we will find it, and we will use it to defeat the Lifedrinker." He fought back a flush of embarrassment, as he realized that his own unfortunate lack of magic would make him of little use in the actual battle against the evil wizard. "Nicci is a powerful sorceress. Do not underestimate her. She used to be called Death's Mistress, and she struck fear across the land."

Victoria's expression turned sour, unimpressed. She seemed a competitive sort. "Death's Mistress? We have no need of further death. Let us hope she can bring *life* back to our fertile valley."

The woman departed with her acolytes, leaving him alone to face the disorganized books, scrolls, and tomes before him. He didn't know where to begin his search for the original spell that had created the Lifedrinker, or where to find an appropriate counterspell.

But he had other priorities as well. If Nathan could restore his own magic, he could fight beside Nicci against the Lifedrinker. Somewhere in the library must be information about how and why he had lost his gift, or perhaps an accurate map showing how to find Kol Adair. Everything was connected.

He walked along the shelves from one side of the great chamber to the other, running his finger across the spines of the leather-bound volumes. He didn't know where to start.

So he carried a volume at random over to a table and took a seat next to an intense young scholar who didn't even look up from her reading. Nathan opened the book and scanned the handwritten symbols on the page, not certain what he was searching for, but sure he would uncover useful information, nevertheless.

CHAPTER 44

While Nathan assessed Cliffwall's countless volumes of preserved magical lore, Nicci decided she needed first-hand knowledge about the Lifedrinker. While she was an accomplished scholar in her own right, she wanted to investigate the Scar with her own eyes.

Bannon was also restless, wandering the silent halls of the giant archive. He practiced with his sword, prancing about in the open halls, because his mentor was too preoccupied in the library. He would dance, slash, and twirl down the corridors, frightening a few distractible scholars as he fought his own shadow, and usually defeated it.

When Nicci proposed a cautious reconnoitering of the Scar to learn about the Lifedrinker, Bannon jumped at the chance. He raised his sword. "I'll go along, Sorceress. Sturdy and I will be your protectors."

Thistle was always at her side, and she sniffed at the young man's eager bravado. "I am Nicci's protector."

"I need no protector, but you are welcome to come along, Bannon Farmer. There may be more dust people to fight." She turned to the orphan girl. "But you will stay here, where it is safe."

"I don't want to be safe. I am safest when I'm with you."

Nicci shook her head. "Bannon and I will go scout, and we'll be back in a day or two. You stay here." Disappointment flashed in the girl's eyes, but she didn't argue further. She darted off to find Nathan and see if he needed her help.

Nicci once again wore her black travel dress, which had been cleaned and mended. The people of Cliffwall provided packs, water, and food for their scouting expedition.

Before she and Bannon set off into the broad desolation, Simon joined them at the outer wall of the plateau, from which they would climb down into the foothills. "Most of those who go to seek the Lifedrinker never come back," he said.

"We don't intend to fight him now," Nicci said. "We are just investigating, checking to see his defenses. And when I return, armed with the intelligence we've gathered, I can help Nathan look for what we need among all those volumes."

She and Bannon left Cliffwall in the early morning, emerging from the opposite side of the plateau onto a steep, winding path. They picked their way down the sheer slope to the foothills, where the vegetation had begun to wither as the Lifedrinker's desolation expanded. The low mesquite trees and piñon pines had bent over, as if in the agony of a long poisonous death. Thorny weeds tore at their clothes as they walked along, descending through the hills. Black beetles scuttled along the ground, while spiders hung forlorn in empty webs.

Much farther out into the valley, the terrain was cracked, lifeless desert. Nicci tried to imagine that broad expanse filled with croplands, thriving villages, and well-traveled roads, all of which had now been swallowed in the dust over the past twenty years. From the vantage of the foothills, the waves of oncoming desolation were as apparent as ripples in a pond.

She narrowed her eyes as she gazed toward the heart of the crater. "The Lifedrinker will be there. We'll get as close as we can for now, gather information, but I will save the real fight for when I know how to kill him."

Bannon squinted toward their destination, then gave a quick nod.

Before they left the last hills, Nicci heard a rustling of shrubs behind her, a loose stone kicked aside, the crack of a dry mesquite branch. Bannon spun, raising his sword, and Nicci prepared to fight.

When the dry boughs of a dead piñon moved aside, Thistle pushed herself through, looking around. Spotting Nicci, the girl smiled. "I knew I would catch up with you sooner or later. I came to help."

"I told you to stay behind," Nicci said.

"Lots of people tell me things. I make up my own mind."

Nicci placed her hands on her hips. "You should not be out here. Go back to Cliffwall."

"I'm coming with you."

"No, you are not."

Thistle clearly wasn't going to listen. "I know these lands. I've lived here all my life. I led you to Cliffwall, didn't I? You would never have been able to find it without me. I can take care of myself—and I can take care of you." She put her hands on her rag skirt, imitating Nicci's stance. Her lips quirked in a defiant smile. "And if I wanted to keep following you, how would you stop me?"

Nicci gave a quick answer. "With sorcery."

The girl huffed. "You would never use sorcery against me."

Thistle's bold confidence brought a wry smile to Nicci's lips. "No, I probably wouldn't. And I'm fully aware of how useful you can be out in the wild, perhaps even more so than Bannon."

The young man flushed. "But I've proved my usefulness in battle. Think of how many dust people I killed back in Verdun Springs, and all the selka before that."

"And you may need to fight and kill more enemies." Nicci didn't want to waste any more time. "Very well. We will go together, scout the Scar, and return quickly. But stay alert. We don't know what other defenses the Lifedrinker might have."

Descending from the last foothills, they headed along cracked canyons that led into the Scar. The breezes swept up white, salty dust from the dry ground, and Bannon coughed as he wiped bitter white powder from his face. Nicci's eyes stung. Her black dress was also smeared with tan and white from all the blowing alkaline powder. She rationed her water, knowing they would find none in the desolation.

The ruined landscape seemed to grow angrier as they continued. The sun pounded down as they emerged from the widening washes of dry rivers that were now just barren, rocky beds. Salt-encrusted boulders protruded from the ground, and all that remained of round lakes were cracked mosaics of dry mud. Dust devils swirled ghostly curls of powder.

Weary in the oppressive environment, the three engaged in little conversation, and paused to rest infrequently. When they sipped a drink, their water tasted bad from the caustic dust on their lips.

Farther along, the cracks in the ground exhaled fumes where steam rose up from underground vents. Nicci smelled the burnt tang of brimstone. Bubbling mud pots looked like raw wounds; bursting and splattering, they emitted the foul stench of rotten eggs. Thistle sprang from rock to rock, picking out a safe path for them.

The stirred debris in the air made the sun appear swollen in the late afternoon, and Nicci felt uneasy about the prospect of camping in the Scar. "It's been hours since we last saw even a dead tree," Bannon said.

"We can find shelter in the rocks," Nicci said. "Or maybe we should just walk through the night. I can make a hand light to guide us."

The girl looked uneasy. "Dangerous things come out at night."

Bannon looked around warily, but the sulfurous steam from fumaroles and bubbling mud pits made the air thick with haze. The sounds would have masked any stealthy movement.

Nicci said, "We can be attacked just as readily during the day."

As they considered their choices, the dry, caked dirt stirred beneath them. Reacting quickly, Nicci pushed Thistle to safety and she herself sprang back as dark, desiccated hands reached out of the dust. Cracks spread apart in the ground, and dust people crawled up from below. Bannon yelled and raised his sword, running toward the attackers.

Nicci let magic boil into her hand. She had battled these things before. She released a surge of fire, igniting the nearest attacker before it could crawl entirely out of the cracked soil.

Jumping onto a flat rock for stability, Bannon swung his sword with a vicious sweep that decapitated three mummified men clad in dirt-encrusted rags. But even headless, the creatures still lunged forward, blindly grasping for victims. Dodging from rock to rock, Thistle ducked under the outstretched claws, and Bannon cleaved a cadaver's torso in two, then hacked off its brittle legs at the knees.

Nicci released a focused hammer blow of wind that shattered the bones and dried sinews of another emerging creature, leaving it in a pile of broken debris half out of the ground. Another push of air knocked the unsteady dust people backward into the bubbling mud pits. The creatures fell into the roiling, churning cauldrons, where they thrashed and sank.

Thistle sprang onto the back of a desiccated creature that advanced toward Nicci from behind. The girl tugged at its shoulders and battered her fists onto its sticklike ribs, stabbed the dry body repeatedly with her knife. The mummified creature broke and fell to the dust.

As Nicci turned to thank her, another pair of dust people crawled up out of the ground, lunging toward Thistle with a clearly focused intent. One was a shriveled woman with a faded red head scarf wrapped around the tufts of wiry hair on her skull. The other, a man, wore the tattered remnants of a leather vest.

Thistle lifted her knife to swing at the new attack, but then she froze in horrified recognition. The dust people stumbled toward her, much too close, hooked hands grasping for the girl. "Aunt Luna? Uncle Marcus!"

Nicci recognized them as well, and she swept in, placing herself in front of the stunned girl. The creatures that had been her aunt and uncle wanted to drag Thistle back with them, but Nicci stood before them. "You can't have her!" Leathery, cadaverous hands touched her arms, her black dress—and Nicci released a furious surge of magic, sparking fire within the inhuman remnants of Marcus and Luna.

The sudden fire burned a hot, purifying white, consuming the remains of the two in an instant. As they reeled away from Nicci, the pair fell into fine gray ash, dropping with a rushing sound that was almost a sigh. Thistle let out a despairing cry.

Panting heavily, the three stood together, poised for more attackers, but the Lifedrinker sent no more dust people after them. The battle was over as swiftly as it had begun. In the distance, they heard scuttling movement, a clatter of pebbles . . . not reanimated corpses this time, but other creatures—armored things with many legs that kept to the shadows.

Thistle clung to Nicci's waist. "The Lifedrinker knows where we are. He is spying on us."

"Are you sure we should keep going out there in the darkness?" Bannon asked. He could barely keep the quaver from his voice.

"It would be a waste to sacrifice ourselves now," Nicci said. "Until we discover a way to cut off the Lifedrinker's magic, we have seen enough. For now."

They made good time retracing their steps toward the rising land at the north end of the vast dead valley, but it was long after dark when they reached the dying forests and remnants of trees in the foothills. The dry grass, dead weeds, and gnarled, leafless trees seemed welcoming by comparison. They were exhausted by the time they found a place to camp.

"At least we have enough wood to build a fire now," Bannon said. "A very large fire."

Still shaken from seeing the remnants of her aunt and uncle, Thistle brought several armloads of dry mesquite and made a pile at their chosen campsite. "It'll be very bright and warm, but won't the Lifedrinker be able to see such a big fire?"

Nicci used her magic to ignite the pile, and the bright fire crackled with intense flames and ribbons of aromatic smoke. "He knows full well where we are. Now at least we will be able to see any attack that comes."

Bannon and Thistle hunkered close to the comforting flames. "Both of you sleep," Nicci said. "I will keep watch."

They bedded down, though they remained restless for many hours. As she sat alone, Nicci listened for sounds beyond the pop and crackle of the burning wood.

The Scar remained silent, an emptiness in the dark that seemed to swallow up sound as well as life. Nicci sensed some other presence out there, however, something prowling in the dying hills around them. Alert, she peered into the blackness beyond the firelight, but could see nothing, hear nothing. Yet she *felt* it . . . something strong and deadly.

Something hunting them.

CHAPTER 45

Surrounded by gifted scholars, Nathan found their dedication refreshing and inspirational. "If I had a thousand years with this grand library, I'd become the greatest wizard who ever lived," he said with a good-natured but weary smile, as Simon brought him another stack of volumes.

"A thousand years . . ." said the scholar-archivist with a shake of his head. He arranged the selected volumes in careful stacks on Nathan's cluttered study table. "I would like nothing more than to spend centuries reading, studying, and learning . . . but alas, I have only a normal life span."

"That was one of the few advantages of being trapped inside the Palace of the Prophets, the webs and spell-forms that prevented us from aging," Nathan said. He looked at the mountains of books brought to him for his review, stacked by subject, some of the passages marked with colorful strings or feathers to separate the pages. "But if the Scar continues to grow and grow, there may not be more than a normal life span left for any of us."

Intent on searching for any useful information about the Lifedrinker, the Cliffwall students pored through book after book, scroll after scroll, highlighting any writings that might bear relevance. Nathan wanted to find the original spell Roland had used to fight his wasting disease, the spell that had transformed him into the Lifedrinker.

During his years in the palace, Nathan had become an extremely fast reader. Even though he'd had all the time in the world, he also had access to thousands and thousands of books, and even forever hadn't seemed like enough time. He could skim a document as fast as he could turn the pages, and he could absorb several thick volumes in an hour.

In only two days here in Cliffwall, he had already finished reading shelves of books, but it would take so much time to learn it all. So much time . . . He had learned very little about the Lifedrinker's draining spell.

Nathan drew his fingers down his chin. "Remind me, did you say that Roland used a spell that was preserved by the memmers?"

"One of the memmers remembered part of it and made certain suggestions. They gave Roland an idea where to look." Simon frowned at an embossed leather volume and set it aside. "We have not yet been able to recover the original text of the spell to study it ourselves. Therefore, we must rely on Victoria's word." When he frowned, the lines in his face made him look much older. "Memories can be faulty. I would prefer independent text verification."

As if summoned, the memmer leader came up with her three lovely acolytes. As she heard him speak, her face darkened with annoyance. Audrey, Laurel, and Sage crowded close behind her, looking indignant on her behalf.

"The memmers are beyond reproach." Victoria stood before the study table piled high with tomes. "You wouldn't have any of these books to study at all, were it not for me. If I had not discovered how to dissipate the camouflage shroud, no one would have access to the archive."

"Nor would Roland," Nathan pointed out, "and we wouldn't be in quite so much trouble."

Simon gathered his dignity and drew himself taller in an attempt to belittle Victoria. "All of us in Cliffwall appreciate your past service. The memmers were important in their day, but you are obsolete now. Gifted and intelligent people have access to the *entire* library now, not just selected volumes memorized generations ago."

Victoria huffed. "Words written on paper are different from words held in the mind." She tapped her temple and leaned close. "It matters not what is written down, but what we *know*."

Simon plainly disagreed. "Knowledge that is not written down cannot be properly shared. How can I study what is inside your mind? How can our scholars draw insights and conclusions if we can't see your thoughts? How can you share properly with Wizard Nathan right now?"

"We will tell him whatever he needs to know," Victoria said.

Nathan raised his hands I exasperation. "Dear spirits, do not quarrel! Cliffwall is a banquet of special lore, and we have a feast before us. Why quibble over a few tidbits?"

Struggling not to let the argument flare, Simon turned to depart. "I will keep gathering suitable volumes for you and let these women tell you the stories they hold in their heads."

Victoria gave the scholar-archivist a condescending frown as he left. "Don't worry about young Simon, Wizard Nathan. He has reached a level of responsibility beyond his capabilities." She sounded sweet and maternal. "Archiving all the volumes in the library is an immense and overwhelming task, and it will take many generations to do properly. Memmers have dealt with the problem of retaining our information for thousands of years, so it is understandable why Simon feels such urgency."

"But there is genuine urgency, madam," Nathan said. "If the Lifedrinker continues to drain the world, none of us has much time left." He ran his fingers through his shoulder-length white hair. "I do need to know what you have memorized, but, as Simon pointed out, I cannot access what is stored inside your head."

Victoria smiled with a patient warmth. "Then we will lead you through it. We shall recite the books you need to read, because we know them by heart."

Nathan could skim words on paper faster than any memmer could speak, but if Victoria and her acolytes sorted through their memorized knowledge and recited only the relevant portions, perhaps it would be worthwhile.

He regarded Audrey, Laurel, and Sage, saw the three different types of beauty. "They are not your actual daughters, though I see how you care for them. You must be very close."

"These dear girls have spent their lives with me. I consider all of my acolytes to be my surrogate sons and daughters." Sadness washed over Victoria's face like a fog closing in. "I never had children of my own, although my husband and I tried very hard. When we wed, Bertram and I dreamed of having a large family, but . . ." Her expression fell further, and she turned away. "But I was barren. We never had children. Three times I found myself pregnant, and we had such hope. I even started making infant clothes . . . but I lost the baby each time. And then Bertram died."

She closed her eyes and heaved a great breath. She gave the three young acolytes a loving look. "So I poured all my maternal instincts into guiding my acolytes, and over the years I have trained a family larger than Bertram and I ever dreamed we could have.

"I have done my duty to preserve the memmers, so that knowledge is passed on from parent to child, independent from what is written down in the archive." She sounded defensive. "I refuse to let go of our heritage. It is we who kept the lore preserved for the centuries when Cliffwall remained hidden." Audrey, Laurel, and Sage, with tears in their eyes, nodded. Victoria swept the three of them into a hug. "Sometimes I wish I had never remembered the spell that dissolved the camouflage shroud." She shook her head.

"You had to," Laurel said.

"It was time," Sage said.

Intrigued, Nathan pushed the stacked books aside. "And how exactly did you reveal the hidden barrier after thousands of years? I thought no one knew how to counter the camouflage spell."

"It was a rare mistake—for the memmers, and for me."

Nathan folded his hands together, raised his eyebrows. "I am listening."

"As we told you, the camouflage shroud was more than just a disguise. It was a barrier, a preservation spell. Cliffwall was sealed behind a barricade of *time*. Not just hidden—it was *gone*.

"But the first memmers were given the knowledge of how to take down that secret barricade when it was time. If no one remembered how to drop the shroud, then the knowledge might as well have been destroyed. So, the key was passed along in our collective memory, generation to generation." She nodded to herself. "After three thousand years had passed, and the wizard wars were long over, the canyon dwellers considered it safe enough to try. But, alas, the release spell we had memorized millennia ago no longer worked."

Victoria put a hand to the center of her chest and drew a shaky breath. "Somewhere along the line, we had remembered it wrong! We truly could not recall the nuances of phrasing. At some point when passing the knowledge from parent to child, from teacher to student, someone must have made an error." She looked away in embarrassment, as if the revelation shamed all memmers.

"Dear spirits," Nathan muttered.

Victoria continued, "We could admit it to no one, though. The isolated canyon people had devoted their lives to keeping the secret—for millennia! They trusted the memmers, they believed in us. We could not tell them we had forgotten! Some stalled for time, making awkward excuses and saying that it wasn't yet time to reveal the archive. But no one knew how to do so! For more than a century, we held out hope that someone would figure out what had gone wrong. The memmers secretly prayed that someone would correct the spell and reveal the library vaults again."

Victoria looked up, met Nathan's azure gaze. "That person was me . . . and it was a mistake. I memorized a spell incorrectly. I uttered an improper combination of syllables in the ancient tongue of Ildakar." She continued in a breathy voice, "And it worked! I was just a girl of seventeen years, being trained by my parents . . . and I got the spell wrong."

Nathan let out a delighted chuckle. "But, dear madam, you accidentally got it *right*. You made a corresponding error, mistakenly saying the sounds properly. The camouflage shroud fell, and you revealed the hidden archive. That is exactly what you wanted, isn't it?"

"Yes." Victoria sounded disappointed. "For millennia, the memmers were powerful and respected, the keepers of inaccessible knowledge. But by throwing open the floodgates and inviting gifted scholars from the outer towns, I may have made us obsolete."

"Perhaps." Nathan briskly rubbed his hands together. "But now everyone has this knowledge. It may help us defeat the Lifedrinker."

Victoria's face remained lined with concern. "Dangerous information for any fool to use! Giving it to people who were not ready, not trained—that was what created the Lifedrinker in the first place."

She grumbled. "My mother was a harsh teacher. She would make me repeat her words over and over again until each spell became part of my soul, every word imprinted in the marrow of my bones. She beat me with a willow switch every time I made an error. She would shriek warnings at me about the dangers a mistake could unleash on the world."

Victoria lifted her shoulders and let them fall. "I remember my father's smile and his patience, but my mother did not believe he took his role seriously enough. She blamed him for teaching me an incorrect phrase, and he just laughed, delighted that the problem of the shroud had been solved—by his own daughter. It was time for celebration, he said. The camouflage shroud was at last gone."

Victoria leaned closer to Nathan, who was captivated by the story. "My mother killed him for it. She threw him over the cliff before he could believe what she was doing. My mother didn't even bother to watch him fall. I heard him scream—and it stopped when he struck the ground.

"My mother railed at me for making my mistake. 'Do you not know how important this is? Do you not see that every word must be perfect? If you do not revere the words, the dangers could be unimaginable!' I was terrified. All I could hear were shouts down on the canyon floor as people rushed to my father's body. But my mother was intent on me. Her eyes were wild, and I could feel her hot breath on my face. 'I killed your father to protect us all. What if he had misquoted a fire spell? What if he mistakenly taught one of us how to breach the veil and unleash the Keeper upon the world?' I had to nod and admit the depth of my father's error. We never mourned him." Tears filled Victoria's eyes.

"But if your error corrected an error, why should you feel guilty?" Nathan asked.

"Because the error itself showed everyone that our perfect memory might not be perfect."

CHAPTER 46

At their makeshift camp, the hot mesquite campfire died to orange coals before dawn, but Nicci did not wake Bannon to change the watch. She needed little sleep, so she remained alert throughout the night, studying the nightmarish outlines of rock formations at the edge of the waning firelight. As soon as Thistle awoke, the girl crawled over to sit next to her. Neither of them said a word, but both stared into the darkness waiting for sunrise.

Bannon yawned, stretched, and got to his feet, brushing dirt and dried twigs from his clothes. Soon enough, they set off, leaving the comforting glow of their campfire embers behind.

As they made their way back toward the sheer wall of the plateau that rose up above the encroaching Scar, Nicci and Bannon picked their way along a wash, while Thistle scuttled ahead with the grace and agility of a darting lizard. They found a trickle of water and followed it up step after step of ocher slickrock. The trickling sounded like music after the dust devils and chemical haze of the desolation. The three spent long moments cupping their hands, filling their palms with drip after drip of cold water, which they splashed on their faces to wipe away the burning alkaline dust.

"Can the Lifedrinker still be watching us?" Thistle asked. "Even here?"

"He could be. There are other dangers, as well," Nicci said. "Something in this world always wants to kill you. Don't forget that."

They moved on up the canyon. Reptiles darted among the rocks overhead, and Thistle glanced up at the ledges, tempted to hunt them, but she kept moving instead.

Bannon trudged through the rocks of the wash, keeping his sword in hand just in case. All night long, Nicci had sensed that predatory presence circling their camp, but she had heard no sound, seen no flashing eyes in the firelight. Now she again felt that oppressive sense of being watched. Following Bannon, she looked around, stared at the rock formations, and wondered if the evil wizard might stage another ambush. But she saw nothing.

Silent and unexpected, something heavy dropped from above and struck her in the back, an avalanche of tawny fur, slashing claws, and loud snarls. The blow knocked Nicci to the ground before she had a chance to release her magic.

Bannon yelled and spun around. Thistle cried out.

Hidden in the ruddy tan of the slickrock walls, two additional feline shapes sprang—huge sand-colored panthers with curved saber-like fangs and claws, like a fistful of sharp daggers.

When the first panther crashed down on Nicci, the blow knocked the wind out of her. She squirmed, trying to fight back. The beast was a dynamo of muscles, its body an engine of attack. It could kill her in mere seconds.

Nicci dodged the first swipe of its paw, but the other paw raked bloody furrows down her back, slicing open her black dress. The panther let out a roaring yowl and tried to clamp its fangs down on her head. Nicci didn't have time or luxury of concentration to find its heart with her magic and stop it dead.

In a desperate defense, she released an unfocused wave of magic, a rippling shock wave of compressed air in every direction. The invisible explosion flung the feline attacker away from her, but the blast seemed oddly diminished. Bleeding badly, Nicci staggered to her feet.

Bannon had pressed his back against the slickrock wall for protection while he jabbed with his sword. One of his blows scored a bloody gash in the ribs of the second panther. Thistle dodged and darted as the third beast tried to trap her, playing with her like a cat with a mouse. Angry at seeing the girl threatened, Nicci reached out and aimed her gift, intending to burst the heart of the attacking panther.

Nothing happened.

Nicci felt the flow of magic go out of her, but somehow her spell bounced off the sand panther like a stone skimming over the surface of a pond. She tried again, also with no effect. She *had* control of her gift—she had not lost it, like Nathan—but this big panther was impervious to her strike.

As the beast prowled in, Nicci saw that its hide was branded with arcane designs, glyphs that were all angles and swooping curves. She recognized it as a spell-form of some sort, perhaps a kind of magical armor.

These were not merely wild beasts.

Nicci crouched to defend herself as the first panther came back to attack. She hurled fire that should have incinerated the big cat, but the magical flames rolled off of its fur. Undaunted, the snarling cat sprang toward her, and Nicci had no time to consider what alternative magic might be effective.

She pulled the long dagger at her side, ready to fight. She realized the branded arcane symbols might give the sand panthers a kind of protection against magic, but surely a sharp knife would cause damage. She sliced the air with her dagger, then sprang to one side as the lunging cat missed her. She did not have time for finesse, nor did she mean to taunt these creatures. She needed them *dead*.

Thistle ducked behind a fallen slab of slickrock and a twisted piñon. Bannon defended himself, wildly flailing with his sword, forgetting the intricate moves that Nathan had taught him. The panther was also a flurry of feral rage.

Nicci watched the big cats move together in an oddly coordinated attack. The three big cats moved in eerie unison. They had separated their prey, and each panther seemed to know what the other two were doing. Although she couldn't read the symbols branded on their hides, she had heard of spell-bonded animals before. These three panthers were a fighting triad, a *troka*, their minds connected to one another to make them a perfect fighting force.

Nicci wondered if the Lifedrinker had sent these predators to attack them, but that didn't seem right. Sand panthers were not part of the Scar, or the original fertile valley here from years ago. They must have been raised and trained somewhere else, by someone else.

Regardless of their origin, the cats were perfect killing machines. The reasons didn't matter. Not now.

She diverted her attention to see Thistle duck under the piñon boughs and scramble out the other side as the cat lunged into the tangled branches. The girl rolled on her back and came up with her own knife in her hands. She wrapped both hands around the hilt as the panther pounced.

Nicci caught her breath, knowing that she couldn't reach the girl in time—and then she realized that Thistle had intentionally lured the overeager predator. As the cat lunged, Thistle brought the knife up under its chin, driving the blade through its jaws, the roof of its mouth, and into its brain. The panther convulsed and shook, then collapsed on top of the scrawny girl, nearly crushing her.

When the big cat fell dead, the other two panthers shuddered and reeled, as if they, too, had suffered a painful blow. They howled in eerie unison.

Bannon used that moment to charge forward, thrusting his sword straight into the rib cage of the second panther. The tawny predator thrashed and roared, opening its mouth wide, but the sword point had pierced the creature's heart and protruded from the opposite side of its chest.

Nicci raked her own knife across the ribs of the last panther, which was momentarily stunned by the deaths of its two spell-bonded partners. The maddened creature slashed at her with its claws, and Nicci sliced again with her knife. The injured beast thrashed its tail and came back in a wild attack, as if ready to throw away its life. The heavy creature drove her to the ground, but Nicci stabbed upward, deep into its belly.

Soaked with blood, Thistle squirmed out from under the body of the panther she had killed and flew like a demon to Nicci's rescue. The girl stabbed the last panther several times with her own knife, and with a great heave, Nicci pushed the dying beast away. She extricated herself and stood covered in blood, both the panther's and her own. The skin of her back had been torn to ribbons.

Bannon was in shock as he slid his sword from the carcass of the panther he had killed. "I'm surprised the Lifedrinker didn't send giant scorpions or centipedes."

Nicci shook her head as she stood bleeding, beginning to feel the fiery pain of her multiple wounds. "I am not certain the Lifedrinker is the cause of this."

The last sand panther was not dead. It lay on the ground heaving great breaths, rumbling with deep pain and bleeding from numerous wounds.

Bannon stepped up behind her, gasping at the deep bloody furrows in her back. "Sorceress! Those wounds! We have to heal them."

Nicci looked down at her scratched arms. "I can heal myself." She bent next to the dying sand panther. "But this one is nearing its end. I should put it out of its misery." She looked around. "With those spell symbols shielding it from magical attacks, I'll have to use my knife."

The dying panther emitted a loud rumble that sounded more forlorn than threatening. Bannon's face fell and his lip trembled. "Do you have to kill it? Can't you heal it, too?"

Nicci narrowed her eyes. "Why would I tend this creature? It tried to kill us."

"What if it was trained to do that? Shouldn't we know where it came from?" Bannon asked. "We already killed the other two, and it's . . ." The words caught in his throat and he choked out the rest. "It's such a beautiful cat. . . ." He couldn't say any more.

As the adrenaline rush faded, Nicci began to feel the raging pain of her own wounds. This panther's claws had torn her back down to the muscle and bone. "It is not a helpless kitten like the ones your father drowned."

"No it's not." Bannon shook his head. "But it is dying, and you can heal it."

Thistle squatted next to the heaving panther and looked up at Nicci with her honey-brown eyes. "My uncle and aunt said that you shouldn't kill unless it is absolutely necessary." Smeared with blood, she looked waifish and forlorn.

Bannon agreed. "And this isn't necessary. Not now. "

Nicci reached out to touch the heaving female cat, cautiously extending her magic to measure the extent of its injuries. The branded spell symbols did not stop her, so she realized the protection must be specifically designed to deflect an attack. She moved her hand to touch the knife wounds she had inflicted. "I can heal it. I can heal *her*," Nicci said, "but you need to know that these three sand panthers were spell-bonded. Her two sister panthers in the *troka* are dead. If we save her to live entirely alone, we may be doing this one no favors."

"Yes we are," Thistle insisted. "Please, Nicci."

Her own wounds and blood loss were making her dizzy, making her weak. She didn't have the strength to argue with the orphan girl.

Nicci touched the panther's deep cuts. As she did so, some of the animal's blood mingled with her own from the gashes in her arms and hands. The blood of two fierce creatures trained and ready to fight . . .

Nicci called up her healing magic, released a flow through her hand into the tawny beast, while also infusing her deepest wounds.

When she did so, Nicci felt a sudden jolt, like the last link being forged in a mysterious chain that connected her with the panther. The chain, the *bond* ran from her heart through her nervous system and her mind, and extended into each of the cat's counterpart systems. Thoughts flooded through her as powerful healing magic surged into both of them, erasing the claw wounds, the knife cuts, the scrapes, the smallest scratches, even the sore muscles.

Yanking her bloody hands away, Nicci staggered backward. Even when she stopped touching the panther, she could sense the animal's presence connected to her. Like a sister. She could not deny it.

"Her name is Mrra," Nicci said in a hushed tone. "I don't know what the word means. It's not really a name, just her self-identity."

The newly healed panther huffed a great breath and rolled over, coiling back onto her feet. The cat's eyes were golden green. The long tail lashed back and forth, in agitation and confusion.

"What just happened?" Bannon asked. "What did you do?"

"My blood mingled with hers. The death of her spell-bonded sisters left a void like a wound inside her. When my magic healed Mrra, it filled that void within me at the same time." Nicci's voice grew breathy, and she was amazed at what she herself had experienced. "Now we are connected, but still independent. Dear spirits!"

The sand panther looked up at her, thick tail thrashing. Nicci looked again at the scarred spell symbols, but in spite of her link to Mrra, she still could not interpret the language. She did, however, understand the residue of pain—the lumpy, waxy scars from when red-hot irons had brutally branded those symbols into the soft tan fur.

Staring at her former prey, Mrra twitched, then dropped her gaze to the bodies of her two sister panthers. With a low growling moan, she turned to pad away, putting distance between herself and the three humans that the *troka* had meant to kill.

Nicci could feel the bond between them stretching, thinning. She couldn't communicate directly, couldn't understand what Mrra might be thinking. She just knew that she, Bannon, and Thistle were safe from further attack. And that Mrra would live now . . . if alone.

But not completely alone: there would always be a shadow of Nicci inside her.

With a thrash of her tail, the sand panther loped into the desolate wilderness, bounding up into the slickrock outcroppings, ledge by ledge.

Thistle stared after the sand panther, while Bannon still held his bloody sword, confused. As Nicci watched the panther go, she felt a strange sense of loss.

In a flash, the beast vanished into the uneven shadows.

CHAPTER 47

As he began to grasp the sheer breadth of the library, Nathan believed the Cliffwall archive might hold the secrets of the entire universe . . . if only he could figure out what he needed and where to find it. He pondered as he nibbled on an oat biscuit that one of the acolytes had brought him from the kitchens.

The problem was, no one understood the entire puzzle. Altogether, the hundreds of archivists and memmers knew only disconnected pieces. It was like trying to find the constellations on a cloudy night when only a few flickers of stars shone through.

Well, the constellations were all wrong now anyway, and everyone had to relearn the universe from scratch.

Nathan finished his biscuit and absently munched on another from the plate. He finished skimming the volume in front of him just as a shy young female scholar delivered more. Mia was one of the students assigned to assist him. About nineteen years old, she had short mouse-brown hair and darting eyes that seemed more accustomed to reading than making contact with other people.

"I found these for you, Wizard Nathan. They might contain viable lines of investigation." She was a daughter of a canyon-dwelling family, and she had grown up learning to read and study. She had been born just after Roland fled Cliffwall and began to drain the life out of the world.

"Thank you, Mia," he said with an appreciative smile. Whenever he asked her to find books or scrolls on a particular subject, she would hurry off and return with possibilities. As he ran his fingers down the words in ancient languages, Mia would often sit quietly beside him, reading books that had captured her own interest, hoping to help.

Now he picked up the top volume and opened the scuffed cover. "Ah, a treatise on enhancing plant growth."

Mia nodded. "I thought it might offer some possible counteraction to the Lifedrinker's magic that drains life. The foundational spell-forms might have some commonalities."

"Excellent suggestion," Nathan said, although he thought it unlikely.

The next volume in the stack was covered in letters he did not recognize, angled symbols and swooping curves of runes. The words seemed to exude a kind of power, and he touched the writing as if he could let the foreign alphabet seep into his fingertips. "Do you recognize this language?" he asked Mia. "It is not High D'Haran, nor any of the languages of the Old World that I know."

The young woman pushed her short hair back from her face and tucked it behind her ears. "Some of our oldest scrolls are written in those letters, but no one can read them anymore. Some say they were part of an ancient library stolen from the city of Ildakar."

Nathan set the volume aside, since the incomprehensible writing rendered it useless to him. He was delighted to see that the next book contained maps of a broad land area, although without any frame of reference. One chart showed a range of mountains extending from rolling foothills to sharp crags. Dotted lines indicated winding, treacherous paths that led up to a summit. The exotic names of peaks and rivers were unfamiliar—until his eyes fixed on a pair of words.

Kol Adair.

He caught his breath. So, his destination truly existed—in that much, at least, the witch woman had been right. He wondered if the broad valley on the map represented the once-fertile basin that had become the Scar.

Nathan felt a desperate longing to have his magic back, if only to help in the fight against the Lifedrinker. Nicci couldn't be required to save the world on her own. Upon beginning this journey, he had not cared overmuch about losing his gift of prophecy, since all the forked paths and dire warnings had caused him nothing but grief. But his gift of magic was such an integral part of him that he had taken it for granted. It made him whole.

He tapped on the map, but his own needs would come later. He set aside the volume and pondered the Lifedrinker's spreading desolation. Nathan went back to his books, still searching for the answer.

Nicci, Bannon, and Thistle reached the sheer rock wall below the mesa, glad to leave the bleak Scar behind. Thistle climbed up the steep slope, easily finding half-hidden trail markers and ledges on the way to the alcove opening high above that led back into the plateau and the archive city.

As she climbed, Nicci looked back the way they had come. The powdery dust whipped across the desolate crater like a miasma. When Bannon stopped beside her at the entry alcove high up on the plateau wall, they all stood together looking out at the devastation. The Lifedrinker was somewhere deep at the center of the crater.

"Are you anxious to go back there, Sorceress?" he asked.

"No," she answered honestly, "but I know we must."

Nicci could still feel a tendril in her mind of a prowling feline presence—a lonely presence. Mrra was out there, roaming the uninhabited wilderness. The spell-bonded cat had spent her life as part of a *troka* with two sister panthers, both now gone. The healing magic had filled that void with Nicci, but she didn't know how to help. . . .

When they returned to the Cliffwall gathering chambers, Nathan hurried out to join them, glad to see them back safe. Hearing about their battles with dust people and sand panthers, he gave Bannon's shoulder a paternal pat. "Did you use the swordcraft I taught you?"

Bannon nodded. "Yes, I remembered everything you showed me."

Nicci remembered how wildly the young man had flailed with his blade, but he had fought the enemies, as needed. She couldn't fault Bannon for that.

"I killed as many as he did," Thistle boasted.

"Of course you did, child," Nathan replied with a wry smile. "And that is exactly what we expect of you. But Bannon is my protégé, and I wanted to make sure he acquitted himself well. As you did."

"Even though you weren't supposed to come along," Nicci said, though her reprimand had no sting. "I'm glad you know how to take care of yourself."

The girl looked up at her. "Am I your protégée, Nicci?"

The idea surprised her. This orphan girl was certainly useful, and eager to help, but Thistle hadn't shown any particular aptitude for the gift. "A protégée in what way? I cannot train you to be a sorceress."

"But my reading is better now. I can help you find books in the library. You said you needed to do a lot of research."

Nicci was surprised to realize she wasn't averse to the idea. "You can help, so long as you don't get in the way."

"I won't!"

When the scholars gathered, Nicci gave a more detailed report of the desolation, the cracked canyons, the fumaroles and mud pots, as well as the Lifedrinker's defenders. She sketched out a map, as best she could remember. "I am sure there will be more powerful guardians closer to the evil wizard's lair. We must be ready." She raised an eyebrow at Nathan and all the eager scholars. "As soon as you find me a weapon I can use to kill him."

Simon lifted his chin. "I am confident the answer resides here in the archives." His fellow scholars gave intent nods and muttered among themselves. "We just have to find the right records."

In the dining hall, they all sat down as servers brought in the evening meal. Thistle ate with her hands—both hands, since she was voraciously hungry. Victoria led her student memmers into the room, taking them to Nathan so they could describe some of the subjects they had committed to memory.

The three beautiful acolytes sat next to Bannon, leaning close and listening to his every word. Audrey, Laurel, and Sage found excuses to feed him morsels of food from his plate: roasted vegetables, freshly baked rolls, skewers of spiced lamb. Warming to his tale, the young man talked with exaggerated gestures. Sage picked up a cloth napkin and dabbed the side of his mouth. His cheeks turned pink.

Audrey giggled. "Look how his freckles stand out when he blushes!"

The comment only made him turn brighter red. "I appreciate your attentions. I don't often have such a . . . beautiful audience." He swallowed hard, then gulped from a goblet of spring water, muttering, "Sweet Sea Mother!"

Victoria stepped up behind Bannon and gave the acolytes an encouraging smile. "I understand your attraction to the young man," she said, as if Bannon weren't there. "I hope you three don't turn out to be barren and childless, as I am."

Bannon blinked. "I—I don't want to stay here and marry anyone." He looked at Nicci as if hoping that she would save him. "We're on a mission."

Nicci regarded him coolly. "After I saved you from the cutthroats in Tanimura, I told you to rescue yourself from then on. You will have to meet this challenge on your own."

Bannon blushed again.

Victoria sounded sad as she stood like a mother hen behind the three young women. "Dry, dusty scrolls cannot possibly make up for carrying a life inside you, or holding a newborn baby. Someday you'll know."

The three acolytes smiled.

Victoria stepped over to Thistle, who was finishing a second handful of grapes. The girl still wore her dusty, raggedy clothes from the journey out into the Scar. "I have good news for you, child." She set a cloth-wrapped parcel onto the table and began to undo the knotted twine that held the edges together. "We have very few young children here in Cliffwall, and certainly no suitable clothes, so therefore I asked a skilled seamstress to make this new for you."

She held up the garment, shaking the fabric to unfold a small, trim dress made to fit Thistle's scrawny form. It had been dyed bright pink.

Thistle stopped chewing a mouthful of grapes. "A new dress?" She frowned uncertainly, not sure how to react. "I've never had a dress like that before."

Victoria continued to smile. "You no longer need to wear rags. You are such a pretty girl, and this will make you even prettier. Do you like the pink? It comes from cliff roses that grow in the canyons."

The dainty dress seemed unsuited for the girl's life of running through the desert and hunting lizards. Thistle looked at Nicci, who responded with a hard honesty. "In general, I dislike the color pink." So much so, in fact, that Nicci had once used Subtractive Magic in a wildly inappropriate fashion just to erase the pink dye from a satiny nightdress she had been made to wear in the Wizard's Keep.

"I think I like my old dress better," Thistle said. "This one is very nice, but I wouldn't want it to get dirty when I follow Nicci on her explorations. We've got the whole world to see after we kill the Life-drinker."

Victoria chuckled. "But, child, you're with us now, here at Cliff-wall. You will stay and be one of my acolytes. I will teach you how to read and understand the spells, and soon enough you will be able to memorize hundreds of books. You will become our newest memmer." She patted the girl's arm.

Nicci felt on edge. "But is that what the girl wants?" Thistle looked back and forth from the matronly memmer woman to the sorceress.

"Of course it is," Victoria said. "I will take you under my wing, child, clean you up, and train you."

Thistle squirmed on her bench. "I want to read better, and I want to learn things, but I won't just stay in Cliffwall. Nicci can teach me while we're out exploring the world. For Lord Rahl. It's an important mission."

Victoria gave a dismissive gesture. "Flights of fancy, child. Better to read adventures than have them for yourself. I can protect you." She gripped the girl's bony shoulders, squeezing hard.

Thistle ducked and slid closer to Nicci, leaving the pink dress on the table. Nicci rose to her feet, on her guard. "Enough, Victoria. The girl is with us."

The memmer woman looked angry, as if unaccustomed to anyone defying her wishes. She made a clucking sound with her tongue. "You know the child needs care and an education. We'll train her how to remember."

Nicci's voice was as hard as forged steel. "Thistle must make her own choice. Her life is her own to control."

"I want to hunt lizards and climb the canyon walls," she interjected. "Nicci promised to take me across the Old World."

Nicci assessed the increased level of tension in the room. The scholars had stopped eating, listening to the escalating verbal battle.

Victoria fixed her gaze on the sorceress. "Are you the girl's mother? By what right do you make decisions for her?"

"No, I am not the girl's mother. I was never meant to be a mother. That was a choice *I* made."

Victoria's mood shifted in an unexpected direction. "And have you ever thought it might be the wrong choice? Why would a beautiful, strong, and obviously fertile woman like yourself choose *not* to create life? I wanted so badly to have children but wasn't able to!" Her voice rose as she grew more incensed. "No one has ever denied me an acolyte before. Who are you to deny me?"

Nicci thought of many answers, but chose the one with the most power. "I am Death's Mistress."

CHAPTER 48

After the satisfying meal in the warm banquet hall, Bannon could still taste the sweetness of the honeyed fruit from dessert. He patted his belly on his way back to his quarters. After sleeping outside in the dying foothills the previous night, he found the simple stone-walled room with its sleeping pallet wonderfully safe and homey. It reminded him of his own room back on Chiriya, when he'd been a young man, when he and his best friend Ian had talked about their dreams . . . before his father had started beating him, before the Norukai slavers took Ian, before the world fell apart.

Bannon closed his eyes and blocked those thoughts. He cleared his mind, breathed in and out, and repainted his memories with bright, if false, colors. Ready for a good night's sleep, he dropped the fabric door curtain for privacy and removed his homespun shirt, which was still encrusted with harsh white powder and dried sand-panther blood. Humming to himself, he tossed the shirt to the side of the room; tomorrow, he would take it to the Cliffwall laundry. In the meantime, he had a spare shirt and trousers, neatly folded on the unused writing desk.

Someone had delivered a fresh basin of water for him, along with a soft rag he could use as a washcloth. It was the sort of thing his mother would have done to take care of him. He dipped the rag in the water and used it to scrub his face. It felt refreshing and wonderful. Someone had even put herbs in the wash water to make his skin tingle. He soaked the rag in the basin again, rinsing out the grit and grime. He squeezed out the excess water, then looked up, startled as the hanging cloth moved aside from the door.

Audrey slipped in, her dark brown eyes glittering. She did not knock or ask to enter. Shirtless, Bannon was instantly embarrassed. He dropped the rag back into the basin. "I'm sorry—" he said, then wondered what he was apologizing for. "I was just washing up."

"I've come to help you," Audrey said with a smile and let the cloth hanging fall back into place.

As she moved toward him, her deep brunette hair was long, loose, and lush. Unlike the white woolen gown she usually wore, her dress seemed tighter than usual, its bodice cinched at her narrow waist and below her breasts to emphasize their swell. "After all you've been through, Bannon Farmer, you shouldn't have to wash yourself."

"I—I'm fine." He felt his cheeks grow warm again. "I've been washing myself all my life. It's not . . . usually a job that requires more than one person."

"Maybe you don't require it," Audrey said, taking the wet rag and dipping it into the herbed water, "but why turn down help? This is a much more pleasurable way to bathe."

All arguments vanished from his mind, and he realized he had no worthwhile objections anyway.

Audrey drew the moist cloth across his chest to wipe away the grit. She moved more slowly than necessary, but her intention was not merely to clean him. She wet the rag again and used it to caress his chest, then down along his flat stomach.

Bannon realized his throat had gone entirely dry. He bent away in further awkwardness as he realized that he had become aroused, prominently pressing out from his canvas trousers.

Audrey discovered it as well. She pressed her hand against his trousers, and a low groan came out of his throat without him even realizing it. He quickly touched her wrist. "There's no need—"

"I insist. I want to make sure you're thoroughly bathed." She undid the rope at his waist to loosen his pants, which had become remarkably tight.

Bannon squirmed. "Please, I—" He stopped and swallowed again.

If anything, his throat had become drier. He wasn't sure whether he was asking her to please stop, or please continue. Audrey reached into his loose pants and used the washcloth to stroke him with its moist softness.

"I want you completely clean," she said, then pushed him back to the pallet, but Bannon's knees were weak and he was ready to collapse anyway. As he lay there looking up at her with shining eyes, Audrey loosened the laces of her bodice, removed it, then slipped out of her white shift, letting the soft wool slide away from her creamy shoulders to expose her ample breasts. The dark circles of her nipples reminded him of the berries she had fed him at the banquet table not long before.

He gasped with wonder at the sight, and she turned to him let him admire the curve of her back, the gentle swell of her perfect buttocks. But Audrey wasn't going away from him. She just wanted to snuff one of the candles, leaving only a single orange flame flickering in its pot. It was enough light for them to see, but most of the time Bannon had his eyes closed. He gasped many more times as she joined him on the pallet, pressing him down on his back. She slid one leg over his waist and straddled him.

When returning to his quarters, Bannon had been exhausted and sleepy, but now sleep was the farthest thing from his mind.

He touched Audrey's skin, felt its warmth, then reached up as she leaned forward, inviting him to cup her breasts. When she shifted her hips to settle on top of him and he slid inside her, he felt as if he had fallen into the embrace of paradise. And it was.

Bannon lost all sense of time, hypnotized by the sensations that Audrey showed him. And when she was done and climbed off of him, she leaned forward to kiss him long and full on the lips, then trailed her lips down his cheek, and his neck. He let out a long, shuddering sigh of ecstasy. He was even more exhausted now and not at all tired. His entire world had changed.

As Audrey picked up the supple white shift and pulled it over her head, his heart already ached for her. "I . . . I don't know what to say."

She giggled. "At least you knew what to do."

"Does this mean that you—you've chosen me? I'm sure I'd be a good husband. I didn't know that I wanted to get married, but you've made me—"

She laughed again. "Don't be silly. You can't marry all of us."

"All?" he asked, not understanding.

After Audrey finished dressing, she came back to his pallet, where he lay drifting and happy, his entire body tingling. She kissed him again. "Thank you," she said, then slipped out of his chambers, darting silently into the corridors.

Bannon's head was spinning. He was sure he would have a foolish grin on his face for days, if not months. He closed his eyes, let out a long sigh, and tried to sleep, but his body was still on fire. He had heard many love poems before, minstrels singing about the yearning of romance, and had not quite understood it. Of course, Bannon remembered his foolish attraction for Nicci, his inept flirtation in giving her the deathrise flower, but he had never dreamed of anything like Audrey. Perfect, beautiful, and *hungry* Audrey.

He lay for an hour, wanting to sleep, but not wanting to let go of a single moment of these cherished memories. He relived in his mind her every touch, imagining the feel of her lips on his cheek, on his mouth, on his chest—everywhere.

He heard a rustle of the fabric door hanging and didn't at first understand what it was, until he raised his head, blinking. Had Audrey come back?

Laurel stood just inside the doorway, her strawberry-blond hair brushed and shining in the faint light of the remaining candle, adorned with a single decorative braid. She responded with a seductive smile, and her green eyes sparkled. Her tongue flicked around the corner of her mouth, and she showed perfect white teeth.

"I see you're still awake." She glided closer to his sleeping pallet as Bannon struggled to sit up. "I hope I'm not disturbing you." As Laurel moved toward him, her hands worked at the tie at her waist, and she slid out of her acolyte's gown like a beautiful naked butterfly emerging from a chrysalis.

Bannon drew in a quick breath. He was alarmed, confused—and aroused again. "Audrey was just—" he said, reaching up, but instead of being pushed away, she met him, took his left hand, and placed it against her breast. It was smaller and firmer than Audrey's. Her nipples were erect.

"Audrey has already had her turn," Laurel said with a smile. "I hope you're not too tired." She reached down, ran her fingers along his belly, then farther down to stroke the corn silk there. She grinned with delight. "I see you're not tired at all." She started kissing him, and now that Bannon knew exactly what to do, he responded with increasing enthusiasm. Given his earlier practice, Bannon decided he might be getting good at this after all.

Laurel was slower and gentler than Audrey, but more intense. She caressed him and showed him how to caress her, wanting to enjoy his entire body, and Bannon proved to be an avid student again. When he tried to rush, feeling the passion build within him, she held him back, strung him along, teased him. Then she rolled him over, slid beneath him on the narrow pallet, drew him down on top of her, and wrapped her arms around his back.

She whispered hotly in his ear, "It's all right. There's no hurry. Sage won't be here until closer to dawn."

CHAPTER 49

After seeing the desolation of the Scar firsthand, Nicci immersed herself in the lore in the wizards' archive, devoting every hour to the piles of old books. And although Thistle tried to help in every way, fetching books she thought looked interesting, bringing food from the kitchens, she was bored.

The girl wished she could offer some assistance, but her skills as a scholar were minimal. When she had helped her friends survive in the wilderness, she'd felt important, useful to be catching lizards, finding water. But, books . . . Thistle didn't know enough about magical lore or ancient languages.

Her aunt and uncle had taught her letters, so she knew how to read some basic words. She took it upon herself to memorize certain key terms that Nicci was interested in—"life," "energy," "Han," "diminish," "drain"—and she would stand in front of the shelves in the great reading rooms, going from spine to spine, book after book, scroll after scroll. Each time she found a likely prospect, she would hurry with it over to Nicci, adding it to the sorceress's reading stack. Nicci always took her offerings seriously, but so far no one had found any revelation about the Lifedrinker's possible weaknesses.

Thistle had always been independent, able to take care of herself. She sensed that Nicci valued her in part because the sorceress appreciated someone who could handle her own problems. Thistle wanted to prove that she could be a valuable member of their group, but she felt left out, without a purpose to serve.

So, she explored the great stone buildings and the tunnels that ran through the heart of the plateau like the worm tracks in a rotting tree. Absorbed in their research, the Cliffwall scholars paid little attention to Thistle.

She avoided Victoria, not wanting to be indoctrinated as a memmer to memorize old books. Once, she came upon one of their rotememorization sessions, with young men and women sitting cross-legged on the stone floor while Victoria read a paragraph aloud and then had them all repeat it word for word. Spotting her, the matronly woman gestured for Thistle to join them, but she ducked away. The older woman's intensity made her uneasy. She didn't want to be locked up here poring over dusty old books all her life. She wanted to stay with Nicci instead. She wanted to share in her adventures.

Thistle found a restless Bannon prowling the tunnels as well, carrying his sword. He commiserated with her. "I wish we could just *do* something." He swung his sword at invisible opponents, though there was little room in the passageway for a satisfying imaginary battle.

"We should go out and fight the evil wizard together," Thistle said.

"You're just a girl."

Thistle scowled. "And you're just a boy."

Bannon huffed. "I'm a man, and I'm a swordfighter. You should have seen how many selka I killed when they attacked the *Wavewalker.*"

"You saw me fight the sand panthers," Thistle said, "and the dust people."

With a sigh, he rested his sword on the stone floor of the tunnel. "Neither of us poses much of a threat to the Lifedrinker. We have to wait until someone learns how to destroy him."

Thistle frowned. "The waiting is driving me crazy."

Bannon went off down the tunnel battling imaginary foes with his sword, but when he came upon Victoria's three beautiful acolytes, he awkwardly stumbled to a halt. As opponents, Audrey, Laurel, and Sage could have hamstrung him with a flirtatious glance. Thistle rolled her eyes.

She made her way through the tunnels to the window on the outer steep slope of the plateau. As she gazed out on the Scar, Thistle's heart ached to see the sweeping devastation and the distant heat shimmer. She longed to know what this beautiful valley must have looked like at one time.

The scholar-archivist Simon found her standing there. "I stare out at it every day," he said. "Each morning I watch the Lifedrinker expand his terrain and suck more and more life out of the world. If you've been here as long as I, you know just how much we've lost."

Thistle looked up at him. "What was it like?"

Simon gestured out the opening. "From here, you could see lakes and rivers. The hills were thick with forests, and the sky was blue, not this dusty gray. There were roads from one end of the valley to the other, connecting the villages. Pastures and crops dotted the countryside." He blew a soft whistle through his teeth. "Sometimes it seems I'm just remembering a dream. But I know it was true."

Thistle felt a tingle of warmth and determination. "We can make it that way again. I know we can."

Simon's voice took on a harder edge. "It should never have happened in the first place—one of our scholars unleashing a spell he couldn't control. Now the valley is gone, the towns dried up—including my old home. The people are all dead." A low groan came out of his throat. "And it's our fault. We have to find some way to fix it."

"I want to help," Thistle said. "There must be something I could do."

He gave her a patronizing smile. "I'm afraid this is a problem best left to the scholars."

Stung, Thistle turned away, muttering a quiet vow that she would help make the world right again. Even after she left, the scholar-archivist continued to stare out at the far-off wasteland.

Forgoing sleep, Nicci read the words of tome after tome until her eyes ached and her skull throbbed from trying to take in so much information. Although she learned a great deal, including many derivations of spells she had used in the past, she did not find the answers she sought. She set aside another volume in impatient disgust.

Now she had a greater grasp of just how dangerous, how devastating the Lifedrinker was, and if she did not stop him, then the world was indeed at stake—she did not underestimate the threat. The Scar would grow and grow, eventually drowning the Old World, then D'Hara.

Now she knew full well why she was here.

During the day, sunshine streamed in through the lensed windows of the towering stone buildings to illuminate the document rooms. During the night she read by the warm yellow light of candles or oil lamps. Nicci turned pages, studied the cryptic ancient languages, and dismissed ten more volumes by morning.

Absorbed in his own research, Nathan could skim and grasp the contents with ease, and he had always been more studious than Nicci. She was a woman of action, trying to save the world. She *had* in fact saved the world by helping Richard Rahl, and saving the world from the Lifedrinker's debilitating spell was exactly what she needed to do next.

Her eyes burned, and her neck and shoulders ached. Needing to clear her head and breathe the open air, Nicci left the archive rooms and emerged from the highest stone tower in the sheltered cave grotto. She looked across the narrow inner canyon, thinking of the people who had lived there undisturbed for centuries. Although it was midmorning, the sun had not yet risen high enough to remove the dark cloak of shadows in the narrow canyons.

She saw sheep grazing near the central stream flanked by blossoming trees in the nut orchards. Nicci inhaled, enjoyed the cool bite of the morning air. A faint breeze blew stray wisps of blond hair around her face.

Nathan stepped out into the open to join her. "Out for a breath of fresh air, Sorceress? Ah, when you look out at the sheltered settlement here, you can almost forget the Scar and the Lifedrinker on the other side of the plateau."

"I can't forget." She glanced over at him. "I need to consider what we should do. I found many tangential spells, but nothing good enough. This morning I've been studying how one might kill a succubus, on the off chance it might prove useful."

Nathan stroked his hands over his white hair. "How does a succu-bus relate to the Lifedrinker?"

"Both of them drain life. A succubus is a kind of witch woman who has the power to absorb vitality through sex. Men find her irresistible, and she tempts them with physical pleasure, trapping them as she drains them to nothing more than a husk." Nicci added with skeptical sarcasm, "The men supposedly die with smiles on their lips, even as their faces shrivel away."

Nathan laughed uneasily. "It would not be wise for a woman as beautiful as yourself to have such magic, Sorceress."

Nicci lifted her chin. "I already have more powerful magic than that. It is all a matter of control—and I do have control. The Life-drinker, however, does not. He drains the vitality of his victim, and in this case his victim is the whole world. In that sense, he is like a succubus."

"Quite extraordinary. And how is a succubus killed, then? What did the old document say?"

"The succubus is responsible for her own demise . . . in a way," Nicci said. "In each of the countless times she lies with a man, there is a very small chance she will get pregnant. If that happens, the succubus is doomed. The child itself, always a daughter, is a powerful entity that gestates and grows, until it absorbs the life from its own succubus mother—doing the same thing to her as she does to men, draining the mother dry until she is nothing but a husk. Then the baby claws its way out of her womb . . . to become the next deadly succubus."

Nathan pursed his lips. "That does not sound like a practical method of killing a succubus if we were to encounter one. There is no other way?"

"According to the legend, the newborn succubus is weak. If one times an attack properly, the baby can be killed, thus terminating the line of succubi."

Nathan looked across the quiet, narrow canyon at a shepherd guid-ing his small flock to a flower-strewn patch of grass. "Although that tale is delightful and fascinating, I fail to see how it can be useful in our situation."

"I don't see how it can help either." She sighed.

Victoria emerged from the tower library with a determined look on her face. Seeing them, she hurried forward. "In our communal discussions, my memmers recalled something important." She focused on Nathan. For the past two days, since Nicci had refused to let her take Thistle as a new acolyte, the matronly woman had given her a cold shoulder. "Because each of us remembers different books, the memmers compared notes, made suggestions."

"And you have remembered something useful?" Nicci asked. "That would be a welcome change."

Victoria's eyes flashed with annoyance, and the wizard quickly broke in, "What is it? The original Lifedrinker's spell?"

Victoria rocked back, lifting her chin. "It is a story about the original primeval forest that once covered the Old World, the pristine wilderness that thrived in perfect harmony with nature. The Eldertree was the first tree in the first forest—a towering and titanic oak that was the most powerful living thing in the entire world. It is a story of creation."

Nicci did not try to hide her disappointment. "How does an ancient myth about a tree help us against the Lifedrinker? He is a present threat, not an old fable."

Victoria's expression darkened. "Because all strands of life are connected, Sorceress. When the primeval forest covered the land, the world had great power and great magic." She addressed her story to Nathan, finding him a more receptive audience. "Even before the wizard wars three thousand years ago, devastating armies swept across the Old World, cutting down trees, razing the last remnants of the original forests. Those evil men cut down the original Eldertree, a task so difficult that it required a hundred powerful wizards and even more laborers. And when the great tree fell, a vital part of the world died.

"But one acorn was saved, one last seed from the Eldertree. As the armies cut down the sweeping forests, they drove all the energy of life back into the Eldertree until at last it was condensed into this single acorn, the final spark of the primeval forest. All the energy of the Eldertree and all its offspring concentrated into that single acorn, stored there, where it could someday be released in an explosion of incomprehensibly powerful life itself."

Nathan sucked in a quick breath of air. "And you think that might be powerful enough to kill the Lifedrinker?"

"It must be," Victoria insisted. "But the more powerful he becomes, the more difficult the task will be. Soon it will be too late. At the moment, I believe that Roland, or what is left of Roland, will be no match for the last spark of the Eldertree."

"Again, how does this help us?" Nicci said. "Do you believe the acorn truly exists? If so, where can we find it? I have read many books and found no mention of the legend or the seed itself."

Nathan also shook his head. "Nothing in my studies either."

"But I *remember*," Victoria said. "It is in one of my memorized books. The acorn of the Eldertree was locked away here in Cliffwall, deep in a vault . . . somewhere over there." She indicated the misshapen tower that was partially melted into a glassy lump at the side of the alcove. "It is still here."

CHAPTER 50

Under Simon's guidance, workers from the other canyon settlements brought their tools to Cliffwall and set to work trying to reach the lower levels of the damaged tower, hoping to find where the Eldertree acorn had been stored. In the cool, dusty underground, some of the access passages had slumped, the stone melting like wax to clog shut the openings, but the determined laborers used hammers and chisels to penetrate the hard slickrock.

A solid wall of vitreous rock had flowed over the opening, sealing off an entire basement level. Laborers were already hard at work, hammering and hauling away the rubble of broken rock. A grime-streaked stonecutter groaned and turned to Simon. "It'll take many days to carve even a small hole through that, sir."

After they followed the workers down into the deep underground passages, ducking and crawling into the damaged vaults, Nathan looked at Nicci. "Sorceress, surely a barricade of solid stone is not too great a challenge for you?"

"No, it is not. Allow me—we are in a hurry." The workers backed away, curious, and Nicci reached out to touch the smooth wall of melted rock. When she released her magic, the stone that had flowed once, now flowed again. She did not need to resort to Subtractive Magic, but was able to work the material like clay, not destroying the rock but simply moving it. She lifted handfuls of fluid stone like a ditch digger slogging through mud. Although she expended a great effort, Nicci succeeded in carving out a tunnel, widening it, lifting the ceiling, and burrowing farther ahead.

After using her magic to move aside ten feet of stone blockage, Nicci began to doubt there truly was another chamber on the other side of the rock. What if the clumsy and untrained wizard had solidified the entire archive with his disastrous accident? Soon, though, she felt the stone grow thin in front of her, then break like an eggshell, and she pushed her way into a dark, claustrophobic vault, exactly where the plans suggested they look. Inside, the air was thick and stale, sealed away for years.

Cupping her hand, Nicci ignited a light spell so she could see the walls dotted with cubbyholes carved into the slickrock. She shone the diffuse glow around the chamber, seeing shadows dance around reverent display shelves that were filled with valuable, mysterious objects, artifacts, sculptures, amulets, all of them covered with dust.

Nathan pushed in behind her, and he straightened, fastidiously brushing stone dust from his borrowed scholar robes. "Dear spirits, this is exactly what we were looking for. Is the Eldertree acorn here?"

Simon and Victoria followed him, and they stared in amazement. "Exactly where my memmers said it would be." She flashed a sharp glance at Nicci. "You should have believed me, Sorceress."

"I prefer to have proof," Nicci said, not responding to the other woman's edgy tone. "Now that I have proof, I believe you."

Impatient, they moved around the museum vault, inspecting the marvelous items that had been sealed away for millennia. They searched among the exotic artifacts, carved vases and small marble figurines, bright glass vials, amulets worked in gold and jewels, fired-clay medallions covered with a jade-green glaze—and a wooden chest no wider than Nicci's hand. She felt drawn to it, sensing an energy in the air, a power barely contained within the small box. When she removed it from the alcove, she felt a warm pulse through her palm. "This holds something very important."

"That is it," Victoria said, pushing closer. "I remember the descriptions from the original writings."

Nicci opened the lid and looked at cushioned folds of purple velvet, which embraced a single acorn that seemed to be made of gold.

Nathan grinned like a young boy. "Quite extraordinary. The Life-drinker will be no match for that. Now we have the weapon we need."

"Yes." Nicci closed the small chest. "I do."

N icci was impatient to leave immediately. "The Lifedrinker's power grows every day. This mission will be more dangerous than our last expedition, but I will go." The scholars could study the other arti-facts down in the vault in due time; if she defeated the evil wizard, they would have all the time in the world. Nicci removed the acorn from its ornate chest, wrapping it in the scraps of purple velvet so she could tuck it into the pocket of her black dress.

As they returned to the main buildings of the archive, Nicci con-sidered what she would need to do before departure. Aside from pack-ing food and water, she didn't need to make other preparations. Bannon and Thistle joined her, as curious scholars gathered around, eager to see the Eldertree acorn.

Victoria looked at Nicci, both stern and uneasy. Her brow fur-rowed as she spoke to the rest of the scholars. "I know she is the most powerful sorceress among us, but I am reluctant to give such a sacred treasure—the essence of life itself—to a woman who calls herself Death's Mistress."

Nicci continued her preparations, ignoring the memmer woman's objection. "It must be done, and I am the one to do it."

With a sidelong glance at Victoria, Simon suggested, "Every person in Cliffwall knows that this is a great battle. We can send scholars and trainee wizards to accompany you. We can be your army against the Lifedrinker."

Nicci looked at the too-young scholar-archivist. "You would all be slaughtered. None of you here is fully trained in magic. The risk is far too great."

Thistle ran up, excited. She had stars in her honey-brown eyes.

"Nicci will do it, I know she will. Do you think it will restore the valley to the way it was?"

"Killing the Lifedrinker will end the spreading blight," she said. She did not want to give the girl unrealistic hopes. "But the wound in the world is severe. It will take some time to recover, even after he is defeated."

"I need to go with you," the girl insisted. "I have to help restore the valley."

Nicci would hear none of it. "Too dangerous. I cannot defend myself and finish my mission if I'm worried about you."

"But you don't need to worry. I *want* to go. I want to help—just like last time."

Nicci crossed her arms. "No, and you will not slip out to follow me. I may have Nathan tie your arms and legs and lock you in a room until I'm gone."

"You wouldn't," the girl said.

"Correct, I wouldn't—but only if you promise me you'll stay behind. That is what I need you to do, because it is the only way I can complete my mission. This is deadly serious."

The girl fumed. "But—"

Nicci raised a hand, leaving no room for doubt. "Or would you rather I blanketed you with a sleep spell, so you do not awake for days?"

"No," the girl mumbled. "I promise I'll stay here." Her voice was low and glum.

"And do you break your promises?"

Thistle seemed insulted. "Never."

Nicci looked long and hard at her, and she believed the girl. "Then I will trust you."

"That child must stay safe, of course," Nathan agreed, "but in a great battle like this, you need someone to fight beside you. The Lifedrinker is an evil wizard, perhaps one of the most powerful you have ever encountered."

"I have killed wizards before," she said.

"Indeed you have, but not a wizard like this. We cannot guess how the Lifedrinker will try to block you. I should come with you, for whatever assistance I can provide."

Nicci raised her eyebrows. "How could you help? Your gift is gone."

He touched the hilt of his ornate sword. "I am an adventurer as well. Magic still resides within me, whether or not I can use it. Maybe if I encounter the Lifedrinker, it will help me to release my powers again."

A chill went through Nicci. "That is what I fear, Nathan Rahl. I know how formidable a wizard you can be, but we cannot risk it."

The old man huffed. "I insist—"

She shook her head. "Think about it. When you tried to heal that victim in Renda Bay, what did your magic do? The wild backlash tore him apart. And when you fought the Adjudicator, the magic backfired again, but fortunately for us, it folded that man's own evil magic back upon himself. But the Lifedrinker is already out of control. If he encounters your wild, chaotic power and it twists further, just imagine the possible consequences." She watched his eyes widen as the realization struck him. She continued, "When I unleash the Eldertree acorn, with so much magic surging through the air, blasting into the Earth—what happens if there is a backlash from your powers? The repercussions could tear you apart . . . or tear the world apart. We dare not risk it."

Nathan gave a reluctant nod and said in a small voice, "I fear you may be right, Sorceress. If I somehow twisted the Lifedrinker's magic and turned it against us but a thousand times worse, there would be no way I could place it back under control. Dear spirits, the damage I could cause . . ."

Nicci squared her shoulders, straightened her back. "I must depend on my own magic, and I can travel quickly." She touched the folds of cloth that wrapped the throbbing golden acorn in her pocket. "Your sword would be welcome, Nathan, but I already have my weapon."

Setting his jaw, Bannon stepped forward. "Then *I* am the one to go along. If you need a sword, you can have mine." He gave her a cocky grin, mostly for the benefit of Audrey, Laurel, and Sage, who also stood listening. "And you already admitted that you never worry about me at all, Sorceress."

Nicci gave him a skeptical frown. "You should not make such a brash offer simply to impress your lovers."

He turned as red as beet soup. "But, I can help! Sweet Sea Mother, you saw how I fought the dust people and the sand panthers. If we are attacked as we approach the Lifedrinker's lair, what if I can buy you the seconds you need to complete your mission? That might mean the difference between success and failure."

Nicci pressed her lips together, assessing the young man. In their battles against seemingly insurmountable enemies, he had indeed killed more than his share of opponents. "I admit, you can sometimes be useful. But know that if you go with me to fight the Lifedrinker, you could face certain death. I will not be able to save you."

"I accept those terms, Sorceress." He swallowed hard, struggling to hide his fear, since he clearly understood the risk in what he was suggesting. "I'm ready to face the danger."

Victoria's acolytes watched him with admiration, which only seemed to increase Bannon's eager determination. Nicci doubted she could change his mind, and she admitted she might need him. "Very well. If nothing else, you may be able to distract a monster at a key moment so that I can keep going."

Audrey, Sage, and Laurel hurried to give Bannon their farewells, and Thistle threw herself against Nicci in a furious hug. "Come back to me. I want to see the world the way it was supposed to be, but I want to see it with you."

Nicci felt awkward, not knowing how to respond to the girl's enthusiastic embrace. "I will restore the world if I can, and then I will come back to you." The next words came out of her mouth before she could think better of it. "I promise."

Thistle looked up at her with her large eyes. "And do you break your promises?"

Nicci gritted her teeth and answered, "Never."

CHAPTER 51

After climbing down the outer wall of the plateau on their way to the Scar, Nicci and Bannon made good time even across the rugged, dead terrain. During their earlier scouting expedition, they had cautiously picked their way, exploring, but now that she possessed the right weapon, Nicci had a clear, firm goal. With the Eldertree acorn, she was on her way to kill the misguided wizard who had caused such appalling damage, had sacrificed countless lives, all because he feared his own death.

Nicci considered the Lifedrinker a monster, an enemy to be defeated at any cost; she did not think of him as a sick and frightened man, a naive scholar playing with dangerous magic. He was not *Roland* in her mind. He was a toxin spreading in every direction. He was a scourge who could destroy the world.

And this was the reason Red had sent her on this journey, accompanying Nathan to find Kol Adair. *Save the world.* She would do her part.

Bannon kept up with her without complaint as they crossed the worsening landscape, and Nicci was impressed with the young man's dogged determination. After emerging from the dying foothills, they made their way on an arrow-straight path across the cracked and rocky Scar. Wind whipped the powdery dust of dry lakes into a salty chemical haze in the air.

Nicci focused ahead. She did not run; she simply did not rest. The barren landscape sparked anger and impatience in her. She picked up the pace, covering miles at a steady clip. Bannon kept looking from side to side, wrinkling his nose in the bitter air. They passed under the shadow of a goblin-shaped pinnacle. Spiky branches of a dead piñon pine protruded from a crack in the rock formation.

Without stopping, Bannon took a cautious sip from his waterskin. A worried frown crossed his face. "Sorceress, is it wise to travel out in the open? Maybe we should try to hide our path so the Lifedrinker doesn't know we are coming for him?"

She shook her head. "He knows where we are. I'm certain he can sense my magic. Skulking in the shadows would only slow us down."

When Bannon offered the waterskin to Nicci, she realized her throat was parched. She drank. The water felt warm, flat, and slippery on her tongue. She handed the waterskin back, and Bannon fastened it at his side, then touched his sword and turned slowly. "I sense that something is watching us."

Extending her gift, Nicci could detect that this desolate place festered with twisted life, the few surviving creatures that had adapted to the Lifedrinker's evil taint. "Many things are watching us, but they don't interest me unless they interfere with our mission." Her lips curled in a hard smile. "If they do, then we will show them their mistake."

Nicci intended to press forward without rest, without making camp, until they reached the heart of the Scar. They had left Cliffwall with the first glimmerings of dawn, and after they had trudged through midday and into the dry afternoon, their pace began to falter. She and Bannon perspired in the relentless heat, and white alkaline dust clung to them, making both of them look white as stone.

Nicci brushed the powder from her face and arms. Her black travel dress was now crusted with the harsh chemical residue.

After the sun set, thermal currents skirled up dust devils, blowing sand and grit into howling veils. As darkness fell, the building dust storm masked the strange stars overhead, but the two plodded on through the night. Near midnight, the raging winds had reached such a crescendo that she could barely hear Bannon behind her, and they grudgingly stopped in the lee of a tall rock. Nicci said, "Rest while you can. We'll stop for no more than an hour."

"I could keep going," he insisted. His lips were cracked, his eyes swollen and red, nearly puffed shut.

"We are too vulnerable if we continue in this blowing storm," Nicci said. "If we can't see, we might fall into a pit, or the Lifedrinker could send dust people to attack us. We will stay here until it calms. It is not my preference, but necessary."

During the brief respite, she released some of her magic to dispel the gritty residue from their chafed faces and burning eyes, but as she used her gift, Nicci felt the magic thrum and recoil inside her. Something else had detected it, tried to grasp it. This deep into the Scar, the Lifedrinker's vitality-sucking power grew more oppressive. She immediately felt him struggling to gain a hold on her, to sap her strength and draw away her powers. Her small use of magic had triggered his response.

The howling wind and whipping sand diminished only slightly after midnight, but Nicci decided they had waited long enough. "We need to go."

Bannon stumbled after her across the parched open terrain. The young man's determined energy had flagged, and it was more than just weariness after the day's long, rugged journey. Nicci could not deny what they saw. The closer they came to the Lifedrinker, the more they both began to weaken from his dark and oppressive thirst. He was draining them as well.

Hours later, the sky became a red haze as the bloated sun rose above the mountains like fire from the funeral pyre of slaughtered victims. Far ahead, Nicci spotted the black center of the crater, a vortex into which the Lifedrinker's potent magic swirled.

"Sweet Sea Mother, we're almost there," Bannon said in a raspy voice. He sounded more relieved than frightened.

"Not close enough." Nicci tried to put on a burst of speed, which only showed her how much the wizard's relentless drain had diminished her. If they didn't confront the enemy soon, she feared she wouldn't have the strength to destroy him, even with the powerful talisman of the Eldertree.

Ahead, the ground became uneven. Slabs of rock tilted at shallow angles, as if restless upheavals continued to stir beneath the surface of the dead valley. Fissures sketched across the land like dark lightning bolts, and tall boulders lay strewn about as if the Lifedrinker's rage of magic had scattered game pieces.

Nicci and Bannon climbed over the sharp rocks, tottering on unstable slabs and leaping across the fissures, from which foul fumes emanated. Even as they journeyed into the increasing heat of the day, the dark lair shimmered like a mirage in the distance. Nicci sensed a prowling presence watching them, closing in, though not yet ready to attack. Although she remained alert, the Lifedrinker was her real enemy, and everything else was just a distraction.

Though her irritated eyes were blurred from the dust, she saw a large shape move across the ground ahead of her, brown and angular. A hissing sound scratched through the air, and a well-camouflaged scaly figure scuttled toward them among the rocks. The creature opened its mouth to reveal moist pink flesh, rows of jagged white fangs, and a forked black tongue: a huge lizard armored with pointed scales, its back crested with a dark sawblade fin. The reptile moved forward on four legs, thrashing a long tail. The creature's hide was mangy with oozing, red sores.

Nicci backed away, and Bannon held up his sword to face the lizard. As it charged at them with a swift skittering gait, Nicci caught more movement to her left and her right. Three more of the giant reptiles emerged from behind rocks or beneath the broken slabs. She had seen the dust-colored lizards that Thistle hunted in the desert, but these were each the size of a warhorse. All were scarred with countless lesions and festering sores.

Bracing himself for the fight, Bannon let out a low whistle. "I always wanted to see a dragon. I've heard legends but—these are real!"

"Not dragons," Nicci said with scorn. "Just lizards." But as the reptiles came closer, flicking their forked tongues and snapping their jaws, she added, "Big lizards."

Beside Nicci, Bannon planted his boots in the dust and held Sturdy in front of him. Two of the lizards stampeded forward, focused on their prey, while the other two crawled on the rock formations around them, flanking Nicci and Bannon. The reptiles moved with a swift grace, warmed by the baking sun and driven by bloodlust.

Nicci held out her hand, curled her fingers. She concentrated on the lizard's chest, found its heart, and as the nearest one bounded toward her, she released a burst of fire. In other battles, she had used her magic to increase the heat inside a tree, flash-boiling the sap and causing the entire trunk to explode. Now she did the same, heating the lizard's heart until the blood burst into steam. The monster staggered and collapsed forward, ploughing a furrow in the rocky sand at Nicci's feet. She knew she could make swift work of all four lizard attackers.

But after killing the first one, she felt a wave of dizziness. By releasing her gift, it was as if she had opened a floodgate to the Lifedrinker. Even from afar, he began to steal her magic, siphoning off her strength.

Long ago, Nicci herself had assimilated the powers of other wizards she had killed, and now the same thing was happening to her. Roland was stealing her life. In a reflexive survival measure, she wove shields to stop the bleeding rupture of power, but she realized she could no longer fight the lizards with magic. She reeled and slumped back against the nearby boulder.

Bannon was busy blocking the second lizard and did not see her stagger. Holding the grip with both hands, he swung his sword with all his weight and strength behind it. When the edge of his blade struck the scaly hide, the sound that rang out was like the tongs and hammer in a blacksmith's shop. He wavered as the blade ricocheted off the lizard's armor, leaving no obvious injury.

The reptile lunged back toward him. Bannon recovered and spun, clattering his sword across the scales, to little effect. When he finally pierced one of the oozing, mangy patches, the lizard did recoil and squirm, but then it kept coming.

Bannon smashed its head so hard that sparks flew. When the lizard opened wide its fang-filled mouth, he pulled back the sword and thrust forward with all of his strength, stabbing Sturdy's tip into the soft pink flesh. He shoved harder, twisting the blade and digging it into the creature's soft palate until it broke through the thin bone and pierced the small brain. As the monster perished, Bannon tore the sword back out, severing the black forked tongue, which fell out and flopped like a dying snake in the blood-soaked dust. The enormous beast twitched and thrashed in a thunderstorm of last nerve impulses.

Bannon spun as the third giant lizard approached from the left, climbing over one of the boulders. Sparing a glance for Nicci, he gasped to see her slumped against the rock as she attempted to recover. "Sorceress!"

Rallying herself, she released a small burst of magic, hoping to stop the creature's heart, but the moment she made the attempt, Nicci felt the voracious Lifedrinker snatch at her magic and her strength like a hunting dog clamping its jaws around a hare. Before it was too late, she cast her protective webs again and closed off the attempt. Dark static swirled around her vision, and she fell against the boulder, but vowed not to give up. She slid the dagger from her side and clutched it in a shaking hand, determined to fight with whatever weapon she had—even teeth and nails if necessary.

"I'll take care of the other two, Sorceress." Bannon charged toward the oncoming lizard, yelling with wordless fury. Again his sword struck sparks from the armored hide. He hammered and hammered with his blade, chipping scales and digging into the lizard's flesh, and he twisted into one of the crusted, patchy sores. When the lizard hissed and snapped at him, Bannon responded with a primal roar of his own.

Nicci had not seen him release such blind rage since battling the Norukai slavers, but something had unleashed his fighting reactions. He was more calculating than a mindless dervish, though. Even if the edge of his blade caused little harm, he raised the sword above his shoulder and drove the point straight into the lizard's eye.

With a gurgling hiss, the monster tried to squirm away, but Bannon pushed forward, driving his sword harder, pushing it in farther. He twisted and screwed the tip so that it turned the creature's eye into a soupy splash of gore. It wasn't enough.

Throwing his full weight into the thrust, he slammed the sword through the bone of the lizard's eye socket and into its head. The monster collapsed. Bannon heaved great breaths and struggled to wrench Sturdy free, but the sword was stuck in the lizard's cranial cavity. He grunted and cursed. "Come on!"

The last of the attacking lizards crawled toward Nicci, cautious. She held out her long dagger, ready for the attack. The monster prepared to spring. She knew its weight and momentum would drive her backward. And she also knew she was too weak to kill it.

Just then she sensed a feral presence, *felt* the ripple of muscles like an echo inside her, experienced the anticipated joy of the attack and the kill. Before the giant lizard could crash down on her, a tawny feline shape bounded from the boulders above. The great cat hurled herself down in a mass of claws and curved fangs and slammed into the distorted lizard, knocking it off balance.

Nicci felt a surge of excitement and relief as she dragged herself to her feet. "Mrra!"

The sand panther mauled the lizard with her long claws, ripping loose mangy patches of scales, exposing open sores. The monster writhed and bucked, but Mrra would not let go. Saberlike fangs chomped down, working into weak spots in the reptile's armor.

Inside her mind, thanks to her connection to the spell-bonded panther, Nicci could feel the bloodlust, the energy, the need to kill this threat . . . this threat to *Nicci*. Mrra was born as a fighter, trained as a fighter, as a killer.

Because she was joined to Mrra, Nicci wanted to tear this monster apart with her bare hands. A feral blood rage sang through her, as it sang through the sand panther. She bounded forward to join the attack. She didn't need magic, just her knife.

Mrra pushed over the thrashing lizard to expose the softer scales in its underbelly just as Nicci reached its head. They seemed to be coordinated, synchronized. The monster clamped its fanged jaws shut, and Nicci drove her sharp dagger beneath the reptile's chin, piercing the thinner skin of its wattled throat. She drove the blade into its head again and again while Mrra tore open the thing's belly and hauled out its flopping entrails. The lizard's gushing blood washed away the caked white powder on Nicci's skin and hands, but she did not feel clean.

Instead, she felt invigorated.

By the time the fourth monster was dead, Nicci shook with exhaustion, but was also afire with the need to go on.

Bannon looked ready to collapse, but he managed an odd grin, giving a respectful look to Mrra. "Good thing I convinced you not to kill the panther, Sorceress."

"I agree." Nicci looked down at Mrra, feeling the powerful inexplicable threads binding them. Her sister panther growled deep in her throat.

Bannon added, "And I told you I could be useful. You need me."

"There are few things I need." Nicci shaded her eyes as she scanned ahead, looking toward the dark vortex still miles away. "Right now, we need to get to the Lifedrinker." She touched the pouch at her side that held the Eldertree acorn. "Before it's too late."

CHAPTER 52

They trudged forward. The Lifedrinker's presence dragged at their bodies like tar, making their movements sluggish, their bodies weak, but Nicci pushed ahead toward the center of the Scar, and the wizard she needed to kill. For Thistle, for this once-fertile valley, for Richard, the D'Haran Empire, and the whole world . . .

"We're almost there, Sorceress," Bannon said in a voice as thin as old paper. "My sword isn't dull yet."

"He will keep trying to stop us, but we don't know how he will attack us next," Nicci said. "Be wary."

The young man managed a hint of cheer in his tone. "And I'll be useful." When she made a noncommittal response, Bannon acted as if she had given him a great compliment.

Mrra stayed with them. The sand panther loped ahead, her tan fur blending into the dusty wasteland. The debris around them turned darker, sharper. The boulders were made of shattered volcanic glass, with every angle as sharp as a knife edge. Sulfurous steam made the air thick and nearly unbreathable, and each step sapped more of their strength.

But as they descended the crumbling, uncertain slope at the heart of the dead valley, Nicci could see their destination ahead. Her target.

The evil wizard's lair resembled an amphitheater with black stelae, spires of rock reaching upward like desperate claws that encircled a central pit. Waves of the Lifedrinker's appetite had frozen into ripples preserved in the blasted stone.

Overhead, thunderclouds strangled the sky, and a web of tortured lightning skittered around—electric whips that cracked across the sky, then stung the tops of the high stelae surrounding the amphitheater. The wind rose to a keening whistle, accompanied by a basso undercurrent of perpetual thunder.

On the ground to their left, a slab of black rock split off to reveal a raw flow of lava beneath. Molten rock like the blood of the world spilled out from a cracked, festering scab.

Bannon staggered back from the furnace air. More obsidian rocks shattered and thrust upward, shifting, twisting. Mrra picked her steps with great caution, her muzzle curled back in a snarl as more lightning flashed overhead. She prowled along, close to Nicci.

Bannon gasped, brushing loose ginger hair out of his eyes. "How can we go on?"

Nicci chose her footsteps carefully as the ground grew more unstable. She climbed over the sharp edges as she pressed toward the Lifedrinker's pit, knowing she would find him there. "How can we not?"

She felt the throbbing, desperate presence ahead, and she wrestled to build shields around her, calling upon her knowledge to protect herself with both Additive and Subtractive Magic. She could not let the Lifedrinker seize her gift, her life. Nicci made use of new spells that she had learned only recently while poring over volume after volume in the Cliffwall archives. It didn't make her entirely safe, but it let her keep moving.

Plodding along in a determined trance, Bannon followed her, step by step. When Nicci turned to encourage him, she was astonished to see his face seamed with wrinkles. His long reddish hair was shot through with streaks of gray. He looked at her in turn, and his hazel eyes went wide with alarm. "Sorceress, you look . . . old!"

Nicci touched her face, and felt wrinkles in her dry skin as if all the years of her long life were catching up with her. The Lifedrinker was stealing the time they had left. "We must hurry," she said. She needed to use the Eldertree acorn before it was too late, before the evil wizard grew any stronger.

Dread built inside her, but it was not a fear for her own life, not despair at the thought that she might be growing old: for Nicci, the greatest fear was that she might *fail* on a quest to which she had given her heart and soul, that she might fail Richard's dreams of a hopeful new order. "I am Death's Mistress," she muttered in a grim whisper. "The Lifedrinker is no match for me."

Mrra hobbled along, and Nicci saw that the cat's big paws left blood smears on the sharp obsidian rocks as she padded forward. But Mrra remained close at hand, ready to fight alongside her surrogate sister panther.

The static in the air thickened, and the background sound near the amphitheater increased to a crackling hiss. Nicci's blond hair rose in a charged corona around her head.

The obsidian rocks ground together, and a belching gasp of brimstone steam coughed upward, nearly choking her. Nicci fixed her gaze to where the circle of ominous sharp spires cast dust-blurred shadows on the ground.

Nicci knew the powerful wizard was inside there. She would stand before him, and she would kill him, even if it cost her last spark of energy.

"Lifedrinker!" she shouted, listening to the deep pervasive thunder in the air. Slashes of lightning whipped through the thunderheads. In a lower voice, she said, *"Roland.* Face me."

The ground shuddered and cracked, and scuttling forms emerged, black-armored creatures with multiple legs, glittering eyes, and segmented front limbs that ended in clacking pincers. Scorpions, each the size of a dog, emerged from underground nests to stand as guardians on top of the black boulders. Each long tail was capped with a wicked stinger that dripped venom.

Beside her, Bannon gave an audible gulp. Nicci recalled that Thistle's parents had been killed by similar creatures.

She stepped forward, remembering her main enemy. She shouted a challenge. "Lifedrinker!"

Suddenly, she remembered what the witch woman had written in the life book: *Future and Fate depend on both the journey and the destination.*

More rocks shifted as the ground convulsed within the circle of towering stelae, and the blackness from the central pit seemed to deepen. Hulking shapes emerged from beneath the ground, withered and desiccated human forms, black with dust. Their sinewy bodies were covered with festering boils, sick open sores that dotted arms and necks, bulges that pushed out the sides of their faces. These horrors were worse than the previous dust people. They stood in a line, blocking Nicci from going closer to the Lifedrinker's lair.

Mrra growled. Bannon raised his sword. "We can cut through them, Sorceress."

The blighted human forms lurched forward, and Nicci drew her knife, careful to restrain her magic, but knowing she might have to use it. With clacking pincers, the scorpions scuttled closer, weaving in and around the desiccated dust people.

Mrra bared her long fangs, and her tail thrashed. Bannon stood at her side. "I'll fight them so you can get close enough, Sorceress." He gulped.

Finally, with a swirl of black static and a slash of angry lightning all around them, the Lifedrinker himself emerged from the darkness.

CHAPTER 53

The ring of distorted pillars surrounded an empty pit like the gullet of a giant buried serpent, a well that sank into the coldest depths of eternity. From this sunken hole, the Lifedrinker's unchecked magic continued to absorb the life from the world.

Climbing out of the inky emptiness from below, the thing that had been Roland emerged. The evil wizard hobbled and lurched, swelled and shrank, a tangled construction of incredible power intertwined with desperate weakness. He had been human once, but very little evidence of his humanity remained.

He stepped out into the crackling air illuminated by slashes of blue-white lightning that racked the thunderheads above. Dust swirled and howled, as if the wind itself were gasping in awe at the Lifedrinker's presence.

He wore what had been the robes of a Cliffwall scholar, but they had frayed and extended into long flapping shrouds that trailed behind him into the deep pit. Dark ripples flowed from his body as his magic stole light itself from the air, drinking, absorbing, draining everything down into the black well. It seemed as if a powerful life lodestone lay at the bottom of the depths—a magical force so great that even the Lifedrinker could not escape its pull.

When the wizard spoke, the words were sucked out of the air along with all other sound, taking Nicci's breath away, stealing more of her energy. "Few come to see me," Roland said. He loomed up, his tattered robes whipping about in the storm of his own energy.

She touched the pocket of her black dress, felt the hard kernel of the Eldertree acorn. She took a step closer, remembering many other terrible foes she had faced, and defeated. "I came to destroy you."

"Yes . . . I know," said the wizard. "Others have tried."

Nicci heard no defiance or arrogance in his voice, just an odd undertone of despair.

His face was long and gaunt, the cheeks sunken, his large eyes red with sickness. Roland's neck was so thin that the tendons stood out like ropes. As the fabric of his flapping robes exposed his bare chest, Nicci was appalled to see his ribs laced with a tangle of swollen growths, as if his torso were composed entirely of tumors. The chaotic protrusions pulsed and throbbed, reservoirs of misdirected life energy that had grown within him and kept growing, desperate for nourishment. The wasting disease had extinguished everything that had been the weak-willed wizard, and controlled him.

His legs were bent, his spine twisted. The Lifedrinker lived because he was a structure of stolen life, a jumble of patched-together flesh, muscle, organs. "Please . . ." he said, in a much quieter voice that surged to a roar. "I hunger . . . I thirst . . . I *need*!" He swayed.

The dust people around the circle of obsidian pillars stood motionless.

Bannon held his sword, but could not conceal that his hands were shaking.

Mrra crouched, growling, but did not move.

The Lifedrinker raised his hands. His fingers were mere sticks covered with a film of skin—no matter how much life he drained from the world, it was not enough, never enough. He curled his hands in a beseeching gesture. "I did not intend this. I don't want this." He heaved a deep breath, and lightning skirled all around them, striking the tops of the obsidian stelae. "I cannot stop this!" the Lifedrinker moaned.

Even as she felt the years and the life draining away from her in the inexorable tug of the evil wizard, Nicci stepped across the uneven ground. "Then I will stop you." She would fight him, hurl him back into the endless pit. The Eldertree acorn might be the most powerful weapon she'd ever held.

But the terrible drain wrung vitality from her muscles and made her thoughts fuzzy.

An uncanny flash flickered in the Lifedrinker's sunken eyes. The tumors that comprised his body writhed like a nest of vipers ready to strike. "No," he said, "I must survive. I have to."

An army of unwieldy but deadly marionettes, the dust people began to move. More than a hundred of them lurched into motion, ready to attack.

Nicci forced herself to move three more steps, and the Lifedrinker did not retreat. He seemed to grow larger, swollen with dark energy, like a man-shaped pustule about to burst from its own evil.

The twisted, festering dust people surged closer. Bannon threw himself between Nicci and the mummified attackers. "I'll clear the way!" He lopped off a desiccated arm at its elbow, then sliced off the head of a second creature. The skin-covered skull rattled onto the blasted ground, its bared teeth still clacking and snapping.

With the oustretched palm of his other hand, the young man shoved another grasping creature, knocking it back into two oncoming foes. Though by now he looked like a greatly aged man himself, Bannon swung and chopped with his sword, splintering ribs, separating shoulders, cleaving body cores. "Complete your mission, Sorceress! Kill the Lifedrinker!"

Nicci could feel herself withering with age and weakness, second by second. She remembered an old crone she had seen long ago in Tanimura hobbling through a market at a snail's pace, as if each step required careful planning and then a rest afterward. Now, Nicci understood how that felt. Her bones were brittle, her joints swollen and aching, the skin on her arms dry and shriveled.

With a snarl, the sand panther also threw herself upon the dust people, shredding the husks of the Lifedrinker's victims as if they were no more than straw and kindling. Mrra's curved fangs ripped the reanimated corpses into scraps of bone and dried flesh.

Behind the dust people, enlarged scorpions moved with angular arachnid speed. In a flash of tawny fur, the big cat dodged the venomous stingers, then bounded onto a rock, leading several scorpions away.

When one of the lashing stingers was about to pierce Mrra's hide, Bannon swung his sword to amputate the segmented tail. Then he skewered the scorpion's hard shell and flung the dying creature into two oncoming dust people.

Snarling, Mrra lunged back into the fray as more desiccated corpses closed in on Nicci, who was fighting her way closer to the Lifedrinker.

The evil wizard jerked his hands, guiding his minions. More dust people crawled up from hiding places beneath the seared ground. For all the attackers that Bannon and Mrra had already savaged, twice as many now joined the fight.

Nicci didn't have much time.

The Lifedrinker's sunken gaze met her cold blue eyes. "Please . . ." he said. "I know I have caused so much harm. I see what I have done, but I *cannot* make it stop! I just wanted to live, wanted to stop the wasting disease from stealing the life inside me. I never wanted this curse."

He raised both of his hands, clenched his clawlike fingers into hard, bony fists. His body swelled with dark ripples of energy, and Nicci felt a sudden flood of debilitating weakness that nearly drove her to her knees.

"I don't know how to shut it off!"

Nicci said in a hoarse voice, "If you found the power within yourself to cause this, then you can find a way to stanch the flow, tie off the wound that is bleeding the world to death. Find it within your own soul."

His voice was hollow with despair. "I drank my own soul long ago. All that remains of me is the *need*!" When he surged again, Nicci knew that the magic had entirely possessed him. The spell had become a living thing in its own right.

An overwhelming army of dust people closed in. More venomous scorpions clattered over the boulders, rushing toward Nicci.

Bannon fought with wild abandon. By now he was an old man with sparse gray hair, yet he still defended her with all his strength, giving the sorceress a chance to make her move. The sand panther also looked old, her fur showing spots of mange, but the branded spell-forms seemed to protect Mrra from the Lifedrinker's deadly appetite.

Nicci herself exhibited many signs of age. The backs of her hands were a tangled map of veins marked with liver spots on skin that had been so creamy and perfect not long ago. Each step she took felt as if she were fighting against a wind of time, age, and weakness.

Behind her, dust people closed around Bannon, but he kept fighting, hacking, chopping them to pieces, even though there were too many. Mrra dove into the fray, trying to protect the swordsman, but a new army of scorpions flowed in, stingers poised and dripping.

Nicci took the final step and reached into her pocket. The Lifedrinker kept draining her magic, and she could not unleash wizard's fire, could not so much as attempt any of her spells. He would only absorb them and then engulf her.

Nicci pulled out the throbbing Eldertree acorn and spoke through gritted teeth. "You. Will. Stop!"

The Lifedrinker swelled even more, looking at his creatures around him. Oddly, he cried as well, "It must stop!" With a surge of his magic, he stole more life from the world, squeezing last drops out of the air, out of the dust—out of the dust people. As he drained his own servants, ten of the mummified corpses twitched and then crumbled into blackened bone powder. The scorpions cracked, shattered, and fell into dust.

The Lifedrinker howled, squirming in the air, raising his hands, as if by triggering this last great call, he had accelerated a magical wildfire, and now a cyclone began to draw down into the endless pit that formed his lair. "Save me," he begged.

Nicci took advantage of that one second of respite. "No. No one can save you, Lifedrinker."

He whispered, "I . . . am . . . *Roland*."

Nicci held out her palm, cupping the last acorn of the Eldertree, and released a simple burst of magic, gathering the air around her in what would otherwise have been a trivial effort. Instead of manipulating the wind to create fists of solid air against an opponent, she used the air to accelerate the acorn forward. The life-infused projectile sped through the air like a quarrel fired from a tightly wound crossbow.

The Lifedrinker screamed, and the acorn plunged into his cavernous mouth, down his throat.

Contained within its hard shell, the last seed of the Eldertree held the concentrated life of the once vast primeval forest. Deep inside the evil wizard, the hard nut cracked and released a flood of life, like a dam bursting in an enormous reservoir. Resurgent energy flared out in an unstoppable explosion of vitality, of renewal, of rejuvenation.

Roland let loose a shriek that seemed to tear open the Scar itself. The evil wizard was an empty pit, an endless appetite that demanded all life, all energy—and the seed from the Eldertree *contained* all life, all energy. The thrashing tumor-strangled wizard was like a man dying of thirst who now found himself drowning in a flash flood.

His evil spell tried to absorb the limitless power geysering from the acorn. The dust storms howled around the curved black pillars; tornadoes of unleashed fury whipped the dry ground, flinging sharp obsidian projectiles in all directions.

Spent, Nicci collapsed mere feet from the edge of the Lifedrinker's pit, unable to move. The battle within the evil wizard continued to build, and he howled with agony. The acorn that had embedded itself inside him blazed and brightened into an inferno of life.

While the Lifedrinker attempted to smother it with ripples of hungry shadows, the remaining dust people collapsed in a rattle of bones and dried skin. The last of the scorpions fell dead, their segmented limbs curling up tight against their armored bodies; their stingers went limp.

Bannon threw the bodies off of him and climbed forward to try to rescue Nicci. He tottered like an ancient man, barely able to survive another hour. Mrra, too, pushed forward, close to the sorceress. Although Nicci was wrung dry and utterly exhausted, she felt the touch of her sister panther in her mind.

The ground shook and rumbled. Stones cracked. Huge boulders fell into the Lifedrinker's pit. The towering stelae creaked, then toppled like felled trees into the hole. The avalanche continued, and the sinkhole slumped, filling with debris. Lightning struck all around.

The raging battle of life continued. The remnant of the Eldertree struggled to produce new life faster than the Lifedrinker could drain it. The bright flare that surged out from the acorn dimmed and flickered away as dark magic continued to fight, but the shadows faded as well, grew patchier, like a mist burning off under a morning sun.

Finally, the evil wizard, the Lifedrinker—Roland—disintegrated, his body gone. All of his death and emptiness turned to dust, and a last bright echo coughed out of the Eldertree acorn, washing over them.

Nicci staggered backward, feeling the warmth like a summer breeze reviving her. Life. Energy. Restoration.

Her joints eased and loosened. Her throat grew less constricted, and when she gasped in a long breath, she smelled a sweetness in the air that she had not experienced since she had first seen the Scar. Nicci raised a hand to her face as the dazzle cleared from her vision, and her skin felt smooth and supple again.

Bannon picked himself up, coughing and shaking. When he turned toward her, Nicci saw that his hair was again thick and red. The wrinkles that had covered his face were gone, leaving only his usual spatter of freckles.

She brushed herself off, and her eyes searched for the place where the Lifedrinker had collapsed, where Roland had lost his battle with the last seed of the original forest.

There, in the middle of the vast dead Scar, stood a sprig of green, the only thing left from all the exuberant power of the Eldertree acorn. A single spindly sapling.

CHAPTER 54

On their long return trek across the desolation, the ominous tension lifted from the air as if the world had heaved a nervous sigh of relief. Though the Scar still remained bleak and desolate, the Lifedrinker's corruption was gone, and his blight would fade from the once-fertile soil. The valley would return, just as Nicci had promised Thistle.

The haze of blown dust and salty powder dissipated, leaving a blue sky scudded with clouds. Bannon looked up with a smile. "I think it might even rain within a day or two, wash the valley clean again." He walked with a jaunty step, obviously proud of himself. He was battered and bruised, with numerous cuts from his last battle, but none the worse for it. "I fought well, didn't I? Made myself worthwhile?"

Though she was not one to shower unnecessary compliments, Nicci did acknowledge the fact. "Yes, you were rather useful when I needed it most."

He beamed.

Mrra stayed with them, ranging widely, wandering out of sight in the rocky canyons, exploring the foothills, and then returning as if to acknowledge her bond with Nicci. The sand panther was a wild creature, though, and as they approached the uplift of the Cliffwall plateau, she seemed restless, sniffing the air. Looking up the striated cliff, Mrra growled; her long tail thrashed.

Nicci gave a brusque nod, which the sand panther seemed to understand. "You can't go in there with us. That is a human place."

Judging by the branded spell markings on her hide, Mrra's previous captivity among humans had not been a pleasant one. With a flick of her tail, the big cat bounded off to vanish into the dry scrub oak and piñon pines.

Nicci and Bannon began the long climb up.

T he people of Cliffwall welcomed them as heroes, which Bannon enjoyed and Nicci tolerated. With a broad grin, the young man patted the sword at his side. "I handled myself well enough. I saved the sorceress too many times to recount."

Nicci was sure he would recount them anyway.

Bannon accepted the fawning attentions of Victoria's three acolytes, who took turns fussing over the scabs and scratches on his cheek, his arms, his hands. They dabbed at the wounds with wet cloths, then cleaned the dust from his forehead, wiping his hair. Bannon touched a cut on his face. "Do you think this one will leave a scar?" he asked, sounding hopeful.

Laurel kissed it. "Maybe so."

Laughing, Thistle ran forward and threw herself on Nicci. "I knew you would survive! I knew you'd save the world."

"And I'm glad you stayed behind, as you promised," Nicci said.

Pleased to hear of their adventure, Nathan stroked his chin. "I wish I had been there, though. It would have been quite a tale to include in my life book."

"We will find other tales, Wizard," Nicci said. "We have a long journey ahead of us yet. Our work here is done."

"Yes, your work is done." He smiled and nodded. "And now that the Lifedrinker has been dispatched, our focus should be on finding Kol Adair, so I can be made whole again—it is quite inconvenient to feel useless! The Cliffwall archives have maps and charts of the world, and Mia will help me sort them right away."

As the ostensible leader of the Cliffwall scholars, Simon was grateful for what Nicci had accomplished. "Even from here, we could feel when the Lifedrinker was defeated. The weight of the world seemed lifted, as if something fundamental had changed." He led the gathered scholars in a loud cheer to thank Nicci and Bannon. "Before we devote our full attentions to learning and cataloging, we should make an expedition to the site of the battle and see this new Eldertree sapling."

Victoria and her memmers nodded in grudging admiration. "Yes, we should all see what remains."

T he following day, nearly fifty people made their way down the narrow, hidden trail from the mesa cliff into the now-quiet Scar.

Full of energy, Thistle trotted along as the group worked their way through the foothills and out into the devastation. The girl was eager to guide them along the easiest path, scouting ahead. "Now I know I'm going to see this valley the way it was meant to be! Someday, I can have my world back, green and growing."

"Maybe even with flower gardens," Nicci said.

She felt that the shadows were lifting from the Scar. They walked at an easy pace all that day, camped for the night, and then set off again the next morning, heading toward the heart of the devastation. Mounds of obsidian glass still protruded from the ground, but the stinking fumaroles had sealed over and the exposed lava hardened. It was only the faintest, first step in the long, painful process of healing.

Finally, near the end of the second day of travel from the Cliffwall plateau, the group of eager travelers gathered at what had been the lair of the Lifedrinker. Nicci and her companions stood with the group, cautiously approaching the crumbling debris that filled the crater.

They paid no attention to the shattered remnants of dust people, the cracked scorpions. Instead, the amazed scholars gathered around the single oak sapling, a delicate tree no taller than Nicci's waist.

"If that is the sapling from the Eldertree, I don't sense any magic from it," Nicci said. "It seems like a normal young tree."

Nathan said, "All of its magic must have burned out in the final battle with the Lifedrinker. This is all that remains, just an oak sapling, but it is alive. That is the important part."

Thistle nudged her way through the crowd so she could look at the spindly little tree that stood so defiant in the desolation.

Victoria seemed disappointed. "That's all? It was . . . the Eldertree!"

"The acorn's outpouring of life was just barely sufficient to win the battle," Nicci said. "The power of life versus the power of death. It was a very close thing. It gave all of its magic to destroy the Lifedrinker—another week or month would have been too late."

While Victoria and her memmers crowded close, the matronly woman let out a sigh. "It is a good thing our memmers recalled the story. Without us, we would not have found the seed of the Eldertree at all, and Roland would still be alive and dangerous."

A flicker of annoyance crossed Simon's face. "Yes, Cliffwall provided the necessary weapon to defeat him, and now we must make up for all the suffering." He raised his voice to address those gathered at the site. "It will be a great deal of work, but we can reclaim this land. The streams and rivers will flow again. With rainfall, we can plant crops and orchards. Many of our scholars came from the towns in this valley, and we can rebuild and replant it."

Understanding the enormity of the problem they faced, the people muttered their agreement.

Nathan placed his hands on his hips, stretching his back. "The Scar can heal. Now that the blight has been eliminated, the natural beauty of the valley will return. It'll just take time." He smiled optimistically. "Maybe only a century or two."

"A century?" Thistle's expression fell. "I'll never see it, then!"

Victoria was grim and determined. She muttered so quietly that only Nicci heard, "It will need to go faster."

CHAPTER 55

The land was dead and desperate. Victoria knew that the harm would take decades, maybe even centuries, to restore . . . if left on its own. That was unforgivable. She could not forget what the self-centered, shortsighted Roland had done, how that pathetic man had killed the land . . . and murdered her dear husband.

But Victoria knew magic, had memorized countless secrets of arcane lore. As the most prominent memmer, she held a wealth of magical information in her mind, and now she searched for a faster solution to revitalize the great valley. The answer was within her—she knew it!

Simon and his scholars could fool themselves that they were experts. They could read books and study spells, but that didn't mean they understood that knowledge. Just because a starving man looked at a pantry filled with food, he did not have the nourishment he required. The memmers, though, had all that information *inside* them, part of their being, their heart, their soul.

Ancient wizards had built this hidden archive to preserve history and lore for all future generations to use. Everything a powerful gifted person could imagine was inside these vaults, written down in volumes, stored on shelves . . . and locked in the minds of the memmers.

That knowledge was part of Victoria.

After the group visited the site of the final battle, the sorceress had seemed so smug, so triumphant about what she had done. Death's

Mistress! Yes, Nicci might have killed the Lifedrinker's ravenous need, but she had not restored life by any means. That was a much more difficult and time-consuming task.

Victoria found the spindly sapling deeply disappointing, even pathetic. Such a small thing, without any magic? She had hoped for much more from the Eldertree. From when she was a young woman, she recalled the rolling hills covered with thick forests, the fertile basin with sweeping croplands and thriving towns. Though the isolated inhabitants of Cliffwall had only rarely left their hidden canyons, they knew the way the real world was supposed to be.

One of the first outsiders brought back to the archive after Victoria had dispelled the camouflage shroud, Roland had been an intense and nervous researcher, an innocuous scholar who read volumes of spells and dabbled with minor magic. He had been quiet and good-natured, and Victoria's husband had considered him a friend.

Early on, Bertram had noticed that Roland was growing gaunt and thin. Victoria now realized those were signs of the wasting disease devouring him from within. But Roland had refused to accept his fate; he had made a bargain with magic he did not comprehend. Without understanding what he was about to unleash, he had turned himself into a bottomless pit of need that siphoned away all life, not just his own.

Victoria winced as she remembered the fateful day she had come upon Roland after he met her husband in the corridor. Desperate, begging for help, he had clasped Bertram's hand, but was unable to control what he unleashed, and the magic kept stealing more and *more* from her poor husband. Bertram could not pull away, could not escape no matter how hard he struggled . . . and the monster Roland purloined his entire life, gorged himself on Bertram's essence.

By the time Victoria saw them, it was too late. Roland fled in terror, and she rushed forward to catch her husband as he collapsed in the corridor. She held him, pressing him against her breast and rocking him back and forth as he faded swiftly. Bertram's skin turned as gray and dry as the old parchments in the archive. His cheeks sank into dark hollows, his eyes shriveled into puckered knots of flesh, his hair fell out in wispy clumps. In her arms, her husband turned into nothing more than a mummified corpse.

From where he had retreated down the corridor, Roland had watched in horror and revulsion. He held up his hands, denying his own deadly touch. "No, no, no!" he screamed.

But after draining all the life energy from Bertram, he did indeed seem stronger, invigorated by what he had stolen. Roland, fast becoming the Lifedrinker, had fled Cliffwall, running into the vast valley. Only later did Victoria learn that he had killed ten other scholars in his frantic, blundering attempts to keep himself strong, trying to get away from the isolated archive.

Now the Lifedrinker was dead, but that was not enough for Victoria. She could not bring Bertram back, but she needed to restore the fertile valley and reawaken life, and she was sure she had the power to do so. Unlike the deluded, inept Roland, she would not make any mistakes. . . .

By the time the expedition returned to the plateau two days later, Victoria knew what she had to do. Sage, Laurel, and Audrey were her three best memmers, but she also had Franklin, Gloria, Peretta, and dozens more students, all of whom were repositories of knowledge. Even now that she had brought down the camouflage shroud and made the wealth of knowledge available to any student who could read, Victoria insisted on keeping the memmer tradition alive. Maybe her acolytes would remember something even more important.

Back inside the great Cliffwall library, Simon insisted on holding a celebration feast, but Victoria could not pretend to be as overjoyed as the others. There was still so much work to do, centuries of work—and that was much too long to wait.

Much as the researchers had scoured the archive for a way to destroy the Lifedrinker, Victoria now sought a *fecundity* spell, some powerful magic to restore everything the evil wizard had taken. If a corrupted spell could steal life away, could not another spell bring it all flooding back? Victoria needed to find that type of magic. Surely some solution lay among all the wisdom preserved here from the ancient wizards.

She spread the word among her memmers, who pondered and sifted through the countless books they had committed to memory. They talked to additional scholars, who combed through now-forgotten volumes from the deepest vaults and dustiest shelves, incorporating that knowledge into their own memory archives.

There had to be a way!

Victoria met privately with her trusted acolytes, keeping her voice low as if they had started a conspiracy. "You are all fertile, all throbbing with life. I can sense it in you. You must create life." She smiled at them, feeling the warmth within her. "And you have gone to Bannon Farmer?"

The three young women looked both eager and embarrassed. "Yes, Victoria," Sage said. "Many times."

"We are trying," Laurel said.

Audrey smiled. "Trying as often as possible."

Sage said, "But none of us is pregnant. Yet."

Victoria sighed and shook her head. "The seed sometimes goes astray, but it will happen in the normal course of things. It is not enough, though. We will have to try something else. The ancient wizards must have known a spell to restore life, magic to encourage growth and rebirth."

"Restore life?" Laurel was astonished by the idea. "You want to bring back the dead?"

"I want to bring back the *world*," Victoria said. "A fertility spell to remove the blight and corruption out in that desolation. I want to bring back the forests and rivers, the meadows and croplands. I want to fill the streams with fish. I want to summon flowers and then bees to pollinate them and make honey. I want the land to thrive again." She drew a breath and looked at her followers. "I refuse to wait decades for that to happen."

While Cliffwall scholars as well as the other canyon villagers engaged in giddy revelry to celebrate the end of the Lifedrinker, Victoria's special memmers meditated, sifting through the vital information in their perfectly preserved memories, searching for some way to accelerate the process.

Victoria spent her every waking moment wrestling with the mountains of words she had locked inside herself. Her head pounded, as if the proper spells were struggling to break free, but she did not have the key to release them. Not yet.

Standing outside under the great cliff overhang in the gathering dusk, she watched shadows fill the finger canyons. Evening lights glimmered from the windows of other alcove settlements across the canyon. Insects buzzed in a low contented music, and she heard the whisper of wings as two night birds swooped by. The world seemed at peace, awakening.

Victoria reflected on the damaged tower that had held the prophecy library. She could remember the terrible day when an inadvertent spell had liquefied the structure and drowned the hapless but foolish apprentice wizard in a flood of stone. Such incidents, even though they were rare, frightened the other scholars from attempting major spells.

Now, standing in the cliff grotto, she looked at the damaged tower with scorn. She had no respect for the clumsy student who had failed to understand the power he unleashed. Another disaster, just like Roland.

Victoria would never allow such a thing. She had higher standards.

As she thought of the mistake that had been made here, something clicked in her mind and she remembered part of an old fertility spell, not just for a woman to have children—perhaps to reawaken the womb of a barren woman, like Victoria herself—but a *creation* spell, a fecundity rite tied to deeper magic that could increase crops, expand herds, rejuvenate forests. She felt the tickle of faint memory, a spell buried deep among so much other knowledge. Victoria tried to sharpen the arcane thoughts at the distant edge of her mind.

She remembered her stern mother, whose angular face looked like the wedge of a hatchet. While her mother had forced Victoria to memorize the lore word for word, she had never bothered to make sure young Victoria *comprehended* what she knew; her mother cared only that she could accurately repeat every line, even if it was in a language neither of them understood. The woman had repeatedly whipped Victoria with a willow switch, raising red welts, spilling blood. Sometimes, she had cuffed her daughter across the face, boxed her ears, or made her bleed from the nose in an attempt to make her try harder to remember, to use her gift and make no mistakes.

Mistakes caused harm. People suffered when an error was made, even an innocent error. Weeping with sincerity, young Victoria had promised her mother she would make no errors. And she had watched that woman shove her good-natured father out of the cliff overhang to his death—a deserved fate, according to her mother, since he had made a mistake, a potentially dangerous mistake.

Victoria could make no mistakes. . . .

Now, once she touched the scattered, ancient spell and followed the memories buried in her past, Victoria could see the words unfurling in her mind. The arcane language, the unfamiliar phrasings, couplets with pronunciations that seemed to defy the letters with which they were written. Victoria remembered the fecundity spell, repeated from generation to generation, passed from memmer to memmer. The thoughts were faint and wispy, frayed from disuse, but she possessed the knowledge. She could use it.

Satisfied, Victoria reentered the main library fortress and hurried to her quarters. Though she had committed everything to memory, she lit her lamp and bent over the low writing desk. On a scrap of paper she began to write, preserving the words she had brought to the forefront of her mind, rolling them over in her mouth, making sure each detail was correct. She spoke the sounds carefully aloud to be sure she got every nuance correct. After she wrote down the fecundity spell, she read it and read it again until she was sure she was right.

Victoria braced herself. She knew what she had to do, and she understood the instructions perfectly.

The land had already been bled dry. What did a little more blood matter?

CHAPTER 56

"Cliffwall served its purpose, exactly as the ancient wizards intended," Simon told Nicci and Nathan, still looking very pleased with himself. After the defeat of the Lifedrinker he seemed more relaxed and focused in his role, back to what he believed his true work should be, though he still looked too young to be the senior scholar-archivist. "Now, at last, our scholars can continue their cataloging and their pure research. There is so much to learn."

The teams of dedicated researchers returned to their everyday work of listing the countless tomes, reshelving volumes by subject, and noting the type of knowledge contained in various disorganized sections. Obviously, decades of work still remained.

Simon looked around with giddy wonder as he tried to encompass the thousands of books shelved haphazardly in the vast library rooms. "The project seems overwhelming, yet for some reason, I feel energized now, more hopeful than I've been in twenty years."

"And well you should feel that way, truth be told," Nathan said. "Simply rediscovering the potential wonders in this library will be an adventure in itself, however. Besides, as you know, all the rules just changed with the star shift. We don't yet understand how much of this information is still accurate, or if everything needs to be relearned, retested, rediscovered."

Simon seemed content. "We are ready, whatever the answer. If your Lord Rahl intends to create a new golden age, then all of this magic can serve humanity."

* * *

Bannon basked in the attention, although one person could handle only so much feasting and dancing. He took a moment to marvel at all that had happened to him in the past month. Despite the horrific ordeals he had endured, the young man realized he now had the life he always wanted.

While battling the selka or the dust people, even facing the Lifedrinker himself, he had been sure he would die. But afterward, the colors of those memories shone bright and vibrant—and they were stories that he could tell until he was a gray-bearded old man, preferably with a wife, many children, and many more grandchildren. In fact, he already wished he could relive some of those adventures.

And love! Here at Cliffwall he had discovered the joys of three beautiful women who adored him and schooled him in the ways of physical pleasure. Though at first Bannon had been embarrassed and awkward, he was an eager student, and now his nights were filled with warm skin and sensuous caresses, whispered laughter and shining eyes. How could he choose a favorite among them? Fortunately, Audrey, Laurel, and Sage were happy to share.

For so many years, he had been trapped in a nightmare, and now he lived a dream that he could never have imagined.

After the late celebrations, Bannon wandered through the Cliffwall complex, searching for the three young women. They had rewarded him most enthusiastically after his triumphant return, but now Victoria had gathered all of her memmers, giving them some very important task that took all of their attention and energy. The lovely young women had expressed their sadness that they couldn't tend to Bannon, claiming other urgent priorities. He hadn't seen them in two days.

Missing Audrey, Laurel, and Sage, Bannon searched the library rooms, the dining hall, and the acolytes' quarters, casually looking for them. He found one of the other memmers, a middle-aged man named Franklin with large, owlish eyes and a square chin. "Victoria took them outside, somewhere in the Scar," Franklin explained. "I think she found the answer they were looking for, something to help the valley return to life."

Bannon gave a solemn nod, not wanting to seem desperate. "It must be important work, then. I'll leave them to it." He went off to his own quarters, hoping they would come back soon.

Thistle was still content to sleep curled on the sheepskin on the floor in Nicci's chamber. "I was worried about you out there," she said. "I didn't want to lose you. I already lost everyone else."

Nicci's brow furrowed. "I promised I'd come back. You should have believed me." While the seamstresses repaired her black travel dress, yet again, she had changed into a comfortable linen gown.

"I did believe you," the girl said, her eyes bright. "I knew you would kill the Lifedrinker. And now I'm ready to go see the rest of the world with you. Will we leave soon?"

Nicci considered the long journey ahead, the unknown lands and the many possible hazards. "You have been through a lot already, and our journey will be full of hardships. Are you sure you want to go?"

On the sheepskin, Thistle sat up in alarm, drawing her scuffed knees to her chest. "Yes! I can hunt, I can help you find the trail, and you know I can fight."

"Someday, people will rebuild Verdun Springs," Nicci said. "Don't you want to go back there? It's your home."

"It's not my home. I lost my home a long time ago. I won't live long enough to see the valley green and lush again, so I want to see what other places are like. You're my new home now." She scratched her mop of hair. "When you leave, I'm going with you again."

Amused by her determination, Nicci readied herself for bed and lay back on her own blanket. "Then I don't think I could stop you." She pulled the blanket over herself, released a hint of magic to snuff out the lamp, and went to sleep.

CHAPTER 57

After the draining, skeletal touch of the Lifedrinker, Nicci slept deeply, plunging into odd dreams.

Though asleep, she ranged far . . . and she wasn't herself. Her mind and her life rode in another body, traveling along on powerful, padded paws. Her muscles thrummed like braided wires as she raced through the night, her long tail lashing behind her, pointed ears cocked and alert for the faintest sounds of prey. The slitted pupils of her gold-green eyes drank in the starlight.

She was Mrra. They were bonded on a deep inner level. Panther sisters. Their blood had intermingled. Nicci had not sought this strange contact in her dreams, but neither did she fear it. She prowled the night, part sorceress, part sand panther. And more.

Lying on the hard pallet inside her chambers, Nicci stirred, twitched, then dropped into a deeper sleep.

Mrra was out hunting, and Nicci hunted with her. They roamed together, and joy sang through her powerful feline body. They raced along for the sheer pleasure of it, not because they were in a hurry. Although hunger gnawed at her belly, she was not starving and she knew she would find food. She always did. With her panther senses, Mrra could catch any scent of prey on the wind, hear the movement of a rodent, see any flicker in the deepest shadows.

And she was free! No longer a prisoner of the handlers. She was wild, as a sand panther was meant to be.

Mrra flowed through the night, exploring the edge of the Scar, which no longer smelled of the festering blight, sour and bitter magic, such as what she had experienced in the great city. This night, the Scar was quiet and Mrra sensed death and silence, but there would also be prey as creatures ventured back into the crumbling wasteland.

Mrra clung to her connection with Nicci. Throughout her life, the sand panther had been spell-bonded with her two sisters, cubs from the same litter, bound inexorably together by the wizard commander, and then turned over to the handlers for training.

Now Mrra's sister panthers were dead, slain in combat—as they were meant to die. Nicci and her companions had killed them, the girl and the young male warrior, but Mrra held no hatred for what the others had done. In the *troka*, the spell-bonded panthers were meant to fight, just as they were meant to eat, breathe, and mate.

The big cat could not think far ahead, did not plan or envision things that might be. Nicci was her bonded partner now. A longing growl rumbled through her chest, and she hoped that she and Nicci could fight together again, side by side. They could tear apart many enemies, just as they had fought the giant lizards or against the Life-drinker.

Mrra bounded onto a slickrock outcropping, where she sat on her haunches under the moonlight, staring across the landscape. Narrowing her golden eyes, twitching her tail, she sniffed the air. Her whiskers vibrated. The hunt was just like a battle, and every day was a battle. Her *troka* had escaped from the great city after killing their handlers, and then the three sister panthers raced into the expansive wilderness and the life they were meant to have.

All three of them had been free, for a time.

As Nicci stirred in her sleep, the dreams became more vivid, the memories more precise. . . .

Violent experiences, razor-sharp recollections of razor-sharp pain. She had been young, and her life was full of mirth and joy as she played with her sister cubs. Then the wizard commander had seized them, forcibly holding the young cubs down while he brought out white-hot irons tipped with spell symbols. Mrra had thrashed, and raked the handlers with her claws, but the leering wizard commander had thrust the searing brand against her hide, burning the symbols into her skin, sizzling the tawny fur. The smoke of burned flesh and hair rose up in a thick cloud, stirred by her feline shriek.

The agony had been unforgettable, and Mrra's pain resonated with the pain of her sister panthers bonded to her, as the spells braided the three into a *troka* so that they shared their minds, their thoughts, and their blood.

That was just the beginning. Once the three panthers were linked by the first blazing symbol, the wizard commander branded more spells into their flesh. And because the three panthers were connected, each one experienced the hideous pain again and again, until their minds were as marred as their beautiful bodies.

After the cats recovered, the handlers began to train them, using hard and painful lessons that involved blood, prey, fear—and more blood. As she and her sister panthers grew stronger, though, Mrra learned to enjoy the tasks. She became faster, deadlier. Her *troka* became the best killers the great city had ever seen.

Mrra's existence became the hunt and the kill. She learned to attack and slay humans inside a gladiatorial coliseum. Some of the prey were terrified and helpless: they ran, but to no avail. Others fell to their knees, weeping and shuddering as the panther claws tore them apart. Some victims were fearsome human warriors, and those provided the best sport, the most challenging battles. Other prey wielded magic, but the symbols branded onto Mrra and her sister panthers deflected the magical attacks.

She remembered the roar of the crowd, the cheers, the howls of bloodlust. With blood-spattered fur, Mrra would lift her head up to the bright sun, and glare at the stands teeming with spectators. She flashed her long, curved fangs and let out her own victorious roar. She remembered the heat of the sun and sand, the taste of the hot blood as it gushed out of a torn throat. Mrra remembered killing victims. Killing warriors. Just *killing*.

Because if she didn't do as she was told, the handlers would cause them pain.

Now free, she prowled around the desolate valley, venturing back to where they had fought and killed the evil wizard. She saw human figures there in the moonlight, four of them, all females who had come out to the lone oak sapling that had grown up at the site of the battle. Sniffing the air, Mrra recognized them as people from the city inside the cliff. An older woman and three young ones.

They were not prey, and therefore held no interest for her.

Mrra ran on into the night, hunting. She picked up the scent of a scrawny antelope that had ventured out of the foothills. The big cat loped onward, picking up speed. Even though the antelope was nearly invisible against the dusty brown landscape, her sharp eyes detected the movement. With a burst of speed and fire through her muscles, she bounded forward.

Even though the panicked antelope tried to run, hooves clattering over the loose rocks, Mrra ran it down and knocked it into the dust. In a flash of fangs, she tore out its throat, then ripped open the antelope's guts while the hooves and the head kept twitching.

The warm blood was delicious, magnificent! She began to feed with a contented, rumbling purr. . . .

In bed, far away, Nicci let out a long satisfied sigh in her sleep.

CHAPTER 58

The great dry valley was intensely silent in the night, brittle with lingering death when it should have been teeming with life. Victoria was offended just to be here. This place should be lush with vegetation, tall grasses, thick forests, and fields of waving grain.

Roland had caused this—stolen all the life, sterilized the land. Even though Nicci had stopped him, that was only part of the solution, and Victoria would not settle for half measures. The others at Cliffwall could congratulate one another, but there was far too much work to do. She would not rest until the job was done, and she could trust no one else to take the necessary measures.

Accompanied by the three loyal young women, she left Cliffwall in the gathering darkness, and together they made their swift expedition across the wasteland out to the site of the Lifedrinker's lair. Laurel, Audrey, and Sage were eager to help, their shining eyes filled with hope. Though the journey took them nearly two days, Victoria had revealed only part of what she intended to do, but these were her acolytes and they would submit to the world's need.

"Our work here is not for personal gain," she said to them. "It will be a triumph for every living man, woman, and child."

At last, at nightfall of the second day, they reached the silent and shuddering area surrounded by fallen obsidian blocks, cluttered with the broken carcasses of giant scorpions and the bony husks of dust people. It was a frightening place, and also a sacred place.

Victoria led them to the lone oak sapling, the frail and fragile tree that had grown from the Eldertree's last acorn.

"It looks so small and weak," Sage said.

"But it has the power of the Eldertree," Laurel said.

"It has the power of the *world*," Victoria corrected. "But its special magic burned away in the battle, and it seems to be just a normal tree now. Nevertheless, it is a tiny spark, a symbol—and we have the power, you three and I, to fan this small flame into a bonfire of life. Are you willing to help?" She looked at the acolytes in turn. "Are you willing to invoke the necessary magic?"

The women nodded without hesitation. Victoria had never had any doubt.

Standing under the moonlight near the thin gray sapling, Victoria loosened the lacings of her dress, then pulled open the collar so that she could remove the garment. She pulled off the drab gown over her head and tossed it aside. The garment fell onto one of the jagged obsidian blocks, and she stood naked in the moonlight, smelling the dusty breezes, experiencing the chill of the darkness.

She turned to her acolytes. "You three must disrobe. You are life. You are pure and fertile. And you must stand as you were born for this sacred process of creation."

The women did as she asked, pulling off their white woolen shifts so that they all stood nude, regal and flawless. Creamy skin glowed in the starlight, their breasts full, their hips rounded. They let their hair flow loose and free.

Audrey's raven locks flowed back like a deeper part of the night, matched by the dark thatch between her legs, while Laurel's strawberry-blond hair looked like gold burning in a slow fire. Sage's nipples were dark and erect in the chill; her breasts were perfectly rounded, flush with the need to create new life.

The power of their beauty took Victoria's words away. These acolytes were the purest personification of female energy, of life itself.

A long time ago, Victoria herself had been just as beautiful. Men had lusted after her, but she had given herself only to Bertram. With a long sigh, she recalled that first time when he had taken her in an

orchard on a night with no moon, while the canyon brook made trickling music, but not loud enough to drown out her gasps of pleasure.
As Bertram stole a kiss, then stole her virginity, they had lain entangled under the soft, fallen leaves, exploring each other. It had been
perfect.

After that night, Victoria had never imagined being satisfied with
any other man. She had found herself pregnant a month later, which
was no surprise since she and Bertram had enjoyed each other many
more times. They spoke the ancient marriage rituals to each other, reciting the words that memmers kept in their minds. But only two
months into their marriage, Victoria lost the baby after hours of agonizing cramps and a gush of blood that produced a small fetus about
the size of her finger. It didn't even look human. And there had been
so much blood.

In her misery, Bertram held her, promised that they would have
many more children. But that had never happened. Discovering that
she was barren had devastated Victoria, one of her greatest disappoint-
ments, one of her greatest failures. She had never given birth to a single
son or daughter, no matter how much she longed for it, no matter how
often she and Bertram tried.

She loved her husband very much, but eventually their physical
pleasure had become more of a duty, and a hopeless one at that. So
Victoria became a surrogate mother to her acolytes and especially these
three perfect, beautiful young women. Victoria claimed that she was
now the true mother to so many more children than she could ever have
had on her own, but she did not convince even herself.

After invoking tonight's ancient, powerful spell, however, she
would be mother to the entire world. Even with the price to be paid,
how could Victoria have any second thoughts?

"Male magic is the magic of conquest and death, of hunting and
killing," she said. Her voice sounded very loud in the silent, secret
place. "Female magic is the magic of life—and our magic is stronger."
She smiled at the three.

Audrey, Laurel, and Sage were flushed as they stood naked together, breathing hard with anticipation. They moved slowly, swaying

their hips, shifting from one foot to the other. Victoria could see that they were aroused. Perhaps enhanced by magic, their own sweat, scent, and inner heat filled the air. Audrey reached down to touch herself and let out a small gasp. Tempted, Laurel and Sage did the same. The night itself was charged with potential, with *life*. Even the oak sapling seemed to tremble.

Victoria's heart ached, and she drove away her growing dread, refusing to let it delay her work, her vital work.

As the three young women stood ready, their eyes half closed, soft groans of pleasure came from deep in their throats. Victoria rummaged in the wadded fabric of her dress and removed the vial she had brought. It was a tincture bottle filled with a deep blue liquid. "You must each drink of this. One swallow should be enough."

Audrey reached out to take it. Her fingers were moist as she removed the cap. "What is it?"

"A vital part of the spell. Drink."

Audrey took a cautious swallow, then passed the bottle on to Laurel, who looked at it. "If you are certain, Victoria . . ."

"I am certain. I have pondered long and hard. We must bring life back to the land, and this is the way we can do it."

Laurel drank without further question; then Sage drained the last of the dark liquid from the bottle.

With a heavy heart, Victoria watched her three acolytes sway, then go limp and collapse to the ground. They were so trusting. . . .

Working quickly, she pulled their naked forms together, propping them up near the Eldertree sapling. Now she could let herself weep, because the girls were unconscious. Hidden in folds of her dress, she had brought strong leather bindings, and she lashed their wrists together, as well as their feet.

The naked young women breathed heavily in their deep drugged sleep, but they would awaken soon, and Victoria had many preparations to make.

Copying what she had memorized in the ancient book and what she had drawn on her scrap of paper for absolute certainty, Victoria scribed a complex spell-form on the ground, etching out the angles and curves of symbols in a long-forgotten language so that the pattern surrounded her acolytes. They were her seeds now; they were the start of new life, the power of which could not be measured.

But there was a cost—there was always a cost. Life required life. Blood required blood.

Victoria shuddered as she finished the pattern, telling herself repeatedly that the benefit was worth the cost. The fecundity spell left no doubt: these three droplets of life would unleash a vivifying downpour. They would restore this verdant valley and heal the wound in the world.

But, oh, Audrey, Laurel, and Sage . . .

Victoria paused to suck in a long shaking breath, and then she let herself sob. Tears flowed down her cheeks. But it had to be done.

When she looked up many minutes later, Victoria saw that the three acolytes had awakened, sooner than expected. Their eyes were still groggy and confused, but the spell required that they had to be conscious, had to be willing. They had already given Victoria their permission.

"What are you doing?" asked Laurel. "What's happening?"

"You're saving us all." With tears pouring down her face, the matronly woman took the knife from her wadded dress and knelt beside the first acolyte.

Sage's eyes went wide, and she squirmed in fear as Victoria drew the razor edge across her throat, spilling a river of blood down her neck and over the swell of her perfect breasts. Her heart kept pumping, gushing out her life's blood onto the achingly sterile ground.

"I'm sorry," Victoria said as she moved to Audrey. Gathering the girl's long dark hair in one hand, she pulled back Audrey's head and slashed her throat.

Laurel looked up at her in defiance, her jaws clenched. She struggled against the leather bonds for just a moment, but her shoulders slumped as she felt her two companions sag in death against her, still bubbling blood across the ground. In a quavering voice, Laurel said, "Tell me it is necessary."

"There is no other way," Victoria answered.

Then Laurel lifted her chin, and Victoria slashed for the third and final time.

When the girls had finished their long wet dying, Victoria wailed with grief. These had been like her daughters, her perfect followers . . . and she'd killed them. But she had done it to bring life.

Now, Victoria worked the spell. The restoration magic unleashed a flood of fecundity strong enough to bring back the forests, the meadows, the grassy plains, the croplands.

Rich blood poured out of the three sacrifices, and Victoria spoke the incantation that she had so perfectly memorized and practiced. The blood flowed like runnels of melted candle wax into the spellforms she had etched there. The liquid glowed a deep red like lava . . . and then the blood changed, darkened, freshened. It turned green and bright as it seeped into the devastated soil, which began to awaken.

Tiny shoots appeared in the brown dust; blades of grass, wideleaved weeds, tangled green branches, bushes, and flowers sprang up.

Victoria stood back and gasped in wonder. The Eldertree sapling grew upward and outward, and more branches unfurled as it rose taller and spread itself. Ferns uncurled like bullwhips and expanded into fanlike fronds. Colorful mushrooms boiled out of the ground, swelled, and burst in an eruption of spores that led to another generation of furiously growing fungi. The ground simmered and crackled as it awakened.

Newborn insects scuttled around, and the night was abuzz with flying creatures—moths with bright feathery wings, beetles with iridescent carapaces.

Victoria stepped back and listened to the rush of life. Inhaling deeply, she smelled moisture, pollen, the perfume of flowers, the resinous scent of fresh trees, the waxy green aroma of leaves. Vines scrambled out of the ground like serpents, following the lines of spilled blood. Roots expanded and thrashed, knitting the broken soil together, raising woody stems and bunches of leaves. Tendrils coiled around the bloodstained bodies of the sacrifices, engulfing the three young women as fertilizer, as trophies.

Victoria stared around herself with wonder. She had never felt so much life before, and she had created this! She had sparked this rebirth. Her rejuvenation spell was powerful enough to overwhelm the damage done by the Lifedrinker.

The verdant forest seemed manic, exploding with life, desperate to reclaim lost territory. Victoria stepped back, proud of what she had done. The scholars at Cliffwall would see the rebirth here, and they would know that Victoria was responsible for it. She stood there naked and pleased, satisfied with her accomplishment. She closed her eyes and let out a sigh of gratitude.

Something seized her ankle. Her eyes flew open and she saw a writhing vine coiling upward, touching her calf. With the speed of a striking viper, it wrapped around her knee and held tight.

She cried out and tried to pull back, but the vine was as unyielding as an iron spring. It tugged in response, dragging her back. Ferns uncurled, bowing over her, closing in. Branches extended toward her, and she struggled to push them away. A curling twig caught her wrist. Vines erupted from the ground, like a swarm of thrashing tentacles that seized her legs. More writhed up to encircle her waist and then tightened.

Victoria screamed and tried to pull away. Roots grabbed her feet, anchoring her. "No! I didn't—!"

As she shouted, a leafy branch thrust into her mouth and pushed into her throat. She gagged and coughed. Fresh green fronds wrapped around her eyes, blindfolding her. She thrashed her head from side to side, choking.

Tendrils thrust into her nostrils, growing deep into her head, while others poked into her ears and explored deeper. She couldn't scream, couldn't see, couldn't breathe. Victoria fought as the vines squeezed tighter.

Then, like the arms of a mighty muscled warrior, the vines pulled her legs apart. She writhed, twisting her hips in a desperate attempt to get away. She felt another vine rising up along her legs, gliding against the side of her thigh, then, with only the slightest hesitation, it plunged between her legs and thrust upward, swelling there, filling her.

The agony throughout her body lasted a long, long time, before the tendrils finally pierced her brain, and her soul was swallowed up in a green darkness.

CHAPTER 59

As Cliffwall stirred with morning activity, Nicci awoke with the taste of blood in her mouth, a delicious coppery flavor that felt warm and hot, but soon faded with the dream memory. She blinked and sat up.

Thistle was beside her, shaking her shoulders. "I was worried about you. You were sleeping so deeply."

Nicci brushed a hand over her eyes, stretched her arms. Her body felt strange. "I am awake now."

"You growled and twitched in your sleep. You must have been having a nightmare."

Flashes of feral memory rose up like tantalizing mist-echoes. "A nightmare, of sorts." She frowned as she tried to remember. "But it wasn't all a nightmare." In fact, the dream in which she hunted with Mrra, in which she had been *part* of Mrra, held a great deal of pleasure. Nicci was strong and exuberant, her instincts singing, every muscle alive as she bounded along, free in the world. Her human lips quirked in a smile.

Thistle knelt beside her pallet with a look of grave concern. "I thought maybe you were dying. I've been trying to wake you up. Your eyes were open, but they were all white, as if you weren't there . . . as if you were somewhere else."

"I was somewhere else," Nicci said. "Gone on a journey. I was with the sand panther, and we were hunting." She lowered her voice, quiet with wonder. "I didn't remember my body here at all."

She went to the low table and splashed her face with water from the basin while she recalled riding inside the sand panther's mind, as if she were an animal dream walker, like Jagang. But while she had dreamed with Mrra, her body here had remained in a deep trance, completely helpless—and that concerned her. Nicci did not like to be vulnerable. She could never allow that to happen again unless she was in a sheltered place, watched over by a guardian.

She straightened her soft shift and combed her blond hair. "If Nathan has found his maps, we will prepare to leave today," she said, hoping to distract the orphan girl. "We have done all we can at Cliffwall."

The girl nodded. "With the Lifedrinker dead, the valley is safe. Someday, I'll return." She flashed a bright, optimistic smile. "The people of Cliffwall will write about this in legends, won't they?"

"I have no wish to be a legend," Nicci said.

They would need packs filled with supplies, fresh travel garments, mended boots. Nicci was still uneasy about having the girl accompany them into unknown dangers, but Thistle certainly was resourceful, fast, clever, independent. Her loyalty and dedication made her a worthy companion, and good companions could be an asset when traveling.

Nicci thought about the great unexplored continent of the Old World, where there were new cities and cultures . . . perhaps with oppressed people, enslaved lands, or ruthless rulers who would need to be brought into line for Lord Rahl's golden age. With a twinge and a shudder, she saw the vivid images from Mrra's mind: the searing white-hot pain as the handlers branded spell symbols into her hide, the great city, the huge coliseum, the wizard commander, the bloodshed.

The great city . . . *Ildakar*. The word came to her, but she couldn't be sure. Was it a name that Mrra had heard but not understood? The sand panther did not comprehend the handlers' speech, only the pain they inflicted. Ildakar . . .

She and Thistle went together to the dining hall, where breakfast was being served as the scholars gathered, ready to dive into another day of research. Simon consulted with two other researchers, comparing notes on an old volume with faded letters. Nathan and Bannon were there already at the morning meal, chatting together.

Seeing Nicci, the wizard gestured them over. "We have what we need, Sorceress. Mia has found ancient maps, which show the landscape as it was three thousand years ago when the documents were hidden behind the camouflage shroud."

"The roads will have fallen away, by now," Nicci said. "Armies swept across the landscape, kingdoms rose and fell. Cities were abandoned, while new ones were built."

Nathan shrugged. "True, but cities are cities, generally built on crossroads and waterways, near productive mines or fertile farmlands. If there was a reason for a city thousands of years ago, the reason is likely still valid." He reached over to tousle Thistle's curly nest of hair, and the girl grinned and reached up to muss his white hair in return, which startled him. He laughed and said to the group, "And if the cities are different and the land has changed, then that is what exploring is all about. Besides, I need my magic back."

"We all need you to have your magic back," Nicci said. "We'll leave as soon as possible. The Lifedrinker is dead, and I have saved the world, so I have fulfilled the witch woman's prediction. Now we go to Kol Adair."

Nathan could barely contain his eagerness. "True, true, my dear sorceress—but what makes you think you will be required to save the world only once?"

With an embarrassed frown, Bannon ate his oat porridge. "Before we go, I really want to say good-bye to Audrey, Laurel, and Sage. We've become very good friends."

The wizard had a twinkle in his azure eyes. "Yes, I suspect very good friends indeed."

Bannon flushed. "But I can't find them. They went away somewhere with Victoria."

Nicci vaguely remembered seeing the group of women through Mrra's eyes in the dream hunting the night before, but she had not seen them since. She said, "If you find them in time, you can say your farewells. But we are leaving." She felt restless, determinted to find Kol Adair for Nathan, but also to continue her mission for Lord Rahl, to move on to other kingdoms, provinces, cities, and towns, all of which needed to know they were now part of the expanded D'Haran Empire.

A mousy young woman dashed into the dining hall, her short brown hair windblown as if she had just run a great distance. Sweat glistened on her forehead. The young scholar, Mia, had often helped Nathan find required tomes in his search for defenses against the Lifedrinker. Now she ran up to the scholar-archivist. "Master Simon, something's happened out in the Scar! I can't even begin to explain it. You must come and see." She looked around the room and also spotted Nathan. "Nathan, you have to see. It's a miracle!"

Simon ran his hands through his mussed brown hair. "What is it?"

In response, Mia led them all into the tunnels through the heart of the plateau, jabbering. "Who could ever have expected this? Wait until you look through the window alcoves. It's remarkable."

The crowds grew larger as they moved through the corridors, following Mia. Simon asked, "Where is Victoria? If it's so important, the memmers should see this as well." He seemed to be trying hard to include them, but no one could remember seeing the matronly woman or her three acolytes. Finally, they reached the window wall that looked out upon the vast valley. From here, they had viewed the extent of the Lifedrinker's spreading devastation, but now they stared out at something exceedingly strange.

Nicci came forward, focused on the sudden, dramatic changes that had occurred overnight.

In the center of the vast, dead valley where the evil wizard had dwelled, the dusty brown had changed. The sandstorms and dust devils were gone, replaced by a green haze over an area of new growth—a burgeoning jungle that arose in the Scar. The vegetation was much more than the lone and defiant Eldertree oak sapling they had left behind. It looked like a storm of plant growth.

And it was clearly spreading.

CHAPTER 60

When the magic revived her, penetrated her, and jolted her, Victoria found herself alive . . . and more than just alive. She was *exploding* with life, seething with an energy that surged through her veins like the runoff from mountain snowmelt. Her muscles writhed, teeming with new creatures. Every droplet of blood, every scrap of skin, every splinter of bone, each hair on her head was alive. She felt as if thousands of swarming bees or termites were energizing her while countless strands of plants bound her together.

Victoria drew an astonished breath. As she inhaled, a furious gale rippled through a dense forest, leaves rushing and rattling, thick boughs swaying against each other, bending in reverence . . . to *her.* She opened her eyes, and light surged in with all the green of the forest, the power of the soil.

By shedding the blood of her sacrificial acolytes, Victoria had worked that ancient spell and unleashed a magic powerful enough to counteract the deadly blight caused by the Lifedrinker. The destructive, selfish fool had brought untold harm to the world, and now Victoria accepted the task of repairing the damage he had done. She was strong enough. Roland had been an embarrassment and a failure because of his improper understanding of powerful spells that he had no business even contemplating.

Victoria could fix it. It was her duty to fix it.

Precious Audrey, Laurel, and Sage had given their lives for the cause, and Victoria realized that she herself had given even more than that. When the awakening forest seized her, co-opted her, she had not understood its intent. She had struggled and screamed, terrified that the writhing explosion of life wanted to kill her. But no, that hadn't been correct at all.

Her spell had awakened an avalanche of exuberant, uncontrollable life, replenishing all that the Lifedrinker had taken, and the magic needed Victoria as a conduit. Even as the vines wrapped around her, plunged into her mouth, and nose, and ears . . . after the writhing plants held her open and assaulted her, the surge of magic was merely trying to make her something *more,* to build her into a woman so filled with the energy of life that she could guide the whole world's reawakening. She would let it flow like a flash flood of fresh growth bursting from the broken dam of Roland's evil sorcery.

When Victoria stood up in the heart of the primeval jungle and extended her arms, she saw that her skin was the mottled green of countless leaves. Her hands were large and powerful, the fingers like small branches. Her muscles were coiled and twisted like sturdy wind-lashed trees. Rising taller, she could feel her limbs creaking as if she were a redwood that towered over the forest. Her vision was shattered and dizzying, as if she saw through countless eyes. She heard the loud hum of bees, saw the colorful flurry of birds, swarms of bright butterflies, fresh blossoms bursting open like a magician's celebratory trick at a wedding party.

Victoria was the embodiment of all this life energy, but she still remained *herself.* With the release of the fecundity spell and the sacrifices she had made, the price she had paid, Victoria contained the sum of fertility—green, vibrant, and feminine. Through her own body and her own soul, she had given birth to life everywhere. In the new forest, she could feel the trees growing and spreading, the perimeter of her reclaimed green territory expanding like a bold army that meant to conquer the Scar, and much more.

This was just the beginning of her work. Victoria would do more than restore the world to the way it had been. Why stop there? Why limit herself at all? After the parade of armies and warlords, after thousands of years of bloody history, mankind had caused tremendous damage.

The spell she had unleashed was extremely powerful, and the magic was as wild and unpredictable as life itself, but for so great a task, Victoria required lieutenants. And she knew exactly where to find them.

Her three acolytes had already given everything. They had believed in her dream and had never questioned her instructions. Even though Simon had insulted her memmers and tried to make her feel irrelevant to the work of Cliffwall, those girls had been utterly loyal. Victoria would reward them now. With the rejuvenated gift so strong within her, she had the power to do anything.

In the swarming, boiling army of life that arose from the desolation, she reached out with her mind and her magic, searching in the dense underbrush, the swelling weeds and shrubbery, the vines that tilled the soil. She found long-forgotten seeds and sparked them awake.

The bodies of Audrey, Laurel, and Sage had become a matrix for the regrowth. Their blood had spilled into the channels Victoria carved in the barren ground, where now the thickest roots and vines swelled, building and strengthening that spell-form. But her acolytes' bodies were more than just fertilizer—they were catalysts.

Victoria found the remains of the young women and rebuilt them, pulling together the strands of their bones, reweaving their muscles, using soft plant tissue to re-create their flesh. She did not intend just to restore the three as they were, however. She would make Audrey, Laurel, and Sage into forest guardians as well. They needed to be strong enough to combat those who would inevitably try to stop her miraculous work.

After she re-created the bodies of the three women as constructs of the living forest, Victoria bent close to the figures and exhaled, blowing the tingle of irresistible life force into the parted lips of first Sage, then Audrey, then Laurel.

The bodies roused, and moved. When their eyes opened, the irises sparkled green as if made from the overlapped carapaces of jewel beetles. The young women breathed hard; they opened their new lips and flicked out pink tongues, exposing sharp white teeth. Their matted hair was lush, like Spanish moss, and they extended their arms and flexed their muscles to show off astonishingly beautiful forms, the perfect embodiments of femininity, of life magic, of the energy of lust and creation.

Awake and aware now, the acolytes looked at Victoria with wonder, admiring what she had become. Victoria could not see her own body, but she felt its power, its ominous beauty, and the potential she contained.

"Victoria," said Sage, but she was no longer Sage; she was but one component of the three-part manifestation of the unstoppable spell.

"Mother," echoed Laurel and Audrey.

Yes, Victoria thought, I am the mother now. The mother of all things.

"We have great work to accomplish. We have the power, the magic, and the will to do what must be done. My original intent was just to restore this valley, make it as fertile and pristine as it once was. Now I know that my ambitions were too limited. I have been given a gift, and I now bear a tremendous responsibility. Through me, you all have the same duty."

She looked at them. "With the acorn from the Eldertree, we have the magic and the spark. It is time to restore the original primeval forest across the Scar and spread it throughout the land, so that the whole world can once again be perfect, as it was when the Creator first manifested his vision."

Victoria's dark green lips curved in a smile. Her three beautiful acolytes nodded. She added, "A world lush and untouched. And without humans to sully it."

CHAPTER 61

After seeing the burgeoning area of growth at the heart of the Scar, a curious and awestruck Simon led another expedition from Cliffwall, rushing out to see what had happened. The people were guardedly optimistic. Life was returning to the great valley.

Simon made his best effort to find Victoria and invite her to join them, but when no one could find her, he heaved a sigh. "We cannot wait. Let us go see this miracle."

As the group descended the plateau wall and headed out across the still-barren landscape, the glimpse of green in the distance made Thistle chatter with excitement. She walked close beside Nicci. "Maybe it won't take so long! Maybe the valley will be green again, just like I dreamed, and I'll have a chance to see it in my lifetime."

"The sorceress gave you all a second chance." Nathan tossed his straight white hair and strode along beside Bannon, who kept his hand near the pommel of his sword, pretending to be alert for dangers.

Nicci glanced back to Nathan. "I helped kill the evil wizard, but do not credit me with this rebirth. It was not my doing."

Nathan said, "Perhaps the Eldertree still had a remnant of energy that the Lifedrinker did not quench after all. That might have triggered this reawakening."

Nicci regarded the verdant haze of forest that had already spread across the desolation. Even from a distance, she could hear a stir of plants and branches, the buzz of life. "So much growth . . ." She frowned at the swell of green ahead of them. "I am concerned unless I understand it."

Nathan raised an eyebrow. "You find fault in an overabundance of life, Sorceress? After so much desolation, this is a good thing, is it not?"

Her eyes narrowed. "Is it?"

Sooner than expected, they reached the edge of the lush vegetation, as if the swath of growth had moved outward at great speed to meet them. The air was humid with vegetation, thick with the smell of grasses, leaves, pollen, and the sickly sweet odor of explosive blossoms.

Thistle gaped. "I've never seen anything like this."

Simon stretched his arms outward to welcome the furiously insistent jungle. "It's marvelous!" Towering ferns unfurled, and trees stretched and cracked, rising impossibly high in such a short period, as if time itself had accelerated to let the forest catch up for all that had been lost to the Lifedrinker.

Branches stretched and strained, unfurling countless leaves. Twigs rustled as they proliferated. Vines swirled back and forth like twitching tentacles. To Nicci's ears, the stir of rampant fertility sounded sinister, restless . . . even dangerous.

The tree trunks enlarged as they grew at a manic pace, groaning with the agony of too much life. The stirring branches sounded like slashing blades. The plants spread a blur of pollen throughout the air. Shrubs and flowers spat seeds, and mushrooms flung spores in all directions. Grasses rose up whispering and hissing.

As the group from Cliffwall stood marveling at the unexpected sight, more shoots sprang up, grasses and weeds extending from the perimeter to reclaim more of the parched desolation. This primeval jungle expanded at a tremendous pace.

"Sweet Sea Mother!" At first, Bannon grinned in amazement, but the awestruck wonder on his face shifted to an expression of concern. "Isn't that a little too fast?"

Bees and beetles hummed and whirred through the air. A dark mist of gnats rose up like a wave.

Simon shouted into the forest, as if he could summon a greater presence. "Thank you! We are grateful for the return of life."

A stirring occurred among the trees and branches, and larger shapes flitted through the green angled shadows: human figures, *female* figures—naked, shapely women whose mottled skin provided perfect camouflage among the leaves. The branches and vines parted to reveal the three women standing before the gathered scholars.

The young women were as lush as the forest itself, their breasts and hips swollen with life, their hair a tangle of matted leaves and moss. They looked alien, their transformed bodies more forest than human. Their features were still recognizable, still familiar.

Bannon gasped. His lips curled in an uncertain smile. "Laurel? Audrey? Sage?"

When the three figures moved forward, the undergrowth flowed along with them. Their eyes flashed an iridescent green. Victoria's acolytes throbbed with fertility, the essence of the forest and life itself. They exuded a wafting and irresistible pull of attractive scent, like an animal in heat. Even Nathan seemed affected by their presence, along with Simon and all the other men in the group. The sexual shimmer pervaded the air.

Bannon breathed heavily. Perspiration covered his skin, and he flushed with longing. The look on his face was one of yearning and impossible separation. "You were gone," he said. "I didn't know where you went. I looked for you."

Laurel said with a vibrant giggle, "We waited for you, Bannon." The other two young women echoed her sentiment.

"We wanted you here."

"With us."

Simon was even more insistent. His mouth was drawn back with male need, his eyes shining, even glazed. At the front of the group, he pushed forward, blocking the others. "So much life, so much hope," he said. "We want you. *I* want you!"

"Yes, come closer," said Sage, fixing her attention on him. "We want you too. We want you all."

Bannon tried to join him, but the scholar-archivist pushed him aside, raising his hands. He didn't even seem aware of what he was doing. "You brought back the forest," Simon cried. "You counteracted the Lifedrinker's curse. It is wondrous!"

The three green forest women reached out to welcome him. "There is enough, enough for all," said Audrey. Their soft and yearning fingers suddenly transformed into pointed wooden spikes. Their nails curved and became the sharpest of thorns.

Drunk on the thick, seductive scent in the air, Simon didn't notice. His eyes were heavy-lidded, his mouth open in a gasp of a smile. When the forest women tore him apart, he didn't even have time to scream. They stabbed him with wooden-spike fingers, raked him open with thorn claws. They sliced and unwrapped his flesh, peeling it away as if stripping the bark from a fallen tree.

Several scholars screamed as they scrambled back. Some let out moans of disbelief. "Simon!" cried Mia.

Releasing a burst of defensive magic, Nicci knocked the rest of her companions away, sweeping them out of reach of the grasping, deadly women.

Bannon shouted in dismay. "Laurel, no! Audrey, Sage!"

Astonishingly, when the forest women tossed Simon's butchered corpse onto the barren ground beyond the fringe of the expanding forest, his blood was like a magical elixir, a potent life-giving spell. As the red droplets soaked into the dead soil, new roots writhed about like earthworms. Shoots of green grass and unfurling leaves lifted upward to form a carpet in the fading shape of a man.

When the young women laughed, it came as the sound of a storm in thick trees.

Nathan and Bannon drew their swords. Nicci stood ready to release her magic if the vicious women lunged after them. "Beware, the attack could come from anywhere." But the three acolytes did not step beyond the edge of the growing forest.

Even Nicci did not expect what they all saw next. Weeds, vines, and thorny brambles continued to erupt from the spilled blood in the pattern of Simon's body, but in the thicker jungle, trees rustled, and the undergrowth backed away as if bowing to a powerful lord. The three deadly forest women respectfully moved apart as a larger form emerged from the forest: a throbbing female titan with skin like bark, leaves, and moss, a naked body with enormous swaying breasts, the broad waist and hips of a gigantic oak, and hair made of vines and ferns. Her face no longer carried even a hint of matronly kindness.

Victoria . . . or, what had once been Victoria.

The fearsome forest woman towered above the gathered people from Cliffwall, and her voice boomed out. "This is my forest, and you are no longer welcome here—nor in this world." She focused her startling, burning eyes on Nicci, who returned the gaze defiantly, not backing down. Victoria added in a mocking tone, "For I am *Life's Mistress*."

Branches cracked. Leaves and branches swelled, and the explosive outpouring of growth continued to spread.

CHAPTER 62

Nicci did not like to retreat under any circumstances, but the insane jungle was too unpredictable and could easily tear the Cliffwall scholars to pieces. As well as Thistle.

She pulled the girl to safety, away from the thrashing forest. The scholars' faces were filled with despair after the slaughter of Simon and the monstrous appearance of Victoria and her acolytes, but she shouted, driving them into action, "Get back!"

Nathan and Bannon helped to herd the Cliffwall people away from the boundary of the deadly jungle, and the others needed little encouragement to run.

Nicci glared at the swollen, transformed figure of Victoria. The green female *thing* had an uncontrolled, hungry magic similar to Roland's—and just like Roland, Victoria would have to be stopped. For this, Nicci suspected they might need a weapon even more powerful than the Eldertree acorn.

And the Sorceress must save the world. Maybe she wasn't done here yet after all.

As the panicked scholars fled back to the uplift of the plateau, Bannon withdrew into a sense of sick denial after what he had seen the three young women do to Simon. "Sweet Sea Mother, they were so beautiful, so loving and kind. I loved them, and they loved me."

"They loved you so much, they wanted your blood," Nicci said. "They would have torn you apart, but Simon paid the price for you."

Bannon shook his head. "We have to save them! They're entangled in an evil spell, but I know their hearts are good. We can bring them back, I know it."

Nicci frowned at him. "Don't delude yourself with unrealistic hopes, Bannon Farmer. Those things are no longer the women you knew. We will certainly have to kill them."

The young man stared at her, his mouth open in disbelief. "No, it can't be. My life was happy, almost perfect for once. . . ."

With an understanding nod, the wizard squeezed his shoulder. "Sometimes outward beauty only masks a darkness inside."

When they finally climbed back up the slope and returned to the hidden archive inside the plateau, Nathan strode directly toward the large library chambers, wasting no time. "Once again, we need to learn about a corrupt, uncontrolled spell," he said, "so we can fight it."

Nicci turned Thistle about, leading her toward their quarters. "I will destroy her, just as I destroyed the Lifedrinker."

The girl hung her head, sniffling. "I just wanted to see my valley restored, but that jungle is almost as bad as the Scar." Her voice hitched as if her throat were full of tears.

"We must eradicate both threats and help the valley return to normal, without being crushed by evil masters," Nicci said. "That is what Lord Rahl stands for." She touched the girl's curly mass of hair, and Thistle looked up at her with complete faith. "That is precisely why we are here."

"I know," Thistle said.

With no clear leaders, the people of Cliffwall turned desperately to Nathan and Nicci for answers. The old wizard buried himself in the archives again, absorbing volume after volume, scroll after scroll, so that he could counteract the dark fecundity that "Life's Mistress" had clumsily unleashed.

Mousy, dedicated Mia hovered by Nathan's side, reading documents with lightning speed, tracing her fingertips over the handwritten lines. She could take in the gist of the text and cull out the important books she felt Nathan should read.

Nicci, though, decided to seek information in a more direct fashion. Because the memmers held the knowledge within their minds, she interrogated Victoria's people face-to-face.

Marching into one of the classroom chambers where the memmers would recite their lessons, she faced them with her hands planted on the curve of her hips. "Victoria commanded you to search for fertility spells, horticulture magic, even restorative lore that could be applied to wildfire damage in forests. One of you must have recalled the dark spell that she used." She narrowed her eyes, looking for an unexpected flush or a wary flinch among the memmers. "Someone pointed her to whatever incantation or blood magic she invoked. I need to know what it was."

"Victoria wanted to save the valley and save us all," said Franklin, blinking his owlish eyes. "She had only the best of intentions. We all wanted to help."

"Best of intentions?" Nicci's glare froze them as if she were a predator about to pounce. "You never learned the Wizard's Second Rule."

Gloria, a plump and earnest young memmer, frowned. Her lower lip trembled. "The Wizard's Second Rule? What is that? Is it in the archives?"

"Any student of magical lore should know it. *The greatest harm can result from the best intentions.* Victoria proved exactly that. Rather than patiently waiting for nature to reclaim the valley, she unleashed even more dangerous magic, and now it is out of control. With her good intentions, Victoria may well have doomed us all, unless we can find a way to stop her."

Gloria swallowed hard. "But how can we undo what she's done?"

"First, we must understand the magic she used, the exact spell she triggered. Did one of you help her to find it?"

The memmers fidgeted uncomfortably in their memorization room. Franklin said, "She hoped one of us might recall something that we had committed to memory, but there were so many possibilities, none of them clear. She wanted to help the valley grow back faster."

Nicci's voice was sharp. "I can tell when you are lying." They feared she was using some rare truth-sensing magic, but she did not need that. She could see their nervous twitches, their averted eyes, the sweat sparkling on their skin. She raised her voice into loud command. "Which spell did Victoria use? Tell me what blood magic she invoked to trigger that wild growth."

Gloria flinched. "It was an ancient fecundity spell, one that could awaken the earth. It was in an obscure language we didn't exactly know how to pronounce or interpret."

Nicci straightened her back. "So she unleashed such a terrible spell without recalling how to say the words?"

"She knew," Franklin said defensively. "We all knew. Memmers remember perfectly from generation to generation."

Nicci pressed harder. "You are saying that what we saw out there in the Scar, that explosive deadly growth, was exactly what Victoria *intended*?"

The memmers were embarrassed. Franklin finally gathered the courage to answer. "We do remember some fertility spells, but we don't know how to counteract them. Very few ancient wizards ever wanted to *stop* life, growth, and prosperity."

"There were some reciprocal spells," Gloria admitted, "but they are dim in our minds, relegated to minutiae. The details were not considered useful, and our ancestors already had so much to remember and preserve."

"Write down whatever you remember, and I will study the information," Nicci said.

Gloria went to a podium in their memorization room, on which an open tome rested on display. During their daily lessons, the acolytes often listened to a speaker, committing line by line to memory. Instead of reading aloud now, Gloria picked up a quill pen, dipped the sharpened end into an inkpot, and began to scratch out words on a scrap of paper. She paused, closed her eyes to summon the details, then wrote more words. She kept her hand on the paper. "This is the spell that Victoria used. I think."

Franklin came forward to study Gloria's letters, corrected one piece of punctuation, altered one word. The memmers gathered around, nodding as they proofread. Once they all agreed on the precise formula and the arcane words, they handed the paper to Nicci.

As she scanned the spell, most of the words were mere gibberish to her. "Nathan might be better informed than I." She tucked the paper into the fold pocket of her dress, then extended a finger, scolding the memmers. "Ransack all the knowledge inside you. Find some way that we can fix the damage Victoria has caused."

From the window alcove on the outer side of the plateau wall, Nicci gazed across the tortured valley, where a crimson sunset deepened like the blood of the sacrifices Victoria had shed. She had given the written spell to Nathan, who read with great eagerness, then deep concern.

"This is every bit as bad as I anticipated. Perhaps worse. The power invoked comes from a language even older than High D'Haran. It will be difficult for us to find a magic powerful enough to overturn it."

"Richard did not send us out to solve simple problems," Nicci pointed out.

"Of course. I just wanted you to appreciate the magnitude of the challenge."

As the red-gold rays of dusk fell over the broad valley, she concentrated on the swarming forest at its core, the primeval jungle that glowed an unhealthy green.

Drawn by the view as well, Bannon joined her, gazing out with a forlorn expression. "First, all life was draining away in the world, and now there's an unstoppable *flood* of life. How do we fight it?"

"We will find a way," Nicci said. "And then I myself will destroy the woman who calls herself Life's Mistress."

"I want to do something, too," Bannon said. "You and Nathan can study all the books to look for a solution. You both understand the magic and can read mysterious languages, but I'm just waiting here, feeling useless. Like I was when we waited for a weapon against the Lifedrinker." He sighed in obvious frustration. "You admitted that I *can* be useful, Sorceress. Isn't there something I could do?"

"Help the farmers harvest crops. Tend the flocks, work the orchards," Nicci suggested. "Learn a skill, perhaps as a carpenter."

Anger flashed across his face. "That's not what I mean! There's got to be some way to save Audrey, Laurel, and Sage." His face was wrenched with helplessness. "I love them."

"And they are hungry for you. Remember what they did to Simon."

His expression grew steely. "We need to understand what is happening out there, Sorceress. You know I can handle myself. I'm going to go on a scout, and I'll come back and tell you what I see."

"That's a foolish risk," Nicci said.

"You've called me a fool before! I want to do this. Don't try to stop me."

"I cannot stop you, Bannon Farmer, but if you are going to expose yourself to such great and unnecessary danger, at least make certain you return with valuable information."

He lifted his chin, relieved that she didn't argue with him further. "I will."

Looking long and hard at him, Nicci added in a softer voice, "And be careful."

CHAPTER 63

Being surrounded by so many books and so much knowledge usually exhilarated Nathan. The secrets and stories contained in those soft, well-worn volumes had made his centuries of captivity a little more tolerable in the Palace of the Prophets. The Sisters' huge library held countless tomes describing magic that Nathan could never use, thanks to the wards, webs, and shields woven throughout the palace architecture, not to mention the iron collar of his Rada'Han. Still, reading the legends, histories, even folktales had brought joy to his tedious existence.

When Lord Rahl's star shift had made all books on prophecy useless and irrelevant, he had offered to let Nathan keep one small library for his own entertainment, perhaps even out of nostalgia, but the wizard soon decided that what he really wanted was not to bury himself in old archives but to go out and live his life, to write his own story. And that was exactly what he did.

He patted the mysterious leather-bound life book the witch woman had given him. Now he had other reading to do. Vital reading.

He let out a weary sigh as dutiful Mia brought him a new stack of volumes. "I have no idea what these contain, Wizard Rahl, but they look interesting." Mia got directly to work, showing him a tome at random. Many of these new books looked waterlogged, scuffed, or tattered. "Somewhere in our archive we'll find a way to stop Victoria. Cliffwall has every answer, if only we can find it."

Nathan chuckled. "Are you suggesting the ancient wizards in the time of Baraccus and Merritt knew all there is to know?"

The studious woman's brow furrowed as if he had questioned her reason for existence. "Why, of course! This is *Cliffwall*. All knowledge was placed here for safekeeping. *All* knowledge."

He drew two fingers down his chin and gave her an indulgent look. "I'm glad you have such faith in the ancients."

Mia nodded. "They were much more powerful than anyone alive now."

"But if they had all that knowledge, then why did they fail?"

She responded with a stern look. "Just because knowledge exists, doesn't mean people know how to *use it*."

"Well, I wish I had your confidence, young woman." Nathan peeled open the cover of the book he had chosen, frowning to see that the pages were swollen and rippled, as if they had been soaked in water and improperly dried. Some of the pages were torn, the ink smudged and unreadable. He brushed clumpy dust off the cover of the next book in the stack. "Where did these volumes come from? Did you dig them out of a hole?"

Mia looked embarrassed. "After the sorceress opened the sealed vault beneath the damaged tower, our laborers used picks and chisels to break into other previously inaccessible chambers. Some of the books had been partly fused into walls, others buried under rubble. No one has looked at them yet, but I wanted you to see them right away, in case they were important."

He picked up a third book, trying to decipher the embossed symbols on the cover. "I thought the damaged tower contained only books on prophecy. I doubt they will help."

"No, the prophecy sections were in the upper levels. In the final days of building Cliffwall, the ancient wizards were in a panic to finish, being hunted down by the forces of Emperor Sulachan. The lower vaults were piled with last-minute additions. No one has seen them except you, Wizard Rahl."

"Then I am absolutely delighted by the opportunity, my dear." He patted the empty chair beside him. "Would you help me study them? I only have two eyes, and together we could read twice as fast."

Mia beamed. "I'd like that." She sat beside him, chose a book at random, and began working her way through the smudged and faded letters.

Deep within the resurgent forest—which was her heart, her very soul—Victoria felt the magic of reawakened life pulsing through her . . . and, by extension, through everything she had made, the burgeoning life that came from the stillborn ground. The tortured Scar had been as painful to her as the stillborn baby that she and Bertram had so wanted to have.

But unlike her bloody and painful miscarriages, Victoria now had the power she had always longed to have: a woman's power to create and nurture life. As proof, she needed only to look out at the flourishing new jungle she had created. The growth charged forth like a wild stampede, but Victoria didn't want to control it, not at all. She wanted it to fill the valley, roll over the mountains, and sweep across the continent, pristine, primeval, and unstoppable.

Life would triumph over death. Her unquenchable victory would overtake all efforts to stop it. "Victory" . . . the very word was in her name. She was Victoria. She was Life's Mistress. Within her, she had a power to rival the Creator Himself.

As she pondered her new role, thickets rose and swirled around her body. Thorny vines and flowers exuded a heady, hypnotic perfume. The trees grew so swiftly they swelled, shattered, and toppled over. And then even the splintered trunks hosted swarming worms and beetle grubs, as well as fungi and molds that churned the fallen tree into mulch, which became fertilizer for more life.

And yet more life.

Her acolytes, who wielded the same energy of vibrant fertility, had gone separately across the primeval jungle. They were stewards of the reawakened life now, nurturing the trees, the insects, the birds, and more. Victoria would see to that. The world would once again be pristine.

As Life's Mistress, she would never be satisfied to merely return this valley to its former baseline, an exploited landscape with enslaved herds and rigidly defined croplands. Victoria understood now what her true role in the world was. All the generations of memmers and their preserved ancient lore had led to this. Victoria could not be content with memorization for its own sake; she had to find those powerful spell-forms, the maps of magic that would let her accomplish what was necessary.

As her unnatural body thrived and the tendrils of her forest conquered the barren territory, her mind unlocked more of what it remembered, revealing esoteric and deadly magic that she could use.

The wizard Nathan and the sorceress Nicci had searched for a way to destroy the Lifedrinker, and she had no doubt they were applying themselves with as much determination to eliminate *her*—and Victoria would not stand for it. She felt the power of life, the power of the Creator, and knew she was stronger than any magic those two adversaries could hurl against her.

Even so, she did not underestimate their abilities.

Although Nicci claimed credit for killing the evil Lifedrinker, Victoria knew that the Eldertree acorn was truly responsible for that triumph. The sorceress was undeniably powerful, nevertheless, and Victoria did not want to be hindered in her sacred work. She already knew that Nicci was a nuisance, interfering where she was not wanted.

Although Nathan Rahl's ability to use magic was minimal, perhaps even imaginary, he was a man with great knowledge and experience, and thus a threat to her as well. There was something about the man, and Victoria did not wish to be sanguine about him, either.

They both must be stopped.

In the thriving thickets, trees, vines, and mushrooms swelled around her like a bubbling life spring. The buzz of swarming flies, bees, and beetles hummed an intense lullaby. As her wisdom and power expanded, Victoria recalled forgotten methods and incantations that the ancient wizards had sealed behind the camouflage shroud, preserved for millennia among the memmers.

With that knowledge, Victoria understood how to create a weapon to eradicate both Nicci and Nathan, perhaps a weapon strong enough to tear down Cliffwall, stone by stone. To activate the magic, Victoria didn't even need to move, because she *was* the forest, all the stirrings within, all the leaves and branches, the wings of insects, the flutter of birds. Everything belonged to her, was part of her.

She released the magic to create her emissary, an assassin, a manifestation of the jungle's primeval power: a *shaksis*. A *shaksis* was a creature molded entirely of debris, the detritus of the forest.

With her mind and her magic, Victoria gathered up fallen branches and gnarled twigs to serve as the bones and framework for the *shaksis*. She wove them together, building a wooden skeleton around which, with whiplike speed, she wound grass blades and dry leaves, forest mulch, and thorny twigs. Fungi inflated to fill out the muscles.

Victoria summoned an army of worms, beetles, maggots, and other crawling creatures to expand the creature's body. By the time the magical construct extended its arms and took tentative steps, its entire form boiled with a thousand points of life.

Two iridescent beetles, each as large as a fist, scuttled along the forest floor and crawled up the thing's body framework. Its rounded head was woven of bent twigs and supple willow, skinned with bark, thatched with dry grasses. Two hollows formed in what should have been its face, and the beetles crawled up the construct's head and nestled into the sockets to serve as surrogate eyes. A splintered branch across its lower face made a gash of a mouth. It clacked and chewed, broken spikes grinding together.

Pale green vines looped around its legs, winding and weaving into its flesh, like blood vessels filled with sap. The *shaksis* creaked as it stepped forward. It folded and unfolded its sharp branchlet fingers, while the two beetles inside its eye sockets stared out with a faceted, malevolent gaze.

Made of the jungle itself, the *shaksis* was Victoria's puppet, her

surrogate, her killer, a soulless thing that was merely an extension of
the primeval forest.

Victoria flashed it a warm and welcoming smile, a maternal smile.
She stroked the uneven chest, feeling the life she had deposited there, a
new child she had created. Into its hollow mind, she placed the details
of its mission—images of the blond sorceress and the pompous old
wizard with straight white hair.

"Find them and kill them," Victoria said. "Go with my blessing."

The animated construct turned and, with a rustle of brittle limbs,
stalked out of the forest toward Cliffwall.

CHAPTER 64

As he scouted through the gathering darkness, Bannon felt brave and important. After all his ordeals, he no longer hid from his past, no longer pretended that those dark memories didn't exist. He was not just Bannon, the son of a man who drank himself into blind violence and abused his family, a bitter man who drowned helpless kittens and beat his own wife to death. No, Bannon was no longer defined by his father.

Standing tall, he marched into the moonlit night on his scouting mission, wending his way through the still-dead foothills. Though the grasses and scrub trees were dry and brittle, he no longer felt the Lifedrinker's poison oozing from the hillsides. This was more like a normal landscape after a long winter: not dead but dormant, waiting to reawaken with spring. Now that the evil wizard was defeated, seeds would germinate, shoots would arise, meadows and forests would creep back.

But Victoria had been too impatient for that natural process. With a sick feeling in the pit of his stomach, Bannon considered the harm she had done with her explosive fecundity spell. Rather than letting the Scar awaken of its own accord, Victoria had effectively dashed icy water into the face of a deeply ill person.

He gritted his teeth as he trudged into the night, making his way toward the expanding jungle boundary. He paused to rest near a moonlit boulder and took out his waterskin to drink while he listened to the vast starlit darkness. He could sense the vibrating power of the proliferating forest and could hear the inevitable sounds of cracking, straining branches, growing trunks, writhing vines, stirring leaves. Combined, it sounded like evil laughter.

A sad shiver ran down his spine. He knew that Audrey, Laurel, and Sage were there in that mass of wild growth, corrupted by Victoria's out-of-control magic. His heart ached for them. He remembered their touch, their kisses, their laughter. He smiled to think of their warm breath in his ears, how he had loved to stroke their hair, touch their bodies. They couldn't be gone now! They were beautiful, wonderful, loving.

Then he fought back a wave of nausea as he recalled what they had done to Simon. If the scholar-archivist had not shoved him out of the way in his eagerness to go forward, *Bannon* would have been the one ripped into ribbons of meat, his blood spilled onto the soil to spawn more of their awful magic.

He pressed his knuckles hard into his eyes, wanting that memory to be just a dream, a nightmare . . . but it was real, in exactly the way his mother's murder had been real, the way he had abandoned Ian to the slavers. It was not a memory he could pretend would ever go away.

Feeling the hairs tingle on the back of his neck, he stepped away from the boulder, alert, sniffing the air. He whirled and looked above him to see Mrra crouched on the rock outcropping, her feline form sandy gold in the moonlight. The big cat let out a growling purr, but Bannon did not feel threatened. The sand panther knew who he was, possibly even understood that he was the one who had begged Nicci to heal her wounds, rather than kill her.

Mrra just sat there watching the night. As Bannon studied the powerful tawny form and the ugly symbols branded onto her hide, he was no longer reminded of the helpless drowned kittens. He was glad he had saved her, and in a sense, he had saved part of himself as well. Those limp, dead kittens had been a symbol of grief and guilt. The Adjudicator had found that agonizing experience inside him and dragged it to the front of Bannon's mind as his damnation.

Running away from Chiriya Island, he had sought a life for himself, not just for adventure but for self-preservation. Since then, he had found all he could have hoped for by joining Nathan and Nicci. He had discovered not just exciting adventures, but friendship, acceptance, and inner strength.

He realized that he had been fooling himself with the illusion of a perfect life, but the things he had discovered since venturing out into the world were so much more. More than anything, he remembered the look of respect and appreciation that Nicci had given him after he helped her kill the Lifedrinker. He had risked his life, given his all, and they had been victorious together. He didn't think his life could get better than that moment. Such thoughts eased his heavy memories of the bad things that had happened to him.

With a swish of her tail, Mrra vanished like a moon shadow into the night. After taking another swig of water, Bannon made his way onward, still hoping against hope that he could save the young acolytes who had so captured his heart, although he feared it might be too late.

The moon had set, and the night held its breath while waiting for the dawn. When Bannon finally reached the edge of the ever-spreading jungle, the demarcation was abrupt, with desolation on one side and a madness of foliage on the other. He could smell the leaves and the resinous wood, the potent aromas of wild vegetation.

Sword raised, Bannon faced the primeval forest, hoping he would not have to go inside. The twitching branches and gnarled, spasming vines unsettled him, but he shored up his courage. Drawing a deep breath, he called out, "I've come for you!" He meant to shout, but it came out as no more than a whisper. His voice cracked.

The vegetation snaked and curled. In the starlight, as his pupils dilated with fear, he spotted more movement, heard a stirring that was more than frenetically growing plants. They had heard him.

Beautiful feminine forms glided between the trunks, branches, and undulating vines. Even with the camouflage of their mottled skin, he could make out the beautiful bodies that were so familiar to him.

He said, "I came to save you."

Though the young women were fundamentally transformed, he still recognized Audrey, Laurel, and Sage. His breath was hot in his mouth, and his pulse raced. He had seen what these forest women could do, and he knew they were monsters . . . yet still he wanted them. Their enhanced scent was thick in the air, making him dizzy.

"Come with me," he begged. "We can go back to Cliffwall. We'll find a spell to make you normal again. Don't you want to be with me?"

They laughed in unison, a musical sound that made all the branches stir. "Don't be silly," said the thing that had been Sage. "We are so much more now. Why don't you come with us? Think of how we could pleasure you with all of our new skills."

Bannon could barely breathe. His vision blurred. They seemed more intensely lovely than he remembered them, more than anyone he'd ever seen, any woman he could imagine. Something about their scent . . .

Flowers suddenly sprang up all around them, a spray of intense violet-and-crimson blossoms that he recognized with a shudder. The deathrise flower! The smell made him dizzy, and in the back of his mind he knew that Nicci must have been wrong about these blossoms, because surely this was the most beautiful, exquisite poison in the world!

Unbidden, he took a step forward. The three young women extended their emerald arms, exuding a mist of attracting chemicals. The lovely, but deadly, flowers bloomed around them.

Tears filled Bannon's eyes, because he *wanted* them so much. He remembered how wonderful they were, how sweet and caring, how innocent, and yet how skilled when they had made love to him.

"We can be together," he said, "if only you'll just—"

Laurel interrupted him. "Yes, we can be together. Always."

"We want you now more than ever," said Audrey. "We are more fertile, more filled with desire."

"We can be everything you want," Sage added. "And you will give us everything we need."

They spread their arms, and their breasts beckoned him. Their dark green nipples looked like flower buds. Bannon yearned for them. He had meant to come and argue, to fight to take them back. The sword felt slick in his hand. Even with its leather grip, his palms were so sweaty, he could barely hold on.

"Come to us, Bannon," said Laurel.

The other two echoed the invitation.

He could not resist. He succumbed, gliding toward the edge of the jungle.

With a great blow, a growling, furred form crashed into him. The full weight of a sand panther knocked him off his feet and tumbled him out of the reach of the vicious forest girls.

The beautiful apparitions snarled, their mouths opening to reveal long woody fangs. Their arms stretched out, coiled with vines, corded muscles, and tendons. Their fingers reached out for him, tipped with hooked thorns. The smooth, perfect green skin on their arms became studded with deadly barbs that dripped with milky venom.

Gasping, Bannon rolled over and tried to catch his breath. The spell was broken. Mrra bounded away, then circled back, snarling. The forest women reached out with a thorn-studded embrace, trying to catch Bannon before he got out of reach.

He instinctively slashed with Sturdy, lopping off one of Audrey's arms. It dropped to the ground, and its severed stump twitched, extended, and grew roots, digging deep into the ground while the arm continued to grope upward for him.

Howling, Audrey raised the stump of her arm, and a new limb grew from the severed end, a tangle of vines, muscles, and blood vessels reemerging to restore her.

Bannon hacked at them, swinging his sword sideways, then up, then back down, splintering the female forms. They did not bleed red, but spilled oozing green sap.

"I wanted to save you," he cried.

The three just laughed as they regrew into contorted new forms with additional branchlike arms that sprang from their shoulders and torsos. Their hair became a wild, marshy tangle of strands.

The sand panther retreated, growling to Bannon. He backed away onto the rocky, desolate ground where the forest avatars could not yet go. From their verdant refuge, they simply glared at him, and Bannon stared back, sobbing. Tears ran down his cheeks. "I thought I loved you."

"We will have you again," the women said in a single rasping voice like dry leaves crackling in a fire. "We will have you forever."

CHAPTER 65

The broad grin on Nathan's face made Nicci immediately suspicious. "I may just know where to find the answer, Sorceress!" The old wizard stopped her in the hallway as she made her way to her chambers, where Thistle was already asleep.

She allowed herself a moment of hope. "You are certain of this spell?"

Nathan's smile faltered. "'Certainty' is an overused term, to be sure. I am confident, let us leave it at that. See here." He set the thick volume on a bench in one of the corridors.

He opened the pages, drew his fingers down a line of archaic text. "It is just a clue, but the best clue we've had. You already gave me the incantation and the spell-form that the memmers think Victoria used, and that provided some excellent parameters for a counterspell or a weapon. We knew the essence of what we were fighting, but not how to do so."

He tapped a stained page where tight handwriting had run together as the ink dissolved. "This gives us somewhere to look, a listing of other books that also shed more light about the Lifedrinker."

"He is no longer a concern," Nicci said. "I killed him."

"Yes, yes, but think of how they are connected. Roland's spell stole too much from the world, and now Victoria's will restore too much. It is all a matter of control, finding a way to modulate the flow of hungry magic, the power of giving and taking."

"Like a valve," Nicci said, unconsciously biting her lower lip. "The

Lifedrinker said he had opened up the magic with his spell, but the flow was too strong. He could not stop himself."

"And neither can Victoria," Nathan said. "Both Roland and Victoria were conduits for the magic. When you destroyed the Lifedrinker, you shut off his flow of death. Now we must destroy Victoria and stop the flow in the opposite direction."

"I couldn't agree more," Nicci said. She looked up as three scholars hurried past them, eager for their dinner. Another middle-aged man strolled by, holding an open book in his hands, reading as he walked. She continued, "I simply need to know how to do it."

Nathan pointed at the stained pages again. "This listing identifies a volume we need to find, and I have reason to believe it is buried in the vault beneath the damaged tower, where those other scattered books were hidden. It is very late now, but we can try to excavate tomorrow."

"And you know where to look?" Nicci asked, thinking of the unexplored maze of damaged rooms and passages underground. "Exactly?"

Nathan smiled. "Mia does."

Though it had left the riotous fecundity of the primeval jungle behind, the *shaksis* could still feel the power of Life's Mistress driving its mission. As the creature walked across the desolate ground on limbs made of twisted vines and leaves, motivated by swarms of worms, spiders, and insects, the *shaksis* kept drawing energy from a distance.

It continued across the desolate Scar through the night. Though parts broke off in the dry rocks and jagged uplifts, the *shaksis* replenished itself with plant matter once it reached the foothills and walked through scrub brush and tangled grasses. The dead vegetation came alive again, whipping around its body, strengthening its limbs, winding like armor around its body core.

Finally, in the darkest hour before dawn, the creature faced the sheer cliff of the plateau uplift. The *shaksis* knew that its two victims were inside the hidden enclave high above.

Because Victoria knew all about Cliffwall, the *shaksis* remembered how to ascend that sheer rock, using the hidden handholds and the faint trail that had isolated the great archive for millennia. The golem of reanimated twigs and vines turned its hollow head upward and stared at the cliff with living-beetle eyes.

An agile person could climb the path to reach the hooded overhang above, but the *shaksis* did not need agility; it had a different kind of power. It reached out with the splayed branches of its hands and touched the stone. With a surge of vibrant life, the fingers grew. Vine tendrils extended and worked their way into the rock, like the roots of a cling- ing windswept tree. The *shaksis* reached with a branchy arm, slapped its hand higher up, and fastened with root tendrils. Its bulging wooden muscles groaned. The vermin infesting its hollow body skittered around, adding energy, squirming.

The *shaksis* pulled itself upward.

A wooden foot found a notch in the rocks and anchored there, while the tendrils released from the first hand, and it climbed higher, stretch- ing and cracking. The insects and grubs made a simmering, humming sound that was lost in the silent gulf of the night.

Staring through scarab eyes, the *shaksis* ascended. It had little room for thoughts in the dried leaves that filled its head. But it held a vivid image of Nicci, of Nathan.

Its targets.

Shouts awakened Nicci from a deep sleep, and she rolled off her pal- let into a fighting crouch, instantly alert and aware. Fortunately, tonight her dreams had not entangled with the sand panther's mind; otherwise she might not have been able to extricate herself quickly enough.

Thistle sprang from her warm sheepskin on the floor and pulled aside the door hanging as more shouts echoed down the corridor, which was lined with shelves of disorganized books. Even where the scholars slept, wall shelves were crammed with old volumes, stacks of scrolls, folded parchments, and documents the students had taken out to read, but not yet reshelved.

Nathan Rahl, exhausted from his studies and eager to ransack the underground vaults the following morning, emerged in rumpled sleeping robes. He fumbled for his ornate sword and drew it from its scabbard, ready to fight, but he had not found the source of the shouting. Nicci joined him.

Then they saw the thing coming toward them, an inhuman soldier made of brambles, wicker, and tangled thorns. It strode forward with a crackle of limbs and an aura of buzzing noises.

One unfortunate scholar emerged from his quarters just as the creature passed. Reacting to a potential target, the thing lashed out. In an instant, its arm grew long spiky thorns, and the limb curved around and impaled the young scholar, whose mouth opened, gaping, then gasping, and finally spurting a gush of blood as the long wooden spikes found his organs. The stalking creature tossed the dead man aside.

Other horrified scholars in the halls screamed; some remained frozen in place, while others fled.

Thistle clung close to Nicci. "What is that monster?"

"I believe it is a *shaksis*," Nathan said. "Made from the detritus of the forest, castaway items from the underbrush."

"What does it want?" cried one of the scholars, dismayed to see the bloody corpse of his comrade still twitching on the floor.

The *shaksis* lurched forward. The buzzing around its body grew louder.

Nicci knew. "Victoria sent the thing. It wants us."

Two bright beetles nestled in the creature's eye sockets turned toward Nicci's voice. Seeing her, the *shaksis* became animated and began to run toward them down the hall.

Turning to face the attacker, Nicci pushed the orphan girl behind her, while Nathan raised his sword. The frightened scholars ducked into their alcoves.

The *shaksis* surged closer, extending arms like wildly growing vines. Its entire body seemed to swarm with small moving bugs and grubs. The reanimated forest creature drove straight toward Nathan and Nicci.

The wizard hacked at the *shaksis* with his sword, as if he were a woodcutter felling an unruly sapling. One of the creature's wooden arms snapped and shattered, then dropped to the stone floor. Insects and worms spilled out like a spray of bizarre, festering blood. The *shaksis* drew back its stump. Twigs, vines, and grasses curled around, extending outward as the limb regrew.

Nathan hacked off its other arm, again wielding his sword like an axe, but this time the *shaksis* regrew even faster. The severed vegetation lashed and whipped, then sprang back into place.

"This will require more than a sword, Wizard." Nicci raised a hand and released a blast of air that rattled into the creature, but it anchored itself, reaching out its branchy arms. It was hollow, woven of wicker, and the breezes whipped and whistled through it. More writhing bugs scuttled across the floor.

"I can't unleash my black lightning or wizard's fire in here," Nicci said. "It would destroy all of the books and the people trapped in the corridor."

The *shaksis* lunged forward, extending its sharp hands. Nathan swept his sword again, letting out a loud grunt with the effort. "There's barely room to swing my blade."

Nicci hammered at the thing with another fist of air. The creature staggered. Books tumbled off the shelves, their pages flapping. In response, the *shaksis* stretched out tangled limbs and seized another scholar who tried to slip away to safety. Vines and thorns curled around the young man, snapped his neck, then tossed his discarded body up against the wall, knocking down an entire shelf of books.

Struggling to control the level of destruction, Nicci called a single bolt of lightning that struck and splintered the thing's thick left leg, rendering it unbalanced. Even though it smoked and smoldered, the tottering creature regrew itself.

Nicci and Nathan stood shoulder-to-shoulder as a barricade, refusing to let the creature past—but it did not want to pass. It wanted to kill them. With a thrashing of uncontrolled branches and dry leaves, along with a buzzing of hungry insects, it pushed back against Nicci's blasts of air. Nathan hacked again, splintering the encroaching branches.

From behind her, Thistle said, "I'll get a torch to light that monster on fire." She darted away, but she didn't get far.

The *shaksis* reacted to her movement, and a long whip of its thorny arm extended. Even though Nicci's magic shoved against the thing's body core, the deadly elongated arm seized Thistle. Sharp finger-thorns pierced the girl's skinny leg and drew blood. She kicked and fought, trying to pull away.

Rage rose within Nicci. She didn't hesitate, did not exercise caution in the confined corridor. This monster had to be stopped. She summoned a ball of flame—normal flame, since wizard's fire could have been catastrophic—and exploded the blaze into the *shaksis*.

Flames immediately caught inside its torso, raging through its skeleton of bent branches and dried vegetation. Roasting insects burst or fled. Worms squirmed out, sizzling. Even as the *shaksis* burned, in a surge of desperation it plodded forward and extended its blazing arms toward Nicci. She shoved back with a blow of solid air and knocked the living inferno against the wall. Some splintered, charred pieces of the forest golem still clattered and twitched, grasping out for any victim.

The forest construct broke into flaming ashes, finally dead. But the embers scattered among the clustered books and stacked scrolls. Because of the speed of her attack and the rush of the air she had unleashed, the volumes quickly caught fire, their pages blackened and curled. Flames raged along the shelves, spreading from one to the next. The fabric door hangings in front of the private quarters also ignited.

Despite her bleeding leg, Thistle ran to their quarters and yanked down the door hanging and tried to put out the spreading fire. Nathan did the same as they yelled for more scholars to help, and they all worked together to stop the inferno.

Nicci released more magic, calling upon the air again, summoning moisture to douse the larger flames. She stole air away to starve the fire until it guttered down to a low smolder.

Cliffwall scholars rushed from other chambers and corridors to aid in quenching the blaze before it could spread to the larger libraries and vaults of books. Seeing their murdered comrades, some of them gasped, halted in their efforts to fight the insidious fire, but others swallowed hard, faced the crisis, and turned their attention to saving the books, the scrolls, the library itself.

One woman, sniffling, struggling to control her weeping, knelt by the first dead and broken scholar. She adjusted his body, his head, and began to pick up the blood-spattered books strewn on the floor from the splintered shelf.

When they had the fire under control, Nicci turned her attention to Thistle and saw that her thigh was bleeding heavily. Without asking, Nicci pressed her palms hard against the deep wound, and released magic to heal the girl and remove the pain.

Thistle laughed with relief. "I knew you'd save me."

The wizard shook his head. His face was smudged with soot. He plucked a squirming beetle grub out of his white hair and crushed it between his fingertips.

Then, just after the ruckus died down, Bannon returned to Cliffwall, gasping and disheveled, weary from an ordeal of his own. His eyes shone with excitement as he pushed his way through the crowded corridor.

"I just got back. Sweet Sea Mother, you won't believe the night I've had!" He ran his hands through his bedraggled red hair, and he finally noticed the destruction and turmoil around him for the first time. "Oh! What happened here?"

CHAPTER 66

The attack of the *shaksis* made clear Victoria's ruthless intent. The next morning, with an odd smile, Nicci nodded with satisfaction. "That means she is afraid of us."

"And well she should be, my dear sorceress," Nathan said as they worked their way into the tunnels beneath the damaged prophecy tower. "I would feel much more confident, though, if we can find the hidden volume that holds the means to destroy her."

"It's down here," Mia said, winding them through the twisted, claustrophobic tunnels.

Down in the dusty vault, where the damaged ceilings were slumped and alarmingly uneven, Mia brought them to a small room where stone walls had melted like candle wax over stacks of books. With an intent expression, the mousy researcher pointed to one thick tome fused partway into the rock. She couldn't hide her excitement. "This one! See the spine? It is exactly the book we're looking for. It matches what was on the list."

Nicci touched the volume and felt its extreme age. "The pages will be difficult to read," she said, "since it is part of the wall."

Nathan gave a futile tug, but could not break the grip of the stone. He looked at her. "Mia has a small amount of the gift, and I would generally encourage her to practice. In fact, under normal circumstances I would just do this myself." He frowned at the trapped book. "But because of the importance, Sorceress, and since you are the only one with the proper control of magic, could you manipulate the stone and release the volume for us?"

"Agreed. This is not an instance where one should resort to dabbling." Nicci ran her fingers over the binding, touched where the pages had seamlessly blended into the stone, and released her magic. A small flow pushed aside the rock, but did not separate the paper and the leather-bound cover from the stone matrix. She concentrated harder, working to extricate the fused elements. "The bond is not easily separable."

"You never shy from difficult things," Nathan said. "You can do it."

"Yes, I can. Just not perfectly."

She moved the fundamental grains of rock and released the locked pages, but some of the fibers remained intertwined. When she finally withdrew the damaged book from its rock prison, some of the pages were still stiff and powdery, as if the last reader had been a sloppy bricklayer with mortar on his hands. Nevertheless, Nathan took the volume from her and pored over the words with an eager Mia close beside him, under the glow of a flickering hand light.

"This is it. This is the deep life spell!" Mia grinned. "Just what we were looking for."

"Good," Nicci said. "Now tell me how we can neutralize Victoria."

Nathan looked at her in alarm. "Dear spirits, it is not so simple as that!"

"It never is. Just tell me what to do."

"This will require some study." Nathan and Mia conferred over the damaged words on the brittle pages. "Ah, yes, that seems clear enough." He looked up at Nicci, explaining, "What Victoria used was a deeply bound life spell, drawn from the bones of the world. That is where Life's Mistress receives her energy, and that is the only way we can stop her." He looked up. "The only way to shut off the valve from her uncontrollable flow of magic."

Mia pulled the book closer to herself and pointed excitedly. "Some words on the bottom of the page are damaged, but the answer is clear." She drew a quick breath. "It's the way we can defeat Victoria."

"I'm pleased to have a clear answer for once." Nicci crossed her arms over her chest. "And what is the weapon?"

"A special bow," Nathan said. "Such an enemy can be destroyed with an arrow, and the archer must be someone with a great command of the gift, a powerful wizard or sorceress."

"That would be me," Nicci said, already anticipating the task. "And I know how to use a bow."

The wizard shook his head. "Alas, it is not so simple as that, Sorceress. The life spell itself is intertwined with the most ancient creatures, the very structure of the world. The arrow must be shot from a special bow—a bow made from the rib bone of a dragon."

Nicci drew in a quick breath of the dusty, still air in the newly opened vault. The magical fire in her hand light flickered. "The rib of a dragon?"

Nathan's voice became troubled as the excitement faded. "Indeed. I can see how that poses a problem."

Mia's disappointment was clear. "Dragons are extinct."

Now that she had a potential answer, though, Nicci refused to give up hope. "*Nearly* extinct."

The scholars gathered in one of the large meeting rooms. A fire of mesquite wood burned in the hearth, sending a warm, savory fragrance into the chamber. Nathan had shown the ancient volume to the intent researchers, and they were all abuzz with the possibility.

"We must take action, and soon." The wizard spoke in a firm, serious tone. "The *shaksis* was only Victoria's first foray against us. I think she meant to catch us in our sleep, but she may also have been testing us. The next attack will certainly be more dangerous."

"And she grows stronger with every inch of territory she claims with that monstrous jungle," Nicci said.

Bannon sat near the hearth, sharpening his sword and brooding. His face was grave. "After what I saw last night, I am convinced there is no other way. Those poor girls . . ." He swallowed hard. "There was no saving them. We have to do what's right. If we don't stop that rampant growth, Victoria will cause as much destruction as the Life-drinker."

"We have to protect Cliffwall." Franklin sounded alarmed. "Should we block off the other side of the plateau? Seal the window alcoves? How do we make sure nothing can get in from the Scar? Like the *shaksis*."

"We know she is coming for us," Mia said.

Nicci nodded. "Blocking the openings would help, but only as a temporary measure. Once Victoria's jungle reaches the cliffs, her vines and heavy tree roots will crack open the mesa itself. We have to stop her before then." She raked her gaze over them. "I don't care how difficult it is. We must kill her."

"And now we know how to do that," Nathan said, "thanks to the lost volume that dear Mia and I found." He smiled over at the attentive female scholar. The other memmers and scholars muttered uncertainly. Having lost both Simon and Victoria, their two factions were adrift, leaderless. "Our powerful sorceress needs to shoot Life's Mistress with an arrow, using a bow made out of a dragon's rib." His voice faltered. "We only need to find a dragon."

Most dragons had been gone for many years, especially in the Old World, and the devastating Chainfire spell had erased even the memory of dragons from humanity for a time, but they still existed. They had to exist.

Bannon let out a sad laugh. "Of course! It's so simple. And once we find a dragon, we just have to slay it and cut a rib from its carcass." He sat down heavily on the hearth. "Sweet Sea Mother, I don't suppose that would take more than a day or two. What are we waiting for?"

"In the last days of the war against the Imperial Order, the witch woman Six flew on a great red dragon in her attacks on the D'Haran army," Nicci said. "The dragon's name was Gregory, but he is far away now, and we would never find him."

Thistle had taken one of the large chairs, curling her knees up on the seat in an awkward but oddly flexible position. She scoffed at the young man, teasing him like a little sister. "We don't need to find and kill a dragon. We just need a dragon *rib*."

Nathan spoke in a professorial tone. "Dear child, dragon ribs come from dragons. How do you expect us to find a rib bone without finding a dragon?"

Thistle gave a groan of frustration. "I mean we don't have to find a live dragon and kill it. We just need to find a rib *bone*. That means we're looking for a dragon *skeleton*."

Bannon looked annoyed. "Sure. That's much easier. They must be lying all over the place."

Nicci had a sudden memory of when she and her hostage Richard had crossed the Midlands as they made their way down to Altur'Rang. On their journey they had found the rotting carcass of a dragon. "I've seen such a skeleton, but it was far up in the Midlands."

"Even if we could find it again, the journey alone would take months, if not years," Nathan said.

The girl groaned again. "That isn't where you'd look for dragon skeletons." She gave an exasperated sigh.

"Where would you propose we look?" Bannon asked.

"Kuloth Vale, of course," she replied, as if he were the uneducated child. "Everyone knows that."

"We are not from here," Nicci said. "What is Kuloth Vale?"

"In my village I grew up hearing stories about the great graveyard of dragons. Kuloth Vale." Thistle looked around the room, and the scholars muttered, clearly expressing concern. Some of them, though, seemed familiar with the tale. Among the memmers, Gloria nodded.

"Kuloth Vale is far away," said Mia, "a sheltered hanging valley in the mountains to the north, and it's a dangerous place. That is where the dragons go to die."

The scholars consulted among themselves. Franklin spoke with his eyes half closed, reciting from memory: "'All dragons have an instinctive bond to the magical place of Kuloth Vale. The bones of hundreds of dragons lie there at rest.'" His voice became ominous. "'No human has ever gone there and returned to tell the tale.'"

"Then how was the tale ever recorded?" Nathan asked.

Gloria nodded gravely. "That is a mystery yet to be explained."

Nicci said, "If you know of this graveyard of dragons, then surely we can find a rib bone and come back swiftly."

Though always eager for an adventure, even Bannon looked doubtful. "Sounds like chasing mist dancers on a foggy night."

But Nicci had heard all she needed to hear. "Our alternative is to wait here while Victoria's jungle keeps spreading, and hope that a dragon happens to fly by so we can kill it and take a rib."

"I see. When you frame the debate in that way, Sorceress, even Kuloth Vale sounds like a preferable alternative," Nathan said.

Thistle looked up at her with an intent gaze. "Kuloth Vale is real. I've heard stories all my life."

Bannon rolled his eyes. "You're not even twelve years old."

Nicci turned to the gathered scholars. "You've been gathering maps to help us on our journey, Wizard. Have you found any that show the location of Kuloth Vale?"

"If no one has ever seen the graveyard of dragons, how could they make a map?" Bannon asked.

"Another unexplained mystery," Franklin said.

Nicci did not give in to frustration. She would follow this lead, knowing it was their best chance. "While we are gone, the rest of you must shore up the defenses of Cliffwall in case Victoria sends more attackers against you." Thistle slid off the chair, stretched her legs, and moved to stand by Nicci.

"The journey to Kuloth Vale will take many days," Mia said, "across unknown terrain."

"We have done that before," Nicci said. "The sooner we leave, the sooner we will return. With a dragon rib."

CHAPTER 67

The sketchy maps from the Cliffwall archives gave them a starting point in their search for the legendary graveyard of dragons, and Nicci and her companions set off with confidence. With full packs and fresh traveling clothes, they moved up through isolated canyons, climbing into the desert highlands, away from the great valley.

Full of energy, Thistle took point as they headed north toward a distant line of rugged gray mountains that looked volcanic in origin. The air was clear and the terrain expansive, which made the distances uncertain.

"Those mountains are many days away," Nathan said, "even if we keep up a good pace."

Nicci kept moving. "Then we should not slow."

The wizard paused to wipe his brow. He withdrew a white kerchief that Mia had shyly given him before their departure, and he looked at it with a curious smile. "Let's see if that dear girl's spell worked." He wiped the cloth across his face, then brightened. "Ah yes, moist and cool and refreshing. She promised me it was a simple, innocuous spell, but I find it quite effective."

Nicci had been there when the quiet young scholar had given Nathan the white rag. Mia promised that the spell would always keep the kerchief cool and moist to ease a traveler's burden. "Simple and innocuous," Nicci agreed. "But no matter how gifted the scholars may be, I am reluctant to see them dabbling with any sort of magic. They are all untrained. Think of the damage they have already done, unaware of what they were doing . . . the melted archive tower, the Lifedrinker, now Victoria and her mad jungle."

"It is just a kerchief, Sorceress . . ." Nathan said.

"And that is how it begins."

Embarrassed, he tucked it away in his pocket, but she did see him using it often during the heat of the afternoon, especially in steep terrain.

They walked all day, taking only brief rests for water and a quick meal. Ranging ahead, Thistle killed several plump lizards to supplement their meals, not because they needed the food, but because she enjoyed the hunt.

By the second day, they left the high desert, and the terrain grew more forested. In the rolling hills they found brooks to refill their waterskins and even a grove of wild plum trees. With the simple joy of finding plentiful fresh fruit, they ate far too many plums, particularly Bannon. That evening, they all suffered from stomach cramps and knotted intestines.

The following day Nicci sensed an animal presence watching them, and she realized that Mrra had trailed them up from the valley. She caught a flash of tawny fur gliding among the low trees in the distance, staying close. Still spell-bonded with Nicci, the big cat followed wherever her sister panther traveled, but maintained her independence.

Nicci was pleased just to know of the animal's presence. She sensed the big cat's need to hunt, and with a distant thrill in her veins, she felt Mrra on the chase, the pounding heart, the taste of iron-hot blood, and the squeal and twitch of fresh prey brought down.

When Nicci led them into a small meadow in late afternoon, they found a bloody deer carcass, freshly slaughtered. Its guts were torn open and the liver had been devoured, but the rest of the meat remained intact. Nathan and Bannon were immediately wary that the predator was still nearby, but Nicci dropped to her knees next to the deer. "Mrra hunted for us. She's had her fill and left the rest for our supper."

The wizard brightened. "Dear spirits, now that's a different story. Let's have a good meal."

While Nicci prepared a fire, Thistle and Bannon worked together to carve out strips of venison to roast over the flames. The girl admitted that it tasted better than her lizards. After the feast, they bedded down on the soft meadow grass, satisfied. The next morning, they wrapped some of the steaks in fresh green leaves, and Nicci worked a simple preservative spell to keep the meat from going bad. They carried the meat in their packs.

Over the next several days they wound through trackless areas and ascended sheer gorges that rose into more rugged terrain, but the sharp, volcanic mountains remained very far away.

"I don't recall hearing of Kuloth Vale in my histories," Nathan mused. He enjoyed talking to Bannon as they walked, although the others listened as well. "But I did read many tales of the Midwar, records of when Emperor Kurgan conquered the south of the continent. General Utros and his invincible armies swept across the land, and city after city fell. He had wizard warriors, as well as hordes of expendable soldiers.

"When he set off to lay siege to the remarkable city of Ildakar, Utros knew he would face extraordinarily powerful magic, so he needed a special weapon." Nathan looked down at Thistle and dropped his voice into a dramatic whisper. "They captured a dragon—a silver dragon." The girl's eyes widened.

"I've never heard of a silver dragon," Bannon said. "Are they special?"

"All dragons are special, my boy—and they have always been rare. Angry red dragons, aloof green dragons, wise gray dragons, evil black dragons. But, General Utros wanted a *silver* dragon."

"Why?" Thistle asked.

"Because silver dragons are the best fighters." Nathan waved a persistent white butterfly away from his face, which fluttered off to seek flowers instead. "But they are not easily tamed or controlled. Utros's warriors did manage to capture one such beast, and they kept it chained and harnessed. The army intended to turn it loose once they reached Ildakar.

"But one night the dragon snapped its bonds and broke free, devouring the harness and then the handlers. It could simply have flown away, but instead the dragon took vengeance. The silver monster ripped through the army camp and slaughtered hundreds of the Iron Fang's soldiers. General Utros barely escaped with his life, though the side of his face was burned, scarred from dragon fire. The silver dragon flew away, leaving his army a shambles, but General Utros would never go back to Emperor Kurgan and admit failure. So he pressed on, hoping to find some other way to conquer Ildakar."

Nathan continued his story as they moved through the forest until they reached the crest of a hill, where they could see the towering black mountains rising closer at last. "But when his armies arrived at Ildakar, Utros found that the entire city had vanished! One of the greatest cities in the Old World, entirely gone."

"How? Where did it go?" Thistle asked.

The wizard shrugged. "No one knows. The legend is fifteen centuries old, so it could just be a story."

"Let's hope that Kuloth Vale is more than just a story," Nicci said.

That night they slept next to a roaring campfire as the winds picked up through the thin trees. Nathan agreed to stand first watch while the rest of them bedded down. Thistle curled up in her blanket, as comfortable on the hard forest floor as she had been in the stone chamber at Cliffwall, although she missed her soft sheepskin.

Nicci lay near the girl. Listening to the crackle of the fire with her eyes closed, she extended her senses, but picked up no immediate danger in the nearby forests. Her mind touched the sand panther, however, and from a distance, Mrra felt the bond as well. The big cat affirmed that they were safe from any threats, so Nicci let herself fall into a deep sleep. . . .

While her body rested, her dreams ranged far, once again inside the mind of her sister panther. Mrra was more content in this sort of terrain than in either the desolate Scar or the unsettling primeval jungle. Here, the hills felt normal, and she experienced true freedom.

As the cat loped along in the night, Mrra's mind was attuned to the world, while also in touch with pristine memories, which Nicci experienced. Mrra remembered her spell-bonded *troka* mates, who would romp together, biting, clawing, pretending to hurt but causing no real damage.

The handlers soon forced stricter, deadlier training upon them. At first, the wild sand panthers resisted, but then they learned to enjoy the fight, the kill. In her dream state, Nicci also experienced the remembered pleasure of clawing her victims, from terrified humans who offered little fight, to horrific monsters created by the fleshmancers for the combat arena.

With singing adrenaline, Mrra remembered a particular beast she and her sister panthers had fought in the gladiator arena before shouting crowds, spectators who demanded blood, demanded death—though Mrra did not understand whose blood they wanted. Under the guidance of the wizard commander, the fleshmancers had altered, manipulated, and *twisted* a powerful bull into a fighting beast with a rack of four sharp, curved horns, a flat armored head, and steel-hard bony hooves that struck sparks from the arena gravel. The monster bull was far more massive than the three cats combined, but the *troka* had to fight it. Mrra and her sister panthers understood that.

As the demon bull charged forward with an ear-shattering bellow that overwhelmed the giddy roar of the crowd, the sand panthers had split apart, each knowing what her sisters were doing. Coordinating their attack, the *troka* circled the giant snorting beast.

The bull lumbered forward, picking up momentum, and Mrra sprang to one side while her sister panthers circled and struck from behind. One raked the beast's left haunch, leaving parallel bloody gouges down its hide. The other cat sprang for the demon bull's throat, but the creature's muscles were like corded steel, and her curved fangs could make only shallow bites.

Mrra stood her ground as the monster thundered forward, too heavy and too swift to stop. She leaped for its head, clawed at its eyes, but the bull knocked her to the ground, nearly crushing her. She felt her ribs crack. Blood burst inside of her. Pain exploded in her mind at the same time that the bull's hot blood poured down upon her from the deep wounds.

Through the spell bond, she experienced her two sister panthers leaping onto the bull's back, using claws and saber teeth to tear deep wounds. With a great bellow, the beast threw them off, striking more sparks with its enhanced hooves as it lashed out in search of a target.

Mrra rolled in the dusty sand, listened to the roaring cheers, ignoring the pain of her broken ribs. *This* was what the handlers wanted her to do. *This* was why she and the entire *troka* existed. Moving as one being, the three panthers attacked again. Even though the bull charged, even though the panthers were already injured, eventually they wore the monster down.

The fleshmancers watched from the stands, scowling with displeasure to see that the specialized combat monster they had created could be defeated by three panthers.

Mrra and her sisters tore the twisted bull into tatters of gore. Its entrails dangled from its stomach, but like a great senseless machine, it still lumbered and charged until it collapsed with a grunt and a spray of dark blood. Its thick pink tongue gasped out of its mouth, and the beast died with a rattling exhale.

Mrra and her sisters stood together, bloody and in pain, their tails thrashing. They looked up, waiting for the handlers to come and retrieve them. Even with the deep-seated agony from her broken bones and gashed hide, Mrra had felt content. The sound that bubbled from her chest was more a purr than a growl, because she had done what the handlers had trained her to do.

She had killed. She had defeated the enemy.

During the late part of the night, while Nathan curled up near the fire and went to sleep, Bannon took second watch. He sat on a fallen log, his sword ready, looking out for his friends and listening for any threats out in the forest.

Nicci slept soundly, lost in dreams. She twitched, and a low sound came from her throat, something like a feline growl. The sorceress was so deep in the dream, she was vulnerable. Nicci had warned them about this, and Bannon did not intend to let her down.

He sat alert, guarding her until Nicci finally awoke at dawn.

CHAPTER 68

After days of hard travel, they finally reached the volcanic mountains. Very little vegetation poked through the crumbly rust-brown soil, and the boulders were porous pumice, honeycombed with fossilized air pockets. Lichen and moss mottled the lava boulders.

Standing on a high ridge, Nathan studied the crude charts from Cliffwall so he could get his bearings. "This way. Almost there." No one questioned his definition of "almost." He wiped his brow with Mia's special kerchief, then tucked it away before setting off, refreshed.

"I hope you're correct," Nicci replied. "We have been gone for too long already, and Life's Mistress will keep growing more powerful back there in the valley." Seeing the breathtaking sweep of the rampant growth, she had no doubt this scourge would grow even faster than the Lifedrinker's desolation. Yet again, she would have to stop an enemy that would threaten Lord Rahl, the D'Haran Empire, the Old World and the New.

After pushing through the untracked mountains, they finally arrived at a saddle that overlooked a stark and secluded hanging valley. The rocky bowl below was guarded by sharp volcanic barricades and towering rock spires, like a walled-off preserve skirted with glaciers and broken cliffs. The black-rock basin held patches of snow and a partially frozen lake among the giant boulders and pinnacles of solidified ash.

Nicci recognized the place instinctively, and she could feel in her heart that this was where they needed to be. "Kuloth Vale," she whispered.

Thistle pointed eagerly. "Look! See the bones?"

Looking closer, Nicci could discern the scattered white skeletons of enormous creatures—dozens of them, lying stark against the desolation.

The sharp breezes blew Nathan's white hair into his face. He wore a satisfied smile. "Dragon bones, all right," he said, as if he were particularly familiar with such things.

Bannon craned his head upward and peered into the sky as if expecting to see the angular silhouette of a circling dragon.

"We have to get down there," Nicci said. She paused to assess the difficult route down into the rocky valley, but Thistle set off like a mountain goat, making her way down the loose rocks. When the scree slid beneath her, she merely hopped to a more stable boulder, and kept descending into the bleak basin.

With the goal finally in sight, Nicci picked her way down the slope without dwelling on the spectacular scenery. Bannon and Nathan followed close behind them, the wizard toiling with great care and the young man offering unwanted help. Behind them, Mrra remained at the top of the ridge, a silhouette in the afternoon light; the panther did not go farther, refusing to enter Kuloth Vale. Nicci knew the big cat would make her own choices.

Among the broken black rocks at the bottom of the bowl, they came upon the first dragon skeleton. Its rib bones had collapsed in like the legs of a dead spider. Time and weather had twisted the vertebrae. Its skull was hollow, and many of its long fangs had fallen loose. Its empty eye sockets stared upward at eternity.

Nathan went to the skeleton and tugged on a curved rib. "Should we just take the first one and go?" He rapped his knuckles on the hollow-sounding ivory. "You could fashion one of these into a bow."

Bannon looked at the wizard in disbelief. "We can't leave yet! We have to explore. This is the lost graveyard of dragons—think of the stories!"

"We need to choose the right bone," Nicci said. "I want to test the size and resiliency of the ribs."

They moved among the grim clutter, exploring the wealth of ribs, vertebrae, and skulls in the final resting place of the last dragons.

The wizard paused beside a towering skeleton to which some shreds of scaled hide still clung. Nicci examined the enormous skull, which was as large as an oxcart. Its long fangs were pitted, possibly rotten with age. The rib bones that curved majestically up from the skeleton were twice her height. Even in this faint remnant, Nicci could feel the power still resident in this great creature. She understood the closely bonded life magic throbbing within the bones. Yes, a bow made from such a rib could hold enough power to quench Victoria's rampant spell.

"This one looks like a black dragon," Nathan said. Each ebony scale was the size of his outstretched hand. "A great dragon, possibly a king among his kind."

Nicci was more pragmatic. "Perhaps so, but this rib is far too large for me to use. We need to find a more appropriate skeleton."

Moving around the upthrust volcanic rock, Bannon paused to inspect another set of collapsed bones. Nathan came up beside him, nodding. "Look there, see the slight differences in the shape of the head and the structure of the wing bones? This was a green dragon, I believe. Note the horn protrusions on its snout? That is how one can identify a green dragon."

Bannon frowned. "Wouldn't you know it's a *green* dragon by the color of its scales?"

"Yes, my boy—but once you are that close, then you face troubles far more pressing than scientific classification."

As they worked their way deeper into the valley, clouds scudded across the sky. They walked among the skeletons, piles of them, as if at one time there had been a great die-off of dragons.

"I wonder when the last one came here." Bannon bent down at another skull, a small one, perhaps that of a young dragon that had perished beside its mother. Even the young dragon was larger than a draft horse.

Thistle scampered ahead to explore among the rocks. She climbed out of sight as she found more and more cluttered bones, ancient generations of fallen dragons.

"Over here, Sorceress!" Nathan called. "Perhaps this one? It's a silver dragon, based on the configuration of its skull and the bony back ridges there. Metaphorically, at least, this one might be best for fighting."

Joining him at the skeleton he had found, Nicci assessed the length and curvature of the rib, extended her arms as if holding an imaginary bow. "A good possibility."

Bannon stepped up with his sword. "If that's the one you want, Sorceress, I can cut the bone free. We'll shape it into a bow when we get back to Cliffwall."

Thistle screamed.

Nicci moved in a flash, bounding over the pitted volcanic rock and dodging the jumbled skeletons. She reached a pumice outcropping from which she could see the girl racing away in terror. Something stirred among the rocks and bones—something enormous.

A pair of angular wings unfolded, and leathery gray skin stretched taut. With a hiss, a serpentine neck scattered the rocks and heaved itself up in a spray of dust and gravel. The piled bones clattered and tumbled away from the half-buried form. It was a reptilian beast with wattled skin at its throat and tendrils drooping from fang-filled jaws. Many of its pewter-colored scales were missing, leaving exposed sections of wrinkled skin.

With the sound of blacksmith's bellows, the dragon inhaled air into its lungs, flapped its broad wings, and lifted itself up. Fire lit its golden eyes. The creature seemed incredibly ancient, but not at all weak.

As it rose up, the gray dragon scattered debris, looming over them. Thistle cringed, directly in its line of sight. She had nowhere to run.

The beast spoke with loud thunder that caused more rocks to tumble from the steep slopes of the vale. "I am Brom!" He flapped his wings backward, making a stir of wind. "I am the guardian. I am the last." The ancient gray dragon snorted, inhaling again to fill his withered, wrinkled hide. "And you are intruders."

CHAPTER 69

As Brom heaved himself up from a pile of bones and volcanic rock, Thistle backed away, her eyes darting, searching for shelter. Throwing herself forward to face the gray dragon, Nicci dug within herself to find magic she could use against the huge beast, sure the girl would be incinerated any moment.

Bannon and Nathan both drew their swords and stood ready, as if they might terrify or intimidate Brom. The wizard seemed defiant, but Bannon was clearly awestruck and terrified.

The gray dragon kept rising from the rubble of skeletons. Dust, boulders, and bones pattered off of his wrinkled hide. Smoke and sparks curled from his mouth as his jaws yawned wide. "I thought I was at my end," Brom rumbled, "but I am still the protector of this place." The great wings flapped back and forth; the thin membranes were blotchy and discolored, and small rips gave the wings a tattered appearance. Nicci doubted the beast could fly anymore.

Brom was unspeakably ancient. Scales fell like loose coins from his hide. Summoning a roar from a bottomless pit of great weariness, the dragon bellowed at them. "Thieves! I must guard the bones of my kind."

When Nathan raised his ornate blade in challenge, he looked laughably insignificant. "We meant no harm to you, dragon, but we will defend ourselves." He swept his sword high, cutting through the air. Bannon followed his mentor's lead, waving Sturdy in an attempt to scare the huge creature.

The gray dragon turned his head and squinted, as if he had trouble seeing. "You are not like other dragon slayers I have encountered. You are much punier. Easy to kill." His serpentine throat swelled like pumping bellows as he coughed gouts of smoke, cinders, and sparks at them.

Just in time, Nicci released a wave of wind that deflected the dragon's sputtering exhalations. She reached the terrified girl and pushed Thistle away from Brom. "Run—find shelter!"

The gray dragon lunged toward them on unsteady limbs.

Foolishly, Bannon leaped forward, and with a great yell, swung his sword down on Brom's foreleg. Sturdy's keen edge cut through the loose, displaced scales and the parchment-thin hide, sinking in to the bone, as if the reptilian leg were nothing more than a fallen log.

Brom let out a roar, sparking more fire from his throat. The ancient dragon thrashed his barbed tail and knocked bones and volcanic rock aside in an explosion of anger and pain. He thrust his long neck forward, questing and snarling, as he squinted his slitted eyes.

Nicci pushed the girl along as they ran, ducking behind pumice towers and huge bones. Even a feeble, decrepit dragon was a formidable opponent. Rattling dry ivory bones around her as she climbed, Thistle reached the giant skeleton of another black dragon just as Brom came up behind her and Nicci.

The beast heaved back his long head and inhaled, building up smoke and cinders. Knowing she had to protect the girl and herself, Nicci tossed Thistle inside the petrified dome of the black dragon's skull and dove in beside the girl.

The gray dragon's blast of smoke and flickering fire pelted the skull, and Nicci felt the shudder of the impact, the wave of forceful wind rocking their shelter, a throb of intense heat. Thistle curled up against her, holding tight as they weathered the attack.

As soon as Brom's blast was over, Nicci heard Nathan call out, "Fight someone your own size, dragon!" He let out a rude laugh. "But since no such opponent is available, you will have to battle us. Today, Bannon and I will become dragon slayers after all."

The young man added his shout, deliriously and foolishly brave. "Come on, old thing—or are you too weary? Is it time for your nap?"

Snorting at the insult, Brom wheeled about, sprinting away from the blackened skull that still sheltered Nicci and the girl. With a roar that sounded more like a trembling sigh, the gray dragon staggered after the two swordsmen. Nathan and Bannon darted about, hacking and hammering at Brom's hind legs and tail, gouging the scales and skin. Thick, dark blood oozed out of the wounds.

Brom snapped his jaws, but Nathan rolled out of the way amid a clatter of long-dried vertebrae. Though the ancient guardian dragon seemed intimidating, many of his teeth had fallen out. Because of his titanic size, Brom toppled rock spires and struck Bannon a glancing blow, knocking him among the debris.

As soon as the dragon had turned away, Nicci pressed Thistle down. "Stay here. You're sheltered, at least for now. You'll be safe enough." Then she emerged to face the ancient dragon herself.

"Be careful, Nicci!" Thistle called after her.

Her normal magic would not be enough against even this weak and decrepit behemoth, and she was forced to draw upon elements of both Additive and Subtractive Magic. In the gray smear of clouds that had closed over the high valley, thunder cracked like an explosion. Nicci pulled down skittering lashes of blue-black lightning. The jagged bolts were wild and rampant. One crashed into the curved rib cage of a sprawling skeleton, but two other branches of lightning struck Brom, ripping through the membrane of his right wing and scoring a deep black wound along his side.

The old dragon let out a smoke-filled roar and thrashed his head from side to side. "No! I am the guardian." Brom stormed toward Nicci, though he could barely see.

Nicci held both hands out in front of her, curling her fingers. She could unleash a ball of wizard's fire and throw it at the dragon, but she had another idea. Better to summon fire *within* the dragon, burn it from the inside out. She could find Brom's heart, and explode it.

In previous battles, she would summon heat and dramatically raise the internal temperature of an object, as she had done with the giant lizards near the lair of the Lifedrinker. Now, searching with her mind, she found the dragon's heart. She could burn it to a cinder.

Facing the giant beast, she remained calm, focused. When Brom lunged, Nicci released her magic, filling the dragon's heart with fire. She would give the ancient beast a swift and merciful death.

Her magical blaze ignited Brom's heart into a furnace—but still the dragon didn't stop.

Instead, as the fire continued to rage within him, building inside his chest cavity, Brom actually flourished, grew, swelled. Losing control of the magic she had triggered, Nicci realized her terrible mistake.

Fire would not burn a dragon's heart to ash. Fire was intrinsic to the very being of such a creature. The intense heat had reignited Brom's heart—not killing him, but *rejuvenating* him, infusing the dragon with a renewed power. His thin skin and rows of ribs became flush again. His wing membranes crackled and healed. His enormous reptilian body grew more threatening.

Fully alive again, Brom flapped his wings to create a gale of wind that knocked Nicci backward. Bannon and Nathan scrambled out of the way, diving for shelter among the volcanic boulders.

The gray dragon turned his head to the sky, spread wide his jaws, and let out a river of bright, intense fire. When Brom swung his head around, his eyes, which had been previously dimmed with age, blazed with a golden intensity.

"Now you have made me strong enough to defeat you!"

CHAPTER 70

As the dragon turned its newly bright-eyed gaze toward them and let out a blast of flames, Bannon dove for shelter behind the tall pumice boulder, dragging a startled Nathan along with him. The roar of heat slammed against the pocked volcanic surface, blackening it.

While a rejuvenated Brom attacked her companions, Nicci summoned lightning again, a blast three times as strong as her first barrage, but now the dragon's pewter scales were like thick armor, and the lightning skittered harmlessly off his back. Full of energy, the guardian dragon coiled his leg muscles, and sprang into the air, creating a great gust with his restored wings.

"This is a sacred place to dragons! You are thieves."

He vomited a wave of fire toward Nicci, and she cast out her hands, releasing magic in a shield of air and mist that deflected the flames. But she staggered under the incinerating onslaught, reinforcing her barrier, straining as the avalanche of flames pounded and pounded. That one defense nearly drained her, and when the fire subsided, she staggered back.

"Grave robbers!" Brom roared from the sky. "You must die."

"No!" Thistle's voice rang out in the odd silence that filled the gap between the dragon's bellow and the blast of his flames. "Brom, listen! That's not why we're here."

Nicci whirled to see that the scrawny girl had climbed on top of the giant dragon skull and now stood waving her hands to draw Brom's attention. "We came because we have to!" Thistle looked tiny and vulnerable out in the open.

The gray dragon swooped above the girl and curled his serpentine neck in preparation for another fire blast.

Nicci screamed, "Thistle! Take cover!"

The girl looked so waifish, so brave, so impossible, that even Brom hesitated. Thistle stood on top of the curve of the monstrous blackened skull, defiant and angry. "We're trying to save the world! My friends and I made a long journey to come here. It's important!"

The dragon's eyes were bright, reflecting a sharp mind now, his full faculties reawakened with the supercharged fire that Nicci had pumped into his heart. "You are a strange creature, tiny one," Brom rumbled. "Very brave and very foolish."

Thistle put her hands on her narrow hips and her raggedy skirt. "I am determined. And I was told that gray dragons are wise." She shot a quick glance over to Nathan, then back to Brom. "You should listen to reason. Don't you want to know why we came here? Aren't you curious?" She huffed, then answered without waiting to hear a response. "An evil woman has unleashed a terrible magic that could swallow up the whole land. It will destroy Kuloth Vale before long . . . and there's only one way to stop it. We need a bone—a dragon's rib." She glared at the gray-scaled beast. "That's why we came here. We'll kill you if we have to. We don't *want* to, but we mean to take what we need. We are trying to save the world."

Intrigued, Brom backflapped his wings and settled his great bulk among the graveyard rubble, close to Thistle. Bannon and Nathan emerged from where they had taken shelter. Their hair was streaked with sweat, their faces smeared with soot and dust.

Nicci held the magic within her, barely restraining herself from releasing another barrage of lightning, though she was not sure it would do any good. She was still weary from her previous defense and doubted she could kill or even stun the reenergized dragon. She realized that attacking now would only put Thistle in greater danger. If gray dragons were the most intelligent of the species, maybe Brom would listen before he lashed out again.

The dragon settled back, extending his wedge-shaped head forward. Smoke curled out of his nostrils as he regarded the spunky girl. Thistle faced him without flinching, even though Brom's hot breath blew back her tangled curls of hair. "Explain yourself, tiny one."

Still standing as tall as she could on top of the scorched dragon skull, Thistle said, "I just want to save my land. First, the Lifedrinker killed my parents, my aunt and uncle, my village, and everything in my valley—and we destroyed him. But now there's an even worse threat, a sorceress who unleashed an explosion of life, and now *that* is taking over the valley. It will destroy everything!" Her voice became a desperate shout. "I just want a normal world. I want the beautiful valley back, the one everyone talks about."

Brom snorted smoke. "A sorceress created *too much* life?" He lifted a now-healed forelimb and used an enormous claw to scratch between his tusk-sized teeth. "I marvel at the concept. Too much life . . ."

He turned his blazing gaze to where Nicci, Bannon, and Nathan stood ready to fight. The dragon addressed them. "I came here to die, as all dragons do at Kuloth Vale . . . but it has been so long. I was the guardian, and I remember their lives. Now you have restored my life." Smoke and cinders curled from his mouth as the gray dragon let out an odd, growling chuckle. "Although I do not believe you meant to." He turned back to Thistle, leaning forward. The dragon's head was so close that she could have reached out and touched his scaled snout. "Now, brave tiny one, what does this have to do with me?"

"Not with you," Thistle said. "But with the bones . . . or just one bone. The only way we can kill the evil woman and stop that flood of life is with a bow made from a dragon's rib. That's why we came here. We mean to take one!"

Nicci carefully edged her way closer to Thistle. She wanted to be in a position to shield the girl with magic if Brom became enraged. Nicci spoke up, in a firm but reasonable tone. "Just one rib, noble dragon. That is all we ask—and it is also what we require."

Bannon spoke up. "There are plenty of bones here, dragon. You won't miss one."

Brom lifted his huge head and flexed his wide leathery wings. "These are the remains of my kind. These are my ancestors."

"The spell is very specific and powerful," Nathan explained. "We would not have come to Kuloth Vale unless we had no choice. Gray dragons are wise, are they not? If we don't stop Life's Mistress, eventually her wave of rampant growth will cover the world, even these high mountains."

Brom simmered for a long moment, pondering deeply. "I understand that it must seem a small thing to you, considering all these bones here, but I must revere the remains of the dragons and do what I have sworn to do. Dragons are honorable creatures." He paused, regarding them one by one with his reptilian gaze. "*I* am an honorable creature."

Now he faced Nicci, his eyes a molten gold. "However, I must acknowledge what you did for me, Sorceress. You gave me life. I was about to perish and become the last set of bones here, and then no dragon would have guarded Kuloth Vale. But with the fire that you placed in my heart, I am alive and powerful again. You have added centuries to my life and purpose." He huffed and seemed to relax. "Perhaps a single rib bone is not an excessive price to ask."

As dusk swallowed Kuloth Vale, the gray creature watched their every move while the companions searched through the graveyard of dragons. Nicci assessed each rib for its suitability. When she found exactly the right one, she ran her fingers along the smooth, ivory surface, bent it slightly, felt it spring back.

Nathan studied the head, the structure of the skull. "That skeleton belonged to a blue dragon. A medium-size one. The bones look undamaged."

Brom loomed above them. A thick membrane flickered across his golden eyes, then slid back beneath the lids. His voice was somber. "Not just any blue dragon, that was Grimney. I remember him well. We were young together, hatched only a century apart. He was always a reckless adventurer, wanting to fly across the seas or soar off to the frozen wastes. He would play in the updrafts of the mountains, taking foolish risks." He snorted a curl of smoke. "Once, Grimney crashed down in a thick forest and became so tangled in tree limbs that he bellowed there for days until other dragons arrived to extricate him. I helped burn the forest to ash so Grimney could pull himself free."

Brom shook his heavy head from side to side. "Another time he flew high, high enough that he hoped to taste the fire of the sun. He came back long afterward, spiraling and flying unevenly. He was never right in the head after that." The gray dragon flapped his wings, then folded them neatly against his back. "I believe it fitting that you use his rib for your quest. Take what you need. Grimney would approve."

Nicci assessed the rib bone one last time to convince herself that it would make the perfect bow to kill Life's Mistress. She used a line of magic to cut the rib free, and the long, curved arc came loose in her hands. "Thank you, Brom."

"Now, leave this place," said the gray dragon. "Much as I enjoy the conversation, it breaks my rules. Take Grimney's rib and do what you must. Honor him—give him one last adventure."

As darkness fell, they climbed up the rocky slopes to get past the wall that bounded the valley, so they could camp outside of Kuloth Vale. When they crossed the pass and began the rugged descent into the thickening darkness, Nicci stopped and turned back to look.

The gray dragon stood on the ridge, spreading his wings. Brom called after them in a loud thrumming voice. "I am the Guardian of the Vale. Do not think we are friends. I will kill you all if you ever intrude again."

Nicci hoped they would never need to return.

CHAPTER 71

It was a long journey back to Cliffwall, but the terrain and the route were familiar to them now. During the initial trip to Kuloth Vale, Nathan had annotated the ancient charts, marking their way and identifying landforms, and also updating his life book.

Determined to get back to the archive, Nicci pressed them to their best possible speed, dreading what damage Victoria had caused while they were away from the isolated canyons. Now, she had the weapon she needed to destroy Life's Mistress. She carried Grimney's curved rib lashed across her shoulders, and she felt the faint tingling power intrinsic to the bone of the magnificent creature, a power resident in life, connected to the world itself.

Leaving the volcanic mountains behind and descending into the gradually opening terrain, she could sense Mrra out in the distance again, watching over them. The sand panther had been unwilling to enter the place of dead dragons, but now she was there to guard them, ranging ahead and scouting, keeping them safe on the way back to Cliffwall.

Knowing they had no time to lose, the companions walked for many miles until the terrain was too dark to see, and even then Nicci was not ready to stop. She would ignite a hand light to lead their way for a few hours longer. They slept when they could, and always set off into the first light of dawn.

When the hills finally gave way to high desert and red-rock canyons, the clear arid air carried the hint of a miasma. Even from a distance, Nicci could see a moist greenish haze beyond the plateau, simmering with primeval forest energy as it spread across the valley toward the cliffs.

Mrra left them again when they entered the network of canyons, not wanting to come too close to people, but Nicci could still feel the big cat out there, watching. Farmers and workers from the outlying settlements in the canyon-wall alcoves welcomed them back while sending runners to report to Cliffwall. When the companions reached the overarching cave grotto that held the primary archive buildings, anxious scholars rushed out to meet them. In the late-afternoon shadows, they gathered to welcome the weary but triumphant travelers as they climbed the steep cliff trail.

"Look, she has the dragon rib!" Gloria called, waving down at them. Beside her, Franklin was relieved. The mousy scholar Mia happily welcomed Nathan, helping him as he climbed up to the cave overhang, followed by Bannon. She chattered about the fascinating and useful books she had read in his absence, and the wizard gave her a warm, paternal pat on the back. "By the way, I used your kerchief while we were traveling, my dear. The spell worked quite well. It was very refreshing and restorative." Mia responded with a glow of pride as he held out the perpetually cool, moist cloth to show her. "A remarkable and useful bit of magic."

Inside the archive complex, a determined Nicci led the way into the main hall, where she unslung the large rib bone and dropped it onto the first table she found, moving aside other books that had been piled there by distracted scholars. "We can now make the weapon we need." She ran her hand over the smooth ivory surface, studying it by the light of the magical torches burning in the main entry hall. The scholars gathered around, breathless and eager to see.

Nicci straightened her shoulders and explained. "This rib belonged to a blue dragon named Grimney. With this bone, I will fashion a powerful bow, and I will be the archer to stop Victoria. We have a chance to stop a scourge that I believe is even greater than the Lifedrinker." She saw the hope in their eyes. "I just have to get ready. Ask the hunters among the canyon dwellers to bring me their best arrows and bowstring. I will prepare everything else here."

Nathan ran his fingers through his pale hair, looking at the scholars, and Mia in particular. "Did you have any troubles while we were away? Did Victoria and her wild jungle attack Cliffwall? Another *shaksis?*"

Franklin's words gushed out, as if he couldn't contain them. "We erected a barricade at the outer wall of the plateau to keep us safe, just as you instructed. For defenses, we built wooden bars and planks across the cliff openings to block any other attacks. We tried to make this place impregnable."

"But that horrendous jungle kept spreading," Gloria added. "It filled the valley, and now even the foothills are exploding with life. Some of her thorn vines reached as far as the plateau wall, and they're climbing the cliffs."

"It keeps spreading and spreading," Franklin said. "Nothing can stop it."

Mia nodded, her forehead furrowed with concern. "All those wooden barricades and bars—we didn't think anything could break through our defenses. But when Victoria's magic touched them, the wood itself burst into life again! It sprouted, then kept growing. Soon, the chamber behind the window alcove was an impenetrable thicket. We tried to cut it back, but there was nothing we could do. It grew too fast."

"When wood didn't work, we used stone bricks to wall off that passage," said Franklin. "It is secure now, unless Victoria can find a way to make the stone come alive."

"That's a good solution," Bannon said.

"But only a *temporary* solution," Nicci said, shaking her head. "Given time, vines and roots can break through even the strongest stone." She stroked the curved dragon rib, imagining how she would use it. "But I will not give Victoria that time."

Mia came up to the wizard, holding a charred book in her hands. The pages were curled and blackened, the cover scorched. "Nathan, I've wanted to show you. We salvaged this volume after the fire from the *shaksis*. I was putting the books away when I found a reference in here to a dragon-bone bow, so I knew it was relevant to the spells we need. Would you help me study them? See if we can make out the words, even though the pages are damaged?" She lowered her head. "I didn't want to use my gift to restore the ink and the paper unless you were here to help me."

"Why, I'd be delighted to supervise, my dear," Nathan said, turning to follow the young scholar. "Do you think we could have some tea while we read? And something to eat?"

Gloria shouted for food and drink to be summoned for all of them. "Where is our hospitality? These people have had a long journey! Victoria never would have—" She cut off her words in embarrassment, realizing what she had said.

Though she was tired and dirty, her black dress tattered, her boots scuffed, Nicci refused to rest. "I have to get to work. I am going back to my quarters to fashion the bow we need."

"I'll help," Thistle said, tagging along. "Show me what to do."

Seeing the eagerness in the girl's eyes, Nicci gestured down the corridor. "Come with me. This requires my magic, but you can watch and be ready to help if I think of anything." Thistle readily agreed and accompanied her with a jaunty step through the stone tunnels until they reached their shared room.

The girl poured water into the washbasin and let Nicci refresh herself by wiping a damp rag over her face and her tired eyes. When she was done, Nicci rinsed the rag and handed it to Thistle. "Now you scrub, at least enough so I can see your face."

"You've seen my face."

"I'd like to see more of it. You may well be a pretty girl, but I have yet to see complete proof."

Thistle gave her a teasing frown. "As long as you don't make me wear a pink dress."

"Never."

Dutifully, Thistle washed her cheeks, forehead, eyes, and nose, scrubbing hard. "Clean enough?"

Nicci saw that the girl had indeed exposed some patches of clean skin, and smeared dust around others. The water in the washbasin was brown with grit. "Clean enough for now. You can sit on your sheepskin and watch me, but quietly. I need to concentrate."

The girl acted as if Nicci had given her a solemn mission. She found a comfortable spot on the sheepskin, tucking her knees under her. When one of the archive workers hurried in with a tray of tea, biscuits, and fruit, Thistle served Nicci, who ate distractedly. The girl, on the other hand, devoured everything that remained.

Laying the long bone across her lap, Nicci sat on her pallet and considered how she would fashion the bow. She ran her palm along the curve of Grimney's rib, found the structure of the bone, and released her magic to reshape it. She softened and then hardened the marrow. She felt the great power already contained in the stiff, curved rib, but added even more power to it.

Working carefully, cautiously, she adjusted the arc, then fashioned a recurve on each end, added flexibility where it was needed, reinforced cracks in the bone structure, sealed the porosity. She concentrated tirelessly, consumed with the task.

Looking up, she saw that Thistle was sound asleep, curled up on the sheepskin. Nicci watched the sleeping girl, noting the relaxed expression on her elfin face, her smooth brow now that she felt safe and at peace.

Nicci knew she needed to kill Life's Mistress, so that she could *keep* the girl safe.

While Thistle dozed, Nicci finished her work. She felt the rib trembling with energy and anger, ready to complete its mission. In his life, the blue dragon Grimney had wanted excitement, had wanted to accomplish great things. Now he would do that.

Touching the new weapon, Nicci thought of how she would bring much-needed death back to the throbbing evil of the primeval forest.

Leaving the other scholars behind, Mia led Nathan into a small, well-lit study room. She carried the burned, damaged book she had found among the volumes salvaged from the *shaksis* fire.

Nathan took a seat and patted the bench beside him. "Now, let's study those records you found. The more we understand, the better chance Nicci has." He knew they could never go back to Kuloth Vale and demand another rib bone from the gray dragon if this one failed. "We'll only have one chance."

He and Mia sat in a small alcove lit by bright candles, leaning close to study the blackened, curled pages of the volume. "I don't know if this is anything significant," she said as she flattened the pages and pointed out lines written in an eclectic dialect. "But it does mention a bow made of a dragon's rib."

"That can't be a coincidence. I never heard that dragon skeletons were particularly useful." He touched his lips. "Though I admit they are certainly impressive."

The young woman frowned at the smudged writing, the scorched paper. "No one noticed this spell before, because we were looking for a spell to block the outpouring of life." She gave him a faint smile. "After you left, I searched for such documents, and another scholar referred me to this book. He was actually researching a cure for impotence." She lowered her voice to a conspiratorial whisper. "It took some doing to get him to admit that."

"A cure for impotence? I suppose that fits with the restoration of life," Nathan quipped. "And is there a counter to it?"

"For his purposes, he did not find the spell he needed, so he placed the book back in the corridor shelves to be returned to the archives in the normal course of work. As it happens, the *shaksis* attacked before the book could be reshelved, and it went missing. Some of these pages are damaged, but I noticed a mention of the dragon-rib bow, and I knew you would want to see it." She pointed to a deep brown spot on the paper. "Look here."

"Indeed. We already knew the power of the bones, my dear girl. It references the weapon we want?"

"Yes, the bow itself and the powerful gifted person required to be the archer. But that is only part of the spell! This section, the damaged part, mentions requirements for the *arrow* as well. We didn't have all the information before."

Nathan's brows pulled together in a troubled frown as a chill ran down his back. "You're certain the arrow has to be special, too? The bow doesn't impart the required magic? I hadn't considered that. How discouraging. What more do we have to do?" He squinted, but the blackened char on the edges had destroyed the ink. He knew Nicci would certainly not want to be delayed. "It's too damaged to read."

"I can attempt to fix that," Mia said, smiling. "I found a trick when I was studying the old books, but I didn't want to try unless you were here. I've never done it before, but I think I understand the magic involved." She traced her fingers along the outside of the pages, then released a tiny trickle of her own gift. To Nathan's delight, the edges of the paper became white again, then tan. The damaged page healed and stiffened, clarifying the ends of sentences that had previously been obscured.

Marveling at what she had done, and how easily, Nathan let out a sigh. "I forgot how many people here are gifted, even if they are untrained." He sniffed. "And *I'm* supposedly the great wizard and prophet."

"It's a simple spell, really," Mia said, embarrassed. "Nothing dangerous."

"Starting a fire is also simple if you have a spark. But without the spark . . ." He shook his head, and focused on the newly restored writing. "Never mind. Now, what does it say?"

Mia concentrated on the words she had just restored. "Hmm, the couplet only refers to a 'properly prepared arrow.' And this section here"—she tapped with a finger—"says, 'Only one kind of poison is appropriate.'"

"Dear spirits, a poison? What kind of poison is it?" Nathan groaned, fearing they would be faced with some other lengthy and difficult quest before they could fight Victoria. "And where are we supposed to find it?"

Mia turned the pages and they scanned the other spells, including the most effective cure for impotence, though they needed the opposite sort of magic to stop Victoria. "In this next line it refers back to the original spell book, and we didn't read all of that, either. I thought we had all the information we needed, but some of those pages were damaged when it was fused with the stone wall."

Nathan gave her an encouraging smile. "You've just demonstrated your proficiency with the new restoration spell. Maybe you can fix those pages, too?"

Mia stood from her seat, ready to do whatever he asked. "Perhaps I can."

Still weary from the journey, he sipped his tea and pondered while the young librarian ran into the archives. She knew where to find what she was looking for and soon returned with the damaged book that Nicci had extracted from the melted stone wall.

Together, they turned the pages, assessing the smears of dust that obscured the ancient writing. Using her gift, Mia held her hands over the pages, squeezed her eyes shut in deep concentration, and worked her fingers over the smeared writing. Some of the stone powder flaked off like dried mud and lifted free in tiny specks of dust, floating away to expose words that had previously been damaged and lumped together.

"I thought we had read the whole spell before," Nathan said, "but this section on the next page . . ." He leaned closer to read what she revealed.

Mia cleared away and freshened the distorted ink, pleased to use her newfound skill. When the letters became dark and clear, Nathan read the precise instruction for preparing the arrow to be shot from a dragon-rib bow, an arrow that could kill the wielder of the uncontrolled fecundity spell.

It was the key to defeating Life's Mistress, the poison that they needed to accomplish their task.

In a long, hoarse whisper, Nathan said, "Oh no."

CHAPTER 72

When she was finished, Nicci considered the dragon-bone bow a work of art, a work of death. The surface of the magic-infused ivory was veined with lines of faint gold that were intrinsic to the dragon itself, threads connected to the world and life.

She couldn't wait to use it against Victoria.

In the Cliffwall canyons, the isolated settlers often hunted with bows of their own making, and the best archers had already provided sturdy bowstrings made of woven sheep gut. At Nicci's request, they had also offered a selection of long arrows fletched with crow's feathers and tipped with splayed iron heads, their razor edges sharpened to a bright silver edge.

After she strung the graceful recurved bow, it thrummed with the energy of one of the world's most magnificent creatures, a dragon tied to the source of life deep within the earth—likely the same source of power that the Eldertree had drawn upon. The bow vibrated in her hand, as if Grimney's spirit was eager to be released for one last quest.

Nicci was ready. The arrows were ready.

She took her weapon and headed through the winding tunnels until she reached a gathering hall for the Cliffwall scholars, deep in the heart of the plateau. She found Nathan already there, his face stricken, his skin ashen. Beside him, the young scholar Mia looked terrified.

She immediately sensed something terribly wrong. Her hand tensed around the bow. "What is it, Wizard?" Nathan opened his mouth, closed it, as if he couldn't find the words. "Tell me." The sharpness in her tone startled the answer out of him.

"The bow isn't enough," Nathan said.

Just then, Bannon entered the room with a jaunty step, full of energy. Thistle accompanied him like a little sister, washed, dressed, and rested now. Bannon's eyes sparkled in anticipation of the great battle that was to come. He seemed too naive to be afraid. "I am ready to fight Victoria! Just like when we destroyed the Lifedrinker together. Will I join you, Sorceress?"

Nicci raised a hand so abruptly that she cut off his words as surely as if she had released a silencing spell.

Thistle's honey-brown eyes went wide at her reaction. Bannon looked around in confusion and saw the expression on Nathan's face. "W-What happened? What's the matter?"

Nathan slid one of the old, damaged books across the table toward them. "A bow made from a dragon's rib is an extremely potent weapon, and you are indeed a powerful sorceress to wield it, but that is only part of what the magic requires to destroy Victoria. There is more . . ." He slowly shook his head. "The price is much greater than we knew."

He opened the stained volume to the pages that Mia had restored with magic. He touched the words with his extended finger. "Read the ancient text yourself, Sorceress. Draw your conclusions." His voice grew much quieter. "The words leave no room for interpretation."

Mia stared at the lines, as if she hoped the letters would change. She slumped heavily into a chair.

Bannon stood straight and determined. "No matter the price, we have to stop Victoria," he blurted out. "After what she did to those poor girls . . ."

Nathan's azure eyes bored into Nicci as he explained. "In order to kill Life's Mistress, not only must you use a bow made of dragon bone, but the arrow itself has to be tipped with the necessary poison—a poison that can sap all vitality from life."

"What poison?" Thistle asked.

Nicci looked down at the page and read the words herself even as the wizard recited, *The loss of a loved one.* He drew a deep breath. "No matter how sharp the arrow is, or how strong the bow might be, in order to kill Victoria, the arrowhead must be coated with the heart's blood of someone that the archer loves, someone the archer kills. And we have already established that *you* must be the archer, Sorceress."

Bannon and Thistle both gasped, and Mia slumped in her seat, her shoulders shaking. Nicci felt deep cold rush through her as she read the spell again, grasped what it said. "This is not acceptable."

Before she could respond, a distant crack resonated through the stone-walled chamber and rumbled through the corridors. Cliffwall scholars hurried down the hall, running to investigate. An old librarian with a long white beard scuttled past the chamber door, his eyes wide with alarm. "The outer wall! Victoria's vines are attacking the plateau defenses."

Followed by the others, Nicci bolted out of the chamber and rushed among the panicked scholars through passageways to the outer wall of the plateau. Thistle ran faster, racing ahead to where a frantic crowd tried to barricade the opening that had been breached by writhing, murderous vegetation. Men and women frantically hauled crates and stone blocks from other rooms, any obstacle to block the passage from the intrusion.

Outside, thick, thorny vines from the explosive primeval jungle had climbed the cliff like an invading army. Tendrils and tentacles thrust into cracks in the rock, pushing, prying, breaking open the defenses. The vines had now burst through the outer chambers previously sealed with stone blocks. The wooden bars the defenders had initially mounted in place had now grown into huge writhing thickets that shoved open the temporary barricade, and the broken stone blocks lay strewn in the hall. Wild vegetation spewed into the formerly impervious archive complex.

Mia cried out in dismay when she saw the infestation of dangerous growth. Thistle dodged and danced away from the grasping vines and branches that surged into the corridor. A whipping tendril scratched her skin, but she slapped it away and scuttled out of reach.

Nathan had not brought his own sword, but Bannon leaped to the attack, using his blade to hack the whipping vines and branches. One woody appendage snapped back and slammed hard against the side of his head, stunning him. The young man reeled and his knees began to buckle.

Nathan rushed in to grab his protégé, and pulled him to safety before the vines could lunge for him. Bleeding from the side of his head, Bannon groaned and dropped his sword with a metallic clatter on the stone floor. Nathan dragged him farther out of reach so that he could check his injury.

Mia, left staring appalled at the horrific growth, did not move quickly enough. Before she could dodge out of the way, a thorn-studded vine lashed around her neck, coiled, and tightened. The sharp spikes plunged into her throat, digging through flesh and blood vessels. Gouts of crimson sprayed out as she screamed and struggled.

Whirling, Nathan howled, "No!" He lunged toward Mia to save her, instinctively lashing out with his hand to summon a blast of magic . . . but nothing happened, not even a flicker. He was helpless.

With an additional jerk and twist, the malicious vine snapped the young woman's neck, then discarded her body against the curved wall.

Nicci knocked the frightened scholars away as she pushed forward, desperate to find something powerful enough to block this incursion. Ignoring Bannon's groans and the wizard's outcry of grief and fury, Nicci thought of how she had manipulated the fused stone down in the vaults, reshaping and moving the rock. Now she called upon the structure of the plateau walls, reshaped the stone as if it were soft candle wax to create an impenetrable curtain across the opening the plants had broken through. Under her guidance, the re-formed slickrock flowed down and severed the writhing vines and branches, sealing off the outer wall of the plateau. The stone solidified, restoring the integrity of the cliff, walling off the incursion of deadly plants. They were safe. For now.

Sobbing, Nathan had dropped to the floor, pulling the dead young scholar against him. Mia bled from the brutal gashes in her neck, soaking the wizard's borrowed robes with red, and her head lolled. He groaned. "She was so smart, so loyal. Dear spirits, if not for Mia we wouldn't have found the other part of the spell. Otherwise, all our efforts would have failed. It's because of her that we have a chance." He looked up at Nicci with reddened eyes. "We have a chance."

Nicci assessed the shocked and frightened scholars. She had no illusions about how difficult this terrible enemy would be. "We need the necessary poison for the arrow." But the task seemed impossible, and dread weighed heavily in the pit of her stomach. The heart's blood of someone she loved? Her voice was cold. "But I love no one."

It was a bleak statement, but true. Her one true love, the only man she would ever love, was Richard Rahl. She had given him her heart with a passion that had now transformed, but had never waned. At first, that love had been dark—the wrong kind of love—but Nicci had an epiphany. She had grown and learned her lesson, eventually accepting that Richard would only ever love Kahlan. Those two belonged together in a special way and could never be separated, *should* never be separated.

Nicci had come to that realization long ago. She still loved Richard with all her heart, but in a different way. Nicci had gone to the Old World to serve him, to explore his new empire, to lay the groundwork for a new golden age . . . even if it meant she had to be far away from him.

She had not believed the words Red had written, about saving the world—for Richard—but now she saw it was true. First the Lifedrinker and now mad Victoria would have swallowed up the world, devastated the D'Haran Empire. Nicci had to do everything necessary to defeat the enemy, but in order to do so she needed the heart's blood of someone she loved.

And it was Richard she loved. She could think of no one else.

Nicci had to be the archer. No one else had the necessary power to face Victoria. Nathan had lost control of his gift, and none of these amateur scholars and dabblers here in Cliffwall even approached Nicci's skill. It must be her.

But . . . someone she loved? Truly loved? Richard . . .

That solution was not possible. She couldn't save the world for Richard, if she had to kill Richard to do so. Oh, if he knew the situation, truly understood what was at stake, Nicci was sure he would immediately agree to the terms—he would offer himself, tear open his shirt to expose his chest so that she could take his heart's blood. He would willingly give Nicci what she needed, the blood poison that would stop Life's Mistress.

But he was on the other side of the world.

And Nicci would never kill Richard, *could* never kill him. The very thought filled her with horror. She remembered how it had destroyed her to stop his heart, to send him to the underworld, so he could rescue Kahlan. He had begged her, and Nicci could not refuse him.

But now . . . Would she sacrifice the world itself, just to keep Richard alive a little longer? It sounded foolish, but she knew she would. Her stomach knotted.

Somewhere, far up in the Dark Lands, Red must be laughing.

The heart's blood of a loved one.

As she listened to the moans of the gathered scholars, she knew they were all terrified, but not as despairing as Nicci was. After the difficult quest to obtain the dragon's rib, and with her own powers as a sorceress, she had expected to have the weapon to kill Victoria.

But it was not enough, and now the last component simply did not seem achievable. She didn't know what to do.

Nathan sat on the floor, staring at Mia's pale, lifeless face. He stroked the mousy brown hair from her forehead. "I am so sorry, my dear." Wearing a stricken expression, he wiped her brow with the always moist, always cool kerchief that she had given him before their journey to Kuloth Vale.

Nicci looked down at Thistle, who was thankfully unharmed from the attack, other than a scratch on her leg.

Suddenly Bannon stood before Nicci, still bleeding from his forehead. He rested the point of his lackluster sword on the floor in front of him. He reached up to wipe a smear of blood from his wound, obviously drawing on his courage. He raised his chin and looked at her. "I am the one, Sorceress." He drew a ragged breath. "It has to be me."

He hooked his fingers in the opening of his shirt and tore it open to expose his chest. "I know you care for me. I saw how you looked at me after we fought the Lifedrinker together. You praised me for how useful

I was. And I have seen what Victoria is doing . . . what she already did to Audrey, Laurel, and Sage." Sad determination filled his eyes. "If I can save the world by giving my life, then I'll gladly do so. Draw your knife, take my heart's blood." He swallowed hard. "It belongs to you anyway." He lifted his head back and closed his eyes, as if bracing himself for a deathblow.

Taken aback, Nicci scowled. "Don't be a fool." She pushed him aside. "That would never work. I have no time for this."

Leaving the crestfallen Bannon behind, she stalked away to the archive chambers, hoping to find a different answer, some other way in one of the spell books. She felt a terrible dread inside.

After all Nicci had endured in her life, what if there was no one she loved?

CHAPTER 73

With the full intensity of a dedicated memmer, Nicci mulled over all the knowledge she possessed, the spells she had been taught, the powers she had stolen from the wizards she killed. There had to be another solution.

Wanting to be alone as she grappled with her thoughts, she went to stand outside under the great overhang of the main cliff grotto. She looked across the hidden, protected canyons to the clustered dwellings in the smaller alcoves scattered up and down the opposite cliffs. All these people had lived sheltered for millennia, guarding this secret archive. They had seemed safe, untouched by the outside world until young Victoria had accidentally brought down the camouflage shroud and revealed the great library after thousands of years.

The knowledge contained in the archive was dangerous enough, Nicci knew, but far worse were those amateur would-be wizards who did not understand the powers they foolishly unleashed.

Now, late in the afternoon, the secluded canyons felt peaceful and quiet, as if unaware of the monstrous flood of life that approached like a destructive wave from the opposite side of the plateau. Nicci had to stop Victoria, who had transformed herself into a monster. She knew how to accomplish the task, how to defeat Life's Mistress, but whether or not the price was too high, Nicci didn't know how to pay it. The answer seemed impossible.

Nicci, a gifted sorceress, had the dragon-rib bow, she had arrows, and she had the will. She was ready to face Life's Mistress and kill her.

But she did not have the necessary poison.

Nevertheless, Nicci refused to accept the impossible. She never had.

Tension filled the halls of Cliffwall as the scholars tried to find some way to help. Nathan mourned the death of Mia, and Nicci knew he would do anything to destroy Victoria and her rampaging fecundity, but he had no magic to offer . . . or if he did, the wild and uncontrolled backlash might cause even more destruction than Victoria.

There had to be something else. . . .

Lost in thoughts, Nicci stared into the brooding canyon silence, where shepherds, farmers, and orchard tenders went about their business as they waited for what came next. Sheltered, peaceful, oblivious . . . A grim weight pressed down on her shoulders. These people all counted on her to save them, because no one else had the ability.

Yet Nicci wasn't sure she had the ability either—the ability to love.

It seemed laughable and tragic that, for all her knowledge, for all the great magic she possessed—and every skill she had learned or power she had stolen—Nicci's great failing was a simple human emotion that any child could produce at will.

Her eyes stung as she looked at the secret canyon where so many people had lived undisturbed for generations. She wanted to preserve this peaceful home for the inhabitants of Cliffwall—and especially for Thistle, who had already endured so much, lost so much.

As a child, Nicci had loved her father, although she had been convinced otherwise. Without understanding the depth of his devotion to his employees, his business, his future, Nicci had watched her father work in the armory. She had observed the workers' respect for him, but she gave him no credit for his skills, thanks to her mother's corrupt influence.

Her mother had made Nicci feel worthless, feeding her the debilitating philosophy of the Order until Nicci choked on it, all the while believing she was being fed a fine feast. Only after Richard pulled the blindfold from her eyes and showed her how to break those lifelong chains had Nicci understood her father's devotion and exactly how much harm the Order had done to him, as well as what they had stolen from her with their twisted philosophy.

But Nicci's father was long gone and the Order defeated, Jagang dead by her own hands, and she could not make up for the past. Instead, she had to look to the future. Now, as part of the new task for Richard that she had taken into her heart, she could save the world from Life's Mistress . . . if only she could find a way to use the weapon she had.

Looking nervous, the memmer Gloria emerged from the front stone gates of the main tower, waving to Nicci. "Sorceress! We've been looking for you."

Nicci felt a tiny spark of hope, ready to grasp at any straw. "Did you find another solution?"

Gloria's round cheeks puffed out as she blew air through her lips. "Why, no, Sorceress. It's just that the orphan girl asked us to look for you, says it's extremely important."

Nicci was instantly alert. "Is Thistle all right?"

"She's waiting in your quarters to talk with you. She said it was urgent, but wouldn't tell any of us, only that we had to find you right away."

Leaving Gloria behind, Nicci rushed back inside the main buildings, hurrying along the corridors. She was worried about the girl. Thistle had watched her village collapse, fought dust people, sand panthers, and a dragon, and if *she* claimed that something was urgent . . .

Or maybe she had remembered some detail that they could use?

Thistle was waiting for her inside their quarters, sitting on the sleeping pallet, her scuffed knees drawn up against her chest. Her body was shaking. When she saw Nicci, her large honey-brown eyes filled with relief, but also fear.

Before Nicci could speak, the girl said, "I've already eaten the seeds. I knew you would try to stop me, but now you can't. It was the only way I could be sure, so now you have to do it."

A chill like a trickle of ice sliced down Nicci's back. She stepped forward. "What do you mean?"

Thistle clutched dried petals and leaves in her hands. Nicci instantly recognized the shriveled plant, the distinctive violet-and-crimson flower, the crumbled stem. The girl held it out to show her. The deathrise flower, the poisonous bloom that Bannon had clumsily given her, not knowing its awful potency. As a sorceress, Nicci had kept it because she knew that such powerful tools were not to be wasted.

Thistle's eyes flashed. Even as Nicci lunged toward her, the girl shoved the rest of the dried petals into her mouth.

Nicci threw herself upon the girl. "Stop!"

Thistle swallowed.

Nicci grabbed the girl's chin and tugged at her jaw, trying to remove any remnants from her mouth, but Thistle kept her teeth clenched together.

"Too late," she mumbled. She was already starting to convulse.

Nicci summoned her magic. Maybe she could force the girl to purge herself. Maybe she could find some way to neutralize the deadly substance.

But Nicci knew that no healing spell could cure the deathrise poison. She remembered Emperor Jagang's tortures, how he had tested variations of the deadly plant in camps that he called Places of Screaming. This was no chilling tale to be whispered over ale in an inn. The deathrise flower was truly the worst possible poison in existence.

If Nicci could kill Jagang all over again, she would.

"There is no cure," Thistle said defiantly. "You told me so yourself." Her mouth was empty now. She had swallowed every bit of the deadly flower.

In anger and despair, Nicci shook the girl's narrow shoulders. "What are you thinking? Why would you do that?"

"To give you no choice," Thistle said. A vicious shudder racked her body, and her voice came out in a gasp. "To make the valley beautiful again, so everyone can live their lives . . . just like I always wished for."

Nicci wrapped her arms around Thistle, as if afraid the girl would try to escape. "That was a stupid, useless gesture. It won't help."

An image flashed through Nicci's mind of Jagang sitting outside his tent to listen to the prolonged agony of the test subjects after they consumed the poison. Some took hours to die, some took days. Even the mildest dose caused eyes to hemorrhage and made blood ooze from ears and nostrils. Some victims writhed so wildly that their convulsions cracked their spines. They screamed until they coughed up their vocal cords in bloody strands. Their skin would swell, their joints burst. Some clawed off their own faces trying to escape the pain.

The orphan girl shuddered in Nicci's arms, and she began to cough. Her skin was already chalky, her lips bloodless. Her mournful honey-brown eyes were bloodshot.

Nicci knew what was going to happen to the poor girl. "There is no cure, child. Why would you do this to yourself?"

"For you," Thistle choked out. "To give you what you need. To make the choice for you." She squirmed and thrashed, and Nicci tried to hold her tight to keep her still. "What you can do—is give me a quick and painless death. End that for me." She looked up. "Take one of the arrows, pierce me through the heart, quick and clean. Before it's too late."

"No!" Nicci called up her magic, tried to find healing spells. She sent power into the girl to keep her strong, but the deathrise poison raged like a wildfire through her body. "I can't!"

"Take my heart's blood. You need it against Victoria."

Nicci glanced over at the razor-sharp, iron-tipped arrows she had left on the writing desk.

"If you love me, you'll save me from what you know is coming," Thistle said. "Kill me. Use the arrow to stab me through the heart."

"No!"

The girl continued in a hoarse voice. "You'll have the blood you need. The necessary poison." As she began convulsing, her small hands clutched Nicci's black dress. "Stop Victoria and save my land."

Nicci was torn, her heart broken. She held the orphan girl, felt her spasms grow worse. She knew the pain was only the start of what would be long hours, possibly even days as Thistle slowly tore herself apart, screaming the whole time.

"I know you love me," Thistle murmured, lifting a trembling hand to touch Nicci's cheek just for a moment.

"No . . ." Nicci whispered, and she wasn't sure the girl even heard her.

Thistle coughed and shuddered, pressing her face against Nicci.

Not wanting to release her hold on the dying girl, Nicci extended her other hand and reached out with magic to pull one of the arrows from its resting place. It slid through the air, across the room, and landed in Nicci's palm. She wrapped her fingers around the shaft, saw the silver sheen of the sharpened edge, the pointed tip.

Thistle could no longer hold back her pain. She convulsed and cried out.

Nicci squeezed her tight, knowing the agony would only grow worse. She held the arrow in her right hand, turning Thistle just slightly with her left arm, finding a vulnerable place in the girl's chest. As tears came to Nicci's deep blue eyes, she drove the arrow forward, taking away the pain as gently as she could.

And when she pulled the arrow out, its tip and the end of its shaft were red with a thick layer of blood from Thistle's heart. The necessary poison.

Nicci bowed her head and unwittingly added even more poison to the bloody arrow—a single tear. The first tear that Nicci had shed in a long time.

Chapter 74

As she stalked through Cliffwall preparing to kill Life's Mistress, Nicci felt like a black shadow filled with razors. Hollow inside, her heart a bottomless pit like what she had seen at the center of the Scar, she clutched the bloody arrow, its sharp tip not at all blunted by the sticky coating. The necessary poison was based on dangerous love, a love that Nicci had never admitted existed.

Now her heart was just a hot wound.

The spunky orphan girl had surrendered her very life, had forced Nicci to do such a terrible thing in order to achieve the victory they all needed. Thistle had seen something in Nicci's heart that the sorceress did not even know she had. She squeezed the arrow tighter, but she forced her muscles to relax, so that her anger would not snap the shaft. She dared not waste this weapon she had acquired at a great, impossible price.

Thistle's blood.

Her normal reaction would have been to deny such feelings, to burn them away or wall them off, but she needed that emotion now because love was the vital component. Love was the poison. In this case, as Victoria would soon discover, love was deadly.

As she prepared to make her way out into the primeval jungle, Nicci saw that she had stained her black dress with the innocent girl's blood. More poison.

She paid no attention to other tense, frightened scholars who huddled in Cliffwall, looking at her as a savior to stop Life's Mistress. Poor Thistle had already paid the price.

Victoria would pay a higher one.

Future and Fate depend on both the journey and the destination.

Bannon met her in the wide hallway, dressed in fresh traveling clothes and carrying his unimpressive sword. His face looked drawn and pale. "I am ready to go with you, Sorceress."

Nathan stood beside him, haggard and distraught, but he had a fire in his azure eyes. "Even if I can't use my magic, Bannon and I are deadly fighters. You know it. We're going with you."

The young man swallowed hard. "Thistle made it possible. We should all do it together."

She looked at them for a long, silent moment, then shook her head. "No, I go alone. This is my battle. Thistle did her part. Now I will do mine." Nicci didn't *dare* need them. She slung the dragon-bone bow over her shoulder, and carried her one blood-tipped arrow. She did not bring spares. This one would be deadly enough. It had to be. "I have everything I need."

After a long, solemn moment, Nathan seemed to understand. He reached out to clasp Bannon's shoulder before the young man could say anything else. "It's not about us, my boy. You've proved yourself over and over. The sorceress needs to do this alone."

Bannon looked helplessly at his sword, as if it had become useless in his hands. When he glanced up and met her eyes, his expression froze at what he saw on her face. He stepped back, swallowing hard. "Our hearts go with you, Sorceress. I know you will succeed."

Nathan drew in a deep breath, let it out slowly. "Nicci herself is the deadliest of weapons."

Traveling through the tunnels, she reached the wall on the far side of the plateau. She had remolded the rock to seal Cliffwall's defenses against the intrusion of the madly growing jungle, but even stone walls could not stop her. Releasing her magic, she shifted the slickrock and shoved it out of her way like soft clay, opening the wall to the outside.

She looked out upon a primeval disaster, an encroaching wall of twisted, thrashing greenery, tangled vines, fungi that grew as tall as houses before exploding into a blizzard of spores. Thunderheads of gnats and flies buzzed around the fetid forest. In order to solve an extreme problem, Victoria had unleashed an even more extreme solution.

Branches stretched out, vines writhed, ferns uncoiled. A haze of pollen and spores thickened the air into a choking miasma. The rustle, crackle, and hiss of all that growth battering against the mesa cliff sounded like an unstoppable army of life. Too much life.

But Nicci was Death's Mistress.

"Make way," she said. She held out both hands and released her magic in a thunderclap of devastation, clearing the path. Wizard's fire rolled out, unquenchable, unstoppable, and the flames charred the grasping branches and thorny vines into ash. Under the onslaught of heat, massive tree trunks exploded and the storm of splinters shredded adjacent monstrous plants.

Once she had blasted a path, Nicci stepped out into the wreckage and made her way across blackened ground, descending the steep slope. In only moments, the scorched earth already stirred and simmered with new shoots bursting forth. Grass blades and vine tendrils whipped up to grasp at Nicci's feet, trying to hold her back or take her prisoner. She sent a thought toward them, the merest taste of vengeful anger, and the new growth shriveled and died.

Then she went hunting.

Victoria would not hide from her. The memmer sorceress, swollen with lush fertility, wanted to kill Nicci. She had already sent the *shaksis* to attack them, and now Nicci would go to the heart of this primeval jungle. She knew what lurked there.

She adjusted the dragon-bone bow on her shoulders and walked forward, her blue eyes focused ahead. Dead things crunched under her boots. The writhing jungle reached out to seize her with clawlike branches and lashing fronds. Nicci summoned the winds, bringing great raging storms of air that blasted the vegetation, snapped trees, stripped leaves off of branches, exploded mushrooms, uprooted ferns. She tore open a path to insure that her progress would be unhindered. Nicci was the eye of a walking storm.

The distance did not matter. She knew her destination, her target.

Expending so much magic should have weakened Nicci, but the anger and hurt inside her were a rejuvenating force. When she had cleared the way far ahead, she stopped the winds and continued deeper into the mad infestation of life. The plants themselves seemed cowed after what she had inflicted upon them.

In that momentary respite, the insects came, a cloud of black, biting gnats, a swarm of stinging wasps, and a thundercloud of dark beetles, tens of thousands of them.

Nicci spared them barely a glance. As the swarms descended upon her, swirling in the air, she released a thought. She did not even need to gesture with her hands as she stopped tens of thousands of minuscule insect hearts. Gnats, wasps, and beetles fell to the ground like a pattering black rain.

Nicci stepped forward, and the jungle fell into a hush. But she knew she wasn't finished. She had not yet won.

Ahead of her, branches and leaves stirred, and three figures emerged, figures that had once been lovely young women. Audrey, Laurel, and Sage. Now they had been possessed and transformed by the forest. Their skin was the mottled green of mixed leaves, their eyes fractured and glinting with many shades of emerald, their mouths filled with sharp white fangs. Their hair was a stir of moss about their heads.

The women closed in to stand in front of Nicci and block her way. She regarded them with a withering stare. "Victoria sent you to stop me? She fears to face me herself?"

The thing that had been Laurel chuckled. "It is not because she fears you. It's because she rewards *us*."

When the forest women spread their arms, long thorns sprouted from their skin. Glistening sap oozed from the thorn tips as if they had become scorpion tails.

"This is a chance for us to test our powers," said Sage.

"And we'll have fun," Audrey said.

Nicci did not touch her dragon-bone bow, leaving her single poisoned arrow in its quiver as the deadly forest women approached. "I don't have time to play," she said.

She unleashed the still-seething magic inside her, manifesting

three writhing spheres of wizard's fire. They rolled forward like miniature suns. Audrey, Laurel, and Sage had time only to reel backward and
throw out their hands in desperate defensive spasms before the trio of
suns exploded, one for each of them. Unstoppable flames engulfed their
green-infested bodies, closing tight, crushing the inhuman women
with incinerating fire. The female figures crumbled to ash that smelled
more like burning wood than burning flesh.

"Death is stronger than life," Nicci said.

She stepped over the ashes of their bones and made her way to the
heart of the forest.

CHAPTER 75

The jungle stopped fighting back, as if it had accepted its own doom, and instead the writhing, simmering forest welcomed her, lured her ahead. Trees bent out of the way, and vines curled aside to clear a path for her. Weeds and spiky shrubs bowed down before Nicci. She walked forward, dressed in black, her blond hair flowing behind her.

She knew Victoria had not surrendered. The open way before her was a green tunnel surrounded by drooping ferns and low, twitching willows. It reminded her of a spiderweb . . . a trap. Nicci's lips curved in a thin smile. Yes, it was a trap—but it was *her* trap, and Victoria would learn the truth soon enough.

The terrain that had been the Scar was unrecognizable, but after a long journey she realized she had reached the center. Twisted obsidian pillars and broken black rock had once risen up from the Lifedrinker's lair here, but now Nicci saw a glade of lush, suffocating green. Trees stretched high overhead, their boughs arching inward like hands clasped in prayer—a prayer directed toward the vicious green *thing* that grew at the center of the glade.

Victoria was no longer the matronly woman who had instructed the memmers, a mentor who took young acolytes under her wing and taught them everything she knew. Victoria was no longer human. She still possessed the knowledge, the tangled spells, the lore that filled all the magic preserved by generations of memory-enhanced people, but she had become something so much more.

The skin of Victoria's naked body was encrusted with a lumpy excrescence of bark. Her legs had planted into the ground, taking root as twin trunks, twisting and coiling with bright green vines gathered into a burgeoning nest of growth where the two legs fused into a single torso-trunk with rounded wooden breasts. Victoria's arms stretched out as thick curved boughs, her fingers a myriad of branches. Her hair spread outward in a panoply of twigs, a thicket of tangled brush. But Victoria's face was still recognizable, if awful, her skin not just wood but suffused with green. Pulsing lines of dark sap ran up her cheeks and along her ears.

Seeing Nicci, Life's Mistress preened like a bird displaying its feathers. Victoria drew strength, pulling energy from the ground where her roots had spread throughout the primeval jungle, where the growth had built up enormous spell-forms to enhance and reinforce the magic. Her mouth opened in a loud, sharp-edged laugh.

Neither showing nor feeling fear, Nicci stepped into the glade, paying no heed to the rustle and whisper of angry branches, of slithering undergrowth. Her enemy was here. Victoria had sent the three forest women to block her, but now she would face Nicci herself.

Nicci stopped in front of Life's Mistress and planted her boots in the soft forest loam. Her black dress clung to her with perspiration, and Nicci touched the drying bloodstain on the fabric. *Thistle's* blood. A reminder.

She spoke in a haughty challenge. "For a woman who wanted to restore life and make the land thrive, you have caused far too much pain and destruction, Victoria."

As her huge trunk body writhed, the layers of thick bark cracked. A bellow came out of the forest woman's mouth. *"I am Life's Mistress!"*

Nicci was unimpressed. "And I cannot let you live."

She unslung the ivory bow from her shoulder and calmly, without taking her eyes from Victoria's monstrous face, bent the curved rib of Grimney, the blue dragon. The bone thrummed with energy, the magic of the earth, the source of creation. The string itself came from the people of Cliffwall, and although it had no magic, it did have the power of human creation, stretched taut, ready for what the weapon had to do. Ready to use life to destroy life.

Victoria's laughter stirred the crouching trees and angry under-brush. "One insignificant sorceress? One bow? One arrow?"

"It will be sufficient," Nicci said. "We found the spell, a magic that draws upon the very power of life. A bone of creation . . . the bone of a dragon." She held the bow, grasped the tense string, and felt Grimney's rib vibrate.

"The bones of the earth," Victoria said, her boughs creaking, her body bending. "The magic inside a dragon's rib?" Her face folded and shifted, as if her mind sorted through all the ancient knowledge of thousands upon thousands of arcane tomes that she and many genera-tions before her had memorized.

Nicci pulled out the arrow, looked at its sharp end and the thick red coating, still sticky. Her throat had gone dry. "And I have an arrow tipped with the necessary poison. The heart's blood of one that I loved, one that I killed." She knocked it on the string. "Thistle's blood."

Victoria suddenly jerked back as Nicci provided the last clue. In her vast mental library of ancient lore, the other woman recalled the spell. One of her trunklike legs ripped itself out of the ground. The boughs whipped, branches cracked.

Nicci did not flinch. "You remember. I wanted you to remember. Thistle deserves that."

A desperate Victoria rallied the primeval jungle to attack. The for-est closed in, the ferns, vines, and wildly growing trees lunging toward Nicci. Thorns, branches, stinging insects swept to the attack, rushing in a desperate last attempt to stop her.

But Nicci had only one thing left to do. She drew back the string of the dragon-bone bow and aligned the arrow. She aimed its blood-dipped point directly between the large rounded growths of Victoria's breasts.

As branches, vines, and thorns thundered down upon her, Nicci loosed the arrow.

She didn't need to use magic to guide the shaft as it flew. The air whistled and sang like a last keening cry, and the razor-sharp point struck home with a loud thump. Poisoned with an innocent girl's blood, the arrow sank into the flesh of the transformed woman.

In Nicci's hands, unable to bear the tension of the bowstring, the dragon's rib snapped in half. It had released its magic, the last energy, the final gift of the blue dragon who had sought adventure in his life long ago. As the attacking jungle froze and quivered, Nicci dropped the now-useless weapon to the ground. It had served its purpose.

The Victoria thing howled with screams so loud that her mouth cracked open. Her head splintered; her branch-limbs writhed in pain, broke, and fell like dead wood to the floor of the glade.

Death spread outward from the center of the arrowhead like a blight of revenge, reclaiming the life that Victoria had stolen. The necessary poison had swiftly penetrated her heart, and the green sorceress crumbled. The bark cracked and festered. Smoking sap-blood oozed out of the wound, spilling in thick, stinking gouts down her rough body.

Victoria had uprooted one of her thick legs, but now the rooted leg shattered like a tree felled in a windstorm. She toppled in a long, slow collapse as her branches tangled in the encroaching trees. Vines whipped up as if to cushion her fall, but instead turned brown and withered.

Around the glade, the supercharged jungle that had swarmed across the open terrain began to shrivel. Trees collapsed, rotted, fell apart. All the extra life—the enforced growth and tortured fecundity that never should have existed—dissolved.

Nicci turned away. The corpse of Life's Mistress had already rotted into mulch, returning to the soil. The balance of magic would be restored and the unnatural forest would die back to its former levels, its *natural* levels.

Nicci had accomplished what she needed to. She had completed her mission, and she had paid the price. There was no reason for her to stay any longer.

She strode back toward Cliffwall as the seething jungle collapsed around her. She didn't give it a second thought.

CHAPTER 76

By the time Nicci returned to the steep uplift at the edge of the plateau, the unnatural jungle had already begun to retreat, a mere shadow of itself—a proper level of vegetation that did not strain the very foundations of life itself.

She felt no joy over her victory, *Thistle's* victory. Nicci had done what was required. Her duty was discharged. She had paid the cost in blood and unexpected love.

She was done.

As the once-burgeoning trees sloughed into rotting vegetation, she saw a dart of movement ahead of her, a tawny shape. Mrra came to join her. Gliding out of the falling trees and collapsing ferns, the sand panther paced alongside, not close enough for Nicci to touch her fur, but she was there, and that was what mattered. Nicci drew strength from their spell bond, and the big cat seemed to need reassurance as well.

When the two reached the sheer mesa wall, Nicci saw that the steep slope had broken and eroded away. The gnarled brown strands of dead vines still clung to the rocks, but Nicci found a way up to the alcoves and the tunnels high above. At the base of the cliff, Mrra let out a low growl, a temporary farewell, and loped off into the foothills. She would be back.

Nicci climbed back up the steep wall, using magic when necessary to move aside crumbling blocks that the aggressive vegetation had broken away from the cliff.

Nathan and Bannon met her as soon as she reentered the tunnels. Crowds from inside Cliffwall also came, excited and amazed. While watching from the alcove windows, they had seen the festering jungle die away.

"We must have a celebration!" someone called.

Nicci didn't see who spoke, didn't even bother to turn in the direction of the voice. "Celebrate among yourselves," she said gruffly. "Do not make me a hero."

Life's Mistress was dead, the enemy vanquished, the blight of twisted life now disappearing. Yes, there was good reason to cheer, but Nicci did not feel like rejoicing. Rather, she found a hard core inside her and held on to that.

She would never be Death's Mistress again. She had left that dark part of her life in the past, and she had promised Richard. She had learned from the terrible things she'd done for Emperor Jagang. Though Thistle's blood had provided the necessary poison to destroy Life's Mistress, Nicci herself did not want to be that vulnerable.

Never again. She had saved the world, and that was enough. Even if Thistle could never see it, the girl would have her beautiful valley back.

The Cliffwall scholars were unsettled by Nicci's response, and Nathan looked at her with a concerned expression. He gave her a slow nod, then lowered his voice. "You don't need to dance and sing, Sorceress, but you did defeat Victoria and stop that terrible threat. You can feel satisfied."

She looked at him for a long moment and then said, "I would rather not allow myself to feel anything at all."

At Nicci's suggestion, although it was obvious to anyone who considered it, they buried the girl out on the edge of the valley where the fresh vegetation, the *healthy* shrubs and plants, had begun to grow again.

It was a somber procession as they wrapped Thistle's small body in the soft sheepskin rug she had loved so much when she slept on the floor in Nicci's quarters. Nicci carried the body herself, and although her heart was heavy as a stone, the girl seemed to weigh almost nothing.

Franklin, Gloria, and many of the other remaining memmers and scholars left Cliffwall, emerging along the steep side of the plateau. They walked until they reached a spot just on the foothills overlooking the valley, which Thistle had so longed to see fertile again.

Nicci halted. "This is the place. This the view Thistle would want. From here, she would have been able to see the restoration of life that she made possible."

As hot tears stung her eyes, Nicci caught a glimpse of Bannon and Nathan, their faces also flooded with grief. Bannon's hazel eyes welled with unshed tears, and even Nathan, who had seen so much sadness and lost so many people during his centuries of life, was deeply affected by the loss of this one spunky and determined little girl.

"Her spirit can tell the Creator how she would like the valley to be," Nathan said. "I'm sure she will make herself heard."

Bannon nodded. "Thistle could be very convincing." His voice cracked.

Nicci could only nod. She felt so full of words, emotions, and ideas that she wanted to express, but they only simmered within her. Thistle would know. That was all Nicci cared about.

With a gesture from her hand, she released a flow of magic that moved the dirt and rocks on the chosen patch of ground. As she had done at the village of Renda Bay, Nicci created a grave, carving out a perfect, comfortable last bed to embrace Thistle's remains.

As the scholars watched solemnly, Nicci laid the girl wrapped in the sheepskin into the open grave. "This is as far as you can go with us," Nicci said. "I know you wanted to travel to see all the new lands we intend to explore, but from here you can watch the valley. I hope it becomes all you ever wanted to see."

Her arms and shoulders felt stiff, and it was because she had forced such tight control on her muscles to keep herself from trembling. Nicci drew a deep breath. She, Bannon, and Nathan looked down at the wrapped form in the grave. With a gesture, Nicci brought the soft loamy dirt back into place, filling it perfectly, leaving an open patch of naked brown earth on top.

"Should we mark the grave somehow?" Gloria asked. "Is there a stone or a wooden post you'd like us to use?"

Nicci thought of what Thistle had said, how she had laughed at the frivolous but wondrous thought. The girl had grown up without seeing anything of natural beauty, watching her aunt and uncle eke out a living in Verdun Springs, trying to grow stunted plants for food.

"Flowers," Nicci said. "Plant beautiful flowers. That's what Thistle would want to mark her grave."

Before she and her companions departed again, Nicci called a gathering inside Cliffwall, speaking to the workers, farmers, and canyon dwellers as well as the memmers and scholars. In a stern voice, she said, "We have only been here for a few weeks, but already we have saved the world—twice! Both times the disasters were caused by your own clumsy ignorance. And, oh, the consequences . . . the price that had to be paid."

She swept her blue-eyed gaze over the gifted researchers, and they trembled with guilt and shame.

She continued, "You are untrained. Thousands of years ago, your people were entrusted to guard this storehouse of knowledge. Dangerous knowledge. Do not consider it a library, but an *armory*—all the books and scrolls here are weapons, and you have seen how easily they can be misused."

"With disastrous results," Nathan said. "For all my objections to the Sisters and their iron collars, at least they devoted themselves to training new wizards back at the Palace of the Prophets. With the lore stored here, you cannot just willy-nilly dabble with spells as if they were toys."

Franklin hung his head. "Perhaps we should devote ourselves only to the work of cataloging, exactly as Simon wanted us to do. That is enough to keep us busy for decades."

Gloria wiped a small tear from the side of her eye. "The memmers can help to match what we know with the volumes we find on the shelves." She drew a deep breath, let it out slowly. "But who will teach us?" She looked hopefully at Nicci and Nathan. "Will you stay?"

Nicci shook her head. "We will depart soon. I have my own mission for Lord Rahl, and the wizard has an important destination." She spoke in a tone of command, the same tone she had used to send tens of thousands of Emperor Jagang's soldiers off to certain death. "But after we go, you must do one thing for me. An important task."

Franklin spread his hands, then gave a respectful bow. "Of course, Sorceress. Cliffwall is in your debt."

"Send emissaries north to D'Hara and tell Lord Rahl about this archive, and about what we have done here. That is knowledge he needs. Once he learns what is here, he will send his own wizards, scholars, experts. They will help you."

"I'm sure Verna would delight in the challenge," Nathan said. "Dear spirits, imagine what the Prelate would do with so much unexplored lore! She needs something to do, now that prophecy is gone. She could bring many Sisters with her." He nodded slowly. "Yes, indeed, you would be in good hands." He narrowed his eyes and added in a scolding tone, "But in the meantime, no more dabbling with spells."

Gloria agreed. "We will put in checks and balances to insure that no disaster like Roland or Victoria ever happens again."

One of the scholars fidgeted, looking at the rest of the uneasy audience. "But how will we find D'Hara?" He was a thin and rabbity young man named Oliver who had a habit of squinting, as if his eyesight had already waned from too much reading by dim candlelight. "I will volunteer to go, to accept the quest . . . so long as I know where I'm going."

Nicci had little patience for the details. "Follow the old imperial roads. Head north. Make your way beyond the Phantom Coast to the main port cities of the Old World. Ask about the Lord Rahl."

"That will be an arduous expedition, Oliver." Franklin sounded uncertain.

"Yes, it will be," Nicci said. "And we require it of you. Sometimes you must do things even though they are hard."

"I will go with Oliver," said a thin young memmer woman, Peretta, with tight ringlets of dark hair. "Not only is it an important mission, but every person here in Cliffwall, whether memmer or traditional scholar, has a mission to gather knowledge. And what could be a better way to seek knowledge than to explore the rest of the world?" She blinked her large brown eyes.

Oliver smiled and nodded at her. "I will be happy to have you."

"You'll both learn much. You'll be great explorers." Nathan patted the leather pouch at his side, which still carried his life book. "I will also want Cliffwall scholars to copy the maps I've drawn along the way, and take a summary of our expedition so far. The people of D'Hara need to know everything they can of the Old World."

Franklin looked at the memmers, then at the rest of the scholars, and he gave a confident nod. "Do you think you can do this, Oliver and Peretta? Will you be ambitious enough to undertake this quest?"

Like a slowly exhaled breath, the audience began nodding and talking. Peretta sniffed. "Of course we will."

Ready to go, Nathan had dressed in fine travel clothes again, his ornate scabbard belted at his waist, his brown cape from Renda Bay, a dark vest and ruffled shirt taken from Cliffwall stores. "After years of reading dusty old legends, some of you must want to become adventurers yourselves." He laughed. "When you return from D'Hara, you will have earned your own place in history."

B efore her unexpected death, Mia had found for Nathan an old chart that clearly showed a place marked *Kol Adair* on the far eastern side of the great valley, over several lines of stark mountains.

Looking at the ancient map, Nathan was concerned at the prospect of crossing over such sheer and jagged crags. "Maybe it won't be so bad. The cartographer could have exaggerated the extremity of the terrain."

"We will know when we get there," Nicci said.

"And we know where we need to go," Bannon added.

The two men bade farewell to the people of Cliffwall, but Nicci said no good-byes; she simply set off, descending the path to the valley floor. They headed eastward into the now-recovering terrain at a brisk pace. Nicci sensed Mrra following them from a distance, and she acknowledged the sand panther's presence through their tenuous bond.

They headed into the unknown.

CHAPTER 77

Leaving Cliffwall behind them, they crossed the wide, wounded valley for days before reaching the eastern foothills. The hills rose toward distant and far more rugged mountains that looked like the ridges on a dragon's spine.

As they traveled, they found the remnants of old roads that had been all but erased by the life-absorbing Roland and by Victoria's raging fecundity. They crossed terrain where once-thriving towns had been emptied and swallowed up. Now, the uninhabited wilderness was breathtaking in its sheer, empty silence.

Although Nicci didn't feel like engaging in conversation, the silence and constant walking gave her too much time for internal reflection. There wasn't a moment when she did not feel the loss of Thistle, but she tried to build up her inner walls and harden the scar. She had lost many people before, others she cared about, especially in the recent battles with Emperor Sulachan and his bloodthirsty, soulless hordes. Cara . . . Zedd . . .

Nicci had killed countless people herself. She was familiar with death, untroubled by blood on her hands. Her conscience was not heavy. She tried to convince herself that the orphan girl was just another death.

Just another death . . .

Topping a sparsely wooded ridge, Nicci, Bannon, and Nathan turned to look behind them. The vast valley now showed patches of healthy green growth and the flowing silver ribbons of streams. But it was neither a madness of life, nor a cracked desolation of death.

Nathan drew a satisfied breath. "You see? That is what we did, Sorceress."

"It is what we set out to do. Now I'm done with the witch woman's prediction." Nicci turned and continued into the hills before she could think about the price they had paid for that achievement.

"Ah, but Sorceress, on such a journey as ours, is one ever truly done with saving the world?"

When they made camp that night, Mrra dragged a mountain-goat carcass into the meadow and dropped it there for their dinner. The sand panther had already fed, and she sat on the fringes of the clearing, watching Bannon cut fresh meat while Nathan built a campfire. "I want to prove I can do this without magic, though the process is certainly a lot less convenient." He sighed. "Soon, though, I will be whole again."

They contoured along streams through the hills, picking the best path that would keep them moving into the rising mountains. Since Bannon had grown up on an island and sailed the ocean, he had little instinct for finding a route through hilly terrain. Nicci led the way.

She scanned the rugged landscape and picked a switchbacked path up the slopes, across open parks, then into thick pine forests. As they gained altitude, the trees became sparser, then stunted. After thrashing through thickets of knee-high alpine willows, the three emerged into open windswept tundra with whistling grasses and low cushions of wildflowers. Mrra bounded on the rocks, ranging ahead to chase waddling marmots.

Bannon was out of breath, panting hard. He bent over, resting his palms on his knees. "The trail is steep, and the air is thin."

Nathan did not commiserate. "I am a thousand years old, my boy, and I'm keeping up with you. Come, Kol Adair is ahead."

"The air will grow thinner still," said Nicci. "Our destination is much higher."

Bannon squinted as the wind whipped his ginger hair like crackling flames around his head. "When I grew up on Chiriya, I never imagined this." He looked in curious amazement at the rugged lichen-covered rocks as they picked their way toward a steep pass ahead. "I've come so far from that place and from that life, not just in the miles I've traveled but in the things we've seen and done." He gave his mentor a wan smile. "All the things you've taught me and all the experiences I've had, Nathan. Maybe this isn't the perfect life that I dreamed about, but I am happy with it."

He turned to Nicci, pressing her for a response. "Do you think I'll ever see the D'Haran Empire for myself? You've told stories about those lands. Could I even meet Lord Rahl someday?"

"D'Hara is a long way from here," Nicci said, pushing toward the top of the steep ridge ahead. "And we are heading in a different direction."

Nathan was more encouraging. "Maybe you'll see it someday, my boy, but why be in a hurry? This world has many lands, many people, and many sights to see." He smiled and quoted what Red had shown him in the life book: "Future and Fate depend on both the journey and the destination."

Because the slope was so steep, they stopped to catch their breath before reaching the summit of the pass. Nathan took out the Cliffwall charts, studied them again, and looked back at the mountains they had just crossed. "We should be close to our destination," he said. "Very close."

When Nicci set off again, her gaze fixed ahead, Bannon and Nathan hurried after her. Mrra ranged among the rocks, frustrated that the fat, furry marmots always managed to duck into shelter before the cat could catch them. Then one of the animals let out a high-pitched squeal as Mrra killed it for a snack.

The ground was hard and packed under Nicci's boots while she worked her way up to the pass, leading the way, steeper and steeper. Finally, when she climbed her last steps to the top, the grand vista opened up before her, and even she stopped in her tracks, awestruck.

They had reached Kol Adair.

CHAPTER 78

P anting and weary, Nathan came to stand at the top of the pass
and inhaled a deep breath of the cold, thin air. The splendor of
the view struck him like a physical blow. "Kol Adair—dear spirits, it's magnificent!"

Since escaping from the Palace of the Prophets, he had witnessed
many sights, experienced grand and dramatic events, but he had never
before beheld a panorama that inspired in him such absolute awe.
From here, they could see forever.

The sun shone down upon the high mountain valley through the
lens of a perfectly transparent blue sky. Regimented black crags spread
out in a fiercely beautiful barrier, their peaks capped with snow. Dramatic couloirs cradled glaciers that dispatched pearly white ribbons
of meltwater over cliffs in a chain of thundering waterfalls. The
cascades sent up a wondrous spray that spawned rainbows. Mountain
lakes in hanging valleys glittered like jewels, the purest turquoise
blue, some crusted with broken white ice still unmelted in mid-
summer.

Bannon plodded up beside him, wheezing, too weary to do anything but stare at his boots. When he lifted his head to take in the
view, though, he gasped.

Nathan continued to drink in the visceral beauty around him. The
sweeping meadows were lush and green, spangled with so many bright
and colorful alpine flowers it looked like a meteor shower of blossoms.
Even from this distance, he could hear the soothing roar of the water-

falls that tumbled down the black cliff faces. Bluebirds darted about in the spray or swooped down to snatch insects among the wildflowers.

On the saddle, Mrra paced around the open terrain, staying close to Nicci. None of the three spoke as they absorbed the sight.

Nathan filled his lungs with the brisk air and extended his arms to his sides, just reveling in the beauty, the uplifting spectacle. Was this what the witch woman Red had wanted him to see? Although he gloried in the vista, Nathan wondered if this very place was supposed to restore his gift. He stretched out his arms, flexed his fingers, wondered if he felt whole again.

Restless and not sure what they were supposed to do now that they had arrived, Nicci wandered across the open, flat area. She explored the low grasses, pincushion mounds of pink flowers, and lichen-spattered boulders.

Nathan knew there had to be something more if the witch woman had sent them here, if the command had been written in an old life book and chiseled in the stones of a cairn a continent away. He had to have come here to Kol Adair for a reason.

Nathan could survive just fine without his gift of prophetic misery, but living without his *magic* was different. He had drawn great satisfaction from the spells he could work, the magical weapons he could wield—and he could have been a valuable asset in fighting both the Lifedrinker and Victoria. When he and Nicci had begun their journey, leaving the People's Palace and heading into the Dark Lands, Nathan had believed that the two of them would be invincible, a wizard and a powerful sorceress. He needed to be able to do his part again. He needed his magic back.

And this was the place he should be. But he felt no different.

"Look, another cairn!" Bannon said. To mark the top of the pass, some other traveler had piled up a tall cairn of stones, even more imposing than the one they had seen on the windswept Phantom Coast. He set off, but plodded slowly because he was out of breath.

Nicci reached the rocks first. She circled slowly, searching for a message such as what they had found before. She stopped, looked at the rocks, and frowned. "Nathan, come here."

Hurrying up to her, he felt a surge of hope, longing to feel his Han again, to control his gift and become a useful wizard once more. He needed to be made whole again!

Nathan looked down at the base of the cairn. Among the stacked rocks, like a grave marker, was a flat stone tablet devoid of pervasive lichens. Words had been chiseled into the flat granite surface: *Wizard, behold what you need to make yourself whole again.*

Nathan felt a surge of delight. He had seen that phrase before. "So the witch woman was here. Red communicated those words. And they're written in my life book . . . just as they were engraved on that other cairn."

"Either Red was here in person, or she foresaw it," Nicci said. "Someone left these words, and the witch woman *knew* about this from the time before prophecy was banished from the world. Kol Adair has been waiting for you for some time, Nathan Rahl."

"But what does it mean?" Bannon asked. "How will you get your magic back?" He turned a hopeful look to the wizard.

Nathan didn't want to admit that he had no idea of the answer. His brows knitted in concentration, and he made a grandiose gesture to indicate the astonishing vista, trying to convince himself. "Perhaps it is something about this place. Look around you, a sight so marvelous that it's enough to wash away the darkness in the world." He gave Nicci a meaningful look. "After killing the Lifedrinker and Victoria, and after the tragic loss of that poor little Thistle, maybe this is what we *all* need to restore ourselves." He closed his eyes and drew in another deep, satisfied breath of the clear air.

Nicci turned from the cairn. "I need more than a pretty view to heal the darkness inside me. I am strong enough to do that for myself. I already have a strong purpose."

Nathan swept his gaze across the waterfalls, hanging valleys, snow-capped peaks. His skin tingled, his pulse raced, and he felt a wondrous energy that he drew from the earth itself.

"This must be a magical place, a nexus of power springing from the world, just as the bones of a dragon carry a certain kind of power,"

Nathan said. "Simply by being here, I do feel myself restored! Yes, dear spirits, this is what I needed. It was worth the entire journey."

He stretched out his palm, cupped his fingers, and concentrated, remembering what it felt like. He reached for his Han and released a flow of magic, intending to call up a ball of flame. He remembered the last time he had attempted such a spell, on the windswept deck of the *Wavewalker*, manifesting only feathery flickers that had scattered away in the breeze. Now, he meant to produce a bright blaze cupped in his hand.

He had reached Kol Adair. His powers should be back.

Nothing happened.

He concentrated harder. Nicci and Bannon watched him. But although he strained, he felt no response from his gift. Nothing.

His heart, which had felt so uplifted in this magnificent place, now sank into dismay. His magic was gone, unraveled and untangled, stripped from him just as his ability of prophecy had gone away.

"What did I do wrong?" he demanded. "Why haven't I been restored? I should be made whole here—look at the words on the cairn! What else do I need to do?" He raised his voice in desperation, knowing that neither Nicci nor Bannon would have an answer for him.

He hung his head. The foundations of the world had changed, and the stars had shifted overhead. "Maybe with the loss of prophecy, Red's prediction is no longer true after all."

CHAPTER 79

Nicci watched the wizard withdraw into disappointment and defeat. His expression looked as bleak as the patches of glaciers across the mountain valley. "Nothing," he said, flexing his fingers.

Nathan Rahl had always been personable, confident, intelligent—a perfect roving ambassador for D'Hara. Nicci had accompanied him on the journey for her own purposes, but along the way she had come to value the wizard's abilities and knowledge. There was more to the former prophet than was immediately obvious from his demeanor and his personal façade.

Together, they had come a great distance and endured many hardships to find Kol Adair, all based on the whim of a witch woman. Yes, this immense, virgin land must be filled with resources, incredible wealth to whet the appetite of any ambitious ruler. But there was no magic here for Nathan. He had not found what Red promised.

Intensely weary, the old wizard folded his legs and sat on the tundra next to the cairn's piled stones. He opened the leather pouch at his side and sadly removed his new life book. "I wonder if she left me another message." When he turned back the cover, he saw only the sketches and journal entries that he himself had written. Hoping for answers, he skimmed the lines, but the words offered no surprises.

Future and Fate depend on both the journey and the destination.

Kol Adair lies far to the south in the Old World. From there, the Wizard will behold what he needs to make himself whole again. And the Sorceress must save the world.

He closed the cover and tucked it away again. "What should I do and where should I go now? I came to Kol Adair. Why haven't I been made whole?" Now he only frowned at the spectacular view. "What more am I supposed to behold?"

Nicci said, "We have the rest of the Old World to explore. Maybe someone else can tell you the answer."

Bannon looked down at the carved words in the granite tablet again, as if he had somehow misread the simple sentence. "'Behold what you need to make yourself whole again.'" He stood up quickly. "Wait, listen to what it says! The witch woman didn't claim you would *be restored* just by coming to Kol Adair. She said this is where you would *see* what you need." The young man's freckled face flushed with excitement. "Maybe we just haven't seen it yet."

Nathan struggled to his feet. "That means we have to look for whatever it is I need, my boy." He pursed his lips. "Maybe some magical artifact, or a spell-form laid out in the rocks here on the pass. The witch woman wouldn't be so obvious."

"A witch woman rarely is," Nicci said.

Nathan was grinning with renewed hope. "Dear spirits, there's still a chance . . . but what are we even looking for?"

Bannon bent down to the large cairn and began searching among the mottled rocks, looking for answers. "Maybe something is hidden here. It's the most obvious thing." He found a loose stone at the base and rolled it aside, surprised to find a second flat slab with more engraved words. "I don't think you're finished yet, Nicci."

She felt a chill as she saw the ominous statement carved years—or centuries—ago, but she already guessed what it would say. *Sorceress, save the world.* "I don't need some ancient writing to tell me what to do," she grumbled.

The cairn held no other messages, no artifacts, no clues. At a loss, standing on the high mountain pass, the companions searched the distance. The grand view encompassed countless miles of breathtakingly beautiful terrain, but nothing at all that might help the wizard regain his magic.

The wind whistled around them, mocking. Nathan's azure eyes sparkled with a hint of desperate tears, and he stared as if the very intensity could make his need come true. "We've come a very long and difficult way to reach this place." He shouted, "I would appreciate instructions that are a little less obtuse!"

Just then the sun shone at an angle from a precise spot up in the sky. The air shimmered on the far side of the mountains like a curtain opening, a veil pulled away—to reveal a sudden, startling vision of a distant plain beyond the mountains.

Catching a quick breath, Nicci thrust out her arm. "Look there! It's a . . . city!"

Nathan and Bannon turned. The sand panther let out a low growl.

Bannon cried, "That looks even bigger than Tanimura. It wasn't there before!"

Nathan looked giddy with excitement. "No, my boy. No, it wasn't. Why didn't we see it?"

Nicci drank in the unbelievable details. The far-off city was a magnificent metropolis, perhaps greater even than Aydindril and Altur'Rang combined. The skyline was a forest of fantastic construction, exotic architecture with high temples and civic buildings, crowded dwellings and elaborate villas. The tall buildings stretched upward, soaring towers built of white stone. Their roofs shone with vibrant enamel tiles; windows flashed with jewel colors of extensive glass mosaics.

The air around the whole city flickered and blurred, seen through a viewing lens that sharpened details into amazing clarity before they grew fuzzy again. It was as if a huge dome shielded the strange metropolis, hiding it—and for just a brief moment, the magic and the vantage from Kol Adair had revealed it to them. The dome was crumbling, fading.

"We are seeing it from here, for the first time." Nathan was breathing hard. "That must be what Red meant! We reached Kol Adair, and from this exact viewpoint, we can see that city. 'Behold what you need to make yourself whole again.'" He turned to Nicci, his smile bright. "We need to go to that city. The answer lies there. It has to."

Nicci had spent most of her time in crowded civilization, and she much preferred a city to the austerities of life on the trail. The flickering mirage intrigued her with its possibilities. "I agree."

Before they set off, the air shimmered again—and the entire majestic metropolis simply vanished. On the other side of the mountains, the land appeared completely empty.

Bannon yelped. "Was it just an illusion?"

"Not an illusion," Nathan insisted. "It can't be an illusion. Maybe the city is hiding itself somehow, camouflaged by a shroud similar to the one that hid Cliffwall for so many centuries." He nodded, convincing himself as much as the others. "But now we know it's there. Come, Sorceress! We still have a long journey ahead of us, but at least we realize where we have to go."

Mrra continued to rumble with an uneasy growl at the sight, but the wizard would not be deterred. He set off, picking his way down the slope from the pass. They would have to cross many mountain valleys and work their way through the stark snowcapped crags before they reached the site of the mysterious vanishing city.

As they came over the next ridge, they found a prominent trail from the south, a clear footpath that wound through the mountains. "This is not a game trail," Nicci said. In one section, the path widened to reveal moss-covered paving stones, an ancient thoroughfare that had been laid down for traffic. But it had obviously been used in recent days.

"A road!" Nathan could not suppress his optimism. "We are on our way now, Sorceress. That was the sign we needed."

Tall, black rocks blocked their view as they descended another convoluted ridge. When they rounded a barren swell, following the narrow road, Nicci stopped as they beheld a startling and repulsive sight. Bannon gasped, sickened.

Set upon tall spikes on either side of the path were four severed heads, the faces partially crow-pecked, but otherwise preserved by an anti-decay spell. The skin on the faces had slackened in death, but their mouths had been horrifically and distinctively scarred—sliced from the corners of the lips all the way back to the hinge of the jaw, then sewn up and healed. Their cheeks were tattooed with scales to give them the appearance of serpent men.

Nicci recognized them from their attack on the poor people of Renda Bay.

Bannon flushed with anger. "Norukai slavers."

"It appears they must have offended someone," Nathan said.

Nicci stepped forward to scrutinize the appalling heads. "The preservation spell masks how long they've been here."

Beneath the first stake rested a blood-spattered placard written in strange symbols that Nicci couldn't read. She did, however, recognize the arcane letters as similar to those branded onto Mrra's hide.

The sand panther growled again, long and low.

Nicci flashed a hard smile and looked along the winding trail that led toward the vanished city. "Yes, that place might be very interesting indeed."

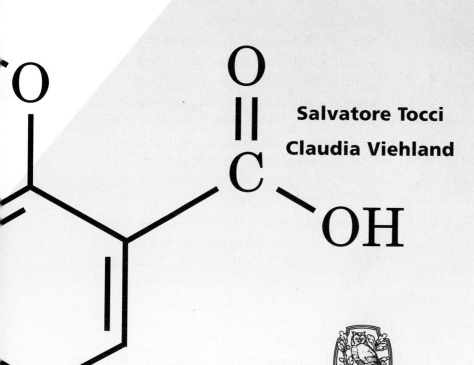

HOLT
Chemistry
VISUALIZING MATTER

Salvatore Tocci
Claudia Viehland

HOLT, RINEHART AND WINSTON

Austin • New York• Orlando • Chicago • Atlanta • San Francisco • Boston • Dallas • Toronto • London

Contributing Writers

Craig Gabler
Chemistry Teacher
Centralia High School
Centralia, WA

Jane Gallion
Author
Guildhouse Productions
Austin, TX

Dave Jaeger
Chemistry Teacher
Will C. Wood High School
Vacaville, CA

Thomas Lindberg
Research Chemist
The Upjohn Company
Kalamazoo, MI

R. Thomas Myers, Ph.D.
Emeritus Professor
of Chemistry
Kent State University
Kent, OH

Suzanne Weisker
Science Teacher and
Department Chair
Will C. Wood High School
Vacaville, CA

Jay A. Young, Ph.D.
Chemical Safety
Consultant
Silver Spring, MD

Acknowledgments

Editorial Director of Math and Science
Richard Monnard

Executive Editor
Ellen Standafer

Project Editors
Mark Grayson
Patty Coffey
Mary Ellen Teasdale

Editorial Staff
Laurie Baker
Jane Martin
Steve Oelenberger

Production
Beth Prevelige
Simira Davis
George Prevelige
Rose Degollado
Nancy Hargis

Design Development
Foca, Inc.
New York, NY

Lab Reviewers
Cheryl Epperson
Chemistry Teacher
Flour Bluff High School
Corpus Christi, TX

David L. Heiserman
Author
Sweethaven
  Publishing Services
Columbus, OH

Marilyn Lawson
Chemistry Teacher/
  Science Department
  Chair
Gregory Portland
  High School
Portland, TX

A. Ruthe Tyson
Supervisor-
  Stanford Teacher
  Education Program
Stanford University
Stanford, CA

Kris Wynne-Jones
Photography Consultant
  Chemistry Teacher
Poly Prep Country
  Day School
Brooklyn, NY

Text Reviewers
George Atkinson, Ph.D.
Associate Professor
  of Chemistry
University of Waterloo
Waterloo, Ontario, Canada

Judith A. Bazler, Ph.D.
Professor of Science
  Education/SMART
  Center Director
Lehigh University
Bethlehem, PA

Ted Branson
Chemistry Teacher
Hug High School
Reno, NV

Elizabeth Briggs
Chemistry Teacher
Ursuline Academy
  of Cincinnati
Cincinnati, OH

Patricia F. Buis, Ph.D.
Assistant Professor
  of Geology
University of Mississippi
Oxford, MS

G. Lynn Carlson, Ph.D.
Senior Lecturer
  in Chemistry
U. of Wisconsin-
  Parkside
Kenosha, WI

James A. Carroll,
  Ph. D.
Assistant Professor
  of Chemistry
University of
  Nebraska-Omaha
Omaha, NE

Tom Custer, Ph.D
Coordinator of Science
Anne Arundel County
  Public Schools
Annapolis, MD

William W. Duff
Chemistry Teacher
Baltimore School
  for the Arts
Baltimore, MD

Joanne Dunlap
Science Teacher
Concord High School
Concord, NH

David A. Ebert
Chemistry Teacher
Johnson Senior
  High School
Saint Paul, MN

David W. Eldridge,
  Ph.D.
Professor of Biology
Baylor University
Waco, TX

Neil Ellis
Chemistry/Physics
  Teacher
Raytown South
  High School
Raytown, MO

Jeffrey L. Engel
Chemistry Teacher
Madison County
  High School
Danielsville, GA

David J. Gamble
Chemistry Teacher
Robbinsdale Cooper
  High School
New Hope, MN

Joe Guthrie
Chemistry/Physics
  Teacher
Mountain View
  High School
Mountain View, CA

Robert Harriss
Professor of
  Environmental
  Chemistry
University of
  New Hampshire
Durham, NH

Smith L. Holt, Ph.D.
Professor of Chemistry
Oklahoma State
  University
Stillwater, OK

Robert Iverson
Chemistry Teacher
Irondale High School
New Brighton, MN

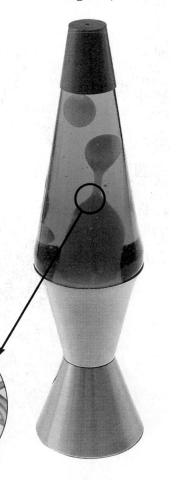

Anthony F. Kardis
Science Department
 Chair
Ladue Horton Watkins
 High School
St. Louis, MO

Shirley M. Kitchens
Chemistry/Physiology
 Teacher
Coronado High School
El Paso, TX

**Samuel P. Kounaves,
 Ph.D**
Associate Professor
 of Chemistry
Tufts University
Medford, MA

Alan Kousen
Science Consultant
Vermont Dept.
 of Education
Montpelier, VT

Janice Lane
Chemistry Teacher
St. Louis Park
 High School
Minneapolis, MN

Valerie Lang
Project Engineer
The Aerospace
 Corporation
Los Angeles, CA

Maureen Lemke
Chemistry Teacher
Navarro High School
Geronimo, TX

Doris I. Lewis, Ph.D.
Professor of Chemistry
Suffolk University
Boston, MA

Timothy Lincoln, Ph.D.
Associate Professor
 of Geology
Albion College
Albion, MI

Mark V. Lorson, Ph.D.
Chemistry Teacher
Jonathan Alder
 High School
Plain City, OH

Celia Marshak, Ph.D.
Chemistry Professor
 Emeritus,
College of Sciences
San Diego State
 University
San Diego, CA

Rachel McCaskill
Chemistry Teacher
Hillsborough
 High School
Tampa, FL

**Michael A. McKinney,
 Ph.D.**
Associate Professor
 of Chemistry
Marquette University
Milwaukee, WI

Audrey Miller, Ph.D.
Professor of Chemistry
University of Connecticut
Storrs, CT

Keith B. Oldham, Ph.D.
Professor of Chemistry
Trent University
Peterborough, Ontario,
Canada

Lance Phillips, Ph.D.
Research Associate
Cornell University
Ithaca, NY

Terry M. Phillips, Ph.D.
Professor of Medicine/
 Immunochemistry
George Washington
 University Med. Ctr.
Washington, DC

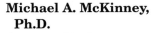

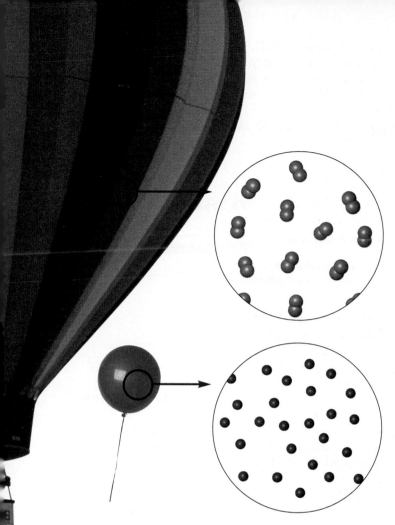

Jean Stanley, Ph.D.
Associate Professor
  of Chemistry
Wellesley College
Wellesley, MA

David C. Taylor, Ph.D.
Professor of Chemistry
Slippery Rock University
Slippery Rock, PA

Richard Treptow, Ph.D.
Professor of Chemistry
Chicago State University
Chicago, IL

Martin VanDyke, Ph.D.
Project Scientist
ACTA Resources, Inc.
Englewood, CO

Carolyn B. Watson
Teacher/Science
  Department Chair
Summerville High School
Summerville, SC

Jeffrey L. Wolfe
Chemistry Teacher
Hamburg Area
  High School
Hamburg, PA

Charles M. Wynn, Ph.D.
Professor of Chemistry
Eastern Connecticut
  State University
Willimantic, CT

**Norbert J. Pienta,
  Ph.D.**
Department of
  Chemistry/
Director of Laboratories
University of
  North Carolina
Chapel Hill, NC

Fred Redmore
Chemistry Instructor
Highland Community
  College
Freeport, IL

Laurie J. Resch
Chemistry Teacher
Coon Rapids High School
Coon Rapids, MN

Patricia A. Richards
Chemistry Teacher
Como Park High School
Saint Paul, MN

**Stanley R. Sandler,
  Ph.D.**
Principal Research
  Scientist
ELF ATOCHEM
  North America, Inc.
King of Prussia, PA

Vicki Sofianek
Chemistry/Biology
  Teacher
Glenelg High School
Glenelg, MD

Stephen Sprinkle
Science Chairman
St. Mary's High School
St. Louis, MO

Table of Contents

Product research

Product
development

Product
production

Water
Hydrogen atom
Oxygen atom

Fructose

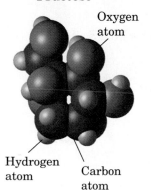

Oxygen
atom

Hydrogen
atom

Carbon
atom

J. J. Thomson's
model of the atom

Niels Bohr's
model of the atom

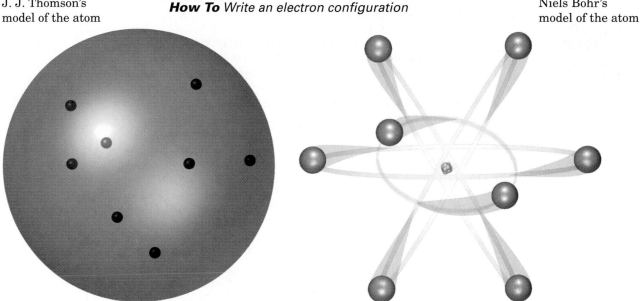

6 —— Atomic number
C —— Symbol
Carbon —— Name
12.011 —— Average atomic mass
[He]$2s^2 2p^2$ —— Electron configuration

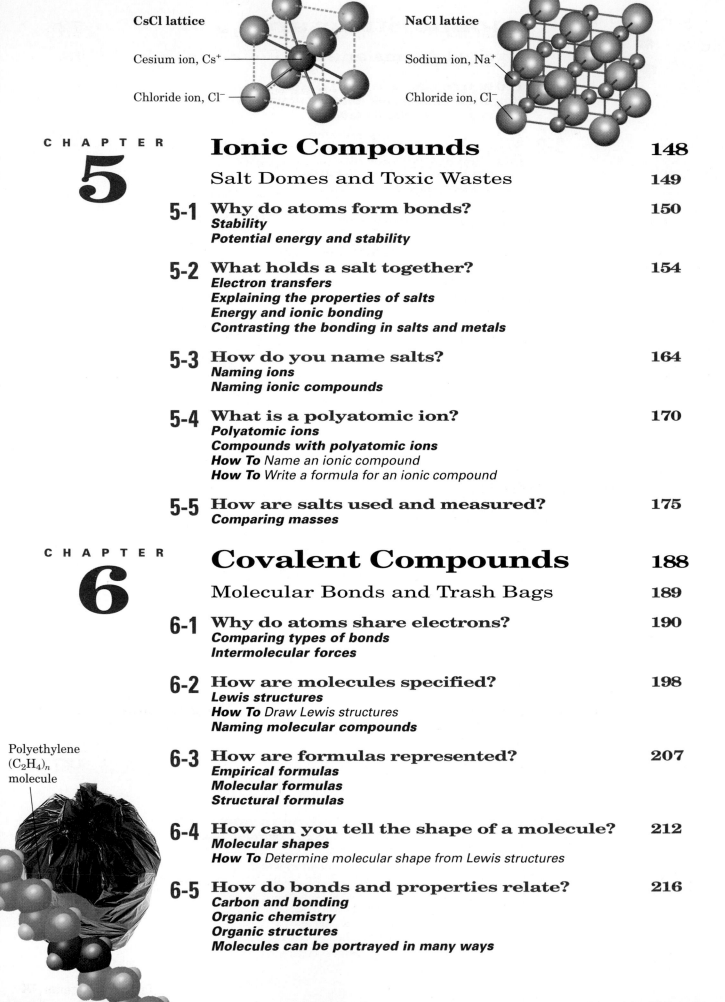

CsCl lattice

Cesium ion, Cs⁺

Chloride ion, Cl⁻

NaCl lattice

Sodium ion, Na⁺

Chloride ion, Cl⁻

Polyethylene
$(C_2H_4)_n$
molecule

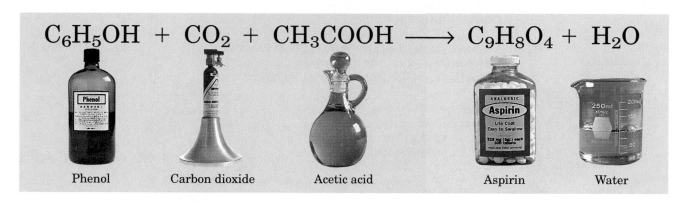

$$C_6H_5OH + CO_2 + CH_3COOH \longrightarrow C_9H_8O_4 + H_2O$$

Phenol   Carbon dioxide   Acetic acid   Aspirin   Water

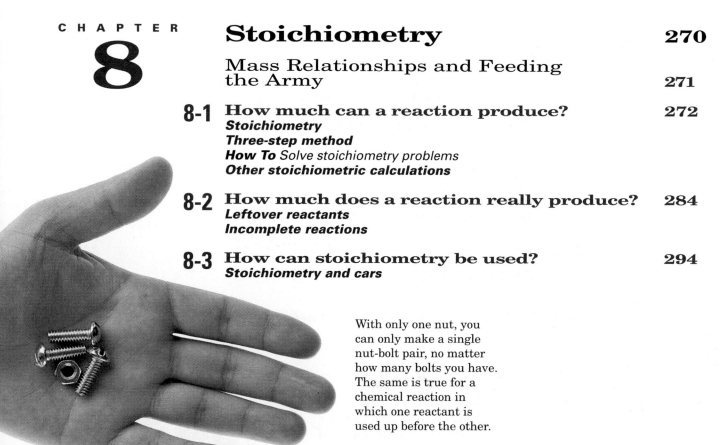

With only one nut, you can only make a single nut-bolt pair, no matter how many bolts you have. The same is true for a chemical reaction in which one reactant is used up before the other.

Calorimeter

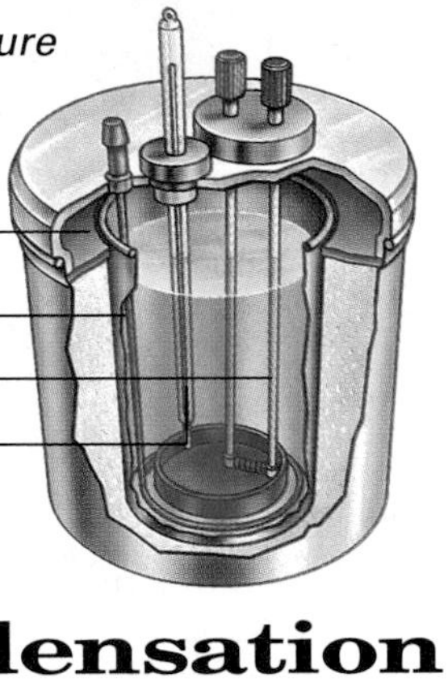

Insulated outer vessel

Stirrer

Heating element

Thermometer

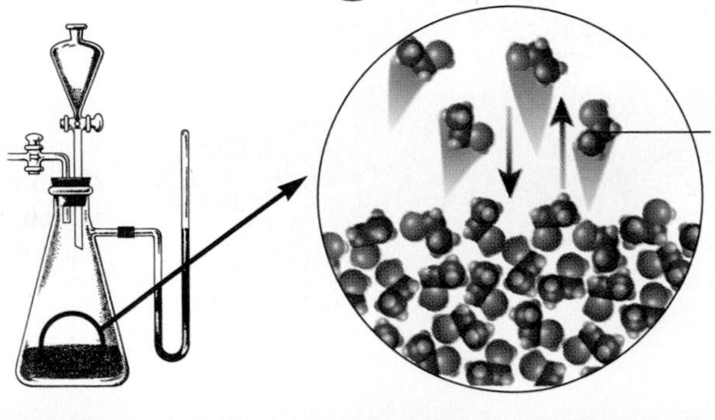

Ethanol molecule, CH_3CH_2OH

Vapor pressure of ethanol at equilibrium

Saltwater solution
Water molecule
Sodium ion, Na^+
Chloride ion, Cl^-

Equilibrium system of NO_2 and N_2O_4
$2NO_2(g) \rightleftarrows N_2O_4(g)$
0°C very light brown
25°C medium brown
100°C dark brown

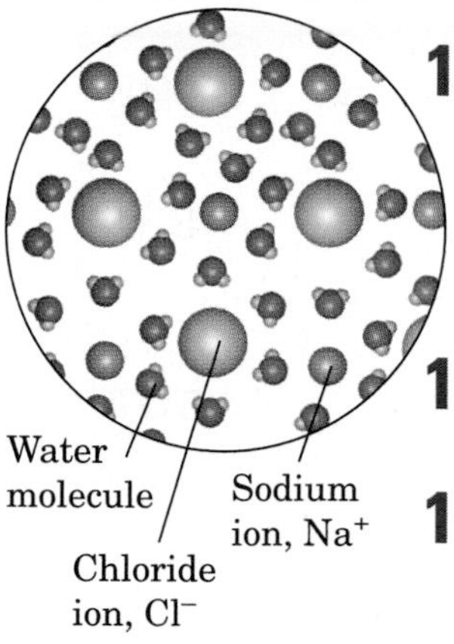

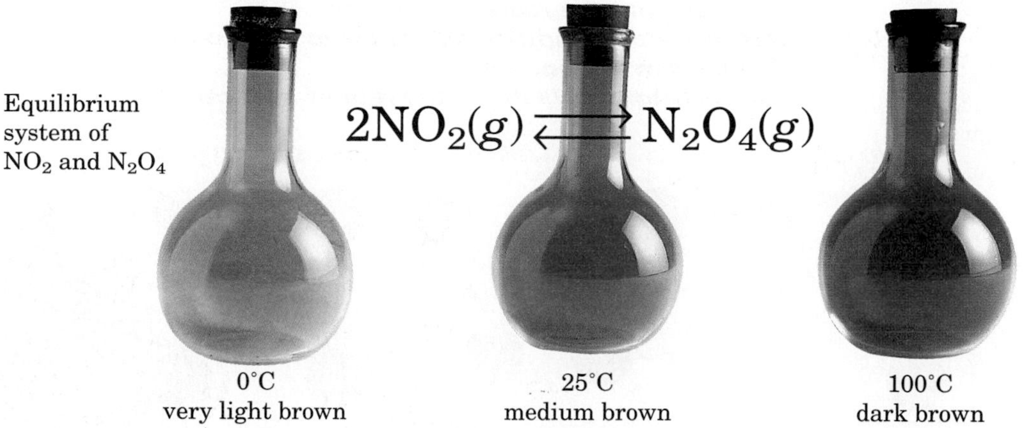

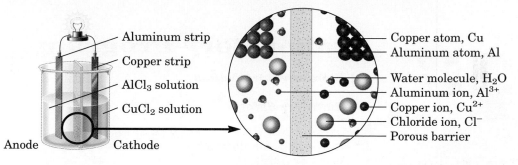

The activity series predicts electrons will flow from Al to Cu. A flow of electricity will light the bulb.

Aluminum strip
Copper strip
$AlCl_3$ solution
$CuCl_2$ solution
Anode   Cathode

Copper atom, Cu
Aluminum atom, Al
Water molecule, H_2O
Aluminum ion, Al^{3+}
Copper ion, Cu^{2+}
Chloride ion, Cl^-
Porous barrier

Electron

Transmutation process of carbon-14 to nitrogen

Carbon-14 nucleus   Nitrogen-14 nucleus

Laboratory Program 642

Laboratory Introduction

Laboratory Safety

Clothing
protection

Laboratory Explorations and Investigations 656

Student preparing for a lab

Hydrated cobalt chloride

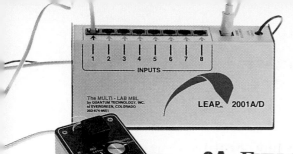

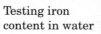

Testing iron content in water

LEAP apparatus with colormeter

Heating water with a Bunsen burner

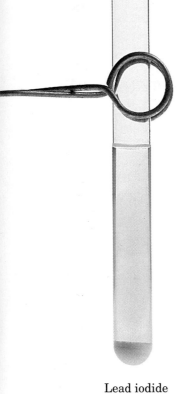

Lead iodide
precipitate

Calculator

Features

![]()

Consumer Focus

Fire hose used
on Class A fires

DNA fingerprint

Science, Technology, and Society

HISTORICAL TIMELINES

Marie S. Curie

Albert Einstein
and
Niels Bohr

Dorothy Hodgkin

Yuan Tseh Lee

The Science of Chemistry

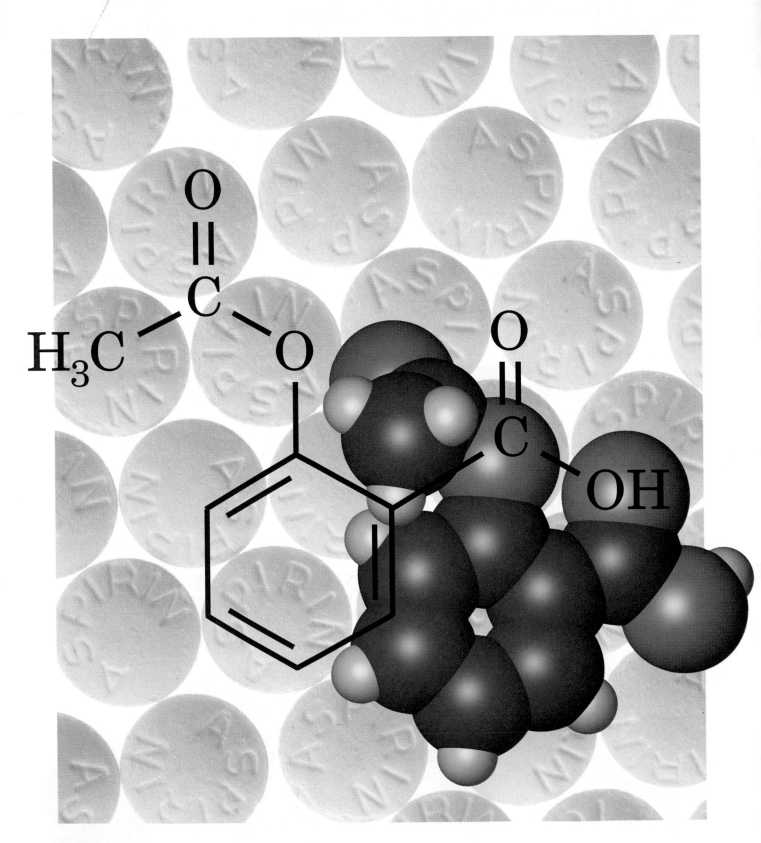

A Wonder Drug

As far back as 2000 years ago, the Greeks and Romans relied upon a substance extracted from plants, particularly the bark of the willow tree, to relieve pain and treat fevers. This plant extract was used to treat various ailments throughout the world, even in North America where Native Americans used a bark extract to treat fever and pain.

In the 1760s, Edward Stone, an English clergyman and naturalist, wrote about how he used "twenty grains of powdered bark dissolved in water, administered every four hours" to treat 50 people suffering from acute, shiver-provoking illnesses. The results, he was happy to report, were excellent. Stone was unaware that his treatment would someday become a common prescription—two aspirin tablets every four hours. Stone was also unaware that his findings would set in motion a chain of events that would evolve into a billion-dollar industry.

Following up on Stone's report, German chemists in the early 1800s isolated a tiny amount of what they felt was the active ingredient in the bark extract and called it salicin, which is related to *Salix*, the genus name for willow. French chemists improved on the extraction process and were able to obtain about an ounce of salicin from three pounds of bark. Salicin could be converted to salicylic acid, the active form of the pain reliever.

Once its identity was known, a compound related to salicylic acid, sodium salicylate, was made available for public use. Unfortunately, sodium salicylate was found to be extremely irritating to the lining of the stomach. Those who took it often suffered stomach irritation or nausea and occasionally developed ulcers.

In the late 1800s, Felix Hoffmann, a German dye chemist, began looking for ways to reduce some of the unpleasant side effects of sodium salicylate. His interest in salicylate compounds came from wanting to help relieve the pain his father experienced from arthritis. His solution to the problem was to synthesize a different derivative of salicylic acid, acetylsalicylic acid.

Each year, Americans consume 30 billion tablets, equaling 16 000 tons of aspirin, at a cost of $2 billion. The story of how aspirin has become the most widely used drug in the world is also a story about chemistry.

You'll begin this course by studying some of the chemistry of aspirin. Along the way, you'll find the answers to some interesting questions.

- *What is aspirin?*
- *How does aspirin work?*
- *How is aspirin similar to other widely used pain relievers?*
- *How does buffered aspirin differ from regular aspirin?*
- *How does name-brand aspirin differ from generic brands?*

The science of chemistry has contributed much to our knowledge of the world and has enabled chemists to make tremendous changes in the way we live. These changes can lead to challenges that we all must face and, at times, to problems that we have yet to solve.

What will I learn in chemistry?

1-1

Section Objectives

Distinguish between the properties of acids and bases.

Classify the activities and fields of working chemists.

Classify compounds as organic or inorganic.

List three ways that the public is protected from chemical hazards.

Explain the difference between chemistry and technology.

Chemistry deals with the properties of chemicals

Although the development of aspirin as a commercial product began in a laboratory, not all chemistry is done in a lab. For example, the swimming pool maintenance person in Figure 1-1 runs tests to decide what **chemicals** must be added to the pool, and how much of each. A gardener runs tests to decide what chemicals will improve vegetable yields or treat plant diseases. An amateur photographer uses an acid stop bath to neutralize a base and stabilize the image on a negative. A baker experiments to determine the right mix of ingredients and temperature to make light and tasty bread. A consumer buying groceries for the week scans food labels for substances that can cause allergic reactions. Researchers throughout the world search for a drug that will be more effective than AZT in the treatment of HIV infections.

It's not just the chemists who need to know something about chemistry. Because chemicals are an integral part of our everyday lives, everyone needs some background in chemistry.

chemical
any substance formed by or used in a chemical reaction

Figure 1-1
Swimming pool maintenance work requires a knowledge of acidity and reactions to keep the pool in the correct chemical balance.

You use chemicals every day

Some people think chemicals cause the problems of pollution, cancer, and toxic waste and that they should be banned. But think for a moment about what that would mean—everything around you is a chemical. Imagine going to the supermarket to find fruits and vegetables grown without any chemical reactions. The produce section would be completely empty! In fact the entire supermarket would be empty because *all* foods contain chemical components. Artificial flavorings, colorings, and preservatives make food taste better, look better, and last longer before spoiling. Without chemicals you would have little to wear because most of your clothing is made of synthetic fibers. Even clothing made of natural fibers is the product of chemical reactions. Finally, consider your own body, which is a highly efficient chemical factory containing thousands of compounds. Aspirin, too, is a chemical.

" I measure the pH to monitor the acid balance in the pool."

Table 1-1
Some Properties of Acids and Bases

Water solutions of acids...	Water solution of bases...
taste sour, conduct electricity	taste bitter and feel slippery
turn blue litmus paper red	turn red litmus paper blue
have pH values less than 7	have pH values higher than 7
react with bases and certain metals to form salts	react with acids to form salts

acid
a class of compounds whose water solutions taste sour, turn blue litmus to red, and react with bases to form salts

pH
a quantitative expression of acidity with the standard for a neutral solution expressed as pH 7

base
a class of compounds that taste bitter, feel slippery in water solution, turn red litmus to blue, and react with acids to form salts

organic compound
any covalently bonded compound containing carbon (except carbonates and oxides)

inorganic compound
all compounds outside the organic family of compounds

Aspirin is classified by its properties

Chemistry focuses on the properties and reactions of matter like aspirin. Aspirin is a white crystalline compound with no odor and a slightly bitter taste. The chemical name for aspirin is acetylsalicylic acid. The term **acid** in the name signifies that it belongs to a group of compounds that have certain chemical properties, which are listed in **Table 1-1**. The degree to which a compound shows these properties is its acidity. Acidity can be expressed numerically as **pH**. In water, acids have pH values below 7. Another class of compounds called **bases** have pH values higher than 7 when in water. Bases have properties that are somewhat opposite of acids, as shown in **Table 1-1**.

The pH of aspirin in water is 2.7. Compare the acidity of aspirin to other familiar substances in **Figure 1-2**. Your stomach is an acidic environment because certain cells in the lining secrete hydrochloric acid, HCl. Hydrochloric acid solutions are more acidic than aspirin. Aspirin irritates the lining of the stomach. People with ulcers or other stomach disorders cannot use aspirin.

Bufferin is a trade name for buffered aspirin. Buffering keeps the pH of a solution somewhat constant even if some acid or base is added. So using buffered aspirin could reduce stomach irritation, but it does not eliminate the problem.

Aspirin can also be classified as an **organic compound** because it contains carbon. Hydrochloric acid is an example of an **inorganic compound** because it does not contain carbon.

Figure 1-2
One way of measuring the pH of a substance is to use pH paper. The color of the paper at each pH is shown along with the pH measurements of some common materials.

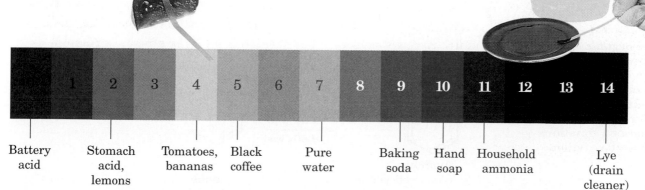

1	2	3	4	5	6	7	8	9	10	11	12	13	14

Battery acid   Stomach acid, lemons   Tomatoes, bananas   Black coffee   Pure water   Baking soda   Hand soap   Household ammonia   Lye (drain cleaner)

Chemical reactions

Felix Hoffmann began working on an alternate salicylic acid compound to relieve his father's arthritic pain. At the time, sodium salicylate was being used and the standard dose was about 6–8 grams per day. The effects of this dosage were causing so much stomach discomfort that Hoffmann's father could no longer take it. Hoffmann searched for information about other known compounds that were related to sodium salicylate but less irritating. After testing the product on his father, he found that acetylsalicylic acid worked best. Hoffmann took his research results to the president of the company where he worked, the Bayer Company. As a result, the first commercial aspirin was marketed by the Bayer Company in 1899. The name *aspirin* was selected for acetylsalicylic acid using the letter *a* from *acetyl* and *spirin* from the *spiraea* plant—a natural source of salicylic acid.

Hoffmann's search of the chemical literature available on salicylate compounds was an important part of his work. A literature search is very often the first step of research chemists trying to create a new product or solve a problem. They often use Chemical Abstracts (CA), which is the most comprehensive on-line source of chemical information in the world. CA includes abstracted versions of articles from over 18 000 scientific journals published throughout the world.

Figure 1-3
Searching the chemical literature is now easier and faster using on-line chemical databases.

synthesis
the process of building compounds from elementary substances through one or more chemical reactions

Aspirin is the product of chemical reactions

You know from previous science courses that compounds like water, H_2O, and sugar, $C_6H_{12}O_6$, are made from chemical reactions. **Figure 1-4** shows one **synthesis** process that is used to make aspirin.

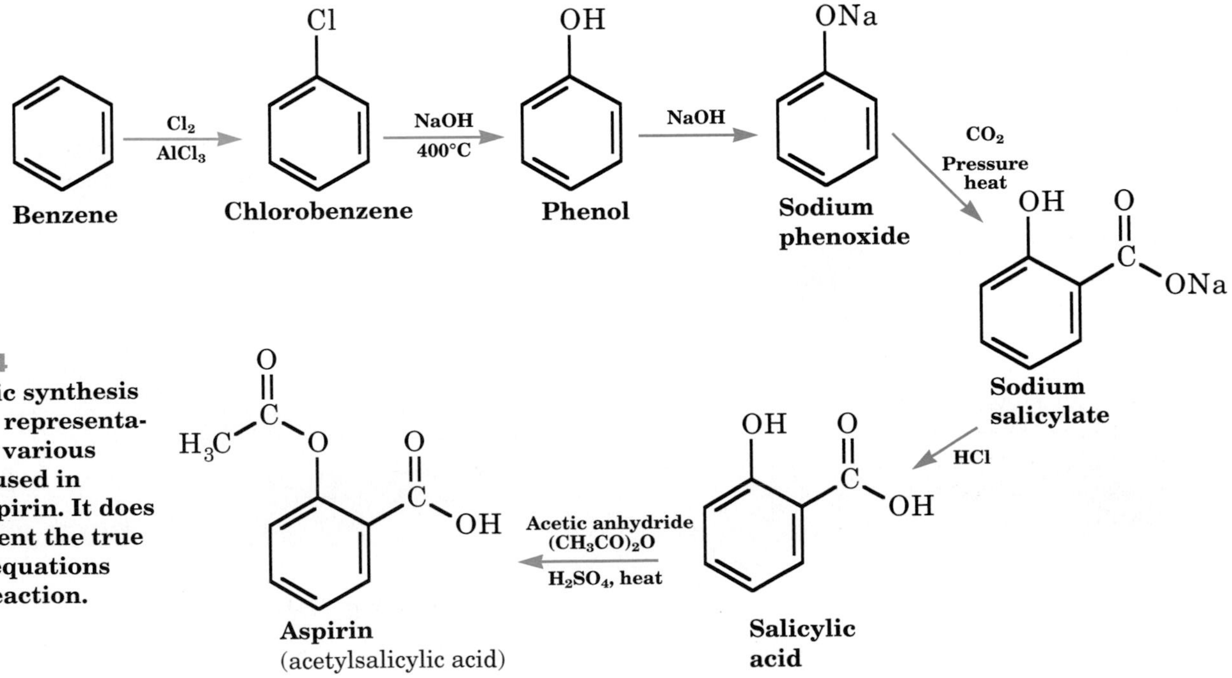

Benzene $\xrightarrow[\text{AlCl}_3]{\text{Cl}_2}$ Chlorobenzene $\xrightarrow[\text{400°C}]{\text{NaOH}}$ Phenol $\xrightarrow{\text{NaOH}}$ Sodium phenoxide $\xrightarrow[\text{heat}]{\text{CO}_2 \text{ Pressure}}$ Sodium salicylate $\xrightarrow{\text{HCl}}$ Salicylic acid $\xrightarrow[\text{H}_2\text{SO}_4,\text{ heat}]{\text{Acetic anhydride (CH}_3\text{CO)}_2\text{O}}$ Aspirin (acetylsalicylic acid)

Figure 1-4
The organic synthesis shown is a representation of the various reactions used in making aspirin. It does not represent the true balanced equations for each reaction.

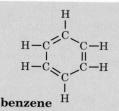

benzene

Figure 1-5a
Benzene is an organic compound with an unusual structure. The carbon atoms are arranged in a ring. Benzene and molecules that react similarly to benzene are called aromatic compounds.

benzene

1-5b
This representation of benzene is an abbreviated structural formula showing carbon–carbon bonds. It is understood that one carbon atom is bonded to one hydrogen atom at each corner of the figure.

benzene

1-5c
This abbreviated structural formula more accurately depicts the bonding between carbon atoms in the ring. One carbon atom is bonded to one hydrogen atom at each corner of the figure.

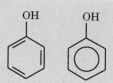

phenol is derived from benzene

1-5d
Structural representations of compounds derived from benzene are abbreviated in these forms to show the benzene ring and the atoms that substitute for hydrogen atoms.

reagent
a chemical used to convert one substance into another substance in a chemical reaction

Synthesizing aspirin involves a number of chemical reactions in which the product of one step is the reactant in the next step. Products of a reaction are always shown to the right of the arrow. Reactants are always shown to the left of the arrow. The information you see printed over each reaction arrow gives the conditions or the **reagents** used for the reaction to occur. The process starts with benzene, C_6H_6, which comes from coal tar and oil. It is a raw material for many familiar products like polystyrene and rubber. Chemists have several ways of representing benzene and compounds like it as shown in **Figure 1-5**

Before a product is made available to the public, its synthesis is studied to determine the difficulties and costs of the process on a large scale. Because there is more than one way to make acetylsalicylic acid, as shown in **Figure 1-6**, alternative methods of production must be evaluated to determine which is most cost effective.

Willow branch

Figure 1-6
Aspirin can also be synthesized starting with salicin in willow bark or methyl salicylate from the wintergreen plant.

Salicin $OC_6H_{11}O_5$ CH_2OH

Hydrolysis and oxidation

Methyl salicylate (oil of wintergreen)

Hydrolysis

Salicylic acid

Addition of acetic anhydride

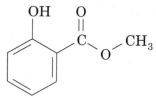

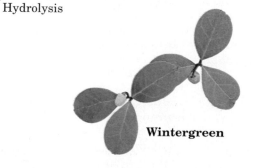

Wintergreen

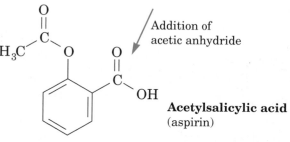

Acetylsalicylic acid (aspirin)

Most production processes begin with a piloting stage before full production begins. **Figure 1-7** shows that there is a dramatic difference between making a substance like nylon on a lab bench and in a manufacturing plant. Nylon production in the United States is about 2.6 billion pounds per year.

Chemists and chemical engineers who work on the large-scale development of a product want to make as much of it as possible, as cheaply as possible. Pilot programs for any new production process allow production chemists to monitor all aspects of the process to ensure that standards for the product can be met safely and economically.

When the product is a drug, the manufacturing process must adhere to the strict safety standards set by the U.S. Food and Drug Administration. Less than 1 out of 10 000 compounds synthesized by drug companies will ever make it to the consumer. Bringing a new drug to market generally takes about 10 years of research and testing before production can begin.

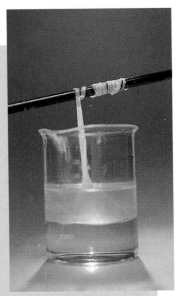

Figure 1-7a
Nylon was first produced on a small scale in 1935 by Dr. Wallace Carothers of Du Pont.

1-7b
The large-scale production of nylon results in a material that can be extruded into fibers for making nylon fabric. Nylon 66 and nylon 6 are the two most widely produced forms. Nylon 6 is prepared from another organic acid called amino-caproic acid.

Large-scale production considerations for chemicals

- What will the raw materials cost?
- Are the raw materials in adequate supply?
- What safety hazards are involved in the synthesis?
- Is it possible to carry out the reaction on a large scale? What kinds of equipment will be needed?
- How long will it take?
- What side reactions could take place? Do they need to be controlled?
- How pure will the product be? What steps must be taken to ensure a certain purity? What standards must be maintained for purity?
- Will the process involve the production and disposal of wastes or pollutants?
- What will it all cost?

Working in the field of chemistry involves the research, development, and production of new materials

The principles of chemistry are the foundation of the chemical industry, a multibillion-dollar business that employs chemists, chemical engineers, and chemical technicians to create new compounds and materials. Though you may think all chemists are research scientists, this aspect is only one of three major categories. **Figure 1-8** gives you some ideas about the variety of things chemists, engineers, and technicians do.

Research chemists work on the design and discovery of new materials. The drugs that will be used to treat or cure diseases like arthritis, diabetes, cancer, and AIDS are being designed and tested by research chemists. Work in this field requires a solid background in using computers. Today's chemists use computers extensively to design compounds, to simulate models of reactions to find out if they will work before going into the lab, and to communicate with other researchers concerning their progress in solving similar problems. To design experiments, researchers must be very familiar with today's sophisticated laboratory equipment.

Chemists, engineers, and technicians working in *development* are concerned with the task of developing full-scale production processes for new compounds and materials. They design the most inexpensive way of producing a compound or material that is also safe and environmentally sound.

Production chemists and technicians ensure that the new compound or material meets the predetermined standards set for its purity and other physical properties.

Jobs for chemists also exist in the areas of chemical sales and marketing, computer-software engineering, patent law, banking and finance, teaching, and technical writing.

Figure 1-8a
Research focuses on the design, discovery, and preparation of new materials and products.

"*I'm working on new methods for making improved coatings and catalytic materials.*"

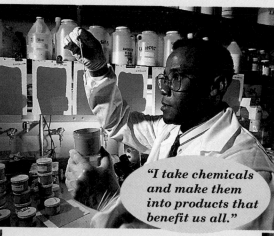

"*I take chemicals and make them into products that benefit us all.*"

1-8b
Development focuses on the creation of methods for producing new products safely and economically.

"*I ensure that the equipment and processes we use deliver products that meet our customers' needs.*"

1-8c
Production focuses on monitoring production processes to ensure that manufacturing and quality specifications are met.

Table 1-2
Top 25 Chemicals in the U.S. (1993)

Rank	Name	Formula	Pounds produced (in billions)
1	sulfuric acid	H_2SO_4	80.31
2	nitrogen	N_2	65.29
3	oxygen	O_2	46.52
4	ethylene	C_2H_4	41.25
5	calcium oxide (lime)	CaO	36.80
6	ammonia	NH_3	34.50
7	sodium hydroxide	$NaOH$	25.71
8	chlorine	Cl_2	24.06
9	methyl *tert*-butyl ether	$C_5H_{12}O$	24.05
10	phosphoric acid	H_3PO_4	23.04
11	propylene	C_3H_6	22.40
12	sodium carbonate	Na_2CO_3	19.80
13	ethylene dichloride	$C_2H_4Cl_2$	17.95
14	nitric acid	HNO_3	17.07
15	ammonium nitrate	NH_4NO_3	16.79
16	urea	CN_2H_4O	15.66
17	vinyl chloride	C_2H_3Cl	13.75
18	benzene	C_6H_6	12.32
19	ethylbenzene	C_8H_{10}	11.76
20	carbon dioxide	CO_2	10.69
21	methanol	CH_3OH	10.54
22	styrene	C_8H_8	10.07
23	terephthalic acid	$C_8H_6O_4$	7.84
24	formaldehyde (37%)	CH_2O	7.61
25	xylene	C_8H_{10}	6.84

Source: *Chemical & Engineering News*, July 1994.

Chemicals production is a major industry

The chemical industry consists of those firms that supply chemical compounds that are raw materials for building other materials. **Table 1-2** is a list of the top 25 chemicals produced in the United States. Sulfuric acid, ranked first, is also the top inorganic chemical. It is the least expensive acid to produce and is therefore a desirable raw material for building other compounds. Its other uses are shown in **Figure 1-9**. Sulfuric acid is produced by burning sulfur and sulfur ores to produce sulfur trioxide, SO_3. Sulfur trioxide is converted to sulfuric acid by adding water.

$$SO_3 + H_2O \longrightarrow H_2SO_4$$

Nitrogen and oxygen, ranked second and third, are the two gases most prevalent in air. Both of these gases are obtained by liquifying air. Nitrogen and oxygen have different boiling points. As the liquid air mixture is warmed, the nitrogen boils off first, leaving the liquid oxygen behind.

Ethylene, ranked fourth, is the top organic chemical on the list. Most ethylene is used in making plastics. Ethylene is also a raw material for the production of ethylene dichloride (ranked 13th), vinyl chloride (ranked 17th), ethylbenzene (ranked 19th), and styrene (ranked 22nd).

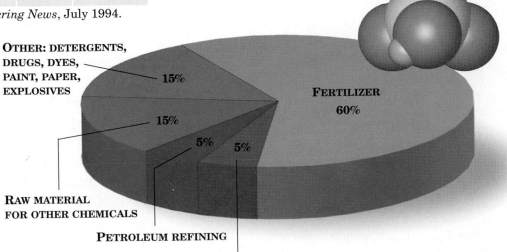

H_2SO_4

Figure 1-9
Most H_2SO_4 is used in fertilizers. When combined with salt, sulfuric acid can be used to make hydrochloric acid. It is a highly corrosive chemical. Outside of a lab about the only time you would encounter it is in the battery of a car.

OTHER: DETERGENTS, DRUGS, DYES, PAINT, PAPER, EXPLOSIVES 15%

15%

RAW MATERIAL FOR OTHER CHEMICALS

PETROLEUM REFINING

METAL PROCESSING

5%

5%

FERTILIZER 60%

Table 1-3
Top 25 Chemical Producers
in the U.S. (1993)

Rank	Name	Sales (in millions $)
1	Du Pont	15 603
2	Dow Chemical	12 524
3	Exxon	10 024
4	Hoechst Celanese	6 347
5	Monsanto	5 540
6	General Electric	5 042
7	Union Carbide	4 640
8	Occidental Petroleum	4 065
9	BASF	4 037
10	Eastman Chemical	3 903
11	Shell Oil	3 875
12	Amoco	3 773
13	ICI Americas	3 565
14	Mobil	3 533
15	Rohm and Haas	3 269
16	Arco Chemical	3 192
17	Miles	3 053
18	Air Products	2 906
19	W. R. Grace	2 895
20	AlliedSignal	2 791
21	Chevron	2 708
22	Ashland Oil	2 586
23	Ciba	2 519
24	Praxair	2 438
25	Phillips Petroleum	2 308

Source: *Chemical & Engineering News*, July 1994.

Figure 1-10
You can see that the top chemical producers are clustered by region. Texas and Louisiana, ranked first and second, occupy the region of the country where most petroleum refineries are found.

The chemical industry produces chemicals

Table 1-3 shows the top 25 chemical producers in the United States ranked by sales in millions of dollars. Some of the companies listed might be familiar to you, especially if you live in one of the top 10 chemical-producing states shown in **Figure 1-10**.

Du Pont (ranked first) has held the top position since the companies were first ranked in 1969. Du Pont is classified as a diversified producer of chemicals, which means that it manufactures chemicals in more than one industrial division. Du Pont supplies industrial organic chemicals, industrial inorganic chemicals, and synthetic organic fibers like nylon and polyester. Dow Chemical (ranked second) is a producer of basic chemicals, and Exxon (ranked third) is a producer of petroleum chemicals. Hoechst Celanese (ranked fourth) is a major producer of synthetic organic fibers, plastics, and resins.

The government regulates chemicals to reduce risk

There is risk associated with using chemicals, just as there is risk in having an operation or crossing a busy street. Government agencies whose policies and guidelines protect the public from some of the hazards of chemicals in industry and at home are listed in **Table 1-4**. Their policies are the result of risk assessment analysis. For example, in 1969 the widely used class of artificial sweeteners called cyclamates was banned because studies suggested that they have the potential to cause cancer. Though they were widely used in foods, the risk of cancer outweighed any potential benefit of using cyclamates to reduce the calorie content of some foods.

Table 1-4
Agencies Regulating Chemicals in the United States

Food and Drug Administration (FDA)

Purpose
Develops and enforces regulations regarding impurities and other hazards in foods, drugs, and cosmetics

Significant activities related to chemistry
- Approves new drugs for public release
- Sets labeling standards for drugs and foods (except meat and poultry)
- Sets regulations for the use of additives
- Inspects food manufacturers for sanitary conditions
- Validates product claims

Environmental Protection Agency (EPA)

Purpose
Works with state and local governments to enforce laws enacted by Congress regarding control of air and water pollution, solid wastes, pesticides, radiation, and toxic substances

Significant activities related to chemistry
- Sets limits for pollutants
- Sets restrictions on use of hazardous substances
- Sets tolerance levels for pesticides in foods; monitors those levels in humans, animals, and food plants

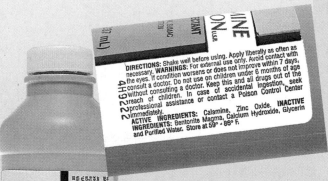

Occupational Safety and Health Administration (OSHA)

Purpose
Develops and enforces regulations regarding safe and healthy work environments

Significant activities related to chemistry
- Conducts site inspections to ensure safe conditions
- Imposes citations and penalties for noncompliance

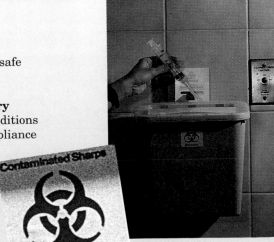
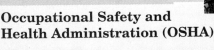

Agency for Toxic Substances and Disease Registry

Purpose
Works with state and federal agencies to collect and disseminate information regarding adverse health effects of hazardous substances in storage or of accidental release of hazardous substances through fire, explosions, or transportation accidents

Significant activities related to chemistry
- Maintains list of areas closed because of toxic contamination
- Assists in treatment of individuals exposed to hazardous substances

Consumer Product Safety Commission

Purpose
Evaluates safety of consumer products

Significant activities related to chemistry
- Enforces labeling of hazards on products
- Bans highly hazardous products

Department of Agriculture

Purpose
Works to maintain and improve agricultural productivity while protecting natural resources; ensures quality of food supply

Significant activities related to chemistry
- Analyzes foods for contaminants and pesticides
- Provides information on nutrient values in foods

Working with chemicals

To minimize your risk when working with chemicals in this course, you will be expected to pay strict attention to chemical labels, Material Safety Data Sheets (MSDS), and safety precautions. Chemists, like the one in **Figure 1-11**, know how important the MSDS is. You will be expected to consult these sheets frequently to understand the risks and hazards of using particular chemicals.

Figure 1-11
People working with chemicals consult MSDS for precautions and hazards.

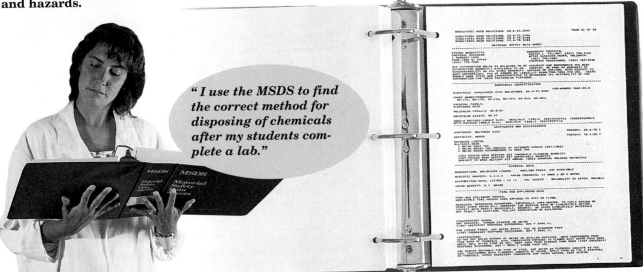

"I use the MSDS to find the correct method for disposing of chemicals after my students complete a lab."

Consumer Focus

Product warning labels

Although aspirin is considered one of the safest over-the-counter drugs, there are still a few unpleasant side effects associated with its use. It may cause nausea or vomiting and may prolong bleeding. For this reason, aspirin should not be used by anyone who has just had a tonsillectomy or oral surgery, or by pregnant women or hemophiliacs. Some people, especially those with asthma, may be allergic to aspirin. Some studies have also shown that children and adolescents with chickenpox or a severe case of flu may develop Reye's syndrome if they take aspirin. Symptoms of Reye's syndrome include sudden vomiting, violent headaches, and unusual behavior. As the condition progresses, it causes swelling of the brain and liver malfunction. More than 1000 children, approximately one-quarter of those diagnosed with the condition, have died from Reye's syndrome. The FDA requires that every container of aspirin sold in the United States have a warning label about Reye's syndrome.

You'll find warning labels on a wide variety of consumer products, such as foods, medicines, cosmetics, toys, cleaning agents, solvents, and paints. When you purchase a product, check the label carefully for warnings.

Technology is using science to solve problems

Chemistry differs from **technology**, which is the use of scientific principles to solve a problem. Determining the structure of aspirin, an analytical process, is chemistry. Using aspirin to relieve pain and reduce fever is technology. Using the structure of aspirin to design other pain relievers is also technology.

Aspirin has a number of technological uses and has become the model for other pain relievers. This is an example of how chemists can take a product, modify it slightly, and come up with another substance with more useful properties and applications.

Because aspirin is a pure compound, there is no difference between the chemical action of name brands and generic brands. However, aspirin can vary from brand to brand in terms of dosage, buffering systems, and the time it takes to act. Some aspirin tablets have special coatings that do not dissolve in the acidic environment of the stomach, and therefore do not cause irritation of the stomach. In spite of these slight variations in brands, there is no difference between the relief you get from a generic brand and a name brand.

You can now buy aspirin-free pain relievers like ibuprofen and acetaminophen. Their structures are shown in **Figure 1-12**. Tylenol and Anacin-3 are brand names for products that both contain acetaminophen. This compound does not prolong bleeding and is less likely to cause stomach upset. Ibuprofen is the compound found in Advil and Nuprin. Like aspirin, ibuprofen may irritate the stomach and prolong bleeding. Stomach irritation can be reduced if products with ibuprofen are taken with food.

technology
the application of scientific knowledge for practical purposes

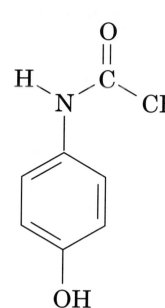

Acetaminophen

Figure 1-12a
Acetaminophen is a derivative of benzene which was shown in Figure 1-5. Notice that it differs from aspirin and ibuprofen in that it contains nitrogen.

1-12b
Ibuprofen is also a derivative of benzene and, like aspirin, it is an acid. The carbon group shown in red on the right side of the molecule is the same group that gives aspirin its acidic properties.

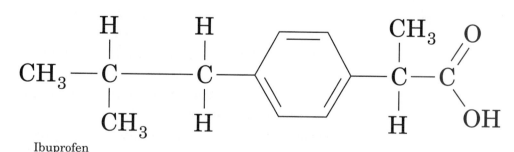

Ibuprofen

Section Review

1. Classify all the compounds in **Table 1-2** as organic or inorganic.
2. Which compounds in **Table 1-2** are acids?
3. List four properties of H_2SO_4.
4. How does technology differ from chemistry?
5. List three ways that you can determine whether an unknown compound is an acid or base.
6. **Story Link**

   What government agency regulates tamper-proof packaging for aspirin?

How do scientists approach problems?

Section Objectives

Describe the processes in the scientific method.

Explain the purpose of controls in an experiment.

Describe the role of models in chemistry.

Distinguish between hypothesis, theory, and law.

Scientific knowledge is gained from experiments

When the early Romans and Greeks discovered how an extract prepared from willow bark could relieve a variety of ailments, they undoubtedly came upon this finding by trial and error. In their search, they must have tried many extracts prepared from a variety of plants. Most extracts were probably useless, and some may even have been lethal. In the end, their success was more the result of chance rather than the product of well-designed plans.

Although these Romans and Greeks placed great reliance on rational thought and logic, they rarely felt it necessary to test their findings or conclusions and were not inclined to experiment. Gradually, experiments became the crucial test for the acceptance of knowledge. Today, experiments are an integral part of research in all sciences, including chemistry. Science is distinguished from other fields of study in that it provides guidelines or methods for conducting research.

The way scientists carry out experiments or investigations is referred to as the *scientific method*. The scientific method is a logical approach to exploring a problem or question that has been raised through observation. In addition, this approach is designed to produce a solution or answer that can be tested, retested, and supported by experimentation. Although different representations are used to describe the scientific method, it consists of the fundamental activities outlined to the left. One distinguishing feature of science that separates it from other fields of study is the last step. The research findings of any study must be reproducible by other scientists for those findings to be valid.

The biggest difference in the way discoveries are really made is in how the question or problem is recognized. Sometimes questions arise from an accidental discovery. In turn, these questions may lead scientists to search for answers in one of several ways. As examples, let's look at how two important drugs were discovered.

Activities of the Scientific Method

Make observations and collect data that lead to a question.

↓

Formulate and objectively test hypotheses by experiments.

↓

Interpret results and revise the hypothesis if necessary.

↓

State conclusions in a form that can be evaluated by others.

Scientific knowledge is sometimes gained by accident

In the 1920s, the British scientist Alexander Fleming was experimenting with bacteria that he was growing in special dishes. Before going on vacation, Fleming decided to leave the dishes as they were and clean them when he returned. When he returned from vacation, he noticed that some of the dishes had become contaminated with a blue mold. But what really caught Fleming's attention was that the bacteria had grown all over the dish except for the area around the mold.

Fleming hypothesized that the mold was secreting a substance that was lethal to the bacteria. He designed experiments to test his idea and found that he was correct. The substance secreted by the mold is what we now know as penicillin.

A similar accidental discovery was made some 40 years later. In this case, Dr. Barnett Rosenberg had been using platinum probes to study the effects of electric fields on living cells. He and his colleagues observed that bacteria did not reproduce near these probes. After conducting extensive experiments, they were able to show that a compound made from platinum formed near the electrodes. This compound, called cisplatin, is shown in **Figure 1-13**. Cisplatin was responsible for the changes in cell reproduction.

Rosenberg then reasoned that because cancer involves uncontrolled cell growth, perhaps cisplatin would be effective in treating cancer. The results of carefully planned experiments showed this reasoning to be correct. Cisplatin was approved by the Food and Drug Administration in 1979 for treatment of certain types of cancer.

The discovery of aspirin, penicillin, and cisplatin show that there is no *one* method that will guarantee an important discovery. However, there is a sequence of events that leads to the formation of a conclusion. That conclusion must be supported by data in order to be valid.

Figure 1-13a
Cisplatin is a compound made from platinum, chlorine, nitrogen, and hydrogen.

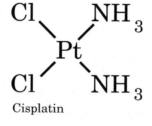

Cisplatin

1-13b
The large cell in the center of the photograph is a cancer cell. Cisplatin affects the DNA of cancer cells to halt uncontrolled reproduction.

The scientific method involves making educated guesses

Recognizing and defining a problem or question stems from observation, as shown in **Figure 1-14**. The discovery of cisplatin and its usefulness in treating cancer resulted from a simple observation—bacteria did not reproduce near the platinum electrodes. That observation led to further experiments and tests.

Once observations have been made, they are analyzed. Scientists start by examining all the relevant information or data they have gathered. They look for related data to establish some relationship or conclusion. Scientists then try to come up with a reasonable explanation for what they have observed. Any explanation they propose must be testable. A reasonable explanation of some observation that can be tested is known as a

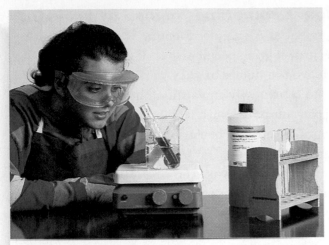

Figure 1-14
Carolyn is testing various food products claiming to be "sugar free" for the presence of sugar. If the test reagent turns from blue to red after reacting with the sample, sugar is present.

hypothesis
a proposition based on certain assumptions that can be evaluated scientifically

hypothesis. Hypotheses are usually written using an *if–then* format that describes a cause-and-effect relationship. A testable hypothesis for Dr. Rosenberg's work with cisplatin is as follows: *If* cisplatin can slow or stop cell reproduction, *then* it could be effective in treating cancer, which is uncontrolled cell growth.

The scientific method involves experiments

An *experiment* is a process carried out under controlled conditions to test the validity of a hypothesis, as shown in **Figure 1-15**. Dr. Rosenberg's work with cisplatin initially involved the question of what was inhibiting the growth of the cells. The most important part of his experimentation was the control of *variables*. Before Rosenberg could come to the conclusion that cisplatin was indeed the reason that the growth of bacteria was affected, he had to measure the effects of all other possible causes. How did he know the effect was not caused by a simple temperature change in the culture medium? How did he know the culture had not been contaminated? How did he know there weren't changes in the amount of electric current? Because platinum is a generally unreactive (inert) element and the concentration of platinum compounds in the culture medium were very low, it initially seemed unlikely that platinum could be causing the cells to stop reproducing.

Figure 1-15
Monica and Desmond are experimenting to determine how to get the largest volume of popped corn from the fewest kernels. They hypothesize that *if* the volume of popped corn increases as the moisture in the kernels increases, *then* soaking the kernels in water should increase the popped volume of a fixed number of kernels.

Figure 1-16
Collaboration between scientists is common in the search for new information.

Rosenberg had to narrow the field of possible variables by keeping them constant. Temperature, current, purity of the platinum, and the contents of the culture medium are some of the many variables that could change from experiment to experiment. By keeping variables constant, researchers can isolate the key variable. It took many experiments over a two-year period for Rosenberg and his team to verify that the formation of cisplatin was the key variable that caused the cell growth to stop.

Rosenberg's initial work spawned further research of the anticancer properties of cisplatin. After years of testing by independent sources to verify the effectiveness of the drug, cisplatin was approved for use in cancer chemotherapy.

Data from experiments can lead to a theory

Any conclusion scientists make must come directly and solely from the data they obtain in their experiments. Many times, scientists discover that they are unable to arrive at a conclusion. In fact, they may discover that the data fail to support their hypothesis. In that case, they must reexamine the question and develop a new hypothesis to be tested.

Any hypothesis that withstands repeated testing may become part of a theory. A **theory** is a broad generalization that is based on observation, experimentation, and reasoning. Because theories are not facts, but rather explanations, they can never be proven. A theory is considered successful if it explains *most* of what is observed and is modified as new information is discovered. For example, you will learn about atomic theory in Chapter 3. The idea that all matter is made of discrete particles called atoms that cannot be further divided was first proposed by Democritus about 400 B.C. Using experimentation in the early 1800s, John Dalton provided the data to support that theory. This theory has been modified as scientists have discovered a number of smaller particles that make up atoms, as illustrated in **Figure 1-17**.

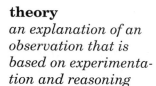
theory
an explanation of an observation that is based on experimentation and reasoning

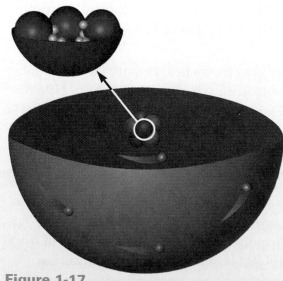

Figure 1-17
The discovery of quarks adds to the theory of atomic structure. A neutron is made of three quarks held together by small particles called gluons.

Top Quark, Last Piece in Puzzle Of Matter, Appears to Be in Place

By WILLIAM J. BROAD

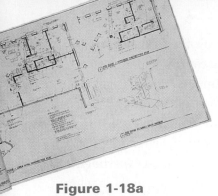

1-18b
The mouse is often used in research as a model for how humans react to drugs and treatments.

Figure 1-18a
Models take many forms. The blueprint is a two-dimensional model.

Aspirin model

1-18c
Chemists today use computers to build molecules for specific uses. They also use simulation models to predict the results of reactions before entering the lab.

Models are like theories

Models play a major role in science. They can take many forms, from actual replicas to written descriptions. **Figure 1-18** shows several types of models. Models can be used in various ways. The structure of acetylsalicylic acid serves as the model for the development of other chemical substances that could also work as painkillers. The wave-particle model describes the behavior of electrons as waves and as particles.

It is important to remember that models are not always exact. The model you see in **Figure 1-18** represents a molecule. The atoms are not hard spheres, nor are they the sizes and colors shown. However, the model does show the geometrical arrangement of the atoms and their relative sizes.

When a model is an explanation, it explains *most* of the observations. Models, like theories, are refined as new information is discovered.

Scientific laws are based on facts

Certain facts in science always hold true. Such facts are labeled as scientific laws. A *scientific law* is a statement or mathematical expression of some consistency about the behavior of the natural world.

For example, motion is described by Newton's laws. Newton's first law states that if there is no net force acting on an object and if the object is at rest, it will stay at rest; and if the object is in motion, it will continue in its motion. This law explains the movement or lack of movement of all matter.

There are a limited number of laws in science compared to the number of theories and hypotheses. Do not confuse a scientific law with either a hypothesis or theory. A hypothesis *predicts* an event. A theory *explains* it. A law *describes* it.

Section Review

7. Give two reasons why chemists publish the results of their experiments.
8. What activities are part of the scientific method?
9. How do models help chemists acquire knowledge about the natural world?
10. You observe that more sugar will dissolve in hot tea than in iced tea. Formulate a hypothesis for this observation. Develop a plan to test your hypothesis.

11. **Story Link**
    How did Felix Hoffmann build on other scientists' work with aspirin?

1-3

How do I learn chemistry?

Section Objectives

List one example of how you can use chemical knowledge.

List the characteristics of a system at equilibrium.

Describe the five themes that will be used in this text.

Make a study plan for this course.

Acquiring scientific knowledge

All of the advancements in communications technology have contributed to a rapid accumulation of scientific knowledge. Scientists depend heavily on the work of other scientists in their search for answers. Think back to Hoffmann's discovery of aspirin as a pain reliever. His original work was based on a literature search of the work done by other chemists on salicylate derivatives. Today that search would be much easier using an online database like Chemical Abstracts.

Rosenberg's work with cisplatin became the basis for further study by the National Cancer Institute and numerous other research facilities around the world working to find more effective cancer-fighting drugs. Today these scientists can easily talk to each other by modem using computer networks like Internet, the world's largest network. More than ever before, the ability to communicate information in an organized, understandable manner is essential to progress.

Figure 1-19a
Scientists communicate their findings through published accounts in scientific journals.

"I use Internet to communicate with my colleagues around the world."

Themes help unify your study

Because so much knowledge has accumulated over the years, chemistry, like any other science, has become a complex subject. However, that doesn't mean that chemistry is difficult to understand or impossible to learn. On the contrary, although understanding chemistry may be a challenge at times, it should never be an obstacle that you can't overcome, especially if you keep a few suggestions in mind. The wealth of information in any subject can be classified using a small number of fundamental ideas.

1-19b
Scientists use computer networks to look up information and confer with other scientists.

The Science of Chemistry | **21**

system
*all the parts that form
a unified whole*

equilibrium
*a reversible reaction in
which the rates of the
forward and reverse
reactions are equal*

The themes in this text can help you organize what initially looks like a lot of unrelated information. Five themes have been selected to cover most of what you will learn this year. You will be given questions and problems throughout the text that will signal you to think about how a theme could be used to link some of the many things you have learned. Use these themes as a reference in your study throughout the year.

Macroscopic observations and micromodels

Chemistry focuses on the observable effects of the behavior of particles like atoms, molecules, and ions. The observable effects are in the macroscopic world and are acquired using the senses. Explaining those observations requires a model of what we believe to be occurring at the particle level. You will see numerous examples of this theme in the text illustrations. When you observe a substance, you'll see a model of its atoms, molecules, or ions, such as the one in **Figure 1-20**. When looking at a solid dissolving in water, you'll see models of the breakdown of the solid's ordered structure. Understanding events on the particle level enhances your ability to explain what you observe and to make predictions.

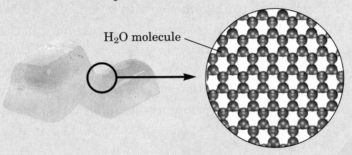

Figure 1-20
Ice consists of an open network of water molecules. Each water molecule is made from oxygen and hydrogen atoms.

H_2O molecule

Systems and interactions

A **system** is a collection of components that define something we choose to study. A system may be as large as the universe or as small as the contents of a test tube as in **Figure 1-21**. One goal of chemistry is to understand interactions within a system.

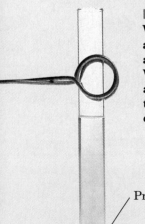

Figure 1-21
When nitric acid is added to the system, a precipitate forms. When ammonia is added to the system, the precipitate disappears.

Precipitate

Equilibrium and change

Equilibrium describes a state or condition of balance. In chemistry, equilibrium describes reversible processes occurring at the same rate. An example of an equilibrium system is shown in **Figure 1-22**, a glass of salt water. When you add salt to water until no more salt dissolves, you have what is called a solubility equilibrium system. Dissolved salt is in equilibrium with solid salt crystals at the bottom of the glass.

The system appears to be in balance at the macroscopic level. However, the equilibrium model explains that dissolved salt is recrystallizing, while solid salt crystals are dissolving.

$$\text{dissolving} \rightleftharpoons \text{recrystallizing}$$

Because both processes occur at the same rate, the system is in equilibrium. Disrupting an equilibrium system usually produces noticeable change.

Conservation

Although you will study numerous examples of change throughout this course, there are some fundamental properties of a system that are conserved, such as mass, energy, and charge. See **Figure 1-23**. Chemistry is more readily understandable and predictable because we know certain things cannot appear and disappear. For example, although mass is rearranged during a chemical reaction, it is conserved.

$$2H_2 + O_2 \rightarrow 2H_2O$$

Hydrogen   Oxygen   Water

Figure 1-23
Conservation of mass for the formation of water is symbolized by a balanced equation. The same number of each type of atom appears on both sides of the arrow.

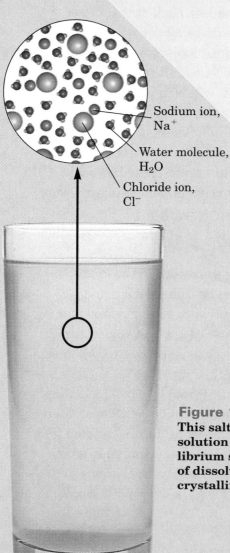

Sodium ion, Na^+

Water molecule, H_2O

Chloride ion, Cl^-

Figure 1-22
This saltwater solution is an equilibrium system of dissolved and crystalline salt.

Classification and trends

From your very first science course, you've been taught to classify. Developing categories based on similar characteristics or patterns of behavior will simplify your study and reduce the need to memorize. In this chapter, you learned that there are two large classes of compounds based on composition—organic and inorganic. You learned about two subclasses of compounds, acids and bases, each of which are characterized by a specific set of properties. If a compound is an acid, like those shown in **Table 1-5**, you can predict that when it is dissolved in water, it will have a pH of less than 7 and will turn blue litmus to red. You will get a lot of practice classifying, and your understanding of classification will be measured by your ability to make reasonable predictions.

Table 1-5
Common Acids and Their Formulas

Acid	Formula
sulfuric	H_2SO_4
nitric	HNO_3
hydrochloric	HCl
acetic	CH_3COOH
formic	HCOOH
phosphoric	H_3PO_4

Themes overlap

You probably recognized that these themes are not unrelated ideas but are interconnected. When describing an equilibrium situation, you look at the interactions of particles in a system and describe the equilibrium in terms of macroscopic observations and micromodels. Do not expect to fully understand all of these ideas at this point in the course. Thinking thematically takes time and requires practice. The Linking Chapters section in the Chapter Reviews will give you some practice.

Study tips
Your notebook as a resource

Good class notes are critical to your success in this course. The following are some guidelines for keeping up your notebook, which will save you time and frustration at exam time.

1. Listen during the lecture, and write down only those things that seem important. Don't try to write down everything.
2. Review your notes after the lecture, and organize them in a manner that allows you to make sense of them when you look back at them later. Revise any unclear explanations while the material is fresh in your mind. If there is still something that you don't understand, highlight the material to remind yourself to ask questions about it the next day in class. Use titles throughout your notes that will help you locate the information you need quickly. Some students rewrite their notes outside of class to keep the material fresh in their minds. Think of your notebook as a second textbook.
3. Keep notes on all the problems worked out in class. Make thorough notes for each step of the solution so the process is clear when you refer to these notes while working homework problems.

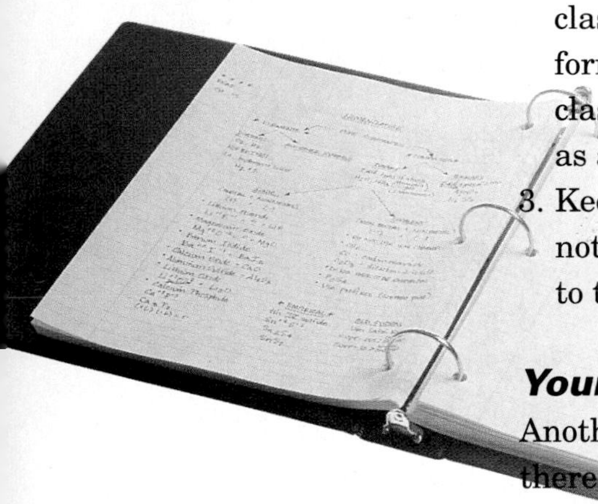

Figure 1-25
Review your class notes right away and keep your materials in good order.

Your work in the lab

Another important part of your study will be your work in the lab. It is there that you will be exposed to the real world of the chemist, and like a chemist, you will be expected to approach your work seriously. You will be assigned a variety of experiments in this course. Some will be practice in a particular technique that you will use later to investigate a problem. Others will reinforce the ideas you learn from the text.

Your success in the lab will depend on your technique. Good technique results in statistically valid data, which result in valid conclusions. Therefore, it is a good idea to be prepared for the day's work before walking into the lab. Know what you are supposed to do before you begin. Ask questions if you are unsure about a procedure. Observe all safety precautions to protect yourself and those working with you. You will find more information about your role in the lab on page 644.

How To

Succeed in learning chemistry

1. Learn the language.

Important terms and their definitions are listed in the margin of this book. Make sure you understand these definitions. Ask your teacher about them if they don't seem to make sense to you. In addition, writing formulas and using mathematical equations are also part of the language of chemistry. The Sample Problems will guide you through both of these skills, and the reviews will give you a lot of opportunity to practice.

2. Learn the material described by the Section Objectives.

Each section opens with a listing of what you are expected to learn. All questions and problems for that section relate to the objectives, so if you can work through the Reviews, you will know that you're ready for the test.

3. Use the illustrations.

The illustrations throughout the text will help you make the connections between what you see in the macroscopic world and micromodels. To practice thinking on the particle level, draw your own pictures to represent concepts or problems.

4. Take notes and review them frequently.

It is wise to review your notes as soon as possible after class. Write down questions on any material you don't understand so that you can ask them during the next class. Each chapter builds on the next, so don't fall behind! Remember that after the exam you can't forget what you've learned—you will use it in the next chapter. Use the Linking Chapters section in each Chapter Review to help reinforce necessary skills as you progress through the course.

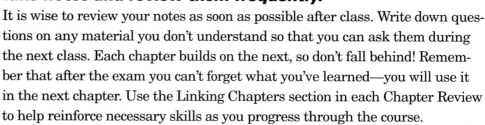

DON'T CRAM FOR THAT EXAM!

5. Work all the problems you can for practice.

Always review the chapter's Sample Problems. If you have difficulty with a problem in the Chapter Review, the Hints refer you back to the Sample Problems. Answers to selected problems are in the back of the book so that you can see if you are on the right track. Never spend more than 15 minutes trying to solve a problem—get help! You won't pass the test if you can't work the problems.

6. Don't cram for an exam.

Section Review

12. What is a system? What is the system for the equilibrium example on page 22?
13. Bring in one example of a news story that you read recently in a newspaper or magazine that demonstrates why knowledge of chemistry is important.
14. Develop a study plan to use in this course.
15. What fundamental properties are conserved during chemical change?
16. List one example of something you did in the last month that involved chemistry.

Conclusion: A Wonder Drug

The story of aspirin is just one of many examples of how chemistry works. Let's go back to the questions posed on page 3 to build on the aspirin story.

What is aspirin? Aspirin is the common name for acetylsalicylic acid, $C_9H_8O_4$. It is a white crystalline compound with no odor and a slightly bitter taste. In moist air, acetylsalicylic acid will break down to form salicylic acid and acetic acid, which smells like vinegar.

How does aspirin work? In the 1970s, chemists working in London observed that many forms of tissue injury in the human body were followed by a release of a group of hormones known as prostaglandins. Prostaglandins are synthesized and released only when cells are injured, and are responsible for the redness, swelling, and fever that accompany an inflammation or infection. These compounds can also cause headache and pain throughout the body.

Chemists have suggested that aspirin somehow blocks the release of prostaglandins, but the details of how aspirin does this still remain a mystery.

How is aspirin similar to other widely used pain relievers? Aspirin has striking structural similarities to both acetaminophen and ibuprofen. All three of these pain relievers are organic compounds with a benzene ring as part of their structure.

How does buffered aspirin differ from regular aspirin? Because aspirin is an acid, it can increase the acidity level of the stomach. Buffers are mixtures that resist changes in pH when small amounts of acid or base are added. Buffers help maintain the stomach's overall acidity level even when some acid is added.

How does name-brand aspirin differ from generic brands? Because aspirin is a pure compound, there is no difference between the chemical action of name brands and generic brands in the body. Aspirin can vary from brand to brand in terms of dosage, buffering systems, and the time it takes to act.

Applying Concepts

1. Classify every compound listed in **Figure 1-4** as organic or inorganic.

Research and Writing

Use the library to find out more about the following.

1. Technology has created some challenges that we all must face and some problems that no one has yet solved. Choose a current event to highlight one such problem that chemists are currently trying to solve.

2. The Food and Drug Administration must approve any drug before it can be made available to the public. Find out how the FDA can determine that a drug is safe without testing it on humans.

Highlights

Key terms

acid	organic compounds
base	pH
chemical	reagent
equilibrium	synthesis
hypothesis	system
inorganic compounds	technology
	theory

Key study strategy
Studying the textbook: The SQ3R method

Survey: Scan the headings throughout the chapter to learn what the chapter is about.

Question: Change each heading in the chapter to a question that you will answer while reading.

Read: Read slowly and with meaning to answer your question. Ask yourself what the author is expecting you to learn from each paragraph.

Recite: Say the answers to your questions out loud whenever possible. If you state your answers clearly, then you know the material and you've made some of it part of your long-term memory.

Review: This strategy also helps move information into your long-term memory. Using concept maps (described in Appendix C) is an active way to review material for long-term retention.

Key ideas

 ### What will I learn in chemistry?

- Chemistry is the study of the structure of matter, its properties, and reactions.
- Chemists classify matter into categories based on common properties, such as organic compounds and inorganic compounds, or acids and bases.
- Chemists work in research, development, and production of new materials.
- Chemistry differs from technology, which is the application of scientific knowledge for practical purposes.
- Because chemicals pose risks to both individual health and the global environment, several government agencies issue policies and guidelines to protect the public from chemical hazards.

 ### How do scientists approach problems?

- Scientists investigate a question or problem by reporting their observations in a way that other researchers can duplicate the conditions and verify the results.
- To explain scientific observations, scientists form a hypothesis, which is then tested by experiments with controlled variables. By changing only one variable at a time, scientists isolate the key variable.
- Theories and models are broad generalizations that explain most of the observations made of a particular phenomenon.
- While hypotheses and theories change with the discovery of new information, a limited number of principles hold true. These principles are scientific laws.

 ### How do I learn chemistry?

- Five themes unify this text: macroscopic observations and micromodels, systems and interactions, equilibrium and change, conservation, and classification and trends.
- A successful study plan for this chemistry course includes learning the language of chemistry, mastering the section objectives, using the illustrations, working all practice problems, taking well-organized notes, and reviewing your notes promptly.

Review and Assess

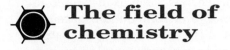

The field of chemistry

R E V I E W

1. List four situations in which you used chemicals today.
2. Your friend mentions that she buys shirts made only of natural materials because she follows a chemical-free lifestyle. How would you respond?
3. The pH values for several products are listed below. Label each as acid, base, or neutral.
   a. grapes: pH = 4.0
   b. orange juice: pH = 3.7
   c. shampoo: pH = 10.0
   d. depilatory (hair remover): pH = 12.0
   e. bread: pH = 5.5
4. Classify each of the following compounds as organic or inorganic.
   a. HCl   **b.** H_2SO_4 **c.** CH_3COOH
   d. $C_{12}H_{22}O_{11}$ **e.** H_2 **f.** CH_3Cl
   g. C_6H_6 **h.** $C_2F_2Cl_2$
5. Describe the stages involved in developing a new chemical product.
6. List three factors that chemists consider before proposing the full-scale production of a substance or product.
7. How does a product warning label differ from Material Safety Data Sheet (MSDS)?

A P P L Y

8. Aspartame is an artificial sweetener produced from the amino acids phenylalanine and aspartic acid.
   a. Predict the pH of phenylalanine and aspartic acid. Is it pH < 7, or pH = 7?
   b. Predict the pH of aspartame. Is it pH < 7, or pH = 7?

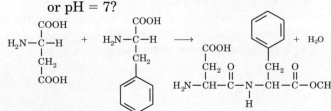

Aspartic acid   Phenylalanine   Aspartame

9. If new government regulations increased the cost of producing sulfuric acid, what industries would be most affected by the higher cost?
10. Classify the following examples as the result of science or technology.
    a. using a microwave oven
    b. determining the formula for a new polymer
    c. driving your car
    d. determining the mass of a white powder
    e. washing with soap
    f. dry cleaning a dress or suit

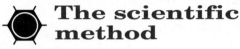

The scientific method

R E V I E W

11. Identify the requirements of a good hypothesis.
12. How does the phrase "cause and effect" relate to the formation of a good hypothesis?
13. Classify these statements as observation, hypothesis, theory, or law.
    a. A system containing many particles will not go spontaneously from a disordered to an ordered state.
    b. The substance is silvery white, fairly hard, and is a good conductor of electricity.
    c. Bases taste bitter and feel slippery in water.
    d. If I pay attention in class, then I will succeed in this course.
14. What components are necessary for an experiment to be valid?
15. Explain the purpose of an experimental control.
16. Explain the relationship between models and theories.

A P P L Y

17. Explain the generalized statement: "No theory is written in stone."

18. a. The table below contains data from an experiment in which an air sample is subjected to different pressures. Propose a hypothesis that could be tested from this set of observations.
  b. What theories can be stated from the data in the table below?
  c. Are the data sufficient for the establishment of a scientific law. Why or why not?

The Results of Compressing an Air Sample

Volume (cm)³	Pressure (kPa)	Volume × Pressure (cm³ × kPa)
100.0	33.3	3330
50.0	66.7	3340
25.0	133.2	3330
12.5	266.4	3330

19. You read in the paper that "experiments have shown that listening to music increases the efficiency of studying." Should you immediately start listening to music as you study? Explain.

Acquiring scientific knowledge

R E V I E W

20. Briefly describe the five themes used to organize the material in this textbook.
21. List at least five study skills that are required to successfully study chemistry.

A P P L Y

22. Name two social concerns that you have that can be better understood with the study of chemistry.
23. In music, the theme is a continually repeated melody that shows up throughout the piece. How do the themes in this book relate to a musical theme?
24. Why are themes important in scientific inquiry?

Alternative assessment

Performance assessment

1. Outline a study strategy for learning the important facts and understanding the concepts for this course. One effective strategy is to get a study partner. Another is to approach your study by assuming that you have to teach someone the material you are expected to learn. Discuss your plans with your teacher and use them throughout the course.
2. Select one of the chemicals in **Table 1-2** that is kept in the chemistry laboratory. Request a copy of the MSDS for that chemical from your teacher. Prepare your own product warning label from the MSDS. Compare your product warning label with the actual product warning label from the manufacturer.
3. Your teacher will provide you with an unknown chemical solution. Design an experiment that will classify the solution as an acid or a base.

Portfolio projects

1. *Chemistry and you*
Make a poster showing the types of product warning labels that are found on products in your home.
2. *Research and communication*
Clip a scientific article from a newspaper or magazine and paraphrase the article. Highlight and define chemical terms. Note the difference between the uses of chemistry and technology that appear in the article.
3. *Chemistry and you*
For one week, practice your observation skills by listing chemistry-related events around you. After your list is compiled, choose three events that are especially interesting or curious to you. Label three pocket portfolios, one for each event. As you progress through the chapters in this textbook, gather information that helps explain these events. Put pertinent notes, questions, figures, and charts in the folders. When you have enough information to explain each phenomenon, write a report and present it in class.

FRIDAY, MARCH 24, 1989

Taming H-Bombs? Scientists Claim Breakthrough In Quest for Fusion Energy— Using Car Batteries

SALT LAKE CITY-Two scientists working at the University of Utah made an unprecedented claim to have achieved a sustained hydrogen fusion reaction, thus harnessing in-laboratory the fusion power of a hydrogen bomb.

The scientists said that with no more equipment than might be used in a freshman chemistry class, they had brought about a fusion reaction in a tube that continued for 100 hours.

tion, they claim, break-

ever, enough hydrogen atoms must be confined into a small enough space so that energy released by a few fusions will trigger other nuclei to fuse. If this happens, the hydrogen fire becomes self-sustaining. If enough fusion reactions are thus ignited, the fire will give off more energy than it took to ignite it, somewhat analogous to a log fire giving off more energy than the match used to start it.

False hopes of fusion reaction raised i

Publish or Perish

A Problem Out of Control?

On March 23, 1989, two chemists, B. Stanley Pons and Martin Fleischmann, claimed that they had produced a sustained thermonuclear fusion reaction, the same process that powers stars and exists briefly in the explosion of hydrogen bombs. This claim was astonishing in light of the fact that nuclear fusion had been pursued by physicists for over 40 years with expenditures of billions of dollars, all without success. Pons and Fleischmann had experimented for less than six years at a total cost of about $100 000. Furthermore, while conventional approaches required temperatures over 10 million kelvins for fusion to occur, Pons and Fleischmann produced fusion at room temperature with simple electrolysis equipment. Although the process they used was not clearly understood at the time, the expectation was that in a few years cold fusion would not only be harnessed to produce energy, but also change the way nuclear physics would be understood.

Neither of these expectations came to pass. Nearly all attempts to repeat the experiment were unsuccessful. In the course of the next few months it was learned that Pons and Fleischmann had never performed any carefully controlled experiments in cold fusion and that the work they had done lacked reproducible data.

The cold fusion incident is a recent but hardly singular case of scientific dishonesty. For centuries improper practices have occurred in the sciences and have ranged from "trimming" actual data (to help them match the desired results) to the complete fabrication of findings.

Why would scientists mislead the public and the scientific community? Many influences can twist the work of reputable and normally honest scientists. One factor is called experimenter bias, which involves emphasizing data that fit an expectation, while overlooking, or sometimes deliberately suppressing data that contradict expectations. Experimenter bias is often unconscious and, as such, does not constitute deliberate deceit. For instance, Gregor Mendel, founder of the modern principles of heredity and genetics, may have classified some peas that were not clearly smooth or wrinkled or green or yellow into categories that gave the correct results. Thus, while Mendel's hypothesis was correct, his data were statistically "too good to be true."

Similarly, reputable scientists in the former Soviet Union and the United States believed in the 1960s that they had successfully formed a polymer (a chain of molecules linked together and the basic chemical form of plastics) out of ordinary water. It was finally determined that "polywater" was nothing more than water contaminated by silicon from the capillary tubes in which it was always observed.

Experimenter bias is embarrassing, but little more. Far more serious is the recent trend of professional self-preservation. As the number of scientists has increased in the last hundred years, so has the competition among them for available funding. The need to maintain a competitive edge has driven a number of scientists to alter data to yield more impressive results or, in some cases, to manufacture results completely. The excuse cited for this behavior is that scientists are overworked and pressed for time, so they draw conclusions of which they are absolutely certain with the intention of actually running the experiment later. All too often, the experimental values turn out to be nowhere near those that have been prematurely reported. This situation is worsened by researchers' fears that competitors may know of their work and may use this knowledge to publish findings first.

Many of these factors seem to have been at play in the cold fusion experiments. Pons, although hard working and dedicated, often worked so fast that he did not catch errors in his methods or analysis. His enthusiasm for new ideas, such as those suggested by Fleischman, may have actually encouraged experimental bias.

Concern over competitors was also involved. Pons and Fleischmann carried out their work at the University of Utah in Salt Lake City, while their principal rival, Steven Jones, was conducting similar experiments less than fifty miles away at Brigham Young University in Provo. The desire of administrators at each school to be the first to announce the ground-breaking work led to the publicizing of results before they had been sufficiently confirmed. Apparently they believed that there was too much at stake for them not to make the announcement.

What can be learned from the cold fusion episode? Obviously, more care must be taken in checking claims before they are published. Ironically, the speed with which cold fusion was debunked arose from the simplicity of the apparatus used. Scientists across the country had cold fusion reactors running within days of the announcement,

and a flood of null results appeared before Pons' and Fleischmann's article was even published. If such efficiency can be employed in evaluating other claims that sound too good to be true, the effects of dishonesty and negligence may be reduced.

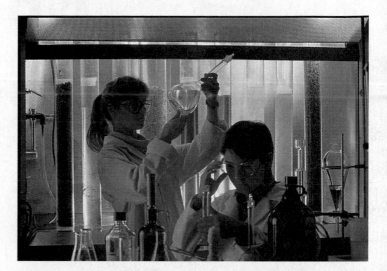

Researching the Issue

1. Martin Fleischmann has said, "If you really don't believe something deeply enough before you do an experiment, you will never get it to work." What are the strengths and weaknesses of this argument?

2. What methods could be used to reduce or eliminate experimenter bias? How could the "double blind" technique, which is often used in psychology, be modified for use in experimental chemistry?

3. Choose one of the following scientists and investigate claims that they misinterpreted or misreported research data. Consider whether the conclusions they reached were valid or invalid.
   a. Isaac Newton   **b.** Sir Cyril Burt
   c. Galileo Galilei   **d.** Robert Millikan
   e. Alexander Gurwitch   **f.** René Blondlot

4. In some cases, test results for products (such as new drugs) have been falsified. What steps might be taken to safeguard against this practice?

5. The following books provide accounts of scientific dishonesty, its causes, and possible solutions.
   Kohn, Alexander. *False Prophets.* Oxford: Basil Blackwell Ltd., 1986.
   Broad, William & Wade, Nicholas. *Betrayers of the Truth.* New York: Simon and Schuster, 1982.

2 Matter and Energy

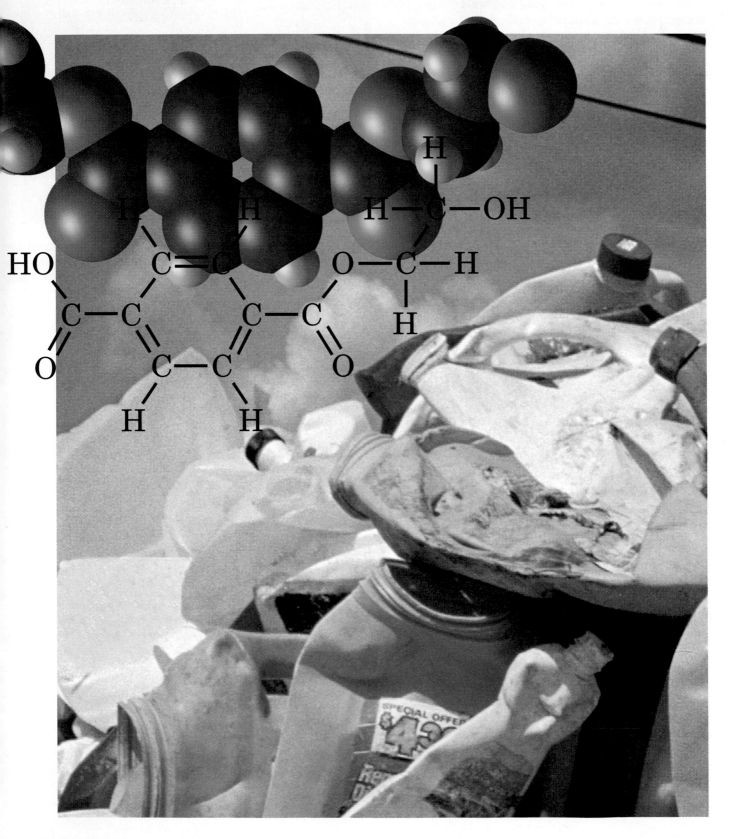

Recycling—Saving Matter and Energy

What happens to a plastic soda bottle that you put in the recycling bin? You could end up wearing it. New technology allows bottles made from PET (polyethylene terephthalate, a kind of plastic) to be converted to polyester. Polyester is a great material for many things, including T-shirts and fleecy jackets.

More likely, however, the plastic soda bottle you want to recycle will never be remade as a useful product. Odds are the bottle will end up in a landfill or incinerator. In the landfill, it will take up valuable space for, perhaps, hundreds of years. In the incinerator, the bottle will be burned, giving off exhaust gases that pollute the air.

On the other hand, when you toss an aluminum can into a recycling bin, the can will almost certainly be recycled. The average aluminum can deposited at a recycling center is melted down, reformed, and back on supermarket shelves in only six weeks.

Recycling aluminum saves energy and raw materials, reduces litter and pollution, saves landfill space, and is profitable too. Every business day, manufacturing companies make more than $2 million by recycling aluminum. When properly sorted by color, glass bottles are also easily and profitably recycled. Energy and raw materials are saved in the process.

What about paper? What happens to those newspapers and old homework pages that you dump in the recycling bin? The prospects for paper recycling are mixed. A lot of paper *is* recycled annually—with great energy and resource savings. For every ton of new paper made from 100% recycled wastepaper, 17 trees, 4100 kilowatt-hours of energy (enough to power the average home for six months), 7000 gallons of water, three cubic yards of landfill space, and taxpayers' dollars are saved. Yet more paper is collected than can actually be recycled. Excess paper piles up at some recycling collection sites with no place to go.

As you study this chapter, you will begin learning some chemistry that explains the successes and failures of current recycling efforts. Look especially for answers to the following questions.

- *How can materials be identified so they can be recycled or disposed of properly?*
- *How can mixtures be separated so that their components can be recycled?*
- *How is energy measured, and what do we mean when we say "recycling saves energy"?*
- *Why can some materials (such as aluminum) be recycled more successfully than others?*

As you will see, recycling is like all other processes of the physical world—it involves the interaction of matter and energy.

What is matter?

2-1

Describing matter

What do the stars, your brain, air, a peanut butter sandwich, and a plastic soda bottle have in common? All of these things are examples of matter. Matter, the "stuff" of which all things in the universe are composed, comes in a fantastic variety of forms.

Matter has mass and volume

Matter is defined as anything that has mass and volume. What do we mean by *mass* and *volume*? **Volume** is simply the amount of space an object occupies. A grapefruit has more volume than a lemon, for example.

The **mass** of an object is a measure of how difficult it is to change the object's state of motion. You can compare masses of different objects by pushing or pulling them. Very massive objects are relatively hard to start or stop moving. Common units of mass are the gram (g), kilogram (kg), and milligram (mg). Mass also indicates the amount of matter in an object; the more massive an object is, the more matter it contains.

Note that mass is similar to weight, although strictly speaking they are not the same thing. The difference is that weight depends on gravity, while mass does not. Since gravity varies from place to place, weight also varies. But mass is constant because it is not determined by gravity.

A balance measures mass

Weight can be measured using a scale. To determine mass you must use a *balance*. In chemistry, you will generally be interested in mass rather than weight, so the balance is standard laboratory equipment. Two types of balances that you may use are the *analytical balance,* shown in **Figure 2-1**, and the *triple beam balance,* shown in **Figure 2-2** on the next page.

Although the term *weigh* is not literally equivalent to "determine the mass of," these expressions are often interchanged. In chemistry, when you hear the word *weigh,* you may actually need to determine mass. Check to be sure.

matter
anything that has mass and volume

volume
the amount of space an object occupies

mass
the quantity of matter in an object

Figure 2-1
The analytical balance is used to measure the mass of very small quantities of substances or to measure with extreme precision. As indicated by this analytical balance, the mass of the copper(I) chloride and flask is 73.3187 g.

Figure 2-2
Mass can also be measured with a triple beam balance, though not as precisely as with an analytical balance. This triple beam balance shows that the mass of the flask and the copper(I) chloride it contains is 73.32 g.

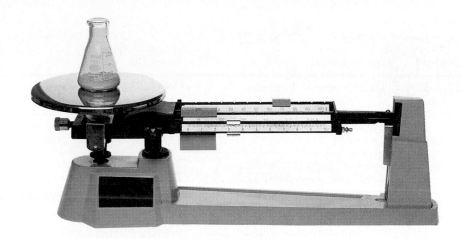

atom
*the basic unit
of matter*

molecule
*a neutral group of
atoms held together by
chemical bonds*

Atoms are basic units of matter

Imagine crushing some coffee beans in a grinder. The beans break into pieces. You keep grinding the beans until you get a fine powder. Each of the tiny grains contains billions and billions of submicroscopic **atoms**.

Matter in and around you is made of atoms. There are over 110 different kinds of atoms in the known universe. Yet, combined in various ways, atoms make up everything you can see, touch, smell, taste, or hear.

Atoms usually do not exist by themselves, but combine to form compounds. Some of these are clusters called **molecules**. A molecule may contain two atoms or two thousand, but in any case the molecule behaves as a unit. **Figure 2-3** shows three of the many kinds of inorganic and organic molecules in an orange. Most materials in your environment, like the orange, are made of many kinds of molecules, which are mixed together. An orange peel, for example, contains more than 100 different kinds of molecules.

Figure 2-3a
One type of inorganic molecule found in an orange is water. It consists of two hydrogen atoms and one oxygen atom.

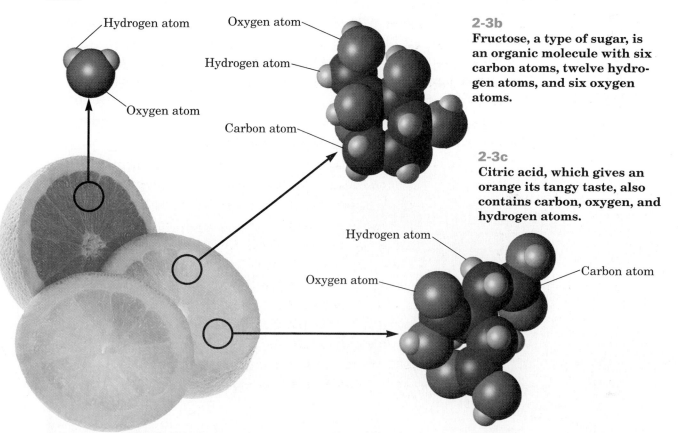

Hydrogen atom

Oxygen atom

Oxygen atom

Hydrogen atom

Carbon atom

2-3b
Fructose, a type of sugar, is an organic molecule with six carbon atoms, twelve hydrogen atoms, and six oxygen atoms.

2-3c
Citric acid, which gives an orange its tangy taste, also contains carbon, oxygen, and hydrogen atoms.

Hydrogen atom

Carbon atom

Oxygen atom

Table 2-1
Properties of Matter

Property	Description	Example
Electrical conductivity	ability to carry electricity	Copper is a good electrical conductor, so it is used in wiring.
Heat conductivity	ability to transfer energy as heat	Aluminum is a good heat conductor, so it is used to make pots and pans.
Density	mass-to-volume ratio of a substance; measure of how tightly matter is "packed"	Lead is a very dense material, so it is used to make sinkers for fishing line.
Melting point	temperature at which a solid changes state to become a liquid	Ice melts to liquid water at the melting point of water.
Boiling point	temperature at which a liquid boils and changes state to become a gas at a given pressure	Liquid water becomes water vapor at the boiling point of water.
Index of refraction	extent to which a given material bends light passing through it	The index of refraction of water tells you how much light slows and bends as it passes through water.
Malleability	ability to be hammered or beaten into thin sheets	Silver is quite malleable, so it is used to make jewelry.
Ductility	ability to be drawn into a thin wire	Tantalum is a ductile metal, so it is used to make fine dental tools.

Properties of matter
Matter can be described by its properties

Chemists describe different types of matter by listing their characteristics, or *properties*. Color, mass, volume, texture, transparency, flammability, and taste are a few of the many properties that are useful for describing matter. **Table 2-1** lists some other useful properties with which you may be less familiar.

Ever since the earliest humans sought flammable materials for making fire, people have been collecting information about properties of matter. Collected data from the history of chemical investigation is compiled in reference books that are easily available to you. A page from a popular chemistry reference book is shown in **Figure 2-4**.

Figure 2-4
Reference books catalog substances and describe them by their properties. This page from The Merck Index (Eleventh Edition, ©1989, Merck & Co., Inc.) gives a description of silver. How many properties in this list are familiar to you?

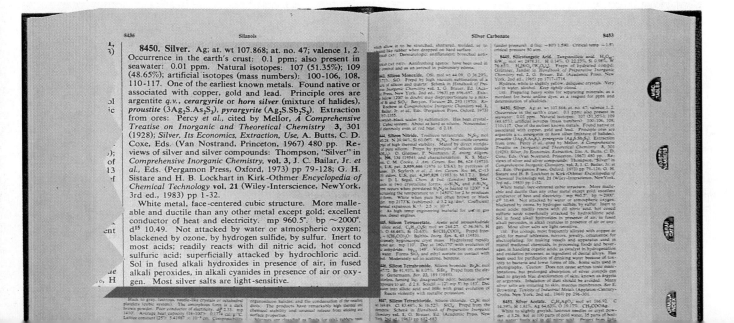

Physical properties are useful for identifying things

Color, texture, shape, and mass can be observed or measured without changing the composition of matter. Properties such as these are called **physical properties**.

You rely on physical properties to identify things all the time. Using color, texture, and mass, it's easy to know which recycling bin a piece of white paper or a brown glass bottle belongs in, for example. Or, look at **Figure 2-5**. Even in a photograph, you can probably identify what material the objects shown are made from by observing some of their physical properties.

Figure 2-5
Can you identify what material these objects are made from? What properties did you use to identify them?

physical properties
properties that can be observed or measured without changing the composition of matter

state
the condition of being a gas, liquid, solid, plasma, or neutron star

State of matter is a physical property

An easily observed physical property is **state**. Solids, liquids, and gases are the three common states of matter. **Figure 2-6** shows the solid, liquid, and gaseous states of water at the molecular level.

Solids have fixed volume and shape. These features result from the way solids are structured on a microscopic level. In the solid state, atoms and molecules are held tightly in a rigid structure but vibrate slightly about fixed positions.

2-6a
Below 0°C, water molecules solidify to form ice. In the solid state, water molecules are held close together in a rigid structure.

2-6c
At 100°C, water becomes water vapor, a gas. Water molecules can move randomly over large distances.

Figure 2-6b
Between 0°C and 100°C, water exists mostly as a liquid. In the liquid state, water molecules are close together, but can move about freely.

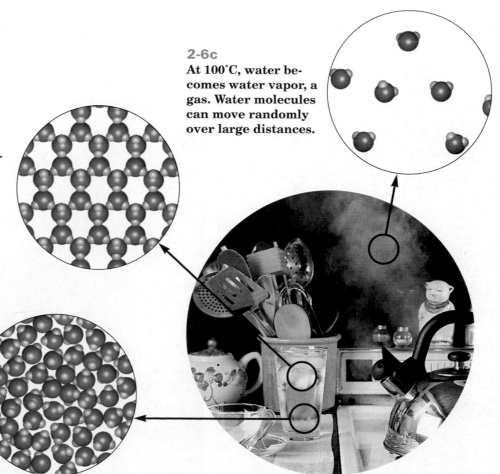

Liquids have a fixed volume but variable shape. The particles in a liquid are not held together in the rigid manner characteristic of solids. Like ball bearings in oil, the particles of a liquid can slip and slide past one another. As a result, the liquid as a whole is able to flow. The distances between adjacent particles are constant on average, so the overall volume of the liquid is fixed.

Gases have no fixed shape or volume and therefore expand to fill any container they occupy. In the gaseous state, a few grams of helium would become evenly distributed in a small flask or throughout a large room. This behavior of gases results from the fact that their particles are not held to one another. Instead, they are free to move about.

At very high temperatures, matter can exist as a *plasma*, a fourth state of matter. In this high energy state, atoms are torn apart into smaller pieces. The sun, stars, much intergalactic matter, and the glowing interiors of fluorescent lights are in the plasma state. A fifth state of matter, that of the *neutron star*, has recently been discovered as well. Little is known about this state at the present time.

Chemical properties tell how substances interact

A material is not fully described by physical properties alone. Left out of the description is how it will behave when it is in contact with other materials. To describe this type of behavior, we refer to **chemical properties**, properties that are observable only when one substance interacts with another.

Reactivity with acid, for example, is a chemical property. Calcium hydroxide, the active ingredient in some antacid medications, such as the one shown in **Figure 2-7**, is very reactive with acids. It is used to neutralize excess hydrochloric acid that forms in your stomach. Reactivity with acid can sometimes have destructive effects, as shown in **Figure 2-8**.

chemical properties
properties that can be observed only when substances interact with one another

Figure 2-7
Some antacids contain calcium hydroxide as the active ingredient. Calcium hydroxide, a base, reacts with hydrochloric acid in your stomach.

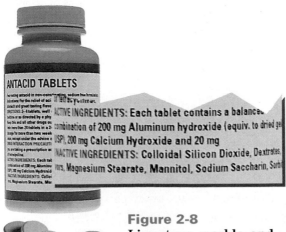

Figure 2-8
Limestone, marble, and concrete all react with acid. Objects made from these materials are therefore harmed by acid rain, which results from air pollution. This Greek statue shows signs of damage by acid rain.

Reactivity with oxygen is another chemical property. **Figure 2-9** shows how a bicycle and an apple react with oxygen.

Intensive properties result from the way matter is structured

Some properties of matter, such as mass, volume, and length, depend on the quantity of matter present. These are called *extensive* properties. But all chemical properties and many physical properties, including melting point, color, density, and texture, do not depend on the amount of matter present. These properties are called *intensive* properties.

For example, consider graphite, the material that makes up your pencil point. Pencil "leads" are made of graphite rather than lead. Graphite is a gray solid at room temperature and has a slippery texture regardless of whether it is in a pencil or a laboratory reagent bottle. Graphite has these intensive properties because of the way its atoms are arranged.

Figure 2-10 shows how the slippery texture of graphite results from its structure.

Figure 2-9a
The iron in this bicycle reacts with oxygen in the air to produce rust.

2-9b
Some kinds of fruit turn brown when they are exposed to the air because they contain compounds that react with oxygen.

Figure 2-10
Graphite consists of sheets of carbon atoms stacked in layers. A pencil can glide across a piece of paper because the carbon layers that make up the point slide over one another easily.

Section Review

1. Draw a picture representing chlorine atoms in the gaseous state.
2. Tell whether the underlined property is a chemical or physical property. <u>Iron is transformed into rust</u> in the presence of air and water.
3. What properties of spinach distinguish it from ice cream?
4. Classify the following properties as physical or chemical and as extensive or intensive: volume, area, flammability, state, odor.
5. **Story Link**

What properties of aluminum distinguish it from glass?

How do matter and energy interact?

2-2

Much of chemistry is about creating new substances to improve food, fuel, health, and fashion. Chemists can put atoms and molecules together in different ways or take them apart. When atoms form molecules, and when molecules change into new ones or break down into atoms, energy is involved. Energy plays an essential role in chemistry. Energy is a broad concept, but a good basic description is that **energy** is the capacity to move or change matter.

energy
the capacity to do work

Forms of energy
Kinetic energy is energy of motion

kinetic energy
energy that moving objects possess by virtue of their motion

Kinetic energy is a type of energy that only moving objects have. A truck rolling down an alley sets objects in its way in motion or changes those objects as it smashes into them. The rolling truck has energy; it can move and change matter. Because the truck's energy arises from its motion, we call its energy *kinetic energy*.

The amount of kinetic energy, *KE*, in an object depends on its mass, *m*, and velocity, *v*. Kinetic energy is easy to calculate from the following equation.

$$\text{kinetic energy} = \frac{1}{2} (\text{mass})(\text{velocity})^2 \qquad KE = \frac{1}{2} mv^2$$

Energy is measured in units of kg·m²/s², or *joules*, J. One joule is about equal to the energy you expend bringing a cheeseburger to your mouth. It is easy to apply the expression for kinetic energy to other situations as well. For example, a typical cheetah has a mass of 60 kg. Its peak speed, or velocity, is about 28 meters per second, m/s. Substituting these numbers into the expression below gives the kinetic energy of the cheetah in **Figure 2-11**.

$$KE = \frac{1}{2} mv^2 = \frac{1}{2} (60 \text{ kg})(28 \text{ m/s})^2 = 2.4 \times 10^4 \text{ J}$$

Figure 2-11
The kinetic energy of a cheetah chasing its prey can be calculated if you know the cheetah's velocity and mass.

The kinetic energy of a typical oxygen molecule in your classroom can also be easily calculated. At room temperature and standard pressure, an average oxygen molecule moves with a speed of about 400 m/s. Its mass is 5.3×10^{-26} kg. Substituting these numbers into the expression for kinetic energy gives us the kinetic energy of an average oxygen molecule.

$$\text{KE} = \frac{1}{2}\, mv^2 = \frac{1}{2}\, (5.3 \times 10^{-26}\text{ kg})(400\text{ m/s})^2 = 4.2 \times 10^{-21}\text{ J}$$

The oxygen molecule's small mass gives it a small kinetic energy.

Potential energy is stored energy

potential energy
energy an object possesses because of its position

Potential energy is energy an object possesses because of its position. It is called *potential* energy because it has the potential, or ability, to make matter move and change once the energy is released.

An object's potential energy corresponds to the amount of force needed to keep it in position. For example, there is potential energy in a compressed spring. As shown in **Figure 2-12**, a force must be applied to the spring to hold it in place.

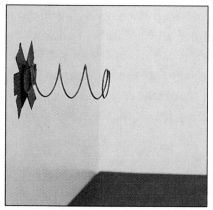

Figure 2-12a
The spring is at rest, neither stretched nor compressed.

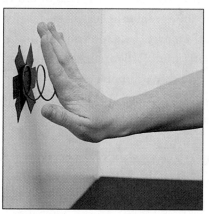

2-12b
The spring is compressed, which gives it potential energy.

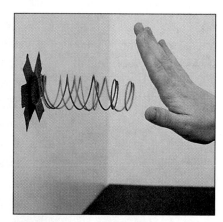

2-12c
Potential energy decreases as the force holding the spring in a compressed position is removed.

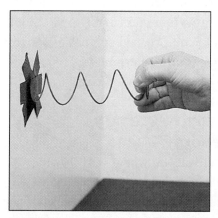

2-12d
The spring is stretched to give it potential energy.

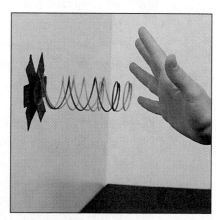

2-12e
Potential energy decreases as the force stretching the spring is removed, and the spring returns to its resting position.

Matter held in an elevated position is subject to the downward force of gravity, so forces are required to keep it in place. Therefore, elevated objects have potential energy. Which has more potential energy, a car parked on a small hill or the same car parked on a high mountaintop?

Potential energy also influences the behavior of atoms and molecules. Strong forces hold these tiny particles together, and as a result, clusters of such particles contain potential energy.

Kinetic and potential energy underlie other energy forms

There are many forms of energy, from wind to solar to nuclear to electric to sound energy. In the *macroscopic* world, the world of objects on a scale large enough to see, it makes sense to speak of these diverse forms of energy. But when you consider matter on the atomic level, you find that these diverse forms of energy are not truly distinct. They are just kinetic energy, potential energy, or combinations of these acting on small-mass particles. Kinetic and potential energy underlie electrical, solar, and the other seemingly different forms of energy that we encounter.

One of the important forms of energy to consider when studying matter is *internal energy*. Internal energy is the sum of all the kinds of energy inside a substance. This includes potential energy associated with the forces between atoms and molecules and kinetic energy due to the motions of atoms and molecules. As the temperature of a substance increases, the motion of its atoms and molecules increases, as does its internal energy.

Figure 2-13
This hydroelectric plant is at Hoover Dam, on the Colorado River in Arizona.

Energy can be transformed

The hydroelectric plant in **Figure 2-13** shows how energy can be *transformed*, or changed from one form into another. Hydroelectric plants transform the potential energy of elevated bodies of water to the kinetic energy of rushing water and finally to electrical energy, which is delivered to homes or industry.

Energy is transformed continually all around you. The internal energy in a flashlight's battery is transformed to electrical energy and then to light energy when you turn the flashlight on, for example. Potential energy held in a compressed spring is transformed to kinetic energy when the compressing force is removed, as shown in **Figure 2-12** on the preceding page.

Relating mass and energy
Mass is a form of energy

In 1905, Albert Einstein shook the world with his discovery of a third fundamental type of energy. The third kind of energy is a familiar quantity—mass! This idea is described in Einstein's famous equation.

$$E = mc^2$$

E represents the energy of an object, m is its mass, and c is the speed of light. Light travels a constant speed of 3×10^8 meters per second, m/s.

law of conservation of energy
the observed fact that in any chemical or physical process, energy is neither created nor destroyed

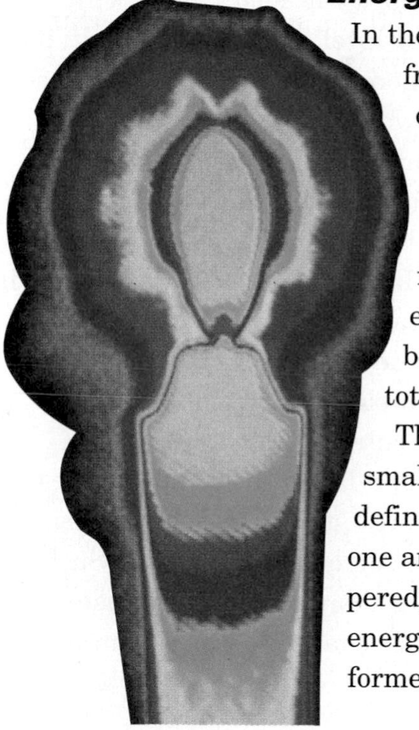

Figure 2-14
Energy is transferred as heat from the flame to the candle and the surrounding air.

Besides being the amount of material in an object or a measure of the difficulty of changing the motion of an object, mass is also a form of energy. One way to look at this is to view the mass of an object as its "energy of being." Consider a basketball. If it is moving, it has kinetic energy. If it is elevated, it has potential energy. Even resting on the ground the basketball has energy, because there is internal energy in its atoms and molecules. But beyond all this, the ball has another kind of energy—mass energy. Its mass energy is not due to its motion or position, nor to the internal energy of its atoms and molecules, but to the very fact of its mass.

Mass, like other forms of energy, can be transformed. In transformations, a small amount of mass corresponds to a huge amount of other kinds of energy. In nuclear reactors, the masses of particles are converted to kinetic energy, which is then transformed to electric energy.

Energy cannot be created or destroyed

In the previous examples, you found that energy can be transformed from one kind to another. Energy is also often transferred between objects. Energy transfer, as heat, happens when things that are at different temperatures are brought into contact, as in **Figure 2-14**.

When energy is transferred or changes form, none can be created or destroyed. The **law of conservation of energy** is the formal statement of this principle. The law of conservation of energy states that energy cannot be created or destroyed; it may be transformed or transferred from one object to another, but the total amount of energy in the universe never changes.

The law of conservation of energy can be applied to closed systems smaller than the entire universe as well. *Closed systems*, or well-defined groups of objects that are free to transfer energy only among one another, demonstrate energy conservation. Chemicals in a stoppered, insulated reaction flask approximate such a system. The total energy of the system does not change even though energy may be transformed or transferred among the atoms and molecules in the flask.

Concept Review

Energy transformation

6. A skier is in motion midway down a slope. Does the skier have kinetic energy, potential energy, or both kinetic and potential energy? Give the reason for your answer.

7. If an arrow is shot from a bow that has 40 J of potential energy, what will the kinetic energy of the arrow be?

8. **Story Link**
Certain trash incineration plants, called *high-technology resource recovery plants*, can use the heat given off by burning trash to produce electricity. This electricity can then be sold to nearby industry or housing developments. Describe the energy transformations that would be likely to occur in this process.

Answers for Concept Review items and Practice problems begin on page 841.

Matter changes
Physical changes do not affect chemical composition

Before glass is recycled, it is crushed so that it will take up less space. This broken glass is called cullet, as shown in **Figure 2-15**. When it arrives at the factory, cullet is melted to the liquid state. The liquid glass is poured into molds in the shapes of new bottles and jars.

In the recycling process, glass undergoes a series of physical changes including melting and crushing. A **physical change** is a change that affects physical properties only. Chemical properties are unaffected. So, in recycling processes that involve only physical changes, recycled glass is chemically identical to glass made from raw materials.

Change of state is a physical change

For a gram of ice to change from the solid to the liquid state—to *melt*—333 J of energy are required. Why is this energy needed? To see why, picture what is happening on the molecular level. For a solid to melt, its atoms or molecules must begin to move vigorously enough to break partially free of their neighbors and break down the solid crystal structure. The atoms and molecules require energy input to increase their own kinetic energy. This energy input is most often supplied as heat.

Boiling, the rapid change of state from liquid to gas, consumes even more energy—2260 J per gram for water. In boiling, atoms or molecules in the liquid state need enough energy to break totally free of one another. Melting and boiling are called **endothermic** changes because they take in energy as heat from the surroundings. Melting and boiling both increase the internal energy of water molecules.

When a gas cools and becomes a liquid or a liquid cools and becomes a solid, it goes from a higher to a lower energy state. The energy given up by the gas or liquid is transferred to its surroundings as heat. Such changes, in which energy is given off rather than taken in by a system, are called **exothermic** changes. Exothermic changes occur when rain forms and liquid water freezes.

Figure 2-15
Glass bottles are crushed to tiny pieces, or cullet, in the recycling process. Crushing is a physical change because the chemical properties of the material are unaltered.

physical change
a change that affects only physical properties

endothermic change
a physical or chemical change in which a system absorbs energy from its surroundings

exothermic change
a physical or chemical change in which energy is released by a system to its surroundings

Figure 2-16
Change of state can be an exothermic or endothermic physical change, depending on the direction of energy flow between an object and its surroundings. When ice melts or liquid water vaporizes, energy is absorbed from the surroundings and endothermic change occurs.

Figure 2-17a
When vinegar and baking soda are combined, the solution *bubbles* and carbon dioxide forms.

2-17b
When sodium sulfide and cadmium nitrate are combined, cadmium sulfide, a yellow *precipitate* forms.

2-17c
When aluminum reacts with iron oxide in the clay pot, *heat and light* are produced. Melted material is collected in the skillet.

2-17d
When phenolphthalein is added to ammonia, a *color change* occurs.

chemical change
a change that produces one or more new substances

Chemical changes alter chemical composition

In a **chemical change**, one or more substances are changed into new ones. This change occurs at the atomic level, where atoms are rearranged without a loss or gain in the total number of atoms.

You learned in Chapter 1 that the substances undergoing chemical change are called reactants and those created in the reaction are called products. **Figure 2-17** shows some of the signs that can indicate a chemical reaction has taken place.

All chemical changes are accompanied by transfers of energy. Like changes of state, chemical changes are either endothermic or exothermic, depending on whether they absorb or release energy. Reactions that produce heat are exothermic. Reactions that absorb heat are endothermic. In an endothermic reaction, the products have more energy than the reactants have. Which reaction shown in **Figure 2-17** is obviously exothermic?

Section Review

9. Which has more internal energy: frozen or liquid orange juice? Explain the reason for your answer.

10. A few substances, such as solid carbon dioxide, or "dry ice," change directly from the solid to the gaseous state in a process called *sublimation*. Is sublimation an exothermic or endothermic physical change? Explain your answer.

11. Observe the photograph of the beakers. In the beaker on the right, an aluminum strip is immersed in nitric acid. In the beaker on the left, a copper strip is immersed in nitric acid. What evidence of a reaction do you see? Can you be sure no reaction is occurring in the beaker on the right?

2-3

How is matter classified?

**Section
Objectives**

*Distinguish between
pure substances
and mixtures on the
particle level.*

*Classify mixtures as
heterogeneous or
homogeneous.*

*Distinguish among
atoms, elements, and
compounds.*

*Explain how
compounds can be
distinguished from
mixtures.*

pure substance
*matter composed of
only one kind of atom
or molecule*

mixture
*a collection of two or
more pure substances
physically mixed
together*

Recyclers classify matter—brown bottles in one
collection bin, clear bottles in another. All materials must be classified and sorted before they
can be deposited at a recycling center. Chemists
have ways of classifying matter too. The categories they use are somewhat different from
those you find at a recycling center, however.

Mixtures and pure substances
Matter can be classified as either a pure substance or a mixture

A **pure substance** is matter made of only one kind of atom or molecule.
Carbon dioxide, hydrogen, and copper are all examples of pure substances. A **mixture**, on the other hand, is a collection of two or more pure
substances physically mixed together that cannot be represented by a
chemical formula.

The proportions of different substances in a mixture can vary. For
instance, chicken soup is a mixture that may contain different relative
amounts of celery, carrots, chicken, pepper, water, and other ingredients,
depending on the recipe.

The properties of mixtures can vary because the proportions of the substances in them can vary. For example, gold is mixed with other metals in
various proportions to obtain materials suitable for different purposes.
Pure gold, which is also called *24 karat* gold, is too soft to keep its shape
in jewelry, so it is mixed with other stronger metals to achieve necessary
strength. The *alloy*, or solid mixture, of gold used in the finest jewelry is
18 karat gold; it contains 18 out of 24 parts, or 75% gold. The remaining
six parts are usually copper, silver, or nickel. For even greater hardness
and strength, 14 karat gold is used. As shown in **Figure 2-18**, 14 karat
gold does not have quite as much of the brilliant gold color that is characteristic of pure gold or even 18 karat gold.

Figure 2-18a
**The gold nugget
contains a pure
substance—gold.
Pure gold, also called
24 karat gold, is too
soft to be used for
jewelry.**

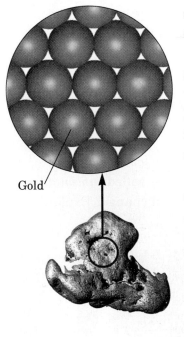

Gold

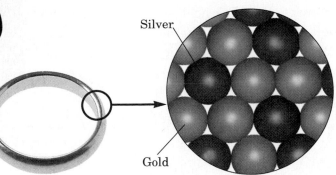

Silver

Gold

2-18b
**A gold-silver alloy rated
as 14 karat gold is 14/24
or 58.3% pure gold. This
mixture is strong
enough to be used for
jewelry. Because 14
karat gold contains a
smaller proportion of
gold than pure gold, its
gold color is less intense.**

A pure substance has specific chemical and physical properties. Any sample of pure water is clear, odorless, will produce bubbles of hydrogen gas if placed in contact with calcium, and has a boiling point of 100°C.* As you might imagine, one rarely finds perfectly pure substances in nature or in the laboratory. Therefore, "pure" is really a relative term. If a given substance is mixed with such a small amount of impurities that the impurities can be ignored, the substance is considered pure.

Mixtures can be further classified

Mixtures can be further classified as heterogeneous or homogeneous. A **homogeneous mixture** is one in which the substances are uniformly distributed. Gasoline, syrup, and saltwater are homogeneous mixtures. All regions of a homogeneous mixture are identical in their composition and their properties. Homogeneous mixtures that consist of substances mixed on the scale of individual particles are called *solutions*. Gasoline, tea, and salt water are all solutions, for example.

A **heterogeneous mixture** contains substances that are not evenly distributed. Some regions of a heterogeneous mixture have different properties from other regions. Heterogeneous mixtures can take many forms. Most of the things you see in **Figure 2-19** are heterogeneous mixtures.

Chemists sometimes also use the term *phase*. A **phase** is any part of a system that has uniform composition and properties. Mixtures contain more than one phase. Oil-and-vinegar salad dressing is a two-phase, heterogeneous mixture.

Many plastic products, such as plastic squeeze containers, are mixtures of molecules which present difficulties for recycling. If squeeze bottles are melted in the recycling process, the plastics run together and cannot be easily separated. The pure plastics in each layer are unrecoverable once they are mixed.

You may be surprised to learn that a plastic squeeze bottle is a heterogeneous mixture. If you examined the bottle microscopically you would see separate layers of different kinds of plastic. Without laboratory testing, there is no way to distinguish between homogeneous mixtures and heterogeneous mixtures that appear uniform to the naked eye.

*Water boils at 100°C at standard pressure. On a mountaintop, where the atmospheric pressure is lower than the standard pressure, water boils at a temperature lower than 100°C.

homogeneous mixture
a mixture containing substances that are uniformly distributed

heterogeneous mixture
a mixture containing substances that are not evenly distributed

phase
any part of a system that has uniform composition and properties

Figure 2-19a
Many of the things you see everyday, such as a mixed salad, oil-and-vinegar dressing, apple juice, and a plastic squeeze bottle are heterogeneous mixtures.

2-19b
A human skin cell is also an example of a heterogeneous mixture.

Homogeneous and heterogeneous mixtures

12. Consider the mixtures below. State which ones are definitely heterogeneous.

    a. gelatin dessert   **b.** iced tea   **c.** concrete

    d. topping on a pizza   **e.** toothpaste   **f.** creamy peanut butter

    g. homogenized milk   **h.** a taco   **i.** chunky peanut butter

13. Mark the following statements true or false.

    a. All homogeneous mixtures appear to have a uniform composition.

    b. All mixtures that appear uniform are homogeneous.

    c. In a solution, no grains or particles are visible.

    d. Solutions are single-phase systems.

14. Draw picture-models representing the following.

    a. the pure substance nitric oxide (nitric oxide molecules contain one nitrogen atom and one oxygen atom)

    b. a homogeneous mixture of the two diatomic gaseous elements, oxygen and nitrogen.

Elements

Elements are the simplest pure substances

elements
the 109 simplest substances from which more complex materials are made

Aluminum, copper, oxygen, and silicon are some elements that may be familiar to you. **Elements** are the simplest pure substances, because they contain only one kind of atom. For example, a piece of elemental silicon contains many billions of atoms, all of which are silicon atoms.

Every element has its own unique set of physical and chemical properties. Once it is purified, gold mined in Africa today is indistinguishable from gold panned in the California gold rush or gold discovered by the Aztecs of Mexico centuries ago. Pure gold, obtained from any source, is the same substance. It is an unreactive, soft metal that melts at 1064°C.*

Chem Fact
Gold is relatively uncommon in the Earth's crust. A million tons of earth contains, on average, only 10 pounds of pure gold. It is estimated that all the gold in the world would make a cube measuring 60 ft. on each edge.

A small number of elements make up most common substances

Although there are 109 different elements, only about a dozen compose the things we notice every day. By far, the most common element is hydrogen. More than 90% of the atoms in the known universe are hydrogen. The two elements oxygen and silicon make up more than 70% of the mass of the Earth's crust. **Figure 2-20** shows the other elements whose masses contribute substantially to the Earth's crust. Living things are composed primarily of four elements: carbon, hydrogen, oxygen, and nitrogen. These four elements combine to create thousands of different molecules needed for life.

Figure 2-20
The pie chart below shows the abundances of various elements in the Earth's crust by mass.

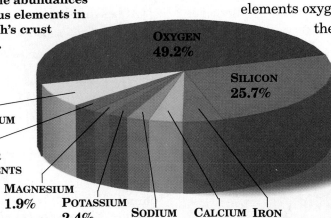

OXYGEN 49.2%
SILICON 25.7%
ALUMINUM 8.1%
OTHER ELEMENTS 2.6%
MAGNESIUM 1.9%
POTASSIUM 2.4%
SODIUM 2.6%
CALCIUM 3.4%
IRON 4.7%

*The melting point is specified at a given pressure.

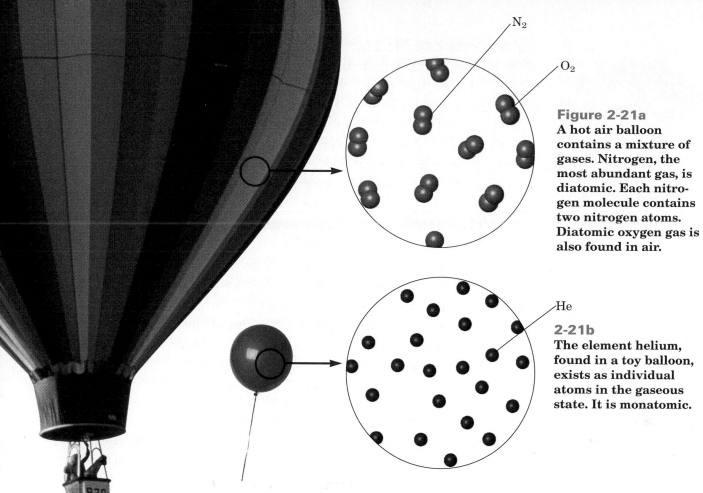

Figure 2-21a
A hot air balloon contains a mixture of gases. Nitrogen, the most abundant gas, is diatomic. Each nitrogen molecule contains two nitrogen atoms. Diatomic oxygen gas is also found in air.

2-21b
The element helium, found in a toy balloon, exists as individual atoms in the gaseous state. It is monatomic.

allotropes
different molecular forms of an element in the same physical state

Elements may consist of single atoms or molecules

An element may be made of individual atoms or molecules. For example, the helium gas in a toy balloon consists of individual atoms, as shown in **Figure 2-21**. If an element consists of molecules, those molecules contain just one type of atom. For example, the element nitrogen, found in air, exists in the molecular state. Each nitrogen gas molecule contains two nitrogen atoms joined together. For this reason, nitrogen is called a *diatomic* gas. Oxygen, another gas found in the air in appreciable amounts, is also diatomic.

Some elements have allotropic forms

A few elements, notably oxygen, phosphorus, sulfur, and carbon, are unusual because they exist as allotropes. **Allotropes** are different molecular forms of an element in the same physical state. One allotrope of oxygen is the diatomic oxygen gas you breathe. *Ozone* is another oxygen allotrope. Ozone molecules contain three atoms each.

The properties of allotropes can vary widely. Diatomic oxygen is a colorless, odorless gas essential to life. Ozone is a toxic, blue gas with a sharp odor. You can smell ozone after an intense thunderstorm. Lightning provides the energy to convert diatomic oxygen to ozone in the atmosphere.

Carbon has several interesting allotropes in the solid state. One allotrope is graphite, the gray solid with a slippery texture that you read about earlier in this chapter. Diamond is another carbon allotrope. The properties of graphite and diamond are, of course, very different.

Figure 2-22a
The buckminster-fullerene molecule is commonly known as a buckyball. It is a carbon allotrope consisting of 60 carbon atoms arranged like a geodesic dome.

2-22b
Buckytubes, discovered in 1991, resemble spiraling honeycombs with pentagons at the ends.

compounds

pure substances composed of two or more different elements

In the 1980s, a carbon allotrope consisting of molecules with 60 carbon atoms was discovered. This allotrope is shaped like the geodesic dome designed by the innovative American philosopher and engineer Buckminster Fuller. For this reason, the 60-carbon molecule shown in Figure 2-22a is called a "buckyball." More recently another allotropic form of carbon, the "buckytube," has been found. A buckytube is shown in Figure 2-22b. Buckyballs and buckytubes exhibit superconductivity (the ability to conduct electricity with no wasted energy).

Compounds
Compounds can be separated into elements

Pure substances that are composed of two or more different elements that are chemically combined are called **compounds**. Compounds are created when atoms of different elements join together in chemical reactions.

Carbon monoxide is an example of a molecular compound. Molecular compounds are made of molecules. Some compounds, such as table salt, are not made of separate molecules. Table salt, or sodium chloride, is an ionic compound. *Ionic compounds*, like molecular compounds, are made of at least two different elements that are chemically joined. However, an ionic compound is not made of discrete molecules. Instead its atoms are distributed in a continuous network. You will learn more about the differences between molecular and ionic compounds in Chapters 5 and 6.

Every compound has a unique set of properties

Because a compound is a pure substance, you know that it has a unique set of chemical and physical properties. You may be surprised to find out, however, that the properties of the compounds are often very different from those of the elements that compose them.

A set of elements can often form more than one compound. Carbon monoxide and carbon dioxide are examples of very different compounds made from carbon and oxygen. Carbon dioxide is used in some fire extinguishers to put out fires, while carbon monoxide burns when ignited. Carbon monoxide is extremely toxic, but carbon dioxide is the gas you exhale in normal respiration.

Compounds can be distinguished from mixtures

It is important to understand the difference between compounds and mixtures. There are three principal differences.

1. Mixtures are never made of only a single compound.
2. The properties of a mixture reflect the properties of the substances it contains, but the properties of a compound often bear no resemblance to the properties of the elements that compose it.
3. Compounds have a definite composition by mass of their combining elements. The iron-sulfur compound pyrite has a definite composition. The mass of pyrite is always 46.55% iron and 53.45% sulfur. In contrast, substances in a mixture can exist in any mass ratio. The sugar in a sugar-water mixture may make up 99% or 1% of the overall mass.

You can see how compounds and mixtures relate to other classes of matter in **Figure 2-23.**

Figure 2-23
Study this figure to understand the relationships among different classes of matter.

Classification of Matter

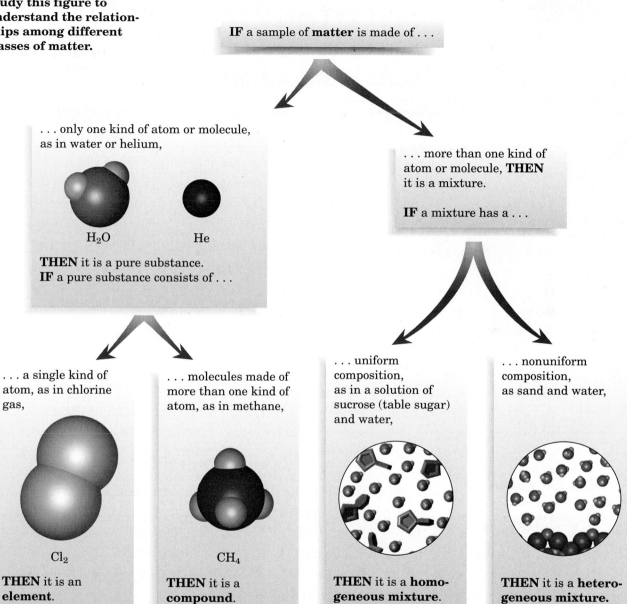

IF a sample of **matter** is made of . . .

. . . only one kind of atom or molecule, as in water or helium,

H_2O He

THEN it is a pure substance.
IF a pure substance consists of . . .

. . . more than one kind of atom or molecule, **THEN** it is a mixture.

IF a mixture has a . . .

. . . a single kind of atom, as in chlorine gas,

Cl_2

THEN it is an **element**.

. . . molecules made of more than one kind of atom, as in methane,

CH_4

THEN it is a **compound**.

. . . uniform composition, as in a solution of sucrose (table sugar) and water,

THEN it is a **homogeneous mixture**.

. . . nonuniform composition, as sand and water,

THEN it is a **heterogeneous mixture**.

Section Review

15. How many different compounds can a pure substance contain?
16. Bronze is a mixture of tin, copper, and zinc. To predict the properties of bronze, what information do you need about tin, copper, and zinc?
17. In what ways will a mixture of copper, oxygen, and sulfur be different from a compound of these three elements?
18. **Story Link**
    Why are the properties of aluminum always the same while the properties of a leaded-glass mixture may vary?
19. **Story Link**
    Why must aluminum and glass be sorted before they can be recycled?

How are substances identified?

Methods of separating mixtures

In order to recycle items in a pile of trash, you separate them by hand, using one or more physical properties to identify various substances. Or, if you need to separate steel cans from aluminum cans, you might use a magnet to identify and isolate them. (Steel is magnetic and aluminum is not.) There are a multitude of ways to separate mixtures. The method to use in a given situation depends on the properties and relative amounts of substances in a mixture.

Mixtures can be separated by physical means

The photographs in **Figure 2-24** and **Figure 2-25** on the next page show some of the many ways to separate a mixture using only physical means. When you *filter, evaporate, centrifuge,* or *decant* a mixture, you bring about only physical changes. The substances you obtain after separation are not chemically changed by the separation process.

Figure 2-24a
Coffee grounds and water are separated by filtration. Liquid and particles smaller than the filter holes pass through the filter. The *filtrate* is collected in the coffee pot.

2-24b
Magnetism can be used to separate magnetic components of a mixture, like iron and steel, from nonmagnetic components.

2-24c
In salt ponds such as this one, sea water evaporates. Sodium chloride, or salt, is left behind. This simple method of salt production is still widely used.

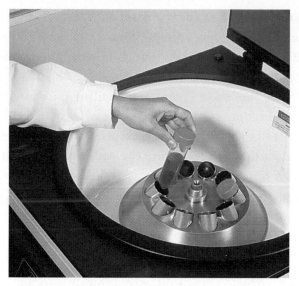

Figure 2-25a
A centrifuge is a tool used to separate matter of different densities. The centrifuge spins rapidly; the resulting centrifugal force pushes dense matter outward. Medical workers often separate the solid matter in blood from the liquid portion. Then tests can be performed on the solid cellular material.

2-25b
To decant a mixture, simply pour the liquids off and leave the solids behind. To do so, the solid contents must be well settled on the bottom of the container.

Chromatography is widely used in industry

Chromatography may be used to separate the components of a solution so that they can be identified. Chromatography works because different substances have different attractions to solvents and other media.

Paper chromatography can be used to separate black ink into the colored dyes it contains, as shown in **Figure 2-26**. How does this work? Water dissolves the ink. The ink-containing water travels up the paper through capillary action. Substances travel at different rates according to the attraction they have for the paper. Those most attracted to the paper travel the slowest. They appear in a relatively low position on the paper. Those that have the least affinity for the paper travel the fastest.

Research laboratories make great use of chromatography. The food industry uses gas chromatography to isolate and identify compounds that give foods their aromas. Some of these pleasant-smelling compounds can be processed for use in artificial flavors and fragrances.

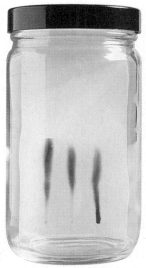

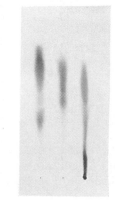

Figure 2-26
Chromatography can separate the dyes in different samples of black ink. First, ink marks are made on absorbant paper. Then, as shown in the middle photograph, solvent in the bottom of the jar rises through the paper, carrying the ink with it. The finished chromatogram, shown at right, displays different dyes found in each of the three black sample inks.

Distillation can be used to purify salt water

Distillation is a method of separating substances that have different boiling points. **Figure 2-27** shows how distillation can be used to obtain pure water from a salt-water solution. Salt-water is placed in the distillation flask, where it is heated to the boiling point. The boiling point of sodium chloride, or salt, is much higher than the temperature at which the solution boils. Thus, the water in the salt-water mixture turns to steam, and rises upward in the distillation flask, leaving the sodium chloride behind. The steam flows through the condenser, a water-cooled glass tube. The steam condenses as it makes contact with the cooled surface of the condenser. The condensed steam is purified water in the liquid state. Pure water is collected in the receiving flask.

In a few locations throughout the world, distillation is used to obtain drinking water from seawater. However, the process requires a great deal of energy and is very expensive, so other ways of obtaining drinking water are preferred. Distillation is used on a wide scale in the petroleum industry to separate crude oil. The separated components of crude oil have many uses. Gasoline, heating oil, lubricants, and the materials from which plastics are made are all obtained from the separation of crude oil.

Figure 2-27a
During the first step of distillation, the salt water solution is heated to the boiling point of water.

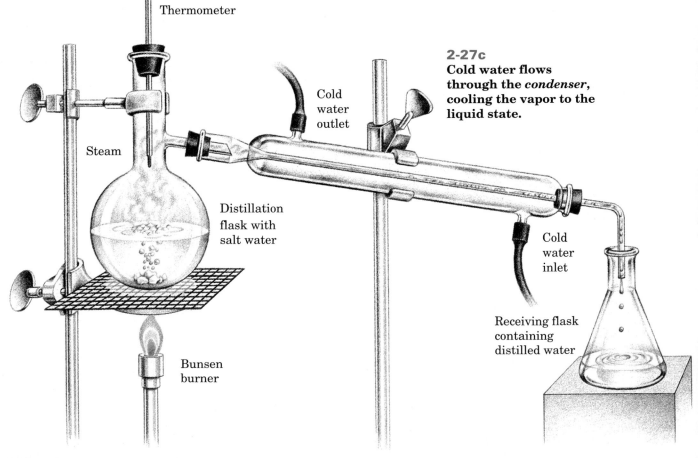

Thermometer

2-27c
Cold water flows through the *condenser*, cooling the vapor to the liquid state.

Steam

Cold water outlet

Distillation flask with salt water

Cold water inlet

Receiving flask containing distilled water

Bunsen burner

2-27b
The solution boils when it reaches its boiling point. Because the boiling point of water is lower from that of salt, pure water vapor rises and moves to the condenser while sodium chloride is left behind.

2-27d
Once the pure water vapor cools, it condenses back to the liquid state.

Density is a constant ratio of mass to volume

A relationship between two quantities, such as mass and volume, can be represented on a graph. For example, consider a set of lead samples of different sizes. The mass and volume of each sample are listed in **Table 2-2**. The pairs of mass and volume values are represented as data points on the graph, as shown in **Figure 2-28**. Note that a straight line can be drawn through the data points. What does this mean?

The rising straight line from left to right indicates that mass increases at a constant rate as volume increases. As the volume of lead doubles, its mass doubles; as the volume triples, mass also triples, etc. In other words, mass is *directly proportional* to volume for lead.

The *slope* of a graph of directly proportional quantities, or the degree to which the graph slants, equals the ratio of the quantity plotted on the vertical axis (*y*) divided by the corresponding quantity plotted on the horizontal axis (*x*). This is mathematically stated as follows.

$$\text{slope} = \frac{y}{x}$$

Note that the slope of the graph of directly proportional quantities is constant. The slope of the mass-versus-volume graph for lead has a constant value of 11.3. Pick any data point on the graph, and divide the mass value by the corresponding volume value, and you will get this result.

Table 2-2
Mass and Volume Data for Samples of Lead

Sample number	Mass (g)	Volume (mL)
1	5.00	0.443
2	15.0	1.33
3	24.0	2.12
4	52.0	4.60
5	64.0	5.66
6	81.0	7.17
7	95.0	8.41
8	101	8.94
9	142	12.6
10	153	13.5

Figure 2-28
Mass and volume are related. As the masses of lead samples increase, so do their volumes.

Mass vs. Volume for Lead Samples

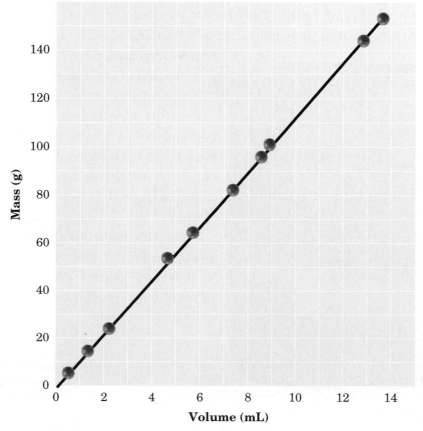

Table 2-3
Densities of Various Substances

Substance	Density (g/mL) at 25°C
aluminum	2.70
carbon dioxide gas (1 atm)	0.00197
copper	8.94
ethyl alcohol	0.789
gold	19.3
hydrogen gas (1 atm)	0.00089
iron	7.86
osmium	22.6
sodium chloride	2.164
sucrose (table sugar)	1.587
water	0.997

The constant slope of a mass-versus-volume graph has a special name—*density*. Density is the ratio of mass to volume, as expressed below.

$$\text{density} = \frac{mass}{volume} \qquad D = \frac{m}{V}$$

Density is usually expressed in units of grams per milliliter, g/mL. Thus, the density of lead is 11.3 g/mL. As noted earlier in this chapter, density can be interpreted conceptually as well as mathematically. In conceptual terms, density is a measure of how tightly matter is packed. **Table 2-3** shows the density of some interesting substances. Osmium, a blue-white metal, is the densest substance on Earth. It is so dense that a piece of osmium the size of a football would be too heavy for you to lift.

Density can be used to identify substances

Because the density of a substance is the same for all samples of it, density can be used to identify substances. For example, suppose you find a bracelet on the street that appears to be silver. You wonder if it could be pure. To find out, you take the bracelet into the lab and measure its mass with a balance—210 g. Next you measure its volume—20.0 mL. The density of the bracelet is calculated as follows.

$$D = \frac{m}{V} = \frac{210\ g}{20.0\ mL} = 10.5\ g/mL$$

Next, you look up the density of silver in a reference table and find that it is 10.5 g/mL. The bracelet you found is silver!

Densities can be used to determine whether a given material will sink or float. A material floats if its density is lower than that of the surrounding medium. The material sinks if its density is greater than that of its surrounding fluid. Ice floats on water because ice has a lower density than water. Check **Figure 2-6** to compare ice and water on the particle level. Ice is less dense than water because it contains fewer H_2O molecules in a given amount of space.

Comparing densities allows you to make interesting predictions about floating and sinking. As shown in **Figure 2-29**, two or more liquids of different densities can be layered if you are careful while pouring them.

Figure 2-29
Substances with lower densities float in or on top of substances with higher densities.

Wood

Corn oil

Red wine vinegar

Glycerine soap

Corn syrup

Recycling codes for plastic products

More than half of the states in the U.S. have enacted laws that require plastic products to be labeled with numerical codes that identify the type of plastic. These codes are shown in **Table 2-4**. Used plastic products can be sorted by these codes and properly recycled or processed. Knowing what the numerical codes mean will give you an idea of how successfully a given plastic product can be recycled. This may affect your decision to buy, or not to buy, particular items.

Table 2-4
Recycling Codes

Recycling code	Type of plastic	Physical properties	Example	Uses
1	polyethylene terephthalate (PET)	usually glossy, tough, rigid; drips when burned; sinks in water	soda bottles	fiberfill for jackets, sleeping bags, carpet
2	high density polyethylene (HDPE)	rough surface, semi-rigid; drips and gives off white smoke when heated	milk containers	furniture, toys, trash cans
3	polyvinyl chloride	very glossy, semi-rigid; does not burn; sinks in water	plastic bags	usually not recycled
4	low density polyethylene (LDPE)	low gloss, flexible; drips and gives off white smoke when burned; floats on water	clear bottles for cooking oils, peanut butter jars, shampoo, liquor	not recycled
5	polypropylene	low gloss, semi-rigid; drips and gives off white smoke when burned	heat-proof containers, insulated clothing, marine rope	not recycled
6	polystyrene (P/S, PS)	glossy, brittle to semi-rigid; does not drip when burned; gives off black smoke when burned; sinks in water unless in the form of foam	fast-food containers	recycled for permanent outdoor furniture such as park benches

Section Review

20. Can iron oxide (rust) be separated into oxygen and iron by chromatography? Why or why not?

21. Ocean water can be made suitable for drinking by boiling the water, and then condensing the vapor back to the liquid state. What is the name of this process?

22. Graph the data in the table to the right to determine the mass of 6.0 mL of iron. Also determine the density of iron by whatever method you choose.

Mass (g)	Volume (mL)
15.6	2.0
27.3	3.5
31.2	4.0
41.3	5.3

23. **Story Link**

You have an unlabeled container that looks like it is made of aluminum. How can you be sure whether it belongs in the aluminum recycling bin?

How should data be reported?

Section Objectives

List the basic SI units and the quantities they describe.

Use metric prefixes to convert metric units.

Distinguish between accuracy and precision in measurement.

Use significant figures in measurements and calculations.

Standard units

Properties are described most exactly in numerical terms. You can describe a person's height, mass, or age in words: tall or short, heavy or light, old or young. But such descriptions are easily misinterpreted because they are inexact and subjective. From a child's perspective, you may be considered "old." A grandparent, however, would probably describe you as quite young.

Numbers make descriptions more exact. You may have used the expression, "On a scale of one to ten, it's about a four," or "On a scale of one to ten, that's a minus two!" These descriptions are still vague because it is unclear what the numbers refer to. This is why standard units are useful.

SI units are used in science

In 1960, the scientific community adopted a subset of the metric system to use as the standard scientific system of measurement units. This is the "Systeme Internationale" (SI). It features seven base units. Combinations of the base units can be used to describe nearly all physical measurements. Although only five are used extensively in chemistry, all seven base units are shown in **Table 2-5**.

Base units and prefixes establish appropriate scale

Any SI unit can be modified with prefixes to match the scale of the object being measured. Meters may be suitable to express a person's height. Millimeters (0.001 m) are more appropriate for measuring the diameter of a living cell. Atoms and molecules are generally measured in picometers or nanometers. The nuclear decay of an atom happens in picoseconds; the blink of an eye takes milliseconds. A human lifetime (assuming 75 years) is about 2.4 gigaseconds. Metric prefixes are given in **Table 2-6**.

Table 2-5
SI Base Units

Quantity	Unit	Symbol
Length	meter	m
Mass	kilogram	kg
Time	second	s
Electric current	ampere	A
Thermodynamic temperature	kelvin	K
Amount of substance	mole	mol
Luminous intensity	candela	cd

Table 2-6
Some SI Prefixes

Prefix	Symbol	Meaning
giga	G	billion
mega	M	million
kilo	k	thousand
deci	d	tenth
centi	c	hundredth
milli	m	thousandth
micro	μ	millionth
nano	n	billionth
pico	p	trillionth

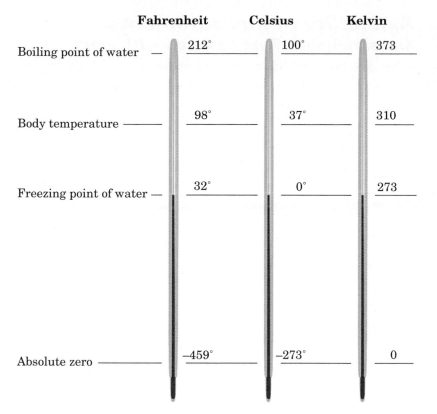

Fahrenheit	Celsius	Kelvin
Boiling point of water — 212°	100°	373
Body temperature — 98°	37°	310
Freezing point of water — 32°	0°	273
Absolute zero — −459°	−273°	0

Figure 2-30
Three different scales are used to measure temperature. The Fahrenheit scale is used to measure temperature on a daily basis in the United States. The Celsius scale is the metric scale used to measure temperature. The Kelvin scale is used in scientific work.

Kelvins are used to measure temperature

You are probably familiar with the Fahrenheit and Celsius temperature scales. Notice that the SI unit of temperature is the **kelvin** (abbreviated K, with no degree symbol). Kelvins are the same size as Celsius degrees, but the zero on each temperature scale does not correspond to the same actual temperature.

The Celsius scale designates zero degrees as the freezing point of water. Absolute zero, or 0 K, is the coldest temperature theoretically possible. **Figure 2-30** compares the Fahrenheit, Celsius, and Kelvin scales. It is simple to convert a temperature from Celsius degrees to kelvins.

$$°C + 273.16 = K, \text{ or } K − 273.16 = °C$$

You will study the basis for the absolute temperature scale in Chapter 10.

Derived units can be obtained for any quantity

Because the seven SI base units cannot measure every observable property, *derived units* are created by multiplying or dividing the seven base units in various ways. The derived unit for area, for example, is the square meter, m^2. It is obtained by multiplying a distance unit by a distance unit, as in the case of a rectangular surface.

$$\text{area units: } m × m = m^2$$

Volume is expressed in the derived SI unit cubic meters, m^3. It is obtained by multiplying length, width, and height.

$$\text{volume units: } m × m × m = m^3$$

In the traditional metric system, the liter, L, is the volume unit. The liter and milliliter, mL, are widely used in scientific work even though the cubic meter is the SI unit. In the health-related fields, the cubic centimeter, cm^3, is often used instead of the milliliter.

Reliability of measurements
Measurements must be made with care

When you measure the mass of an object or its volume or length, you obtain a number with units. How accurate is this number? How close to the true value will the measurement be? No experimentally obtained value is exact because all measurements are subject to errors—instrument errors, method errors, and human errors.

If a measuring device is not calibrated (or scaled) correctly, instrument errors will be introduced. For instance, a scale may be printed incorrectly on a graduated cylinder. Or a balance may stick and not read small masses correctly. Also, measurements must be made using a standard, or agreed-on, method. Reading the volume of the liquid in a graduated cylinder must be done the same way every time, as shown in **Figure 2-31**. Can you see why?

Human error can occur by chance or through bias. People inevitably make mistakes, even when care is taken. Human errors can also be caused by sheer carelessness. Experimenters usually have some idea about what answer they would like to see; this introduces bias. Recognizing one's own biases is an important part of research. But because it is impossible to detect all of one's own biases, experimental work can never be completely free of them.

Accuracy differs from precision

There are two things to consider when making and reporting a measurement: accuracy and precision. The **accuracy** of a measurement is the extent to which it approaches the true value and is free from error. The **precision** of a measurement is how exactly or sharply stated the measurement is. A measurement made on a very fine scale is more precise than a coarse measurement made with a blunt instrument. An analytical balance measures mass with greater precision than a triple beam balance, as **Figure 2-2** shows. **Figure 2-32** illustrates the difference between accuracy and precision.

Figure 2-31
The position of the meniscus indicates this volume should be read as 50.0 mL of solution.

accuracy
the extent to which a measurement approaches the true value of a quantity

precision
the degree of exactness or refinement of a measurement

Figure 2-32
Precision relates to exactness. Accuracy relates to how close a measurement is to the true value.

Good accuracy,
good precision

One accurate result,
poor precision overall

Poor precision,
poor accuracy

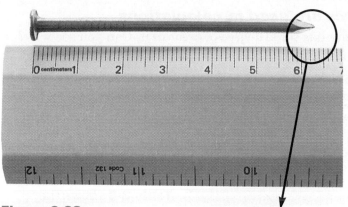

Figure 2-33
By comparing the length of the nail to the scale on the ruler, you can see that the nail is more than 6.3 cm but less than 6.4 cm long. To report this measurement in significant figures, report *6.3*, which you have actually measured, plus the next digit, which you estimate. The final measurement, correctly reported to three significant figures, is 6.35 cm.

Measurements must be reported to the correct number of significant figures

If a measurement is reported with either too many or too few digits, it is not possible to tell how precise the measurement really is. To indicate precision, significant figures are used. Significant figures are those digits in a measurement that have actually been measured by comparison with a scale, plus one estimated digit. For example, if you were measuring temperature with a thermometer marked in intervals of 1°C, you would report the temperature to the nearest tenth of a degree—25.1°C, for example. The procedure for expressing a measurement in significant figures is shown in **Figure 2-33**. Note that the number of significant figures you obtain is limited by how finely divided your measuring scale is.

As the fourth rule in **Table 2-7** indicates, you cannot tell whether zeros to the right of a nonzero number but to the left of a decimal are significant just by looking at a measurement. But there are two ways to write such numbers so that you can tell whether such zeros are significant.

1. Put a decimal point after zeros that are significant.
2. Use scientific notation.

For example, if all the zeros in the measurement 1100 m are significant, you can write the measurement as either 1100. m or in scientific notation, as 1.100×10^3 m. (For more information on how to use scientific notation, please see **Appendix B**.)

Table 2-7
Rules for Determining Whether Zeros Are Significant

Rule	Examples
1. Zeros appearing between nonzero digits are significant.	a. 40.7 L has three significant figures. b. 87 009 mi. has five significant figures.
2. Zeros that appear in front of nonzero digits are not significant.	a. 0.095 897 m has five significant figures. b. 0.0009 kg has one significant figure.
3. Zeros at the end of a number and to the right of a decimal are significant.	a. 85.00 g has four significant figures. b. 9.000 000 000 has 10 significant figures.
4. Zeros at the end of a number but to the left of a decimal may or may not be significant. If such a zero has been measured or is the first estimated digit, it is significant. On the other hand, if the zero has not been measured or estimated but is just a placeholder, it is *not* significant.	a. 2000 m may contain from one to four significant figures, depending on how many zeros are placeholders.

Significant figures are used in calculations

Each measured quantity has some degree of error in it. Can you see why? When measurements are added, subtracted, multiplied, or divided, small errors may either cancel each other or add up to a larger error. To avoid the possibility of adding extra error, significant figures are used in calculations.

The procedure for obtaining significant figures in addition and subtraction is different from the procedure used for multiplication and division. **Table 2-8** shows the procedure for each. See Appendix B for more examples of calculations with significant figures and for information on rounding numbers.

Table 2-8
Rules for Using Significant Figures in Calculations

Operation	Rule	Example
Addition or subtraction	The answer can have no more digits to the right of the decimal point than there are in the measurement with the smallest number of digits to the right of the decimal point.	$\begin{array}{r} 3.95 \\ 2.879 \\ +\ 213.6 \\ \hline 220.429 \end{array}$ $\xrightarrow{\text{round off}}$ 220.4
Multiplication or division	The answer can have no more significant figures than there are in the measurement with the smallest number of significant figures.	$\begin{array}{r} 12.257 \\ \times\ 1.162 \\ \hline 14.2426 \end{array}$ $\xrightarrow{\text{round off}}$ 14.24

Now can you put together all the rules for using significant figures to perform a laboratory task such as determining the density of, say, a sugar cube? This is how you might go about the task: Measure the mass of the sugar cube with a triple beam balance. Following the procedure for correct measuring summarized in **Figure 2-33**, you determine that the mass of the cube is 2.08 g. Now determine the volume of the sugar cube. To do this, you can measure the length of one of the cube's edges. Your ruler shows the length is 1.1 cm. The volume of a cube can be found from the following expression.

$$\text{Volume} = \text{length (cm)} \times \text{length (cm)} \times \text{length (cm)}$$

If you apply the rules for multiplying with significant figures listed in **Table 2-8**, you find that the volume of a sugar cube, correctly expressed, is 1.3 cm^3, or 1.3 mL. Now use your measurements, the expression for density, and the rules in **Table 2-8** to determine the density of a sugar cube and report the result in the correct number of significant figures.

$$D = m\,/\,V = 2.08 \text{ g}/1.3 \text{ mL} = 1.6 \text{ g/mL}$$

The exercises below will give you more practice with significant figures.

Concept Review

Calculating with significant figures

24. Express the following calculations in the proper number of significant figures.
  a. 129/29.2   **b.** 30.8/45.0   **c.** 0.098/45.4   **d.** 3.45/0.78
  e. 1.551 × 3.260 × 4.9001   **f.** 3.02 × 500. × 0.0023

25. A 102 kg boulder is falling at a velocity of 20. m/s. How much kinetic energy does the boulder possess?

26. A block of rock salt has a mass of 10.7 g. Each edge of the block has a length of 5.00 cm. What is the density of the rock salt?

$$6.25$$
$$\times\ 4.75$$
$$3125$$
$$43750$$
$$250000$$
$$\overline{29.6875}$$

Answer: 29.7

Figure 2-34
A calculator does not round an answer to the correct number of significant figures. In this case, the answer should have only three significant figures.

Calculators do not increase the precision of calculated values

A calculator often exaggerates the precision of your calculations by reporting too many digits. The calculator in **Figure 2-34** was used to calculate the area of a room 6.25 m long and 4.75 m wide. Because the length and width have three significant figures, the area must also have three significant figures. The correctly rounded product is 29.7 m². Compare this answer with the number that the calculator reports. The answer provided by the calculator is misleading. It implies that we know the size of the room to a greater degree of precision than we actually do.

Section Review

27. a. Convert 302°C to kelvins.
  b. Convert 185 K to degrees Celsius.
28. Suggest appropriate SI units and prefixes for measuring the following objects.
  a. the length of a textbook
  b. the volume of a bathtub (about 30 gallons of water)
  c. the mass of an eyelash
  d. the volume of an aluminum can
29. Speed is calculated from length and time according to the following equation. What derived SI unit is used to describe speed?
  speed = distance / time
30. A quarter (25¢) has a mass of about 5.65 g. Express this mass in milligrams, nanograms, and kilograms.
31. Round each of these measurements to three significant figures.
  a. 24.590   **b.** 24.353   **c.** 3.002   **d.** 956.789   **e.** 67.963

Conclusion: Recycling—Saving Matter and Energy

Throughout this chapter, you have been learning about matter and energy and applying your knowledge to recycling. In the introduction, you were asked to keep several questions in mind. Look at these questions again.

How can materials be identified so they can be disposed of properly? As you have seen, materials can be identified by measuring density and other physical and chemical properties and comparing the results to published data. Also, some plastics can be identified by recycling codes.

How can mixtures be separated so that their components can be recycled? Distillation, filtration, evaporation, and magnetic separation are often useful. For most of your solid household recyclables, however, separation by hand is still the most practical method. Better yet, set up bins for different types of recyclables so that you do not have to sort waste materials that have been mixed together.

How is energy measured, and what do we mean when we say "recycling saves energy"?

In scientific work, energy is usually measured in joules or in the SI base units $kg \cdot m^2/s^2$. To "save" energy is to transfer and transform it wisely, for we know from the law of conservation of energy, that the total amount of energy in the universe can never change.

Why can some materials (such as aluminum) be recycled more successfully than others? You've considered many scientific answers to this question. One reason aluminum and glass can be easily recycled is that these materials can be melted and remolded without altering their chemical compositions. But plastic products are often mixtures of various plastics that mingle together when heated and cannot then be purified.

Recycling involves economics as well as science. The economic reality is that without consumer demand for recycled products, there will be no supply of them because manufacturers cannot stay in business. For recycling to work, there must be reliable consumer demand. How can you help make this happen?

Applying Concepts

1. Why might wearing polyester clothing be a way to support recycling?
2. "Nothing is ever really thrown away." Explain, in scientific terms, what this statement means.

Research and Writing

Use community resources to research the following questions.

1. New plastic soda bottles cannot now be made from used ones. Why not? What research efforts are underway to meet this challenge?
2. Why is some recycled paper stockpiled at recycling collection centers? How will the United States government's recent pledge to buy more recycled paper impact the paper-recycling industry?

Highlights

Key terms

accuracy

allotropes

atom

chemical change

chemical properties

compounds

elements

endothermic change

energy

exothermic change

heterogeneous mixture

homogeneous mixture

kinetic energy

law of conservation of energy

mass

matter

mixture

molecule

phase

physical change

physical properties

potential energy

precision

pure substance

state

volume

Key ideas

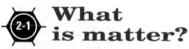 **What is matter?**

- Matter is anything that has mass and volume.
- Chemical properties can be observed only when one substance interacts with another. Physical properties can be observed without changing the chemical composition of a substance.
- The relative positions and motions of atoms or molecules determine physical state.

 How do matter and energy interact?

- Kinetic energy is the energy of motion, and potential energy is stored energy. These give rise to other forms of energy.
- Energy can change form but cannot be created or destroyed.
- Changes in which a system absorbs energy are endothermic changes. Changes in which a system releases energy are exothermic changes.

 How is matter classified?

- Pure substances contain only one type of atom or molecule.
- Uniformly distributed mixtures are homogeneous; uneven mixtures are heterogeneous.
- Compounds, unlike mixtures, are pure substances with a definite composition.

 How are substances identified?

- Components of a mixture can be separated and identified by comparing their properties to a standard.

How should data be reported?

- There are seven SI base units. Other SI measurements are derived from these base units.
- Accuracy expresses how close a measured value is to the true value, and precision expresses the exactness of a measurement.

Key problem-solving approach:
SI conversions

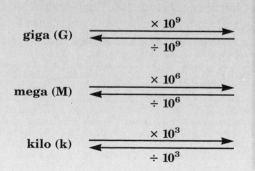

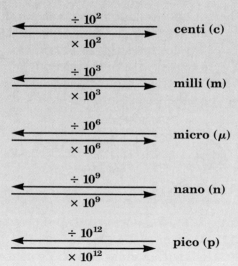

Base Unit*

meter, m
second, s
ampere, A
kelvin, K
mole, mol
candela, cd

*Kilogram, the base unit for mass, does not appear in this list because it has a different set of conversion values (1 kg = 1000 g).

Review and Assess

The nature of matter

REVIEW

1. **a.** What is matter?
   b. How do weight and mass differ?
   c. What is the building block of matter?
2. **a.** Name three physical properties.
   b. Define *chemical property*, and give an example.
3. Differentiate between intensive and extensive properties. Give an example of each.
4. Describe the five states of matter.

APPLY

5. An astronaut plans to bring home a massive moon-rock collection. Mission control on Earth wants to know the mass of the collection in advance. Why can't the astronaut use a scale to obtain the data requested by mission control?
6. Pick an object you can see right now. List three physical properties of the object that you can observe. Can you also observe a chemical property of the object? Explain.
7. Compare the physical and chemical properties of salt and sugar. What properties do they share? Which properties could you use to distinguish between salt and sugar?
8. A student checks the volume, melting point, and shape of two unlabeled samples of matter and finds that the measurements are identical. From this he concludes that the samples have the same composition. What is wrong with his thinking?
9. Draw three atomic-level models representing the three common states of matter.

Matter and energy

REVIEW

10. Define *kinetic energy*, and give an example.
11. Determine the kinetic energy of a bowling ball with a mass of 4.55 kg as it rolls down an alley at 3.20 m/s.

12. Define *potential energy*, and give an example of an object that possesses it.
13. Give an example of energy transformation that you witnessed today.
14. What is the relationship between mass and energy?
15. State the law of conservation of energy.
16. Differentiate between an exothermic and an endothermic process.
17. Label the following processes as endothermic or exothermic changes.
    a. evaporating water
    b. condensing water vapor
    c. cooling bath water
    d. evaporating perspiration

APPLY

18. Show that an object with a mass of 8.00 kg can have the same kinetic energy as an object with a mass of 32.0 kg.
19. Explain how a skateboard resting on the ground contains energy. If the skateboard were moving, would it have more energy than it did at rest? Explain.
20. Water evaporates from a puddle on a hot, sunny day faster than on a cold, cloudy day. Explain this phenomenon in terms of interactions between matter and energy.
21. Label each of the following as a physical or a chemical change.
    a. Coffee beans are processed in a grinder.
    b. Carbonated soda pop loses its fizz.
    c. A short-order cook fries an egg.
    d. Water expands when frozen, decreasing its density.
    e. Heated calcium carbonate decomposes and releases carbon dioxide gas.
    f. Rain droplets high in the atmosphere form hail.
    g. Hydrogen peroxide decomposes into water and oxygen gas in the presence of light.

The classification of matter

22. Indicate whether the substances below are compounds or elements.
   a. SO_2 **b.** S_8 **c.** C_{60} **d.** CH_4
23. Differentiate between pure substances and mixtures. Give examples of each.
24. Compare and contrast the properties of homogeneous and heterogeneous mixtures.
25. Tell which of the following items are heterogeneous mixtures. Tell which items could be homogeneous mixtures.
   a. copper penny   **b.** bean burrito
   c. paint   **d.** diamond
   e. plastic wrap   **f.** sea water
   g. blood   **h.** tea
26. Give an example of each type of solution.
   a. liquid solvent/ liquid solute
   b. liquid solvent/solid solute
   c. solid solvent/solid solute
27. Name three elements that exist as molecules.
28. How are atoms and molecules related to one another?

29. Choose a mixture. Tell how its properties compare with the properties of the pure substances that compose it.
30. Identify each phase in the following mixtures.
   a. chunky peanut butter   **b.** soda pop
   c. a sponge
31. Diamond and graphite are both allotropic forms of carbon. Why do their physical properties differ?

 # Separation and identification

32. Describe four different methods of separating mixtures. Give an example of a mixture that could be separated using each of the separation techniques you described.
33. a How would you describe density to a friend unfamiliar with the concept?
   b. State the mathematical expression for density.
   c. Is density an intensive or extensive property?

34. Describe how different substances can be distinguished by density.
35. Calculate the volume of 2.00 g of a substance with a density of 4.54 g/mL.

36. For each pair below, indicate the substance with the greater density. Explain your answer.
   a. rubber stopper and cork
   b. ice cube and water
   c. rubber stopper and automobile tire
37. Substances A and B are colorless, odorless liquids that are nonconductors and flammable. The density of substance A is 0.97 g/mL; the density of substance B is 0.89 g/mL. Are A and B the same substance? Explain.
38. A forgetful student leaves an uncapped watercolor marker on an open notebook. Upon returning, she discovers the leaking marker has produced a rainbow of colors on the top page.
   a. Is the ink a pure substance or a mixture? How do you know?
   b. What separation technique is involved?

 # Reporting data

39. a. Why are measurements often more useful than word descriptions?
   b. There are two parts to every measurement. One of these is the numerical part. What is the other necessary part of every measurement?
40. Distinguish between *precision* and *accuracy*.
41. a. What is an SI base unit?
   b. Name the five most common base units used in chemistry and the quantity that each represents.
   c. Explain what derived units are. Give an example of one.
42. What is the purpose of significant figures?
43. a. Contrast human and instrument error.
   b. Describe a situation where each type of error could have disastrous results.
44. a. If you add a series of numbers, how many significant figures can the sum have?
   b. If you multiply a series of numbers, how many significant figures can the product have?

45. Perform the following calculations, and the express answers in the correct number of significant figures.
  a. $12.4 \times 7.943 + 0.0064$
  b. $(246.83 / 26.3) - 1.349$
  c. $0.1273 - 0.000008$

46. Express normal body temperature (37.0°C) in terms of the Kelvin scale.

47. Give the appropriate prefix and base unit for each of the indicated measurements.
  a. thickness of a dime
  b. length of a highway
  c. volume of a thimble
  d. mass of a staple
  e. diameter of a hamburger

48. What derived units are appropriate for expressing the following?
  a. kinetic energy
  b. density
  c. potential energy
  d. speed
  e. pressure
  f. the rate of water flow

49. Why can a measured number never be exact?

50. Why is the Kelvin temperature scale more convenient than the Celsius scale when investigating low-temperature superconducting materials?

51. Is it possible for a number to be too small or too large to be expressed adequately in the metric system? Explain your answer.

52. a. The inch was originally defined as the distance between the knuckles and thumb of King Edgar (A.D. 959–975). Discuss the practical limitations of this early unit of measurement.
  b. Invent a length unit of your own that is practical and accurate. Discuss how your unit avoids the problems created by King Edgar's early version of the inch.

Linking chapters

1. *Scientific laws*
  The law of conservation of energy is a scientific law rather than a scientific theory. What does this tell you about how conservation of energy can be applied?

2. *Succeeding in chemistry*
  Review the guidelines for success stated on page 25. Write a summary of how you have applied each step in your study of Chapter 2. Be specific in your answers; for example, describe what you learned by looking at particular illustrations.

3. *Chemical reactions*
  Describe the organic synthesis of aspirin (which you studied in Chapter 1) in terms of the following vocabulary terms from Chapter 2: atom, molecule, compound, element, pure substance, mixture, and chemical change.

4. *Scientific method*
  State a hypothesis that you could test using a separation technique such as distillation, chromatography, or filtration. Also explain how the separation technique would help you prove or disprove the hypothesis.

5. Theme: *Systems and interactions*
  Use the diagram below to answer the following questions.
  a. Is the change from **a** to **b** a physical or chemical change?
  b. Is the mixture in **b** homogeneous or heterogeneous?
  c. What method would you use to separate mixture **b** into its pure substances?

a.

b.

USING TECHNOLOGY

1. *Graphics calculator*
   Density can be graphically represented as a straight line with a positive slope when the x value denotes volume and the y value denotes mass. Set the x-range of your calculator at 0–60 and the y-range at 0–160. Select the $\boxed{y =}$ key, and enter the function $y = 2.70x$.
   a. Press $\boxed{GRAPH}$ and use the $\boxed{TRACE}$ mode to estimate the volume of aluminum (density of 2.70 g/mL) for the following masses: 15.0 g, 75.0 g, and 125 g.
   b. Calculate the true volumes of these masses. Note the accuracy of your calculations.
   c. Enlarge the range by a factor of 4. Estimate the volumes using the $\boxed{TRACE}$ mode. Repeat this step after reducing the range by a factor of 4. What happens to your calculator's precision when you change the range?

2. *Computer art*
   Use a computer art program to model each of the concepts listed below.
   a. Illustrate the particles of a substance changing state from solid to liquid to gas.
   b. Represent a chemical reaction in which one atom and one molecule react to produce two molecules.
   c. Draw models of homogeneous and heterogeneous mixtures on the particle level.

Alternative assessment

Performance assessment

1. Using what you know about separation techniques, construct an experiment to separate a mixture of water, salt, sand, and oil. Outline your procedure and show it to your teacher. When the teacher approves the outline, obtain the mixture and test the procedure.
2. Your teacher will make several unknown samples of pure metals available to you. Describe to your teacher exactly how you will gather information about the densities of the metals. When your procedure is approved, test the metals, and use chemistry reference books to identify them.
3. Using the *Handbook of Chemistry and Physics,* compile a list of the physical and chemical properties of several substances available in your lab. Use a computer flowchart program to outline the procedures you could follow to identify the substances.
4. Describe as completely as possible all of the physical properties of a simple household object. Highlight any subjective parts of your description. Compare language to numerical data as a basis for useful scientific description.

Portfolio projects

1. *Chemistry and you*
   Describe in a journal the types of matter you come in contact with daily. Separate these into large categories, such as pure substances and mixtures, and then break them down into smaller groups, such as elements, compounds, solutions, and alloys. When done, total the entries in each category. With a chart or graph, relate the relationship between your totals and the relative abundance of these substances on Earth.
2. *Chemistry and you*
   a. Using outside resources, trace the history of antimatter research from the hypothesis of its existence through experimental proofs to plans for the space station construction of Astromag (Particle Astrophysics Magnet Facility).
   b. Collect information on possible uses of the energy produced by collisions of matter with antimatter.
3. *Chemistry and you*
   We often don't notice expressions of commonplace measurements. What units do you use each day without thinking about them? Keep a record of all units that you use in a one day. Comment on the difficulties you might encounter if standard units did not exist.

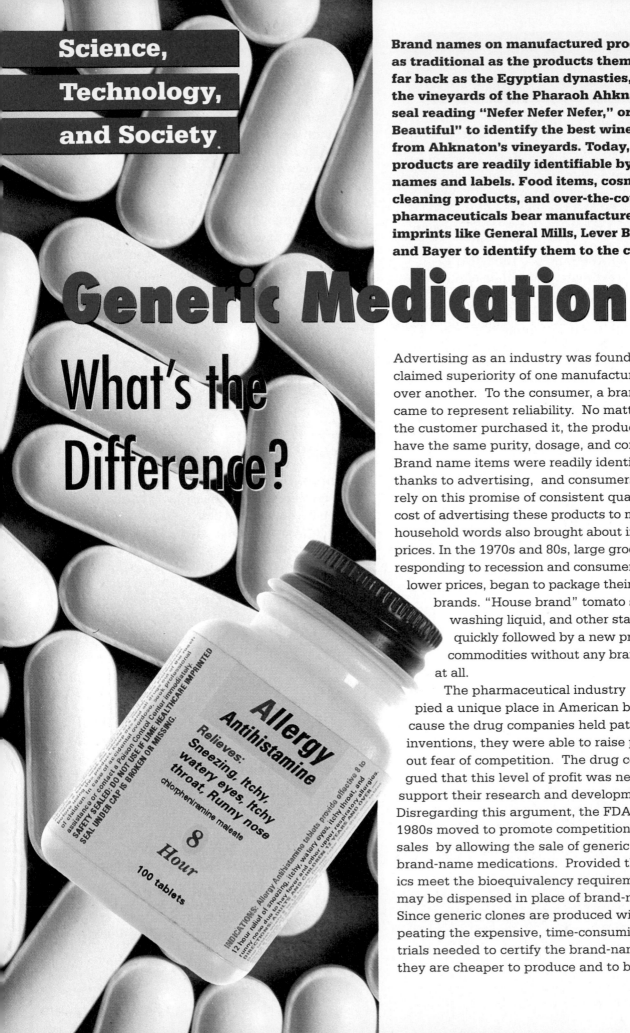

Brand names on manufactured products are as traditional as the products themselves. As far back as the Egyptian dynasties, wine from the vineyards of the Pharaoh Ahknaton bore a seal reading "Nefer Nefer Nefer," or "Thrice Beautiful" to identify the best wine to emerge from Ahknaton's vineyards. Today, many products are readily identifiable by their names and labels. Food items, cosmetics, cleaning products, and over-the-counter pharmaceuticals bear manufacturer's imprints like General Mills, Lever Brothers, and Bayer to identify them to the customer.

Generic Medication

What's the Difference?

Advertising as an industry was founded on the claimed superiority of one manufacturer's product over another. To the consumer, a brand name came to represent reliability. No matter where the customer purchased it, the product would have the same purity, dosage, and contents. Brand name items were readily identifiable, thanks to advertising, and consumers came to rely on this promise of consistent quality. But the cost of advertising these products to make them household words also brought about increased prices. In the 1970s and 80s, large grocery chains, responding to recession and consumer demand for lower prices, began to package their own brands. "House brand" tomato sauce, dishwashing liquid, and other staples were quickly followed by a new product line, commodities without any brand names at all.

The pharmaceutical industry long occupied a unique place in American business. Because the drug companies held patents on their inventions, they were able to raise prices without fear of competition. The drug companies argued that this level of profit was necessary to support their research and development efforts. Disregarding this argument, the FDA in the mid-1980s moved to promote competition in drug sales by allowing the sale of generic clones of brand-name medications. Provided these generics meet the bioequivalency requirement, they may be dispensed in place of brand-name drugs. Since generic clones are produced without repeating the expensive, time-consuming clinical trials needed to certify the brand-name drug, they are cheaper to produce and to buy.

Allergy
Antihistamine

Relieves:
Sneezing, Itchy, watery eyes, Itchy throat, Runny nose

chlorpheniramine maleate

8

Hour

100 tablets

Drug manufacture, unlike the production of other generic items, is supervised by the FDA. Generic drugs must be rigorously tested and approved before sale, and must be chemically identical to the name brand. The FDA's supervisory role was particularly important in the early days of generic drug manufacture, as some companies cut corners to rush their products onto the market. The scandal resulting when a few generic drug companies resorted to bribery and substitution to gain FDA approval for their products caused even more stringent procedures to be put in place. These regulations ensured that generics, were exactly equivalent, but much less costly. The FDA currently approves about 200 generic drugs annually, and a staff of nearly 50 chemistry reviewers tests and reviews all such drugs before they are approved for sale.

A drug's bioequivalence rating guarantees that there is no real difference in the chemical composition of the drug, nor in its action in the body. For example, you know that aspirin has the formula $C_9H_8O_4$. No matter what brand of aspirin you buy, the chemical composition of the drug is still $C_9H_8O_4$. In actual practice, a brand-name version of thioridazine, called Mellaril, produced by Sandoz, Inc., was analyzed with its generic equivalent. The variations found between the brand-name and generic drug were as many as you would find between different lots of thioridazine, according to a regulatory letter from the FDA to Sandoz. Because all drugs are inherently variable in individual patients, a statistical variation of plus or minus 20 percent is standard, and is the basis for bioequivalency. The average statistical variation for generics is a mere 3.5 percent, giving generic drugs only a minute difference from the original, and consumers an average 52.8 percent break in the purchase price of generics over brand-name prescriptions.

Today, generic drugs account for 60 to 85 percent of the market for new prescriptions in the United States. More and more, providers are offering consumers a choice of pharmaceuticals when they fill their prescriptions. Continuing education courses are giving pharmacists information and techniques for educating consumers on the use of generic drugs, and overcoming their fears about bioequivalency. Mindful of rising health care costs, employer benefit specialists in companies encourage their members to choose generics over prescription medications to save money, an advantage to both the company and its employees.

As expiration dates on patents for dozens of brand-name medications grow closer, generic drug manufacturers hasten to develop generic equivalents and some, such as Merck and Co., have formed subsidiaries to supply the generics market with bioequivalent drugs of their own manufacture. Merck's West Point Pharmaceutical Division produces the generic equivalent of Dolibid, Merck's brand-name anti-inflammatory on which the patent expired in 1989.

Drug Topics magazine reported in March, 1994, that there are at least 170 vendors of generic drugs in the United States, offering about 2000 economically priced products. Six such firms have formed a consortium to investigate generic drug manufacturing opportunities in Russia, where there has been a critical shortage of drugs and vaccines. The consortium, MIR Pharmaceuticals, Inc., is conducting a feasibility study of cost and problems associated with setting up an FDA-standard drug manufacturing facility in Russia. There are some $60 billion in drug patents due to expire within the next five years, which will make these substances fair game for manufacture in generic forms.

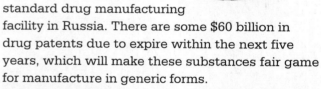

Generics are here to stay. Reputable companies produce them, doctors prescribe them by checking a box on the prescription blank. Grateful consumers use them to affordably maintain their health.

Researching the Issue

1. How long does a new medication remain under patent?

2. When a generic equivalent comes on the market, how does the FDA ensure that it is identical to a name brand medication?

3. How are generics manufactured outside the United States regulated for purity?

4. How long does it typically take to bring generic substitutes to market after the patent on a drug expires?

5. State your views as to who should make the decision to prescribe a generic medication—the patient, the doctor, the pharmacist?

3 | Atomic Structure

Excited Atoms and the Fourth of July

The national anthem blasts through loudspeakers, and the show is about to begin. It's July 4th, and hundreds have come to watch the fireworks display. Crack! A rocket flares and red stars burst forth. Kaboom!

A dazzling white chrysanthemum-shaped shower of light fills the sky. The show continues, but wait, something is missing. You've seen red and white fireworks, but what about blue?

You may see a burst of blue, but it will not be as brilliant as the red, white, orange, green, gold, pink, and yellow displays. Today's pyrotechnic technology has not yet produced a bright, eye-popping blue. The search for one keeps fireworks manufacturers scrambling.

Fireworks, originally invented in China, have used a similar basic design for hundreds of years. The design consists of a shell that fits inside a cannon-like mortar; black powder beneath the shell that is a mixture of 15 parts charcoal, 10 parts sulfur, and 75 parts potassium nitrate; and a fuse that feeds into the powder. When the fuse is lit, the powder ignites and explodes, producing gas that expands behind the trapped shell, thrusting it high into the sky. When it reaches a safe altitude, a time-delayed fuse lights within the shell, setting off chemical reactions between an oxygen source and a fuel within the shell. These reactions release tremendous energy and create the spectacular effects you witness.

Some recent advances would astound pyrotechnicians of the past, however. For example, fireworks can be ignited indoors at rock concerts and other entertainment events. Some fireworks turn off and on in midair with intermittent color. Fuses can be lit by remote with computer-timed switches, improving fireworks safety. But despite all these advances, there are still no really good blue fireworks. Why not?

Bill Page, the resident chemist at Astro Pyrotechnics fireworks manufacturing firm, answers the question. The colors of fireworks, Page explains, are generated by atoms or molecules that are present in the gaseous state when the chemical contents of shells react. Different elements, either in the elemental state or combined in compounds, produce different colors. Compounds of strontium produce red fireworks, aluminum compounds produce bright white light, barium compounds produce green light, and sodium atoms produce yellow light. A copper compound, copper chloride, is the best producer of blue light yet identified. But copper chloride is unstable at high temperatures.

A brilliant blue display may be achieved someday by Bill Page or some other pyrotechnic chemist—maybe by you. To get started, consider the following questions.

- *What is light, and how do various colors of light differ?*
- *What is going on at the level of atoms and molecules when fireworks produce colored light?*
- *How does the instability of copper chloride at high temperatures interfere with its ability to emit blue light?*

The answers to these questions, as you will see, involve atomic structure.

How are the elements organized?

3-1

Properties of elements relate to atomic structures

As early as 400 B.C., Greek philosophers proposed that matter is made of atoms, extremely small particles that cannot be broken down into anything smaller. The word *atom* actually comes from the Greek word for "indivisible." Today, the atom is still recognized as a fundamental unit of matter. But scientists know that the atom is actually divisible and contains dozens of subatomic particles. Three of these particles are of major importance in chemistry: protons, neutrons, and electrons.

All atoms have similar structures. Protons and neutrons cluster together to form a central core, or *nucleus.* Electrons inhabit the space surrounding the nucleus. Beyond this basic similarity, however, there is variation among the structures of different elements. One variation is the number of protons. Each of the 109 chemical elements has a characteristic number of protons. For example, silicon atoms, such as those shown in **Figure 3-1**, contain 14 protons. Neon atoms contain 10 protons each, while oxygen atoms have 8 protons. As you will discover later in this chapter, electrons are arranged differently in atoms of different elements.

The structures of different elements vary, but not in a wild or random fashion. The structures differ in gradual and regular ways. For example, a hydrogen atom contains one proton, helium has two protons, lithium has three protons, and so on, up to element 109. The number of protons in atoms increases steadily in increments of one proton.

The properties of an element depend on its structure. Thus, you might infer that the behavior of elements also varies gradually from one element to the next. This is indeed the case. The orderly variation in the structure and properties of atoms is represented in the *periodic table of the elements*, a complete chart of all the elements in the known universe.

Figure 3-1a
Individual silicon atoms are visible in this image, provided by a scanning tunneling microscope. Silicon atoms are semiconductors—their electrical conductivity is between that of the metals and nonmetals.

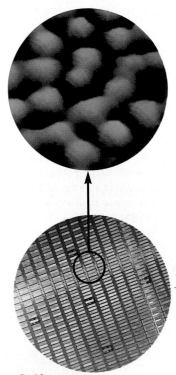

3-1b
This wafer of pure silicon will be used to fabricate integrated circuits.

3-1c
Computers are built from integrated circuits or "computer chips." Integrated circuits take advantage of the semiconductivity of silicon— a property that reflects the structure of silicon atoms.

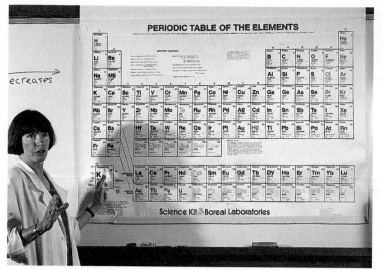

Figure 3-2
The periodic table is an organized display of all the chemical elements.

The periodic table shows all the elements

The periodic table is shown in **Figure 3-2**. It contains a complete listing of all known elements and the chemical symbols that represent them. The symbol for chlorine is Cl, for example. Hydrogen has the symbol H and silicon has the symbol Si.

The symbols for the elements consist of either one, two, or three letters, as shown in **Table 3-1** on the next page. In the case of a single letter, the symbol is always a capital letter. In the case of symbols with two and three letters, only the first letter is capitalized. Elements represented by symbols containing three letters have not been officially named. These three-letter symbols will be changed when the International Union of Pure and Applied Chemistry (IUPAC) gives the elements official names.

It is easy to see that the symbols for chlorine, hydrogen, and silicon are logical. But you may wonder how the names and symbols of some elements could possibly relate to each other. For example, tungsten, which is used to make light bulb filaments, has the symbol W. The key to the apparent mismatch is that tungsten was discovered in Germany and named from the German word *Wolfram*.

Other elements are named in honor of a person or after the place where the element was discovered. Curium (Cm), for example, is a radioactive element named in honor of Marie and Pierre Curie, the discoverers of radioactivity. Californium (Cf) was discovered in California. Can you identify where francium and berkelium were discovered?

The periodic table is organized by properties

group
a series of elements that form a column in the periodic table

The periodic table is arranged so that elements with similar properties fall within the same **group**. Group 1, the column of elements at the left edge of the periodic table, contains the following elements: lithium, sodium, potassium, rubidium, cesium, and francium. All of the Group 1 elements have low densities, low melting points, and good electrical conductivity. As **Figure 3-3** shows, Group 1 elements are shiny until they react with air and are soft enough to be cut with a knife. They also react violently with cold water.

Figure 3-3
Sodium is soft enough to be cut with a knife. It is shiny until it reacts with oxygen in air to form a dull surface.

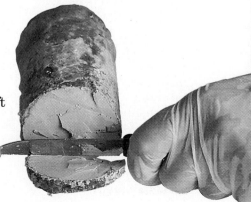

Table 3-1
Element Names and Symbols

Element	Symbol	Atomic number	Atomic mass	Element	Symbol	Atomic number	Atomic mass
actinium	Ac	89	227.0278	neon	Ne	10	20.1797
aluminum	Al	13	26.981539	neptunium	Np	93	237.0482
americium	Am	95	243.0614	nickel	Ni	28	58.6934
antimony	Sb	51	121.757	niobium	Nb	41	92.90638
argon	Ar	18	39.948	nitrogen	N	7	14.00674
arsenic	As	33	74.92159	nobelium	No	102	259.1009
astatine	At	85	209.9871	osmium	Os	76	190.23
barium	Ba	56	137.327	oxygen	O	8	15.9994
berkelium	Bk	97	247.0703	palladium	Pd	46	106.42
beryllium	Be	4	9.012182	phosphorus	P	15	30.973762
bismuth	Bi	83	208.98037	platinum	Pt	78	195.08
boron	B	5	10.811	plutonium	Pu	94	244.0642
bromine	Br	35	79.904	polonium	Po	84	208.9824
cadmium	Cd	48	112.411	potassium	K	19	39.0983
calcium	Ca	20	40.078	praseodymium	Pr	59	140.90765
californium	Cf	98	251.0796	promethium	Pm	61	144.9127
carbon	C	6	12.011	protactinium	Pa	91	231.03588
cerium	Ce	58	140.115	radium	Ra	88	226.0254
cesium	Cs	55	132.90543	radon	Rn	86	222.0176
chlorine	Cl	17	35.4527	rhenium	Re	75	186.207
chromium	Cr	24	51.9861	rhodium	Rh	45	102.90550
cobalt	Co	27	58.93320	rubidium	Rb	37	85.4678
copper	Cu	29	63.546	ruthenium	Ru	44	101.07
curium	Cm	96	247.0703	samarium	Sm	62	150.36
dysprosium	Dy	66	162.50	scandium	Sc	21	44.9655910
einsteinium	Es	99	252.083	selenium	Se	34	78.96
erbium	Er	68	167.26	silicon	Si	14	28.0855
europium	Eu	63	151.965	silver	Ag	47	107.8682
fermium	Fm	100	257.0951	sodium	Na	11	22.989768
fluorine	F	9	18.9984032	strontium	Sr	38	87.62
francium	Fr	87	223.0917	sulfur	S	16	32.066
gadolinium	Gd	64	157.25	tantalum	Ta	73	180.9479
gallium	Ga	31	69.723	technetium	Tc	43	97.9072
germanium	Ge	32	72.61	tellurium	Te	52	127.60
gold	Au	79	196.96654	terbium	Tb	65	158.92534
hafnium	Hf	72	178.49	thallium	Tl	81	204.3833
helium	He	2	4.002602	thorium	Th	90	232.0381
holmium	Ho	67	164.93032	thulium	Tm	69	168.93421
hydrogen	H	1	1.00794	tin	Sn	50	118.710
indium	In	49	114.818	titanium	Ti	22	47.88
iodine	I	53	126.90447	tungsten	W	74	183.84
iridium	Ir	77	192.22	unnilquadium	Unq	104	261.11
iron	Fe	26	55.847	unnilpentium	Unp	105	262.114
krypton	Kr	36	83.80	unnilhexium	Unh	106	263.118
lanthanum	La	57	138.9055	unnilseptium	Uns	107	262.12
lawrencium	Lr	103	262.11	unniloctium	Uno	108	265
lead	Pb	82	207.2	unnilennium	Une	109	266
lithium	Li	3	6.941	uranium	U	92	238.0289
lutetium	Lu	71	174.967	vanadium	V	23	50.9415
magnesium	Mg	12	24.3050	xenon	Xe	54	131.29
manganese	Mn	25	54.93805	ytterbium	Yb	70	173.04
mendelevium	Md	101	258.10	yttrium	Y	39	88.90585
mercury	Hg	80	200.58	zinc	Zn	30	65.39
molybdenum	Mo	42	95.94	zirconium	Zr	40	91.224
neodymium	Nd	60	144.24				

period

a series of elements that form a horizontal row in the periodic table

The rows of the periodic table are called **periods**. Elements close to each other in the same period are more similar than those farther apart in the same period. For example, the properties of the elements of Group 1 vary significantly from those of Group 17, but are somewhat similar to those observed in the Group 2 elements. Consider the elements potassium, calcium, and bromine. Potassium and calcium, as members of Group 1 and Group 2 respectively, share properties not possessed by bromine, a member of Group 17.

Concept Review

Using chemical names and symbols

1. Write the chemical symbols for the following elements.
   - **a.** lithium
   - **b.** barium
   - **c.** chromium
   - **d.** phosphorus
   - **e.** plutonium
   - **f.** sulfur

2. State the name of each of the following elements, which are represented by their symbols.
   - **a.** H
   - **b.** Cl
   - **c.** Fe
   - **d.** Cf

Regions of the periodic table
The periodic table contains regions of similar elements

The periodic table is like a map of the United States. It features individual elements (states), groups (the Pacific coastal or Rocky Mountain states), and periods (the Corn Belt or Sun Belt states). Just as the United States can be divided into regions (the northeast or the southwest), so can the periodic table. **Table 3-2** shows the four regions of the periodic table—metals, nonmetals, metalloids, and noble gases.

**Table 3-2
Regions of the Periodic Table**

■ Metals
■ Metalloids
■ Nonmetals
■ Noble gases

1	2	3	4	5	6	7	8	9	10	11	12	13	14	15	16	17	18
1 H																	2 He
3 Li	4 Be											5 B	6 C	7 N	8 O	9 F	10 Ne
11 Na	12 Mg											13 Al	14 Si	15 P	16 S	17 Cl	18 Ar
19 K	20 Ca	21 Sc	22 Ti	23 V	24 Cr	25 Mn	26 Fe	27 Co	28 Ni	29 Cu	30 Zn	31 Ga	32 Ge	33 As	34 Se	35 Br	36 Kr
37 Rb	38 Sr	39 Y	40 Zr	41 Nb	42 Mo	43 Tc	44 Ru	45 Rh	46 Pd	47 Ag	48 Cd	49 In	50 Sn	51 Sb	52 Te	53 I	54 Xe
55 Cs	56 Ba	57 La	72 Hf	73 Ta	74 W	75 Re	76 Os	77 Ir	78 Pt	79 Au	80 Hg	81 Tl	82 Pb	83 Bi	84 Po	85 At	86 Rn
87 Fr	88 Ra	89 Ac	104 Unq	105 Unp	106 Unh	107 Uns	108 Uno	109 Une									

58 Ce	59 Pr	60 Nd	61 Pm	62 Sm	63 Eu	64 Gd	65 Tb	66 Dy	67 Ho	68 Er	69 Tm	70 Yb	71 Lu
90 Th	91 Pa	92 U	93 Np	94 Pu	95 Am	96 Cm	97 Bk	98 Cf	99 Es	100 Fm	101 Md	102 No	103 Lr

Figure 3-4
Iron is the most abundant, widely used, and least expensive metal. The earliest iron artifacts date to 3000 B.C.

26
Fe

Properties and Uses of Selected Metals

Silver

Silver, like other metals, has excellent reflective properties (luster). It is therefore used to plate mirrors. Silver is also ductile and malleable so it can be hammered, molded, or drawn into shape for jewelry.

Mercury

Mercury is the only metal that is a liquid at room temperature. Because mercury conducts heat and expands and contracts evenly with temperature change, it has long been used in thermometers.

Titanium

Titanium is strong, has low mass, and resists corrosion. It is therefore used in high performance jet engines and missiles. Also, because it does not react with flesh or bone, titanium is used to make surgical pins.

Metals form the largest region of the table

The largest region of the periodic table contains elements classified as **metals**. Note that this region is shaded blue in **Table 3-2**. Metals are excellent conductors of heat and electricity. They also share other distinguishing properties that make them useful in technology, as shown in **Figure 3-4**. Metals are also generally lustrous, ductile, and malleable.

Nonmetals are the second largest region of the table

If you recall the properties of metals, you can probably guess what properties nonmetals have just from their name. **Nonmetal** elements have varying properties but are generally poor conductors of heat and electricity. Most are gases or are brittle solids at room temperature. One nonmetal, iodine, is shown in **Figure 3-5**. Where are the nonmetals located in the periodic table, **Table 3-2**?

metal
any of a class of elements that generally are solid at room temperature, have a grayish color and shiny surface, and conduct electricity

nonmetal
any chemical element that is neither a metal, metalloid, or a noble gas

53
I

Figure 3-5
Iodine is a nonmetal. Tincture of iodine, a mixture of alcohol and iodine, is a familiar antiseptic used to treat cuts and scrapes.

Properties and Uses of Selected Nonmetals

Selenium

Selenium is used in light-sensitive devices such as copy machines because its electrical conductivity increases in response to light shining on it. Its various forms range from a metallic gray solid to one with a red glassy appearance.

Phosphorus

Phosphorus is known for phosphorescence—the most common form glows in the dark. Other forms are used in fireworks and matches. Most phosphorus is used to produce fertilizer. Phosphorus is very toxic and must be handled carefully.

Carbon

Carbon atoms join with other atoms to form strong structural units. Carbon atoms combine with one another to create diamonds, which are so hard that they can be used in cutting tools. Carbon combines quickly with oxygen at high temperatures.

Properties and Uses of Selected Metalloids

Tellurium

Tellurium has some properties of metals and some of nonmetals. Pure tellurium has a metallic luster yet, like a nonmetal, it is easily ground into a powder. It is a relatively rare element found in the Earth's crust.

Germanium

Germanium is a brittle, crystalline solid that retains its luster in air. Germanium is also an important semiconductor. It is slightly more conductive than silicon so circuits fabricated with germanium operate faster than silicon.

Arsenic

Arsenic is a gray solid that tarnishes in air. When oxidized it has a garlic odor. Because it is very toxic, it has been used as a pesticide. Arsenic is also used in electronics fabrication because of its metalloid properties.

Figure 3-6
Boron, a metalloid, conducts electricity only at high temperatures. The mineral borax, which contains boron, is widely used in laundry and cleaning products.

metalloid
an element having properties of metals as well as nonmetals

noble gas
an element that exists in the gaseous state at normal temperatures and is nonreactive with other elements

Metalloids have properties of both metals and nonmetals

By now you realize that metals appear toward the left in the periodic table and nonmetals appear toward the right. Sandwiched in between these two regions are the **metalloids**. Locate the metalloids in the periodic table, **Table 3-2**. As the name suggests, a metalloid is an element that has some properties of metals and others of nonmetals. Several metalloids, most importantly silicon and germanium, are used in semiconducting devices, because their moderate electrical conductivity is just right for this delicate operation. Boron, shown in **Figure 3-6**, is another useful metalloid.

Noble gases are on the far right of the periodic table

Several elements are extremely unreactive or inert—they rarely form compounds with other elements. Such elements compose a group known as the **noble gases**. Krypton, used to make the lighting shown in **Figure 3-7**, is a noble gas. Find the noble gas region of the periodic table, **Table 3-2**. Which of the elements found in this group do you recognize?

Properties and Uses of Selected Noble Gases

Figure 3-7
Krypton is used in lighting products. Some krypton is used as an inert atmosphere for light bulbs. Mixed with argon, it is used in fluorescent lamps.

Neon

Neon emits brilliant red light when stimulated by electric current so it is useful for advertising signs. Neon is a monatomic gas. It is the fourth most abundant element in the universe.

Helium

Helium is a light, nonreactive gas so it is used in both weather balloons and toy balloons. It is plentiful, inexpensive, and harmless. Helium has the lowest melting point of any element.

Radon

Radon is an odorless, colorless, tasteless radioactive gas. It is emitted from certain rocks underground, and can accumulate in homes and basements. Overexposure to radon can cause cancer.

Consumer Focus

Essential elements

Of the more than 100 elements in the universe, 33 are essential to your health. These elements are highlighted in red in **Table 3-3**. Carbon, hydrogen, oxygen, and nitrogen are present in the largest amounts. Together, they make up 96% of your body mass. These elements are the major components of proteins, carbohydrates, lipids, and nucleic acids. Such compounds provide the structural materials your body needs for energy and for growth and repair.

Calcium, phosphorus, potassium, chlorine, sodium, and magnesium are the major minerals. They have a variety of important functions. For example, calcium is needed for your blood to clot when you bleed, and for your muscles to contract when you move. Other minerals help build hormones.

Some elements are called *trace elements* because only very small amounts—100 mg or less per day—are required. Trace elements include iron, manganese, copper, iodine, zinc, cobalt, chromium, nickel, silicon, tin, and vanadium.

To be sure you are getting enough of the major minerals and trace elements, you can take a multivitamin/mineral supplement. You should check with your doctor before taking such a supplement and take only the recommended dosage. These substances can be very toxic if you overdose. A spoonful of arsenic oxide, for example, is lethal, as you might know from mystery novels.

A healthy diet is safer than a supplement. If you eat a diet rich in animal protein, legumes, nuts, fruits, and vegetables, you are probably getting all the elements you need. Leafy, green vegetables are one especially good source of minerals and trace elements. The standard advice "eat your spinach! " is based on good science as well as common sense.

Table 3-3
Elements Needed for Health

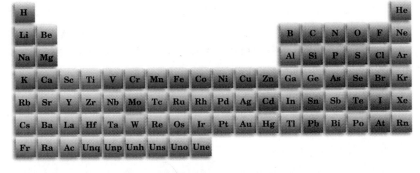

Section Review

3. Why are the properties of each element unique?

4. Which of the following elements would most likely have similar properties: zinc, copper, lead, and mercury? Explain the reason for your answer.

5. Name the elements represented by each of the following symbols: Br, Ni, Ag, Sn, Es, C, and Kr.

6. Identify each of the following elements as either a metal, nonmetal, metalloid, or noble gas: radon, carbon, selenium, cesium, antimony, and boron.

7. Assume that a new element was recently discovered. This element has a shiny luster and conducts electricity only moderately. In which of the four major categories would you place this element? Defend your choice.

3-2

What is the basic structure of an atom?

Section Objectives

Infer the existence of atoms from the laws of definite composition, conservation of mass, and multiple proportions.

List the five basic principles of Dalton's atomic theory.

Describe models of the atom.

Compare and contrast the properties of electrons, protons, and neutrons.

Explain the particle-wave nature of electrons.

Describe the quantum model of the atom.

Building the atomic model

Figure 3-8b shows a nuclear weapon exploding. Because the "atom bomb" and atomic energy have had such a huge impact on modern life, the present era has been described as the "atomic age." In such an age, many people take the existence of atoms for granted. But no one has ever directly seen an atom. Scientists infer their existence from an enormous amount of evidence.

To infer is to draw a conclusion based on observations that you make or evidence that you gather. For example, you may have had a cup of coffee or tea this morning. After one sip, you may have realized you had too much sugar in it. Even if you had the most powerful microscope, you could search and never find a trace of sugar. But you know it's there. So you sometimes accept things, or infer their existence, without ever actually seeing them, as long as you have some evidence for their existence. In the case of the coffee or tea, you know that sugar is in it because it tastes sweet. Similarly, scientists accept atoms without actually seeing them. But scientists, too, require evidence to support their inferences. There is plenty of experimental evidence for atoms, as you will see.

Figure 3-8a
This internationally recognized symbol warns of the presence of radioactivity. Radioactivity is produced by unstable atoms.

3-8b
The tremendous energy of the atomic nucleus is exploited by the atomic bomb. The first bomb was built in Los Alamos, New Mexico, as part of the "Manhattan Project."

3-8c
Nuclear power plants tear atoms apart, thereby releasing the atom's enormous energy for use in homes and industry.

Figure 3-9a
Table sugar (sucrose) is composed of 42.1% carbon, 51.4% oxygen, and 6.5% hydrogen. Table sugar contains exact proportions of these elements . . .

Evidence supporting the atomic theory

Recall that the idea that matter is made from atoms can be traced to Greek philosophers as far back as 400 B.C. But the ancient Greeks were better theorists than experimenters. Experimental results supporting the existence of atoms did not appear until more than 2000 years later in eighteenth-century Europe. There, early chemistry investigators—the first true chemists—noticed certain characteristics shared by all chemical compounds. Their observations of compounds and chemical reactions led to three laws that describe how compounds are formed.

1. Law of definite composition

The law of definite composition states that a compound contains the same elements in exactly the same proportions by mass regardless of the size of the sample or source of the compound. **Figure 3-9** illustrates this law.

3-9b
. . . regardless of the size of the sample or source of it.

2. Law of conservation of mass

The law of conservation of mass states that when two or more elements react to produce a compound, the total mass of the compound is the same as the sum of masses of the individual elements. The law of conservation of mass is illustrated in **Figure 3-10**.

Figure 3-10
The total mass of a system remains the same whether elements are combined, separated, or rearranged.

Combination of atoms:

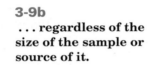

S	+	O_2	$\longrightarrow$	SO_2
Sulfur atom		Oxygen molecule		Sulfur dioxide molecule
32 mass units	+	32 mass units	=	64 mass units

Separation of atoms:

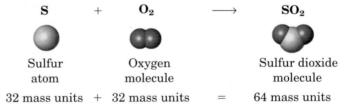

$2HgO$	$\longrightarrow$	Hg	Hg	+	O_2
2 mercury(II) oxide molecules		2 mercury atoms			1 oxygen molecule
434 mass units	=	402 mass units		+	32 mass units

Rearrangement of atoms:

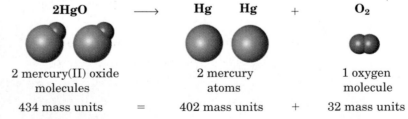

H_2CO_3	$\longrightarrow$	H_2O	+	CO_2
1 carbonic acid molecule		1 water molecule		1 carbon dioxide molecule
62 mass units	=	18 mass units	+	44 mass units

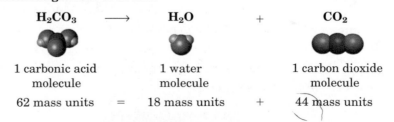

3. Law of multiple proportions

The law of multiple proportions applies to different compounds made from the same elements. It states that the mass ratio for one of the elements that combines with a fixed mass of the other element can be expressed in small whole numbers. **Figure 3-11** illustrates the law of multiple proportions.

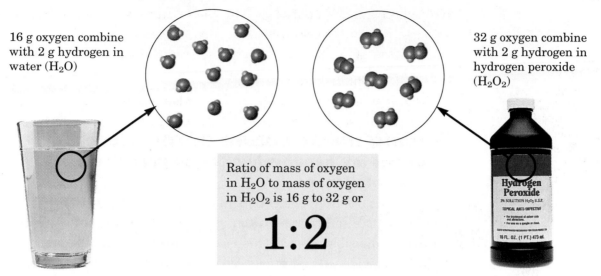

16 g oxygen combine with 2 g hydrogen in water (H_2O)

32 g oxygen combine with 2 g hydrogen in hydrogen peroxide (H_2O_2)

Ratio of mass of oxygen in H_2O to mass of oxygen in H_2O_2 is 16 g to 32 g or

1:2

Figure 3–11
Water and hydrogen peroxide are both formed from the elements hydrogen and oxygen. The ratio of the masses of oxygen in these two compounds is 1:2.

Dalton's atomic theory includes five principles

Taken together, these three laws represent much of the quantitative data obtained by chemists in the 1700s. But as useful as these laws were, no one realized their true potential until the English chemist John Dalton showed that, collectively, the laws demonstrate the existence of atoms.

Dalton argued that the three experimental laws could not be explained without assuming that all compounds are made from tiny particles such as atoms. This reasoning led to the development of the modern theory of the atom. Dalton's early atomic theory, published in the early 1800s, includes five basic principles.

1. All matter is made of indivisible and indestructible atoms.
2. Atoms of a given element are identical in their physical and chemical properties.
3. Atoms of different elements have different physical and chemical properties.
4. Atoms of different elements combine in simple, whole-number ratios to form chemical compounds.
5. Atoms cannot be subdivided, created, or destroyed when they are combined, separated, or rearranged in chemical reactions.

Dalton's proclamation attracted much interest from other chemists, who conducted experiments to test the new theory. While some exceptions to Dalton's atomic theory were eventually discovered, the theory itself has never been discarded, only modified and expanded as the world of the atom was explored.

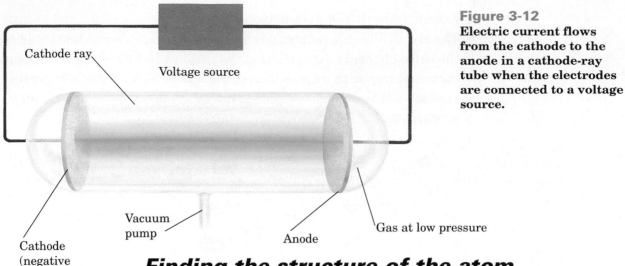

Figure 3-12
Electric current flows
from the cathode to the
anode in a cathode-ray
tube when the electrodes
are connected to a voltage
source.

Cathode ray

Voltage source

Vacuum pump

Anode

Gas at low pressure

Cathode (negative electrode)

Finding the structure of the atom
Electrons are negatively charged particles that have a small mass

Experiments by several scientists in the middle of the nineteenth century led to a major alteration to Dalton's atomic theory. The atom was found not to be indivisible after all. Instead, it consists of smaller particles.

The first evidence that atoms consist of smaller particles was obtained by researchers whose main interest was electricity rather than the structure of the atom. These researchers studied the flow of electric current in glass tubes such as the one shown in **Figure 3-12**. Notice the metal disks called *electrodes* that are placed at each end of the tube. When the electrodes were connected to a source of voltage and most of the gas was removed from the tube, current flowed in the tube, and the remaining gas began to glow. A glowing beam always originated at the negative electrode, or **cathode**, and traveled toward the positive electrode, or **anode**. For this reason, the glowing beams were named *cathode rays*, and the apparatus in which they were observed became known as a *cathode-ray tube*. Today, cathode-ray tubes have various practical applications, including television sets, computer monitors, and radar screens, as shown in **Figure 3-13**.

Researchers observed that a small paddle wheel placed in the paths of cathode rays rolled from the cathode toward the anode. This suggested that the rays must be composed of small, individual particles that could push the paddle wheel down the tube.

cathode
a negative electrode through which current flows

anode
a positive electrode through which current flows

Figure 3-13
Cathode rays "paint" the pictures on television screens and computer CRT (cathode-ray tube) screens.

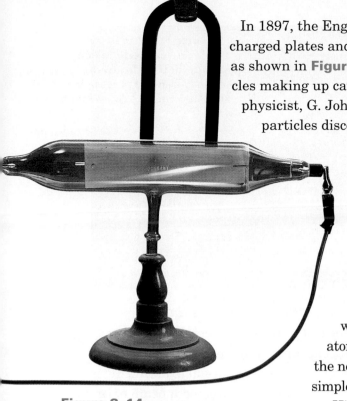

In 1897, the English physicist J. J. Thomson discovered that electrically charged plates and magnets deflected the straight paths of cathode rays, as shown in **Figure 3-14**. The direction of deflection shows that the particles making up cathode rays must be negatively charged. The English physicist, G. Johnstone Stoney named the small, negatively charged particles discovered in the cathode ray tube experiments *electrons*.

Experiments were later performed to determine the charge and mass of the electron. The electron was discovered to have a mass nearly 2000 times smaller than the mass of the smallest atom, hydrogen. The lightness of electrons implied that atoms must contain other, heavier matter to account for most of their mass.

There was additional evidence that atoms are made up of other, yet-to-be-identified kinds of matter. Atoms were known to be electrically neutral. This meant that an atom must contain some positively charged matter to balance the negative charges of its electrons. Thomson developed a simple early model of the atom based on all this information. His model of the atom, which is shown in **Figure 3-15**, was named the "plum pudding model" because it resembled plum pudding, a British dessert that consists of a ball of sweet bread with pieces of fruit embedded in it. Thomson envisioned the atom as a ball of positive charge with negatively charged electrons embedded inside.

Figure 3–14
Note the deflection of the cathode ray. Magnets near the cathode-ray tube cause the beam to be deflected as shown. The direction of the deflected beam with respect to the north and south poles of the magnets indicates that the particles making up the beam have a negative charge.

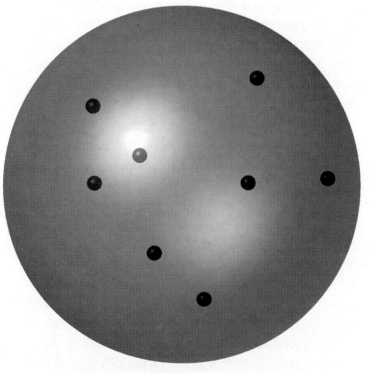

Figure 3–15a
J. J. Thomson's model of the atom featured negatively charged electrons embedded in a ball of positive charge.

3-15b
Thomson's model of the atom is often called the plum pudding model of the atom. Can you see the resemblance?

Figure 3–16
In Rutherford's famous experiment, small positively charged particles were targeted at a thin foil of gold atoms. Note how the gold atoms scatter these small particles.

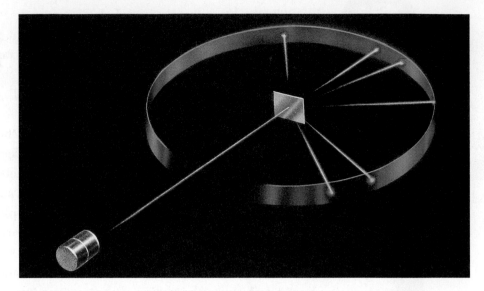

Each atom has a positively charged inner core

A student of J. J. Thomson, Ernest Rutherford, assembled a research team to perform an experiment that ultimately disproved the plum pudding model of the atom. This now-famous "gold-foil experiment" is represented in **Figure 3-16**. Rutherford's team directed a beam of tiny positively charged particles, called *alpha particles*, at a very thin gold foil sheet. The team measured the angles at which the alpha particles were deflected from their straight-line paths as they emerged from the foil. This procedure was much like determining the shape of an object hidden under a table by rolling marbles at it, as shown in **Figure 3-17**.

The researchers discovered that most of the alpha particles they shot at the foil passed straight through it. Rutherford reasoned that these alpha particles went straight through because they were traveling through empty regions of the foil. The researchers also observed that some particles did not pass straight through the foil but were slightly deflected. But what really surprised the scientists were the alpha particles that were actually scattered back.

Rutherford reasoned that the deflections resulted from electrical repulsion between the positively charged alpha particles and the positively charged matter contained in the atom. However, if the positive charge were spread out within the atom as the plum pudding model described, the backward scattering of the alpha particles would not have been possible. The positive charge and the mass must be concentrated within atoms to scatter the alpha particles backward. Rutherford had discovered the positively charged core of the atom. The tiny central region of the atom was named the **nucleus**, from the Latin word meaning "little nut." Electrons, Rutherford supposed, traveled in the space surrounding the nucleus in a way similar to the motion of the planets around the sun.

nucleus

the central region of an atom made up of protons and neutrons

Figure 3–17

Marbles are rolled at a hidden object. The shape of the object can be determined from the directions of the scattered marbles.

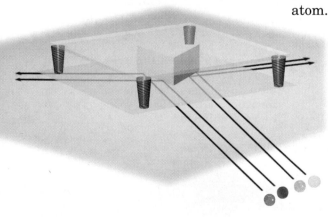

Figure 3-18
If the nucleus of an atom were the size of a marble, then the whole atom would be the size of a football stadium.

The nucleus, then, is the dense central portion of the atom that contains all of its positive charge and nearly all of its mass but occupies only a small fraction of its volume. By measuring the fraction of alpha particles that were deflected and their angles of deflection, the radius of the nucleus was calculated to be at least 10 000 times smaller than the radius of the whole atom. To put this relationship in perspective, examine **Figure 3-18**.

Electrons occupy energy levels within an atom

Classical physics predicted that, because all accelerating charged particles radiate energy, the circulating electrons in Rutherford's planetary model must also radiate energy. As electrons radiated, their energy would be lost, and they would not be able to stay in orbit. The electrons would spiral toward the nucleus and collapse into it. The atom would be destroyed in a billionth of a second. Yet most atoms were known to remain stable for thousands of years. Clearly, something was wrong with Rutherford's model of the atom.

In 1913, a young Danish physicist named Niels Bohr came up with a new model that addressed the deficiencies of Rutherford's model of the atom. Bohr proposed that electrons in an atom can reside only in certain **energy levels**. The rungs of a ladder are similar to the energy levels within an atom, as shown in **Figure 3-19**. A person can move up or down the ladder only by standing on its rungs; it is impossible to stand between them. Similarly, the Bohr model of an atom postulated that an electron can reside only in certain energy levels within an atom, as shown in **Figure 3-20** on the next page.

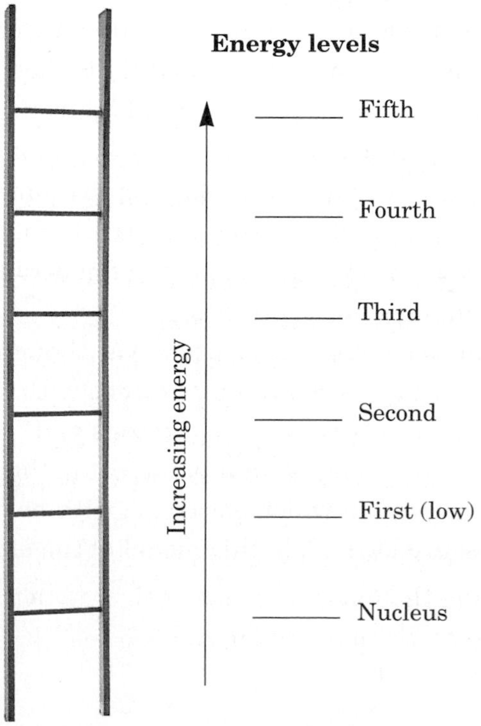

energy level or principal energy level

a specific energy or group of energies that may be possessed by an electron in an atom

Energy levels

Increasing energy →

_____ Fifth

_____ Fourth

_____ Third

_____ Second

_____ First (low)

_____ Nucleus

Figure 3-19
The energy levels of electrons within an atom are like the rungs of a ladder. Just as you cannot stand between the rungs of a ladder, electrons can reside only in certain energy levels in an atom.

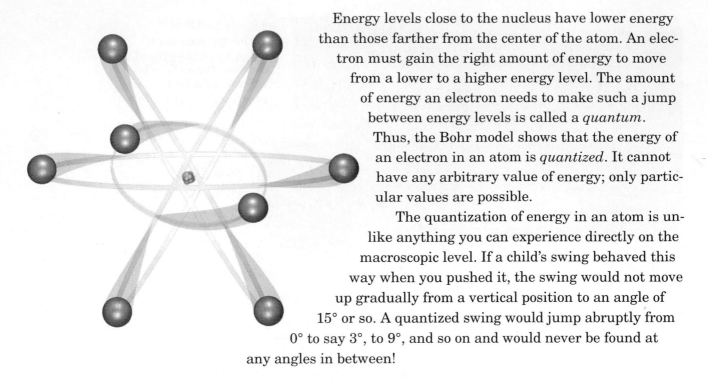

Energy levels close to the nucleus have lower energy than those farther from the center of the atom. An electron must gain the right amount of energy to move from a lower to a higher energy level. The amount of energy an electron needs to make such a jump between energy levels is called a *quantum*.

Thus, the Bohr model shows that the energy of an electron in an atom is *quantized*. It cannot have any arbitrary value of energy; only particular values are possible.

The quantization of energy in an atom is unlike anything you can experience directly on the macroscopic level. If a child's swing behaved this way when you pushed it, the swing would not move up gradually from a vertical position to an angle of 15° or so. A quantized swing would jump abruptly from 0° to say 3°, to 9°, and so on and would never be found at any angles in between!

Figure 3-20
The model of the atom proposed by Niels Bohr included quantized energy levels for the electrons. Although the Bohr model has been revised in part, the quantum concept of the atom is still considered valid today.

Neutrons add mass to the nucleus

The positively charged nuclear particles that repelled the alpha particles in Rutherford's experiment were found to be quite heavy. The mass of one such particle is almost 2000 times that of an electron. Scientists call these heavy particles *protons*.

The mass of the proton presented a dilemma because the masses of all atoms besides hydrogen were known to be larger than the total mass of their protons and electrons. Clearly there must be yet another particle that contributed to the mass of an atom. The search for a third subatomic particle was soon underway. This particle, however, proved to be more difficult to detect than either electrons or protons because it was electrically neutral. Some 30 years after the discovery of electrons, Irene Joliot-Curie (daughter of the famous Pierre and Marie Curie) discovered that when beryllium was bombarded with alpha particles, a beam with high penetrating power was formed. A British scientist, James Chadwick, found that this penetrating beam was made of particles that had approximately the mass of protons. Also, the beam was not deflected by electric or magnetic fields. Chadwick deduced that the beam was composed of neutrons—neutral particles that have mass equal to that of protons.

With the discovery of the neutron, the picture of an atom was thought to be complete. An atom consists of a nucleus containing protons with positive charges and neutrons with no electrical charge. Protons and neutrons together make up nearly all the mass of an atom. Most of the volume of an atom consists of empty space in which electrons, with negative charges and insignificant mass, are located. Is this model of the atom still accepted as truly complete?

Figure 3-21a
The bright-line emission spectrum is unique to each element, just like a fingerprint is unique to each person. The bright-line emission spectrum for calcium . . .

3-21b
. . . is easily distinguished from the bright-line emission spectrum for mercury.

ground state
the lowest energy state of a quantized system

excited state
the condition of an atom in a state higher than the ground state

The modern view of the atom
Electrons can be described as particles or waves

Electrons were first recognized as particles because they were seen to push a paddle wheel down a cathode-ray tube. Other experiments on the light emitted by energized, gaseous atoms also indicate that electrons are particles.

When all electrons are in the lowest possible energy levels, an atom is said to be in its **ground state**. When the atom absorbs energy so that its electrons are boosted to higher energy levels, the atom is said to be in an **excited state**. Experiments on gaseous atoms showed that they absorb energy from an electric discharge to reach excited states. Later, the gaseous atoms return to the ground state by emitting the energy they had absorbed, now in the form of light.

The light emitted by an element when its electrons return to a lower energy state can be viewed as a *bright-line emission spectrum,* shown in **Figure 3-21**. The bright-line emission spectrum is obtained by passing the light that an element emits through a prism to separate the various colors it contains. Each colored band represents the light energy released by an electron when it returns from a high energy state to a lower one. The energy of each band of colored light is equal to the difference between the original and final energy levels of the electron.

Sunlight, when passed through a prism, produces the *visible spectrum*— all the colors of light that can be perceived by the human eye, as shown in **Figure 3-22**.

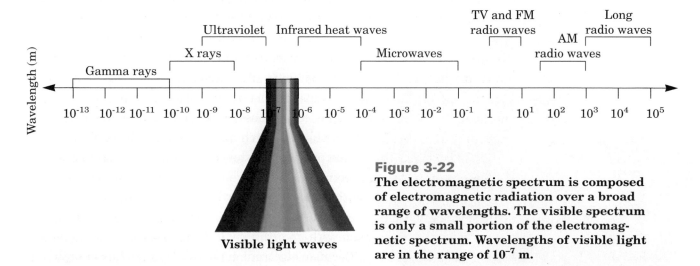

Visible light waves

Figure 3-22
The electromagnetic spectrum is composed of electromagnetic radiation over a broad range of wavelengths. The visible spectrum is only a small portion of the electromagnetic spectrum. Wavelengths of visible light are in the range of 10^{-7} m.

electromagnetic spectrum
the total range of electromagnetic radiation, ranging from the longest radio waves to the shortest gamma waves

The visible spectrum is a small portion of the larger **electromagnetic spectrum**. The electromagnetic spectrum consists of the various classes of electromagnetic waves: microwaves, radio waves, X rays, gamma rays, infrared radiation, and ultraviolet radiation, in addition to visible light. All electromagnetic waves are essentially the same—they are electromagnetic vibrations traveling through space in the form of waves. However, the *wavelength* and *frequency* of different kinds of electromagnetic waves differ, as **Figure 3-23** shows. The wavelength of a wave is the distance between two identical points on the wave. Frequency is the number of wavelengths that pass a certain point in a given period of time—usually a second. Wavelength and frequency are inversely related.

Figure 3-23
The frequency and wavelength of a wave are inversely related. As wavelength increases, frequency decreases. The higher the energy of a wave, the shorter its wavelength and the higher its frequency.

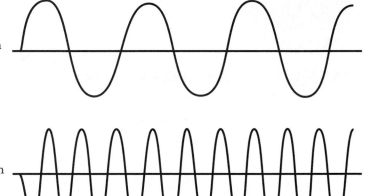

Red light
Low frequency
Long wavelength

Blue light
High frequency
Short wavelength

All electromagnetic waves are created by accelerating charged particles. The radio waves that transmit the signals that a radio picks up are produced by the motions of electrons up and down along an antenna wire. The visible spectrum is produced by the "jumping" and "falling" of electrons in atoms. In "falling" from a state of higher energy to a lower state, the electron moves closer to the nucleus. Electrons, then, have properties of particles, as evidenced by their behavior in cathode-ray tubes and their ability to "jump" and "fall" among high- and low-energy orbitals.

Electrons also have properties of waves. However, electrons have tiny wavelengths, on the order of 10^{-10} m. Thus, electron waves are much smaller than visible light waves. Because of this, the wave behavior of electrons can be observed only on the scale of very small objects—such as atoms. The electron microscope provides evidence of the wave behavior of electrons. The image in **Figure 3-24** was taken with an electron microscope, which uses electron waves to explore details of matter too small to be seen with an ordinary light microscope.

Because electrons have dual properties of both particles *and* waves, a new model for atomic structure had to be developed. This model was produced by quantum theory.

Figure 3-24
This electron micrograph shows the germination of two grains of pollen at a magnification of 1100×.

quantum theory
the field of physics based on the idea that energy is quantized and that this has significant effects on the atomic level

orbital
a region of an atom in which there is a high probability of finding electrons

Figure 3-25a
This probability plot shows the hydrogen atom in its ground state. The electron is most likely to be found in regions where the dots are closest together.

3-25b
This probability plot shows hydrogen in an excited state. The region where the electron is most likely found is no longer spherical.

Quantum theory provides a modern picture of the atom

The description of the atom that is built on the wave properties of electrons is the **quantum theory**. The quantum theory uses the complex mathematical equations of *quantum mechanics* that describe waves. The quantum mechanical model of the atom is an essentially mathematical one, and it cannot be represented by anything that exists in the macroscopic world.

Like the Bohr model, the quantum mechanical model predicts quantized energy levels for electrons. Unlike the Bohr model, however, the quantum mechanical model that scientists use today does not describe the exact path an electron takes around the nucleus. It is concerned with the *probability*, or likelihood, of finding an electron in a certain position.

When all of the probable locations of an electron are plotted as points on a graph, they indicate a region where the electron can be found, as **Figure 3-25** shows. Such regions are called **orbitals**. Each orbital can be occupied by up to two electrons. Note that the boundaries of an orbital are fuzzy because the probability of finding an electron changes gradually throughout the region. Regions with the densest concentrations of points are areas where the probability of finding electrons is highest. Due to their fuzzy boundaries and gradual shading, orbitals are sometimes called "electron clouds." Just as the blade of a fan could be anywhere within its blurred path, the electron could be anywhere within an electron cloud. The quantum mechanical model of the atom is therefore often called the "electron cloud model."

It is conventional to draw a surface around the model of an electron cloud to designate where an electron can be found 90% of the time, as shown in **Figure 3-26**. With this helpful technique, it is possible to simplify the representation of electron orbitals while maintaining a basically accurate picture of the atom.

The position and velocity of an electron can be measured, but the precision of these measurements is limited. The quantum theory shows that regardless of how sophisticated technology becomes, it will never be possible to measure both the electron's position and its velocity simultaneously. This fact is known as the *Heisenberg uncertainty principle*: you can never know exactly where an electron is if you know exactly how fast it is moving. Conversely, you can never know exactly how fast an electron is moving if you know exactly where it is. The quantum theory shows that there is a limit to what we can know about events inside an atom.

Figure 3-26
The exact location of an electron cannot be determined. Instead, electron orbitals indicate the areas where electrons have the highest probability of being located. Though orbitals have fuzzy boundaries, it is conventional to draw closed surfaces over them that show where the electron has a 90% probability of being found. The cloud model of hydrogen in its ground state is most often represented as a closed sphere, as shown here.

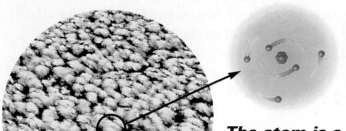

3-27b
The modern atomic model describes the atom as a central cluster of neutrons and protons surrounded by electrons that travel in orbitals.

Figure 3-27a
The scanning tunneling microscope allows scientists to "see" the surface of boron atoms.

The atom is a scientific model

John Dalton showed that the existence of atoms can be inferred from experimental evidence. Now, with the scanning tunneling microscope, there is even better evidence that atoms exist, as **Figure 3-27a** shows.

However, no one really knows what the internal structure of an atom looks like. Because scientists cannot look directly at an atom, the best they can do is design clever experiments to probe the atom's inner design. From these experiments, the scientists build a model to account for the experimental findings, as shown in **Figure 3-27b**.

The model of the atom has been revised many times. Dalton's indivisible spheres were replaced with the plum pudding model, which was replaced by Rutherford's model of the atom, the Bohr model, and finally the electron cloud model. Each model was built on experimental data. Once the model was created, it served as a springboard for further experiments designed to test it. When the experimental tests revealed flaws, the model was revised.

Models play a key role in science. As you have seen in the case of the atom, models provide guidelines for research that leads to new knowledge. Models also help simplify and organize phenomena that would otherwise be too complex to understand.

Current experimental research in atomic physics and chemistry may show that flaws exist in the model of atomic structure that scientists accept today. Nonetheless, the current model, like its predecessors, has greatly advanced our understanding of the structure of atoms and our ability to predict how they will behave.

Section Review

8. How might you infer that it has rained without actually having seen the rain? How is this like the belief that atoms exist?
9. What laws first enabled scientists to infer the existence of atoms?
10. Which of Dalton's five principles still apply to the structure of an atom?
11. How are models useful in understanding atomic structure?
12. Describe the major differences between electrons, protons, and neutrons.
13. What evidence supports the particle nature of electrons? the wave nature of electrons?
14. How does the quantum theory's depiction of atomic structure differ from the Bohr model?

How do the structures of atoms differ?

Chem Fact
Although scientists in Nazi Germany possessed the theoretical know-how to produce an atomic bomb, their progress was slowed by several key practical deficiencies. One was their inability to produce the required amounts of water with hydrogen atoms that have the heavy deuterium nucleus. This *heavy water* was needed to control the rate of nuclear reactions. American scientists, on the other hand, did find ways to produce large amounts of heavy water.

Atomic number and mass number

If all atoms consist of electrons, protons, and neutrons, then how are the atoms of one element different from those of another element? As you know, atoms differ not in the kinds of subatomic particles they contain, but in how many of each kind there are.

Each element has an atomic number

The number of protons in the nucleus of an atom is known as its **atomic number**. Hydrogen, which has atomic number 1, contains one proton in its nucleus. Oxygen has atomic number 8 and contains eight protons. The periodic table lists the atomic number of each element. **Figure 3-28** shows the hydrogen and oxygen blocks of the periodic table. Notice that the atomic number of each element is given.

If you know an element's atomic number, you also know how many electrons are contained in an electrically neutral atom of that element. Such an atom must contain the same number of electrons as protons. Thus, nitrogen, with atomic number 7, has seven protons and seven electrons.

Figure 3-28
The periodic table lists each element's name, symbol, and atomic number. Atomic mass and electron configuration—which you will learn about in this chapter—are also given on most periodic tables.

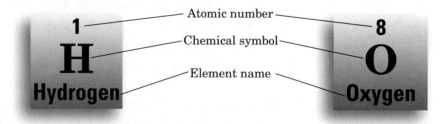

atomic number
the number of protons in the nucleus of an atom

isotope
one of two or more atoms having the same number of protons but different numbers of neutrons

Isotopes of the same element have different mass numbers

The number of protons that an element contains is fixed, so all atoms of the same element have the same atomic number. However, the number of neutrons can vary. Atoms of the same element that have the same number of protons but different numbers of neutrons are called **isotopes**.

Consider the simplest element, hydrogen. Three isotopes of hydrogen exist. They are named *protium, deuterium,* and *tritium*. Each hydrogen isotope contains one proton in its nucleus. But protium contains no neutrons, while deuterium has one neutron, and tritium has two. Despite their differences, isotopes have very similar chemical properties. Can you see why this is true?

mass number
the total number of protons and neutrons in the nucleus of an atom

In addition to having an atomic number, each element also has a mass number. The **mass number** is the total number of protons and neutrons in the atomic nucleus.

An isotope is represented by its chemical symbol with two additional numbers written to the left of it. The mass number is written as a superscript, and the atomic number is written as a subscript.

A second way to represent isotopes is to use both the element's name and mass number. Deuterium, for example, is described as hydrogen-2 and tritium as hydrogen-3. Two isotopes of oxygen are oxygen-16 and oxygen-18. **Table 3-4** shows how to represent isotopes.

Table 3-4
Isotopes of Hydrogen

Name	Number of neutrons	Symbol	Representation
protium	0	^1_1H	hydrogen-1
deuterium	1	^2_1H	hydrogen-2
tritium	2	^3_1H	hydrogen-3

The number of neutrons in an element is easy to find

If you know the atomic number of an element, you know how many protons and electrons it contains. If you also know the mass number, you can determine how many neutrons the element contains.

For example, consider the element sodium. It has the atomic number 11 and a mass number of 23. From its atomic number, you can quickly determine that a sodium atom has 11 protons and 11 electrons. To determine the number of neutrons, simply subtract the atomic number from the mass number. Sodium has $23 - 11$, or 12, neutrons.

Labeling electrons in atoms
Quantum numbers are used to differentiate among electrons

In quantum theory, each electron in an atom is assigned a set of four quantum numbers. Three of these numbers, like coordinates on a map, give the location of the electron. The fourth quantum number describes the orientation of an electron in an orbital.

The first quantum number, called the *principal quantum number*, is represented by the letter n. This number describes the energy level that the electron occupies. The principal quantum number is assigned a positive integer starting with 1 ($n = 1, 2, 3, 4, \ldots$). Generally speaking, the larger the value of n, the farther away from the nucleus and the higher the energy of the electron. For example, an electron for which $n = 2$ occupies a higher energy level than an electron for which $n = 1$.

Figure 3-29 shows various energy levels of the hydrogen atom and their relative spacing with respect to the nucleus. These are not distances.

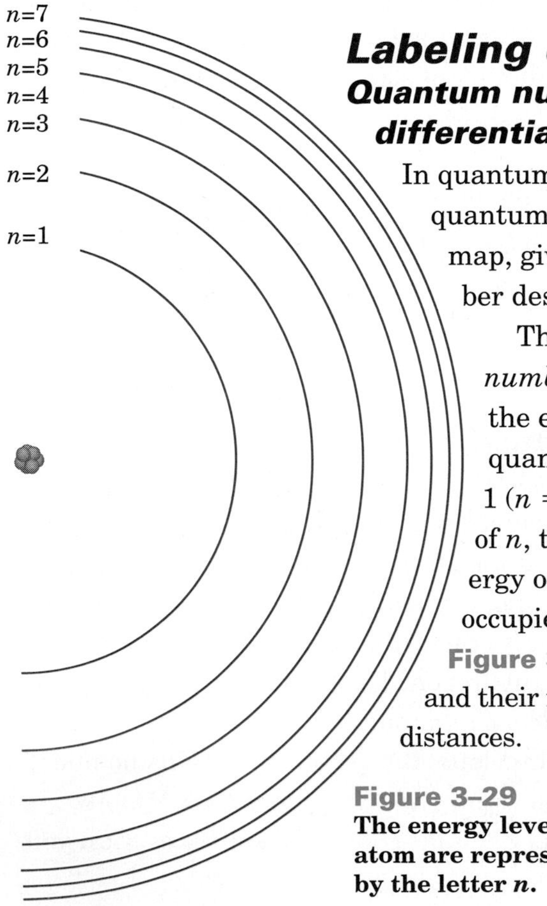

$n=7$
$n=6$
$n=5$
$n=4$
$n=3$
$n=2$
$n=1$

Figure 3–29
The energy levels of an atom are represented by the letter n.

Table 3-5
Letter Designations for Values of ℓ

ℓ	Letter
0	s
1	p
2	d
3	f

Quantum numbers are also used to describe the shapes of atomic orbitals. A second quantum number is designated by the letter ℓ. It provides a code for the shapes of orbitals.

Values of ℓ are often expressed as letters rather than numbers. **Table 3-5** shows number values of ℓ along with their letter designations. The lowest energy orbital in each energy level is designated as s. It has a spherical shape as shown in **Figure 3-30**. There is only one s orbital allowed in each energy level. There are three orbitals designated p in each energy level. Each p orbital is shaped like a dumbbell. The p orbitals have greater energy than s orbitals within a particular energy level. Orbitals designated d and f have more complex shapes and still higher energy. Notice the shapes of d orbitals, shown in **Figure 3-30**.

As you can see below, orbitals (other than s orbitals) can be oriented in a number of different ways. A p orbital can exist in one of three possible orientations, for example. A third quantum number, the magnetic quantum number, is designated m_ℓ. The value of m_ℓ tells you the electron's position by designating the spatial orientation of the orbital that the electron occupies.

Electrons that have the same values of n and ℓ but not necessarily m_ℓ are said to be in the same **sublevel** of the atom. The $2p$ sublevel contains a maximum of three orbitals, $2px$, $2py$, $2pz$. These orbitals are oriented along the x, y, and z axes respectively.

sublevel

one orbital or a group of orbitals within an energy level which have the same value of ℓ

Figure 3-30a
The s orbital is shaped like a sphere.

3-30b
A single p orbital is shaped rather like a dumbbell. It can be oriented in one of three directions.

3-30c
A single d orbital can assume any of the forms represented here. Notice that four of the five possible d orbital shapes are the same, but they are oriented differently in space.

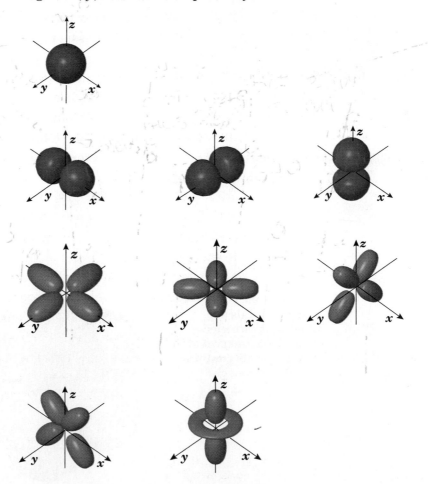

Table 3-6
Number of Electrons Accommodated in Electron Energy Levels and Sublevels

Principal energy level	Sublevels available	Number of orbitals in sublevel $(2\ell + 1)$	Number of electrons possible in sublevel $[2(2\ell + 1)]$	Total electrons possible for energy level $(2n^2)$
1	s	1	2	2
2	s	1	2	8
	p	3	6	
3	s	1	2	18
	p	3	6	
	d	5	10	
4	s	1	2	32
	p	3	6	
	d	5	10	
	f	7	14	
5	s	1	2	50
	p	3	6	
	d	5	10	
	f	7	14	
	g*	9	18	
6	s	1	2	72
	p	3	6	
	d	5	10	
	f*	7	14	
	g*	9	18	
	h*	11	22	

*These orbitals are not used in the ground state of any known element.

To describe the motion of an electron, there is a fourth quantum number, m_s, called the spin quantum number. This number labels the orientation of the electron. Electrons in an orbital spin in opposite directions. These directions are arbitrarily designated as $+ 1/2$ and $-1/2$.

No two electrons have an identical set of four quantum numbers. This statement, first made by the German chemist Wolfgang Pauli, is appropriately referred to as the Pauli exclusion principle. The Pauli exclusion principle ensures that no more than two electrons can be found within a particular orbital. There is also a maximum number of electrons allowed in each sublevel and principal energy level. **Table 3-6** summarizes the possible sublevels and orbitals that can be found in each principal energy level. Also note that the maximum numbers of electrons in orbitals, sublevels, and principal energy levels can be calculated from expressions involving quantum numbers.

So far you have learned that the way to designate a single electron in an atom is to use its quantum numbers. All elements except hydrogen contain more than one electron, as illustrated in **Figure 3-31**. To represent all of the electrons in an atom, you can use the Pauli exclusion principle along with quantum numbers to write an overall electron configuration for the element.

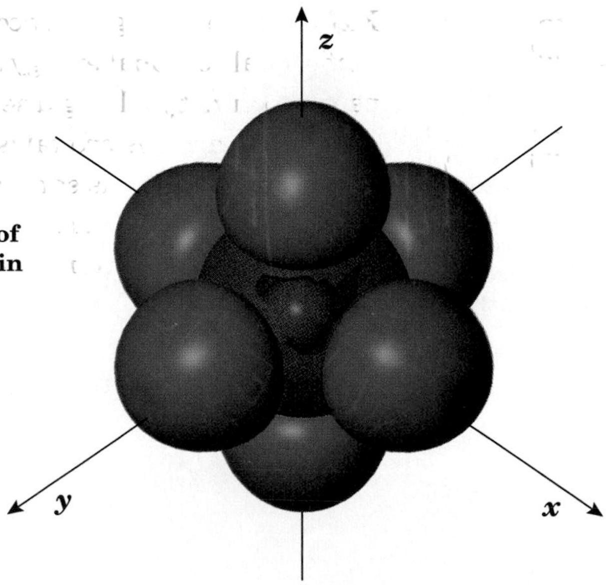

Figure 3-31
This model shows a carbon atom. Its 1s and 2s orbitals are filled with two electrons each and two of its 2p orbitals contain one electron each.

Orbital diagrams and electron configurations are models for electron arrangements

Orbital diagrams are used to show how electrons are distributed within sublevels and to show the direction of spin. In an orbital diagram, each orbital is represented by a box, and each electron is represented by an arrow. The direction of spin is represented by the direction of the arrow. The orbital diagram for hydrogen, which contains one electron, would be represented as follows.

1s

An electron configuration is an abbreviated form of the orbital diagram. The electron configuration for hydrogen would be $1s^1$. The coefficient 1 indicates that the sole electron occupies the first energy level, and the superscript 1 indicates that one electron occupies the s orbital within that first energy level.

How do you write the orbital diagram and electron configuration for boron? The atomic number of boron is 5. It has 5 electrons; this means there are electrons in the first and second energy levels. There are two electrons in the first ($n = 1$) principal energy level, both in an s orbital. There are three electrons in the second principal energy level, two in an s orbital and one in a p orbital. The electron configuration for boron can be written $1s^2 2s^2 2p^1$. The orbital diagram can be written as follows.

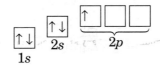

Neon, with 10 electrons, could be represented with the electron configuration $1s^2 2s^2 2p^6$ or with the following orbital diagram.

Hund's rule
the most stable arrangement of electrons is that with the maximum number of unpaired electrons, all with the same spin direction

Electrons are arranged in accordance with **Hund's rule**, which states that orbitals of equal energy are each occupied by one electron before any pairing occurs by adding a second electron. In this way, repulsion between electrons in a single orbital is minimized. All electrons in singly occupied orbitals must have the same spin. When two electrons occupy an orbital they have opposite spins.

You can write electron configurations yourself as long as you keep in mind the maximum number of electrons allowed in each orbital and the order in which orbitals are filled. For an atom in the ground state, electrons fill the orbitals beginning with the lowest energy orbital before filling orbitals with successively higher energies.

Figure 3-32

Electrons fill orbitals in the order indicated by the arrow. Note that there is some overlap of energy levels. The 3*d* orbitals actually have higher energy than the 4*s* orbital and the 7*s* orbital has lower energy than the 6*d* orbital, for example.

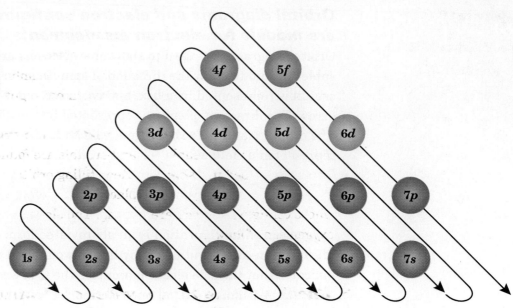

Figure 3-32 shows a sequence model that can be used to write electron configurations. Notice that principal energy levels do not always fill in order. You can see in **Figure 3-33**, which shows the energy distribution of orbitals, that there are areas where principal energy levels overlap. Notice that even though the 3*d* orbital is in a lower principal energy level, it is higher in energy than the 4*s*. Therefore a 4*s* orbital generally fills before a 3*d* orbital.

The electron configuration for gallium, $1s^2 2s^2 2p^6 3s^2 3p^6 4s^2 3d^{10} 4p^1$, shows why you need to understand **Figure 3-32** and **Figure 3-33** to write its orbital diagram.

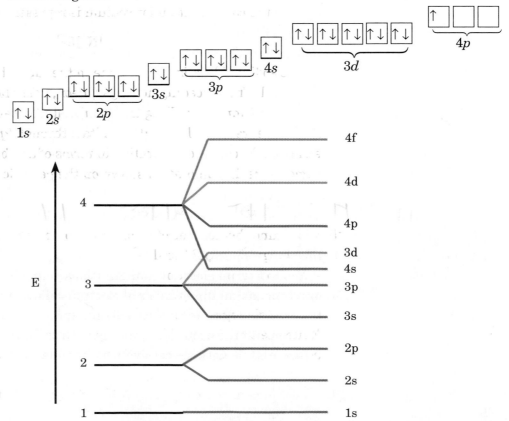

Figure 3-33

Energy generally increases as *n*, the principal energy level, increases. It is possible, however for the lowest sublevel of *n* = 4 to be below the highest sublevel of *n* = 3. This occurs in potassium and calcium atoms, where successive electrons enter the 4*s* rather than the 3*d* sublevel.

1. Locate the element whose electron configuration you wish to write in the periodic table.

For example, locate oxygen. Use the atomic number to determine the number of electrons in one atom. Oxygen has eight electrons.

2. Fill orbitals in the proper order with electrons.

Keep in mind which sublevels and orbitals are found in each energy level. This is described in **Table 3-6**. Keep filling orbitals using the order shown in Figure 3-32 until you have placed all the electrons of the element whose configuration you are writing. The electron configuration for oxygen is as follows.

$$1s^2 2s^2 2p^4$$

3. Check that the total number of electrons in the electron configuration equals the atomic number.

For oxygen, the total number of electrons shown in the electron configuration is 2 + 2 + 4, or 8. This is equal to the atomic number of oxygen.

Electron configurations can be written in terms of noble gases

The electron configuration for every element can be found on the periodic table on pages 110–111. Notice that the configurations are abbreviated to save space even further. For example, the electron configuration for sodium, Na, could be written as $1s^2 2s^2 2p^6 3s^1$. On the periodic table, you can see the configuration for sodium is represented as follows.

$$[Ne]3s^1$$

The sodium block is the first one in the table that shows filling of the 3s orbital. The preceding noble gas, neon, ends the row in the previous period by completely filling the 2p orbital. You can use the symbol for neon to represent all the filled orbitals through 2p. When you express an element's electron configuration in terms of a noble gas, you are using the same abbreviated notation shown on the periodic table.

Section Review

15. Determine the number of electrons, protons, and neutrons in each of the following: $^{235}_{92}U$, $^{106}_{46}Pd$, and $^{133}_{55}Cs$.

16. What do the quantum numbers n, ℓ, m_ℓ, and m_s represent?

17. Write the electron configurations for phosphorus and nickel. Then draw the orbital diagrams for these elements.

18. Write the complete electron configurations for magnesium, sulfur, and potassium. Then write their electron configurations using the symbols for the noble gases.

19. What element is represented by $[Ne]3s^2 3p^6$? What does it have in common with Ne?

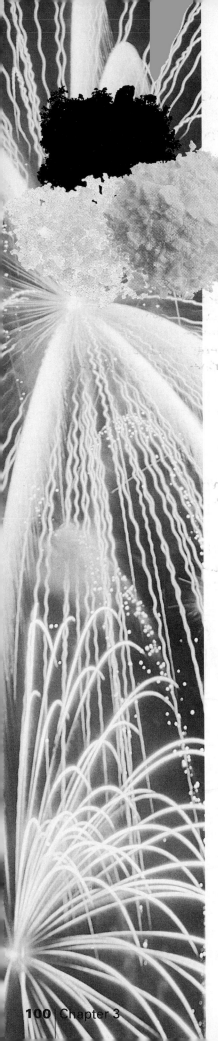

Conclusion: Excited Atoms and the Fourth of July

hat is light, and how do various colors of light differ? Visible light consists of electromagnetic radiation having wavelengths between 3.8×10^{-7} m and 7.8×10^{-7} m. The longest visible waves appear red, shorter waves appear blue, and the shortest visible waves are violet.

What is going on at the level of atoms and molecules when fireworks produce colored light? The colors are generated either by atoms or molecules present in the gas state when a firework shell explodes. In the former case, *atomic emission* occurs: atoms are excited so that their electrons are bumped from the ground state to a higher energy state. The electrons quickly return to the ground state, shedding the energy they had absorbed as light of a specific wavelength. Sodium is a potent atomic light emitter. Sodium atoms heated to more than 1800°C give off yellow light with a wavelength of 5.89×10^{-7} m. The process is so efficient that it tends to overwhelm other atomic or molecular light emissions in a fireworks explosion. Yellow fireworks explosions are the easiest to produce and, consequently, are very popular.

As with atomic emission, *molecular emission* involves a transition from a ground state to an excited one. Gaseous molecules radiate light when they are heated to a temperature high enough to reach an excited state; the electrons in their atoms must absorb energy to receive an energy boost. Then electrons fall to a lower energy state, and light of a particular wavelength is emitted.

How does the instability of copper chloride at high temperatures interfere with its ability to emit blue light? Copper chloride is unstable—it decomposes into copper and chlorine atoms—at a temperature only slightly higher than that at which it emits light. Therefore, if the temperatures generated by the exploding shell and reacting chemicals are not precisely controlled, copper chloride crystals absorb so much heat energy that they break apart and never emit blue light.

Applying Concepts

1. Fireplace logs that burn various colors are available in many supermarkets. How might a manufacturer treat a log so that it burns with a bright yellow flame? a green flame? a red flame?
2. Why do different elements produce light of different colors?

Research and Writing

Use the library to find out more about the following.

1. By what process do hand-held sparklers emit light? How does this process differ from atomic and molecular emission?
2. Describe three applications of pyrotechnic technology, other than fireworks.

Highlights

Key terms

anode	mass number
atomic number	metal
cathode	metalloid
electromagnetic spectrum	metalloid noble gas
energy level	nonmetal
excited state	nucleus
ground state	orbital
group	period
Hund's rule	quantum theory
isotope	sublevel

Key ideas

How are the elements organized?

- The periodic table organizes all known elements according to atomic structure so that elements with similar properties fall within the same group.
- The periodic table can be divided into four regions of elements with similar characteristics: metals, metalloids, nonmetals, and noble gases.

What is the basic structure of an atom?

- Three laws support the existence of the atom: the law of definite composition, conservation of mass, and multiple proportions.
- Atoms consist of particles with positive and negative charges. The positive charge is confined to a central nucleus that accounts for most of the atom's mass but has a radius 10000 times smaller than that of the whole atom.
- The nucleus also contains neutrons, particles with no charge.
- Electrons, particles with a negative charge and a mass 2000 times smaller than the mass of hydrogen, travel about the nucleus. Discrete amounts of energy are released or absorbed when electrons move from one energy level to another.
- Quantum theory describes the wave nature of electrons.

How do the structures of atoms differ?

- The atomic number is the number of protons contained in each atom of that element. The mass number is the total number of protons and neutrons in an atom.
- A unique set of four quantum numbers describes each electron in an atom. The Pauli exclusion principle states that no two electrons can have the same four quantum numbers.

Key problem-solving approach: Determining electron configurations

Determine the number of electrons in the atom. Then, use the diagram on the right to determine the order for filling. Finally, fill the orbitals using the energy level diagram at the bottom as a guide.

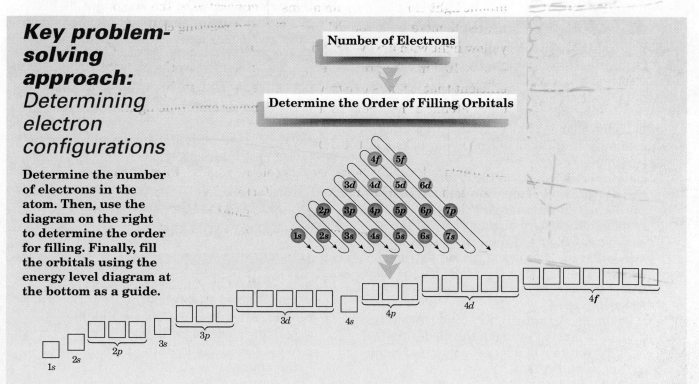

Review and Assess

Classifying the elements

REVIEW

1. What is the basis for the organization of the periodic table?
2. **a.** What are the four regions of the periodic table?
   b. Describe the general characteristics of each region.
3. Propose a reason why sodium, Na; copper, Cu; and lead, Pb; have symbols that do not relate directly to their names.
4. Complete the following table.

Element	Symbol	Region of the table
aluminum		
	C	
fluorine		
iron		
	Pb	
	Ag	

APPLY

5. One substance used in dental alloys is gray-ish white, shiny, and a poor conductor of electricity.
   a. In what region of the periodic table would this element be found?
   b. If this element has chemical properties similar to those of silicon, what is its name?
6. Carbon is the chemical basis for all life on the Earth. Lead is a poison that can cause muscle deterioration and brain damage. Although these two elements are in the same group, some of their properties are very different. Propose a reason for this.
7. Identify the region of the periodic table that would include an element suitable for the following uses.
   a. An element that slightly conducts electricity and is used to make the diodes that allow you to run a battery-powered radio from a wall socket

b. A highly reactive gas that helps to purify drinking water
c. A highly unreactive gas enclosed in lightbulbs to prevent the filament from evaporating
d. An electrical conductor that connects the electrodes in a hearing aid to its battery

8. Explain why a cold soft drink would warm up to room temperature much faster in a tin cup than in a ceramic cup, made mostly of SiO_2.

Atoms in compounds

REVIEW

9. Identify the law that explains why the water in a raindrop falling on Phoenix, Arizona, and the water flowing through the Nile Delta in Egypt both contain two hydrogen atoms for every oxygen atom.

APPLY

10. Ibuprofen, $C_{13}H_{18}O_2$, that you take for headaches is manufactured in Michigan and contains 75.69% carbon, 8.80% hydrogen, and 15.51% oxygen. If you are vacationing in Europe, how do you know that the ibuprofen you buy at a store in Munich, Germany, is the same as the chemical you buy at home?
11. Relate the law of definite composition to the law of multiple proportions.

Models of the atom

REVIEW

12. **a.** What flaws exist in Dalton's model of the atom?
    b. What flaws exist in Thomson's plum pudding model of the atom?
    c. What flaws exist in Rutherford's model of the atom?

d. What flaws exist in Bohr's model of the atom?

e. Do any flaws exist in the modern quantum model of the atom? Explain.

13. For each letter in the diagram below describe what happens to the alpha particles. Explain what can be inferred about the structure of the atom from each instance.

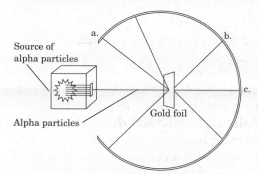

14. **a.** Which of Dalton's principles was contradicted by the work of J. J. Thomson?

b. Which of Dalton's principles was contradicted by the bombs that were dropped on Hiroshima and Nagasaki, Japan?

c. Which of Dalton's principles is contradicted by a doctor using radioactive isotopes to trace chemicals in the body?

d. Do any of Dalton's principles still hold completely true today? If so, which ones hold true?

15. Identify the models illustrated below.

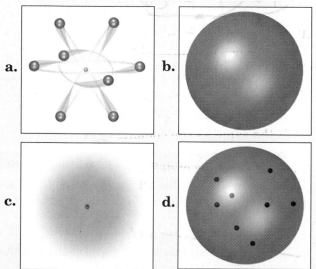

16. Which of the following did Rutherford's experiments suggest?

a. Atoms contain negatively charged electrons.

b. Electrons travel around the nucleus.

c. Atoms contain a positively charged nucleus.

d. Alpha particles exist.

17. What is the relationship between bright-line emission spectra and Bohr's atomic model?

18. Is it possible to verify the current model of the atom by direct observation? Explain.

APPLY

19. What atomic model explains why light from excited gases gives off a bright-line spectrum?

20. If a lightning bolt strikes your power lines while your color television is running, your screen may become magnetized, causing the color to become unbalanced. This problem can be fixed with a magnetic instrument known as a degausser.

a. Refer to the diagram below to explain how you know that the ray creating the picture on screen is composed of charged particles.

b. How is this related to the development of the plum-pudding atomic model?

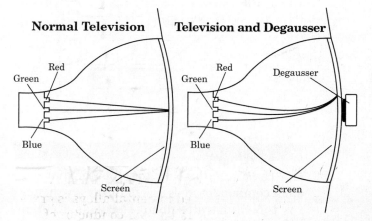

21. Regarding his famous gold foil experiment, Rutherford said, "It is about as incredible as if you had fired a fifteen-inch shell at a piece of tissue paper, and it came back and hit you." Why was Rutherford so amazed by the results of his experiment?

22. How were the atomic models developed when no one had seen the atom?

23. How are the frames that run through a movie projector similar to the quantum concept?

 **Parts of the atom**

24. Why is it necessary to use quantum mechanics to describe electrons?
25. How is the location of an electron within an atom described?
26. Write nuclear symbols for the isotopes of uranium with the following numbers of neutrons.
    a. 142 neutrons
    b. 143 neutrons
    c. 146 neutrons
27. Three isotopes of oxygen are listed below. Identify how many protons, neutrons, and electrons are in each atom.
    a. $^{16}_{8}O$ **b.** $^{17}_{8}O$ **c.** $^{18}_{8}O$
28. Complete the table below.

Isotope	Number of protons	Number of electrons	Number of neutrons	Atomic number
carbon–12				
carbon–14				
tin–119				
tin–120				
lithium–7				
sodium–23				

A P P L Y

29. Use the diagram below to indicate what each component of J. J. Thomson's cathode-ray tube illustrates about electrons. Explain your answer.

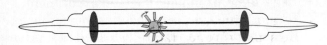

30. How is an atom like a city?
31. How does Heisenberg's uncertainty principle make it impossible to know completely the exact structure of an atom?
32. **a.** Differentiate between an orbit and an orbital.
    b. How do these words relate to the correct description of electrons in an atom?
33. What would happen to poisonous chlorine gas if the following alterations were made?
    a. A proton is added to each atom.
    b. An electron is added to each atom.
    c. A neutron is added to each atom.

34. In the diagram on the right, indicate which subatomic particles would be found in areas **a** and **b**.

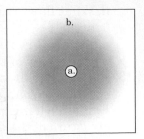

 **Designating electrons**

35. Complete the following table about quantum numbers.

Type	Symbol	Values	Description
principal			
orbital shape			
magnetic			
spin			

36. What do the electron configurations of the noble gas elements have in common?
37. The element sulfur has an electron configuration of $1s^2 2s^2 2p^6 3s^2 3p^4$.
    a. What does the superscript *6* refer to?
    b. What does the letter *s* refer to?
    c. What does the coefficient *3* refer to?
38. Why does the Pauli exclusion principle include the word *exclusion*?
39. Write the electron configuration for calcium, a nutrient essential to healthy bone growth and development.
40. Write the electron configuration for copper which is used in pennies.

A P P L Y

41. Use the symbols for the noble gases to write the electron configurations for the following elements.
    a. Zr   **b.** U   **c.** Rn
42. Identify the element with each of the following electron configurations.
    a. $1s^2 2s^2 2p^2$
    b. $1s^2 2s^2 2p^6 3s^2 3p^1$
    c. $1s^2 2s^2 2p^6 3s^2 3p^6 4s^2 3d^{10} 4p^6 5s^1 4d^{10}$
43. Why are noble gases used to abbreviate electron configurations?
44. How are quantum numbers like an address?

Linking chapters

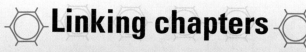

1. Theme: *Conservation*
A Japanese company recently developed a signboard that uses no wiring and no power source. The characters are illuminated by absorbing surrounding light and then radiating different colors. Use the concept of a quantum to explain how this sign can emit light with no power source.

2. Theme: *Micromodels*
Explain the different macroscopic observations that led to the following.
a. the discovery of the nucleus
b. the quantum concept
c. the discovery of electrons

3. Theme: *Classification and trends*
Scientists are continually attempting to create new elements. If more elements were created past number 109, would they all be metals? Explain.

USING TECHNOLOGY

1. *Computer art*
Use a computer art program to illustrate the orbitals in electron configurations using the diagram on page 98 as a model. Draw and write the configurations for C, Na, and Ti.

2. *Computer program*
Write a spreadsheet program that will sum up the exponents for any electron configuration you write.

Alternative assessment

Performance assessment

1. Your teacher will provide you with ionic substances containing the following ions: Na^+, Li^+, Be^{2+}, Mg^{2+}, K^+, Ca^{2+}, and Sr^{2+}. Develop criteria to judge the identity of the different ions. Show your criteria and safety precautions to your teacher for approval.

2. Use the safety appendix to write the necessary precautions for performing flame tests and for working with open flames. Your teacher will give you an unknown ion to identify.

3. Organize the characteristics of metals, nonmetals, metalloids, and noble gases on a poster. Your teacher will provide you with several unknown elements. Classify them by the characteristics noted on your poster.

Portfolio projects

1. *Research and communication*
Research several elements that have a symbol that is inconsistent with their English name. Some examples include silver (Ag), gold (Au), and mercury (Hg). Compare the reasoning for these names to the reasoning for symbols and names that coincide.

2. *Cooperative activity*
Build your own full-scale model of a particular isotope of an atom. Be sure to use a wide open area for this project. Look up the radius of the nucleus and atom, and build the atom with relative sizes. Discover how far away another atom would be if the atoms existed in the solid state.

3. *Chemistry and you*
Heisenberg's uncertainty principle applies to atomic-sized systems. However, it reminds us that uncertainty exists elsewhere. Write a description of instances in your life when major uncertainty existed. Could uncertainty have been avoided in any of these situations?

4. *Research and communication*
"Neon" signs actually use substances other than neon, which provides a bright red light. Research the different colors used for these signs. Determine the chemicals that are utilized. Design your own sign, and identify which gases you would use to achieve the desired color scheme.

CHAPTER 4

Periodicity

Periodic Trends and a Medical Mystery

George Decker seemed to be in perfect health. He was 35 years old, did not smoke, and had no history of serious illness. But one day after cooking something on his stove, Decker began to cough, wheeze, and gasp for air. His girlfriend rushed him to the hospital for treatment.

Tests revealed that Decker had pneumonia in both lungs. Pneumonia is an inflammation of lung tissue. Normally the lungs are as light and airy as cotton candy. Tiny air sacs called alveoli provide the lungs with oxygen-rich air. Pneumonia, however, causes the air sacs to become filled with white blood cells and cellular debris, making breathing difficult. Most pneumonias are caused by organisms such as bacteria, fungi, or viruses. But tissue samples taken from Decker's lungs showed no evidence of microorganisms. What caused Decker to develop pneumonia was a mystery.

Decker's condition became worse. The air sacs in his lungs continued to fill up with solid materials. As a result, his lungs thickened so much that they could not hold enough oxygen to sustain life. Eventually, Decker died.

A pathologist was called in to perform an autopsy. The autopsy revealed that Decker's lungs, as expected, were heavy and thick. But still no trace of pneumonia-causing microorganisms was found. Baffled, the pathologist scrutinized Decker's hospital records. What caught his attention was the fact that Decker had just finished cooking when he began having breathing problems. What Decker had been cooking—in fact what he had cooked many times before—turned out to be what caused the pneumonia.

By talking to Decker's employer, the pathologist discovered that Decker collected old gold and silver dental fillings. Both gold and silver dental fillings are not pure but are actually mixtures of metals. Gold fillings consist primarily of gold mixed with palladium. Silver dental fillings are composed of silver and mercury, with added copper or other metals. Decker would take the fillings home, place them in a pot, and cook them on his stove to extract the precious metals. The pure gold and silver could be sold for a sizable profit. Decker had been employed in a metal shop where his job was to pour molten aluminum into casts to form ingots. His experience at work provided him with the know-how to extract the gold and silver from dental fillings. But Decker's ignorance about certain physical and chemical properties of the metals he was working with proved fatal.

In this chapter, you will explore the elements, including the metals used in dental fillings, that form the periodic table. Then you will be able to answer the following questions.

- *What properties of elements can be determined from the periodic table?*
- *How do trends in the periodic table explain George Decker's death?*

Periodic trends are not only interesting and important to your study of chemistry, but as you will see, they can even be a matter of life and death!

What makes a family of elements?

Section Objectives

Describe how the modern periodic table is organized.

State the periodic law.

Explain why elements in the same family of the periodic table have similar properties.

Describe characteristic properties of the alkali metals, alkaline-earth metals, transition metals, actinides, lanthanides, halogens, and noble gases.

Relate the properties of various elements to their electron configurations.

Families of elements

How could you tell if two people you have never seen before are members of the same biological family? Chances are you would look for physical features that they have in common. Or the way that two people behave might provide a clue as to whether they are related. Both people might have similar facial expressions or share certain striking mannerisms. Thus, both physical and behavioral traits can indicate whether people are related. The same is true for elements. Elements that are members of the same family of the periodic table share structural and behavioral characteristics.

Figure 4-1
These elements belong to different families of the periodic table. Their properties and atomic structures vary widely. As the periodic table shows, however, there is order and regularity—or *periodicity*—in this variation.

Dmitri Mendeleev invented the periodic table

As **Figure 4-1** shows, the properties of elements vary widely. But the elements do not differ from one another in a random fashion. Their properties vary in an orderly way. Because of this, they can be grouped as families of similar elements whose properties vary only slightly from one to the next. Though other chemists had proposed groupings for some elements, it was not known before 1871 that this kind of regularity—or *periodicity*—among the elements was so widespread.

Dmitri Mendeleev, a Russian chemistry professor, discovered periodicity one evening while he sat writing a chemistry book for his students. To organize his thoughts about the elements, Mendeleev wrote the name of each element on a separate card along with its properties. He shuffled the cards about on his desk looking for patterns among them. To his delight, he discovered that when the elements were put in rows such that atomic mass increased from left to right, columns of elements with similar properties could be built. **Figure 4-2** shows the organization of the elements as originally conceived by Mendeleev. Notice the gaps in the table for elements with masses of 45, 68, 70, and 180.

Figure 4-2
Mendeleev's table grouped elements with similar properties into columns called "groups" or "families." Elements are arranged in order of increasing atomic mass.

Mendeleev's Organization of the Known Elements

			Ti = 50	Zr = 90	? = 180	
			V = 51	Nb = 94	Ta = 182	
			Cr = 52	Mo = 96	W = 186	
			Mn = 55	Rh = 104,4	Pt = 197,4	
			Fe = 56	Ru = 104,4	Ir = 198	
		Ni = Co = 59	Pd = 106,6	Os = 199		
H = 1			Cu = 63,4	Ag = 108	Hg = 200	
	Be = 9,4	Mg = 24	Zn = 65,2	Cd = 112		
	B = 11	Al = 27,4	? = 68	Ur = 116	Au = 197?	
	C = 12	Si = 28	? = 70	Sn = 118		
	N = 14	P = 31	As = 75	Sb = 122	Bi = 210?	
	O = 16	S = 32	Se = 79,4	Te = 128?		
	F = 19	Cl = 35,5	Br = 80	J = 127		
Li = 7	Na = 23	K = 39	Rb = 85,4	Cs = 133	Tl = 204	
		Ca = 40	Sr = 87,6	Ba = 137	Pb = 207	
		? = 45	Ce = 92			
		?Er = 56	La = 94			
		?Yt = 60	Di = 95			
		?In = 75,6	Th = 118?			

Table 4-1
Some Elements Predicted by Mendeleev

Predicted elements	Element and year discovered	Properties	Predicted properties	Observed properties
Ekaaluminum	gallium 1875	density of metal	6.0 g/mL	5.96 g/mL
		melting point	low	30°C
		oxide formula	Ea_2O_3	Ga_2O_3
Ekaboron	scandium 1877	density of metal	3.5 g/mL	3.86 g/mL
		oxide formula	Eb_2O_3	Sc_2O_3
		solubility of oxide	dissolves in acid	dissolves in acid
Ekasilicon	germanium 1886	melting point	high	900°C
		density of metal	5.5 g/mL	5.47 g/mL
		color of metal	dark gray	grayish white
		oxide formula	EsO_2	GeO_2
		density of oxide	4.7 g/mL	4.70 g/mL
		chloride formula	$EsCl_4$	$GeCl_4$

Mendeleev postulated that the gaps represented missing elements. He predicted that the gaps would be filled by elements not yet discovered. He also predicted the properties of these missing elements. **Table 4-1** shows three "missing" elements, along with some of their properties, that were discovered just as Mendeleev predicted.

The modern periodic table is based on the periodic law

In addition to gaps, Mendeleev's table contained some irregularities. In a few cases, putting elements in order of increasing mass placed elements in columns where they did not seem to fit. Their properties were not similar to those of the other elements in the same family. Mendeleev assumed these irregularities were due to errors in atomic mass measurement. Yet these mass measurements were subsequently shown to be quite accurate.

Forty years later, the young English scientist Henry Moseley removed the irregularities in Mendeleev's table. Moseley discovered that each element has a unique nuclear charge and, therefore, a different atomic number. When Moseley arranged the elements in order of increasing atomic number, rather than according to atomic mass as Mendeleev had done, the irregularities disappeared. Hence, in today's version of the periodic table, elements are placed in order of increasing atomic number.

The most common form of the periodic table used by scientists today is shown in **Table 4-2**, on the next two pages. It is based on the **periodic law**, which states that the physical and chemical properties of the elements are periodic functions of their atomic numbers.

periodic law
properties of elements tend to change with increasing atomic number in a periodic way

Table 4-2
Periodic Table of the Elements

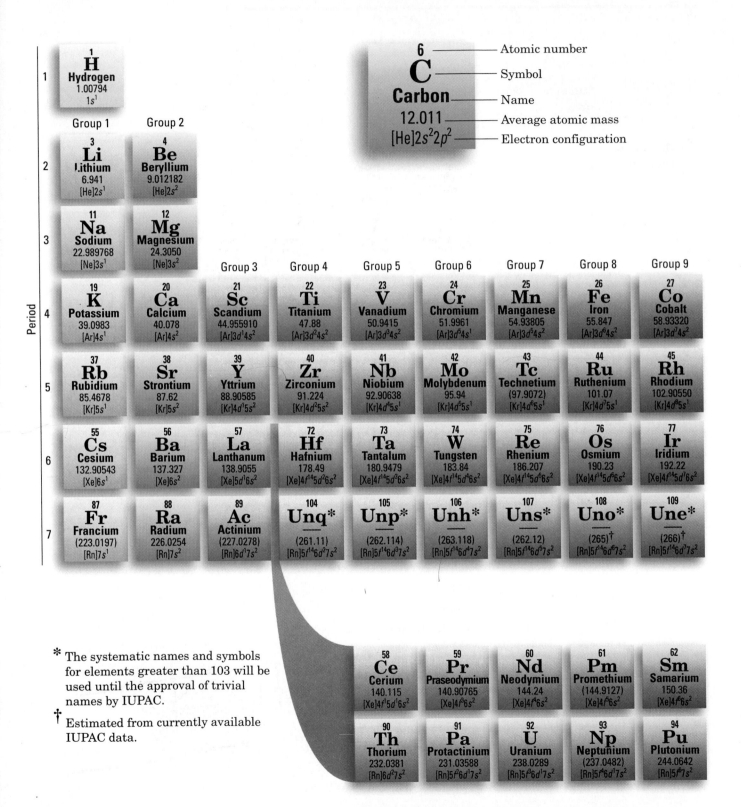

* The systematic names and symbols for elements greater than 103 will be used until the approval of trivial names by IUPAC.

† Estimated from currently available IUPAC data.

Atomic masses listed in this table reflect the precision of current measurements. However, atomic mass measurements throughout the text have been rounded to two places to the right of the decimal.

Metals

- Alkali metals
- Alkaline-earth metals
- Transition metals
- Other metals

Metalloids

- Metalloids

Nonmetals

- Halogens
- Other nonmetals

Noble gases

- Noble gases

							Group 18
							2 **He** Helium 4.002602 $1s^2$

		Group 13	Group 14	Group 15	Group 16	Group 17	
		5 **B** Boron 10.811 $[He]2s^22p^1$	6 **C** Carbon 12.011 $[He]2s^22p^2$	7 **N** Nitrogen 14.00674 $[He]2s^22p^3$	8 **O** Oxygen 15.9994 $[He]2s^22p^4$	9 **F** Fluorine 18.9984032 $[He]2s^22p^5$	10 **Ne** Neon 20.1797 $[He]2s^22p^6$
		13 **Al** Aluminum 26.981539 $[Ne]3s^23p^1$	14 **Si** Silicon 28.0855 $[Ne]3s^23p^2$	15 **P** Phosphorus 30.973762 $[Ne]3s^23p^3$	16 **S** Sulfur 32.066 $[Ne]3s^23p^4$	17 **Cl** Chlorine 35.4527 $[Ne]3s^23p^5$	18 **Ar** Argon 39.948 $[Ne]3s^23p^6$

Group 10	Group 11	Group 12					
28 **Ni** Nickel 58.6934 $[Ar]3d^84s^2$	29 **Cu** Copper 63.546 $[Ar]3d^{10}4s^1$	30 **Zn** Zinc 65.39 $[Ar]3d^{10}4s^2$	31 **Ga** Gallium 69.723 $[Ar]3d^{10}4s^24p^1$	32 **Ge** Germanium 72.61 $[Ar]3d^{10}4s^24p^2$	33 **As** Arsenic 74.92159 $[Ar]3d^{10}4s^24p^3$	34 **Se** Selenium 78.96 $[Ar]3d^{10}4s^24p^4$	35 **Br** Bromine 79.904 $[Ar]3d^{10}4s^24p^5$
							36 **Kr** Krypton 83.80 $[Ar]3d^{10}4s^24p^6$
46 **Pd** Palladium 106.42 $[Kr]4d^{10}5s^0$	47 **Ag** Silver 107.8682 $[Kr]4d^{10}5s^1$	48 **Cd** Cadmium 112.411 $[Kr]4d^{10}5s^2$	49 **In** Indium 114.818 $[Kr]4d^{10}5s^25p^1$	50 **Sn** Tin 118.710 $[Kr]4d^{10}5s^25p^2$	51 **Sb** Antimony 121.757 $[Kr]4d^{10}5s^25p^3$	52 **Te** Tellurium 127.60 $[Kr]4d^{10}5s^25p^4$	53 **I** Iodine 126.90447 $[Kr]4d^{10}5s^25p^5$
							54 **Xe** Xenon 131.29 $[Kr]4d^{10}5s^25p^6$
78 **Pt** Platinum 195.08 $[Xe]4f^{14}5d^96s^1$	79 **Au** Gold 196.96654 $[Xe]4f^{14}5d^{10}6s^1$	80 **Hg** Mercury 200.59 $[Xe]4f^{14}5d^{10}6s^2$	81 **Tl** Thallium 204.3833 $[Xe]4f^{14}5d^{10}6s^26p^1$	82 **Pb** Lead 207.2 $[Xe]4f^{14}5d^{10}6s^26p^2$	83 **Bi** Bismuth 208.98037 $[Xe]4f^{14}5d^{10}6s^26p^3$	84 **Po** Polonium (208.9824) $[Xe]4f^{14}5d^{10}6s^26p^4$	85 **At** Astatine (209.9871) $[Xe]4f^{14}5d^{10}6s^26p^5$
							86 **Rn** Radon (222.0176) $[Xe]4f^{14}5d^{10}6s^26p^6$

63 **Eu** Europium 151.965 $[Xe]4f^76s^2$	64 **Gd** Gadolinium 157.25 $[Xe]4f^75d^16s^2$	65 **Tb** Terbium 158.92534 $[Xe]4f^96s^2$	66 **Dy** Dysprosium 162.50 $[Xe]4f^{10}6s^2$	67 **Ho** Holmium 164.93032 $[Xe]4f^{11}6s^2$	68 **Er** Erbium 167.26 $[Xe]4f^{12}6s^2$	69 **Tm** Thulium 168.93421 $[Xe]4f^{13}6s^2$	70 **Yb** Ytterbium 173.04 $[Xe]4f^{14}6s^2$	71 **Lu** Lutetium 174.967 $[Xe]4f^{14}5d^16s^2$
95 **Am** Americium (243.0614) $[Rn]5f^77s^2$	96 **Cm** Curium (247.0703) $[Rn]5f^76d^17s^2$	97 **Bk** Berkelium (247.0703) $[Rn]5f^97s^2$	98 **Cf** Californium (251.0796) $[Rn]5f^{10}7s^2$	99 **Es** Einsteinium (252.083) $[Rn]5f^{11}7s^2$	100 **Fm** Fermium (257.0951) $[Rn]5f^{12}7s^2$	101 **Md** Mendelevium (258.10) $[Rn]5f^{13}7s^2$	102 **No** Nobelium (259.1009) $[Rn]5f^{14}7s^2$	103 **Lr** Lawrencium (262.11) $[Rn]5f^{14}6d^17s^2$

Mass numbers in parentheses are those of the most stable or most common isotope.

The periodic table can be used to determine the electron configuration of each element

The periodic table contains a wealth of information about each element. Examine the key to **Table 4-2** for the information it gives about carbon: atomic number, symbol, name, atomic mass, and electron configuration. Notice that a shorthand form is used to show electron configuration.

Perhaps the most important thing to notice about the periodic table is the similarity of electron configurations of elements in most families. Look at the periodic table to see this for yourself. Recall from Chapter 3 that the electron configuration of an element determines its chemical behavior. Do you see why elements of the same family have similar properties? Their chemical properties are similar because their electron configurations are similar, as the periodic table shows.

Family characteristics
Group 18 elements are the noble gases

You were introduced to the Group 18 elements in Chapter 3. You learned that these elements, listed in **Figure 4-3a**, have a special name: *noble gases*. The noble gases were called the *inert gases* because they were thought to be unreactive. No stable compounds of three noble gases—helium, neon, and argon—have ever been prepared. The other noble gases—xenon, krypton, and radon—have very low reactivity because in recent years a few compounds have been made from them.

Noble gas atoms are characterized by electron configurations featuring full *s* and *p* orbitals in the highest principal energy level. From the low reactivity we observe in noble gases, we can infer that the noble gas electron configuration is very *stable*, or resistant to change. Indeed, we observe that when atoms of other groups lose or gain electrons to form compounds, they achieve an electron configuration like that of the noble gases. The stability of the element in the compound increases compared to the stability of the element alone.

Despite the low reactivity of the noble gases, they have many uses. Neon and argon, for example, are used in advertising signs. And helium, which is not flammable because it is unreactive, is the preferred lighter-than-air gas used in airships and weather balloons.

Figure 4-3a
The noble gas family is on the right side of the periodic table and consists of gaseous, unreactive elements.

4-3b
Noble gas elements are used in making lighted signs and displays.

2
He
Helium
4.002602
$1s^2$

10
Ne
Neon
20.1797
$[He]2s^22p^6$

18
Ar
Argon
39.948
$[Ne]3s^23p^6$

36
Kr
Krypton
83.80
$[Ar]3d^{10}4s^24p^6$

54
Xe
Xenon
131.29
$[Kr]4d^{10}5s^25p^6$

86
Rn
Radon
222.0176
$[Xe]4f^{14}5d^{10}6s^26p^6$

alkali metals
highly reactive metallic elements which form alkaline solutions in water, burn in air, and belong to Group 1 of the periodic table

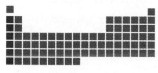

Figure 4-4a
The alkali metals are located on the left edge of the periodic table.

4-4b
Potassium is stored in oil to prevent it from reacting with moisture and oxygen in air.

3
Li
Lithium
6.941
[He]2s^1

11
Na
Sodium
22.989768
[Ne]3s^1

19
K
Potassium
39.0983
[Ar]4s^1

37
Rb
Rubidium
85.4678
[Kr]5s^1

55
Cs
Cesium
132.90543
[Xe]6s^1

87
Fr
Francium
(223.0197)
[Rn]7s^1

Group 1 is also known as the alkali metals

Group 1 elements, listed in **Figure 4–4a**, are soft, highly reactive metals. They are so soft that they can be cut with a knife. Once cut, their shiny surfaces dull quickly as they react with oxygen in air. In the laboratory, alkali metals are usually stored under oil or kerosene to protect them from moisture and oxygen in air. As you can see from **Figure 4-4b**, when added to cold water, an alkali metal reacts vigorously.

In ancient times, people discovered that ashes mixed with water produce a slippery solution that can remove grease. In the Middle Ages such solutions were named *alkaline*, after the Arab word for ashes, *al-qali*. We now know that the ashes that produce alkaline solutions contain compounds of the Group 1 elements. The Group 1 elements are called the **alkali metals** because they produce alkaline solutions and because they have metallic properties.

The reactivity of alkali metals results from their characteristic electron configurations, which feature a single electron in the highest energy level. When an alkali metal atom loses this single electron, the next-lowest energy level becomes the outer shell. This energy level has the same electron configuration as the noble gases. Thus, by losing a single electron, an alkali-metal atom achieves the stable, nonreactive electron configuration of the noble gases.

The alkali metals share many physical properties, as **Table 4-3** shows. Additionally, due to their metallic nature, solid alkali metals are good conductors of electricity.

The single electron can easily be bumped off an alkali metal atom when electrical energy is applied. In the gaseous state at high voltages, the motion of dislodged electrons makes up electric current flow. Sodium vapor, for example, conducts electricity. When an electric current passes through sodium vapor, sodium atoms emit energy in the form of orange-yellow light. Light of this color penetrates fog very well. Therefore, sodium vapor is used in street lamps and in fog lights on cars.

Table 4-3
Physical Properties of Alkali Metals

Element	Melting point (°C)	Boiling point (°C)	Density (g/cm³)	Atomic radius (pm)
lithium	179	1336	0.53	152
sodium	98	883	0.97	186
potassium	64	758	0.86	227
rubidium	39	700	1.53	248
cesium	28	670	1.90	265
francium	27	677	unknown	unknown

The lightest alkali metal is lithium. Although it has only one electron in its outer energy level just as the other alkali metals do, it is less reactive. The reason for this has to do with the small size of lithium atoms. Because it is a small atom, the outer electron and the nucleus are relatively close to one another. Consequently the electron is held tightly and is not readily removed. This makes lithium just right for certain applications, including an experimental electric car. The car gets its energy from a lithium-based battery. Lithium compounds are used in medications for psychological depression, though the biochemical processes that account for its success are not yet fully understood.

alkaline-earth metals
reactive, metallic elements which belong to Group 2 of the periodic table

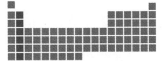

Figure 4-5a
The alkaline-earth metals are the second column of elements from the left edge of the periodic table.

4
Be
Beryllium
9.012182
[He]$2s^2$

12
Mg
Magnesium
24.3050
[Ne]$3s^2$

20
Ca
Calcium
40.078
[Ar]$4s^2$

38
Sr
Strontium
87.62
[Kr]$5s^2$

56
Ba
Barium
137.327
[Xe]$6s^2$

88
Ra
Radium
(226.0254)
[Rn]$7s^2$

Group 2 is also known as the alkaline-earth metals

Group 2 elements are known as the **alkaline-earth metals**. They are all harder, denser, stronger, and have higher melting points than the alkali metals. Check Figure 4-5a to see what elements belong to Group 2. How are their electron configurations similar to each other? How do their electron configurations compare with those of Group 1 elements?

The alkaline-earth metals are all reactive. However, they are not as reactive as the Group 1 metals. Why is this so? Group 2 metals are less reactive because they have to lose two electrons to achieve a noble gas electron configuration, while the alkali metals have to lose only one electron.

Consider the alkaline-earth metal magnesium. If the surface of an object made from magnesium is exposed to air, it reacts with the oxygen in air to form the compound magnesium oxide. The magnesium oxide serves as a protective layer that prevents the remaining magnesium metal from corroding. Also, magnesium is lighter than other structural metals, yet still very strong. For all of these reasons, magnesium has a wide variety of practical applications, from the building of aircraft and missiles to the manufacture of ladders and tools.

4-5b
Emeralds contain the Group 2 element beryllium.

Figure 4-6
The Taj Mahal in India was commissioned in 1632 by emperor Shāh Jahān as a tomb for his wife. The central structure and domes are made of pure white marble, which contains calcium.

The best known alkaline-earth metal is calcium. Calcium-containing compounds, such as those in limestone and marble, are common in the Earth's crust. Marble was used in the construction of the Taj Mahal, shown in **Figure 4-6**, on the previous page, because it is hard and durable.

Consumer Focus

Calcium supplements

Calcium plays an important role in bone formation. Too little calcium in the diet, especially during periods of bone growth, may lead to soft bones that break easily. Milk is a well-known source of calcium. Fortunately, most children in the United States get enough calcium by drinking milk and eating a balanced diet to avoid noticeably weak bones.

However, many Americans suffer the disabling effects of weak bones later in life. More than 25 million people have osteoporosis, a disease that primarily affects people over 50, in which the bones lose mass, and break easily. Osteoporosis-related hip fractures are an especially serious problem for many elderly Americans. Osteoporosis also carries an expense to society of over $10 billion a year.

Medical investigators agree that the best way to prevent osteoporosis in later life is for children and young adults to consume more calcium. Additional calcium consumed during the childhood and teenage years leads to development of more massive bones. People who start off with stronger, more massive bones can withstand the loss of bone mass that inevitably occurs with aging better than those who start off with weaker bones. The need for extra calcium is greatest between ages 9 and 18 when young people lay down 37 percent of their adult bone mass.

To obtain the calcium they need, many people take calcium supplements in tablet or liquid form. However, investigations have shown that some calcium supplements are potentially dangerous because they contain lead, a poisonous metal that can destroy brain cells and stunt growth.

If you think you may need more calcium, check the level in **Table 4-4** then monitor your diet. Eat plenty of calcium-rich foods, such as dairy products and broccoli. If you want to take a supplement, choose a product that has been approved by the Food and Drug Administration. And remember: Never exceed the recommended dosage without proper medical supervision.

Table 4-4
Optimal Daily Intake of Calcium*

Group		Optimal Daily Intake (in milligrams of calcium)
Children		800
Teenagers		1200 to 1500
Men	25–50	800
	51–65	1000
	over 65	1500
Women	25–50	1000
	51–65	1500
	pregnant and nursing	1900

*Optimal Daily Intake values are the amounts of calcium needed to build and maintain bone mass in order to prevent disease.

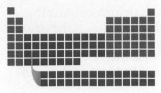

Figure 4-7a
The transition elements are found in the middle of the periodic table.

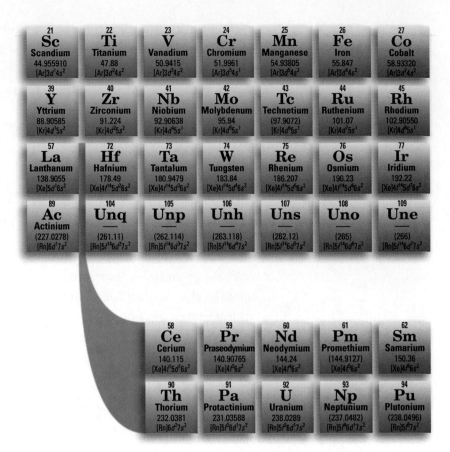

21 Sc Scandium 44.955910 [Ar]$3d^14s^2$	22 Ti Titanium 47.88 [Ar]$3d^24s^2$	23 V Vanadium 50.9415 [Ar]$3d^34s^2$	24 Cr Chromium 51.9961 [Ar]$3d^54s^1$	25 Mn Manganese 54.93805 [Ar]$3d^54s^2$	26 Fe Iron 55.847 [Ar]$3d^64s^2$	27 Co Cobalt 58.93320 [Ar]$3d^74s^2$
39 Y Yttrium 88.90585 [Kr]$4d^15s^2$	40 Zr Zirconium 91.224 [Kr]$4d^25s^2$	41 Nb Niobium 92.90638 [Kr]$4d^45s^1$	42 Mo Molybdenum 95.94 [Kr]$4d^55s^1$	43 Tc Technetium (97.9072) [Kr]$4d^65s^1$	44 Ru Ruthenium 101.07 [Kr]$4d^75s^1$	45 Rh Rhodium 102.90550 [Kr]$4d^85s^1$
57 La Lanthanum 138.9055 [Xe]$5d^16s^2$	72 Hf Hafnium 178.49 [Xe]$4f^{14}5d^26s^2$	73 Ta Tantalum 180.9479 [Xe]$4f^{14}5d^36s^2$	74 W Tungsten 183.84 [Xe]$4f^{14}5d^46s^2$	75 Re Rhenium 186.207 [Xe]$4f^{14}5d^56s^2$	76 Os Osmium 190.23 [Xe]$4f^{14}5d^66s^2$	77 Ir Iridium 192.22 [Xe]$4f^{14}5d^76s^2$
89 Ac Actinium (227.0278) [Rn]$6d^17s^2$	104 Unq (261.11) [Rn]$5f^{14}6d^27s^2$	105 Unp (262.114) [Rn]$5f^{14}6d^37s^2$	106 Unh (263.118) [Rn]$5f^{14}6d^47s^2$	107 Uns (262.12) [Rn]$5f^{14}6d^57s^2$	108 Uno (265) [Rn]$5f^{14}6d^67s^2$	109 Une (266) [Rn]$5f^{14}6d^77s^2$

58 Ce Cerium 140.115 [Xe]$4f^15d^16s^2$	59 Pr Praseodymium 140.90765 [Xe]$4f^36s^2$	60 Nd Neodymium 144.24 [Xe]$4f^46s^2$	61 Pm Promethium (144.9127) [Xe]$4f^56s^2$	62 Sm Samarium 150.36 [Xe]$4f^66s^2$
90 Th Thorium 232.0381 [Rn]$6d^27s^2$	91 Pa Protactinium 231.03588 [Rn]$5f^26d^17s^2$	92 U Uranium 238.0289 [Rn]$5f^36d^17s^2$	93 Np Neptunium (237.0482) [Rn]$5f^46d^17s^2$	94 Pu Plutonium (238.0496) [Rn]$5f^67s^2$

4-7b
Which one of these iron buckets was galvanized?

transition elements
metallic elements that have varying properties and belong to Groups 3 through 12 of the periodic table

Groups 3 through 12 contain the transition elements

Elements in Groups 3 through 12 are called the **transition elements**. Like the elements belonging to Groups 1 and 2, the transition elements are all metals. However, the transition elements are not as reactive as elements belonging to Groups 1 and 2. With the exception of mercury, the transition metals are harder, denser, and have higher melting points than the Group 1 and 2 metals.

Check **Figure 4-7a** to see that there are many irregularities in the electron configurations of the transition elements. Unlike Group 1 and 2 elements, the transition elements do not all have the same number of electrons in their highest occupied energy level. Many of them have two electrons in the *s* sublevel of their highest occupied energy level, but some have only one, and palladium has none. Because the transition elements are filling the *d* orbitals with electrons, they are sometimes called *d*-block elements.

While looking at the transition elements, you probably recognized a number of them, including iron and zinc. Zinc is one of industry's most useful metals. Large amounts of it are used to *galvanize* iron products, or coat them with a protective layer of zinc. The galvanized bucket shown in **Figure 4-7b** will not rust. Zinc is more reactive than iron, so zinc is oxidized (reacts to form a compound containing oxygen) before iron.

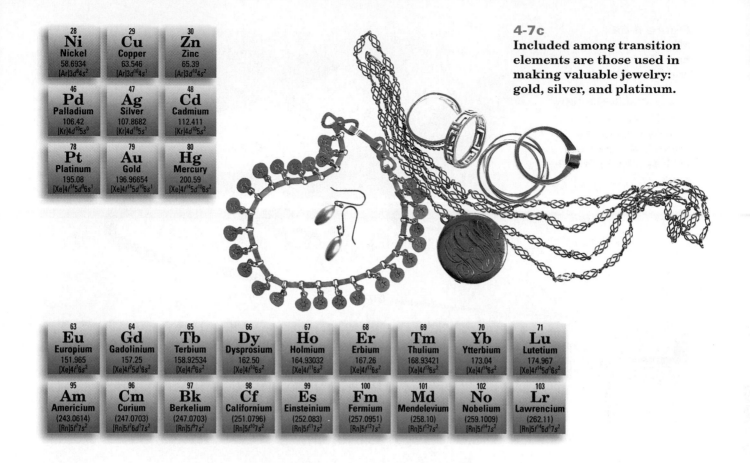

4-7c
Included among transition elements are those used in making valuable jewelry: gold, silver, and platinum.

lanthanides
shiny, metallic elements with atomic numbers 58 through 71 that fill the 4f orbitals

As you learned in Chapter 3, parts of two periods of transition elements are placed toward the bottom of the periodic table to keep the table conveniently narrow. These rows of elements are referred to as the lanthanides and actinides. The **lanthanides** include elements 58 through 71. The name of element 57 will give you a clue as to how the lanthanides got their name. Check the periodic table to identify the two groups of elements on either side of the lanthanides. Examine the periodic table again to verify the similarities of their electron configurations.

The lanthanides are shiny, reactive metals. Some have practical uses. For example, compounds of some lanthanide metals are used to make the phosphor dots in television tubes. When bombarded by a beam of electrons, the phosphors emit light of various colors. These colors combine to create the brilliant images you see on a color television screen.

actinides
metallic elements with atomic numbers 90 through 103 that fill the 5f orbitals

Elements 90 through 103 constitute the **actinides**. The name of element 89 tells you how the actinides got their name. In the unique case of the actinides, nuclear structure is of more practical importance than electron configuration. All of the actinides have an unstable arrangement of protons and neutrons in the nucleus. All actinides have radioactive forms. Perhaps the best-known actinide is uranium. Its nuclear disintegration provides the energy for power plants, submarines, and aircraft carriers.

Figure 4-8a
Main-block elements have diverse properties and uses. The blimp exploits the low density and nonreactivity of helium. Living things, such as the iguana, are made of carbon-based proteins.

4-8b
The main-block elements are those found in the long columns on the left and right sides of the periodic table.

2 **He** Helium 4.002602 $1s^2$

5 **B** Boron 10.811 $[He]2s^22p^1$	6 **C** Carbon 12.011 $[He]2s^22p^2$	7 **N** Nitrogen 14.00674 $[He]2s^22p^3$	8 **O** Oxygen 15.9994 $[He]2s^22p^4$	9 **F** Fluorine 18.9984032 $[He]2s^22p^5$	10 **Ne** Neon 20.1797 $[He]2s^22p^6$
13 **Al** Aluminum 26.981539 $[Ne]3s^23p^1$	14 **Si** Silicon 28.0855 $[Ne]3s^23p^2$	15 **P** Phosphorus 30.973762 $[Ne]3s^23p^3$	16 **S** Sulfur 32.066 $[Ne]3s^23p^4$	17 **Cl** Chlorine 35.4527 $[Ne]3s^23p^5$	18 **Ar** Argon 39.948 $[Ne]3s^23p^6$
31 **Ga** Gallium 69.723 $[Ar]3d^{10}4s^24p^1$	32 **Ge** Germanium 72.61 $[Ar]3d^{10}4s^24p^2$	33 **As** Arsenic 74.92159 $[Ar]3d^{10}4s^24p^3$	34 **Se** Selenium 78.96 $[Ar]3d^{10}4s^24p^4$	35 **Br** Bromine 79.904 $[Ar]3d^{10}4s^24p^5$	36 **Kr** Krypton 83.80 $[Ar]3d^{10}4s^24p^6$
49 **In** Indium 114.818 $[Kr]4d^{10}5s^25p^1$	50 **Sn** Tin 118.710 $[Kr]4d^{10}5s^25p^2$	51 **Sb** Antimony 121.757 $[Kr]4d^{10}5s^25p^3$	52 **Te** Tellurium 127.60 $[Kr]4d^{10}5s^25p^4$	53 **I** Iodine 126.90447 $[Kr]4d^{10}5s^25p^5$	54 **Xe** Xenon 131.29 $[Kr]4d^{10}5s^25p^6$
81 **Tl** Thallium 204.3833 $[Xe]4f^{14}5d^{10}6s^26p^1$	82 **Pb** Lead 207.2 $[Xe]4f^{14}5d^{10}6s^26p^2$	83 **Bi** Bismuth 208.98037 $[Xe]4f^{14}5d^{10}6s^26p^3$	84 **Po** Polonium (208.9824) $[Xe]4f^{14}5d^{10}6s^26p^4$	85 **At** Astatine (209.9871) $[Xe]4f^{14}5d^{10}6s^26p^5$	86 **Rn** Radon (222.0176) $[Xe]4f^{14}5d^{10}6s^26p^6$

main-block elements
elements that represent the entire range of chemical properties and belong to Groups 1, 2, and 13 through 18 in the periodic table

Main-block elements include groups 13 through 18

Along with elements in Groups 1 and 2, those in Groups 13 through 18 are called **main-block elements**. The main-block elements shown in **Figure 4-8b** are also called the *representative elements* because they represent a wide range of chemical and physical properties.

Within Groups 13 to 18, properties vary systematically. For example, these elements include metals, metalloids, nonmetals, and noble gases. You are probably familiar with many of the elements found in Groups 13 to 18, including carbon, nitrogen, oxygen, aluminum, tin, and lead. Two of the elements, silicon in Group 14 and oxygen in Group 16, account for four of every five atoms found near the surface of the Earth.

halogens

elements that combine with most metals to form salts and that belong to Group 17 of the periodic table

Two families of elements within Groups 13 through 18 have special names. The Group 18 elements, as you know, are also called the *noble gases*. The elements of Group 17 are known as the **halogens**. The halogens combine easily with metals, especially the alkali metals, to form compounds known as *salts*. *Halogen* is derived from Latin and means *salt-former*. Common table salt is made of a halogen, chlorine, in chemical combination with an alkali metal, sodium.

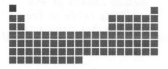

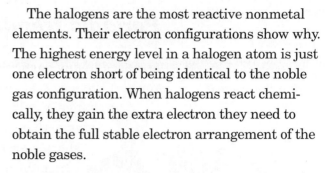

Figure 4-9a
Hydrogen sits apart from the other elements in the periodic table.

The halogens are the most reactive nonmetal elements. Their electron configurations show why. The highest energy level in a halogen atom is just one electron short of being identical to the noble gas configuration. When halogens react chemically, they gain the extra electron they need to obtain the full stable electron arrangement of the noble gases.

One element forms its own chemical family

The element that "sits" by itself in the periodic table is the most common element in the universe—hydrogen. Hydrogen is usually considered to be a chemical family by itself because it behaves unlike any other element.

The cloud model for hydrogen shown in Figure 4-9 has one electron. Hydrogen reacts very rapidly with most other elements, including oxygen, as you can see in Figure 4-10. Because it reacts so easily, hydrogen in its free state is rare, while compounds containing hydrogen are very common. Water is the most abundant hydrogen compound. Combined with carbon and oxygen, hydrogen is present in fats, proteins, and carbohydrates. The main industrial use of hydrogen is to combine it with nitrogen to make ammonia. Large quantities of ammonia, in turn, are used in the production of fertilizers.

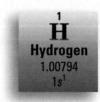

4-9b
The single electron of hydrogen occupies the orbital volume shown by the blue sphere outside the nucleus. This structure gives hydrogen unique properties and puts this element in a family of its own.

Figure 4-10
When hydrogen reacts with oxygen in the space shuttle, enough energy is released to lift the shuttle into orbit.

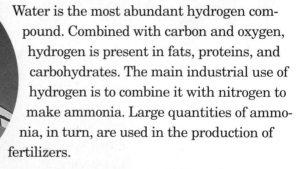

Section Review

1. State the periodic law.
2. Why do the elements belonging to a particular group exhibit similar chemical behavior?
3. How do the alkali metals differ from the alkaline-earth metals?
4. Explain what the transition metals have in common with respect to their electron configurations.
5. What features do all of the halogens have in common?

What trends are found in the periodic table?

Section Objectives

Describe the trends seen in the periodic table with respect to atomic radius, ionization energy, electron affinity, and electronegativity.

Relate trends of the periodic table to the atomic structures of the elements.

Periodic trends

Figure 4-11
How could you arrange these people to reveal a trend in their ages?

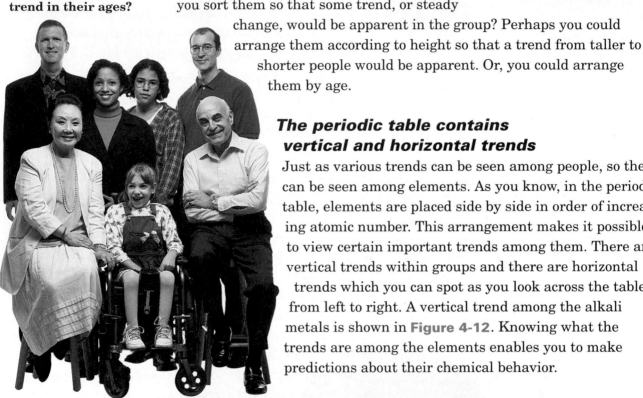

The people shown in **Figure 4-11** are not arranged in any particular manner. How would you sort them so that some trend, or steady change, would be apparent in the group? Perhaps you could arrange them according to height so that a trend from taller to shorter people would be apparent. Or, you could arrange them by age.

The periodic table contains vertical and horizontal trends

Just as various trends can be seen among people, so they can be seen among elements. As you know, in the periodic table, elements are placed side by side in order of increasing atomic number. This arrangement makes it possible to view certain important trends among them. There are vertical trends within groups and there are horizontal trends which you can spot as you look across the table from left to right. A vertical trend among the alkali metals is shown in **Figure 4-12**. Knowing what the trends are among the elements enables you to make predictions about their chemical behavior.

Figure 4-12
Chemical reactivity increases from top to bottom in Group 1 elements, as shown in the reactions of lithium, sodium, and potassium with water.

Lithium

Sodium

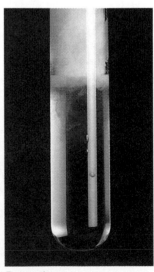

Potassium

Atomic radius increases within a family

atomic radius
one-half of the distance from center to center of two like atoms

Recall that the nucleus of an atom occupies only a small fraction of its volume. Electrons outside the nucleus determine the atom's boundaries. These electrons travel in regions that are pictured as "clouds." Imagine how difficult it would be to measure the size of a real cloud. The same is true of measuring the size of an atom. Its outer boundaries are fuzzy and variable—just like those of a cloud.

Chemists calculate **atomic radius** in several ways. The radii of some atoms are determined by measuring the distance between centers of like atoms that are joined together in a diatomic molecule. Other measurements are taken from bond lengths of atoms in compounds. Data in tables can vary because there is no firm agreement on these measurements. Use **Figure 4-13** to calculate atomic radii. Note that atoms are represented as simple spheres when atomic size is calculated this way. This is an oversimplification, but a useful one. In many instances, atoms are best represented as spheres for the sake of simplicity.

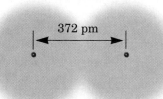

Sodium atoms

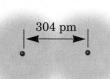

Lithium atoms

Figure 4-13
The distances between centers of like atoms joined as molecules are shown. Use this data to calculate the atomic radius for both a lithium atom and a sodium atom. Use units of picometers, pm.

Do atomic radii show a periodic trend? **Table 4-5** shows the atomic radii of main-block atoms. Notice that, generally, *atomic radius increases as you progress down through the elements in each group*. If you check the electron configurations of elements in the periodic table, you'll see that as you move down any group, another principal energy level is added. It is easy to see that as principal energy levels are added, the atomic radius gets bigger because electrons are added to energy levels farther away from the nucleus.

Table 4-5
Comparing Atomic Radii*

1	2		13	14	15	16	17	18
1 **H** 37								2 **He** 50
3 **Li** 152	4 **Be** 112		5 **B** 85	6 **C** 77	7 **N** 70	8 **O** 73	9 **F** 72	10 **Ne** 71
11 **Na** 186	12 **Mg** 160		13 **Al** 143	14 **Si** 118	15 **P** 110	16 **S** 103	17 **Cl** 100	18 **Ar** 98
19 **K** 227	20 **Ca** 197		31 **Ga** 135	32 **Ge** 122	33 **As** 120	34 **Se** 119	35 **Br** 114	36 **Kr** 112
37 **Rb** 248	38 **Sr** 215		49 **In** 167	50 **Sn** 140	51 **Sb** 140	52 **Te** 142	53 **I** 133	54 **Xe** 131
55 **Cs** 265	56 **Ba** 222		81 **Tl** 170	82 **Pb** 146	83 **Bi** 150	84 **Po** 168	85 **At** (140)	86 **Rn** (141)

*Radius in picometers

shielding effect
the reduction of the attractive force between a nucleus and its outer electrons due to the blocking effect of inner electrons

Figure 4-14
Energy levels are shown as hollow spheres and electrons are shown as moving spheres in this representation of the lithium atom. Electrons in intermediary energy levels interfere with the attraction between the nucleus and outer energy level electrons.

There is another reason why atomic size increases within a family. Descending within a group, the number of occupied orbitals between the nucleus and the outermost energy level increases. The added inner electrons reduce the attraction between the outer electrons and the nucleus. This **shielding effect** allows the outer electrons to be farther away from the nucleus, such that the size of the atom increases.

Atomic size decreases from left to right across a period

As **Table 4-5** shows, the atomic radii of elements follow another periodic trend. *Atomic radii generally decrease as you move across a period from left to right.* Why is this so?

In crossing a period from left to right, each atom gains one more proton and one more electron. No principal energy levels are added, so electrons enter the same energy level. As the number of protons increases across a period, the positive charge of the nucleus increases. As a result, the nucleus exerts a greater pull on all of the electrons in the atom. Hence, as electrons are added within a period, they are pulled closer to the nucleus, and atomic size decreases. When atomic radii are plotted against atomic number, as in **Figure 4-15**, this periodic trend becomes clear.

Notice from the graph in **Figure 4-15** that this trend is less pronounced in periods where there are many electrons between the nucleus and outermost energy level. As you move from left to right in a period, one proton is added to the nucleus and one electron is added to the outer energy level. As you proceed from left to right in the period, the effective positive charge increases gradually. Therefore, the electrons are pulled closer to the nucleus. As the electrons are pulled closer to the nucleus, they get closer to each other and repulsions occur. Finally, a stage is reached where the electrons won't come closer, and the size of the atom tends to level off.

Figure 4-15
Because elements in Period 2 have fewer electrons between their nuclei and outermost energy levels compared to those in Period 5, the shielding effect is less. Thus the decrease in atomic size across Period 2 is more pronounced than across Period 5.

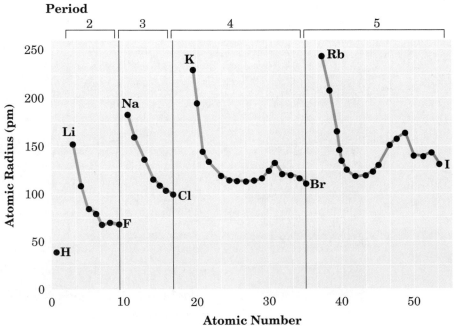

Atomic Radii of Sample Elements

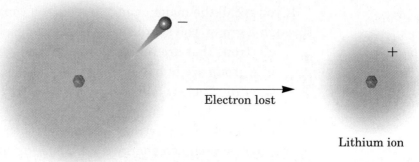

Figure 4-16
When enough energy is absorbed by a lithium atom, the atom loses an electron to become a positive ion.

Electron lost

Lithium ion

Lithium atom

Ionization energy follows a periodic trend

Recall that atoms are normally electrically neutral. However, an atom may lose or gain electrons to become an electrically charged **ion**. Imagine you can reach into an atom, hold the nucleus with one hand, and remove the outermost electron, creating an ion. The energy you would use to remove the electron is the **ionization energy** of the atom. For any element (A), the process of removing an electron, shown in **Figure 4-16**, can be represented as follows.

$$\textbf{A + energy} \longrightarrow \textbf{A}^+ + e^-$$

In the process shown above, a neutral atom absorbs energy equal to its ionization energy. As a result, the neutral atom acquires a positive charge and becomes a positive ion. The ionization energies of elements display periodic trends. **Figure 4-17** shows what happens to ionization energy as you move across a period. **Figure 4-18** on the next page summarizes the trend: *Ionization energy generally decreases as you move down a group of elements but increases across a period.*

Figure 4-17
Ionization energies of main-block elements belonging to the first four periods are shown. The periodic trend in ionization energy is the opposite of that for atomic size. This makes sense if you think about changes in electron configuration that occur in groups and periods.

Ionization Energies of Sample Elements

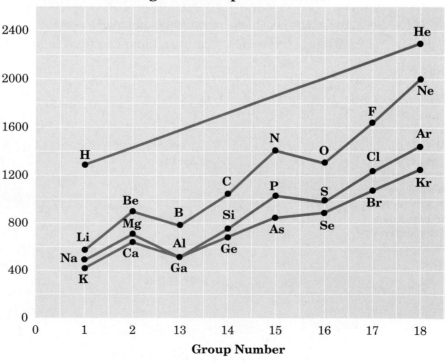

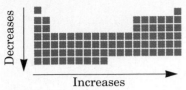

Figure 4-18
Ionization energy generally decreases from top to bottom and increases from left to right across the periodic table.

If you recall the major change in electron configuration as you proceed through a group, you should see why the ionization energy decreases. The electrons that are removed from atoms of each succeeding element in a group are in higher energy levels. Therefore, they are farther from the nucleus and more easily removed. In addition, the shielding effect has an impact. As you move down a group of elements, more and more electrons lie between the nucleus and the electrons in the highest occupied energy level. These additional electrons help to shield the outermost electrons from the attractive forces of the nucleus.

But why does the ionization energy generally increase as you move through a period from left to right? Recall that as you move through a period, the nuclei of succeeding elements exert more pull on their electrons. This stronger pull means that more energy is required to remove an electron. This is similar to what happens when someone tries to pull away something you are holding. The harder you hold onto it, the more difficult it is to remove.

Electron affinity decreases within a family and increases within a period

electron affinity
the energy change that accompanies the addition of an electron to an atom in the gas phase

The ability of an atom to attract and hold an extra electron is its **electron affinity**. Electron affinity is measured as the energy change that occurs when an electron is added to an atom as shown in **Figure 4-19**. For an atom of any element (A), the attraction of an electron can be represented as in the following equation. Note that when an atom gains an extra electron, it acquires a negative charge and becomes a *negative ion*.

$$A + e^- \longrightarrow A^- + \text{energy}$$

Electron affinity can have either a positive or negative numerical value. A negative value indicates that an atom releases energy when it gains an electron. A positive electron affinity means that energy must be added to the atom for the electron to be added. Thus, the more negative its electron affinity is, the more easily an atom can take in an extra electron.

Figure 4-19
A fluorine atom gains an electron to become a negatively charged ion. Fluorine gives off energy in the process. Therefore, the electron affinity of fluorine has a negative value.

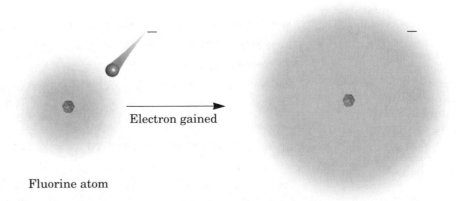

Electron gained

Fluorine atom

Fluoride ion

Table 4-6
Electron Affinity Values (in kJ/mol)

Group 1	2		13	14	15	16	17
1 H −73							
3 Li −60	4 Be 0		5 B −27	6 C −154	7 N −7	8 O −141	9 F −329
11 Na −53	12 Mg 0		13 Al −42	14 Si −134	15 P −72	16 S −200	17 Cl −349
19 K −48	20 Ca 0		31 Ga −29	32 Ge −120	33 As −77	34 Se −195	35 Br −325
37 Rb −47	38 Sr 0		49 In −29	50 Sn −107	51 Sb −101	52 Te −190	53 I −295
55 Cs −45	56 Ba 0		81 Tl −19	82 Pb −35	83 Bi −91	84 Po −183	85 At −270

By studying **Table 4-6**, you can see that *electron affinity values generally become more negative as you move from left to right across a period.* This trend can be explained by changes in nuclear charge, atomic radius, and shielding effect. From left to right across a period, nuclear charge increases, atomic radius decreases, and the shielding effect remains constant, so the attractive force that the nucleus can exert on another electron increases.

From top to bottom within a group, electron affinity tends to become less negative. Again, nuclear charge, atomic radius, and the shielding effect account for the observed trend. As you go down a group the effective nuclear charge increases. This effect is more than offset by the larger size. The result is decreased attraction for an added electron which results in a decreased electron affinity.

Electronegativity decreases within a family and increases within a period

electronegativity
the tendency for an atom to attract electrons to itself when it is combined with another atom

The **electronegativity** of an atom is the tendency of an atom to attract electrons to itself when it is chemically combined with another element. Electronegativity is expressed in terms of a relative scale with arbitrarily selected standard units. Fluorine, the most electronegative element, is assigned an electronegativity value of 4.0. Electronegativity values for the other elements are calculated in relation to this value. **Figure 4-20**, on the next page, shows the general electronegativity trend of the periodic table. The actual values can be found on **Table 11-3**, page 418. The noble gases are not included in these figures because they do not form a significant number of chemical compounds.

Figure 4-20
Electronegativity values tend to decrease down a group and increase across a period.

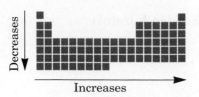

As **Figure 4-20** shows, electronegativity follows a periodic trend: *electronegativity values generally decrease going down a group and increase going across a period*. The least electronegative element is cesium, found toward the lower left corner of the table. The most electronegative element is fluorine, located in the upper right corner of the periodic table (excluding the unreactive noble gases).

Table 4-7 summarizes the periodic trends in atomic radius, ionization energy, shielding effect, and electronegativity. You will see the importance of these trends in the chapters that follow as you study how elements react to form compounds.

Table 4-7
Summary of Periodic Trends

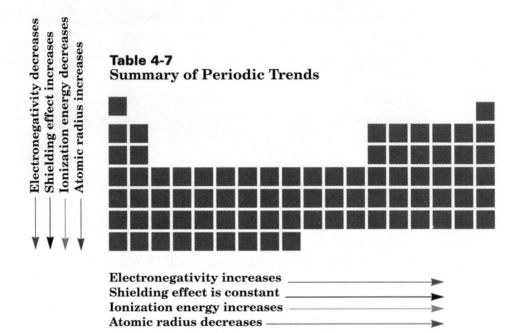

Electronegativity increases ⟶
Shielding effect is constant ⟶
Ionization energy increases ⟶
Atomic radius decreases ⟶

Section Review

6. Why is it difficult to measure the size of an atom?
7. How do metals and nonmetals generally compare with respect to their ionization energies and electronegativities?
8. What trends are evident in atomic radius, ionization energy, and electronegativity as you proceed down a group of elements? How do each of these trends progress as you move across a period?
9. When an atom loses an electron to become an ion, what happens to its electric charge? To its size? When an atom gains an electron to become an ion, what happens to its charge? To its size?
10. **a.** Arrange the following atoms to show a trend of increasing atomic radius: potassium, carbon, rubidium, iodine, fluorine, and lithium.
    b. Arrange these elements in terms of increasing electronegativity values: fluorine, nitrogen, calcium, germanium, oxygen, and bromine.
    c. Arrange these elements in order of increasing ionization energy: beryllium, helium, krypton, and cesium.

4-3

How are elements created?

Section Objectives

Distinguish between naturally occurring and synthetic elements.

Describe how the naturally occurring elements are formed.

Explain the term nuclear reaction.

Explain how scientists use particle accelerators to create synthetic elements.

The origins of naturally occurring elements

You have learned much about the uses of the elements. You have also learned how to read the periodic table to obtain information about the properties and structures of elements. But two fundamental questions remain: Where do the elements come from? How were they created?

Natural and synthetic elements are created in different ways

Of the over 110 elements currently known, only elements up to number 92, uranium, occur naturally.[*] The remaining elements in the periodic table are all *synthetic*. These elements are made by teams of research scientists working in vast laboratories around the world. One such laboratory, the Stanford Linear Accelerator, is 3 km long and is shown in Figure 4-21.

The origins of both natural and synthetic elements are equally fascinating. While the creation of synthetic elements requires technology and human ingenuity on the grandest scale, the naturally occurring elements were forged in violent unions of matter and energy in deep space. With the exception of hydrogen and trace amounts of other light elements, all of the natural elements found on Earth were manufactured in the interiors of stars that exploded long before our solar system came into being. Hydrogen was created as an immediate consequence of the Big Bang, the initial explosion that is believed to have launched the universe.

[*] Four elements with atomic numbers less than 92 are not truly naturally occurring. These elements are: Fr, Pm, Tc, and At. Technetium (Tc) is produced in the laboratory and does not exist naturally. The other three elements exist naturally in minute amounts, but samples are obtained from artificial sources.

Figure 4-21
The Stanford Linear Accelerator Center is a national facility for research in subatomic physics. It is located at Stanford University in California and includes several particle accelerators. Particle accelerators are the largest machines on Earth. Synthetic elements are created in particle accelerators during energetic collisions of small particles.

Elements are created through nuclear fusion

Stars form when clouds of dust and hydrogen gas condense under the influence of gravity. As stellar material condenses, pressure builds and temperatures within a young star reach millions of degrees. The spectra of stars show that they are composed chiefly of hydrogen and helium. The star nearest the Earth, the sun, is a great ball of hydrogen and helium gas that glows because of its high temperature in the same way that a burning coal glows when it is "red hot."

If the stars' high temperatures and resulting glow were simply the result of the gravitational contraction of stellar material, the stars would shine for only about 30 million years. Yet, rocks have been found on Earth indicating that the solar system is at least 4 billion years old. So, from what source do the stars derive the energy they need to shine for such a long time?

The principal source of stellar energy is *nuclear fusion*. Nuclear fusion occurs when the nuclei of two or more atoms join together, or *fuse*, to form the nucleus of a larger atom. The basic fusion process in most stars typically follows this pattern: four hydrogen nuclei combine to produce one helium nucleus, represented in **Figure 4-22**. Nuclear fusion is one kind of **nuclear reaction**. In a nuclear reaction, an atomic nucleus gains or loses protons, thereby becoming a different element.

nuclear reaction
a reaction that involves a change in the nucleus of an atom, as opposed to a chemical reaction which involves changes to the arrangement of electrons that surround the nucleus

The mass of the helium nucleus formed in the nuclear fusion process, however, is slightly less than the mass of the four hydrogen nuclei that went into it. The small amount of "missing" mass is converted to energy according to Einstein's famous equation: $E = mc^2$. Hence the mass of combining nuclei, which is converted to energy in the nuclear fusion process, supplies the enormous energy that stars use to shine.

Nuclear fusion is not only the principal source of energy for stars, but also the process by which elements heavier than hydrogen are created. Most of the helium in the universe, as noted above, was produced inside stars as hydrogen nuclei undergo nuclear fusion. The sun alone converts about 400 million tons (3×10^{14} g) of hydrogen into helium every second.

Figure 4-22a
Nuclear fusion in the sun has provided the Earth with energy for billions of years. Fusion reactions also create elements heavier than hydrogen.

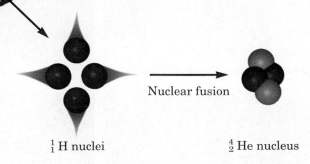

Nuclear fusion

$^1_1$ H nuclei $^4_2$ He nucleus

4-22b
The single helium nucleus has less mass than the four hydrogen nuclei from which it is formed. The small amount of mass "lost" during fusion is converted to energy.

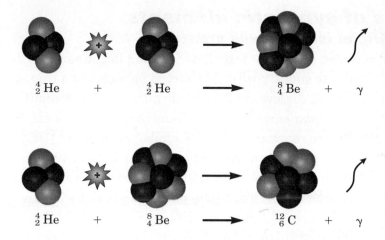

Figure 4-23
Carbon-12 is formed in stars through these nuclear reactions.

Fusion reactions other than the fusion of four hydrogen nuclei to create a helium nucleus also occur. Depending on the temperature of a star, its mass, and the stage of its development, many other fusion reactions may take place. For example, the fusion reactions illustrated in **Figure 4-23** can occur at temperatures above 10^8 K. This process is important only in stars hotter than the Earth's sun. Note that in the first part of the process, two helium nuclei fuse to produce an isotope of beryllium (as well as electromagnetic energy in the form of gamma rays, which are symbolized by the lowercase Greek letter gamma, γ). In the second step, the newly created beryllium isotope fuses with a helium nucleus to produce a carbon-12 isotope.

When a star uses up all of the elements that fuel its nuclear fusion, the star is no longer stable, and it dies in a last, great explosion. The elements forged within the star are flung into space. When planets eventually condense from this material, they take up the rich array of elements found in the stellar debris. Elements heavier than Fe are produced by supernovas.

The relative abundances of the elements found in the universe have been calculated from meteorites that have fallen from space and from other sources. The results are shown graphically in **Figure 4-24**. This graph closely matches the relative abundance of elements found in stars. The close match is strong evidence that the elements distributed throughout the universe are the remnants of stars that have long since exploded.

Figure 4-24
Hydrogen is the most abundant element in the universe. Which is the least abundant natural element?

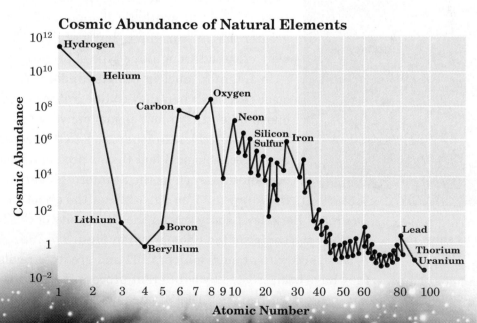

Cosmic Abundance of Natural Elements

The origins of synthetic elements
The first artificial isotope was created in 1919

In Chapter 3, you read about how scientists working in the early 1900s shot extremely small, positively charged particles at a thin sheet of gold foil and discovered the atomic nucleus. These small particles, called *alpha particles*, are fast-moving helium nuclei. Alpha particles are represented by the symbol for helium: $_2^4\text{He}$.

In 1919, alpha particles were used in another important experiment on atomic nuclei. This time, alpha particles were targeted at nitrogen atoms. The alpha particles reacted with the nitrogen nuclei. As a result, an oxygen isotope was created. This experiment was the first instance in which one element was transformed into another in the laboratory. This transformation of nitrogen is represented by the following equation.

$$_7^{14}\text{N} + _2^4\text{He} \longrightarrow _8^{17}\text{O} + _1^1\text{H}$$

Besides oxygen, what other product was made by bombarding nitrogen with alpha particles?

Elements heavier than uranium are synthetic

Today, scientists change one element into another by bombarding nuclei with various small particles, such as protons, neutrons, alpha particles, and beta particles (which are fast-moving electrons). The bombarding particles, known collectively as "nuclear bullets," undergo nuclear reactions with the nuclei at which they are aimed. Many isotopes of the naturally occurring elements—as well as numerous *synthetic* elements—have been made this way. Indeed, all of the synthetic elements with atomic numbers greater than 92 (uranium) but less than 101 (mendelevium) were created through this type of process.

In order for "nuclear bullets" and nuclei to undergo a nuclear reaction when they collide, rather than just bounce off one another, they must be moving very fast and have a lot of energy. Accelerating particles to the required speeds is a major technological feat that is accomplished by particle accelerators, such as the Stanford Linear Accelerator shown in **Figure 4-21** on page 127, or the cyclotron located at Lawrence Berkeley Laboratory on the University of California campus, which is the source of the photograph in **Figure 4-25a**.

Elements with atomic numbers 101 and greater are also synthetic, but they have been created by a different process. To make these elements, accelerators hurl entire nuclei at one another. For example, nobelium, atomic number 102, is created by crashing together carbon and curium nuclei. This reaction is represented by the following equation.

$$_6^{12}\text{C} + _{96}^{244}\text{Cm} \longrightarrow _{102}^{254}\text{No} + 2_0^1n$$

Figure 4-25a
Numerous synthetic elements were originally created by scientists working at Lawrence Berkeley Laboratory on the University of California campus. Some of these Berkeley scientists are shown here.

4-25b
These tracks show the paths taken by colliding particles in the bubble chamber of a particle accelerator. Such bubble chamber tracks are used to detect particles created in collisions.

Unq
Credit for the discovery of this radio-active synthetic metal will eventually be assigned to Russian scientists at the Joint Institute for Nuclear Research at Dubna, or to scientists at the University of California at Berkeley, depending on which team can provide the best evidence of having created this element.

Une
On August 29, 1982, element 109 was made and identified by scientists at the Heavy Ion Research Laboratory, in Darmstadt, West Gemany.

Mendelevium
Synthesized in 1955 by G. T. Seaborg, A. Ghiorso, B. Harvey, G. R. Choppin, and S. G. Thompson at the University of California, Berkeley; named in honor of the inventor of the periodic table.

Curium
Synthesized in 1944 by G. T. Seaborg, R. A. James, and A. Ghiorso at the University of California, Berkeley; named in honor of Marie and Pierre Curie.

Californium
Synthesized in 1950 by G. T. Seaborg, S. G. Thompson, A. Ghiorso, and K. Street, Jr. at the University of California, Berkeley; named in honor of the state of California.

Nobelium
Synthesized in 1958 by A. Ghiorso, G. T. Seaborg, T. Sikkeland, and J. R. Walton; named in honor of Alfred Nobel, discoverer of dynamite and founder of the Nobel Prize.

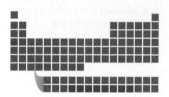

Figure 4-26
All the highlighted elements are synthetic. Those shown in red were created by colliding moving particles with stationary targets. The elements shown in blue were created by colliding nuclei.

Though other discoveries have been reported, the discovery of element 109 has been thoroughly verified and accepted. Element 109 is extremely unstable. Only three atoms of element 109 have ever been produced, and they existed for only a short time, only 0.0034 second, just long enough to be spotted and identified.

Today, scientists are attempting to create some "superheavy" elements that may be more stable than element 109. Why should these superheavy elements be stable? To understand why, you need to know that protons and neutrons are arranged in alternating shells within an atomic nucleus. Each shell can contain no more than a certain maximum number of particles. When its shells are filled, a nucleus is stable. If a nucleus contains unfilled shells, it is unstable and breaks apart spontaneously.

If element 114 were created, calculations show that the shells in its nucleus would be filled. Therefore, element 114 should be stable. Look at a periodic table to see that there is an empty spot where element 114 could fit, under lead in Group 14. But can element 114 exist? No one knows for sure. More experiments are needed to find out.

Section Review

11. Define the term *naturally occurring element*. Where are the naturally occurring elements found in the periodic table?
12. How are the naturally occurring elements created?
13. What evidence is there that the elements are made in stars?
14. What is a synthetic element?
15. Describe the two types of processes scientists use to create synthetic elements.

Can atoms be counted or measured?

Section Objectives

Explain the relationship between atomic mass and atomic mass units.

Use a periodic table to determine the average atomic mass for an element.

Use the mole as a counting unit for large numbers of atoms.

Solve problems with conversions between moles, Avogadro's number, and molar mass.

Calculate the mass of a single atom.

Finding mass measurements in the periodic table

Mendeleev initially arranged the periodic table according to atomic masses. Although Moseley changed this so that the table is now arranged according to atomic number, the periodic table is still your first source for information on the masses of atoms. You learned in Chapter 3 that the mass of an atom can be expressed as its mass number. But a mass number indicates the total number of protons and neutrons present, not their actual mass. Usually, mass is expressed in mass units.

Atomic mass is expressed in atomic mass units

Measured in grams, the masses of atoms are extremely small. A carbon-12 atom, for example, has a mass of only 1.99×10^{-23} g. Such extremely small numbers can be a nuisance in calculations. Therefore, instead of using actual atomic masses, chemists find it more convenient to work with relative atomic masses. In determining relative atomic masses, one atom is arbitrarily chosen as the standard and assigned a value. The masses of all the other atoms are then expressed in relation to this standard value. Relative scales are easy to establish and use, as you can see from examining **Figure 4-27**.

Figure 4-27
In establishing a relative scale, a standard is selected and everything is then compared to this standard. What is the standard used in this illustration?

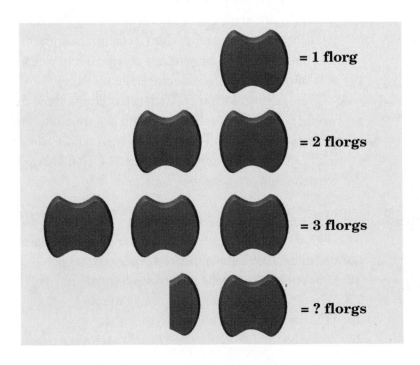

= 1 florg

= 2 florgs

= 3 florgs

= ? florgs

atomic mass unit
one-twelfth the mass of the carbon-12 isotope

In establishing the relative scale for atomic masses, scientists agreed upon the carbon-12 atom as the standard. A single carbon-12 atom, which has an actual mass of 1.99×10^{-23} g, was arbitrarily assigned the value of 12 atomic mass units. Based on this, one **atomic mass unit** is exactly 1/12 of the mass of a carbon-12 atom. So, in terms of the actual mass values of atoms, one atomic mass unit equals 1.66×10^{-24} g.

The atomic mass unit is represented by the symbol *amu*. The atomic mass of a carbon-12 atom is therefore 12 amu. Hydrogen-1, which has 1/12 of the mass of carbon-12, has an atomic mass of 1 amu. The atomic masses of all the other elements are expressed in the same way—relative to the atomic mass arbitrarily assigned to carbon-12. The mass of an atom expressed in atomic mass units (amu) is called the **atomic mass**.

atomic mass
the mass of an atom in atomic mass units

The periodic table lists average atomic mass

If you check the atomic mass given for either carbon or hydrogen on a periodic table, you'll notice something odd. The value listed for carbon is 12.01, not just 12; that for hydrogen is 1.00794, not simply 1. In fact, most of the atomic masses listed in the periodic table are not whole numbers. Most atomic masses in the periodic table are not whole numbers because the mass listed for any element is the weighted average of the masses of all its naturally occurring isotopes.

Weighted averages, like relative scales, are not complicated. Your teacher uses a weighted average when calculating the average for a set of grades for a class. The same procedure is used for determining the average atomic mass of an element. Just as a weighted grade average depends on two factors (students and grades), the average atomic mass depends on two factors—in this case, the mass and relative abundance of each isotope. Consider the example of copper. Its average atomic mass is computed below.

Sample Problem 4A
Calculating average atomic mass

Copper has two naturally occurring isotopes: copper-63 and copper-65. The relative abundance of copper-63 is 69.17%; the atomic mass of copper-63 is 62.94 amu. The relative abundance of copper-65 is 30.83%; its atomic mass is 64.93 amu. Determine the average atomic mass for copper.

Calculate

• **Use a weighted average such that the atomic mass of each isotope is multiplied by its relative abundance. The sum of these products is divided by 100.**

$$\frac{(69.17 \times 62.94 \text{ amu}) + (30.83 \times 64.93 \text{ amu})}{100} = \text{Average atomic mass of copper} = 63.55 \text{ amu}$$

Practice 4A

Answers for Concept Review items and Practice problems begin on page 841.

1. Calculate the average atomic mass for silicon if 92.21% of its atoms have a mass of 27.98 amu, 4.70% have a mass of 28.98 amu, and 3.09% have a mass of 29.97 amu.

2. Calculate the average atomic mass of oxygen. Oxygen has three naturally occurring isotopes: oxygen-16 with a mass of 15.99 amu; oxygen-17 with a mass of 17.00 amu; and oxygen-18 with mass of 18.00 amu. The relative abundances are 99.76%, 0.038%, and 0.20%, respectively.

Table 4-8
Counting Units

Units	Example
1 dozen eggs	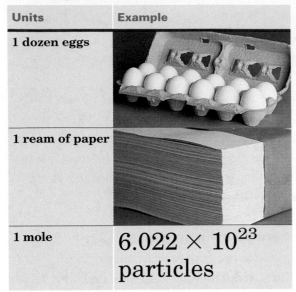
1 ream of paper	
1 mole	6.022×10^{23} particles

mole
the fundamental SI unit used to measure the amount of a substance

Avogadro's number
6.022×10^{23}, the number of particles in a mole

The mole
A mole is a huge number

All calculations involving atoms so far have dealt with terms that are defined in relation to infinitesimally small particles: atomic number relates to the number of protons; mass number relates to the number of protons and neutrons; and the atomic mass unit standard relates to an isotope of carbon. Rather than always working on the atomic scale, chemists often find it useful to work with a unit that represents a large collection of atoms. Such a unit serves as a bridge between the invisible world of atoms and the macroscopic world of materials and objects. This unit is called a *mole* and is abbreviated *mol*. How big is a mole?

A **mole** is a collection of $6.022\ 137 \times 10^{23}$ particles, as shown in **Table 4-8**. The mole is usually rounded to 6.022×10^{23}. You may wonder why 6.022×10^{23} particles was chosen as the counting unit for atoms or molecules. What is so special about this number? The answer is that there is exactly 1 mol of atoms in the atomic mass of an element when that mass is expressed in grams. For example, the atomic mass of carbon-12 is 12.00 amu. At the same time, 1 mol, or 6.022×10^{23}, carbon-12 atoms has a mass of 12.00 g.

In recognition of the value and importance of this number, scientists named it in honor of Amedeo Avogadro (1776–1856), an Italian scientist whose ideas were crucial to the early development of chemistry, as explained in **Figure 4-28**. **Avogadro's number** is the number of particles, $6.022\ 137 \times 10^{23}$, in exactly 1 mol of a pure substance.

To appreciate how large Avogadro's number is, imagine that all 5 billion people on Earth were to do nothing but count the atoms in 1 mol of an element. If each person counted at the rate of one atom per second, it would take about 4 million years to count all of the atoms in that 1 mol!

Figure 4-28
Avogadro's number was determined by a German physicist nine years after Avogadro's death. Count Amedeo Avogadro was a lawyer whose interests turned to mathematics and physics. He later became a professor of these subjects. Avogadro was the first to propose the concept of molecules. Unfortunately, the significance of Avogadro's ideas was not recognized until after his death.

Figure 4-29
One mole of iron has a mass of 55.85 g and contains 6.022×10^{23} iron atoms. The mass shown represents a mole of Fe and the mass of the watch glass.

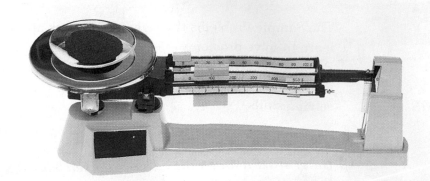

Moles can be converted to number of atoms and vice versa

Avogadro's number is useful as a factor in converting from a given number of moles to the equivalent number of atoms. The conversion works just like when you change a quantity like 20 dozen eggs to the equivalent number of individual eggs. If 1 dozen is 12, then 20 dozen is 20×12. The conversion of 5 mol to the equivalent number of atoms works the same way. If 1 mol is equivalent to 6.022×10^{23} atoms, then 5 mol would contain $5(6.022 \times 10^{23})$ atoms.

If you were given a number of atoms and needed to find the number of moles, you would again use Avogadro's number. The reverse calculation works the same way as when you have 350 objects and you want to express this value in dozens. If 1 dozen is 12, then you divide the total number of objects by 12 to determine the number in dozens.

$$\frac{350}{12} = 29.2 \text{ dozen}$$

To convert the number of atoms to moles you divide the number of atoms by Avogadro's number. For example, if you have 1×10^{10} atoms, you would divide by 6.022×10^{23} to get the number of moles. **Figure 4–30** shows another way to look at these conversions. The relationship of 1 mol to 6.022×10^{23} atoms can be written as two equivalent unit factors.

$$\frac{6.022 \times 10^{23} \text{ atoms}}{1 \text{ mol}} \qquad \frac{1 \text{ mol}}{6.022 \times 10^{23} \text{ atoms}}$$

Factors like the ones in **Figure 4–30** are helpful because you can keep track of units as a way of checking your work. You generally multiply the factor that has the correct units for the answer in the numerator by the given quantity. You can see how this process works in the feature and Sample Problems that follow.

Figure 4-30
By using Avogadro's number, 6.022×10^{23}, you can determine moles from number of atoms and number of atoms from moles.

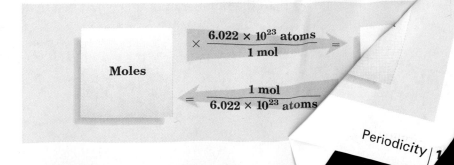

The Sample Problems throughout this book are set up to help you learn to solve problems effectively. The process for solving most Sample Problems is divided into three steps. Each step emphasizes a specific se... of activities for you to follow that will help you develop your problem-solving skills.

How To

Use the sample problems in this text

1. List what you know

Don't start using your calculator yet. The biggest mistake tha... beginning chemistry students make is taking numbers from ... lem statement and using the calculator before they know wh... problem means.

• Read the problem twice.
• Organize the information given in the problem statement. What... What are you asked to find?
• List any conversion factors you might need such as Avogadro's or molar masses from the periodic table.

2. Set up the problem

Don't start using your calculator yet.

• First, analyze what needs to be done to get the answer. Ide... given in the problem that is your starting point. Write the ... for your answer. Then determine the relationships needed for your answer.
• Write down your setup with all the conversion factors. C... the units cancel each other. If they all cancel to give you ... for your answer, the setup is probably correct.

3. Calculate and verify

• Make an estimate of your answer by rounding the n... and making a quick calculation. Another way of ma... to look at the conversion factors in your setup and answer should be larger or smaller than the begin...
• Work through your setup from Step 2. In the exa... require multiple calculations, the numbers are ... steps.
• When you finish your calculations, round off t... number of significant figures.
• Verify your answer to make sure it is *reason... make a conversion of grams to moles and t... larger than the number of grams, you nee...

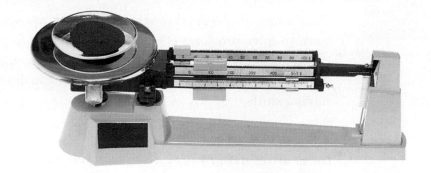

Figure 4-29
One mole of iron has a mass of 55.85 g and contains 6.022×10^{23} iron atoms. The mass shown represents a mole of Fe and the mass of the watch glass.

Moles can be converted to number of atoms and vice versa

Avogadro's number is useful as a factor in converting from a given number of moles to the equivalent number of atoms. The conversion works just like when you change a quantity like 20 dozen eggs to the equivalent number of individual eggs. If 1 dozen is 12, then 20 dozen is 20×12. The conversion of 5 mol to the equivalent number of atoms works the same way. If 1 mol is equivalent to 6.022×10^{23} atoms, then 5 mol would contain $5(6.022 \times 10^{23})$ atoms.

If you were given a number of atoms and needed to find the number of moles, you would again use Avogadro's number. The reverse calculation works the same way as when you have 350 objects and you want to express this value in dozens. If 1 dozen is 12, then you divide the total number of objects by 12 to determine the number in dozens.

$$\frac{350}{12} = 29.2 \text{ dozen}$$

To convert the number of atoms to moles you divide the number of atoms by Avogadro's number. For example, if you have 1×10^{10} atoms, you would divide by 6.022×10^{23} to get the number of moles. **Figure 4–30** shows another way to look at these conversions. The relationship of 1 mol to 6.022×10^{23} atoms can be written as two equivalent unit factors.

$$\frac{6.022 \times 10^{23} \text{ atoms}}{1 \text{ mol}} \qquad \frac{1 \text{ mol}}{6.022 \times 10^{23} \text{ atoms}}$$

Factors like the ones in **Figure 4–30** are helpful because you can keep track of units as a way of checking your work. You generally multiply the factor that has the correct units for the answer in the numerator by the given quantity. You can see how this process works in the feature and Sample Problems that follow.

Figure 4-30
By using Avogadro's number, 6.022×10^{23}, you can determine moles from number of atoms and number of atoms from moles.

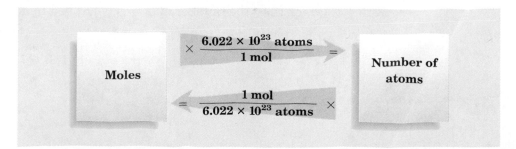

The Sample Problems throughout this book are set up to help you learn to solve problems effectively. The process for solving most Sample Problems is divided into three steps. Each step emphasizes a specific set of activities for you to follow that will help you develop your problem-solving skills.

1. List what you know

Don't start using your calculator yet. The biggest mistake that beginning chemistry students make is taking numbers from a problem statement and using the calculator before they know what the problem means.

- Read the problem twice.
- Organize the information given in the problem statement. What is given? What are you asked to find?
- List any conversion factors you might need such as Avogadro's number or molar masses from the periodic table.

2. Set up the problem

Don't start using your calculator yet.

- First, analyze what needs to be done to get the answer. Identify the value given in the problem that is your starting point. Write the units needed for your answer. Then determine the relationships needed to get from the given value to the answer.
- Write down your setup with all the conversion factors. Check to see how the units cancel each other. If they all cancel to give you the units needed for your answer, the setup is probably correct.

3. Calculate and verify

- Make an estimate of your answer by rounding the numbers in the setup and making a quick calculation. Another way of making an estimate is to look at the conversion factors in your setup and decide whether your answer should be larger or smaller than the beginning value.
- Work through your setup from Step 2. In the examples in this book that require multiple calculations, the numbers are not rounded between steps.
- When you finish your calculations, round off the answer to the correct number of significant figures.
- Verify your answer to make sure it is *reasonable*. For example, if you make a conversion of grams to moles and the number of moles you get is larger than the number of grams, you need to double-check your work.

Sample Problem 4B
Converting moles to number of atoms

Determine how many atoms are present in 2.5 moles of silicon.

❶ List what you know
- moles of Si = 2.5
- number of atoms Si = **?**
- Avogadro's number = 6.022×10^{23} atoms in one mole

❷ Set up the problem
- Use Figure 4-30, to determine which factor will take you from moles to the number of atoms.

$$\frac{6.022 \times 10^{23} \text{ atoms}}{1 \text{ mol Si}}$$

- Multiply the number of moles by this factor.

$$2.5 \text{ mol Si} \times \frac{6.022 \times 10^{23} \text{ atoms Si}}{1 \text{ mol Si}} = \textbf{?}$$

❸ Calculate and verify
- Solve and cancel like units in the numerator and denominator.

$$2.5 \text{ mol Si} \times \frac{6.022 \times 10^{23} \text{ atoms Si}}{1 \text{ mol Si}} = 1.5 \times 10^{24} \text{ atoms Si}$$

- The answer has the correct units and is more than Avogadro's number of atoms, which makes sense because you started with more than one mole.

Sample Problem 4C
Converting number of atoms to moles

Convert 3.01×10^{23} atoms of silicon to moles of silicon.

❶ List what you know
- number of atoms Si = 3.01×10^{23}
- moles of Si = **?**
- Avogadro's number = 6.022×10^{23} atoms in one mole

❷ Set up the problem
- Use Figure 4-30 to determine which factor will take you from the number of atoms to moles.

$$\frac{1 \text{ mol}}{6.022 \times 10^{23} \text{ atoms}}$$

- Multiply the number of atoms by this factor.

$$3.01 \times 10^{23} \text{ atoms Si} \times \frac{1 \text{ mol Si}}{6.022 \times 10^{23} \text{ atoms Si}} = \textbf{?}$$

❸ Calculate and verify
- Solve and cancel like units in the numerator and denominator.

$$3.01 \times 10^{23} \text{ atoms Si} \times \frac{1 \text{ mol Si}}{6.022 \times 10^{23} \text{ atoms Si}} = 0.500 \text{ mol Si}$$

- The answer has the correct units and is less than 1 mol, which makes sense because you started with less than Avogadro's number of atoms.

Practice 4B

1. How many atoms are present in 3.7 moles of sodium?

2. How many atoms are present in 155 moles of arsenic?

4C

3. How many moles of xenon are equivalent to 5.66×10^{26} atoms?

4. How many moles of silver are equivalent to 2.888×10^{15} atoms?

Moles can be converted to mass and vice versa

The relationship between moles and mass is appropriately referred to as the *molar mass*. The **molar mass** is the mass in grams of 1 mol of a substance. One mole of carbon-12 atoms, for example, has a molar mass of 12.000 g. Because a random sample of an element includes isotopes, the molar mass for an element is the same as its average atomic mass. For example, one molar mass of carbon is 12.01 g. The periodic table provides the molar mass value for each element.

molar mass
the mass in grams of one mole of a given substance

Figure 4-31
By using the molar mass of an element, you can convert between moles and the mass in grams of an element.

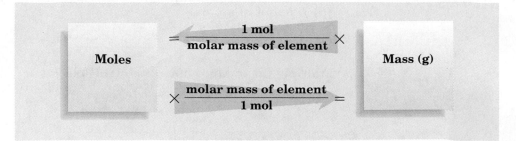

Like Avogadro's number, molar mass can be used as a conversion factor in chemical calculations. **Figure 4-31** shows the relationship between moles and the mass in grams of an element. Consider a problem where you must determine the mass in grams of 3.50 mol of the element copper. First, you must check the periodic table to see that the average atomic mass for copper is 63.55 amu. This means that the molar mass of copper is 63.55 g. (Note: we have rounded to two decimal places to the right of the decimal point.) Next, you set up the problem, using the molar mass as a conversion factor, as shown below.

Sample Problem 4D
Converting moles to mass

Determine the mass in grams of 3.50 moles of the element copper.

❶ List what you know
- moles of Cu = 3.50 mol
- mass of Cu = **?**
- molar mass of copper = 63.55 g

❷ Set up the problem
- Use **Figure 4-31** to determine which factor will take you from the number of moles to the number of grams.

$$\frac{63.55 \text{ g Cu}}{1 \text{ mol Cu}}$$

- Multiply the number of moles by this factor.

$$3.50 \text{ mol Cu} \times \frac{63.55 \text{ g Cu}}{1 \text{ mol Cu}} = \text{?}$$

❸ Calculate and verify
- Solve and cancel like units in the numerator and denominator.

$$3.50 \text{ mol Cu} \times \frac{63.55 \text{ g Cu}}{1 \text{ mol Cu}} = 222 \text{ g Cu}$$

- The answer has the units specified by the problem. An answer of more than 63.55 g (the molar mass) makes sense because you started with more than 1 mol.

Sample Problem 4E
Converting mass to moles

Determine the number of moles represented by 237 g of copper atoms.

❶ List what you know
- mass of Cu = 237 g
- moles of Cu = **?**
- molar mass of copper = 63.55 g

❷ Set up the problem
- Use Figure 4-30 to determine which factor will take you from the number of grams to moles.

$$\frac{1 \text{ mol Cu}}{63.55 \text{ g Cu}}$$

- Multiply the number of grams by this factor.

$$237 \text{ g Cu} \times \frac{1 \text{ mol Cu}}{63.55 \text{ g Cu}} = \mathbf{?}$$

❸ Calculate and verify
- Solve and cancel like units in the numerator and denominator.

$$237 \text{ g Cu} \times \frac{1 \text{ mol Cu}}{63.55 \text{ g Cu}} = 3.73 \text{ mol Cu}$$

- The answer has the units specified by the problem. An answer of more than 1 mol makes sense because you started with more than the molar mass of copper.

Practice 4D

1. Find the mass in grams of 8.6 moles of bromine atoms.

2. Find the mass in grams of 7.55 moles of silicon atoms.

4E

3. How many moles are in 38 g of carbon atoms?

4. How many moles are in 2 g of hydrogen atoms?

The average mass of atoms can be calculated from molar mass

Figure 4-32
Using the relationships in Figure 4-30 and Figure 4-31, you can build this model for calculating the mass of a single atom.

Now that you know how to convert between moles, Avogadro's number, and molar mass, you can calculate the mass of a single atom of any element, as shown by the model in **Figure 4-32**. For example, the mass in grams of a single silicon atom can be calculated as shown on the next page.

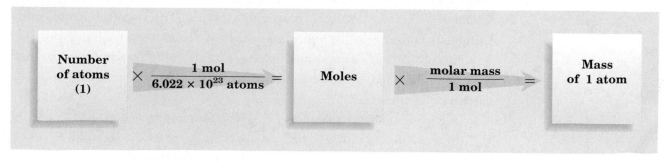

Number of atoms (1) × $\dfrac{1 \text{ mol}}{6.022 \times 10^{23} \text{ atoms}}$ = Moles × $\dfrac{\text{molar mass}}{1 \text{ mol}}$ = Mass of 1 atom

**Sample
Problem
4F**
*Finding the
mass of an
atom*

Find the mass of a single silicon atom.

❶ List what you know
- molar mass of silicon = 28.09 g
- Avogadro's number = 6.022×10^{23} atoms in one mole
- mass of one silicon atom = **?**

❷ Set up the problem
- You know the number of atoms in 28.09 g. You can divide the mass by the number of atoms to get the mass per atom. Or you can express the relationships above as factors that will give g/atom as an answer.

$$\frac{28.09 \text{ g Si}}{1 \text{ mol Si}} \qquad \frac{1 \text{ mol Si}}{6.022 \times 10^{23} \text{ atoms Si}}$$

❸ Calculate and verify
- Solve and cancel like units in the numerator and denominator.

$$\frac{28.09 \text{ g Si}}{1 \text{ mol Si}} \times \frac{1 \text{ mol Si}}{6.022 \times 10^{23} \text{ atoms Si}} = 4.665 \times 10^{-23} \text{ g/atom Si}$$

- The answer has the units specified by the problem. A very small value for mass makes sense because you are calculating the mass of a single atom.

Practice 4F

1. Find the average mass of hydrogen atoms in grams.
2. Find the average mass of europium atoms in grams.

More than 99% of the mass of a silicon atom is due to the protons and neutrons in its nucleus. The electrons that occupy most of the volume of the atom contribute very little to its mass. However, their number and arrangement determine most of the chemical behavior of atoms, which you will learn more about in the following chapter.

**Section
Review**

16. Why was the relative scale of atomic masses established?
17. Distinguish among atomic mass, atomic mass unit, and average atomic mass.
18. What do isotopes of the same element have in common? How are they different?
19. Write the isotopic symbols for argon-36, argon-38, and argon-40.
20. Element X has two naturally occurring isotopes. The isotope with mass number 10 has a relative abundance of 20%. The isotope with mass number 11 has a relative abundance of 80%. Use these figures to estimate the average atomic mass for element X. State the atomic number and true identity of element X.
21. Calculate the mass in grams of each of the following.
    a. 1.38 mol N   **b.** 6.022×10^{23} atoms of Ag   **c.** 2.57×10^8 mol S
22. Calculate the number of atoms present in each of the following.
    a. 2 mol Fe   **b.** 40.1 g Ca   **c.** 4.5 mol boron-11
23. Calculate the average mass in grams of Pt atoms.

Conclusion: Periodic Trends and a Medical Mystery

Now that you have completed the chapter, reconsider the introductory questions and the mysterious death of George Decker.

What properties of the elements can be determined from the periodic table? Atomic radius, ionization energy, electron affinity, and electronegativity values are some trends you have studied. Also, melting point and boiling point vary in a periodic manner. Melting points generally increase as you move across from Group 3 to Group 6. Then, beginning with Group 7, melting points start to decrease. At Group 12, melting points drop dramatically and then continue to decrease across the table.

How do trends in the periodic table explain George Decker's death? Gold fillings contain gold and palladium. As the periodic trend in melting points would predict, gold melts at a lower temperature than palladium. To separate these metals, Decker heated them to the melting point of gold and then removed the pure liquid gold.

George Decker applied a similar process to silver fillings, with deadly results. Silver fillings contain silver, copper, and mercury. To separate silver from copper, this mixture must be heated to 962° C, the melting point of silver. This temperature is not only higher than the melting point of mercury, it is also higher than the *boiling point* of mercury. Thus, mercury evaporates before copper and silver can be separated. And mercury vapors are deadly.

Gaseous mercury atoms, once they are inhaled, enter red blood cells and are then transported throughout the body. Mercury is fairly difficult to oxidize, as its position in the periodic table shows. But once in body cells, enzymes supply the energy needed to oxidize mercury. Mercury ions create chaos by reacting with numerous substances in the body. This causes tissue damage and inflammation that result in pneumonia.

Applying Concepts

1. Assume that Decker had inhaled a total of 0.375 mol of mercury. How many atoms of mercury is this?
2. How many years would it take to count all the mercury atoms that Decker inhaled if all 250 million people in the United States were to count them at a rate of one atom per second?

Research and Writing

Use the library to find out more about the following.

1. You learned that the metals used in dental fillings are all transition metals. Report on other practical uses these transition metals have.
2. In the process of discovering elements, some early chemists actually tasted them or inhaled their vapors. Profile one such scientist, and describe the consequences of his or her dangerous laboratory practices.

CHAPTER

Highlights 4

Key terms

actinides	ion
alkali metals	ionization energy
alkaline-earth metals	lanthanides
atomic mass	main-block elements
atomic mass unit	molar mass
atomic radius	mole
Avogadro's number	nuclear reaction
electron affinity	periodic law
electronegativity	shielding effect
halogens	transition elements

Key ideas

 What makes a family of elements?

- According to the periodic law, properties of elements are periodic functions of their atomic numbers.
- In the periodic table, elements are ordered left to right by increasing atomic number. Elements with similar properties are grouped vertically in families.
- Elements of the same family have similar characteristic properties because they have similar electron configurations. For example, noble gases are unreactive because they have full *s* and *p* orbitals in the highest energy level.

 What trends are found in the periodic table?

- The atomic radius of the elements decreases as you move left to right across a period and increases down a periodic table group.
- Ionization energy, electron affinity, and electronegativity generally increase as you move left to right across a period and decrease as you move down a group.

 How are elements created?

- Naturally occurring elements (atomic numbers 1–92) were formed in the interior of stars. Synthetic elements (atomic numbers above 93) are made by research scientists.
- All elements larger than helium are formed by nuclear reactions in which nuclei gain or lose protons to become different elements.
- Synthetic elements are made in particle accelerators, which launch particles at speeds fast enough to generate nuclear reactions.

Can atoms be counted or measured?

- An atomic mass unit is 1/12 of the mass of a carbon-12 atom. The atomic mass of an atom is the mass of that atom expressed in atomic mass units.
- Chemists represent large collections of atoms using moles. One mole is equal to 6.022×10^{23} particles.
- The mass in grams of one mole of a substance is called the molar mass.

Key problem-solving approach:
Using Avogadro's number

When solving molar conversion problems, begin at the box with the appropriate units. Follow the calculation pathway to the desired units.

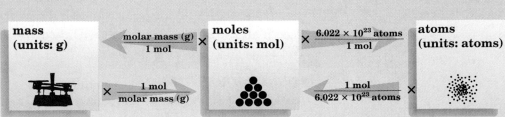

Review and Assess

Organization of the periodic table

REVIEW

1. How do chemists use the periodic law to classify elements?
2. Yttrium, which follows strontium, has an atomic number one greater than strontium. Barium is 18 atomic numbers after strontium, but falls directly beneath it in the periodic table. Does strontium share more properties with yttrium or barium? Explain your answer.
3. a. What determines the vertical arrangement of the periodic table?
   b. What determines the horizontal arrangement of the periodic table?
4. All halogens are highly reactive. What causes this similarity among the halogens?
5. a. What property do the noble gases share?
   b. How does this property relate to the electron configuration of the noble gases?
6. Why is beryllium, a highly reactive metal, placed in Group 2?
7. Use the periodic table to describe the properties of the following elements.
   a. bromine, Br   b. barium, Ba
   c. xenon, Xe   d. tungsten, W
   e. rubidium, Rb   f. neptunium, Np
   g. promethium, Pm
8. Argon differs from both chlorine and potassium by one proton each. Compare the reactivity and electron configurations of these three elements.
9. a. How do the electron configurations of the transition metals differ from the electron configurations of the metals in Groups 1 and 2?
   b. How do the electron configurations of the actinide and lanthanide series differ from the electron configurations of the other transition metals?
10. a. What groups make up the main-block elements?
    b. Why are the main-block elements also called the representative elements?

11. a. Why is hydrogen in a family by itself?
    b. Some periodic tables place hydrogen above the alkali metals, and some place it above the halogens. Explain the reasoning behind both of these placements.

APPLY

12. Compare the modern periodic table to Mendeleev's periodic table in **Figure 4-2**.
    a. List the differences between Mendeleev's periodic table and the modern table.
    b. Identify the discrepancies in Mendeleev's table that were rectified in Moseley's table.
13. While at an amusement park, you inhale helium from a balloon to make your voice squeaky. A friend says this practice is dangerous because the helium will react with your blood and produce toxic compounds. Is your friend correct? Explain.
14. a. What is happening to the sodium atom shown in the diagram below?
    b. How will the electron configuration of the atom change when the atom becomes an ion?
    c. Would a potassium atom behave in a similar way? Explain.

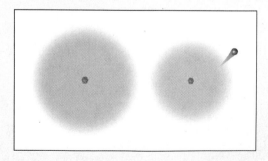

15. Why would you never expect a Ca^+ or Na^{2+} ion to exist?
16. Calcium ions, Ca^{2+}, play an important role in muscle relaxation. Potassium ion, K^+, is also found in your body. Why is there no danger of K^+ and Ca^{2+} reacting with each other?

17. You read a science fiction story about an alien race of silicon-based life-forms. Use information from the periodic table to hypothesize why the author chose silicon over other elements. (Hint: life on Earth is carbon based.)

Periodic trends

18. **a.** Why don't scientists define atomic radius as the radius of a single electron cloud?
    b. What periodic trends occur for atomic radius?
19. **a.** Use an analogy of a football team's offensive line protecting the quarterback to explain the shielding effect of electrons.
    b. How does the shielding effect alter atomic size?
20. How does the periodic trend in atomic radius relate to the addition of electrons?
21. Define ionization energy, electron affinity, and electronegativity.
22. **a.** What periodic trends exist for ionization energy?
    b. How does this trend relate to different energy levels?
23. What happens to electron affinity values as you move left to right across a period?

24. **a.** Examine the graph below. Explain the patterns you see among the transition metals and among the nonmetals.

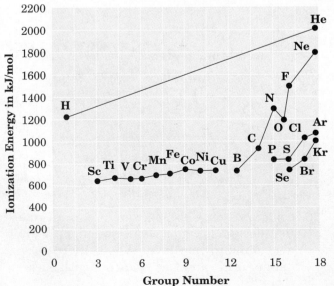

b. Which element on this graph would be the best conductor of electricity?
c. What possible reasons might exist for not using certain elements as conductors?

25. Identify which trends in the diagrams below describe atomic radius, ionization energy, or electronegativity.

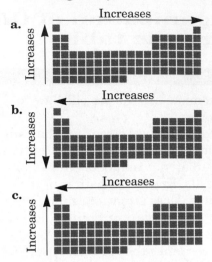

26. **a.** The number of nonmetals in each group increases as you move across the periodic table from Group 13 to Group 18. Using the concept of atomic size, explain this observation.
    b. Will there ever be a metallic noble gas? Explain.
27. How do the trends in atomic radius relate to the following?
    a. ionization energy
    b. electronegativity
28. Name three periodic trends you encounter in your life.

Creating the elements

29. When two elements are involved in a nuclear reaction, a different element is created. How does this happen?
30. How does the nuclear fusion process appear to create energy? Is energy really created?
31. What two significant features characterize the elements with an atomic number of 93 or greater?
32. Cite two reasons why hydrogen is involved in the most common nuclear fusion reaction.

33. Compare the two charts below.
   a. Why are the most abundant elements in Earth's crust not the most abundant in the universe?
   b. Explain how the elements in stars formed the elements in Earth's crust.

Elemental Abundance in Universe   **Elemental Abundance on Earth**

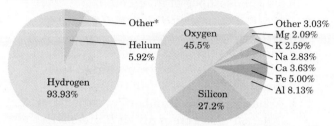

*Oxygen 0.075%, Carbon 0.047%, Nitrogen 0.0094%, Neon 0.0087%, Magnesium 0.0042%, Silicon 0.0030%, Other 0.0027%.

34. Irene Joliot Curie created the first artificial radioactive isotope, phosphorus-30, in 1934 when she bombarded aluminum-27, a shiny metal with conductive properties, with helium nuclei. The resulting product was a nonmetal with completely different properties. What caused the change in properties?

35. In 1987, Russian scientist Yury Organessian claimed to have synthesized element 110 using two different reactions. Predict the element that he used to bombard the starting elements in each reaction.
   a. starting with uranium, U, nuclei
   b. starting with thorium, Th, nuclei

36. Years ago, many people dreamed of transforming lead, an abundant metal, into gold, a rare and highly prized metal. Could gold be made from lead using the nuclear processes described in this chapter?

Atomic mass units

37. a. How is the carbon-12 atom used to define atomic mass units?
   b. How are atomic mass units and atomic mass related?

38. Why is the atomic mass of nitrogen 14.0067 and not 14.?

39. What needs to be determined before the atomic mass of an element can be verified?

Answers to items in a black square begin on page 841

40 The lithium found in a hearing aid battery has two naturally occurring isotopes. Lithium-6 has a mass of 6.015121 amu and an abundance of 7.42%. Lithium-7 has a mass of 7.016003 amu and an abundance of 92.58%. Calculate the atomic mass of lithium. (Hint: see Sample Problem 4A.)

41. Silver found in jewelry has two naturally occurring isotopes. Silver-107 has a mass of 106.905092 amu and an abundance of 51.35%. Silver-109 has a mass of 108.904757 amu and an abundance of 48.65%. Calculate the atomic mass of silver. (Hint: see Sample Problem 4A.)

42. Create your own relative scale that is similar to the atomic mass unit.

43. a. Several elements in the periodic table have atomic masses very close to a whole number. What is the likely cause?
   b. What could be the cause of atomic masses that are not close to an integer?

The mole

44. a. How are moles related to atomic mass?
   b. How is Avogadro's number related to moles?

45. How would you determine the number of atoms in 2 mol of gallium?

46. How is molar mass related to average atomic mass?

47 How many atoms of oxygen enter your lungs when you inhale 5.00×10^{-2} mol of oxygen atoms? (Hint: see Sample Problem 4B.)

48. How many atoms are in the 6.75×10^{-2} mol of mercury within the bulb of a thermometer? (Hint: see Sample Problem 4B.)

49 How many moles of gold are in 1.00 L of sea water if there are 1.50×10^{17} atoms in the sample? (Hint: see Sample Problem 4C.)

50. How many moles are in a copper penny containing 1.80×10^{21} atoms? (Hint: see Sample Problem 4C.)

51 A neon sign contains 4.50×10^{-2} mol of Ne gas. How many grams of gas are in that sign? (Hint: see Sample Problem 4D.)

52. How many grams are in the 2.00 mol phosphorus used to coat your television screen? (Hint: see Sample Problem 4D.)

53 A cup of hot chocolate contains 35.0 mg sodium. How many moles of sodium are in the chocolate? (Hint: see Sample Problem 4E.)

54. One cup of whole milk contains 290. mg calcium. How many moles of calcium are in the drink? (Hint: see Sample Problem 4E.)

55 Element 106, has a molar mass of 263.12 g/mol. What is the average mass of a single atom of element 106? (Hint: see Sample Problem 4F.)

56. Element 107, is produced by bombarding bismuth with chromium. What is the average mass of the chromium atom used to produce element 107? (Hint: see Sample Problem 4F.)

APPLY

57. Relate the mole to two other counting units.

58. The mass of one mole of toy poodles is 9.00×10^{27} g. What is the mass of a single toy poodle?

59. In 1986, the national debt was 2.00×10^{12} dollars. How many moles of dollars is this?

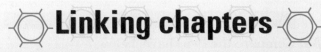

Linking chapters

1. **Theme: *Classification and trends***
   Explain the nature of the observations that Dmitri Mendeleev used to first construct his periodic table.

2. ***Allotropes***
   How do the allotropes of an element differ from the isotopes of an element?

3. ***Electron configuration and quantum numbers***
   a. How does the electron configuration of all alkali metals differ from that of the halogens?
   b. What quantum numbers are the same for the last electron in all alkaline-earth metals?
   c. What quantum numbers are the same for the last electron in all noble gases?

4. **Theme: *Classification and trends***
   a. What trends were first used to classify the elements?
   b. What trends were discovered after the elements were classified in the periodic table?

USING TECHNOLOGY

1. ***Graphics calculator***
   Calculations from moles to grams can be done on the graphics calculator using a simple program. Press [PRGM] [▶] [▶] [ENTER] to open a new program from the program menu. Name the program "MOLES TO G." Then enter the following program. Prompt M: "MX" ⟶ Y1 (Keystrokes: [PRGM]; [▶] [▼] [ENTER]; [M]; [ENTER]; " [M] [X] "; [STO]; [Y-VARS]; [ENTER]; [ENTER]; [QUIT].) To run the program, press [PRGM]; [ENTER]; [ENTER] and enter the molar mass of your element. Press [GRAPH] and use the [TRACE] function to read the appropriate y-value that corresponds to the x-value of moles.
   a. How many grams of Fe are in 210. mol?
   b. How many grams of S are in 13.0 mol?
   c. How many grams of P are in 1.25 mol?

Alternative assessment

Performance assessment

1. Your teacher will give you a notecard that identifies the electronegativity, ionization energy, and electron affinity of an element. Identify the element by analyzing these periodic trends.
2. You are given a sample of an unknown element. Design a set of procedures that you could use to determine if the unknown is a metal, nonmetal, or metalloid. Organize your procedures in the form of a flow chart like the one you saw in Chapter 2 for classifying matter.

2. *Graphics calculator*

Write a similar program to convert grams to moles. Open a new program, and name it "G TO MOLES." Enter the following program. Prompt M: "(F(1,M))X": $\longrightarrow$ Y1 (Keystrokes: PRGM; ▶; ▼; ENTER; M; ENTER; "; ((; 1; ÷; M;); X; "; STO; Y-VARS; ENTER; ENTER; QUIT.) To run the program, press PRGM; ENTER; ENTER; and enter the molar mass of your element. Press GRAPH and use the TRACE function to read the appropriate *y*-value that corresponds to the *x*-value of mass.

 a. How many moles of carbon are in 25.0 g?
 b. How many moles of lead are in 135 g?
 c. How many moles of gold are in 55.0 g?

3. *Computer spreadsheet*

Create a computer spreadsheet that will calculate the number of atoms, the number of moles, and the mass of a sample when the given quantity is atoms, moles, or grams.

Portfolio projects

1. ***Research and communication***
Research some methods chemists might initially have used to arrive at Avogadro's number. Then compare these methods with modern methods. What other element besides carbon has been used as a basis for the mole? Study the reasons for basing all measurements on carbon.
2. ***Cooperative activity***
Construct your own periodic table or obtain one of the posters available that shows related objects in a periodic arrangement like vegetables or fruits. Describe the organization of the table and the trends it exemplifies. Use this table to make predictions about your subject matter.
3. ***Chemistry and you***
Many minerals in food are elements. They are essential to your health. Examine the product labels of foods that you eat. Determine which elements are represented in your food and what their function is in the body. Make a poster of foods that are good sources of the minerals you need.
4. ***Research and communication***
Research the use of nuclear power. Analyze the most common method of utilizing nuclear fuel. Research the waste products and the efficiency of the energy production. Have a class debate concerning the use of nuclear power. Be sure to address the concerns of waste disposal, safety, and availability of the fuel source.

CHAPTER 5

Ionic Compounds

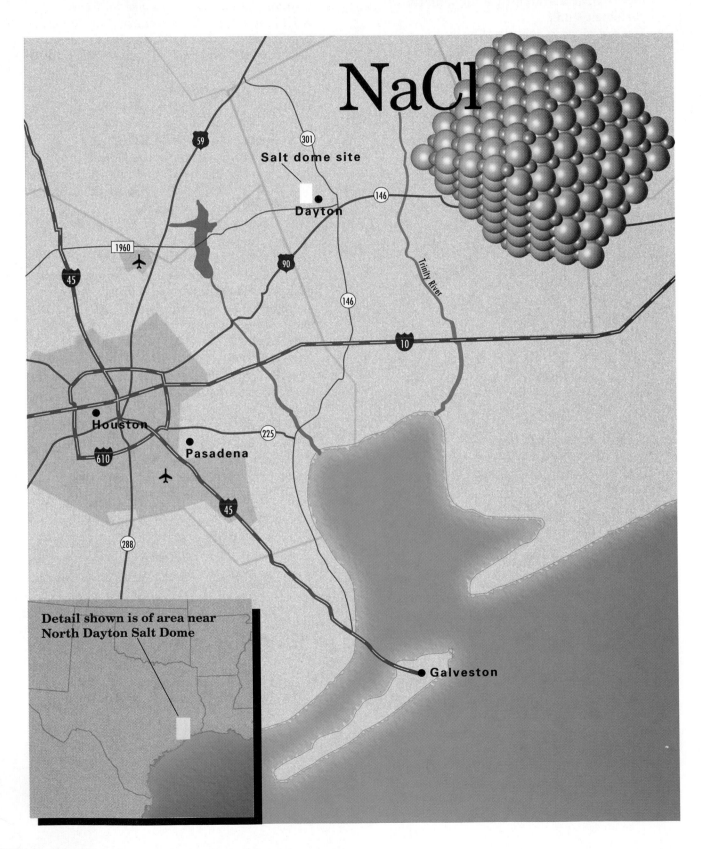

NaCl

59

301

Salt dome site

146

Dayton

1960

90

146

45

Trinity River

10

Houston

225

610

Pasadena

45

288

Galveston

Detail shown is of area near
North Dayton Salt Dome

Salt Domes and Toxic Wastes

In the early 1990s, a scientific showdown took place in Texas. Scientists and engineers with a disposal firm proposed a plan to store toxic wastes hundreds of meters underground, while other scientists argued that the plan was too risky. How could nearby residents and the state government know who to believe?

Many communities are facing a disposal crisis. Toxic compounds containing lead, mercury, and arsenic are used in making many products, including car batteries, fluorescent light bulbs, and thermometers. When these products are discarded, they can't be put into ordinary landfills because the toxins slowly seep into the ground water, poisoning the water supply for plants, animals, and people. If they are burned, metals are released into the atmosphere, poisoning the air. Finding a safe way to dispose of these toxic wastes has seemed impossible.

In 1990, Hunter Industrial Facilities, Inc. applied for a permit to bury toxic wastes near Houston, Texas, in a new way that they claimed was safe. Hunter's scientists and engineers proposed drilling a hole to gouge out narrow, deep caverns 250 m beneath the surface. Toxic wastes would be combined with ash and cement to form solid pellets, which would be dumped down the shaft. Then, the shaft opening would be sealed with reinforced concrete.

Because of their immense size, each cavern could hold the contents of up to 4 million barrels of toxic wastes. But the claims for safety were based neither on the size nor depth of the caverns, but rather on what the walls of these caverns would be made of—salt, NaCl.

Similar salt domes have served for years as storage sites for oil and gas. In the United States, potentially explosive natural gases, such as propane, are currently stored in more than 1000 caverns in 26 states. A nuclear device that was one-third the size of the atomic bomb dropped on Hiroshima was detonated in a dome in Mississippi. No measurable radiation has leaked into nearby drinking water supplies, even after 20 years.

While some scientists believed that the unique properties of salt will provide a safe storage area for toxic wastes, other scientists opposed the idea. They did not believe that the salt domes would adequately confine the wastes. Many of their arguments against the project near Houston were also based on the chemical properties of salt.

To understand how scientists can be on both sides of this controversy, you need to understand how each group interpreted the properties of salts when answering the following questions.

- *Would the salt react and combine dangerously with the hazardous wastes, and leak into the areas surrounding the domes?*
- *Could outside influences cause a break in the salt cavern walls?*

Why do atoms form bonds?

Section Objectives

Explain why the atoms of noble gases have chemical stability.

Recognize that most isolated atoms achieve stability by forming chemical bonds.

Relate chemical stability, energy, bond formation, and the octet rule.

Compare the bond energies of various chemical compounds, including salts.

Stability

In considering the question of why atoms form bonds, the best place to start may be to examine what is special about those atoms that generally do not form bonds. In Chapter 4, you learned that the noble gases, the members of Group 18, have one thing in common—chemically, they are very unreactive. They exist as individual atoms, and they rarely form chemical bonds.

Most other elements behave very differently from the noble gases. Potassium, for example, is a very reactive metal. Potassium reacts violently with a variety of substances, including the oxygen present in air. Potassium also reacts violently with water, as shown in **Figure 5-1**. One product of this reaction is a compound dissolved in the beaker which is more chemically stable than the potassium metal; unlike the original potassium metal, it does not react with water or air. The forces of attraction that held the atoms in the water molecules and the atoms in the potassium metal together are broken, and the atoms of each are attracted in new ways to form new substances that are chemically more stable. These forces of attraction are called *chemical bonds*.

Chem Fact
Some potassium compounds are used as salt substitutes for low-sodium diets. However, overuse of such compounds can lead to muscular weakness and heart attacks.

Figure 5-1
Potassium metal is chemically unstable. When dropped in water, bonds between the potassium atoms and within the water molecules are broken, and new bonds between atoms are formed to make a new, more stable substance.

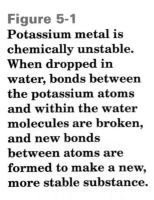

Filled energy levels make noble gas atoms stable

To understand why noble gas atoms do not form bonds under ordinary circumstances, examine **Table 5-1**. What do you notice about the number of electrons in the outermost energy levels of each noble gas? You may recall from Chapter 3 that the s and p orbitals of the outermost occupied energy level (except when it is the first one) are filled when they contain eight electrons.

Helium, with only two electrons, contains the maximum number that can be found in its only energy level. (Recall from Chapter 3 that the first energy level holds only two electrons.) The other noble gases also have eight electrons filling the s and p orbitals in their outermost occupied energy levels. They do not have room for additional electrons in their outermost s and p orbitals. Eight electrons in outer levels help make atoms stable.

Table 5-1
Electron Orbital Notations for Three Noble Gases

Noble gas	Helium, He	Neon, Ne	Argon, Ar
Third energy level			↑↓ 3s ↑↓ ↑↓ ↑↓ 3p
Second energy level		↑↓ 2s ↑↓ ↑↓ ↑↓ 2p	↑↓ 2s ↑↓ ↑↓ ↑↓ 2p
First energy level	↑↓ 1s	↑↓ 1s	↑↓ 1s

Table 5-2
Electron Orbital Notations for Argon and Potassium

Element	Argon, Ar	Potassium, K
Fourth energy level		↑ 4s
Third energy level	↑↓ 3s ↑↓ ↑↓ ↑↓ 3p	↑↓ 3s ↑↓ ↑↓ ↑↓ 3p
Second energy level	↑↓ 2s ↑↓ ↑↓ ↑↓ 2p	↑↓ 2s ↑↓ ↑↓ ↑↓ 2p
First energy level	↑↓ 1s	↑↓ 1s

The octet rule predicts reactivity of atoms

The presence of eight electrons in the outermost energy level is known as a *stable octet*. An extremely useful rule in chemistry is based on stable octets. The most likely reactions are those that yield products whose atoms have stable octets. Once an atom has a stable octet, it does not form bonds as easily, and it is said to be *less reactive*.

On the other hand, an atom that does not have eight electrons filling the s and p orbitals in the outermost level is said to be *more reactive* because it will form chemical bonds with other atoms to achieve a stable octet.

Now look at the electron orbital notation for potassium in **Table 5–2**. Notice that it differs from that of argon by a single electron. It is this single electron that makes potassium so reactive. If a potassium atom loses this electron, the electron orbital notation of the resulting particle is the same as that of argon. It is also more stable, like argon. The reactivity shown by potassium in losing an electron to achieve a noble gas notation follows an observed principle called the **octet rule**.

Other numbers and arrangements of electrons can also contribute some stability to atoms, especially in the case of the transition metals and other atoms with unfilled d orbitals. However, the octet rule is the best indicator of stability for the main-block elements.

octet rule
main-block elements form bonds by rearranging electrons so that each atom has a stable octet in its outermost energy level

Potential energy and stability

When potassium is dropped in water, it changes from a metal that is chemically unstable into part of a compound that is more stable. But more is going on than just the rearrangement of electrons and atoms. You can also tell from **Figure 5-1** that this chemical change is very exothermic.

Although atoms gain stability by forming a chemical bond, keep in mind that they do lose something—energy. When two atoms form a chemical bond, energy is released. As you can see in **Figure 5-2**, when the individual potassium atoms lose electrons and attain a stable octet in the reaction with water, they release some energy in the form of heat and light, and a lower potential energy level is attained.

The change in energy in this reaction is important because it is *easily quantifiable and measurable*. Energy is the ability to do work. But changes in stability are harder to measure and quantify. Chemical stability can be considered the inability to cause a chemical change—the opposite of energy. Thus, a measurement of a change in energy can be a useful indicator for a change in stability.

You may know that natural changes that result in a decrease of potential energy are favored. For example, water tends to flow downhill and never uphill. The potassium compound in the beaker in **Figure 5-1** will not revert to potassium metal and water without an input of energy. Another way to examine these examples is to say that changes that maximize stability are favored. Thus, bond formation for most individual atoms, except the noble gases, is a process that is favored. By rearranging electrons so that atoms acquire eight electrons in the outermost energy level, these atoms become more stable.

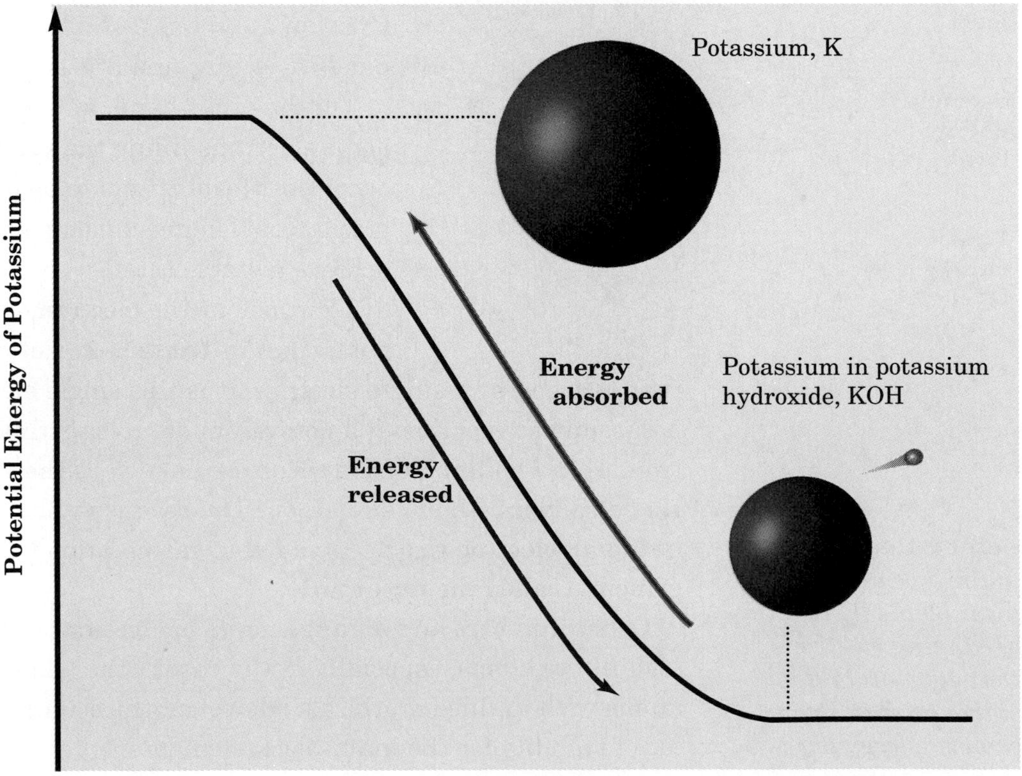

Figure 5-2
A potassium atom is reactive because it has an electron beyond an octet. When added to water, potassium forms bonds to achieve an octet. In the new substance, potassium hydroxide, the potassium is more stable and has a lower potential energy.

Atoms Release Energy and Gain Stability in Bonding

Potassium, K

Energy absorbed

Energy released

Potassium in potassium hydroxide, KOH

Potential Energy of Potassium

Breaking bonds requires energy

It takes energy to overcome the forces of attraction in a bond and separate the atoms. The energy required to break a chemical bond is known as **bond energy** and is measured in kilojoules per mole (kJ/mol).

Atoms that are held by a strong bond are very stable and have a low energy state. Therefore, large amounts of energy must be supplied to bring the compound to a high enough energy state to break the bond.

Conversely, atoms held by a weak bond (low bond energy) are not as stable and have a higher energy state. Relatively little energy is required to break apart these atoms.

bond energy
the energy required to change the atoms in one mole of bonds from a bonded state to an unbonded state

Electron transfers create charged particles

In many chemical reactions, an atom may give up electrons from its outermost energy level. Other atoms will accept these additional electrons to fill their outermost levels.

Recall that atoms are electrically neutral because they have the same number of protons and electrons. If an atom gives up or accepts electrons, it will have an imbalance of electric charges.

As a result of donating and accepting electrons, particles with positive and negative charges are formed. These positive and negative charges will bring the particles together to form one type of bond. *Salts*, such as those described in the beginning of the chapter, contain this type of bond.

Section Review

1. Explain why atoms of the noble gases do not easily form bonds, unlike most other atoms.
2. State the octet rule. Explain its relationship to bond formation.
3. What happens to the energy and stability of an atom when it forms a chemical bond?
4. How could each of the following atoms achieve a stable octet?
   a. calcium, Ca   **b.** oxygen, O   **c.** iodine, I   **d.** xenon, Xe
5. Identify the particle below that has lost an electron. What charge does this particle now have? Which particle has gained an electron? What will the charge be on this particle?

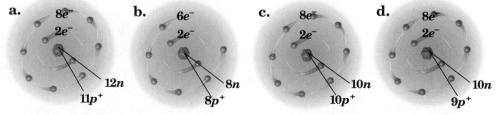

6. **Story Link**

   Why are the high bond energies of salts used as an argument by some scientists to support the plan to bury toxic wastes in salt domes?

What holds a salt together?

Section Objectives

Describe how sodium and chlorine atoms achieve stable octets by forming a chemical bond with one another.

Distinguish among ions, cations, and anions.

Explain how an ionic bond is formed.

Describe the properties of ionic compounds, including the crystal lattice structure of salts.

Summarize the energy changes that occur when an ionic compound is formed.

Electron transfers

Chem Fact
Sodium chloride makes up more than 60% of the particles dissolved in human blood plasma.

Sodium is a reactive Group 1 metal, much like the potassium metal discussed earlier. Chlorine, a Group 17 nonmetal, is a poisonous gas composed of pairs of chlorine atoms bonded together. When the two are placed together, a violent exothermic reaction occurs, leaving behind a white residue, as shown in **Figure 5-3**. This compound, formed from two dangerous elements, is something you probably eat every day—table salt. Chemists call it *sodium chloride* instead of salt because the word *salt* could be used to describe any one of thousands of different compounds. Yet all salts have something in common. They are formed from atoms in the same way and therefore share certain properties.

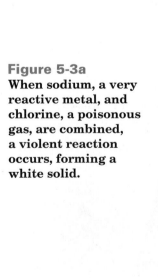

Figure 5-3a
When sodium, a very reactive metal, and chlorine, a poisonous gas, are combined, a violent reaction occurs, forming a white solid.

5-3b
The solid crystals that form are sodium chloride, the salt used to enhance the flavor of foods.

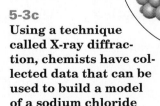

5-3c
Using a technique called X-ray diffraction, chemists have collected data that can be used to build a model of a sodium chloride crystal.

All salts are made of charged particles formed by donating electrons. Sodium chloride is an excellent example of how such a bond forms and how the nature of this bond determines the properties of a salt. Sodium chloride consists of cube-shaped crystals that are hard and brittle. **Figure 5-4** shows a photograph of sodium chloride taken with a high-powered microscope. Sodium chloride must be heated to 801°C before it melts and to 1413°C before it boils. Like many other salts, sodium chloride dissolves in water, and when dissolved or molten, it conducts electricity. To understand why salts have such similar properties, recall what you know about energy, stability, the octet rule, and the electron orbital notations of sodium and chlorine.

Figure 5-4
This scanning electron micrograph of sodium chloride has been magnified 840×. (Note: the colors seen are an artifact of the electron micrograph process.)

Sodium atoms lose electrons to achieve stable octets

Look at the electron orbital notations shown in **Table 5-3**. How could the sodium atom most easily achieve a stable octet? You may suggest that the sodium atom could take on seven additional electrons or lose the one electron in its outermost level. Removing one electron requires plenty of energy, but still much less energy than gaining seven. By removing this one electron, the sodium atom would then have a different arrangement of electrons. In effect, the former highest energy level would be stripped away if this electron were removed.

After losing an electron, sodium's electron configuration is $1s^2 2s^2 2p^6$. There's another element that has this same configuration in its natural state without having to lose an electron. Check a periodic table or table of electron configurations to identify this element. In what group is this element found?

Table 5-3
Comparing a Sodium Atom With a Sodium Ion

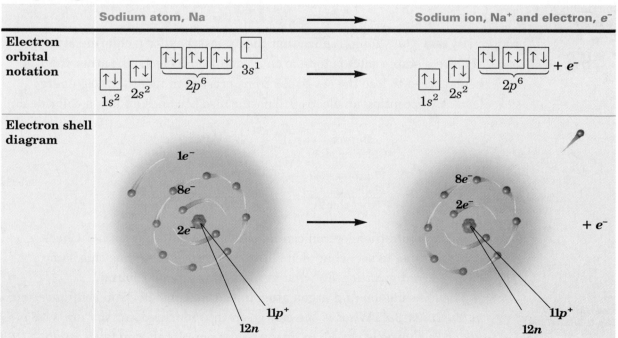

Recall that atoms of the noble gases, with the exception of helium, have stable octets in their natural state. A sodium atom, however, achieves a stable octet by having an electron stripped away, thus revealing its next lower energy level with its eight electrons.

Before	**After**
Sodium atom	Sodium ion
11 protons (+)	11 protons (+)
11 electrons (−)	10 electrons (−)
0 net charge	1+ net charge

In losing an electron, sodium loses a negative charge. As a result, sodium is no longer neutral; the number of protons does not equal the number of electrons. The particle with a 1+ charge produced when the Na atom loses an electron is called an ion. Any ion with a positive charge is called a **cation**. Metals tend to form cations.

cation
ion with a positive charge

Chlorine atoms gain electrons to achieve stable octets

Although chlorine is found in nature as Cl_2, the bond can be broken by light, heat, or electrical energy, yielding two individual Cl atoms. How would you describe the electron configuration of the chlorine atom shown in **Figure 5-5**? How would this chlorine atom achieve a stable octet?

Figure 5-5
Look at the electron orbital notation and electron shell diagram of a chlorine atom. How many additional electrons does it need to achieve a stable octet?

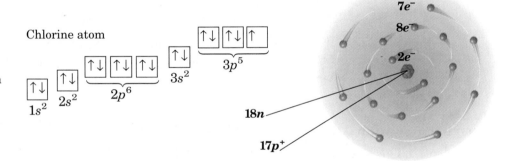

By now you should realize that the easiest way for a chlorine atom to achieve a stable octet is to take on an additional electron, rather than being forced to lose the seven electrons present in its outermost energy level. By accepting an electron, chlorine also becomes an ion, a chloride ion.

Before	**After**
Chlorine atom	Chloride ion
17 protons (+)	17 protons (+)
17 electrons (−)	18 electrons (−)
0 net charge	1− net charge

What would the electron configuration of a chloride ion be? Check a periodic table to see what element in its natural state has this same electron configuration. In what group is this element found?

The chloride ion and argon atom have the same electron configuration, $1s^2 2s^2 2p^6 3s^2 3p^6$. What is the charge on the chloride ion? Any ion with a negative charge is called an **anion**. Most nonmetals can form anions.

anion
ion with a negative charge

Oppositely charged ions attract and bond to each other

ionic bond
bond formed by the attraction of oppositely charged ions

The force of attraction between the 1+ charge on a sodium ion and the 1– charge on a chloride ion is called an **ionic bond**. *All salts are held together by ionic bonds.*

The structures of salts show that the attractions are between more than just a single cation and a single anion. This attraction is so great that many sodium and chloride ions are pulled together in a tightly packed structure. The tight packing of the ions causes pieces of salt to have a distinctive crystal shape, such as the one shown in **Figure 5-6**.

Figure 5-6
In a sodium chloride crystal, each sodium ion is surrounded by six chloride ions. Similarly, each chloride ion is surrounded by six sodium ions.

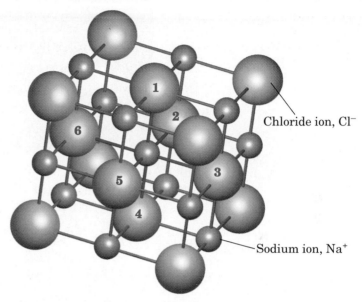

Chloride ion, Cl⁻

Sodium ion, Na⁺

How many chloride anions surround each sodium cation? How many sodium cations, in turn, surround each chloride anion? When these ions come together, the oppositely charged ions are closer together than similarly charged ones. As a result, the attraction between oppositely charged ions is much greater than the repulsion between ions with the same charge. In addition, because the forces extend even further into the crystal, the force of attraction for ions in a crystal is 1.76 times as strong as for a single Na^+—Cl^- pair.

ionic compound
chemical compound composed of cations and anions combined so that the total positive and negative charges are equal

In NaCl and other compounds with ionic bonds, the amount of charge from cations equals the amount from anions, so that the compound itself is electrically neutral. Any chemical compound that has such a balance of oppositely charged ions is called an **ionic compound**.

Explaining the properties of salts
Salts are made of ions

salt
an ionic compound containing cations other than H⁺ and anions other than OH⁻ or O²⁻

Now that you have studied a specific salt, sodium chloride, and the types of bonds that hold it together, you can use what you already know to predict and understand the properties of other **salts**.

To conduct an electric current, a substance must have charged particles that can move about freely. Recall that the particles in a solid have some vibrational motion, but remain in relatively fixed locations. Thus, ionic solids such as salts are not good electric conductors because the ions cannot move very much, except to vibrate.

However, if the ions could move about, ionic compounds would become good conductors. If a crystal is melted, the ions that make up the crystal can move past each other. No longer held in rigid positions by ionic bonds, these ions can move about freely, as shown in **Figure 5–7**, and thus conduct electricity. Similarly, when a crystal dissolves, its ions are no longer held tightly in a crystal and can therefore conduct electricity.

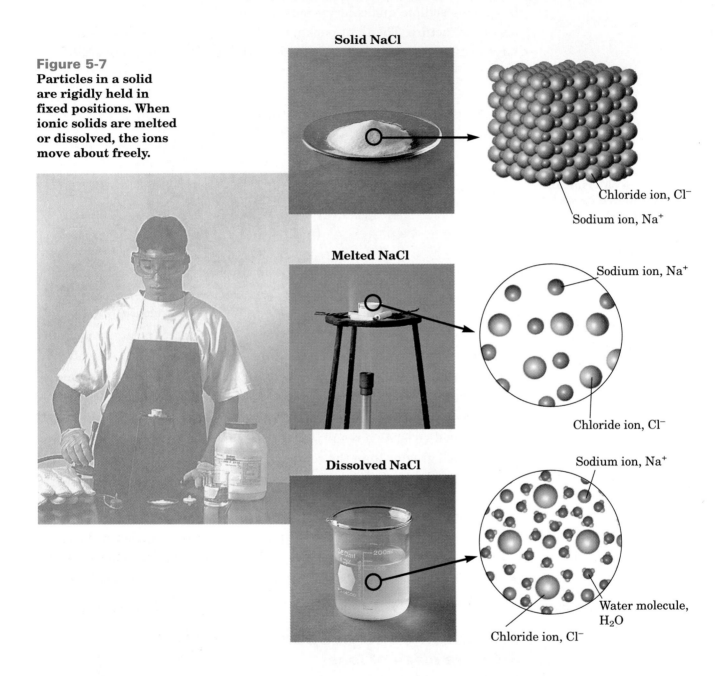

Figure 5-7
Particles in a solid are rigidly held in fixed positions. When ionic solids are melted or dissolved, the ions move about freely.

Solid NaCl

Chloride ion, Cl⁻
Sodium ion, Na⁺

Melted NaCl

Sodium ion, Na⁺
Chloride ion, Cl⁻

Dissolved NaCl

Sodium ion, Na⁺
Water molecule, H₂O
Chloride ion, Cl⁻

Salts have ordered packing arrangements

The ions in a salt form repeating patterns, with each ion held rigidly in place by strong attractive forces that bond it to several oppositely charged ions. No matter which ions are present, the order in which they are packed is repeated throughout the salt. The pattern found in the arrangement of ionic compounds is called a **crystal lattice**.

crystal lattice
three-dimensional arrangement of atoms or ions in a crystal

NaCl lattice

CsCl lattice

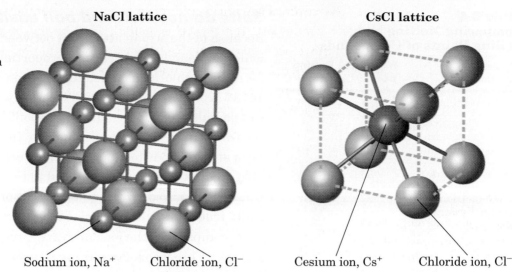

Sodium ion, Na⁺   Chloride ion, Cl⁻   Cesium ion, Cs⁺   Chloride ion, Cl⁻

Not all salts, however, have the same crystal lattice structure as sodium chloride. In cesium chloride, CsCl, each cation is surrounded by *eight* anions instead of *six* anions, as shown in **Figure 5–8**. Despite this difference, both sodium chloride and cesium chloride crystals have a structural similarity. The crystals of both salts are made of simple repeating ionic units that yield shapes which are cubic.

unit cell

the simplest portion of a crystal lattice that portrays the three-dimensional structure of the entire lattice

The simplest repeating unit of a crystal is known as a **unit cell**. Both sodium chloride and cesium chloride crystals are classified as part of a cubic crystal system. However, the unit cells making up the cubic crystals of sodium chloride differ from those in cesium chloride. These two salt crystals have different numbers of nearest neighbors because their ions have different sizes. Cesium ions are larger than sodium ions. The larger cesium ions have room for more chloride ions around them, thus causing a cesium chloride unit cell to have a slightly different spatial arrangement.

Examine **Figure 5–9**, which shows three different ways that atoms can be arranged in the unit cells to form a cubic crystal system. For sodium chloride, if you look at either the chloride ions alone or the sodium ions alone, each type forms a face-centered cubic unit cell. For cesium chloride, the ions of cesium form a simple cubic arrangement intertwined with a simple cubic arrangement of chloride ions.

Figure 5-9
The unit cells of crystals with a cubic shape can have one of three possible arrangements of particles.

Simple cubic

Body-centered cubic

Face-centered cubic

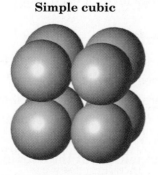

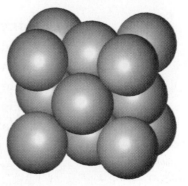

Table 5-4
Comparing Melting and Boiling Points of Compounds

Compound	Melting point (°C)	Boiling point (°C)
calcium iodide	784	1100
carbon tetrachloride	−23	77
hydrogen fluoride	−83	19.5
hydrogen sulfide	−85.5	−61
iodine monochloride	27	97
magnesium fluoride	1261	2239
methane	−182	−164

Salts do not melt and boil easily

Because of the strong attraction between their ions, all ionic compounds share certain properties. The boiling point for sodium chloride is much higher than that for water—1413°C compared with 100°C. Similarly, most other ionic compounds have high melting and boiling points, as you can see from **Table 5-4**. Because the ions in such a compound form strong bonds to a number of different ions, a considerable amount of energy is required to break them apart, as would be required for the salts to melt or boil. This is especially true for small ions formed by atoms. However, in some compounds, the ions are very large, and the forces of attraction are weaker, resulting in lower boiling points.

Salts are hard and brittle

Like most other salts, table salt is fairly hard and brittle. Both properties are shared by ionic compounds with small ions because of the bonding between ions.

No matter which unit cell a crystal has, ions are arranged in a repeating pattern, forming layers. As long as the layers stay in a fixed position relative to one another, the ionic compound will be hard because it will take a lot of energy to break all of the bonds between the ions.

However, if a force moves one layer slightly, ions with the same charge will be next to each other. What would happen as a consequence of such a realignment of ions? When a force is large enough to reposition the ions, the repulsive forces between two layers cause them to break apart.

Energy and ionic bonding
Energy can be released or absorbed when ions form

Removing electrons from atoms requires an input of energy. Recall from Chapter 4 that this energy is known as ionization energy. The ionization energy to remove one electron from each atom in a mole of sodium atoms is 495.8 kJ/mol. On the other hand, adding electrons to atoms releases energy. This energy release results from the affinity certain atoms have for electrons. A mole of chlorine atoms, for example, releases 348.6 kJ/mol when an electron is added to the outermost energy level of each atom.

Forming ions is only one part of bonding

If adding an electron to a chlorine atom cannot supply enough energy to remove an electron from a sodium atom, why does an ionic bond form?

Forming an ionic bond actually involves several steps, which are shown in **Figure 5-10** on the next page. The chief driving force for the reaction is the last step in the formation of an ionic compound, in which the ions come together to form the crystal lattice. Keep in mind that the starting materials are sodium atoms and chlorine gas, which is in the form of pairs of bonded chlorine atoms. The final product consists of sodium chloride salt crystals.

Energy Changes in NaCl Formation

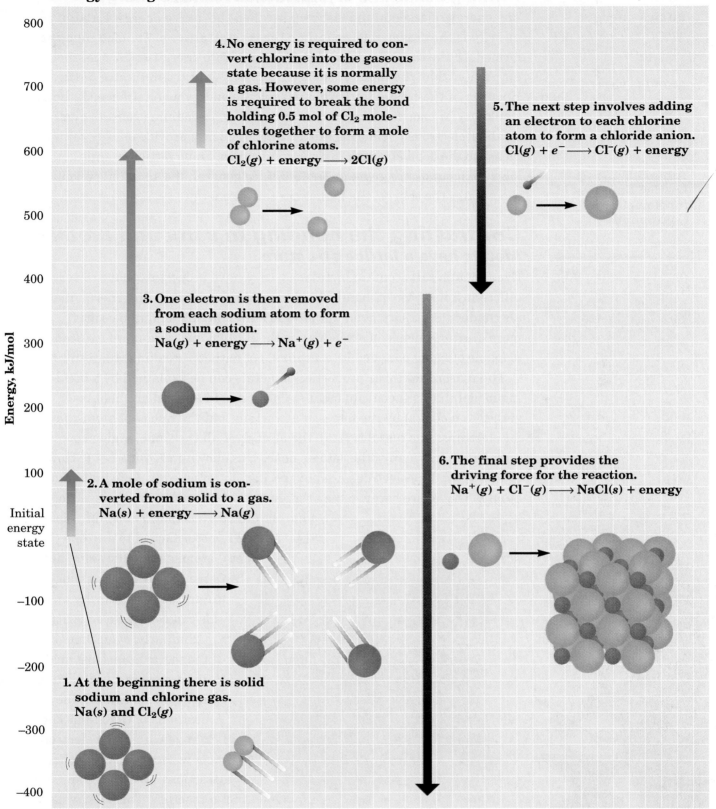

Energy, kJ/mol (y-axis)

800
700
600
500
400
300
200
100
Initial energy state
−100
−200
−300
−400

4. No energy is required to convert chlorine into the gaseous state because it is normally a gas. However, some energy is required to break the bond holding 0.5 mol of Cl_2 molecules together to form a mole of chlorine atoms.
$Cl_2(g) + energy \longrightarrow 2Cl(g)$

5. The next step involves adding an electron to each chlorine atom to form a chloride anion.
$Cl(g) + e^- \longrightarrow Cl^-(g) + energy$

3. One electron is then removed from each sodium atom to form a sodium cation.
$Na(g) + energy \longrightarrow Na^+(g) + e^-$

6. The final step provides the driving force for the reaction.
$Na^+(g) + Cl^-(g) \longrightarrow NaCl(s) + energy$

2. A mole of sodium is converted from a solid to a gas.
$Na(s) + energy \longrightarrow Na(g)$

1. At the beginning there is solid sodium and chlorine gas.
$Na(s)$ and $Cl_2(g)$

Figure 5-10
Of the steps involved in making sodium chloride, steps 2–4 are endothermic, and the last two are exothermic. Combining the steps and the energy changes provides the net reaction, which is exothermic. In other words, the final energy state of NaCl is lower than the initial energy state of the reactants.

lattice energy
energy released when a crystal containing one mole of an ionic compound is formed from gaseous ions

Table 5-5
Lattice Energies for Some Ionic Compounds

Compound	kJ/mol
LiCl	861.3
LiBr	817.9
LiI	759
NaCl	787.5
NaBr	751.4
NaI	700
CaF_2	2634.7
MgO	3760
MgS	3160
CaO	3385
CaS	2775

Forming bonds in a crystal lattice releases energy

The energy released in the last step is called the lattice energy. **Lattice energy** is the energy released when the crystal lattice of an ionic solid is formed. In the case of sodium chloride, the lattice energy is 787.5 kJ/mol, far greater than the input of energy in steps 2, 3, and 4 in **Figure 5-10**. However, if the crystal lattice did not release energy when it formed, there would not be enough energy solely from step 5 for sodium atoms to give up their electrons to chlorine atoms. Lattice energy provides a way to measure the bond strength in ionic compounds. Some lattice energies of ionic compounds are given in **Table 5-5**. In general, the smaller the ion, or the greater the charge, the higher the lattice energy.

Contrasting the bonding in salts and metals
Metals have a lattice structure

Even though salts contain metal ions, they have properties that are very different from those of metal atoms bonded to each other. In general, metals conduct electricity, even in the solid state. Metals tend to be softer, more *ductile* (capable of stretching without breaking), and more *malleable* (capable of being pounded into a thin sheet without breaking) than salts.

The reasons for these properties of metals can be explained by a bonding model that is specific to metals. The atoms in a metal are held together in a crystal by the forces of attraction that the nuclei of atoms have for electrons. In a metal crystal, the atoms are all the same, and each metal atom has many other atoms nearby, as shown in **Figure 5-11**. However, the bonding electrons are not specifically attached to each individual atom in the lattice because the orbitals in the outermost energy levels of adjacent atoms overlap. The bonding electrons are not attached to any one metal atom, as in ionic salts, but are free to move throughout the crystal. This is why metals can conduct electricity. Similarly, even though the metal atoms are held in somewhat fixed positions in the crystal, the positions of the atoms can change within the electron pool without breaking the attractions that hold the metal together. This is why metals can be bent or stretched without shattering.

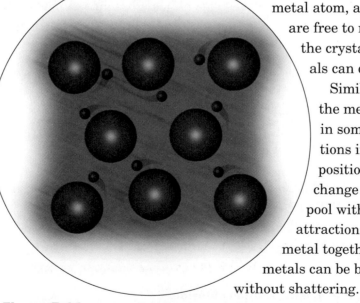

Figure 5-11
The ability of metals to be hammered into shape depends on the softness that results from the bonding among the metal atoms.

7. Which of the particles shown below are cations? Give reasons for your answers.

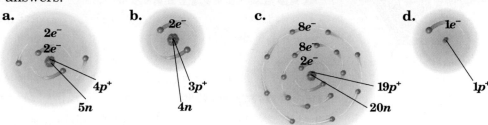

a. $2e^-$ $2e^-$ $4p^+$ $5n$

b. $2e^-$ $3p^+$ $4n$

c. $8e^-$ $8e^-$ $2e^-$ $19p^+$ $20n$

d. $1e^-$ $1p^+$

8. Which of the particles shown below are anions? Give reasons for your answers.

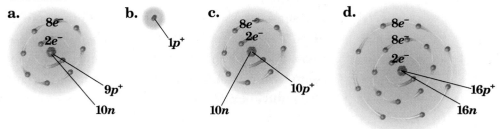

a. $8e^-$ $2e^-$ $9p^+$ $10n$

b. $1p^+$

c. $8e^-$ $2e^-$ $10p^+$ $10n$

d. $8e^-$ $8e^-$ $2e^-$ $16p^+$ $16n$

9. Give the charges for ions formed from elements of the following groups.
   a. Group 1   **b.** Group 2   **c.** Group 16   **d.** Group 17

10. Draw the electron shell notations for the ions of the following elements: magnesium, oxygen, and bromine. Indicate whether each is a cation or anion.

11. Suggest a reason why the structure of a unit cell of LiF differs from that of a unit cell of LiCl.

12. **Table 5-4** on page 160 lists several compounds along with their boiling points. Which ones would you classify as ionic compounds?

13. With the knowledge that ionic compounds are both hard and brittle, which of the compounds shown below would you classify as ionic? Explain your answers.

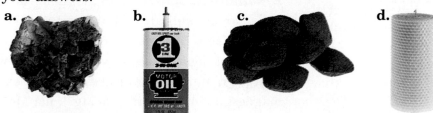

a.   **b.**   **c.**   **d.**

14. What role does lattice energy play in forming an ionic compound?

15. Name two properties of metals, and explain each in terms of the bonding model for metals.

16. **Story Link**
    Explain how the hardness of salts can be used to argue in favor of the salt-dome toxic-waste plan.

17. **Story Link**
    Explain how the brittleness of salts can be used to argue against the salt-dome toxic-waste plan.

How do you name salts?

Naming ions

A salt may be any one of thousands of chemical compounds. So how do chemists describe which salt they're discussing or working with in the laboratory?

Chemists use a system to write and to name the ions and the salts they form. This system is based on the chemical symbols listed in the periodic table. By using this system, chemists have a uniform standard to represent chemical compounds. The system makes communication easier, saves time, and simplifies calculations.

monatomic ion
cation or anion formed from a single atom

Monatomic ions are made from a single atom

Many elements found in the main groups on the periodic table form ions with noble gas notations by either losing or gaining electrons. In fact, the periodic table can be helpful in determining how these elements form ions. For example, Group 1 metals lose one electron to produce cations with a 1+ charge. Group 2 metals lose two electrons to produce cations with a 2+ charge.

On the other side of the periodic table, Group 16 nonmetals form ionic compounds by gaining two electrons to produce anions with a 2– charge. Finally, Group 17 nonmetals gain one electron to form anions with a 1– charge. Group 18 elements usually don't form ions.

Any ion formed when an atom gains or loses electrons is known as a **monatomic ion**. To write the chemical symbol for a monatomic ion you must indicate both the symbol for the element and its charge. **Table 5-6** lists the chemical symbols and charges for several monatomic ions. Notice how the symbol is written for an ion with a charge greater than either 1+ or 1–. For example, the symbol for the magnesium ion is written as Mg^{2+}, not Mg^{+2} or Mg^{++}.

The system for naming chemical substances, whether ions or compounds, is known as nomenclature. The nomenclature for monatomic ions is straightforward. A monatomic cation is named using the element's name followed by *ion*. Na^+ ion is *sodium ion* and Mg^{2+} ion is *magnesium ion*.

A monatomic anion is named by dropping the ending of the element's name and adding the suffix *-ide*. Cl^- ion is *chloride ion*, S^{2-} ion is *sulfide ion*, and N^{3-} ion is *nitride ion*.

Table 5-6
Common Monatomic Ions

Positive charge	Ion name
1+	cesium ion, Cs^+ lithium ion, Li^+ potassium ion, K^+ rubidium ion, Rb^+ sodium ion, Na^+
2+	barium ion, Ba^{2+} calcium ion, Ca^{2+} magnesium ion, Mg^{2+} strontium ion, Sr^{2+}
3+	aluminum ion, Al^{3+}

Negative charge	Ion name
1–	bromide ion, Br^- chloride ion, Cl^- fluoride ion, F^- iodide ion, I^-
2–	oxide ion, O^{2-} sulfide ion, S^{2-}
3–	nitride ion, N^{3-}

The octet rule cannot always predict charges

Determining how an element forms an ion is not always as easy as checking a periodic table and applying the octet rule. Some ions, especially those of transition metals, can reach stability without noble gas configurations. In addition, some elements can form ions in more than one way. For example, iron may lose either two or three electrons, and copper may lose either one or two electrons. In such cases, you will have to refer to a table that lists ions having more than one charge. **Figure 5-12** lists most of the elements that have more than one common charge or that are difficult to predict.

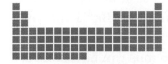

Ti^{2+} Ti^{3+} Ti^{4+}	V^{2+} V^{3+} V^{4+} V^{5+}	Cr^{2+} Cr^{3+} Cr^{6+}	Mn^{2+} Mn^{3+} Mn^{4+} Mn^{7+}	Fe^{2+} Fe^{3+}	Co^{2+} Co^{3+}	Ni^{2+} Ni^{3+}	Cu^{+} Cu^{2+}	Zn^{2+}	Ga^{3+}
Zr^{4+}	Nb^{3+} Nb^{5+}	Mo^{6+}	Tc^{4+} Tc^{6+} Tc^{7+}	Ru^{3+}	Rh^{3+}	Pd^{2+} Pd^{4+}	Ag^{+}	Cd^{2+}	In^{3+} Sn^{2+} Sn^{4+}
Hf^{4+}	Ta^{5+}	W^{6+}	Re^{4+} Re^{6+} Re^{7+}	Os^{3+} Os^{4+}	Ir^{3+} Ir^{4+}	Pt^{2+} Pt^{4+}	Au^{+} Au^{3+}	Hg_2^{2+} Hg^{2+}	Tl^{+} Tl^{3+} Pb^{2+} Pb^{4+}

Figure 5-12
Many metals can form ions with more than one charge.

Nomenclature for ions that can have other charges

How do chemists name ions with more than one common charge? Different names are needed, and to solve this problem, chemists use a system involving Roman numerals to indicate charge. Copper can form compounds containing either Cu^{+} ions or Cu^{2+} ions. The former is written as copper(I) ion and is read as *copper one ion*. The latter is written as copper(II) ion and is read as *copper two ion*. Roman numerals are not used for atoms that always form ions with the same charge. For example, the Mg^{2+} is never referred to as *magnesium(II) ion*, because magnesium only forms ions with that charge.

Concept Review

Symbols for monatomic ions

18. How would you write the symbol for the ion formed when an oxygen atom gains two additional electrons?
19. How would you write the chemical symbol for the ion formed when a phosphorus atom gains three electrons?
20. How would you write and name the ions for tin?
21. For each group below, list only those ion charges that all members of the group can form.
    a. Group 5   **b.** Group 7   **c.** Group 9   **d.** Group 11   **e.** Group 12

Answers for Concept Review items and Practice problems begin on page 841.

Naming ionic compounds
Binary compounds are made from two elements

Recall that table salt is made of ions of two elements—sodium and chlorine. Ionic compounds consisting of two elements are known as **binary compounds**. Naming binary compounds is easy—you just combine the names of the two ions. The cation is written first and named first. For example, the ionic compound composed of a cesium ion (Cs^+) and a chloride ion (Cl^-) is called cesium chloride. A barium ion (Ba^{2+}) and an oxide ion (O^{2-}) compose barium oxide.

Writing chemical formulas for binary ionic compounds can be simple or somewhat more involved, depending on which two ions are combined. Recall that an ionic compound, although composed of charged ions, is neutral because the total charge of the cations equals the total charge of the anions. Consequently, in sodium chloride, Na^+ ions and Cl^- ions are present in a 1:1 ratio. For every sodium ion with a single positive charge, there is a chloride ion with a single negative charge. Thus, the positive and negative charges cancel each other. Similarly, in barium oxide, Ba^{2+} ions and O^{2-} ions are present in a 1:1 ratio. The formulas are written as NaCl and BaO to show that in each compound the cation and anion are present in a 1:1 ratio. Notice that in writing the chemical formula, the cation is always written first. The absence of subscript numbers alongside the chemical symbols implies that there is one of each ion in the formula, a 1:1 ratio. Also notice that the charges are not usually written as a part of the formula.

binary compound
compound composed of two elements

Figure 5-13
Iron(II) iodide is a binary compound with a 1:2 ratio of iron to iodide ions.

Cation symbol
(iron)

Anion symbol
(iodine)

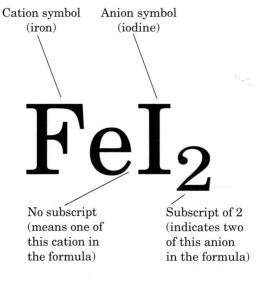

No subscript
(means one of this cation in the formula)

Subscript of 2
(indicates two of this anion in the formula)

Ionic compounds have balanced charges

Remember that in an ionic compound, the charges balance to produce a neutral compound. If you are given the ions in an ionic compound and their charges, you can determine which subscripts will be needed to write the formula. The key is to determine the total number of positive and negative charges necessary for each ion in the formula. This number is the least common multiple of the charges of the individual ions.

For example, if an ionic compound contains manganese(IV) ions, Mn^{4+}, and oxide ions, O^{2-}, the least common multiple of the charges would be four. Because the total number of charges necessary for each ion in the formula is four, it will require one manganese(IV) cation for four positive charges, and two oxide anions for four negative charges. The correct formula for the compound is MnO_2.

How would you write the formula for the binary compound made from iron(II) ions, Fe^{2+}, and iodide ions, I^-? Obviously, you need twice as many iodide ions, each with a 1− charge, to balance the iron(II) ions, each with a 2+ charge. Therefore, the ratio of Fe^{2+} ions to I^- ions must be 1:2. The formula must show this ratio. As shown in **Figure 5-13**, this is done by using a subscript to the right of the symbol for iodine, indicating twice as many I^- ions as Fe^{2+} ions: FeI_2.

Sample Problem 5A
Writing ionic formulas

What is the formula for aluminum oxide?

❶ List
- Symbol for aluminum ion from **Table 5-6:** Al^{3+}
- Symbol for oxide ion from **Table 5-6:** O^{2-}

❷ Set up
- Write the symbols for the ions, side by side, with the cation first.

$$Al^{3+}O^{2-}$$

❸ Solve
- **Find the least common multiple of the ions' charges.**
  The least common multiple of three and two is six—to get a neutral compound, you would need a total of six positive charges and six negative charges.
- **To get six positive charges:** you need two Al^{3+} ions because $2 \times 3+ = 6+$.
- **To get six negative charges:** you need three O^{2-} ions because $3 \times 2- = 6-$. Therefore, the ratio of Al^{3+} to O^{2-} should be 2:3.
- **The formula would then be written as follows.**

$$Al_2O_3$$

Practice 5A

Answers for Concept Review items and Practice problems begin on page 841.

1. Determine the formulas for the ionic compounds shown below.

a.

Calcium chloride

b.

Iron(II) oxide

c.

Magnesium oxide

Chemical formulas must reflect actual composition of compounds

The formula for sodium chloride is always written as NaCl and never as $NaCl_2$, and the formula for calcium fluoride is always shown as CaF_2 and never as Ca_2F_4. The reason in each case is different.

In the case of sodium chloride, why does the crystal show a 1:1 ratio of Na and Cl and not a 1:2 or 1:3 ratio? After all, the more chloride ions that bind to sodium ions, the greater the lattice energy. In fact, the lattice energy that would be produced by $NaCl_2$ could be as much as three times that produced by NaCl, if sodium could form an Na^{2+} ion.

But Na^{2+} ions and $NaCl_2$ do not form naturally. To understand why, recall that sodium loses a single $3s$ electron to attain a stable octet. To remove an additional $2p$ electron and create an Na^{2+} ion would dismantle the stable octet. You already know that a decrease in stability results from an input of energy. But if the energy required to remove an additional electron is less than that released when the lattice is formed, it could still happen.

Table 5-7
Ionization Energies for Sodium, Magnesium, and Aluminum

Element	Ionization Energy (kJ/mol)			
	First	Second	Third	Fourth
sodium	496	4562	6910	9543
magnesium	738	1451	7733	10 543
aluminum	578	1817	2745	11 577

In Chapter 4, ionization energy was described as the amount of energy required to remove the outermost electron from a mole of neutral atoms. Chemists have also measured and recorded how much energy it takes to remove additional electrons from the ion formed. These other ionization energies, such as the second, third, and fourth ionization energies, are shown for sodium, magnesium, and aluminum in **Table 5-7**.

As you can see, the amount of energy required to remove a $2p$ electron from a sodium ion (the second ionization energy) is almost 10 times greater than that required to remove the sole $3s$ electron. The amount of energy released if Na^{2+} ions formed a crystal lattice with Cl^- ions does not come close to that needed to remove the $2p$ electron. There is simply not enough energy to make $NaCl_2$. Similarly, Mg^{3+} and Al^{4+} require too much energy to occur naturally. *Chemical formulas should always describe compounds that can really exist.*

Ionic formulas show the smallest ratio of ions

In the case of CaF_2, however, there is enough energy to make Ca_2F_4. Why isn't it correct to write Ca_2F_4 as the formula for calcium fluoride? After all, it's just as stable as CaF_2. Ca_2F_4 is a neutral compound, as can be verified by calculating the total charge for the calcium ions ($2 \times 2+ = 4+$) and for the fluoride ions ($4 \times 1- = 4-$). To understand why writing the formula of calcium fluoride as Ca_2F_4 is incorrect, consider the crystal shown in **Figure 5-14**.

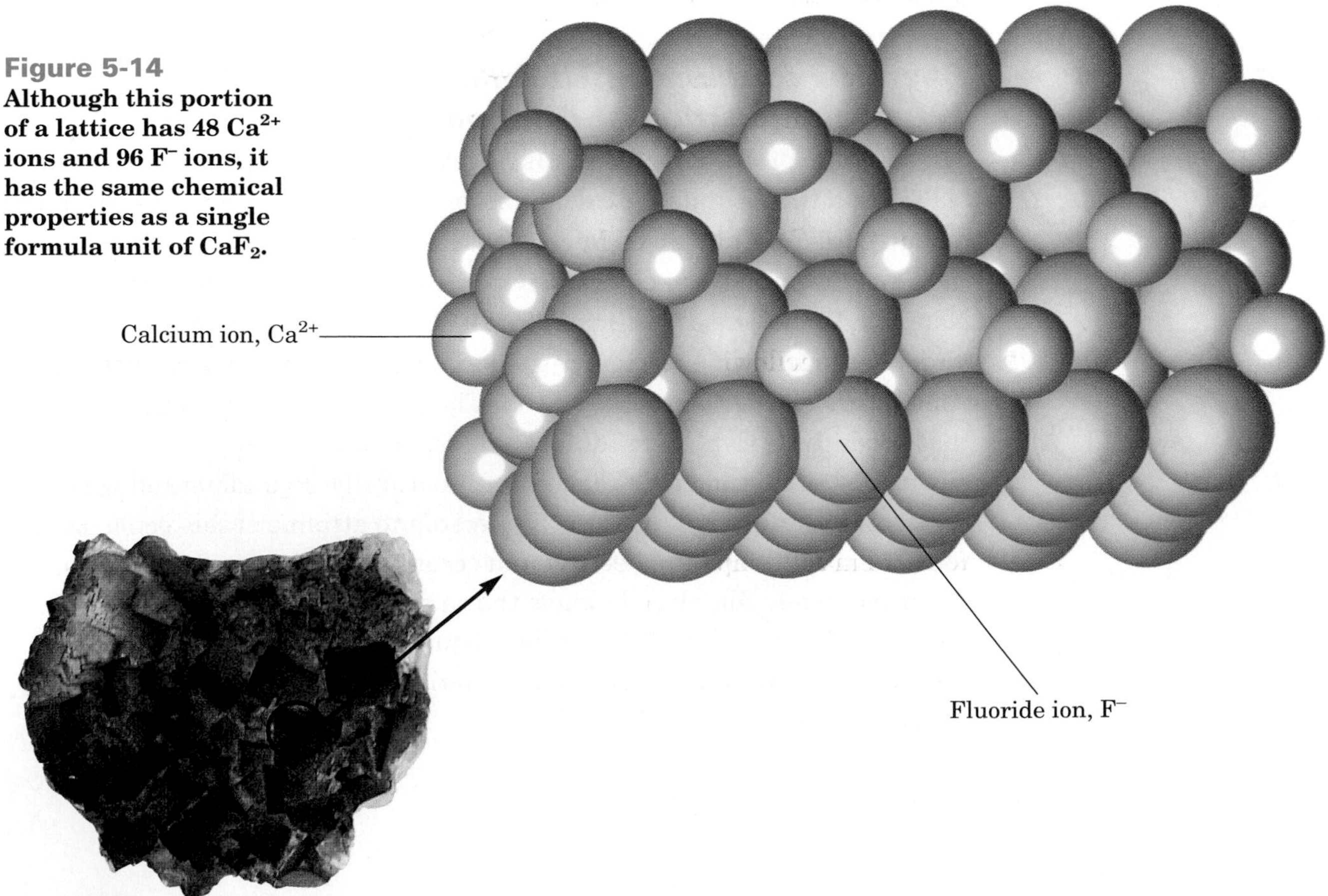

Figure 5-14
Although this portion of a lattice has 48 Ca^{2+} ions and 96 F^- ions, it has the same chemical properties as a single formula unit of CaF_2.

Calcium ion, Ca^{2+}

Fluoride ion, F^-

As you may recall, ionic compounds are composed of ions arranged in an orderly, repeating pattern. The model of a calcium fluoride crystal, shown in **Figure 5-14**, could be described as $Ca_{48}F_{96}$ because there are 48 Ca^{2+} ions and 96 F^- ions shown in the model. However, if the crystal were cut into two pieces (each representing $Ca_{24}F_{48}$), each smaller crystal would have the same physical and chemical properties as the larger crystal.

Because either of those formulas describes a compound with similar chemical properties (as do others such as $Ca_{12}F_{24}$, Ca_3F_6, and even CaF_2), you should *express all ionic formulas as the lowest whole-number ratio of the atoms that form the compound*, rather than using such large numbers. In this way, everyone will use the same formula for the same compound no matter how much of it is present. This "simplest" formula is also known as the **empirical formula**.

In the case of calcium fluoride, the formula must be written as CaF_2 because the lowest whole-number ratio is 1:2. CaF_2 is the simplest formula for calcium fluoride. CaF_2 also represents the **formula unit** for calcium fluoride. One formula unit of sodium chloride is one sodium ion plus one chloride ion (NaCl).

empirical formula
simplest whole-number ratio of atoms that matches the relative ratio found in a chemical compound

formula unit
simplest collection of atoms from which a compound's formula can be established

Section Review

22. Many chemical compounds have common names. Give the chemical names for each of the following.
    a. lime, CaO   **b.** alumina, Al_2O_3 **c.** calcite, $CaCO_3$
    d. chalcocite, Cu_2S **e.** magnesia, MgO

23. What are the names of the following monatomic ions?
    a. Cr^{3+} **b.** Co^{2+} **c.** H^+ **d.** Pb^{4+}

24. Write formulas for the ionic compounds formed from the following.
    a. magnesium and iodine   **b.** rubidium and sulfur
    c. Fe^{3+} and O^{2-} **d.** Pb^{2+} and O^{2-}

25. Name the following pairs of compounds.
    a. $SnCl_2$, $SnCl_4$ **b.** MnO, MnO_2 **c.** FeO, Fe_2O_3

26. Give the chemical names for each of the following ionic compounds.
    a. KCl   **b.** CaI_2 **c.** Li_2O **d.** Cu_2O

27. Rewrite the following to represent the correct formula unit for each compound.
    a. CaBr   **b.** Ag_2I_2 **c.** NaO_2 **d.** Al_4Br_{12}

28. Element Z can form ions with either a 1+ or 2+ charge. Element Y can form ions with either a 2– or 3– charge. Write all of the possible formulas for the binary compounds that can be formed from these two elements.

5-4

What is a polyatomic ion?

Distinguish between monatomic and polyatomic ions.

Identify polyatomic ions in formulas and in compound names.

Use the proper rules for naming and writing formulas for ionic compounds containing polyatomic ions.

Polyatomic ions

The student shown in **Figure 5-15** works at a garden center. While stocking the fertilizer display, he notices that fertilizer contains potassium compounds, nitrogen compounds, and phosphorus compounds. From his study of chemistry, he recognizes these to be ionic compounds.

Most of the potassium is in the form of K_2CO_3. The formula for the compound that supplies nitrogen is NH_4NO_3. The phosphorus is contained in $Ca(H_2PO_4)_2$. These ionic compounds have formulas that are much more complicated than the binary compounds you saw in the previous section. However, with a few additional rules, they can be almost as easy to decipher and understand.

Each of these salts contains a special type of ion. Unlike monatomic ions, these ions are not composed of a single element. Rather, they are **polyatomic ions** that are formed from two or more elements. A polyatomic ion consists of two or more atoms that act as a single ion. Because they act as single ions, they are given special names.

polyatomic ion
ion made of two or more atoms bonded together that function as a single ion

Figure 5-15
Fertilizer contains compounds such as K_2CO_3, NH_4NO_3, and $Ca(H_2PO_4)_2$. All of these are made of polyatomic ions.

Polyatomic ions can be cations or anions

Compounds made of polyatomic ions also contain cations and anions. The only difference is that a polyatomic ion is made of two or more atoms. To write or name formulas with polyatomic ions, you must still begin by determining which parts of a compound are cations and which are anions.

K_2CO_3 contains potassium, a Group 1 metal that almost always forms cations with a 1+ charge. Since ionic compounds are neutral, the remainder of the formula must balance the two positive charges from the two potassium ions in the K_2 part of the formula. Therefore, CO_3 must be a polyatomic anion with a charge of 2–, as shown in **Figure 5-16**.

Figure 5-16a
This potassium carbonate formula unit . . .

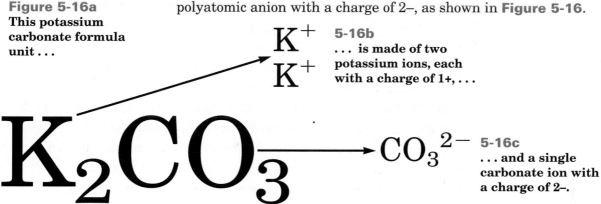

5-16b
. . . is made of two potassium ions, each with a charge of 1+, . . .

5-16c
. . . and a single carbonate ion with a charge of 2–.

Compounds with polyatomic ions must be neutral

Fertilizer also contains ammonium nitrate, NH_4NO_3, which has two polyatomic ions—ammonium and nitrate. Look at **Table 5-8** and you will see that the ammonium ion is written as NH_4^+. The charge on the ion is 1+. The nitrate ion has the formula NO_3^-, and the charge on this ion is 1–.

To balance the anion and cation charges in the formula for ammonium nitrate, you will need one of each ion. In this way, the single positive charge of the ammonium cation is balanced by the single negative charge of the nitrate anion, resulting in a neutral compound. Thus, the formula for the compound should be written as NH_4NO_3, indicating that the ions are present in a 1:1 ratio.

For polyatomic ions, it is important to understand that although the charges are written to the right of the formula, the charge applies to the ion as a whole and not to any individual element. For example, the 1– charge on NO_3^- applies to the whole ion, and not just to the oxygen atoms.

Table 5-8
Some Polyatomic Ions

Negative charge	Ion name and formula	
1–	acetate ion, $C_2H_3O_2^-$	hydrogen sulfate ion, HSO_4^-
	bromate ion, BrO_3^-	hydroxide ion, OH^-
	chlorate ion, ClO_3^-	hypochlorite, ClO^-
	chlorite ion, ClO_2^-	nitrate ion, NO_3^-
	cyanide ion, CN^-	nitrite, NO_2^-
	dihydrogen phosphate, $H_2PO_4^-$	perchlorate, ClO_4^-
	hydrogen carbonate ion (bicarbonate ion), HCO_3^-	permanganate, MnO_4^-
2–	carbonate ion, CO_3^{2-}	oxalate ion, $C_2O_4^{2-}$
	chromate ion, CrO_4^{2-}	peroxide ion, O_2^{2-}
	dichromate ion, $Cr_2O_7^{2-}$	sulfate ion, SO_4^{2-}
	hydrogen phosphate, HPO_4^{2-}	sulfite ion, SO_3^{2-}
3–	arsenate ion, AsO_4^{3-}	phosphate ion, PO_4^{3-}

Positive charge	Ion name and formula
1+	ammonium ion, NH_4^+
2+	dimercury(I) ion, Hg_2^{2+}

Parentheses group polyatomic ions

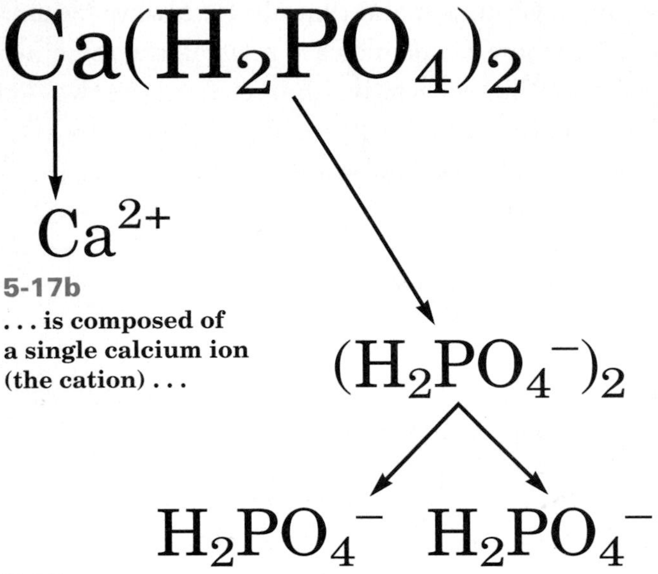

Figure 5-17a
This calcium dihydrogen phosphate formula unit . . .

$$Ca(H_2PO_4)_2$$

The third compound found in this fertilizer seems complicated: $Ca(H_2PO_4)_2$. The number of subscripts may seem intimidating, but it can be deciphered if you remember that polyatomic ions act as a unit. There-fore, *to show more than one polyatomic ion, parentheses are used*. The subscripts attached to the parentheses refer to everything within the parentheses.

This compound contains a calcium ion, Ca^{2+}. From **Table 5-8**, you see that $H_2PO_4^-$ is a dihydrogen phosphate ion with a 1– charge. In the complete formula, the subscript *2* at the end of the parentheses means that each for-mula unit contains two dihydrogen phosphate ions (everything inside the parentheses), as shown in **Figure 5-17**. In this way, the charges balance to give a neutral compound. Even though these polyatomic ions are large and complex, they are arranged in a crystal lattice just like ions in binary ionic compounds.

$$Ca^{2+}$$

5-17b
. . . is composed of a single calcium ion (the cation) . . .

$$(H_2PO_4^-)_2$$

$$H_2PO_4^- \quad H_2PO_4^-$$

5-17c
. . . and two dihydrogen phosphate ions (the anions).

Compounds with polyatomic ions
A set of rules explains the naming of polyatomic ions

Ionic compounds containing polyatomic ions are named in the same manner as binary ionic compounds. The cation name is listed first, followed by the anion name.

Look again at **Table 5-8**. Do you notice something unusual about some of the polyatomic ions listed in this table? In some cases, two different polyatomic ions are formed by the same two elements. For example, chlo-rine and oxygen atoms can combine to form either ClO_3^- ions, ClO_2^- ions, or ClO^- ions . Sulfur can combine with oxygen to form either SO_3^{2-} ions or SO_4^{2-} ions.

You may have noticed that one of the two atoms in every case was oxygen. In naming these compounds, the ions with larger numbers of oxy-gen atoms are named with the *-ate* ending, and the ions with smaller numbers of oxygen atoms are named with the *-ite* ending. Notice that the ending does not tell you how many oxygen atoms are present in the poly-atomic ion.

The rules for writing formulas for ionic compounds involving poly-atomic ions are similar to those for binary compounds. When a polyatomic ion has a subscript, the use of parentheses is necessary to make it clear that the subscript refers to the whole ion, as with $Ca(H_2PO_4)_2$. Parenthe-ses are not needed if only a single polyatomic ion is used in the formula, as with K_2CO_3 and NH_4NO_3. On the other hand the formula for ammo-nium sulfate, $(NH_4)_2SO_4$, requires the use of parentheses. Note that parentheses can be used with polyatomic cations or anions.

Chem Fact
Calcium sulfate, $CaSO_4$, is an ingredient in plaster and wall-board; calcium sulfite, $CaSO_3$, is used as a preservative in some fruit juices.

Sample Problem 5B
Writing formulas with polyatomic ions

Write the formula for ammonium carbonate.

❶ List
- Symbol for ammonium ion: NH_4^+
- Symbol for carbonate ion: CO_3^{2-}

❷ Set up and solve
- Write the symbols for the ions, side by side, with the cation first.

$$NH_4^+ \; CO_3^{2-}$$

- To get a neutral ionic compound, you need two ammonium ions, each with a 1+ charge, for every carbonate ion with a 2– charge. To show this 2:1 ratio, you would write the formula as follows.

$$(NH_4)_2CO_3$$

Practice 5B

1. Write formulas for the following.

   a. aluminum sulfate   b. magnesium hydroxide   c. copper(II) acetate

   d. hydrogen peroxide   e. iron(III) sulfide   f. lead(II) phosphate

Rules for naming and writing ionic formulas

At this point you may feel that naming and writing the formulas for ionic compounds are complicated processes. However, the same basic steps apply, whether the ionic compound is polyatomic or not. By working your way through the steps you will be led in the right direction for naming a particular ionic compound.

How To
Name an ionic compound

Identify the cation and anion, using **Table 5-6**, **Figure 5-12**, and **Table 5-8**.

IF the cation . . .

. . . is a metal that **can have more than one charge,** such as copper, which can form either Cu^+ or Cu^{2+} ions, . . .

THEN determine the cation charge in this formula, using **Figure 5-12** as a guide.

THEN write the **cation name first, using Roman numerals** for the charge,

and **THEN** write the **anion name last**.

$Cu(NO_3)_2$ is copper(II) nitrate.

. . . is either a **polyatomic ion,** such as ammonium, NH_4^+, or a metal that can have **only one charge,** such as sodium, Na^+, . . .

. . . **THEN** write the **cation name first,**

and **THEN** write the **anion name last**.

NH_4Cl is ammonium chloride.
NaOH is sodium hydroxide.

Similarly, writing a formula for an ionic compound involves a series of steps that remain the same for all ionic compounds. By working your way through the steps, you will be led through the rules governing the writing of the formula for a particular ionic compound.

Write a formula for an ionic compound

Identify the cation and anion names in the compound name.

Write the symbols for the cation and anion side by side.

IF the cation name . . .

. . . is followed by Roman numerals, as in lead(IV) chloride, **THEN** assign that amount of charge to the cation, such as Pb^{4+}, and determine the anion charge, based on **Table 5-6** or **Table 5-8**.

. . . **is not followed by Roman numerals**, **THEN** determine the ions' charges, based on **Table 5-6** or **Table 5-8**.

And **THEN** find the **least common multiple** of the ions' charges. For example, in aluminum oxide, the least common multiple of the charges for Al^{3+} and O^{2-} would be 6.

IF polyatomic ions . . .

. . . **are not present**, use **subscripts** to indicate how many of each ion would be necessary to have the amount of charge designated by the least common multiple.

Aluminum oxide is Al_2O_3.
  $2 \times 3+ = 6+$
  $3 \times 2- = 6-$
Lead(IV) chloride is $PbCl_4$.
  $1 \times 4+ = 4+$
  $4 \times 1- = 4-$

. . . **are present**, use **subscripts and parentheses** to indicate how many of each ion would be necessary to have the amount of charge designated by the least common multiple.

Iron(III) acetate is $Fe(C_2H_3O_2)_3$.
  $1 \times 3+ = 3+$
  $3 \times 1- = 3-$
Magnesium hydroxide is $Mg(OH)_2$.
  $1 \times 2+ = 2+$
  $2 \times 1- = 2-$

Section Review

29. What is the main difference between monatomic and polyatomic ions?
30. Name the following compounds.
   a. $NaNO_3$ **b.** $Ca(NO_2)_2$ **c.** $Fe(OH)_3$ **d.** $AlAsO_4$ **e.** $(NH_4)_2SO_4$
31. Write the formulas for the following compounds.
   a. iron(II) chlorate   **b.** sodium bicarbonate
   c. mercury(I) acetate   **d.** ammonium hydroxide
   e. copper(II) phosphate   **f.** aluminum oxalate

How are salts used and measured?

Section Objectives

Use chemical formulas to determine the molar mass of an ionic compound.

Determine the percentage composition of an element.

Interpret the chemical formula for a hydrated crystal.

Comparing masses

Salts have many uses. You already know that sodium chloride is used in food and is used to melt ice and snow on roads. You may not realize that sodium chloride, like many other salts, is also a valuable starting material for many other useful substances, as shown in **Table 5-9**.

If you are using sodium chloride to make chlorine gas, you need to know how many sodium and chloride ions you have because the number of chloride ions will determine how much chlorine gas can be made. As you have read, salts are made of ions arranged in a crystal lattice, a three-dimensional pattern. In the case of NaCl, each Na^+ ion is surrounded by six Cl^- ions, and each Cl^- ion is surrounded by six Na^+ ions. But if you have a 55 g sample of sodium chloride, how can you count the number of NaCl units you have if you can't tell which Na^+ ion goes with which Cl^- ion?

Although chemists rarely deal with individual NaCl pairs, calculations are treated as if they did because the 1:1 ratio of Na^+ ions to Cl^- ions will be true for all samples of NaCl. Similarly, because the ratio of ions in a formula unit for any ionic compound will be the same for all samples of that compound, most calculations with salts and other ionic compounds are done as if the compound were actually a pile of individual formula units, rather than an interconnected crystal lattice.

Table 5-9
Some Uses of NaCl in Chemical Synthesis

Reactants	Products	Uses
NaCl, H₂O	NaOH	chemical manufacturing, paper production, water treatment, petroleum refining, soap manufacturing
	Cl₂ gas	chemical manufacturing, water treatment, paper bleach, bleach manufacturing
NaCl, CaCO₃	Na₂CO₃	glass manufacturing, soap, detergent, water softener, paper production, photography
	CaCl₂	drying agent, glue manufacturing, ice and snow melter, concrete
NaCl, H₂SO₄	Na₂SO₄	chemical reagent, dyeing and printing
	HCl gas	chemical reagent, steel manufacturing, metal cleaners, chemical manufacturing, food processing, oil recovery

A pure substance has a specific molar mass

A formula such as $CaCl_2$ can represent either one Ca^{2+} ion and two Cl^- ions or a mole of Ca^{2+} ions and two moles of Cl^- ions. The **molar mass**, expressed in grams, of a compound can be calculated from the molar masses of the elements. To determine the molar mass of an ionic compound, you must add the individual molar masses of all the atoms shown in the formula. Although ions may have slightly different masses than their corresponding atoms, such differences are small enough that they can be disregarded. Molar masses of compounds with polyatomic ions are calculated the same way.

molar mass
sum of the molar masses of all atoms represented by 1 mol of formula units

---

Sample Problem 5C
Calculating molar mass

The subscript 2 means that in every mole of compound there are 2 moles of NO_3^- ions, each containing 1 mole of N and 3 moles of O atoms.

What is the molar mass of barium nitrate, $Ba(NO_3)_2$?

❶ List
- **Interpret the formula.**

  Every mole of the compound contains 1 mol of Ba, 2 mol of N, and 6 mol of O.

- **Check the periodic table for the molar mass of each element.**

  Ba molar mass: 137.33 g/mol

  N molar mass: 14.01 g/mol

  O molar mass: 16.00 g/mol

❷ Set up

- $1 \text{ mol Ba} \times \dfrac{137.33 \text{ g Ba}}{1 \text{ mol Ba}} = \text{mass of 1 mol Ba}$

- $2 \text{ mol N} \times \dfrac{14.01 \text{ g N}}{1 \text{ mol N}} = \text{mass of 2 mol N}$

- $6 \text{ mol O} \times \dfrac{16.00 \text{ g O}}{1 \text{ mol O}} = \text{mass of 6 mol O}$

❸ Estimate and calculate

- **Estimate by adding the individual molar masses rounded off to the nearest whole number.**

137:	137
+ (2 × 14):	+28
+ (6 × 16):	+96
	261

- **Add the actual masses calculated using the setups from Step 2.**

Mass of 1 mol Ba	=	137.33 g
Mass of 2 mol N	=	28.02 g
Mass of 6 mol O	=	96.00 g
Molar mass of $Ba(NO_3)_2$ =		261.35 g/mol

Practice 5C

1. Calculate the molar mass of the following compounds.

   a. $KClO_3$ b. $Ca(H_2PO_4)_2$ c. $(NH_4)_2SO_4$

   d. sodium hydrogen carbonate   e. potassium dichromate

   f. magnesium perchlorate

Describing mass relationships within a compound

If you were in the business of making chlorine, you would want to know exactly what mass of chlorine you could make from a given mass of sodium chloride. If you needed a lot of salt to produce a very small amount of chlorine, your business wouldn't be very profitable. One way to determine this would be to look at the *percentage composition* of NaCl.

To determine percentage composition, remember that the molar mass is 100% of the mass represented by the formula. The percentage of each element in the compound is simply the molar mass of the element divided by the molar mass of the whole compound and multiplied by 100.

$$\frac{\text{mass of element in compound}}{\text{total mass of compound}} \times 100 = \text{percentage by mass of element}$$

For example, sodium chloride is 39.34% sodium and 60.66% chlorine.

Sample Problem 5D
Determining percentage composition from a formula

Copper(I) sulfide is found in nature as the mineral chalcocite, a copper ore. What is the percent composition of pure chalcocite?

❶ List
- **Compound name:** copper(I) sulfide
- **From the periodic table, you can determine that the formula is Cu₂S.**
  Cu molar mass: 63.55 g/mol
  S molar mass: 32.07 g/mol

❷ Set up
- **Find the molar mass for Cu₂S.**

Mass of 2 mol Cu:	127.10 g
Mass of 1 mol S:	+ 32.07 g
Molar mass of Cu₂S:	159.17 g/mol

- **Use the molar masses of Cu and S to set up calculations of percentage composition for each element in the compound.**

$$\text{percentage Cu} = \frac{\text{mass of 2 mol Cu}}{\text{molar mass of Cu}_2\text{S}} \times 100 = \frac{127.10 \text{ g Cu}}{159.17 \text{ g Cu}_2\text{S}} \times 100$$

$$\text{percentage S} = \frac{\text{mass of 1 mol S}}{\text{molar mass of Cu}_2\text{S}} \times 100 = \frac{32.07 \text{ g S}}{159.17 \text{ g Cu}_2\text{S}} \times 100$$

❸ Calculate and verify
- **Calculate the percentage composition for each element by using the setups from Step 2 and rounding to the correct number of significant figures.**

  79.85~~173308~~% = 79.85% Cu
  20.148~~26915~~% = 20.15% S

- **To check your work, be sure the sum of the percentages is very close to 100%.**

Practice 5D

1. Chalcopyrite has the formula CuFeS₂. What is the percentage composition of this compound?

2. Will you get more copper from the same mass of pure chalcopyrite or pure chalcocite? Explain your answer.

Chalcopyrite

Formulas can be determined from composition data

When a new chemical substance is discovered, its discoverers often do not know its formula or its composition. Analytical chemists use chemical reactions to break down the compound into its elements and analyze the mass of each element present. From this information they can calculate the chemical formula of the compound. As with most other chemistry calculations, the key is to convert the percentages by mass into amounts by *moles*. Then, compare the mole amounts to find the simplest whole-number ratio. The best way to do this is to divide each amount in moles by the smallest of the mole amounts. This will give a coefficient of one for the atoms present in the smallest amount. After this step, additional multiplication may be necessary to achieve whole numbers of atoms. These numbers will be the coefficients in the formula.

Sample Problem 5E

Determining formula from composition data

In percentage problems, it is often convenient to assume you are working with a 100. g sample of the substance.

As part of a science fair project, Antonio is analyzing the contents of fresh alkaline batteries. He has determined that one ingredient is a black powdery compound, of 63% manganese and 37% oxygen. What is the compound's formula?

❶ List
- percentage Mn: 63%
- percentage O: 37%

❷ Set up
- Find the moles of manganese and oxygen present.

$$63 \text{ g Mn} \times \frac{1 \text{ mol Mn}}{54.94 \text{ g Mn}} = 1.146705497 \text{ mol Mn} = 1.1 \text{ mol Mn}$$

$$37 \text{ g O} \times \frac{1 \text{ mol O}}{16.00 \text{ g O}} = 2.3125 \text{ mol O} = 2.3 \text{ mol O}$$

❸ Calculate
- To determine the simplest ratio of moles in the compound, select the smallest number of moles, and divide other numbers of moles by it.

$$\frac{1.1 \text{ mol Mn}}{1.1} = 1.0 \text{ mol Mn}$$

$$\frac{2.3 \text{ mol Mn}}{1.1} = 2.1 \text{ mol O}$$

1.0 mol Mn: 2.1 mol O is nearly the same as 1 mol Mn: 2 mol O.

- Write the formula using the smallest whole number ratio of oxygen to manganese.

$$MnO_2$$

Practice 5E

1. While analyzing a dead alkaline battery, Antonio finds a compound of 70% manganese and 30% oxygen. What is its formula?

2. Find the formula for an ingredient of rechargeable batteries that has the following percentage composition: 21.9% O, 1.4% H, and 76.7% Cd.

Percentage composition tells how much water is in a hydrate

Some salts have the ability to bind water molecules within their lattice structure. These compounds are known as hydrated crystals. The anhydrous salts are used as drying agents because they can absorb so much water as they form hydrated crystals. Others change color when hydrated and can serve as moisture indicators. As shown in **Figure 5-18**, the desiccant packed with a camera lens or most electronic equipment contains silica gel, a hydrate of SiO_2. In fact, many pure anhydrous salts will absorb moisture from the air to form hydrates.

The copper sulfate shown in **Figure 5-19** is an example of a salt that can form a hydrate. In copper sulfate pentahydrate, for every formula unit of copper sulfate, five molecules of water are trapped, as seen in the formula $CuSO_4 \cdot 5H_2O$. Notice that when writing the formula for a hydrate, a number is placed in front of the formula for water. This number indicates how many units of water are present for every formula unit of the crystal.

Another hydrate is sodium carbonate decahydrate, $Na_2CO_3 \cdot 10H_2O$. In problems with hydrates, it is important to remember that 25.0 g of Na_2CO_3 contains more sodium carbonate formula units than 25.0 g of $Na_2CO_3 \cdot 10H_2O$. In the anhydrous salt, all 25.0 g are Na_2CO_3, but in the hydrate, the *$\cdot 10H_2O$* in the formula tells you that water makes up some of the 25.0 g, with the remainder being Na_2CO_3.

Figure 5-18
When you unpack a new camera lens, CD player, or television, the box usually contains one or more packets of desiccant. The packet absorbs moisture in the air so that the equipment will not be damaged.

Figure 5-19a
Anhydrous copper sulfate, $CuSO_4$, is a white powder, . . .

5-19b
. . .but when water is added, a blue hydrate, $CuSO_4 \cdot 5H_2O$, is formed.

Figure 5-19c
Anhydrous cobalt chloride has a lavender or blue color, . . .

5-19d
. . . but when water is added, the red or pink hydrate, $CoCl_2 \cdot 6H_2O$, is formed.

Sample Problem 5F
Percentage composition of hydrates

What percentage of hydrated sodium carbonate, $Na_2CO_3 \cdot 10H_2O$, is Na_2CO_3?

❶ List

- Determine the molar mass of Na_2CO_3.

$$2 \text{ mol Na} \times \frac{22.99 \text{ g Na}}{1 \text{ mol Na}} = 45.98 \text{ g}$$

$$1 \text{ mol C} \times \frac{12.01 \text{ g C}}{1 \text{ mol C}} = 12.01 \text{ g}$$

$$3 \text{ mol O} \times \frac{16.00 \text{ g O}}{1 \text{ mol O}} = 48.00 \text{ g}$$

Molar mass of $Na_2CO_3 = 105.99$ g/mol

- Determine the mass of 10 mol H_2O.

$$20 \text{ mol H} \times \frac{1.01 \text{ g H}}{1 \text{ mol H}} = 20.2 \text{ g}$$

$$10 \text{ mol O} \times \frac{16.00 \text{ g O}}{1 \text{ mol O}} = 160.0 \text{ g}$$

Mass of 10 mol H_2O = 180.2 g

- Determine the molar mass of $Na_2CO_3 \cdot 10H_2O$.

$$
\begin{array}{ll}
 & 105.99 \text{ g for 1 mol } Na_2CO_3 \\
+ & 180.2 \text{ g for 10 mol } H_2O \\
\hline
 & 286.2 \text{ g/mol for } Na_2CO_3 \cdot 10H_2O
\end{array}
$$

❷ Set up

- Set up the percentage.

$$\text{percentage } Na_2CO_3 = \frac{\text{molar mass of } Na_2CO_3}{\text{molar mass of } Na_2CO_3 \cdot 10H_2O} \times 100$$

❸ Estimate and calculate

- Calculate the answer.

$$\text{percentage } Na_2CO_3 = \frac{105.99}{286.2} \times 100 = 37.03354298\% = 37.03\% \ Na_2CO_3$$

Practice 5F

1. How many grams of hydrated sodium carbonate would be needed to supply the same number of formula units of Na_2CO_3 as 86.3 g of anhydrous sodium carbonate? (Hint: use the percentage calculated in Step 3 above.)

2. Anhydrous $CaCl_2$ is used as a drying agent because it forms hydrates such as $CaCl_2 \cdot 6H_2O$. How many grams of $CaCl_2$ would it take to absorb 33.5 g of water if all of it were converted to $CaCl_2 \cdot 6H_2O$?

Section Review

32. Find the molar mass of each of the following.
    - **a.** calcium acetate
    - **b.** iron(II) phosphate
    - **c.** $Al(ClO_3)_3$
    - **d.** Na_2CO_3

33. Find the percentage composition of each of the following.
    - **a.** zinc sulfate
    - **b.** $Fe_2(SO_4)_3$
    - **c.** $CuSO_4 \cdot 5H_2O$

34. Gram for gram, which will absorb more water: anhydrous $CaCl_2$ forming $CaCl_2 \cdot 6H_2O$ or anhydrous $Co_3(PO_4)_2$ forming $Co_3(PO_4)_2 \cdot 8H_2O$? Explain your answer.

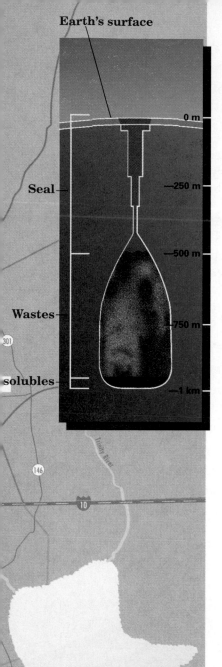

Earth's surface

0 m

Seal

250 m

500 m

Wastes

750 m

solubles

1 km

Conclusion: Salt Domes and Toxic Wastes

Remember the properties of salts as you examine the arguments for and against burying toxic wastes in salt domes.

Would the salt react and combine dangerously with the hazardous wastes and leak into the areas surrounding the domes? Those proposing the plan said there would be no dangerous reaction because the wastes would be sealed in airless caverns. To be sure that no air would leak in, nitrogen gas was to have been pumped in to check for leaks. Without oxygen, the wastes should be less reactive. The atoms in a salt have already achieved stable octets and should be nonreactive.

In addition, those in favor of the plan said that the crystal lattice would form an impenetrable barrier that would prevent the toxic wastes from escaping.

However, opponents of the project pointed out that even stable, nonreactive atoms or compounds can combine under certain circumstances. The salt in some domes may have impurities that are difficult to detect and that may weaken the crystal lattice. Also, wastes may react differently from the pure compounds stored in other salt domes.

Could outside influences cause a break in the salt cavern walls? The many salt domes currently in use have not leaked yet. Although salts are brittle under normal conditions, salt domes are under such high pressure that the salt can "flow" when it deforms, instead of cracking.

Storage caverns are usually built away from the edges and top of a salt dome, so most of the salt would have to dissolve in water before a leak would occur. Right now, this dissolving is an extremely slow geologic process because there is water only near the Earth's surface.

However, in 1993 the Texas Natural Resource Conservation Commission ruled against granting the permit. Hunter appealed the decision to the Texas Attorney General but lost the appeal as well.

Applying Concepts

1. A typical salt dome is about 620 m in diameter and 2.0×10^3 m deep. If the density of the salt, NaCl, is 2.2 g/cm³, how many grams of NaCl are there? How many moles of the salt is this?
2. If 1.0 L of water is needed to dissolve 350 g of NaCl, how many liters of water would it take to dissolve the entire dome?

Research and Writing

Use the library to find out the following.
1. What other ideas are being suggested for the storage of hazardous wastes? Who should pay for taking care of the wastes?
2. Research the number and average size of salt domes in the United States and the amount of toxic wastes produced annually. If the domes were used to store wastes, how long would it take to fill them?

Highlights

Key terms

anion

binary compounds

bond energy

cation

crystal lattice

empirical formula

formula unit

ionic bond

ionic compounds

lattice energy

molar mass

monatomic ion

octet rule

polyatomic ion

salt

unit cell

Key ideas

 ### Why do atoms form bonds?

- Atoms without filled outermost energy levels will form chemical bonds to achieve a stable octet.
- An input of energy is needed to break chemical bonds between atoms. Energy is released when bonds form between atoms.

 ### What holds a salt together?

- The opposite charges of anions and cations attract, forming a tightly packed substance of bonded ions called a crystal lattice, which determines the properties of ionic compounds.
- A salt will form if the energy released to create anions and form the crystal lattice is greater than the energy absorbed to create cations.

 ### How do you name salts?

- Ionic compounds are named by joining the cation and anion names.
- The subscripts in the formula for an ionic compound indicate the lowest electrically neutral whole-number ratio of cations to anions.

What is a polyatomic ion?

- Polyatomic ions are two or more atoms bonded together and functioning as a single unit.
- Parentheses are used to group polyatomic ions in a chemical formula with a subscript.

 ### How are salts used and measured?

- Molar mass can be calculated from the chemical formula of a compound.
- The percentage composition gives the mass percentages of the elements within a compound.

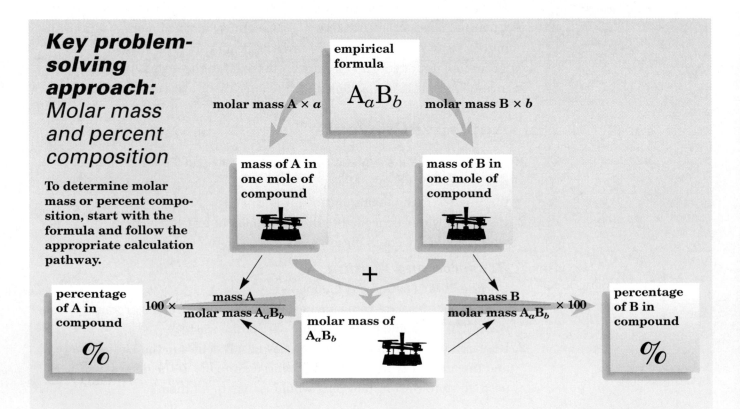

Key problem-solving approach: *Molar mass and percent composition*

To determine molar mass or percent composition, start with the formula and follow the appropriate calculation pathway.

empirical formula

$$A_aB_b$$

molar mass A × a

molar mass B × b

mass of A in one mole of compound

mass of B in one mole of compound

+

percentage of A in compound

%

$100 \times \dfrac{\text{mass A}}{\text{molar mass } A_aB_b}$

molar mass of A_aB_b

$\dfrac{\text{mass B}}{\text{molar mass } A_aB_b} \times 100$

percentage of B in compound

%

Review and Assess

Bond formation

REVIEW

1. Predict the reactivity of atoms of the following elements. Explain your predictions. (Hint: write the electron configuration for each atom.)
   a. lithium, Li **b.** helium, He **c.** nitrogen, N
2. When a certain substance is dropped into water, no reaction is apparent. How would you describe the stability and energy of the atoms making up this substance?
3. How might atoms of the following elements achieve stability?
   a. Magnesium, Mg (atomic number 12)
   b. Bromine, Br (atomic number 35)
   c. Oxygen, O (atomic number 8)
   d. Iodine, I (atomic number 53)
   e. Aluminum, Al (atomic number 13)
   f. Nitrogen, N (atomic number 7)
4. What happens to the energy level and stability of two bonded atoms when they are separated and become individual atoms?
5. Propose a reason why magnesium forms Mg^{2+} ions and not Mg^{6-} ions.
6. Complete the table below.

Atom	Ion	Noble gas configuration
S		
Be		
I		
Rb		
O		
Sr		
F		

7. Cadmium and chlorine can combine to form cadmium(II) chloride, $CdCl_2$, which is used in the production of television picture tubes. Identify the effect of the following on this reaction.
   a. stability of the products compared to the reactants
   b. energy

APPLY

8. Which has greater potential energy, a noble gas or a metal? Explain your answer.
9. With the exception of technetium, all elements with an atomic number less than 93 are naturally occurring. Do you expect to be able to find all of these elements as pure substances? Explain.
10. Your lab partner believes that all ions are stable. How would you explain what is wrong with his belief?
11. Why are most metals found in nature as ores that need refining and not as pure metals?
12. A classmate insists that sodium gains a positive charge when it becomes an ion because it gains a proton. Explain this student's error.
13. Which diagram below illustrates the electron shell diagram for a potassium ion found in the nerve cells of your body? (Hint: potassium's atomic number is 19.)

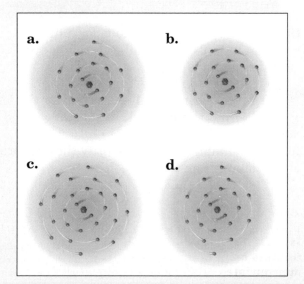

a.   b.

c.   d.

14. Free radicals are atoms with electrons that are not in pairs; thus, they do not have an octet. Some people believe that these free radicals are responsible for cancer, the effects of aging, and the depletion of the ozone layer. What would cause these free radicals to be so environmentally dangerous?

Structure and properties of ionic compounds

15. Determine the ratio of cations to anions for the following compounds.
   a. strontium chloride, an ingredient in fireworks
   b. rubidium chloride, an ingredient in gasoline
   c. aluminum chloride, an ingredient in wood preservatives
   d. barium oxide, a substance used in making detergents for lubricating oils
   e. aluminum oxide, an ingredient in some dental cements
   f. aluminum nitride, a substance used in making semiconductors

16. Why do ionic compounds ordinarily have such high melting and boiling points?

17. Under the right conditions, ionic substances can conduct electricity very well. Describe these conditions, and explain why an ionic substance would be a poor choice as a conductor for a computer circuit board.

18. Does a cube of salt have a different unit cell than powdered salt? Explain your answer.

19. The electron configurations for a lithium atom is $1s^2 2s^1$. The configuration for an iodine atom is $1s^2 2s^2 2p^6 3s^2 3p^6 4s^2 3d^{10} 4p^6 5s^2 4d^{10} 5p^5$. Write the electron configurations for the ions that form lithium iodide, a substance used in photography.

20. Use the table below to identify the chemicals as ionic or non-ionic.

21. Label the drawings below as representing solid, liquid, or solution. State whether the substance pictured will or will not conduct electricity.

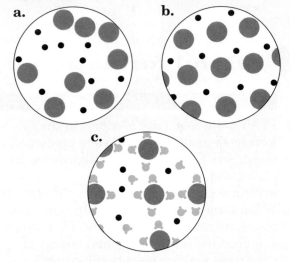

22. Sodium chloride can be prepared by reacting sodium metal with chlorine gas. Another way to prepare it is to combine sodium hydroxide and hydrochloric acid and allow any water present to evaporate. Will the method of preparation affect the unit cell and crystalline structure of NaCl?

23. Although metals and salts have similar lattice structures, metals make good materials for electrical wiring. Why aren't salts used instead?

24. The equations below show the energy changes that are necessary for calcium bromide, $CaBr_2$, to be formed from the elements calcium and bromine. Is formation of $CaBr_2$ an exothermic or endothermic process? Explain.

$$Ca(s) + 8.5 \text{ kJ} \longrightarrow Ca(g)$$

$$Ca(g) + 1735 \text{ kJ} \longrightarrow Ca^{2+}(g) + 2e^-$$

$$Br_2(g) + 193 \text{ kJ} \longrightarrow 2Br(g)$$

$$2Br(g) + 2e^- \longrightarrow 2Br^-(g) + 650 \text{ kJ}$$

$$Ca^{2+}(g) + 2Br^-(g) \longrightarrow CaBr_2(s) + 2176 \text{ kJ}$$

Substance	State at room temperature	Conducts electricity at room temperature	Melting point (°C)	Conducts electricity as a liquid
KI	solid	no	680	yes
Fe	solid	yes	1535	yes
$AlPO_4$	solid	no	1460	yes
CH_4	gas	no	−182.6	no
NaBr	solid	no	755	yes
$C_6H_{12}O_6$	solid	no	83	no

Formulas and nomenclature

25. Complete the table below, and then use it to answer the following questions.

Element	Ion	Name of ion
barium	Ba^{2+}	
chlorine		chloride ion
chromium	Cr^{3+}	
fluorine	F^-	
manganese		manganese(II) ion
oxygen		oxide ion

a. Give the formula for an ingredient of electrical batteries containing manganese and chlorine.

b. Give the formula for a compound containing chromium and fluorine used to treat silk.

c. Give the formula for a compound containing barium and oxygen used to manufacture lubricating oil detergents.

26. Why are there no rules for naming Group 18 ions?

27. Refer to **Table 5-7**. Explain the large break that appears between different ionization energies for different elements.

28. Why is the strontium nitrate found in roadside emergency flares represented as $Sr(NO_3)_2$ rather than SrN_2O_6?

29. What is the difference between the chlorite ion and the chlorate ion? (Hint: refer to **Table 5-8**)

30. Give the name, formula, and charge for the ions found in the following compounds.
a. $NaClO$ **b.** $(NH_4)_2CO_3$
c. K_2HPO_4 **d.** $CuCN$
e. FeC_2O_4 **f.** $MnC_2H_3O_2$
g. Hg_2SO_4

Answers to items in a black square begin on 841

31 Give formulas for the following compounds.
a. aluminum fluoride, used in ceramics
b. magnesium oxide, an antacid
c. calcium sulfide, used in luminous paints
d. strontium bromide, an anticonvulsant
  (Hint: see Sample Problem 5A.)

32. Give formulas for the following compounds.
a. cadmium(II) bromide, used in process engraving
b. palladium(II) chloride, used in some photographic toning solutions
c. vanadium(V) oxide, an ingredient in yellow glass
d. cobalt(II) sulfide, used as a catalyst
  (Hint: see Sample Problem 5A.)

33 Give formulas for the following compounds.
a. potassium hydrogen phosphate, an ingredient in nondairy creamers
b. strontium nitrate, an ingredient in red safety flares
c. lithium sulfate, an antidepressant
d. magnesium dihydrogen phosphate, used to make wood fireproof.
  (Hint: see Sample Problem 5B.)

34. Give formulas for the following compounds.
a. ammonium acetate, a meat preservative
b. mercury(I) nitrate, used to blacken brass
c. titanium(III) sulfate, used as a stain remover
d. chromium(III) phosphate, a green pigment
  (Hint: see Sample Problem 5B.)

35. Determine the subscripts that are most likely in the formulas for ionic substances of the following elements.
a. an alkali metal and a halogen
b. an alkaline-earth metal and a halogen
c. an alkali metal and a member of Group 16
d. an alkaline-earth metal and a member of Group 16

36. Use **Figure 5-12** to provide all possible formulas for the ionic compounds listed.
a. iron chloride   **b.** copper oxide
c. tin fluoride

37. Explain what is wrong with each of the following chemical formulas.
a. $RbCl_2$ **b.** $Ge_{12}S_{24}$ **c.** $NaCs$ **d.** $NaNe$

38. Explain the error contained in each of these descriptions of barium sulfide.
a. Ba_2S **b.** BaS_2 **c.** Ba_2S_2

39. How many atoms of each element are contained in a single formula unit of iron(III) formate, $Fe(CHO_2)_3 \cdot H_2O$, a compound used as a preservative in fodder?

Molar mass and percentage composition

40. When purifying metals from mined ores, why is it important to know the percentage composition of the ore?

41. Potassium chlorate, $KClO_3$, decomposes to give oxygen, O_2, and potassium chloride, KCl. How many grams of oxygen can be produced by the decomposition of 150. g of $KClO_3$? The percentage composition for $KClO_3$ is 28.93% Cl, 31.91% K, and 39.17% O.

42. What is the percentage composition of ammonium nitrate, NH_4NO_3, a common fertilizer?

43. How would you go about determining the formula for a compound containing only barium, sulfur, and oxygen?

44. Which of the following molar masses should be used in problems with hydrated copper sulfate, $CuSO_4 \cdot 5H_2O$?
  a. 159.62 g/mol   **b.** 177.64 g/mol
  c. 249.72 g/mol   **d.** 339.82 g/mol

45 What is the molar mass of barium carbonate? (Hint: see Sample Problem 5C.)

46. While working at a toothpaste factory, you are instructed to add 200. mol of SnF_2, an ingredient to prevent tooth decay, to a batch of product. If you know the molar mass of SnF_2, you can determine the number of grams needed. What is the molar mass of SnF_2? (Hint: see Sample Problem 5C.)

47 Iron pyrite, FeS_2, is a a shiny golden crystal often called fool's gold. What is the molar mass of iron pyrite?
(Hint: see Sample Problem 5C.)

48. Tin(IV) oxide, SnO_2, is the ingredient that gives fingernail polish its characteristic luster. What is the percentage composition of SnO_2? (Hint: see Sample Problem 5D.)

49 Some antacids use compounds of calcium, a mineral that is often lacking in the diet. What is the percentage composition of calcium carbonate, a common antacid ingredient? (Hint: see Sample Problem 5D.)

50. A superconductor has the formula $YBa_2Cu_3O_7$. What is the percentage composition of the substance? (Hint: see Sample Problem 5D.)

51 During winter vacation, you work at a ski resort covering icy sidewalks with a substance containing 26.2% N, 7.5% H, and 66.3% Cl. What is the formula for this compound? (Hint: see Sample Problem 5E.)

52. Magnetite is an iron ore with natural magnetic properties. It contains 72.4% Fe and 27.6% O. What is the formula for magnetite? (Hint: see Sample Problem 5E.)

53 Phosphorus forms two oxides. One has 56.34% P and 43.66% O. The other has 43.64% P and 56.36% O. What are the empirical formulas for these compounds? (Hint: see Sample Problem 5E.)

54. What percentage of hydrated cobalt(II) chloride, $CoCl_2 \cdot 6H_2O$, which is used as a humidity indicator, is $CoCl_2$? (Hint: see Sample Problem 5F.)

55 What percentage of blue-violet hydrated chromium(III) sulfate, $Cr_2(SO_4)_3 \cdot 18H_2O$, a paint pigment, is $Cr_2(SO_4)_3$? (Hint: see Sample Problem 5F.)

56. Soil in several regions has a reddish tinge due to the presence of iron in the form of limonite, $Fe_2O_3 \cdot 3/2 H_2O$. What percentage of limonite is water? (Hint: see Sample Problem 5F.)

57. Which iron ore has more pure iron per kilogram of ore, Fe_2O_3 or Fe_3O_4?

58. Which substance, anhydrous cobalt chloride, $CoCl_2$, or anhydrous magnesium chloride, $MgCl_2$, will absorb the most water per gram if both form a hexahydrate with six moles of water per mole of salt?

59. What percentage of ammonium carbonate, $(NH_4)_2CO_3$, an ingredient in smelling salts, is the ammonium ion, NH_4?

60. Which should yield a higher percentage of pure aluminum per gram, aluminum phosphate or aluminum chloride?

61. Aluminum chlorohydrate is an ingredient used in some antiperspirants. In its anhydrous form, it has 30.93% Al, 45.86% O, 20.32% Cl, and 2.89% H.
  a. What is the empirical formula for aluminum chlorohydrate ?
  b. Aluminum chlorohydrate forms a hydrated compound with 2.00 mol H_2O / 1.00 mol compound. What is the percentage composition of the hydrate?

Linking chapters

1. *Electron configurations*
   Scientists have been able to create fluoride compounds with the noble gases krypton and xenon. However, fluorine will not form compounds with helium or neon.
   a. Use the different electron configurations of the noble gases to explain why some can form compounds.
   b. Could fluorine form a compound with radon? Explain.

2. *Periodic trends*
   Use **Table 5-7** to predict trends of first, second, third, and fourth ionization energies for the following series of elements.
   a. K, Ca, Ga
   b. Li, Na, K
   c. Cs, Ba, Tl

USING TECHNOLOGY

1. *Graphics calculator*
   Ionic substances have high melting points. The periodic trends of melting points can be used to predict the properties of different substances. Press $\boxed{\text{WINDOW}}$ and set Xmin = 0, Xmax = 10, Xscl = 1, Ymin = 0, Ymax = 1000, and Yscl = 100. Press $\boxed{\text{STAT}}$ $\boxed{4}$ on your calculator and clear lists L_1 and L_2. Then press $\boxed{\text{STAT}}$ $\boxed{1}$ and enter the values 1, 2, 3, and 4 in L_1. Enter the following melting points in L_2: 712°C for $MgCl_2$, 772°C for $CaCl_2$, 868°C for $SrCl_2$, and 963°C for $BaCl_2$. Press $\boxed{\text{STAT}}$ $\boxed{\blacktriangleright}$ $\boxed{3}$ for two-variable statistics. Set Xlist = L_1, Ylist = L_2 and Freq = 1. Press $\boxed{\text{STAT}}$ $\boxed{\blacktriangleright}$ $\boxed{5}$ $\boxed{\text{ENTER}}$ $\boxed{\text{Y=}}$ $\boxed{\text{VARS}}$ $\boxed{5}$ $\boxed{\blacktriangleright}$ $\boxed{\blacktriangleright}$ $\boxed{7}$ to calculate a line for the data. Then press $\boxed{\text{ZOOM}}$ $\boxed{9}$ to display the graph. Press $\boxed{\text{TRACE}}$ and use the arrow keys to answer the following questions.
   a. What trend is displayed?
   b. $BeCl_2$ has a melting point of 405°C. Is this likely to be an ionic substance like the others? Explain.
   c. Predict the melting point of the ionic substance $RaCl_2$.

✓ Alternative assessment

Performance assessment

1. Your instructor will give you a notecard with one of the following formulas on it: $NaC_2H_3O_2 \cdot 3H_2O$, $MgCl_2 \cdot 6H_2O$, $LiC_2H_3O_2 \cdot 2H_2O$, and $MgSO_4 \cdot 7H_2O$. Design an experiment to determine the percentage of water by mass in the hydrated salt described by the formula. Be sure to explain what steps you will take to ensure that the salt is completely dry. If your teacher approves your design, obtain the salt. What percentage of water does it contain?

2. Devise a set of criteria that will allow you to classify the following substances as ionic or non-ionic: $CaCO_3$, Cu, H_2O, NaBr, and C (graphite). Show your criteria to your instructor. If it is approved, obtain some of the listed substances. Are these substances ionic or non-ionic?

Portfolio projects

1. *Research and communication*
   Create your own model of an ionic bond in the form of an analogy, picture, mechanical model, or computer program. Present your model to the class, and explain the ways in which your model does or does not match experimental observations.

2. *Chemistry and you*
   Ions play an important physiological role in your body. Select one such ion, and write a report detailing its function. Be sure to include recent medical information.

3. *Cooperative activity*
   Keep the ingredients labels from all of the food products you eat in one day. Make a list of all of the salts contained in each one. Compile a master list for the whole class, identifying which salts were eaten by the most people. Research the properties and uses of the salts that were most frequently eaten, and as a class, create an information poster describing the functions of these compounds.

4. *Research and communication*
   Many people follow low-sodium diets. However, they still desire a flavor enhancer like common table salt. Research the different types of salt substitutes and the physiological effects of each. Determine which is the safest salt substitute, and organize your information into a report.

6

Covalent Compounds

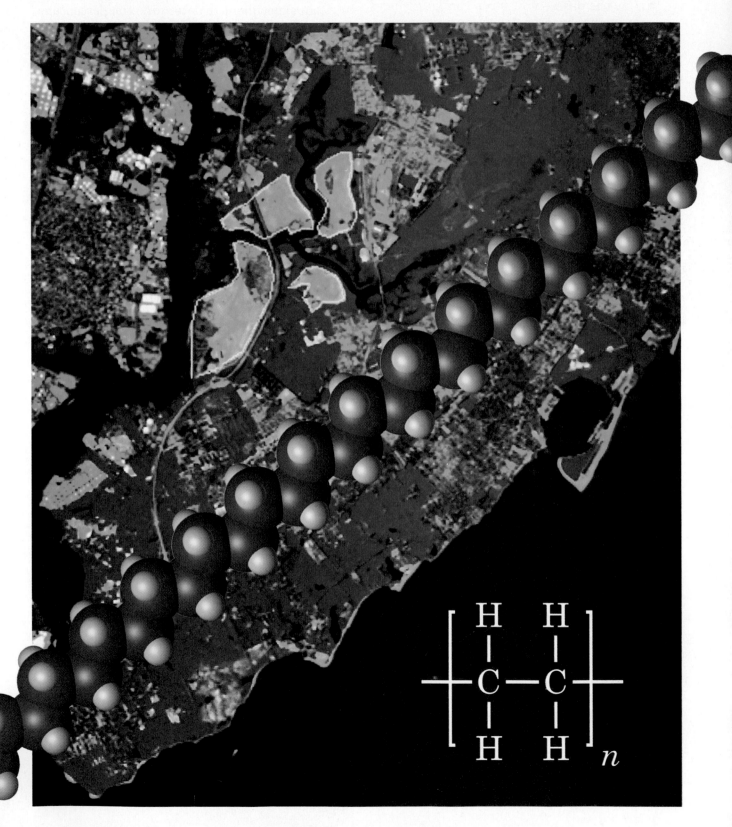

Molecular Bonds and Trash Bags

What is the largest structure ever made by humans? It's not the Great Wall of China, which extends for a total of 6300 km and can even be seen by astronauts at an altitude of 1000 km. It is actually the Fresh Kills landfill in Staten Island, New York, shown from a satellite, at left.

Although a landfill is not a structure in the same way as the Great Wall, this site does represent the largest collection of materials ever accumulated for a single purpose by humans. Begun in 1948 atop a swamp, the Fresh Kills landfill receives nearly 13 000 metric tons of garbage every day. As a result, it covers nearly 20 km^2 and holds 6.5×10^7 m^3 of refuse.

Eventually, it will tower over 130 m at its tallest point. If this much trash were stacked on a thousand football fields, it would pile up as high as a 21-story building.

Landfills such as Fresh Kills are so big because Americans produce a lot of garbage. Some studies have found that on average each American family of four produces 9 kg of garbage per day, or 3.5 metric tons per year. Even if the waste isn't hazardous, there are basically only three ways of dealing with all this garbage—burn it, recycle it, or bury it.

Burying garbage has been the most commonly used method since humans first started producing trash. But today, places to bury garbage are quickly filling up. Since 1978, some 14 000 landfills in the United States have been filled up and shut down. The opening of new landfills is not keeping pace with the closing of old ones. As populations increase, some communities face garbage crises, with nowhere to put their refuse.

Many people say that minimizing the amount of garbage produced is the best solution; that way, there would be less to bury. Moreover, the garbage that does get buried should be biodegradable so that microorganisms can break it down quickly once it's in a landfill. Biodegradable products would also take up less space as they decompose in landfills.

Trash bags have become a target in the search for biodegradable materials because Americans use a lot of them. For example, just raking all of the leaves from a single 23 m maple tree can fill 10 large plastic bags. But the plastic trash bags are made from polyethylene, a material that does not break down easily.

Chemically, this type of plastic consists of carbon and hydrogen atoms bonded together to form long chains, often as long as 7000 carbon-hydrogen units. These carbon-hydrogen units are very stable—they are hard to break.

Scientists are seeking ways to change polyethylene so that it will break down more easily in landfills, yet still hold up to daily use.

But before looking at how scientists are trying to accomplish this task, you need to understand how compounds such as plastics are built from individual atoms. Questions you will need to explore include the following.
- *What is the composition of the material currently being used in trash bags?*
- *How do bags labeled as biodegradable differ?*

Why do atoms share electrons?

6-1

Section
Objectives

Compare and contrast the properties of substances with covalent and ionic bonds.

Identify the forces acting on two covalently bonded atoms.

Explain the changes that occur in stability and energy as a covalent bond forms.

Use electronegativity values to determine the nature of a chemical bond.

Distinguish between intermolecular bonds and covalent and ionic bonds.

Comparing types of bonds

Hydrogen and oxygen are stable separately, but when combined, all it takes is a spark to create a violent explosion, as shown in **Figure 6-1**. Afterward, only tiny droplets of moisture are left. By applying some of what you learned in Chapter 5, you can explain much of what is happening in such an explosion.

You know that breaking bonds requires energy. The initial spark provides the energy to break the bonds that already exist in oxygen gas and hydrogen gas. But after that small input of energy, there is a huge release of energy, and a new product is formed—water. The release of energy suggests two things: first, new bonds are being formed as atoms are rearranged; and second, the product made by rearranging atoms, water, is lower in energy and more stable than the reactants, hydrogen and oxygen.

So far, this seems like the same situation as with ionic compounds described in Chapter 5, but water has very different properties than salts, as can be seen in **Table 6-1**. These different properties are shared by many other substances as well.

Figure 6-1a
Hydrogen is a colorless gas that is relatively stable on its own, . . .

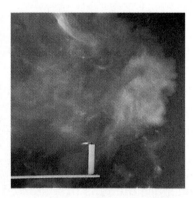

6-1b
. . . but in the presence of oxygen, a spark or small flame can cause an explosion, with the production of water.

Table 6-1
Properties of Salt, Water, Iodine, and Hydrogen

Substance	Physical state (at room temperature)	Melting point	Boiling point	Electrical conductivity
NaCl	solid	high (801°C)	high (1413°C)	high (when melted or dissolved)
H₂O	liquid	low (0°C)	low (100°C)	very low (for pure water)
I₂	solid	low (113.5°C)	low (184.3°C)	very low
H₂	gas	very low (−259.3°C)	very low (−252.8°C)	very low

Molecular compounds have covalent bonds

Based on the differences in **Table 6-1**, it seems that the bonds in water must be different from those in salt. Lower melting and boiling points for water suggest that the attractions among particles are weaker than those in salt. The fact that pure liquid water does not conduct much current suggests that there are few ions present. To explain the properties of compounds like water, iodine, and hydrogen (all of which have some similar properties), you need a new bonding model.

The properties of water can be explained by considering a bond made through electron sharing. In a **covalent bond**, atoms do not lose or gain electrons. Instead, they share pairs of electrons to achieve stability, often by filling their outer energy levels so that they have stable octets.

Can the covalent model explain why the properties of these compounds with covalent bonds differ so much from those with ionic bonds? Why are the melting and boiling points of molecular compounds so much lower than those of salts?

The force that holds together two atoms in a covalent bond can be as strong as the force between an individual cation and anion. However, in an iodine molecule, the two iodine atoms are covalently bonded only to each other and not to any other iodine atoms. Compare the structures of sodium chloride and iodine in **Figure 6-2**. Notice that even though iodine and salt are both solids, iodine exists as individual molecules, whereas NaCl exists as an extended crystal lattice. Each ion in the salt lattice is bonded to six adjacent ions. Because covalent compounds are often in the form of individual molecules, they are called **molecular compounds.**

covalent bond
bond formed when atoms share pairs of electrons

molecular compound
substance consisting of atoms that are covalently bonded

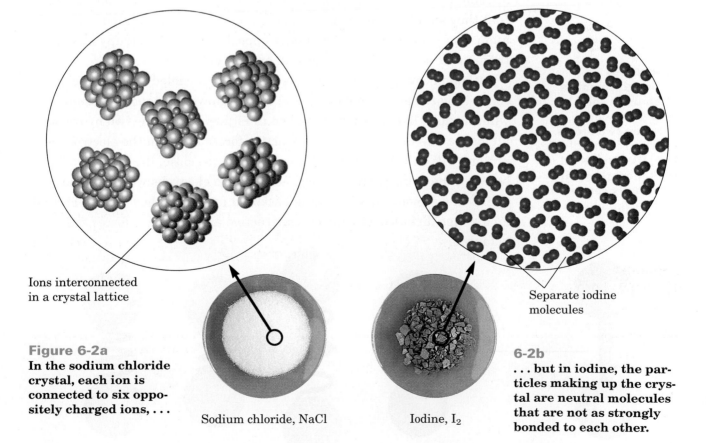

Ions interconnected in a crystal lattice

Figure 6-2a
In the sodium chloride crystal, each ion is connected to six oppositely charged ions, . . .

Sodium chloride, NaCl

Separate iodine molecules

6-2b
. . . but in iodine, the particles making up the crystal are neutral molecules that are not as strongly bonded to each other.

Iodine, I$_2$

Forces of electric attraction make a covalent bond

Why are atoms attracted and held together in a covalent bond? Consider all of the forces in the simplest covalent bond, that between two hydrogen atoms. An attractive force occurs between the electron on the first hydrogen atom and the proton on the second hydrogen atom. However, a repulsive force would also occur—the two electrons would repel each other, as would the two protons. At first, you might think that these attractive and repulsive forces would cancel each other, causing the two individual atoms to remain separate. But experiments have shown that most hydrogen exists as two atoms bonded together.

As you can see in **Figure 6-3**, the distance between two protons is greater than the distance between a proton and either electron. Similarly, the two electrons are each closer to the two protons than they are to each other. Consequently, there is an attraction between an electron of one atom and the proton of the second atom and another attraction between the first atom's proton and the second atom's electron. Taken together, the attractions are much greater than the repulsions between the two protons and between the two electrons. This net attraction holds the two hydrogen atoms together and is the basis of the covalent bond that forms between them.

Another reason that attractive forces between atoms can overcome the repulsive forces is that another factor besides charge becomes important. You learned in Chapter 3 that the two electrons sharing an orbital must have different values for the spin quantum number. For convenience, they are said to have opposite "spins," even though the term does not mean that they spin in opposite directions. A pair of electrons shared between atoms in a stable covalent bond have opposite spins and occupy less space than a pair of electrons in an orbital on only one atom.

Although covalent bonds are often drawn or modeled as rigid sticks connecting the atoms, a more useful model shows the bond to be somewhat flexible, like a spring, as shown in **Figure 6-4**. If the two hydrogen atoms start to move apart, the attractive forces between the electrons and protons will pull them back. If the atoms are too close, the repulsive forces between the two protons and between the two electrons will push them apart. The atoms actually vibrate back and forth, but they vibrate around an average distance, at which the attractive and repulsive forces are balanced.

Figure 6-3
When two hydrogen atoms come into contact, the particles within one atom attract and repel particles within the other atom. When these forces balance, a bond forms.

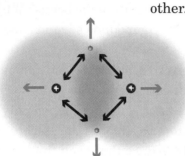

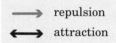

→ repulsion
↔ attraction

Figure 6-4
Although chemists often use a solid bar to represent a bond between two atoms, bonds are actually flexible. If compressed or stretched, they will eventually return to their original size.

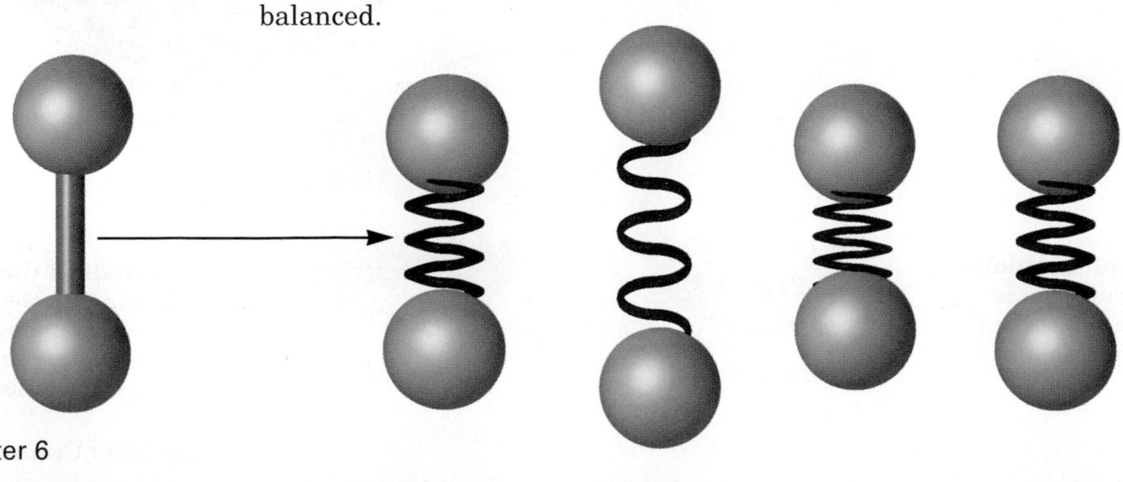

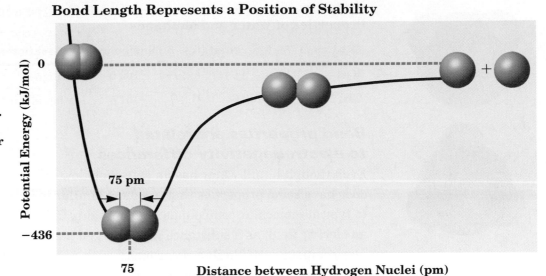

Figure 6-5
A bond forms when atoms are a certain distance from each other. At this distance, the atoms are in a low energy state. If they are closer together or farther apart, they will be in an unstable situation.

Bond Length Represents a Position of Stability

Potential Energy (kJ/mol)

0

75 pm

−436

75

Distance between Hydrogen Nuclei (pm)

Bond length and energy are inversely related

Another way to consider this model is to examine the potential energy levels for two hydrogen atoms at different distances, as shown in **Figure 6-5**. At what point on the graph do the two atoms have the most stability? This point, representing the lowest potential energy level on the graph, also represents the average distance between the two atoms when they are covalently bonded. Atoms that are farther apart than this distance tend to get closer because of the attractive forces, and atoms that are closer together than this distance tend to get farther apart because the repulsive forces grow stronger.

The two bonded atoms vibrate back and forth, but as long as their energy remains near this minimum potential energy level, they are covalently bonded to each other. The average distance that separates them is known as their **bond length.**

Because hydrogen atoms are more stable when bonded than when isolated, energy is released as the bond between them is formed. **Table 6-2** lists the bond lengths and bond energies for various atoms connected by covalent bonds. Keep in mind that bond lengths are never really fixed values because the atoms vibrate. Bond lengths can also vary depending on what other bonds are present in a molecule. The bond lengths listed in **Table 6-2** represent average values. Bond energy is the energy required to break a chemical bond to produce individual atoms, each keeping its own electrons.

Bond energy is the best indicator of the strength of the force of attraction in a bond. In general, the closer two atoms are, the greater the bond energy that is required to separate them, but there are exceptions to this rule. Large atoms usually have longer bond lengths and lower bond energies than smaller atoms. As a result, it is often easier to break a bond between two large atoms than between two small atoms.

Refer again to the graph shown in **Figure 6-5**. Trace the line on the graph that represents the separation of the two covalently bonded hydrogen atoms. Notice that 436 kJ of energy are needed to make a mole of hydrogen molecules so unstable that their bonds break.

bond length
average distance between the nuclei of two bonded atoms

Table 6-2
Average Bond Lengths and Energies

Bond	Length (pm)	Energy (kJ/mol)
H—H	75	436
H—C	109	418
H—Cl	127	432
H—Br	142	366
C—O	143	341
C—C	154	332
H—I	161	298
C—Cl	177	326
C—Br	194	276
Cl—Cl	199	243
Br—Br	229	193
I—I	266	151

Table 6-3
Properties of Water and Methane

Substance	Melting point (°C)	Boiling point (°C)	Reaction to electric field
H_2O	0.0	100.0	aligned
CH_4	−182.6	−161.4	not aligned

Bond properties are related to electronegativity differences

Even though liquid water has an extremely low electrical conductance, it does have some properties that are more similar to ionic compounds than to typical molecular compounds like methane, CH_4. Water will respond to an electric field, as a substance with charged particles will. Unlike molecular compounds of similar molar mass, such as methane, which has very low boiling and melting points, water remains a liquid for a much larger temperature range. See **Table 6-3**.

Once more, these properties can be explained by expanding the model used for bonding. Few chemical compounds are either totally *molecular* or totally *ionic*. These terms actually refer to the extremes at either end of a continuous spectrum of bonding. The bonds in many compounds, like water, have some features of both types of bonds. For example, even though electrons are shared between the hydrogen and oxygen atoms in a water molecule, they are not shared evenly. In each bond, the oxygen atom attracts the electrons much more than the hydrogen atom does. Because the electrons are unequally shared, the molecule behaves as if each oxygen atom has a partial negative charge, and each hydrogen atom has a partial positive charge.

To determine whether this uneven sharing will be very small or so large that the substance is made of fully charged ions, you can compare the atom's relative ability to pull electrons in a bond toward itself. You learned in Chapter 4 that electronegativity is a periodic property. The electronegativity table, **Table 6-4**, is an attempt to summarize observations and measurements of how strongly certain atoms attract electrons while in a covalent bond.

Table 6-4
Electronegativity Values

1 **H** 2.1																	
3 **Li** 1.0	4 **Be** 1.5											5 **B** 2.0	6 **C** 2.5	7 **N** 3.0	8 **O** 3.5	9 **F** 4.0
11 **Na** 0.9	12 **Mg** 1.2											13 **Al** 1.5	14 **Si** 1.8	15 **P** 2.1	16 **S** 2.5	17 **Cl** 3.0
19 **K** 0.8	20 **Ca** 1.0	21 **Sc** 1.3	22 **Ti** 1.5	23 **V** 1.6	24 **Cr** 1.6	25 **Mn** 1.5	26 **Fe** 1.8	27 **Co** 1.8	28 **Ni** 1.8	29 **Cu** 1.9	30 **Zn** 1.6	31 **Ga** 1.6	32 **Ge** 1.8	33 **As** 2.0	34 **Se** 2.4	35 **Br** 2.8
37 **Rb** 0.8	38 **Sr** 1.0	39 **Y** 1.2	40 **Zr** 1.4	41 **Nb** 1.6	42 **Mo** 1.8	43 **Tc** 1.9	44 **Ru** 2.2	45 **Rh** 2.2	46 **Pd** 2.2	47 **Ag** 1.9	48 **Cd** 1.7	49 **In** 1.7	50 **Sn** 1.8	51 **Sb** 1.9	52 **Te** 2.1	53 **I** 2.5
55 **Cs** 0.7	56 **Ba** 0.9	57 **La** 1.1	72 **Hf** 1.3	73 **Ta** 1.5	74 **W** 1.7	75 **Re** 1.9	76 **Os** 2.2	77 **Ir** 2.2	78 **Pt** 2.2	79 **Au** 2.4	80 **Hg** 1.9	81 **Tl** 1.8	82 **Pb** 1.8	83 **Bi** 1.9	84 **Po** 2.0	85 **At** 2.2
87 **Fr** 0.7	88 **Ra** 0.9	89 **Ac** 1.1															

0–0.9   1.0–1.9   2.0–2.9   > 2.9

Atoms with large electronegativity values, such as fluorine, chlorine, and oxygen, tend to attract electrons in a bond more strongly than atoms with low electronegativity values, such as sodium, magnesium, and lithium. The greater the difference in electronegativities between two atoms, the more ionic character the bond they form will have.

Consider cesium fluoride, CsF, as an example. The electronegativity value for Cs is 0.70; that for F is 4.00. The difference between these two electronegativity values is 3.30. **Figure 6-6** indicates that this bond has properties that are much more like those of ionic bonds, rather than those of covalent bonds. When the difference in electronegativities between two atoms in a bond is much greater than 2.1, the bond is classified as mostly ionic.

Next, consider the example of the bond formed between silicon and oxygen. Because oxygen has an electronegativity value of 3.5 and silicon's value is 1.8, the difference is 1.7. This difference places it near the threshold of being classified as an ionic bond. Use **Figure 6-6** to describe the nature of the bond between silicon and oxygen.

Figure 6-6
Differences in electronegativity can be used as a rough measure to predict the properties of the bond. In general, the greater the electronegativity differences, the more ionic properties the bond will have.

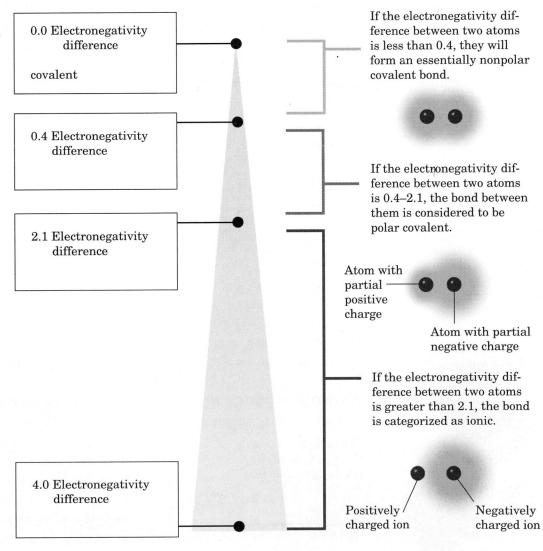

0.0 Electronegativity difference

covalent

0.4 Electronegativity difference

2.1 Electronegativity difference

4.0 Electronegativity difference

If the electronegativity difference between two atoms is less than 0.4, they will form an essentially nonpolar covalent bond.

If the electronegativity difference between two atoms is 0.4–2.1, the bond between them is considered to be polar covalent.

Atom with partial positive charge

Atom with partial negative charge

If the electronegativity difference between two atoms is greater than 2.1, the bond is categorized as ionic.

Positively charged ion

Negatively charged ion

Can you think of an example in which the difference in electronegativities between two atoms would be exactly zero? Obviously, when the two atoms that bond are of the same element, no difference in electronegativity exists. This means that both hydrogen atoms in a hydrogen molecule have an equal attraction for the electrons they share. When a covalent bond forms between two atoms with equally shared electrons, the bond is said to be a **nonpolar covalent bond.**

nonpolar covalent bond
covalent bond in which the bonding electrons are shared equally between the two bonding atoms

Covalent bonds with uneven electron sharing are polar

When atoms of different elements bond, the sharing can never be truly equal. As an example, consider carbon and oxygen. The oxygen atom, with an electronegativity of 3.5, will have a greater affinity for the electrons than will the carbon atom, with an electronegativity of 2.5. One of several reasons why is that the oxygen atom has more protons than the carbon atom, but they have an equal number of electron energy levels.

Because the attractive force for bonding electrons is not equal, the electrons will not be shared equally. When a covalent bond forms with unequally shared electrons, the bond is said to be a **polar covalent bond.** The uneven sharing causes the more electronegative atom to have a partial negative charge. The other atom will have a partial positive charge.

polar covalent bond
covalent bond in which the bonding electrons are more strongly attracted by one of the bonding atoms

Intermolecular forces
Weak attractions also form between molecules

All atoms and molecules attract each other. But the **intermolecular forces** between molecules or atoms are usually not as strong as covalent or ionic bonds because they *do not* involve transferring or sharing electrons. One good measure of the strength of intermolecular forces in a substance is the boiling point. The more strongly the particles are attracted, the higher the boiling point will be. For *nonpolar* substances, the attraction is a weak one, roughly in direct proportion to the number of electrons. The forces between nonpolar substances are called *London forces.*

intermolecular forces
attraction resulting from forces between molecules

If the molecules are *polar,* then there is an additional force because the positive end of one molecule attracts the negative end of a nearby molecule, and so on. This is called the *dipole force.* The more polar the molecule, the stronger the dipole force. The farther apart molecules are, the weaker the dipole force. Thus, large polar molecules which cannot get as close to each other tend to have a weaker force of attraction than smaller ones.

Hydrogen bonds are strong intermolecular forces

Water has many unique properties that are not shared by similar substances such as hydrogen sulfide, H_2S, as shown in **Table 6-5**. The much higher melting and boiling points shown for water indicate that water molecules have a particularly strong polar-polar attraction for each other, much stronger than the attractions between H_2S molecules.

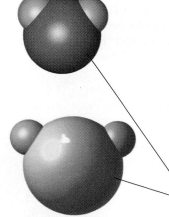

Table 6-5
Properties of Water and Hydrogen Sulfide

Substance	Melting point (°C)	Boiling point (°C)
H_2O	0.0	100.0
H_2S	−85.5	−60.3

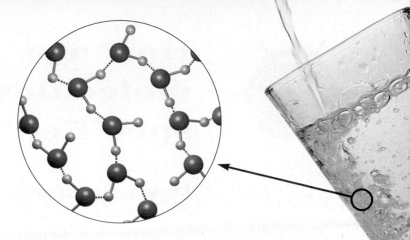

Figure 6-7
Many of water's unique properties are a result of the hydrogen bonds that form between different water molecules.

hydrogen bond
attraction occurring when a hydrogen atom bonded to a strongly electronegative atom is also attracted to another electronegative atom, often of a different molecule

These especially strong intermolecular forces are called **hydrogen bonds**. Hydrogen bonds can form when hydrogen, the smallest atom, is bonded within a molecule to fluorine, oxygen, or nitrogen (the smallest and most electronegative atoms). Because of the small size of the hydrogen atoms, the partial positive charge on the hydrogen atom of one molecule is able to come very close to the partial negative charge of a different electronegative atom, as shown in **Figure 6-7**. As with other bonds, the closer the opposite charges are to each other, the stronger the attraction between them is.

The name *hydrogen bond* is confusing because, like other intermolecular forces, these types of attraction are considerably weaker than chemical bonds between atoms. Hydrogen bonding is an important factor in many of the chemical reactions that make life possible. The DNA strands in your cells' genes are able to match up time and time again because of hydrogen bonds. Hydrogen bonding also enables enzymes to attract and latch onto the chemicals they change to make energy for life.

Section Review

1. Describe the attractive and repulsive forces that occur as two atoms are brought closer together.
2. What happens to the stability and energy of two atoms as they form a covalent bond?
3. List three differences between molecular and ionic compounds, and explain how they relate to the differences in bond types.
4. Use **Figure 6-6** and electronegativity values from **Table 6-4** to classify the bonds between the following.
   a. Cs and Br   **b.** H and S   **c.** Ca and O   **d.** Si and Cl
5. Compare the behavior of bonding electrons in a nonpolar covalent bond with that of bonding electrons in a polar covalent bond.

6. **Story Link**
   Recall that the chemical compound in plastic—polyethylene—consists of many units with carbon-hydrogen bonds. Use **Figure 6-6** and electronegativity values from **Table 6-4** to determine the type of these bonds.

6-2

How are molecules specified?

Section Objectives

Draw Lewis structures to show the arrangement of valence electrons among the atoms in a molecular compound.

Recognize exceptions to the octet rule and the limitations of Lewis structures.

Determine the oxidation number for each atom in a molecular compound.

Use both prefixes and Roman numerals to name molecular compounds.

Lewis structures

Electronegativity differences provide only limited information about the nature of a bond between two atoms. To develop a model that explains how some atoms combine, you can use dots to represent the **valence electrons** that are involved in bond formation.

Each hydrogen atom, with an electron configuration of $1s^1$, has only one valence electron. This valence electron is shown in **Figure 6-8**. The lone valence electron can also be represented by a single dot.

H·

Using a pair of dots to represent the pair of valence electrons shared in a bond, a hydrogen molecule would be drawn as follows.

H : H

Note that the two dots are placed between the two hydrogen atoms to indicate that they are shared by both atoms. Hydrogen does not share more than two electrons.

Next, consider a chlorine atom, with the electron configuration $1s^2 2s^2 2p^6 3s^2 3p^5$, as shown in **Figure 6-9**. Chlorine has 17 electrons, but 2 electrons are in the first energy level, and 8 are in the second energy level. The 7 electrons in the third and outermost energy level are the valence electrons. Thus, a structure for chlorine can be drawn as follows.

: C̈l ·

If there are two chlorine atoms, each would need just one additional electron to satisfy the octet rule. Neither can take an electron from the other, so they share. These atoms can achieve stability by sharing a pair of electrons to form a covalent bond as shown.

: C̈l : C̈l :

Identify the two dots that represent the pair of electrons that are shared. Notice that each chlorine atom also has electrons that are not part of the bond; they are called **unshared pairs.** How many unshared pairs does each chlorine atom have?

The use of these pairs of dots to indicate shared and unshared pairs makes it easier to check whether an atom has a stable octet. If the symbol is surrounded by an unshared or shared pair on the left, top, right, and bottom, the atom represented has a stable octet.

---

valence electron
electron present in the outermost energy level of an atom

Figure 6-8
A hydrogen atom and its single valence electron can be represented by the letter *H* and a dot.

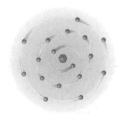

Figure 6-9
A chlorine atom has 17 electrons, 7 of which are valence electrons. The chlorine nucleus and the inner 10 electrons can be represented by the symbol Cl. The 7 valence electrons can be represented by 7 dots.

unshared pair
pair of electrons that is not involved in covalent bonding, but instead belongs exclusively to one atom

When drawing electron-dot diagrams, the pair of dots representing a shared pair or covalent bond can also be shown by a long dash, representing a **single bond**.

single bond
sharing of one pair of electrons between two atoms

$$H : H \qquad H — H$$

$$: \overset{..}{\underset{..}{Cl}} : \overset{..}{\underset{..}{Cl}} : \qquad : \overset{..}{\underset{..}{Cl}} — \overset{..}{\underset{..}{Cl}} :$$

Lewis structure
diagram showing the arrangement of valence electrons among the atoms in a molecule

A **Lewis structure** represents a chemical formula: the nuclei and inner-shell electrons are represented by the element's atomic symbol, and covalent bonds are represented by pair of dots or by dashes. Unshared pairs are represented by pairs of dots adjacent to only one atomic symbol. Lewis structures, which can be drawn for either ionic or molecular compounds, can help you understand how atoms engage in bonds.

How To
Draw Lewis structures

1. **Determine the total number of valence electrons in the compound.**
   This involves nothing more than adding the valence electrons of each atom. Consider the example of HCl. By now, you should realize that hydrogen has one valence electron, while chlorine has seven.

   Total number of valence electrons: $1 + 7 = 8$

2. **Arrange the atoms' symbols to show how they are bonded and show valence electrons as dots.**
   Be sure to distribute the paired dots so that the octet rule is followed, except in the case of hydrogen.

   $$: \overset{..}{\underset{..}{Cl}} : H$$

3. **Compare the number of valence electrons used in the structure to the number available from step 1.**
   There are two electrons in the covalent bond and six around the chlorine atom that are not shared.

   Total number of electrons shown: $2 + 6 = 8$

4. **Change to a single dash each pair of dots that represents two shared electrons.**

   $$: \overset{..}{\underset{..}{Cl}} — H$$

5. **Be sure that all atoms, with the exception of hydrogen, follow the octet rule.**
   The hydrogen atom has two valence electrons, and the chlorine atom is surrounded by eight valence electrons. The octet rule is satisfied.

Lewis structures can involve many atoms

When drawing a Lewis structure for a molecule with more than two atoms, you must first decide how to arrange the atoms. Keep in mind the following guidelines.

- Hydrogen and halogen atoms usually bond to only one other atom in a molecule and are usually on the outside or end of a molecule.
- The atom with the smallest electronegativity is often the central atom.
- When a molecule contains more atoms of one element than the others, these atoms often surround the central atom.

Sample Problem 6A
Lewis structures

Draw the Lewis structure for iodomethane, CH_3I.

❶ Calculate the total number of valence electrons

1 C atom with 4 electrons = $1 \times 4 = 4$
3 H atoms with 1 electron = $3 \times 1 = 3$
1 I atom with 7 electrons = $1 \times 7 = \underline{7}$
14 valence electrons

❷ Arrange the atoms

- **Follow the guidelines to determine the central atom.** It is most likely that carbon is in the middle of the structure.

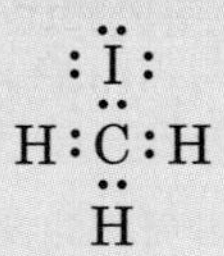

$$
\begin{array}{c}
:\overset{\displaystyle ..}{\underset{\displaystyle ..}{I}}: \\
H:\overset{\displaystyle }{\underset{\displaystyle ..}{C}}:H \\
H
\end{array}
$$

❸ Compare the number of electrons used with the number of valence electrons available

- All of the 14 available valence electrons were used.

$7 \times 2 = 14$ electrons

❹ Change dots to dashes where appropriate

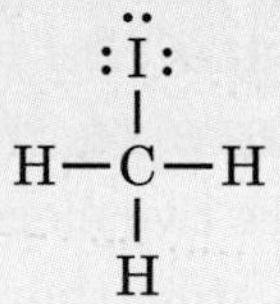

$$
\begin{array}{c}
:\overset{\displaystyle ..}{I}: \\
| \\
H-C-H \\
| \\
H
\end{array}
$$

❺ Check to see that the octet rule has been followed

Practice 6A

Answers for Concept Review items and Practice problems begin on page 841.

1. Draw the Lewis structures for iodine monochloride, ICl, and hydrogen bromide, HBr.

2. Try drawing the Lewis structures for dichloromethane, CH_2Cl_2, and methanol, CH_3OH.

3. Draw a Lewis structure for cyclohexane, C_6H_{12}. (Hint: the carbon atoms form a six-membered ring.)

Figure 6-10
Astronomers believe that liquid ethane, C_2H_6, covers the surface of Titan, Saturn's largest moon.

Two atoms can share more than one electron pair

Because carbon has four valence electrons in its outermost energy level, it can form bonds with up to four atoms to satisfy the octet rule. In the molecule of ethane, C_2H_6, shown in **Figure 6-10**, each carbon atom has bonded with another carbon atom and three hydrogen atoms. Each hydrogen atom is bonded to a carbon atom and shares one pair of electrons with the carbon atom.

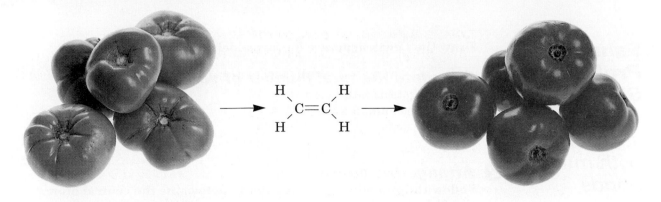

Figure 6-11a
Ethene, C_2H_4, also called ethylene, is a hormone found in most plants. Tomatoes release ethylene as they ripen.

6-11b
In turn, this ethylene causes other tomatoes to ripen more quickly. The produce industry uses ethylene as a ripening agent because often fruit must be picked before it is ripe for shipping purposes.

double bond
covalent bond formed by the sharing of two pairs of electrons between two atoms

triple bond
covalent bond formed by the sharing of three pairs of electrons between two atoms

Figure 6-12a
Spelunkers exploring caves often use carbide lamps. In these lamps, calcium carbide, CaC_2, reacts with water to form ethyne, C_2H_2.

In addition to carbon, other elements, including, nitrogen, oxygen, and occasionally sulfur, can share more than one pair of electrons with other atoms to satisfy the octet rule. For example, if two carbon atoms share two pairs of electrons (four electrons total) instead of just one pair, a double covalent bond or **double bond** can form. The molecule of ethene shown in **Figure 6-11** consists of two carbon atoms that have formed a double bond and four hydrogen atoms.

Two carbon atoms are also able to share three pairs of electrons. The molecule with two carbon atoms that have formed a **triple bond** and two hydrogen atoms is called ethyne, shown in **Figure 6-12**. Although the names for ethane, ethene, and ethyne may not seem very different, the substances have very different Lewis structures, characteristics, and uses. Nitrogen also can form triple bonds, as in nitrogen gas, N_2, and hydrogen cyanide, HCN.

If no arrangement of single bonds provides an appropriate Lewis structure, it could be that the molecule contains multiple bonds. Sample Problem 6B shows how to deal with such molecules.

$$H-C\equiv C-H$$

6-12b
When burned in air, ethyne, also called acetylene, produces a bright white flame.

Sample Problem 6B
Lewis structures with multiple bonds

Draw the Lewis structure for formaldehyde, CH_2O.

❶ Calculate the total number of valence electrons

2 H atoms with 1 electron = 2
1 C atom with 4 electrons = 4
1 O atom with 6 electrons = 6

12 valence electrons

❷ Arrange the atoms
- Follow the guidelines given earlier to determine the central atom.

It is most likely that carbon is in the middle of the structure. Place the other atoms around carbon. It seems like it would be easy to add shared and unshared pairs as shown, but it is important to check this approach.

$$H:\ddot{\underset{\cdot\cdot}{C}}:\ddot{\underset{\cdot\cdot}{O}}:$$
$$H$$

❸ Compare the number of electrons used to the number of valence electrons available
- electrons used: 14
- valence electrons available: 12

Obviously, something is wrong with this Lewis structure. Two electrons must be eliminated without violating the octet rule. *Whenever too many electrons have been used, try connecting atoms with a double bond or other multiple bond.*

In this case, by removing two unshared electrons from both the carbon and oxygen atoms and by forming a double covalent bond between carbon and oxygen, only 12 electrons are used. Now the number used equals the number available.

$$H:\underset{\cdot\cdot}{C}::\underset{\cdot\cdot}{O}:$$
$$H$$

- electrons used: 12
- valence electrons available: 12

❹ Change dots to dashes where appropriate
- Carbon forms two single bonds and one double bond, for a total of four covalent bonds.

$$H-C=\ddot{\underset{\cdot\cdot}{O}}:$$
$$|$$
$$H$$

❺ Check to see that the octet rule is not violated
Remember that the double bond represents four electrons shared by carbon and oxygen. As a result, the octet rule has been followed.

Practice 6B

1. Draw the Lewis structures for the following molecules.
   a. carbon dioxide, CO_2 b. tetrachloroethene, C_2Cl_4
   c. nitrogen, N_2 d. hydrogen cyanide, HCN

2. Benzene, C_6H_6, contains a ring of six carbon atoms. Draw one possible Lewis structure for benzene.

3. Benzoic acid, C_6H_5COOH, contains a benzene ring, but one of the hydrogen atoms has been replaced with a —COOH group. Draw a Lewis structure for benzoic acid.

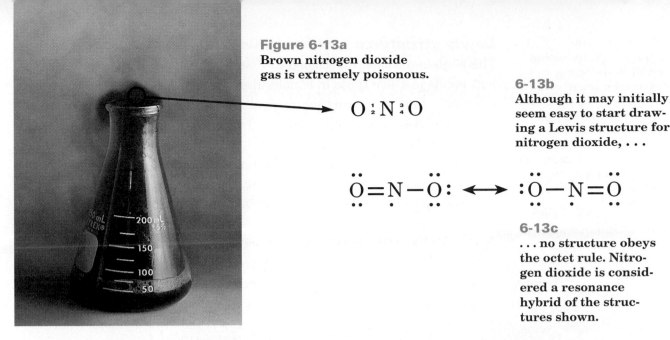

Figure 6-13a
Brown nitrogen dioxide gas is extremely poisonous.

$$O : N : O$$

6-13b
Although it may initially seem easy to start drawing a Lewis structure for nitrogen dioxide, . . .

$$\ddot{O} = N - \ddot{O} : \longleftrightarrow : \ddot{O} - N = \ddot{O}$$

6-13c
. . . no structure obeys the octet rule. Nitrogen dioxide is considered a resonance hybrid of the structures shown.

Sometimes no single Lewis structure is correct

At some point you may come across a molecule like NO_2, as shown in **Figure 6-13a**, which has 17 valence electrons. As shown in **Figure 6-13b**, you can arrange the 3 atoms and 4 of the electrons with no trouble. However, no matter how you try, the 13 remaining electrons cannot be placed so that each atom has 8 valence electrons, even if you use double bonds. Instead, you get two equivalent structures.

In each of the structures shown in **Figure 6-13c**, a single electron is left unpaired on the nitrogen atom, which does not have a stable octet. Since there were an odd number of electrons to begin with, this situation is unavoidable. From Chapter 3 you know that, ordinarily, atoms have paired electrons. Atoms with unpaired electrons are somewhat unstable, although they can exist. Similarly, situations without an octet are unstable, but they too are possible. *Before such a rule-breaking structure is considered accurate, either an octet must be impossible, or experimental measurements must indicate that a non-octet structure is more likely.*

Note also that the double bond is on the left in one of the structures in **Figure 6-13c** and on the right in the other. The fact that the two structures are equally likely indicates that neither structure alone is correct. This is not uncommon. Even some other molecules that obey the octet rule can have several possible Lewis structures, each of which is equally likely.

Such molecules are evidence that Lewis structures are merely models that cannot accurately portray all cases. When more than one Lewis structure for a molecule can be drawn, the molecule is said to be a *resonance hybrid.* Originally, chemists believed that the molecule resonated between the different structures, like a plucked guitar string vibrating back and forth. Now, however, chemists treat the molecule as if it had a structure that was the *average* of these structures. Measurements show that in NO_2, the N—O bonds are identical, with bond lengths between those of single and double bonds. The fact that the NO_2 molecule has an odd electron is evidence of an important rule: molecules that exhibit resonance are more stable than one would predict from each of the contributing Lewis structures.

Chem Fact
Nitrogen dioxide, NO_2, is a compound that gives smog its brownish color. The presence of an unpaired electron is one factor contributing to its reactivity.

Figure 6-14a

An ammonium cation is formed when a hydrogen ion is combined with an ammonia molecule. Smelling salts often contain an ionic compound composed of an ammonium cation and a carbonate anion.

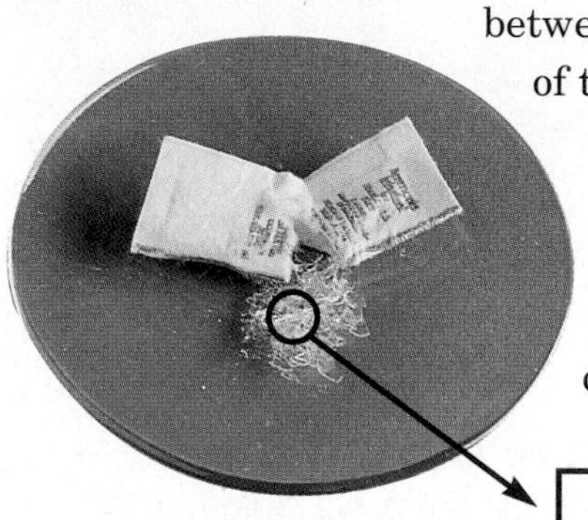

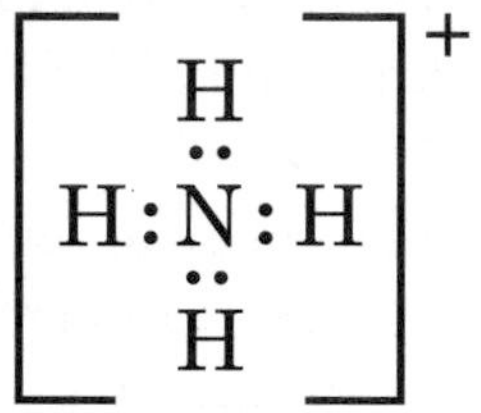

6-14b

The brackets around the Lewis structure of a polyatomic ion, such as ammonium, indicate that the ion has a charge, in this case a positive one.

Chem Fact
In 1993, more than 16 billion kg of ammonia were produced in the United States, mostly for use in fertilizers. Ammonia ranks sixth among the most-produced chemicals.

Lewis structures can be drawn for polyatomic ions

The polyatomic ions you studied in Chapter 5 are held together by covalent bonds just like those in a molecular compound. The only difference in drawing a Lewis structure for a polyatomic ion is that you must alter the number of electrons to reflect the total charge of the polyatomic ion.

The ammonium cation, which is contained in the smelling salts shown in **Figure 6-14**, is prepared from an ammonia molecule and a hydrogen ion, which is only a proton. In this case, a covalent bond is formed between the hydrogen ion and the unshared pair on the nitrogen atom of the ammonia molecule.

Unlike other bonds, in which each atom provides one electron to a pair that is later shared, the nitrogen atom provides both of the electrons that form one of the four covalent bonds in NH_4^+. This special type of bond is called a *coordinate covalent bond*. Once the coordinate covalent bond is formed, it is indistinguishable from the other covalent bonds in the ammonium cation even though the nitrogen atom contributed both of the shared electrons.

$$\left[\begin{array}{c} H \\ H : N : H \\ H \end{array} \right]^+$$

In Lewis structures for polyatomic ions, brackets are put around the polyatomic ion to indicate that the charge is for the polyatomic ion as a whole, not for a specific atom.

If you check the periodic table, you'll see that nitrogen normally has five valence electrons, while each hydrogen usually has only one valence electron to contribute in forming a bond. This equals nine electrons. But since the charge on the polyatomic cation is 1+, it must be missing one of these nine electrons.

For *cations,* the positive charge is due to a smaller number of electrons, so you must *subtract* the charge from the count of electrons. For *anions,* the negative charge is due to additional electrons, so you must *add* the charge to the number of electrons.

1 N atom with 5 valence electrons:	$1 \times 5 =$	5 electrons
4 H atoms with 1 valence electron each:	$4 \times 1 =$	+ 4 electrons
total electrons (if a neutral substance):		9 electrons
charge of 1+ means 1 less electron:		−1 electron
total electrons for the polyatomic cation:		8 electrons

The calculated number, eight electrons, matches the eight electrons shown in the Lewis structure for the ammonium ion in **Figure 6-14b**.

Concept Review

Resonance and polyatomic ions

7. Try drawing two resonance hybrid structures for SO_2.
8. Draw the Lewis structures for ClO_3^- and SO_4^{2-}.
9. Draw two of the resonance structures for CO_3^{2-}.

Answers for Concept Review items and Practice problems begin on page 841.

Naming molecular compounds

Although there are several steps to writing the Lewis structures for molecular compounds, naming a compound is relatively straightforward, especially for compounds made of only two elements. Such compounds can be named in one of two ways, both of which are similar to the methods used to name the salts that were described in Chapter 5, as shown in **Figure 6-15**.

Figure 6-15
Chemists had to invent a system for naming compounds that symbolically portrayed both the similarities and the differences in compounds such as these.

$$P_2O_3$$

diphosphorus **tri**oxide
phosphorus(III) oxide

$$P_2O_5$$

diphosphorus **pent**oxide
phosphorus(V) oxide

Table 6-6
Prefixes for Naming

Prefix	Number of atoms
mono-	1
di-	2
tri-	3
tetra-	4
penta-	5
hexa-	6
hepta-	7
octa-	8
nona-	9

One naming system uses prefixes, roots, and suffixes

Chemists often name molecular compounds using the system of prefixes shown in **Table 6-6**. Prefixes and suffixes are usually attached to root words of the elements in a compound. For example, the two oxides of carbon, CO and CO_2, are named carbon monoxide and carbon dioxide, respectively. The first element named is usually the one with the lowest electronegativity value. The first word in the compound name is the first element's name. If the molecule contains only one atom of the first element given in the formula, the prefix *mono-* is omitted in naming that element. For example, no prefix is used with carbon in either compound. The root *oxy-* is given the *-ide* ending, just as for anions in an ionic compound. A prefix is used to tell you how many oxygen atoms each compound has.

The Stock system of naming uses oxidation numbers

Another way to name molecular compounds resembles the Stock system. Using the method from Chapter 5, Cu^+ ions form copper(I) chloride, $CuCl$, while Cu^{2+} ions form copper(II) chloride, $CuCl_2$.

Covalently bonded atoms *do not* give and take electrons but rather *share* them, so these atoms do not obtain full positive or negative charges like ions do. However, because the sharing is often unequal, the atom with the greatest attraction for electrons will pull the shared electrons toward itself, giving it a fractional negative charge. The atom that has less of an attraction for the electrons will have a slight positive charge. However, now we act as if the entire charge has been transferred. This charge is known as the **oxidation number** of the atom and can be used in naming the molecular compound.

oxidation number
apparent charge assigned to an atom based on the assumption of complete transfer of electrons

Oxidation numbers can also be used as tools for analyzing reduction-oxidation reactions, a special type of chemical reaction that will be studied further in Chapter 15. For now, learning a little about how to assign oxidation numbers will help you name and identify molecular compounds.

Figure 6-16a

To balance the –2 oxidation number of the oxygen atom in carbon monoxide, the carbon atom must have an oxidation number of +2.

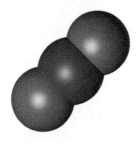

6-16b

In CO_2, the oxidation number of oxygen is also –2. Because there are two oxygen atoms in each molecule, this carbon atom must have an oxidation number of +4.

Determining oxidation numbers from a formula

When most atoms bond with oxygen, the oxygen atom attracts the shared pair of electrons more strongly than the other atoms do. These two electrons, along with their negative charges, spend most of the time near the oxygen atom. *As a result, oxygen is usually assigned an oxidation number of −2.* Similarly, hydrogen atoms do not have a high electronegativity, and the electron they donate in bonding usually spends most of the time around the other atom in the bond. *Thus, hydrogen is usually assigned an oxidation number of +1.* Other atoms tend to have oxidation numbers similar to the charges they have when in ionic compounds because that is often the number needed to complete an octet. The element with the higher electronegativity will have a negative oxidation number. For example, in NH_3, N is −3 and H is +1.

Before using Roman numerals to name a molecular compound, you need to determine the oxidation number for each atom. This can be tricky because some elements can have more than one oxidation number, depending on the other atoms in the compound. *The sum of the oxidation numbers in a neutral compound must equal zero. For a polyatomic ion, the sum must be equal to the charge on the ion.* Using this knowledge and the rules of thumb for the oxidation numbers of hydrogen, oxygen, and the halogens, you can predict the oxidation numbers of most other atoms in a compound or polyatomic ion.

As an example, consider CO and CO_2, the molecules shown in **Figure 6-16**. Using Roman numerals to represent the oxidation numbers, CO could be named carbon(II) oxide, and CO_2 could be named carbon(IV) oxide. But like many common covalent compounds, CO and CO_2 are usually named using the prefix method—carbon monoxide and carbon dioxide.

Section Review

10. Write the number of valence electrons for atoms with the following electron configurations.
    a. $1s^2 2s^2$ **b.** $1s^2 2s^2 2p^6 3s^2 3p^4$ **c.** $1s^2 2s^2 2p^6 3s^2 3p^5$
11. Draw Lewis structures for the following.
    a. bromine, Br_2 **b.** ozone, O_3
    c. sulfur trioxide, SO_3 **d.** hydronium ion, H_3O^+
12. Using the system of prefixes, name the following molecular compounds.
    a. SiO_2 **b.** SO_2 **c.** CF_4 **d.** N_2O_3
13. Give the oxidation numbers of each atom in the following compounds.
    a. PBr_5 **b.** PBr_3 **c.** H_2SO_4 **d.** SO_3 **e.** CCl_4
14. Write formulas for the following compounds.
    a. dinitrogen tetroxide **b.** phosphorus trichloride
    c. dinitrogen pentoxide

15. **Story Link**
    Try drawing the Lewis structure of the $C_{12}H_{26}$ molecule, which is like a fragment of polyethylene. The carbon atoms form the "backbone" of this compound. Visualize what 7000 carbon-hydrogen units might look like. This may help you understand why plastic does not break down very easily.

6-3

How are formulas represented?

Section Objectives

Given composition data, determine the empirical and molecular formulas of a molecular compound.

Given the molecular formula, determine the structural formula for a molecular compound.

Empirical formulas

How many different ways could you describe what happened at a basketball game? You could tell someone the final score, give a detailed scoring history for the game, or even videotape it. Any one of these ways would give someone an idea of what the game was like. Each way, though, would provide the person with different information.

How many different ways could you describe the glucose in the sports drink that the basketball player in **Figure 6-17** is drinking? You may not think there are as many ways to describe a simple molecular compound as there are to describe a basketball game, but chemists do have a number of ways to represent a molecule. Moreover, each way provides different information about the molecule. You have seen two possible ways to represent a molecule—Lewis structures and chemical formulas.

In fact, chemists can write the formula for the same molecular compound in various ways. The simplest formula, or *empirical formula,* consists of the symbols for the elements combined with subscripts showing the smallest whole-number ratio of the atoms. For example, CH_2O is the empirical formula for glucose, $C_6H_{12}O_6$. Formulas for ionic compounds are really empirical formulas showing the smallest whole-number ratio of ions.

Figure 6-17a
The formula for the glucose molecule found in this sports drink . . .

$$C_6H_{12}O_6$$
$$(CH_2O)_6$$

6-17b
. . . can be shown a number of different ways.

Empirical formulas are determined experimentally

Chemists sometimes have to determine the empirical formula for a compound recently discovered in nature. Similarly, after chemists synthesize a new compound, they often analyze it to obtain its empirical formula and check their work. They do this by analyzing composition data to determine what elements are present and their percentage by mass, just as was discussed in Chapter 5. By translating these mass percentages into mole ratios, chemists can determine the empirical formula for the compound, as shown in Sample Problem 6C on the next page.

Sample Problem 6C

Calculating empirical formulas from percentage composition

Chemical analysis of 2-propanol, also known as isopropanol or rubbing alcohol, indicates that it is 60.0% C, 13.4% H, and 26.6% O. What is its empirical formula?

❶ List what you know
- **60.0% C means:** 60.0 g C in every 100. g of compound
- **13.4% H means:** 13.4 g H in every 100. g of compound
- **26.6% O means:** 26.6 g O in every 100. g of compound
- **molar mass for C:** 12.00 g/1 mol C
- **molar mass for H:** 1.01 g/1 mol H
- **molar mass for O:** 16.00 g/1 mol O

❷ Set up conversion from mass to moles
- To convert mass to moles, multiply by the reciprocal of the molar mass to cancel *g*, leaving *mol* in the numerator. Remember to follow significant figure rules.

$$60.0 \text{ g C} \times \frac{1 \text{ mol C}}{12.00 \text{ g C}} = 5.00 \text{ mol C}$$

$$13.4 \text{ g H} \times \frac{1 \text{ mol H}}{1.01 \text{ g H}} = 13.26732673 \text{ mol H} = 13.3 \text{ mol H}$$

$$26.6 \text{ g O} \times \frac{1 \text{ mol O}}{16.00 \text{ g O}} = 1.6625 \text{ mol O} = 1.66 \text{ mol O}$$

At this point, the formula could be written as $C_5H_{13.3}O_{1.66}$, but empirical formulas have whole numbers for subscripts.

❸ Compare amounts of each element in moles
- **The empirical formula is the simplest whole-number mole ratio of the atoms. Divide the moles of each element by the moles of the element with the smallest amount to find a whole-number ratio.**

1.66 is the smallest value.

$$\frac{1.66 \text{ mol O}}{1.66} = 1.00 \text{ mol of O}$$

$$\frac{5.00 \text{ mol C}}{1.66} = 3.012048193 \text{ mol C} = 3.01 \text{ mol of C.}$$

$$\frac{13.3 \text{ mol H}}{1.66} = 8.012048193 \text{ mol H} = 8.01 \text{ mol of H.}$$

For every 1.00 mol of O, there are 3.01 mol of C and 8.01 mol of H.

The formula contains atoms in this ratio: 1 O : 3 C : 8 H.

- **The empirical formula for isopropanol must be C_3H_8O.**

Often, the numbers do not always divide out perfectly because of slight errors of measurement or rounding, but they are usually close enough for a reasonable guess.

❹ Verify your work
- Use the empirical formula and molar masses to calculate the percentage composition of a single mole of isopropanol. Does it match the values from the problem?

Practice 6C

1. What is the empirical formula of a compound that contains 26.56% potassium, 35.41% chromium, and 38.03% oxygen?

2. Determine the empirical formula for a compound that contains 5.717 g of O and 4.433 g of P.

3. What would be the empirical formula for a compound that contains 32.38% sodium, 22.65% sulfur, and 44.99% oxygen?

Molecular formulas

molecular formula
gives type and actual number of atoms in a chemical compound

Empirical formulas can be compared to the score of a basketball game. They just give you an idea of what is in the compound by indicating the simplest whole-number ratio of atoms. But they do not tell you exactly how many atoms of each element are present in a molecule of the compound. For that information, you would need a **molecular formula.** A molecular formula can be compared to a detailed scoring history of the game. Just as a play-by-play will give you a better idea of which players scored the most baskets, the molecular formula will give you a better idea of the molecule's properties based on exactly how many of each atom there will be in a molecule.

With some compounds, the empirical formula is the same as the molecular formula. Such is the case with water, H_2O. But for most compounds, the two formulas are not the same. Consider the three molecular compounds in **Table 6-7**. The first compound is toxic and causes cancer. The second gives vinegar its sour taste. The third is a type of sugar found in sports drinks and other foods. All three compounds have the same empirical formula, CH_2O, but because each has a different molecular formula, they each have very different properties.

Chem Fact
Formaldehyde, CH_2O, is used as a disinfectant, for hardening photographic gels and plates, to improve dyeing on fabrics, and to make polymers.

Molecular formulas are determined from molar mass

Notice that in **Table 6-7** the molecular formulas are multiples of the empirical formulas.

$$x \text{ (empirical formula)} = \text{molecular formula}$$

Note that x can be any whole number. For formaldehyde, x is 1; for acetic acid, x is 2; and for glucose, x is 6. A similar relationship exists between the molar masses of the empirical formula and that of the compound. If you know both the empirical formula mass and the molecular formula mass, you can determine the number by which you must multiply the empirical formula to get the molecular formula for a compound.

$$\frac{\text{molecular formula mass}}{\text{empirical formula mass}} = x$$

Table 6-7
Comparing Empirical and Molecular Formulas

Compound	Empirical formula	Molecular formula	Molar mass (g)	Representation
formaldehyde	CH_2O	CH_2O (1 times empirical formula)	30.03	
acetic acid	CH_2O	$C_2H_4O_2$ (2 times empirical formula)	60.06	
glucose	CH_2O	$C_6H_{12}O_6$ (6 times empirical formula)	180.18	

The empirical formula of a compound containing phosphorus and oxygen was found to be P_2O_5. Experiments show that the molar mass of the compound is 283.89 g/mol. What is the molecular formula of the compound?

❶ List what you know

- empirical formula: P_2O_5
- molar mass of unknown compound = 283.89 g/mol
- 1 mol P = 30.97 g P
- 1 mol O = 16.00 g O
- Determine the formula mass for the empirical formula, P_2O_5. Be sure to follow significant figure rules.

2 mol P	= 2 × 30.97 g P	=	61.94 g
5 mol O	= 5 × 16.00 g O	=	80.00 g
empirical formula mass		=	141.94 g/mol

❷ Set up the problem

- Use the equation from page 209 to solve for *x*, the factor relating the empirical and molecular formulas.

$$x = \frac{\text{molecular formula mass}}{\text{empirical formula mass}} = \frac{283.89 \text{ g/mol}}{141.94 \text{ g/mol}} = 2.0001 \approx 2$$

- Once *x* has been calculated, multiply the empirical formula by it to get the molecular formula.

$$x(\text{empirical formula}) = 2(P_2O_5) = P_4O_{10}$$

❸ Verify your work

- Calculate the formula mass for the molecular formula, and compare it to the experimental formula mass given in the problem.

Practice 6D

1. Determine the molecular formula of a compound having an empirical formula of CH and a molar mass of 78.11 g/mol.

2. A compound has the following composition: 76.54% C, 12.13% H, 11.33% O. If its molar mass is 282.45 g/mol, what is its molecular formula?

polymer
large molecule made of many repeated small subunits, each of which is a small molecule or group of atoms

Polymers are large molecules made of repeating units

To understand the structure of the polyethylene in trash bags, take a closer look at the name of the material. The name *polyethylene* can be broken down into two parts: *poly*, which means "many," and *ethylene*, which is the name for a molecule with the molecular formula C_2H_4. Thus, polyethylene means "many C_2H_4," an accurate description of the molecule is shown in **Figure 6-18**. Polyethylene is a typical **polymer**, a substance composed of many repeating groups of atoms. The units that link to form a polymer are called *monomers*. For example, C_2H_4 is the monomer for polyethylene.

Many of the molecules that make life possible, such as DNA, proteins, and starch, are also polymers made of different types of monomers. Polymers with many useful properties can also be made in a lab or factory, using a variety of different monomers. The one thing all these natural and artificial polymers have in common is that they are all held together with covalent bonds. These bonds allow the polymer molecules to resist being broken down.

Figure 6-18
The molecular formula for polyethylene, the material used to make trash bags, can be written as $(C_2H_4)_n$, with *n* as large as 3500.

Structural formulas

structural formula
indicates the spatial arrangement of atoms and bonds within a molecule

Molecular formulas tell you what types of atoms are present and the number of each that are in the compound. But to know how the atoms are connected together, you need a **structural formula.** A structural formula can be compared to a videotape of a basketball game. Just as the videotape will give you a thorough idea of where each player was during the game, a structural formula will give you much more detailed information about the positions of atoms within a molecule.

Properties depend on atoms and arrangement

Compare the empirical, molecular, and structural formulas of the two molecules shown in **Table 6-8**. Both have the same kinds and number of atoms. The only difference is the way they are arranged. Yet this small structural difference makes a huge difference in their chemical properties. Diethyl ether was once used as an anesthetic, while 1-butanol can be used to dissolve varnish. Structural formulas are similar to Lewis structures, but unshared pairs of electrons are not shown. A dash represents a single bond shared between two atoms.

Table 6-8
Comparing 1-Butanol and Diethyl Ether

Compound	Empirical formula	Molecular formula	Structural formula	Melting point (°C)	Boiling point (°C)	Density (g/mL)
1-butanol	$C_4H_{10}O$	$C_4H_{10}O$	$\begin{array}{c} \text{H H H H} \\ \mid \ \mid \ \mid \ \mid \\ \text{H—C—C—C—C—OH} \\ \mid \ \mid \ \mid \ \mid \\ \text{H H H H} \end{array}$	−90	117	0.810
diethyl ether	$C_4H_{10}O$	$C_4H_{10}O$	$\begin{array}{c} \text{H H} \quad \text{H H} \\ \mid \ \mid \quad \mid \ \mid \\ \text{H—C—C—O—C—C—H} \\ \mid \ \mid \quad \mid \ \mid \\ \text{H H} \quad \text{H H} \end{array}$	−116.3	34.6	0.713

Section Review

16. Determine the empirical formula for each of the following.
    a. a compound containing 63.50% Ag, 8.25% N, and 28.25% O
    b. a compound found to contain 111.16 g of Fe and 63.84 g of S
17. Determine the molecular formula for each of the following.
    a. a compound with a molar mass of 86.17 g/mol that contains 83.62% carbon and 16.38% hydrogen
    b. a compound with a molar mass of 92.01 g/mol that contains 0.608 g of nitrogen and 1.388 g of oxygen
18. Draw a structural formula for each of the following molecules.
    a. C_2H_2 b. CCl_4 c. C_2H_6O (2 possible structures)

19. **Story Link**

    The molecular formula for the polyethylene used in trash bags can be as much as 3500 times its empirical formula. What is the molar mass for such a polyethylene molecule?

How can you tell the shape of a molecule?

Chem Fact
The sense of smell is related to a sense organ that distinguishes the shapes of molecules.

Molecular shapes

Although you have learned a lot about the structures of molecules, you have not really studied their three-dimensional orientation or molecular geometry. Shape is an important factor in determining the chemical properties of a molecule. Hemoglobin, a polymer contained in your red blood cells, transports oxygen to all parts of your body. If a genetic mutation causes the shape of hemoglobin to change, the result could be sickle cell anemia, as shown in **Figure 6-19**. This condition is often so serious that children who inherit the disorder from both parents seldom live past the age of two.

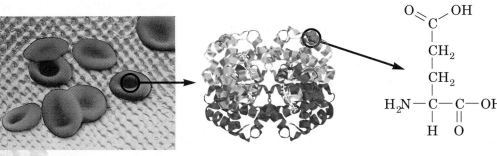

Figure 6-19a
The round, doughnut-like shape of healthy red blood cells is determined by the hemoglobin molecules in the cell.

6-19b
Hemoglobin consists of four chains; two are called alpha chains, and two are called beta chains.

6-19c
Each of the chains contains about 141–146 amino acid subunits, such as the glutamic acid monomer shown here.

Blood flowing through a vein

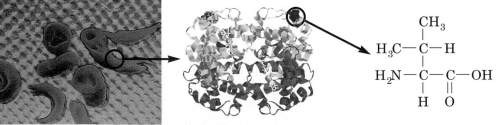

6-19d
Because of their shape, sickle cells clog small blood vessels so that not as much oxygen reaches body cells.

6-19e
The sickled cell shape is the result of the slight changes in the shape of hemoglobin molecules found in red blood cells.

6-19f
These changes in the shape of hemoglobin are caused by a genetic mutation, in which another amino acid, valine, is substituted for one of the glutamic acid monomers in each of the beta chains.

Figure 6-20
Molecules with only two atoms, such as H₂, can only have one shape.

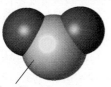

Figure 6-21
Even though carbon dioxide and sulfur dioxide have the same number of atoms, they have different shapes.

Carbon dioxide

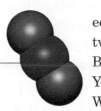

Sulfur dioxide

VSEPR (Valence Shell Electron Pair Repulsion) theory *system for predicting molecular shape based on the idea that pairs of electrons orient themselves as far apart as possible*

Shapes cannot be predicted from molecular formulas

Molecules with relatively simple molecular formulas also have simple shapes. In molecules with only two atoms, such as the H₂ molecule shown in **Figure 6-20**, only one shape is possible. But for molecules of more than two atoms, molecular shapes become more complicated. In such cases, you need to know more than their molecular formulas.

There is usually no obvious relationship between the molecular formula of a compound and its shape. Consider the two molecules carbon dioxide, CO_2, and sulfur dioxide, SO_2. Both contain three atoms, two of which are oxygen atoms. Yet they have different shapes, as shown in **Figure 6-21**. With such similarities in their atomic makeup, why is CO_2 linear, while SO_2 is bent? The answer lies in the arrangement of the valence electrons, especially unshared pairs.

After performing many tests that were designed to detect the shape of different molecules, scientists built a theory that summarized their findings. **VSEPR theory** states that electrostatic repulsion between the valence-level electron pairs causes these pairs to be oriented as far apart as possible. This positioning of pairs represents the most stable arrangement because it will take an input of energy to overcome the repulsive forces and push the electron pairs closer together. Although useful predictions about shape can be made with this theory, there is evidence that this theory does not provide a good description of electron cloud behavior.

How To

Determine molecular shape from Lewis structures

Figure 6-22
According to VSEPR theory, a molecule with two electron clouds around a central atom is most likely to be arranged in a straight line, as shown in this model of carbon dioxide.

1. Draw the Lewis structure for the molecule.

2. Count the number of electron clouds surrounding the central atom.

- Each single bond counts as an electron cloud.
- Each multiple bond generally counts as a single electron cloud.
- Each nonbonding electron pair must be considered an electron cloud. These aid in determining the geometry, but only bonded atoms are included in the shape.

3. Apply the appropriate geometry based on the number of electron clouds.

- **Two electron clouds: linear**
  Consider the case of CO_2, which has the following Lewis structure.

$$\overset{..}{O} = C = \overset{..}{\underset{..}{O}}$$

Each double bond is counted as a single electron cloud, even though it contains four electrons. The orientation that will keep the two electron clouds on either side of the carbon atom as far apart as possible is the straight-line arrangement, shown in **Figure 6-22**. For molecules with only two electron clouds surrounding the central atom, this is the likeliest geometry, with a bond angle of 180°.

How To continued on following page . . .

- **Three electron clouds: trigonal planar**

  Now consider the Lewis structure for sulfur trioxide, SO_3.

$$:\overset{..}{O}:$$
$$|$$
$$\overset{..}{O}=S-\overset{..}{\underset{..}{O}}:$$

  SO_3 has three electron clouds surrounding the central atom. The most likely arrangement for this molecule is shown in **Figure 6-23**. This shape is called a "trigonal planar" arrangement of electron pairs.

- **Four electron clouds: tetrahedral**

  The situation for molecules with four electron clouds, like methane, CH_4, is somewhat trickier because instead of having a planar shape that can be drawn on a paper like the others, it has a three-dimensional shape called a *tetrahedron*. Several different views of a tetrahedron are shown in **Figure 6-24**. The shape can be described as a tripod with a fourth leg sticking straight up. Such an arrangement of electron pairs will yield bond angles of 109.5°.

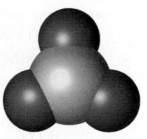

Figure 6-23
When a molecule consists of a central atom surrounded by three other atoms, as in SO_3, a trigonal planar arrangement is most likely.

4. *Adjust bond angles to account for unbonded pairs*

The SO_2 molecule shown in **Figure 6-21** has one unbonded pair and two bonds to oxygen atoms. As a result, it has three electron clouds and falls into the "trigonal planar" category, with angles between the electron pairs of about 120°. However, an unshared pair of electrons occupies more space than a shared pair. As a result of their greater size, the force of repulsion between unshared pairs is slightly greater than the repulsive force between shared pairs. Consequently, the electrons shared between each O atom and the central S atom are pushed together, causing the bond angle for SO_2 to be 119.5°, instead of 120°. The shape is based only on the atoms, so it is described as *bent*. A similar effect is observed for double and triple bonds, because their electron clouds take up more space than the electron clouds for a single-bond pair.

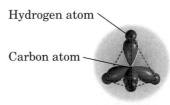

Hydrogen atom

Carbon atom

Figure 6-24a
A tetrahedral shape can't be shown accurately with a planar structural formula.

6-24b
The true shape can only be shown by a three-dimensional model, or . . .

6-24c
. . . in other ways that emphasize its three-dimensionality, such as with wedge-shaped bonds that seem to recede or protrude from the plane of the page.

6-24d
Another way to portray the tetrahedral shape shows the location of the orbitals of the atoms within the molecule.

Although this presentation of VSEPR theory can be very useful in predicting the shape of compounds made from main-block elements, it does not explain the rules for molecules that have more than an octet of valence electrons. In addition, VSEPR theory does not always work for some complex molecules. However, this simplified discussion should explain the shapes of most of the molecules in this chemistry text.

Sample Problem 6E
Predicting molecular shapes

Determine the shape and approximate bond angles for the following compounds: NH_3 and H_2O.

① Draw Lewis structures

$$H:\overset{\cdot\cdot}{N}:H$$
$$H$$

$$H:\overset{\cdot\cdot}{\underset{\cdot\cdot}{O}}:$$
$$H$$

② Count the electron clouds
- NH_3 has three bonds to H atoms and one unbonded pair: four electron clouds
- H_2O has two bonds to H atoms and two unbonded pairs: four electron clouds

③ Apply the proper VSEPR geometry
- Both atoms will have a tetrahedral arrangement of electron clouds, giving bond angles of about 109.5°.

④ Account for unbonded pairs
- For ammonia, consider the tetrahedron that is similar to a tripod with a fourth leg sticking straight up. If the unbonded electron pair is assigned the position of the leg sticking up, the shape that is left is pyramidal, or a pyramid with three triangular sides and a triangular base.

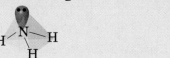

- For water, the shape will be bent. This will be true regardless of which two legs of the tetrahedron the two unbonded pairs are assigned to.

- Due to the effects of the unbonded pairs, ammonia and water both have bond angles slightly less than 109.5°. (Ammonia has bond angles of 107.3°, and water has an angle of 104.5°.)

Section Review

20. How might changing the shape of a molecule affect its properties?
21. Predict the molecular shape of Br_2 and HBr.
22. What is the relationship between the VSEPR theory and molecular shape?
23. Predict the molecular shapes of SCl_2, PI_3, and NCl_3.
24. What is the angle for the C—C—C bond in C_3H_8? Using this information, explain why organic structural formulas often show chains of carbon atoms as zigzag lines instead of straight lines.

How do bonds and properties relate?

Carbon and bonding

Remember that carbon generally forms four bonds and has the Lewis structure shown in **Figure 6-25**. When it forms single bonds, the compounds will reflect a tetrahedral geometry. Everything you see in **Figure 6-26** contains substances with carbon atoms bonded to one another. Carbon often forms long chain compounds, giving rise to a wide variety of compounds with different properties. The differences in properties are related to the ways that carbon atoms are bonded.

·C·

Figure 6-25
Because a carbon atom has four valence electrons, it can form bonds with up to four other atoms.

6-26b
The proteins, carbohydrates, fats, and nucleic acids that make up your body contain many carbon atoms.

6-26c
This plastic ruler is made of polyethylene, which contains carbon and hydrogen.

Figure 6-26a
All paper is composed of cellulose. Cellulose contains carbon, oxygen, and hydrogen.

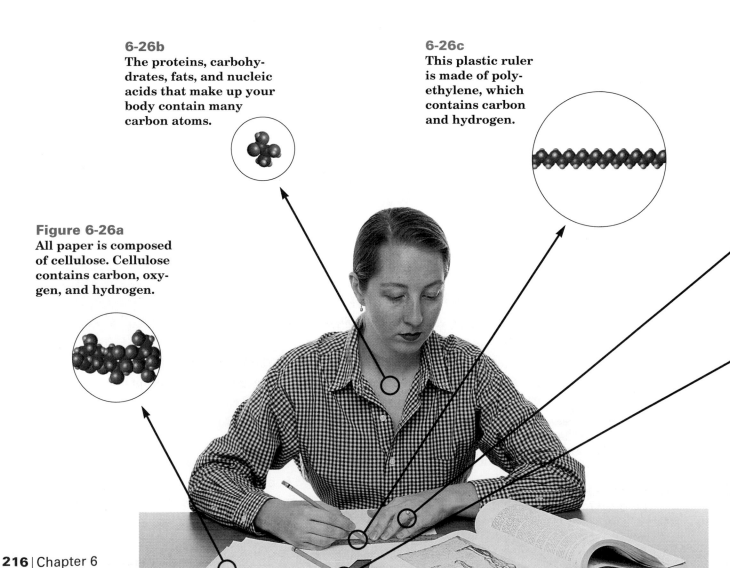

Carbon can form covalent networks

Some of the properties of diamond and graphite are shown in **Table 6-9**. You might expect each substance to have properties similar to molecular compounds, because the carbon-carbon bonds in each are nonpolar covalent. But graphite and diamond each have some properties of molecular substances and some properties that are unusual for molecular compounds. Although graphite is soft like most molecular substances, it conducts electricity and has a high melting point. Diamond is hard, like an ionic crystal, but it is not as brittle.

Table 6-9
Properties of Diamond and Graphite

Property	Diamond	Graphite
Mohs' hardness scale rating	10 (top of scale)	0.5–1
Density	3.51 g/mL	2.23 g/mL
Melting point	(changes to graphite)	(sublimes at 3652°C)
Conductivity	low	high

Unlike compounds consisting of individual molecules, graphite and diamond are examples of network solids, in which all atoms are covalently linked to others, somewhat like the crystal lattice of ionic compounds. Because every atom is bonded to several other atoms, melting requires enough energy to break all of these bonds.

Figure 6-26d shows the bonding between the carbon atoms in diamond. Each carbon atom in diamond is bonded to four other carbon atoms in three dimensions, at tetrahedral angles. This tetrahedral arrangement creates a network of covalently bonded carbon atoms that gives diamond its great strength and hardness. This arrangement also makes diamond denser than graphite.

Notice that in graphite, as shown in **Figure 6-26e**, the atoms are arranged in layers. Each carbon atom is covalently bonded to three other carbon atoms in a layer forming a strongly bonded covalent network of carbon atoms. London forces exist between layers, which can slide over each other. The ability of the layers to slide over one another not only accounts for graphite's tendency to crumble but also makes graphite a good lubricant, especially at temperatures that are too high for lubricating oils and petroleum jellies. Some of the bonding electrons on each carbon atom are very mobile, allowing graphite to conduct electricity, just as metals do.

6-26d
Diamond's hardness is due to the many strong covalent bonds in its network structure.

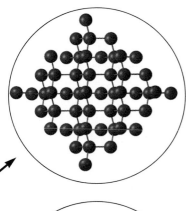

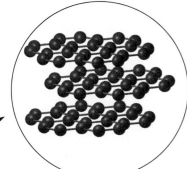

6-26e
The soft and crumbly properties of graphite stem from the relative weakness of the London forces between different layers of carbon atoms.

organic compound
compound containing carbon

Organic chemistry
Organic compounds are important to life

The molecules found in all living things—proteins, carbohydrates, nucleic acids, and lipids—all contain "backbones" that include carbon atoms linked together. In addition, other atoms can be bonded to these carbon backbones, forming a special category of compounds known as **organic compounds**.

Organic compounds, with few exceptions, are molecular compounds that contain carbon and, usually, hydrogen. Other atoms, such as oxygen, nitrogen, sulfur, and phosphorus, are also frequently found in organic compounds. More than 6 000 000 organic compounds have been identified and named.

Hydrocarbons are the simplest organic compounds

Hydrocarbons are composed of only hydrogen and carbon. Gasoline is a mixture of hydrocarbons, including octane. Hydrocarbons are grouped into categories based on the bonding between carbon atoms. The simplest hydrocarbons are those whose carbon atoms are connected in a long chain by single covalent bonds. These hydrocarbons are called *alkanes,* and they are a large part of all petroleum products. The suffix *-ane* is a part of their name and indicates that only single bonds are present. The names and formulas of the first 10 straight-chain alkanes are shown in **Table 6-10**. The names of most other organic compounds are based on these names.

Table 6-10
Names of Alkanes

Number of carbon atoms	Name of alkane	Molecular formula	Structural formula	Melting point (°C)	Boiling point (°C)
1	methane	CH_4		−182	−161
2	ethane	C_2H_6		−172	−88
3	propane	C_3H_8		−187.7	−42.1
4	butane	C_4H_{10}		−138.4	−0.5
5	pentane	C_5H_{12}		−129.7	36.1
6	hexane	C_6H_{14}		−95	69
7	heptane	C_7H_{16}		−90.6	98.4
8	octane	C_8H_{18}		−56.8	125.7
9	nonane	C_9H_{20}		−51	150.8
10	decane	$C_{10}H_{22}$		−29.7	174.1

Functional groups determine properties of organic molecules

functional group
group of atoms that determines an organic molecule's chemical properties

Most organic compounds, especially those used by living things, consist of carbon atoms that are covalently bonded to other types of atoms, especially oxygen and nitrogen atoms. Combinations of carbon, hydrogen, oxygen, and nitrogen atoms can also form groups known as **functional groups.** Many properties of organic chemicals depend on functional groups, so organic compounds are classified by the functional groups they contain. **Table 6-11** gives an overview of some common functional groups.

The compounds in each class have similar chemical properties. For example, almost all alcohols can lose a water molecule, H_2O, to form an *alkene,* a compound containing a double bond.

The way a compound is named provides clues about its functional groups and its structure. For example, heptanol is a derivative of heptane, a 7-carbon alkane. The *-ol* ending tells you that this compound is an alcohol and contains the —OH functional group that is characteristic of all alcohols. Because of this functional group, heptanol has physical and chemical properties that are more similar to other alcohols than to the heptane from which it is derived.

Table 6-11
Some Common Organic Functional Groups

Name	Chemical symbol	Naming suffix or prefix	Example	Properties and uses
Alcohol	—C—OH	*-ol*	H_3C—C—CH_3 with OH and H (isopropanol)	some properties similar to water, able to form hydrogen bonds, useful precursor for many compounds
Ether	—C—O—C—	*ether*	H_3C—C—O—C—CH_3 (diethyl ether)	volatile solvents used in anesthetics, no hydrogen bonding
Aldehyde	—C—H with ‖O	*-al*	C with H, H and ‖O (methanal or formaldehyde)	reactive compounds formed by oxidizing alcohols, used to preserve tissues and in polymers, no hydrogen bonding
Organic acid	—C—OH with ‖O	*-oic acid* or *-ate* for ionized form	H_3C—C—OH with ‖O (ethanoic acid or acetic acid)	usually weakly acidic compounds, formed by oxidizing aldehydes, combined with glycerol in fats, strong hydrogen bonding
Ketone	—C— with ‖O	*-one*	H_3C—C—CH_3 with ‖O (acetone)	polar solvents used in paints and textile processing, no hydrogen bonding
Amine	NH_2—C— , —C— with NH and —C— , —C— with N—C— and —C—	*-amine, amino-, -ine,* or *azo-*	H—C—H with N(H,H) and H (methylamine)	slightly basic compounds with some similarities to ammonia, often have unpleasant, fishy smell, weak hydrogen bonding

To name an organic chemical, you simply take the prefix from the alkane name for the hydrocarbon with the same number of carbons. Then you add a suffix that describes the compound's functional group.

Some organic molecules contain more than one type of functional group. Amino acids, which are the building blocks of proteins in living things, are a good example. One part of the molecule has an amine group, and another part has an organic acid group. Amino acids have the characteristics of both amines and organic acids. One end is weakly basic, and the other end is weakly acidic.

Organic structures
Carbon atoms can also form ring structures

Carbon atoms that covalently bond to one another can also form ring struc-

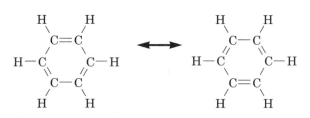

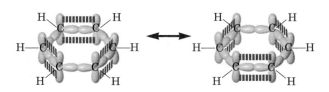

Figure 6-27a
Benzene has two possible resonance structures.

6-27b
Because the electrons involved in the double bonds are contained in orbitals that all touch each other, each resonance structure is equally likely.

tures. These rings are like pieces of the carbon network in graphite. Benzene, C_6H_6, is one of the most important organic compounds consisting of a ring of carbon atoms. Notice that the double bonds in this structure can be validly drawn in either of the ways shown in **Figure 6-27a**. Benzene is an example of a resonance hybrid. It has these resonance structures because of the arrangement of the orbitals in the benzene molecule. The electrons involved in double bonds are in orbitals that extend above and below the plane of the molecule. These orbitals are so close, they actually overlap.

Organic structures are often abbreviated

When chemists draw structural formulas for organic molecules, they often use a short-hand notation that leaves out the carbon and hydrogen atoms in the main part of the molecule and shows only carbon-carbon bonds. You can figure out how many hydrogen atoms and carbon-hydrogen bonds there are by remembering that carbon tends to form four bonds. Atoms other than hydrogen are always shown. The zigzag pattern of the carbon chain indicates where two tetrahedrally oriented C—C bonds are joined at a carbon atom. Although organic structures may not seem useful for smaller molecules, they are very helpful when it comes to more complicated molecules such as the one shown in **Figure 6-28**. Because some atoms aren't shown, the functional groups are easier to recognize.

Figure 6-28a
The chemical name for aspirin is acetylsalicylic acid.

6-28b
Because the complete structural formula for acetylsalicylic acid is complex, . . .

6-28c
. . . chemists usually draw its organic structure instead. Note that it is an aromatic compound.

Molecules can be portrayed in many ways

So far, you have seen a variety of different ways to portray atoms, ions, and molecules, from Lewis structures to three-dimensional views of molecules. Each structure has aspects that accurately describe some aspects of the bonded atoms, but like all models, each has its shortcomings, some of which are described in **Table 6-12**. One disadvantage shared by all of these models is that they attempt to portray the three-dimensional structure of atoms on a flat page. Another disadvantage is that these models cannot show motion. All molecules are constantly moving. Not only do molecules move from one place to another, but bonds within each molecule are constantly stretching, compressing, bending, and twisting. Today, molecular modeling of some large molecules is done on computers so that chemists can look at a molecule from a variety of angles and in motion.

Table 6-12
Advantages and Disadvantages of Molecular Models

Type of representation	Example	Advantages	Disadvantages
Chemical formula	C_6H_6	shows relative numbers of each kind of atom in a molecule or formula unit	does not show bonds, atom sizes, or actual shape
Lewis structure		shows arrangement of valence electrons in a molecule	does not show actual shape of molecule or atom sizes; electron position is not definite as is implied; larger molecules can be too complicated to show
Structural formula		shows arrangement of all atoms and bonds in a molecule; less complicated than Lewis structures	does not necessarily show actual shape of molecule or atom sizes; ignores unbonded pairs; larger molecules can be too complicated to show
Organic structure		shows arrangements of carbon chains in organic molecules; less complicated than structural formulas	does not necessarily show actual shape of molecule or atom sizes; does not show all atoms and bonds
Electron-cloud model		shows shape of molecule; shows probability clouds of electrons in each molecule, including nonbonding pairs	difficult to label individual atoms; larger molecules can be too complicated to show; bonds are not clearly indicated
Space-filling model		shows three-dimensional shape of molecule; shows most of the space taken by electrons in each molecule; less complicated than electron-cloud models	uses false colors to differentiate among elements; bonds are not clearly indicated; parts of large molecules may be hidden

Sample Problem 6F
Deciphering organic structures

Unlike most other protein monomers, tryptophan cannot be manufactured by the human body, so it must be available in the diet. For this reason, tryptophan is called an essential amino acid. What is the molecular formula of tryptophan?

❶ Place carbon atoms at all unmarked bond angles

❷ Place hydrogen atoms in C—H bonds so that each carbon has four bonds

❸ To determine the molecular formula, count the number of each type of atom
$C_{11}H_{12}N_2O_2$

Section Review

25. Explain why graphite is very soft, while diamond is extremely hard, even though both are made entirely of carbon atoms in covalent networks.

26. Compare and contrast the structures of an alcohol, an aldehyde, and an organic acid, all of which contain oxygen and hydrogen in their functional groups.

27. Explain how organic structures of molecules can make functional groups easier to identify.

28. Classify these organic molecules by identifying their functional groups. Then, calculate the molar mass of each.

    a. asparagine   **b.** cinnamaldehyde

Conclusion: Molecular Bonds and Trash Bags

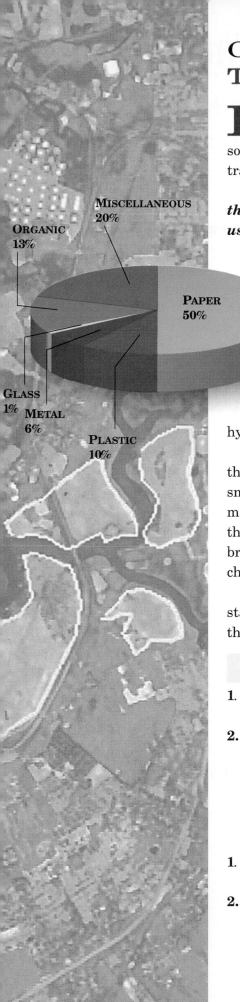

ORGANIC 13%

MISCELLANEOUS 20%

PAPER 50%

GLASS 1%

METAL 6%

PLASTIC 10%

From your study of molecular bonds, you can now examine some of the problems in making trash bags that biodegrade.

What is the composition of the material currently being used in trash bags? Trash bags are made of polyethylene, a polymer that can consist of more than 3500 subunits arranged in long chains.

Polyethylene is a hydrocarbon, meaning it is composed of atoms of hydrogen and carbon only.

Because most of the chemicals that living things use for food are smaller organic chemicals or have many functional groups, most of their enzymes are not useful in breaking down large hydrocarbon chains like polyethylene.

Even if bacteria in the landfill start to decompose polyethylene, they must start at either end of the long molecule, slowly breaking off only one of the 7000 carbon atoms in the chain at a time. As a result, it takes a very long time for an entire polyethylene molecule to be broken down.

How do bags labeled as biodegradable differ? Chemists have recently made it possible for bacteria to attack polyethylene at more places than just the edges of the bag. To accomplish this, they make the bags out of a mixture of cornstarch and polyethylene.

Bacteria consider these cornstarch molecules to be a "tasty treat." Most living things have developed enzymes that allow them to use starch and other compounds with many —OH functional groups as energy sources.

When the bacteria consume these cornstarch molecules, a "hole" in the bag is left behind. This, in turn, leaves behind smaller pieces of polyethylene, which are easier to break down.

Applying Concepts

1. How many points of attack would there be if 25 starch molecules were equally spaced among 3500 units of ethylene monomers?
2. When microorganisms break down polyethylene, they usually change it into several shorter molecules known as fatty acids. Fatty acids are organic acids containing long hydrocarbon chains. Draw the structural formula for a fatty acid with the formula $C_9H_{19}COOH$.

Research and Writing

Use the library to find out more about the following.

1. Research the properties of cornstarch. Give a reason why biodegradable trash bags are not made entirely of cornstarch instead of polyethylene.
2. Check to see what compounds, other than cornstarch, are being considered as possible candidates to make trash bags biodegradable. What tests are used to measure these against bags made of regular polyethylene and polyethylene with cornstarch?

Breakthroughs in Carbon Chemistry

1765

Karl Scheele discovers prussic acid, the first of several carbon compounds that he will discover and isolate over the next 20 years. His work marks the beginning of the serious study of organic substances.

1772

Antoine Lavoisier shows that diamond, being a form of carbon, burns.

1828

Friedrich Wöhler forms an organic compound (urea) from inorganic compounds, proving that living matter is not needed for organic synthesis.

1848

Louis Pasteur separates tartaric acid into two optical isomers, molecules that are physically identical except for their effect on polarized light.

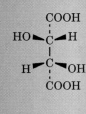

1926

Hermann Staudinger discovers that polymers, the basic material of plastics, consist of long chains of single molecules (monomers).

1933

While trying to react benzaldehyde and ethylene under high pressure, **R.O. Gibson** accidentally discovers polyethylene.

1935

Nylon is first synthesized at Du Pont by **Wallace Carothers** and his coworkers.

1937

Robert B. Woodward partially synthesizes the hormone estrone. During his remarkable career he will synthesize a number of complex molecules, including strychnine, chlorophyll, cortisone, and vitamin B$_{12}$.

1938

Du Pont chemist **Roy Plunkett** accidentally discovers that tetrafluoroethylene polymerizes to a white inert solid, that is later named Teflon.

1856

William Henry Perkin creates the first synthetic dye (mauve) using aniline from coal tar, thus beginning the modern dye industry.

1858

Archibald Scott Couper and **Friedrich August Kekulé** each propose that carbon is tetravalent (forms four bonds) and bonds to other carbon atoms to form chains.

1865

F. A. Kekulé suggests that benzene (the basic molecule in all aromatic hydrocarbons) consists of a ring of six carbon atoms connected by alternating double and single bonds. He claims that the idea came to him in a dream.

1874

Jacobus van't Hoff and **Joseph Le Bel** each propose that the bonds of a tetravalent carbon atom point to the corners of a tetrahedron with the carbon atom at the center. This three-dimensional molecular model accounts for the optical isomers of tartaric acid discovered by Pasteur.

1879

Vladimir Markovnikov synthesizes cyclobutane, a molecule containing four carbon atoms in a ring. This overthrows the belief that a cyclic compound is limited to a ring of six carbon atoms.

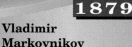

1880

Friedrich Beilstein publishes the first *Handbook of Organic Chemistry*, a compilation of information on organic chemistry that is still being published today.

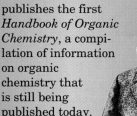

1985

R. E. Smalley and his colleagues, after vaporizing graphite, identify a hollow, spherical form of pure carbon consisting of 60 carbon atoms. Because it resembles the geodesic domes designed by architect Buckminster Fuller, Smalley names it buckminsterfullerene. The extremely stable molecule provides the basis for the new field of fullerene chemistry.

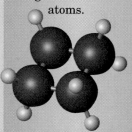

1945

Dorothy Hodgkin, by means of X-ray diffraction, determines the structure of penicillin, thus providing a crucial step towards its synthesis. During the next 25 years she will determine the structures of vitamin B_{12} and insulin.

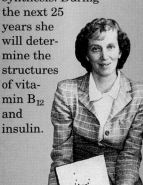

1949

Derek Barton proposes his theory of conformational analysis in which he shows that the three-dimensional shape of a molecule determines both its physical properties and its behavior in chemical reactions.

1957

John Sheehan and his coworkers synthesize penicillin after a nine-year effort.

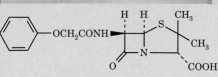

Highlights

 How are molecules specified?

- A Lewis structure models the valence electron arrangement in a molecule. In most molecules, each atom is surrounded by an octet of electrons. Some molecules have more than one valid Lewis structure.
- Molecules are named using either prefixes or Roman numerals.

 How are formulas represented?

- Empirical formulas show the smallest whole-number ratio of atoms. Molecular formulas are multiples of empirical formulas. Structural formulas show the spatial arrangement of atoms in molecules.

 How can you tell the shape of a molecule?

- VSEPR theory states that electron pairs are as far apart as possible. This theory can be used to predict the molecular shape.

 How do bonds and properties relate?

- Carbon, with its ability to form four bonds, can form molecules and covalent networks in a variety of shapes.
- Organic compounds can be named and identified by functional groups, which are groups of atoms responsible for the molecule's properties.

Key terms

bond length	organic compound
covalent bond	oxidation number
double bond	polar covalent bond
functional group	polymer
hydrogen bond	single bond
intermolecular forces	structural formula
Lewis structure	triple bond
molecular compound	unshared pair
molecular formula	valence electrons
nonpolar covalent bond	VSEPR theory

Key ideas

 Why do atoms share electrons?

- Covalent bonds form as atoms share pairs of electrons.
- The higher the electronegativity difference, the more ionic the bond character.
- Intermolecular forces, such as hydrogen bonds, dipole forces, and London forces, link molecules to each other.

Key problem-solving approach: *Calculations with percentage composition*

When solving problems involving percentage composition, empirical formula, or mass, select the variable that is given from the options near the top of this diagram. Then follow the calculation pathway to the required answer quantity shown among the options near the bottom of the diagram.

percentage composition by mass

%

$100 \times \dfrac{1}{\text{total mass}} \times$

mass of each element (units: g)

empirical formula subscripts

A_xB_y

$\times \dfrac{1 \text{ mole}}{\text{molar mass (g)}}$

$\times \dfrac{1 \text{ mole}}{\text{molar mass (g)}}$

no conversion necessary

amount of each element (units: mol)

$\times \dfrac{\text{molar mass (g)}}{1 \text{ mole}}$

$\times \dfrac{1}{\text{smallest amount}}$

percentage composition by mass

%

$100 \times \dfrac{1}{\text{total mass}} \times$

mass of each element (units: g)

empirical formula subscripts

A_xB_y

Review and Assess

Chemical bonds

REVIEW

1. **a.** How does a covalent bond differ from an ionic bond?
   b. How do molecular compounds differ from ionic compounds?
2. **a.** Draw and label the forces that affect atoms in a covalent bond.
   b. Explain why bonding electrons are able to come relatively close to each other.
   c. Why is a spring a better model than a stick for a covalent bond?
3. **a.** Which is likely to have the higher bond energy: an O—C bond in HO—CH_3 with a bond length of 141 pm or an O—C bond in HO—C_6H_5 with a bond length of 136 pm?
   b. Which is likely to have the longer bond length: an H—O bond in H—OH with a bond energy of 498 kJ/mol or an H—O bond in H—OC_2H_5 with a bond energy of 436 kJ/mol?
4. Why are bond lengths given in average, not exact, values?
5. **a.** Explain why the melting and boiling points of molecular compounds are usually lower than those of ionic compounds.
   b. Which will have the lower boiling point, HF or HCl? (Hint: HF is more polar than HCl, and is a smaller molecule.)
6. **a.** Why are intermolecular forces weaker than covalent or ionic bonds?
   b. How does a hydrogen bond develop between two molecules?
7. What type of bonds do line segments *ab*, *cd*, and *de* represent in the figure below?

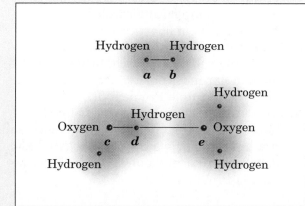

APPLY

8. Which graph below represents the inverse relationship between bond length and bond energy?

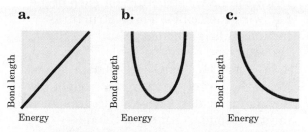

a. **b.** **c.**

9. Use **Table 6-4** and electronegativity differences to determine whether the bonds between the following pairs of elements are ionic, polar covalent, or nonpolar covalent.
   a. Na—F **b.** K—Cl **c.** N—O
   d. H—I **e.** Al—O **f.** S—O
   g. Cl—Br
10. When a positively charged plastic comb is brought close to a stream of water, the water is deflected by the comb. Using the electronegativity difference between hydrogen and oxygen, explain why this phenomenon occurs.
11. Arrange the following pairs from strongest to weakest attraction.
    a. polar molecule and polar molecule
    b. nonpolar molecule and nonpolar molecule
    c. polar molecule and ion
    d. ion and ion

Lewis structures

REVIEW

12. Determine the number of valence electrons in Mg, K, and Al. Draw the electron-dot diagram for each.
13. Using atoms *A* and *B*, draw a Lewis structure for a diatomic molecule containing each of the following types of bonds. (Hint: assume that each atom has an octet, and remember to show unbonded pairs.)
    a. single bond **b.** double bond
    c. triple bond
14. What term is used when molecules have more than one valid Lewis structure?

Answers to items in a black square begin on page 841

15 Draw the Lewis structure for each of the following molecules. (Hint: see Sample Problem 6A.)
  a. NF_3 **b.** $GeCl_4$ **c.** CH_3OH

16. Draw the Lewis structure for each of the following molecules. (Hint: see Sample Problem 6A.)
  a. PCl_3 **b.** CCl_2F_2 **c.** CH_3NH_2

17 Draw the Lewis structure for each of the following molecules. These structures include multiple bonds. (Hint: see Sample Problem 6B.)
  a. O_2 **b.** CS_2 **c.** C_2H_5COOH

18. Draw the Lewis structure for each of the following molecules. These structures include multiple bonds. (Hint: see Sample Problem 6B.)
  a. N_2 **b.** CH_3COCH_3 **c.** CH_3CHO

A P P L Y

19. Draw the Lewis structure for each of the molecules below.
  a. a refrigerant with one C atom and four F atoms
  b. a photographic chemical with three H atoms, one N atom, and one O atom
  c. a natural-gas ingredient with two C atoms and six H atoms

20. Draw the Lewis structure for each of the following polyatomic ions.
  a. OH^- **b.** H_3CCOO^- **c.** BrO_3^-

21. Write a possible Lewis structure for SF_6, which does not follow the octet rule.

22. NO_3^- has several resonance structures. Draw two.

23. Explain what is wrong with the following structures, then correct each one.

  a. 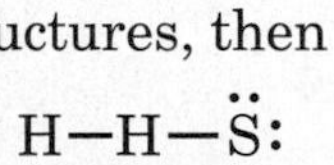 H—H—S̈:

  b. 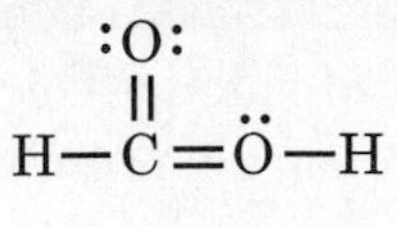
  :O:
  ‖
  H—C=Ö—H

  c.
  :C̈l:
  ‖
  N
  :C̈l⟋   ⟍C̈l:

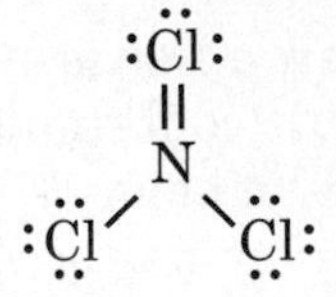

Names and formulas of molecular compounds

24. Give the oxidation number for each atom in the following compounds.
  a. H_3PO_4 **b.** CO_2 **c.** As_2O_5 **d.** HNO_3

25. Using the system of prefixes, name the following molecular compounds.
  a. SF_4 **b.** SF_6 **c.** P_2O_5 **d.** XeF_4

26. Write formulas for the following molecular compounds.
  a. bromine(III) fluoride
  b. carbon(IV) chloride
  c. carbon(IV) oxide
  d. nitrogen(V) oxide
  e. phosphorus pentachloride

27. What is the empirical formula for each of the following compounds?
  a. $C_{12}H_{24}O_6$ **b.** Hg_2I_2 **c.** C_6H_6

28. a. How is a structural formula different from a molecular formula?
  b. How is a molecular formula related to an empirical formula?

29. a. Name three objects that a classmate is wearing or using that are made of polymers.
  b. Why is the formula for polyethylene sometimes written $(C_2H_4)_n$?

30. Which formula—empirical, molecular, or structural—is most useful in determining the chemical properties of a molecule? Explain your answer.

31 Chemical analysis of citric acid shows that it contains 37.51% C, 4.20% H, and 58.29% O. What is its empirical formula? (Hint: see Sample Problem 6C.)

32. Chemical analysis of tetraethyl lead, an additive once used in gasoline, shows that it contains 29.71% C, 6.22% H, and 64.07% Pb. What is its empirical formula? (Hint: see Sample Problem 6C.)

33 What is the molecular formula of the molecule that has an empirical formula of CH_2O and a molar mass of 120.12 g/mol? (Hint: see Sample Problem 6D.)

34. What is the molecular formula of *para*-dichlorobenzene, an ingredient in moth balls that has a molar mass of 147.00 g/mol and an empirical formula of C_3ClH_2? (Hint: see Sample Problem 6D.)

35. In each of the following, element X forms a molecular compound with the formula shown. What is a likely oxidation number for X in each compound?
  a. XF **b.** Na_2XO_4 **c.** XCl_2 **d.** H_2XO_3

36. A 175.0 g sample of a flavor enhancer, monosodium glutamate (MSG), contains 56.15 g C, 9.43 g H, 74.81 g O, 13.11 g N, and 21.49 g Na. What is its empirical formula?

 ## Molecular shapes

37. Explain why VSEPR theory predicts molecular shapes with the largest bond angles possible.

38. Name the molecular shapes shown below.
  a.   **b.**   **c.**

39 Draw the shape and approximate bond angles for the following molecules. (Hint: see Sample Problem 6E.)
  a. CCl_4 **b.** $BeCl_2$ **c.** PH_3

40. Draw the shape and approximate bond angles for the following polyatomic ions. (Hint: see Sample Problem 6E.)
  a. NO_2^- **b.** NO_3^- **c.** NH_4^+

41. Use the following Lewis structures to help you describe the molecular shape of **a**, **b**, and **c**. (The Lewis structure does not necessarily represent the geometry of the molecule.)

  a. H—C≡C—H

  b. :B̈r—P̈—B̈r:
              |
           :B̈r:

  c. :C̈l—Ö—C̈l:

 ## Organic compounds

42. a. Why does carbon form more compounds than chlorine does?
  b. Why is diamond hard and strong?
  c. Why is graphite slippery?

43. Use **Table 6-10** to name the following alkanes.
  a. C_7H_{16} **b.** C_4H_{10} **c.** $C_{10}H_{22}$ **d.** C_3H_8

44. Use **Table 6-11** to identify the type of functional group from the name for each of the following organic compounds.
  a. propanol **b.** acetic acid **c.** propanal
  d. hexanone **e.** butanamine

45. Classify the functional groups of the organic compounds shown below.

46. Compare the advantages of structural formulas with those of chemical formulas.

47. a. Which alkanes are gases at room temperature, 25°C? (Hint: use **Table 6-10**.)
  b. Which do you predict will boil first: $C_{12}H_{26}$ or $C_{15}H_{32}$?

48 The organic structure for proline, an amino acid, is shown below. Draw its structural formula. (Hint: see Sample Problem 6F.)

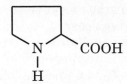

49. The organic structure for vitamin A is shown below. Draw its structural formula. (Hint: see Sample Problem 6F.)

H₃C   CH₃

50. Name the following organic compounds.

a. [structure] OH

b. [structure] NH₂

c. [structure with O double bond] OH

d. Write molecular formulas for the compounds shown in **a, b**, and **c.**

51. Name the following organic compounds.

a. [structure with O]

b. [structure with O] H

c. [structure] OH

d. Write molecular formulas for the compounds shown in **a, b**, and **c.**

52. Draw structures for the following.
a. butanoic acid, found in butter
b. nonanol, used in making artificial lemon oil
c. 2-pentanone, a solvent (Hint: the number tells you which carbon the functional group is attached to.)
d. Write molecular formulas for the compounds in **a, b**, and **c.**

Linking chapters

1. *Molar mass*

Find the molar mass for each of the following polyatomic ions.

a. $\left[\begin{array}{c} :\ddot{O}: \\ | \\ :\ddot{O}-S-\ddot{O}: \\ | \\ :\ddot{O}: \end{array}\right]^{2-}$ b. $\left[\begin{array}{c} :O: \\ \| \\ :\ddot{O}-N-\ddot{O}: \end{array}\right]^{1-}$

c. $\left[\begin{array}{c} :\ddot{O}: \\ | \\ :\ddot{O}-Cl-\ddot{O}: \\ | \\ :\ddot{O}: \end{array}\right]^{1-}$ d. $\left[:C\equiv N:\right]^{1-}$

2. Theme: *Classification and trends*

The table below shows different bond energies for single, double, and triple bonds.
a. Which is the shortest type of bond?
b. Predict how the N—O bond would compare to the N═O bond in terms of bond energy and bond length.

	Carbon and carbon	Oxygen and oxygen	Carbon and oxygen	Carbon and nitrogen
Single	347 kJ/mol	142 kJ/mol	360 kJ/mol	305 kJ/mol
Double	611 kJ/mol	498 kJ/mol	728 kJ/mol	615 kJ/mol
Triple	837 kJ/mol	N/A	N/A	891 kJ/mol

USING TECHNOLOGY

1. *Graphics calculator*

The relationship between bond length and bond energy can be shown graphically. Select the WINDOW key on your calculator, and use the following range: Xmin = 50, Xmax = 300, Xscl = 50, Ymin = 100, Ymax = 500, Yscl = 50. Enter the statistics from **Table 6-2** using the STAT mode:
a. Press STAT 1 and enter the data from **Table 6-2** in lists L₁ and L₂.
b. Press STAT ▶ 5 ENTER to compose a best-fit line.
c. Press Y= VARS 5 ▶ ▶ 7 to copy the equation, and press GRAPH to draw. What general relationship exists between bond length and bond energy?

Alternative assessment

Performance assessment

1. Devise a set of experiments to study how well biodegradable plastics break down. If your teacher approves your plan, conduct a class experiment to test the procedure on products labeled "biodegradable."
2. Your teacher will make available un-labeled samples of the organic chemicals listed in the table below. Develop an experiment to identify each of the unknown chemicals using the properties listed in **Table 6-11** as a guide. If your teacher approves your plan, identify the unknown substances.

Chemical	Structure	Functional group
Benzoic acid		organic acid
Ethyl alcohol		alcohol
Hexane diamine		amine

   d. Press TRACE ► to move the cursor along the best-fit line. Predict the bond lengths of the H—S bond (368 kJ/mol), C—N bond (305 kJ/mol), and N—O bond (230 kJ/mol).
   e. Press STATPLOT ENTER and set Plot 1 "On" for a scatterplot with "Xlist"= L_1 and "Ylist" = L_2. Then press GRAPH to compare your original data points to the best-fit line. Press TRACE and use the arrow keys to determine which two data points are farthest from the line. Describe what limitations there are on the general relationship between bond length and bond energy.
2. *Computer presentation*
   Using presentation software, create a tutorial that explains how to draw Lewis structures and provides plenty of practice.

Portfolio projects

1. *Chemistry and you*
   Inventory the food you consume in a single day. Compare the content labels from those foods, and then list the most commonly used chemicals in them. With the aid of your teacher and some reference books, try to classify the organic chemicals by their functional groups.
2. *Research and communication*
   Many everyday materials could be reused or recycled. However, recyclable products are continually deposited into landfills like the one at Fresh Kills in the story at the beginning of chapter. Research the waste-management methods of your community. Write local waste-management officials to find out what has been done to reduce the amount of landfill space needed for the community's refuse. With your class, organize a plan to publicize the recycling programs available.
3. *Cooperative activity*
   As a class or small group, research preservatives for various foods. Examine their chemical structure. Determine a way to test for organic functional groups of possibly hazardous preservatives.
4. *Research and communication*
   Covalently bonded solids such as silicon, an element used in computer components, are harder than pure metals. Research theories that explain the hardness of covalently bonded solids and their usefulness in the computer industry. Present your findings to the class.
5. *Chemistry and you*
   Because margarine spreads are now used more often than margarine sticks and contain a smaller percentage of fat than margarine sticks (80% fat) or butter, baking recipes are being changed to specify butter instead of margarine. Research the percentage of fat in margarine spreads available to you. Test the effect of using spreads with varying percentages of fat in a recipe. What is the minimum percentage of fat that will still provide adequate results? Try several recipes. Are some recipes more sensitive to ingredient changes than others?

7

Chemical Equations

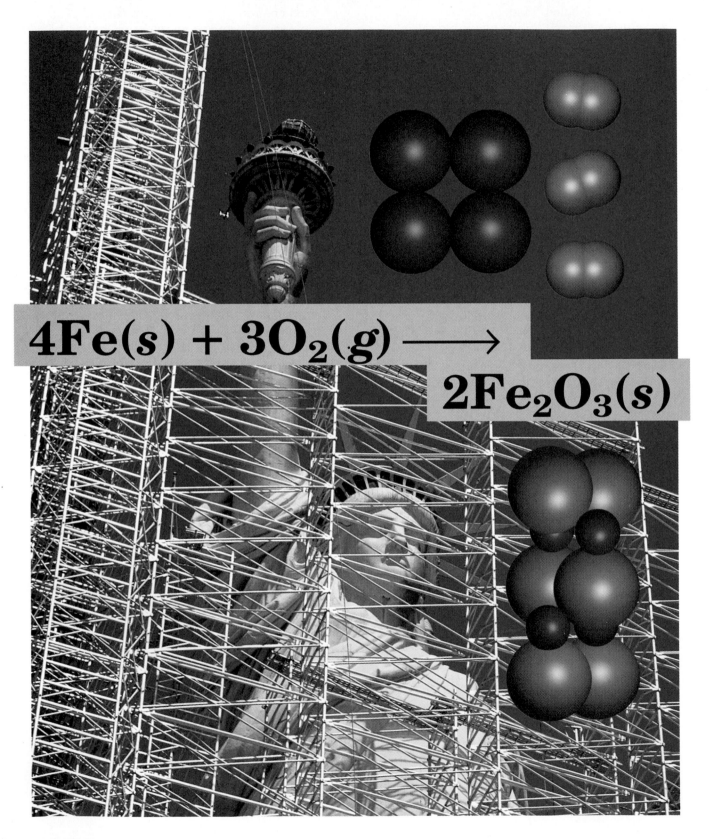

$$4Fe(s) + 3O_2(g) \longrightarrow$$

$$2Fe_2O_3(s)$$

Reactivity and the Statue of Liberty

Several people climbed inside the Statue of Liberty

even though it was closed to visitors that day in 1985. One

man pointed an unusual tool at the inside of the statue. White powder shot

out of the tool, scouring the interior surface. What was he doing? Why?

The man was not a vandal bent on destroying the statue. He was part of a team working with the National Park Service on an $85-million project to restore the 100-year-old statue and museum.

The tool was a combination blaster/vacuum cleaner that used sodium hydrogen carbonate, $NaHCO_3$, to remove a layer of tar from the inside of the statue. The tar was supposed to have kept salt water from leaking into the statue, where it could make contact between the statue's copper outer shell and its iron internal support framework. But over time the tar deteriorated, and the statue leaked.

A team of workers led by architect John Robbins, architectural conservator Fran Gale, and metallurgist Norman Nielson had searched for something rough enough to remove the tar but gentle enough to avoid damaging the copper skin, which is only slightly thicker than a penny. Before deciding on $NaHCO_3$, the team tried ground walnut shells, corncobs, glass beads, rice, and even sugar. Scouring all 300 sheets of copper in the statue required 40 tons of $NaHCO_3$.

When the statue was built in 1886, the French sculptor Frederic Bartholdi chose copper because of its softness and malleability, the same properties that make it difficult to clean. After being hammered into shape, the sheets were riveted together and hung on an iron structure, an internal tower surrounded by an armature framework of 1800 iron bars. The structure was designed by the French engineer Alexandre-Gustave Eiffel, who also designed the famous tower in Paris that bears his name. Iron was the strongest and most flexible material available at a reasonable cost.

Copper and iron, like other metals, can react to form ionic compounds. The green coating, or *patina*, on the outside of the statue resulted when the copper reacted to form several green copper compounds, including CuO, $CuSO_4 \cdot 3Cu(OH)_2$, and $CuSO_4 \cdot 2Cu(OH)_2$. These compounds do not dissolve well in water, and they therefore protect the remaining copper from reacting with substances in precipitation and the air.

The iron supports had also reacted to form a series of hydrates, such as $Fe_2O_3 \cdot 3H_2O$, which is often referred to as iron(III) hydroxide, because of its empirical formula, $Fe(OH)_3$. This compound is also commonly known as "rust." It is a weak, flaky compound that crumbles easily. Some of the iron bars had rusted to only one-half of their original thickness.

- *Why did the iron support beams corrode so much, while the thin copper skin did not?*
- *How could future corrosion be prevented?*

In this chapter, you will study reactions and how they can be controlled, information that will enable you to answer these questions.

What is a chemical reaction?

7-1

Section Objectives

Explain what a chemical reaction is.

Distinguish between evidence that suggests a chemical reaction may have occurred and conclusive proof of a chemical change.

Use a word equation to describe a chemical reaction.

Explain why some reactions are endothermic and others are exothermic.

Relate conservation of mass to the rearrangement of atoms in a chemical equation.

Explain why reactants must be brought into contact for a reaction to occur.

Chemical change

You can't avoid chemical reactions. You see them taking place all the time—in rusting iron, in leaves that change color in the fall, in milk that turns sour, and in exhaust fumes emitted from cars. Chemical reactions are happening not only all around you, but also inside of you. Digestion and respiration each involve chemical reactions.

A *chemical reaction* is simply a chemical change—the process by which one or more substances are changed into one or more different substances. In any chemical reaction, the original substances are known as *reactants,* while the resulting substances are called *products.* One chemical reaction that you probably see quite often is shown in **Figure 7-1**.

Figure 7-1
Chemical changes occur as a match burns.

Evidence of a chemical change

To understand what is involved in a chemical reaction, consider **Figure 7-1**. When a safety match is struck against a matchbook cover, several observations can be made. Heat and light are released in the form of flames; the substance on the match head is enveloped in the flames and changes color; and a puff of unpleasant-smelling smoke rises from the match. In addition, a hissing noise can be heard.

Light ——————

Heat ——————

Formation of gas ——

Change in color ——

Figure 7-2
The formation of a solid precipitate when two solutions are mixed is an indication of a chemical change.

How do you know what has happened to the match? It appears to have undergone a chemical change because the products left at the end appear very different from the reactants present at the beginning. The same is true of the solutions shown mixing in **Figure 7-2**. In general, the changes that are noticeable in **Figure 7-1** and **Figure 7-2** are evidence that a chemical reaction *may have occurred*.

But this kind of evidence only suggests that a chemical change may have occurred. It cannot be considered absolute proof that a chemical change has taken place. For proof, you need to analyze the products to verify that their *physical and chemical properties* are different from those of the reactants.

For example, a change in heat energy would certainly be involved in the melting of ice. However, analysis of the water that forms would reveal that it has the same chemical properties as the ice that melted. Consequently, you can be certain that no chemical reaction takes place in the melting of ice, even though there is a noticeable change in heat.

Chemical reactions release or absorb energy

Why are heat, light, and noise all considered evidence that a chemical change may have occurred? Each indicates an energy change. Most reactions either release or absorb energy. Consider the reaction discussed at the beginning of Chapter 6, in which hydrogen and oxygen react to produce water in an exothermic reaction. This exothermic reaction can be described by the following word equation, which names the reactants and the products.

$$\underbrace{\text{Hydrogen} + \text{Oxygen}}_{\text{Reactants}} \longrightarrow \underbrace{\text{Water} + \text{Energy}}_{\text{Products}}$$

Recall from Chapter 2 that according to the law of conservation of energy, energy cannot be created or destroyed. So where does the energy that this reaction produces come from?

In Chapter 6, the energy changes in the chemical reaction were linked to breaking and forming bonds. Energy, in the form of a spark, is needed to start the process of breaking the covalent bonds in the hydrogen and oxygen molecules. When new bonds form among the atoms to produce the water molecules, energy is released in the form of heat and light.

But in the case of exothermic reactions such as the synthesis of water, the bonds holding the products together are stronger than those in the reactants. Recall from your study of chemical bonding in Chapters 5 and 6 that the stronger a bond is, the more energy that is released when the bond is formed. In addition, the atoms in the bond are more stable once the bond is formed. In this case, more energy is released in bond formation than was absorbed to break bonds, and the overall reaction is exothermic. The great majority of chemical reactions in nature are exothermic.

Figure 7-3
Breaking down water in electrolysis requires an input of energy that is the same size as the output of energy from the synthesis reaction of water.

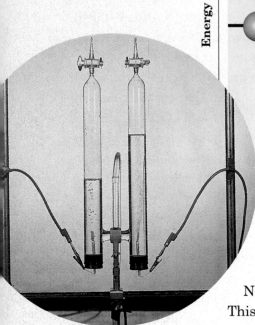

Energy and the Water Reaction

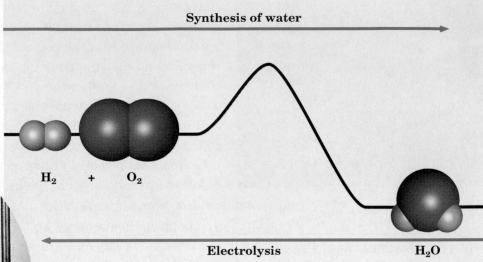

But under the right conditions, endothermic reactions can occur. One necessary condition is that an adequate amount of energy must be available as indicated by the following word equation.

$$\text{water} + \text{energy} \longrightarrow \text{hydrogen} + \text{oxygen}$$

Notice that this reaction is the opposite of the exothermic reaction. This reaction is known as *electrolysis* because electrical energy is added to water to break it down. The same amount of energy that was released when the water molecules were formed must be absorbed, as shown in **Figure 7-3**. Then, as hydrogen and oxygen molecules form again, the same amount of energy that was absorbed to break the bonds in these molecules will be released. The net result will be that the same amount of energy released in making the water will be absorbed in breaking it down again.

Atoms are rearranged in a chemical change

Recall from Chapter 2 the law of conservation of mass—mass is never created or destroyed. But where does the new substance with new properties formed in a chemical reaction come from? Where does the old substance go?

In ordinary chemical changes, atoms do not change into other atoms; nor do they appear or disappear. *The bonding patterns among the atoms are merely rearranged.* Consider the word equation for the match reaction.

$$\text{potassium chlorate} + \text{phosphorus} \longrightarrow$$
$$\text{potassium chloride} + \text{phosphorus(V) oxide} + \text{energy}$$

In the match-head reaction, bonds are broken, atoms are rearranged, and then new bonds are formed. Both sides of the equation contain potassium, chlorine, phosphorus, and oxygen atoms (oxygen is in potassium chlorate and phosphorus(V) oxide). There are no types of atoms in the products that are not found in the reactants.

Particles must collide for a chemical reaction to occur

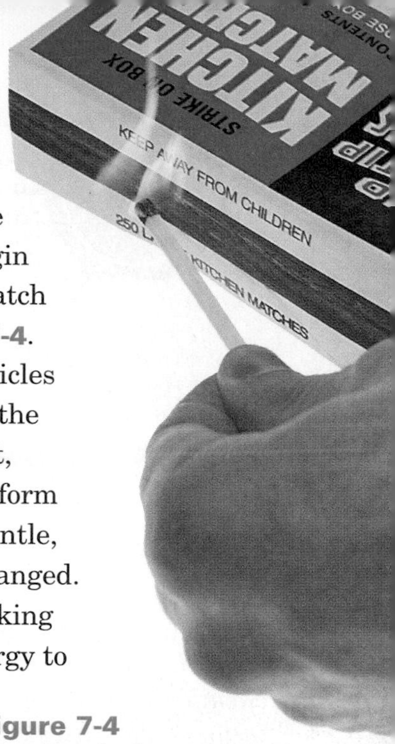

Chem Fact
In "strike anywhere" matches, all the ingredients are on the match head. Some commonly used ingredients are P_4S_3, $KClO_3$, and $K_2Cr_2O_7$.

Consider what happens when a safety match is lit. One reactant is on the match head. The other is on the matchbook's striking surface. The reaction will not begin unless the two are brought together by striking the match head across the striking surface, as shown in **Figure 7-4**.

When the reactants are brought together, their particles collide. If these collisions happen with enough energy, the existing bonds in the reactants can be broken. In effect, such collisions leave behind unbonded atoms that can form new bonds and make products. If the collision is too gentle, the molecules will simply bounce off one another unchanged. The reason that the match must be slid across the striking surface is that the heat from friction is a source of energy to get the reaction started.

Some unwanted reactions can be prevented by knowing what happens when reactants are brought together. Matches are kept inside a matchbook or box to isolate them from the striking surface on the outside. The chances of inadvertently lighting a match are thereby greatly reduced.

Figure 7-4
The chemical reactants for igniting safety matches are potassium chlorate, $KClO_3$, on the match head and phosphorus, P_4, on the striking surface.

Section Review

1. What is a chemical reaction?
2. What is the only way to prove that a chemical reaction has occurred?
3. In photosynthesis, plants make oxygen and sugars from carbon dioxide, water, and the energy from sunlight. Write a word equation for this process.
4. Decide whether the reactions that occur in each of the following situations are exothermic or endothermic. Explain your choice.
   a. the "burning" of gasoline in a car's engine
   b. the creation of oxygen and sugars from carbon dioxide and water by plants through photosynthesis
   c. fireworks exploding in the sky
5. When an orange substance is heated, it reacts by giving off nitrogen gas, green crystals of chromium(III) oxide, and water vapor. What atoms were contained in the original substance?
6. Explain which would be good places to store potassium.
   a. in the bottom of a sealed jar of mineral oil
   b. in the air near an open window
   c. in a glass jar that contains only oxygen
7. **Story Link**
   In the description of the Statue of Liberty, what evidence was given that chemical reactions had occurred?

How are reactions written?

Accurate chemical equations

Reactions can be described with word equations, but it is more convenient to use the chemical symbols and formulas for elements and compounds. In Chapters 5 and 6 you learned that a correctly written formula matches the actual composition of the bonded atoms. Similarly, a correctly written **chemical equation** describes exactly which and how many atoms are rearranged during the course of a reaction.

chemical equation
symbols that describe a chemical reaction and indicate identities and relative amounts of reactants and products

Atoms and mass are conserved in chemical reactions

The word equation for the water reaction is shown in **Table 7-1**. Beneath the word equation is a formula equation for the same reaction. The molecular models are also shown.

Imagine the reaction of the hydrogen molecules and oxygen molecules, portrayed by the models in **Table 7-1**. First, the reactants must collide so that the bonds holding them together can be broken. Only then can the individual atoms in the reactants form new bonds to make water molecules.

Look again at the models for the formula equation in **Table 7-1**. How many of each type of atom will there be when all of the bonds in these reactants are broken? How many are there in the product, once the new bonds are formed?

Table 7-1
Different Ways to Write the Water Reaction

Representation	Reactants	Yield (or "produce")	Product
Word equation	hydrogen + oxygen	$\longrightarrow$	water
Formula equation	H_2 + O_2	$\longrightarrow$	H_2O
Molecular models	⚬⚬ + ⬤⬤	$\longrightarrow$	⬤

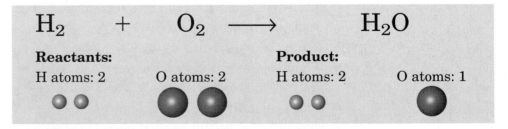

$$H_2 \quad + \quad O_2 \longrightarrow \quad H_2O$$

Reactants:
H atoms: 2   O atoms: 2

Product:
H atoms: 2   O atoms: 1

There are *two* oxygen atoms in the reactants but only *one* in the product. One of the oxygen atoms has apparently disappeared, in violation of the law of conservation of mass, as shown in **Figure 7-5** on the next page. *But this is not what has actually happened.* Measuring the masses of the product and the reactants shows that they remain the same. Somehow the formula equation must be adjusted so that it does not appear as if an oxygen atom simply disappeared. The law of conservation of mass must be taken into consideration.

Figure 7-5
One hydrogen molecule and one oxygen molecule can form one water molecule, but there is an oxygen atom in the reactants that is not accounted for in the products.

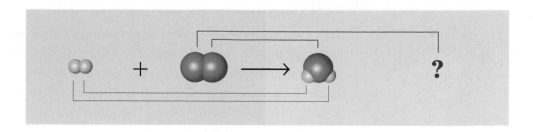

Coefficients indicate amounts of reactants and products

When trying to write a correct equation, DO NOT change the products or reactants either by adding new ones or by changing the subscripts and identities of the formulas in the equation.

The difficulty with the equation can be solved by adjusting the numbers of particles to get equal numbers of each atom on either side of the arrow. To balance both of the oxygen atoms, you would need *two* water molecules, each containing one oxygen atom, as shown in **Figure 7-6**.

Figure 7-6
The extra oxygen atom can be accounted for by showing *two* water molecules as products, but now there are more hydrogen atoms in the product than in the reactants.

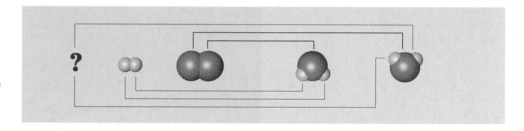

This can be done by writing the number *2* in front of the formula for the water molecule.

$$H_2 \quad + \quad O_2 \quad \longrightarrow \quad 2H_2O$$

Numerals placed in front of a formula in this way are called **coefficients**. Just as a subscript indicates the number of atoms within a molecule or formula unit, a coefficient indicates the relative number of molecules, formula units, or atoms required for a complete reaction. Because a coefficient refers to an entire unit, such as molecules or formula units, *you should never insert a coefficient between the elements in a chemical formula.* Is the addition of a coefficient to the product, water, enough to solve the conservation of mass problem in this equation?

coefficient
numeral used in a chemical equation to indicate relative amounts of reactants or products

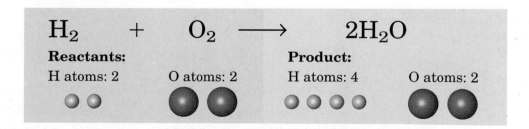

$$H_2 \quad + \quad O_2 \quad \longrightarrow \quad 2H_2O$$

Reactants:

H atoms: 2   O atoms: 2

Product:

H atoms: 4   O atoms: 2

The equation is still not balanced. But if two more hydrogen atoms are added on the reactant side, the numbers of atoms on both sides of the equation will match. Adding *two* more hydrogen atoms is the same as adding *one* more hydrogen molecule, giving a total of *two* hydrogen molecules in the reactants. This is an acceptable way to adjust the equation because hydrogen molecules are already listed as reactants. *No new reactants or products are being added.* Only the relative amounts have changed.

Now the law of conservation of mass is no longer being violated, as shown in **Figure 7-7**. No atoms are left unaccounted for, and all of the reactants and products are a part of the reaction.

Notice that if no number is written as a coefficient on a final balanced equation, the number is understood to be 1. In the hydrogen-oxygen equation, for example, one oxygen molecule is reacting.

Figure 7-7
The properly balanced equation has the same number of each type of atoms in the reactants and the products.

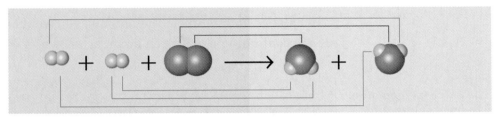

Coefficient
(number of formula
units in reaction)

Subscript
(number of atoms
in formula unit)

$$2H_2 \quad + \quad O_2 \quad \longrightarrow \quad 2H_2O$$

Reactants:

H atoms: 4   O atoms: 2

Product:

H atoms: 4   O atoms: 2

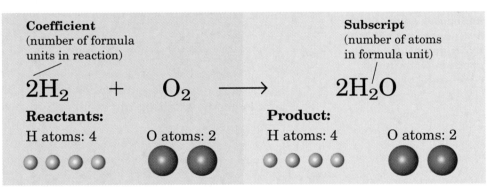

At first, you may think something has been lost because three molecules of reactants produce only two molecules of product. But compare this to the building of a car, as shown in **Figure 7-8**. Many parts, including four wheels, one engine, and one frame, are required to make only one car, but that doesn't mean something is lost in the product. Before and after the car is made, the number and types of specific *parts* are equal, but the *overall number* of separate objects need not be the same.

Figure 7-8
A car contains the same total number and types of parts whether it is being built or taken apart. Similarly, the products of a chemical equation must contain the same number and types of atoms.

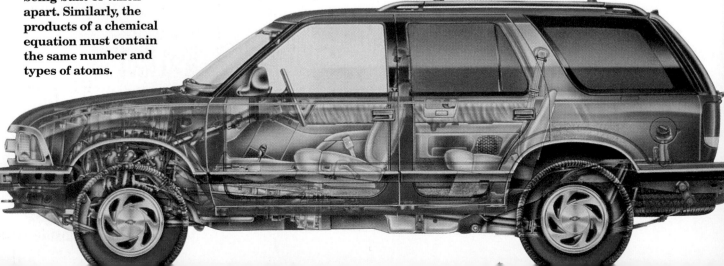

For this reason, conservation of mass is tested by checking the amounts and types of *atoms* (not molecules) that are present. This process of inserting coefficients to satisfy the law of conservation of mass is referred to as "balancing an equation."

Balancing a formula equation turns it into a *chemical equation*. A chemical equation uses symbols and formulas to show the reactants and products and indicates the relative amounts by using coefficients.

How To

Write a balanced chemical equation

Chemical equations are sometimes more complex than the example you've just studied. But there is a step-by-step approach that can make balancing equations easier. These steps are outlined for the reaction in a safety match. This process is called balancing by inspection.

1. Write the word equation, showing all of the reactants and products.

phosphorus + potassium chlorate $\longrightarrow$

potassium chloride + phosphorus(V) oxide

2. Write the correct symbols and formulas for all of the reactants and products.

In effect, change the word equation into a formula equation. When doing so, recall what you learned in Chapters 5 and 6 about formula writing. You may need to consult reference works for some formulas. Be sure to leave space to insert the coefficients.

$$?P_4 \ + \ ?KClO_3 \ \longrightarrow \ ?KCl \ + \ ?P_2O_5$$

3. Count the number of atoms of each element for both sides of the equation.

List the kinds and numbers of atoms on each side of the equation.

Left side (reactants)	**Right side** (products)
P atoms: 4	P atoms: 2
K atoms: 1 ✓	K atoms: 1 ✓
Cl atoms: 1 ✓	Cl atoms: 1 ✓
O atoms: 3	O atoms: 5

4. Insert coefficients for atoms of one element at a time so that the law of conservation of mass is satisfied.

For each element, the total number will be the least common multiple of the amounts on each side of the unbalanced equation. This number may be split among different reactants if they contain the same element. Balancing all of the reactant and product coefficients requires a process of trial and error.

How To continued on the following page . . .

Table 7-2
Tips for Balancing Equations

Step	Rule
1	First, balance the types of atoms that appear in only one reactant and only one product.
2	Balance the remaining types of atoms one at a time.
3	Balance H atoms and O atoms after most of the other elements have been balanced.
4	If the same polyatomic ions appear on both sides of the equation, treat them as if they were single units, like monatomic ions.

The tips shown in **Table 7-2** may help organize your thinking. In this reaction, all atoms appear in only one reactant and one product. The only valid suggestion is to leave the O atoms until the end. Starting with phosphorus, there are four atoms in the reactants and two in the products. Adding a coefficient of 2 to the products will help balance the equation.

$$?P_4 \ + \ ?KClO_3 \ \longrightarrow \ ?KCl \ + \ 2P_2O_5$$

Left side (reactants)   **Right side** (products)

P atoms:	4 ✓	P atoms:	4 ✓
K atoms:	1 ✓	K atoms:	1 ✓
Cl atoms:	1 ✓	Cl atoms:	1 ✓
O atoms:	3	O atoms:	10

5. Repeat steps 3 and 4 until the law of conservation of mass holds for all of the elements in the equation.

It now appears that only the oxygen atoms are out of balance. Use the coefficient 10 for the reactant side, and multiply the coefficient already on the product side by 3, so that the least common multiple, 30, is the number of oxygen atoms on each side of the equation. *Do not be concerned if adding coefficients causes an imbalance in other atoms that were previously balanced.*

$$?P_4 \ + \ 10KClO_3 \ \longrightarrow \ ?KCl \ + \ 6P_2O_5$$

Left side (reactants)   **Right side** (products)

P atoms:	4	P atoms:	12
K atoms:	10	K atoms:	1
Cl atoms:	10	Cl atoms:	1
O atoms:	30 ✓	O atoms:	30 ✓

The coefficient for the KCl product will be 10 since that will balance the potassium and chloride ions in the reactant. This will balance most of the reactants and products.

$$?P_4 + 10KClO_3 \rightarrow 10KCl + 6P_2O_5$$

Left side (reactants)	Right side (products)
P atoms: 4	P atoms: 12
K atoms: 10 ✓	K atoms: 10 ✓
Cl atoms: 10 ✓	Cl atoms: 10 ✓
O atoms: 30 ✓	O atoms: 30 ✓

The last coefficient to be readjusted is for phosphorus. *Note that it may take several adjustments before the right combination of coefficients is found to balance the whole equation.*

$$3P_4 + 10KClO_3 \rightarrow 10KCl + 6P_2O_5$$

Left side (reactants)	Right side (products)
P atoms: 12 ✓	P atoms: 12 ✓
K atoms: 10 ✓	K atoms: 10 ✓
Cl atoms: 10 ✓	Cl atoms: 10 ✓
O atoms: 30 ✓	O atoms: 30 ✓

6. **Make sure that there are equal numbers of atoms of each element on both sides of the equation.**

Yes, the law of conservation of mass has been satisfied. If it hasn't, try working through these steps again.

Sample Problem 7A
Balancing chemical equations

Cellular respiration is the process that your body uses to get energy from the food you eat. In cellular respiration, sugars such as glucose, $C_6H_{12}O_6$, react with oxygen. The net result is an increase of energy and the production of carbon dioxide and water. Write the balanced chemical equation for cellular respiration.

❶ Write the word equation

$$\text{glucose} + \text{oxygen} \longrightarrow \text{carbon dioxide} + \text{water}$$

❷ Write the formula equation

$$?C_6H_{12}O_6 + ?O_2 \longrightarrow ?CO_2 + ?H_2O$$

❸ Count the number of atoms for each element

Left side (reactants)	Right side (products)
C atoms: 6	C atoms: 1
H atoms: 12	H atoms: 2
O atoms: 8	O atoms: 3

❹ Insert coefficients for atoms of one element at a time

Begin with carbon, because it appears in only one reactant and one product.

$$C_6H_{12}O_6 + ?O_2 \longrightarrow 6CO_2 + ?H_2O$$

Left side (reactants)	Right side (products)
C atoms: 6 ✓	C atoms: 6 ✓
H atoms: 12	H atoms: 2
O atoms: 8	O atoms: 13

*Remember when no coefficient is written, as for $C_6H_{12}O_6$, **one** formula unit is involved.*

Sample Problem 7A continued on the following page . . .

⑤ Repeat steps 3 and 4 until the law of conservation of mass holds for the equation

Work with hydrogen next, because it appears in only one reactant and one product.

$$C_6H_{12}O_6 + \textbf{?}O_2 \longrightarrow 6CO_2 + 6H_2O$$

Left side (reactants)	Right side (products)
C atoms: 6 ✓	C atoms: 6 ✓
H atoms: 12 ✓	H atoms: 12 ✓
O atoms: 8	O atoms: 18

Work with oxygen last, because it is in more than one of the reactants and more than one of the products.

$$C_6H_{12}O_6 + 6O_2 \longrightarrow 6CO_2 + 6H_2O$$

Left side (reactants)	Right side (products)
C atoms: 6 ✓	C atoms: 6 ✓
H atoms: 12 ✓	H atoms: 12 ✓
O atoms: 18 ✓	O atoms: 18 ✓

⑥ Make sure that there are equal numbers of atoms of each element on both sides of the equation

Practice 7A

Answers for Concept Review items and Practice problems begin on page 841.

1. Balance the following equations.

   a. $CaSi_2 + SbCl_3 \longrightarrow Si + Sb + CaCl_2$ **b.** $C_2H_2 + O_2 \longrightarrow CO_2 + H_2O$

   c. $Al + CH_3OH \longrightarrow (CH_3O)_3Al + H_2$

2. When calcium is added to water, calcium hydroxide and hydrogen gas are formed. When calcium hydroxide is heated, water and calcium oxide are the products. Write balanced chemical equations that describe this series of changes.

Section Review

8. Explain the differences among a word equation, formula equation, and chemical equation.

9. Use diagrams of particles to explain why four atoms of silver can produce only two formula units of silver sulfide, even with an excess of sulfur atoms.

10. Indicate which of the numbers in the following equation are coefficients and which are subscripts. Which can be adjusted to balance an equation? Why?

$$3H_2SO_4 + 2Al \longrightarrow Al_2(SO_4)_3 + 3H_2$$

11. Rewrite the following word equations as formula equations.
    a. Hydrogen reacts with chlorine to produce hydrogen chloride gas.
    b. Aluminum and iron(III) oxide react to produce aluminum oxide and iron.
    c. Potassium chlorate decomposes to yield potassium chloride and oxygen.
    d. Calcium hydroxide and hydrochloric acid react to produce calcium chloride and water.

12. Balance the equations you wrote for item **11**.

13. **Story Link**
    Write balanced equations for the following word reactions.
    a. Copper and oxygen make copper(II) oxide.
    b. Iron and oxygen make iron(III) oxide.

What information is in an equation?

Section Objectives

Use information from a chemical equation to describe the energy change involved in a reaction.

List states of matter for reactants and products.

Interpret a chemical equation in terms of the relative number of molecules involved and the moles of reactants and products.

Derive mole ratios from a balanced chemical equation.

Use mole ratios and ΔH values to calculate energy changes in reactions.

Equations as instructions

Equations are like chemical recipes in that they describe a process that makes something new out of the ingredients. You've already seen that equations can tell you about the identities of products and reactants. Therefore, it is important to be sure the formulas are written correctly so that these substances are correctly identified. But equations contain much more information.

The ingredients label on the cookie package shown in **Figure 7-9** identifies the ingredients in cookies, but it is not a recipe. Using only this list would make it very difficult to actually make cookies. The list doesn't tell you that the cookies need to bake in the oven, nor does it tell you at what temperature the oven must be set. The order in which the ingredients should be mixed is not specified. Perhaps most important, the amounts of each ingredient are missing. Cookies containing more salt than flour would not be very tasty.

A recipe contains information about the amounts and forms of the ingredients, the order in which they are to be added, all of the instructions needed to make the cookies, and an indication of how many cookies can be made using the amounts given. Like a recipe, many chemical equations contain more than just the identities of the reactants and products. When read properly, the equations contain clues about whether the reaction they describe will occur, how to make the reaction occur, and how much of the reactants and products will be involved.

Figure 7-9
To make the cookies, you need a recipe with instructions, not just a list of ingredients. Like a recipe, a chemical equation can contain instructions about how to make reactions happen.

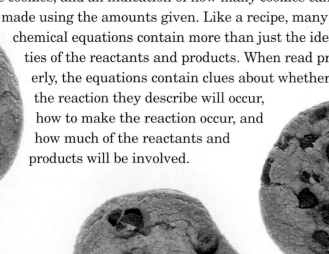

INGREDIENTS: ENRICHED WHEAT FLOUR (CONTAINS NIACIN, REDUCED IRON, THIAMINE MONONITRATE [VITAMIN B₁], RIBOFLAVIN [VITAMIN B₂], SWEET CHOCOLATE DROPS (SUGAR, CHOCOLATE, COCOA BUTTER, DEXTROSE, AND SOY LECITHIN–AN EMULSIFIER), VEGETABLE SHORTENING (PARTIALLY HYDROGENATED SOYBEAN AND/OR COTTONSEED OILS), SUGAR, BROWN SUGAR, HIGH FRUCTOSE CORN SYRUP, SALT, BAKING SODA, WHEY, NATURAL AND ARTIFICIAL FLAVOR AND COCOA (PROCESSED WITH ALKALI).

Figure 7-10a
The energy released by the synthesis reaction for two moles of water is as much energy used in 7.5 minutes of walking up stairs, . . .

7-10b
. . . 14.5 minutes of basketball, . . .

Energy changes in equations

You have seen that energy can be produced in exothermic reactions and absorbed in endothermic reactions.

Exothermic: $2H_2 + O_2 \longrightarrow 2H_2O + 572\ \text{kJ}$
Endothermic: $2H_2O + 572\ \text{kJ} \longrightarrow 2H_2 + O_2$

The most common reactions in chemistry are exothermic. Endothermic ones can occur, but they are less likely or require special conditions. Notice that the special condition required in the reaction of water to form hydrogen and oxygen is an input of 572 kJ of energy, usually in the form of electricity. This is the same amount of energy in the activities shown in Figure 7-10.

Another way that energy changes are indicated is in terms of ΔH, the amount of heat energy released or absorbed when the reaction takes place at normal atmospheric pressure. Positive ΔH values indicate an endothermic reaction, in which energy is absorbed. Negative ΔH values indicate an exothermic reaction, in which energy is released. Such values are often designated as amounts of energy per mole of a product or reactant. Thus, the ΔH values are half of the heat energy values noted in the first set of equations, which were for two moles of water. In cases in which energy amounts are measured per mole of a substance, fractional coefficients may be used. Note that the coefficient refers to *one-half of a mole* of oxygen, *not* one-half of a molecule.

7-10c
. . . or 16.5 minutes of swimming.

Exothermic: $H_2 + \frac{1}{2}O_2 \longrightarrow H_2O$

$$\Delta H = -286\ \text{kJ/mol}\ H_2O$$

Endothermic: $H_2O \longrightarrow H_2 + \frac{1}{2}O_2$

$$\Delta H = +286\ \text{kJ/mol}\ H_2O$$

One way to remember the meaning of positive and negative ΔH values is to consider them as a part of a recipe: *the ΔH value contains part of the instructions on how to get the reaction to happen.* If ΔH is a positive number, energy must be added to the reactants and absorbed as the reaction takes place. If ΔH is a negative number, energy will be lost by the reactants, and this energy will be released.

In the example of the synthesis of water, because the ΔH has a negative value, 286 kJ of energy are lost by the reactants and released as heat when the reaction occurs. In the reaction that breaks down water into hydrogen and oxygen, the positive ΔH value indicates that the 286 kJ of energy must be added to the reactants for the reaction to take place.

Reaction conditions in equations

Having all of the substances listed in an equation is not always enough to be certain the reaction will occur. Often, reactions require special conditions. It could be that the reactant substances must be gases, or that the reaction requires high pressure. Without such conditions, some reactions won't occur at all. Others will occur, but will take place so slowly that they are not useful. In addition to the chemical formulas for the reactants and products, chemical equations often contain symbols that indicate the states of matter for the reactants and products. Other notations in an equation, usually over the reaction arrow, can indicate special conditions that are required for the reaction to happen efficiently. **Table 7-3** lists the notations or symbols that are commonly used in chemical equations. Using these notations, the balanced equation for the safety match reaction discussed earlier in the chapter can be written as shown below.

$$3P_4(s) + 10KClO_3(s) \xrightarrow{\text{heat (friction)}} 10KCl(s) + 6P_2O_5(s)$$

Table 7-3
Symbols Used in Chemical Equations

Reactants and Products		Reaction Conditions	
Symbol	**Meaning**	**Symbol**	**Meaning**
(s) or (cr)	solid or crystal	$\longrightarrow$	"produces" or "yields," indicating result of reaction
(l)	liquid	$\rightleftharpoons$	reaction in which products can re-form into reactants; final result is a mixture of products and reactants
(g)	gas	$\xrightarrow{\Delta}$ or $\xrightarrow{\text{heat}}$	reactants are heated
(aq)	in aqueous solution (dissolved in water)	$\xrightarrow{1.0 \times 10^8 \text{kPa}}$	pressure at which reaction is carried out
$\downarrow$	solid precipitate product forms	$\xrightarrow{0°C}$	temperature at which reaction is carried out
$\uparrow$	gaseous product forms	$\xrightarrow{\text{Pd}}$	chemical formula of a catalyst added to speed up a reaction
		$\xrightarrow{e^-}$	electrolysis

Figure 7-11a
The cellular respira-
tion reaction that
breaks down glucose is
used as an energy
source by animals,
such as this dog ...

Quantitative relationships
Equations reveal the numbers of formula units involved

Take another look at the equation for cellular respiration introduced in Sample Problem 7A.

$$C_6H_{12}O_6(aq) + 6O_2(g) \longrightarrow 6CO_2(g) + 6H_2O(l) + energy$$

This reaction is used by living things to release stored energy. **Figure 7-11** shows where this reaction takes place at the cellular level in both plants and animals. The coefficients used to balance the equation serve not only to satisfy the law of conservation of mass, but also to *predict* the amount of each reactant that is required to produce a certain amount of product. The coefficients in a chemical equation tell you the relative numbers of formula units of reactants and products in the reaction. For example, the equation for cellular respiration tells you that *one* molecule of glucose, $C_6H_{12}O_6$, reacts with *six* molecules of oxygen, O_2, to produce *six* molecules of carbon dioxide, CO_2, and *six* molecules of water, H_2O. Another way to read the equation is in terms of *moles*. This approach will give you all of the information you see in **Table 7-4**.

As you can see from **Table 7-4**, mass is conserved in terms of grams. **Figure 7-12** on the next page demonstrates how atoms are conserved. Remember that the numbers of moles and molecules do not necessarily remain the same on both sides of the equations, because the molecules are being created and destroyed as the atoms are rearranged. In this case, one big molecule, $C_6H_{12}O_6$, is being used to create many smaller molecules, $6CO_2$ and $6H_2O$.

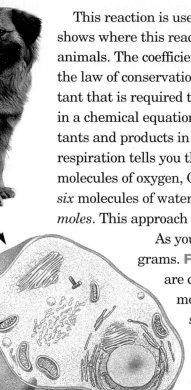

Mitochondrion:
site of cellular
respiration
reaction

Animal cell

Table 7-4
Information From a Balanced Chemical Equation

Equation:	$C_6H_{12}O_6$	$+ 6O_2$	$\longrightarrow$	$6CO_2$	$+ 6H_2O$
Moles	1	+ 6	$\longrightarrow$	6	+ 6
Molecules	$(6.02 \times 10^{23}) \times 1$	$+ (6.02 \times 10^{23}) \times 6$	$\longrightarrow$	$(6.02 \times 10^{23}) \times 6$	$+ (6.02 \times 10^{23}) \times 6$
Mass (grams)	180.18×1	$+ 32.00 \times 6$	$\longrightarrow$	44.01×6	$+ 18.02 \times 6$
Total mass (grams)	180.18	+ 192.00	$\longrightarrow$	264.06	+ 108.12

7-11b
... and plants, such as
this golden pothos vine.

Mitochondrion:
site of cellular
respiration
reaction

Plant cell

$$C_6H_{12}O_6 \quad + \quad 6O_2 \quad \longrightarrow \quad 6H_2O \quad + \quad 6CO_2$$

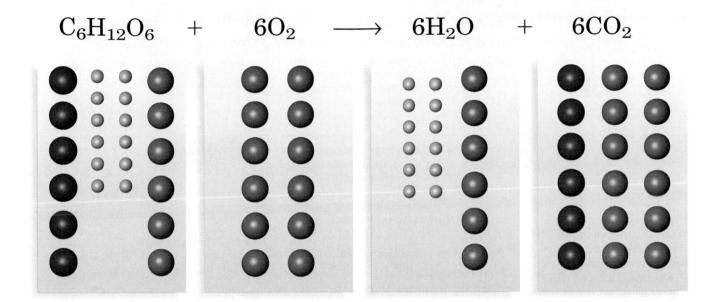

Figure 7-12
Atoms are neither created nor destroyed in the cellular respiration reaction. They are only rearranged to form new products.

Balanced equations show proportions

What would happen if you had *two* molecules of glucose instead of *one*? What would be required to ensure that the reaction went to completion? To answer this question, consider the models of the reactants and products shown in **Figure 7-12**. One way to determine the outcome would be to run the reaction one molecule at a time. The first glucose molecule would require six O_2 molecules and would produce six CO_2 molecules and six H_2O molecules. As the second molecule reacted, it would require an additional six O_2 molecules and would produce six more CO_2 molecules and six more H_2O molecules. In short, the reaction of two glucose molecules would require and produce 12 molecules of each of the other reactants and products, as shown in **Table 7-5**. For three glucose molecules, another six of each of the other molecules will be required for a complete reaction giving a total of 18 molecules of each type. A similar calculation can be made for four glucose molecules, which require 24 molecules of each type. Look closely at the proportions of reactants and products. You should be able to detect a pattern in the table. How many molecules of each reactant and product will be necessary for five glucose molecules?

Table 7-5
Amounts for Additional Molecules of Glucose

| | Amount Consumed | | Amount Produced | |
	$C_6H_{12}O_6$	O_2	H_2O	CO_2
First glucose molecule	1 molecule	6 molecules	6 molecules	6 molecules
Two glucose molecules	2 molecules	12 molecules	12 molecules	12 molecules
Three glucose molecules	3 molecules	18 molecules	18 molecules	18 molecules
Four glucose molecules	4 molecules	24 molecules	24 molecules	24 molecules

Ratio for one banana split is 1:1:1:3:1

Ratio for four banana splits is 4:4:4:12:4

1 cherry
1 squirt of whipped cream
1 spoon of hot fudge
3 scoops of ice cream
1 banana

4 cherries
4 squirts of whipped cream
4 spoons of hot fudge
12 scoops of ice cream
4 bananas

Figure 7-13
Whether one is making one banana split or four banana splits, the proportions of the ingredients remain the same.

4:4:4:12:4 ratio is the same as 1:1:1:3:1 ratio

Rather than counting all of the reactants and products or running the reaction one molecule at a time, it is easier to imagine that the entire equation has been multiplied by two. If you wanted to know how much of the reactants and the products would be required and produced by 64 glucose molecules, you would multiply the entire equation by 64. This situation is similar to the situation shown in **Figure 7-13**.

$$C_6H_{12}O_6 + 6O_2 \longrightarrow 6CO_2 + 6H_2O \text{ (equation)}$$

$$2C_6H_{12}O_6 + 12O_2 \longrightarrow 12CO_2 + 12H_2O \text{ (equation} \times 2)$$

$$64C_6H_{12}O_6 + 384O_2 \longrightarrow 384CO_2 + 384H_2O \text{ (equation} \times 64)$$

Relative amounts in equations can be expressed in moles

You have already seen how to interpret the cellular respiration reaction in terms of molecules. In addition, the equation for the cellular respiration reaction also indicates that 1 mol of $C_6H_{12}O_6$ reacts with 6 mol of O_2 to produce 6 mol of CO_2 and 6 mol of H_2O. This can be expressed as a ratio of reactants and products.

$$1 \text{ mol } C_6H_{12}O_6 : 6 \text{ mol } O_2 : 6 \text{ mol } CO_2 : 6 \text{ mol } H_2O$$

Thus, for any pair of molecules or formula units, a *mole ratio* can be determined by comparing the coefficients from the balanced chemical equation. For example, the mole ratio of glucose to carbon dioxide would be 1:6 because glucose's coefficient is 1 and carbon dioxide's coefficient is 6.

$$1 \text{ mol } C_6H_{12}O_6 : 6 \text{ mol } CO_2$$

What other mole ratios can you establish for this reaction? Be sure to express mole ratios in the lowest whole-number ratios.

Mole ratios can be multiplied just like equations. They can also be used like conversion factors to compare amounts of substances. In this way, you can determine exactly how much of a reactant is needed for the reaction or how much of a product can be expected. For example, 3 mol of $C_6H_{12}O_6$ would create 18 mol of CO_2.

$$3 \text{ mol } C_6H_{12}O_6 \times \frac{6 \text{ mol } CO_2}{1 \text{ mol } C_6H_{12}O_6} = 18 \text{ mol } CO_2$$

Energy is usually expressed in amounts per mole

The reaction shown below is used by living things to release stored energy. But how much energy can it release? The ΔH value for this reaction is given along with the balanced equation.

$$C_6H_{12}O_6(aq) + 6O_2(g) \longrightarrow 6CO_2(g) + 6H_2O(l)$$

$$\Delta H = -2870 \text{ kJ/mol glucose}$$

Because this ΔH value is expressed in terms of *kJ/mol of glucose,* it can be treated as part of a mole ratio. For every mole of glucose, 2870 kJ of heat energy will be released.

$$2870 \text{ kJ} : 1 \text{ mol } C_6H_{12}O_6 : 6 \text{ mol } O_2 : 6 \text{ mol } CO_2 : 6 \text{ mol } H_2O$$

Thus, you can calculate how much energy is provided by a reaction that produces 24 mol of H_2O or any other amount of any product or reactant.

$$24 \text{ mol } H_2O \times \frac{2870 \text{ kJ}}{6 \text{ mol } H_2O} = 11\ 480 \text{ kJ}$$

Section Review

14. Which of the following equations represent exothermic reactions?

a. $H_2(g) + Cl_2(g) \longrightarrow 2HCl(g) + 185 \text{ kJ/mol } H_2$

b. $Al_2O_3(s) + 1675.7 \text{ kJ} \longrightarrow 2Al(s) + \frac{3}{2}O_2(g)$

c. $C(s) + H_2O(g) \longrightarrow CO(g) + H_2(g)$
$\Delta H = +131.3 \text{ kJ/mol}$

d. $SnCl_2(s) + Cl_2(g) \longrightarrow SnCl_4(s)$
$\Delta H = -186.2 \text{ kJ/mol } SnCl_4$

15. Explain the states of the reactants and products and the other conditions that are described by each of the following equations.

a. $2KClO_3(s) + 156 \text{ kJ} \xrightarrow{\text{heat}} 2KCl(s) + 3O_2(g)$

b. $CaCO_3(s) \xrightarrow{\Delta} CaO(s) + CO_2(g)$
$\Delta H = +178.1 \text{ kJ/mol}$

c. $NH_4NO_3(s) \xrightarrow{200°C} N_2O(g) + 2H_2O(g)$
$\Delta H = -100. \text{ kJ/mol}$

d. $N_2(g) + 3H_2(g) \xrightarrow[10^7 \text{ Pa, 500°C}]{\text{Ru, C catalyst}} 2NH_3(g)$
$\Delta H = -92.0 \text{ kJ/mol } N_2$

16. Identify all possible mole ratios in each of the reactions in item **15**.

17. Using the mole ratios in item **16**, determine how many moles of each product could be formed given the following reactant amounts.

a. reaction **a** with 16.0 mol $KClO_3$

b. reaction **b** with 6.00 mol $CaCO_3$

c. reaction **c** with 7.00 mol NH_4NO_3

d. reaction **d** with 9.00 mol H_2

18. For each of the reactions in item **15** and amounts in item **17**, calculate how many kilojoules of energy would be involved. Also indicate whether the change would be exothermic or endothermic.

7-4

How can reactions be used?

Section Objectives

Categorize reactions as belonging to one (or more) of five basic types of chemical reactions.

Write chemical equations representing each type of chemical reaction.

Use an activity series to predict whether a given reaction will occur and what its products will be.

Write total and net ionic equations for double displacement reactions.

Putting reactions to work

You already know that chemical reactions involve rearrangements of atoms to produce substances with new properties. Sometimes a reaction is desirable, especially if the new substances have special uses because of their properties. For example, aspirin can be made in a multi-step process from acetic acid, carbon dioxide, and phenol, a highly toxic compound. This synthesis is summarized in Figure 7-14.

Figure 7-14
Chemical reactions can be used to make products that have useful properties that are different from those of the reactants.

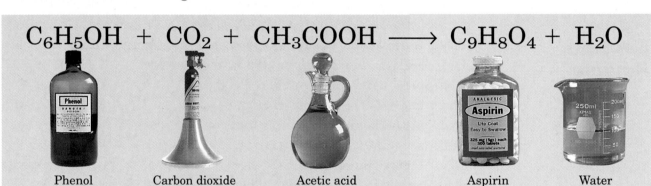

$$C_6H_5OH + CO_2 + CH_3COOH \longrightarrow C_9H_8O_4 + H_2O$$

Phenol   Carbon dioxide   Acetic acid   Aspirin   Water

Another reason for wanting a reaction to proceed is to use the energy it releases. The reaction between methane and oxygen produces the energy for a Bunsen burner's flame to boil water or melt glass.

Conversely, some reactions are undesirable, and the goal is to prevent them from occurring. Sometimes the same reactants can lead to several different reactions with different products, only one of which is useful.

The key to understanding and controlling all reactions lies in grouping together reactions that follow similar patterns, just as elements with similar properties were classified together.

combustion
exothermic reaction that usually involves oxygen to form the oxides of the elements in a reactant

Oxygen combines with other elements in combustion

Most reactions that are used for energy are **combustion** reactions, which usually involve the production of oxide compounds. The heat from the phosphorus and potassium chlorate safety match reaction from Section 7-1 is great enough to ignite the sulfur on the match head, which undergoes combustion to produce sulfur dioxide. Combustion reactions are exothermic, releasing a large amount of heat and light.

$$S_8(s) + 8O_2(g) \longrightarrow 8SO_2(g) + energy$$

Oxide of reactant

Figure 7-15
The complete combustion of any hydrocarbon, such as methane, yields carbon dioxide and water.

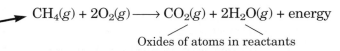

Another example of a combustion reaction is the reaction between methane and oxygen in a Bunsen burner, as shown in **Figure 7-15**. Note that the carbon from methane makes carbon dioxide, and the hydrogen makes water (hydrogen oxide). This production of water occurs when any hydrocarbon is burned.

$$CH_4(g) + 2O_2(g) \longrightarrow CO_2(g) + 2H_2O(g) + energy$$

Oxides of atoms in reactants

When a match is lit and the phosphorus and sulfur reactions get the cardboard or wood core of the match lit, the cellulose in the matchstick begins to burn. Cellulose is a polymer chain of glucose units. The following equation represents the combustion of 20 glucose units, but cellulose chains can be thousands of units long.

$$(C_6H_{10}O_5)_{20} + 120O_2 \longrightarrow 120CO_2 + 100H_2O + energy$$

Oxides of atoms in reactants

Although the combustion reaction indicates that the only products are water and carbon dioxide, ashes usually remain after a match burns. The equation is not often followed exactly. Combustion is incomplete, and some carbon that has not reacted with oxygen remains. Also, some carbon monoxide, CO, is produced in incomplete combustion. For wood or cardboard to burn so that only carbon dioxide and water are produced, the temperature must be high. *Remember that not all reactions are complete and special conditions are often required to maximize the reaction.* For combustion reactions, the higher the temperature, the more likely it is to be complete.

In all of the combustion examples in this section, binary oxides are formed. **Table 7-6** lists common oxides of nonmetals, some of which are formed in combustion reactions. The more complete the reaction, the more likely it is that the oxides near the bottom of the table will be formed.

Chem Fact
If gas furnaces or car engines aren't well ventilated, CO can form from incomplete combustion. The symptoms of CO poisoning are headaches, nausea, and difficulty sensing and thinking.

Table 7-6
Oxides of Some Nonmetals

Carbon	Nitrogen	Phosphorus	Sulfur
carbon(II) oxide (carbon monoxide), CO	nitrogen(I) oxide, N_2O	phosphorus(III) oxide, P_2O_3 (or P_4O_6)	sulfur(IV) oxide, SO_2
carbon(IV) oxide (carbon dioxide), CO_2	nitrogen(II) oxide, NO	phosphorus(V) oxide, P_2O_5 (or P_4O_{10})	sulfur(VI) oxide, SO_3
	nitrogen(III) oxide, N_2O_3		
	nitrogen(IV) oxide, NO_2 (or N_2O_4)		
	nitrogen(V) oxide, N_2O_5		

Concept Review

Predicting the products of combustion

19. Many stoves and water heaters get energy by burning natural gas, a mixture that contains propane, C_3H_8. Write a balanced equation for the combustion of propane to form CO_2 and H_2O.

Answers for Concept Review items and Practice problems begin on page 841.

Fire extinguishers

The key to most firefighting strategies is to control the combustion reaction by separating the reactants, fuel and oxygen, so that the molecules can no longer collide and react. Different types of fuels require different types of firefighting methods. Most fire extinguishers display codes indicating which types of fires they can put out.

Water, used on Class A fires involving solid fuels such as wood, cools the fuel so that it does not react as readily. The steam that is produced helps to displace the oxygen in the air around the fire. A Class B fire, in which the reactant is a liquid or gas, is put out best by a fire extinguisher containing CO_2 gas. Because CO_2 is more dense than O_2, it forms a layer underneath the O_2, cutting off the oxygen supply for the combustion reaction.

Class C fires involving a "live" electric circuit can also be extinguished by CO_2. Liquid water cannot be used, or there will be a danger of electric shock. Some Class C fire extinguishers contain a dry chemical which smothers the fire by interrupting the chain reaction that is occurring. For example, a competing reaction may take place with the contents of the fire extinguisher and the intermediates of the reaction. Class C fire extinguishers usually contain compounds such as ammonium dihydrogen phosphate, $(NH_4)H_2PO_4$, or sodium hydrogen carbonate, $NaHCO_3$.

Finally, Class D fires involve burning metals. These fires cannot be extinguished with CO_2 or water because they may react with some hot metals. For these fires, non-reactive dry powders are used to cover the metal and keep it separate from the oxygen in the air. One kind of powder contains finely ground sodium chloride crystals mixed with a special polymer that allows the crystals to adhere to any surface, even vertical ones. Another is finely ground graphite powder, which not only cuts off the oxygen supply but also absorbs heat.

Most fire extinguishers can be used with more than one type of fire. Check the fire extinguishers in your home and school for these codes. Be sure you know which kinds of fires they can put out.

Synthesis and decomposition reactions
Compounds are made in synthesis reactions

So far in this book, you have examined several synthesis reactions, in which a new compound is made from several reactants. For example, in Chapter 5, the reaction in which sodium metal and chlorine gas form sodium chloride crystals was discussed in great detail.

In this chapter, the reaction of sulfur in a match head with oxygen from the air to form a new compound, sulfur dioxide, was referred to as a combustion reaction. But this reaction involves atoms of two elements forming molecules of a new compound. Therefore, the sulfur-oxygen reaction can be described as either a synthesis reaction or a combustion reaction. *Some reactions can fit more than one category.*

The compound formed in a synthesis reaction can be made from more than one element as reactants, or it can be made from smaller molecules. As in the photosynthesis reaction, *the key feature of a synthesis reaction is that one of the compounds produced is larger or more complex than any of the reactant substances.*

$$6CO_2(g) + 6H_2O(l) \longrightarrow C_6H_{12}O_6(aq) + 6O_2(g)$$

More complex compound

Chem Fact
The production of one component of acid rain involves a series of synthesis reactions, starting with sulfur impurities in coal and other fuels, that form sulfuric acid.

$$2SO_2(g) + O_2(g) + 2H_2O(l) \longrightarrow 2H_2SO_4(aq)$$

Sample Problem 7B
Predicting products of a synthesis reaction

Write a balanced chemical equation for the synthesis reaction between lithium metal and liquid bromine.

❶ List what you know
- **reactants:** $Li(s) + Br_2(l)$
- **reaction type:** synthesis
- **product(s):** **?**

❷ Identify the products
- **Because it is a synthesis reaction, a compound containing the same atoms as the reactants will be among the products. Use information about compounds and formulas to determine the likeliest product.**

From Chapter 4, you know that Li is a metal and Br is a nonmetal.

From Chapters 5 and 6, you know that this combination is likely to form a salt with ionic bonds. When ionic bonds are formed, Li tends to form Li^+ ions, and Br_2 tends to form Br^- ions. The salt produced is probably LiBr.

❸ Write and balance the equation
- **Write a formula equation, and then balance it.**

$$\text{?}Li(s) + \text{?}Br_2(l) \longrightarrow \text{?}LiBr(s)$$

$$2Li(s) + Br_2(l) \longrightarrow 2LiBr(s)$$

- **Check to see that the question has been answered properly.**

Practice 7B

1. Write a balanced equation for the synthesis reaction between carbon, C, and sulfur, S_8.

2. Write a balanced equation for the synthesis reaction that produces iron(III) oxide.

polymerization
chemical reaction in which many simple molecules combine in chains to form a very large molecule

Polymerization reactions are a form of synthesis

Plants use the glucose produced in photosynthesis both as an energy source and as material to help build their structure. Plants and wood are made mostly of cellulose. To make cellulose, glucose molecules produced in photosynthesis are bonded to form long chains. The same reaction occurs over and over again, bonding one glucose molecule to another and gradually building up long, strong fibers of cellulose composed of thousands of glucose units, as shown in **Figure 7-16**.

Figure 7-16
The molecule that plants such as sunflower plants use to build their structural frameworks is cellulose, a polymer of glucose. In the structural formula for $C_6H_{12}O_6$, carbon atoms are represented by every unlabeled vertex.

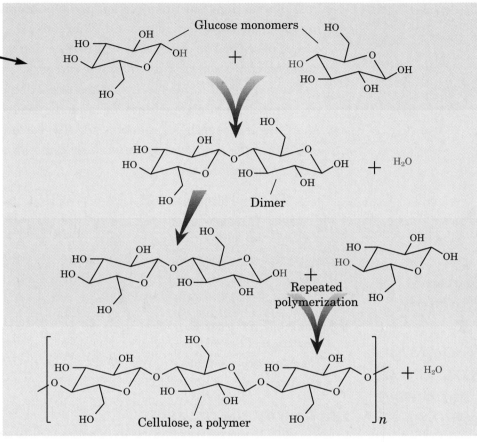

This type of reaction is called **polymerization**. In such reactions, many similar repeating units, known as *monomers*, are linked to form very large molecules, called *polymers*. In the cellulose-building reaction, the glucose molecules are the monomers, and the cellulose chains are the polymers.

In living things, polymerization reactions are responsible for building many molecules of life, especially protein and DNA. Chemists can also synthesize many polymers. The polyethylene used to make trash bags is a polymer. Other artificially made polymers include the examples shown in **Figure 7-17**.

Polystyrene foam (Styrofoam) in the helmet

Polyethylene terephthalate (Dacron) in the shirt

Nylon-66 polyamide (nylon) in the shorts

Polyethylene (plastic) in the water bottle

Styrene-butadiene rubber (rubber) in the tires

Polytetrafluoroethylene (Teflon) in the lubricants

Figure 7-17
Natural and artificial polymers are used in many consumer products.

In most polymers, like polyethylene and cellulose, the monomers are all identical. In other cases, such as proteins, different monomers may be combined. Although the amino acid monomers that make up proteins appear to be very different, each one has an amino functional group and an organic acid functional group, so the monomers all link in the same way, forming a "backbone" of carbon, nitrogen, and oxygen atoms. A polymer with three amino acids is called a *tripeptide*.

Arginine + Phenylalanine + Glycine ⟶ Tripeptide + Water

Compounds are broken down during decomposition

When $NaHCO_3$ is heated, it is broken down, and its atoms are rearranged to form three products. Such reactions, in which a compound is broken into different parts, are known as **decomposition** reactions.

decomposition
chemical reaction in which a single compound is broken down to produce two or more simpler substances

$$2NaHCO_3(s) \longrightarrow Na_2CO_3(s) + H_2O(g) + CO_2(g)$$

Reactant compound broken into several products

Metal carbonates decompose to yield CO_2. Some metal oxides decompose to yield O_2. Other common products of decompositions include H_2 and N_2.

The electrolysis of water is another decomposition reaction. Like most decomposition reactions, this reaction is endothermic. The energy required for this reaction may be supplied by a battery. Remember that the hydrogen and oxygen are produced in a 2:1 ratio, which you can predict by looking at the coefficients of the products in the balanced equation.

$$2H_2O(l) \longrightarrow 2H_2(g) + O_2(g)$$

More than one product, each less complex

A decomposition reaction can yield products that are elements, as in the case of the electrolysis of water, or products that are less complex substances than the reactants, as in the $NaHCO_3$ reaction.

The key feature of a decomposition reaction is that a reactant compound is broken into two or more less complex formula units.

Figure 7-18
Aluminum undergoes a displacement reaction with solutions of copper compounds to form copper metal and a solution of an aluminum compound. Some of the copper metal adheres to the aluminum foil, and the rest falls to the bottom of the beaker.

(labels, top circle)
Aluminum atom
Water molecule
Chloride ion, Cl⁻
Copper ion, Cu^{2+}

(labels, bottom circle)
Aluminum atom
Water molecule
Aluminum ion, Al^{3+}
Copper atom

single-displacement
chemical reaction in which one element replaces another element in a compound

Chem Fact
In electrical wiring in buildings, it is dangerous to join copper and aluminum wiring because of the metals' tendency to undergo this type of reaction.

Displacement reactions
Elements trade places in single-displacement reactions

When hydrogen gas is needed in the lab, the reaction of zinc and hydrogen chloride is used.

$$Zn(s) + 2HCl(aq) \longrightarrow ZnCl_2(aq) + H_2(g)$$

One way to think of this reaction is as a **single-displacement** reaction. Before the reaction begins, atoms of zinc are in the elemental form, and atoms of hydrogen are combined in a compound with chlorine. After the reaction, the atoms of hydrogen are in the elemental form, and atoms of zinc are combined in a compound with chlorine. In effect, the zinc atoms and hydrogen atoms switch places.

Single displacements can also occur with elements other than hydrogen. For example, if a piece of aluminum foil is scraped and then added to a solution of copper(II) chloride, reddish copper metal starts to form on the aluminum foil, and some falls to the bottom of the container. Aluminum is displacing copper in the compound, leaving behind copper metal, as shown in **Figure 7-18**.

$$2Al(s) + 3CuCl_2(aq) \longrightarrow 2AlCl_3(aq) + 3Cu(s)$$

Recall the example of potassium and water from Chapter 5. When the two are combined, there is a violent reaction, a gas is formed, and a solution remains. The equation for the reaction shows that potassium is displacing some of the hydrogen atoms in water, producing hydrogen gas and an ionic compound, potassium hydroxide, that dissolves in water. The heat released by the reaction is great enough to ignite the hydrogen so that it undergoes combustion with oxygen in the air.

$$2K(s) + 2HOH(l) \longrightarrow 2KOH(aq) + H_2(g)$$ — Single-displacement reaction

$$2H_2(g) + O_2(g) \longrightarrow 2H_2O(g)$$ — Combustion reaction

Figure 7-19a
Potassium reacts vigorously with water in a single-displacement reaction.

7-19b
Copper does not react with water, as predicted by the activity series.

activity series
arrangement of elements in the order of their tendency to react with water and acids

Table 7-7
Activity Series

Element	Reactivity
Li Rb K Ba Ca Na	react with cold H_2O and acids, replacing hydrogen
Mg Al Mn Zn Cr Fe	react with acids or steam, but usually not liquid water, to replace hydrogen
Ni Sn Pb	all react with acids, but not water, to replace hydrogen
H_2 Cu Hg	all react with oxygen to form oxides
Ag Pt Au	mostly unreactive

Halogen	Reactivity
F_2 Cl_2 Br_2 I_2	listed from most reactive to least reactive

An activity series summarizes and predicts reactions

Recall what happened when the piece of potassium was dropped in water. A rapid single displacement occurred as potassium replaced hydrogen in a compound. **Figure 7-19** shows what happens when a piece of copper, another metal, is dropped into water—nothing. No bubbles of hydrogen gas are formed. The single-displacement reaction does not occur.

$$Cu(s) + 2H_2O(l) \longrightarrow \text{no reaction}$$

Being able to write a chemical equation, therefore, does not necessarily mean that the reaction will actually take place.

Years of scientific experiments involving single-displacement reactions have been summarized in the **activity series**. The activity series is a list of elements organized according to their tendency to react (their "activity"). The more readily an element reacts with other substances, the greater its activity.

The more active elements tend to be more stable in a compound than in elemental form. If a more active element, such as potassium, and a compound containing a less active element, such as H_2O (which contains hydrogen), are brought together, the more active element will replace the less active element in the compound. In the activity series in **Table 7-7**, the elements are arranged in order of activity, with the most active element at the top. In general, any element can displace those below it from compounds but not those above it. There are a few exceptions to these rules, but this basic pattern is the most important thing to remember.

For example, potassium is near the top of the list, far above hydrogen. It can replace hydrogen in most compounds, including water. This confirms our observation of a violent reaction when potassium is added to water. But copper is farther down on the list, below hydrogen. It cannot replace hydrogen in compounds. This is why we observed no reaction when copper was added to water.

Figure 7-20a
If not galvanized, an iron nail will soon rust.

7-20b
After a nail is galvanized, the zinc layer corrodes preferentially because it is more active than iron. As a result, zinc(II) hydroxide, $Zn(OH)_2$ is formed.

Chem Fact
Most metals are like zinc, copper, and aluminum, all of which form an oxide layer that tends to protect the rest of the metal. Iron is the only commonly used metal that is susceptible to continued rusting in the presence of air and water.

The activity series enables you to predict results for many reactions. With the activity series, you could have predicted the result of adding aluminum foil to the copper chloride solution. Aluminum is above copper in the activity series and can replace it from compounds.

The activity series can help predict not only single-displacement reactions, but also some synthesis and decomposition reactions. In general, active metals undergo synthesis easily, but their compounds do not tend to undergo decomposition. Compounds of less active metals undergo decomposition easily, but are more difficult to synthesize. For example, calcium metal reacts so quickly with the oxygen in air that it forms an oxide tarnish while you watch. But copper wire can remain exposed to air for many years before forming copper oxide.

Controlling reactions with the activity series

Along with predicting whether a reaction will occur, the activity series also provides indications of how easily and quickly the reaction will proceed. For example, nickel can replace tin, which is immediately below it in the activity series, but the reaction is not as violent and fast as the reaction of potassium replacing hydrogen in water. Potassium and hydrogen are far apart on the activity series.

In general, the farther apart two elements are on the activity series, the more likely the higher one will replace the lower one in compounds.

Similarly, synthesis reactions with potassium metal occur much faster than those with nickel or tin.

Knowledge of the activity series can be used to prevent *corrosion,* the synthesis reaction in which metals form oxides and hydroxides. Iron is often galvanized to protect it from rusting by coating it with a thin layer of zinc, as shown in **Figure 7-20**. The iron will react only after most of the zinc has reacted. A similar approach is used to prevent corrosion in underground pipes, ship hulls, and cars.

Concept Review

Using the activity series to predict reactions

20. If a single-displacement reaction would occur between $H_2O(l)$ and the following metals, write a balanced chemical equation for the reaction.
    a. Ba   **b.** Rb   **c.** Zn
21. If a synthesis reaction would occur between $O_2(g)$ and the following metals, write a balanced chemical equation for the reaction.
    a. Au   **b.** Mn   **c.** Pb

Sample Problem 7C
Using the activity series

Write a balanced chemical equation for the reaction that will occur if the following substances are mixed together.

Cu(*s*)

Zn(NO$_3$)$_2$(*aq*)

Cu(NO$_3$)$_2$(*aq*)

Zn(*s*)

❶ Check the activity series for the more reactive metal
- The metal higher on the activity series in **Table 7-7** is most likely to displace the other.

Zinc is higher than copper. This means that zinc metal will form a zinc compound as a product, displacing copper in a compound. So the zinc metal and copper nitrate will be the reactants.

$$Cu(NO_3)_2(aq) + Zn(s) \longrightarrow Cu(s) + Zn(NO_3)_2(aq)$$

❷ Check other combinations of reactants for reactions
Cu will not react with Cu(NO$_3$)$_2$, nor will Zn react with Zn(NO$_3$)$_2$. Because Cu is lower than Zn on the activity series, Cu will not react to replace Zn in Zn(NO$_3$)$_2$. No other combination of reactants will result in a reaction.

Practice 7C

Using **Table 7-7**, arrange the following reactions in order of decreasing tendency to occur. Indicate which would not occur at all. For those reactions that would occur, predict the products that would be formed.

1. Zn(*s*) + CuCl$_2$(*aq*) $\longrightarrow$

2. Mg(*s*) + Pb(NO$_3$)$_2$(*aq*) $\longrightarrow$

3. Ni(*s*) + Al$_2$(SO$_4$)$_3$(*aq*) $\longrightarrow$

4. Cu(*s*) + AgNO$_3$(*aq*) $\longrightarrow$

double-displacement
chemical reaction in which two elements in different compounds exchange places

In double-displacement reactions, atoms are exchanged between compounds

In **Figure 7-21**, two colorless solutions are being mixed. Where they mix, a bright yellow cloud is formed. This is a **double-displacement** reaction. The colorless solution in the graduated cylinder contains potassium iodide. The solution in the beaker contains lead(II) nitrate. There are actually two products formed: the solid, yellow ionic compound lead(II) iodide, PbI$_2$, and potassium nitrate, KNO$_3$, which dissolves easily in water and can't be seen in **Figure 7-21**.

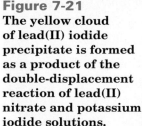

$$2KI(aq) + Pb(NO_3)_2(aq) \longrightarrow PbI_2(s) + 2KNO_3(aq)$$

Figure 7-21
The yellow cloud of lead(II) iodide precipitate is formed as a product of the double-displacement reaction of lead(II) nitrate and potassium iodide solutions.

From this equation, it appears that the atoms within the reactants have been exchanged to form the products. The main reason the reaction occurs so dramatically is that one of the products is a solid that does not dissolve in water. Because the compound does not dissolve in water, there is little chance for the ions in PbI$_2$ to collide with K$^+$ and NO$_3^-$ ions and re-form KI and Pb(NO$_3$)$_2$.

In Chapter 5, you learned that when ionic compounds such as KI and $Pb(NO_3)_2$ dissolve, the solutions actually contain mixtures of ions.

$$KI(aq) = K^+(aq) + I^-(aq)$$

$$Pb(NO_3)_2(aq) = Pb^{2+}(aq) + 2NO_3^-(aq)$$

Thus, the real reaction is better indicated by individually listing all of the ions in the reactants and products in a total ionic equation.

$$2K^+(aq) + 2I^-(aq) + Pb^{2+}(aq) + 2NO_3^-(aq) \longrightarrow$$

$$PbI_2(s) + 2K^+(aq) + 2NO_3^-(aq)$$

When these four ions are mixed, two of them, Pb^{2+} and I^-, bond to form a solid. The other two ions, K^+ and NO_3^-, are on both sides of the total ionic equation. Because they remain unchanged in the reaction, they are called *spectator ions*. Total ionic equations can be long and difficult to decipher, so double-displacement reactions are often written using *net ionic equations*, which indicate only the ions involved in the reaction. Spectator ions, such as K^+ and NO_3^-, are omitted.

$$2I^-(aq) + Pb^{2+}(aq) \longrightarrow PbI_2(s)$$

The precipitate, lead(II) iodide, PbI_2, is responsible for the yellow cloud produced when the solutions mix.

Double-displacement reactions always involve the formation either of a molecular compound such as water or the creation of a gas or precipitate.

You have already learned a little about acids and bases and their properties. You may even know that they are "opposites" that can *neutralize* each other. If equally acidic and basic solutions are combined, the resulting solution will have properties of neither acids nor bases. But why have the properties changed?

Consider the reaction that occurs when a person takes an antacid product to settle an upset stomach caused by the secretion of too much acid by the cells lining the stomach.

$$Mg(OH)_2(aq) + 2HCl(aq) \longrightarrow MgCl_2(aq) + 2H_2O(l)$$

Antacids contain bases, such as magnesium hydroxide, to neutralize the hydrochloric acid produced by the stomach, as shown in **Figure 7-22**.

Figure 7-22
After taking an antacid for indigestion, double displacement reactions provide the relief you get. The stomach acid (modeled here by an acid solution in a beaker) reacts with antacid to make a salt and water, substances with neutral pH.

pH paper indicates pH of 1

Before

pH paper indicates pH of 6

After

But remember that if you combine $Mg(OH)_2$ and HCl in a solution, you are really combining solutions containing four different ions. Not only that, but the hydroxide anion and hydrogen cations react to form water. All that remains when an acid has completely reacted with a base in a double-displacement reaction is water and a salt.

Recall from Chapter 5 that a salt is a compound made when atoms donate and accept electrons to become ions and bond together. A salt can also be defined as a product of a double-displacement reaction between an acid and a base. In fact, there is no detectable difference between a solution made from the double-displacement neutralization reaction and one made by dissolving magnesium chloride in water.

The net ionic equation for the neutralization reaction includes only the hydroxide anion and hydrogen cation because they are changed into a water molecule by the reaction.

$$H^+(aq) + OH^-(aq) \longrightarrow H_2O(l)$$

Section Review

22. Balance the following equations, and identify which of the five types of reactions each represents.
    a. $Cl_2(g) + KBr(aq) \longrightarrow KCl(aq) + Br_2(l)$
    b. $CaO(s) + H_2O(l) \longrightarrow Ca(OH)_2(aq)$
    c. $AgNO_3(aq) + K_2SO_4(aq) \longrightarrow Ag_2SO_4(s) + KNO_3(aq)$
    d. $NH_3(g) + O_2(g) \xrightarrow{\text{Pt}} NO(g) + H_2O(g)$
    e. $H_2SO_4(aq) + KOH(aq) \longrightarrow K_2SO_4(aq) + H_2O(l)$

23. Write balanced chemical equations for the following reactions.
    a. synthesis of sulfuric acid, H_2SO_4, from water and sulfur trioxide
    b. combustion of butane, C_4H_{10}
    c. decomposition of potassium chlorate to form potassium chloride and oxygen
    d. single-displacement reaction for zinc and copper(II) sulfate
    e. double-displacement reaction for silver nitrate and sodium chloride

24. Explain how to use an activity series to predict chemical behavior.

25. Predict whether the following reactions would occur. For each that would, complete and balance the equation.
    a. $Ni(s) + H_2O(l) \longrightarrow$
    b. $Br_2(l) + KI(aq) \longrightarrow$
    c. $Mg(s) + Cu(NO_3)_2(aq) \longrightarrow$
    d. $FeO(s) \longrightarrow$
    e. $Ba(s) + O_2(g) \longrightarrow$

26. Write both the total ionic and net ionic equations for each of the following.
    a. Potassium chloride and silver nitrate solutions react to yield the ionic compound potassium nitrate, which dissolves, and silver chloride, which is insoluble.
    b. When copper(II) chloride reacts with ammonium phosphate in aqueous solutions, soluble ammonium chloride forms, and copper(II) phosphate precipitates out of the solution.

Conclusion: Reactivity and the Statue of Liberty

At the beginning of this chapter, you read about problems associated with the restoration of the Statue of Liberty.

Why did the iron support beams weaken so much, while the copper skin did not? When the tar coating wore away, the salt water acted as an electrical conductor between the copper and iron. Because copper is below iron in the activity series, iron will corrode preferentially, just like zinc on a galvanized nail. The copper will not begin to react until nearly all of the iron reacts.

How could future corrosion be prevented? During restoration, the iron bars had to be replaced a few at a time so that the statue was not left unsupported. Two alloys, or mixtures of metals, were used to replace the rusted iron. One of them, ferallium, is a very strong steel-aluminum alloy that resists corrosion. It was used to connect the framework to the statue's structural tower. The original iron framework was designed with many twists and turns, so 316L stainless steel, which is more flexible than ferallium but also is corrosion-resistant, was used as a replacement.

The bars of the structure were also painted with sealants to prevent corrosion. First, an undercoat containing potassium silicate and zinc dust was applied. On top of that, an epoxy polyamide polymer was used. The sealants had to be water based, or fumes could build up to toxic or explosive levels within the statue. They also had to stick to each other and to the bars. Finally, the top coat needed to be resistant to graffiti.

To keep the copper shell from touching the new frame, a layer of solid polytetrafluoroethylene (Teflon) was inserted between them.

Finally, the cracks between the copper sheets needed to be sealed to keep out the sea spray. A silicone sealant used in construction was chosen because it is long lasting, withstands changes in temperature, and doesn't corrode or discolor the statue's copper skin.

Applying Concepts

1. Using the activity series, explain why zinc dust is an important part of the undercoat for the structure.
2. The top coat of paint on the steel framework is composed of the monomers shown in the equation below. Write a formula for the product. (Hint: only the ends of each molecule will react.)

$$HOOC(CH_2)_nCOOH + H_2N(CH_2)_nNH_2 \longrightarrow \mathbf{?} + H_2O$$

Research and Writing

Use the library to find out more about the following.

1. Report on a chemical or a process used in a specific restoration project.
2. Some chemistry technology can be used on artworks or documents. Report on how such techniques are used to detect forgeries.

Highlights

• The mass, number, and types of atoms remain the same on both sides of a balanced equation.
• Coefficients indicating amounts of reactants and products can be adjusted to balance a chemical equation. Subscripts within a chemical formula cannot be changed.

Key terms

activity series

chemical equation

coefficient

combustion

decomposition

double-displacement

polymerization

single-displacement

Key ideas

 ### What is a chemical reaction?

• A chemical reaction involves rearrangements of atoms from the reactants into new substances, the products.
• The only way to prove that a change was a chemical change is to demonstrate that the new substances produced have different properties from those of the reactants.
• An exothermic reaction releases energy to the environment because the bonds holding the products together are stronger than the bonds holding the reactants together.

 ### How are reactions written?

• A formula equation uses atomic symbols to describe the rearrangement of atoms of the reactants to form the products in a chemical reaction.

 ### What information is in an equation?

• Notations in a chemical equation can indicate special conditions required for a reaction to occur, as well as the states of matter for the substances in the reaction.
• Chemical equations describe energy changes in a reaction. ΔH indicates the amount of energy released or absorbed as heat for each mole of product or reactant.
• The coefficients in a balanced equation indicate the relative amounts required for each substance. They can be interpreted in terms of formula units or as a mole ratio.

 ### How can reactions be used?

• Five basic types of chemical reactions include combustion, synthesis, decomposition, single-displacement, and double-displacement.
• Polymerization reactions are synthesis reactions that build large molecules from many repeated units.
• An activity series predicts single-displacement reactions. Any element on the list will displace those below it in compounds.
• Double-displacement reactions can be represented by net ionic equations indicating only the ions that are changed by the reaction.

Key problem-solving approach:
Reaction types

To classify a chemical reaction, compare the reaction to the description of each of the five basic reaction types. The proper description points to the reaction type and an example of that reaction.

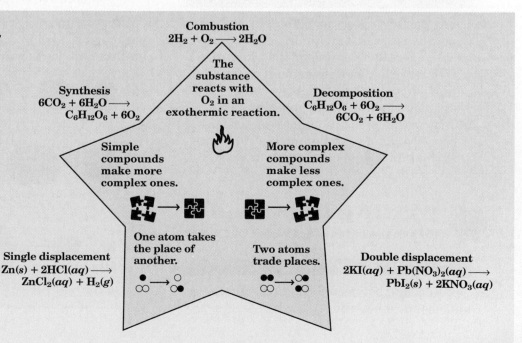

Combustion
$2H_2 + O_2 \longrightarrow 2H_2O$

The substance reacts with O_2 in an exothermic reaction.

Synthesis
$6CO_2 + 6H_2O \longrightarrow$
$C_6H_{12}O_6 + 6O_2$

Decomposition
$C_6H_{12}O_6 + 6O_2 \longrightarrow$
$6CO_2 + 6H_2O$

Simple compounds make more complex ones.

More complex compounds make less complex ones.

One atom takes the place of another.

Two atoms trade places.

Single displacement
$Zn(s) + 2HCl(aq) \longrightarrow$
$ZnCl_2(aq) + H_2(g)$

Double displacement
$2KI(aq) + Pb(NO_3)_2(aq) \longrightarrow$
$PbI_2(s) + 2KNO_3(aq)$

Review and Assess

The nature of chemical reactions

REVIEW

1. Calcium oxide, CaO, is an ingredient in cement mixes. When water is added, CaO reacts to form calcium hydroxide, $Ca(OH)_2$, which can be used as an egg preservative. The properties of CaO are different from those of $Ca(OH)_2$.
   a. Write a word equation for this exothermic chemical reaction.
   b. Are the bonds stronger in the reactants or the products? Explain your answer.
   c. What evidence is there that this is a chemical reaction?

2. Use the concepts of bond energy and stability to explain why most naturally occurring chemical reactions are exothermic.

3. A student writes the following statement in a lab report: The atoms of the reactants are destroyed, and the atoms of the products are created; energy is also created.
   a. Explain the scientific inaccuracies in the student's statement.
   b. How could the student correct the inaccurate statement?

APPLY

4. Using particle theory, explain why liquids generally react faster than solids, and why gases generally react faster than liquids.

5. a. Use particle theory to explain why gasoline pumps contain labels warning against smoking while pumping gas.
   b. Why is this precaution not a major concern around a solid flammable substance such as a block of candle wax or wood?

Writing balanced chemical equations

REVIEW

6. Differentiate between formula equations and chemical equations.

7. Why must coefficients, and not subscripts, be changed to balance a chemical equation?

8. The white paste that lifeguards rub on their noses to prevent sunburn contains zinc oxide, $ZnO(s)$, as an active ingredient. Zinc oxide is produced by burning zinc sulfide.

$$2ZnS(s) + 3O_2(g) \longrightarrow 2ZnO(s) + 2SO_2(g)$$

   a. What is the coefficient for sulfur dioxide?
   b. What is the subscript for oxygen gas?
   c. How many atoms of oxygen react?
   d. How many atoms of oxygen appear in the sulfur dioxide molecules?

9. Balance the following equations.

   a. $CaH_2(s) + H_2O(l) \longrightarrow Ca(OH)_2(aq) + H_2(g)$

   b. $CH_3CH_2C{\equiv}CH(g) + Br_2(l) \longrightarrow$
   $\qquad\qquad\qquad CH_3CH_2CBr_2CHBr_2(l)$

   c. $Pb(NO_3)_2(aq) + NaOH(aq) \longrightarrow$
   $\qquad\qquad\qquad Pb(OH)_2(s) + NaNO_3(aq)$

10. Translate the following word equations into balanced formula equations.

   a. silver nitrate + potassium iodide $\longrightarrow$
   $\qquad\qquad$ silver iodide + potassium nitrate

   b. nitrogen dioxide + water $\longrightarrow$
   $\qquad\qquad$ nitric acid + nitrogen monoxide

   c. silicon tetrachloride + water $\longrightarrow$
   $\qquad\qquad$ silicon dioxide + hydrochloric acid

11. Molecular models of chemical reactions are pictured below. Correct the drawings to reflect balanced equations.

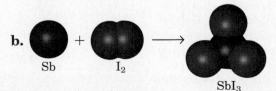

a. CH_4 O_2 CO_2 H_2O

b. Sb I_2 SbI_3

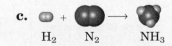

c. H_2 N_2 NH_3

Answers to items in a black square begin on page 841.

12 Carbon tetrachloride is used as an intermediate chemical in the manufacture of other chemicals. It is prepared by reacting chlorine gas with methane. Hydrogen chloride is also formed in this reaction. Write the balanced chemical equation for the production of carbon tetrachloride. (Hint: see Sample Problem 7A.)

13. Sodium hydroxide is produced commercially by the electrolysis of aqueous sodium chloride. Hydrogen and chlorine gases are also produced. Write the balanced chemical equation for the production of sodium hydroxide. (Hint: see Sample Problem 7A.)

APPLY

14. Iron chloride, $FeCl_3$, is a chemical used in photography. It can be produced by reacting iron and chlorine. Identify the chemical equation that is balanced, and explain what is wrong with the two that are not.
a. $Fe(s) + Cl_3(g) \longrightarrow FeCl_3(s)$
b. $2Fe(s) + 3Cl_2(g) \longrightarrow 2FeCl_3(s)$
c. $Fe(s) + 3Cl_2(g) \longrightarrow Fe2Cl_3(s)$

15. What product is missing in the following equation?

$$MgO + 2HCl \longrightarrow MgCl_2 + \mathbf{?}$$

16. How many moles of HCl can be made from 6.15 mol of H_2 and an excess of Cl_2?

Decoding chemical equations

REVIEW

17. What is the significance of the positive or negative sign before the ΔH value in a chemical reaction?

18. Aluminum sulfate, $Al_2(SO_4)_3$, is used in fireproofing fabrics and the manufacture of antiperspirants. It can be formed from a reaction with H_2SO_4.

$$Al_2O_3(s) + 3H_2SO_4(aq) \longrightarrow$$
$$Al_2(SO_4)_3(aq) + 3H_2O(l)$$

a. How many moles of $Al_2(SO_4)_3$ would be produced if 6 mol of H_2SO_4 reacted with an excess of Al_2O_3?
b. How many moles of Al_2O_3 are required to make 2 mol of H_2O?
c. If 588.0 mol of Al_2O_3 react with excess H_2SO_4, how many moles of each of the products would be produced?

19. Sucrose, $C_{12}H_{22}O_{11}$, is the sugar used to sweeten many foods. Inside the body it is broken down to produce H_2O and CO_2.

$$C_{12}H_{22}O_{11} + 12O_2 \longrightarrow 12CO_2 + 11H_2O$$
$$\Delta H = -5.65 \times 10^3 \text{ kJ}$$

a. List all of the ratios that can be derived from this equation.
b. Three teaspoons (0.0695 mol) of table sugar are mixed in a glass of iced tea. How much energy will the person drinking this iced tea gain from the sugar?

20. Copper(II) nitrate, $Cu(NO_3)_2$, is used to give a dark finish to items made of copper metal, making them appear antique. Copper(II) nitrate can be produced by reacting copper metal with nitric acid. Complete the following table which analyzes this reaction.

$$3Cu(s) + 8HNO_3(aq) \longrightarrow$$
$$3Cu(NO_3)_2(aq) + 4H_2O(l) + 2NO(g)$$

Equation	Cu	HNO$_3$	Cu(NO$_3$)$_2$	H$_2$O	NO
Moles					
Formula units					
Molar mass (g/mol)					
Total mass (g)					
State of matter					

21. 1,3-butadiene gas is an intermediate in the production of synthetic rubber, which is widely used in many products, from electrical insulation to car tires. This gas can be obtained by putting butane gas under high pressure and heat. Refer to the diagram below to answer the following questions.
a. Is this reaction exothermic or endothermic?
b. If 236.5 kJ of heat are absorbed, what would be ΔH for the reaction?
c. Write the full equation for the reaction, along with the ΔH value.

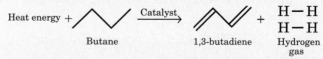

22. Why do you breathe hard during exercise?

Classifying chemical reactions

REVIEW

23. Explain the difference between single-displacement and double-displacement reactions.

24. Use **Table 7-7** to predict which metal would be the best to plate components of a boat to prevent corrosion.
    a. Rb **b.** Cr **c.** Ba

25. Use **Table 7-7** to predict which metal would be the best choice as a container for concentrated acid.
    a. Sn **b.** Mn **c.** Pt

26. How do total and net ionic equations differ?

27. Which ions in a total ionic equation are called spectator ions? Why?

28. The saline solution used to soak contact lenses is primarily NaCl dissolved in water. Which of the following ways to designate the solution is incorrect?
    a. NaCl(aq) **b.** NaCl(s)
    c. Na$^+$(aq) + Cl$^-$(aq)

29. What are some of the characteristics of each of these five common chemical reactions?
    a. combustion
    b. synthesis
    c. decomposition
    d. single-displacement
    e. double-displacement

PRACTICE

30 Write the balanced chemical equation for the synthesis of the antacid magnesium oxide from magnesium metal and oxygen gas. (Hint: see Sample Problem 7B.)

31. Write the balanced chemical equation for the synthesis of the pollutant nitrogen dioxide from nitrogen monoxide and oxygen gas. (Hint: see Sample Problem 7B.)

32 Write a balanced chemical equation for the reaction that will occur if the following ingredients are mixed together. (Hint: see Sample Problem 7C.)

Pb(s), PbCl$_2$(aq), Zn(s), and ZnCl$_2$(aq)

33. Write a balanced chemical equation for the reaction that will occur if the following ingredients are mixed together. (Hint: see Sample Problem 7C.)

Rb(s), RbNO$_3$(aq), Zn(s), and Zn(NO$_3$)$_2$(aq)

APPLY

34. What other reaction type(s) can be used to categorize combustion reactions? Explain.

35. Terephthalic acid and ethylene glycol, shown below, can combine to synthesize a single monomer of the polyethylene terephthalate polymer used in film production. During the reaction, a molecule of water is formed. Write the balanced formula equation for this reaction.

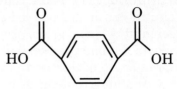

Terephthalic acid

Ethylene glycol

36. Use **Table 7-7** to predict whether the following reactions are possible.

a. Ni(s) + MgSO$_4$(aq) ⟶
    NiSO$_4$(aq) + Mg(s)

b. 6Li(s) + Al$_2$(SO$_4$)$_3$(aq) ⟶
    3Li$_2$SO$_4$(aq) + 2Al(s)

c. Ba(s) + 2H$_2$O(l) ⟶ Ba(OH)$_2$(aq) + H$_2$(g)

37. **a.** Write the total and net ionic equation for the reaction in which the antacid Al(OH)$_3$ neutralizes stomach acid.
    b. Identify the spectator ions in this reaction.
    c. What would be the advantages of using Al(OH)$_3$ as an antacid rather than NaHCO$_3$, which undergoes the following reaction with stomach acid?

NaHCO$_3$(aq) + HCl(aq) ⟶
    NaCl(aq) + H$_2$O(aq) + CO$_2$(g)

38. When heated, tungsten metal usually forms an oxide compound in a synthesis reaction. Light-bulb filaments are made of tungsten. Use the information in the diagram to explain why the light-bulb filament does not form an oxide compound.

Tungsten filament

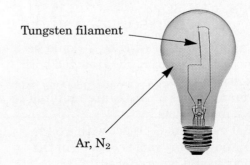

Ar, N$_2$

1. *Conservation of energy*
   When wood is burned, energy is released in the forms of heat and light. Explain why this change does not violate the law of conservation of energy.

   $$[C_6H_{10}O_5]_n + 6nO_2 \longrightarrow 5nH_2O + 6nCO_2$$

2. *Structural formulas*
   Neoprene is a polymer used to make shoes and gloves.
   a. Identify the monomer in this portion of a neoprene molecule by drawing its Lewis structure.
   b. What is the empirical formula of neoprene?

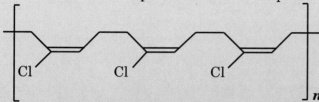

3. **Theme:** *Classifications and trends*
   Although cesium is not included in the activity series in **Table 7-7**, where would you expect it to appear based on its position in the periodic table?

USING TECHNOLOGY

1. *Graphics calculator*
   In a given chemical equation, the ΔH value can be expressed as part of a mole ratio. This ratio can be graphically represented as the slope of a straight line. The graph can be used to predict how much energy is transferred when a given amount of substance reacts. The combustion of 1.00 mol of methane, CH_4, has a ΔH of $-890.$ kJ. Using the $\boxed{WINDOW}$ function, set the x-range from 0 to 20 with a scale of 2 and the y-range from $-20\,000$ to 0 with a scale of 2000. Select the $\boxed{Y=}$ key and enter the function $Y_1 = \boxed{(-)}\,890\,\boxed{X, T, \theta}$, which is $y = -890x$. (Hint: use the negative key, not the subtraction key.) Press $\boxed{GRAPH}$ and use the $\boxed{TRACE}$ mode to estimate the kilojoules released when the following amounts of methane are burned.
   a. 5.00 mol **b.** 8.00 mol **c.** 15.00 mol

Performance assessment

Design an experiment to test different antacids on the market. Include $NaHCO_3$, $Mg(OH)_2$, $CaCO_3$, and $Al(OH)_3$ in your data. Discover which one neutralizes the most acid and what byproducts are formed. Show your experiment to your teacher for approval. If your experiment is approved, obtain the necessary chemicals from your teacher and test your procedure.

Portfolio projects

1. *Chemistry and you*
   For one day, record situations that show evidence of a chemical change. Identify the reactants and the products, and determine whether there is proof of a chemical reaction. Classify each of the chemical reactions according to the five common reaction types in the chapter.

2. *Chemistry and you*
   Research safety tips for dealing with fires. Create a poster or brochure about fire safety that explains both these tips and their basis in science.

3. *Research and communication*
   Much of the energy used in the United States comes from the combustion of hydrocarbon fuels. Other sources of energy are available, however, including the sun, wind, and water. As a group, research either hydrocarbon fuels or alternative fuels. Analyze the reactions involved in using and producing the fuel. For example, solar power produces no byproducts; however, the production of solar panels should be considered. Have the class debate which power source is the safest, the most economical, the most efficient, and the most convenient.

4. *Research and communication*
   Many products are labeled biodegradable. Choose several biodegradable items on the market, and research the decomposition reactions involved. Be sure to take into account any special conditions that must occur for the substance to biodegrade. Present your information to the class to help inform the students about what products are best for the environment.

CHAPTER 8 | Stoichiometry

$$Mg(s) + 2H_2O(l) \longrightarrow$$
$$\text{heat energy} + Mg(OH)_2(s) + H_2(g)$$

Mass Relationships and Feeding the Army

At dinnertime, the soldiers were miles from the nearest field kitchen.

They each pulled out a meal pouch, inserted it into a small bag, and

added water from a canteen to the bag. The contents grew warm, and

within 15 minutes, they were eating hot meals.

The dinner is one of the U.S. Army's "Meal, Ready-to-Eat," or MRE, rations. Each MRE is a complete main dish within a pouch made of aluminum foil and plastic. In 1985, researchers at the Army's Natick Research, Development, and Engineering Center in Massachusetts invented a new way to heat MREs using a special "Flameless Ration Heater," or FRH.

Each FRH is a plastic sleeve containing a paperboard-covered pad with holes in it. Within the pad are metal particles embedded in a polymeric matrix. The metal contains a 90% magnesium and 10% iron alloy, a homogeneous mixture of the two elements. The entire assembly has a mass of 20.0 g, of which about 8.1 g are magnesium. A little NaCl is also included.

Most people think of water as being used to cool things, but in this case, the water reacts with magnesium in an exothermic single-displacement reaction. The energy released by this reaction in the FRH warms the meal to 60°C.

$$Mg(s) + 2H_2O(l) \longrightarrow Mg(OH)_2(s) + H_2(g) + 353 \text{ kJ}$$

According to the activity series, this reaction ordinarily doesn't occur. But when Fe, a less active metal, is in contact with it, Mg corrodes preferentially, just like the zinc coating on galvanized iron. The cardboard pad keeps the water and magnesium in contact. Earlier models of the FRH used more than 60 mL of water, but the latest version requires only 45 mL.

The necessity of heating meals with equipment that is lightweight and easy to use is one shared by the Army and people involved in outdoor activities such as camping and backpacking.

A heater similar to the FRH is also available for campers. It uses the synthesis reaction that combines calcium oxide and water.

$$CaO(s) + H_2O(l) \longrightarrow Ca(OH)_2(s) + 64.4 \text{ kJ}$$

Before the FRH, the Army issued bars of trioxane, $C_3H_6O_3$, to warm meals. The bars, which came in 15 g and 30 g sizes, were burned. Complete combustion of a 30 g bar releases about 500 kJ of energy.

MREs could not be heated directly by burning trioxane. Instead, the burning trioxane heated a metal cup of water containing the MRE pouch.

- *Why was the magnesium-water reaction of the FRH chosen over the other methods?*
- *Why is there a difference between the amount of water that is added and the amount of water that the reaction requires?*

To answer these questions, you need to understand how the amounts and masses of substances in a reaction compare. In this chapter, you will learn to predict the amount of reactant needed for a reaction, and you will apply these principles to determine the most effective way to heat an MRE.

How much can a reaction produce?

Stoichiometry

stoichiometry
mass and quantity relationships among reactants and products in a chemical reaction

In Chapter 7, you learned that reactions can be used to make new products, to break down reactants, or to provide a source of energy. But the predictions you made in Chapter 7 relate only to the *identities* and *relative amounts* of the products and reactants. It is also very useful to predict exactly *how much mass* of a substance will be involved in a reaction. Such predictions are a part of chemistry known as **stoichiometry**.

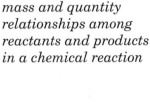

Isoamyl acetate

Figure 8-1
Isoamyl acetate is the compound primarily responsible for a banana's fruity flavor. It is used in a variety of artificially flavored products.

Making chemicals by the kilogram

The makers of artificial flavors for items such as banana ice cream or banana-flavored bubble gum need to use stoichiometry when they make the banana flavoring. The substance providing most of the taste and smell of bananas is actually a single compound known as 3-methylbutyl acetate, or isoamyl acetate. The structure of this compound is shown in **Figure 8-1**. Isoamyl acetate is a member of a group of organic compounds known as esters. Esters are among the organic chemicals responsible for the aromas and flavors of fruits. The ester functional group is indicated in red on the structure in **Figure 8-1**.

Because there are so many compounds in a banana, it is difficult to isolate and purify natural flavoring. It is actually more cost-efficient to synthesize isoamyl acetate in the lab and use it as an artificial banana flavoring. The equation for the synthesis reaction is shown below. The flavor chemicals shown in **Figure 8-2** on the following page are also often synthesized as artificial flavors in the lab.

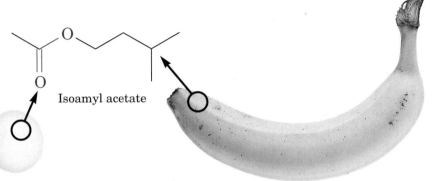

Acetic acid   Isoamyl alcohol   Isoamyl acetate   Water

Ethyl butyrate

Ethyl acetate

4-(4-hydroxyphenyl) 2-butanone
or raspberry ketone

OH

Benzaldehyde

Figure 8-2
Many flavors and aromas are due to organic chemicals such as esters, aldehydes, alcohols, and ketones.

Consider the following question: *If a flavoring manufacturer has 45.0 kg of isoamyl alcohol and enough acetic acid to react with all of it, what is the maximum number of kilograms of banana flavoring that can be made?* Questions that deal with amounts in reactions are examples of *reaction stoichiometry*. Using what you have read so far in this chapter and what you learned in Chapters 2, 5, 6, and 7, you *already know everything necessary* to find the answer to this question. Reaction stoichiometry is simply a new way to apply skills such as writing chemical formulas, calculating formula masses, and converting from mass to moles.

Organize what you already know

When solving a problem like this one, a good way to start is to make a table or list of all of the information given in the problem, as well as what answer you are trying to find. *Remember to include units for all quantities.* This will help you later when you are trying to decide how to solve the problem. The sections of **Table 8-1** highlighted in pink include this starting material. The red question mark in the table indicates the answer that is sought. Problems like this one are often known as *mass-mass problems* because the data given is a mass amount and the answer sought is also a mass amount.

Start by figuring out more than just what the problem tells you. In Chapter 6, you learned how to get the molecular formulas for the reactants and products from the organic structures shown on the previous page for isoamyl alcohol and acetic acid.

In Chapter 5, you learned how to use the periodic table to calculate the molar masses of these reactants and products. Such calculations are called *composition stoichiometry* because they describe the mathematical relationships among the elements that make up a substance. The results are shown in the rest of **Table 8-1**. *For almost all chemistry problems of this type, you will need the molar masses of the substances involved.*

Table 8-1
Some Data for the Banana-Flavoring Problem

Reactants	Amount	Formula	Molar mass
isoamyl alcohol	45.0 kg	$C_5H_{11}OH$	88.17 g/mol
acetic acid	excess	CH_3COOH	60.06 g/mol

Products	Amount	Formula	Molar mass
isoamyl acetate	**?** kg	$CH_3COOC_5H_{11}$	130.21 g/mol
water	not given	H_2O	18.02 g/mol

The last piece of information that you need is the balanced chemical equation for the reaction. In Chapter 7, you learned that a balanced chemical equation can provide you with the mole ratios for the substances in the reaction so that you can compare relative amounts. In the balanced equation for isoamyl acetate synthesis, no coefficients are written. This means that all of the coefficients are equal to 1, so all of the mole ratios are 1:1.

$$C_5H_{11}OH(l) + CH_3COOH(l) \xrightarrow{\text{HCl}} CH_3COOC_5H_{11}(l) + H_2O(l)$$

One mole of isoamyl alcohol and one mole of acetic acid react to make one mole of isoamyl acetate and one mole of water. *For almost all chemistry problems, you need a balanced chemical equation so that you can find the mole ratios.*

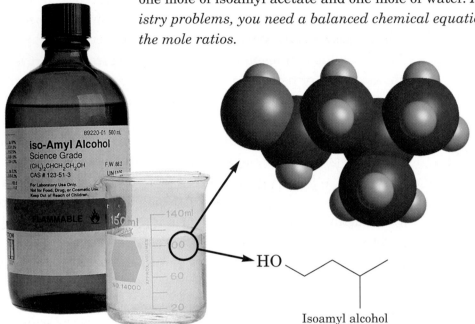

Isoamyl alcohol

Figure 8-3
Isoamyl alcohol, one of the reactants in the banana-flavoring synthesis reaction, has many uses. It is used as a solvent and in synthesizing artificial silk, lacquers, and other materials. Recall that the —OH functional group is characteristic of an alcohol.

Use conversion factors on data from the problem

1. Check the units given

Right now, all of your data is in grams except the amount actually given in the problem, 45.0 kg. Having data with units that do not match is a clue that you need to convert the units—in this case, from kilograms to grams. Recall from Chapter 2 that such conversions can be achieved by multiplying by a conversion factor that connects the units—for example, 1000 g equals 1 kg. But how do you know which factor to use?

$$\frac{1000 \text{ g}}{1 \text{ kg}} \text{ or } \frac{1 \text{ kg}}{1000 \text{ g}} \text{ ?}$$

The correct factor is the one that has the units you already have, *kg*, on the bottom and the units you want to have, *g*, on the top—the factor on the left. Remember that when the value from the problem is multiplied by this conversion factor, the unwanted units, *kg*, cancel and leave the desired units, *g*.

$$45.0 \text{ kg} \times \frac{1000 \text{ g}}{1 \text{ kg}} = 4.50 \times 10^4 \text{ g isoamyl alcohol reactant}$$

2. Determine the mole ratio

You want to know the amount of isoamyl acetate product from the given amount of reactant. In Chapter 7, you learned that the mole ratio provides information about the relative amounts of the reactants and products shown in **Figure 8-3** on the previous page and **Figure 8-4**. From the balanced chemical equation for the reaction, you know that for every mole of isoamyl alcohol used in the reaction, a mole of isoamyl acetate will be produced. But right now you know the amount of isoamyl alcohol only as a mass in *grams*. To compare amounts of reactant and product, you must first convert the amount of the reactant to *moles*. Use the molar mass as the conversion factor to make this change. *Grams* belong on the bottom of the conversion factor because you want to cancel it out, leaving the desired units, *mol*.

$$\frac{88.17 \text{ g}}{1 \text{ mol isoamyl alcohol}} \quad \text{or} \quad \frac{1 \text{ mol isoamyl alcohol}}{88.17 \text{ g}}$$

$$4.50 \times 10^4 \text{ g} \times \frac{1 \text{ mol}}{88.17 \text{ g}} = 510. \text{ mol isoamyl alcohol}$$

3. Use the mole ratio to calculate moles

Now you can use the mole ratio to calculate the amount of product that can be made from a reactant. In this problem, the calculation is not very difficult because it involves a 1:1 mole ratio. However, it can be tricky with more difficult reactions. Be certain that the mole ratio is written like a conversion factor that cancels the given units and leaves the units of the substance of interest.

$$510. \text{ mol isoamyl alcohol} \times \frac{1 \text{ mol isoamyl acetate}}{1 \text{ mol isoamyl alcohol}} = 510. \text{ mol isoamyl acetate}$$

4. Use molar mass to calculate grams

Finally, you know the amount of isoamyl acetate produced in this reaction. But check the problem and your data list on page 273. You were asked for the number of *kilograms* of isoamyl acetate, not the number of *moles*. Once again, some conversions are needed. First, convert the moles of isoamyl acetate to grams using the molar mass, as in Chapter 5. Then, convert from grams to kilograms using the correct conversion factor, as in Chapter 2.

$$510. \text{ mol} \times \frac{130.21 \text{ g}}{1 \text{ mol}} \times \frac{1 \text{ kg}}{1000 \text{ g}} = 66.4 \text{ kg isoamyl acetate product}$$

Figure 8-4
Besides being used as a flavoring agent, isoamyl acetate is also used as an ingredient in air fresheners, as a solvent, and as an ingredient in the manufacture of artificial leather, artificial pearls, and waterproof varnishes.

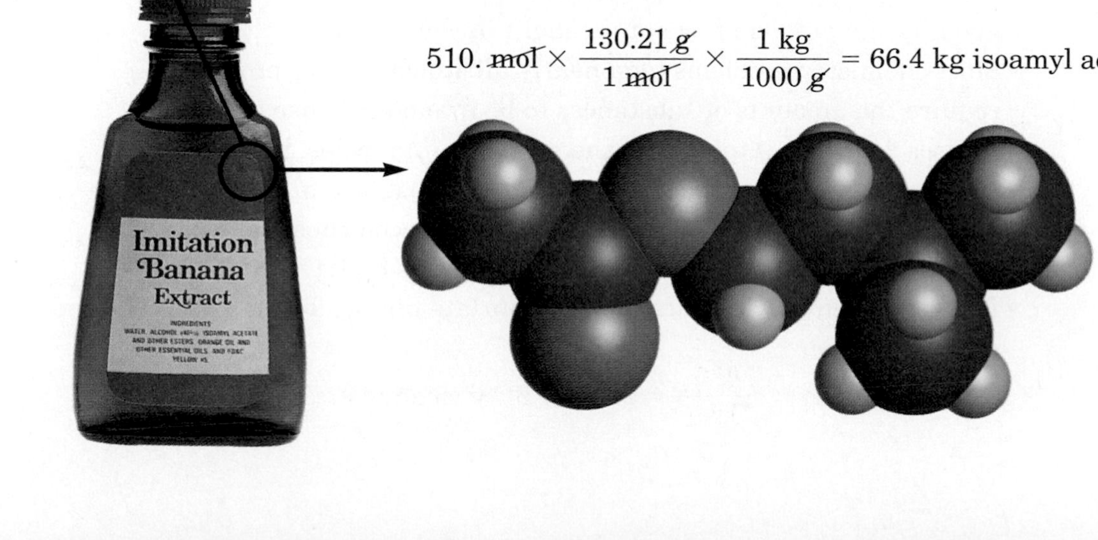

Isoamyl acetate

Imitation Banana Extract

Three-step method

In solving stoichiometry problems, it is important to think about what the problem means and not just to multiply and divide the given values with your calculator. In Chapter 4 you learned about the three-step method used in solving the Sample Problems. Because the ability to solve stoichiometry problems is crucial to your success in chemistry, the method is repeated here for you to review before working with the Sample Problems that follow. As you work through your homework problems, it may be useful to refer to this page for ideas. The Sample Problems that follow can also provide helpful hints.

Remember that the *best way to convert from one substance to another is to relate the reaction stoichiometry* **in moles**. If your data from the problem is in grams, convert it to moles first.

How To

Solve stoichiometry problems

1. List what you know

🔲 *Don't start using your calculator yet.*
- Read the problem twice.
- Organize the information from the problem statement in a list or table.
- Identify what you are asked to find, and write down the units for the answer.
- For all substances you will be working with, write the formulas, and determine the molar masses. Check a periodic table if necessary.
- If there is a reaction, write an equation for it, making sure that it is balanced so that you'll have the correct mole ratios.
- List any conversion factors that you might need, such as molar masses, mole ratios, and unit conversions.

2. Set up the problem

🔲 *Don't start using your calculator yet.*
- First, analyze what needs to be done to get to the answer. See if there is any information not in the problem that you need for the answer.
- Identify which value given in the problem can be used as a starting point. Write it on the left side of a sheet of paper. On the right side of the paper, write an equals sign and then a question mark with the units of the answer. Fill in the conversion factors necessary to convert from what is given in the problem to what is sought in the answer.
- Most chemistry problems (and nearly all stoichiometry problems) require the amounts of substances to be in moles, so use the molar masses from step **1** to convert the amounts into moles, if necessary.
- If you need to change from amount of one substance to a different substance, use mole ratios derived from the balanced chemical equation. Remember that the mole ratio may not always be 1:1.
- Be sure to convert the data into appropriate units, such as *grams* instead of *kilograms*.

- A plan that works for solving most reaction stoichiometry problems is summarized in **Figure 8-5**.
- When you have finished writing down your plan with all of the conversion factors, check to see how the units cancel each other. If they all cancel to give you the units you need for the answer, the setup is probably correct.

Figure 8-5
Most stoichiometry problems involve converting an amount into moles and using the mole ratio to calculate a corresponding amount of another substance in the reaction.

Solving Mass-Mass Stoichiometry Problems

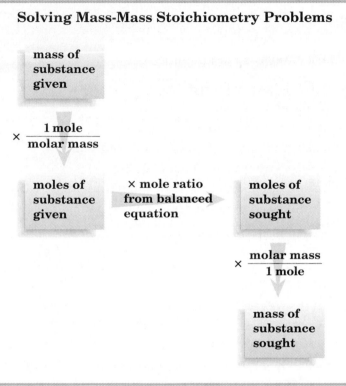

3. Estimate and calculate

Don't start using your calculator yet.

- First, estimate your answer. One way to do this is to round off the numbers in the problem setup and make a quick calculation. Another way is to compare conversion factors in the setup and decide whether the answer should be bigger or smaller than the beginning value.
- Then, begin your calculations by working through the problem setup you made in step **2**. **In the examples in this book, numbers are not rounded off between steps in calculations.**
- When you have finished your calculations, *remember that you still don't have the correct answer.* You must round off and make sure that the answer has the correct number of significant figures.
- Always report the answer with the correct units, not just as a number.
- Compare your answer with the estimate. If they are not close, check all of your work.
- Make sure your answer is reasonable. For example, if you began with 5.3 mg of one reactant, and your answer is that it will make 725 g of a product, you know that you need to double-check all of your work.

Methyl salicylate, also known as "oil of wintergreen," is most often made in a synthesis reaction between methanol and salicylic acid. How many grams of salicylic acid are needed to produce 325 g of methyl salicylate, provided there is plenty of methanol available?

Salicylic acid + CH_3OH $\xrightarrow{HCl}$ Methyl salicylate + H_2O
        Methanol   Water

---

❶ List what you know

These facts were taken from the problem statement.

- **reactants:** salicylic acid, methanol
- **products:** methyl salicylate, water
- **mass of methyl salicylate produced:** 325 g
- **mass of salicylic acid needed:** ❓ g

These molar masses were calculated from the periodic table.

- **formula and molar mass of salicylic acid:** $C_7H_6O_3$, 138.13 g/mol
- **formula and molar mass of methyl salicylate:** $C_8H_8O_3$, 152.16 g/mol

---

❷ Set up the problem

- To convert from the amount of product to the amount of reactant needed, first convert to moles and use the mole ratio to link the two amounts.

$$325 \text{ g } C_8H_8O_3 \times \underset{a}{\frac{1 \text{ mol } C_8H_8O_3}{152.16 \text{ g } C_8H_8O_3}} \times \underset{b}{\frac{1 \text{ mol } C_7H_6O_3}{1 \text{ mol } C_8H_8O_3}} \times \underset{c}{\frac{138.13 \text{ g } C_7H_6O_3}{1 \text{ mol } C_7H_6O_3}} =$$

$$❓ \text{ g } C_7H_6O_3$$

Always remember to work stoichiometry problems by calculating with moles. Notice that all of the factors cancel to give you the units of the answer, g $C_7H_6O_3$.

ⓐ First, convert the given mass of the product into moles. The reciprocal of the molar mass (mol/g) of the product must be used in order to cancel the mass of $C_8H_8O_3$ and leave the amount of $C_8H_8O_3$ in moles.

ⓑ Next, to convert moles of product into moles of reactant, multiply by the mole ratio (1:1) from the balanced chemical equation.

ⓒ Last, convert the moles of reactant into mass using the molar mass of the reactant.

---

❸ Estimate and calculate

- Before calculating, round off the numbers in the setup to make an estimate.

$$300 \times \frac{1}{150} \times \frac{1}{1} \times \frac{140}{1} \approx 280$$

- Use your calculator to work through the setup. Be sure to round to the correct number of significant figures, which is three.

$$325 \text{ g } C_8H_8O_3 \times \frac{1 \text{ mol } C_8H_8O_3}{152.16 \text{ g } C_8H_8O_3} \times \frac{1 \text{ mol } C_7H_6O_3}{1 \text{ mol } C_8H_8O_3} \times \frac{138.13 \text{ g } C_7H_6O_3}{1 \text{ mol } C_7H_6O_3} =$$

$$❓ \text{ g } C_7H_6O_3$$

The answer is reasonably close to the estimate.

Calculator answer: 2.950331887×10^2

Answer to three significant figures: 295 g $C_7H_6O_3$

Practice 8A

Answers for Concept Review items and Practice problems begin on page 841.

1. **Tin(II) fluoride, also known as stannous fluoride, is added to some dental products to help prevent cavities. How many grams of tin(II) fluoride can be made from 55.0 g of hydrogen fluoride, HF, if there is plenty of tin?**

$$Sn(s) + 2HF(aq) \longrightarrow SnF_2(aq) + H_2(g)$$

2. **Fluorescein is a reddish powder used as a coloring agent in some cosmetics, such as shampoo. It is made by combining phthalic anhydride with resorcinol. If a cosmetics company starts with 25.00 kg of resorcinol, how many kilograms of fluorescein can they produce, assuming that there is plenty of phthalic anhydride?**

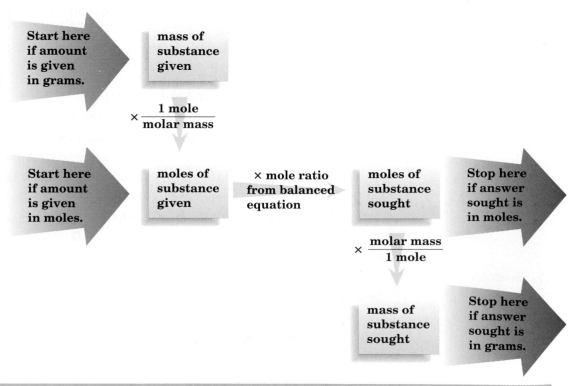

Two resorcinol   One phthalic anhydride   One fluorescein   Two water

Other stoichiometric calculations
Problems with amounts in moles

Some stoichiometry problems involve data or answers in mole amounts instead of mass amounts. These problems can be solved with an approach similar to that used to solve the problems having both data and answers in mass, but with a shortcut. There are fewer steps because one or both molar mass conversions are unnecessary, as shown in **Figure 8-6**, which has many of the same steps as **Figure 8-5**. If both the answer and the given data are in moles, the only conversion factor necessary to solve the problem is the mole ratio.

Figure 8-6
If a stoichiometry problem involves amounts in moles, solving the problem has fewer steps than problems with amounts in grams.

Solving Stoichiometry Problems With Moles or Grams

Start here if amount is given in grams. → mass of substance given

$$\times \frac{1 \text{ mole}}{\text{molar mass}}$$

Start here if amount is given in moles. → moles of substance given → × mole ratio from balanced equation → moles of substance sought → Stop here if answer sought is in moles.

$$\times \frac{\text{molar mass}}{1 \text{ mole}}$$

mass of substance sought → Stop here if answer sought is in grams.

Sample Problem 8B
Mole-mass stoichiometry

Because oxygen is already given in a mole amount, the molar mass of O_2 is unnecessary.

The human body needs at least 1.03×10^{-2} mol O_2 every minute. If all of this oxygen is used for the cellular respiration reaction that breaks down glucose, how many grams of glucose does the human body consume each minute?

$$C_6H_{12}O_6(s) + 6O_2(g) \longrightarrow 6CO_2(g) + 6H_2O(l)$$

❶ List
- amount of O_2 used each minute: 1.03×10^{-2} mol O_2
- molar mass of $C_6H_{12}O_6$: 180.18 g/mol
- mole ratio: 1 mol $C_6H_{12}O_6$:6 mol O_2
- mass of glucose needed each minute: **?** g

❷ Set up
- First, analyze what needs to be done to get the answer. You are given moles of oxygen, so you can convert to moles of glucose using the mole ratio. Then, you can use the molar mass to determine the mass in grams of the glucose.

$$1.03 \times 10^{-2} \text{ mol } O_2 \times \frac{1 \text{ mol } C_6H_{12}O_6}{6 \text{ mol } O_2} \times \frac{180.18 \text{ g } C_6H_{12}O_6}{1 \text{ mol } C_6H_{12}O_6} = \text{?} \text{ g } C_6H_{12}O_6$$

❸ Estimate and calculate
- Before calculating, round off the numbers in the setup to make an estimate.

$$0.01 \times \frac{1}{6} \times \frac{180}{1} \approx 0.3$$

Then use your calculator to work through the setup. Be sure to round to the correct number of significant figures, which is three.

The answer is reasonably close to the estimate.

Answer to three significant figures:

$$1.03 \times 10^{-2} \text{ mol } O_2 \times \frac{1 \text{ mol } C_6H_{12}O_6}{6 \text{ mol } O_2} \times \frac{180.18 \text{ g } C_6H_{12}O_6}{1 \text{ mol } C_6H_{12}O_6} = 0.309309 \text{ g } C_6H_{12}O_6$$

Practice 8B

1. Use the information in Sample Problem 8B to determine how many grams of carbon dioxide would be produced each minute.

2. Use the information in Sample Problem 8B to determine how many grams of water would be produced each minute.

Using density with stoichiometry

Remember that the key to solving any reaction stoichiometry problem is to always calculate in moles. Once the number of moles is determined, conversion factors such as molar mass can be used to convert to the mass in grams. Similarly, once the mass is known, the density of a substance can be used to convert from mass to volume.

Recall from Chapter 2 that density is defined as the mass of a substance per unit volume, expressed mathematically as $D = m/V$. Once again, the key is to use the density value to set up a conversion factor that will cancel the units in the measurement you have and leave the units of the measurement for the answer, as shown in Sample Problem 8C. Once more, you already know everything you need to solve such problems from your study of concepts earlier in the book.

In the space shuttles, the CO_2 that the crew exhales is removed from the air by a reaction within canisters of lithium hydroxide. On average, each astronaut exhales about 20.0 mol of CO_2 daily. What volume of water will be produced when this amount of CO_2 reacts with an excess of LiOH? (Hint: the density of water is about 1.00 g/mL.)

$$CO_2(g) + 2LiOH(s) \longrightarrow Li_2CO_3(aq) + H_2O(l)$$

❶ List
- **amount of CO_2:** 20.0 mol CO_2
- **density of H_2O:** 1.00 g/mL
- **molar mass of H_2O:** 18.02 g/mol
- **mole ratio:** 1 mol CO_2:1 mol H_2O
- **volume of H_2O produced:** **?** mL

❷ Set up
- First, analyze what needs to be done to get the answer. You are given moles of CO_2, so you can convert to moles of water using the mole ratio. Then, use the molar mass to find out the mass of water.

$$20.0 \text{ mol } CO_2 \times \frac{1 \text{ mol } H_2O}{1 \text{ mol } CO_2} \times \frac{18.02 \text{ g } H_2O}{1 \text{ mol } H_2O} \times \underline{\quad\quad} = \textbf{?} \text{ mL } H_2O$$

- Next, convert from mass of H_2O to volume of H_2O using the density as the conversion factor. The correct conversion factor will have **g H_2O** in the denominator and **mL H_2O** in the numerator.

$$20.0 \text{ mol } CO_2 \times \frac{1 \text{ mol } H_2O}{1 \text{ mol } CO_2} \times \frac{18.02 \text{ g } H_2O}{1 \text{ mol } H_2O} \times \frac{1 \text{ mL } H_2O}{1.00 \text{ g } H_2O} = \textbf{?} \text{ mL } H_2O$$

❸ Estimate and calculate
- Before calculating, round off the numbers in the setup to make an estimate.

$$20 \times \frac{1}{1} \times \frac{18}{1} \times \frac{1}{1} \approx 360$$

- Then, use your calculator to work through the setup. Be sure to round to the correct number of significant figures, which is three.

Answer to three significant figures: 360. mL H_2O

Practice 8C

1. The reaction that causes cake batter to rise involves the production of CO_2 from $NaHCO_3$. How many liters of CO_2 gas will be created when 15.0 g $NaHCO_3$ are heated? (Note: at baking temperature, the density of CO_2 is about 1.10 g/L.)

$$2NaHCO_3(s) \longrightarrow H_2O(g) + Na_2CO_3(s) + CO_2(g)$$

2. A common ingredient used in some sunscreens is *p*-aminobenzoic acid, or PABA, which can absorb some of the ultraviolet radiation of the sun. It is made from *p*-nitrobenzoic acid, which is a solid with a density of 1.58 g/mL. The reaction actually has several intermediate steps but can be summarized as shown below. What is the maximum mass of PABA that can be made from 500. mL of *p*-nitrobenzoic acid crystals?

Calculating the number of atoms or formula units

Just as molar mass, density, and mole ratios can be used as conversion factors in problems, Avogadro's number, 6.022×10^{23}, can be used to calculate the number of atoms or formula units participating in a reaction. Again, the two points to remember are the same as with other stoichiometry problems.

- Be certain that you work with moles.
- Make sure that you set up the conversion factors so that the quantity sought is in the numerator and the quantity given is in the denominator.

Figure 8-7 summarizes the approaches that can be taken in stoichiometric calculations. Notice that several steps are the same as in **Figure 8-5** and **Figure 8-6**.

Solving Many Types of Stoichiometry Problems

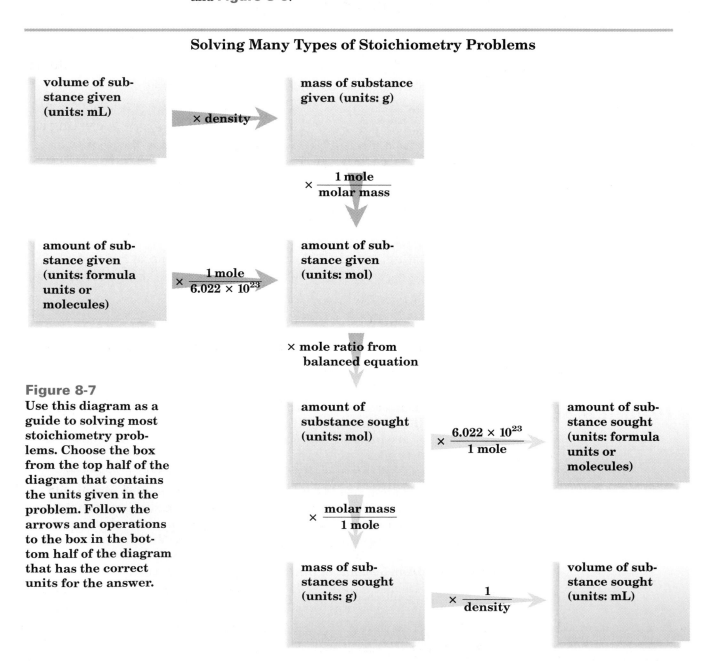

Figure 8-7
Use this diagram as a guide to solving most stoichiometry problems. Choose the box from the top half of the diagram that contains the units given in the problem. Follow the arrows and operations to the box in the bottom half of the diagram that has the correct units for the answer.

1. Why do you need to use moles to solve stoichiometry problems? Why can't you just convert from grams to grams?

2. Write and solve two problems, one involving composition stoichiometry and the other pertaining to reaction stoichiometry.

3. Use the three-step method to solve the following problems based on the equation shown, which shows the use of the reactant hydrazine, N_2H_4, as a propellant for a rocket. For each problem, assume that you start with 1200. kg of N_2H_4 and that it is completely used up by the reaction.

$$2N_2H_4(l) + (CH_3)_2N_2H_2(l) + 3N_2O_4(g) \longrightarrow 6N_2(g) + 2CO_2(g) + 8H_2O(l)$$

   a. Calculate how many moles of N_2O_4 are needed.
   b. Calculate how many grams of $(CH_3)_2N_2H_2$ are needed.
   c. Calculate how many molecules of N_2 are produced.
   d. Calculate how many liters of H_2O are produced. The density of water is 1.00 g/mL.

4. Oxygen, O_2, was discovered by Joseph Priestley in 1774 when he decomposed mercury(II) oxide, HgO, into its constituent elements by heating it. How many moles of oxygen could Priestley have produced if he had decomposed 216.59 g of mercury(II) oxide?

5. Aspirin is made by reacting salicylic acid with acetic anhydride.

$$\underset{\substack{\text{Salicylic}\\\text{acid}}}{C_7H_6O_3} + \underset{\substack{\text{Acetic}\\\text{anhydride}}}{C_4H_6O_3} \xrightarrow{\text{HCl}} \underset{\text{Aspirin}}{C_9H_8O_4} + \underset{\text{Acetic acid}}{CH_3COOH}$$

What is the maximum mass of aspirin that can be produced from 251.7 g of salicylic acid?

6. **Story Link**
   Each FRH contains 8.1 g magnesium. Assuming this magnesium reacts completely, how many grams of hydrogen gas are produced?

7. **Story Link**
   At the temperature within an FRH, 60°C, the density of hydrogen gas is 0.081 g/L. How many liters of H_2 gas are produced by an FRH?

8. **Story Link**
   Calculate the amount of heat energy produced per gram of reactants added for the magnesium, calcium oxide, and trioxane reactions. If the mass of the reactants were the deciding factor, which reaction would be most effective? (Hint: refer to page 271, and remember to include the mass of water necessary for the first two reactions.)

9. **Story Link**
   How much of each reactant would be necessary to create a camping-food warmer that would provide the 575 kJ necessary to warm a dinner for four hikers? (Hint: refer to page 271, and set up conversion factors relating energy and amount of each reactant.)

How much does a reaction really produce?

Section Objectives

Distinguish between a limiting reactant and an excess reactant.

Identify the limiting reactant in a problem, and calculate the theoretical yield.

Distinguish between theoretical yield and actual yield.

Given the actual yield and the quantity of the limiting reactant, calculate the percent yield.

Use percent yield to calculate actual yield.

Leftover reactants

You now know how to use mole ratios and other conversion factors to figure out how much of a product should be produced by a chemical reaction. So far, such reactions and calculations have described an *ideal situation*. Some assumptions were made: there was always enough of the other reactants so that none would be left over, and all reactions went to completion, producing only the products indicated in the equation. There were no competing reactions.

Figure 8-8
With only one nut, you can only make a single nut-bolt pair, no matter how many bolts you have. The same is true for a chemical reaction in which one reactant is used up before the other.

These assumptions are useful when trying to learn how reactions and equations work and how to make predictions from them. But to treat real reactions accurately, you must take additional factors into account, such as the amounts of all reactants and the completeness of the reaction.

Reactants combine in specific whole-number ratios

Have you ever tried to assemble a bicycle only to discover that you didn't have enough nuts for the bolts that were supplied, as shown in **Figure 8-8**? For every bolt, you needed a nut. In other words, the shortage of nuts limited what you could do. Or have you ever been in a car that ran out of gas? The car needed both gas and oxygen from the air to run, so once the gas was gone, it wouldn't run, no matter how much oxygen was present.

A similar limitation occurs in all chemical reactions. When a chemical reaction occurs, the reactants are not always present in amounts equal to their mole ratios. For example, reconsider the reaction used to make the banana-flavored ester, isoamyl acetate.

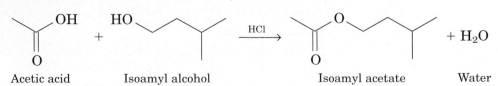

Acetic acid   Isoamyl alcohol   Isoamyl acetate   Water

According to this equation, for every mole of acetic acid, a mole of isoamyl alcohol is needed. What would happen if there were 20 mol of acetic acid and only 1 mol of isoamyl alcohol? How much isoamyl acetate could be made?

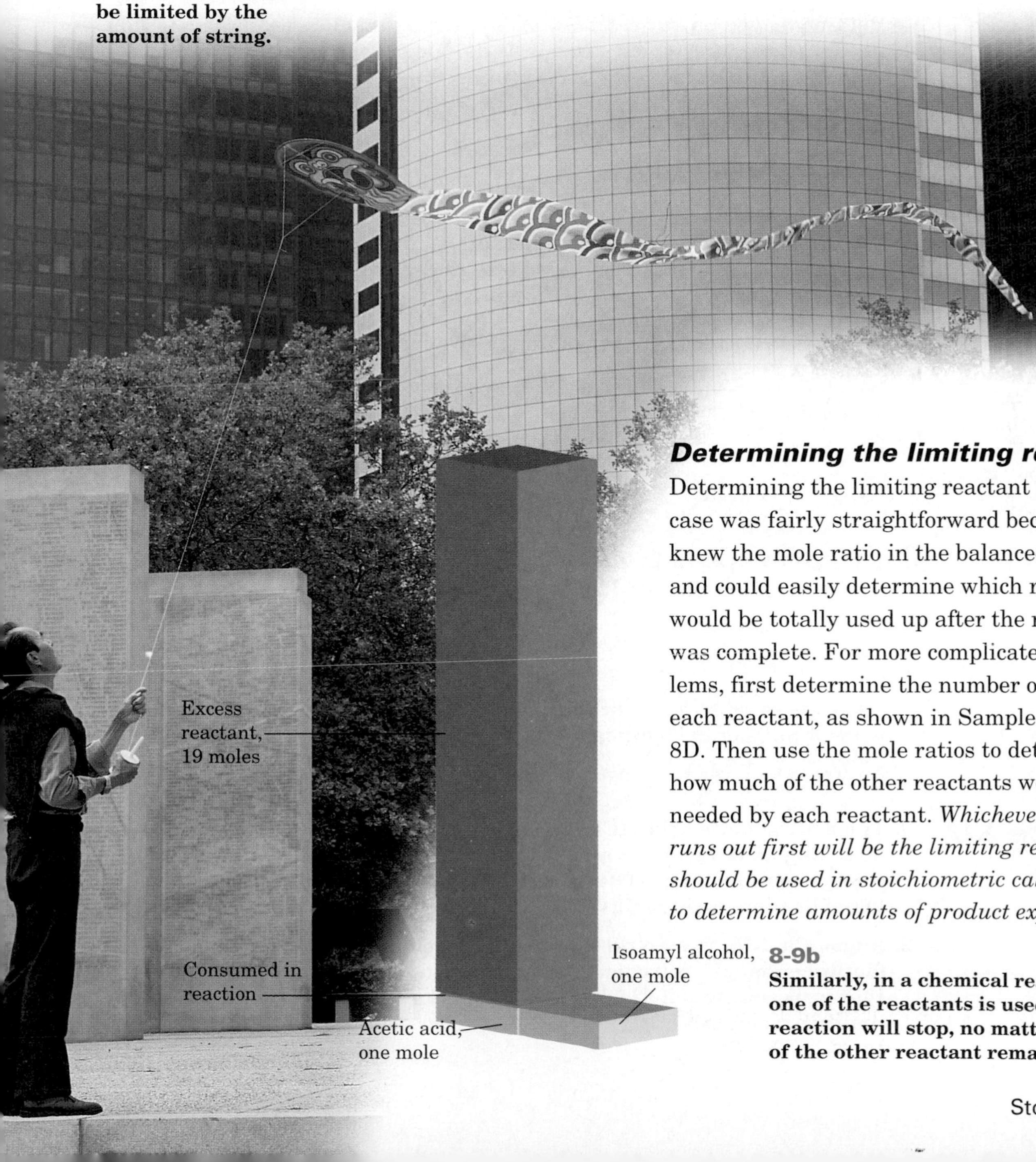

Figure 8-9a
**Flying a kite can be an
analogy for a reaction
with limiting reactants.
No matter how strongly
the wind blows, the
height of the kite will
be limited by the
amount of string.**

One mole of acetic acid will react with one mole of isoamyl alcohol. After that, the isoamyl alcohol reactant would be used up, and none would be available to react with the other 19 moles of acetic acid. Obviously, the reaction would stop after forming only one mole of each product even if there were 20 moles of one reactant at the start. An excess of this reactant would be left over, as shown in **Figure 8-9**.

An **excess reactant** is the reactant that is not completely used up in a chemical reaction. In the preceding paragraph, acetic acid was the excess reactant. There will be some of this reactant left over when the reaction is complete. On the other hand, isoamyl alcohol is known as the limiting reactant. A **limiting reactant** is a reactant that is used up first and thus limits the amount of other reactants that can participate in a chemical reaction to make products. (Sometimes, chemists refer to it as the *limiting reagent*.)

Excess
reactant,
19 moles

Consumed in
reaction

Acetic acid,
one mole

Isoamyl alcohol,
one mole

Determining the limiting reactant

Determining the limiting reactant in this case was fairly straightforward because you knew the mole ratio in the balanced equation and could easily determine which reactant would be totally used up after the reaction was complete. For more complicated problems, first determine the number of moles of each reactant, as shown in Sample Problem 8D. Then use the mole ratios to determine how much of the other reactants would be needed by each reactant. *Whichever reactant runs out first will be the limiting reactant and should be used in stoichiometric calculations to determine amounts of product expected.*

8-9b
**Similarly, in a chemical reaction, once
one of the reactants is used up, the
reaction will stop, no matter how much
of the other reactant remains.**

Stoichiometry | **285**

Sample Problem 8D
Determining the limiting reactant

Carbon monoxide can be combined with hydrogen to produce methanol, CH_3OH. Methanol is used as an industrial solvent, as a reactant in synthesis, and as a clean-burning fuel for some racing cars. If you had 152.5 kg CO and 24.50 kg H_2, how many kilograms of CH_3OH would be produced?

❶ List
- balanced chemical equation for reaction: $CO(g) + 2H_2(g) \longrightarrow CH_3OH(l)$
- amount of CO: 152.5 kg CO
- amount of H_2: 24.50 kg H_2
- molar mass of CO: 28.01 g/mol
- molar mass of H_2: 2.02 g/mol
- molar mass of CH_3OH: 32.05 g/mol
- amount of CH_3OH produced: **?** kg CH_3OH

❷ Set up
- Before you can do any calculations to convert reactants to products, you need to determine which reactant is the limiting reactant. First, figure out how many moles of each reactant are present.

$$152.5 \text{ kg CO} \times \frac{1000 \text{ g}}{1 \text{ kg}} \times \frac{1 \text{ mol CO}}{28.01 \text{ g CO}} = 5.444 \times 10^3 \text{ mol CO present}$$

$$24.50 \text{ kg H}_2 \times \frac{1000 \text{ g}}{1 \text{ kg}} \times \frac{1 \text{ mol H}_2}{2.02 \text{ g H}_2} = 1.213 \times 10^4 \text{ mol H}_2 \text{ present}$$

It does not matter which of the two reactant amounts you choose. If you started with CO first, you would find that 1.089×10^4 mol of H_2 were needed. Because the amount of H_2 needed was less than the amount present, CO will be the limiting reactant.

- Then, for one of these reactant amounts, figure out how much of the first reactant would be needed to use up all of the second reactant. Compare this with the amount actually present.

$$1.213 \times 10^4 \text{ mol H}_2 \times \frac{1 \text{ mol CO}}{2 \text{ mol H}_2} = 6.065 \times 10^3 \text{ mol CO needed}$$

Because the amount of CO needed to use up the H_2 is larger than the amount of CO present, the CO will be the limiting reactant.

- Use the limiting reactant to set up the stoichiometric calculation.

$$5.444 \times 10^3 \text{ mol CO} \times \frac{1 \text{ mol CH}_3\text{OH}}{1 \text{ mol CO}} \times \frac{32.05 \text{ g CH}_3\text{OH}}{1 \text{ mol CH}_3\text{OH}} \times \frac{1 \text{ kg}}{1000 \text{ g}} = \textbf{?} \text{ kg CH}_3\text{OH}$$

❸ *Estimate and calculate*
- Before calculating, round off the numbers in the setup to make an estimate.

$$5500 \times \frac{1}{1} \times \frac{30}{1} \times \frac{1}{1000} \approx 165$$

- Use your calculator to work through the setup. Be sure to round to the correct number of significant figures, which is four.

Answer to four significant figures: 174.5 kg CH_3OH

Practice 8D

1. The hydrochloric acid, HCl, secreted in your stomach can be neutralized by taking an antacid like aluminum hydroxide, $Al(OH)_3$. This is a double-replacement reaction. If 34.0 g HCl are secreted and 12.0 g $Al(OH)_3$ are taken, is there enough $Al(OH)_3$ to react with all of the HCl?

2. Ammonia, NH_3, is used throughout the world as a fertilizer. To manufacture ammonia, nitrogen, N_2, is combined with hydrogen, H_2, in a synthesis reaction. If 92.7 kg N_2 and 265.8 kg H_2 are used, which is the limiting reactant?

Cost is a factor in selecting the limiting reactant

When any chemical reaction is actually carried out in industry, the least abundant reactant, which is often more expensive, is the limiting reactant. The most abundant reactant, which is usually cheaper, is the excess reactant. In this way the expensive reactant will be completely used up and not wasted, while some of the cheaper reactant will be left over.

In addition to being a way to maintain cost-efficiency, this principle can be used to control which reactions happen. One example is the production of the cider and cider vinegar shown in **Figure 8-10** from apple juice. At first, the original apple juice is kept where there is no oxygen. When no oxygen is present, the microorganisms in the apple juice cannot use the cellular respiration reaction as a source of energy. Instead, they use an alternative pathway in which the glucose is fermented, or broken down, into molecules of ethanol. The resulting solution is hard cider.

In the next step in the production of apple cider vinegar, the presence of plenty of oxygen is used as a means to control another reaction. Once the ethanol in hard cider is exposed to air, it slowly reacts with atmospheric oxygen to produce acetic acid, resulting in cider vinegar. Because the oxygen in the air costs nothing and is abundant, the makers of cider vinegar pump air through hard cider as they make it into vinegar. In this way, oxygen is not the limiting reactant. The ethanol is the limiting reactant, so it will be entirely consumed in the reaction.

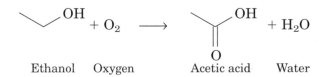

| Ethanol | Oxygen | Acetic acid | Water |

Similarly, the manufacturers of banana flavoring discussed at the beginning of the chapter tend to use acetic acid as the excess reactant because it costs much less than isoamyl alcohol. For example, acetic acid costs about $11.00 for 500 mL (525 g). But 500 mL (406 g) of isoamyl alcohol costs about $16.00. When compared mole for mole, isoamyl alcohol is almost three times as expensive as acetic acid. With an excess of acetic acid, none of the more expensive isoamyl alcohol is wasted by being leftover.

Incomplete reactions
Measuring what a chemical reaction actually produces

Although equations tell you what *should* happen, they can't always tell you what *will* happen. For example, a reaction will stop once the limiting reactant has been used up, regardless of how much of the other reactants is present.

Sometimes reactions don't match equations in other ways. The amount expected from stoichiometry calculations is called the **theoretical yield**. But, in some cases, the **actual yield**, the amount of product actually created, is not what was expected—it can be much less than the theoretical yield. But how can this be? For an example, reconsider the banana-flavoring problem.

Figure 8-10
Makers of cider vinegar use special tanks and equipment to pump air through hard cider so that oxygen, O_2, is the excess reactant.

theoretical yield
calculated maximum amount of product possible from a given amount of reactant

actual yield
measured amount of product actually produced from a given amount of reactant

Table 8-2
Predictions and Measurements for Isoamyl Acetate Synthesis

Reactants	Formula	Mass	Amount present	Amount needed for reaction
isoamyl alcohol	$C_5H_{11}OH$	500. g	5.67 mol (limiting reactant)	5.67 mol
acetic acid	CH_3COOH	1.25×10^3 g	20.8 mol	5.67 mol

Products	Formula	Amount expected	Theoretical yield (mass expected)	Actual yield (mass produced)
isoamyl acetate	$CH_3COOC_5H_{11}$	5.67 mol	738 g	454 g
water	H_2O	5.67 mol	102 g	62.8 g

When a worker at the flavoring factory mixes 500. g of isoamyl alcohol and 1.25×10^3 g of acetic acid, the stoichiometry calculations that account for isoamyl alcohol being a limiting reactant give the results summarized in the second half of **Table 8-2**. But when the actual yield is measured, it is much less than was expected. What went wrong? Of course, the first things to check are the calculations and measurements. But even after checking them, the amounts come out the same. In science, calculations and theories are useful only as ways to predict actual measurements and observations.

In this case, the calculations were not wrong, but they were based on an assumption that was not supported by the observations. Stoichiometric calculations like the ones in **Table 8-2** assume that a reaction will use up all of the limiting reactant to make the products indicated in the equation.

But in cases such as the one shown in **Table 8-2**, the reaction does not completely use up the reactants to make only the products in the equation. If it had, there would be more water and isoamyl acetate present at the end. What happened here? In this case the problem is the equation for the reaction. Although the balanced chemical equation is correct by itself, it describes only part of what is going on. Reactions other than the synthesis of isoamyl acetate are also occurring and producing other products. In fact, the main reaction in competition with the synthesis reaction is a decomposition reaction that is the reverse of the synthesis reaction. In other words, the products are re-forming the reactants, as shown below. The net effect is that at the end of the reaction, instead of having only products, the result is a mixture of products and reactants.

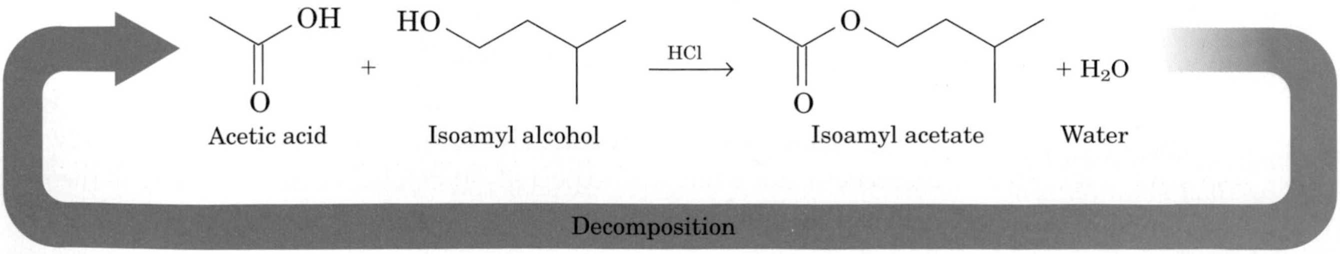

Acetic acid   +   Isoamyl alcohol $\xrightarrow{HCl}$ Isoamyl acetate   + H_2O Water

Decomposition

Percent yield is a way to describe reaction efficiency

If the reaction creates a mixture of products and reactants, how can any worthwhile predictions be made about the results of this reaction? Suppose a worker in the flavoring factory kept track of the results of several attempts to make isoamyl acetate. The results are shown in **Table 8-3**.

As you can see, the results are reasonably consistent—the actual yield and the theoretical yield occurred in roughly the same proportion each time. A good way to express this is with **percent yield**, which describes how much of the theoretical yield is actually produced.

percent yield
ratio of actual yield to theoretical yield, multiplied by 100

$$\text{percent yield} = \frac{\text{actual yield}}{\text{theoretical yield}} \times 100$$

The percent yield figures for the values shown in **Table 8-3** are 61.5%, 62.5%, 61.2%, 61.2%, and 62.1%. These values are all reasonably close, but why aren't they equal? Along with the possibility that competing side reactions will lower the actual yield and the percent yield, some of the product may be lost, especially if it is a gas or has to be purified from a mixture. As a result, the percent yield figures are usually averaged over several different trials. For this set of values, the average is 61.7%.

The use of these different ways to describe yields is similar to the use of statistics to describe how frequently a player scores in sports. For example, if you try 20 layups during a basketball game, your theoretical yield is 40 points. That is the maximum number of points you could get from the 20 layups. However, if you make only 10 of those shots, your actual yield is 20 points. Your shooting percentage, or percent yield, is 50%. The batting average shown on the back of baseball cards like the one in **Figure 8-11** is similar to percent yield because it is a ratio of the number of hits to the number of times at bat.

Chemists cannot predict percent yields by looking at a balanced equation or by performing stoichiometric calculations. Precise percent yields must be measured experimentally. However, after closely observing many different reactions, experienced chemists can recognize patterns and reaction types that allow them to make pretty good estimates of percent yield.

Table 8-3
Data From Several Trials of Isoamyl Acetate Synthesis

Mass of isoamyl alcohol used (g)	Theoretical yield of isoamyl acetate (g)	Actual yield of isoamyl acetate (g)
500.	738	454
500.	738	461
500.	738	452
500.	738	452
500.	738	458

Figure 8-11
A baseball player's batting average can be considered similar to a percent yield, because it is a ratio of the number of hits achieved to the number of hits possible.

Sample Problem 8E
Calculating percent yield

A student is synthesizing aspirin by adding 200. g of salicylic acid to an excess of acetic anhydride. Calculate the percent yield if 96.0 g of aspirin are produced. (Hint: before you can determine the percent yield, you must first calculate the theoretical yield of aspirin based on the amount of the limiting reactant supplied.)

Salicylic acid   Acetic anhydride   Aspirin, acetylsalicylic acid   Acetic acid

① List
- amount of limiting reactant: 200. g $C_7H_6O_3$
- molar mass of reactants: 138.13 g/mol $C_7H_6O_3$
  102.10 g/mol $C_4H_6O_3$
- molar mass of products: 180.17 g/mol $C_9H_8O_4$
  60.06 g/mol $C_2H_4O_2$
- mole ratio: 1 mol $C_7H_6O_3$:1 mol $C_9H_8O_4$
- actual yield: 96.0 g $C_9H_8O_4$
- theoretical yield: **?** g $C_9H_8O_4$
- percent yield: **?** %

② Set up
- **Before you can calculate percent yield, you must calculate theoretical yield by using the molar masses and mole ratios as conversion factors.**

$$200. \text{ g } C_7H_6O_3 \times \frac{1 \text{ mol } C_7H_6O_3}{138.13 \text{ g } C_7H_6O_3} \times \frac{1 \text{ mol } C_9H_8O_4}{1 \text{ mol } C_7H_6O_3} \times \frac{180.17 \text{ g } C_9H_8O_4}{1 \text{ mol } C_9H_8O_4} =$$

$$\textbf{?} \text{ g } C_9H_8O_4$$

Calculator answer: 260.8701947 g $C_9H_8O_4$

Properly rounded answer: 261 g $C_9H_8O_4$

- **Calculate percent yield from the actual and theoretical yields.**

$$\frac{96.0 \text{ g actual}}{261 \text{ g theoretical}} \times 100 = \textbf{?} \% \text{ yield}$$

③ Estimate and calculate
- **Check the initial calculation of theoretical yield, and estimate the percent yield by rounding off the numbers.**

$$200 \times \frac{1}{140} \times \frac{1}{1} \times \frac{180}{1} \approx$$

$$\frac{10}{7} \times 180 \approx 270$$

$$\frac{90}{270} \times 100 \approx 33\%$$

- **When calculating, be sure to use the correct number of significant figures.**

Calculator answer: 36.7816092

Properly rounded answer: 36.8% yield

Practice 8E

1. **One step in making *para*-aminobenzoic acid, PABA, an ingredient in some suntan lotions, involves replacing one of the hydrogen atoms in a toluene molecule with an —NO₂ group, directly opposite the —CH₃ group. Calculate the percent yield if 550. g of toluene added to an excess of nitric acid provides 305 g of the nitrotoluene product.**

		H₂SO₄		
CH₃	+ HNO₃	→	CH₃ ... NO₂	+ H₂O
Toluene	Nitric acid		*p*-nitrotoluene	Water

2. **One reason for the low yield in the reaction shown above is a competing side reaction that produces another nitrotoluene product, but one which cannot be used to make PABA. After 550. g of toluene reactant were used with an excess of nitric acid, 468 g of this other product remained. Calculate its percent yield.**

		H₂SO₄		
CH₃	+ HNO₃	→	CH₃ NO₂	+ H₂O
Toluene	Nitric acid		*o*-nitrotoluene	Water

Percent yield figures can be used to predict actual yield

Once the percent yield has been measured, chemists can use it to evaluate the efficiency of a chemical reaction. Just as a basketball player would like to have the highest possible shooting percentage, a chemist would like to have the maximum percent yield. If the percent yield is too low, the chemist might be able to make changes in reaction conditions to increase the actual yield. Such changes will be explored in later chapters.

Perhaps more important, once the percent yield has been measured for the reaction, it can be used as a conversion factor in stoichiometry to make predictions about any reaction, *even those that do not go to completion*. For example, the chemical equation for the synthesis of isoamyl acetate can be written to include the percent yield, as shown below. With this information, the actual yield of the reaction can be calculated.

Acetic acid	Isoamyl alcohol	Isoamyl acetate: 61.7%	Water

After calculating the theoretical yield of the reaction in the usual way, you can use the percent yield as a conversion factor. The easiest way to do this is to write it as a number of grams of actual yield per 100 g of theoretical yield.

$$61.7\% \text{ yield} = \frac{61.7 \text{ g actual yield}}{100 \text{ g theoretical yield}} \times 100$$

For example, 150. g of isoamyl alcohol should provide a theoretical yield of 221 g of isoamyl acetate. But you know from the equation with the percent yield to expect only about 61.7% of that isoamyl acetate to actually be formed.

$$221 \text{ g theoretical yield} \times \frac{61.7 \text{ g actual yield}}{100 \text{ g theoretical yield}} = 136 \text{ g actual yield}$$

Sample Problem 8F
Using percent yield

A more efficient way to prepare the molecule that was used to produce PABA for suntan lotions involves a slightly different starting material, known as isopropylbenzene. This reaction usually has a 91.2% yield. How many grams of the product, *para*-nitro-isopropylbenzene, can you expect if 775 g of isopropylbenzene react with an excess of nitric acid?

Isopropylbenzene $+ HNO_3$ Nitric acid $\xrightarrow{H_2SO_4}$ NO_2 *p*-nitro-isopropylbenzene $+ H_2O$ Water

① List

• This is a case in which a table for organizing data is useful.

Substance	Formula	Molar mass	Mass present	Mole ratio
isopropylbenzene	C_9H_{12}	120.21 g/mol	775 g	1
para-nitro-isopropylbenzene	$C_9H_{11}NO_2$	165.21 g/mol	**?** g	1

Percent yield: 91.2%

② Set up

• First, set up the calculation for the theoretical yield.

$$775 \text{ g } C_9H_{12} \times \frac{1 \text{ mol } C_9H_{12}}{120.21 \text{ g } C_9H_{12}} \times \frac{1 \text{ mol } C_9H_{11}NO_2}{1 \text{ mol } C_9H_{12}} \times \frac{165.21 \text{ g } C_9H_{11}NO_2}{1 \text{ mol } C_9H_{11}NO_2}$$

$$\times \text{———} = \textbf{?} \text{ g } C_9H_{11}NO_2$$

• Then, use the percent yield as a conversion factor to calculate actual yield.

$$775 \text{ g } C_9H_{12} \times \frac{1 \text{ mol } C_9H_{12}}{120.21 \text{ g } C_9H_{12}} \times \frac{1 \text{ mol } C_9H_{11}NO_2}{1 \text{ mol } C_9H_{12}} \times \frac{165.21 \text{ g } C_9H_{11}NO_2}{1 \text{ mol } C_9H_{11}NO_2}$$

$$\times \frac{91.2 \text{ g actual}}{100 \text{ g theoretical}} = \textbf{?} \text{ g } C_9H_{11}NO_2$$

③ Estimate and calculate

• Round the numbers to make an estimate.

$$800 \times \frac{1}{120} \times \frac{1}{1} \times \frac{165}{1} \times (0.9) \approx 990$$

• Calculate, and round to the correct number of significant figures.

Calculator answer: 971.3869728

Correctly rounded answer: 971 g $C_9H_{11}NO_2$

10. Titanium(IV) oxide, TiO_2, is used as a pigment in paints and as a whitening and coating agent for paper. It can be made by reacting O_2 with $TiCl_4$.

$$TiCl_4(s) + O_2(g) \longrightarrow TiO_2(s) + 2Cl_2(g)$$

a. If 4.5 mol of $TiCl_4$ react with 3.5 mol of O_2, identify both the limiting and excess reactants.

b. How many moles of excess reactant will remain if the reaction goes to completion?

c. How many moles of each product should be formed if the reaction goes to completion?

11. How much nitric acid, HNO_3, is produced when NO_2 gas is bubbled under pressure through 100. g of H_2O? (Hint: assume the reaction goes to completion.)

$$3NO_2(g) + H_2O(l) \longrightarrow 2HNO_3(aq) + NO(g)$$

12. When phosphorus burns in the presence of oxygen, P_4O_{10} is produced. In turn, P_4O_{10} reacts with water to produce phosphoric acid, which is one of the compounds found in acid precipitation.

$$P_4O_{10}(g) + H_2O(l) \longrightarrow H_3PO_4(aq)$$

a. Write a balanced chemical equation for this reaction.

b. When 100. g of P_4O_{10} are reacted with 200. g of H_2O, what is the theoretical yield of phosphoric acid?

c. If the actual yield is 126.24 g of H_3PO_4, what is the percent yield for this reaction?

13. If 50.0 g of benzaldehyde react with an excess of acetaldehyde to make cinnamaldehyde and the percent yield is 84.5%, how many grams of cinnamaldehyde will be produced?

Benzaldehyde   Acetaldehyde   Cinnamaldehyde   Water

14. Suggest two reasons why theoretical yields are rarely achieved in chemical reactions.

15. Story Link

When using an FRH, soldiers add 45 mL of water. How much water is theoretically necessary for the reaction of the 8.1 g of magnesium in the FRH? (Hint: the density of water is 1.0 g/mL.)

16. Story Link

Using your answer to item **15**, state whether water or magnesium is the limiting reactant.

8-3

How can stoichiometry be used?

Stoichiometry and cars

So far in your study of stoichiometry, you have examined a number of chemical reactions with practical applications—from banana flavoring to cosmetics to aspirin. But stoichiometry's practical importance goes beyond factories and laboratories. When you drive a car, you are depending on stoichiometry to keep you safe and make the car work efficiently with the smallest possible impact on the environment.

Air-bag design depends on stoichiometric precision

Air bags are designed to protect occupants in a car from injuries during a high-speed front-end collision, as shown in **Figure 8-12**. When inflated, they gently slow down the occupants of a car so that they do not strike the steering wheel, windshield, or instrument panel as hard as they would without the air bag. Stoichiometry and the principles of reactions studied in Chapter 7 are used by air-bag designers to make certain that air bags do not under-inflate or over-inflate. Bags that under-inflate do not provide enough protection for the occupants, and bags that over-inflate can cause injury or may even rupture, making them useless. To adequately protect occupants, air bags must fully inflate within one-tenth of a second after impact. The systems that make an air bag work this quickly are shown in **Figure 8-13** on the next page. A front-end collision transfers energy to a crash sensor that signals the firing of the ignitor, which is similar to a small blasting cap. The ignitor provides heat energy to start a reaction in a mixture called the *gas generant*, which forms a gaseous product. The ignitor also raises the temperature and pressure within the reaction chamber, a metal vessel, so that the reaction occurs at a rate fast enough to fill the bag before the occupant strikes it. This reaction chamber releases the gas into the bag while a high-efficiency filter keeps the reactants and the solid products away from the occupant.

Figure 8-12
When used in combination with seat belts, air bags can lessen the severity of injuries in the event of a front-end collision.

For most current systems, the gas generant is a solid mixture of sodium azide, NaN_3, plus an oxidizer. The gas that inflates the bag is almost entirely nitrogen gas, N_2, which is produced in the following decomposition reaction.

$$2NaN_3(s) \longrightarrow 2Na(s) + 3N_2(g)$$

However, this reaction alone cannot inflate the bag fast enough, and the sodium metal produced is a dangerously reactive substance. Oxidizers such as ferric oxide, Fe_2O_3, are included in the gas generant so that they can immediately react with the sodium metal in a single-displacement reaction. This exothermic reaction also raises the temperature more than a hundred degrees so that the gas fills the bag faster.

$$6Na(s) + Fe_2O_3(s) \longrightarrow 3Na_2O(s) + 2Fe(s)$$

But even sodium oxide is unsafe because it is an extremely basic substance. Eventually, it reacts with carbon dioxide, CO_2, and moisture from the air to form sodium hydrogen carbonate, or baking soda.

$$Na_2O(s) + 2CO_2(g) + H_2O(g) \longrightarrow 2NaHCO_3(s)$$

The volume of gas needed to fill an air bag of a certain volume depends on the amount of gas available and the density of the gas. Gas density, in turn, depends on temperature. To calculate the amount of gas generant necessary, air-bag designers must know the stoichiometry of the reactions and account for energy changes in the reaction, which may change the temperature, and thus the density, of the gas.

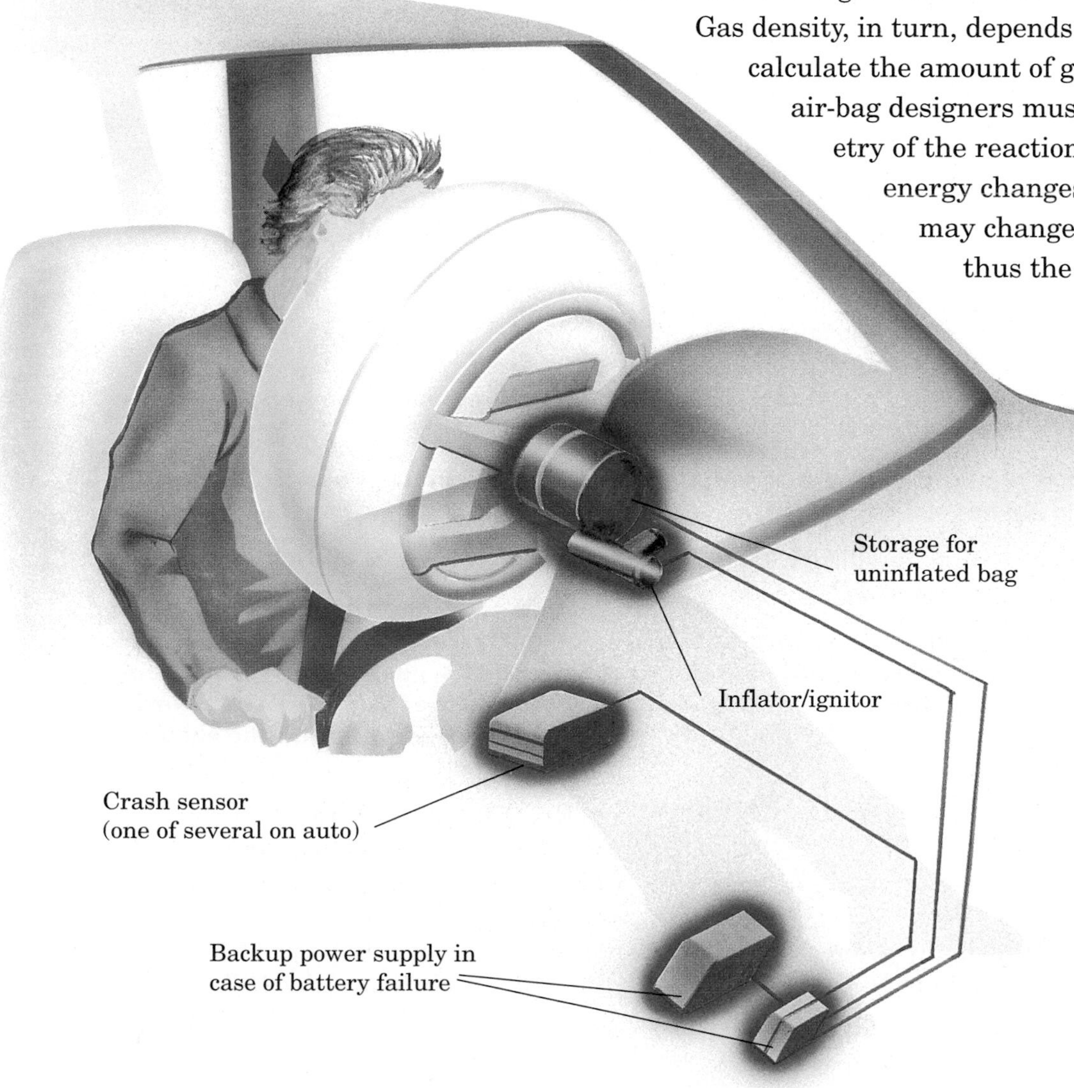

Storage for uninflated bag

Inflator/ignitor

Crash sensor (one of several on auto)

Backup power supply in case of battery failure

Figure 8-13
When a crash occurs, a switch in the sensor closes, and electricity from the battery or the backup power supply flows to the inflator behind the steering wheel. The ignitor within the inflator heats up rapidly, igniting the gas generant to start the sodium azide decomposition reaction. The nitrogen gas that is made inflates the air bag.

Sample Problem 8G

Stoichiometry and density: air bags

Assume that 65.1 L of N_2 gas are needed to inflate an air bag to the proper size. How many grams of NaN_3 must be included in the gas generant to generate this amount of N_2? (Hint: the density of N_2 gas at this temperature is about 0.916 g/L.)

❶ List
- balanced chemical equation: $2NaN_3(s) \longrightarrow 2Na(s) + 3N_2(g)$
- volume of N_2: 65.1 L N_2
- density of N_2: 0.916 g/L
- molar mass of NaN_3: 65.02 g/mol
- molar mass of N_2: 28.02 g/mol
- mole ratio: 2 mol NaN_3: 3 mol N_2
- mass of reactant: **?** g NaN_3

❷ Set up
- First, the product amount must be converted from a volume to a mass using density and then from a mass to amount in moles using molar mass. Next, the mole ratio is used to determine moles of reactant needed. Then, the mass of reactant is calculated using molar mass as a conversion factor.

$$65.1 \text{ L } N_2 \times \frac{0.916 \text{ g } N_2}{1 \text{ L } N_2} \times \frac{1 \text{ mol } N_2}{28.02 \text{ g } N_2} \times \frac{2 \text{ mol } NaN_3}{3 \text{ mol } N_2} \times \frac{65.02 \text{ g } NaN_3}{1 \text{ mol } NaN_3} = \text{?} \text{ g } NaN_3$$

❸ Estimate and calculate
- Round off to make an estimate.

$$66 \times \frac{1}{1} \times \frac{1}{30} \times \frac{2}{3} \times \frac{66}{1} \approx$$

$$\frac{22}{10} \times \frac{44}{1} \approx 96.8$$

- Calculate, and round to the correct number of significant digits.

Calculator answer: 92.2495035 g

Properly rounded answer: 92.2 g NaN_3

Practice 8G

1. How much Fe_2O_3 must be added to the gas generant for this amount of NaN_3?

2. Calculate the mass of sodium hydrogen carbonate produced in the air-bag reaction.

3. The density of $NaHCO_3$ is 2.20 g/mL. What volume of $NaHCO_3$ is produced by the reaction?

4. How many grams of sodium hydrogen carbonate and acetic acid would be needed to inflate the same air bag with CO_2 gas? CO_2 gas has a density 1.57 times that of N_2 gas at this temperature. (Hint: in other words, 1.57 times as many grams of CO_2 will be required to inflate the same air bag.)

$$NaHCO_3(s) + CH_3COOH(aq) \longrightarrow CH_3COONa(aq) + H_2O(l) + CO_2(g)$$

| Sodium hydrogen carbonate | Acetic acid | Sodium acetate | Water | Carbon dioxide |

5. How many grams of water and sodium acetate would be produced by the reaction of $NaHCO_3$ and CH_3COOH to fill an air bag with CO_2?

Engine efficiency depends on reactant proportions

Even if you never have to depend on the stoichiometric calculations that are planned by air-bag designers, any time you drive a car, you are using stoichiometry to control how fast the car moves.

You may already know that a car's engine "burns" gasoline to make the engine run and the car move. The faster the engine runs, the more quickly you will use up the gasoline. But how does the liquid in the gas tank make the engine run? Why does pressing on the accelerator make it run faster? What happens when an engine is "flooded" by having too much gas in it before it is started?

The answers to all these questions require a knowledge of stoichiometry and of the combustion reaction in which gasoline burns. Because the main purpose for the combustion of gasoline is to provide energy, it will be included as one of the products in the following word equation.

$$\text{gasoline} + \text{air} \longrightarrow \text{carbon dioxide} + \text{water} + \text{energy}$$

Actually, this word equation does not identify the reactants very well. Gasoline is not a single chemical but a mixture of many different hydrocarbons, each containing between 5 and 12 carbon atoms.

On average, the gasoline used for automobiles can be treated as if it were pure isooctane (2,2,4-trimethylpentane), whose structure is shown in **Figure 8-14**. This molecule has a molar mass that is about the same as the weighted average of the molecules within the gasoline.

In addition, the only component of air that the gasoline uses in combustion is oxygen, which is only 20.9% of air by volume. So, a satisfactory way to portray the combustion reaction would be to indicate the actual proportions of the reactants and products in the following balanced chemical equation.

$$2C_8H_{18}(g) + 25O_2(g) \longrightarrow 16CO_2(g) + 18H_2O(g) + 10\,900\ \text{kJ}$$

The two reactants must be mixed in a mole ratio that is close to the one shown in the balanced chemical equation for efficient combustion. If too much excess reactant is leftover, the engine will not perform well and may even stop firing.

Figure 8-14
Isooctane, one of the components found in gasoline, has some properties as a pure substance that are similar to those of the mixture, gasoline.

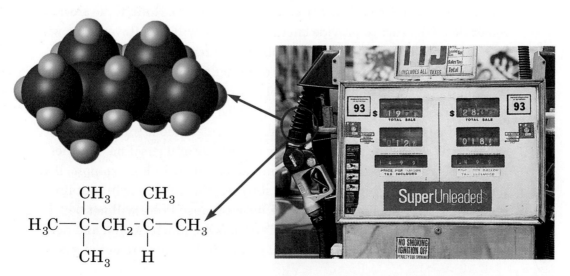

**Engine running at
normal speeds**

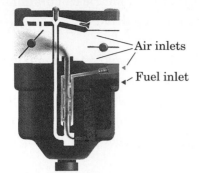

Engine starting

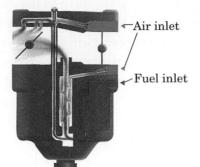

← Air inlet

← Fuel inlet

Engine idling

←Air
inlet

←Fuel
inlet

←Air inlets

←Fuel inlet

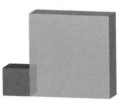

1:16 fuel-air ratio by mass
(1:13.2 isooctane-oxygen mole ratio)

1:2 fuel-air ratio by mass
(1:1.7 isooctane-oxygen mole ratio)

1:9 fuel-air ratio by mass
(1:7.4 isooctane-oxygen mole ratio)

Figure 8-15a
**Under ordinary running con-
ditions, an engine's fuel-air
ratio is maintained at 1:16 by
the carburetor, instead of the
1:12.5 stoichiometric mole
ratio, so that the mixture is
slightly lean, meaning that
gasoline is the limiting reactant. Oxygen is in excess.**

8-15b
**When an engine is starting,
the mixture is very rich, a
1:2 ratio of fuel to air. Oxygen is the limiting reac-
tant, and gasoline is in
excess.**

8-15c
**When an engine is idling, the
reaction mixture is kept rich
at a 1:9 fuel-air ratio, meaning
that oxygen is the limiting
reactant. In this way, there
will always be plenty of fuel
for the combustion reaction.**

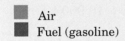

Air
Fuel (gasoline)

Either a carburetor, as shown in **Figure 8-15**, or a fuel-injection
system, depending on the car's year and model, is responsible for feeding
gasoline and air to the engine in variable but precise mixtures.

As an engine runs under ordinary conditions, the fuel-air ratio is kept
relatively close to the 1:12.5 mole ratio for the balanced equation. For
maximum fuel economy, gasoline is the limiting reactant by a slight
amount. In such a "lean" mixture, it is more likely that all of the gasoline
molecules will react to provide energy and none will be leftover. This will
also minimize pollution due to incomplete combustion.

Other conditions, such as starting or idling, require "rich" combinations
with a greater relative amount of fuel so that there is enough fuel to
support combustion. The excess gasoline also cools the engine.

As you push down on the gas pedal when an engine is idling, it opens
the throttle valve, increasing the flow of both air and gasoline. If either
reactant is restricted too much, the engine might stall. For example, if you
pump the gas pedal too much before starting, the mixture will contain
almost entirely gasoline and may not burn because there will not be
enough oxygen. On the other hand, if there is too much oxygen and not
enough gasoline, the engine will stall just as if the car were out of gas.

Sample Problem 8H
Stoichiometry calculations: air–fuel ratio

How many liters of air must react with 1.000 L of isooctane in order for combustion to occur completely? At 20°C, the density of isooctane is 0.6916 g/mL, and the density of oxygen is 1.331 g/L. (Hint: remember to use the percentage of oxygen in air.)

❶ List
- A table will help organize the data.

Reactant	Formula	Molar mass	Density	Volume	Mole ratio
isooctane	C_8H_{18}	114.26 g/mol	0.6916 g/mL	1.000 L	2
oxygen	O_2	32.00 g/mol	1.331 g/L	**?** L	25

Percentage oxygen in air: 20.9% oxygen

Volume of air needed: **?** L

❷ Set up
- First, the volume of isooctane must be converted to mass and then to moles. Then, the mole ratio is used to convert to moles of oxygen. The moles of oxygen must be converted to mass and then to volume of oxygen. Then, the percentage of oxygen in air is used to convert to volume of air.

$$1.000 \text{ L } C_8H_{18} \times \frac{1000 \text{ mL}}{1 \text{ L}} \times \frac{0.6916 \text{ g } C_8H_{18}}{1 \text{ mL } C_8H_{18}} \times \frac{1 \text{ mol } C_8H_{18}}{114.26 \text{ g } C_8H_{18}} \times$$

$$\frac{25 \text{ mol } O_2}{2 \text{ mol } C_8H_{18}} \times \frac{32.00 \text{ g } O_2}{1 \text{ mol } O_2} \times \frac{1 \text{ L } O_2}{1.331 \text{ g } O_2} \times \frac{100 \text{ L air}}{20.9 \text{ L } O_2} = \textbf{?} \text{ L air}$$

This problem looks complicated, but if you break down the process into smaller pieces, it is not difficult to understand.

❸ Estimate and calculate
- Round off to make an estimate.

$$1 \times 1000 \times 0.7 \times \frac{1}{115} \times \frac{25}{2} \times 32 \times \frac{1}{1.33} \times 5 \approx$$

$$700 \times \frac{5}{46} \times 32 \times \frac{3}{4} \times 5 \approx 700 \times \frac{25}{46} \times 24 \approx$$

$$350 \times 25 = 8750$$

- Calculate, and round off correctly.

Rounded answer: 8.704×10^3 L air

Practice 8H

1. Indicate whether the following fuel-air ratios are too rich in fuel. Then indicate what volume of the limiting reactant would need to be added to bring them to the proper stoichiometric ratio.
   a. 3.000 L of isooctane: 35 000. L of air
   b. 24.75 L of isooctane: 2.00×10^5 L of air
   c. 57.3 mL of isooctane: 400. L of air

2. Rather than isooctane alone, a better model for the complex mixture in gasoline would be a 9:1 molar mixture of isooctane and n-heptane, C_7H_{14}.
   a. Write balanced chemical equations for the combustion of isooctane and n-heptane.
   b. If the density of the isooctane-heptane mixture is 0.6908 g/mL, how many liters of air are needed for the complete combustion of 1.000 L of the mixture?

Table 8-4
Clean Air Act Targets for 1996 Air Pollution*

Pollutant	Cars	Light trucks	Motorcycles
hydrocarbons	0.25 g/km	0.50 g/km	5.0 g/km
carbon monoxide	2.1 g/km	2.1–3.1 g/km, depending on truck size	12 g/km
oxides of nitrogen (NO_2)	0.25 g/km	0.25–0.68 g/km, depending on truck size	not regulated

*Note: excludes standards for diesel-powered vehicles. EPA standards for cars and light trucks are actually measured in grams per mile at 75°F.

Car designers use stoichiometry to control pollution

Automobiles are the primary source of air pollution in many parts of the world. To reduce the amount of photochemical smog and other pollution caused by automobile exhaust, Congress passed the Clean Air Act in 1968. This act was amended in 1990 to set new, more restrictive emission control standards for automobiles driven in the United States. **Table 8-4** lists the latest standards for exhaust pollution, which are issued by the U.S. Environmental Protection Agency.

But where do all of these pollutants come from if the combustion of gasoline produces only carbon dioxide, water, and energy? Although the equation for the combustion of isooctane shows most of what happens when gasoline burns, it does not show the whole story. For example, if the fuel-air mixture is improperly balanced and there is not enough oxygen, as when a car is started, some carbon monoxide will be produced instead of carbon dioxide. In cold weather, cars need even more fuel to start than usual, and more carbon monoxide is formed.

If combustion is incomplete, or if gasoline fumes leak out of the tank, hydrocarbons can be released into the atmosphere. In addition, in the high-pressure and high-temperature environment of the engine, nitrogen oxides are formed from the nitrogen and oxygen in air.

One of the Clean Air Act standards limits the amount of nitrogen oxides, especially NO_2, that a car can emit. Such compounds can combine with water in the atmosphere to produce acids that are a part of acid rain. In addition, these compounds can react with unburned hydrocarbons to produce irritating chemicals. Because these chemicals are produced in reactions that are catalyzed by the energy from the sun's ultraviolet light, they form what is referred to as photochemical smog. Photochemical smog can make your eyes burn, and it can be harmful for people with respiratory or heart problems. As you can see in **Figure 8-16**, photochemical smog is easy to detect around many cities. However, it is caused by very small amounts of pollutants. The typical percentage of pollutants in smoggy air is about 0.003%.

Figure 8-16
Smog is a problem for many cities in the United States. It not only is unpleasant to look at, but also can make breathing difficult for many people.

Formation of photochemical smog begins when NO_2 molecules absorb light. The NO_2 decomposes as it absorbs this energy and produces oxygen atoms and nitrogen(II) oxide molecules. In turn, the oxygen atoms produced by the NO_2 decomposition react with oxygen molecules in the air to produce ozone.

$$NO_2(g) \xrightarrow{\text{ultraviolet light}} NO(g) + O(g)$$

$$O_2(g) + O(g) \longrightarrow O_3(g)$$

You may already know that ozone in the upper atmosphere serves as a protective shield against the sun's ultraviolet rays. But closer to the Earth, ozone is a very reactive molecule that can crack rubber, corrode metals, and damage living tissues. In addition, ozone can undergo a complex series of reactions with any hydrocarbons that are not completely burned by a car's engine. The products of these reactions also contribute to photochemical smog.

Automobile manufacturers use stoichiometry to predict when adjustments will be necessary to keep exhaust emissions within legal limits. Moreover, car manufacturers must be sure that all of these stoichiometric concerns are met without raising costs to the point where the manufacturers begin to lose their share of the consumer market.

Because the units in **Table 8-4** are *grams per kilometer*, auto manufacturers must first take into account how much fuel the vehicle will burn in order to move a certain distance. Automobiles with better gas mileage will use less fuel per kilometer. If the reaction progresses in the same way, according to stoichiometry, more fuel-efficient cars should also have slightly lower emissions per kilometer.

Most cars have catalytic converters that treat the exhaust before it is released to the air. The platinum, palladium, or rhodium found in these converters, as shown in **Figure 8-17**, assists in the decomposition of NO_2 into N_2 and O_2, harmless gases already found in the air. Catalytic converters also decrease emissions of CO and hydrocarbons. But catalytic converters perform at their best in warm weather and when the ratio of air and fuel in the engine is very close to the proper stoichiometric ratio. Newer model cars include on-board computers and oxygen sensors to make sure that the proper ratio is maintained so that the engine and the catalytic converter work at top efficiency.

Figure 8-17
The catalytic converters used in automobiles effectively decrease nitrogen oxides, carbon monoxide, and hydrocarbons in exhaust, unless the converter is exposed to leaded gasoline or conditions of extreme heat.

Catalytic converter containing ceramic pellets coated with platinum, palladium, or rhodium catalysts

The contents of gasoline can also be adjusted to decrease pollution. Volatile hydrocarbon compounds like benzene easily evaporate into the air. Some newer blends of gasoline use fewer volatile organic compounds. The addition of ethanol, C_2H_5OH, to fuel can help fuel burn with lower CO levels. Many cities in the United States are required to use these blends of gasoline as part of the Clean Air Act in an effort to improve the air quality.

Sample Problem 8I
Calculating yields: pollution

How much ozone could be produced from 3.50 g of NO_2 contained in a car's exhaust? (Hint: first calculate how much O is produced from NO_2. Then, use this value to calculate how much O_3 is produced.)

❶ List
- **amount of reactant: 3.50 g NO_2**
- **molar mass for NO_2: 46.01 g/mol**
- **molar mass for O_3: 48.00 g/mol**
- **amount of products: ?g O_3**
- **balanced equations:** $NO_2(g) \longrightarrow NO(g) + O(g)$
  $$O_2(g) + O(g) \longrightarrow O_3(g)$$

❷ Set up
- **First, convert the mass of NO_2 into moles so that the mole ratio can be used to calculate moles of O. Then, use the mole ratio for the second equation to calculate moles and then grams of O_3.**

$$3.50 \text{ g } NO_2 \times \frac{1 \text{ mol } NO_2}{46.01 \text{ g } NO_2} \times \frac{1 \text{ mol } O}{1 \text{ mol } NO_2} \times \frac{1 \text{ mol } O_3}{1 \text{ mol } O} \times \frac{48.00 \text{ g } O_3}{1 \text{ mol } O_3} = \textbf{?}\text{g } O_3$$

❸ Estimate and calculate
- **Round off to make an estimate.**

$$3.5 \times \frac{1}{46} \times \frac{1}{1} \times \frac{1}{1} \times \frac{48}{1} \approx 3.5$$

- **Calculate the answer, and round to the correct number of significant figures.**

Calculator answer: 3.651~~380135~~

Correct answer: 3.65 g O_3

Section Review

17. Calculate how many liters of N_2 gas would be produced if 22.4 g of NaN_3 were placed inside an air-bag ignitor.
18. Determine how many grams of O_2 must be provided by a car's carburetor or fuel-injection system so that 528.7 g of C_8H_{18} would be completely combusted.
19. Calculate how many grams of O_2 could react with 18.3 g of O produced from the NO_2 emitted in a car's exhaust.
20. How many grams of O_3 would be produced by the O_2 and O in item **19**?
21. Assume that 74.0 g of isooctane must be combusted to drive a car for 1.0 km. What is the theoretical yield of carbon monoxide, if it is assumed that all of the carbon atoms in the isooctane form CO?
22. Check the data listed in **Table 8-4**. Using your answer from item **21**, what is the maximum percent yield of CO permitted by law to be released in this car's exhaust?

Conclusion: Mass Relationships and Feeding the Army

At the beginning of this chapter, you learned about how the Army invented a new way to make sure that soldiers get hot meals.

Why was the magnesium-water reaction of the FRH chosen over the other methods? Soldiers have a great deal of equipment to carry. The less mass devoted to warming equipment, the better. Soldiers also operate under hectic conditions. The simpler the method is to use, the better.

From the story, you know that the reaction of 1 mol of Mg produces more than five times as much energy as the reaction of 1 mol of CaO. When equal masses are compared, the advantage is even greater.

But mole for mole and gram for gram, trioxane releases far more energy than does the Mg reaction. Why was this method discarded?

Trioxane must be used outside, it must be lit with matches or a lighter, and it takes longer to heat a meal, which makes it difficult to use in dangerous situations. On the other hand, an FRH can be used safely in vehicles, tents, ships, planes, and buildings.

Why is there a difference between the amount of water that is added and the amount of water the reaction requires? To warm a meal in the FRH, 45 mL of water are added, even though the balanced chemical equation requires only 12 mL.

Water is an excess reactant. Thus, the more expensive magnesium will be the limiting reactant that is completely consumed in the reaction.

Another reason for the extra water is to provide efficient heat transfer over a larger area. Also, the paperboard and the porous pad soak up some of the water, so it is not available for the reaction.

The designers of this system balanced many competing concerns. If too little water is added, the reaction will not go to completion, some magnesium will be wasted, and not as much energy will be generated. On the other hand, excess water absorbs heat that could be warming the meal.

Applying Concepts

1. Before the development of the FRH, soldiers heated their meals using the combustion reaction of trioxane, shown at right. Write the balanced chemical equation for this reaction.

Research and Writing

Use the library to find out more about the following.

1. In many wars, food poisoning contributes substantially to the number of casualties. Compare the percentages for several wars. Give a reason for any pattern you find.

2. Check the listings for portable stoves in a catalog of camping goods. Determine what fuels they use, and write balanced chemical equations for the reactions.

FRH

Highlights

How much does a reaction really produce?

- Once the limiting reactant has been used up, no more product can be formed, no matter how much of the other reactant(s) remains.
- The theoretical yield is the calculated maximum amount of product possible from a given amount of reactants.
- The actual yield is the amount of product experimentally measured after the reaction of a given amount of reactants.
- Percent yield, 100 times the ratio of actual yield to theoretical yield, describes reaction efficiency.

Key terms

actual yield

excess reactant

limiting reactant

percent yield

stoichiometry

theoretical yield

Key ideas

How much can a reaction produce?

- Reaction stoichiometry compares the mass and quantity of substances in a chemical equation. Composition stoichiometry describes the relationship among the elements within a substance.
- Stoichiometry problems can be solved with conversion factors created from mole ratios, molar masses, density, and Avogadro's number.

How can stoichiometry be used?

- Stoichiometry can be used by automobile designers to maximize a car's safety and performance, while minimizing its environmental impact.

Key problem-solving approach:
Stoichiometry calculations

When solving stoichiometry problems, select the variable given in your problem from the options near the top of this diagram. Then, follow the calculation pathway that leads to the proper units for the answer near the bottom of this diagram.

volume of substance A (units: mL)

$\times$ density $\left(\frac{g}{mL}\right)$

mass of substance A (units: g)

amount of substance A (units: formula units)

$\times \dfrac{1 \text{ mole}}{\text{molar mass (g)}}$

$\dfrac{1 \text{ mole}}{6.022 \times 10^{23} \text{ formula units}}$

amount of substance A (units: mol)

$\times$ mole ratio

amount of substance B (units: mol)

$\times \dfrac{6.022 \times 10^{23} \text{ formula units}}{1 \text{ mole}}$

$\times \dfrac{\text{molar mass (g)}}{1 \text{ mole}}$

volume of substance B (units: mL)

$\times \dfrac{1}{\text{density } (^g/_{mL})}$

mass of substance B (units: g)

amount of substance B (units: formula units)

Review and Assess

 Stoichiometry

1. Explain the difference between reaction stoichiometry and composition stoichiometry.
2. Why is a balanced chemical equation required to solve stoichiometry problems?
3. A student encounters a stoichiometry problem. He quickly glances over it, punches the numbers into a calculator, and obtains an answer. Explain why the student's method is unlikely to yield the correct answer. What should he have done differently?
4. How do stoichiometry problems that provide data or require answers in mass amounts differ from stoichiometry problems that provide data or require answers in mole amounts?
5. A reaction between hydrazine, N_2H_4, and dinitrogen tetroxide, N_2O_4, has been used to launch rockets into space. The reaction produces nitrogen gas and water vapor, as shown in the unbalanced equation below.

$$N_2H_4(l) + N_2O_4(l) \longrightarrow N_2(g) + H_2O(g)$$

   a. Write the balanced chemical equation for the reaction.
   b. What is the mole ratio of N_2H_4 to N_2?
   c. What is the mole ratio of N_2O_4 to H_2O?
   d. How many moles of water will be produced from 14 000 mol of hydrazine used by a rocket?

PRACTICE

Answers to items in a black square begin on page 841.

6 In your body, cell metabolism produces carbon dioxide, which is promptly combined with water to form carbonic acid, H_2CO_3. The carbonic acid is released into the blood, where enzymes speed up its decomposition into water and carbon dioxide. The carbon dioxide is later released from your lungs. How many grams of carbon dioxide would you exhale after 0.250 g of H_2CO_3 decomposes? (Hint: see Sample Problem 8A.)

7. Various processes, including gasoline combustion in automobiles and industrial burning of fossil fuels, can result in the production of sulfur dioxide, SO_2. This can undergo a series of reactions with oxygen and water in the air to eventually form sulfuric acid as shown in the equation below. This acid mixes with moisture to form acid precipitation. If 0.500 g of sulfur dioxide from pollutants reacts with excess water and oxygen found in the air, how many grams of sulfuric acid can be produced? (Hint: see Sample Problem 8A.)

$$2H_2O(l) + O_2(g) + 2SO_2(g) \longrightarrow 2H_2SO_4(aq)$$

8 Oxygen gas can be produced by decomposing potassium chlorate using the reaction below. If 125 g of $KClO_3$ are heated and decompose completely, how many moles of oxygen gas are produced? (Hint: see Sample Problem 8B.)

$$2KClO_3(s) \longrightarrow 2KCl(s) + 3O_2(g)$$

9. Ethanol is considered a clean fuel because it burns in the presence of excess oxygen to produce carbon dioxide and water with fewer trace pollutants than some hydrocarbons found in gasoline. If 5.00 mol of water are produced during the combustion of ethanol, how many grams of ethanol were present at the beginning of the reaction? (Hint: see Sample Problem 8B.)

Ethanol   3 Oxygen   2 Carbon dioxide   3 water

10 Oxygen gas and water are produced by the decomposition of hydrogen peroxide. If 10.0 mol H_2O_2 decompose, how many liters of oxygen will be produced? Assume the density of oxygen is 1.429 g/L. (Hint: see Sample Problem 8C.)

$$2H_2O_2(aq) \longrightarrow 2H_2O(l) + O_2(g)$$

11. One of the intermediate steps in the production of nitric acid is the reaction between ammonia and oxygen. If 25.0 mol of ammonia gas react with excess oxygen, how many liters of NO will be produced? Assume the density of NO is 1.340 g/L. (Hint: see Sample Problem 8C.)

$$4NH_3(g) + 5O_2(g) \longrightarrow 4NO(g) + 6H_2O(g)$$

A P P L Y

12. Hydrogen gas can be produced by adding an active metal, such as zinc, to hydrochloric acid. A student reports that for every kilogram of zinc reacted, 1.0 kg of hydrogen gas is evolved. Is this correct? Explain why or why not.

$$Zn(s) + 2HCl(aq) \longrightarrow ZnCl_2(aq) + H_2(g)$$

13. Explain what, if anything, is wrong with the setups shown below, which are for problems relating to the production of ammonium hydrogen phosphate, a common fertilizer.

$$H_3PO_4(aq) + 2NH_3(g) \longrightarrow (NH_4)_2HPO_4(aq)$$

a. $10.00 \text{ g NH}_3 \times \dfrac{1 \text{ g (NH}_4)_2\text{HPO}_4}{2 \text{ g NH}_3} =$

$20.00 \text{ g (NH}_4)_2\text{HPO}_4$

b. $10.00 \text{ g NH}_3 \times \dfrac{17.04 \text{ g NH}_3}{1 \text{ mol NH}_3} =$

170.4 mol NH_3

c. $10.00 \text{ L NH}_3 \times \dfrac{0.761 \text{ g NH}_3}{1 \text{ L NH}_3} \times$

$\dfrac{1 \text{ mol NH}_3}{17.04 \text{ g NH}_3} = 0.447 \text{ mol NH}_3$

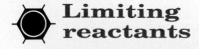 **Limiting reactants**

R E V I E W

14. Differentiate a limiting reactant from an excess reactant.
15. Do all reactions have a limiting reactant? Explain.

16. Answer the following questions about the production of zinc citrate, $Zn_3(C_6H_5O_7)_2$, an ingredient in toothpaste.

$$3ZnCO_3(s) + 2C_6H_8O_7(aq) \longrightarrow$$
zinc(II) carbonate   citric acid

$$Zn_3(C_6H_5O_7)_2(aq) + 3H_2O(l) + 3CO_2(g)$$
zinc(II) citrate   water   carbon dioxide

a. How many moles of $ZnCO_3$ are needed to react with 1 mol $C_6H_8O_7$?
b. If there is 1 mol $ZnCO_3$ and 1 mol $C_6H_8O_7$, which is the limiting reactant?
c. How many moles of $ZnCO_3$ and $C_6H_8O_7$ are required to produce 20.0 mol $Zn_3(C_6H_5O_7)_2$?
d. If there are 6.0 mol $ZnCO_3$ and 10.0 mol $C_6H_8O_7$, which is the limiting reactant?

P R A C T I C E

17 When copper metal is added to silver nitrate solution, silver metal and copper(II) nitrate are produced. If 100. g of copper metal are added to a solution containing 100. g of silver nitrate, how many grams of silver metal will be produced? (Hint: see Sample Problem 8D.)

18. A fruit-scented air freshener can be made by reacting butanoic acid with methanol to produce methyl butanoate and water. How many grams of methyl butanoate can be produced if 50.0 g of butanoic acid react with 40.0 g of methanol? (Hint: see Sample Problem 8D.)

[Structural diagram: Butanoic acid + H₃C—OH (Methanol) ⟶]

Butanoic acid   Methanol

[Structural diagram: Methyl butanoate + water]

Methyl butanoate   Water

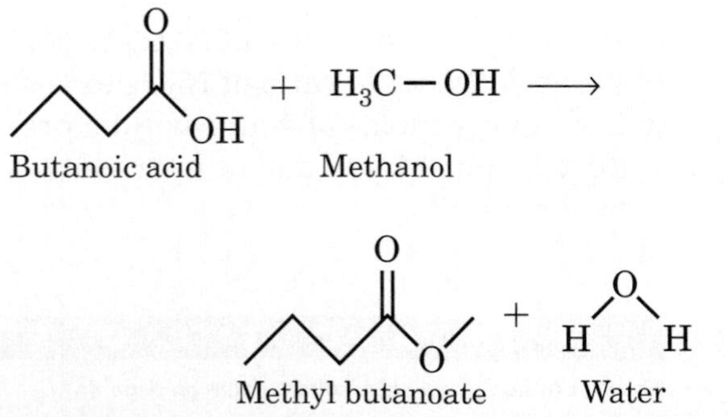

A P P L Y

19. Identify the limiting reactant and the excess reactant in the following situations.
a. firewood burning in a campfire
b. stomach acid breaking down food
c. sulfur compounds from the air tarnishing silver
d. NO_2 reacting with water vapor to produce acid rain

20. A perfume manufacturer needs to produce large supplies of nitrobenzene for the creation of different fragrances. The nitrobenzene can be made by reacting benzene with nitric acid in the presence of a catalyst. If benzene costs \$1.75/mol and nitric acid costs \$0.57/mol, which should the perfume manufacturer choose to be the limiting reactant?

Percent yield

R E V I E W

21. a. Differentiate theoretical yield from actual yield.
   b. How is actual yield determined?
   c. How is theoretical yield determined?
22. Why do many chemical reactions produce less than the amount of product predicted by stoichiometry?

P R A C T I C E

23 Magnesium is obtained from sea water. $Ca(OH)_2$ is added to sea water, precipitating $Mg(OH)_2$. This is filtered out, and reacted with HCl to produce $MgCl_2$. This is dried, fused, and electrolyzed, producing Mg and Cl_2 as shown in the equation below. If 185.0 g of magnesium are recovered from 1000. g of magnesium chloride, what is the percent yield for this reaction? (Hint: see Sample Problem 8E.)

$$MgCl_2(l) \longrightarrow Mg(s) + Cl_2(g)$$

24. The combustion of methane produces carbon dioxide and water. Assume that 2.00 mol CH_4 are burned in the presence of excess oxygen. What is the percent yield if the reaction produces 80.0 g CO_2? (Hint: see Sample Problem 8E.)

$$CH_4(g) + 2O_2(g) \longrightarrow CO_2(g) + 2H_2O(g)$$

25 Coal gasification is a process that converts coal into methane gas. If this reaction has a percent yield of 85.0%, how much methane can be obtained from 1250 g of carbon? (Hint: see Sample Problem 8F.)

$$2C(s) + 2H_2O(l) \longrightarrow CH_4(g) + CO_2(g)$$

26. If the percent yield for the coal gasification process in item 25 is increased to 95.0%, how much methane can be obtained from 2750 g of carbon? (Hint: see Sample Problem 8F.)

A P P L Y

27. A sandpaper company uses silicon carbide, SiC, to make its product. Reacting silicon dioxide with graphite yielded 30.0 kg of SiC. The theoretical yield is 998 mol. What is the percent yield?
28. a. Can actual yield ever exceed theoretical yield? Explain.
   b. In the lab, you run an experiment that appears to have a percent yield of 115%. Propose possible reasons for this result.

Practical uses of stoichiometry

R E V I E W

29. Use stoichiometry to explain the following problems that a lawn mower may have.
   a. A lawn mower fails to start because the engine floods.
   b. A lawn mower stalls after starting cold and idling.
30. Use stoichiometry to explain why a 4.00 kg firework would produce more light than a 2.00 kg firework containing the same proportion of reactants.

P R A C T I C E

31 Phosphate baking powder is a mixture of starch, sodium hydrogen carbonate, and calcium dihydrogen phosphate. When mixed with water, phosphate baking powder releases carbon dioxide gas, causing a dough or batter to bubble and rise.

$$2NaHCO_3(aq) + Ca(H_2PO_4)_2(aq) \longrightarrow$$
$$2Na^+(aq) + Ca^{2+}(aq) + 2HPO_4{}^{2-}(aq) +$$
$$2CO_2(g) + 2H_2O(l)$$

If 0.750 L of CO_2 is needed for a cake and each kilogram of baking powder contains 168 g of $NaHCO_3$, how many grams of baking powder must be used to generate this amount of CO_2? The density of CO_2 at baking temperature is about 1.25 g/L. (Hint: see Sample Problem 8G.)

32. The addition of yeast can make bread rise because the yeast produces CO_2 from glucose, $C_6H_{12}O_6$, according to the equation below. Assume that 0.50 L of carbon dioxide is required for a loaf of bread. How many grams of $C_6H_{12}O_6$ must be broken down by yeast to produce this amount of CO_2? The density of CO_2 at baking temperature is about 1.25 g/L. (Hint: see Sample Problem 8G, and balance the equation.)

$$C_6H_{12}O_6(s) \longrightarrow C_2H_5OH(l) + CO_2(g)$$

33 Plaster of Paris, $CaSO_4 \cdot 1/2\,H_2O$, has many uses, including castings and dental cement. It can be obtained by heating gypsum, $CaSO_4 \cdot 2H_2O$. How many liters of water vapor evolve when 5.00 L of gypsum are heated at 110°C to produce plaster of Paris? At 110°C the density of $CaSO_4 \cdot 2H_2O$ is 2.32 g/mL, and the density of water vapor is 0.581 g/L. (Hint: see Sample Problem 8H.)

$$2CaSO_4 \cdot 2H_2O(s) \longrightarrow$$
$$2CaSO_4 \cdot \tfrac{1}{2}H_2O(s) + 3H_2O(g)$$

34. Builders and dentists must store plaster of Paris, $CaSO_4 \cdot 1/2\,H_2O$, in airtight containers to prevent it from absorbing water vapor and changing back into gypsum, $CaSO_4 \cdot 2H_2O$. If 7.50 kg of plaster of Paris absorbed excess water vapor, what volume of gypsum would form? The density of $CaSO_4 \cdot 2H_2O$ is 2.32 g/mL. (Hint: see Sample Problem 8H.)

$$2CaSO_4 \cdot \tfrac{1}{2}H_2O(s) + 3H_2O(g) \longrightarrow$$
$$2CaSO_4 \cdot 2H_2O(s)$$

35 A common additive to motor oil is the substance *p-tert*-butylphenol. It is produced by two reactions, starting with the reactants chlorobenzene and sodium hydroxide. How many moles of *p-tert*-butylphenol could be produced if 500. g of NaOH are available? (Hint: see Sample Problem 8I.)

Step 1:

Step 2:

36. Gold can be recovered from sea water by reacting the water with an active metal such as zinc, which is refined from zinc oxide. The zinc displaces the gold in the water. What mass of gold can be recovered if 2.00 g of ZnO and an excess of sea water are available? (Hint: see Sample Problem 8I.)

$$2ZnO(s) + C(s) \longrightarrow 2Zn(s) + CO_2(g)$$
$$2Au^{3+}(aq) + 3Zn(s) \longrightarrow$$
$$3Zn^{2+}(aq) + 2Au(s)$$

A P P L Y

37. Explain the stoichiometry involved in blowing air on the base of a dwindling campfire to keep the coals burning.

38. Why would it be unreasonable for an amendment to the Clean Air Act to call for 0% pollution emissions from cars with combustion engines?

39. While working in a lab to synthesize acetaminophen, a common pain reliever, you discover that the amount of reactants planned for the reaction was based on the assumption that the entire theoretical yield would be produced. What should you do to be certain that as much acetaminophen as was expected is actually made? Explain.

Linking chapters

1. *Recognizing reaction types*
Determine the conversion factors needed for the following problems. Be sure to write a balanced equation first.
a. How many grams of oxygen gas are evolved from the decomposition of a known amount of water in moles?
b. How many moles of hydrochloric acid are needed to completely react with a known mass of zinc in a single-displacement reaction?
c. How many moles of calcium carbonate are produced in a double-displacement reaction between a known mass of calcium nitrate and potassium carbonate?

2. Theme: *Equilibrium and change*
In some synthesis reactions, part of the product decomposes into reactants. How is the reversal similar to the dissolving and recrystallizing of sugar in iced tea that illustrated equilibrium and change in Chapter 1?

1. Graphics calculator

The ratios used in stoichiometry can be expressed as the slope of a straight line graph. For example, the complete combustion of ethanol is represented below.

$$C_2H_5OH(g) + 3O_2(g) \longrightarrow$$
$$2CO_2(g) + 3H_2O(g)$$

$\Delta H = -1368$ kJ

For every mole of ethanol, 1368 kJ of energy are released. The mole ratio is 1368 kJ:1 mol C_2H_5OH. By graphing a function with this slope, you can predict how much energy can be obtained from any amount of ethanol. Select the $\boxed{\text{WINDOW}}$ key on your calculator, and set Xmin to 0, Xmax to 20, and Xscl to 2. Set Ymin to 0, Ymax to 30 000, and Yscl to 3000. Select the $\boxed{\text{Y}=}$ key and enter the function $Y_1 = (1368 \div 1)$ $\boxed{\text{X,T,}\Theta}$. This represents the equation $y = 1368x$, with y equal to energy and x equal to number of moles ethanol. Press $\boxed{\text{GRAPH}}$ and use the $\boxed{\text{TRACE}}$ mode to estimate the energy released during the combustion of the following amounts of ethanol.

a. 5.5 mol **b.** 18 mol **c.** 0.75 mol

2. Computer spreadsheet

Percent yield will allow you to predict what the actual yield of an experiment will be. Create a spreadsheet that will calculate the actual yield from any percent yield and theoretical yield.

Alternative assessment

Performance assessment

1. Design an experiment to measure the percent yields for the reactions listed below. If your teacher approves your design, acquire the necessary materials, and carry out your plan to obtain percent yield data.

   a. $Zn(s) + 2HCl(aq) \longrightarrow ZnCl_2(aq) + H_2(g)$

   b. $2NaHCO_3(s) \xrightarrow{\Delta}$
   $$Na_2CO_3(s) + H_2O(g) + CO_2(g)$$

   c. $CaCl_2(aq) + Na_2CO_3(aq) \longrightarrow$
   $$CaCO_3(s) + 2NaCl(aq)$$

   d. $NaOH(aq) + HCl(aq) \longrightarrow$
   $$NaCl(aq) + H_2O(l)$$

   (Note: use only dilute NaOH and HCl, less concentrated than 1.0 mol/liter.)

2. Your teacher will give you an index card specifying a volume of a gas. Reactants to make the gas will also be listed. Describe exactly how you would make the gas from the reactants. Include a method of collecting the gas without allowing it to mix with air. Then specify how much of each reactant you need. Choose a limiting reactant and explain your choice. If your teacher approves your plan, obtain the necessary materials and make the gas. (Hint: look up the density of the gas in a chemical handbook.)

Portfolio projects

1. Research and communication

Research the composition of gasoline sold in your area. Contact a gasoline company to discover what formulations are used. Investigate whether the mixtures change by season or by geographic area. Find out if your area has any guidelines regarding gasoline additives that reduce air pollution. Present your findings to the class.

2. Cooperative activity

Investigate corporate, governmental, or private use of alternative fuel sources for vehicles. Hold a class debate to compare the costs and environmental effects of these alternative fuels.

3. Chemistry and you

Visit a car maintenance shop to find out how you can help reduce air pollution by increasing your car's efficiency. Make a checklist of tasks to perform regularly to help meet this goal.

4. Research and communication

Research the production of the following pollutants: methane, CH_4; mercury, Hg; lead, Pb; chlorine, Cl_2; and sulfur oxides, SO_x. Determine the stoichiometry involved in the production of each of these chemicals. Contact the EPA, and gather information on what you can do to help reduce pollution by these chemicals.

CHAPTER 9

Causes of Change

$$2H_2 + O_2 \longrightarrow 2H_2O$$

Energy and Low-Emission Cars

Would you like a car like this one? The car looks like many other sports cars of the same model available from dealers around the country. It can go from 0 to 60 mph in 10.5 s. But it's different—very different. And as much as you might love to drive or own such a car, unfortunately you can't—at least not yet.

This car is different not because of its shape or its stereo, but because of what is under the hood. It has a 1300 cm^3, 120 horsepower, two-rotor engine that doesn't use gasoline—it is powered instead by hydrogen.

Scientists have long been searching for alternative sources of energy to replace petroleum products that produce toxic emissions and that will eventually be exhausted. As an alternative for gasoline, scientists and engineers have experimented with solar-powered and battery-powered vehicles.

However, with current technology, solar-powered vehicles can be unreliable because they can't run unless the sun has been shining. Battery-powered vehicles are expected to be more expensive than gasoline-powered cars because the batteries are made of expensive and heavy materials. In addition, pollution can be created when the electricity needed to recharge the batteries is generated.

As a fuel, hydrogen's big advantage is that it produces very low toxic emissions. When gasoline is used, several undesirable products, including hydrocarbons and oxides of nitrogen and carbon, are released into the atmosphere.

These compounds cause acid precipitation, contribute to photochemical smog, and promote the "greenhouse effect." When pure hydrogen is burned, however, no hydrocarbons or carbon oxides are emitted. The levels of nitrogen oxides are also diminished.

For the moment, only a few of these cars will be produced as prototypes. Mass production is still years or even decades away.

With all these advantages, why aren't hydrogen cars available now? One challenge is the expense of producing and distributing the huge supplies of hydrogen that will be needed. Another is the high cost of producing the car.

Even if a cost-effective method of producing hydrogen were available, the problem of safe storage would remain. Hydrogen is hard to store because it is a very reactive gas. In the presence of a spark, it combines easily and rapidly with oxygen, resulting in an explosive reaction that releases a large quantity of energy.

In this chapter, you will study the driving forces that cause reactions to occur so that you can answer the following questions.

- *What drives the hydrogen combustion reaction?*
- *How can this reaction be controlled so that it does not happen accidentally?*

How does energy affect change?

Section Objectives

Distinguish between heat and temperature.

Explain how a calorimeter measures changes in energy.

Explain what is meant by the caloric content of foods.

Calculate the amount of heat energy released or absorbed in a chemical reaction or physical change.

List examples of different heats of reaction.

Use heats of reaction in stoichiometric calculations.

Heat in physical changes

If an ice cube is left out on a table at room temperature, no one is surprised that it melts and changes into water. No matter how long the water sits on the table, it will not become ice again as long as it is held at room temperature. If an ice cube and glass of water are left in a freezer at −10°C, the ice cube will not melt, and the water in the glass will freeze.

In other words, the physical change of melting and freezing can be considered a reversible change, one that does not happen in only one direction. The direction of the change of state can be reversed merely by adjusting the temperature. The change from water to ice (and back again) can be summarized by the following equation.

$$H_2O(l) \rightleftharpoons H_2O(s)$$

Pure water has a melting/freezing point of 0°C. Below 0°C, freezing will occur, and the equation written above runs from left to right. Eventually, only solid will remain. Above 0°C, melting will occur, and the equation runs from right to left so that only liquid remains.

Melting and boiling occur at specific temperatures

To understand why changing the temperature will affect the state of matter of water, you need to know the difference between heat energy and temperature. Consider the experiment shown in **Figure 9-1**. Two beakers are placed on hot plates. One contains a single ice cube; the other contains eight ice cubes. Times and temperatures are measured as each beaker is heated, with the hot plates set on medium. This way, the hot plates deliver the same amount of energy to each beaker each second.

Figure 9-1a
In this experiment, one beaker containing eight ice cubes . . .

9-1b
. . . and another containing only one ice cube were both heated.

Table 9-1
Data from Ice Cube Experiment

Beaker with one ice cube		Beaker with eight ice cubes	
Temperature	Time (s)	Temperature	Time (s)
0°C (start)	0	0°C (start)	0
0°C (ice disappears)	25	0°C (ice disappears)	190
25°C	33	25°C	250
50°C	41	50°C	310
75°C	49	75°C	370
100°C (water begins boiling)	57	100°C (water begins boiling)	429
100°C (water disappears)	226	100°C (water disappears)	1701

In each case, the solid ice cubes melt, making liquid water. Eventually, the liquid boils, forming gaseous steam until there is nothing left in the beakers. The data are summarized in **Table 9-1** and represented by the graph shown in **Figure 9-2**.

Because the hot plates deliver heat at a constant rate, similar time intervals represent similar amounts of heat transferred by the hot plates. The quantity of heat transferred in the first 30 s is the same as the heat transferred between 200 s and 230 s.

First, compare the differences between the data for one ice cube and for eight ice cubes. From the graph, you can tell that the temperature at which melting and boiling occur are the same, regardless of the amount of ice used. But the wide difference in time indicates that different amounts of heat were needed. Each sample of ice melted at 0°C, but only 25 s of heat were required to completely melt the lone ice cube. A much longer time, 190 s, was required to melt eight ice cubes completely. The amount of heat that the hot plate transferred during 57 s was enough to melt the water in one ice cube and bring it to boiling, but not enough to melt the eight ice cubes entirely. In fact, the eight ice cubes required about eight times as much heat to be transferred before they boiled. Yet boiling occurred at the same temperature, 100°C, for both samples of ice.

Figure 9-2
When ice is heated, its temperature does not change until all of it has melted. Then the temperature rises steadily until it reaches the boiling point, rising no further until all of the water has boiled away.

Temperature vs. Time Data from Ice Cube Experiment

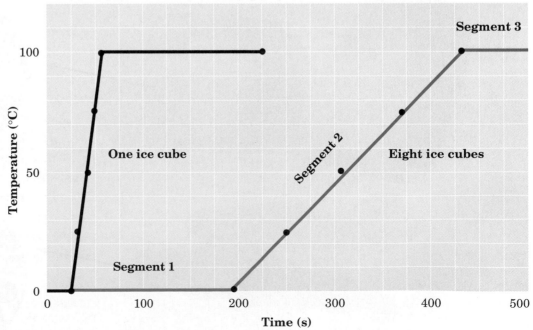

Next examine the shape of the plots. Both plots have the same basic shape: flat, then slanted upward, and then flat again. Because the plot for the eight ice cubes is larger, we will examine its shape in further detail. What happens in the three different parts of the plot?

In the first segment, heat was transferred for 190 s, but the temperature of the sample did not change at all—it remained at 0°C until there was no ice present. The heat that was transferred during the next 190 s raised the temperature of the sample, now entirely liquid water, by almost 80°C. The upward slope of the second segment shows that, as heat was transferred, the temperature of the water increased. At 429 s the temperature reached 100°C, and boiling began, as indicated in the third segment of the graph. Once more, the temperature held steady during boiling, despite the large amounts of heat being added.

Modeling melting, heating, and boiling

But why is the temperature constant during melting or boiling? You know from Chapter 2 that ice is a solid, consisting of a rigid arrangement of water molecules in a crystal. The molecules vibrate but cannot move from one place to another. Liquid water consists of water molecules that are still attracted to one another but not rigidly held together. They are able to move from one position to another as well as vibrate.

For ice to melt, energy must be added to cause the vibrations to increase enough so that the molecules can break loose from their positions in the ice crystal. Because temperature is a measure of the average kinetic energy of the particles in a substance, temperature will increase only after the forces holding the ice crystals together are overcome. When the particles are free to move, the heat energy that is added is converted to energy of motion for the particles. No matter how much heat energy is transferred, the temperature will not rise above 0°C until all of the solid melts.

Figure 9-3
As ice absorbs energy from the surroundings, the vibrations of the molecules in the lattice increase. When the force of the vibrations is greater than the force of attraction between molecules in the lattice, the lattice breaks down to form liquid water, a process you see as melting.

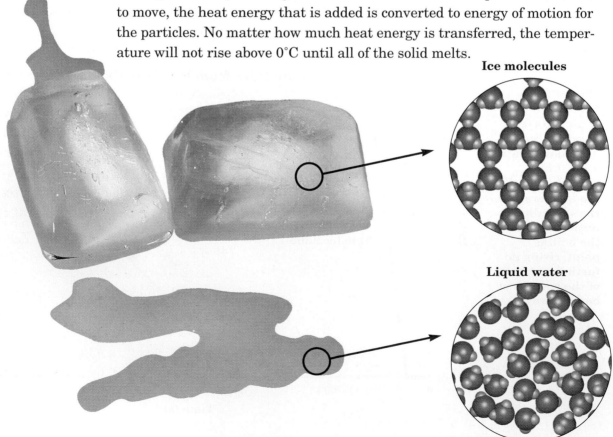

Ice molecules

Liquid water

temperature
a measure of the average kinetic energy of random motion of the particles in a sample of matter

heat
the total of kinetic energy of random motion of molecules, atoms, or ions in a substance

specific heat capacity
the amount of heat energy required to increase the temperature of one gram of a substance by one degree Celsius

Once all of the ice was melted, the heat energy transferred by the hot plate caused an increase in the temperature of the sample. During this process, the temperature climbed steadily until it reached the boiling point. As you learned in Chapter 2, gases consist of individual molecules with only weak attractions for each other. For boiling to occur, the molecules needed more energy, which was transferred as heat by the hot plate, to overcome the intermolecular forces holding the liquid water molecules together. The high-energy water molecules were moving so rapidly that they moved right out of the pan and into the air as a gas. Because heat energy was used to overcome the intermolecular forces, none was available to raise the temperature past 100°C.

Heat and temperature are different

The temperatures at melting and boiling were the same for one ice cube or eight ice cubes. *Temperature is a measure of the average kinetic energy of random motion of the particles in a substance.*

The beaker with eight ice cubes required more heat to reach the melting and boiling temperatures because it had more particles in it. *Heat is a measure of the total amount of energy transferred from an object of high temperature to one of low temperature.* The energy was transferred from the hot plate to the water molecules in the beaker. A change in temperature, which means a change in average kinetic energy values, is usually accompanied by a transfer of energy in the form of heat. However, the more particles there are, the greater the amount of heat that must be transferred to raise the average kinetic energy, the temperature, of all the particles.

Specific heat capacity relates temperature changes to heat changes

Table 9-2
Specific Heat of Selected Substances

Substance	Specific heat capacity, c_p (J/g·°C at 25°C unless noted)
water, $H_2O(l)$	4.180
ethanol, $C_2H_5OH(l)$	2.438
methane, $CH_4(g)$	2.200
isooctane, $C_8H_{18}(l)$	2.093
ice, $H_2O(s)$ at −5°C	2.077
steam, $H_2O(g)$ at 100°C	2.042
aluminum, $Al(s)$	0.897
table salt, $NaCl(s)$	0.865
graphite, $C(s)$	0.714
iron, $Fe(s)$	0.449
silver, $Ag(s)$	0.235
mercury, $Hg(l)$	0.139
tungsten, $W(s)$	0.132

The **specific heat capacity** of a substance is the amount of heat energy required to raise the temperature of one gram of that substance by one degree Celsius. Its symbol is c_p. The p in the symbol stands for "at constant pressure." The specific heat capacity can vary if pressure is not kept constant. It can also vary at different temperatures, but for most purposes, it is reasonable to assume the specific heat capacity remains constant.

Specific heat capacity is a physical property of matter. Each pure substance has a characteristic specific heat capacity. Scientists have measured and recorded specific heat capacities for many substances, including those shown in **Table 9-2** Specific heat capacities must be measured; they cannot be determined from a chemical formula.

Figure 9-4
Metals typically have low heat capacities. When a sterling silver spoon is left in a cup of hot tea, it rapidly reaches the temperature of the tea.

Substances with low specific heat capacities require less energy to feel hot than those with high specific heat capacities. For example, a piece of silver changes temperature faster than a piece of iron with the same mass. For this reason, a sterling silver spoon such as the one shown in **Figure 9-4** will warm up more quickly that a stainless steel one containing mostly iron.

If the temperature change and the mass of the substance undergoing the change are given, the specific heat capacity can be used to calculate the change in heat. The symbol for "change in" is the Greek letter delta, Δ. Thus, the change in temperature can be symbolized as Δt.

change in heat = change in temperature × mass × specific heat capacity

$$\text{change in heat} = \Delta t \times m \times c_p$$

Sample Problem 9A
Specific heat capacity

Imagine that you're working outdoors on a hot, humid day. If you drink four glasses of ice water at 0°C, how much heat energy is transferred as this water is brought to body temperature? Assume that each glass contains 250. g of water and that your body temperature is 37°C.

① List
- mass of 4 glasses of water: $m = 4 \times 250. \text{ g} = 1.00 \times 10^3 \text{ g H}_2\text{O}$
- change in water temperature: $\Delta t = 37°C - 0°C = 37°C$
- specific heat capacity of water: $c_p = 4.180 \text{ J/g·°C}$
- quantity of heat energy transferred: **?** J

② Set up
- Use the specific heat capacity equation to calculate the amount of heat energy transferred.

$\Delta t \times m \times c_p = \text{change in heat energy}$

$(37°\cancel{C})(1.00 \times 10^3 \text{ g})(4.180 \text{ J/g·}\cancel{°C}) = \text{?} \text{ J}$

③ Estimate and calculate
- **Round off to make an estimate.**

$40 \times 1000 \times 4 \approx 1.6 \times 10^5 \text{ J}$

- **Calculate, and round off correctly.**

Calculator answer: 1.5466×10^5

Rounded answer: $1.5 \times 10^5 \text{ J} = +150 \text{ kJ}$

Practice 9A

Answers for Concept Review items and Practice problems begin on page 841.

1. How much heat energy is released to your body when a cup of hot tea containing 200. g of water is cooled from 65°C to body temperature, 37°C?

2. How much heat energy is needed to raise the temperature of a 425 g aluminum baking sheet from room temperature, 25°C, to a baking temperature of 200°C?

Amounts of heat transferred can be measured

Melting and boiling also involve energy transfer, just like changing the temperature of the liquid water did. The amounts of energy required for melting, heating, and boiling various substances have been measured, as shown in **Table 9-3**.

Table 9-3
Molar Heat Data for Some Substances

Name	Symbol	Description	Examples		
			Mercury, Hg	Ethanol, C_2H_5OH	Water, H_2O
Heat of fusion	ΔH_{fus}	Energy needed to melt one mole	+2.29 kJ/mol mp = −38.8°C	+5.02 kJ/mol mp = −114.1°C	+6.00 kJ/mol mp = 0.0°C
Heat change for 1.0°C		Energy needed to raise temperature of one mole by 1.0°C	2.80×10^{-2} kJ/mol	1.12×10^{-1} kJ/mol	7.53×10^{-2} kJ/mol
Heat of vaporization	ΔH_{vap}	Energy needed to boil one mole	+59.1 kJ/mol bp = 357°C	+38.6 kJ/mol bp = 78.3°C	+40.6 kJ/mol bp = 100.0°C

Using this table, you can predict how much heat energy would be required to repeat the ice cube experiment for exactly one mole of water molecules. First, enough energy must be added to melt the ice, changing it into liquid water. This amount is the heat of fusion, 6.00 kJ/mol. Then, the liquid water must be heated from 0.°C to 100.°C. From **Table 9-3**, the amount of energy, or heat change, required for 100°C is 100 times 7.53×10^{-2} kJ/mol, or 7.53 kJ/mol. Last, the liquid water at 100.°C must be converted to steam at 100.°C, requiring the heat of vaporization, 40.6 kJ/mol. Adding these values (6.00 kJ/mol + 7.53 kJ/mol + 40.6 kJ/mol) gives you a prediction that the total amount of heat energy transferred during the experiment is 54.1 kJ/mol of H_2O. **Figure 9-5** shows how to calculate the amounts of heat energy needed for each step in a heating curve.

Figure 9-5
Differing amounts of heat energy are required in the different parts of the process going from heating ice to heating steam.

Calculating Energy Changes for Various Parts of a Heating Curve

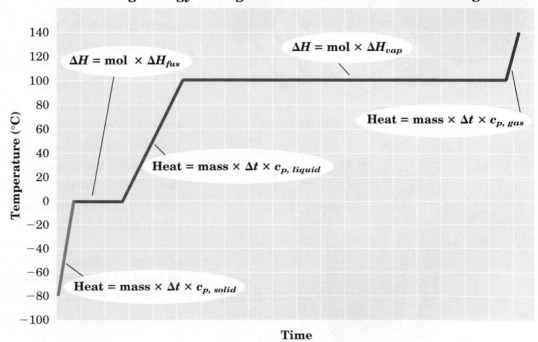

Heat in chemical changes
Energy can be interconverted into other forms

Isooctane combustion can be used as a model for the burning of gasoline. The equation for this reaction includes an energy change of 10 990 kJ.

$$2C_8H_{18}(l) + 25O_2(g) \longrightarrow 16CO_2(g) + 18H_2O(l) + 10\ 990\ kJ$$

But how was this amount determined? Although chemical handbooks list energy changes for many such chemical reactions and physical changes, these energy values were first determined by measuring them experimentally.

Changes in heat reflect the movement of energy from one system to the surroundings. Energy released during the combustion of isooctane is in the form of heat and moves from the fuel and oxygen to the products and their surroundings, including the engine and the air. Some of this energy can be transferred into other forms, such as the kinetic energy that moves the pistons which turn the car's axle. Similarly, heat energy moves from the water in an ice tray to the air inside a freezer as it freezes. *Such interconversions are possible whether the energy was generated by a physical change or a chemical change.*

Measuring changes in heat energy

If the transfer of energy between a system and its surroundings occurs only in the form of heat, the changes in energy can be easily measured. A device to measure heat energy is known as a *calorimeter*. **Figure 9-6** shows the basic parts of one type of calorimeter. This calorimeter can be used to measure the specific heat capacity of materials, by measuring the water's temperature change as a warm object is placed in the calorimeter.

Another type of calorimeter, a *bomb calorimeter*, can be used to measure changes in heat energy during combustion reactions. A substance to be oxidized is placed in a "bomb," a chamber in the center of the calorimeter, along with excess oxygen. An electrical heating element initiates the reaction.

Calculating the amount of heat energy for the change involves the same procedure whichever calorimeter is used. By multiplying the temperature change by the mass of water present and by its specific heat capacity, you can calculate the amount of heat energy involved in the change occurring within the calorimeter.

$$\text{change in heat} = \text{change in temperature} \times \text{mass } H_2O \times \text{specific heat capacity of } H_2O$$

$$\text{change in heat} = \Delta t_{H_2O} \times m_{H_2O} \times c_{p,H_2O}$$

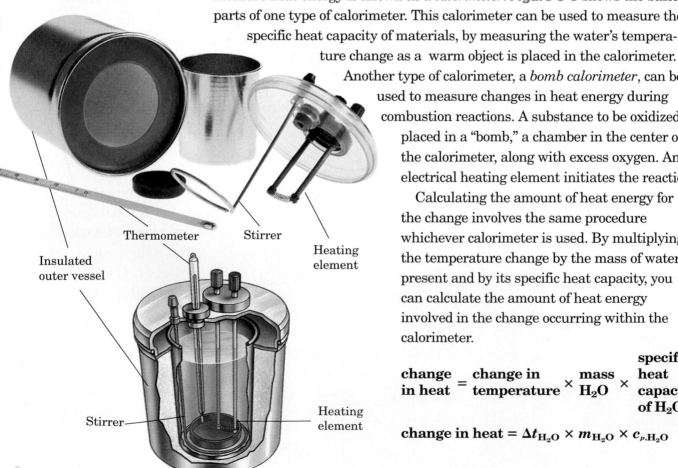

Figure 9-6
The heat energy released by a change taking place in the calorimeter can be measured by determining how much warmer it makes the surrounding water.

Thermometer   Stirrer

Heating element

Insulated outer vessel

Stirrer

Heating element

Table 9-4
Energy and Nutrient Breakdown of Some Foods*

Food and measure	Calories	Grams carbohydrate	Grams protein	Grams fat
Apple, 1 medium	81	21.1	0.3	0.5
Cheeseburger, 4.1 oz.	310	31.2	15.0	13.8
Cola soft drink, 6 oz.	72	19.0	0	0
French fries, 3.4 oz.	320	36.3	4.4	17.1
Potato, baked, 7.1 oz.	220	51.0	4.7	0.2
Potato chips, 1 oz.	150	15.0	1.0	10.0
Pretzels, 1 oz.	110	22.0	2.0	2.0
Yogurt with fruit, 8 oz.	240	43.0	9.0	3.0
Yogurt, low-fat frozen, 3 oz.	100	22.0	4.0	0.8

*These figures have been rounded and represent average values.

You get energy from carbohydrates, proteins, and fats

The substances your body needs in order to grow and maintain life come from the nutrients in food. There are six classes of nutrients in food—carbohydrates, proteins, lipids, water, vitamins, and minerals. Of these, carbohydrates, proteins, and fats are major sources of energy for the body.

The energy content of food is calculated from data collected by burning the dry food sample in a bomb calorimeter. Your body does not burn food as efficiently as the calorimeter, so the data from calorimetry must be adjusted slightly. **Table 9-4** gives the energy content of some foods expressed in Calories.

Table 9-5
Energy Content of Carbohydrates, Proteins, and Fats

Nutrient	Cal/g	kJ/g
Carbohydrate	4	17
Protein	4	17
Fat	9	38

Up to this point you have been using energy measurements expressed in kilojoules. So what does it mean that one medium, plain baked potato supplies about 220 Calories? Most reference tables for foods give information in dietary Calories (which are kilocalories) rather than kilojoules. One dietary Calorie equals the following.

$$1 \text{ Cal}^* = 4.184 \text{ kJ}$$

Using this conversion, the energy of the baked potato is equivalent to 920 kJ. Using this same conversion, a cheeseburger at 310 Calories supplies 1297 kJ of energy. **Table 9-5** gives the caloric equivalent of 1 g of the three energy nutrients. These are standard general conversion factors that can be used to estimate the energy content of a typical diet, but not of a specific food. Notice that fats provide more energy per gram than carbohydrates and proteins. Fats are the energy storage compounds in the body.

*The large Calorie is written with a capital C and is equivalent to 1000 cal or 1 kcal.

Sample Problem 9B

Calorimetry calculations with food

A nutritional chemist burns one pulverized peanut with a mass of 0.887 g in a bomb calorimeter. The calorimeter contains 2.50 kg of water, and its temperature increases from 25.0°C to 27.0°C as the peanuts burn. What is the energy content of the peanuts?

❶ List
- mass of water: 2.5 kg = 2.50×10^3 g
- change in temperature: 27.0°C − 25.0°C = 2.0°C
- specific heat capacity of water: 4.180 J/g·°C
- heat energy transferred: **?** kJ

❷ Set up
- Use the specific heat capacity equation to calculate the amount of heat energy transferred.

$\Delta t \times m \times c_p$ = change in heat energy

$(2.0°\cancel{C})(2.50 \times 10^3 \cancel{g})(4.180 \cancel{J}/\cancel{g}\cdot\cancel{°C}) \left(\dfrac{1 \text{ kJ}}{1000 \cancel{J}} \right) = $ **?** kJ

❸ Estimate and calculate
- Round off to make an estimate.

$5000 \times 4 \times \dfrac{1}{1000} \approx 20$

- Calculate and round off correctly.

Calculator answer: 20.9

Rounded answer: +21 kJ

Practice 9B

1. What is the energy content of a 1.28 g sample of oatmeal that raises the temperature of 2.50 kg of water within a calorimeter from 25.0°C to 27.2°C?

2. Predict the final temperature of 2.50 kg of water within a calorimeter if the water is at 25.0°C before a 1.8 g piece of dried peach with an energy content of 18.5 kJ is burned.

heat of reaction
the amount of heat energy absorbed or released during a chemical change

Stoichiometry and heat calculations

Certain physical and chemical changes are frequently used as energy sources, and chemists have recorded the amounts of heat energy involved in these changes in reference works such as chemical handbooks. This way, the change in heat energy can be determined without measuring it yourself. These listings are sometimes referred to as tables of *heats* of whatever process is being monitored. For example, a term used to describe the energy associated with a chemical reaction is **heat of reaction**. Heat energies involved in specific types of reactions can also have special names, as shown in **Table 9-6**.

Table 9-6
Transfers of Heat for Different Types of Changes

Heat	Symbol for a mole	Description
Heat of reaction	ΔH_r or ΔH_{rxn}	heat energy absorbed or released during a reaction
Heat of formation	ΔH_f^0	heat energy absorbed or released during synthesis of one mole of a compound from its elements at 298 K and 1 atm of pressure*
Heat of solution	ΔH_{sol}	heat energy absorbed or released when a substance dissolves in a solvent
Heat of combustion	ΔH_{comb}	heat energy released when a substance reacts with oxygen to form CO_2 and H_2O

*Because elements are not synthesized from themselves, their ΔH_f^0 is defined to be zero.

Heat refers to the total flow of energy during a chemical or physical change. The greater the quantity of the substance undergoing a change, the more heat will be transferred. For example, the heat of combustion for methane is 891 kJ/mol.

$$CH_4(g) + 2O_2(g) \longrightarrow CO_2(g) + 2H_2O(l) \; \Delta H_{comb} = -891 \text{ kJ}$$

For 10.0 mol of methane, 8910 kJ of heat (10 times the heat of combustion) will be produced.

$$10CH_4(g) + 20O_2(g) \longrightarrow 10CO_2(g) + 20H_2O(l) \; \Delta H_{comb} = -8910 \text{ kJ}$$

For 100. mol of methane, 89 100 kJ of heat will be produced.

$$100CH_4(g) + 200O_2(g) \longrightarrow 100CO_2(g) + 200H_2O(l) \; \Delta H_{comb} = -89\,100 \text{ kJ}$$

Because the amount of heat energy transferred is expressed in terms of kJ/mol of one of the products or reactants, this amount can be used in stoichiometry problems as if it were another mole ratio, as shown in Sample Problem 9C.

Sample Problem 9C
Stoichiometry and heat transfers

What are the minimum masses of oxygen and gasoline that must be delivered by the carburetor or fuel-injection system to a car's engine in order for it to generate the 5000. kJ of energy needed to pass a slow-moving truck? (For this problem, assume that the gasoline is entirely isooctane, as shown in the equation.)

$$2C_8H_{18}(l) + 25O_2(g) \longrightarrow 16CO_2(g) + 18H_2O(l) \; \Delta H_{comb} = -1.099 \times 10^4 \text{ kJ}$$

❶ List
- **change in heat:** $\Delta H = -1.099 \times 10^4$ kJ
- **total energy needed:** 5000. kJ
- **molar masses of reactants:** 114.26 g C_8H_{18}/mol
  - 32.00 g O_2/mol
- **mass of C_8H_{18}:** ❓ g C_8H_{18}
- **mass of O_2:** ❓ g O_2

❷ Set up
- **First, determine the proportionality factor for the reaction. The reaction shown in the problem produces more energy than you need. Because energy is a product, it can be treated as a limiting factor in the reaction.**
  1.099×10^4 kJ > 5000. kJ

- **Therefore, determine the mole amounts of each reactant that would be required to provide that much energy, starting with isooctane.**
  $$5000. \text{ kJ} \times \frac{2 \text{ mol } C_8H_{18}}{1.099 \times 10^4 \text{ kJ}} = 0.9099 \text{ mol } C_8H_{18}$$

- **Perform a similar calculation to determine the necessary amount of oxygen.**
  $$5000. \text{ kJ} \times \frac{25 \text{ mol } O_2}{1.099 \times 10^4 \text{ kJ}} = 11.37 \text{ mol } O_2$$

Sample Problem 9C continued on following page...

- **Now calculate the masses of C_8H_{18} and O_2 using the molar masses.**

  0.9099 mol C_8H_{18} × 114.26 g/mol = **?** g C_8H_{18}

  11.37 mol O_2 × 32.00 g/mol = **?** g O_2

❸ **Estimate and calculate**

- **Round off to make an estimate.**

  $1 \times 114 \approx 114$ g C_8H_{18}

  $11 \times 32 \approx 352$ g O_2

- **Calculate, and round off correctly.**

  Calculator answer: 1.03965174×10^2 g C_8H_{18}

  $\qquad\qquad\qquad$ 3.6384×10^2 g O_2

  Rounded answer: $\quad$ 104.0 g C_8H_{18}

  $\qquad\qquad\qquad$ 363.8 g O_2

Practice 9C

1. Most automobile engines are only about 25% efficient, meaning that only 25% of the energy released by the combustion reaction is used for movement. Using this efficiency, what masses of oxygen and isooctane would need to be delivered to the engine for the car's kinetic energy to increase by 5000. kJ?

2. Chemical reactions such as respiration help provide energy for movement and keep your body warm. On average, each person in the United States consumes 110. g of sugar daily. If all of this sugar is assumed to be glucose, how much heat energy from glucose is transferred to one person through respiration each day?

$$C_6H_{12}O_6(s) + 6O_2(g) \longrightarrow 6CO_2(g) + 6H_2O(l) \quad \Delta H_{rxn} = -2870 \text{ kJ}$$

Section Review

1. What is the difference between heat and temperature?

2. Identify each of the following symbols: ΔH_{fus}, ΔH_{rxn}, and ΔH_{vap}.

3. How much energy is released by a reaction that raises the temperature of 1.00 kg of water in a calorimeter from 25.0°C to 27.0°C?

4. A swimming pool measures 6.0 m × 12.0 m and has a uniform depth of 3.0 m. The pool is full of water at a temperature of 20.°C. How much heat energy must be released by the pool's heater to raise the water temperature to 25°C?

5. Gaseous butane, C_4H_{10}, is burned in cigarette lighters. Write the balanced chemical equation for the combustion of butane. Butane's heat of combustion is 2.878×10^3 kJ/mol. How many kilojoules of heat would be provided by the combustion of 10.0 g of butane?

6. Use **Table 9-4** and **Table 9-5** to calculate the number of kilojoules provided by the fat in one serving of each of the following foods.

   a. french fries $\qquad$ **b.** potato chips $\qquad$ **c.** pretzels $\qquad$ **d.** cheeseburger

7. Use **Table 9-4** to calculate the calories from fat in an 8 oz. serving of frozen yogurt versus the same size serving of yogurt with fruit.

8. **Story Link**

   Is more energy released when 428 g of H_2 or 428 g of isooctane, C_8H_{18}, react with an excess of oxygen?

   $$2H_2(g) + O_2(g) \longrightarrow 2H_2O(l) \quad \Delta H_{comb} = -571.6 \text{ kJ}$$

   $$2C_8H_{18}(l) + 25O_2(g) \longrightarrow 16CO_2(g) + 18H_2O(l) \quad \Delta H_{comb} = -10\,990 \text{ kJ}$$

How does enthalpy drive changes?

Section Objectives

Explain the relation among heat of reaction, enthalpy change, and stability.

Interpret an energy diagram of the reaction pathway for an exothermic reaction.

Explain the relationship between activation energy and chemical changes.

Use the kinetic molecular theory to explain why some exothermic reactions do not require an input of energy.

Use Hess's law to solve problems involving physical and chemical changes.

Driving forces

The melting of ice on a tabletop is an example of a **spontaneous change**. Spontaneous changes occur primarily in one direction. Once ice melts, it won't refreeze unless the temperature changes. In other words, ice melting is not reversible at room temperature.

There are several important ideas to keep in mind about spontaneous changes. First, spontaneity does not mean that a reaction occurs quickly. For example, even though ice melts spontaneously at 1°C, the change usually takes place very slowly. Another related point is that some spontaneous reactions occur only when a small amount of energy is added to the system. The combustion of a gasoline-air mixture is a spontaneous change. Even though an outside influence, a spark, as shown in **Figure 9-7**, must be provided to get the reaction going, once the combustion has occurred, the reaction is not reversible under ordinary conditions. No one has ever observed carbon dioxide and water vapor in the air spontaneously re-forming oxygen and isooctane or other components of gasoline.

However, some reactions can be reversed if conditions change. For example, a large drop in temperature will induce freezing instead of melting. In reality, many chemical changes are like the ice-to-water physical change: they are reversible, depending upon the conditions. Some reactions that are spontaneous and appear to be complete under normal conditions can be reversed if the conditions are changed to an extreme.

So far, you have explored some details of how reactions and other changes release or absorb heat. But why do some reactions happen, and others don't? Are there ways to induce reactions that wouldn't take place otherwise?

The answers to these questions rely upon a model that will describe the driving forces, or underlying tendencies, that cause or resist change.

Heat transfers are an important part of the model of driving forces. But to understand how to use heat flow and temperature to predict and control reactions, a more complete model is necessary.

spontaneous change *a change that will occur because of the nature of the system, once it is initiated*

Chem Fact
The change of diamond to graphite is a spontaneous reaction under normal conditions, but it is extremely slow.

Figure 9-7

Under most conditions, the burning of gasoline in air is a spontaneous change. Once the sparkplug in an engine fires, the reaction will proceed on its own.

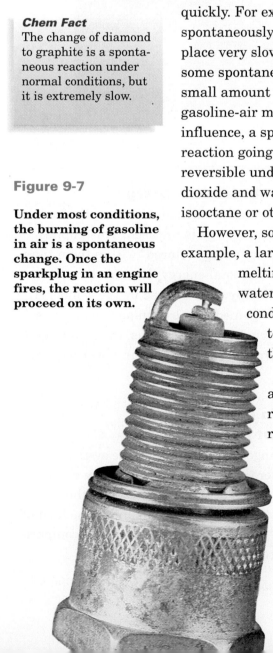

Causes of Change | **323**

Exothermic Reaction $C_{12}H_{22}O_{11}(s) \xrightarrow{H_2SO_4} 12C(s) + 11H_2O(l)$

Before   **After**

Figure 9-8a
The total enthalpy of any substance can never be calculated or measured, but the *change* in enthalpy can be measured. This reaction is exothermic, and energy is released. The products must have less enthalpy than the reactants have.

Endothermic Reaction $Ba(OH)_2 \cdot 8H_2O(s) + 2NH_4NO_3(s) \longrightarrow$
$2NH_3(aq) + 10H_2O(l) + Ba(NO_3)_2(aq)$

Before   **After**

9-8b
This reaction absorbs so much heat that the condensation on the flask freezes it to the block of wood. The products have more enthalpy than the reactants have.

Enthalpy is the total of a substance's energy

In an exothermic change, such as the combustion of isooctane, the heat of reaction is negative, indicating heat energy is released. This implies that somehow the reactants have more energy "stored" within them than the products do. The name given to the total energy that substances contain at constant pressure is **enthalpy**, represented by the symbol H. Any information about enthalpies is gained only by comparing systems before and after a change, as shown in **Figure 9-8**. Thus, the actual total enthalpy of a substance, whether product or reactant, can never be measured or calculated directly.

enthalpy
total energy content of a system

Enthalpy change is equal in magnitude to heat of reaction at constant pressure

For most physical and chemical changes, the enthalpy of the system before the change is different from that after the change. This **enthalpy change** is represented by the symbol ΔH. In fact, at constant pressure, the enthalpy change for a chemical change is the same amount as the heat of reaction. Thus, ΔH can be read as "enthalpy change," which is a comparison of the total enthalpies of the products and the reactants.

enthalpy change
heat energy released or absorbed when a physical or chemical change occurs at constant pressure

$$\Delta H = H_{products} - H_{reactants}$$

Chemical equations sometimes include the value of ΔH. Exothermic reactions are assigned negative ΔH values, and endothermic reactions have positive ΔH values.

Exothermic

$$C_6H_{12}O_6(s) + 6O_2(g) \longrightarrow 6CO_2(g) + 6H_2O(l) \qquad \Delta H = -2870 \text{ kJ}$$

Endothermic

$$6CO_2(g) + 6H_2O(l) \longrightarrow C_6H_{12}O_6(s) + 6O_2(g) \qquad \Delta H = +2870 \text{ kJ}$$

Compare the enthalpies of a sample of water before and after condensation, as shown in **Figure 9-9**. As water vapor, the water molecules are widely separated. For the sample as a whole, this corresponds to a high enthalpy state. After condensing into a liquid, the molecules are much closer to each other, which corresponds to a lower enthalpy state. The difference in enthalpy between these two states equals the amount of heat change during the process, the heat of vaporization. Thus, the condensation of water vapor releases heat. The enthalpy decreases.

$$H_2O(g) \longrightarrow H_2O(l) \qquad \Delta H = -40.6 \text{ kJ/mol}$$

Figure 9-9
Condensation is an exothermic process. Gaseous water molecules come together on the cool surface of the man's glasses, forming a liquid, which results in a lower enthalpy state.

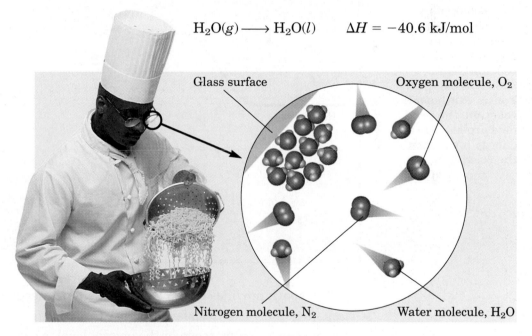

Glass surface

Oxygen molecule, O_2

Nitrogen molecule, N_2

Water molecule, H_2O

Decreasing enthalpy drives some spontaneous changes

A reaction that liberates energy is more likely to occur than one that does not. This is one of the underlying *driving forces* for chemical and physical changes. In general, changes that involve a decrease in enthalpy are favored. The more energy released by an exothermic reaction, the greater the decrease in enthalpy, and the more likely it is that the reaction will be spontaneous.

Because energy is released in all exothermic reactions, the products of an exothermic reaction have a lower energy state than that of the reactants and are more stable from an energy perspective. This was true of the potassium and water reaction described in Chapter 5 and of the combustion of hydrogen described in Chapter 6.

Reaction pathways
Most reactions need energy to get started

The combustion of isooctane in gasoline is a strongly exothermic reaction. If such a change in enthalpy is a driving force for chemical reactions, why doesn't isooctane react instantly when stored in a can with air? Why is a spark necessary to ignite the gasoline and oxygen?

From the discussion in Chapter 6 of the combustion of H_2 and O_2 to make H_2O, you already know the answer. If new bonds are to form to make products, the reactants must be brought together. Because of the electrons surrounding atoms, the reactants tend to repel each other, requiring energy to overcome these forces. This initial input of energy is called **activation energy**. The symbol for activation energy is E_a or E_{act}.

One way to explore this idea is to examine a reaction pathway, which shows the relationship between energy and the progress of the reaction. The reaction pathway shown in **Figure 9-10** is the general pattern for all exothermic reactions.

activation energy
the minimum amount of energy that must be supplied to a system to start a chemical change

Figure 9-10
A reaction pathway shows how the relative energy levels of the reactants and products compare. For an exothermic reaction, the products are at a lower energy level than the reactants.

Exothermic Reaction Pathway

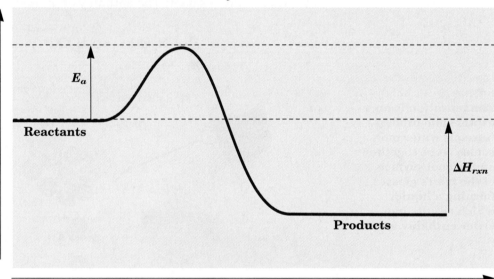

The spark provides initial activation energy needed to bring the reactants together. The transfer of energy from the spark to the reaction system causes an increase in the energy level, as shown by the peak on the reaction pathway. Energy is released as the products separate. The released energy is able to serve as activation energy for other reactant molecules. The net change in bond energy between the reactants and the products is the heat of reaction, or the enthalpy change.

Using reaction pathways

Use **Figure 9-10** to answer the following questions.

Concept Review

9. Explain whether ΔH_{rxn} would change if E_a were increased, but the reactants and the products remained at the same enthalpy levels.
10. Explain why the reverse reaction is less likely than forward reaction. (Hint: what is E_a for the reverse reaction?)

Answers for Concept Review items and Practice problems begin on page 841.

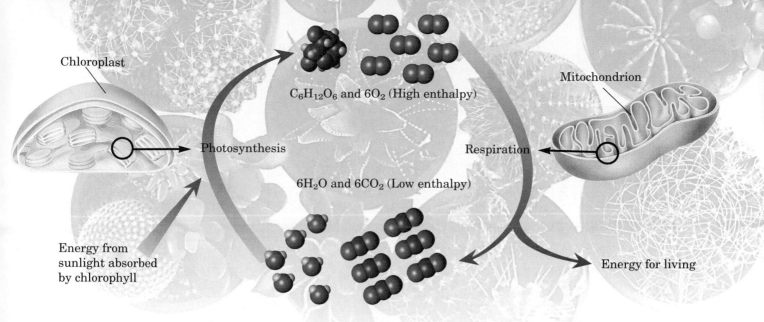

Chloroplast

$C_6H_{12}O_6$ and $6O_2$ (High enthalpy)

Photosynthesis

Mitochondrion

Respiration

$6H_2O$ and $6CO_2$ (Low enthalpy)

Energy from sunlight absorbed by chlorophyll

Energy for living

Figure 9-11
Photosynthesis is an endothermic reaction taking place in a chloroplast. Respiration is an exothermic reaction taking place in a mitochondrion. Both require activation energy.

Endothermic changes require a source of energy

In general, exothermic changes are favored over endothermic changes, but many endothermic changes can take place. For example, plants use the endothermic photosynthesis reaction to make sugar. This sugar, when decomposed through cellular respiration, provides the energy that plants and other living things need to live, as shown in **Figure 9-11**. You may remember that the equations for these two reactions are the reverse of one another. *The change in enthalpy of the reverse reaction will be numerically equal to that of the forward reaction, but the sign will be changed.*

Photosynthesis: $6CO_2(g) + 6H_2O(l) \longrightarrow C_6H_{12}O_6(s) + 6O_2(g)$ $\Delta H = +2870$ kJ

Respiration: $C_6H_{12}O_6(s) + 6O_2(g) \longrightarrow 6CO_2(g) + 6H_2O(l)$ $\Delta H = -2870$ kJ

How is it that photosynthesis, an endothermic reaction, can occur, even though the driving force of enthalpy favors the opposite reaction? You know that plants require sunlight to survive. This sunlight is the source of the energy for the photosynthesis reaction. Endothermic reactions occur if there is a sufficient source of energy available.

In plants, chlorophyll molecules absorb energy from sunlight and transform it into chemical energy that can be used to overcome several activation energy barriers and to drive the complex series of reactions that constitute photosynthesis.

Energy is unevenly distributed among particles

If reactions need activation energy to get started, how is it that some spontaneous reactions, like the reaction of potassium and water to form potassium hydroxide, proceed without added energy, whereas some, like the isooctane combustion reaction, do require added energy?

$$2K(s) + 2H_2O(l) \longrightarrow 2KOH(aq) + H_2(g) \qquad \Delta H = -393 \text{ kJ}$$

Actually, the only difference between the potassium-water reaction and other reaction pathways is that the activation energy for the potassium reaction is lower, as shown in **Figure 9-12** on the next page.

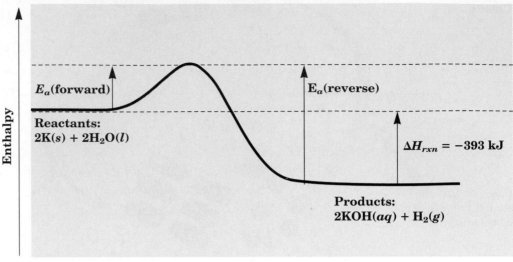

Figure 9-12
The reaction pathway for the potassium-water reaction requires little activation energy, so it is easy to get started once the reactants are in contact.

Reaction Pathway for Potassium-Water Reaction

Enthalpy

E_a(forward)

E_a(reverse)

Reactants:
$2K(s) + 2H_2O(l)$

$\Delta H_{rxn} = -393$ kJ

Products:
$2KOH(aq) + H_2(g)$

Reaction Progress

From the kinetic molecular theory, you already know that particles, such as molecules, atoms, and ions, are constantly in motion and possess different amounts of energy, depending on how rapidly they are moving. This, in turn, is related to their temperature. The higher the temperature of the substance, the faster, on average, the particles are moving.

Even though a sample of matter, such as a chunk of potassium, has a characteristic average energy that depends on its temperature, not all of its particles have that same energy. Most have an energy close to that of the average, but some have more, and some have less. That is why the graph of kinetic energy versus number of particles has the shape similar to a normal distribution curve: a peak in the middle with a "shoulder" on each side. This situation is summed up in **Figure 9-13**. In Chapter 14, you will see exactly how changing the temperature can change the shape of this curve.

Distribution of Kinetic Energy Among Particles

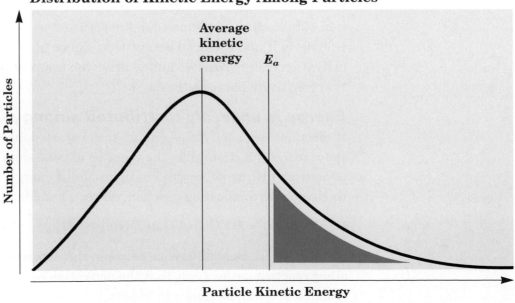

Figure 9-13
In any sample of particles, some will have kinetic energies higher than the necessary activation energy for a reaction. These particles will react immediately.

Number of Particles

Average kinetic energy

E_a

Particle Kinetic Energy

According to the law of conservation of energy, particles can convert their energy of motion into other forms of energy, including the activation energy necessary to make a reaction happen. If the activation energy has the value indicated by the line marked E_a on the horizontal axis of the graph, the molecules represented by the shaded zone already have enough energy to react. This explains why heat, light, or a spark is not needed for the reaction to occur—some of the particles have enough activation energy to begin the reaction without requiring any additional input of energy.

If the reaction is exothermic, as the first particles react, more energy is released as the products are formed. The potassium and water particles that didn't have enough energy to react absorb this energy in the form of heat, which increases their motion and kinetic energy. Some of these particles now have enough energy to react and release still more energy. This process continues until nearly all of the particles have reacted.

Calculating enthalpy changes
Combining enthalpy changes using Hess's law

Any two processes that start with the reactants in the same condition and finish with the products in the same condition will involve the same enthalpy change. This statement is the basis of **Hess's law,** which states that the overall enthalpy change in a reaction is equal to the sum of the enthalpy changes for the individual steps in the process. If the heats of reaction for each of these smaller reactions are known, then they can be combined to give the heat change for the overall reaction.

Hess's law

the total enthalpy change for a chemical or physical change is the same whether it takes place in one or several steps

How can you predict the enthalpy change for the decomposition of 5.00 mol of ice to produce hydrogen gas and oxygen gas from the resulting water?

$$2H_2O(s) \longrightarrow 2H_2(g) + O_2(g)$$

So far in this chapter, several different values for enthalpy changes associated with water have been discussed; they are summarized in **Table 9-7**. According to the principle behind Hess's law, if the products and reactants are the same for two reactions, the overall enthalpy change will be the same. In effect, it doesn't matter whether the ice decomposes into hydrogen and oxygen gas directly or melts first. Either way, you will be starting with ice and ending with hydrogen and oxygen, so the net enthalpy change will be the same. The enthalpy changes in **Table 9-7** can be considered to be individual steps that are each a part of a greater overall change. Enthalpy changes for steps can be added together to describe a net enthalpy change. This addition can occur whether the enthalpy changes are for physical changes or for chemical changes.

Table 9-7
Some Enthalpy Changes Involving H$_2$O

Reaction	Enthalpy change (kJ)
$2H_2(g) + O_2(g) \longrightarrow 2H_2O(l)$	$\Delta H_{rxn} = -571.6$
$2H_2O(l) \longrightarrow 2H_2(g) + O_2(g)$	$\Delta H_{rxn} = +571.6$
$H_2O(l) \longrightarrow H_2O(g)$	$\Delta H_{vap} = +40.6$ (at 100°C)
$H_2O(s) \longrightarrow H_2O(l)$	$\Delta H_{fus} = +6.00$ (at 0°C)

The last equation in **Table 9-7** is the only one that begins with ice, like the net reaction on the previous page. If it is multiplied by two, it will match the amount of ice in the net reaction. The second equation in **Table 9-7** is the only one containing the products, hydrogen and oxygen gas, that are also the products of the net reaction. If you add these equations and cancel substances that appear in the same form and same amount on both sides of the equations, you get the following result.

$$2H_2O(s) \longrightarrow 2H_2O(l) \qquad\qquad \Delta H_{fus} = \ +12.00 \text{ kJ}$$
$$2H_2O(l) \longrightarrow 2H_2(g) + O_2(g) \qquad\qquad \Delta H_{rxn} = +571.6 \text{ kJ}$$

$$2H_2O(s) + 2H_2O(l) \longrightarrow 2H_2O(l) + 2H_2(g) + O_2(g) \quad \Delta H_{total} = +583.6 \text{ kJ}$$

This equation matches the net reaction. Thus, decomposing ice involves the same net energy as first melting it and then decomposing the liquid water. But the question asked how much enthalpy was released when *5.00 mol H_2O*, not *2.00 mol H_2O*, reacted. A simple stoichiometry calculation provides the answer.

$$\frac{583.6 \text{ kJ}}{2.00 \text{ mol } H_2O} \times 5.00 \text{ mol } H_2O = 1460 \text{ kJ}$$

Another way of interpreting Hess's law states that the enthalpy change of a reaction is equal to the enthalpy of formation of the products minus the enthalpy of formation of the reactants, when stoichiometric relationships are taken into account.

$$\Delta H_{rxn} = \text{sum of } \Delta H^0_{f,\ products} - \text{sum of } \Delta H^0_{f,\ reactants}$$

This approach treats a reaction as if all of the reactants were decomposed into elements. Then, those elements proceed to form the bonds needed to make the products. The superscript zero indicates standard conditions.

Figure 9-14
In football, as in Hess's law, only initial and final conditions matter. If a football team gains 15 yards on a pass play but has a 10-yard penalty, the team's field position is no different than if the team had gained only 5 yards during the play.

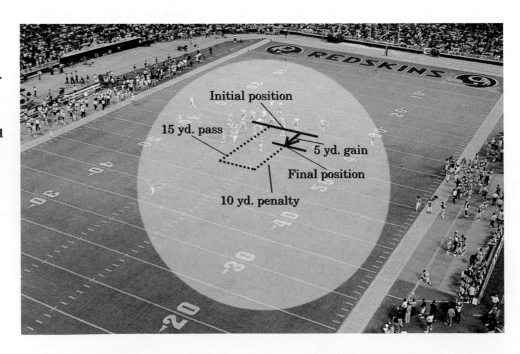

Sample Problem 9D
Heats of formation and Hess's law

The Romans used CaO as a mortar for building. CaO was mixed with water to produce $Ca(OH)_2$, which reacted slowly with CO_2 in air to form limestone, $CaCO_3$. This reaction is represented as follows.

$$Ca(OH)_2(s) + CO_2(g) \longrightarrow H_2O(g) + CaCO_3(s)$$

Determine the ΔH value for this reaction using the data given below.

Substance	ΔH_f^0 (kJ/mol)	Substance	ΔH_f^0 (kJ/mol)
$Ca(OH)_2$ (s)	−986.1	$H_2O(g)$	−241.8 kJ
$CO_2(g)$	−393.5	$CaCO_3(s)$	−1206.9 kJ

❶ List
- Reactants:

  1 mol $Ca(OH)_2(s)$: $\Delta H_f^0 = -986.1$ kJ
  1 mol $CO_2(g)$: $\Delta H_f^0 = -393.5$ kJ

- Products:

  1 mol $H_2O(g)$: $\Delta H_f^0 = -241.8$ kJ
  1 mol $CaCO_3(s)$: $\Delta H_f^0 = -1206.9$ kJ

- Heat of reaction: $\Delta H_{rxn} = $ **?** kJ

❷ Set up
- According to Hess's law, the sum of the ΔH_f^0 values for the products minus the sum of the ΔH_f^0 values of the reactants will give the net ΔH value for the reaction.

  [sum of ΔH_f^0 values for products] − [sum of ΔH_f^0 values for reactants] = **?** kJ

  $[(-241.8 \text{ kJ}) + (-1206.9 \text{ kJ})] - [(-986.1 \text{ kJ}) + (-393.5 \text{ kJ})] = $ **?** kJ

❸ Estimate and calculate
- Round off to make an estimate.

  $[(-240) + (-1200)] - [(-990) + (-390)] \approx$

  $[-1440] - [-1380] \approx -60$

- Calculate, and round off correctly.

  $\Delta H_{rxn} = -69.1$ kJ/mol

Practice 9D

1. Under extreme pressure, graphite can be converted to diamond. Because both are forms of pure carbon, each undergoes combustion to make carbon dioxide. Given the following heats of reaction for the combustion reactions, calculate the enthalpy change for converting graphite to diamond.

   $C(graphite) + O_2(g) \longrightarrow CO_2(g)$ $\Delta H_{rxn} = -393.5$ kJ/mol C
   $C(diamond) + O_2(g) \longrightarrow CO_2(g)$ $\Delta H_{rxn} = -395.4$ kJ/mol C

2. Calculate the heat of reaction for changing 1.00 mol of silica, SiO_2, that has been extracted from sand into the pure silicon that is needed to make computer chips. Use the following data.

   $SiO_2(s) + 2C(s) \longrightarrow$ impure $Si(s) + 2CO(g)$ $\Delta H_{rxn} = +689.9$ kJ
   impure $Si(s) + 2Cl_2(g) \longrightarrow$ pure $SiCl_4(g)$ $\Delta H_{rxn} = -657.0$ kJ
   pure $SiCl_4(g) + 2Mg(s) \longrightarrow 2MgCl_2(s) +$ pure $Si(s)$ $\Delta H_{rxn} = -625.6$ kJ

11. Nitrogen dioxide, $NO_2(g)$, has a heat of formation of 33.1 kJ/mol. Dinitrogen tetroxide, $N_2O_4(g)$, has a heat of formation of 9.1 kJ/mol. Which compound is likely to have the highest enthalpy? What is the enthalpy change for synthesizing N_2O_4 from NO_2?

12. Draw and label an energy pathway for a typical exothermic reaction.

13. Describe the sources of activation energy in each of the following reactions.

  a. A match is struck against a match cover and bursts into flame.

  b. When exposed to ultraviolet light, hydrogen and chlorine combine to form hydrogen chloride.

  c. Vinegar and baking soda react instantly to make carbon dioxide and sodium acetate solution.

14. Use Hess's law to calculate the heat of combustion of carbon monoxide to form carbon dioxide, given that the heat of formation for carbon monoxide is -110.5 kJ/mol and that of carbon dioxide is -393.5 kJ/mol. (Hint: remember that the heat of formation represents the enthalpy needed to synthesize a substance from its elements at 298 K and 1 atm. Under those conditions, oxygen is already in the form of oxygen molecules, so no synthesis reaction is necessary. Thus, its heat of formation is defined to be 0.)

15. Is the activation energy greater than, equal to, or less than the change in enthalpy of an endothermic reaction? (Hint: examine **Figure 9-10**, the energy diagram for an *exothermic* process.)

16. The diagram below represents the interpretation of Hess's law for the following reaction.

$$Sn(s) + 2Cl_2(g) \longrightarrow SnCl_4(l)$$

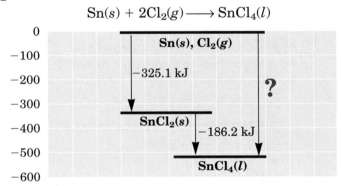

Use the diagram to determine the ΔH for each step and the net reaction

$$Sn(s) + Cl_2(g) \longrightarrow SnCl_2(l) \qquad \Delta H = \text{?}$$

$$SnCl_2(s) + Cl_2(g) \longrightarrow SnCl_4(l) \qquad \Delta H = \text{?}$$

$$\overline{Sn(s) + 2Cl_2(g) \longrightarrow SnCl_4(l) \qquad \Delta H = \text{?}}$$

17. Use the data in **Table 9-7** to construct a diagram like that in item **16** to graphically show the decomposition of ice to form gaseous hydrogen and oxygen. Your diagram should include the enthalpy change for each step along with the total enthalpy change for the net reaction.

18. The activation energy needed for a particular reaction can be reduced by using a catalyst. How would a reduction of E_a affect ΔH_{rxn}?

How does entropy drive changes?

Section Objectives

Define entropy, and provide examples of high- and low-entropy situations.

Explain the relation between a change in entropy and stability.

Use standard entropy values in calculations.

Entropy and stability

You learned in Chapter 2 that solids have a very specific and rigid arrangement that is less flexible than the arrangement of liquids. Thus, an ice cube left on a countertop spontaneously changes from an ordered substance (a solid) to a less-ordered substance (liquid). The tendency in nature is to more disorder. The measure of the degree of disorder is called **entropy**. For a system that can exist in two states, the one with higher entropy or disorder tends to be more stable. Usually, it is far easier to go from the low-entropy state to the high-entropy state. For example, it is easy to imagine throwing an intact jigsaw puzzle on the floor and having the pieces get mixed up. However, one rarely can throw a jumbled puzzle on the floor and have all the pieces bounce into place. Examples of high and low entropy states are shown in **Figure 9-15**.

entropy
a measure of the randomness or disorder of a system

Low entropy

High entropy

Figure 9-15
By comparing the photographs you can see changes from low entropy to high entropy. Melted ice, the broken pitcher, and the jumbled jigsaw puzzle all represent an increase in the disorder of the system.

Entropy is given the symbol S. All physical and chemical changes involve a change in entropy, or ΔS. Although entropy is often described in terms of randomness or disorder, a better way to understand it is in terms of the number of ways a substance can be arranged. For example, there is only one way to assemble the pieces of a jigsaw puzzle correctly to form a completed picture. But there are a great number of ways to arrange the pieces when they are just thrown in a box.

Another example of a physical change with an increase in entropy is the sugar-water system shown in **Figure 9-16**. Immediately after sugar is added, the system is initially very ordered. All the sugar molecules are in one region at the bottom of the pitcher. All the water molecules are in a different region, the rest of the pitcher. Eventually, the two types of molecules spontaneously form a more disordered system, in which sugar and water molecules are homogeneously mixed.

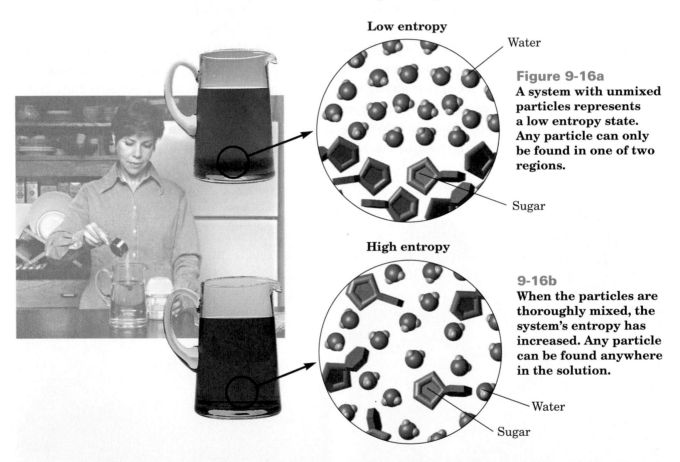

Low entropy

Water

Figure 9-16a
A system with unmixed particles represents a low entropy state. Any particle can only be found in one of two regions.

Sugar

High entropy

9-16b
When the particles are thoroughly mixed, the system's entropy has increased. Any particle can be found anywhere in the solution.

Water

Sugar

Entropy's effects increase with temperature

If equal amounts of sugar are added to a glass of cold water and a glass of hot water, the sugar will dissolve more rapidly in the hot water. Why? The liquid water molecules possess kinetic energy, and as they move randomly, they collide with the sugar molecules and mix with them. The ongoing collisions of water and sugar molecules help sugar dissolve. The hot water has more kinetic energy and faster moving molecules than the cold water has. There are more collisions between water and sugar molecules in hot water than in the cold water.

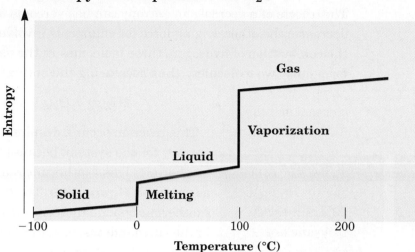

Entropy vs. Temperature for H$_2$O

Entropy changes for chemical changes can be predicted

From what you know about entropy, you can make some educated guesses about how entropy will affect chemical reactions. The key is to remember that high entropy situations, which are randomized and disordered or which have more possibilities for arrangement, are generally preferred or are more stable, as long as other factors are kept equal.

Solids are very low in entropy, and liquids are higher in entropy, as shown by the graph in **Figure 9-17**. Gases are much higher in entropy than liquids because gas particles are farther apart. Chemical changes that produce gases are favored when entropy is the main consideration. Not only are the particles less ordered in a gas, but when there is more than one gaseous product, they will mix homogeneously. If liquids are formed, they may or may not mix, depending upon whether they can dissolve. When only solids are formed, they cannot mix easily. When a reaction results in more particles, there are more ways they can be arranged. These considerations are illustrated in **Figure 9-18**.

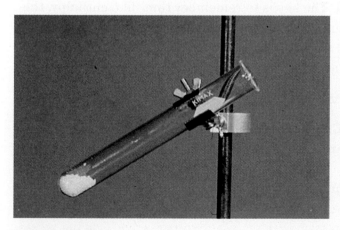

Figure 9-18a
The decomposition of ammonium nitrate, NH$_4$NO$_3$(s), involves a change from a low-entropy system with one solid reactant . . .

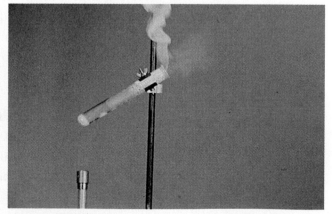

9-18b
. . . to a high-entropy system with two gaseous products and one liquid product.

Entropy's effects can be overcome

The effects of a decrease in entropy can be overcome if enough enthalpy decrease, the other driving force for change, is involved. For example, in the combustion of hydrogen, three molecules in the gaseous state react to form only two molecules, thus decreasing the entropy.

$$2H_2(g) + O_2(g) \longrightarrow 2H_2O(g)$$

This reaction occurs, despite the decrease in entropy for the system, because the reaction is exothermic. This exothermic reaction releases heat, as shown in **Figure 9-19**. The heat released by an exothermic change increases the particle motion in the surroundings, resulting in an increase in entropy in the system and surroundings combined that is greater than the decrease in entropy in the system alone.

The same concept explains how refrigerators and air conditioners work. They make a specific system cooler and lower in entropy, but only by heating the surroundings and increasing the entropy there.

 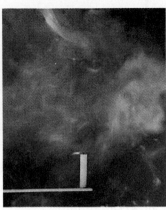

Figure 9-19
Although the combustion of hydrogen creates a product with lower entropy than the reactants, the reaction occurs because the heat energy released by the reaction causes a larger increase in the entropy of the surroundings: the air and balloon.

Entropy can be quantified

Unlike enthalpy, absolute values of entropy can be measured. Entropy involves thermal motion. Absolute zero, or 0 K ($-273°C$), is the temperature at which all motion in solids ceases (except for zero-point vibrations, whose energy cannot be utilized for anything) and the entropy is considered to be zero. Changes in entropy can be measured in comparison with this zero baseline, and chemistry handbooks contain tables of entropy values for elements and compounds.

Entropy has units of J/K. Like enthalpy, entropy can be used in stoichiometric calculations or Hess's law changes if the entropy values are given in units of J/K•mol. The key is to remember that, like enthalpy, the net entropy change is equal to the sum of the entropies of the products minus the sum of the entropies of the reactants when stoichiometric relationships are taken into account.

$$\Delta S = S_{products} - S_{reactants}$$

For example, at 100.°C, the entropy of liquid water is 87 J/K•mol, and that of steam is 196 J/K•mol. The entropy change, ΔS, is equal to the difference between the two. The positive value of ΔS indicates that entropy increases as water evaporates or boils.

$$H_2O(l) \longrightarrow H_2O(g)$$

$$\Delta S = S_{products} - S_{reactants}$$

$$\Delta S = 196 \text{ J/K•mol} - 87 \text{ J/K•mol} = +109 \text{ J/K•mol}$$

Sample Problem 9E
Entropy calculations

Calcium carbonate, $CaCO_3$, decomposes into calcium oxide and carbon dioxide. What is the entropy change for this reaction?

$$CaCO_3(s) \longrightarrow CO_2(g) + CaO(s)$$

Substance	S (J/K·mol)
$CaCO_3(s)$	+92.9
$CO_2(g)$	+213.8
$CaO(s)$	+38.2

❶ List
- The necessary pieces of data are already shown in the table.

❷ Set up
- The sum of the S values for the products minus the sum of the S values of the reactants will give the net ΔS for the reaction.

[sum of S values for products] − [sum of S values for reactants] = **?** J/K·mol

[(38.2 J/K·mol) + (213.8 J/K·mol)] − [92.9 J/K·mol] = **?** J/K·mol

❸ Estimate and calculate
- **Round off to make an estimate.**

[40 + 210] − [90] ≈ [250] − [90] ≈ 160

- **Calculate, and round off correctly.**

ΔS = +159.1 J/K·mol

Because this reaction involves a single solid reactant producing two products, one of which is gaseous, the answer should be a large positive number, reflecting an increase in entropy.

Practice 9E

1. What is the entropy change for converting graphite to diamond? Is this likely to be a spontaneous change?

   graphite: S = +5.7 J/K·mol
   diamond: S = +2.4 J/K·mol

2. Calculate the entropy change for the single replacement reaction that occurs at 25°C between copper chloride crystals and iron metal. (Hint: remember to adjust the entropy values to account for the mole ratios in the balanced equation.)

   $$3CuCl_2(s) + 2Fe(s) \longrightarrow 2FeCl_3(s) + 3Cu(s)$$

Substance	S (J/K·mol)
$CuCl_2(s)$	+108.1
$Fe(s)$	+27.3
$FeCl_3(s)$	+142.3
$Cu(s)$	+33.2

Section Review

19. Give two examples of a change in entropy. Indicate whether the change is an increase or decrease in entropy of the system.

20. What kind of change in entropy promotes a spontaneous physical or chemical change?

21. Describe what happens to the entropy of ice as it melts to form water, the water is heated, and the water boils to form water vapor.

22. The entropy of 2-propanol (also known as isopropyl alcohol or rubbing alcohol) is 309.2 J/K·mol in the gaseous state (at 25°C), and the entropy change for evaporation at this temperature is 128.1 J/K·mol. What is the entropy for liquid 2-propanol?

How do entropy and enthalpy affect change?

9-4

Section Objectives

Summarize the conditions that favor a spontaneous chemical reaction.

Define free energy.

Calculate the change in free energy to predict whether a reaction will occur spontaneously.

Describe how chemical reactions can be controlled.

Entropy and enthalpy

So far, you've learned about two driving forces that can affect chemical and physical changes—entropy and enthalpy. Most changes involve both enthalpy and entropy. It is the interplay of these two driving forces that determines whether or not a physical or chemical change will actually happen. Changes that are spontaneous are often referred to as *thermodynamically favored*. It is important to remember that even spontaneous changes can take a long time to occur. What the terms *spontaneous* and *thermodynamically favored* mean is that the opposite change will not occur unless reaction conditions change.

Predicting the combined effects of entropy and enthalpy

When entropy and enthalpy oppose each other, the dominant one determines the outcome. But how do you know which will predominate? One way to find out is to make some observations.

Think of what happens when ice melts. The water molecules go from a solid, in which they are held in a rigid pattern within a crystal, to a liquid, in which they are free to move. This is an endothermic process that produces disorder because the increased freedom of movement in the liquid state means that there are more ways to arrange the molecules than there are in a solid, as shown in **Figure 9-20**. The change in entropy encourages melting, but the change in enthalpy discourages it. The observation that this change happens spontaneously only if the temperature is above 0°C signifies that the entropy change is dominant over the enthalpy change at higher temperatures.

Solid ice

Figure 9-20a
Melting is endothermic, but involves an increase in entropy. Melting is favored at higher temperatures.

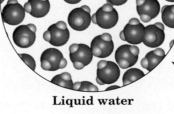

Liquid water

9-20b
Condensation is exothermic, but involves a decrease in entropy. Condensation is favored at lower temperatures.

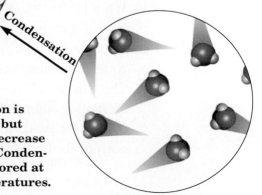

Gaseous steam

Table 9-8
Relating Enthalpy and Entropy to Spontaneity

ΔH	ΔS	Spontaneity	Example
− value Exothermic	+ value (disordering)	Always spontaneous	$2K(s) + 2H_2O(l) \longrightarrow 2KOH(aq) + H_2(g)$
− value Exothermic	− value (ordering)	Spontaneous at *lower* temperatures	$H_2O(g) \longrightarrow H_2O(l)$
+ value Endothermic	+ value (disordering)	Spontaneous at *higher* temperatures	$H_2O(s) \longrightarrow H_2O(l)$
+ value Endothermic	− value (ordering)	Never spontaneous	$16CO_2(g) + 18H_2O(l) \longrightarrow 2C_8H_{18}(l) + 25O_2(g)$

Now think of what happens when steam condenses. At the beginning, the system has high entropy. The particles in a gas have a great freedom of movement, so there are many ways in which they can be arranged. But when the system becomes liquid, the particles have less freedom of movement because they are closer together. As a result, the system has less entropy. The change in entropy discourages condensation, but the exothermic change in enthalpy favors it. This change is observed to happen spontaneously at normal atmospheric pressure, but only if the temperature is below 100°C. This observation indicates that enthalpy is the stronger driving force at lower temperatures. **Table 9-8** summarizes the thermodynamic spontaneity of possible combinations of enthalpy and entropy changes.

Chem Fact
The discussion assumes that enthalpy and entropy remain constant with temperature. This is not technically true, but unless there is a change of state, the effects of temperature on values of ΔH and ΔS are small enough that they can be disregarded.

Free energy
Free energy is a combination of entropy and enthalpy

Depending on the temperature, either entropy or enthalpy can be the cause of a change. How can you tell which will make a change happen?

A quantity that relates enthalpy and entropy in a way that indicates which predominates is **free energy**. Think of free energy as the quantity of energy that is available or stored to do useful work or to cause a change. The free energy of a system is represented by the letter G, in honor of the American chemist J. Willard Gibbs, who developed the equation to predict whether a reaction will occur spontaneously. This equation is used to calculate the change in free energy, represented by ΔG. If the value of ΔG is negative, the change is spontaneous. If it is positive, the change will not occur spontaneously. If ΔG is zero, this is an indication that neither the forward nor the reverse reaction is thermodynamically favored; the final result will be a state of dynamic equilibrium, with a mixture of products and reactants.

free energy
a quantity of energy related to the capacity of a system to do work, which can be used to predict spontaneity

$$\Delta G = \Delta H - (T\Delta S)$$

ΔG: positive value means change is not spontaneous

ΔG: negative value means change is spontaneous

Recall that ΔH represents the enthalpy change, T represents the temperature expressed in kelvins, and ΔS denotes the entropy change.

Remember that *when making free energy calculations, the temperature must be in kelvins.* Instructions for converting temperatures were given in Chapter 2. Also remember that ΔS values are given in J/K•mol or J/K and ΔH values are in kJ/mol or kJ. Be certain to convert ΔS values from J/K into kJ/K.

Sample Problem 9F
Calculating free energy changes

Graphite and steam can react to produce water gas, a fuel which is a mixture of several gases, but mostly of carbon monoxide and hydrogen gas. When water gas is made industrially, the reaction is carried out at temperatures near 900°C. Are the products or reactants favored at this temperature? (Hint: assume that ΔH and ΔS are constant at all temperatures.)

$$H_2O(g) + C(graphite) \longrightarrow CO(g) + H_2(g) \quad \Delta H = +135.5 \text{ kJ} \quad \Delta S = +148.8 \text{ J/K}$$

❶ List
- **temperature:** 900°C + 273 = 1173 K
- **enthalpy change:** +135.5 kJ
- **entropy change expressed in kJ/K:** $148.8 \text{ J/K} \times \dfrac{1 \text{ kJ}}{1000 \text{ J}} = 0.1488 \text{ kJ/K}$
- **free energy change:** ❓ kJ

❷ Set up
- **To determine the answer, you must calculate the value for the free energy change for the reaction at 900°C and check whether or not it is negative. If it is negative, the reaction will be spontaneous, and the products will be favored.**

$$\Delta G = \Delta H - T\Delta S = \text{❓ kJ}$$

$$\Delta G = 135.5 \text{ kJ} - \left(1173\,K \times \frac{0.1488 \text{ kJ}}{K}\right) = \text{❓ kJ}$$

❸ Estimate and calculate
- **Round off to make an estimate.**
  $135 - (1200 \times 0.150) \approx 135 - 180 \approx -45$

- **Calculate, and round off correctly.**
  Calculator answer: $135.5 - 174.5424 = -39.0424$

  Correctly rounded answer: -39.04 kJ

  Because the free energy change is negative, the reaction is spontaneous, and the products are favored.

Practice 9F

1. Holding the temperature of the reactants in the water-gas reaction at 900°C is expensive. What is the lowest temperature that the manufacturers could use and still have the reaction be spontaneous? (Hint: assume that ΔS and ΔH do not change and $\Delta G = -0.1$ kJ.)

2. Calculate ΔG for the following reaction at 25°C. Is the reaction spontaneous?

   $C(s) + O_2(g) \longrightarrow CO_2(g) \qquad \Delta H^0 = -393.5$ kJ/mol $\Delta S^0 = +3.0$ J/K•mol

3. A sample of ammonium chloride, NH_4Cl, is at 25°C. What must be done to make the decomposition reaction spontaneous?

   $NH_4Cl(s) \longrightarrow NH_3(g) + HCl(g) \quad \Delta H^0 = +176$ kJ/mol $\quad \Delta S^0 = +285$ J/K•mol

4. The thermite reaction used in some welding applications has the following enthalpy and entropy changes at 25°C. Assuming ΔS and ΔH are constant, calculate ΔG at 175°C.

   $Fe_2O_3(s) + 2Al(s) \longrightarrow 2Fe(s) + Al_2O_3(s) \qquad \Delta H^0 = -851.5$ kJ/mol
   $\Delta S^0 = +38.5$ J/K•mol

Comparing free energy changes

Values for free energy changes are similar to entropy and enthalpy in that they are usually tabulated as an amount *per mole*. As a result, these values can often be used in stoichiometric calculations. Additionally, if a reaction can be broken into two smaller reactions, its total free energy change will be equal to the sum of the component free energy changes.

For example, at 25°C, ΔG for the combustion of gaseous hydrogen to make water vapor is -228.6 kJ/mol. For the condensation of water vapor at 25°C to form liquid water, ΔG is -8.5 kJ/mol. The ΔG value involved in the change when making liquid water from gaseous hydrogen and oxygen is the sum of these two values, -237.1 kJ/mol.

$$H_2(g) + \tfrac{1}{2}O_2(g) \longrightarrow H_2O(g) \qquad \Delta G = -228.6 \text{ kJ/mol}$$
$$\underline{H_2O(g) \longrightarrow H_2O(l) \qquad\qquad \Delta G = \quad\, -8.5 \text{ kJ/mol}}$$
$$H_2(g) + \tfrac{1}{2}O_2(g) \longrightarrow H_2O(l) \qquad \Delta G = -237.1 \text{ kJ/mol}$$

Controlling reactions
How to influence what happens in a reaction

Any factor that affects the change in free energy of a reaction will influence how the reaction or change proceeds. One of the factors in the free energy equation is temperature. The reasons why temperature can have this effect, described earlier in this section, are clear if you examine the equation closely.

As shown in **Figure 9-21**, at low temperatures, the $T\Delta S$ part of the equation is smaller and will have less of an influence on the value of the free energy change. At high temperatures, the opposite is true. In cases where the effects of enthalpy and entropy changes tend to force the reaction in different directions, the temperature can be the factor that determines how a reaction will occur.

Figure 9-21
At lower temperatures, particles are moving slowly, and free energy is determined mostly by the enthalpy change. At higher temperatures, particles are moving faster, and the contribution of the entropy change becomes a more important factor than the enthalpy change.

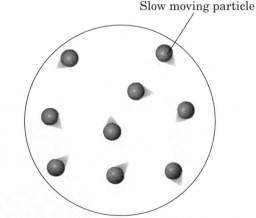

Low temperatures—small T value
means less randomness

$$\Delta G = \Delta H - T\Delta S$$
ΔH plays larger role

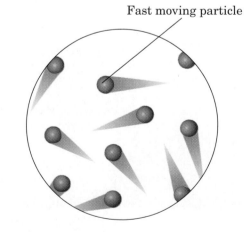

High temperatures—large T value
means more randomness

$$\Delta G = \Delta H - T\Delta S$$
$T\Delta S$ plays larger role

Just as water will freeze below 0°C and ice will melt above 0°C, many chemical reactions occur in one direction at low temperatures and in the other direction at high temperatures. For example, consider the reaction of an oxygen atom, O, combining with a molecule of oxygen, O_2, to produce ozone, O_3, as shown in **Figure 9-22**. When present in the lower atmosphere, ozone is a pollutant that can cause smog. However, in the stratosphere, ozone provides a blanket that absorbs the sun's ultraviolet radiation.

$$O_2(g) + O(g) \longrightarrow O_3(g) \qquad \Delta H = -106.5 \text{ kJ} \qquad \Delta S = -127.4 \text{ J/K}$$

At room temperature, 298 K, the effects of the enthalpy change are dominant, and the exothermic synthesis reaction is spontaneous, as indicated by the negative value for the free energy change of the reaction.

$$\Delta G = \Delta H - T\Delta S$$

$$\Delta G = -106.5 \text{ kJ} - (298 \text{ K})(-0.1274 \text{ kJ/K})$$

$$\Delta G = -106.5 \text{ kJ} - (-38.0 \text{ kJ}) = -68.5 \text{ kJ}$$

But at higher temperatures such as 1000. K, the reverse is true. The effects of the entropy change, which favor the decomposition of one molecule into an atom and a molecule, are dominant, and the reverse reaction is spontaneous. Then the value of the free energy change is positive.

$$\Delta G = \Delta H - T\Delta S$$

$$\Delta G = -106.5 \text{ kJ} - (1000. \text{ K})(-0.1274 \text{ kJ/K})$$

$$\Delta G = -106.5 \text{ kJ} - (-127.4 \text{ kJ}) = +20.9 \text{ kJ}$$

It is even possible to calculate the temperature at which neither reaction will be thermodynamically favored. At this temperature, ΔG will have the value of zero. For this to be true, ΔH and $T\Delta S$ must be equal so that you have zero left after subtracting. You already know from the two previous calculations that this temperature must be somewhere between 298 K and 1000. K. (Again, assume ΔH and ΔS are constant to get an approximate answer.)

$$\Delta G = \Delta H - T\Delta S = 0 \text{ kJ}$$

$$T\Delta S = \Delta H \text{ if } \Delta G = 0$$

$$T = \frac{\Delta H}{\Delta S} \quad \frac{-106.5 \text{ kJ}}{-0.1274 \text{ kJ}} = 836 \text{ K}$$

$$= 563°C$$

Figure 9-22a
Ozone can form as a result of electrical sparks such as lightning. The lightning provides the energy necessary to form O atoms from molecules. Ozone synthesis is thermodynamically favored over decomposition near room temperature. Ozone near the surface of the Earth is harmful.

9-22b
Ozone in the stratosphere shields Earth from ultraviolet radiation. At these altitudes, ozone reacts with pollutants such as chlorine from chlorofluorocarbons in a different reaction that favors decomposition.

Temperature is not the only reaction condition that can affect the spontaneity of a reaction. Anything that changes the values of the enthalpy and entropy changes will have an effect upon the value of the free energy change. Earlier, it was mentioned that enthalpy change is equal to the heat of reaction, provided that the pressure is held constant. Pressure changes will have an effect on the enthalpy change, which will in turn affect the free energy change of the reaction. If this effect is big enough, it can affect the spontaneity. Other factors, such as the nature of the reactants, can also affect the energy and spontaneity of a reaction.

Section Review

23. Using **Table 9-8**, predict what conditions, if any, are needed to make the following changes spontaneous.
    a. exothermic reaction with an increase in entropy
    b. enthalpy and entropy are both increased
    c. enthalpy and entropy are both decreased
24. Define *free energy,* and explain how a change in free energy is calculated.
25. From the following values, compute the ΔG value for each reaction, and predict whether each reaction will occur spontaneously.

Reaction	ΔH (kJ)	Temperature	ΔS (J/K)
1	+125	293 K	+35
2	−85.2	127 K	+125
3	−275	500°C	+450

26. How might you induce an endothermic reaction that does not usually occur spontaneously?

27. **Story Link**
For use in cars, hydrogen gas can be prepared in several ways, such as by the decomposition of water or hydrogen chloride.

$$2H_2O(l) \longrightarrow 2H_2(g) + O_2(g)$$
$$2HCl(g) \longrightarrow H_2(g) + Cl_2(g)$$

Use the following data to determine whether these reactions can occur spontaneously. Assume that ΔH and ΔS are constant.

	ΔH_f° (kJ/mol)	S° (J/K·mol)
$H_2O(l)$	−285.8	+70.0
$H_2(g)$	0	+130.7
$O_2(g)$	0	+205.1
$HCl(g)$	−92	+187
$Cl_2(g)$	0	+223.1

9-5

What are your energy needs?

Section Objectives

Describe the factors that affect daily energy requirements.

Estimate daily energy expenditure.

Estimate daily caloric intake.

Interpret food labeling for nutrient content.

Evaluate your diet against recommended guidelines.

Calculating your energy needs

As a living organism, your body requires energy to carry out the processes that keep you alive. Every movement you make involves the contraction of muscles and requires energy. Even when you are asleep, your body uses energy to keep you breathing and your heart beating. Obviously, the more you move, the more energy you need. In this section, you'll find out how much energy it takes to keep you going. Using this information and what you learned about the energy content of foods in Section 9-1, you can determine whether your energy requirements balance your energy intake.

basal metabolic rate
one's resting energy expenditure measured in the morning, at least 12 hours after the last meal

Estimating your metabolic rate

Your daily energy needs are determined by three factors—basal metabolic rate, activity level, and the thermic effect of food. By calculating the energy equivalents of these three factors, you can determine your daily energy needs.

Basal metabolic rate (BMR) includes the energy needed for all life sustaining reactions except the digestion and absorption of food. BMR is not constant but varies with factors like age, gender, stress level, and general health. To measure basal metabolic rate accurately, measurements must be taken before any activity or intake of food. The measurements collected under these controlled conditions give the **resting metabolic rate** (RMR). A resting metabolic rate is a basal metabolic rate measured after five to six hours of no food or exercise. BMRs and RMRs usually differ by less than 3%. Estimated RMRs for the general population are given in **Table 9-9**.

resting metabolic rate
energy expended by a person at rest in a thermally neutral environment

Table 9-9
Energy Expended at Resting Metabolic Rate (Cal/day)

Body mass	Male age 10–18	18–30	30–60	>60	Body mass	Female age 10–18	18–30	30–60	>60
50 kg (110 lb.)	1526	1444	1459	1162	50 kg (110 lb.)	1356	1231	1264	1121
57 kg (125 lb.)	1648	1551	1540	1256	57 kg (125 lb.)	1441	1334	1325	1195
64 kg (140 lb.)	1771	1658	1621	1351	64 kg (140 lb.)	1527	1437	1386	1268
70 kg (155 lb.)	1876	1750	1691	1423	70 kg (155 lb.)	1600	1525	1438	1331
77 kg (170 lb.)	1998	1857	1772	1526	77 kg (170 lb.)	1685	1628	1499	1404
84 kg (185 lb.)	2121	1964	1853	1621	84 kg (185 lb.)	1771	1731	1560	1478
91 kg (200 lb.)	2243	2071	1935	1716	91 kg (200 lb.)	1856	1833	1621	1552

Table 9-10
Estimating Energy for Activity Level
(in Relation to Resting Metabolic Rate)

Activity level	Activity factor
Resting (sleeping, reclining)	RMR × 1.0
Very light (seated and standing activities, painting, driving, lab work, typing, sewing, ironing, cooking, playing cards, playing a musical instrument)	RMR × 1.5
Light (walking on a level surface, garage work, carpentry, house cleaning, child care, golf, sailing, table tennis)	RMR × 2.5
Moderate (walking 3.5–4 mph, weeding and hoeing, carrying a load, cycling, skiing, tennis, dancing)	RMR × 5.0
Heavy (walking uphill with a load, chopping wood, manual digging, basketball, climbing, football, soccer)	RMR × 7.0

Source: Adapted from *Recommended Dietary Allowances*, 10th Edition

Figure 9-23
You can find calorie information based on serving sizes in the nutritional facts panel on food packages.

Thermic effect of food is estimated as a percentage of caloric intake

You can use **Table 9-10** to estimate the effects of activity on daily energy requirements. The table provides a realistic estimate as long as you don't exaggerate your activity level.

The thermic effect of food is the energy required for digestive processes. *Ten percent of the total caloric intake is an accepted figure for estimating the thermic effect of food.* Accurate measurement of this effect depends on the percentages of carbohydrates, fats, and proteins consumed. Fat is stored more efficiently than carbohydrate and protein.

Determining caloric intake

You can find data just about anywhere on the caloric equivalents of most of the foods you eat. Fortunately, most of the packaged food you get from the grocery store provides a lot of nutritional information. The cans in **Figure 9-23** each have labels in the style now mandated by the Food and Drug Administration (FDA).

Keep a food diary for a day. Use Calorie data on each of the foods you eat to determine your caloric intake for that day. The food diary and labels are also useful in doing a dietary analysis of how your caloric consumption is subdivided into carbohydrates, proteins, and fats.

How To

Estimate your energy expenditure

1. Use **Table 9-9** to estimate your RMR for 24 hours. Convert this value to Cal/h.
2. Use **Table 9-10** to calculate your activity level in Calories. Divide the day into the number of hours for your various levels of activity. For each level of activity, multiply the time by the factor from **Table 9-10** and by the RMR in Cal/h calculated in step **1**.
3. Determine the thermic effect of food by estimating total caloric intake (use food value tables) and multiplying by 0.10.
4. Add the results of steps **2** and **3** to get your total energy expenditure.

Reading food labels

The FDA's standardization of nutritional labeling has made it possible to compare the nutritional compositions of similar foods, and it is also easier to determine how a particular food affects your daily caloric intake and how it matches sound dietary guidelines.

1. Serving size—The amounts listed now more closely approximate the amounts people eat. Serving sizes have been standardized for the same types of foods to allow for easy comparison.

2. Calories from fat—The fat Calories are based on grams of fat multiplied by the Calories per gram for fat (9 Cal/g).

3. Percent daily values—This section provides a breakdown of the nutrient content with respect to a 2000 Cal diet. Thus, 8 g of fat represent 12% of the recommended daily fat intake for someone on a 2000 Cal diet.

4. Total fat—A sum and breakdown of the fat content by degree of saturation are given.

5. Vitamin and mineral content—This breakdown allows you to compare foods as sources of vitamins and minerals. It also helps you in determining whether your diet provides enough of these nutrients. A value of 10% means the food is a "good source" of that nutrient. Values of 20% and higher mean that the food is "high" in that nutrient.

6. Dietary recommendations based on percent daily values—This information has been standardized to reflect caloric consumption at realistic levels. These values can be used to calculate recommendations at other caloric levels.

7. Calories per gram—The energy equivalent of these nutrients is constant and independent of the type of food.

1.
2.
3.
4.
5.
6.
7.

Section Review

28. Name three factors that determine your daily energy needs.

29. You gain 1 lb. for every 3500 Cal you consume over what you expend. Assume your energy intake and expenditures are in balance and then you decide to add a bag of potato chips to your lunch every day. How long will it take you to gain 1 lb.? (Hint: use **Table 9-4**.)

30. Assume your energy intake and expenditures are in balance and then you decide to walk for one hour each day. If an hour of walking requires 370 Cal, how long will it take you to lose 1 lb.?

31. A typical fast-food lunch consisting of a cheeseburger, french fries, and a large soft drink has the following nutritional breakdown.

Protein	32.9 g
Carbohydrate	124.2 g
Fat	46.3 g

  a. Calculate the total number of Calories in this lunch.

  b. How does this nutrient content compare to the daily recommendations for someone on a 2000 Cal diet?

  c. How long would you have to walk to burn the Calories in this lunch?

Conclusion: Energy and Low-Emission Cars

At the beginning of this chapter, you explored hydrogen-powered cars. ***What drives the hydrogen combustion reaction?*** All chemical reactions that occur are driven by one or both of two forces: an increase in entropy or a decrease in enthalpy. The exothermic combustion reaction is driven by a large decrease in enthalpy even though entropy decreases because three molecules ($2 H_2$ and $1 O_2$) combine to form only two molecules ($2 H_2O$).

How can this reaction be controlled so that it does not happen accidentally? It would be difficult to maintain the extreme conditions necessary for the reaction to be non-spontaneous. Instead, the hydrogen is absorbed within a compound, a metal hydride containing hydrogen, manganese, and titanium, until it is needed. Hydrogen fits within the relatively widely-spaced metal atoms, where it is more stable.

The absorption of hydrogen is strongly exothermic. As the vehicle is refueled, water is circulated around the storage tanks to absorb the heat.

The reverse process, the release of hydrogen, is endothermic. To provide the energy necessary, coolant water that has absorbed heat from the engine is circulated around the storage tank.

One "tankful" of the metal hydride fuel provides only about half of the mileage provided by a full tank of gas. Because of the complicated fuel system, a hydrogen-powered car costs at least one-and-a-half times as much as its gasoline-powered counterpart.

The only place where humans depend on hydrogen for energy is in space. The energy supplied by the combustion of hydrogen is used by spacecraft such as the space shuttle.

Despite the remaining obstacles, engineers at several car companies believe that use of hydrogen-powered cars will be common someday.

Applying Concepts

1. Which of the following is the most efficient fuel, in terms of energy output per unit mass of fuel?

Fuel	ΔH_{comb} (kJ/mol) at 298 K
methane	+891
methanol	+726
propane	+2219
1-propanol	+2021

Research and Writing

Use the library to find out more about the following.

1. Some car manufacturers are experimenting with compressed natural gas (CNG) as an alternative fuel. What advantages and disadvantages does CNG offer compared to gasoline and hydrogen gas?

Highlights

Key terms

activation energy	heat of reaction
basal metabolic rate	Hess's law
enthalpy	resting metabolic rate
enthalpy change	specific heat capacity
entropy	spontaneous change
free energy	temperature
heat	

Key Ideas

 ### How does energy affect change?

- Heat and temperature are not the same thing. Heat is the measure of total energy transferred from one system to another; temperature is the measure of average kinetic energy in a sample of matter.
- The specific heat capacity for a substance describes how much heat energy is required to cause a temperature change.
- Heat of reaction—the energy released or absorbed during a chemical reaction or a physical change—is measured with a calorimeter.
- The amount of heat involved in a physical or chemical change can be expressed as a ratio in stoichiometric calculations.

 ### How does enthalpy drive changes?

- When heat is released during a change, enthalpy is decreased. Decreasing enthalpy drives most chemical reactions.
- All reactions require activation energy, which can be provided by adding energy to the system or by converting the kinetic energy a substance already has.
- Total changes in enthalpy can be calculated by adding together the enthalpy changes for each part of a reaction.

 ### How does entropy drive changes?

- Entropy, a measure of the disorder of a system, increases with increasing temperature.
- A higher entropy level in a reaction results in a more stable product.

 ### How do entropy and enthalpy affect change?

- Entropy and enthalpy values can be mathematically combined with temperature to describe the free energy of a system and predict whether the reaction is spontaneous.

 ### What are your energy needs?

- Resting metabolic rate (RMR) is the amount of energy needed to keep the body running at its most basic level.
- The thermic effect of food is the energy needed for the chemical reaction of digestion.

Key problem-solving approach: *Calculations involving energy*

When solving energy calculations, begin at the top by writing the balanced equation. Then, follow the arrows to calculate the desired quantity.

reactants products

$$A + B \longrightarrow X + Y$$

Enthalpy
$$\Delta H_{rxn} = (\Delta H_{fX} + \Delta H_{fY}) - (\Delta H_{fA} + \Delta H_{fB})$$
$+ \Delta H$ = endothermic
$- \Delta H$ = exothermic

Entropy
$$\Delta S_{rxn} = (S_X + S_Y) - (S_A + S_B)$$
$+ \Delta S$ = disordering
$- \Delta S$ = ordering

$$\times \frac{1\,kJ}{1000\,J}$$

Free Energy
$$\Delta G = \Delta H_{rxn} - T\Delta S_{rxn}$$
$+ \Delta G$ = nonspontaneous
$- \Delta G$ = spontaneous

Review and Assess

 Heat and energy

REVIEW

1. What is the difference between heat and temperature?
2. How is heat of solution related to heat of reaction?
3. Indicate whether the change occurring in the following situations is due to specific heat capacity, heat of fusion, or heat of vaporization.
   a. a pot of boiling coffee
   b. ice cream melting on a hot day
   c. a burner on the stove heating up
4. Which illustration below shows the energy flow during an exothermic reaction, and which shows the energy flow during an endothermic reaction?

   a. $CH_4 + O_2 \longrightarrow CO_2 + H_2O$

   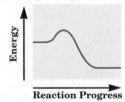

   b. $H_2O + CO_2 \longrightarrow C_6H_{12}O_6 + O_2$

   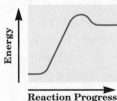

5. A man with a mass of 80 kg requires 2500 Cal/ day to keep his body working efficiently. What is his required daily energy in kJ?
6. Complete the following table.

Food and measure	kJ	Calories
carrot, 1, trimmed	50.2	
jelly doughnut, 1		220.
whole milk, 1 cup	656.9	
rice cake, 1		60.0

PRACTICE

Answers to items in a black square begin on page 841.

7. If you fill a bathtub with 200. kg of water at 44°C, how much heat energy is lost as the water cools to a temperature of 21°C? (Hint: see Sample Problem 9A.)
8. On a cold winter day with a temperature of 4°C, you pick up a penny from the ground and put it in your pocket. If the penny has a mass of 1.85 g, how much heat energy must be transferred to the coin to warm it to your body temperature, 37°C? The specific heat of copper is 0.385 J/g•°C. (Hint: see Sample Problem 9A.)
9. A nutritional chemist burns a saltine cracker in a calorimeter containing 2.50 kg of water. The temperature increases from 25.0°C to 29.8°C. What is the energy content of the cracker in Calories and in kilojoules? (Hint: see Sample Problem 9B.)
10. Predict the final temperature of 2.50 kg of water in a calorimeter if the water is at 25.00°C before 0.5 oz. of noodles containing 54.0 Cal are burned. (Hint: see Sample Problem 9B.)
11. When suffering from a fever, your body temperature rises from 37°C to 40°C, using 787 kJ of energy in the process. Assume that your body burns only glucose to raise your temperature. How many grams of glucose are consumed?

$$C_6H_{12}O_6(s) + 6O_2(g) \longrightarrow$$
$$6H_2O(l) + 6CO_2(g)$$

$\Delta H = -2870$ kJ/mol
(Hint: see Sample Problem 9C.)

12. A mountain climber, wanting a drink of water, must melt the snow from the mountain with a propane burner. How many grams of propane would the mountain climber have to use to generate the 33.5 kJ needed to melt the snow for 100 mL of water if her burner heats with 50% efficiency?

$$C_3H_8(g) + 5O_2(g) \longrightarrow 4H_2O(l) + 3CO_2(g)$$

$\Delta H = -2220$ kJ
(Hint: see Sample Problem 9C.)

13. An ounce of peanuts has more Calories than an ounce of celery. If equal masses of peanuts and dried celery were burned in separate calorimeters, how would the temperature of the water inside one calorimeter compare to the temperature of the water in the other?

14. Refer to **Table 9-3** to answer the following questions.
    a. How much energy is required to change 1 mol of ice at 0°C to steam at 100°C?
    b. How much energy is required to change 1 mol of liquid mercury at –38.8°C to mercury vapor at 357°C?
    c. How much energy is required to boil 5.00 mol of ethanol at 78.3°C?

15. Name the type(s) of heat data needed by the following people to complete their jobs.
    a. a pool operator who needs to regulate water temperature of a heated swimming pool
    b. a steel mill worker who needs to regulate the heat of the melting furnace

16. Refer to **Table 9-3** and draw and label a temperature vs. heat curve for 1 mol Hg being heated from a solid at –38.8°C to a gas at 357°C.

17. The concrete that surrounds a swimming pool takes less time to heat up than the water in the pool on a hot summer day. What can you infer about the specific heat capacity values for concrete and water?

18. During an exothermic change, energy is lost from the reaction system and gained by the surroundings as heat. The opposite happens in an endothermic change. Explain how the use of both processes controls the temperature of your home. (Hint: for each process, carefully consider what the system is and what the surroundings are.)

Enthalpy changes

19. What is the difference between enthalpy and an enthalpy change?

20. What is the relationship between enthalpy and spontaneous reactions?

21. Why do some exothermic reactions appear to require no added activation energy?

22. Use the following terms to label the energy diagram for the production of phosgene, $COCl_2$, a chemical used in the production of organic supplies: activation energy, ΔH, reactants, products.

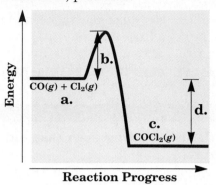

23 In the engine of your car, nitrogen and oxygen can combine to form nitrogen oxides, chemicals that contribute to pollution. Below is a reaction that forms nitrogen dioxide from previously formed nitrogen monoxide. Determine the ΔH value for this reaction using the heats of formation given. (Hint: see Sample Problem 9D.)

$$2NO(g) + O_2(g) \longrightarrow 2NO_2(g)$$

Substance	ΔH^o_f (kJ/mol)
$NO(g)$	+90.2
$O_2(g)$	0
$NO_2(g)$	+33.2

24. Pentane, the smallest hydrocarbon found in gasoline, can be synthesized from 2-pentanol and hydrogen gas in a multistep process. Determine the ΔH for this reaction using the heats of formation given for the equation below. (Hint: see Sample Problem 9D.)

$$C_5H_{11}OH(l) + H_2(g) \longrightarrow C_5H_{12}(l) + H_2O(l)$$

Substance	ΔH^o_f (kJ/mol)
$C_5H_{11}OH(l)$	–365.2
$H_2(g)$	0
$C_5H_{12}(l)$	–173.5
$H_2O(l)$	–285.8

APPLY

25. Some fire extinguishers work by evolving an unreactive gas, like CO_2, that smothers the flame. The contents also work as a cooling agent. Using your knowledge of activation energy, explain the importance of including a cooling agent in fire extinguishers.

26. The gasification of coal is a method of producing methane. The entire reaction has four separate steps, with heats of reaction of + 188 kJ, –54 kJ, –221 kJ, and –75 kJ, respectively. What is the ΔH of this entire reaction for the gasification of coal?

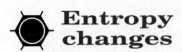 **Entropy changes**

REVIEW

27. Give three examples of each of the following conditions.
  a. high entropy   **b.** low entropy

28. Which provides a greater number of ways to arrange particles: a high-entropy or low-entropy system?

29. Why can absolute values of entropy be calculated while absolute values of enthalpy cannot be?

30. What is the difference between entropy units and enthalpy units?

PRACTICE

31 Solid iron will slowly oxidize into iron oxide, Fe_2O_3, if it is left untreated in the open air. What is the entropy change for this reaction? (Hint: see Sample Problem 9E.)

$$4Fe(s) + 3O_2(g) \longrightarrow 2Fe_2O_3(s)$$

Substance	S (J/K·mol)
$Fe(s)$	27.3
$O_2(g)$	205.2
$Fe_2O_3(s)$	87.4

32. Ammonium nitrate is a common fertilizer that can become a powerful explosive when it undergoes rapid decomposition. What is the entropy change for this reaction? (Hint: see Sample Problem 9E.)

$$2NH_4NO_3(s) \longrightarrow$$
$$2N_2(g) + 4H_2O(g) + O_2(g)$$

APPLY

33. Oil of citronella, a volatile liquid, is often burned to repel insects. For each molecule of oil of citronella, several molecules of carbon dioxide and water are produced. Identify whether entropy increases or decreases in this reaction, and list three pieces of evidence for this change in entropy.

34. Predict whether ΔS of the changes in the following examples is positive or negative.
  a. A chemist heats a chemical in order to determine its melting point.
  b. A petroleum distillery fractionally distills crude oil by boiling off different volatile hydrocarbons.
  c. The condensation of water vapor on a humid day causes a glass to appear to sweat.

35. Which graph shown below depicts the mathematical relationship between S and temperature for a system which is not undergoing a chemical reaction or a phase change?

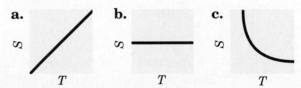

 Free energy

REVIEW

36. What types of enthalpy and entropy changes always give rise to a spontaneous change?

37. What free-energy condition must occur for a reaction to be spontaneous?

38. Name three reaction conditions that can control a reaction by affecting its spontaneity.

39. Is a solution of a substance representative of a high-entropy system or a low-entropy system compared to the pure substance and pure solvent?

40. What, if anything, is wrong with the following setups for calculating free energy for this reaction?

$$2Na(s) + Cl_2(g) \longrightarrow 2NaCl(s)$$

$\Delta H = -822.4$ kJ/mol
$\Delta S = -181.5$ J/K•mol

a. $\Delta G = -822.4$ kJ/mol − (298 K) (−181.5 J/K•mol)

b. $\Delta G = -822.4$ kJ/mol − (323 K) (−181.5 J/K•mol) (1 kJ/1000 J)

c. $\Delta G = -822.4$ kJ/mol − (15°C) (−181.5 J/K•mol) (1 kJ/1000 J)

d. $\Delta G = -181.5$ J/K•mol − (273 K) (−822.4 kJ/mol) (1000 J/1 kJ)

41. At high temperatures does enthalpy or entropy usually have a greater effect on a reaction's free energy? Explain your answer.

P R A C T I C E

42 Titanium chloride, $TiCl_4$, is an intermediate chemical formed in the production of titanium metal, a substance used extensively in aerospace technology. Will the reaction for the production of $TiCl_4$ be spontaneous if it is carried out at 100.0°C? Show your work. (Hint: see Sample Problem 9F.)

$$TiO_2(s) + 2Cl_2(g) \longrightarrow TiCl_4(l) + O_2(g)$$

$\Delta H = +140.5$ kJ
$\Delta S = -38.9$ J/K

43. Will the combustion of benzene, an alternative fuel, be spontaneous if the temperature is 25°C? Show your work. (Hint: see Sample Problem 9F.)

$$2C_6H_6(l) + 15O_2(g) \longrightarrow$$
$$12CO_2(g) + 6H_2O(l)$$

$\Delta H = -6535$ kJ
$\Delta S = -439.1$ J/K

A P P L Y

44. Draw a graph with ΔH on the x-axis and ΔS on the y-axis. In each quadrant of the graph, indicate what conditions, if any, are necessary to make a reaction spontaneous for each combination of positive and negative ΔH and ΔS values.

45. Gold can be dissolved using nitrosyl chloride, NOCl. The entropy change for the spontaneous reaction to make NOCl at a low temperature is negative. Is the enthalpy positive or negative?

Energy and your body

R E V I E W

46. What does the human body's basal metabolic rate represent?

47. What happens to your energy requirements as your activity level increases?

48. How does the thermic effect of food differ from BMR?

A P P L Y

49. Support the following statements, using what you know about metabolism and the thermic effect of food.
a. Men have a higher BMR than women.
b. A person living in Alaska has a higher BMR than a person living in Florida.

50. Use **Table 9-9** and **Table 9-10** to answer the following questions.
a. A 16-year-old, 50 kg girl rides her bicycle for 2 h. How many Cal/h does she expend?
b. About how many Calories do you expend in 1 h of cleaning your room?
c. A 24-year-old, 84 kg basketball player plays for 30 min. How many Cal/h does he expend?

51. How long could a 30-year-old 75 kg cyclist ride using the energy from a meal with 50.1 g protein, 145.3 g carbohydrate, and 29.7 g fat?

 Linking chapters

1. Bond energy
Energy diagrams show the relative bond energies of reactants and products. How does the concept of enthalpy relate to bond energy?

2. Chemical reactions
For a chemical reaction to take place, particles must collide with each other. Gasoline-air mixtures don't react at cool temperatures, but do react at warmer temperatures. What other requirement is there for reaction collisions?

3. Theme: *Systems and interactions*
Inside a calorimeter, two systems interact. What are these two systems, and how do they interact?

4. Theme: *Equilibrium and change*
Oxygen forms ozone, and at the same time, the ozone decomposes to form oxygen. At 836°C the reaction of oxygen gas to form ozone has a ΔG value of zero. Which of these reactions, if any, is absent?

1. Graphics calculator

Free energy can be predicted by examining a graph of the free energy equation. This function can be graphed on a calculator. Press PRGM ▶ ▶ ENTER to open a new program from the program menu on your graphics calculator, and give it a name. Then enter the following program.

    :Prompt H,S
    :"H–(X/1000)S" → Y₁.

Remember to use the "ALPHA" key for entering the letters. (Keystrokes: PRGM ; ▶ ; 2 ; H,S; ENTER ; "H–(X÷1000)S"; STO ; 2nd ; Y-VARS ; ENTER ; ENTER). The temperature at which ΔG will be zero is the value of x at the y-intercept. Run the program by pressing 2nd ; QUIT ; PRGM ; select the program by pressing ENTER ; ENTER . Enter the desired ΔH and ΔS values, press GRAPH , and then TRACE until $y = 0$. Determine the temperature at which the following reactions will have free energy values of zero. (Hint: see owner's manual to reset the WINDOW function to show the correct parts of the graph.)

a. $C_7H_8(l) \longrightarrow C_7H_8(g)$
$\Delta H = +38.0$ kJ/mol
$\Delta S = +99.7$ J/K•mol

b. $PCl_3(g) + Cl_2(g) \longrightarrow PCl_5(g)$
$\Delta H = -87.9$ kJ/mol
$\Delta S = -170.25$ J/K•mol

c. $H_2(g) \longrightarrow 2H(g)$
$\Delta H = +435.9$ kJ/mol
$\Delta S = +98.74$ J/K•mol

Alternative assessment

Performance assessment

1. Design an experiment to measure the heat capacities of zinc, copper, and iron. If your teacher approves your design, obtain the materials needed. When finished, compare your experimental values to values from a chemical handbook or reference source.

2. Develop a procedure to measure the ΔH of a reaction. If your teacher approves, test your procedure by measuring the ΔH value of the following reaction. Determine the accuracy of your method by comparing your ΔH to the accepted ΔH value.

$$NaC_2H_3O_2(s) \longrightarrow Na^+(aq) + C_2H_3O_2^-(aq)$$

Portfolio projects

1. Chemistry and you

During the course of a week, keep a journal of the different reactions you encounter. Estimate the sign and order of magnitude for ΔH, ΔS, and ΔG values for the reactions.

2. Research and communication

Conduct research on different mechanisms that lower the entropy of a system. Decide which are most effective. Present your findings to the class.

3. Research and communication

The chapter story covers several alternative fuels for cars. Conduct research on the public and private uses of these fuels in both automobiles and other combustion engines. Determine which ones can be used and produced with the least environmental impact. Present your findings to the class.

4. Chemistry and you

Evaluate your own diet based on information found in **Table 9-4**, **Table 9-5**, **Table 9-9** and **Table 9-10**. You may also want to research such diet issues as starchy carbohydrates versus sugary carbohydrates, complete versus incomplete proteins, and saturated versus unsaturated fats. Determine a realistic weekly plan of diet and exercise that will help you balance energy needs and food consumption. Try this plan and report to the class how you feel after one week.

5. Chemistry and you

Evaluate the labels of serveral different types of pet food. Explain which one you believe to be most nutritious and give your reasons.

CHAPTER 10

Gases and Condensation

Ascent Into the Ozone

In the still air, the sun begins to rise above the horizon. The busy team of scientists, awake for hours, monitors atmospheric conditions to be sure they are right. Today looks like a great day for the research team—today, there will be a launch.

As the sun rises, a growing silver form appears in the distance. A strange hissing sound fills the air. The shape, now recognizable as a huge balloon, takes form as it inflates with helium.

The ground crew continues to monitor atmospheric conditions as other scientists turn their attention to the expanding balloon. When the top of the partially inflated balloon extends about 250 m into the air, it is ready for launch. Though the balloon is only a small fraction of the size it will be when completely inflated, it still is capable of lifting a payload of telescopes, cameras, and recording equipment with a total mass of over 700 kg. With the data provided by these instruments, scientists can derive a clearer picture of what is happening to the upper atmosphere.

When the lead lines are removed, the balloon will ascend to about 38 500 m above Earth's surface. This mission, like many others before it, involves collecting data on the ever-changing ozone layer in the atmosphere. After collecting data for several days, the payload instruments will be retrieved by scientists when the payload falls back to Earth. The data collected will become part of the monthly log scientists use to make predictions about the ozone layer.

With the advent of satellites you might expect the use of balloons to be obsolete. Though satellites are used to record atmospheric composition data and meteorological conditions, balloons offer several advantages over satellites. Balloons are far less expensive to build and to launch. The cost of launching a satellite includes the price of the satellite itself and the rocket used to propel it into orbit. Another advantage of using balloons to measure the ozone layer is that the balloon can collect data from within the layer, while a satellite can merely provide data from an aerial perspective above the layer.

The principles used in launching balloons were discovered nearly 150 years ago and are the subject of this chapter. In studying these ideas, you will find that there are simple answers to seemingly complicated questions like the following.

- *Why is the balloon only partially inflated at launch?*
- *How do scientists know how much to inflate the balloon?*
- *Why are scientists monitoring the ozone layer?*
- *What gases are thought to be responsible for changes in the ozone layer?*
- *What's being done to protect the ozone layer?*

What are characteristics of gases?

10-1

Section Objectives

Describe the general properties of gases.

Describe the role of Earth's atmosphere in trapping radiant energy.

Identify the causes of ozone depletion over Antarctica.

Explain the assumptions of kinetic molecular theory.

Explain the energy distribution diagram for a gas at different temperatures.

Describe the four variables that define a gaseous system.

Describe how a barometer is used to measure pressure.

Properties of gases

Gases are the least complex state of matter. In elementary school you learned that gases can be compressed and that they expand to fill their containers. This means that the volume of a gas is variable. Recall that both solids and liquids have essentially fixed volumes and cannot be easily compressed because there is very little space between particles, as shown in the models in **Figure 10-1**. Therefore, gases typically have very low densities compared with liquids and solids. In fact, at standard conditions 1 mol of oxygen gas (32.0 g) has a volume of roughly 22 400 mL compared with 1 mol of water (18.0 g) with a volume of 18.0 mL or 1 mol of aluminum metal (27.0 g) with a volume of 10.0 mL.

Figure 10-1
Though all three substances are similar in mass, the volume occupied by the gas is substantially greater than that of the solid or liquid. Gases are easily compressed because there is so much space between particles compared to a solid or liquid.

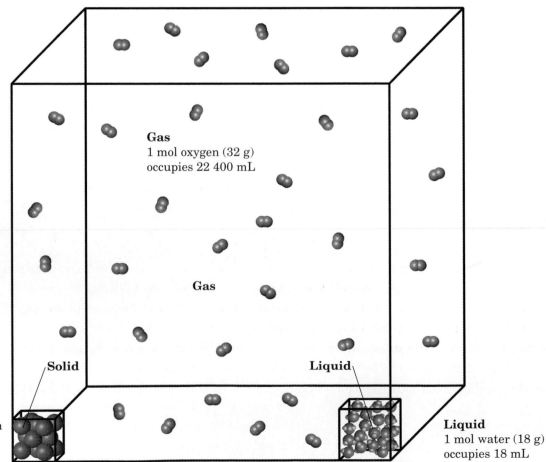

Gas
1 mol oxygen (32 g)
occupies 22 400 mL

Gas

Solid

Liquid

Solid
1 mol aluminum (27 g)
occupies 10 mL

Liquid
1 mol water (18 g)
occupies 18 mL

Table 10-1
Composition of Dry Air at Sea Level

Gas	Formula	Percentage by volume
nitrogen	N_2	78.084
oxygen	O_2	20.948
argon	Ar	0.934
carbon dioxide	CO_2	0.033
neon	Ne	0.001 82
helium	He	0.000 52
methane*	CH_4	0.000 2
krypton	Kr	0.000 1
hydrogen	H_2	0.000 05
carbon monoxide*	CO	0.000 01
xenon	Xe	0.000 008
ozone*	O_3	0.000 002
ammonia*	NH_3	0.000 001
nitrogen dioxide*	NO_2	0.000 000 1
sulfur dioxide*	SO_2	0.000 000 02

* Denotes components with variable concentrations.

The atmosphere is a sea of gases

The molecular composition of the atmosphere provides the perfect conditions for life to exist on Earth. For example, the oxygen we breathe is generally abundant in supply. The atmosphere provides protection from the sun, and it helps keep Earth at a comfortable temperature. **Table 10-1** is a listing of the gases found in our atmosphere.

How does this layer of gases keep the Earth warm? More than half of the sun's radiant energy that is directed toward Earth is absorbed by the surface. **Figure 10-2** shows a model for what happens to this energy as it passes through the atmosphere. Some of the radiant energy never reaches Earth's surface because it is deflected back into space by clouds and particles in the atmosphere. Some of the radiant energy that does penetrate the atmosphere will be reflected into space after striking materials on the ground such as snow and concrete. Earth radiates most of this absorbed energy back into the atmosphere as infrared radiation, which accomplishes a very important task—it warms our atmosphere.

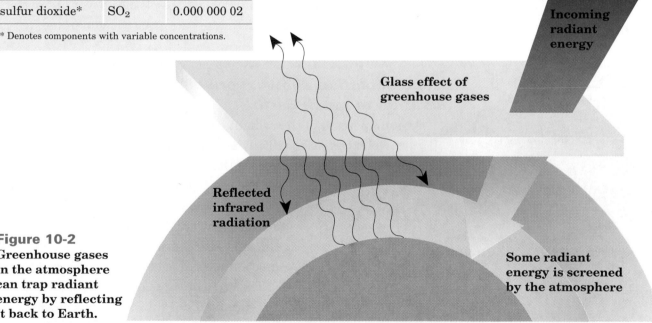

Figure 10-2
Greenhouse gases in the atmosphere can trap radiant energy by reflecting it back to Earth.

Incoming radiant energy

Glass effect of greenhouse gases

Reflected infrared radiation

Some radiant energy is screened by the atmosphere

greenhouse effect
an increase in the warming effects of infrared radiation absorption brought about by an increase in levels of carbon dioxide and other greenhouse gases in the atmosphere

Greenhouse gases trap radiant energy

The absorption of infrared energy and the trapping of radiant energy by molecules in the atmosphere is a mechanism known as the **greenhouse effect**. This effect is caused largely by the presence of carbon dioxide. However, levels of water, methane, and ozone also contribute to trapping radiant energy much like the glass on a greenhouse. They hold in the heat by trapping radiant energy that passes through the atmosphere. As the levels of greenhouse gases in the atmosphere increase, the temperature of the Earth could increase as well.

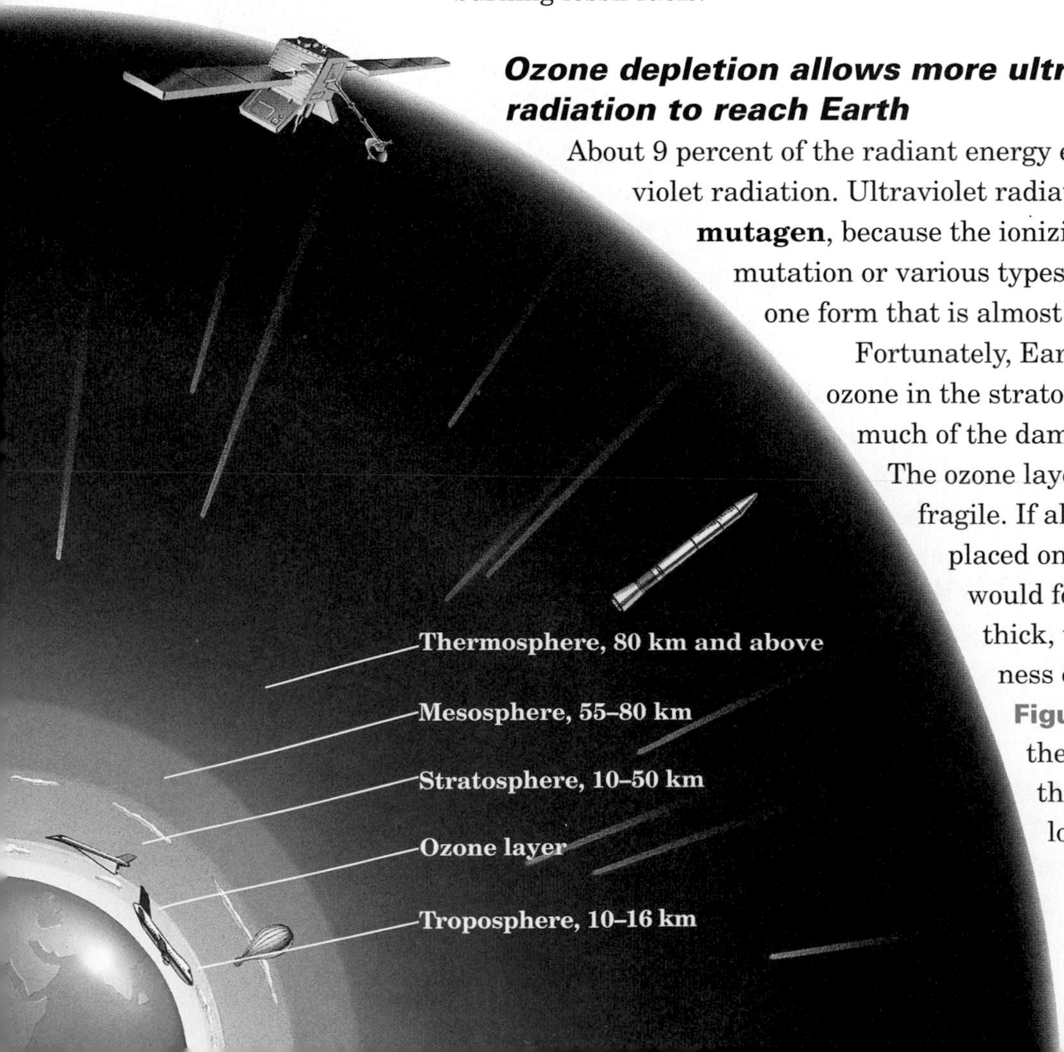

Figure 10-3
The atmosphere is divided into five regions. The troposphere is that region closest to Earth where all our weather patterns form. The ozone layer is part of the stratosphere. Satellites can be found in the thermosphere. Rockets also ascend into the thermosphere. Balloons can be found in the stratosphere. The SST travels in the stratosphere at about 15 km. Jet aircraft travel in the troposphere at about 12 km from Earth.

The 1980s produced a decade-long warming trend, ending with 1990 being the warmest year on record. The possibility that this trend will continue has raised concerns about global warming—the idea that the average global temperature could increase by as much as 3°C during the next 100 years.

An increase of 3°C over 100 years may not seem to be cause for too much concern. However, some computer models predict that an average global temperature increase from 17°C to 20°C could trigger massive droughts in inland regions and cause catastrophic floods in coastal areas as glaciers and polar caps melt. The weather could also become unpredictable.

Carbon dioxide levels are rising in the atmosphere

What is causing this warming effect? During the past century, human activities have been largely responsible for nearly a 15 percent increase in the CO_2 level of the atmosphere. One of these activities is burning rain-forest lands, which not only increases CO_2 from the combustion process, but reduces the amount of plant life on Earth that can consume CO_2 for photosynthesis.

However, it is the burning of fossil fuels, not rain forests, that releases the most CO_2 into the atmosphere. Many everyday activities involve the combustion of fossil fuels. Driving a car, cooking on an outdoor grill or gas stove, using a power lawn mower, and using a gas clothes dryer all involve combustion processes that release CO_2. Most electricity is generated by burning fossil fuels.

Ozone depletion allows more ultraviolet radiation to reach Earth

About 9 percent of the radiant energy emitted by the sun is ultraviolet radiation. Ultraviolet radiation is classified as a **mutagen**, because the ionizing radiation can cause a mutation or various types of skin cancers, including one form that is almost always fatal.

Fortunately, Earth is shielded by a layer of ozone in the stratosphere that screens out much of the damaging ultraviolet radiation. The ozone layer is extremely thin and fragile. If all the ozone molecules were placed on the Earth's surface, they would form a layer only 3 mm thick, which is about the thickness of the cover on this book! **Figure 10-3** shows a model for the parts of the atmosphere so that you can see the relative location of the ozone layer.

Thermosphere, 80 km and above

Mesosphere, 55–80 km

Stratosphere, 10–50 km

Ozone layer

Troposphere, 10–16 km

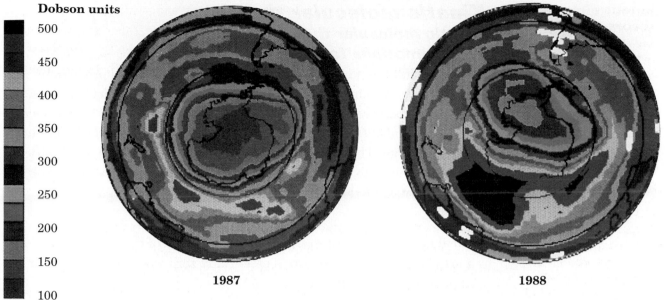

Dobson units

500
450
400
350
300
250
200
150
100

1987   1988

Figure 10-4
These satellite photos show the difference in ozone levels over the Antarctic for 1987 and 1988. Low levels of ozone are represented by shades of pink, as shown by the color scale on the left.

chlorofluoro-carbons
a family of organic compounds in which the hydrogen atoms have been replaced by fluorine and chlorine

A hole in the ozone occurs normally over the Antarctic on a yearly cycle as shown in **Figure 10-4**. Nearly all the ozone in the lower stratosphere disappears for about six weeks in September and October each year. In the years between 1977 and 1984, scientists found ozone levels decreased by more than 40 percent each spring. Further study showed that organic chlorine compounds called **chlorofluorocarbons** (CFCs), like the ones shown in **Figure 10-5**, are causing the ozone to break down. CFCs are gases used primarily as coolants in air-conditioning systems and refrigerators, and as propellants for aerosol sprays. When released, these gases drift up to the stratosphere where energy from ultraviolet light is able to break the bond holding a chlorine atom to a CFC molecule. The Cl atom produced is a free radical atom that reacts with an ozone molecule to form oxygen and a chlorine–oxygen free radical. *Free radicals* are highly reactive particles with an unpaired electron, as shown in the following equation.

$$Cl\cdot + O_3(g) \longrightarrow :\overset{\cdot\cdot}{\underset{\cdot\cdot}{Cl}}:\overset{\cdot\cdot}{\underset{\cdot\cdot}{O}}\cdot + O_2(g)$$

Free radical   Free radical

As a result of this reaction, the ozone hole gets larger each fall. In 1993, the region of the ozone hole spread to over 23 million square kilometers, almost the size of the entire North American continent.

To halt the destruction of the ozone layer, 74 nations signed the Montreal Protocol that calls for ending the production of all CFCs by 1996. However, CFCs now in use will continue to accumulate in the stratosphere until the year 2005. Scientists estimate that it will be the year 2060 before the chlorine concentration returns to the level it was in the 1970s when the ozone hole was first discovered.

Figure 10-5
Freon 11 and Freon 12 were commonly used chlorofluorocarbon compounds. Freon 11 is a liquid below 23.7°C. Freon 12 is a gas at room temperature, 25°C.

```
        Cl                          Cl
        |                           |
Cl — C — Cl                 F — C — Cl
        |                           |
        F                           F
Trichlorofluoromethane      Dichlorodifluoromethane
Freon 11                    Freon 12
```

kinetic molecular
theory
*the theory that
explains the behavior
of gases at the molecu-
lar level*

ideal gas
*a model that effectively
describes the behavior
of real gases at condi-
tions close to standard
temperature and pres-
sure; a gas for which
the product of the pres-
sure and volume is
proportional to the
absolute temperature*

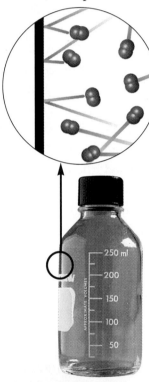

Figure 10-6
Gas particles travel in
straight lines until they
collide with each other
or the walls of their
container.

Figure 10-7
Although a Super Ball
bounces much higher
than a tennis ball or
basketball, even the
Super Ball does not un-
dergo elastic collisions.
However, we assume
collisions of ideal gas
particles are elastic.

Kinetic molecular theory
Kinetic molecular theory is based on assumptions for an ideal gas

You know that the purpose of models in science is to make predictions. A model should explain the facts we know and correctly predict events that have not yet occurred. The **kinetic molecular theory** (KMT) was developed in the mid-1800s and is still extremely useful as a model for predicting gas behavior. This theory is based on assumptions about a theoretical gas often referred to as the **ideal gas**. The ideal gas is a model in itself and is described by the following statements, which are also the basis of KMT.

1. Ideal gas particles are so small that the volume of the individual particles if they were at rest is essentially zero when compared with the total volume of the gas.
2. Ideal gas particles are in constant, rapid, random motion, moving in straight lines in all directions until they collide with other particles, as shown in the model in **Figure 10-6**.
3. There are no attractive or repulsive forces between particles, and collisions between particles are elastic.
4. The average kinetic energy of the particles is directly proportional to the absolute temperature (measured in kelvins).

When we say that the volume of the particles at rest must be almost zero, we don't mean that the volume is actually zero. It is just so small that it's negligible compared with the volume that the moving gas particles occupy. When you realize that a few drops of perfume can evaporate to fill a whole room, the "zero volume" part of this assumption makes sense. However, if gas particles really had no volume, the liquid or solid formed when they condensed would also have no volume! This assumption is not perfectly true.

Moving gas particles have kinetic energy. The average velocity of oxygen molecules is calculated to be about 400 m/s at 298 K. This calculation is based on the kinetic energy equation, which relates kinetic energy to one-half of the mass multiplied by the square of the velocity.

$$KE = \frac{1}{2}mv^2$$

Collisions between ideal particles are described as "elastic" because we assume that total energy is conserved; no energy is emitted when two gas particles collide, and none is lost (on average) when particles collide with the walls. If the collisions were not considered elastic, the colliding particles would continuously lose energy, slow down, and eventually stop, but this doesn't happen. Collisions between ordinary objects are not elastic. For example, a ball loses some of its kinetic and potential energy on each bounce. Not even "Super Balls" bounce with totally elastic collisions, as shown in **Figure 10-7**.

The assumption that gas particles do not attract each other is not realistic. Most particles have some degree of electrical attraction for other particles. However, the strength of that attraction depends on the mass and distance between the particles. Most common gases are composed of small molecules that are very far apart compared with those of a solid or liquid. The attraction between gas particles is so weak that at normal temperatures and pressures the particles are moving too quickly to be affected. If the molecules are pushed close together and slowed down enough, the attractive forces between particles begin to affect the particles' behavior, and condensation occurs. All gases eventually condense into liquids with a measurable volume when subjected to high enough pressure and low enough temperature. However, the ideal gas defined by our model never condenses, no matter how much we compress or cool it.

Figure 10-8
At the same temperature all four gases have the same average kinetic energy. Each gas has a distribution of molecular speeds. The shape of each curve varies because the molecular mass of each gas differs. Light gases (He) have more molecules moving at high speeds than the heavier gases (O_2 and N_2).

Speed Distribution for Four Gases at the Same Temperature

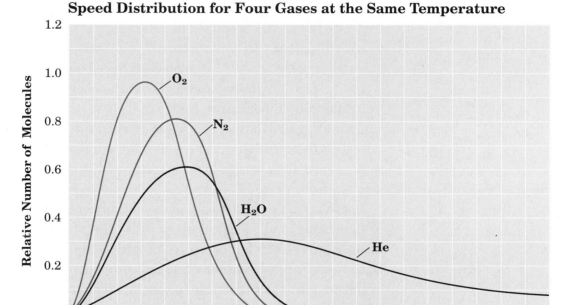

Four variables describe a gas
The temperature of a gas determines the average kinetic energy of the particles

An important aspect of the kinetic theory of gases is that the average kinetic energy of the particles depends on the temperature of the gas. Experiments in the late 1800s led to the discovery that not all gas particles of the same substance travel at the same speed. **Figure 10-8** shows how speed is distributed in four different samples of gas molecules all at the same temperature. The average kinetic energy of all four gases is the same, however the curves differ in shape. You should notice that the steepest curve is for O_2, the gas with the largest molecular mass. The most flattened curve is He, the gas with the lowest molecular mass. The data points used in making each curve were calculated from an equation called the Maxwell-Boltzmann energy distribution. Notice that the curve for each gas is not symmetrical.

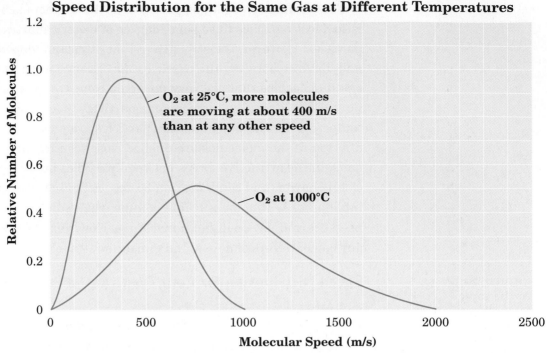

Speed Distribution for the Same Gas at Different Temperatures

O₂ at 25°C, more molecules are moving at about 400 m/s than at any other speed

O₂ at 1000°C

Relative Number of Molecules

Molecular Speed (m/s)

In **Figure 10-9** you see speed-distribution curves for the same gas at two different temperatures. Notice that these curves are not symmetrical and that the distribution gets broader when the temperature is increased. Although there will always be a few high-energy molecules and a few low-energy ones, the average kinetic energy will be directly proportional to the temperature.

Because many properties of gases depend on the temperature of the system being studied, calculations with gases should include a specified temperature. If the temperature is expressed in degrees Celsius, you will need to convert it to absolute temperature in kelvins. In Section 10-2 you will learn why the conversion to absolute temperature is necessary. Remember from Chapter 2 that 0 K differs from 0°C by 273 (it's actually 273.16). *For calculations in this text we will round the conversion value to 273.*

$$K = °C + 273.$$
$$T = t + 273.$$

The symbol T is used to represent absolute temperature; the symbol t represents Celsius temperature.

The volume of a gas is derived from linear measurements

Volume is not one of the SI base units but is derived from linear measurements using the following equation.

$$\text{volume } (V) = \text{length} \times \text{width} \times \text{height}$$

Gas volumes can be expressed in traditional metric units such as liters (L) and milliliters (mL) or in SI units such as cubic meters (m^3) or cubic centimeters (cm^3). Because the volumes of most containers used to hold gases are not easily determined, gas volume measurements are often made by the volume displacement of water.

The pressure of a gas is the force of its particles exerted over an area

You can't see wind, but you can feel its force as it pushes against you. Air pushes against the walls of a tire and rushes out if you open the valve to release it. **Pressure**, *P*, is defined as a force exerted over a specified area.

$$\text{pressure} = \frac{\text{force}}{\text{unit area}}$$

In relation to gases, pressure is a measure of the total force exerted by the moving particles of a gas as they collide with the walls of the container. In **Figure 10-6** you saw a model for particles colliding with the walls of a container. Each collision exerts a force. The sum of all the forces over the surface area of the container is the pressure exerted by the gas. Because each collision contributes to the total pressure, the pressure is proportional to the number of collisions. As the number of collisions increases, the pressure increases.

Why does pumping air into a car tire increase the pressure in the tire? Adding more particles increases the number of collisions on the inside surface of the tire, which increases the pressure in the tire.

The atmosphere exerts a pressure on Earth

The atmosphere that surrounds Earth is a sea of air—a mixture of gases that exerts a force on the surface of the Earth. This force is measured by its effect on the height of a mercury column in a tube, as in **Figure 10-10**. The level of mercury in the column rises or falls depending on the force exerted by gas molecules in air on the mercury surface. This force can be seen on a small scale with the model in **Figure 10-11**. The column of air exerts a force over a certain area of the Earth, creating atmospheric pressure. One standard atmosphere is defined as the pressure of the atmosphere that will support a column of mercury that is 760 mm high.

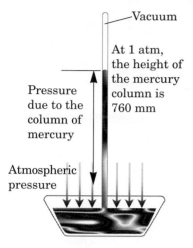

Vacuum

At 1 atm, the height of the mercury column is 760 mm

Pressure due to the column of mercury

Atmospheric pressure

Figure 10-10
Although water could be used in a barometer, the atmosphere would support a column of water about 10.3 m high, which is too high to be practical. Mercury has a density 13.7 times greater than water, so the mercury barometer is less than 1 m high.

Figure 10-11
Molecules in air collide with Earth's surface, creating pressure. The pressure exerted by the air is equivalent to one atmosphere when a column of air exerts a force of 101 325 newtons (N) over a one square meter area of Earth.

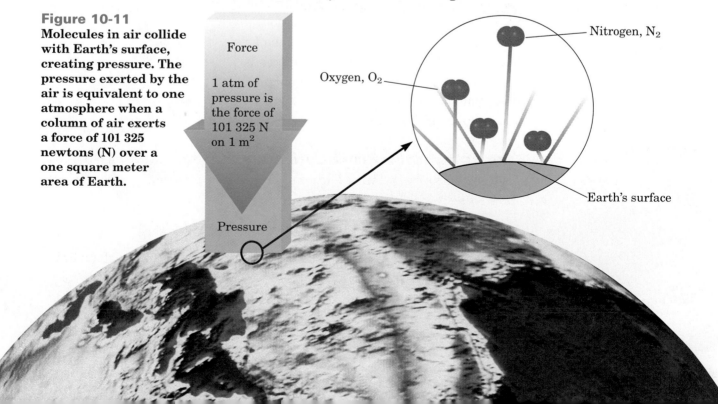

Force

1 atm of pressure is the force of 101 325 N on 1 m²

Pressure

Nitrogen, N₂

Oxygen, O₂

Earth's surface

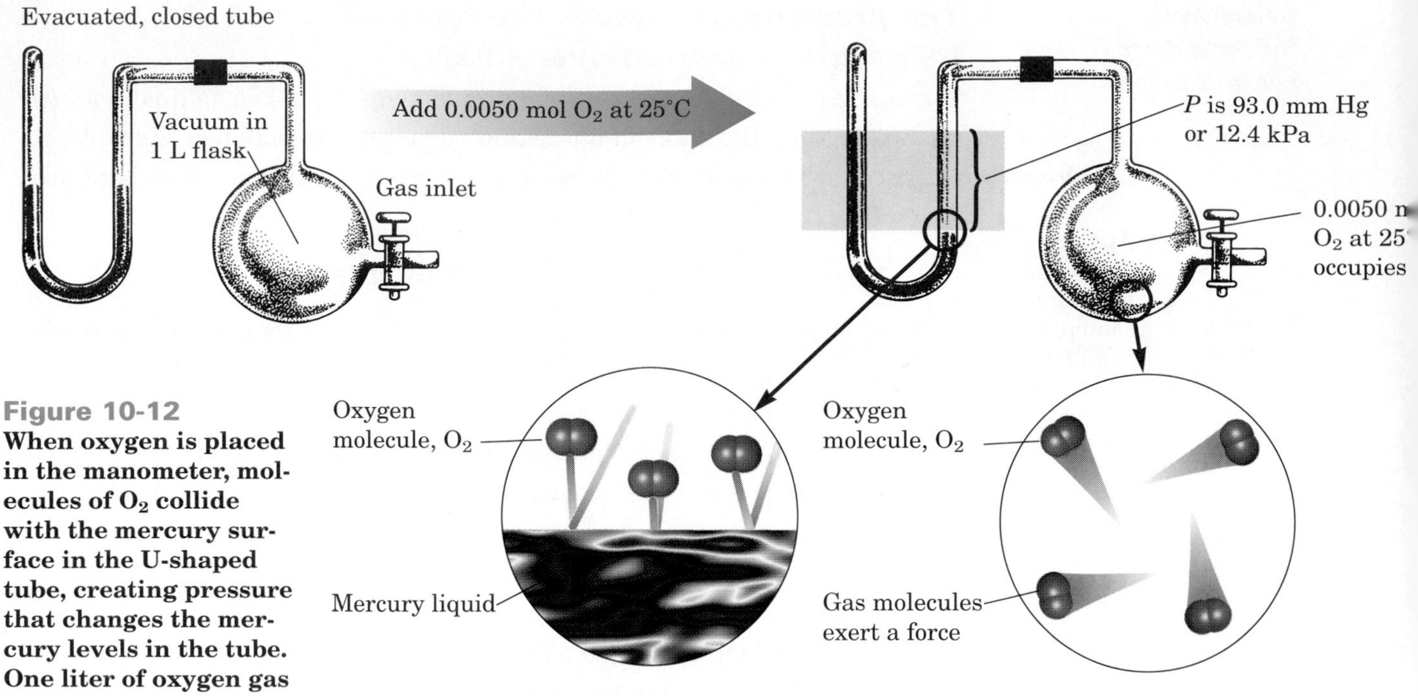

Evacuated, closed tube

Vacuum in 1 L flask

Gas inlet

Add 0.0050 mol O_2 at 25°C

P is 93.0 mm Hg or 12.4 kPa

0.0050 m O_2 at 25 occupies

Oxygen molecule, O_2

Mercury liquid

Oxygen molecule, O_2

Gas molecules exert a force

Figure 10-12
When oxygen is placed in the manometer, molecules of O_2 collide with the mercury surface in the U-shaped tube, creating pressure that changes the mercury levels in the tube. One liter of oxygen gas at 25°C exerts a pressure of 93 mm Hg or 12.4 kPa.

To measure the pressure of a gas inside a container an instrument called a manometer is used. **Figure 10-12** shows a model for how the manometer works. An instrument used to measure the pressure of air inside your bicycle or car tires is a pressure gauge. A pressure gauge measures the *difference* between the pressure inside the tire and the pressure exerted by the atmosphere outside the tire. These simple gauges are calibrated in units of pounds per square inch (psi). Although psi is not a metric unit, it reminds us that pressure is a force (the pound is a unit of weight—the force of gravity acting on a mass) applied over a surface area (square inches).

Figure 10-13
A tire gauge measures the difference between atmospheric pressure and the internal pressure of air in the tire.

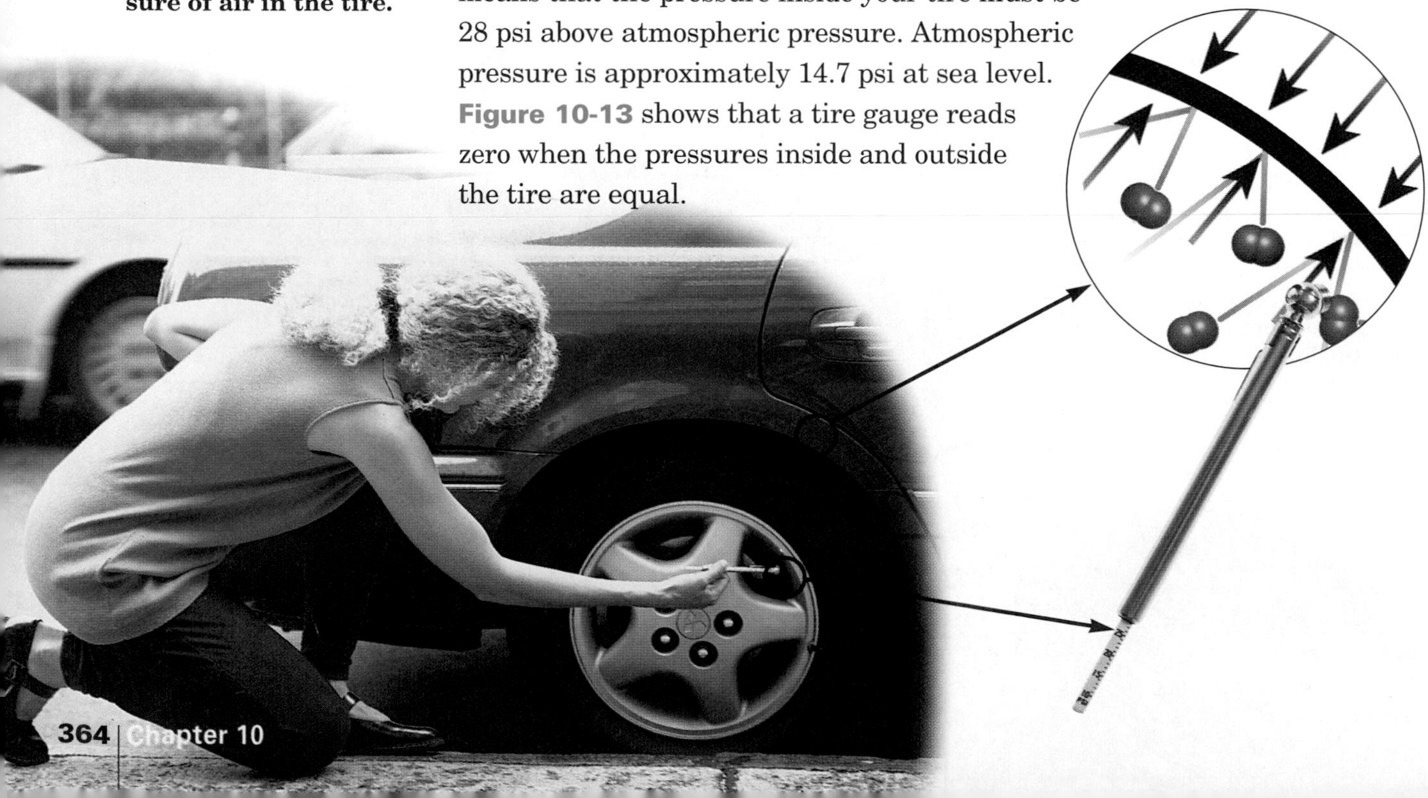

The same force can be applied over a large or small area, but it would result in considerably different pressure. When a mechanic says you need "28 pounds of air" in your tires, this is not the weight of the air at all! This means that the pressure inside your tire must be 28 psi above atmospheric pressure. Atmospheric pressure is approximately 14.7 psi at sea level. **Figure 10-13** shows that a tire gauge reads zero when the pressures inside and outside the tire are equal.

Table 10-2
Pressure Units

Unit	Abbreviation	Definition	Equivalence to one atmosphere
atmospheres	atm	1 atm is the pressure that supports a column of mercury 760 mm high.	
bars	bar	1 bar is a force of 100 000 N/m².	1.013 bar
millimeters of mercury	mm Hg	1 mm Hg is the pressure that supports a column of mercury 1 mm high at 0°C.	760 mm Hg
pascals	Pa	1 Pa is the force of 1 N/m².	1.01325×10^5 Pa or 101.325 kPa
pounds per square inch	psi	1 psi is the force of 1 lb/in².	14.7 psi
torr	torr	1 torr is the pressure that supports a column of mercury 1 mm high at 0°C.	760 torr

In addition to atmospheres, a variety of units are used to express pressure as shown in **Table 10-2**. The SI unit for pressure, the one we will use most often, is derived from base units and is called the **pascal**, Pa. Atmospheres will be used frequently as well—bars and millibars are generally used in meteorology only.

pascal
a unit of pressure equal to the force of 1 N/m²

Standard temperature and pressure are used for comparison purposes

To study the effects of changing temperature and pressure on a gas, it is useful to have a standard for comparison. Scientists have specified a set of standard conditions, giving them the name **standard temperature and pressure**, or **STP**. STP represents a pressure and temperature that are fairly easy to reproduce in any laboratory throughout the world.

standard temperature and pressure (STP)
standard conditions for a gas of 0°C and 1.0000 atm

$$STP = 0°C \text{ and } 1.0000 \text{ atm}$$

Because there are other units used to describe pressure, as shown in **Table 10-2**, STP is equivalent to the following.

$$STP = 273.16 \text{ K and } 101.325 \text{ kPa}$$
$$STP = 273.16 \text{ K and } 1.0000 \text{ atm}$$
$$STP = 273.16 \text{ K and } 760.0 \text{ mm Hg}$$
$$STP = 273.16 \text{ K and } 760.0 \text{ torr}$$

Millimeters of mercury, mm Hg, was once generally accepted as the unit of pressure. However, it seemed odd to use a length measurement (mm) to express a derived quantity, force per unit area. A unit called torr gradually replaced mm Hg for this reason, though you will still see mm Hg used. One millimeter of Hg is equivalent to one torr. When a problem specifies STP conditions, select the pressure value with units that match the other pressure units given in the problem.

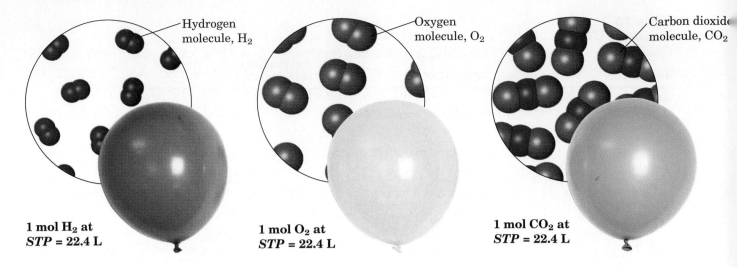

Hydrogen molecule, H_2

Oxygen molecule, O_2

Carbon dioxide molecule, CO_2

1 mol H_2 at
STP = 22.4 L

1 mol O_2 at
STP = 22.4 L

1 mol CO_2 at
STP = 22.4 L

Figure 10-14
Equal numbers of moles of gas at STP have equal volumes.

Gases with equal volumes under the same conditions have equal numbers of particles

In the early 1800s, Amedeo Avogadro was one of several scientists studying the behavior of gases. Some important fundamental relationships in chemistry were determined from this study. Avogadro's experiments led him to hypothesize that *equal volumes of gases under the same conditions have equal numbers of molecules*, which is represented by the model in **Figure 10-14**. Though this sounds simple, it is a very important hypothesis, and it applies only to gases. **Avogadro's principle** allows you to say that two balloons of the same size at the same temperature and pressure contain the same number of gas particles. This statement will hold true for any two gases, no matter what their identity!

From Avogadro's hypothesis, we reason that the volume of a gas at a given temperature and pressure is directly proportional to the quantity of the gas in moles. This means that as the number of moles increases, the volume increases. **Figure 10-15** shows a graph of this proportionality.

Avogadro's principle
equal volumes of different gases under the same conditions have the same number of molecules

molar volume
the volume of one mole of a substance at STP

Figure 10-15
The graph shows there is a direct relationship between the volume and quantity of gas. Whenever the quantity of gas is increased, the volume will increase.

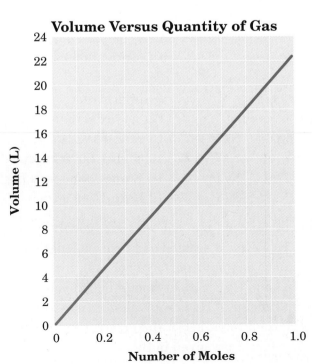

Volume Versus Quantity of Gas

Volume (L)

Number of Moles

Remember that the *amount* of gas is measured in moles, not grams.

Because gases are often compared at *STP*, the volume of one mole of gas at *STP* is called the **molar volume**. At *STP*, the molar volume of any gas is approximately 22.4 L. Notice that the slope of the graph in **Figure 10-15** is 22.4. Because the graph shows a direct relationship and the graph line passes through the origin, the following mathematical relationship holds.

$$\frac{\text{volume}}{\text{number of moles}} = k \text{ (constant)}$$

Non-CFC air conditioning

In keeping with the limits set for CFC's by the Montreal Protocol, car manufacturers have developed new air-conditioning systems that use a hydrofluorocarbon, 1,1,1,2 tetrafluoroethane, called R-134a, as the refrigerant instead of the traditional R-12 (dichlorodifluoromethane).

R-134a has low toxicity and appears to have little effect on the ozone layer. However, the chemical differences between R-12 and R-134a result in some major problems for consumers.

The major disadvantage is that the properties of R-134a make it such that it *cannot* be used in an air-conditioning system that was built for R-12 because R-12 and R-134a are chemically incompatible. In addition R-134a systems operate at slightly higher pressures and are slightly less efficient than R-12 systems. Therefore, R-134a requires a complete redesign of the existing air-conditioning system including all new compressors, evaporators, and condensers that are engineered to operate at higher pressures with a less efficient coolant.

Recharging and flushing an existing R-12 air-conditioning system is expensive because R-12 is now more costly and limited in supply.

Servicing an R-134a system won't exactly be inexpensive, because service equipment also had to be re-engineered. Because non-CFC air conditioning is a new area, consumers should have work performed at a reputable service station by knowledgeable mechanics.

1. Why are atmospheric scientists concerned about burning fossil fuels?
2. Give two physical properties that clearly distinguish gases from liquids or solids.
3. Determine the density in g/mL of a 0.70 g sample of oxygen gas that occupies 5.0 L. Compare the density of oxygen gas to the density of water, assuming both substances are at *STP*.
4. What part of a CFC reacts with ozone?
5. List three ways that an ideal gas differs from a real gas.
6. If a tire gauge reads 20.0 psi, what is the actual pressure in the tire expressed in psi?
7. Describe the relationship between molecular energy and temperature.
8. What does it mean to say that the barometric reading in the room is 756 mm Hg?
9. What are the four variables discussed in this section that can be used to describe a gas quantitatively?

10. **Story Link**
    How high above the Earth will the helium balloon have to ascend before it reaches the ozone level in the stratosphere?
11. **Story Link**
    The density of helium at *STP* is 0.1875 g/L. If the balloon filled with helium at *STP* has a volume of 1.5×10^9 L, what mass of helium is in the balloon?

What behaviors are described by the gas laws?

Gas laws

You will now study a series of mathematical relationships that relate the four variables described in the last section to kinetic molecular theory. Each of the four variables is represented by a symbol.

P = pressure exerted by the particles
V = volume occupied by the particles
T = temperature in kelvins of the particles
n = number of moles of the particles

These symbols define the mathematical expressions known as the gas laws. Using the gas laws, you can make predictions about how the volume of a fixed amount of gas will respond to changes in pressure and temperature.

Charles's law provides a basis for absolute temperature

You already know that heating a gas will make it expand. The particles move faster when they are heated and push with more force against the walls of their container. When a balloon is inflated at room temperature, the walls expand until the pressures inside and outside the balloon are about equal. We can use the balloon shown in **Figure 10-16** to determine how much the volume of a fixed amount of gas changes for each degree that the temperature changes.

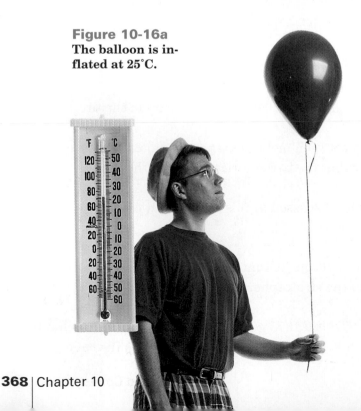

Figure 10-16a
The balloon is inflated at 25°C.

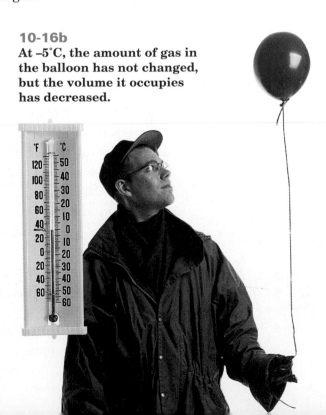

10-16b
At –5°C, the amount of gas in the balloon has not changed, but the volume it occupies has decreased.

Table 10-3
Volume–Temperature Data for a Gas at Constant Pressure

Temperature (°C)	Volume (mL)
273	1094
100	747
10	568
1	545
0	545
−1	546
−73	403
−173	199
−223	100

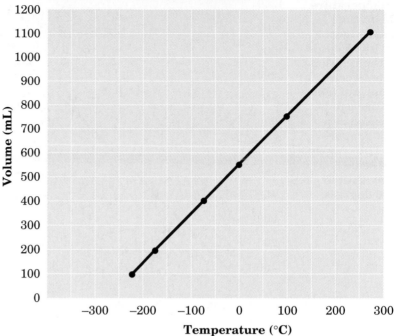

Volume vs. Temperature for a Fixed Amount of Gas at Constant Pressure

Figure 10-17
The graph of the data from Table 10-3 shows volume increases with temperature.

Table 10-3 shows some data for an experiment in which a fixed amount of gas in an expandable container is warmed and cooled. The volume of the gas changes in response to the changes in temperature. The pressure exerted by the gas is kept constant at 101.3 kPa so that you can study the effects of temperature on volume.

The data indicate that as temperature decreases, the volume of the gas decreases. When the temperature drops from 0°C to −223°C, the volume drops from 545 mL to 100 mL. And, as temperature increases, the volume of the gas increases. A graph of the data in **Table 10-3** is shown in **Figure 10-17**. Notice that while the points are such that you can draw a best-fit line for the data, the relationship is not a direct proportion because the best-fit line does not pass through the origin. If you extend the line so that it intercepts the *x*-axis, the temperature at that point is −273°C. A direct proportion would mean that volume varies directly as temperature if there is some constant *k* such that

$$V = kT$$

If you examine the data in **Table 10-3**, you see that you cannot find a consistent value for *k* such that the equation holds true for every set of data points. If we change the temperature scale such that the *x*-intercept at −273 now becomes zero, the data can be replotted to produce a graph that represents a direct proportion. **Figure 10-18** on the next page shows that graph with the *x*-axis relabeled. The temperature scale has been shifted such that −273°C is now equal to 0; the graph now represents a direct proportion. The new temperature scale differs from the Celsius scale by a constant of 273 and is called the **absolute temperature scale**. Remember that the actual difference between the absolute and Celsius scales is 273.16.

absolute temperature scale
a temperature measurement made relative to absolute zero—the lowest possible temperature

Figure 10-18
By changing the temperature scale on the graph so that the *x* intercept is at 0, the relationship between volume and temperature can be expressed as a direct proportion. The temperature scale is merely shifted 273.16 degrees.

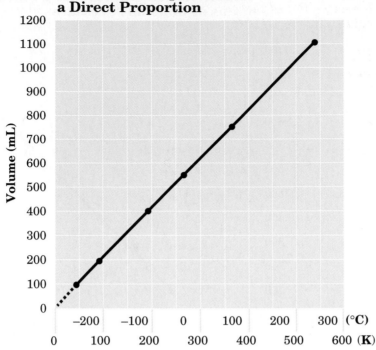

Volume vs. Temperature as a Direct Proportion

Table 10-4
Volume–Temperature Data for a Gas at a Constant Pressure

Volume (mL)	Temperature (˚C)	Temperature (K)	*V/T*
1094	273	546	2.00
748	100	373	2.01
568	10	283	2.01
545	1	274	1.99
545	0	273	2.00
546	−1	272	2.01
403	−73	200	2.02
199	−173	100	1.99
100	−223	50	2.00

Absolute zero in kelvins is the lowest possible temperature. Why? Theoretically, any temperature lower than 0 K (−273.16°C) would represent a negative volume. In **Table 10-4** the original data has been changed to reflect the new temperature scale and the mathematical relationship for a direct proportion, which is expressed mathematically as follows.

$$\frac{\text{volume } (V)}{\text{temperature } (T)} = \text{constant } (k)$$

$$\frac{V}{T} = k$$

If volume divided by temperature is a constant, we can equate this ratio for gases under two different sets of conditions. The initial set of conditions is labeled V_1 and T_1, and another set of conditions is labeled V_2 and T_2.

$$\frac{V_1}{T_1} = k \text{ and } \frac{V_2}{T_2} = k$$

The initial and final conditions can be set equal to each other.

$$\frac{V_1}{T_1} = \frac{V_2}{T_2}, \text{ where } P \text{ is constant}$$

Charles's law
the volume of a gas at constant pressure is directly proportional to the absolute temperature

This relationship is often called **Charles's law**, though it is the work of the French chemists Jacques Charles and Joseph Gay-Lussac that resulted from their interest in ballooning.

Sample Problem 10A
Solving volume–temperature problems

A sample of gas occupies 24 m³ at 100. K. What volume would the gas occupy at 400. K?

❶ List
- $V_1 = 24 \text{ m}^3$
- $T_1 = 100. \text{ K}$
- $T_2 = 400. \text{ K}$
- $V_2 = \textbf{?}$
- Temperature increases, which means the volume should increase also.

❷ Set up
- Use Charles's law and solve for V_2.

$$\frac{V_1}{T_1} = \frac{V_2}{T_2} \text{ therefore, } \frac{24 \text{ m}^3}{100. \text{ K}} = \frac{V_2}{400. \text{ K}}$$

❸ Estimate and calculate

$$V_2 = 24 \text{ m}^3 \times \frac{400. \text{ K}}{100. \text{ K}}$$

- Note that the ratio of temperatures is greater than 1, which means the final volume will be greater, as predicted.

$$V_2 = 96 \text{ m}^3$$

Practice 10A

Answers for Concept Review items and Practice problems begin on page 841.

1. Gas in a balloon occupies 2.5 L at 300. K (about room temperature). At what temperature will the balloon expand to 7.5 L?

2. The balloon from item 1 is dipped into liquid nitrogen that is at a temperature of 80. K. What volume will the gas in the balloon occupy at this temperature?

Figure 10-19
To study the effects of pressure on volume, a fixed amount of gas can be placed in a syringe. Increasing the pressure on the syringe compresses the gas to the point where its internal pressure equals the external pressure.

Boyle's law describes a pressure-volume relationship

We can use a syringe to study the effect of pressure on the volume of a gas. A fixed amount of gas is trapped in the syringe. If you push on the plunger, as in **Figure 10-19**, you are compressing the trapped gas particles into a smaller space. In the smaller space, the particles collide with the walls more often, and more collisions result in a higher pressure.

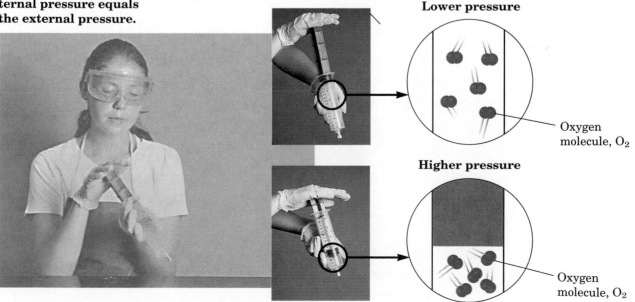

Lower pressure

Oxygen molecule, O_2

Higher pressure

Oxygen molecule, O_2

Table 10-5
Pressure–Volume Data

Pressure (kPa)	Volume (mL)	PV
100	500	50 000
150	333	49 950
200	250	50 000
250	200	50 000
300	166	49 800
350	143	50 500
400	125	50 000
450	110	49 500

Boyle's law
the volume of a gas at constant temperature is inversely proportional to the pressure

If you push with a fixed pressure, the volume inside will decrease until the pressure inside the syringe equals the total pressure (applied and atmospheric) outside it. When the pressures are equal, the plunger won't move any farther. You can measure the volume changes as you increase the pressure on the gas. To note how these two conditions affect each other, you need to keep the temperature of the system constant.

Table 10-5 shows pressure-volume data for an experiment of this type working with a larger volume of gas. Looking at these data, you see that an increase in pressure results in a decrease in volume. You should also notice that the product of each pair of pressure and volume measurements stays essentially constant, within the precision of the data.

Because the product of pressure times volume is a constant, it means that PV under one set of conditions equals PV for another set of conditions as long as the temperature and the amount of gas remain constant. This relationship was identified by Robert Boyle and is known as **Boyle's law**. Boyle's law is represented by the following equation.

$$PV = k$$

Graphing the data in **Figure 10-20** gives a hyperbola, which is representative of an inverse proportion. As one variable increases, the other decreases proportionately. A treatment similar to Charles' law is:

$$P_1V_1 = P_2V_2, \text{ where } T \text{ is constant.}$$

Figure 10-21 on the next page shows a graph of the same data with pressure on the x-axis and the reciprocal of volume ($1/V$) on the y-axis. Note that we now have a straight-line graph passing through the origin, which means that P and $1/V$ are directly proportional.

Figure 10-20
The pressure versus volume graph represents an inverse relationship—as pressure increases, volume decreases.

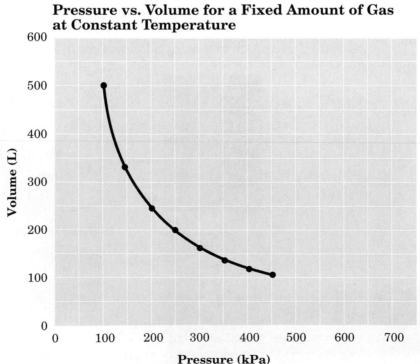

Pressure vs. Volume for a Fixed Amount of Gas at Constant Temperature

Figure 10-21
When pressure data is graphed with the reciprocal of volume (1/V), the graph shows that pressure and the reciprocal of volume are directly proportional.

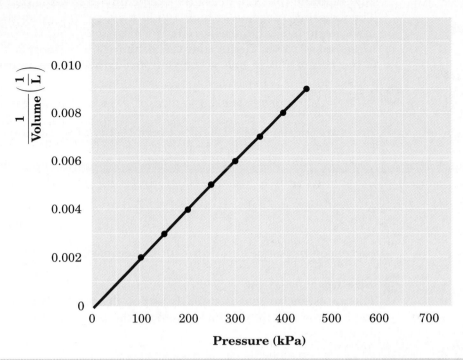

Pressure vs. the Reciprocal of Volume

y-axis: $\dfrac{1}{\text{Volume}}\left(\dfrac{1}{L}\right)$

x-axis: Pressure (kPa)

Sample Problem 10B
Solving pressure–volume problems

The gas in a balloon has a volume of 4 L at 100 kPa. The balloon is released into the atmosphere, and the gas in it expands to a volume of 8 L. What is the pressure on the balloon at the new volume?

❶ List
- $V_1 = 4$ L
- The volume expands, and V_2 is 8 L.
- $P_1 = 100$ kPa
- $P_2 = \;?$
- Because the gas expands, the pressure decreases.

❷ Set up
- Use Boyle's law to determine P_2.

$$P_1V_1 = P_2V_2, \text{ and } P_2 = \frac{P_1V_1}{V_2}$$

- Multiply pressure by the ratio of volumes that will give a pressure decrease.

$$P_2 = 100 \text{ kPa} \times \frac{4\ \cancel{L}}{8\ \cancel{L}}$$

❸ Estimate and calculate
- The volume ratio is 1:2, so we would expect the final pressure to be half the original pressure.

$P_2 = 50$ kPa, which is consistent with the estimate.

Practice 10B

1. The gas in a 10.0 L container exerts a pressure of 100. kPa. What pressure is needed to compress the gas to 2.0 L while keeping the temperature constant?

2. If the pressure of a 2.5 m³ sample of a gas is 1.5 atm, what volume will the gas occupy if the pressure is changed to 7.5 atm?

Sample Problem 10C
Boyle's law for divers

Divers know that the pressure exerted by the water increases with depth. The pressure increases about 100 kPa every 10.2 m, so that at 10.2 m below the surface, the pressure is 201 kPa; at 20.4 m, the pressure is 301 kPa, and so forth. Given that the volume of a balloon is 4.0 L at *STP*, what is the volume 50. m below the water's surface at the same temperature?

① List
- P_1 = 101.3 kPa
- Pressure increases by 100 kPa every 10.2 m of water depth.
- V_1 = 4.0 L
- *T* is constant
- distance = 50. m
- P_2 = ?
- V_2 = ?
- Increased pressure should result in decreased volume.

② Set up
- The pressure increases steadily as you descend. If the pressure increases 100 kPa for 10.2 m, you can calculate the pressure increase per meter of depth.

$$\frac{100 \text{ kPa}}{10.2 \text{ m}} = 9.8 \text{ kPa/m, which is rounded to } 10 \text{ kPa/m}$$

- At 50. m, the total pressure, P_2, is equal to the pressure at the surface, which is 101.3 kPa, plus the pressure from the increase in depth for 50 m.

$$P_2 = 101.3 \text{ kPa} + (50. \text{ m} \times 10 \frac{\text{kPa}}{\text{m}}) = 600 \text{ kPa}$$

- Use Boyle's law to determine V_2.

$$(101.3 \text{ kPa})(4.0 \text{ L}) = (600 \text{ kPa})(V_2)$$

$$V_2 = 4.0 \text{ L} \times \frac{101.3 \text{ kPa}}{600 \text{ kPa}}$$

③ Estimate and verify
- V_2 should decrease as predicted because the pressure ratio is less than 1.

$$4.0 \text{ L} \times \frac{101.3 \text{ kPa}}{600 \text{ kPa}} = 0.67532 \text{ L, calculator answer}$$

$$V_2 = 0.70 \text{ L, rounded answer}$$

Practice 10C

1. A 2.0 L balloon at a pressure of 1.0 atm on Earth's surface ascends 10 km into the atmosphere, where the pressure is 0.27 atm. What is the volume of the balloon at that altitude (assuming the temperature stays the same)?

2. What happens to the volume of a 4 L balloon inside a sinking boat that descends to the bottom of a lake 10.0 m below the surface?

3. A flask containing 155 cm^3 of hydrogen was collected at a pressure of 22.5 kPa. Under what pressure would the gas have a volume of 90.0 cm^3 at constant temperature?

4. If the pressure exerted on a 300. mL sample of hydrogen gas at constant temperature is increased from 0.500 atm to 0.750 atm, what will be the final volume of the sample?

5. A helium balloon has a volume of 5.0 L at a pressure of 1.0 atm. The balloon is released and reaches an altitude of 6.5 km at a pressure of 0.50 atm. If the gas temperature remains the same, what is the volume of the balloon?

Dalton's law applies to mixtures of gases

If you put 1 mol of oxygen and 1 mol of nitrogen into a flask, the total pressure in the flask is the sum of the pressures exerted by each gas. Each gas exerts pressure just as if the other one were not present, as shown by the model in **Figure 10-22**. Though this idea might seem odd, it makes sense when you think of the gas mixture as the total number of particles. A mole of each gas will have 6.022×10^{23} particles. If you put both gases in one container, there are twice the number of particles. The 2 mol (total) of gas exert twice as much pressure as either one did alone, assuming a fixed volume and temperature. Therefore, in a mixture of gases, the total pressure is the sum of the partial pressures, which describes a relationship known as **Dalton's law of partial pressures**. **Partial pressures** are the pressures due to each gas in the mixture. For a mixture of gases labeled *a*, *b*, and *c*, the partial pressure equation would be written as follows.

$$P_{total} = P_a + P_b + P_c$$

Dalton's law of partial pressures
the total pressure in a gas mixture is the sum of the partial pressures of the individual components

partial pressures
the pressure of an individual gas in a gas mixture that contributes to the total pressure of the mixture

Figure 10-22
If samples of oxygen and nitrogen gas in separate containers are mixed, the pressure exerted by the gas mixture is the sum of the pressures exerted by each gas individually. At the same temperature the energy of both gases is the same. Therefore, they exert the same pressure.

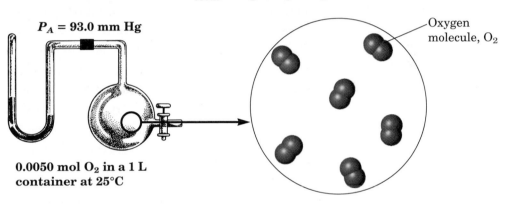

$P_A = 93.0$ mm Hg

0.0050 mol O_2 in a 1 L container at 25°C

Oxygen molecule, O_2

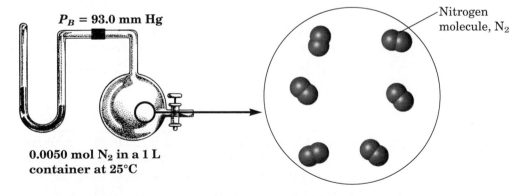

$P_B = 93.0$ mm Hg

0.0050 mol N_2 in a 1 L container at 25°C

Nitrogen molecule, N_2

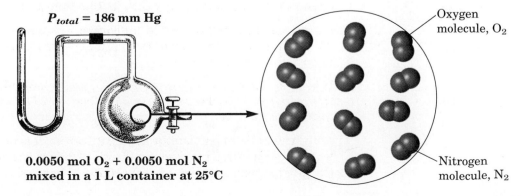

$P_{total} = 186$ mm Hg

0.0050 mol O_2 + 0.0050 mol N_2 mixed in a 1 L container at 25°C

Oxygen molecule, O_2

Nitrogen molecule, N_2

Figure 10-23
Hydrogen can be collected by water displacement by reacting zinc with sulfuric acid. The hydrogen gas produced displaces the water in the gas collecting bottle where it is mixed with water vapor.

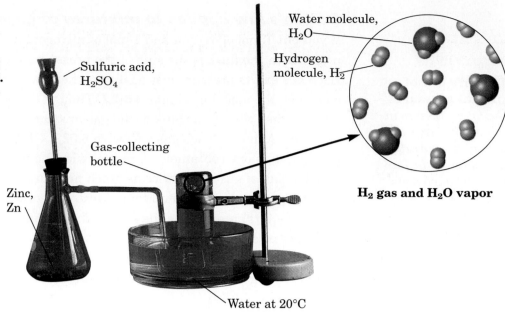

H₂ gas and H₂O vapor

Dalton's law is most often used to calculate the pressure of a gas collected over water. **Figure 10-23** shows such a setup for collecting hydrogen. The collection flask contains hydrogen gas and some water vapor that adds to the total pressure. Therefore, to find the pressure of the hydrogen alone, you need to subtract the pressure due to the water vapor, which can be found in **Table 10-6**. For example, the system above is at 20°C. The total pressure of the gases in the collecting bottle can be adjusted so that it is the same as the air pressure in the room. If the pressure reading for the room is 98.2 kPa, then the pressure exerted by the hydrogen gas is calculated as follows.

98.2 kPa	total pressure
− 2.3 kPa	pressure of H_2O at 20°C
95.9 kPa	pressure of H_2 at 20°C

Table 10-6
Vapor Pressure of Water at Various Temperatures

Temperature (°C)	Pressure H₂O (kPa)	Temperature (°C)	Pressure H₂O (kPa)
0	0.61	55	15.75
5	0.87	60	19.93
10	1.23	65	25.02
15	1.71	70	31.18
20	2.34	75	38.56
25	3.17	80	47.37
30	4.25	85	57.82
35	5.63	90	70.12
40	7.38	95	84.53
45	9.59	100	101.32
50	12.34	105	120.79

Sample Problem 10D
Dalton's law of partial pressure for gas collected over water

Hydrogen gas is collected over water at a total pressure of 95.0 kPa. The volume of hydrogen collected is 28 mL at 25°C. What is the partial pressure of hydrogen gas?

❶ List
- P_{total} = 95.0 kPa
- The flask contains both hydrogen and water vapor.
- From Table 10-6, $P_{water\ vapor}$ at 25°C is 3.17 kPa
- V = 28 mL

❷ Set up

$P_{total} = P_{hydrogen} + P_{water\ vapor}$

95.0 kPa = $P_{hydrogen}$ + 3.17 kPa

❸ Estimate and verify
- The partial pressure of hydrogen alone must be less than the total pressure.

$P_{hydrogen}$ = 91.8 kPa

Practice 10D

1. A gas is collected by water displacement at 50°C and a barometric pressure of 95.00 kPa. What is the pressure exerted by the dry gas?

2. Oxygen gas is collected by water displacement from the reaction of Na_2O_2 and water. The O_2 displaces 318 mL of water at 23°C and 1.0000 atm. What is the pressure of the dry O_2?

Mole fractions are used in determining partial pressures

The partial pressure of any gas in a mixture can be calculated using the **mole fraction** of that gas in the mixture. A mole fraction can be represented mathematically as follows.

mole fraction
the number of moles for an individual substance compared with the total number of moles in the mixture expressed as a ratio

$$\text{mole fraction of gas A} = \frac{\text{moles of gas A}}{\text{total number of moles of gas}}$$

For example, if gas A contributes one-fifth of the total number of particles, we say that the mole fraction of gas A is 0.2. The partial pressure of gas A is one-fifth, or 0.2, times the total pressure.

The tissues and cells in your lungs cannot absorb oxygen efficiently unless this gas exerts a pressure above 14 kPa. At sea level, the pressure due to oxygen in the atmosphere is typically about 20 kPa. At high altitudes oxygen is still about 20% of the total number of moles, so the mole fraction of O_2 at any altitude is about the same. What changes at high altitudes is the partial pressure of O_2. The partial pressure of oxygen at high altitudes is lower than at sea level. The partial pressure of O_2 is 0.2 times the total pressure. If the partial pressure falls well below 14 kPa, oxygen is not absorbed as efficiently. This is why novice climbers often experience "altitude sickness" from insufficient oxygen. Lightheadedness and shortness of breath are two common symptoms of this illness. People who live at high altitudes become acclimated by producing more red blood cells to carry oxygen. Pilots in fighter jets, which are not pressurized as much as passenger jets, must breathe supplemental oxygen to ensure that the partial pressure of oxygen is about 20 kPa.

Gases diffuse to fill their containers

We notice the expansion of some gases through our sense of smell. When you open a bottle of household ammonia, it doesn't take long for the odor of ammonia gas, NH_3, to fill the room. If you spill a little paint thinner or take hot cookies out of the oven, within a moment or two the odor is recognizable throughout the room. Gaseous molecules of the compounds responsible for the smell are traveling at high speeds in all directions and are mixing quickly with the air in a process called **diffusion**. Mixtures of gases do not separate but stay uniformly mixed, as shown by the models in **Figure 10-24**. The most familiar example of a gaseous mixture is air. All the particles in the mixture are in motion. Experiments show that light molecules move faster than heavy ones. However, because they move randomly, gases stay mixed even if they have different molecular masses. Otherwise, the atmosphere would be in layers: carbon dioxide, oxygen, nitrogen, argon, water vapor, and helium.

The diffusion model explains how odors travel across a room. The rapidly moving particles are constantly colliding with other particles, which causes their movement to be an erratic zigzag kind of pattern, as you saw in the particle model in **Figure 10-6** on page 360.

diffusion

the process by which particles disperse from regions of higher concentration to regions of lower concentration

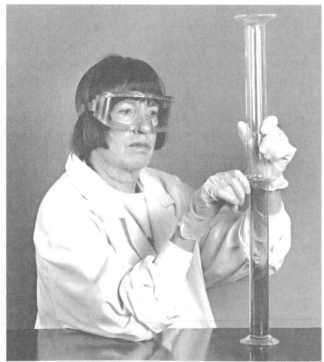

Figure 10-24
Bromine vapor diffuses up the glass cylinder until it hits the partition. The volume above the partition is filled with air. However, once the partition is removed, the vapor continues to move up the tube. Its particles collide with those in air until it uniformly fills the space.

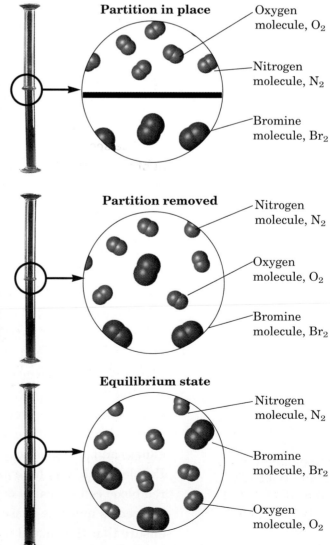

Partition in place
Oxygen molecule, O_2
Nitrogen molecule, N_2
Bromine molecule, Br_2

Partition removed
Nitrogen molecule, N_2
Oxygen molecule, O_2
Bromine molecule, Br_2

Equilibrium state
Nitrogen molecule, N_2
Bromine molecule, Br_2
Oxygen molecule, O_2

Figure 10-25
At the same temperature hydrogen molecules travel faster than nitrogen molecules because they are lighter. As a result, if a hole is made in the barrier, more hydrogen molecules will pass through the hole in a given time than will nitrogen molecules. Hydrogen molecules effuse at a faster rate (particles per second) than nitrogen molecules.

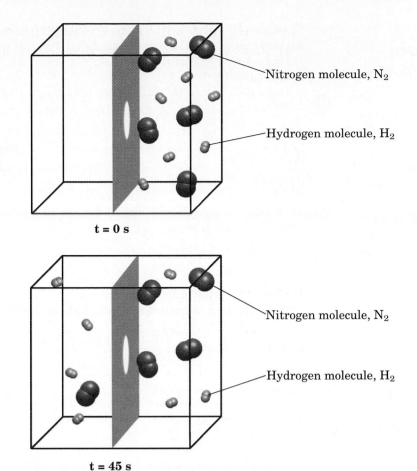

Nitrogen molecule, N_2

Hydrogen molecule, H_2

t = 0 s

Nitrogen molecule, N_2

Hydrogen molecule, H_2

t = 45 s

Graham's law applies to the rate at which gases diffuse and effuse

If we compared the rates at which different gases diffuse, we would find that the speed is related to the molecular mass of the gas. Gases with light particles diffuse quickly. So we would predict that at the same temperature, helium (4.00 g/mol) would diffuse faster than krypton (83.80 g/mol).

The same relationship also applies to the phenomenon called **effusion**, which is shown by the model in **Figure 10-25**. Once a gas particle finds a hole in the apparatus, it escapes. The relative rates at which two gases labeled A and B effuse from the same container under identical conditions of temperature and total pressure depend only on their relative masses. In Section 10-1, you learned that heavy molecules and light molecules have the same average kinetic energy at the same temperature. If kinetic energy is represented by $1/2\ mv^2$, then we can equate the kinetic energy of gas A and gas B by the following relationship.

$$\frac{1}{2}m_A v_A{}^2 = \frac{1}{2}m_B v_B{}^2$$

Rearranging this equation gives a mathematical relationship referred to as **Graham's law of effusion**.

$$\frac{v_A}{v_B} = \sqrt{\frac{m_B}{m_A}}$$

effusion
the motion of a gas through an opening into an evacuated chamber

Graham's law of effusion
the rates of effusion for two gases are inversely proportional to the square roots of their molar masses at the same temperature and pressure

Sample Problem 10E
Comparing molecular speeds

An oxygen molecule travels at about 480 m/s at room temperature. How fast would a molecule of sulfur trioxide, SO_3, travel at the same temperature?

❶ List
- $m_{O_2} = 32.00$ g/mol
- $m_{SO_3} = 80.07$ g/mol
- $v_{O_2} = 480$ m/s
- $v_{SO_3} = ?$

❷ Set up
- Use Graham's law.

$$\frac{v_{SO_3}}{480 \text{ m/s}} = \sqrt{\frac{32.00 \text{ g/mol}}{80.07 \text{ g/mol}}}$$

❸ Estimate and calculate
- SO_3 is heavier, so its velocity should be slower than that of oxygen.

$$v_{SO_3} = 480 \text{ m/s} \sqrt{\frac{32.00 \text{ g/mol}}{80.07 \text{ g/mol}}} = 3.0 \times 10^2 \text{ m/s}$$

Sample Problem 10F
Determining molecular masses

An unknown gas effuses through an opening at a rate 3.53 times slower than nitrogen gas. What is the molecular mass of the unknown gas?

❶ List
- N_2 moves 3.53 times faster than the unknown gas.
- If v represents the velocity of the unknown gas speed, then the velocity of $N_2 = 3.53v$
- $m_{N_2} = 28.02$ g/mol
- mass of the unknown, $m_x = ?$

❷ Set up
- Use the equation for Graham's law.

$$\frac{v_{N_2}}{v_x} = \sqrt{\frac{m_x}{m_{N_2}}} \qquad \frac{3.53v}{v} = \sqrt{\frac{m_x}{28.02 \text{ g/mol}}}$$

- Square both sides of the equation to simplify the expression.

$$\frac{(3.53v)^2}{v^2} = \frac{m_x}{28.02 \text{ g/mol}} \qquad 3.53^2 = \frac{m_x}{28.02 \text{ g/mol}}$$

$$m_x = (28.02 \text{ g/mol})(3.53^2)$$

❸ Estimate and calculate
- The molecular mass of the unknown gas is greater than that of N_2 because its velocity is less than that of nitrogen.

$$m_x = (28.02 \text{ g/mol})(3.53^2) = 3.49 \times 10^2 \text{ g/mol}$$

Practice 10F

1. Given that neon gas travels at 400 m/s at a given temperature, calculate the rate of diffusion for butane, C_4H_{10}, at the same temperature.

2. Hydrogen sulfide, H_2S, has a very strong rotten egg odor. H_2S particles travel at about 450 m/s. Methyl salicylate, $C_8H_8O_3$, has a wintergreen odor. Benzaldehyde, C_7H_6O, has an almond odor. If vapors for these three substances were released at the same time from across a room, which would you smell first, and why?

12. A container contains 20.0 g of oxygen at 40.0 kPa. Twenty grams of neon are added to the container.
    a. Calculate the mole fraction of each gas.
    b. Calculate the partial pressure of neon and the total pressure of the gas mixture.
    c. Explain why the pressure exerted by oxygen does not change when neon is added to the container.

13. A certain mass of gas occupies 2.0 L at 60 kPa. What pressure allows the gas to expand to 6.0 L?

14. A 3.5 L sample of a gas has a temperature of 227°C and a pressure of 160 kPa.
    a. What is the new volume if the gas is held at the same pressure but cooled to 27°C?
    b. What is the new pressure if the gas is held at the same volume but heated to 500°C?
    c. What is the new volume if the gas is adjusted to *STP*?

15. What temperature will increase the pressure of a gas in a 450 mL container from 60 kPa at 300 K to 320 kPa?

16. A gas occupies 4.7 m^3 at 250 Pa.
    a. What is the gas volume at 4800 Pa?
    b. What is the gas volume in liters at 1.0 atm?

17. Think about what happens to a gas bubble that enters the bloodstream of a diver at 50 m below the surface. What happens to the volume of the bubble as the diver ascends to the surface and the pressure is reduced?

18. Using the ideas of the kinetic molecular theory, which of the following gases is best for filling automobile tires: CO_2, air, or He? Explain your answer.

19. Why do your ears sometimes pop when you drive down a steep incline or descend in an airplane?

20. Inexpensive balloons filled with air deflate within a few days because the pores in the walls of the balloons are larger than most of the molecules that are found in air. Explain why helium-filled balloons collapse more quickly than those filled with air.

21. **Story Link**
    At 40 km above the Earth, the pressure is about 2.87×10^2 Pa. A helium balloon launched from Earth's surface, at 1.000 atm of pressure, has a volume of 30.0 m^3. What would be the volume of the balloon at 40 km? You can assume that the temperature of the He stays constant.

22. **Story Link**
    Half of the gas in a 20.0 L tank of helium at 35°C and 1050 kPa is released into a weather balloon while keeping the temperature constant and the balloon pressure at 100. kPa. What is the volume of the weather balloon?

How do the gas laws fit together?

Combining the gas laws

You have thus far studied a series of relationships that can be used to predict the behavior of a gas under changing conditions. Each relationship includes at least one of the four variables we use to measure changes in a gas—pressure, P; volume, V; temperature, T; and number of moles, n. Mathematically, it should be possible to combine all the gas laws you studied in the last section to build an equation in which pressure, volume, temperature, and the number of moles can vary.

The ideal gas law relates all four gas variables

The connection among P, V, n, and T exists in the mathematical combination of Boyle's law, Charles's law, and Avogadro's law. This gas law, called the **ideal gas law,** is most often used when the amount of the gas may change. It is represented mathematically by the following equation.

$$PV = nRT$$

R is a proportionality constant. The value you use for R in calculations depends on the units given for pressure and volume in a problem. Because we use kilopascals and liters most of the time in this text, the value of R that you will use most often is the following.

$$R = \frac{8.314 \text{ L} \cdot \text{kPa}}{\text{mol} \cdot \text{K}}$$

R can also be expressed as

$$R = \frac{0.0821 \text{ L} \cdot \text{atm}}{\text{mol} \cdot \text{K}}$$

ideal gas law
the equation of state for an ideal gas in which the product of the pressure and volume is proportional to the product of the absolute temperature and the amount of gas expressed in moles

Sample Problem 10G
Ideal gas law

A sample of carbon dioxide with a mass of 0.250 g was placed in a 350 mL container at 400. K. What is the pressure exerted by the gas?

❶ **List**
• There is no change of conditions for the gas, so this is a straightforward "equation of state" problem.

• $P = $ **?**

• $V = 350$ mL

• $T = 400.$ K

• $n = $ to be calculated from 0.250 g, and the formula mass, 44.01 g/mol, of CO_2

• $R = 8.314$ L·kPa/mol·K

Sample Problem 10G continued on page 383

❷ Set up

- **The mass in grams must be converted into an amount in moles.**

$$\text{mol } CO_2 = \frac{0.250 \text{ g } CO_2}{44.01 \text{ g/mol } CO_2} = 5.68 \times 10^{-3} \text{ mol } CO_2$$

- **The volume unit must be compatible with the value of R used, therefore the volume must be converted from milliliters to liters.**

1 mL = 0.001 L

350 mL = 0.35 L

- **Use the ideal gas law equation.**

$$PV = nRT$$

- **Substitute the values given in the problem into the equation.**

$(P)(0.35 \text{ L}) = (5.68 \times 10^{-3} \text{ mol})(8.314 \text{ L·kPa/mol·K})(400. \text{ K})$

❸ Calculate

- **Solve for pressure by dividing each side of the equation by the volume to simplify the equation.**

$$P = \frac{(5.68 \times 10^{-3} \text{ mol})(8.314 \text{ L·kPa/mol·K})(400. \text{ K})}{(0.35 \text{ L})}$$

$P = 54 \text{ kPa}$

Practice 10G

1. A 500 g block of dry ice (solid CO_2) vaporizes to a gas at room temperature. Calculate the volume of gas produced at 25°C and 975 kPa.

2. Calculate the volume of 1 mol of CO_2 at *STP*.

3. Average lung capacity for humans is about 4.0 L. At 37°C (body temperature) and 110 kPa, how many moles of oxygen gas could your lungs hold?

4. If 40 g of methane, CH_4, is confined to 2500 mL at 200°C, what pressure does it exert?

5. At what temperature will 7.0 mol of helium gas exert a pressure of 1.2 atm in a 25.0 m³ tank?

The general gas law is derived from the ideal gas law

The ratio of PV/nT equals the ideal gas constant R. Thus, for the same gas under two sets of conditions it is possible to write the following expressions.

$$R = \frac{P_1V_1}{n_1T_1} \text{ and } R = \frac{P_2V_2}{n_2T_2}$$

Because both equations equal R, then both expressions can be set equal to each other. And if the amount of gas, n, does not change, n can be cancelled from both equations, and the expression is simplified to get the following.

$$\frac{P_1V_1}{T_1} = \frac{P_2V_2}{T_2}$$

This relationship is often referred to as the *general gas law* or *combined gas law*. It is often used in calculations for determining the volume of a gas at *STP*.

Sample Problem 10H
Using the combined gas law

A helium balloon with a volume of 410. mL is cooled from 27°C to –27°C. The pressure on the gas is reduced from 110. kPa to 25. kPa. What is the volume of the gas at the lower temperature and pressure?

❶ List
- P_1 = 110. kPa P_2 = 25. kPa
- V_1 = 410. mL V_2 = **?**
- T_1 = 27°C = 300 K T_2 = –27°C = 246 K

- The temperature decreases, so the volume should decrease; at the same time, the pressure decreases, so the gas expands. The effects are opposites but do not necessarily cancel each other completely.

❷ Set up
- Because the amount of gas does not change, use the combined gas law equation.

$$\frac{P_1 V_1}{T_1} = \frac{P_2 V_2}{T_2}$$

$$\frac{(110.\ kPa)(410.\ mL)}{(300\ K)} = \frac{(25.\ kPa)(V_2)}{(246\ K)}$$

❸ Estimate and verify
- The pressure ratio is larger than the temperature ratio, so the pressure reduction will have a greater effect on the volume than the increase in temperature. The new volume should be larger than 400 mL.

$$V_2 = 410.\ mL \times \frac{246\ K}{300\ K} \times \frac{110.\ kPa}{25.\ kPa}$$

$$V_2 = 1.5 \times 10^3\ mL$$

Practice 10H

1. A gas occupies 2.0 m^3 at 100. K, exerting a pressure of 100. kPa. What volume would the gas occupy at 400. K if the pressure is increased to 200. kPa?

2. An 8.00 L sample of neon gas at 25°C exerts a pressure of 900 kPa. If the gas is compressed to 2.00 L and the temperature is raised to 225.°C, what will the new pressure be?

3. A sample of methane that initially occupies 850. mL at 500. Pa and 500. K is compressed to a volume of 700. mL. To what temperature will the gas need to be cooled to lower the pressure of the gas to 200. Pa?

4. A sample of carbon dioxide occupies 45 m^3 at 750 K and 500 kPa. What is the volume of this gas at *STP*?

Gas stoichiometry
Gas volumes can be determined from mole ratios in balanced equations

Avogadro's work showed us that the mole ratio of two gases at the same temperature and pressure is the same as the volume ratio. This relationship greatly simplifies the calculation of the volume of product or reactant in a chemical reaction involving gaseous reactants and products. For example, how many moles of hydrogen would react with 4 mol of nitrogen according to the following equation?

$$3H_2(g) + N_2(g) \longrightarrow 2NH_3(g)$$

The mole ratio of hydrogen to nitrogen from the chemical reaction is 3 to 1, so the proportion is 3 mol H_2 to 1 mol N_2.

$$\frac{3 \text{ mol } H_2}{1 \text{ mol } N_2} = \frac{x \text{ mol } H_2}{4 \text{ mol } N_2} \qquad x = 12 \text{ mol } H_2$$

This ratio is also equivalent to the volume ratio. If the question had been, What volume of hydrogen would react with 4 liters of nitrogen? the approach would be the same. Because temperature and pressure are not specified, it is assumed that they are constant and that the mole ratio will be the same as the volume ratio.

$$\frac{3 \text{ mol } H_2}{1 \text{ mol } N_2} = \frac{x \text{ L } H_2}{4 \text{ L } N_2} \qquad x = 12 \text{ L } H_2$$

Sample Problem 10I
The ideal gas equation and stoichiometry

How many liters of hydrogen gas will be produced at 280. K and 96.0 kPa if 40.0 g of sodium react with excess hydrochloric acid according to the following equation?

$$2Na(s) + 2HCl(aq) \longrightarrow 2NaCl(aq) + H_2(g)$$

❶ List
- $V = ?$
- $P = 96.0$ kPa
- $n =$ to be calculated from mole ratio by converting 40.0 g Na to moles
- **molar mass of Na** = 22.99 g/mol
- $R = 8.314$ L·kPa/mol·K
- $T = 280.$ K

❷ Set up
- First, use the mole ratio in the chemical equation to determine the number of moles of hydrogen that can be produced. Second, use the ideal gas law to calculate the volume of the hydrogen under the temperature and pressure conditions given. The mole ratio between sodium and hydrogen is 2 to 1.

$$\frac{40.0 \text{ g Na}}{22.99 \text{ g/mol}} = 1.74 \text{ mol Na}$$

$$1.74 \text{ mol Na} \times \frac{1 \text{ mol } H_2}{2 \text{ mol Na}} = 0.870 \text{ mol } H_2$$

- Then use the ideal gas equation.

$$(96.0 \text{ kPa})(V) = (0.870 \text{ mol } H_2)(8.314 \text{ L·kPa/mol·K})(280. \text{ K})$$

❸ Estimate and verify

$$V = \frac{(0.870 \text{ mol } H_2)(8.314 \text{ L·kPa/mol·K})(280. \text{ K})}{(96.0 \text{ kPa})}$$

$$V = 21.1 \text{ L of } H_2$$

- The answer of about 20 L is reasonable because it is close to the volume of 1 mol at *STP*.

Magnesium metal will "burn" in carbon dioxide to produce elemental carbon and magnesium oxide.

$$2Mg(s) + CO_2(g) \longrightarrow 2MgO(s) + C(s)$$

What mass of magnesium will react with a 250 mL container of carbon dioxide gas at 77°C and 65 kPa?

❶ List
- P = 65 kPa
- V = 250 mL = 0.25 L
- $n = ?$
- R = 8.314 L·kPa/mol·K
- t = 77°C, therefore, T = 350 K
- molar mass of Mg = 24.30 g/mol

❷ Set up
- Like Sample Problem 10I, this is a two-part problem. Start by determining the amount of CO_2 in the container using the ideal gas equation. Then you must use the mole ratio and formula mass of magnesium to calculate the mass of magnesium needed. The amount of CO_2 is calculated from the ideal gas equation.

$$PV = nRT$$

$$(65 \text{ kPa})(0.25 \text{ L}) = (n)(8.314 \text{ L·kPa/mol·K})(350 \text{ K})$$

$$n = \frac{(65 \text{ kPa})(0.25 \text{ L})}{(8.314 \text{ L·kPa/mol·K})(350 \text{ K})}$$

$$n = 5.6 \times 10^{-3} \text{ mol CO}_2$$

❸ Estimate and verify

$$5.6 \times 10^{-3} \text{ mol CO}_2 \times \frac{2 \text{ mol Mg}}{1 \text{ mol CO}_2} \times \frac{24.30 \text{ g Mg}}{1 \text{ mol Mg}} = 0.27 \text{ g Mg}$$

Practice 10I

1. The formation of hydrogen chloride occurs in the following reaction.
$$H_2(g) + Cl_2(g) \longrightarrow 2HCl(g)$$

   If 3.0 L of H_2 are used, how many liters of HCl can be produced? What do you have to assume to answer this question?

2. Ammonia and oxygen react to form nitrogen monoxide and water, as shown by the following equation.
$$4NH_3(g) + 5O_2(g) \longrightarrow 4NO(g) + 6H_2O(l)$$

   Assume that the temperature and pressure stay constant at 350. K and 100. kPa.
   a. What volume of O_2 is needed to burn 15 L of ammonia?
   b. How many moles of H_2O are produced when 3.50 mol of NH_3 burn?
   c. How many grams of H_2O are produced when 15 L of NH_3 burn?

10J

3. Solid LiOH has been used in spacecraft to remove exhaled CO_2 from the environment as shown by the following equation.
$$2LiOH(s) + CO_2(g) \longrightarrow Li_2CO_3(s) + H_2O(l)$$

   How many grams of LiOH must be used to absorb the carbon dioxide that exerts a partial pressure of 5.0 kPa at 15°C in a space laboratory that is 4.0 m × 2.5 m × 8.0 m?

23. A sample of carbon dioxide has a mass of 35.0 g and occupies 2.5 L at 400 K. What pressure does the gas exert?

24. What volume is occupied by 0.45 g of nitrogen measured at 100 kPa and 25°C?

25. A sample of nitrogen gas exerts 2.5 atm at 250 K.
    a. What is the density of the gas, expressed in g/L?
    b. What is the density of the gas, in g/L, if the pressure is increased to 5.0 atm?

26. How many moles of sulfur dioxide, SO_2, are contained in a 4.0 L container at 450 K and 5 kPa?

27. During a chemical reaction, nitrogen gas was collected by displacement of water at 17°C. The gas displaced 75.0 mL of water, and the atmospheric pressure was 97.25 kPa.
    a. What was the pressure of the nitrogen alone?
    b. How many moles of nitrogen were collected?
    c. What mass of nitrogen was collected?

28. A 10.0 L tank of helium gas is filled to a pressure of 400 psi. Assuming no loss of gas, how many balloons, each containing 4.0 L of helium at 100 kPa, could you fill?

29. Solid iron(III) hydroxide decomposes to produce iron(III) oxide and water vapor. If 0.75 L of water vapor are produced at 227°C and 1.0 atm,
    a. how many grams of iron(III) hydroxide were used?
    b. how many grams of iron(III) oxide are produced?

30. Assume that 13.5 g of Al(s) react with HCl(aq) according to the following balanced equation at *STP*.

$$2Al(s) + 6HCl(aq) \longrightarrow 2AlCl_3(aq) + 3H_2(g)$$

    a. How many moles of Al react?
    b. How many moles of H_2 are produced?
    c. How many liters of H_2 are produced at *STP*?

31. Air is 20.9% oxygen by volume.
    a. How many liters of air are needed to complete the combustion of 25.0 L of octane vapor, $C_8H_{18}(g)$?
    b. What volume of each product is produced?

32. Methanol, CH_3OH, is made by causing carbon monoxide and hydrogen gases to react at high temperature and pressure. If 450. mL of CO and 825 mL of H_2 react,
    a. which reactant is in excess?
    b. how much of that reactant remains when the reaction is complete?
    c. what volume of $CH_3OH(g)$ is produced?

33. A 4.0 L tank of helium at the carnival supply store is intended to fill 100 balloons to a volume of 3.0 L each at 25°C and 745 torr. These values take into account a 4% loss of gas when the balloons are being filled. What must the original pressure inside the tank be if it is filled at 0°C?

10-4

What conditions will cause a gas to condense?

Section Objectives

List the conditions under which gases deviate from ideal behavior.

Relate attractive forces to boiling point, volatility, and surface tension.

Interpret a phase diagram, and describe the significance of the triple point.

Relate volatility and vapor pressure.

Relate vapor pressure and temperature.

Describe sublimation.

Define boiling point in terms of vapor pressure.

Forces of attraction

All the mathematical equations you have used to make predictions of the conditions for gases are based on the kinetic molecular theory. The predictions we make using these mathematical models come relatively close to reality under most conditions. However, gases deviate from ideal behavior when the molecules are close. For example, 1 mol of CO_2 at 100 atm (10 132 kPa) and 50°C has a predicted volume of about 265 mL. However, if this gas is subjected to those conditions in the laboratory, the actual volume is measured at about 130 mL. Why is the actual volume so much smaller than predicted? Let's go back to the assumptions of the kinetic molecular theory of gases presented on page 360. There we identified two assumptions that were not exactly true for real gases.

1. The volume of the gas particles is negligible.
2. There are no attractive forces between particles.

The CO_2 described above is under high pressure and is compressed into a small volume. Similar deviations between predicted and actual gas volumes occur at low temperatures. At low temperatures, gas particles slow down. At high pressures, gas volumes are reduced, the gases still differ from the ideal because of particle size, as shown in **Figure 10-26**. In both cases the conditions are such that particle size and the attractive forces between particles significantly affect particle volume.

If the temperature is low enough and the pressure is high enough, the attractive forces between particles will be so strong that the gas will condense to form a liquid or solid.

Figure 10-26
The ratio of *PV/nRT* for any ideal gas is one, which is represented by the dashed line. Using actual measurements for real gases, you see that they deviate from the ideal.

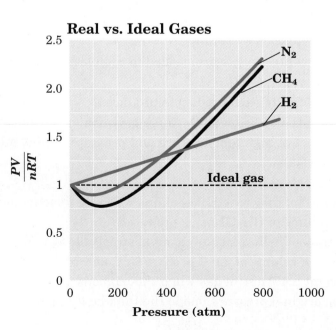

Real vs. Ideal Gases

N₂

CH₄

H₂

Ideal gas

$\frac{PV}{nRT}$

Pressure (atm)

Vapor pressure increases with temperature

A common gas that condenses easily is water vapor. You can see water vapor condense on any cold surface, such as a window. For example, your mirror fogs after a hot shower, and your glasses fog when you come in from the cold.

Even though water exists as a liquid at room temperature and standard pressure, you know that in an open container, water evaporates over a period of time until it finally "disappears." The water vapor formed during evaporation is like any other gas in that it exerts pressure and expands and contracts with temperature. You may have noticed, however, that in a closed system, water does not appear to evaporate.

In a closed container, water will evaporate until the air in the container is said to be *saturated* with water vapor. When the air is saturated with vapor, the vapor condenses to a liquid as fast as the liquid evaporates, and the two processes of evaporation and condensation continue at equal rates.

$$\text{evaporation} \rightleftharpoons \text{condensation}$$

equilibrium vapor pressure
a measure of the tendency of the particles of a liquid substance to enter the gas phase at a given temperature

This equation represents an equilibrium system. The pressure due to the water vapor reaches a maximum value (at a given temperature), called the **equilibrium vapor pressure.** The equilibrium vapor pressure at any given temperature is an actual measurement taken from an apparatus like the one shown in **Figure 10-27**.

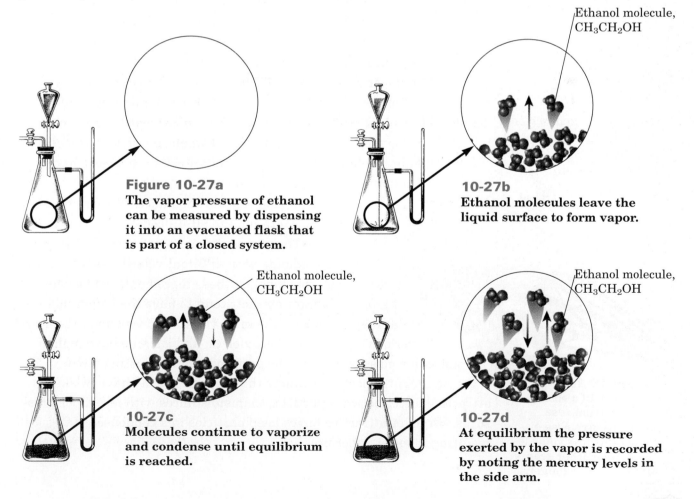

Figure 10-27a
The vapor pressure of ethanol can be measured by dispensing it into an evacuated flask that is part of a closed system.

Ethanol molecule, CH_3CH_2OH

10-27b
Ethanol molecules leave the liquid surface to form vapor.

Ethanol molecule, CH_3CH_2OH

10-27c
Molecules continue to vaporize and condense until equilibrium is reached.

Ethanol molecule, CH_3CH_2OH

10-27d
At equilibrium the pressure exerted by the vapor is recorded by noting the mercury levels in the side arm.

As the temperature of the water increases, its maximum vapor pressure increases. **Figure 10-28** shows how vapor pressure increases with temperature. When the vapor pressure reaches the atmospheric pressure, the liquid begins to boil. The temperature at which boiling occurs is called the boiling point.

Figure 10-28a
A liquid boils when its vapor pressure equals the pressure of the atmosphere. If the pressure in a room is about 1 atm (760 mm Hg) each liquid boils at its normal boiling point.

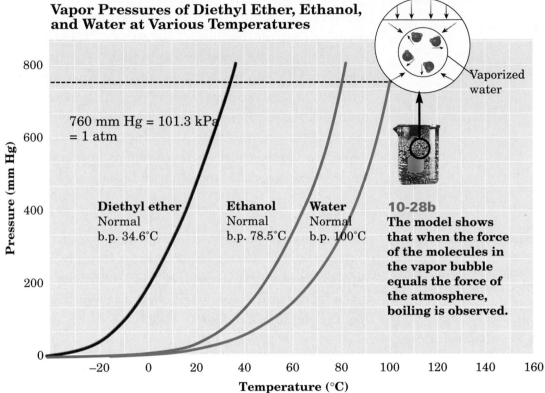

Vapor Pressures of Diethyl Ether, Ethanol, and Water at Various Temperatures

760 mm Hg = 101.3 kPa = 1 atm

Diethyl ether
Normal
b.p. 34.6°C

Ethanol
Normal
b.p. 78.5°C

Water
Normal
b.p. 100°C

Force of atmosphere

Vaporized water

10-28b
The model shows that when the force of the molecules in the vapor bubble equals the force of the atmosphere, boiling is observed.

Volatile substances have high vapor pressures

Like density, vapor pressure is a characteristic property of a substance. Substances that have high vapor pressures at low temperatures are described as **volatile**. You can generally recognize volatile substances by odor because they vaporize easily. For example, gasoline, turpentine, moth balls, acetone (the substance in nail-polish remover), and ethanol are volatile substances.

Perfumes include volatile substances to carry the scent. Perfumes can contain up to 90% alcohol, which evaporates very quickly. The essence of most perfumes is a blend of several ingredients with different volatilities to make the scent last over time. Of these ingredients, citrus oils, herbs, and flower extracts tend to have the lowest molecular masses and are the most volatile, so you smell them first. Flower oils from roses, lilies, violets, and jasmine have higher molecular masses and give the perfume a longer lasting scent.

As you might expect, substances that vaporize easily have weaker attractive forces between particles than substances with low vapor pressures. Stronger attractive forces keep particles in a condensed state, resulting in lower vapor pressures.

volatile
a term used to describe a substance that is readily vaporized at low temperature

Figure 10-29
The scent of a rose is isolated from rose petals to give rose oil. Rose oil is less volatile than some other scents and thus lasts longer.

Figure 10-30

The phase diagram for water can be used to predict the physical state of water at different pressures and temperatures. Note that this diagram is not drawn to scale.

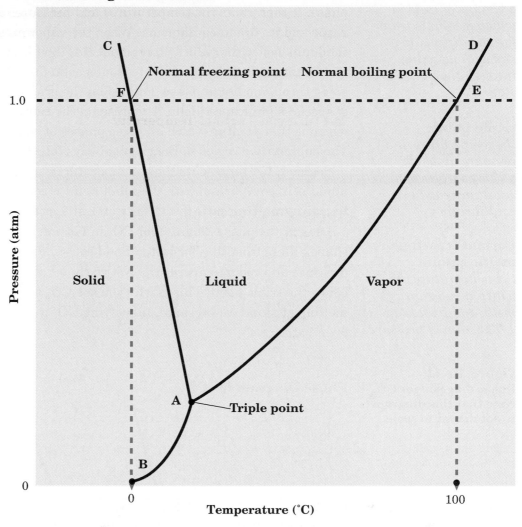

Phase Diagram for Water

Normal freezing point   *Normal boiling point*

Pressure (atm)

Solid   Liquid   Vapor

Triple point

Temperature (°C)

Phase diagrams relate temperature and pressure to physical state

A **phase diagram** is a graph that shows the pressures and temperatures at which different phases of a substance are at equilibrium with each other. Look at **Figure 10-30**, the phase diagram for water. Each line segment on the graph has been given a label. Point *E* corresponds to the boiling point of water at 1 atm (101.3 kPa). At the boiling temperature, the liquid and vapor are in equilibrium with each other. Segment *AD* is the vapor pressure–temperature curve for the liquid phase. Any point along segment *AD* represents the change of state from a liquid to a vapor and the boiling point of water at the corresponding pressure. You can now see why boiling point is more correctly defined as the temperature at which the vapor pressure equals the external or atmospheric pressure. If the pressure is greater than 1 atm, water boils at a higher temperature. If the pressure is less than 1 atm, water boils at a lower temperature. The **normal boiling point** (which you see listed in reference tables) represents the boiling point of a substance at 1 atm, or 101.3 kPa.

phase diagram
a graphic representation of the relationships between the physical state of a substance and its pressure and temperature

normal boiling point
the temperature at which a substance boils at 1.0000 atm of pressure

sublimation

a change of state in which a solid is transformed directly to a gas without going through the liquid state

triple point

the temperature and pressure at which all three states of a substance exist in equilibrium

normal freezing/ melting point

the temperature at which a substance melts and freezes at 1.0000 atm of pressure

Segment BA is the vapor pressure–temperature curve for the solid phase. It represents the temperatures and pressures at which water vapor and ice are in equilibrium. When the vapor pressure above the solid falls below the values on segment BA, then ice will sublime. **Sublimation** is a change of state from a solid directly to a gas without going through a liquid phase. Point A on the graph denotes coordinates of special significance. Point A represents the **triple point** of water— which is that point in which all three phases of water exist in equilibrium. The sublimation region of the graph always falls below the triple point.

Segment CA represents those temperatures and pressures at which the liquid is in equilibrium with the solid. Point F corresponds to the **normal freezing/melting point**, 0°C, for water at 1 atm (101.3 kPa).

Look at the phase diagram for CO_2 in **Figure 10-31**. Note how the shape differs from that for water. Solid carbon dioxide sublimes at normal pressure and room temperature. Notice that 1 atm on the y-axis falls well below the triple point. This is why you see CO_2 subliming rather than melting at standard pressure. Liquefying CO_2 would require a pressure of over 5 atm.

Figure 10-31
**Phase diagram for CO_2.
Note that this diagram is not drawn to scale.**

Phase Diagram for CO_2

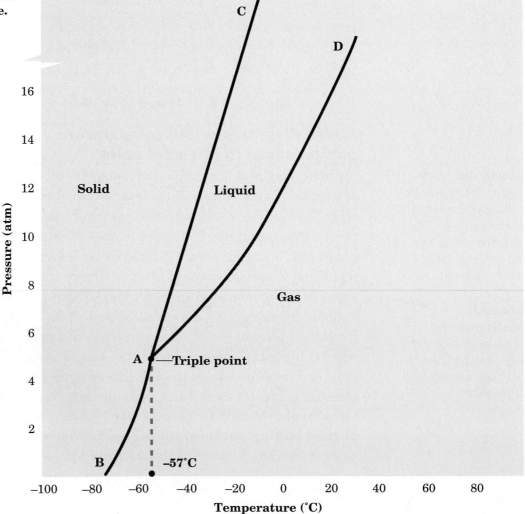

surface tension
the measure of a liquid's tendency to decrease its surface area to a minimum

Figure 10-32a
The weight of the needle is supported by the surface tension of . . .

Attractive forces in liquids result in surface tension

The forces between particles in liquids and solids are stronger than those in gases. The forces among particles on the surface are especially interesting. In **Figure 10-32** you see an example of the strength of these forces shown by the **surface tension** of water. The model shows that particles within the liquid are affected by forces of attraction from all sides. In contrast, particles on the surface are pulled only by particles in the same plane and below. Because the forces among particles at the surface are distributed unevenly, the surface can support objects that exert a small force over a large area.

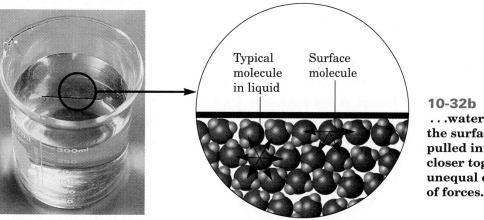

Typical molecule in liquid

Surface molecule

10-32b
. . .water molecules at the surface which are pulled inward and closer together by the unequal distribution of forces.

Section Review

34. Under what conditions do real gases behave differently than ideal gases?

35. For each of the following situations predict whether the attractive forces between particles are weak or strong.
  a. low boiling point   **b.** low volatility
  c. low surface tension   **d.** high vapor pressure
  Use **Figure 10-30** and **Figure 10-31** to answer items **36** and **37**.

36. Estimate the physical state of water under the following conditions.
  a. 0.75 atm and 50°C   **b.** 1 atm and 80°C   **c.** 0.25 atm and 100°C

37. Estimate the physical state of carbon dioxide under the following conditions.
  a. 10 atm and 50°C   **b.** 1 atm and 80°C
  c. 10 atm and –80°C   **d.** 10 atm and 0°C

38. When heated at standard pressure, I_2 sublimes. What does this mean? Look up the melting points of the halogens in a handbook. Explain the differences in melting point in terms of attractive forces.

39. A chunk of dry ice, CO_2, with a mass of 400 g at 78.5°C, sublimes to a gas at 1.0 atm.
  a. If the pressure is held constant, what is the volume of CO_2 at 22°C?
  b. If the dry ice sublimed in a trash bag with a volume of 25 L at 22°C, what would be the pressure of the gas?

Conclusion: Ascent Into the Ozone

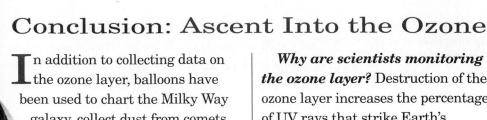

In addition to collecting data on the ozone layer, balloons have been used to chart the Milky Way galaxy, collect dust from comets and meteorites, and photograph the sun. New balloons are being designed to lift a 100 cm telescope into the atmosphere to explore the center of our galaxy. These new balloons have volumes of over 1 million m^3 and are able to lift payloads of over 3500 kg.

Why is the balloon only partially inflated at launch? The volume of the balloon increases as it ascends into the atmosphere and the pressure on the balloon decreases. If the balloon were completely inflated at the launch site, there would be no room for the expanding helium as the balloon ascended, and the pressure of the gas inside the balloon would cause it to burst.

How do scientists know how much to inflate the balloon? They calculate the mass and volume of gas needed at launch based on the volume they want the balloon to have at its cruising altitude.

Why are scientists monitoring the ozone layer? Destruction of the ozone layer increases the percentage of UV rays that strike Earth's surface, which can result in an increased incidence of mutations and skin cancers.

What gases are thought to be responsible for changes in the ozone layer? Chlorofluorocarbons, or CFCs, break down in the stratosphere to form chlorine that reacts with ozone to form oxygen gas. One chlorine atom is capable of reacting with as many as 10 000 ozone molecules. Halons, which are organic compounds containing bromine and nitrogen oxides, have also been shown to react with ozone molecules in the stratosphere.

What's being done to protect the ozone layer? The Montreal Protocol stipulates the following.

- 100% phaseout of CFCs, CCl_4, and CH_3CCl_3 by 1996
- Production freeze of CFCs by 1996; 100% phaseout by 2030
- Halons phased out in 1994
- Production freeze of methyl chloride for 1995.

Applying Concepts

1. The refrigerant released when fixing a typical automobile-air-conditioning system contains CCl_2F_2. If 365 g of CCl_2F_2 are released into the atmosphere from one air-conditioning unit, calculate the mass of chlorine atoms made available to react with ozone.
2. Calculate the number of chlorine atoms released in that 365 g sample.
3. If one chlorine atom can destroy up to 10 000 ozone molecules, calculate the number of ozone molecules destroyed by the chlorine atoms from item **2**.

Research and Writing

Use the library to find out more about the following.

1. Hydrochlorofluorocarbons, HCFCs, are being considered as alternatives to CFCs. HCFCs will react in the troposphere before reaching the stratosphere and the ozone layer. Find out why these compounds will also be phased out by the Montreal Protocol.

Highlights

Key terms

absolute temperature scale	Graham's law of effusion	normal freezing point
Avogadro's principle	greenhouse effect	partial pressure
Boyle's law	ideal gas	pascal
Charles's law	ideal gas law	phase diagram
chlorofluoro-carbons	kinetic molecular theory	pressure
Dalton's law of partial pressures	molar volume	STP
diffusion		sublimation
effusion	mutagen	surface tension
equilibrium vapor pressure	normal boiling point	triple point
		volatile

Key problem-solving approach: Using gas laws

The ideal gas law can be used to solve gas law problems involving a single gas under changing conditions. Match the situation described by the problem with the arrow that represents those conditions. Follow the path to the correct relationship.

Boyle's law

$$PV = k$$

Charles's law

$$\frac{V}{T} = k$$

P and *V* change
n, R, T are constant

Ideal gas law

$$PV = nRT$$

T and *V* change
P, n, R are constant

P, V, and *T* change
n and *R* are constant

General gas law

$$\frac{PV}{T} = k$$

Key ideas

10-1 What are characteristics of gases?

- Gases have variable volumes and very low densities.
- When released into the atmosphere, some gases lead to environmental problems such as the greenhouse effect and ozone depletion.
- The kinetic molecular theory is a model of gas behavior based on assumptions about a theoretical gas known as an ideal gas.
- The pressure, temperature, volume, and number of moles of a gas are four variables that define a gaseous system.

10-2 What behaviors are described by the gas laws?

- Charles's law explains the direct relationship between the volume and temperature of a gas.
- Boyle's law explains the indirect relationship between the volume and pressure of a gas.
- Dalton's law relates the partial pressures of the individual gases in a gas mixture to the total pressure of the mixture.
- Graham's law states that the effusion rates for two gases are inversely proportional to the square roots of their molar masses at the same temperature and pressure.

10-3 How do the gas laws fit together?

- The ideal gas law relates pressure, volume, temperature, and moles of a gas.
- The general gas law relates pressure, volume, moles, and temperature of a gas sample under two sets of conditions.

10-4 What conditions will cause a gas to condense?

- The behavior of real gases deviates from ideal at very high pressures and very low temperatures.
- The attractive forces between particles in a liquid affect the boiling point, volatility, and surface tension of that liquid.
- A phase diagram, a graph relating the physical state of a substance to its pressure and temperature, shows the triple point, and the conditions that result in sublimation.
- A substance with a high volatility has a high vapor pressure at low temperatures.

Review and Assess

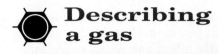

Describing a gas

REVIEW

1. **a.** What assumption does the kinetic molecular theory make about the volume of an ideal gas particle?
   b. Describe the motion of an ideal gas particle.
2. How does the combustion of a fossil fuel contribute to the greenhouse effect?
3. Use **Figure 10-9** and the graphs below to answer the following questions.
   a. What would happen to the shape of **Graph A** if the temperature of the gas increased from 300 K to 1000 K?
   b. Estimate the average molecular speed for the gas in **Graph B**.
   c. Is **Graph C** an accurate representation of molecular speed? Explain

Graph A

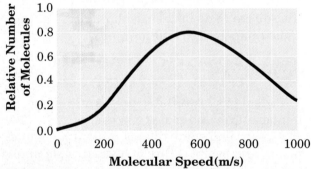

Graph B

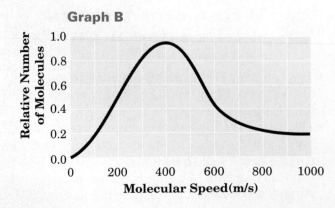

Graph C

4. **a.** List the four variables used to describe a gas.
   b. Why must a specific temperature be stated when working with gas data?
5. **a.** Briefly describe how a barometer works.
   b. Why is mercury used instead of water to measure air pressure?
6. How do the molar volumes of the atmospheric gases in **Table 10-1** compare at STP?

APPLY

7. What technologies have been affected by the Montreal Protocol, which was signed by 74 nations?
8. A ball is dropped from a distance of 2.0 meters above the floor.
   a. If the collision is elastic, how high will the ball bounce?
   b. If the collision is inelastic, will the ball bounce higher or lower than 2.0 meters?
9. Gas companies often store their fuel supplies in liquid form in large storage tanks. Liquid nitrogen is used to keep the temperature low enough for the fuel to remain condensed in liquid form. Although continuous cooling is expensive, storing a condensed fuel as a liquid is still more economical than storing it as a gas. Give one reason why storing a liquid is more economical than storing a gas.

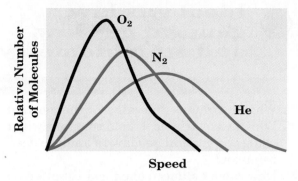

Speed

10. Use the graph above to answer the following questions.
  a. If all three gases are at the same temperature, which one has the highest molar mass and which one has the lowest molar mass?
  b. If the three graphs represent one gas at three different temperatures, which represents the lowest temperature and which curve represents the highest temperature?
11. Below is a diagram of two instruments, a mercury barometer and a water barometer. Which instrument is measuring a higher pressure? Explain.

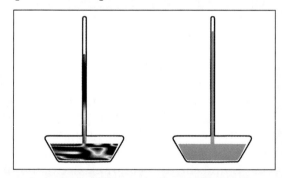

Charles's law and Boyle's law

REVIEW

12. a. Describe the relationship between the volume and temperature of the gas in **Table 10-4**.
  b. List reasons why the values in the *V/T* column of **Table 10-4** are not exactly the same.
  c. How do the values in the *Temperature (°C)* column compare with those in the *Temperature (K)* column of **Table 10-4**?
  d. Which gas law is verified by the data in **Table 10-4**?
13. What type of relationship between pressure and volume does Boyle's law express?

PRACTICE

Answers to items in black squares begin on page 841.

14. A child receives a balloon filled with 2.30 L of helium from a vendor at an amusement park. The temperature outside is 311 K. What will be the volume of the balloon when the child brings it home to an air-conditioned house at 295 K? (Hint: see Sample Problem 10A.)
15. A 1.5 L pocket of air with a temperature of 295 K rises in the air. What will be the volume of the air pocket if the temperature is decreased to 275 K and the pressure is not changed? (Hint: see Sample Problem 10A.)
16. A small 2.00 L fire extinguisher has an internal pressure of 506.6 kPa at 25°C. What volume of methyl bromide, the fire extinguisher's main ingredient, is needed to fill an empty fire extinguisher at standard pressure if the temperature remains constant? (Hint: see Sample Problem 10B.)
17. A child brings an inflatable ball on a small plane. Before take-off, the 2.00 L ball has a pressure of 101.3 kPa. The pilot flies the plane at an altitude where the air pressure is 75.0 kPa. What is the volume of the ball at this altitude if the temperature in the plane does not change? (Hint: see Sample Problem 10B.)
18. At a deep sea station 200. m below the surface of the Pacific Ocean, workers live in a highly pressurized environment. How many liters of gas at STP on the surface must be compressed to fill the underwater environment with 2.00×10^7 L of gas at 20.0 atm? Assume that temperature remains constant. (Hint: see Sample Problem 10C for information.)
19. A child carries a ball with a volume of 4.00 L from the surface of a pool to the bottom of the deep end. The pressure on the surface is 100. kPa. To what volume will the ball shrink when the pressure at the bottom of the pool is 135. kPa? Assume that temperature is constant. (Hint: see Sample Problem 10C.)

APPLY

20. Use the kinetic molecular theory to explain Charles's law.
21. Use Charles's law to explain the danger of throwing an aerosol can into a fire.
22. In a science fiction story, the main character visits a planet where the temperature is less than absolute zero. Use Charles's law to explain why this temperature is unrealistic.
23. Use Boyle's law to explain why "bubble wrap" pops when you squeeze it.

Dalton's law and mole fractions

24. How are mole fractions used to find partial pressures of gas mixtures?
25. Gas is collected in the laboratory by bubbling it through water and trapping it in a container. How can you determine the pressure of the dry collected gas?
26. **a.** Why is it important to know the temperature of water when collecting a gas over it?
    b. How will the pressure of the dry gas change if the temperature of the water is increased?
27. Use the diffusion process to explain how a gaseous emission travels through the air.
28. Differentiate between diffusion and effusion.
29. What ratios are compared in Graham's law?

30 Use **Table 10-6** to determine the partial pressure of oxygen collected over water if the temperature is 20.0°C and the total gas pressure is 98.0 kPa. (Hint: see Sample Problem 10D.)
31. The barometer at an indoor pool reads 105.00 kPa. If the temperature in the room is 30.0°C, what is the partial pressure of the "dry" air? (Hint: see Sample Problem 10D.)
32 A nitrogen molecule travels at 500. m/s at room temperature. What is the velocity of a helium molecule at the same temperature? (Hint: see Sample Problem 10E.)
33. A carbon dioxide molecule travels at 45.0 m/s at a certain temperature. What is the velocity of an oxygen molecule at the same temperature? (Hint: see Sample Problem 10E.)
34 Chlorine gas effuses through an opening at a rate 1.59 times slower than nitrogen gas. What is the molecular mass of chlorine gas? (Hint: see Sample Problem 10F.)
35. An unknown gas effuses through an opening at a rate 1.62 time slower than oxygen gas. What is the molecular mass of the unknown gas? (Hint: see Sample Problem 10F.)

36. How do the velocities of neon molecules and krypton molecules compare when both gases are at the same temperature?

 Ideal gas law, general gas law, and stoichiometry

37. What determines the value for the constant R?
38. Which gas variable is held constant when using the general gas law to analyze gas behavior?
39. How can a balanced chemical equation be used to determine the volume of a gas that will be produced from the reaction?

40 Suppose you have a 500. mL container that contains 0.0500 mol of oxygen gas at 25°C. What is the pressure inside the container? (Hint: see Sample Problem 10G)
41. How many grams of oxygen gas in a 10.0 L container exert a pressure of 97.0 kPa at a temperature of 25.0°C? (Hint: see Sample Problem 10G.)
42 A helium balloon has a volume of 500. mL at STP. What will be its new volume if the temperature is increased to 325 K and its pressure is increased to 125 kPa? (Hint: see Sample Problem 10H.)
43. The air in a balloon has a volume of 3.00 L and exerts a pressure of 101. kPa at 300.0 K. What pressure does the air in the balloon exert if the temperature is increased to 400.0 K and the air is allowed to expand to 15.0 L? (Hint: see Sample Problem 10H.)
44 How many liters of hydrogen gas can be produced at 300.0 K and 104 kPa pressure if 20.0 g of sodium metal are reacted with water? (Hint: see Sample Problem 10I.)

$$2Na + 2H_2O \longrightarrow 2NaOH + H_2$$

45. How many liters of hydrogen gas can be produced at 290. K and 99.0 kPa if 17.0 g of potassium metal are reacted with water? (Hint: see Sample Problem 10I.)

$$2K + 2H_2O \longrightarrow 2KOH + H_2$$

46 Magnesium will burn in oxygen to form magnesium oxide as represented by the following equation.

$$2Mg + O_2 \longrightarrow 2MgO$$

What mass of magnesium will react with a 500.0 mL container of oxygen at 150°C and 70.0 kPa? (Hint: see Sample Problem 10J.)

47. One industrial method for producing nitric acid involves dissolving nitrogen dioxide in water.

$$3NO_2(g) + H_2O(l) \longrightarrow 2HNO_3(l) + NO(g)$$

What mass of water will react with a 1000.0 mL container of nitrogen dioxide at 25.0°C and 60.0 kPa? (Hint: see Sample Problem 10J.)

A P P L Y

48. A plastic weather balloon is filled with 90.0 L of hydrogen gas at ground level, where the pressure is 99.0 kPa and the temperature is 20.0°C. The balloon will burst if its volume exceeds 300.0 L. Can the balloon rise above the altitude of Mount Everest where the pressure drops to 32.1 kPa and the temperature decreases by 64.4°C?

49. Calculate the density of helium at standard temperature and pressure using the ideal gas law equation. Check your answer with a reference source of gas densities.

50. Suppose a certain automobile engine has a cylinder with a volume of 500.0 mL that is filled with air (21% oxygen) at a temperature of 55°C and a pressure of 101.0 kPa. What mass of octane must be injected to react with all of the oxygen in the cylinder?

$$2C_8H_{18}(l) + 25O_2(g) \longrightarrow$$
$$16CO_2(g) + 18H_2O(g)$$

 Condensation and liquids

R E V I E W

51. Why do gases deviate from ideal gas behavior?

52. Use the following graph of the vapor pressure of water versus temperature to answer the following questions.
  a. At which point(s) does water boil at standard atmospheric pressure?
  b. At which point(s) is water only in the liquid phase?
  c. At which point(s) is water only in the vapor phase?
  d. At which point(s) is liquid water in equilibrium with water vapor?

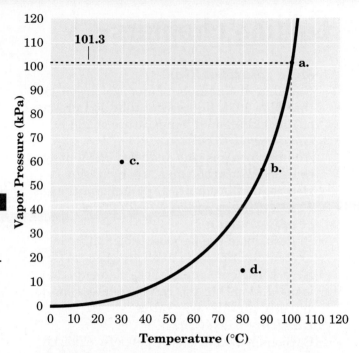

A P P L Y

53. Use the phase diagram for oxygen to determine what phase transition would occur if the following changes occurred.
  a. At point **a**, pressure is decreased, and temperature remains constant.
  b. At point **b**, temperature is decreased, and pressure is constant.
  c. At point **c**, pressure is increased, and temperature is the same.

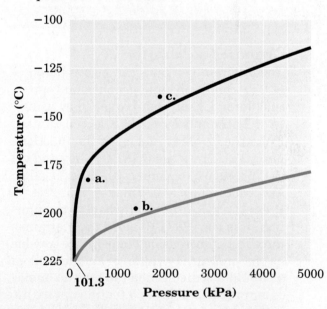

54. From the phase diagram for oxygen, determine the physical state under the following conditions.
  a. 2000 kPa and −180°C
  b. 3000 kPa and −120°C

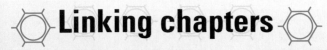

Linking chapters

1. *Mole relationships*
   Calculate the number of atoms of argon gas that fill a 1.0 L fluorescent tube at a pressure of 100.0 kPa and a temperature of 298 K.

2. *Empirical formula*
   An unknown gas was analyzed and found to contain 82% carbon and 18% hydrogen. Determine the empirical formula for the gas.

3. *Properties related to electron configuration*
   In Period 2 of the periodic table, nitrogen, oxygen, fluorine, and neon are gases at STP. Neon is the only one of these elements that is not diatomic in the gaseous state. How do you explain this observation?

4. *Limiting reactants*
   Carbon monoxide is only partially oxidized; further oxidation of carbon monoxide produces carbon dioxide.

   $$2CO(g) + O_2(g) \longrightarrow 2CO_2(g)$$

   Suppose that 500.0 mL of CO at 101 kPa and 15°C is reacted with 500.0 mL of O_2 at the same pressure and temperature. Which gas would be the limiting reactant?

5. **Theme:** *Macroscopic observations and micromodels*
   As a car travels down the road, the air pressure inside the tires may increase. Prepare a model that illustrates what happens to the tires as the car moves.

6. *Stoichiometry*
   Calculate the volume of gas released at STP from the reaction in a car airbag, when 92.0 g of NaN_3 decomposes according to the following reaction.

   $$2NaN_3(s) \longrightarrow 2Na(s) + 3N_2(g)$$

7. *Micromodels*
   Draw a micromodel for each of the following.
   a. balloon filled with helium
   b. balloon filled with air
   c. balloon filled with oxygen

USING TECHNOLOGY

1. *Graphics calculator*
   The different gas laws can be compared at STP conditions and graphed on your calculator. Graph Gay-Lassac's law using $P_2 = 1$ atm and $T_2 = 273$ K as constants. Press the $\boxed{Y=}$ key and enter the function $y = x/273$. Press the $\boxed{WINDOW}$ key and set the $\boxed{WINDOW}$ to Xmin $= 0$, Xmax $= 500$, Xscl $= 50$, Ymin $= 0$, Ymax $= 2.5$, Yscl $= 1$. Press the $\boxed{GRAPH}$ key to display the function. Use the $\boxed{TRACE}$ mode to determine the effect of increasing temperature (x value) on the pressure (y value) of an enclosed gas.
   a. Would a sealed scuba tank with a maximum stress point of 5.0 atm rupture after warming to 315 K?
   b. Will a glass bulb with a stress point of 1.5 atm shatter if it is heated to 150°C?

2. *Computer art*
   Using a computer art program, sketch how gas particles in a closed system may act when the pressure, temperature, volume, or the number of gas particles is changed. Use the kinetic molecular model as a guide.

3. *Computer spreadsheet*
   Create a spreadsheet that will run calculations using the general gas law equation or ideal gas law equation.

Alternative assessment

Performance assessment

1. Design an experiment to measure the molar mass of the gas found inside a disposable butane lighter. Measure the mass and volume of the gas at a known temperature and pressure. Use the ideal gas law equation $PV = nRT$ to find molar mass. Compare your answer with the known molar mass of butane. Try different brands of lighters to compare results. Other reactions that produce a gas can also be used.

2. Match the microviews below with the appropriate description. Microviews can be matched more than once.
   a. model for neon gas
   b. model for chlorine gas
   c. model for gas mixture
   d. model for gas collected over water
   e. model for a pure gas
   f. model for a volatile liquid

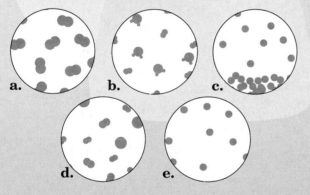

3. Match the graphs below with the appropriate description. Graphs can be matched more than once.
   a. a graph showing a directly proportional relationship
   b. a graph with a slope = 0
   c. a graph showing an inversely proportional relationship
   d. a graph with a constant slope

Portfolio projects

1. *Research and communication*
   For more than 300 years, gases have been an important part of the evolution of chemistry and physics. Research the important contributions of the following scientists.
   a. Robert Boyle (1627–1691)
   b. Jacques Charles (1746–1823)
   c. Joseph Gay-Lussac (1778–1850)
   d. Stanislao Cannizzaro (1826–1910)
   e. Amedeo Avogadro (1776–1856)
   f. James Clerk Maxwell (1831–1879)

2. *Chemistry and you*
   Locate a hot air balloon group to discuss with them how the gas laws are used to fly their balloons. The group may be willing to give a demonstration. Report your experiences to your class.

3. *Chemistry and you*
   Industrial gases are shipped in canisters of various colors that are specific to the gas. Find out what color code is used for each gas.

4. *Research and communication*
   Some commercial gases are produced by the liquification and fractionation of air. Find out how these processes are used to separate a mixture into its component gases.

5. *Chemistry and you*
   Commercial dry cake mixes will generally have two sets of preparation instructions. Go to the grocery store and look at some boxed, dry cake mixes. What is the purpose for having two sets of instructions? How do they differ and why do they differ?

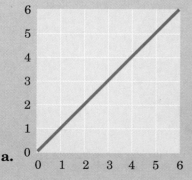

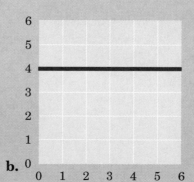

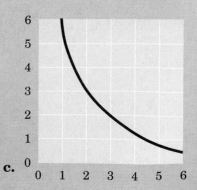

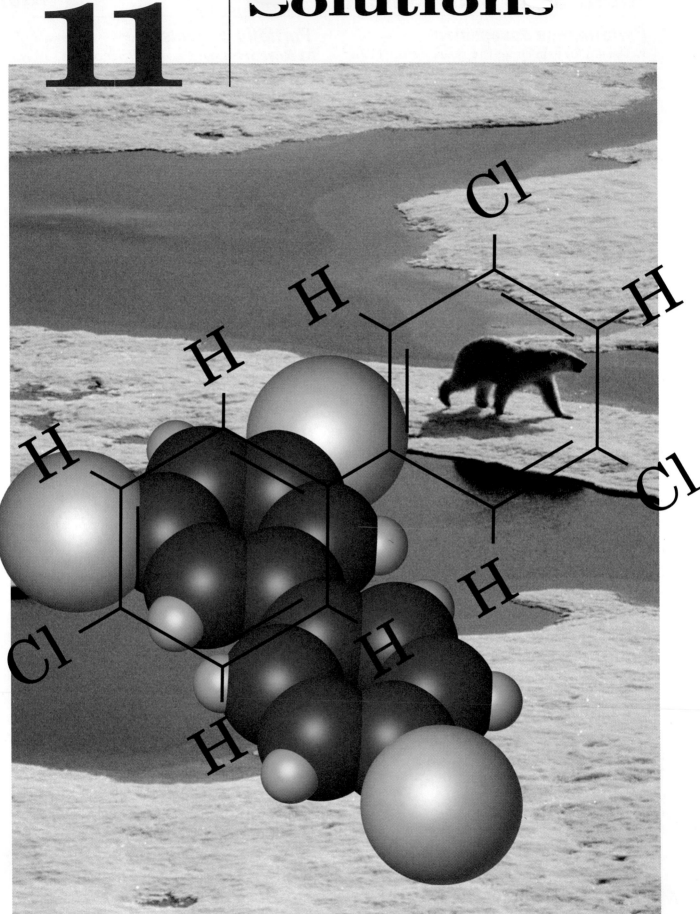

Solubility and the Arctic Bear Hunt

In northern Canada, a helicopter hovers over the snow.

Dr. Malcolm Ramsay leans out of the doorway to keep a polar bear in

sight. As Ramsay braces and aims his rifle, the bear lumbers through

the snow trying to escape. Ramsay fires, and the bear runs faster.

Ramsay, who is an ecologist, signals the pilot to land in a clearing. He unloads his equipment, then shields his face from the helicopter-driven snowstorm as the pilot departs. By the time Ramsay reaches the bear, the tranquilizer-filled dart has done its job, and the animal lies quietly in the snow.

Ramsay begins a physical examination that will take hours. With a net, ropes, and a tripod, the bear is winched into the air to be weighed. Large syringes are filled with blood samples. A tooth is extracted; its growth rings will tell the animal's age. An electronic instrument records the body's resistance to electricity, which is an indication of the bear's muscle-to-fat ratio. A sample of fat tissue is taken. By the time the bear begins to stir, Ramsay has packed his gear and is waving to the returning helicopter. The polar bear will resume its migration to Hudson Bay, generally unharmed by the encounter.

The tissue samples are sent to a laboratory for analysis. The results Ramsay gets from the lab are worrisome. The bear's fat tissue contains polychlorinated biphenyls, better known as PCBs. This family of synthetic organic compounds has been used industrially in electrical and mechanical equipment for decades. Originally scientists believed that PCBs were biologically inert, but in the 1970s they discovered that laboratory animals exposed to PCBs had higher than normal rates of birth defects and liver cancer.

Ramsay has found that the concentration of PCBs in the bear's fat tissue is 8 ppm (parts per million). So far, this concentration of PCBs has caused the bear no apparent harm. But scientists are concerned about the polar bears because the way that PCBs dissolve in fat makes it possible for the concentration to increase in the bears even if the amount of PCBs in the environment does not change.

Ramsay, along with other scientists, is working to answer some puzzling questions.

- *How did the PCBs get into the Hudson Bay ecosystem when there is very little industry in the bay area?*
- *Why did PCBs end up in the bear's fat?*

These questions can be answered by research that requires a knowledge of how oily chemicals mix and dissolve. In this chapter, you will explore the principles of chemical solubility, and then you will apply those principles to answer some of the questions that environmentalists have about PCBs.

What is a solution?

Section Objectives

Distinguish between solutions and suspensions.

Given various types of solutions, determine the solute and solvent.

Interpret solubility graphs and tables.

Distinguish among unsaturated, saturated, and supersaturated solutions.

Solutions are mixtures

In Chapter 2 a solution was defined as a homogeneous mixture. Every day, people use solutions such as mouthwash, diet soda, window cleaner, and gasoline. Most of the chemicals people use at home or on the job are solutions. Most of the chemicals you use in your chemistry lab are in solution because reactions often occur faster in solution. In this chapter, you will examine the properties of solutions in detail.

Solutions are stable, homogeneous mixtures

A student working in a pet shop is asked to prepare some water for a saltwater aquarium. She fills an aquarium with fresh water, then adds the proper amount of Instant Ocean salt crystals to the aquarium, as shown in **Figure 11-1**, and stirs. After stirring, the student can no longer see salt particles that are distinct from the water. No matter how long she waits, the salt will not spontaneously separate itself from the water. The salt has dissolved to form a stable, homogeneous mixture—the particles of each substance are evenly dispersed throughout the mixture.

Figure 11-1a
Fresh water is stable and homogeneous.

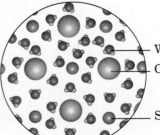

11-1b
The saltwater mixture is stable and homogeneous because mixing occurs between molecules and ions.

Before mixing

Fresh water

Water molecule

After mixing

Saltwater solution

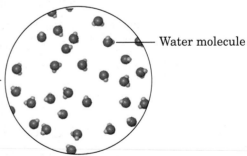

Water molecule

Chloride ion, Cl⁻

Sodium ion, Na⁺

Suspension particles will settle

The sculptor in **Figure 11-2** uses water to join the sides of a clay vase to its bottom. As she dips her fingers into the water, it turns gray-brown. The clay-water mixture seems uniform. However, if the container sits overnight, the next day she will see a muddy layer at the bottom with clear water above. Because the ingredients of this mixture show visible cloudiness and separate spontaneously, it is *not* a solution. This kind of mixture is called a **suspension**. In a suspension, the particles remain thoroughly mixed while the liquid is being stirred, but later they settle to the bottom. Unlike the salt crystals, the clay does not dissolve in water.

suspension
mixture that appears uniform while being stirred, but separates into different phases when agitation ceases

Figure 11-2a
Initially, the clay-water mixture seems homogeneous like a solution.

11-2b
Over time, however, the mixture separates into two distinct layers because the larger clay particles do not remain evenly dispersed with the water molecules.

Before settling

Suspension seems homogeneous

Water molecule

Clay particle

After settling

Suspension particles settle out

Water molecule

Clay particle

Describing solutions
The solute dissolves in the solvent

solvent
the material dissolving the solute to make the solution

solute
the material dissolved in a solution

miscible
indicates liquids or gases that will dissolve in each other

immiscible
indicates liquids or gases that will not dissolve in each other

The simplest solutions have two ingredients—the solvent and the solute. The **solvent** is usually present in a larger amount than the solute, and chemists think of the **solute** as dissolving in the solvent. In the first example, in which a student prepared a saltwater aquarium, sea salt was the solute, and water was the solvent.

Most solutions are combinations of a *solid* solute with a *liquid* solvent, but solutions of other states are possible. Many liquids dissolve, at least partially, in other liquids. Antifreeze, for example, dissolves in water. If two liquids can mix in any proportions (like antifreeze and water), they are said to be **miscible**. If they can't mix, they are **immiscible** (like vegetable oil and water). *Miscibility* is just another term that chemists sometimes use for the ability of liquids or gases to make solutions.

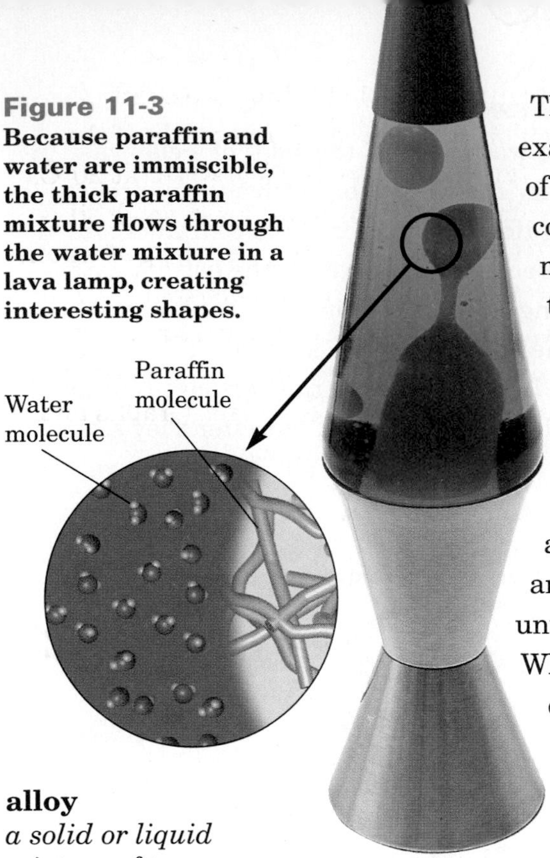

Figure 11-3
Because paraffin and water are immiscible, the thick paraffin mixture flows through the water mixture in a lava lamp, creating interesting shapes.

Water molecule

Paraffin molecule

alloy
a solid or liquid mixture of two or more metals

soluble
can be dissolved in a particular solvent

insoluble
does not dissolve appreciably in a particular solvent

Figure 11-4
The copper(II) nitrate in the test tube on the left is soluble in water. The copper(II) acetate in the center test tube is partly soluble in water. The copper(II) hydroxide in the test tube on the right is insoluble in water. (The black ring visible in the right test tube is a small amount of copper(II) oxide, formed as copper(II) hydroxide decomposes upon heating.)

The contents of the lava lamp shown in **Figure 11-3** are an example of immiscibility. A light bulb concealed in the base of the lamp illuminates and heats a glass container that contains two immiscible liquids. Heat from the light bulb melts the thick paraffin mixture so that it oozes and flows through the colored water like melted candle wax.

Gases can also be solutes in a liquid solution. A bottle of soda gets its fizz from carbon dioxide gas dissolved in water. Fish depend on the small amount of dissolved oxygen that is in water.

Solvents are not always liquid. Can a solid dissolve in another solid? No, and yes. If you combine a piece of copper and a piece of gold, they will not mix; but if they are heated until they melt, gold and copper will dissolve in each other. When cooled, they form a solid mixture of metals, which is called an **alloy**. By mass, gold coins are usually 10% copper and 90% gold. Gases always dissolve in each other. For example, air is a solution of gases including nitrogen, oxygen, argon, and carbon dioxide.

Solubility is the maximum that can dissolve

Salt is said to be *soluble* in water because the solid salt seems to disappear if enough water is added; no solid is left on the bottom of the container. By looking at **Figure 11-4**, you can see that a solute may be **soluble**, partly soluble, or **insoluble** in a particular solvent.

The terms *soluble*, *partly soluble*, or *insoluble* are vague—there are no precise dividing lines among the three categories. When more precision is needed, the exact amount of a solute can be measured and expressed numerically. For example, at 20°C (about room temperature), 36.0 g of sodium chloride is the most that will normally dissolve in 100 g of water.

solubility

the maximum amount of a chemical that will dissolve in a given amount of a solvent at a specified temperature while the solution is in contact with some undissolved solute

When a solution holds the maximum amount of solute, the exact amount that has dissolved is called the **solubility**. For example, if the solubility of lithium iodide, LiI, is 165 g of LiI per 100 g of water at 20°C, 165 g is the *most* LiI that can dissolve in 100 g of water when solid LiI is present. *Any* quantity less than 165 g of LiI can dissolve in 100 g of water.

Temperature can have a great effect on solubility, as shown in **Figure 11-5**. This is why solubility values always include a temperature. For most solid solutes, as temperature increases, the solubility increases. For most gases, such as sulfur dioxide, SO_2, the opposite is true. Graphs and solubility tables are useful planning tools for making solutions.

Figure 11-5
Notice that most ionic compounds, but not all, have solubilities in water that increase as temperature increases. The opposite is true for gases such as sulfur dioxide, SO_2.

Temperature-Solubility Relationships*

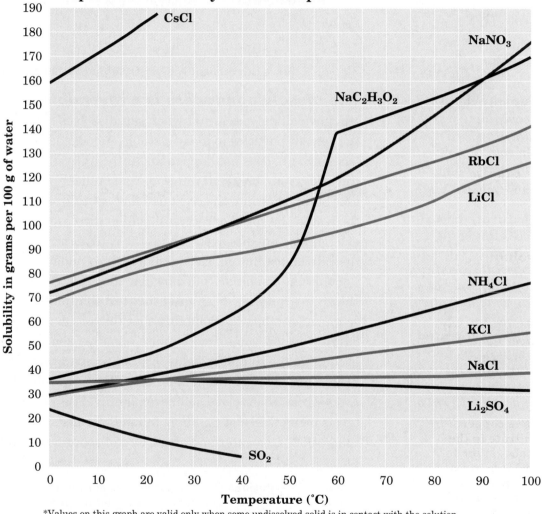

*Values on this graph are valid only when some undissolved solid is in contact with the solution. For SO_2, values are valid when pressure due to SO_2 and water vapor is 101.325 kPa.

Concept Review

Using solubility graphs

Use **Figure 11-5** to answer the following questions.

1. What is the solubility of lithium chloride at 60°C?
2. Does rubidium chloride or sodium nitrate have a greater solubility at 0°C? at 70°C?
3. Which solute's solubility in water is most temperature dependent: sodium nitrate, potassium chloride, or sodium chloride?

Answers for Concept Review items and Practice problems begin on page 841.

Saturation and Solubility

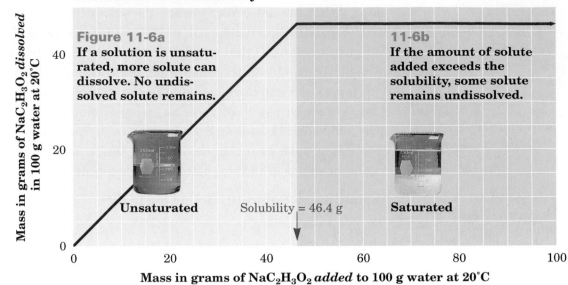

Mass in grams of NaC$_2$H$_3$O$_2$ dissolved in 100 g water at 20°C

40

20

0

Figure 11-6a
If a solution is unsaturated, more solute can dissolve. No undissolved solute remains.

11-6b
If the amount of solute added exceeds the solubility, some solute remains undissolved.

Unsaturated

Solubility = 46.4 g

Saturated

0   20   40   60   80   100

Mass in grams of NaC$_2$H$_3$O$_2$ *added* to 100 g water at 20°C

---

unsaturated
containing less than the standard amount of solute specified by the solubility at a given temperature

saturated
containing the standard amount of solute specified by the solubility at a given temperature

supersaturated
containing more than the standard amount of solute specified by the solubility at a given temperature

The dissolving process is a reversible reaction

You have already seen that when salt dissolves in water, its ions mix with the solvent particles to make a stable, homogeneous mixture. But this uniform mixture does not happen instantly. At first, the ions on the edge of the salt crystal break off into water and quickly dissolve. Some of these ions bump back into the crystal and recrystallize. As more ions dissolve in the water, the speed of recrystallization increases. At the solubility value, enough ions are dissolved so that the rate of recrystallization is equal to the rate of dissolution. Even if more salt is added, no more will dissolve.

Solutions can be classified by how they relate to the solubility value, as shown in **Figure 11-6**. In **unsaturated** solutions, the amount of solute is so much less than the solubility that the dissolving is complete. In a **saturated** solution, some excess solute remains, and the amount that dissolves is equal to the solubility value for that temperature. **Supersaturated** solutions are able to contain more than the usual solubility, as long as there is no excess undissolved solute remaining. **Figure 11-7** explains these terms using the Heat Solution, a hand warmer. The Heat Solution contains 100 mL of water and about 60 g of sodium acetate, NaC$_2$H$_3$O$_2$.

Figure 11-7a
At 100°C, 60 g of NaC$_2$H$_3$O$_2$ will dissolve completely in the 100 mL of water contained in a Heat Solution pack.

11-7b
When the solution is cooled to 20°C, NaC$_2$H$_3$O$_2$ does not recrystallize . . .

11-7c
. . . unless the solution is disturbed. Clicking the disk in the center of the pack triggers rapid exothermic recrystallization.

11-7d
The heat pack can be re-used if it is heated above the saturation point again.

Unsaturated → Cooling → **Supersaturated** → Crystallization → **Saturated** → Heat to re-use

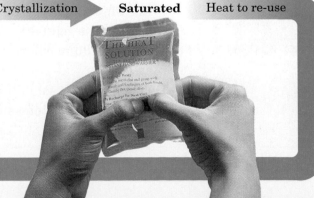

Figure 11-8a
On a 35°C day in New Mexico with a low relative humidity (37%), perspiration will evaporate quickly, cooling the body.

Low relative humidity

Unsaturated air; rapid evaporation

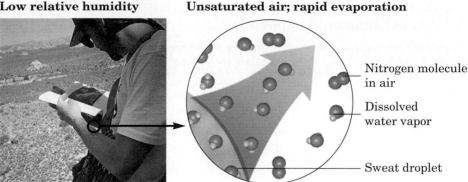

- Nitrogen molecule in air
- Dissolved water vapor
- Sweat droplet

11-8b
On a 35°C day in Louisiana with a high relative humidity (92%), perspiration evaporates more slowly because moisture condenses from the air almost as fast as it evaporates from the body.

High relative humidity

Saturated air; slow evaporation

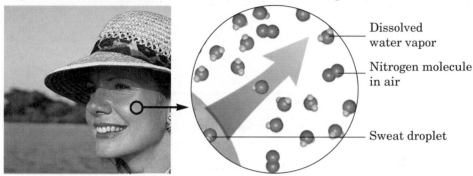

- Dissolved water vapor
- Nitrogen molecule in air
- Sweat droplet

An example of saturation is the relative humidity figure given in the weather report. At any given temperature the air can hold a certain amount of water in the form of gaseous vapor. As long as the relative humidity is less than 100%, the air is unsaturated because it holds less than the maximum amount of water vapor. **Figure 11-8** shows why the air feels "sticky" when it is very hot, and the relative humidity is high. When the relative humidity reaches 100%, the air is saturated and can hold no more water vapor in solution. If more water is present, it will come out of solution as fog, rain, dew, frost, or other precipitation.

Actual practice shows that solutions contain more dissolved solute than the usual solubility limits. This can be achieved by carefully cooling a nearly saturated solution. Such supersaturated solutions are not breaking the rules. Solubility was defined as the maximum that can dissolve *when the solution is in contact with undissolved solute*. The supersaturated solution no longer holds any undissolved solute. Supersaturated solutions are not very stable. If you disturb the solution, you will see rapid crystallization of solids or bubbling of gases.

Some substances don't dissolve

It is easy to get the *misimpression* that all substances dissolve in water. You know that copper, zinc, and iron do not dissolve in water and are classified as insoluble. Some metal salts dissolve slightly but, for practical purposes, are also classified as insoluble in water. **Table 11-1** on the next page summarizes the solubility of many compounds and can be very useful. For example, if an experiment requires silver ions, it would be a waste of time to try to use silver chloride, but silver nitrate would serve your purpose very well.

Chem Fact
Many tests for analyzing dissolved metal ions make use of solubility principles. A sample is mixed with reagents that form an insoluble solid precipitate with some metal ions.

Table 11-1
Solubility of Common Compounds

Compounds containing these ions are **soluble** in water . . .		. . . unless they also contain these ions, which make them **insoluble**.
ammonium	NH_4^+	
potassium	K^+	
sodium	Na^+	
acetate	$C_2H_3O_2^-$	Fe^{3+}, Al^{3+}, Hg_2^{2+}
chlorate	ClO_3^-	
chloride	Cl^-	Ag^+, Hg_2^{2+}, Pb^{2+}
nitrate	NO_3^-	
sulfate	SO_4^{2-}	Ca^{2+}, Ba^{2+}, Pb^{2+}, Sr^{2+}, Hg_2^{2+}

Compounds containing these ions are **insoluble** in water . . .		. . . unless they also contain these ions, which make them **soluble**.
carbonate	CO_3^{2-}	K^+, Li^+, Na^+, NH_4^+
hydroxide	OH^-	K^+, Li^+, Ba^{2+}, Na^+
oxide	O^{2-}	
phosphate	PO_4^{3-}	K^+, Na^+, NH_4^+
silicate	SiO_3^{2-}	K^+, Na^+
sulfide	S^{2-}	K^+, Na^+, NH_4^+
sulfite	SO_3^{2-}	K^+, Na^+, NH_4^+

Section Review

4. Identify the following as solutions or suspensions.
   a. muddy river water   **b.** orange juice
   c. chlorinated water in a swimming pool

5. Name the solute(s) and solvent in these solutions.
   a. carbonated water   **b.** sugar water

6. Categorize the following solutions as saturated, unsaturated, or super-saturated. (Hint: refer to **Figure 11-5**.)
   a. 38 g of NaCl stirred into 100 g of water at 99°C, then cooled to 25°C
   b. 50 g of NaCl added to 100 g of water, with some left undissolved on the bottom
   c. 10 g of NaCl stirred into 100 g of water

7. Use **Table 11-1** to determine whether the following compounds are soluble in water.
   a. copper(II) sulfate   **b.** copper(II) sulfite
   c. iron(III) chloride   **d.** aluminum acetate

8. If you mixed silver nitrate with water, would it dissolve? If you mixed potassium chloride with water, would it dissolve? If you mixed the contents of these two combinations, would anything settle to the bottom?

9. Using **Table 11-1** and **Figure 11-5**, place the following compounds in order from most soluble to least soluble: $LiCl$, NH_4Cl, $PbCl_2$, $CsCl$, $NaCl$.

What does concentration mean?

Section Objectives

Relate various ways of expressing concentration data.

Recognize that units of concentration represent a ratio.

Use units of molarity in stoichiometric calculations.

Describe the procedure for making solutions of different molarities.

Concentration as a ratio

concentration
ratio of solute to solvent or solution

To describe saturation precisely, a quantitative measure is needed—units that measure **concentration**. The important feature of all concentration measures is the ratio expressed. There are many ratios that express how much of some substance is present. Certain expressions are favored in medicine, others in pollution control, and others in biological research, as described in **Table 11-2**. Because chemists are concerned with the interaction of substances, they must know not only how much is present, but also how the amount compares, molecule for molecule, with another chemical.

Table 11-2
Concentration Units

Name	Abbr.	Units	Uses
grams/100. g	g/100. g	$\dfrac{\text{g solute}}{100.\ \text{g solvent}}$	solubility descriptions, medical products
mass percent or "weight percent"	%	$\dfrac{\text{g solute}}{100.\ \text{g solution}}$	biological research
parts per million	ppm	$\dfrac{\text{g solute}}{1\ 000\ 000.\ \text{g solution}}$ *	small concentrations
parts per billion	ppb	$\dfrac{\text{g solute}}{1\ 000\ 000\ 000.\ \text{g solution}}$ *	very small concentrations, as in pollutants or contaminants
parts per trillion	ppt	$\dfrac{\text{g solute}}{1\ 000\ 000\ 000\ 000.\ \text{g solution}}$ *	extremely small concentrations, as in isotopes used as tracers in medicine
molarity	M	$\dfrac{\text{mol solute}}{\text{L solution}}$	laboratory chemistry, where the solute may undergo a chemical change according to a mole ratio
molality	m	$\dfrac{\text{mol solute}}{\text{kg solvent}}$	calculation of special properties such as boiling-point elevation and freezing-point depression

*volume for gases

Molarity

molarity
concentration unit, expressed as moles of solute per liter of solution

The mole is the unit used to count atoms and molecules and to relate the amounts of reactants and products in chemical reactions. The mole is also the basis of the concentration measurement called **molarity**.

$$\text{molarity} = \frac{\text{moles solute}}{\text{liters of solution}} \qquad M = \frac{\text{mol}}{L}$$

Even though molarity is just *one* method of measuring concentration, it can be represented by *four* labels: *molarity*, *molar*, *M*, and *mol/L*. These labels all indicate the concentration of a solution as a ratio of moles of solute per liter of solution.

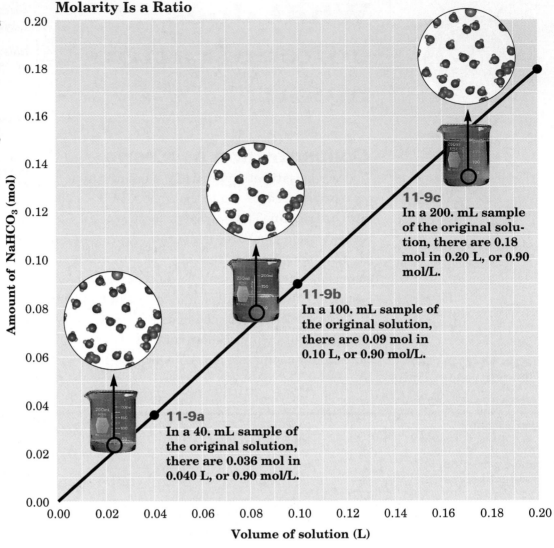

Figure 11-9

If several samples of different volumes are taken from the same solution, the moles of solute and liters of solution are in direct proportion. The ratio (molarity) is a constant, as you can see by selecting any point along the line.

Molarity Is a Ratio

Amount of NaHCO$_3$ (mol) (y-axis)

Volume of solution (L) (x-axis)

11-9c
In a 200. mL sample of the original solution, there are 0.18 mol in 0.20 L, or 0.90 mol/L.

11-9b
In a 100. mL sample of the original solution, there are 0.09 mol in 0.10 L, or 0.90 mol/L.

11-9a
In a 40. mL sample of the original solution, there are 0.036 mol in 0.040 L, or 0.90 mol/L.

Determining molarity

It is easy to calculate molarity when the volume of solution is exactly 1.0 L. Of course, most situations involve more or less than 1.0 L of solution. Keep in mind that molarity is a *ratio*, the moles of solute *divided by* the liters of solution. Once you make a 0.9 M solution, the ratio of amount of solute to volume of solution is *constant*, regardless of how much of the solution you sample. This idea is shown in **Figure 11-9**.

Before calculating the molarity of a solution, be sure the amount of solute and the volume of solution are expressed in the proper units.

$$\frac{\textbf{mol solute}}{\textbf{L solution}}$$

To prepare a solution of a given concentration, if you just mix a liter of solvent and the proper amount of solute in moles, the final solution will have a volume slightly greater or smaller than 1.00 L depending on the attractive forces among the solute and solvent particles. The definition of molarity is based on the number of moles in the final volume of the solution. To make a solution that contains exactly 1.00 L when finished, it is necessary to follow the very specific procedure shown on the next page.

Prepare a 0.5000 molar solution

Start by calculating the mass of $CuSO_4\cdot5H_2O$ needed. To make this solution, each liter will require 0.5000 mol of $CuSO_4\cdot5H_2O$. To convert this amount to a mass, multiply by the molar mass of $CuSO_4\cdot5H_2O$.

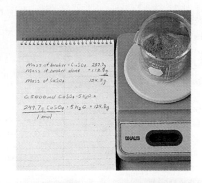

Add some solvent to the $CuSO_4\cdot5H_2O$ to dissolve it, then pour it into a 1.000 L volumetric flask.

Rinse the weighing beaker with more solvent, and pour it into the flask until the solution nears the neck of the flask.

Put the stopper in the flask, and swirl it thoroughly.

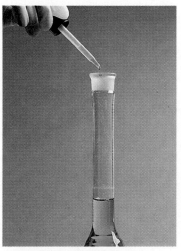

Carefully fill exactly to the 1.000 L mark with more solvent.

Restopper, and invert at least 10 times to ensure complete mixing.

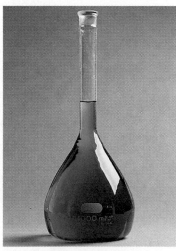

The resulting solution has 0.5000 mol of solute dissolved in 1.000 L of solution—a 0.5000 M concentration.

Sample Problem 11A
Calculating molarity

What is the molarity of a potassium chloride solution that has a volume of 400. mL and contains 85.0 g of KCl?

❶ List
- solution volume: 400. mL
- solute mass: 85.0 g KCl
- solute molar mass: $\dfrac{74.55 \text{ g KCl}}{1 \text{ mol KCl}}$
- solution concentration: **?** M KCl $= \dfrac{? \text{ mol KCl}}{\text{L}}$

❷ Set up
- Because the units of molarity are mol/L, the mass must be converted to an amount in moles and the volume of solution must be converted to liters.

$$\overset{\text{ⓐ}}{\dfrac{85.0 \text{ g KCl}}{400 \text{ mL}}} \times \overset{\text{ⓑ}}{\dfrac{1000 \text{ mL}}{1 \text{ L}}} \times \overset{\text{ⓒ}}{\dfrac{1 \text{ mol KCl}}{74.55 \text{ g KCl}}} = \dfrac{? \text{ mol KCl}}{\text{L}}$$

ⓐ Molarity is moles of solute per volume of solution. Place the solute quantity over the solution amount, even though they are not in the correct units yet.

ⓑ Multiply by a conversion factor that will cancel the *mL* to give units of *L* in the denominator.

ⓒ Use the conversion factor from the molar mass that will cancel the mass of KCl to give the amount in moles.

❸ Estimate and calculate
- Before calculating, round off the numbers in the setup, and solve the math in your head.

$$\dfrac{85}{400} \times \dfrac{1000}{1} \times \dfrac{1}{75} \approx \dfrac{17}{6} \approx \text{almost } 3$$

The answer is close to the estimate.

- Use your calculator to find the actual answer, rounding to the correct number of significant figures, which is three.

$$\dfrac{2.850\cancel{435949} \text{ mol KCl}}{\text{L}} = 2.85 \text{ M}$$

Sample Problem 11B
Variations with molarity: mass of solute

Sodium thiosulfate, $Na_2S_2O_3$, is used in developing photographic film. It is known to photographers as hypo or "fixer." How many grams of $Na_2S_2O_3$ are needed to make 100.0 mL of a 0.250 M solution?

❶ List
- solution volume: 100.0 mL
- solution concentration: 0.250 M $Na_2S_2O_3$
- solute mass: **?** g $Na_2S_2O_3$
- solute molar mass: $\dfrac{158.12 \text{ g } Na_2S_2O_3}{1 \text{ mol } Na_2S_2O_3}$

❷ Set up
- First, analyze what needs to be done to get the answer. You are trying to find out the mass in grams, and you are given a volume. First convert the volume to amount in moles using molarity.

$$\dfrac{100.0 \text{ mL}}{1} \times \dfrac{1 \text{ L}}{1000 \text{ mL}} \times \dfrac{0.250 \text{ mol } Na_2S_2O_3}{1 \text{ L}} = 0.0250 \text{ mol } Na_2S_2O_3$$

Note that this step is just like the mole-mass conversions from Chapter 3.

Then the number of moles can be converted to mass using the molar mass.

$$0.0250 \; \cancel{\text{mol Na}_2\text{S}_2\text{O}_3} \times \frac{158.12 \text{ g Na}_2\text{S}_2\text{O}_3}{1 \; \cancel{\text{mol Na}_2\text{S}_2\text{O}_3}} = ? \text{ g Na}_2\text{S}_2\text{O}_3$$

- Check the two steps to be sure that all units cancel except the proper unit for the answer, *g Na₂S₂O₃*.

❸ *Estimate and calculate*

- Use your calculator to find the precise answer. Round off to the correct number of significant figures.

$$0.0250 \; \cancel{\text{mol Na}_2\text{S}_2\text{O}_3} \times \frac{158.12 \text{ g Na}_2\text{S}_2\text{O}_3}{1 \; \cancel{\text{mol Na}_2\text{S}_2\text{O}_3}} = 3.953 = 3.95 \text{ g Na}_2\text{S}_2\text{O}_3$$

- Check the reasonableness of the answer.

The number $\dfrac{0.250 \text{ mol Na}_2\text{S}_2\text{O}_3}{1 \text{ L}}$ is the same as $\dfrac{\frac{1}{4} \text{ mol Na}_2\text{S}_2\text{O}_3}{1 \text{ L}}$.

A quarter of the molecular weight (160 g) would be about 40 g. Because the solution is one-tenth of a liter, we only need one-tenth of that amount, about 4.0 g.

Sample Problem 11C
Variations with molarity: solution stoichiometry

How many mL of a 0.500 M solution of copper(II) sulfate, CuSO₄, are needed to react with an excess of aluminum, Al, to provide 11.0 g of copper?

❶ *List*

- **solution concentration of reactant:** 0.500 M CuSO₄
- **mass of product:** 11.0 g Cu
- **solution volume:** *?* mL CuSO₄ solution
- **balanced equation for reaction:**
  $3\text{CuSO}_4(aq) + 2\text{Al}(s) \rightarrow 3\text{Cu}(s) + \text{Al}_2(\text{SO}_4)_3(aq)$
- **molar mass of CuSO₄:** 159.62 g/mol
- **molar mass of Cu:** 63.55 g/mol
- **mole ratio:** 3 mol CuSO₄:3 mol Cu

Because Al is in excess, it is not a factor in solving the problem.

❷ *Set up*

- You are trying to find the solution volume from the mass of a substance in a reaction. The amount of Cu produced is given in grams. By converting it to moles, you can determine the number of moles of CuSO₄ needed because the mole ratio of Cu to CuSO₄ is 3 to 3.

$$\frac{11.0 \text{ g Cu}}{1} \times \frac{1 \text{ mol Cu}}{63.55 \text{ g Cu}} \times \frac{3 \text{ mol CuSO}_4}{3 \text{ mol Cu}} \times \underline{\quad} \times \underline{\quad} = ? \text{ mL CuSO}_4 \text{ solution}$$

- Convert the amount in moles to a volume, using the reciprocal of molarity.

$$\frac{1 \text{ L solution}}{0.500 \text{ mol CuSO}_4}$$

- Then, convert *L of solution* to *mL of solution*.

$$\frac{11.0 \; \cancel{\text{g Cu}}}{1} \times \frac{1 \; \cancel{\text{mol Cu}}}{63.55 \; \cancel{\text{g Cu}}} \times \frac{3 \; \cancel{\text{mol CuSO}_4}}{3 \; \cancel{\text{mol Cu}}} \times \frac{1 \; \cancel{\text{L solution}}}{0.500 \; \cancel{\text{mol CuSO}_4}} \times \frac{1000 \text{ mL solution}}{1 \; \cancel{\text{L solution}}}$$

Check that all units cancel, except the answer unit, mL solution.

$$= ? \text{ mL CuSO}_4 \text{ solution}$$

Sample Problem 11C continued on next page . . .

❸ Estimate and calculate

- **Round off, and estimate.** $\dfrac{10}{1} \times \dfrac{1}{60} \times \dfrac{3}{3} \times \dfrac{1}{0.5} \times \dfrac{1000}{1} \approx 300$

- **Use the calculator, and record the proper significant figures.** Because the starting value, 11.0 g Cu, has only three significant figures, the answer should also have three.

$$\dfrac{11.0 \text{ g } \cancel{Cu}}{1} \times \dfrac{1 \text{ mol } \cancel{Cu}}{63.55 \text{ g } \cancel{Cu}} \times \dfrac{3 \text{ mol } \cancel{CuSO_4}}{3 \text{ mol } \cancel{Cu}} \times \dfrac{1 \cancel{\text{ L solution}}}{0.500 \text{ mol } \cancel{CuSO_4}} \times \dfrac{1000 \text{ mL solution}}{1 \cancel{\text{ L solution}}}$$

$$= 346.\cancel{1847107} \text{ mL} = 346 \text{ mL } CuSO_4 \text{ solution}$$

Practice 11A

Answers for Concept Review items and Practice problems begin on page 841.

1. What is the molarity of a sodium hypochlorite bleach that contains 125 g NaOCl in 2.00 L of solution?

2. How many milliliters of a 0.375 M solution of sodium hydrogen carbonate, $NaHCO_3$, are needed to provide 15.3 g of $NaHCO_3$?

3. How many liters of a 2.50 M solution of acetic acid, CH_3COOH, are needed to provide 256 g of acetic acid?

11B
4. How many grams of copper sulfate pentahydrate, $CuSO_4 \cdot 5H_2O$, will be needed to make 75.0 mL of 0.250 M solution?

5. How many kilograms of table sugar (sucrose: $C_{12}H_{22}O_{11}$) will be needed to make 3.50 L of a 1.15 M solution?

11C
6. The calcium phosphate used in fertilizers can be made according to the following unbalanced equation.

$$H_3PO_4(aq) + Ca(OH)_2(s) \longrightarrow Ca(H_2PO_4)_2(aq) + H_2O(l)$$

How many grams of each product would there be if 7.50 L of 5.00 M phosphoric acid reacted with an excess of calcium hydroxide?

7. The workers at a hazardous waste collection site have collected 12.5 L of solution from an automobile battery that contains a trace of lead(II) ions. They add an excess of sodium hydroxide to make insoluble lead hydroxide, which will not leach into ground water. If the completed reaction provides 0.285 g of lead(II) hydroxide, what was the initial molar concentration of the lead(II) ions in the solution?

Section Review

10. What is the molar concentration of these solutions?
    a. 0.0750 moles of $NaHCO_3$ in a volume of 115 mL of solution
    b. 0.750 moles of $NaC_2H_3O_2$ in a volume of 115 mL of solution

11. **a.** If a solution has 3.0 mol of solute in 2.0 L of solution, what is its molar concentration?
    b. How many moles would there be in 350 mL of solution?

12. Methanol can react according to the following equation.

$$CH_3OH(l) + HBr(aq) \longrightarrow CH_3Br(g) + H_2O(l)$$

If there are exactly 2.25 mol of CH_3OH, how many liters of 0.500 M HBr will be needed?

13. Describe in your own words exactly how you would prepare 1.00 L of a 0.85 molar solution of formic acid, HCOOH.

14. **Story Link**
    On page 403, you read that Dr. Ramsay's tests on bear fat revealed a PCB concentration of 8 ppm. How many milligrams of PCB would there be in 35 g of this bear fat?

11-3

Why do some things dissolve?

Section Objectives

Determine polarity of solutes using electronegativity and molecular geometry.

Describe the solvation process.

Explain the solubility of ionic solutes and polar solutes in water.

Explain the insolubility of nonpolar solutes in water.

Testing solubility

Chem Fact
Toluene, once common in school labs, is now considered a dangerous chemical. In 1991, the EPA urged industry to cut toluene emissions in half by 1995.

Some substances dissolve, while others do not. The easiest way to determine whether something will dissolve is to add it to a solvent and watch what happens. **Figure 11-10** shows a series of situations with one solute and two solvents. The solute is lithium chloride, LiCl, a white solid. One solvent is toluene, $C_6H_5CH_3$, a clear liquid with a slight petroleum odor; the other is the most popular solvent in chemistry—water, H_2O. Lithium chloride and water are the only pair that dissolve.

Will it dissolve? Using models to explain why

The model for explaining solubility is based on the very simple idea of attractions between particles. Lithium chloride is composed of ions with large electrical charges, which attract each other strongly. Water is composed of polar molecules with a slightly positive end and a slightly negative end.

Figure 11-10
When water and lithium chloride, LiCl, are mixed, LiCl dissolves. When toluene and LiCl are mixed, LiCl does not dissolve. When toluene and water are mixed, they form two immiscible layers.

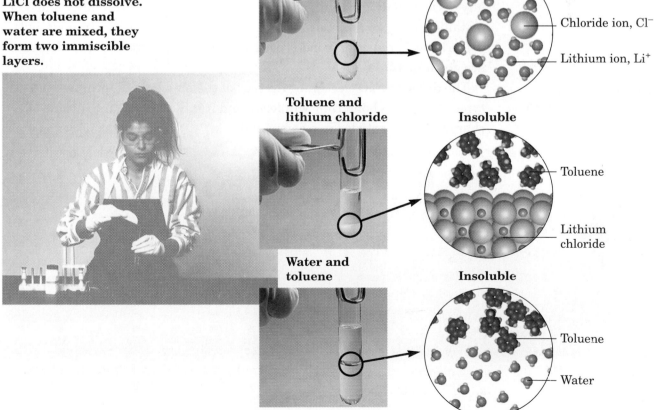

Water and lithium chloride — Soluble — Water, Chloride ion, Cl^-, Lithium ion, Li^+

Toluene and lithium chloride — Insoluble — Toluene, Lithium chloride

Water and toluene — Insoluble — Toluene, Water

Nevertheless, the attraction between ions such as lithium and chloride and water molecules is strong enough that the water molecules can pull the ions away from the solid crystal. This attraction causes lithium chloride to dissolve in water.

What happens when lithium chloride and toluene are mixed? Toluene molecules carry essentially no electrical charge, so they are not strongly attracted to the ions in the crystal. But ions within the crystal are attracted strongly to each other. In the absence of any similar attraction, the ions remain embedded in the solid crystal.

In the third example you saw the combination of the two solvents, toluene and water. There is very little attraction between the molecules of toluene and water, but this factor alone is not why the liquids do not dissolve. The real obstacle is the attraction that each water molecule has for other water molecules. Imagine a single water molecule about to penetrate the layer of toluene. Ahead of it are toluene molecules for which the water molecule has very little attraction or repulsion. Behind the water molecule, however, are water molecules with partial electrical charges that attract each other. These other molecules pull the water molecule back into the water layer.

Predicting attractions

To predict whether two substances will dissolve, you must first predict attractions by determining whether the particles contain electrical charges. This process begins with investigating the types of chemical bonds. In Chapter 6 you learned that there are several fundamental types of bonds, including ionic, polar covalent, and nonpolar covalent. We will examine these to see how each affects solubility. Because metallic substances usually dissolve only in other metals, you will not consider solubility and metallic bonds. You may also recall from Chapter 6 that electronegativity is the key to predicting bond type. The electronegativities of the elements are given in **Table 11-3**.

The difference in electronegativities of the elements determines the type of chemical bond they will form, and it indicates the magnitude of charge on the particles in a compound.

**Table 11-3
Electronegativity
Values**

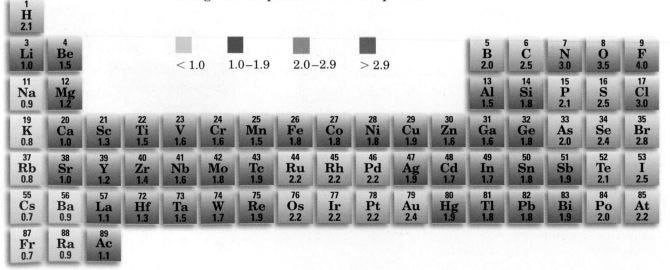

Ionic bonds have strong attractions

Two elements will form an ionic bond when the difference in the electro-negativities is 2.1 or more. This type of bond does not result in molecules but in ionic crystals composed of millions of rows of alternating positive and negative ions.

The particles that make up an ionic crystal have full electrical charges. In many cases the charges are 1+ and 1−, but some are stronger, such as the 2+ and 3+ charges on the Mg^{2+} ion and Al^{3+} ion. All these ions have very strong attractions for other charged ions and molecules with partial charges, and this attraction will determine how they dissolve.

Nonpolar covalent bonds have no charges

Two atoms will form a nonpolar covalent bond when the difference in the electronegativities is in the range of 0 through 0.4. Because the atoms in a nonpolar covalent bond share the electrons equally, neither is more positive or negative than the other. Nonpolar covalent bonds, as the name suggests, carry no electrical charge. In the absence of other attractions, nonpolar molecules will dissolve in each other.

Polar covalent bonds have weak charges

Two atoms will form a polar covalent bond when the difference in the electronegativities is in the range of 0.4 through 2.1. When chlorine, which has an electronegativity of 3.0, bonds with hydrogen, which has an electronegativity of 2.1, the atoms share electrons unequally. Because the shared electrons spend more time near the nucleus of the chlorine atom than the hydrogen atom, the chlorine atom carries a slight negative charge, and the hydrogen atom carries a slight positive charge. These partial charges are represented by δ− and δ+ in **Figure 11-11**. They are not as strong as the full negative and positive charges on ions, but they are strong enough to attract other particles with charges, such as other polar molecules and ions. Thus, you would expect molecules held together by polar covalent bonds to dissolve ionic compounds and each other.

Testing predictions in the lab

The model of solubility based on attractions and differences in bond type has led to several generalizations about solubility. So far, you expect that polar covalent molecules and ions will dissolve together because they contain charges that can attract. You saw an example of this when the LiCl dissolved in water in **Figure 11-10**. Similarly, you could predict that ions and polar covalent molecules will not dissolve in molecules such as toluene that contain nonpolar covalent bonds and no charges. The experiments in **Figure 11-10** support this prediction.

But are these rules enough to predict all cases? What would happen if you mixed water with carbon tetrachloride, CCl_4? Both contain polar covalent bonds, so you predict they will dissolve. But if you try this in the lab, the results may surprise you: they *don't* dissolve, as shown in **Figure 11-12**.

Figure 11-11
This model for a polar covalent bond shows an electron cloud that is more dense near the chlorine nucleus, resulting in partial charges.

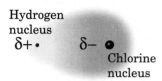

Hydrogen
nucleus
δ+ •   δ− •
                Chlorine
                nucleus

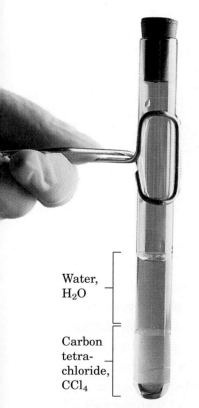

Water,
H_2O

Carbon
tetra-
chloride,
CCl_4

Figure 11-12
Even though carbon tetrachloride, CCl_4, and water, H_2O, both have polar covalent bonds, they do not dissolve in each other.

Any scientist's first instinct is to double-check and make sure that the chemicals are not contaminated and that the procedure was carried out properly. Even when double-checked repeatedly, CCl_4 and H_2O do not dissolve. The prediction was incorrect.

In this case the theory is not totally wrong, but it is incomplete. It turns out that the type of bond is not the only factor that determines solubility. The shape of the molecule is also important.

Molecular shape affects polarity

In a molecule with only two atoms, such as HCl, the atoms can be arranged in only one way—a straight line. However, if a molecule has three atoms, more than one arrangement is possible, as you may recall from your study of molecular shapes in Chapter 6.

A molecule of hydrogen sulfide, H_2S, is arranged in a V shape (bent), whereas a molecule of carbon dioxide, CO_2, has a straight-line (linear) configuration. Both of these molecules, shown in **Figure 11-13**, contain polar covalent bonds. You might expect that both of them would act like particles containing charges and dissolve easily in water. But nearly three times more H_2S dissolves in water than CO_2! Having polar covalent bonds is not enough to ensure solubility. *The molecule must also be polar overall.*

Figure 11-13a
Molecules that contain three atoms can be arranged in two different ways. H_2S exists in a V-shaped (bent) arrangement, . . .

$\delta+$

Hydrogen
nucleus

$\delta+$

Hydrogen
nucleus

$\delta-$

Sulfur
nucleus

11-13b
. . . but CO_2 exists in a straight-line (linear) arrangement.

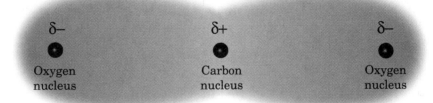

$\delta-$

Oxygen
nucleus

$\delta+$

Carbon
nucleus

$\delta-$

Oxygen
nucleus

Determining effective poles

Examine the models of the CO_2 and H_2S molecules. Each molecule appears to have three different partial charges. But a nearby molecule or ion does not distinguish among all of the individual charges within another small molecule. It is affected by only an overall partial positive charge at one part of the molecule and an overall partial negative charge elsewhere. These average overall charges are called "effective poles."

H_2S and CO_2 have different solubilities resulting from the locations of their effective poles. To determine the location of the effective poles in a molecule, draw its structure with the correct shape, and then connect all of the partial positive charges. The center of the line or shape they form will be the effective positive pole. Do the same for the negative charges to determine the effective negative pole.

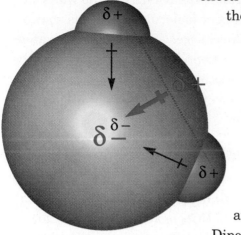

Figure 11-14
Other negative charges are attracted to an H₂S molecule as if it had an effective positive pole midway between its two hydrogen atoms.

δ   Partial charge
δ   Effective pole
→   Bond dipole
→   Molecular dipole

Figure 11-15
Other charges are not attracted or repelled by a CO₂ molecule because the effective poles are at the same place and cancel each other.

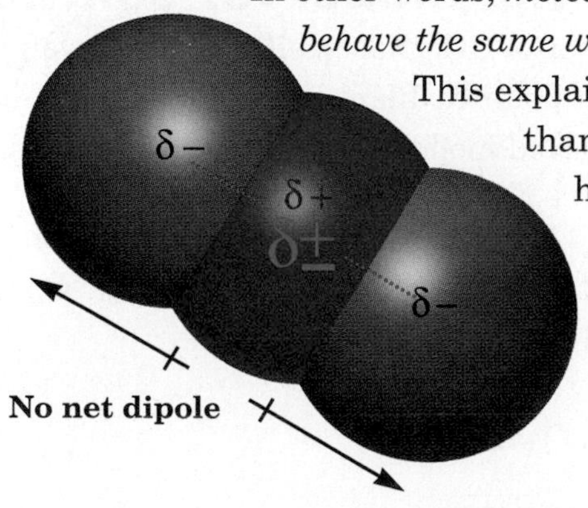

Try this first with the molecule of H_2S shown in **Figure 11-14**. When you connect the two partial positive charges, you get a straight line. The effective positive pole will be at the midpoint of the line connecting the hydrogen atoms. In **Figure 11-14**, and in the molecules on the next few pages, *partial charges are shown in black, and effective poles are shown in blue*. Although the effective positive pole may seem to be a "phantom" on one edge of the sulfur atom, the molecule will behave as though it had a single partial positive charge centered there.

All of the partial negative charges are on the center of the sulfur atom, so the effective negative pole is also there. Such a molecule is called a molecular *dipole*, because its two effective poles are on opposite sides of the molecule. Dipoles are indicated by an arrow pointing from positive to negative. Dipoles can also be drawn for individual bonds. The molecular dipole is the sum of the individual bond dipoles. In **Figure 11-14** and in the molecules on the next few pages, *bond dipoles are shown in black and molecular dipoles are shown in blue*.

If this polar H_2S molecule is approached by an anion or the negatively charged end of another molecular dipole, the positive portion of H_2S will be attracted, and the negative portion of H_2S will be repelled. These forces help a particle containing negative charges to dissolve in H_2S molecules.

Effective poles can cancel each other

Now consider the locations of effective poles on the CO_2 molecule shown in **Figure 11-15**. The midpoint of the line connecting the two partial negative charges is at the same place as the partial positive charge. In this molecule, the negative and positive effective poles are at the same point.

If a CO_2 molecule is approached by a negative charge, the negative charge will be attracted by the positive effective pole located at the center of the carbon atom. However, it will also be repelled by the negative effective pole, which is also located at the center of the carbon atom. These forces will cancel each other completely. The net effect will be as if the molecule had no effective poles at all.

Examine the bond dipoles in **Figure 11-15**. Because they point in opposite directions, they cancel each other. There is no molecular dipole. In other words, *molecules whose poles are at the same location behave the same way as molecules with nonpolar covalent bonds*. This explains why CO_2 is much less soluble in H_2O than H_2S is. Even though all three molecules have the same type of bonds, CO_2 molecules are *nonpolar* overall, and H_2O and H_2S molecules are dipoles.

No net dipole ✕

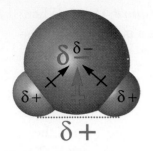

Figure 11-16
Electronegativity differences indicate that the bonds in water are polar covalent with partial charges on each end.

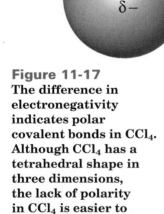

Figure 11-17
The difference in electronegativity indicates polar covalent bonds in CCl₄. Although CCl₄ has a tetrahedral shape in three dimensions, the lack of polarity in CCl₄ is easier to visualize using a two-dimensional square.

Reexamining water and carbon tetrachloride

Are the differences in H_2O and CCl_4 solubility also due to differences in overall polarity? To find out, first determine the polarity of the water molecule. Make a diagram with the correct bent molecular shape, as shown in **Figure 11-16**. All of the partial negative charges are on the oxygen atom, *so the effective charge will be at the same point.* "Average" the two positive charges. The effective positive charge is located in the space between the two hydrogen atoms. Because this space is not at the same location as the effective negative pole, water is a dipole.

Next, examine the molecule of carbon tetrachloride, CCl_4. We know from Chapter 6 that the shape of CCl_4 is a tetrahedron, with four bond angles of 109.5°. But this shape is three dimensional and is difficult to draw accurately on paper. *When determining polarity of molecules with four bond angles of 109.5° such as the CCl_4 molecule, the essential point, that CCl_4 is a symmetrical molecule, is more easily conveyed by representing the molecule as a square*, as in **Figure 11-17**.

Because CCl_4 contains four identical bonds, you must average the locations of the four negative charges to find the location of the effective negative pole. As before, connect the negative partial charges, forming a square. The effective negative pole is at the center of the square, on the central carbon atom.

The partial positive charges are also all on the central carbon atom, so the effective positive pole is there as well. Because the molecule is symmetrical, the effective positive and negative poles are at the same location and cancel each other.

As a result, the molecule cannot attract another charged particle or repel it. This makes CCl_4 a nonpolar molecule overall, with very little attraction for charges.

Now that you know the true nature of carbon tetrachloride, you can make a prediction that actually matches what happens. Water and carbon tetrachloride should not dissolve, because H_2O is a dipole. Even though carbon tetrachloride has polar bonds, the molecule as a whole is nonpolar. In other words, CCl_4 behaves more like the toluene molecules discussed at the beginning of this section than like water. The features of polar covalent bonds are given in **Figure 11-18** on the next page.

Completing the model for solutions

Now that the behavior of CCl_4 has been explained, you can add what you've learned about polar covalent bonds and dipoles to the model of solutions. This improved model can be used to predict solubilities for many substances.

Figure 11-18
Molecules with polar covalent bonds can be either polar or non-polar overall, depending on the location of their effective poles.

Predicting Polarity

IF the difference in electronegativity for bonded atoms is between . . .

. . . **0.4 and 2.1**,

THEN the bonds are **polar covalent**, as in the following.
$$\overset{\delta+}{C}\!-\!\overset{\delta-}{Cl} \text{ and } \overset{\delta+}{H}\!-\!\overset{\delta-}{O}$$

IF the effective poles . . .

. . . **are** in the same position,

THEN the molecule has **no** molecular dipole and no effective charges.

And **THEN**, the molecule is **nonpolar**, as in CCl_4.

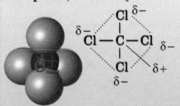

. . . are **not** in the same position,

THEN the molecule will be a **dipole** with effective charges, as in H_2O.

Predicting dipoles

Use these steps for a molecule with polar covalent bonds.
1. For each polar covalent bond, place a $\delta-$ on the atom with higher electronegativity and a $\delta+$ on the atom with lower electronegativity.
2. Place a $\delta+$ at the position of the effective positive pole by averaging the locations of the individual positive poles.
   - The average location of two poles is the midpoint of the line connecting the partial positive charges.
   - The average location of three poles is the center of the triangle formed by connecting the partial positive charges.
   - The average location of four or more poles is the center of the shape formed by connecting the partial positive charges.
3. Place a $\delta-$ at the position of the effective negative pole by averaging the locations of the individual negative charges using the method in step 2.
4. If the effective positive pole is in a different location than the effective negative pole, the molecule is a dipole that can attract charges. Otherwise, the molecule is nonpolar.

Predict solubility

1. Determine bond type by calculating electronegativity difference and selecting range.

2. Indicate charges as needed on a structure of the substance. Check for dipoles if needed.

3. Identify particle types and charges. Determine solubility.

IF the difference in electronegativities for bonded atoms is between . . .

. . . **0.0 and 0.4,**

THEN the bonds are **nonpolar covalent,** as in CH_4.

. . . **0.4 and 2.1,**

THEN the bonds are **polar covalent.**

IF the effective poles . . .

. . .**2.1 and 4.0,**

THEN the bonds are **ionic.**

And **THEN,** . . .

. . . **are** in the same position,

THEN the molecule has **no** molecular dipole and no effective charges.

And **THEN,** the molecule behaves as if it were **nonpolar,** as in CCl_4.

. . . **are not** in the same position,

THEN the molecule will be a **dipole** with effective charges, as in H_2O.

. . . the particles are **ions** with **full charges** in a crystal lattice, as in NaCl.

And **THEN,** because there is **no** net separation of charge on the particles, the substance will be

• **soluble** in **nonpolar** solvents
• insoluble in polar solvents

And **THEN,** because there is a net **separation of charge** on the particles, the substance will be

• **soluble** in **polar** solvents
• insoluble in nonpolar solvents

Overall polarity of molecules determines solubility

In this chapter you have focused on three types of substances: nonpolar molecules, molecular dipoles, and ionic crystals. Nonpolar molecules with either polar or nonpolar bonds carry no overall charge. When it comes to solubility, the full charges of ions and the partial charges of dipoles are grouped together because they attract each other. You can use the presence or absence of charges to predict whether one chemical will dissolve in another. Chemists sometimes summarize this rule by saying "like dissolves like."

• Many charged substances (ions and dipoles) will dissolve in other charged substances. (Some exceptions are described in **Table 11-1** on page 410.)
• A nonpolar substance will dissolve in another nonpolar substance.
• A polar or charged substance will not dissolve in a nonpolar substance. These principles are summarized in the feature above, which can be used to help predict a substance's solubility.

Sample Problem 11D
Analyzing molecules for polarity

The structure of tetrachloroethylene is shown here. Use the electronegativity data in **Table 11-3** and the feature on page 424 to determine if C_2Cl_4 is a molecular dipole. Describe its solubility.

For C_2Cl_4, the difference in electronegativities for bonded atoms is between . . .

1. Determine bond type by calculating electronegativity difference and selecting range.

There are two types of bonds in this molecule: the C≡C double bond and the C—Cl single bond.

. . . **0.0 and 0.4** for the C═C bond $(2.5 - 2.5 = 0.0)$.

So **THEN** the C═C bonds are **nonpolar covalent.**

. . . **0.4 and 2.1** for the C—Cl bonds $(3.0 - 2.5 = 0.5)$.
So **THEN** the C—Cl bonds are **polar covalent.**

$$\delta^-Cl \quad\quad Cl\ \delta^-$$
$$\delta^+C═C\ \delta^+$$
$$\delta^-Cl \quad\quad Cl\ \delta^-$$

For C_2Cl_4, the effective poles **are** in the same position.

2. Indicate charges as needed on a structure of the substance.

*Using the rules for effective poles, the effective negative pole is at the center of the rectangular shape formed by the chlorine atoms. The effective positive pole is halfway between the two carbon atoms. Both poles are at the same place, so there is **no molecular dipole**.*

So **THEN**, C_2Cl_4 has **no** molecular dipole and no effective charges.

And **THEN**, C_2Cl_4 behaves as if it were **nonpolar** covalent.

(**IF** they **were not** in the same position,

THEN the molecule would be a **dipole**, with effective charges.)

3. Identify particle types and charges to determine solubility.

The molecule as a whole is nonpolar, even though it contains polar covalent bonds. It will behave as a nonpolar substance.

And **THEN**, because there is **no** net separation of charge on the particles, C_2Cl_4 will be

• **soluble** in **nonpolar** solvents
• **insoluble** in polar solvents

(And **THEN**, because there would be a net **separation of charge** on the particles, it would be

• **soluble** in **polar** solvents
• **insoluble** in nonpolar solvents)

Practice 11D

1. The structure of boron trichloride, BCl_3, is shown at right. Use **Table 11-3** and the feature on page 424 to determine if BCl_3 is polar.

2. Sulfur dioxide, SO_2, is represented at right. Use **Table 11-3** and the feature on page 424 to determine whether it will dissolve in water.

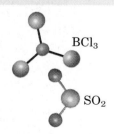

BCl_3

SO_2

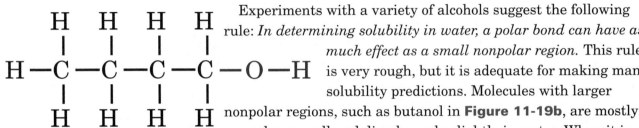

Figure 11-19a
Ethanol has both a polar region (shown in color) and a nonpolar region. It is polar overall.

Molecules with two types of bonds

There are many larger molecules that contain some regions with polar covalent bonds and other regions with nonpolar covalent bonds. Ethanol (ethyl alcohol), shown in **Figure 11-19a**, is a good example. The molecule contains one C—C bond, one C—O bond, one O—H bond, and five C—H bonds. Electronegativity calculations show that the C—C bond and the five C—H bonds are nonpolar, whereas the C—O and O—H are polar. The two polar bonds do not cancel each other, so the region around the oxygen is negative, and the region around the hydrogen next to the oxygen is positive. The remainder of the molecule is nonpolar.

Ethanol is found in beer, wine, and other alcoholic beverages. Because it mixes well with water, you might guess that the entire molecule is polar overall even though part of the molecule contains nonpolar bonds. The two polar bonds can create a dipole that can attract other polar molecules.

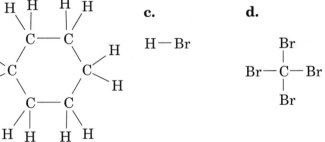

11-19b
Because butanol's nonpolar region is much larger than its polar region, it is nonpolar overall.

Experiments with a variety of alcohols suggest the following rule: *In determining solubility in water, a polar bond can have as much effect as a small nonpolar region.* This rule is very rough, but it is adequate for making many solubility predictions. Molecules with larger nonpolar regions, such as butanol in **Figure 11-19b**, are mostly nonpolar overall and dissolve only slightly in water. When it is important to know a chemical's precise solubility, you must either look it up in a chemical handbook or test it by adding small amounts to a solvent.

Section Review

15. For each of the compounds shown below, determine the particle type as described in the feature on page 424.

a.

KF (*s*)

b.

c.

H—Br

d.

Br—C—Br with Br above and Br below

16. Use your answers from item **15** to answer the following questions. Would you expect compounds **a** and **b** to dissolve in each other? Would you expect compounds **b** and **d** to dissolve in each other? Estimate each compound's solubility in water.

17. Explain how water molecules can attract ions.

 18. Story Link
Analyze the PCB molecule shown on page 402. Is the molecule polar or nonpolar?

19. Story Link
Why does the PCB molecule have a greater solubility in fats and oils? (Hint: fats and oils are mostly nonpolar substances.)

11-4

Can insoluble substances mix?

Section Objectives

Describe the role of emulsions in mixing nonpolar solutes with water.

List the chemical characteristics of an emulsifying agent.

Relate the action of soaps and detergents to the properties of an emulsifying agent.

Overcoming insolubility

You have probably heard the saying, "Oil and water don't mix." It's true. You can demonstrate it the next time you prepare dinner by making oil and vinegar salad dressing.

In a small bottle or carafe, add olive oil to a depth of about 3 cm, then add about 15 mL (3 teaspoons) vinegar, which is a solution of acetic acid and water. You will see the vinegar sink through the oil and collect at the bottom, as in **Figure 11-20**. This observation indicates two things.

1. Vinegar sinks because it is more dense than olive oil.
2. The two liquids are immiscible (insoluble).

Continue adding vinegar until you have about half as much vinegar as oil. If you cap the carafe and shake well, you will see a turbulent mixture of oil and vinegar. What you *can't* see are millions of microscopic droplets of vinegar surrounded by oil. This mixture is called an **emulsion**. The droplets formed in an emulsion are colloidal particles. They are smaller than the particles in a suspension, but larger than the particles in a solution.

This salad-dressing emulsion is a temporary condition. As soon as you stop shaking the container, the droplets of oil begin to rise, the vinegar sinks, and the layers of each re-form. Clearly, the olive oil and vinegar do not dissolve.

emulsion
colloidal-sized droplets (about 100 nm wide) of one liquid suspended in another liquid

Figure 11-20
Oil and vinegar will mix if shaken vigorously. However, the particles of oil and vinegar do not make a homogeneous solution.

To complete your salad dressing, you may wish to add small amounts of salt, chopped onion, mustard powder, pepper, or other spices. Shake the carafe to form an emulsion just before pouring the dressing. This will ensure that you get all of the flavors: vinegar, olive oil, and the spices that dissolve in each solvent.

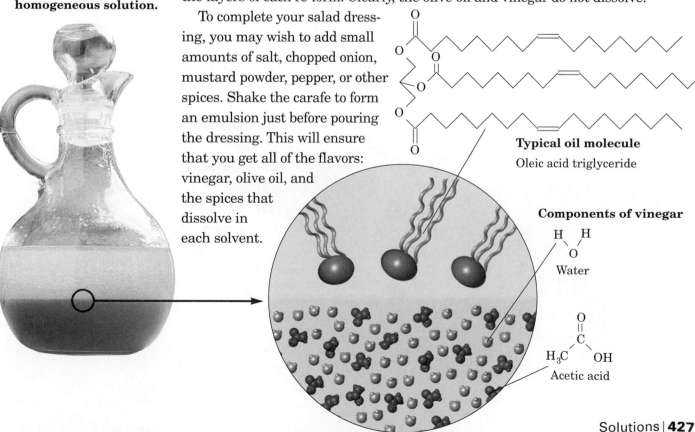

Typical oil molecule
Oleic acid triglyceride

Components of vinegar

H H
O
Water

O
‖
C
H₃C   OH
Acetic acid

Emulsions: making oil and water mix

The next time you are at the grocery store, look at the commercial oil and vinegar salad dressings. You will see two types. The traditional type has distinct layers. The newer type, shown in **Figure 11-21**, has no layers because the oil and vinegar have been mixed in such a way that they stay mixed. The secret of the new style is the addition of a chemical that keeps the oil and vinegar in an emulsion.

Lecithin, which is found in all living organisms, is a family of several similar molecules that stabilize emulsions. Lecithin is obtained commercially by extracting it from soybeans. As you can see in **Figure 11-21**, lecithin molecules have three major branches. The two longer branches are nonpolar, but the shorter, third branch is polar.

When lecithin is added to pure water or pure oil, it dissolves in oil but not in water. Its real value, however, lies in its ability to attract and dissolve in both oil and water when these solvents are present together. Each molecule of lecithin dissolves partly in the oil and partly in the water, linking two immiscible liquids. Lecithin stabilizes emulsions, preventing the layers from re-forming. Lecithin is an **emulsifying agent**.

It is often said that emulsifying agents make oil and water mix. It is more accurate to say that when oil and water are vigorously agitated, they mix to form an emulsion and that the emulsifying agent keeps the oil and water mixed. Some other emulsifying agents found in food are shown in **Table 11-4** on the next page.

Chem Fact
The proteins in eggs are used as emulsifiers in most baking recipes.

emulsifying agent
stabilizes an emulsion that would otherwise separate into different phases

Figure 11-21
An oil and vinegar emulsion can be stabilized by adding an emulsifying agent, such as lecithin. The emulsifying agent acts as a bridge between the oil and the watery vinegar to make them mix.

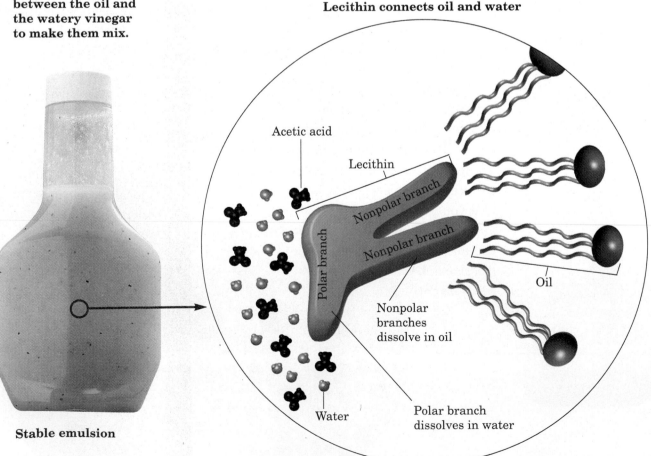

Lecithin connects oil and water

Acetic acid

Lecithin

Nonpolar branch

Nonpolar branch

Polar branch

Oil

Nonpolar branches dissolve in oil

Water

Polar branch dissolves in water

Stable emulsion

Table 11-4
Some Common Food Emulsifiers*

Emulsifying agent types	Other names used in labeling	Uses
Arabic gum	acacia, Australian gum, gum senegal	beverages, candy, chewing gum
Carrageenan (dried seaweed plant)	chondrus, genugel, Irish gum, Irish moss gelose, pellugel, viscarin	artificially sweetened jellies and jams, cheese products, chocolate products, dessert gels, ice cream
Glycerides		baked goods, frozen desserts, fudge, ice cream, lard, margarine, peanut butter, whipped topping
Polysorbates	capmul, glycosperse, liposorb, monitan, monooleate or mono-stearate, polyoxyethylene sorbitan, polysorban 60 or 80	baked goods, barbecue sauce, chewing gum, cottage cheese, cream fillings, dried gelatin mix, frozen desserts, ice cream, icings, margarine, pickles, salad dressings, shortenings, vitamin supplements
Sodium stearoyl lactylate		baked good mixes, dehydrated potatoes, imitation cheese, snack dips, toppings, waffles
Sorbitan c	arlacel, crill, durtan, emsorb, sorbon, sorbitan monostearate, sorgen, span	cakes, fillings, icings, whipped topping
Tragacanth gum		baked goods, citrus beverages, condiments, fruit fillings, oils, relishes, salad dressings
Xanthan gum		baked goods, batter or breaded mixes, beverages, canned chili, desserts, jams, jellies, milk products, pizza topping mixes, salad dressings, stews (canned or frozen)

*Note: many of these emulsifiers also serve several other purposes in foods.

Soap is an emulsifying agent

Have you ever been dirty from working outside? If you washed your hands with water alone, you were probably only partly successful, as most of the dirt remained. To get really clean, plain water is not enough. You have to use soap and water, for reasons relating to emulsions.

Perspiration is a mixture of water and oils. Water cools your body by evaporation; oils keep your skin soft. However, over a period of time, the oils accumulate and coat your skin with an oily layer in which flakes of old skin, dirt, and bacteria become embedded.

Oil and water are immiscible, so the water may never remove the oil and dirt on your skin. To remove all of the dirt, you must first emulsify the oil by scrubbing, then stabilize it with an emulsifying agent like soap. Only then can the soap-and-oily-dirt emulsion be rinsed away from your skin by more water.

Figure 11-22
When you wash with soap, you create an emulsion of oil droplets dispersed in water and stabilized by soap.

Water

Oil

Nonpolar end of soap dissolves in oil

Charged end of soap dissolves in water

When you wash with soap, as shown in **Figure 11-22**, one end of the soap molecule dissolves in the oil while the other end dissolves in the surrounding water. The oil droplet stays suspended in the water and can be easily washed away.

Soap was apparently discovered thousands of years ago, and soap making is one of the oldest chemical industries. The two critical ingredients are lye, NaOH, or potash, KOH, and oils or fat. The North American settlers shown in **Figure 11-23** made their own potash by making a hole in the bottom of a barrel, filling the barrel with wood ashes, pouring water into the barrel, and then collecting the mild solution of potash that dripped from the bottom. Fat from slaughtered cows or pigs was combined with the potash, and then heated and stirred in a large kettle. The mixture was poured into a wooden frame, where it hardened into soap.

Figure 11-23
The steps in soap making are shown here, from making potash in the barrel at the right, boiling it with fat in the kettle in the middle, and cutting the soap into blocks at the left.

Although the settlers didn't know it, the chemical reaction that took place broke down the fat molecules into smaller molecules with charged and nonpolar ends, as shown in **Figure 11-24** on the next page. Such molecules make an effective emulsifying agent. Today, most soaps are made from vegetable oils instead of animal fat. One company was so pleased with the soap they made from palm and olive oils they named it Palmolive.

Animal fat molecule + 3 potash formula units (KOH) ⟶ 3 soap molecules + propanetriol (glycerine)

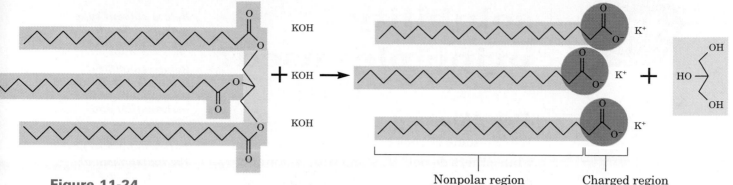

Figure 11-24
To make soap, an animal fat molecule reacts with potassium hydroxide (potash) to produce three soap molecules and a glycerine molecule.

Nonpolar region   Charged region

"Hard" water destroys soap's emulsifying abilities

Even though soap has been used for centuries, it is not the ideal cleaning agent. If you get your water from an underground source, you may have "hard" water, which contains high concentrations of calcium and magnesium ions. In hard water, Ca^{2+} and Mg^{2+} cations are strongly attracted to the anionic end of soap. When cations attach to the anionic soap, they form an insoluble compound. You may have seen this scum in the form of bathtub rings. If you use soap and hard water in the washing machine, the scum clings to fabric and makes the clothes look dingy.

Detergents emulsify better in hard water

In the 1930s, chemists developed soap substitutes that work in hard water without forming insoluble compounds. They added other chemicals that enhance the basic cleaning power of the substitutes, and they named the mixture "detergent." Today, almost all laundry products are detergents.

To replace soap, chemists turned to a class of synthetic compounds that have long molecules with one end that is charged and soluble in water and another end that is nonpolar and insoluble.

Like soap, these compounds, called surface active agents, or **surfactants,** act at the surface that separates oil and water. In a detergent, a surfactant plays the same role as soap in stabilizing emulsions of oil in water. **Figure 11-25** shows the structure of one surfactant.

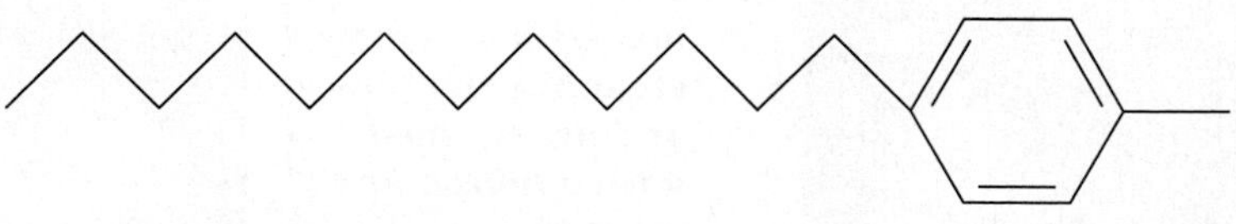

surfactant
a compound that stabilizes an emulsion by acting at the surface between two immiscible substances

Figure 11-25
Sodium dodecyl-benzene sulfonate is an anionic surfactant. This ionic compound does not make an insoluble scum with calcium or magnesium ions.

SO_3^- Na^+

Section Review

20. How does an emulsion differ from a homogeneous mixture?
21. Explain why a substance containing only ionic bonds would not be a good emulsifier for mixtures of water and oil.
22. Contrast the behavior of soap and detergent in pure and "hard" water.

How are solubility principles used?

Dry cleaning

Why do some clothes need to be dry cleaned, while others do not? Washing with water and detergents cleans most clothes just fine. But there are three situations in which dry cleaning may be necessary: if your clothes have a stubborn stain, such as ink or rust; if you have spilled something greasy on your clothes; and if the label recommends it.

Certain fabrics, especially silk and wool, do not respond well to water. They may shrink, take on stubborn wrinkles, or lose their shape. To avoid these effects, they must be cleaned without water.

Cleaners use solubility principles to remove stains

Dry cleaners are experts at removing stubborn stains. Some dry cleaners will ask you which food was spilled on a garment. Knowing the composition of the stain helps them decide how to treat it. Removing a stain, such as oil or grease, that doesn't dissolve in water involves two steps, as shown in **Figure 11-26**. First, the stain is treated with a substance that loosens the stain when the area is brushed. The stain is removed when the garment is washed in a mechanical dry cleaner.

If a garment has a water-soluble stain, it is first treated with a stain remover that is specific for that stain. The stain is then flushed away with a steam gun. The garment is allowed to dry, and then it is placed in the dry-cleaning machine to remove any other stains that are insoluble in water. *Dry cleaning does involve liquids.* The process uses a nonpolar solvent, tetrachloroethylene (perchloroethylene), instead of water.

Figure 11-26a
These pants have a spaghetti sauce stain on them, so this man is loosening the stain by brushing liquid solvent into the spot.

11-26b
The pants are then loaded into a dry-cleaning machine and are washed with a nonpolar solvent.

Dry cleaning is said to have started in 1825, when a kerosene lamp was knocked over onto a greasy tablecloth at the house of a dye-factory owner, Jean-Baptiste Jolly. When the cloth dried, the area of the kerosene spill was noticeably cleaner. In the early decades of dry cleaning, some firms dipped the clothes first in kerosene and then in gasoline, both excellent degreasers. But they are also dangerous to use because they are very flammable.

A good dry-cleaning solvent must be nonpolar so that it can dissolve oil and grease, which trap the water-insoluble particles in the cloth fibers. Tetrachloroethylene, C_2Cl_4, shown in **Figure 11-27**, is favored because it is a versatile solvent of oil, grease, and alcohols; it is not flammable; and it is volatile, so it can be recycled. When the solvent is pumped from the dry-cleaning machine, it contains a certain amount of dissolved oils from clothes. It can be reused up to 200 times, but if it is reused excessively it stops taking oil out and starts putting it into the clothes. The solvent can be recycled by distillation: when heated, C_2Cl_4 vaporizes, leaving the oils behind; when cooled, the C_2Cl_4 vapors condense to form the clean solvent.

Tetrachloroethylene is a suspected carcinogen, and the United States Occupational Safety and Health Administration has said that dry-cleaning workers should not inhale air containing more than 200 ppm of the solvent.

Figure 11-27
The most commonly used dry-cleaning solvent is tetrachloroethylene, C_2Cl_4.

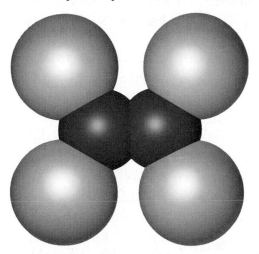

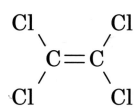

Consumer Focus

Stain removal

When you remove stains, you can see solubility principles in action. Beverage stains can be very stubborn because they contain so many different compounds. To remove stains of coffee, soft drinks, or wine, experts suggest the following series of solvents.

Prepare a 1.0 L solution of warm water and about 5 mL of hand dishwashing detergent, made acidic with about 20 mL of vinegar. Soak and occasionally agitate the fabric in this solution for about 30 min.

Rinse with water. Soak in ethanol or isopropanol (sold as rubbing alcohol) for 15 min. Rinse with water. Soak for 30 min. in a solution of about 20 mL of enzyme-containing laundry detergent mixed with about a quart of warm water. If any stain remains, mix a solution of one part chlorine bleach (by volume) to about four parts of water. Test the fabric to be sure the bleach won't change the color, and then soak the fabric in the bleach solution for 2 min. Rinse with water.

Gas solubility

If you look at an unopened soda bottle, the liquid inside has no bubbles. But what happens once you open an ice-cold soda bottle? First, there is a hissing sound of gas escaping. Then you can see bubbles rising in the liquid. When you first taste it, there is plenty of "fizz" and it is tart. Later, after it is warm, it tastes "flat."

Why does this happen? Where did the bubbles come from? What can you do to keep soda from going flat? If you apply what you already know about gases and solutions, you can answer these questions and others. You may already know that the bubbles in soda are due to carbon dioxide gas, CO_2. Because the bubbles are not visible in the unopened soda bottle, shown in **Figure 11-28a**, you know the bottle's contents, including the CO_2, are a solution that is stable and homogeneous. Part of the CO_2 reacts with water to form carbonic acid, H_2CO_3, which gives the soda a tart taste.

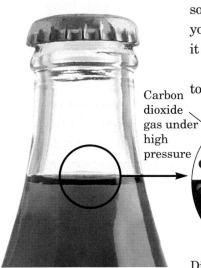

Carbon dioxide gas under high pressure

Dissolved carbon dioxide molecule

Figure 11-28a
There are no bubbles in an unopened bottle of soda because carbon dioxide is dissolved in the liquid.

11-28b
When the bottle cap is removed, the pressure inside the bottle decreases rapidly. Carbon dioxide escapes due to the lower solubility of CO_2.

Carbonation depends on pressure

From Chapter 10, you know that if gas escapes from a container, such as a soda bottle, the pressure is lowered. After this decrease in pressure, the bubbles of CO_2 are seen coming out of the solution.

Chemists have figured out the details of the relationship between pressure and gas solubility. Henry's law sums up the basic idea: *the amount of gas dissolved in a solvent is proportional to the partial pressure of that gas over the solvent.* In an unopened soda bottle, there is a higher partial pressure of CO_2 in the neck of the bottle, above the liquid, than there is in the air outside of the bottle. When the bottle is opened, the CO_2 escapes into the air, and the partial pressure of CO_2 in the bottle's neck soon equals that of the CO_2 in the air. As a result of this decrease in the partial pressure of CO_2, the solubility of CO_2 in the soda is reduced, the solution becomes supersaturated, and the excess CO_2 bubbles out of solution, as shown in **Figure 11-28b**.

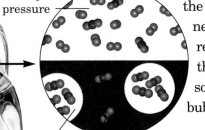

Air at atmospheric pressure

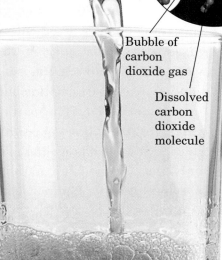

Bubble of carbon dioxide gas

Dissolved carbon dioxide molecule

Gas solubility decreases with increased temperature

After the soda bottle is open and the soda gets warmer, it has fewer bubbles and tastes flat. Similarly, if you compare the taste of a newly opened warm soda with that of a newly opened cold soda, the warm soda will taste flat.

Warm soda is flat because there is less CO_2 dissolved in it. Chemists have found that other dissolved gases follow a similar pattern: *solubility decreases with increasing temperature.* Recall from **Figure 11-5** on page 407 that this pattern is the *opposite* of what you know about most solid solutes, which dissolve better in hot solvents.

Gas solubility and diving

The principles of gas solubility are used in a variety of situations other than soda bottles. Knowledge of these principles is a life-or-death matter for the underwater diver shown in **Figure 11-29**.

When divers are underwater, they are subject to more pressure than at the surface. As a result, the pressure of the air that they breathe must be increased to force the air out of the air tank and into their lungs.

The diver's blood is a water-based mixture. Gases such as oxygen are carried by hemoglobin molecules within the blood cells in this solution. But some oxygen and other gases, such as nitrogen, which makes up most of air, can dissolve in the blood just like carbon dioxide in soda.

If a diver breathing pressurized air rises to the surface too quickly, decompression sickness, called "the bends," can result, causing intense pain and possibly even death.

Figure 11-29
Underwater divers breathing pressurized air must return to the surface gradually to prevent "the bends."

The sudden decrease from high air pressure to normal air pressure is similar to the decrease that takes place when you open a soda bottle. Gases, such as nitrogen, that dissolve in blood, body fluids, and nonpolar fat bubble out of solution. Such bubbles in the blood can block blood flow in smaller blood vessels, press on tissues, and affect nerve impulses.

Most deep-sea divers prevent "the bends" by breathing a mixture that contains helium instead of compressed air, which contains nitrogen. Because helium is less soluble than nitrogen, less of it dissolves in the body tissues. Then, if they have to return to the surface rapidly, there will be less gas bubbling out of solution.

Concept Review

Solubility of gases and carbonation

23. Explain why the carbon dioxide in the air is not enough to recarbonate an opened bottle of soda.

24. What can you do to keep soda from getting flat? Explain how your suggestions work.

Vitamins and solubility

Vitamins act to control chemical reactions within the body. Some vitamins promote the occurrence of specific chemical reactions that are a part of metabolism. Other vitamins prevent harmful reactions that could cause damage to the body. Without vitamins, the beneficial reactions do not occur, and deficiency diseases develop.

The body needs only small quantities of vitamins, about 0.4 g per kilogram of food that you eat. Essential vitamins are not made in the body; therefore, you must get them from the food you eat or by taking vitamin supplements. Not getting enough vitamins can make you sick, but so can getting too much. The reasons relate to solubility.

Vitamin C dissolves in water

People on poor diets have suffered from scurvy at least since the time of the Crusades, nearly 1000 years ago. Soldiers and sailors were especially susceptible to scurvy, which causes fatigue and bleeding of the gums and prevents wounds from healing. Some ships' captains claimed that lemon juice would prevent the disease.

The first controlled study of the effects of diet on scurvy was in 1747 when James Lind, a doctor in the British Royal Navy, compared the reactions of sailors suffering from scurvy when given cider, garlic, mustard, vinegar, ocean water, oranges, or lemons. The sailors who received citrus fruits recovered. We now know that citrus fruits, such as those in **Figure 11-30**, are rich in vitamin C. The structure of this important molecule is shown in **Figure 11-31**.

Researchers have found that vitamin C has several vital functions, but none is more important than its role in the synthesis of collagen. Collagen is the protein that makes up tendons, gives strength to teeth and bones, and, most importantly, knits endothelial cells together to make blood vessels.

To synthesize collagen where it is needed, vitamin C must be distributed throughout the body. Vitamin C is easily transported by the blood because it is water soluble. Important information about vitamin C and other water-soluble vitamins is shown in **Table 11-5** on the next page.

Healthy people have 5 mg or more of vitamin C per liter of blood plasma. Scurvy symptoms appear when this concentration falls to 1.5 mg/L. If an adult consumes the recommended dietary amount, 60 mg per day, the concentration in the blood plasma reaches about 8 mg/L.

But some people prefer to take a lot of vitamin C. Is it possible to take too much? Probably not. When intake increases, the vitamin C level rises to about 15 mg/L of plasma, but then the kidneys begin excreting the vitamin faster. Most people's blood concentration will not exceed 20 mg/L even if they consume 10 or 20 times the recommended amount. Your kidneys are so good at regulating water-soluble vitamins that overdosing on vitamin C is very unlikely.

Figure 11-30
Lemons, oranges, grapefruits, and limes are rich sources of vitamin C.

Chem Fact
1 cup canned orange juice:
86 mg vitamin C

1 baked potato with skin:
26 mg vitamin C

Figure 11-31
Vitamin C's most common form is ascorbic acid, shown here. Because ascorbic acid contains almost as many polar bonds as nonpolar bonds, it is very soluble in water but insoluble in fat and oil.

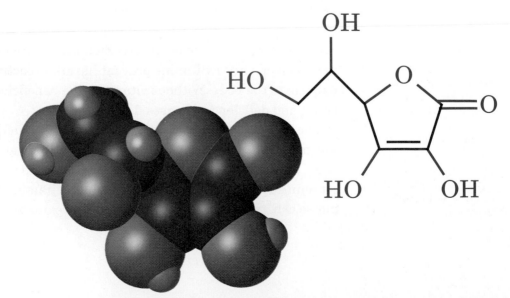

Table 11-5
Some Water-Soluble Vitamins

Vitamin	Chemical formula	Molecular mass (g/mol)	Reference daily intake (RDI)*
Folic acid	$C_{19}H_{19}N_7O_6$	441.40	180 µg
Vitamin B$_1$ (thiamine mononitrate)	$C_{12}H_{17}N_5O_4S$	327.36	1.2 mg (1200 µg)
Vitamin B$_2$ (riboflavin)	$C_{17}H_{20}N_4O_6$	376.36	1.4 mg (1400 µg)
Niacin	$C_6H_5NO_2$	123.11	1.6 mg (1600 µg)
Vitamin B$_6$ (pyridoxine hydrochloride)	$C_8H_{12}ClNO_3$	205.64	1.4 mg (1400 µg)
Vitamin B$_{12}$ (cyanocobalamin)	$C_{63}H_{88}CoN_{14}O_{14}P$	1355.38	2.0 µg
Vitamin C (ascorbic acid)	$C_6H_8O_6$	176.12	60 mg (60 000 µg)

*The RDI is the average intake recommended for individuals by the U. S. Food and Drug Administration.

Vitamin A dissolves in oils and fats

For decades, children have been told, "Eat your carrots so you'll have good eyes." There is some truth to the saying because carrots, and some other vegetables, contain carotenes that your body easily converts into vitamin A, which is shown in **Figure 11-32**. If you don't get enough vitamin A, you may lose your ability to see at night—a disorder called night blindness.

Vitamin A affects vision because your body uses it to make one of the vital light-sensitive molecules in the retina. Vitamin A is also needed for normal growth of skin, respiratory tract, cornea, and other epithelial tissues.

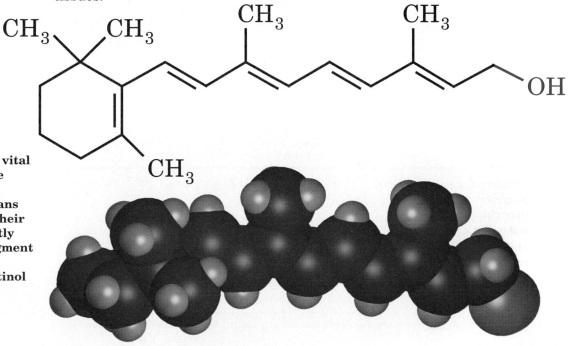

Figure 11-32
Vitamin A is also known as retinol because it plays a vital role in helping the retina of your eye detect light. Humans get about half of their vitamin A indirectly from the plant pigment carotene, which consists of two retinol molecules linked together.

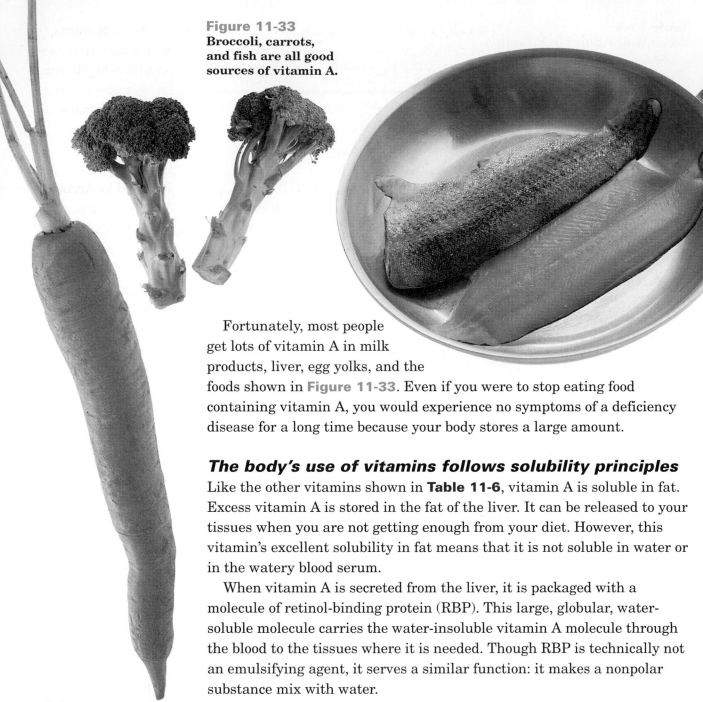

Figure 11-33
Broccoli, carrots, and fish are all good sources of vitamin A.

Fortunately, most people get lots of vitamin A in milk products, liver, egg yolks, and the foods shown in **Figure 11-33**. Even if you were to stop eating food containing vitamin A, you would experience no symptoms of a deficiency disease for a long time because your body stores a large amount.

The body's use of vitamins follows solubility principles

Like the other vitamins shown in **Table 11-6**, vitamin A is soluble in fat. Excess vitamin A is stored in the fat of the liver. It can be released to your tissues when you are not getting enough from your diet. However, this vitamin's excellent solubility in fat means that it is not soluble in water or in the watery blood serum.

When vitamin A is secreted from the liver, it is packaged with a molecule of retinol-binding protein (RBP). This large, globular, water-soluble molecule carries the water-insoluble vitamin A molecule through the blood to the tissues where it is needed. Though RBP is technically not an emulsifying agent, it serves a similar function: it makes a nonpolar substance mix with water.

Table 11-6
Some Fat-Soluble Vitamins

Vitamin	Chemical formula	Molecular mass (g/mol)	Reference daily intake (RDI)*	Toxicity level
Vitamin A (retinol)	$C_{20}H_{30}O$	286.44	875.0 µg	> 15 000 µg/day
Vitamin D (cholecalciferol and related compounds)	$C_{27}H_{44}O$	384.62	6.5 µg	> 5000 µg/day
Vitamin E (α-tocopherol)	$C_{29}H_{50}O_2$	430.69	9.0 mg (9000 µg)	> 600 mg/day (> 600 000 µg/day)

*The RDI is the average intake recommended for individuals by the U. S. Food and Drug Administration.

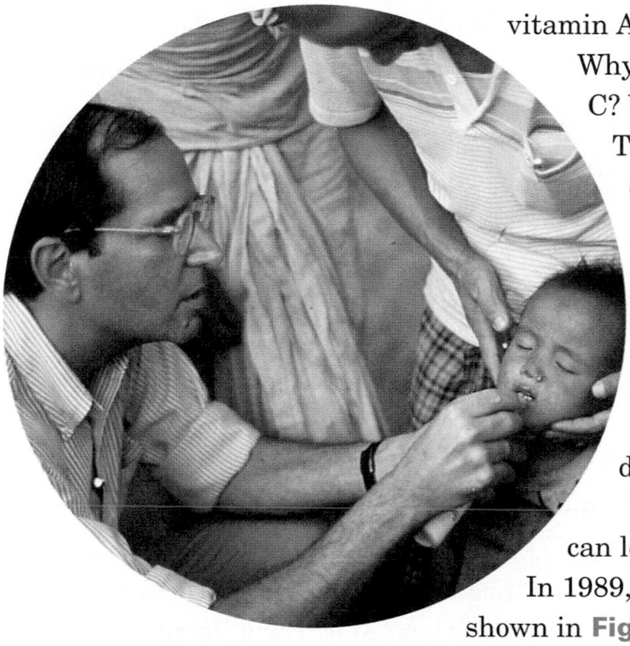

Figure 11-34
In Indonesia, Alfred Sommer examines a child for signs of vitamin A deficiency. Because vitamin A is fat soluble, it can be stored in the liver for long periods. Sommer believes that two vitamin A capsules per year, at a cost of one cent each, could prevent most cases of xerophthalmia.

Normally, because vitamin A is present in food only in small amounts, it is not possible to get too much. But sometimes people become enthusiastic about improving their diet and start taking large quantities of vitamin supplements or tablets. Large doses of vitamin A, taken for many weeks, can overload the storage capacity of the liver and raise the concentration of the vitamin throughout the body to toxic levels. Toxicity symptoms include dry, rough skin, cracked lips, hair loss, birth defects, headaches, and muscle and joint pain.

A bizarre case of extreme vitamin A poisoning was reported by Arctic explorers who killed and ate a polar bear. Members of the expedition who ate the bear's liver became very ill, and three of them lost patches of skin. Much later, scientists discovered that polar bear liver is extremely rich in vitamin A. A single quarter-pound (113 g) serving provides enough vitamin A to meet an adult's dietary requirement for 2.5 years!

Why is it possible to overdose on vitamin A but not vitamin C? Vitamin A is fat soluble; vitamin C is water soluble. The kidneys remove chemicals that are toxic or too concentrated from the blood. You would expect, therefore, that the kidneys would remove excesses of both vitamins A and C. But while the kidneys do a meticulous job of regulating small water-soluble molecules, they are far less effective in processing large molecules, including many proteins. This means that vitamin A is only gradually metabolized, or broken down by chemical reactions within the cells.

When vitamin A is completely absent from the diet, it can lead to blindness and hasten death by other ailments. In 1989, experts such as research physician Alfred Sommer, shown in **Figure 11-34**, estimated that 500 000 children in underdeveloped nations are blinded annually by xerophthalmia, a disintegration of the cornea due to the lack of vitamin A.

Section Review

25. Which compound would be the most effective dry-cleaning agent? Explain your answer.

    a. isopropanol, CH_3CH-CH_3 with OH

    b. acetic acid, CH_3C-OH with O

    c. cyclohexane, C_6H_{12}

26. What would you do to remove the dissolved gases in a sample of water?

27. Many fruit juices contain vitamin C. Why don't any contain substantial amounts of vitamin A?

28. Vitamin E is a long, chainlike molecule with several hydrocarbon rings on one end. Its formula is $C_{29}H_{50}O_2$. Would you expect levels of vitamin E to be easily controlled by the kidneys? Why?

29. **Story Link**

    Bears, like people, are mammals. Given what you've learned about the kidneys, explain why PCBs aren't flushed from the bears' bodies.

Solutions **439**

Conclusion: Solubility and the Arctic Bear Hunt

Range of polar bear

Baltic Sea

Hudson Bay

At the beginning of this chapter you followed Dr. Malcolm Ramsay as he examined a polar bear and took samples of its fat tissue to determine PCB content. This story posed some puzzling questions about the properties of PCBs. Look at those questions again.

How did the PCBs get into the Hudson Bay ecosystem when there is very little industry in the bay area? In past decades, the Baltic Sea was used as an ocean dump for PCBs and other wastes. It is likely that much of the discarded material remains in the mud at the bottom of the ocean. Because PCBs are slightly soluble in water, a small fraction of the PCBs dissolves and circulates in the ocean water.

Some PCBs are ingested by plankton, tiny marine animals. The plankton are eaten by larger plankton, which are eaten by fish. In addition to getting PCBs in their food, fish absorb some PCBs directly from the water. You may recall that oxygen is a nonpolar molecule and therefore has very low solubility

in water. One liter of ocean water contains only about 3×10^{-4} mol of O_2, whereas the air we breathe contains 9×10^{-3} mol of O_2 per liter. This means that as fish process very large quantities of water through their gills, they extract PCBs as well as oxygen from the water.

Once PCB molecules are ingested by a fish, they diffuse out of the fish's watery blood, dissolve in the oily liver, and stay there. Over time, the concentration of PCBs in the liver increases. In effect, fish serve as vacuum cleaners, picking up low-concentration PCBs from the water and storing them to produce far higher concentrations in their bodies.

Why did the PCBs end up in the bear's fat? When a seal eats a fish, the oil-soluble PCBs end up in the seal's oily blubber in concentrations that are even higher than those in fish. From there, it is just another step in the food chain to a polar bear's fat. The animals that are the most likely to have PCBs concentrated in their fatty tissues are polar bears. They are at the top of the food chain and live a long time.

Applying Concepts

1. What is the empirical formula of the PCB molecule on page 402?
2. Do you think this compound will float or sink in water? To estimate the density of the PCB molecule shown on page 402, find its molecular mass, and compare it with the molecular mass of biphenyl. Biphenyl, the related double-ring molecule with no chlorine atoms, has a density that is almost the same as water.

Research and Writing

Use the library to find out more about the following.

1. How can further buildup of PCBs in bears be prevented?
2. How can the harmful effects of PCBs already in bears be reduced?
3. What are the current procedures for PCB disposal?

Highlights 11

Key terms

alloy	solubility
concentration	soluble
emulsifying agent	solute
emulsion	solvent
immiscible	supersaturated
insoluble	surfactant
miscible	suspension
molarity	unsaturated
saturated	

Key problem-solving approach:
Calculations with molarity

When solving molarity problems, select the variable given in your problem from the options near the top of this diagram. Then, follow the calculation pathway that leads to the proper units for the answer near the bottom of this diagram.

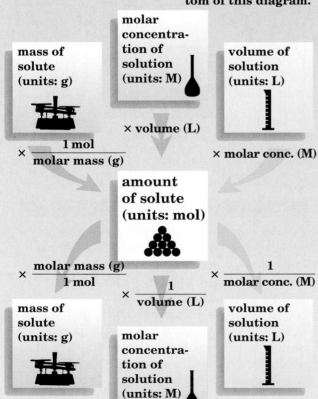

mass of solute (units: g)

molar concentration of solution (units: M)

volume of solution (units: L)

× volume (L)

$\times \dfrac{1 \text{ mol}}{\text{molar mass (g)}}$

× molar conc. (M)

amount of solute (units: mol)

$\times \dfrac{\text{molar mass (g)}}{1 \text{ mol}}$

$\times \dfrac{1}{\text{volume (L)}}$

$\times \dfrac{1}{\text{molar conc. (M)}}$

mass of solute (units: g)

molar concentration of solution (units: M)

volume of solution (units: L)

Key ideas

 ### 11-1 What is a solution?
- Solutions stay mixed; suspensions will settle.
- A solute is dissolved in a solvent to make a solution.
- Solubility is the amount of a solute that will ordinarily dissolve in a solvent at a certain temperature.
- A solution can be described qualitatively by whether it contains more solute than the solubility (supersaturated), as much solute as the solubility (saturated), or less solute than the solubility (unsaturated).

 ### 11-2 What does concentration mean?
- A common concentration measure in chemistry is molarity, which is the moles of solute per liter of solution.

 ### 11-3 Why do some things dissolve?
- Polar solvents dissolve ionic and polar solutes by attracting them into the solvent. Nonpolar substances will not dissolve in water.
- The polarity of a molecular substance can be predicted by determining the polarity of the individual bonds and the effective poles of the particle.

 ### 11-4 Can insoluble substances mix?
- An emulsion is a mixture of two insoluble substances. Ordinarily, emulsions will form two phases on standing.
- Emulsifying agents stabilize emulsions by dissolving partly in a polar droplet and partly in a nonpolar droplet. This linking prevents the droplets from recombining to form two phases.

 ### 11-5 How are solubility principles used?
- Dry cleaning uses nonpolar solvents to dissolve solutes such as oily dirt and greasy stains without harming delicate fabrics.
- Gases are more soluble at increased pressures and lower temperatures.
- Vitamins can be water soluble (polar) or fat soluble (nonpolar). Water-soluble vitamins are regulated by the kidneys. Fat-soluble vitamins link with special proteins to travel in the blood.
- Fat-soluble vitamins are stored in the liver.

Review and Assess

Properties of solutions

1. **a.** What is a solution?
   b. Identify and define the two components of a solution.
   c. Give two examples of common solutions.

2. **a.** How does a suspension differ from a solution?
   b. Give two examples of common suspensions.

3. **a.** What is meant by the solubility of a substance?
   b. What condition(s) must be specified in citing solubility levels?

4. Use **Figure 11-5** to determine the solubility of each of the following, in grams per 100 g of H_2O.
   a. KCl at 10°C   **b.** $NaNO_3$ at 60°C
   c. Li_2SO_4 at 30°C

5. Use **Figure 11-5** to determine the temperature at which the solubility of NH_4Cl is 60 g NH_4Cl/100 g H_2O.

6. Use **Table 11-1** to determine which of the following lead compounds are insoluble.
   a. lead(II) chloride   **b.** lead(II) carbonate
   c. lead(II) sulfide   **d.** lead(II) acetate
   e. If you needed to make a solution of Pb^{2+}, which of the above solutes would you use? Why?

7. The drawings below represent macroscopic and microscopic views of a solution being made by adding increasing amounts of solute. Match the microscopic and macroscopic views and label them *pure solvent*, *unsaturated*, or *saturated*.

a.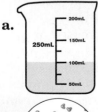

b.

c.

d.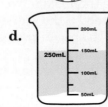

e.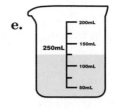

f.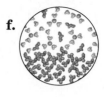

8. Use **Figure 11-5** to decide whether each description represents a saturated or unsaturated solution.
   a. 40 g of KCl added to 100 g of H_2O at 50°C
   b. 120 g of NH_4Cl added to 100 g of H_2O at 80°C
   c. 100 g of RbCl added to 100 g of H_2O at 55°C

9. What is a supersaturated solution?

10. In each of the diagrams shown below, the same amount of sodium acetate has been added to different solutions of sodium acetate. Indicate whether each of the original solutions was unsaturated, saturated, or supersaturated.

5.0 g of $NaC_2H_3O_2$

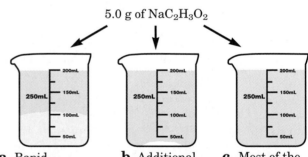

a. Rapid recrystallization of more than the additional amount

b. Additional amount remains undissolved

c. Most of the additional amount dissolves

11. Put these mixtures in order of increasing particle size: muddy water (settles after a few hours), sugar water, ketchup (settles after a few days), sand in water (settles rapidly), salt water.

12. If a saturated solution of $NaNO_3$ in 100 g of H_2O at 60°C is cooled to 10°C, approximately how many grams of the solute will precipitate out of the solution? (Use **Figure 11-5**.)

13. Why would you feel more uncomfortable on a hot, humid day than on a hot, dry day?

14. Plot a solubility graph for $AgNO_3$ with the data below. Plot grams of solute (in increments of 50) per 100 g of H_2O on the vertical axis and the temperature in degrees Celsius on the horizontal axis.

   a. Estimate the solubility of $AgNO_3$ at 30°C, 55°C, and 75°C.

   b. At what temperature would the solubility of $AgNO_3$ be 275 g per 100 g of H_2O?

   c. If 98.5 g of $AgNO_3$ were added to 100 g of H_2O at 10°C, would the resulting solution be saturated or unsaturated?

Grams solute per 100 g H₂O	Temperature (°C)
122	0.
216	20.
311	40.
440	60.
585	80.
733	100.

☀ Concentration and molarity

R E V I E W

15. Describe in detail how you would make 250. mL of a 0.500 M solution of NaCl with equipment found in your chemistry lab.

16. **a.** How many moles and grams of NaOH are in 1.00 L of a 2.50 M NaOH solution?

   b. To make 1.00 L of 2.50 M NaOH, will you need more than 1.00 L of H_2O, less than 1.00 L of H_2O, or exactly 1.00 L of H_2O? Explain your answer.

17. You are determining the concentration of a solution of salt water by evaporating different samples and measuring the mass of salt that remains. Your data are shown below. Calculate the average molar concentration of the original solution.

Sample volume (mL)	Mass of NaCl (g)
25	2.9
50.	5.6
75	8.5
100.	11.3

18. The actual molarity of the solution in item **17** is determined to be 2.00 M. Calculate the percent error in the data.

Answers to items in a black square begin on page 841.

19 Determine the molarity of each of the following solutions. (Hint: see Sample Problem 11A.)
   a. 3.5 mol $NaNO_3$ in 1.0 L of solution
   b. 5.0 mol KOH in 2.0 L of solution
   c. 0.20 mol Na_2S in 0.25 L of solution

20. Determine the molarity of each of the following solutions. (Hint: see Sample Problem 11A.)
   a. 0.25 mol $FeCl_3$ in 2.0 L of solution
   b. 0.015 mol $KMnO_4$ in 350 mL of solution
   c. 3.5×10^{-4} mol $NaC_2H_3O_2$ in 25 mL of solution

21 How many moles of each solute would be required to prepare each of the following solutions? (Hint: see Sample Problem 11B.)
   a. 1.0 L of a 4.0 M $AgNO_3$ solution
   b. 2.50 L of a 0.500 M HCl solution
   c. 400. mL of a 0.250 M HNO_3 solution

22. How many moles of each solute would be required to prepare each of the following solutions? (Hint: see Sample Problem 11B.)
   a. 30.0 mL of a 0.0100 M H_3PO_4 solution
   b. 5.0 mL of an 18 M H_2SO_4 solution
   c. 250. mL of a 1.00×10^{-4} M CH_3OH solution

23 Determine the molarity of each of the following solutions. (Hint: see Sample Problem 11A.)
   a. 20.0 g of NaOH in enough H_2O to make 2.00 L of solution
   b. 14.0 g of NH_4Br in enough H_2O to make 150. mL of solution
   c. 65.0 g of $CuCl_2$ in enough H_2O to make 300. mL of solution

24. Determine the molarity of each of the following solutions. (Hint: see Sample Problem 11A.)
   a. 3.50 g CCl_4 in enough C_6H_{12} to make 500. mL of solution
   b. 0.150 g $CuSO_4 \cdot 5H_2O$ in enough H_2O to make 25.0 mL of solution
   c. 3.00×10^{-4} g $AlCl_3$ in enough H_2O to make 2.00 mL of solution

25 How many grams of each solute would be required to make each of the following solutions? (Hint: see Sample Problem 11B.)
   a. 1.00 L of a 1.50 M NaCl solution
   b. 2.25 L of a 3.50 M NaOH solution
   c. 750.0 mL of a 2.50 M K_2SO_4 solution

26. How many grams of each solute would be required to make each of the following solutions? (Hint: see Sample Problem 11B.)
   a. 1.50 mL of a 0.300 M $Ca(NO_3)_2$ solution
   b. 25 mL of a 1.5 M LiCl solution
   c. 3.00×10^{-4} L of a 2.50×10^{-2} M $C_6H_{12}O_6$ solution

27 What mass of each product results if 750. mL of 6.00 M H_3PO_4 react with an excess of $Ca(OH)_2$ according to the following equation? (Hint: see Sample Problem 11C.)

$$2H_3PO_4(aq) + 3Ca(OH)_2(aq) \longrightarrow$$
$$Ca_3(PO_4)_2(s) + 6H_2O(l)$$

28. A yellow pigment in some artists' oil paints is cadmium sulfide. How much cadmium sulfide would be made if 350. mL of 2.00 M $(NH_4)_2S$ reacted with 400. mL of 1.50 M $Cd(NO_3)_2$ according to the following equation? (Hint: see Sample Problem 11C.)

$$(NH_4)_2S(aq) + Cd(NO_3)_2(aq) \longrightarrow$$
$$2NH_4NO_3(aq) + CdS(s)$$

A P P L Y

29. You have 500 mL of a 0.5 M NaOH solution. For an experiment, you need 0.1 M NaOH. Describe how you would make 100 mL of a 0.1 M NaOH solution from the 0.5 M NaOH.

30. The owner's manual for an outboard motor gives the proportion for mixing gasoline and oil as 100 to 1. You have 2.5 L of gasoline. How much oil do you need to mix with this much gasoline?

31. A shipment of shark meat was destroyed after it was found to contain 1.76 ppm methyl mercury, $[HgCH_3]^+$, which is higher than the legal limit of 1.00 ppm.
  a. If a shark has a mass of 12.5 kg, what mass of methyl mercury is present in the shark?
  b. What is the maximum number of grams of methyl mercury the shark meat could contain and still be safe?

32. Heavy exposure to lead or lead salts is toxic. To prevent lead poisoning, the current standard for lead in paint is 600. ppm, though some older paints had concentrations of 5.00×10^4 ppm. On average, a bucket of paint has a mass of 900. g.
  a. Calculate the maximum mass of lead in a bucket of new paint.
  b. Calculate the mass of lead in a bucket of old paint, based on the concentration given.

Solubility and polarity

R E V I E W

33. a. Explain what is meant by the chemists' expression "like dissolves like."
  b. Explain why another factor must be taken into account when polar covalent bonds are present.
34. Explain why water is a good solvent for both polar molecules and ionic crystals.
35. Copy the table below onto another piece of paper. Then, using the procedure outlined in the feature on page 424, fill in the blank spaces in this table.

Sub-stance	Electro-negativity difference	Bond type	Structural formula	Particle type	Solu-bility in water
NaBr					yes
N_2				nonpolar molecule	
SO_2			O–S=O		
$CaCl_2$		ionic			
C_2H_6	2.5 – 2.1 = 0.4				

P R A C T I C E

36 Butane, C_4H_{10}, is added to carbon disulfide, CS_2. Will the butane dissolve? (Hint: see Sample Problem 11D.)
37. Cesium chloride, CsCl, is added to cyclohexane, C_6H_{12}. Will the cesium chloride dissolve? (Hint: see Sample Problem 11D.)

A P P L Y

38. For the compounds shown below, determine the number and ratio of polar and nonpolar bonds, then estimate each compound's solubility in H_2O.

  a. Ethylene glycol

  b. Myristic acid

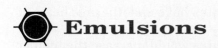 **Emulsions**

39. Explain why it is inaccurate to say that emulsifying agents actually make insoluble chemicals dissolve.

40. Give two examples of emulsifying agents, and explain how each performs its function.

41. Explain why detergents are better emulsifying agents than soaps, particularly in hard water.

A P P L Y

42. Butter contains about 80% oily butterfat and 16% water. During the process of making butter, it is churned, or stirred very quickly, for a long period of time. Explain why the churning step is necessary.

43. Which of these substances would make the best emulsifying agent? Explain your answer.

a. $CaCO_3 \cdot 6H_2O$

b. $(CH_3)_3C - O - C_2H_5$ **c.**

d. $\left[(CH_3)_2 - \underset{\underset{C_2H_5}{|}}{N} - (CH_2)_{15}CH_3 \right]^+ Br^-$

Applications of solubility

R E V I E W

44. What are the chemical characteristics of a good dry-cleaning solvent? How do they differ from those of an emulsifying agent?

45. Using the data below, plot a solubility graph for the following gases with grams of solute per 100 g of H_2O on the vertical axis and temperature in degrees Celsius on the horizontal axis. Then answer the questions at the top of the next column.

Gas	20°C	30°C	40°C	50°C	60°C
CO_2	0.169	0.126	0.097	0.076	0.058
H_2S	0.38	0.30	0.24	0.19	0.15
Cl_2	0.73	0.57	0.46	0.39	0.33

a. Estimate the solubility of each gas at 45°C.

b. At what temperature would the solubility of Cl_2 be 0.50 g per 100 g of H_2O?

c. If a solution contains 0.100 g of CO_2 in 100 g of H_2O at 35°C, is it unsaturated, saturated, or supersaturated?

d. Assuming that other gases follow the pattern of these three gases, should you heat or cool water if you are trying to dissolve a gas in it?

46. What do vitamins do in the body?

47. Name one source of vitamin A and one of vitamin C.

48. Explain the role of solubility in accounting for the fact that you are more likely to overdose on vitamin A than on vitamin C.

49. How does vitamin deficiency differ from vitamin toxicity?

P R A C T I C E

50 Ascorbic acid, vitamin C, has the formula $C_6H_8O_6$. What is the molarity of a plasma solution of ascorbic acid if the concentration is 5.0 mg/L? (Hint: see Sample Problem 11A.)

51. A cup (250 mL) of whole milk contains about 0.4 mg of riboflavin, $C_{17}H_{20}N_4O_6$. What is the molarity of riboflavin in the milk? (Hint: see Sample Problem 11A.)

A P P L Y

52. Some laundry detergents have enzyme additives. What role could these enzymes play in cleaning?

53. Crayon companies recommend treating wax stains on clothes by spraying them with WD-40 lubricant, applying dishwashing liquid, and then washing them. Explain why.

54. To produce clear ice cubes instead of cloudy ones, should hot or cold water be used? Explain your answer.

55. Some industrial plants use water from nearby rivers as a coolant. When that water is returned to the river, it is a few degrees warmer. Explain how this practice could cause a fish kill. (Hint: fish use the oxygen dissolved in water.)

Linking chapters

1. Double-replacement reactions

Use **Table 11-1** to predict whether any precipitate will form when the following solutions are mixed. If a precipitate does form, what would you expect it to be?

a. KOH and $NaNO_3$ **b.** $CaCl_2$ and H_2CO_3
c. Na_2S and $FeBr_3$

2. Molarity of a gas

Air is a solution of nitrogen, oxygen, and other gases. A 5.00 L sample of air contains 20.9% oxygen by volume. The density of oxygen is 1.429 g/L. What is the molarity of oxygen in the air sample?

3. Gas stoichiometry

When small amounts of hydrogen gas are required in a laboratory, chemists frequently use a reaction similar to the one shown.

$$2HCl(aq) + Zn(s) \longrightarrow ZnCl_2(aq) + H_2(g)$$

If 0.250 M HCl is used along with an excess of zinc, how many milliliters of solution will be required to generate the following amounts of hydrogen gas?

a. 0.0375 mol H_2
b. 12.5 mL of H_2 at 2.50 atm and 310 K
c. 101 mL of H_2 at 0.750 atm and 15°C

4. Endothermic and exothermic processes

The table to the right shows the heats of solution when the solutes are dissolved in H_2O. Use it to answer the following.

a. Which solutes have endothermic heats of solution?
b. Which solutes would increase the temperature of the solvent?
c. Which solutes would dissolve better in hot solvents? Cite reasons for your answer.

Solute	Heat of solution (kJ/mol)
hydrogen chloride, HCl	−74.84
potassium chloride, KCl	+17.22
potassium hydroxide, KOH	−57.61
potassium nitrate, KNO_3	+34.89
silver nitrate, $AgNO_3$	+22.59
sodium chloride, NaCl	+3.88
sodium hydroxide, NaOH	−44.51
sodium nitrate, $NaNO_3$	+20.50

5. Classification and trends

Use the table for item **4** to answer these questions.

a. The heat of solution for rubidium chloride, RbCl, isn't given in the table. Predict how its heat of solution compares to potassium chloride, KCl. (Hint: examine the chart closely, looking for patterns, and also examine a periodic table.)
b. Arrange the following compounds in order of their heats of solution, beginning with the most exothermic: NaF, LiF, RbF, KF.

USING TECHNOLOGY

1. Graphics calculator

Molarity can be graphically represented as a straight line with a positive slope. A 0.500 M solution of NaOH can be graphed using the function $y = 0.5x$, where x equals the volume of the solution in liters. Select the $\boxed{y =}$ key of the graphics calculator, and enter the function.

a. Press $\boxed{\text{GRAPH}}$ and use the $\boxed{\text{TRACE}}$ mode to estimate the number of moles of NaOH in 300. mL of solution, 750. mL of solution, and 75.0 mL of solution.
b. Calculate the mass of NaOH in each solution sample using the mole estimates you found in item **a**.

2. Graphics calculator

Use the graphics calculator to graph the mole amounts and volumes in a 1.00 M solution of $CuCl_2$. Use the graph to estimate how you would prepare 1.00 M solutions of $CuCl_2$ with the following volumes.

a. 350. mL **b.** 150. mL
c. 3.00 L **d.** 750. mL

3. Computer art

Using a computer art program, sketch the particles involved in the process of dissolving a solid in water. Include views showing the initially pure water, the addition of the solid, the solid beginning to dissolve, and the final state, in which the solid is completely dissolved to form an unsaturated solution.

Alternative assessment

Performance assessment

1. Design an experiment to identify an unknown substance that is CsCl, RbCl, LiCl, NH₄Cl, KCl, or NaCl. (Hint: examine the solubility graph, **Figure 11-5**.) If your instructor approves your design, get a sample from the instructor, and carry out your plan to identify it.

2. Your instructor will give you an index card describing a solution required in a lab. Describe exactly how you would make the solution. If your instructor approves your plan, obtain what you need from the instructor, and make the solution.

3. The more concentrated an aqueous solution of ethylene glycol is, the more dense it will be. Mechanics make use of this fact when they check the antifreeze in a car's radiator. Using the data for ethylene glycol solutions shown below, graph density vs. concentration. Then, determine the concentration of a solution with a density of 1.030 g/mL. What density would you predict for a 2.50 M solution?

Concentration (M)	Density (g/mL)
0.65	1.003
1.30	1.008
3.30	1.024
7.50	1.057

4. *Computer spreadsheet*
Many reagent chemicals used in the lab are sold in the form of concentrated aqueous solutions, as shown in the table below. Different volumes are diluted to 1.00 L to make less concentrated solutions. Create a spreadsheet that will calculate the volume of concentrated reagent needed to make 1.00 L solutions of any molar concentration that you enter.

Reagent	Concentration (M)
H_2SO_4	18
HCl	12.1
HNO_3	16
H_3PO_4	14.8
CH_3COOH	17.4
NH_3	15

Portfolio projects

1. *Chemistry and you*
For one week, record instances in which you used a mixture of some type. Identify whether each is a solution, suspension, emulsion, or a heterogeneous mixture. If possible, identify the different parts of each mixture.

2. *Research and communication*
Emergency response teams working with oil spills use chemical and physical properties of oil and water along with solubility principles to prevent spills from spreading and to clean them up. Research the techniques used, and explain why they work. Present your findings to the class.

3. *Cooperative activity*
Find out how waste motor oil is collected in your community and where it goes after it is collected. Hold a class debate on whether the community's procedure is safe for the environment. If you find that the procedure is safe, work with your classmates to produce a publicity campaign to promote the use of oil recycling facilities. If you find that it is not safe, create a pamphlet to make the public aware of why recycling oil is important, and how other communities have succeeded.

4. *Chemistry and you*
Keep a seven-day diary of what you eat. Consult a table of food values to determine what your vitamin intake is and whether it matches or exceeds the RDIs for the vitamins listed in **Table 11-5**.

5. *Chemistry and you*
Read the labels of three different over-the-counter vitamin supplements sold at your local pharmacy. Copy the amount of vitamin A supplied in one tablet. What dosage of each supplement could cause vitamin A toxicity? (Hint: to convert IUs to µg, multiply by 0.025.)

6. *Research and communication*
There are many arguments for and against the use of vitamin supplements. Find out what they are. What is the role of the FDA in the regulation of vitamin supplements? Prepare the arguments for or against increased regulation of vitamin supplements, and present them in a class debate.

Cancer and Chemicals

Who Influences Research?

About 182 000 women in the United States will be found to have breast cancer this year. Already 1.8 million women have been diagnosed with the disease and perhaps another 1 million have it but do not know it yet. Standard medical treatments have had little impact on the long-range outcome of the disease: 25 percent of women with breast cancer die within 5 years of their diagnosis. Forty percent die within 10 years. The death rate from metastatic breast cancer—disease that has spread to other parts of the body—has remained unchanged for more than 40 years.

However, what has changed is a woman's chance of developing breast cancer at some time in her life. In 1940, that chance was 1 in 20. The National Cancer Institute estimates that today, by the time a woman is 85 years old, her chance is 1 in 8. Scientists have identified several factors that appear to increase a woman's chance of developing breast cancer.

Altogether known risk factors like heredity account for just 20–30% of all breast cancers. The majority of women with the disease have none of these. As a result, some researchers now think that exposure to some chemicals may be responsible. One group of compounds is highly suspected—organochlorines. Organochlorines include DDT and other pesticides; PCBs, and polyvinyl chloride (PVC). About 11 000 different organochlorines are manufactured and used by industries. Others are formed as by-products of industrial processes like bleaching paper pulp, disinfecting wastewater, and burning garbage containing plastics and other chlorinated materials. Organochlorines are highly toxic, slow to degrade, and they accumulate in fatty breast tissue. Studies have found 177 different organochlorines in samples of fat, blood, semen, and mother's milk in residents of the United States and Canada.

A 1993 study by Mary S. Wolff and co-workers at Mt. Sinai Hospital in New York found that women who get breast cancer had blood levels of DDE, a residue of DDT, that were 35 percent higher than those in women without the disease. Women with 19 parts per billion (ppb) DDE had four times the cancer risk of women with 2 ppb DDE. Although DDT use in the United States was banned in

1972, trace amounts remain in food and soil. Also, the pesticide is still manufactured here and sold to other countries with less strict environmental laws. DDT sprayed on crops in these countries has been found to be carried huge distances in air and water.

Before 1976, the breast cancer death rate among Israeli women under age 44 was unusually high. At the same time, high concentrations of three pesticides—DDT, BHC, and lindane—were found in women's breast milk and in Israeli milk and dairy products. In 1976, use of the three pesticides was banned. By 1978, DDT levels in breast milk dropped 43%, lindane dropped 90%, and BHC dropped 98%. Less than a decade later, the breast cancer rate for Israeli women under age 44 fell 30%. In the time period studied, Israel was the only one of 28 countries in which the death rate from breast cancer actually declined.

Federal law requires the National Cancer Institute to expand its research program on preventing cancers caused by exposures to carcinogens. But at a congressional budget hearing in October of 1993, NCI Director Samuel Broder testified that the NCI spent only 1% of its almost $2 million budget on environmental cancer studies, and he gave no indications that the NCI planned to shift its priorities. NCI research will continue to emphasize the treatment and cure of cancer. Of the part of the budget given to researching causes of the disease, the two areas to receive the most emphasis will remain the links to diet and smoking.

Many health specialists have criticized this approach. They want additional funds devoted to research into identifying carcinogens and studying the link between exposure and the incidence of cancer. Some critics have speculated that the ties between the chemical companies and the organizations devoted to cancer research are too close. These critics point to the interlocking relationships among cancer researchers, policy makers, and industry representatives. They question appointments such as that in the 1980s of Armand Hammer, then president of Occidental Petroleum, to a position as chair of the President's Cancer Advisory Board.

The fear often expressed by critics is that lawmakers may be unduly influenced by lobbyists for the chemical industry. Critics also worry that chemical companies have a vested interest in protecting their own industry. Will chemical companies be willing to support research that may identify their products as probable causes of cancer?

Industry spokespeople, on the other hand, claim a role in helping to identify and solve the problem of carcinogens. They argue that the funds donated by the chemical companies for research are essential to finding both the causes and treatment of cancer. The chemical companies view their involvement as stemming from a natural, communal interest—not as a conflict of interest. From this viewpoint, everyone involved is focused on the problem but working from a different perspective.

The issue is complicated, but it is clear that the value of scientific research is its ability to confirm or deny the link between a substance and the incidence of cancer. The problem of how this research will be funded and directed is the issue. To be effective, a researcher needs a degree of independence, and critics of the current policy worry that researchers will be reluctant to "bite the hand that feeds them." As long as chemical companies are directly involved, many health specialists worry that the objectivity of the research may be compromised.

Researching the Issue

1. Go to the library and find at least 5 books and/or magazine articles on the subject of how cancer research should be funded or directed. Write a statement that summarizes the debate, and list evidence from your reading that should be considered in making a judgment.

2. Find the structural formula for the hormone estrogen. In what ways are organochlorines structurally similar to estrogen?

3. If you were a researcher, what guidelines would you develop to protect the integrity of your research? Write a position statement to be given to potential contributors indicating how they could and could not interact with your research.

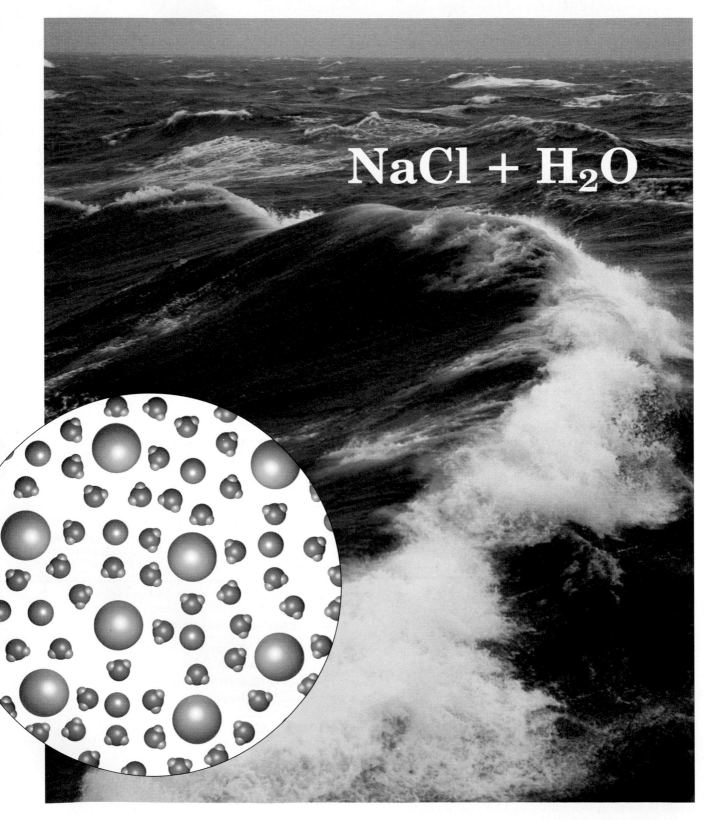

$$NaCl + H_2O$$

Sea Water and Equilibrium

Boating accidents at sea leave people with water all around them but none to drink. Sea water harms the body's equilibrium system, so a person must drink desalinated water to keep from becoming very ill.

The three people, two men and a woman, were experienced sailors. One August evening, they left from South Carolina in a 38 ft (11.6 m) sailboat, which they were to deliver to Rhode Island. Reports of a tropical storm brewing about 500 mi (805 km) to the south posed no problem for their area. By the time the storm moved north, this crew and their ship should have reached port. It didn't happen that way.

The seas were calm the first night, but by the next day the winds had picked up. The storm had developed into a hurricane and had overtaken the vessel, which was more than 100 mi (160.9 km) from shore. Disaster struck the boat and its crew as winds exceeded 100 mph (44.7 m/s). Waves picked up the vessel and slammed it down on its side. Water poured into the boat. Within seconds, the three crew members filled a canvas bag with food, water, and supplies; then they scrambled into a life raft.

Waves crashed down on them and flipped the raft several times. The supplies were lost, and the raft threatened to sink. The three people quickly drank the only water they had so that they could use the container to bail out the sea water and try to keep the raft afloat. The following day, the winds died down and the waves dropped to 20 ft (6.1 m).

The three people took stock of their situation. They had some flares and two paddles, but no radio, food, or water. On the sixth day at sea, the thirsty crew began to fantasize; the men talked about eating watermelons, and the woman dreamed of chocolate shakes. On the 11th day at sea, all three were severely dehydrated and near death. They knew, however, that even though they were surrounded by water, they couldn't drink it. If they did, it would definitely make their medical condition even worse.

You will learn in this chapter why drinking sea water would increase dehydration. Questions you should consider while you study this chapter include the following.

- *How would drinking sea water affect the aqueous equilibrium in the body?*
- *Can sea water be made safe to drink?*
- *How do you know when water is safe to drink?*

Unfortunately, the stranded sailors had no means of making the sea water drinkable, and because it never rained, they could not collect any water to drink. Suffering from severe dehydration on their 11th day at sea, the crew was finally rescued by a Coast Guard helicopter near noon.

What happens in an aqueous solution?

Section Objectives

Describe how conductance can be measured.

Distinguish among the properties of nonelectrolytes, weak electrolytes, and strong electrolytes.

Describe the theory of ionization.

Compare and contrast the dissociation of ionic and molecular compounds in aqueous solutions.

List two colligative properties, and explain how each can be demonstrated.

Conductance

As you know from what you have studied in previous chapters, when a substance dissolves in water, the result is an aqueous solution that is a homogeneous mixture. Is there a way to further classify solutions in terms of solutes? Think back to Chapters 5 and 6, where you learned about ionic and molecular compounds. One way to further classify solutions is by whether or not they conduct electricity.

Some solutions conduct electricity

The measurement of a solution's ability to conduct electricity is known as **conductance**. You have probably seen an apparatus similar to that shown in **Figure 12-1** to measure conductance. The apparatus uses the solution being tested as a "continuance" of the wires carrying the electric current to complete the circuit. When a solution contains charged particles that can continue "carrying" the electricity, the bulb will light. This type of solution contains an **electrolyte**.

conductance
the measurement of a solution's ability to conduct electrical energy

electrolyte
any substance that, when it is dissolved in a solution, will conduct an electric current by means of movement of ions

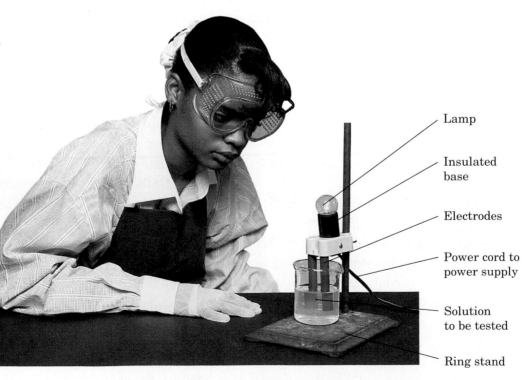

Figure 12-1
The space between the electrodes in the conductivity apparatus prevents the conductance of electricity. The presence of ions in a solution being tested provides the path for conductance.

Lamp

Insulated base

Electrodes

Power cord to power supply

Solution to be tested

Ring stand

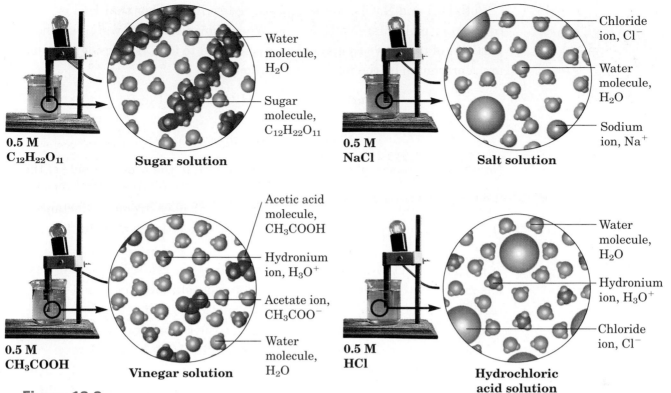

0.5 M C₁₂H₂₂O₁₁ — **Sugar solution**
- Water molecule, H_2O
- Sugar molecule, $C_{12}H_{22}O_{11}$

0.5 M NaCl — **Salt solution**
- Chloride ion, Cl^-
- Water molecule, H_2O
- Sodium ion, Na^+

0.5 M CH₃COOH — **Vinegar solution**
- Acetic acid molecule, CH_3COOH
- Hydronium ion, H_3O^+
- Acetate ion, CH_3COO^-
- Water molecule, H_2O

0.5 M HCl — **Hydrochloric acid solution**
- Water molecule, H_2O
- Hydronium ion, H_3O^+
- Chloride ion, Cl^-

Figure 12-2
For solutions at the same concentration, the brightness of the bulb is an indication of the strength of the electrolyte.

weak electrolyte
a compound that experiences only a small degree of dissociation in an aqueous solution

strong electrolyte
a substance that is completely or largely dissociated in an aqueous solution

nonelectrolyte
a substance that, when dissolved in an aqueous solution, will not conduct an electric current

Vinegar, which is a dilute acetic acid solution, is considered a **weak electrolyte** because it displays low conductance, lighting the bulb dimly. Salt, or sodium chloride, is considered a **strong electrolyte** because it exhibits high conductance in aqueous solution, lighting the bulb brightly. When a solution does not contain charged particles to continue "carrying" the electricity, the bulb will not light up. The solute in this type of solution is called a **nonelectrolyte**. An example of a nonelectrolyte is sugar. When dissolved in distilled water, sugar produces no measurable conductance in the apparatus with the light bulb. How do you think tap water would compare to the solutions shown in **Figure 12-2** in terms of conducting electricity?

A simple way to compare the strength of electrolytes is to use the conductivity apparatus to measure the conductance of various solutions at the same concentration. By comparing the brightness of the bulb under these conditions, you can determine which substances are weak or strong electrolytes. The strength of an electrolyte depends on its tendency to form ions in a solution at a specific concentration. Weak electrolytes form solutions with few ions. Acetic acid is a weak electrolyte. A water solution of acetic acid contains acetic acid molecules, water molecules, acetate ions, and hydronium ions, as shown in **Figure 12-2**. Because the solution contains both molecules and ions, it can be represented by the following equation.

$$CH_3COOH(aq) + H_2O(l) \rightleftharpoons CH_3COO^-(aq) + H_3O^+(aq)$$

The double arrow shows that both reactants and products exist in the solution and that the conversion to ions is not complete. In fact, about 99% of the acetic acid remains as molecules.

Both HCl and NaCl are strong electrolytes. Remember that HCl is covalent or molecular. NaCl is ionic. When they dissolve in water, all the particles of those two compounds are converted to ions. These conversions are represented by the following equations.

$$HCl(aq) + H_2O(l) \longrightarrow H_3O^+(aq) + Cl^-(aq)$$

$$NaCl(s) \xrightarrow{H_2O} Na^+(aq) + Cl^-(aq)$$

Note that the reaction arrow is written pointing to the products side of the equation to represent a complete reaction for the formation of ions. Strong electrolytes form more ions in the solution and display strong conductance. HCl actually reacts with water to form an ion called the **hydronium ion**, H_3O^+.

hydronium ion
a hydrogen ion covalently bonded to a water molecule, written as H_3O^+

Keep in mind that the use of the term "strong" as related to electrolytes has nothing to do with their concentration in a solution. The use of the term "weak" as related to electrolytes has nothing to do with dilute solutions. For example, HCl is a strong electrolyte in solution, whether the solution is very concentrated (10 M) or very dilute (0.000 001 M). A very dilute solution, however, has low conductance. On the other hand, CH_3COOH is a weak electrolyte in solution, no matter how concentrated or dilute the solution.

Tap water conducts electricity

The instructions with a hair dryer or electric shaver warn you about the danger of dropping it into a tub or sink of water. When using extension cords outdoors, you are cautioned to keep them away from water. Obviously, electricity and water are a hazardous combination that, at times, can prove fatal. **Figure 12-3** provides a reminder of this danger.

Have you ever wondered why water is something you should avoid when you're dealing with electricity? Actually, it's not the water that's the problem. It's what's in the water. You have already learned that water is a good solvent. Unlike distilled water, which does not conduct enough electricity to light the bulb in the conductivity apparatus, tap water contains various dissolved salts and minerals. The "harder" the water, the more salts and minerals it contains. Although these dissolved salts and minerals generally do not give tap water high conductance, remember that it is still a conductor of electricity. That's why you have to be careful when using electricity near water.

Although it doesn't display high conductance, tap water can still conduct enough electric current to injure or kill someone. As you enjoy the pool, lake, or beach when a thunderstorm is in the area, be sure to keep in mind that chlorinated water, ground water, and salt water are very good conductors of electricity. Make sure you get out of the water during a storm; don't think that lightning can harm you only if it is extremely close.

Figure 12-3
An electrical appliance is dangerous when it comes in contact with water because it can cause severe electric shock.

Electrolytes and sports drinks

Whenever you work hard or participate in sports activities, you sweat and need to drink water to replace the lost fluids. Sweat is more than just water. It has a salty taste. As you saw with the conductivity tests, salt is an electrolyte. If you take salt tablets when you sweat a lot, you also need to remember to drink lots of water.

You may have seen commercials showing professional athletes drinking sports drinks, which combines electrolytes in a flavored drink to solve the problem of replenishing fluids lost while sweating. Look at labels when you shop for something to quench your thirst after exercising vigorously. Check the label for electrolytes such as potassium ions (K^+), sodium ions (Na^+), and calcium ions (Ca^{2+}).

The fluid in your body's tissues is an aqueous electrolytic solution. The electrolytes serve important roles in various physiological functions, including nerve impulse conduction and muscle contraction.

At rest, a nerve cell uses "ion pumps" to maintain a high concentration of Na^+ ions outside the cell and K^+ ions inside. These ions do not diffuse through the membrane when the nerve cell is at rest.

However, when the cell is stimulated, ions pass through the cell membrane, moving Na^+ ions inside and K^+ ions outside the nerve cell. When the cell returns to its resting state, Na^+ ions are again "pumped" out and the K^+ ions are "pumped" in, readying the cell for the next stimulus.

Muscle contractions also depend on the movement of ions. When muscle cells are stimulated, Ca^{2+} ions go into the cells and cause protein fibers to slide together, resulting in a muscle contraction. When Ca^{2+} ions move back outside the cells, the muscle relaxes.

Obviously, your nerves and muscles need electrolytes. When you sweat, you also lose electrolytes (that salty taste). If you replenish your lost fluids *and electrolytes* with a sports drink, be careful. Too much, like too little, can be dangerous. In fact, some people have to watch their intake of certain electrolytes, especially Na^+ and Ca^{2+}. Some problems include high blood pressure and kidney problems.

Consult a doctor for your particular needs, and check labels accordingly.

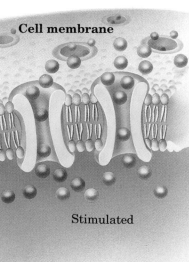

Cell membrane

Na^+

K^+

At rest

Stimulated

theory of ionization
the explanation of the process by which electrolytes break apart in solution in the form of freely moving ions that can conduct an electrical current

Figure 12-4a
When a soluble salt dissolves, it dissociates.

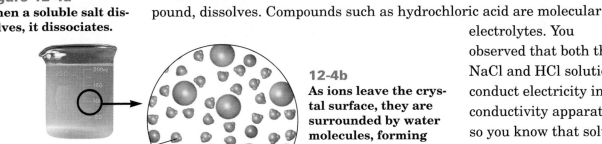

Water molecule, H₂O
Sodium ion, Na⁺
Chloride ion, Cl⁻

12-4b
As ions leave the crystal surface, they are surrounded by water molecules, forming hydrated ions.

Ions in solution
All electrolytes form ions in water

The ability of solutions to conduct an electric current is explained by the **theory of ionization**, which states that electrolytes in solution break apart to form ions. These ions, or charged particles, move freely in the solution and, consequently, conduct an electric current.

Chemists recognize that electrolytes can be either ionic or molecular compounds. You know that ions are released when salt, an ionic compound, dissolves. Compounds such as hydrochloric acid are molecular electrolytes. You observed that both the NaCl and HCl solutions conduct electricity in the conductivity apparatus, so you know that solutions of both ionic and molecular compounds can be electrolytes.

Ionic compounds dissociate in water

Figure 12-4 illustrates what happens when sodium chloride, or table salt, dissolves in water. At the surface of a salt crystal, the positive ends of water molecules attract Cl⁻ ions, while the negative ends attract Na⁺ ions. Attractive forces between water and the ions are just about as strong as forces holding the ions in the crystal, so ions are drawn away from the crystal surface and into solution. In this case there is a fairly large increase in entropy. The free energy change is negative. The process by which water molecules surround each ion as it moves into solution is known as **hydration**, and the ions are said to be *hydrated*.

As ions become hydrated and diffuse into solution, other ions in the crystal become exposed to water. These ions will also move away from the crystal surface, and, eventually, the entire crystal dissolves.

The separation of ions that occurs when an ionic compound dissolves in water is called **dissociation**. The dissociation process for NaCl can be shown by the following chemical equation.

$$NaCl(s) \longrightarrow Na^+(aq) + Cl^-(aq)$$

Energy is involved in the dissociation process

The dissociation of an ionic compound requires the addition of energy to separate ions at the crystal surface and to separate water molecules. Energy is liberated when the ions are hydrated because hydration is a process in which opposite charges are drawn together.

As you can see from **Table 12-1**, dissociation can be either an endothermic or exothermic process. The heat of solution for a solution with water as the solvent depends on the solute ions involved because the energy needed to separate water molecules is always the same.

hydration
the process by which water molecules surround each ion as it moves into solution

dissociation
a process using energy to separate a compound into ions in water

Table 12-1
Enthalpy of Solution

Substance	Enthalpy of solution (kJ/mol)
AgNO₃	+22.77
CuSO₄	−67.81
KCl	+17.58
KClO₃	+42.03
KNO₃	+35.7
KOH	−54.59
LiCl	−35.0
Li₂CO₃	−12.8
NaCl	+4.27
NaOH	−41.6
NH₄NO₃	+25.5

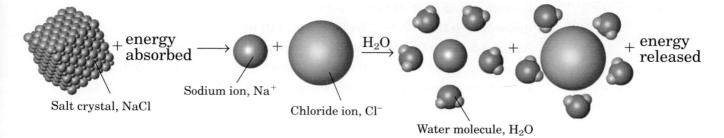

Salt crystal, NaCl

Sodium ion, Na⁺

Chloride ion, Cl⁻

Water molecule, H₂O

Figure 12-5
Individual ions are separated from the solid lattice by energy before they are hydrated by water molecules.

Table 12-2
Heat of Hydration

Ion charge	Radius (picometers)	Heat of hydration (kJ/mol)	Trend
Li⁺	65	523	hydration energy decreases as the radius increases
Na⁺	96	418	
Cl⁻	181	361	
Ca²⁺	168	293	hydration energy increases as the charge increases (and the radius decreases)
Mg²⁺	65	1940	
Al³⁺	55	4690	

Figure 12-5 shows that energy is required to separate ions from the lattice. Energy is released when hydrated ions are released from the lattice. The heat of solution represents the net energy change for these two processes. In all cases where the enthalpy change is positive, an increase in entropy causes the process to be spontaneous. But how can the entropy of solution be negative? Small ions form a tightly arranged group with the molecules such that there is actually an increase in order when the ions dissolve.

As you can see in **Table 12-2**, more energy is usually released in the hydration of ions that are smaller or higher in charge. Notice that although the Mg^{2+} ion is about the same size as the Li^+ ion, the Mg^{2+} ion, with its higher charge, releases almost four times as much energy when hydrated as the Li^+ ion does.

Molecular compounds may also dissociate in water, involving energy in the process

Most molecular electrolytes are polar covalent molecules. Unlike ionic compounds, polar covalent electrolytes *react* with water. Consider what happens to acetic acid, a polar covalent molecule, when it is mixed with water, as shown in **Figure 12-6**. Though you might expect the more concentrated solution to be a better conductor, that is not the case. Why?

Figure 12-6a
The conductivity of a solution is determined by the degree of dissociation rather than by the solution's concentration.

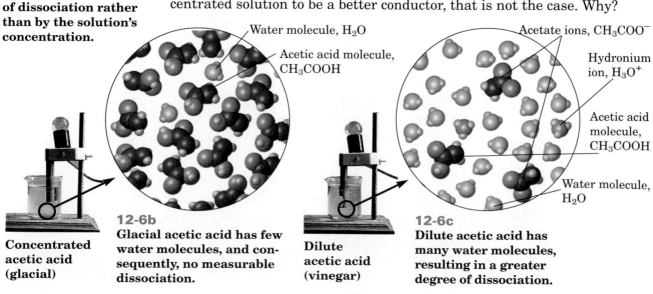

Water molecule, H₂O

Acetic acid molecule, CH₃COOH

Acetate ions, CH₃COO⁻

Hydronium ion, H₃O⁺

Acetic acid molecule, CH₃COOH

Water molecule, H₂O

Concentrated acetic acid (glacial)

12-6b
Glacial acetic acid has few water molecules, and consequently, no measurable dissociation.

Dilute acetic acid (vinegar)

12-6c
Dilute acetic acid has many water molecules, resulting in a greater degree of dissociation.

Concentrated (glacial) acetic acid (17 M) contains relatively few water molecules in the solution, as shown in **Figure 12-6b**. These few water molecules cannot bring about any measurable dissociation of acetic acid molecules. However, in the dilute solution of acetic acid (0.1 M), many more water molecules are present, as shown in **Figure 12-6c**. The negative ends of these water molecules exert enough force to break a covalent bond in the acetic acid molecule and form the hydronium ion, H_3O^+. Acids, as a group, form hydronium ions in water solutions.

As you can see in **Figure 12-7**, there are two arrows in the equation for the formation of the hydronium ion, indicating a *reversible reaction*. The arrows in both directions indicate that the reaction can go both ways. You will learn more about this in the next section.

When molecular compounds form charged particles in solution, the process is also referred to as dissociation. The dissociation of ionic and molecular compounds is different. When an ionic compound dissolves, the ions, which are already present, are released and become dissociated from each other. When a molecular compound dissolves in water, ions that were not originally present in the undissolved compound form from the reaction of the compound with water.

Figure 12-7a
A hydronium ion is formed when a hydrogen ion from an acid covalently bonds to an oxygen atom in a water molecule.

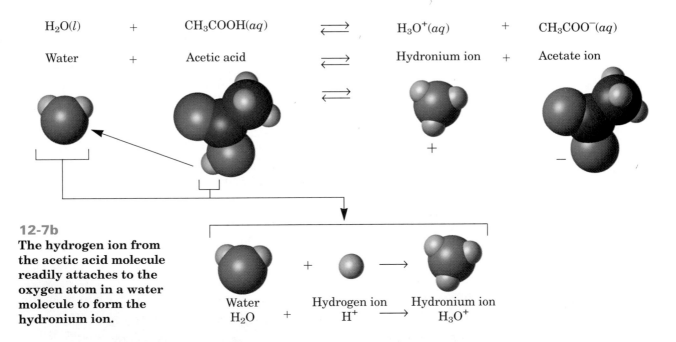

$H_2O(l)$ + $CH_3COOH(aq)$ $\rightleftharpoons$ $H_3O^+(aq)$ + $CH_3COO^-(aq)$

Water + Acetic acid $\rightleftharpoons$ Hydronium ion + Acetate ion

12-7b
The hydrogen ion from the acetic acid molecule readily attaches to the oxygen atom in a water molecule to form the hydronium ion.

Water H_2O + Hydrogen ion H^+ $\rightarrow$ Hydronium ion H_3O^+

Concept Review

Writing dissociation equations and predicting energy requirements

1. Write equations to show the dissociation of the following compounds.
   a. $CaCl_2$ **b.** $Al_2(SO_4)_3$
2. Predict whether more energy would be released by the hydration of $MgCl_2$ or $AlCl_3$. Explain your answer.
3. Write equations for the dissociation of the following compounds.
   a. HCl **b.** H_2CO_3 **c.** Na_2CrO_4 **d.** NH_4NO_3

Answers for Concept Review items and Practice problems begin on page 841.

Figure 12-8
An ice cream maker uses an ice-salt-water mixture to provide a temperature that is colder than ice and water alone.

Colligative properties
Solutes can change some properties of a solvent

When you cook pasta or vegetables in boiling water, recipes generally call for the addition of salt to the water. While this is done simply to flavor the food being cooked, the addition of salt has a slight effect on the boiling process. The boiling point of water is 100°C at normal air pressure of 1 atm, or 101.3 kPa. Once water boils vigorously, its temperature stays relatively constant at 100°C. The temperature does not continue to rise as boiling continues. Adding salt to the water elevates its boiling point. Water with a little salt in it boils at a slightly higher temperature than pure water. Food will cook somewhat faster in salted water because the temperature is slightly higher than in plain water.

A similar effect is noted with the freezing point of water. However, in the case of freezing, the effect is in the opposite direction. Water freezes at 0°C at normal air pressure of 1 atm, or 101.3 kPa. No matter how much ice you have, its temperature stays relatively constant until it melts. When you are making homemade ice cream, as in **Figure 12-8**, salt is mixed with the ice that surrounds the ice cream tub to reduce the temperature at which water freezes. The temperature of the ice-salt mixture drops below 0°C, which is better for making ice cream.

These two properties of solutions, the boiling-point elevation and the freezing-point depression, are known as *colligative properties*. Any property which is determined by the number of particles in solution is known as a **colligative property**. Colligative properties depend only on the concentrations of solute particles rather than the identity of the actual solute. Colligative properties, which include osmotic pressure, freezing-point depression, and boiling-point elevation, change with the amount of solute added to the solvent. Let's look at a model now to explain why these changes occur.

Recall from Chapter 10, and **Figure 10-28**, that the boiling point of a liquid is the temperature at which the vapor pressure of the liquid equals the atmospheric pressure. Adding salt, or any nonvolatile solute, lowers the vapor pressure such that more heat energy must be added to raise the vapor pressure of the liquid phase to that of the atmospheric pressure, thereby elevating the boiling point of the solvent.

Recall that the freezing point of a substance is the temperature at which the vapor pressures of the liquid and solid are equal. Refer to the phase diagram for water, **Figure 10-30**. Because salt lowers the vapor pressure of water, the vapor pressures of water and ice can only be equal at a temperature lower than that for pure water. Therefore, salt is said to depress the freezing point of water.

colligative property
a physical property that is dependent on the number of particles present rather than on the size, mass, or characteristics of those particles

Colligative properties depend on solute particle concentration

Any solute, including nonelectrolytes such as sugar, will affect the colligative properties of a solution. The effect depends on the number of solute particles that dissolve in a given amount of solvent. The more solute particles in solution, the greater the lowering of the freezing point or the raising of the boiling point for the solution. For example, adding 100 formula units of NaCl to water will have about twice the effect on a colligative property as adding 100 molecules of $C_{12}H_{22}O_{11}$ to water.

Examine **Figure 12-9** to discover the reason for this difference. The following equations show why the number of solute particles that form in solution depends on the chemical nature of the solute.

$$C_{12}H_{22}O_{11} \xrightarrow{\text{H}_2\text{O}} C_{12}H_{22}O_{11} \text{ (one particle)}$$

$$NaCl \xrightarrow{\text{H}_2\text{O}} Na^+ + Cl^- \text{ (two particles)}$$

$$CaCl_2 \xrightarrow{\text{H}_2\text{O}} Ca^{2+} + 2Cl^- \text{ (three particles)}$$

Figure 12-9
Colligative properties depend on the number of particles formed by the solute in the solution. Comparison of each substance shown illustrates this concept.

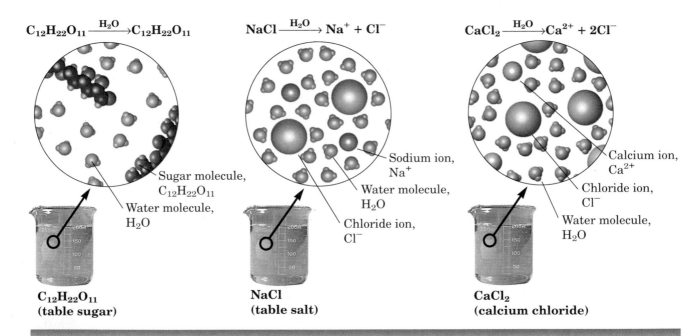

$C_{12}H_{22}O_{11} \xrightarrow{\text{H}_2\text{O}} C_{12}H_{22}O_{11}$

Sugar molecule, $C_{12}H_{22}O_{11}$
Water molecule, H_2O

$C_{12}H_{22}O_{11}$ (table sugar)

$NaCl \xrightarrow{\text{H}_2\text{O}} Na^+ + Cl^-$

Sodium ion, Na^+
Water molecule, H_2O
Chloride ion, Cl^-

NaCl (table salt)

$CaCl_2 \xrightarrow{\text{H}_2\text{O}} Ca^{2+} + 2Cl^-$

Calcium ion, Ca^{2+}
Chloride ion, Cl^-
Water molecule, H_2O

$CaCl_2$ (calcium chloride)

Section Review

4. Would you get a higher boiling point by adding one mole of table sugar or one mole of table salt to equal masses of water?

5. Describe what would happen if an insoluble salt were added to the water in the conductance apparatus shown in **Figure 12-1**.

6. Explain the conductance of concentrated and dilute acetic acid solutions.

7. State the theory of ionization for both ionic and molecular compounds.

8. Describe the process of dissolving ionic and molecular compounds in water.

9. **Story Link**
   Name some substances dissolved in sea water. Which might be worth reclaiming? What might lie undissolved on the ocean floor?

10. **Story Link**
   Explain why the three people stranded for 11 days on a raft had to be concerned about electricity from lightning during a thunderstorm.

What is an equilibrium system?

Completion and reversible reactions

When you look at the components of a chemical reaction, you are looking at how compounds and elements recombine to form products. **Figure 12-10** illustrates an example of this process. In studying reactions, you may have observed changes such as the formation of a precipitate or the evolution of a gas. These types of reactions are described as going to completion. Two examples are shown in the following equations.

$$NaHCO_3(aq) + HC_2H_3O_2(aq) \longrightarrow NaC_2H_3O_2(aq) + CO_2(g) + H_2O(l)$$
Formation of a gas

$$NaCl(aq) + AgNO_3(aq) \longrightarrow AgCl(s) + NaNO_3(aq)$$
Formation of a precipitate

Figure 12-10
Some ions in solution can form a precipitate in a reaction that goes to completion.

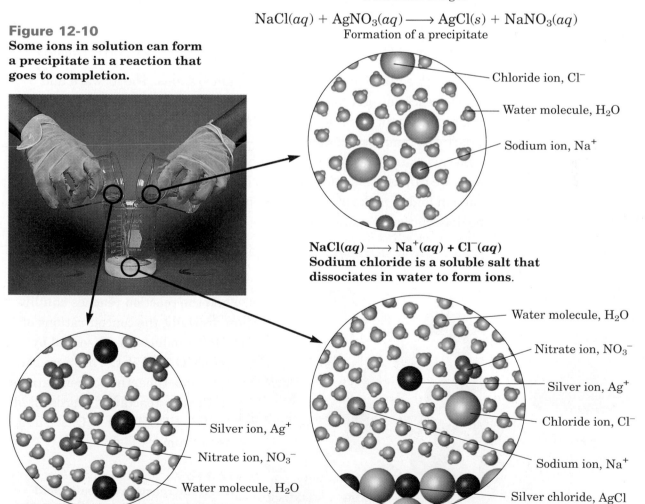

$$NaCl(aq) \longrightarrow Na^+(aq) + Cl^-(aq)$$
Sodium chloride is a soluble salt that dissociates in water to form ions.

Chloride ion, Cl^-
Water molecule, H_2O
Sodium ion, Na^+

Water molecule, H_2O
Nitrate ion, NO_3^-
Silver ion, Ag^+
Chloride ion, Cl^-
Sodium ion, Na^+
Silver chloride, $AgCl$

Silver ion, Ag^+
Nitrate ion, NO_3^-
Water molecule, H_2O

$$AgNO_3(aq) \longrightarrow Ag^+(aq) + NO_3^-(aq)$$
Silver nitrate is a soluble salt that dissociates in water to form ions.

$$Ag^+(aq) + Cl^-(aq) \longrightarrow AgCl(s)$$
Silver chloride is an insoluble salt that forms when Ag^+ ions can react with Cl^- ions.

Reversible reactions reach equilibrium

Some reactions do not run to completion. Instead, the products that are formed in a chemical reaction may re-form the original reactants. If the reactants and products are kept in a closed system where nothing can escape, the reactions may go in either direction. The following are examples of reversible reactions.

$$H_2(g) + I_2(g) \rightleftharpoons 2HI(g)$$

$$2NO_2(g) \rightleftharpoons N_2O_4(g)$$

Notice that the arrows go in both directions, indicating a reversible reaction. Reversible reactions explain why some cold and hot packs can be reused. By reversing the reactions, the reactants are re-formed, and the reactions can occur again, either absorbing or releasing heat energy.

Another example of a reversible reaction is the recharging of a battery. The interior of the automobile battery has lead plates, lead(IV) oxide plates, and a sulfuric acid solution, H_2SO_4. When the battery is used, the forward reaction occurs, releasing energy in the form of electricity. The reverse reaction occurs when electricity from an outside source is fed into the circuit. This reversible reaction is represented by the following equation.

$$Pb(s) + PbO_2(s) + 2H_2SO_4(aq) \rightleftharpoons 2PbSO_4(s) + 2H_2O(l) + energy$$

Reversible reactions may be equilibrium systems. The forward and reverse reactions occur at equal rates, and there are no overall changes as long as the conditions remain the same. At equilibrium, the total amount of particles remains constant.

Because our model of a system at equilibrium has constant concentrations, we can use this information to determine the completeness of the reaction and to make predictions. Consider the reaction that represents the dissociation of acetic acid.

$$CH_3COOH(aq) + H_2O(l) \rightleftharpoons CH_3COO^-(aq) + H_3O^+(aq)$$

Figure 12-11a
This beaker contains an aqueous solution of acetic acid in water.

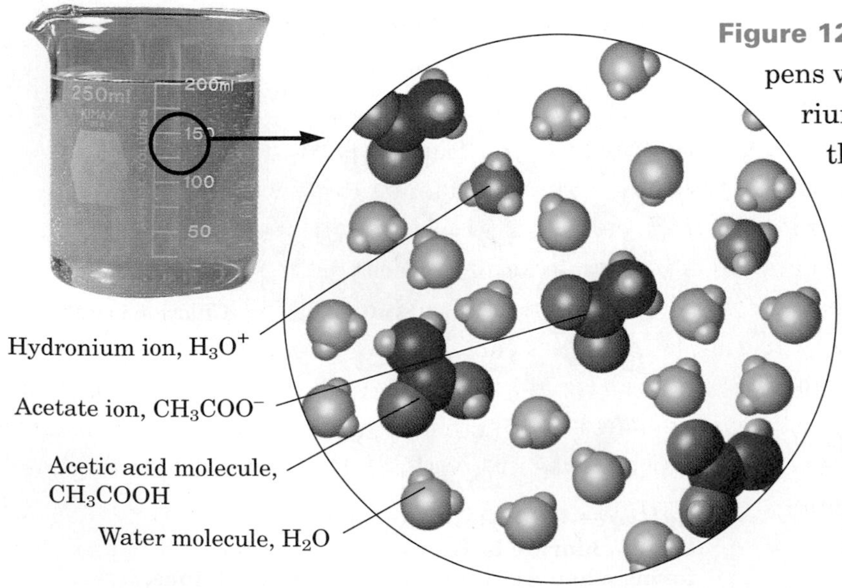

Hydronium ion, H_3O^+

Acetate ion, CH_3COO^-

Acetic acid molecule, CH_3COOH

Water molecule, H_2O

Figure 12-11 shows a model of what happens when the reaction reaches equilibrium. Initially, the concentrations of the two products, represented by CH_3COO^- and H_3O^+, are zero. At the same time, the concentrations of the two reactants, represented by CH_3COOH and H_2O, are at a maximum.

12-11b
When the reaction of acetic acid and water reaches equilibrium, the system contains CH_3COOH, H_2O, H_3O^+, and CH_3COO^-.

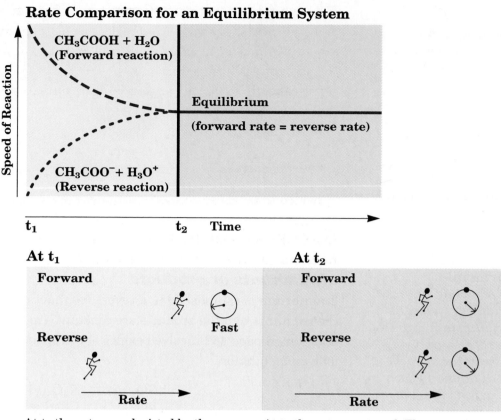

Rate Comparison for an Equilibrium System

$CH_3COOH + H_2O$
(Forward reaction)

Equilibrium
(forward rate = reverse rate)

$CH_3COO^- + H_3O^+$
(Reverse reaction)

Speed of Reaction

t_1 t_2 Time

At t_1

Forward

Reverse

Fast

Rate

At t_1 the rates are depicted by the forward reaction going fast and the reverse reaction starting from zero.

At t_2

Forward

Reverse

Rate

At t_2 the rates are equal. They remain equal at all times greater than t_2.

Over time, as shown in **Figure 12-12**, the rate of the forward reaction decreases as the reactants are used up. Meanwhile, the rate of the reverse reaction increases as the products are formed. When the two reaction rates become equal, equilibrium of the system is established. At equilibrium, the individual concentrations of the reactants and the products undergo no further changes as long as conditions remain the same. However, chemical activity continues to occur even when equilibrium is reached. Although the macroscopic properties no longer change (the system appears unchanged), the forward and reverse reactions are still occurring. In other words, the reaction does not stop at equilibrium, but maintains a constant concentration or ratio of reactants to products. The reactants continue forming products, and, at the same rate, the reverse reaction continues, with the products forming reactants. That's why any chemical equilibrium system is really a dynamic process, not a static one.

To understand the difference between a dynamic and static process, imagine that you and a friend are each holding a baseball. With each of you just holding your own baseball, the situation can be described as static. But if you throw the balls back and forth, action occurs; the situation is described as dynamic. If you continue to throw the baseballs, your situation continues to be dynamic.

0°C
Very light brown

25°C
Medium brown

100°C
Dark brown

$$N_2O_4(g) \rightleftharpoons 2NO_2(g)$$

**Le Châtelier's
principle**
*a principle stating
that if a system at
equilibrium is dis-
turbed by applying
stress, the system
will adjust in such
a way as to counter
the stress*

System equilibria
Equilibria can favor the formation of reactants or products

Equilibrium is established in a reversible reaction when the amounts of the reactants and the products are constant. An example of a reversible reaction on page 462 involved oxides of nitrogen as represented by the following equation.

$$2NO_2(g) \rightleftharpoons N_2O_4(g)$$
Brown   Colorless

Figure 12-13 shows this equilibrium system at three different temperatures. At 25°C, the system at equilibrium is a medium color of brown, but when cooled to 0°C, the color of the solution in the flask is lighter. We infer that some of the brown NO_2 is no longer there and that more of the N_2O_4 has formed. At 100°C, you can see that the contents of the flask are darker. We infer that more of the brown NO_2 has formed at the higher temperature.

Because our model involves a reversible reaction, we can use it to explain the color changes that were observed. The color lightens at 0°C because there is more N_2O_4 than at 25°C. Therefore, the reduction in temperature must cause the reaction to shift from its original equilibrium state to favor the forward reaction. But why does this shift occur?

Stresses alter equilibrium

When a system is at equilibrium, it will stay that way until something changes this condition. In the reaction between NO_2 and N_2O_4, the condition that changed is temperature. An important principle, developed by the French chemist Henri Louis Le Châtelier, shown in **Figure 12-14**, enables us to predict how changes in a system at equilibrium will affect the status of the system. **Le Châtelier's principle** states that when a system at equilibrium is disturbed by applying stress, it attains a new equilibrium position to accommodate the change and relieve the stress. Examples of stress that can be used to change a system at equilibrium include changes in concentration, temperature, or pressure.

Temperature affects equilibrium systems

Temperature changes can cause equilibrium shifts. Consider the reaction between NO_2 and N_2O_4 as the temperature is decreased from 25°C to 0°C. The exothermic process at 25°C is shown by the following equation.

$$2NO_2(g) \underset{\text{at 25°C}}{\rightleftharpoons} N_2O_4(g) + 58.8 \text{ kJ}$$

$$\underline{2NO_2 \underset{\text{at 25°C}}{\rightleftharpoons} N_2O_4}$$

Le Châtelier's principle states that a system will react to relieve any stress placed on it. In the previous reaction, energy is one of the products. Therefore, by lowering the temperature, one of the products (energy) is being removed. As the temperature continues to drop, the system reacts in such a way as to relieve the stress. To accomplish this, more NO_2 is converted to N_2O_4.

When the rate of the forward reaction is greater than the rate of the reverse reaction, the forward arrow can be shown as longer than the reverse arrow. As the gas becomes lighter, the equation is written as follows.

$$\underset{\text{Shift to the right}}{\overset{\text{Brown} \qquad \text{Colorless}}{2NO_2(g) \underset{\text{at 0°C}}{\rightleftarrows} N_2O_4(g)}}$$

$$\underline{2NO_2 \underset{\text{at 0°C}}{\rightleftarrows} N_2O_4}$$

The system reaches a new equilibrium state at the new temperature, with constant macroscopic properties. As long as this temperature is maintained, the gas in the flask will remain a light brown. The rates of the forward and reverse reactions are again equal.

On the other hand, by increasing the temperature to 100°C, more heat energy is added to the system. It reacts in such a way as to relieve the stress, and absorbs some of the heat. The equilibrium shifts left and forms more brown NO_2.

When the reverse reaction is favored, that arrow can be shown as longer. As the gas becomes darker brown, the equation is written as follows.

$$\underset{\text{Shift to the left}}{\overset{\text{Brown} \qquad \text{Colorless}}{2NO_2(g) \underset{\text{at 100°C}}{\rightleftarrows} N_2O_4(g)}}$$

$$\underline{2NO_2 \underset{\text{at 100°C}}{\rightleftarrows} N_2O_4}$$

The reaction reaches a new equilibrium state for the system at the new temperature, with constant macroscopic properties. As long as this temperature is maintained, the gas in the flask will remain a dark brown.

Pressure changes may alter gaseous equilibrium systems

According to the equation at the top of this page, 2 mol of NO_2 react to produce 1 mol of N_2O_4. When this equilibrium mixture is subjected to an increase in pressure, it relieves the stress by favoring the reaction that produces fewer gas molecules. Fewer gas molecules will exert less pressure. Observations show that an increase in pressure will cause the system to shift to the right forming more N_2O_4 molecules. Conversely, a decrease in pressure will favor the reaction that produces the most gas molecules, so the system shifts to the left, forming more NO_2 molecules.

Figure 12-15
The effects of a reversible reaction can be observed in certain sunglasses. When more light energy is added, the forward reaction is favored, forming more silver atoms (the darker color).

Practical use of Le Châtelier's principle

Have you ever worn sunglasses like the pair shown in **Figure 12-15**? If you have, then you know that in bright light they get darker. The lenses of these glasses contain the ionic compound AgCl. In the presence of light energy, AgCl decomposes, as shown by the following equation.

$$AgCl(s) + energy \rightleftharpoons Ag° + Cl°$$

Notice that this reaction is a decomposition and not a dissociation. The difference is that neutral atoms are formed in an AgCl decomposition. Ions are formed from an AgCl dissociation. In the reverse reaction, the Ag° and the Cl° atoms react to form AgCl(s). When more energy is added, a stress is placed on the system. To relieve this stress, the forward reaction is momentarily favored, shifting the equilibrium to the right, as shown by the following equation.

$$AgCl(s) + energy \xrightleftharpoons{} Ag° + Cl°$$

As the system adjusts to reach a new equilibrium, more Ag° atoms are formed. The Ag° atoms make the lenses darker and reduce the amount of sunlight that can penetrate them.

With less light energy, the equilibrium shifts to the left as indicated by the following equation.

$$AgCl(s) + energy \xrightleftharpoons{} Ag° + Cl°$$

When this happens, fewer Ag° atoms are present, and the lenses lighten and allow more light to pass through them.

complex ions
an ion having a structure in which a central atom or ion is bonded by coordinate bonds to other ions or molecules (called ligands)

Complex ion equilibria
Changes in concentration alter equilibrium systems

Complex ions are composed of a central metal ion combined with a specific number of other ions or polar molecules. For example, $[Zn(NH_3)_4]^{2+}$, shown in **Figure 12-16**, is a complex ion. The formation of a complex ion generally involves a reversible reaction that reaches equilibrium. Complex ions are interesting because many are colored, and their reactions can be tracked by color changes. In this section, you will see how changing the concentration of a reactant or product in a complex-ion equilibrium system also follows Le Châtelier's principle.

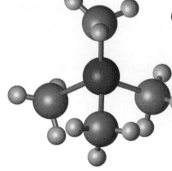

Figure 12-16
In this complex ion, the ammonia molecules are the ligands bonded to the central zinc ion.

Table 12-3
Examples of Complex Ions

Complex ion	Color
$[Co(NH_3)_5Cl]^{2+}$	violet
$[Co(NH_3)_5H_2O]^{3+}$	red
$[Co(NH_3)_6]^{3+}$	yellow-orange
$[Co(CN)_6]^{3-}$	pale yellow
$[Ni(NH_3)_6]^{2+}$	blue-violet
$[Cu(NH_3)_4]^{2+}$	blue-purple
$[Cu(H_2O)_4]^{2+}$	green-blue
$[Fe(CN)_6]^{4-}$	yellow
$[Fe(CN)_6]^{3-}$	red
$[Fe(SCN)(H_2O)_5]^{2+}$	deep red

ligand

a functional group, atom, or molecule that is attached to the central atom of a complex ion

In our example, zinc is the central metal ion that is bonded to four ammonia molecules. The molecules (or ions) that are bonded to the central metal atom are often referred to as **ligands**. Some common *ligands* are ions such as Cl^-, F^-, and CN^-, or polar molecules such as NH_3 and H_2O. More examples of complex ions are listed in **Table 12-3**.

Figure 12-17 shows a solution containing a complex ion of nickel. As you can see, this particular complex ion consists of a Ni^{2+} ion with six water molecules and produces the green color in the solution. When an excess of a concentrated ammonia solution is added to this green solution, a blue-violet color forms. This blue-violet color is characteristic of another complex ion of nickel. Ammonia molecules have replaced the water molecules that surround the nickel ion, as shown by the following equation.

$$[Ni(H_2O)_6]^{2+}(aq) + 6NH_3(aq) \rightleftharpoons [Ni(NH_3)_6]^{2+}(aq) + 6H_2O(l)$$

Green   Colorless   Blue-violet   Colorless

Each metal complex ion has a distinct color that makes it easy to identify which ion is present in a higher concentration in the solution. This reaction for complex ions is reversible and eventually reaches equilibrium. However, the equilibrium can be shifted in either direction, depending on which stress is applied. For example, if more NH_3 is added to the aqueous solution, the stress forces the equilibrium to shift to the right. Thus the color of the system will change to blue-violet. How can you get the system to change to green?

Some other aqueous equilibria reactions involving complex ions are shown below.

$$[Zn(H_2O)_4]^{2+} + H_2O \rightleftharpoons [Zn(H_2O)_3(OH)]^+ + H_3O^+$$

Colorless   Colorless

$$[Cu(H_2O)_4]^{2+} + 4NH_3 \rightleftharpoons [Cu(NH_3)_4]^{2+} + 4H_2O$$

Light blue   Deep blue-purple

$$[Cr(H_2O)_3Cl_3] + 3H_2O \rightleftharpoons [Cr(H_2O)_6]^{3+} + 3Cl^-$$

Green   Violet

$$[Co(H_2O)_6]^{2+} + 4Cl^- \rightleftharpoons [CoCl_4]^{2-} + 6H_2O$$

Pink   Deep blue

Figure 12-17
The color of the nickel complex makes it easy to see which complex ion is favored in the solution. This reaction can be reversed by adding more water to the nickel ammonia complex to return it to the green solution.

$$6NH_3(aq) + [Ni(H_2O)_6]^{2+}(aq) \rightleftharpoons [Ni(NH_3)_6]^{2+}(aq) + 6H_2O(l)$$

Practical uses of complex ions: weather prediction and stain removal

Figure 12-18
The color changes on the treated cloth for a simple weather indicator are shown for both dry and humid conditions.

Have you ever seen a weather indicator that appears blue when the weather is supposed to stay dry and turns pink when it is supposed to rain? The simple little item involves some interesting chemistry. The color changes are shown in **Figure 12-18**. The weather indicator has a piece of fabric or paper that has been soaked in a solution of cobalt(II) chloride, $CoCl_2$. When the moisture in the air is low, the cobalt(II) chloride forms a tetrahedral complex, $[CoCl_4]^{2-}$, that is blue. When the humidity is high, the $[CoCl_4]^{2-}$ reacts with water and forms a complex ion that has six water molecules attached to cobalt, $[Co(H_2O)_6]^{2+}$, and that ion appears pink. The color change in the weather indicator can be explained by Le Châtelier's principle and the following chemical equation.

$$[CoCl_4]^{2-} + 6H_2O \rightleftharpoons [Co(H_2O)_6]^{2+} + 4Cl^-$$
$$\text{Blue} \qquad\qquad \text{Pink}$$

Rust stains are difficult to remove from fabrics in regular washing but can be bleached out with an oxalic acid solution. Iron oxide combines with oxalic acid to form a complex ion, $[Fe(C_2O_4)_3]^{3-}$, as shown by the following equation.

$$Fe_2O_3(s) + 6H_2C_2O_4(aq) + 3H_2O(l) \rightleftharpoons 2[Fe(C_2O_4)_3]^{3-}(aq) + 6H_3O^+(aq)$$
$$\text{Rust} \qquad \text{Oxalic acid} \qquad\qquad\qquad \text{Complex ion}$$

The complex ion is soluble and can be washed off the fabric with detergent. Oxalic acid works in a similar manner to remove some iron-based ink stains on fabrics, which would not ordinarily wash out with detergents alone. Lemon juice, containing citric acid, can usually produce the same results as oxalic acid.

Section Review

11. Explain why the following reaction runs to completion rather than being reversible.

$$H_2CO_3(aq) \rightarrow H_2O(l) + CO_2(g)$$

12. When a hot, saturated solution of salt is allowed to cool, any excess salt could recrystallize as the solution cools. Explain what is happening in terms of the solution equilibrium if the salt does recrystallize.

13. Using the equations for complex ions (on page 467), make a hypothesis about how each system would change under the following conditions.
    a. Adding NH_3 to the copper complex ion system.
    b. Removing $[CoCl_4]^{2-}$ from the cobalt complex ion system.
    c. Adding $AgNO_3$ to the chromium complex ion system. (Hint: check your solubility table.)
    d. Adding water to the zinc complex ion system.
    e. Adding a base to the zinc complex ion system.

 14. **Story Link**
    What would be one way to separate water from salt that would be an example of a reaction that goes to completion? Explain the process.

How is equilibrium measured?

The equilibrium constant K_{eq}

Look again at the reaction of acetic acid and water.

$$CH_3COOH(aq) + H_2O(l) \rightleftharpoons$$

$$CH_3COO^-(aq) + H_3O^+(aq)$$

At equilibrium, the reactants continue to form the products, and the products are reacting to re-form the reactants at the same rate. So, even though reactions continue to occur at equilibrium, the rates are equal and effectively cancel each other out, resulting in no net chemical change. Consequently, the equilibrium concentrations of reactants and products remain constant. At equilibrium, the forward rate ($rate_f$) equals the reverse rate ($rate_r$), with the equilibrium point based on a specific temperature and pressure.

Doug never thought joining the circus would be this hard!

K_{eq} quantitatively describes equilibrium

When working with equilibrium systems, we make calculations involving the concentrations of the products and the reactants. We express the concentration of a substance by placing it in brackets. For example, to specify the concentration of OH^- ions in water as 1.0×10^{-7} M, you write it as $[OH^-] = 1.0 \times 10^{-7}$ M. When solving equilibrium problems, the formula or numerical value for a compound or ion is enclosed in brackets to represent a concentration expressed in mol/L or M.

The following is the reaction for acetic acid and water.

$$CH_3COOH(aq) + H_2O(l) \rightleftharpoons CH_3COO^-(aq) + H_3O^+(aq)$$

The rate of the forward reaction ($rate_f$) can be expressed using the product of the constant, k_f, and the concentrations of the reactants.

$$rate_f = k_f\,[CH_3COOH][H_2O]$$

The term k_f is a constant for the forward reaction and depends on the size and kind of ion or molecule involved in the reaction. The concentrations of the reactants are enclosed in brackets.

Similarly, the rate of the reverse reaction ($rate_r$) can be expressed by the following equation.

$$rate_r = k_r\,[CH_3COO^-]\,[H_3O^+]$$

The term k_r is a constant for the reverse reaction and depends on the size and kind of ion or molecule involved in the reaction. The concentrations of the products are enclosed in brackets.

Chem Fact
Over two-thirds of the acetic acid manufactured is used in the production of either vinyl acetate or cellulose acetate.

Because the two rates are equal at equilibrium, you can show the two equations as equal.

$$\text{rate}_f = \text{rate}_r$$

We can substitute the expressions in the equation as follows.

$$k_f\,[CH_3COOH][H_2O] = k_r\,[CH_3COO^-][H_3O^+]$$

At this point, we can simplify all of these ideas into a workable equation. If you divide both sides by the same expression, $k_r\,[CH_3COOH][H_2O]$, you get an expression that can then be simplified to the following equation.

$$\frac{k_f}{k_r} = \frac{[CH_3COO^-][H_3O^+]}{[CH_3COOH][H_2O]}$$

You can then rewrite this equation as the final relationship for the equilibrium expression because the ratio k_f/k_r is also a constant.

$$K_{eq} = \frac{[CH_3COO^-][H_3O^+]}{[CH_3COOH][H_2O]}$$

equilibrium constant, or K_{eq} *for a reversible reaction, a number expressing the relationship between the mathematical product of the molar concentrations of the products divided by the mathematical product of the molar concentrations of the reactants, each raised to the power of its coefficient in the balanced equation*

K_{eq} is known as the **equilibrium constant**. The equilibrium constant is the ratio (at equilibrium) of the mathematical product of the concentrations of the products to the mathematical product of the concentrations of the reactants.

Each concentration is raised to the power of its coefficient in the equation

A chemical equation can be written in the following general form.

$$\mathbf{aA + bB \rightleftharpoons cC + dD}$$

The equilibrium constant for this equation is written as follows.

$$\mathbf{K_{eq} = \frac{[C]^c[D]^d}{[A]^a[B]^b}}$$

Note that the products, represented as C and D, appear in the numerator of the expression, while the reactants, represented as A and B, appear in the denominator. Also notice that each concentration is raised to the power equal to the coefficient of the substance in the equation. Each coefficient in a chemical equation becomes a superscript in the equilibrium constant expression for that equation. When a reaction occurs in dilute aqueous solution, the concentration of water is omitted. The $[H_2O]$ is almost constant and does not need to be included in the K_{eq} calculation.

Determining K_{eq} for substances at equilibrium

In chemistry, we can express the equilibrium constant for any chemical reaction using the general equation. For example, the K_{eq} expression for the formation of ammonia can be determined from its equation as follows.

$$N_2(g) + 3H_2(g) \rightleftharpoons 2NH_3(g)$$

$$K_{eq} = \frac{[NH_3]^2}{[N_2][H_2]^3}$$

Table 12-4
Equilibrium Constants

Equation	K_{eq} value	Temperature
$N_2O_4(g) \rightleftharpoons 2NO_2(g)$	5.6×10^{-3}	0°C
	5.9×10^{-3}	25°C
	8.3×10^{-1}	55°C
$CO_2(g) + H_2(g) \rightleftharpoons CO(g) + H_2O(g)$	2.0	1120°C
	4.40	1727°C
$N_2(g) + O_2(g) \rightleftharpoons 2NO(g)$	4.5×10^{-31}	25°C
	6.7×10^{-10}	627°C
	1.7×10^{-3}	2027°C
$CH_3COOH + H_2O \rightleftharpoons H_3O^+ + CH_3COO^-$	1.8×10^{-5}	25°C
$2HI(g) \rightleftharpoons H_2(g) + I_2(g)$	1.5×10^{-2}	350°C
	1.8×10^{-2}	425°C
	2.2×10^{-2}	1123°C

The actual value for a particular K_{eq} is found experimentally. A chemist analyzes the equilibrium mixture and calculates the concentrations of all substances involved in the reaction. When determining the K_{eq} value for a particular reaction, the chemist must also specify the temperature under which the concentrations are measured. The K_{eq} value will change if the temperature changes. **Table 12-4** gives some values for equilibrium constants. You can see that the same reactions have different values at different temperatures.

Concept Review

Writing equilibrium expressions

15. You can write an equilibrium expression for any reaction that is balanced by using the general equation for the equilibrium constant. Write equilibrium expressions for the following reactions.
   a. $HOCl(aq) \rightleftharpoons H^+(aq) + ClO^-(aq)$
   b. $[Cu(H_2O)_4]^{2+}(aq) + 4NH_3(aq) \rightleftharpoons [Cu(NH_3)_4]^{2+}(aq) + 4H_2O(l)$
16. Write equilibrium expressions for all reactions listed in **Table 12-4**.

Figure 12-19
An example of equilibrium is a descent down the face of a cliff, involving a double-rope system secured above the person in a method called "rappelling."

Using the value of K_{eq} to determine which direction is favored in a reaction

Rappelling, shown in **Figure 12-19**, is an example of opposing forces maintaining an equilibrium. If the two rope forces are equal, there is no movement for the climber. This situation is similar to having a K_{eq} value of one in a chemical equation. For a K_{eq} value of one, the product of the concentrations of the products (the numerator) and the product of the concentrations of the reactants (the denominator) have the same value. (Remember, these equilibrium concentrations are raised to the correct powers.)

What does a K_{eq} value that is greater than one tell you about which reaction is favored at equilibrium? In reactions that have K_{eq} values larger than one, the forward reaction is favored. For reactions that have K_{eq} values smaller than one, the reverse reaction is favored. Consequently, by knowing the value of K_{eq} for a reaction, you know which reaction is favored. Using known values of K_{eq}, we can make calculations and predictions about equilibrium systems without having to do lab work or make actual measurements.

Carbon dioxide and carbonic acid are part of a biochemical equilibrium system

Respiration is an essential function of living organisms. Carbon dioxide given off by your cells during respiration diffuses into your blood, where some of it combines with water to form the compound carbonic acid, H_2CO_3.

$$CO_2(g) + H_2O(l) \rightleftharpoons H_2CO_3(aq)$$

In turn, H_2CO_3 reacts with the water that makes up most of the plasma of your blood. The equation for this reaction is written as follows.

$$H_2CO_3(aq) + H_2O(l) \rightleftharpoons H_3O^+(aq) + HCO_3^-(aq)$$

This process is illustrated in **Figure 12-20**, showing how your breathing and blood plasma pH level are part of a biochemical equilibrium system.

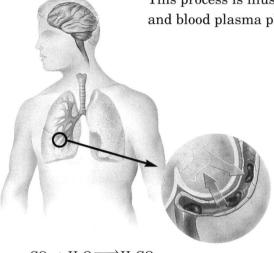

$$CO_2 + H_2O \rightleftharpoons H_2CO_3$$
$$H_2CO_3 + H_2O \rightleftharpoons H_3O^+ + HCO_3^-$$

Figure 12-20a
In solution, carbonic acid exists in equilibrium with H_2O and CO_2. However, this equilibrium can be altered, depending on the nature of the stress.

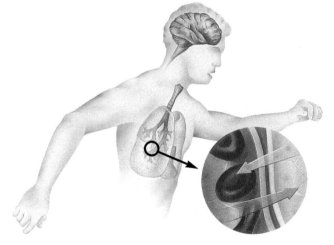

$$CO_2 + H_2O \rightleftharpoons H_2CO_3$$
$$H_2CO_3 + H_2O \rightleftharpoons H_3O^+ + HCO_3^-$$

12-20b
If you exercise vigorously, more CO_2 is produced in your body. An increase in the concentration of CO_2 will place stress on the first equation, forcing the equilibrium to shift to the right so that the formation of H_2CO_3 will be favored. As the concentration of H_2CO_3 increases, stress is placed upon the second equation, forcing the equilibrium to shift to the right so that more H_3O^+ and HCO_3^- are produced.

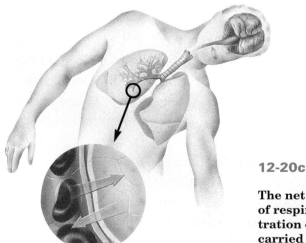

$$CO_2 + H_2O \rightleftharpoons H_2CO_3$$
$$H_2CO_3 + H_2O \rightleftharpoons H_3O^+ + HCO_3^-$$

12-20c

The net result of an increase in your rate of respiration is an increase in the concentration of both the H_3O^+ and HCO_3^- ions carried in your blood. The pH level of your blood plasma decreases due to the increased hydronium ion concentration. Your brain sends a message to exhale CO_2 more rapidly in order to return the system to its original state.

Your body is sensitive to even small changes in the pH level of your blood plasma. When a drop in the pH level is detected, your brain responds by sending a signal to increase your rate of breathing. The faster you breathe, the more CO_2 you exhale. By exhaling more CO_2, the initial stress of an increased CO_2 concentration is reduced, and the original equilibrium will be reestablished.

Suppose, however, that someone is hyperventilating. As a result of breathing very rapidly, the person exhales CO_2 at a very rapid rate, shifting both equilibria reactions to the left. As a result, the concentration of both H_3O^+ and HCO_3^- ions drops, and the pH level of the blood plasma rises. Your body responds by constricting the cerebral blood vessels, which reduces the flow of blood to your brain and causes dizziness. When normal breathing is restored, as depicted in **Figure 12-21**, the pH level returns to normal, and there is no longer a feeling of dizziness.

Figure 12-21
Hyperventilation can cause dizziness. A person with this condition should sit down and attempt to restore normal breathing by lowering the head and breathing slowly into cupped hands or a small paper bag.

Sample Problem 12A
Calculating K_{eq} for the carbonic acid system at equilibrium

At a temperature of 25°C, the following concentrations of the reactants and products for the reaction involving carbonic acid and water are present: $[H_2CO_3] = 3.3 \times 10^{-2}$ M, $[H_3O^+] = 1.1 \times 10^{-5}$ M, and $[HCO_3^-] = 7.1 \times 10^{-1}$ M. The $[H_2O]$ is not considered because it is constant. What is the K_{eq} value for the following reaction at equilibrium in a dilute aqueous solution?

$$H_2CO_3(aq) + H_2O(l) \rightleftharpoons H_3O^+(aq) + HCO_3^-(aq)$$

❶ List
- $[H_2CO_3] = 3.3 \times 10^{-2}$ M
- $[H_3O^+] = 1.1 \times 10^{-5}$ M
- $[HCO_3^-] = 7.1 \times 10^{-1}$ M
- $K_{eq} = \ ?$

❷ Set up
- Write the K_{eq} expression for this reaction.

$$K_{eq} = \frac{[H_3O^+][HCO_3^-]}{[H_2CO_3]}$$

- Substitute the given values.

$$K_{eq} = \frac{[1.1 \times 10^{-5}][7.1 \times 10^{-1}]}{[3.3 \times 10^{-2}]}$$

❸ Estimate and calculate
- A rough estimate of the answer is approximately 2.5×10^{-4}.

$$K_{eq} = \frac{[1.1 \times 10^{-5}][7.1 \times 10^{-1}]}{[3.3 \times 10^{-2}]} = 2.4 \times 10^{-4}$$

- The K_{eq} value for this reaction is 2.4×10^{-4}, which is consistent with the rough estimate.

Sample Problem 12B

Calculating concentrations using the equilibrium constant

Ammonia gas is extremely soluble in water. An aqueous solution of ammonia is known as ammonium hydroxide.

$$NH_3(g) + H_2O(l) \rightleftharpoons NH_4^+(aq) + OH^-(aq)$$

K_{eq} for this reaction equals 1.8×10^{-5} at a temperature of 298 K. If the equilibrium concentration of NH_3 is 6.82×10^{-3} M, calculate the concentration of ammonium ion at equilibrium. The concentration of H_2O is constant and need not be included in the K_{eq} calculations.

❶ List
- $K_{eq} = 1.8 \times 10^{-5}$
- $[NH_3] = 6.82 \times 10^{-3}$ M
- $[NH_4^+] = [OH^-] = $ **?**

❷ Set up
- Write the K_{eq} expression for this reaction.

$$K_{eq} = \frac{[NH_4^+][OH^-]}{[NH_3]}$$

- Substitute the known values in this equation.

$$1.8 \times 10^{-5} = \frac{[NH_4^+][OH^-]}{[6.82 \times 10^{-3}]}$$

- Then solve for $[NH_4^+][OH^-]$.

$$[NH_4^+][OH^-] = (1.8 \times 10^{-5})(6.82 \times 10^{-3})$$

❸ Estimate and calculate
- Rounding the numbers for estimation, you get 14×10^{-8}.

$$[NH_4^+][OH^-] = (1.8 \times 10^{-5})(6.82 \times 10^{-3}) = 1.2 \times 10^{-7} \text{ M}$$

- The concentration of each ion, $[NH_4^+]$ and $[OH^-]$, is found by taking the square root of 1.2×10^{-7} M. (The concentrations of the two ions are equal.)

$$[NH_4^+] = \sqrt{1.2 \times 10^{-7} \text{ M}}$$

- The concentration of ammonium ion at equilibrium is 3.5×10^{-4} M.

Practice 12A

Answers for Concept Review items and Practice problems begin on page 841.

1. For the following reaction, equilibrium is established at a certain temperature when the following concentrations are present: [CO] = 0.010 mol/L, [H_2O] = 0.020 mol/L, [CO_2] = 0.012 mol/L, and [H_2] = 0.012 mol/L. Calculate the K_{eq} value for this reaction.

$$CO(g) + H_2O(g) \rightleftharpoons CO_2(g) + H_2(g)$$

2. For the system involving N_2O_4 and NO_2 at equilibrium at a temperature of 100°C, the concentration of N_2O_4 is 4.0×10^{-2} mol/L, and the concentration of NO_2 is 1.2×10^{-1} mol/L. What is the K_{eq} value for the reaction to form NO_2?

12B 3. Methanol can be prepared by the reaction of H_2 and CO at high temperatures, according to the following equation.

$$CO(g) + 2H_2(g) \rightleftharpoons CH_3OH(g)$$

What is the concentration of $CH_3OH(g)$ if [H_2] = 0.080 mol/L and [CO] = 0.025 mol/L at 700 K, and $K_{eq} = 290$?

4. Using a K_{eq} value of 1.7×10^6 at 2027°C for the following reaction, what is the equilibrium concentration of nitrogen monoxide when the concentrations of nitrogen and oxygen at equilibrium are 1.8×10^{-3} mol/L and 4.2×10^{-4} mol/L, respectively?

$$N_2(g) + O_2(g) \rightleftharpoons 2NO(g)$$

The solubility-product constant K_{sp}

K_{sp} is an equilibrium constant for slightly soluble ionic substances

Recall from Chapter 11 that solubility refers to the maximum amount of a solute that will dissolve per unit volume of a solvent under various conditions. In Chapter 11, solubility was expressed in units of grams of solute per 100 g of water. As you will see in this section, solubility can also be expressed in terms of equilibrium expressions.

In Chapter 11, you learned that salts differ in degree of solubility in water; some are highly soluble, some are only slightly soluble, and others are almost insoluble. Actually, most "insoluble" salts will dissolve to some extent in water and are more accurately described as being *very slightly soluble*. In such cases, an extremely small quantity of the salt saturates the solution, usually less than 0.1 g of salt per 100 g of water.

An example of a slightly soluble salt is barium sulfate, $BaSO_4$. The equation for this salt in aqueous equilibrium is the following.

$$BaSO_4(s) \rightleftharpoons Ba^{2+}(aq) + SO_4^{2-}(aq)$$

The K_{eq} expression is written as shown by the following equation.

$$K_{eq} = \frac{[Ba^{2+}][SO_4^{2-}]}{[BaSO_4]}$$

However, the concentration of $BaSO_4$ in the solid state is a constant. Consequently, this equation can be simplified and written as follows.

$$K_{eq} = [Ba^{2+}][SO_4^{2-}]$$

This is the solubility of a pure solid ionic compound, so the equilibrium constant is called the **solubility-product constant**, or K_{sp}. The expression now reads as follows.

$$K_{sp} = [Ba^{2+}][SO_4^{2-}]$$

Each ion concentration is raised to the power of its coefficient in the equation

The equation for a slightly soluble ionic substance in a saturated solution can be written in the following general form.

$$A_aB_b(s) \rightleftharpoons aA^+ + bB^-$$

The general equation for the solubility-product constant, K_{sp}, is as follows.

$$K_{sp} = [A^+]^a[B^-]^b$$

Look at the K_{sp} values in **Table 12-5**. The K_{sp} value for a slightly soluble salt reveals the relative solubilities of its ions. Compounds with larger K_{sp} values are more soluble than those with smaller K_{sp} values.

solubility-product constant, or K_{sp} *the equilibrium constant for a solid in equilibrium with its ions in a saturated solution; used for substances that are described as "insoluble" because they are only very slightly soluble*

Table 12-5
Solubility-Product Constants at 25°C

Salt	K_{sp}
Ag_2CO_3	8.45×10^{-12}
Ag_2CrO_4	1.12×10^{-12}
Ag_2S	1.09×10^{-49}
$AgBr$	5.35×10^{-13}
$AgCl$	1.77×10^{-10}
AgI	8.51×10^{-17}
$Al(OH)_3$	1.98×10^{-31}
$BaSO_4$	1.07×10^{-10}
$Ca_3(PO_4)_2$	2.07×10^{-33}
$CaSO_4$	7.10×10^{-5}
CuS	1.27×10^{-36}
$Fe(OH)_3$	2.64×10^{-39}
FeS	1.59×10^{-19}
$MgCO_3$	6.82×10^{-6}
$MnCO_3$	2.24×10^{-11}
$Ni_3(PO_4)_2$	4.73×10^{-32}
PbS	9.04×10^{-29}
$PbSO_4$	1.82×10^{-8}
$SrSO_4$	3.44×10^{-7}
$ZnCO_3$	1.19×10^{-10}
ZnS	2.93×10^{-25}

Keep in mind that the K_{sp} expression has limited applications. The K_{sp} equation can be very useful for calculating the concentrations of ions formed from slightly soluble salts. However, K_{sp} cannot be applied successfully to salts that are more soluble. These simple equations do not hold when concentrations of ions are high, as is the case of highly soluble salts.

Sample Problem 12C
Calculating concentrations using K_{sp}, the solubility-product constant

Refer to the instruction book for your calculator to find out how to determine the square root of a number with an exponent.

Consider the dissociation of the salt CaF_2.

$$CaF_2(s) \rightleftharpoons Ca^{2+}(aq) + 2F^-(aq)$$

At a temperature of 298 K, the concentration of Ca^{2+} ions is 2.2×10^{-4} M, and K_{sp} for CaF_2 is 1.46×10^{-10}. Calculate the concentration of F^- in the solution.

❶ List
- $K_{sp} = 1.46 \times 10^{-10}$
- $Ca^{2+} = [2.2 \times 10^{-4}]$
- $F^- = \mathbf{?}$

❷ Set up
- Write the K_{sp} expression for the reaction.
$$K_{sp} = [Ca^{2+}][F^-]^2$$

- Substitute the known values into this equation.
$$1.46 \times 10^{-10} = [2.2 \times 10^{-4}][F^-]^2$$

- Rearrange to solve for $[F^-]^2$.
$$[F^-]^2 = \frac{1.46 \times 10^{-10}}{2.2 \times 10^{-4}}$$

- Solve for $[F^-]$ by determining the square root of the expression.
$$[F^-]^2 = 0.664 \times 10^{-6} \qquad \text{(determine the square root)}$$

❸ Estimate and calculate
- To approximate the square root, change the value to 67×10^{-8}, which has a square root of roughly 8×10^{-4}.
$$[F^-]^2 = 0.664 \times 10^{-6} \qquad \text{(determine the square root)}$$

$$[F^-] = 8.1486195 \times 10^{-4}, \text{ which is rounded to } 8.1 \times 10^{-4}$$

$$[F^-] = 8.1 \times 10^{-4}$$

- The F^- ion concentration is 8.1×10^{-4} M.

Practice 12C

1. What is the K_{sp} value for $Co_3(PO_4)_2$ if the concentrations at equilibrium and standard temperature are determined to be 1.60×10^{-6} M for Co^{2+} ions and 2.24×10^{-9} M for PO_4^{3-} ions?

2. At 298 K, the K_{sp} value for barium carbonate is 2.58×10^{-9}. What is the concentration of barium ions in a saturated solution of this salt? The concentration of CO_3^{2-} ions is 7.12×10^{-5} M, and the dissociation equation is as follows.
$$BaCO_3(s) \rightleftharpoons Ba^{2+}(aq) + CO_3^{2-}(aq)$$

3. The K_{sp} value for silver carbonate is 8.14×10^{-12} at 298 K. The concentration of carbonate ions is 2.85×10^{-6} M; what is the concentration of silver ions?

Common ion effect
Practical uses of equilibrium constants

Barium sulfate, $BaSO_4$, is an insoluble salt, which means that very little of it will actually dissolve in solution. Doctors use $BaSO_4$ as an X-ray contrast medium. The patient ingests solid $BaSO_4$ powder that is suspended in water and will appear as light areas on the X-ray film. By studying these light areas, like those shown in **Figure 12-22**, doctors can diagnose problems in the patient's digestive tract. Doctors must make sure that almost no Ba^{2+} ions are present to dissolve in a person's body fluids because Ba^{2+} ions are poisonous. Knowing the solubility-product constant (K_{sp}) for $BaSO_4$, calculations are made to determine the amount of $BaSO_4$ needed for the procedure. To ensure that the concentration of Ba^{2+} ions will not exceed the safety level, a soluble salt such as Na_2SO_4, which also contributes SO_4^{2-} ions, is added to increase the SO_4^{2-} ion concentration and reduce the Ba^{2+} ion concentration.

Na_2SO_4 dissociates as shown by the following equation.

$$Na_2SO_4(s) \longrightarrow 2Na^+(aq) + SO_4^{2-}(aq)$$

Increasing the concentration of Na_2SO_4 results in an increase in the concentration of SO_4^{2-} ions in the solution. These SO_4^{2-} ions affect the chemical reaction involving the dissociation of $BaSO_4$. Examine the following equation.

$$BaSO_4(s) \rightleftharpoons Ba^{2+}(aq) + SO_4^{2-}(aq)$$

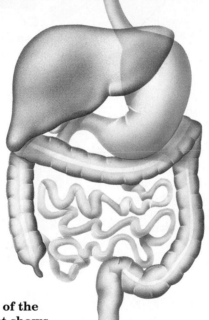

Figure 12-22a
The light areas on an X ray of the digestive tract show the insoluble barium sulfate.

12-22b
This drawing of the digestive tract shows the same area that is shown in the X ray.

common ion
an ion that comes from two or more substances making up a chemical solution

An increase in the SO_4^{2-} ions shifts the equilibrium to the left, and this shift causes Ba^{2+} ions to combine with SO_4^{2-} ions, forming solid $BaSO_4$. By having $BaSO_4$ precipitate out of solution, there is a lower concentration of Ba^{2+} ions in the solution. Adding the Na_2SO_4 has the effect of reducing the concentration of Ba^{2+} ions in the solution. Because SO_4^{2-} ion is present in both $BaSO_4$ and Na_2SO_4, sulfate is the **common ion** present in both substances dissolved in the solution.

common ion effect
a process in which an ionic compound becomes less soluble upon the addition of one of its ions by adding another compound

The displacement of an equilibrium caused by the presence of more than one source for a reactant or product ion is called the **common ion effect**. Remember from Le Châtelier's principle that changing the concentration of ions can have an effect on the equilibrium of the system. In **Figure 12-23,** Na_2SO_4 is added to the saturated solution of $BaSO_4$. The increase in the concentration of SO_4^{2-} ions causes the equilibrium to shift to the left so that less $BaSO_4$ dissolves in the presence of the common ion, thereby causing a decrease in the Ba^{2+} ion concentration in the solution.

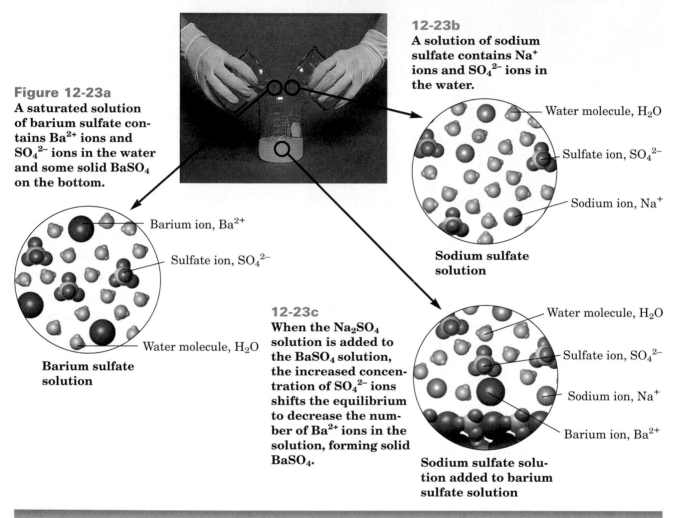

Figure 12-23a
A saturated solution of barium sulfate contains Ba^{2+} ions and SO_4^{2-} ions in the water and some solid $BaSO_4$ on the bottom.

Barium ion, Ba^{2+}
Sulfate ion, SO_4^{2-}
Water molecule, H_2O
Barium sulfate solution

12-23b
A solution of sodium sulfate contains Na^+ ions and SO_4^{2-} ions in the water.

Water molecule, H_2O
Sulfate ion, SO_4^{2-}
Sodium ion, Na^+
Sodium sulfate solution

12-23c
When the Na_2SO_4 solution is added to the $BaSO_4$ solution, the increased concentration of SO_4^{2-} ions shifts the equilibrium to decrease the number of Ba^{2+} ions in the solution, forming solid $BaSO_4$.

Water molecule, H_2O
Sulfate ion, SO_4^{2-}
Sodium ion, Na^+
Barium ion, Ba^{2+}
Sodium sulfate solution added to barium sulfate solution

Section Review

17. What information does the K_{eq} value for a reaction provide?
18. Write the K_{eq} expression for each of the following reactions.
    a. silver chloride in an aqueous solution
    b. the dissociation of lead(II) nitrate in aqueous solution
    c. $NiSO_4(aq) + 6H_2O(l) \rightleftharpoons [Ni(H_2O)_6]^{2+}(aq) + SO_4^{2-}(aq)$
19. Why does the concentration of undissolved salt not appear in the K_{sp} expression?
20. Write the solubility-product expression for the slightly soluble salt aluminum hydroxide, $Al(OH)_3$.
21. Calculate K_{sp} for the following hypothetical reaction.
    $$A_2B_3(s) \rightleftharpoons 2A^{3+}(aq) + 3B^{2-}(aq)$$
    The equilibrium concentration of A^{3+} is 2.7×10^{-3} M, and the concentration of B^{2-} is 1.1×10^{-6} M.

Conclusion: Sea Water and Equilibrium

The chapter began with a story about three people who were stranded without drinkable water. Even though your body contains between 55% to 65% fluid by weight, losing just 2% makes you feel extremely thirsty, and death is inevitable with a 20% loss. The people rescued had lost nearly 20% of their body fluids.

The principles learned in this chapter can be used to answer the questions presented in the story.

How would drinking sea water affect the aqueous equilibrium in the body? Body fluids contain ions. Normally, water flows across cell membranes into areas with a higher concentration of dissolved electrolytes, including Na^+, Cl^-, Ca^{2+}, Mg^{2+}, and K^+ ions. Drinking sea water, with its high concentration of some of these ions, causes an electrolytic imbalance.

As a result, water would move out of cells. Brain cells would shrink, causing seizures, coma, and then death. Hospital care is required to restore normal electrolyte balance.

Can sea water be made safe to drink? Many substances dissolved in sea water are electrolytes. The methods used to remove these substances include ion exchange and electrodialysis membranes. The latter method makes use of salt's electrolytic properties to collect ions along a membrane in an electric field. The ions are separated from sea water, making it salt-free and safe to drink.

How do you know when water is safe to drink? You can have water samples tested at city water treatment plants. Many substances come into contact with water before it goes to a processing plant. Various processes remove such substances before it becomes available to the public. Chemists approve community water supplies.

Applying Concepts

1. Sea water contains a high concentration of Na^+ and Cl^- ions formed from the dissociation of NaCl. A reference for K_{sp} values does not list NaCl. What does that tell you about NaCl?
2. When people suffer from dehydration, their hearts must beat harder to maintain circulation. Why?

Research and Writing

Use the library to do the following.

1. Prepare a report to show how aqueous equilibrium processes are involved in the formation of stalagmites and stalactites in caves.
2. Sea water contains many salts and minerals. Research what is being done to extract minerals from the oceans.
3. Some people stranded at sea have survived for more than 100 days. Report on what methods they used to obtain drinkable water.

Highlights

• Both electrolytes and nonelectrolytes can affect colligative properties, such as boiling point elevation and freezing point depression, which depend on the number of particles in solution.

What is an equilibrium system?

• Reactions go to completion when products include such things as the formation of a precipitate or the evolution of a gas.
• Reactions that are reversible can re-form the reactants. When the forward and reverse reactions occur at equal rates, the reaction is at equilibrium.
• A system stays at equilibrium until conditions change. Le Châtelier's principle explains that stress, including temperature, pressure, and change in concentration, can shift equilibrium.

How is equilibrium measured?

• The equilibrium constant K_{eq} is a number that expresses the relationship between the concentrations of substances in a reversible reaction at a given temperature.
• The solubility-product constant K_{sp} is the equilibrium constant for a solid in equilibrium with its ions in a saturated solution of a slightly soluble salt.
• Adding a common ion to a solution can shift the equilibrium to reduce the concentration of a substance in solution.

Key terms

colligative property
common ion
common ion effect
complex ions
conductance
dissociation
electrolyte
equilibrium constant
hydration
hydronium ion

Le Châtelier's principle
ligand
nonelectrolyte
solubility-product constant
strong electrolyte
theory of ionization
weak electrolyte

Key ideas

What happens in an aqueous solution?

• Substances that can conduct electricity when they dissolve in a solution are called electrolytes.
• Electrolytes form ions in a solution. Strong electrolytes undergo large dissociation; weak electrolytes undergo small dissociation.
• Electrolytes are either ionic or molecular compounds that dissociate in water.

Key problem-solving approach:
Equations using constants

For an equilibrium problem, analyze the type of equilibrium presented. Follow the arrows in the diagram to determine the proper equilibrium expression to use.

Sample Equation
$$aA + bB \rightleftharpoons cC + dD$$

Equilibrium problem

Slightly soluble salt in water

Other reversible reactions

Solubility product constant (K_{sp})

Equilibrium constant (K_{eq})

Problem will use

Problem will use

$$K_{sp} = [C]^c[D]^d$$

$$K_{eq} = \frac{[C]^c[D]^d}{[A]^a[B]^b}$$

Review and Assess

Properties of aqueous solutions

REVIEW

1. **a.** What property identifies all electrolytes?
   b. How could you safely determine whether an unknown aqueous solution contains an electrolyte?
2. Rate the solutions below from most conductive to least conductive.
   a. 1.0 M KOH solution
   b. 10. M ammonia solution
   c. 5.0 M glucose solution
3. **a.** How does a strong electrolyte differ from a weak electrolyte?
   b. Distinguish between the use of the terms *strong* and *weak* with the terms *dilute* and *concentrated* in describing solutions containing electrolytes.
   c. Which of the following solutes would show conductivity properties when dissolved in water: $NaCl$, KCl, $C_{12}H_{22}O_{11}$, $Mg(NO_3)_2$, CCl_4, and $Al_2(SO_4)_3$?
4. **a.** Describe the hydration process on the particle level for an ionic compound in water.
   b. Describe the dissociation process on the particle level for a molecular compound in water.
5. What determines whether a dissociation is endothermic or exothermic?

APPLY

6. When you touch an appliance that has a short circuit, an electric current travels through your body, giving you a shock. What feature of the human body allows this to happen?

7. Sports medicine utilizes heats of solution in hot and cold packs. Many of these products work by dissolving an ionic substance in water. Study **Table 12-1**, and suggest the best substances to use for hot packs and for cold packs. Explain the reasons for your choices.

8. Suggest a method for making water boil at 100°C in high-altitude areas.
9. In northern Utah the temperature falls well below freezing in the winter. Would you expect the Great Salt Lake to be safe for ice skating? Explain your answer.
10. Rank the following substances from greatest to least ability to change the colligative properties of water. Explain your reasons.
    a. NaOH   **b.** $C_6H_{12}O_6$ **c.** $AlBr_3$

Solutions in equilibrium

REVIEW

11. **a.** Compare the rate of the forward reaction to the rate of the reverse reaction for a solution as it approaches equilibrium.
    b. Compare the rate of the forward reaction to the rate of the reverse reaction for a solution in equilibrium.
12. **a.** How does Le Châtelier's principle relate to reversible reactions?
    b. Does Le Châtelier's principle affect reactions that go to completion?
13. Use **Figure 12-12** to answer the following questions.
    a. What is happening to the rate of formation of H_3O^+ before the system reaches equilibrium?
    b. When is the rate of the forward reaction the greatest?
    c. How would the addition of sodium acetate, $NaCH_3COO$, affect the equilibrium described in the figure?
14. Draw two diagrams that depict the difference between the microscopic and macroscopic events that occur when a reaction is at equilibrium.
15. Identify the ligands in the following complex ions.

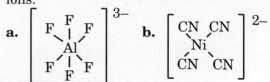

c.

$$\left[H_3N{-}Ag{-}NH_3 \right]^+$$

d.

$$\left[\begin{array}{ccc} & H_2O & \\ NH_3 & | & NH_3 \\ & Co & \\ NH_3 & | & NH_3 \\ & H_2O & \end{array} \right]^{3+}$$

Quantitative equilibrium

A P P L Y

16. Identify the stress on each reaction below.
   a. the color of a shirt changing according to the heat surrounding it
   b. the chemical in a pool test kit turning red in response to the chloride ions in the water
   c. a mood ring changing color when you get angry

17. A home economics teacher instructs the class to add several teaspoons of sugar to their homemade lemonade and then stir until the sugar stops dissolving. Is this instruction chemically correct? Explain.

18. Ethyl acetate, $CH_3COOC_2H_5$, is used to make artificial silk and is prepared by reacting acetic acid, CH_3COOH, and ethanol, C_2H_5OH. Water is also produced in this reaction.
   a. Write the balanced equation for this reaction.
   b. If the production of ethyl acetate is not sufficient, what would increase the yield?
   c. Why is it a good idea to remove ethyl acetate as it forms?

19. Identify which of the following reactions will go to completion. Give a reason for your answer.
   a. dripping water depositing limestone in caves
   b. CO_2 bubbles forming as hydrochloric acid reacts with limestone
   c. saline solution dissolving all of the mineral deposits on a contact lens

20. Carbonated beverages contain carbonic acid in solution. The end result of the dissociation of this acid is represented by the following equation.

$$H_2CO_3(aq) \rightleftharpoons H_2O(l) + CO_2(g)$$

   What changes would cause a shift to the right?

21. Use Le Châtelier's principle and the reaction below to answer the following questions.

$$2SO_2(g) + O_2(g) \rightleftharpoons 2SO_3(g)$$

   a. SO_2 reacts with oxygen to form SO_3. How can you minimize the amount of SO_2 that re-forms?
   b. How can you produce oxygen from this reaction?
   c. How can you ensure that the amount of SO_3 formed remains unchanged?

22. Although the K_{eq} value is known as the equilibrium constant, **Table 12-4** shows that one substance can have several different K_{eq} values. Why is it still called a constant?

23. Predict the concentration(s) of the reactants and the products in the decomposition reaction of ammonium bisulfide when K_{eq} is greater than 1, less than 1, and equal to 1.

$$NH_4HS(s) \rightleftharpoons NH_3(g) + H_2S(g)$$

24. Use **Table 12-4** to determine whether the following equations favor the forward or the reverse reaction at the given temperature.
   a. $2HI(g) \rightleftharpoons H_2(g) + I_2(g)$ at 350°C
   b. $N_2(g) + O_2(g) \rightleftharpoons 2NO(g)$ at 25°C
   c. $CH_3COOH(l) \rightleftharpoons H^+(aq) + CH_3COO^-(aq)$ at 25°C
   d. $N_2O_4(g) \rightleftharpoons 2NO_2(g)$ at 0°C
   e. $N_2O_4(g) \rightleftharpoons 2NO_2(g)$ at 55°C

25. Why can the term *insoluble* be a misleading description for most salts that do not appear to dissolve in water?

26. Write equilibrium constant expressions for the following reactions.
   a. $2NO_2(g) \rightleftharpoons N_2O_4(g)$
   b. $[Cu(NH_3)_4]^{2+} \rightleftharpoons Cu^{2+}(aq) + 4NH_3(aq)$
   c. $AgCl(s) \rightleftharpoons Ag^+(aq) + Cl^-(aq)$

27. Relate Le Châtelier's principle to the common ion effect.

P R A C T I C E

Answers to items in a black square begin on page 841.

28. Vinegar, a solution of acetic acid, CH_3COOH, and water, is used in varying concentrations for different household tasks. If the concentration of the acetic acid solution at equilibrium is 3.00 M, the H_3O^+ concentration at equilibrium is 7.22×10^{-3} M, and the CH_3COO^- concentration is 7.22×10^{-3} M, what is the K_{eq} value for acetic acid? (Hint: see Sample Problem 12A.)

$$CH_3COOH(aq) + H_2O(l) \rightleftharpoons H_3O^+(aq) + CH_3COO^-(aq)$$

29. Aniline, $C_6H_5NH_2$, is a weak base. If the concentration of aniline is 6.00 M at equilibrium, and the concentrations of both $C_6H_5NH_3^+$ and OH^- are 5.08×10^{-5} M, what is the K_{eq} value for aniline? (Hint: see Sample Problem 12A.)

$$C_6H_5NH_2(l) + H_2O(l) \rightleftharpoons$$
$$C_6H_5NH_3^+(aq) + OH^-(aq)$$

30 Benzoic acid, C_6H_5COOH, is a slightly soluble acid used in food preservation. K_{eq} for benzoic acid is 6.30×10^{-5} at 25°C. For a solution of benzoic acid that has an equilibrium concentration of 2.00 M, what are the concentrations of H_3O^+ and $C_6H_5COO^-$? (Hint: see Sample Problem 12B.)

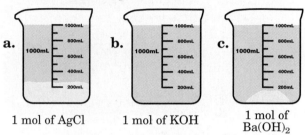

31. Phenol, C_6H_5OH, is used as a disinfectant in many household cleaning solutions. If the equilibrium concentration of phenol is 1.61×10^{-3} M, what are the concentrations of H_3O^+ and $C_6H_5O^-$? K_{eq} for phenol is 1.60×10^{-10} at 25°C. (Hint: see Sample Problem 12B.)

32 Aluminum hydroxide, $Al(OH)_3$, is used in the process of waterproofing fabrics. If the Al^{3+} concentration is 2.63×10^{-9} M, what is the concentration of OH^-? The K_{sp} value for $Al(OH)_3$ is 1.30×10^{-33} at 288 K. (Hint: see Sample Problem 12C.)

33. Silver sulfide, Ag_2S, is an ingredient used to make ceramics. If the Ag_2S in your dog's ceramic water dish dissolves in the water, giving a Ag^+ concentration of 4.93×10^{-17} M, what concentration of S^{2-} will be in your dog's water? The K_{sp} value for Ag_2S is 6.00×10^{-50} at 288 K. (Hint: see Sample Problem 12C.)

A P P L Y
---

34. What is wrong with the following expression for K_{eq}?

$$NH_3(g) + O_2(g) \rightleftharpoons NO(g) + H_2O(g)$$

$$K_{eq} = \frac{[NH_3][O_2]}{[NO][H_2O]}$$

35. Lactic acid, $HC_3H_5O_3$, a by-product of cell metabolism, causes your muscles to ache shortly after vigorous exercise. Write an equilibrium equation for the dissociation of lactic acid in muscle tissue.

36. The figure below shows the results of adding different chemicals to distilled water.
   a. Which substance(s) is (are) completely soluble in water?
   b. Is it correct to say that AgCl is completely insoluble? Explain.

a. 1000mL 1 mol of AgCl
b. 1000mL 1 mol of KOH
c. 1000mL 1 mol of $Ba(OH)_2$

37. Pb^{2+} in drinking water can result in nerve damage. Trace amounts of Pb^{2+} in a water supply system can be detected by increasing the concentration of Cl^- ions to form $PbCl_2$ as a precipitate. Assuming that all of the chemicals listed in the table below are equally available at low cost, which would be most useful in testing for Pb^{2+} in your water supply? Explain.

Name	Formula	K_{sp}
silver chloride	AgCl	1.77×10^{-10}
lead sulfate	PbS	9.04×10^{-29}
sodium chloride	NaCl	high solubility
lead sulfate	$PbSO_4$	1.82×10^{-8}

38. a. Are any of the K_{sp} values listed in the table above greater than 1?
   b. Explain this observation.

Linking chapters

1. **Saturated solutions**
   a. Relate the behavior of sparingly soluble salts to the concept of saturation.
   b. How does Le Châtelier's principle explain the behavior of a saturated solution that forms more solid solute precipitate when a common ion is added?

2. **Percent yield**
   Using Le Châtelier's principle, explain how to increase the percent yield of a reversible chemical reaction.

3. **Free energy**
   a. What does the equilibrium constant have in common with free energy?
   b. What is the ΔG of a reaction at equilibrium?

4. **Bond energy**
   Heat of solution occurs when an ionic substance dissolves in water. Explain the energy transfers involved in the heat of dissociation and heat of hydration that result in the heat of solution.

5. **Theme: *Equilibrium and change***
   a. If a process is in equilibrium, does this mean there are no changes?
   b. If a reversible reaction favors the formation of the products, are any reactants being re-formed?

USING TECHNOLOGY

1. **Graphics calculator**
   Equations using the equilibrium constant can be analyzed using a quadratic equation and a graphics calculator. The amount of product formed can be predicted from the beginning amount of reactant. For example, predict how many H_3O^+ and CHO_2^- ions will be formed from 3.00 M formic acid.

   $$HCHO_2 + H_2O \rightleftharpoons H_3O^+ + CHO_2^-$$

   $$K_{eq} = 1.8 \times 10^{-4}$$

   First, write out the equilibrium equation with [$HCHO_2$] as $3.00 - x$ (the original concentration less the dissociated ions), [H_3O^+] as x, and [CHO_2^-] as x. Then, solve the equation for zero. You should get the quadratic equation $x^2 + (1.8 \times 10^{-4})x - 5.4 \times 10^{-4} = 0$. Press the Y= key and enter the quadratic equation. Then press GRAPH and use the TRACE key to find the value of the x-intercept. This will equal the concentration of H_3O^+ and the concentration of CHO_2^-. [$HCHO_2$] will be 3.00 minus the x-intercept.

   a. What concentrations of H_3O^+ and CHO_2^- will result from 3.00 M $HCHO_2$?
   b. What concentrations of H_3O^+ and CHO_2^- will result from 5.00 M $HCHO_2$?
   c. What concentrations of H_3O^+ and ClO_2^- will result from the dissociation of 3.00 M $HClO_2$? (Hint: K_{eq} for $HClO_2$ is 1.2×10^{-2}.)

2. **Data analysis**
   Data analysis equipment can measure the concentrations of specific ions in solution. The H_3O^+ concentration of a solution can be analyzed using a pH meter. First, calculate the theoretical [H_3O^+] for the reaction of each of the following acids with water using the K_{eq}. Analyze your data by organizing a table ranking the acids from highest [H_3O^+] to the lowest [H_3O^+].

Acid	K_{eq}
3.00 M HCN	$K_{eq} = 4.0 \times 10^{-10}$
3.00 M HF	$K_{eq} = 6.7 \times 10^{-4}$
3.00 M HOCl	$K_{eq} = 2.95 \times 10^{-8}$
3.00 M HC$_2$H$_2$ClO$_2$	$K_{eq} = 1.35 \times 10^{-3}$
3.00 M HNO$_2$	$K_{eq} = 5.13 \times 10^{-4}$

Alternative assessment

Performance Assessment

1. Your instructor will give you an index card with a specific equilibrium reaction on it. Describe how you would alter the reaction to produce either more of the products or more of the reactants. Show your method to your instructor. If your method is approved, obtain the necessary materials from your instructor, and perform the experiment.

2. Devise an experiment to test the conductance properties of certain substances that are soluble in water. Show your experimental procedure to your instructor for approval. When your procedure is approved, test the conductance properties of the following substances.
   a. glucose, $C_6H_{12}O_6$
   b. potassium permanganate, $KMnO_4$
   c. aspartame, $C_{14}H_{18}N_2O_5$
   d. calcium saccharin, $CaC_{14}H_8N_2O_6S_2$

3. Study the colligative properties of different substances. Develop a procedure to test the effect of both ionic and molecular substances in solution on boiling point and freezing point. Show your procedure to your instructor for approval. When your procedure is approved, obtain the following materials to test your experiment and complete the table below. CAUTION: *Ethanol and acetone are flammable. Do not use around an open flame.*

Solvent	Solute	Concentration	Property	Effect
Water	NaCl		freezing point	
Water	sucrose		freezing point	
Ethanol	NaCl		boiling point	
Ethanol	sucrose		boiling point	
Acetone	NaCl		boiling point	
Acetone	sucrose		boiling point	

Portfolio projects

1. ***Research and communication***
   Analyze your daily intake of foods. Identify the substances as ionic or molecular. Study the physiological effects of each substance, and indicate which are the most helpful to your body. Use this information to choose foods rich in the vitamins and solutes that you need. Make a poster of your findings.

2. ***Research and communication***
   Colligative properties are often used in the production of automobile supplies. The most familiar example is antifreeze. Research the development of antifreeze and the different substances used to obtain its properties. Study the weather in your area to determine the best type of antifreeze and the most appropriate concentration to use. Make a chart to present your results.

3. ***Cooperative activity***
   As a group, develop a unique method of demonstrating the difference between static and dynamic equilibrium. Show how Le Châtelier's principle will work for one and not the other. Perform your demonstration for the rest of your class. If possible, perform your demonstration for a different science class that has not yet been introduced to the concept of dynamic equilibrium.

4. ***Chemistry and you***
   Study the many uses of complex ions. Analyze products you use that contain complex ions. Write an essay that explains how your life might be different without complex ions.

5. ***Research and communication***
   Many different pollutants are in the form of ions dissolved in water. Industries must remove these ions from the water to avoid exposing the environment to harmful chemicals. Research the use of solubility principles and equilibrium to clean up the chemicals listed below. Write a report about the effect that these chemicals have on our environment.
   a. Pb^{2+}
   b. Hg_2^{2+} and Hg^{2+}
   c. Cl^-
   d. SO_4^{2-}
   e. PO_4^{3-}

13 | Acids and Bases

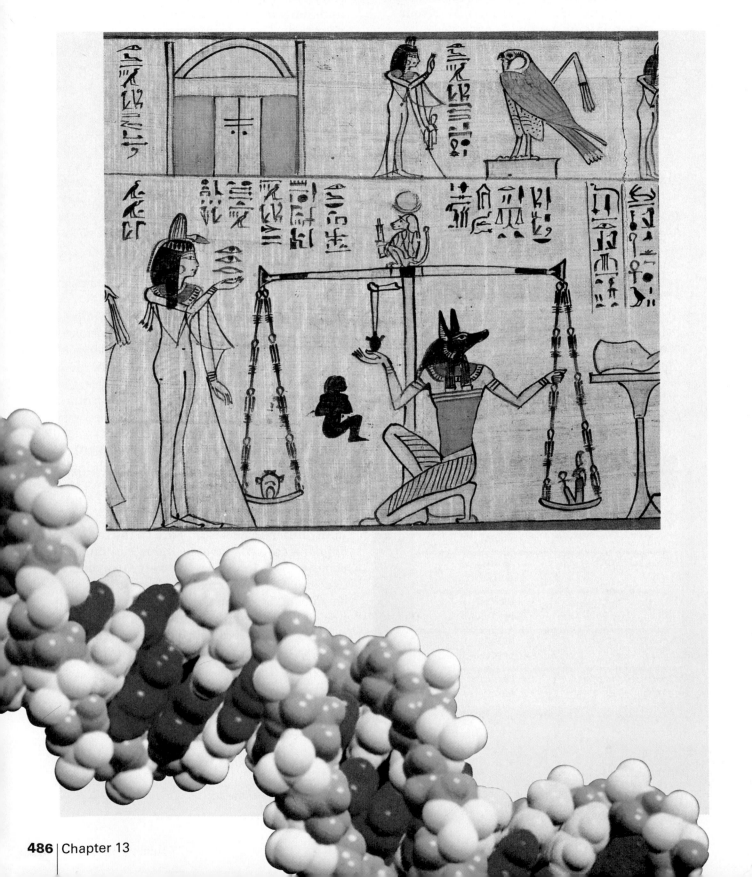

Ancient Acids

With a sterile scalpel, Svante Pääbo scraped tissue from an ancient mummy. This was the end of his long quest for permission to test an idea that first came to him when he was a student in Sweden in the early 1980s. Now he finally had access to 23 of the best-preserved mummies in the state museums in Berlin, Germany.

As a student, Pääbo had wondered whether the techniques that were being used to study the genetic material of living organisms could be applied to dead organisms. He also wanted to know if it was possible to extract DNA from dead tissue like the skins of human mummies preserved in museums throughout the world. But getting tissue samples from archaeological specimens isn't easy. Most museum curators refused to give Pääbo permission, knowing that he would have to destroy a part of the specimen in order to study its genetic material.

Deoxyribonucleic acid, DNA, has been called the master molecule of life. It is the primary component of your chromosomes, and it serves as the carrier of the hereditary information stored in your genes. For 50 years, scientists have been studying the DNA of living organisms, trying to understand how it controls the activities of the cell. Only recently have Svante Pääbo and other scientists begun to study DNA from dead and even extinct organisms. Such DNA is known as ancient DNA. Ancient DNA is recovered from ancient bones, organisms frozen in the Arctic tundra, or creatures trapped in amber.

An insect preserved in amber for 125 million years was the basis for a popular book and movie in which dinosaurs were brought back from extinction. But it's the ancient DNA of our human ancestors that most intrigues scientists like Pääbo. Scientists of this new breed are known as molecular archaeologists. The mummies of people who lived in Egypt more than 4400 years ago provided molecular archaeologists with their first look at ancient human DNA. A human brain that survived intact for nearly 7000 years in a Florida sinkhole was a source of even more ancient DNA.

By studying DNA from sources like these, scientists hope to shed new light on the pathways of human development at the molecular level. The work is painstaking and often frustrating. Precious samples of rare DNA can easily be contaminated by something as simple as a skin cell sloughed off a researcher's body. Also, because there is so little DNA to work with, it is not always possible to repeat experiments in order to establish confidence in the results. Nevertheless, molecular archaeologists are excited about successes they have had with ancient plant and animal DNA and are optimistic that their new field will add another dimension to the study of human origins.

In this chapter, you will explore some of the chemical characteristics of a group of compounds that includes DNA—acids. Recall that DNA's full name is deoxyribonucleic acid. From what you learn in this chapter, you will be able to answer the following questions.
- *What makes DNA an acid?*
- *Is DNA a strong or weak acid?*
- *Why have some ancient DNA fragments been preserved better than others?*

To answer this last question, you will need to take a look at the second group of compounds that are examined in this chapter—bases.

13-1

What are acids and bases?

Section Objectives

Describe the characteristic properties of aqueous acids and bases.

Distinguish between the Arrhenius and Brønsted definitions of acids and bases.

Describe how some compounds can function as both a Brønsted acid and a Brønsted base.

Explain the difference between a strong acid and a weak acid and between a strong base and a weak base.

Identify conjugate acid-base pairs.

Relate the reactions of anhydrides to acid rain.

Acids and bases

Have you ever had difficulty swallowing an aspirin tablet? If you have, then you know how unpleasant aspirin tastes. You learned in Chapter 1 that aspirin is acetylsalicylic acid. When this acid dissolves in saliva, it tastes sour. To mask the sour taste, manufacturers of children's aspirin add both natural and artificial sweeteners. The foods and beverages shown in **Figure 13-1** also contain acids and you know that some of these taste sour too. A sour taste is a characteristic property of all acids in aqueous solution.

Acids have distinctive properties

In addition to a sour taste, most acids share several other properties. For example, many aqueous acids react with carbonate in rocks to produce carbon dioxide gas as they dissolve the rock. Acids react with some metals to produce hydrogen gas, as you can see in **Figure 13-2**. Because the metal reacts with the acid to replace hydrogen, the acid must contain hydrogen. In fact, many acids contain hydrogen.

Figure 13-3 shows that aqueous acid solutions conduct electricity. You learned in Chapter 12 that conductivity depends on the presence of ions in solution. Both acids in **Figure 13-3** form ions in solution, but one acid forms more ions than the other. The degree to which an acid dissociates determines whether it is strong or weak.

Figure 13-1
Fruits contain citric acid, lactic acid, and ascorbic acid. Carbonated cola drinks contain benzoic acid and sorbic acid. Teas contain tannic acid.

Figure 13-2
Sulfuric acid reacts with zinc to produce hydrogen gas.

Figure 13-3
Strong acids, like hydrochloric acid on the left, dissociate completely and are therefore better conductors, as shown by the brightly lit bulb on the left. Weak acids, like acetic acid on the right, partially dissociate, so the bulb on the right is dimly lit.

Table 13-1
Some Strong and Weak Acids

Strong acids	Weak acids
chloric acid, $HClO_3$	acetic acid, CH_3COOH
hydrobromic acid, HBr	boric acid, H_3BO_3
hydrochloric acid, HCl	hydrocyanic acid, HCN
hydroiodic acid, HI	hydrofluoric acid, HF
nitric acid, HNO_3	hydrosulfuric acid, H_2S
perchloric acid, $HClO_4$	hypochlorous acid, HClO
periodic acid, HIO_4	nitrous acid, HNO_2
permanganic acid, $HMnO_4$	oxalic acid, $H_2C_2O_4$
sulfuric acid, H_2SO_4	phosphoric acid, H_3PO_4
tetrafluoroboric acid, HBF_4	sulfurous acid, H_2SO_3

Any acid that dissociates completely in aqueous solution is considered a *strong acid*. Hydrochloric acid is a common strong acid. Because HCl is less dangerous than other strong acids, it is used for tough cleaning jobs. *Weak acids* are dissociated only partially in aqueous solutions. Because relatively few ions form, weak acids exhibit poor conductivity. **Table 13-1** lists the names of some strong and weak acids.

Bases have distinctive properties

Recall from Chapter 1 that you learned about some of the characteristics of bases. They taste bitter and feel slippery. They cause litmus to change from red to blue and they show pH values between 7 and 14. Bases also react with acids to form salts. Household ammonia, used for cleaning, is a base. If you have ever used household ammonia, you know it feels slippery. **Figure 13-4** shows some common household products that consist of aqueous solutions of bases.

Figure 13-4
Some household cleaning products contain bases and are able to dissolve grease and oil.

Another important property of acids and bases is their ability to neutralize each other. This means that each loses its characteristic properties (such as sour taste or slippery feeling) as a result of neutralization. You will learn more about neutralization later in this chapter.

Table 13-2
Some Strong and Weak Bases

Strong bases	Weak bases
barium hydroxide, $Ba(OH)_2$	ammonia, NH_3
calcium hydroxide, $Ca(OH)_2$	aniline, $C_6H_5NH_2$
potassium hydroxide, KOH	potassium carbonate, K_2CO_3
sodium hydroxide, NaOH	sodium carbonate, Na_2CO_3
trisodium phosphate, Na_3PO_4	trimethylamine, $(CH_3)_3N$

The degree to which a base forms ions in aqueous solutions determines whether it is a strong or weak base. Any base that dissociates completely is a *strong base*. On the other hand, a *weak base* dissociates only partially in aqueous solution. Because relatively few ions are present, a weak base is not a good conductor of electricity. **Table 13-2** lists the names of some strong and weak bases.

Figure 13-5
Svante August Arrhenius, 1859–1927, received the Nobel Prize in 1903 for his work on the theory of electrolytic dissociation.

hydroxide ion
the OH⁻ anion

Arrhenius definitions of acids and bases
Acids in water produce H⁺; bases in water produce OH⁻

In the 1880s, the Swedish chemist Svante Arrhenius, shown in **Figure 13-5**, introduced the theory of ionization, which you learned in Chapter 12. This theory states that in aqueous solutions both molecular and ionic compounds can break apart to form ions. Arrhenius found that his theory of ionization explained the behavior of acids and bases.

Arrhenius reasoned that the characteristic properties of acids are the properties of hydrogen ions in solution. Thus, an Arrhenius acid is defined as any compound that contains hydrogen and dissociates in aqueous solution to form H^+ ions. Nitric acid dissociates completely, as shown by the following equation.

$$HNO_3(aq) \longrightarrow H^+(aq) + NO_3^-(aq)$$

Arrhenius also reasoned that the characteristic properties of bases are the properties of OH^- ions in solution. An Arrhenius base is any compound that contains OH^- ions and dissociates to produce OH^- ions in aqueous solution. For example, as potassium hydroxide dissolves in water, it dissociates as shown by the following equation.

$$KOH(s) \xrightarrow{\ H_2O\ } K^+(aq) + OH^-(aq)$$

The OH^- ion is known as the **hydroxide ion**. You should not confuse the hydroxide ion, OH^-, with the hydroxyl group, —OH. You learned in Chapter 6 that the hydroxyl group is a functional group that forms a covalent bond to carbon in the organic compounds known as alcohols.

If you look in **Table 13-2**, you see several compounds that do not include the hydroxide ion in the formula. Ammonia is probably the most common weak base. Though its formula does not include the hydroxide ion, ammonia reacts with water to form hydroxide ions, as shown by the following equation.

$$NH_3(aq) + H_2O(l) \longrightarrow NH_4^+(aq) + OH^-(aq)$$

Bottles of ammonia water are frequently labeled as ammonium hydroxide.

The class of organic bases known as *amines* are related to ammonia in structure. Trimethylamine, $(CH_3)_3N$, reacts similarly to ammonia when added to water, as shown by the following equation.

$$H_3C-\underset{\underset{\displaystyle CH_3}{|}}{N}-CH_3 + H_2O \longrightarrow \left[H_3C-\underset{\underset{\displaystyle CH_3}{|}}{\overset{\overset{\displaystyle H}{|}}{N}}-CH_3 \right]^+ + OH^-$$

In the Arrhenius theory, neutralization is the reaction of $H^+(aq)$ and $OH^-(aq)$ to form water, as shown by the following equation.

$$H^+(aq) + OH^-(aq) \longrightarrow H_2O(l)$$

Acid and base anhydrides
Some oxides react with water to produce acids

You've heard the saying "What goes up must come down." This expression certainly applies to gases emitted on Earth that rise into the atmosphere. Recall from Chapter 10 that gases are produced by the burning of fossil fuels. Some 80% of all the energy used in the United States is obtained by burning fossil fuels. Coal and oil burned by power plants and gasoline burned by cars release sulfur oxides. These sulfur oxide compounds react with moisture in the atmosphere to produce acids.

$$SO_2(g) + H_2O(l) \longrightarrow H_2SO_3(aq)$$
Sulfurous acid

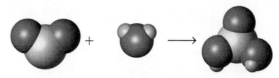

$$SO_3(g) + H_2O(l) \longrightarrow H_2SO_4(aq)$$
Sulfuric acid

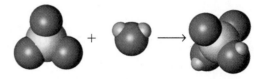

acid anhydride
an oxide that forms an acid when reacted with water

Substances such as SO_2 and SO_3 belong to a class of compounds called acid anhydrides. An **acid anhydride** is an oxide that reacts with water to form an acid. When fossil fuels are burned, the combustion reactions produce some acid anhydrides and other oxides that are released into the atmosphere, where they form acids that fall back to Earth in the form of acid precipitation. Acid anhydrides are usually oxides of nonmetals in the upper right portion of the periodic table.

An oxide of nitrogen also plays a part in increasing the acidity of rainfall. Nitrogen dioxide is also released into the atmosphere as a product of the burning of fossil fuels. It reacts with water in the atmosphere to produce nitric acid, as shown by the following equation.

$$3NO_2(g) + H_2O(l) \longrightarrow NO(g) + 2HNO_3(aq)$$
Nitric acid

Even though the equation shows an oxide forming an acid, NO_2 is not an acid anhydride. You'll notice that when the sulfur oxides react with water, they form acids exclusively. In the reaction of nitrogen dioxide and water, we get an acid along with nitrogen oxide. The oxides of nitrogen that are acid anhydrides are N_2O_5 and N_2O_3. They react with water as shown by the following equations.

$$N_2O_5(s) + H_2O(l) \longrightarrow 2HNO_3(aq)$$
$$N_2O_3(g) + H_2O(l) \longrightarrow 2HNO_2(aq)$$

Pollutants cause acid rain

Normally, the pH of rainwater is about 5.5. However, the acids formed in the atmosphere can lower this pH to 3. The most acidic rainfall in the United States occurred in Wheeling, West Virginia, where the pH was measured at 1.5. Acid rain is such a large-scale environmental problem because it is difficult to control. The areas producing the pollutants that cause acid rain usually don't experience its effects. Pollutants that are released from factories in highly industrialized areas may travel hundreds of miles, carried by the wind, before they fall back to Earth. In the United States, the heavy burning of fossil fuels in the industrialized Midwest produced very acidic rainfall in the Northeast and Canada. **Figure 13-6** illustrates how acids formed in industrial areas can have an effect many miles away.

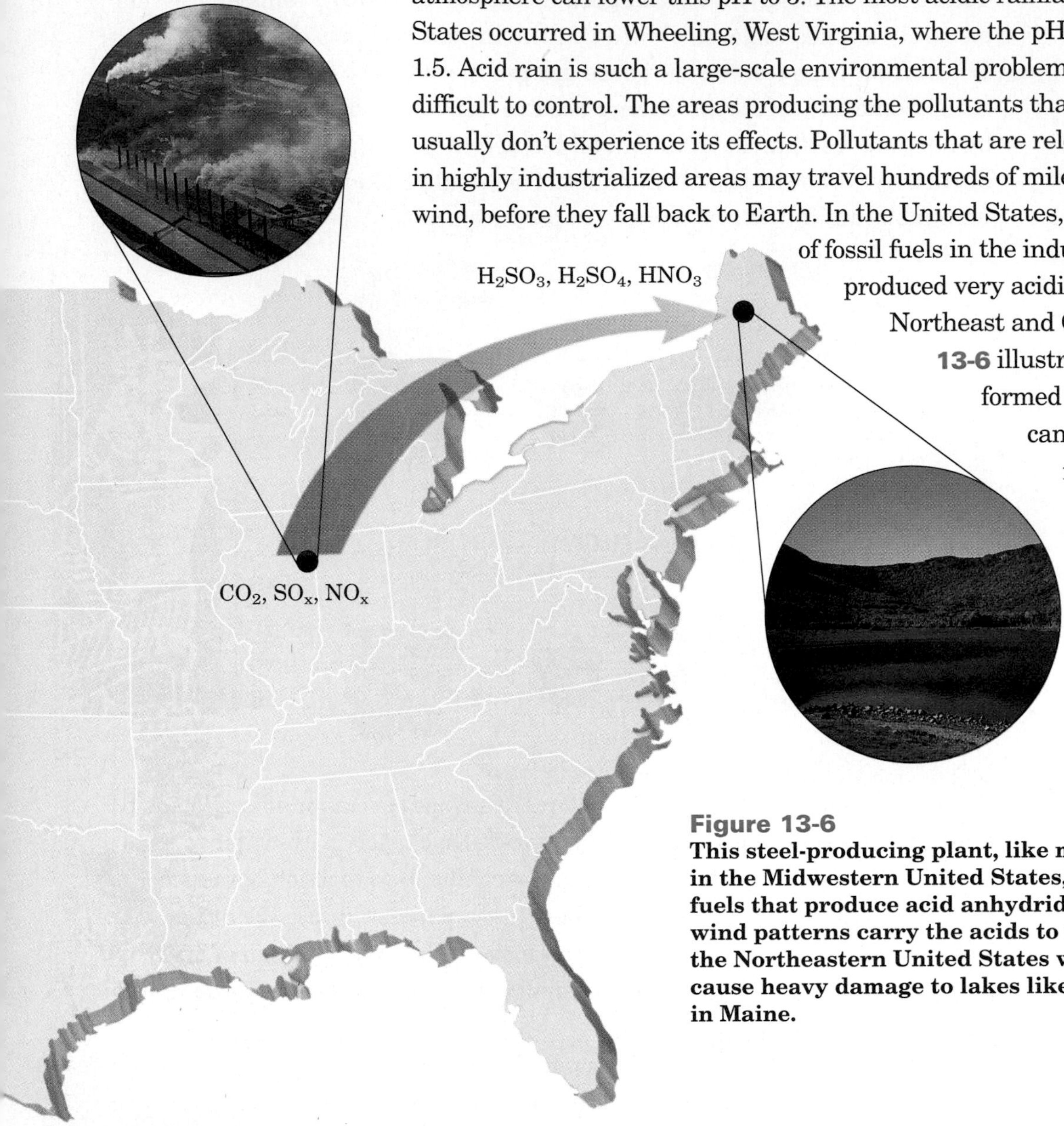

H_2SO_3, H_2SO_4, HNO_3

CO_2, SO_x, NO_x

Figure 13-6
This steel-producing plant, like many others in the Midwestern United States, burns fossil fuels that produce acid anhydrides. Prevailing wind patterns carry the acids to Canada and the Northeastern United States where they cause heavy damage to lakes like this one in Maine.

Figure 13-7
The calcium carbonate in seashells is decomposed by the action of an acid.

Modeling the damaging effects of acid precipitation

What happens when a piece of chalk or a seashell is placed in an acid? Chalk and seashells are made of calcium carbonate. Recall that one property of acids is their reaction with carbonates. You can see in **Figure 13-7** how calcium carbonate reacts with the hydronium ion in aqueous acids. The equation for this reaction is shown as follows.

$$CaCO_3(s) + 2H_3O^+(aq) \longrightarrow Ca^{2+}(aq) + CO_2(g) + 3H_2O(l)$$

Calcium carbonate in marble buildings and statues reacts slowly with acidic rainwater. Notice in **Figure 13-8a** on the next page how acids affect marble. The impact of acid precipitation is widespread. In addition to damaging marble, it is causing fish to die in major lakes and rivers. Acid rain also causes food crops to grow more slowly and forests to be thinned out, as shown in **Figure 13-8c**.

Figure 13-8a
Marble structures such as this statue in Brooklyn, New York, are slowly decomposing from acid precipitation.

13-8b
Acid rain has reduced the pH of this lake in the Adirondack Mountains of New York to the point where the lake can no longer support life.

13-8c
This area in Vermont is beginning to show the effects of acid rain. Notice the reddish areas on many of the evergreens.

Recent measurements show a decline in acid precipitation

In 1990 the Acid Rain Control Program was passed as an amendment to the Clean Air Act of 1970. By the year 2000, the program calls for SO_2 emissions by industry and power plants to be reduced to about 15 million tons a year, less than half the amount emitted in 1980. Improvements in the air quality have already been observed.

Solving the problem with base anhydrides

base anhydride
an oxide that forms a base when reacted with water

To counteract the effect of acid precipitation on aquatic life, calcium oxide, commonly known as lime, is sometimes added to ponds and lakes. Calcium oxide, CaO, belongs to a class of compounds called base anhydrides. A **base anhydride** is an oxide that reacts with water to form a base. When calcium oxide is added to water, the base calcium hydroxide, $Ca(OH)_2$, is produced.

$$CaO(s) + H_2O(l) \longrightarrow Ca(OH)_2(s)$$

Calcium hydroxide is also called "slaked" lime. It is a strong base, but it is only slightly soluble in water. In aqueous solution, the slightly soluble $Ca(OH)_2$ dissociates to form Ca^{2+} and OH^- ions.

$$Ca(OH)_2(s) \longrightarrow Ca^{2+}(aq) + 2OH^-(aq)$$

Because this solution contains OH^- ions, it can neutralize acidic solutions.

How can you predict whether an oxide is a basic anhydride or an acidic anhydride? In general, oxides of metals in groups 1 and 2 produce bases when they react with water. For example, magnesium oxide, MgO, produces magnesium hydroxide, $Mg(OH)_2$, in aqueous solution. Oxides of nonmetals often produce acids in water solution. Carbon dioxide reacts with water to form carbonic acid, H_2CO_3.

Types of acids
Monoprotic and polyprotic acids differ in relative number of ionizable hydrogen ions

Figure 13-9a
Hydrochloric acid is classified as a monoprotic, binary acid.

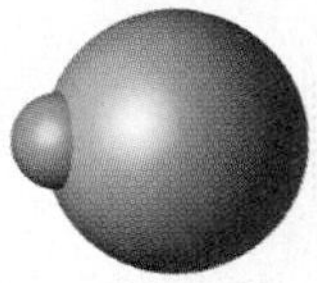

Compare the moles of acid with the moles of base for the reactions of HCl, $H_2C_2O_4$, and H_3PO_4 shown below.

$$HCl(aq) + KOH(aq) \longrightarrow KCl(aq) + H_2O(l)$$

$$H_2C_2O_4(aq) + 2KOH(aq) \longrightarrow K_2C_2O_4(aq) + 2H_2O(l)$$

$$H_3PO_4(aq) + 3KOH(aq) \longrightarrow K_3PO_4(aq) + 3H_2O(l)$$

H_3PO_4 is a weak acid and HCl is a strong acid (shown in **Figure 13-9**). However, one mole of H_3PO_4 will react with three times more base than one mole of HCl does. See the mole ratios in the above equations. H_3PO_4 has three hydrogen ions per molecule to react with the OH^- ions of a base. Acids that can supply more than one hydrogen ion per molecule are called *polyprotic* acids. Acids that can supply only one hydrogen ion per molecule, like hydrochloric acid, are *monoprotic* acids. Notice that it is common to write acidic hydrogens first in the formula for inorganic acids. Can you explain why H_2SO_4 and $H_2C_2O_4$ are *diprotic* acids? Why is acetic acid, $HC_2H_3O_2$, a monoprotic acid?

Figure 13-9b
Phosphoric acid is classified as a polyprotic, ternary acid.

Binary and ternary acids differ in the number of elements per molecule

Acids can also be categorized by numbers of constituent elements. For example, HCl is a binary acid. A *binary* acid is an acid composed of only two elements, one of which is hydrogen. Some other binary acids are HBr, HI, HF, H_2S, H_2Se, and H_2Te. Acids that contain hydrogen and two other elements, like H_2SO_4 and H_3PO_4, are known as *ternary* acids.

Figure 13-9c
The carboxyl group of acetic acid is highlighted in red. Acetic acid is a monoprotic, ternary, carboxylic acid.

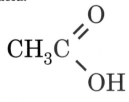

Carboxylic acids all contain the carboxyl group

In Chapter 1 you encountered a number of acids that were organic compounds. Organic acids contain the carboxyl group and for that reason organic acids are often called carboxylic acids. Acetic acid is the most familiar carboxylic acid. It is shown in **Figure 13-9c**.

Concept Review

Anhydrides and types of acids

1. Write equations for the formation of NaOH and $HClO_4$ from their anhydrides, Na_2O and Cl_2O_7.
2. Which of the acids listed in **Table 13-1** are monoprotic, ternary acids?
3. Use the periodic table to predict whether the following anhydrides will form acids or bases in water: Cs_2O, TeO_3, I_2O_5, and SrO.

Answers for Concept Review items and Practice problems begin on page 841.

Brønsted acids and bases
Acids donate H⁺ ions; bases accept H⁺ ions

Chemists came to realize that H^+ ions are protons, and protons cannot exist in aqueous solution. Also, the fact that an ammonia solution is a base is explained by describing ammonia as ammonium hydroxide. However, anhydrous ammonia can neutralize HCl.

$$NH_3(g) + HCl(g) \longrightarrow NH_4Cl(s)$$

Therefore, NH_3 must be a base. These observations led to a change in the definition of acids and bases. In the 1920s, the Danish chemist Johannes Brønsted and the English chemist Thomas Lowry independently suggested a new definition. A *Brønsted acid* is a hydrogen ion donor, and a *Brønsted base* is a hydrogen ion acceptor.

To understand the definition of a Brønsted acid, consider the reaction of acetic acid with water.

$$\underset{\text{Acetic acid}}{CH_3COOH(aq)} + \underset{\text{Water}}{H_2O(l)} \rightleftharpoons \underset{\text{Acetate ion}}{CH_3COO^-(aq)} + \underset{\text{Hydronium ion}}{H_3O^+(aq)}$$

Acetic acid, CH_3COOH, is an organic acid. The equation shows that a hydrogen ion, H^+, is transferred from the –COOH group on acetic acid to water. You can visualize this transfer more clearly with the help of electron-dot diagrams.

Brønsted acid   Brønsted base

Because CH_3COOH donates a hydrogen ion, it acts as a Brønsted acid. Notice that H_2O accepts a hydrogen ion and is therefore the Brønsted base in this reaction.

Another example of a Brønsted base can be seen in this equation for the reaction between ammonia and water.

$$NH_3(aq) + H_2O(l) \rightleftharpoons NH_4^+(aq) + OH^-(aq)$$

In this reaction a hydrogen ion, H^+, is transferred from H_2O to NH_3. Again, you can picture this transfer with the help of electron-dot diagrams.

Brønsted base   Brønsted acid

Because NH_3 accepts the hydrogen ion, it functions as a Brønsted base. Notice that in this reaction H_2O donates a hydrogen ion and acts as a Brønsted acid.

Amphiprotic compounds
Some compounds can behave both as Brønsted acids and Brønsted bases

amphiprotic
having the property of behaving as an acid and base

If you define acids and bases according to the Arrhenius definitions, you can be sure that an acid will always behave as an acid and a base will always behave as a base. This is true because, in Arrhenius's definition, acids contain ionizable hydrogen, and bases produce OH^- in solution. The Brønsted definitions expand the class of substances that are called bases. The OH^- ion is only one of many bases according to the new definition. This leads to some interesting consequences. Take another look at the two electron-dot representations on page 495. In the first reaction H_2O is a Brønsted base, while in the second reaction H_2O is a Brønsted acid. Any substance that can act as either an acid or a base according to the Brønsted definition is described as **amphiprotic**.

Concept Review

Identifying Brønsted acids and bases

4. In the following equations, identify which reactant is the Brønsted acid and which reactant is the Brønsted base.
   a. $CH_3NH_2(aq) + H_2O(l) \rightleftharpoons CH_3NH_3^+(aq) + OH^-(aq)$
   b. $HSO_4^-(aq) + H_2O(l) \rightleftharpoons H_3O^+(aq) + SO_4^{2-}(aq)$
5. In the following reactions, identify whether H_2O behaves as a Brønsted acid or a Brønsted base.
   a. $HClO_4(aq) + H_2O(l) \longrightarrow H_3O^+(aq) + ClO_4^-(aq)$
   b. $H_2O(l) + SO_3^{2-}(aq) \rightleftharpoons HSO_3^-(aq) + OH^-(aq)$

Conjugate acid-base pairs
Reaction of a Brønsted acid and base produces the conjugate base and acid

In Chapter 12 you learned about the equilibrium system between H_2CO_3 and H_2O in the plasma of your blood.

$$H_2CO_3(aq) + H_2O(l) \rightleftharpoons H_3O^+(aq) + HCO_3^-(aq)$$

Compare that equilibrium system with the reactions of the carbonate ion and the hydrogen carbonate ion with an acid.

$$CO_3^{2-}(aq) + H_3O^+(aq) \rightleftharpoons HCO_3^-(aq) + H_2O(l)$$

$$HCO_3^-(aq) + H_3O^+(aq) \rightleftharpoons H_2CO_3(aq) + H_2O(l)$$

Notice that the second reaction is the reverse of the equilibrium system in your blood. In that system, H_2CO_3 donates a hydrogen ion, so it is a Brønsted acid. Water accepts the hydrogen ion, so it is a Brønsted base. But take another look at the equations. The product formed after H_2CO_3 donates a hydrogen ion is the hydrogen carbonate ion, HCO_3^-.

Notice that in the second reaction the hydrogen carbonate ion acts as a Brønsted base, accepting a hydrogen ion from H_3O^+. The hydrogen carbonate ion, HCO_3^-, is called the conjugate base of the acid H_2CO_3, and

H_2CO_3 is called the conjugate acid of the base, HCO_3^-. A **conjugate base** is the ion or molecule that is formed when a Brønsted acid has given up a hydrogen ion. A **conjugate acid** is the ion or molecule that is formed when a Brønsted base accepts a hydrogen ion.

Now identify the product formed when H_2O, acting as a base, accepts a hydrogen ion from H_2CO_3. The H_3O^+ ion that is formed is the conjugate acid of the base H_2O. The hydronium ion, H_3O^+, now has a hydrogen ion to donate and is a Brønsted acid in the reverse reaction. The relationship between an acid and its conjugate base and between a base and its conjugate acid can be seen by labeling each reactant and product as shown in the following examples.

conjugate base
the particle formed when an acid has donated a H^+ ion

conjugate acid
the particle formed when a base has accepted a H^+ ion

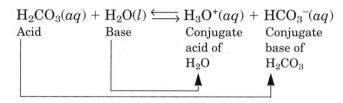

$$H_2CO_3(aq) + H_2O(l) \rightleftharpoons H_3O^+(aq) + HCO_3^-(aq)$$
Acid — Base — Conjugate acid of H_2O — Conjugate base of H_2CO_3

$$NH_3(aq) + H_2O(l) \longrightarrow NH_4^+(aq) + OH^-(aq)$$
Base — Acid — Conjugate acid of NH_3 — Conjugate base of H_2O

Section Review

6. Explain how the Arrhenius definitions of acids and bases differ from the Brønsted definitions.

7. What is an amphiprotic substance?

8. CH_3COOH is a monoprotic acid, yet the formula shows four hydrogen atoms. Why is acetic acid classified as a monoprotic acid?

9. In the following reactions, label the conjugate acid-base pairs.
   a. $H_3PO_4(aq) + NO_2^-(aq) \rightleftharpoons HNO_2(aq) + H_2PO_4^-(aq)$
   b. $CN^-(aq) + HCO_3^-(aq) \rightleftharpoons HCN(aq) + CO_3^{2-}(aq)$
   c. $HCN(aq) + SO_3^{2-}(aq) \rightleftharpoons HSO_3^-(aq) + CN^-(aq)$
   d. $H_2O(l) + HF(aq) \rightleftharpoons F^-(aq) + H_3O^+(aq)$

10. Predict whether an aqueous solution of Na_2O is acidic or basic.

11. **Story Link**

    DNA contains four different organic bases. The structural formulas for two of them are shown below. Identify the sites in each compound where hydrogen ions could be accepted.

How are weak acids and bases compared?

Dissociation constants

The equilibrium constant for the reaction of an aqueous weak acid with water is known as the **acid-dissociation constant**, or K_a. Consider the equilibrium established by acetic acid in vinegar. The equation for the equilibrium system is written below.

acid-dissociation constant
a quantity derived from the ratio of the concentrations of the products and reactants at equilibrium for a weak acid equilibrium system

$$CH_3COOH(aq) + H_2O(l) \rightleftharpoons CH_3COO^-(aq) + H_3O^+(aq)$$

The equilibrium expression for this reaction is written as follows.

$$K_a = \frac{[CH_3COO^-][H_3O^+]}{[CH_3COOH]}$$

The concentration of H_2O does not appear in the equilibrium expression. The essentially constant concentration of water has already been incorporated into the numerical value of K_a.

K_a and K_b values can be used to compare acid and base strength

At 25°C, the acid-dissociation constant, K_a, for acetic acid has been experimentally determined to be 1.76×10^{-5}. The K_a value for acetic acid can be compared with K_a values for other weak acids as a measure of their relative strengths. **Table 13-3** lists some acid-dissociation constants.

Table 13-3
Selected Acid-Dissociation Constants

Acid name	Acid formula	Reaction temperature (°C)	K_a
acetic	CH_3COOH	25	1.75×10^{-5}
arsenic	H_3AsO_4	18	5.62×10^{-3}
boric	H_3BO_3	20	7.3×10^{-10}
citric	$H_3C_6H_5O_7$	20	7.10×10^{-4}
formic	$HCOOH$	20	1.77×10^{-4}
hydrogen peroxide	H_2O_2	25	2.4×10^{-12}
nitrous	HNO_2	12.5	4.6×10^{-4}
selenous	H_2SeO_3	25	3.5×10^{-2}
sulfurous	H_2SO_3	18	1.54×10^{-2}

Table 13-4
Selected Base Dissociation Constants

Base name	Base formula	Reaction temperature (°C)	K_b
ammonia	NH_3	25	1.77×10^{-5}
aniline	$C_6H_5NH_2$	25	4.27×10^{-10}
asparagine	$C_4H_4O_3(NH_2)_2$	20	1.63×10^{-12}
dimethylamine	$(CH_3)_2NH$	25	5.4×10^{-4}
pyridine	C_5H_5N	25	1.77×10^{-9}
silver hydroxide	$AgOH$	25	1.0×10^{-2}
trimethylamine	$(CH_3)_3N$	25	6.45×10^{-5}

Similarly, equilibrium constants can be determined for weak bases in aqueous solution. These are called **base-dissociation constants**, or K_b. Some are shown in **Table 13-4**.

Look at the equation for the equilibrium system in a bottle of aqueous ammonia used for cleaning. The base-dissociation constant expression would be written as follows.

$$NH_3(aq) + H_2O(l) \rightleftharpoons NH_4^+(aq) + OH^-(aq)$$

$$K_b = \frac{[NH_4^+][OH^-]}{[NH_3]}$$

base-dissociation constant
a quantity derived from the ratio of the concentrations of the products and reactants at equilibrium for a weak base equilibrium system

The equation for the base-dissociation constant for an organic base follows the same pattern. The dissociation equation of trimethylamine and the equation for its K_b are written as follows.

$$(CH_3)_3N(aq) + H_2O(l) \rightleftharpoons (CH_3)_3NH^+(aq) + OH^-(aq)$$

$$K_b = \frac{[(CH_3)_3NH^+][OH^-]}{[(CH_3)_3N]}$$

pH and [H₃O⁺]
The concentration of H₃O⁺ in solution can be measured

The pH is a number that is derived from the concentration of hydronium ions in solution. Defined in mathematical terms, **pH** is the negative logarithm (to the base 10) of the H_3O^+ concentration.

pH
the negative logarithm of the hydronium ion concentration of an aqueous solution; used to express acidity

$$pH = -log[H_3O^+]$$

For example, if the H_3O^+ concentration in a solution equals 1.0×10^{-12} M, then the pH of the solution is calculated as follows.

$$pH = -log[1.0 \times 10^{-12}]$$

Using a calculator to determine the log of 1.0×10^{-12}, you get −12. Therefore the pH is as follows.

$$pH = -log[1.0 \times 10^{-12}] = -(-12) = 12$$

The neutral point on the pH scale, pH 7, is neither acid or base. However, any solution with a pH of 7 has equal concentrations of H_3O^+ ion and OH^- ion. Let's look at pure water, which has a pH of 7, to see how this is possible.

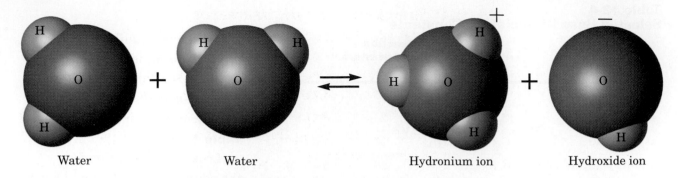

Water   Water   Hydronium ion   Hydroxide ion

Figure 13-10
The reaction of two molecules produces a hydronium ion and a hydroxide ion. Even pure water at pH 7 contains a small concentration of each of these ions.

Water itself can dissociate

In Chapter 11, you learned that water acts as a solvent in dissolving various solutes. In Chapter 12, you learned that water can bring about the dissociation of both ionic and molecular compounds in solution but pure water does not conduct electricity. Yet there are some ions in pure water. The ions are present in such small quantities, however, that they cannot be detected by a simple conductivity apparatus. You learned that water is an amphiprotic compound. It can act as an acid or base, both of which are quite weak. Water has a very slight tendency to react with itself, which can be described as a Brønsted acid-base reaction. One of the reacting water molecules is a weak acid, the other is a weak base. In **Figure 13-10** you can see how two water molecules interact to produce ions. A hydrogen ion is transferred from one water molecule to another water molecule, forming a hydronium ion and a hydroxide ion. These ions can conduct an electric current, but because they are present in such small quantities, a sensitive measuring instrument known as a microammeter is needed to detect their presence.

Measurements taken with sensitive instruments show that pure water contains 1.0×10^{-7} mol of H_3O^+ ions per liter of solution. This concentration is consistent with a pH measurement for pure water of 7, because when pH is calculated from the H_3O^+ ion concentration you get the following.

$$pH = -log[1.0 \times 10^{-7}] = -(-7.0) = 7.0$$

The calculation shows that the pH of pure water matches the actual measurement of the pH.

If you look again at **Figure 13-10**, you can see that for every H_3O^+ ion formed when water dissociates, one OH^- ion is also formed. Thus pure water contains 1.0×10^{-7} mol of OH^- ions per liter along with 1.0×10^{-7} mol of H_3O^+ ions per liter. The H_3O^+ ion is a Brønsted acid and OH^- ion is a Brønsted base. Pure water contains equal concentrations of the acid and base and, therefore, water is said to be neutral. So if the pH of any solution at 25°C equals 7, then the solution is neutral, and that solution has a H_3O^+ ion concentration that is equal to 1.0×10^{-7} M. That same solution also has a OH^- ion concentration equal to 1.0×10^{-7} M.

As [H₃O⁺] increases, the pH decreases

When an acid is added to pure water, the concentration of H_3O^+ ions will increase to a value greater than 1.0×10^{-7} M. If an acid added to pure water causes $[H_3O^+]$ to increase to 1.0×10^{-5} M, then the pH will equal 5. Notice that the H_3O^+ ion concentration increased by a factor of 100, from 1.0×10^{-7} M to 1.0×10^{-5} M and the pH decreased by two units, from 7 to 5. Each one-unit change in the pH represents a ten-fold change in the H_3O^+ ion concentration.

As [H₃O⁺] decreases, the pH increases

The addition of a base to pure water causes the concentration of H_3O^+ ions to drop below 1.0×10^{-7} M, and the pH rises. For example, if the addition of NaOH causes $[H_3O^+]$ to decrease from 1.0×10^{-7} to 1.0×10^{-9}, the pH increases from 7 to 9.

Each pH value represents a relationship between [H₃O⁺] and [OH⁻]

The pH of a solution does not tell you whether the solution contains a strong or a weak acid. It tells you the concentration of hydronium ions from which you can calculate the concentration of OH⁻ ions in the solution as well. You can determine the pH of an aqueous solution in several ways. Examine **Figure 13-11** and compare the pH values that were obtained by testing various solutions with a pH meter. Each pH value represents a specific hydronium ion concentration. Even the most acidic solutions contain some hydroxide ions too. You can see in **Figure 13-11** how an increasing hydronium ion concentration results in a decreasing hydroxide ion concentration. At every pH the following relationship holds.

$$[H_3O^+][OH^-] = 10^{-14}$$

Figure 13-11
A pH meter measures pH to a greater degree of precision than pH paper. The pH value of various common substances are shown along with their pH paper indicator color. The relationship between [H₃O⁺] and [OH⁻] is shown for each pH value. Notice as [H₃O⁺] increases, [OH⁻] decreases and vice versa.

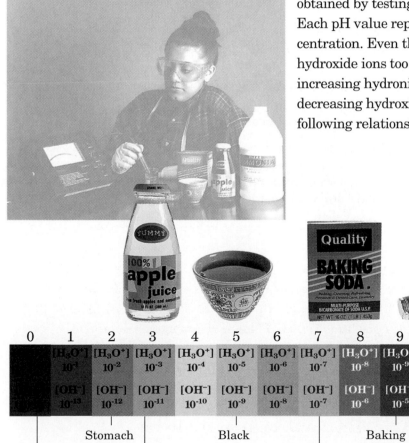

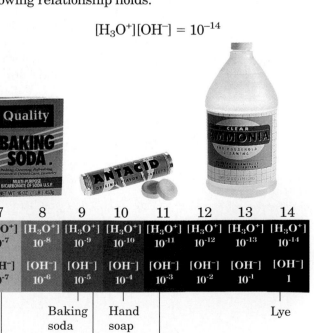

0	1	2	3	4	5	6	7	8	9	10	11	12	13	14
[H₃O⁺] 10⁻⁰	[H₃O⁺] 10⁻¹	[H₃O⁺] 10⁻²	[H₃O⁺] 10⁻³	[H₃O⁺] 10⁻⁴	[H₃O⁺] 10⁻⁵	[H₃O⁺] 10⁻⁶	[H₃O⁺] 10⁻⁷	[H₃O⁺] 10⁻⁸	[H₃O⁺] 10⁻⁹	[H₃O⁺] 10⁻¹⁰	[H₃O⁺] 10⁻¹¹	[H₃O⁺] 10⁻¹²	[H₃O⁺] 10⁻¹³	[H₃O⁺] 10⁻¹⁴
[OH⁻]	[OH⁻] 10⁻¹³	[OH⁻] 10⁻¹²	[OH⁻] 10⁻¹¹	[OH⁻] 10⁻¹⁰	[OH⁻] 10⁻⁹	[OH⁻] 10⁻⁸	[OH⁻] 10⁻⁷	[OH⁻] 10⁻⁶	[OH⁻] 10⁻⁵	[OH⁻] 10⁻⁴	[OH⁻] 10⁻³	[OH⁻] 10⁻²	[OH⁻] 10⁻¹	[OH⁻] 1

Stomach acid   Black tea   Baking soda   Hand soap   Lye

Battery acid   Apple juice   Pure water   Antacid   Household ammonia

Sample Problem 13A
Calculating pH

Refer to the instruction booklet for your calculator to find out how to determine the log of an exponential number.

What is the pH of a 0.0001 M solution of HCl, a strong acid?

❶ List
- HCl is completely dissociated.
- $[H_3O^+]$ of a 0.0001 M HCl solution = 0.0001 M or 1.0×10^{-4} M
- pH = **?**

❷ Set up
- Write the equation for pH.
  pH = $-log[1 \times 10^{-4}]$
- Use your calculator to determine the log of 1.0×10^{-4}.
  The log of 10^{-4} is -4.

❸ Calculate
  pH = $-(-4) = 4.0$

Sample Problem 13B
Calculating pH

What is the pH of a solution if $[H_3O^+] = 3.4 \times 10^{-5}$ M?

❶ List
- $[H_3O^+] = 3.4 \times 10^{-5}$ M
- pH = **?**

❷ Set up
- Write the equation for pH.
  pH = $-log[3.4 \times 10^{-5}]$

❸ Calculate and verify
- Use your calculator to determine the log of 3.4×10^{-5}.
  pH = $-log[3.4 \times 10^{-5}] = -(-4.4685)$, which is rounded to $-(-4.5) = 4.5$

  The pH of a 1.0×10^{-5} M acid solution is 5. Thus the pH of a solution containing a greater concentration of H_3O^+ ions would be more acidic and have a pH less than 5. Therefore, a pH of 4.5 is reasonable.

Sample Problem 13C
Calculating $[H_3O^+]$

Refer to the instruction booklet for your calculator to find out how to determine the antilog of a number.

The pH of a solution is measured with a pH meter and determined to be 9.00. What is the H_3O^+ ion concentration?

❶ List
- pH = 9.00
- $[H_3O^+]$ = **?**

❷ Set up

  $9.00 = -log[H_3O^+]$
  $-9.00 = log[H_3O^+]$
  $antilog(-9.00) = [H_3O^+]$

❸ Calculate
- Use your calculator to determine the antilog of -9.00.
  $[H_3O^+] = 1.00 \times 10^{-9}$ M

Sample Problem 13D
Calculating [H₃O⁺]

Refer to the instruction booklet for your calculator to determine the antilog of a number.

The pH of a solution is measured with a pH meter and determined to be 7.52. What is the H_3O^+ ion concentration?

❶ List
- $pH = 7.52$
- $[H_3O^+] =$ **?**

❷ Set up

$7.52 = -log\,[H_3O^+]$

$-7.52 = log\,[H_3O^+]$

$antilog(-7.52) = [H_3O^+]$

❸ Calculate
- Use your calculator to find the antilog of –7.52.
  $[H_3O^+] = 3.01995 \times 10^{-8}$ M which is rounded to 3.02×10^{-8} M

Sample Problem 13E
Calculating the pH of a basic solution

What is the pH of a 0.025 M NaOH solution?

❶ List
- Concentration of NaOH: 0.025 M
- pH: **?**

❷ Set up
- This problem differs from the previous ones because you are starting with a base and the concentration represents the concentration of OH^- ions in the solution. Start by determining $[H_3O^+]$ of the solution.

- For any solution
  $[H_3O^+][OH^-] = 10^{-14}$

- In this problem $[OH^-] = 0.025$ M.

- Therefore,
  $[H_3O^+] = \dfrac{10^{-14}}{[0.025]} = \dfrac{10^{-14}}{2.5 \times 10^{-2}} = 0.40 \times 10^{-12} = 4.0 \times 10^{-13}$

- Now calculate pH. Start with the following equation.
  $pH = -log[4.0 \times 10^{-13}]$

- Use your calculator to determine the log of 4.0×10^{-13}.
  The log of 4.0×10^{-13} is -12.3979, which is rounded to -12.4.

❸ Calculate
  $pH = -(-12.4) = 12.4$

Practice 13A

Answers for Concept Review items and Practice problems begin on page 841.

13A
1. Determine the pH of the following solutions of strong acids.
   a. 0.00001 M HNO_3 b. 0.01 M HNO_3

13B
2. Determine the pH of the following solutions.
   a. 2.50×10^{-6} M HNO_3 b. 8.750×10^{-4} M HCl

13C
3. Determine $[H_3O^+]$ of the following solutions.
   a. drain cleaner with a pH of 13.0   b. ammonia with a pH of 11.0

13D
4. Determine $[H_3O^+]$ of the following solutions.
   a. human blood with a pH of 7.4   b. apple juice with a pH of 3.5

13E
5. Determine the pH of the following base solutions.
   a. 0.0005 M KOH   b. 2.80×10^{-4} M NaOH

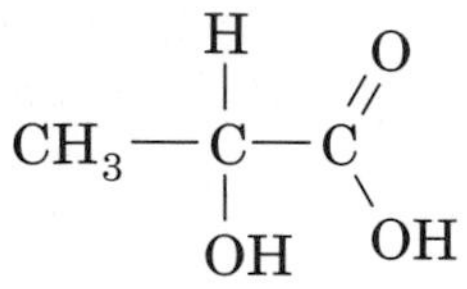

Figure 13-12
Lactic acid is a carboxylic acid, as shown by the carboxyl group in its structural formula.

Calculating dissociation constants
Using pH to calculate K_a

Have you ever gone to your refrigerator for milk only to find that it had turned sour? The sour taste comes from lactic acid, a monoprotic organic acid that is present in sour milk. Lactic acid reacts with water as shown by the following equation.

$$CH_3CHOHCOOH(aq) + H_2O(l) \rightleftharpoons H_3O^+(aq) + CH_3CHOHCOO^-(aq)$$
Lactic acid   Lactate ion

Sample Problem 13F
Calculating the dissociation constant for an acid

Assume that enough lactic acid is dissolved in sour milk to give a solution concentration of 0.100 M lactic acid. A pH meter shows that the pH of the sour milk is 2.43. Calculate K_a for the lactic acid equilibrium system.

❶ **List**
- The lactic acid concentration is initially 0.100 M. However at equilibrium the lactic acid concentration will be less than 0.100 M. The amount that it is reduced depends on the amount of lactic acid that dissociates.
- $[CH_3CHOHCOOH] < 0.100$ M
- pH = 2.43
- $[H_3O^+] = [CH_3CHOHCOO^-]$
- $K_a = \dfrac{[H_3O^+][CH_3CHOHCOO^-]}{[CH_3CHOHCOOH]} = ?$

❷ **Set up**
- To solve for K_a, you need to know the equilibrium concentration of each substance in the K_a expression. From the pH, you can calculate the value of $[H_3O^+]$, which is also the value of $[CH_3CHOHCOO^-]$.

$$2.43 = -log[H_3O^+]$$
$$-2.43 = log[H_3O^+]$$
$$antilog(-2.43) = [H_3O^+]$$

- Use your calculator to determine the antilog of –2.43.
  $[H_3O^+] = 3.71535 \times 10^{-3}$ M, which is rounded to 3.72×10^{-3} M

- According to the equation, H_3O^+ and $CH_3CHOHCOO^-$ are present in a 1:1 molar ratio. Thus,
  $[CH_3CHOHCOO^-] = 3.72 \times 10^{-3}$ M

- The lactic acid concentration at equilibrium equals the initial concentration of lactic acid minus the amount that dissociates. According to the equation, there is a 1:1 ratio between the amount of H_3O^+ formed and the amount of lactic acid that dissociated. Thus if 3.72×10^{-3} M of H_3O^+ are formed in this reaction, then 3.72×10^{-3} M of lactic acid must have dissociated. Thus $[CH_3CHOHCOOH]$ present at equilibrium is found as follows.
  0.100 M $- 0.00372$ M $= 0.09628$ M $= 9.6 \times 10^{-2}$ M

- You now have all the concentrations to substitute in the equilibrium expression for K_a.

❸ **Calculate**

$$K_a = \frac{[H_3O^+][CH_3CHOHCOO^-]}{[CH_3CHOHCOOH]} = \frac{(3.72 \times 10^{-3})(3.72 \times 10^{-3})}{(9.6 \times 10^{-2})} = 1.4 \times 10^{-4}$$

Practice 13F

1. Calculate K_a for lactic acid if a 0.2800 M solution has a pH of 2.21.

2. Most berries have a tart taste because they contain benzoic acid. Calculate the concentration of benzoic acid molecules in berries with a pH of 4.96. The concentration of benzoate ions is 0.0140 M, and K_a for benzoic acid is 6.3×10^{-5}. The equation for the equilibrium reaction is written as follows.

$$C_6H_5COOH(aq) + H_2O(l) \rightleftharpoons C_6H_5COO^-(aq) + H_3O^+(aq)$$

Dissociation constant of water
Calculating the [OH⁻] or [H₃O⁺] of an aqueous solution

You learned that pure water dissociates only slightly, as shown by the following equation.

$$H_2O(l) + H_2O(l) \rightleftharpoons H_3O^+(aq) + OH^-(aq)$$

K_w is the symbol used to represent the equilibrium constant of this reaction.

$$\boldsymbol{K_w = [H_3O^+][OH^-]}$$

In pure water, $[H_3O^+]$ and $[OH^-]$ equal 1.00×10^{-7} M. By substituting these values into the equilibrium expression, you can determine K_w for water.

$$K_w = [1.00 \times 10^{-7}][1.00 \times 10^{-7}] = 1.00 \times 10^{-14}$$

dissociation constant for water
the ion product constant for water that is equal to 1.00×10^{-14}

The **dissociation constant for water**, K_w, at 25°C is 1.00×10^{-14}. You have already used K_w to calculate the concentration of H_3O^+ ions in base solutions to determine their pH. This same idea is used to calculate the concentration of OH^- ions if you know $[H_3O^+]$.

Sample Problem 13G
Calculating [OH⁻]

The pH of sea water is 8.3. What is [OH⁻] of sea water?

❶ List
- pH = 8.3
- $[H_3O^+][OH^-] = 1.00 \times 10^{-14}$
- $[OH^-] = ?$

❷ Set up
$$8.3 = -log[H_3O^+]$$
$$-8.3 = log[H_3O^+]$$
$$antilog(-8.3) = [H_3O^+]$$

❸ Calculate
- Use your calculator to determine the antilog of −8.3.
  $[H_3O^+] = 5.01187 \times 10^{-9}$ M, which is rounded to 5.0×10^{-9} M

- Substitute all values into the expression for K_w.
  $1.00 \times 10^{-14} = [5.0 \times 10^{-9}][OH^-]$

  $$[OH^-] = -\frac{1.00 \times 10^{-14}}{5.0 \times 10^{-9}} = 2.0 \times 10^{-6} \text{ M}$$

Practice 13G

1. Calculate [OH⁻] for the following solutions.

   a. 0.001 M HNO₃   b. milk with a pH of 6.7
   c. 1.5×10^{-4} M KOH   d. soap with a pH of 10.8
   e. strawberries with a pH of 3.5   f. lemon juice with a pH of 2.3

Polyprotic acids

pH and K_a values of polyprotic acid solutions

You learned that polyprotic acids can donate more than one hydrogen ion. For example, carbonic acid can donate two hydrogen ions, as shown by the following equations.

$$H_2CO_3(aq) + H_2O(l) \rightleftharpoons H_3O^+(aq) + HCO_3^-(aq)$$

$$HCO_3^-(aq) + H_2O(l) \rightleftharpoons H_3O^+(aq) + CO_3^{2-}(aq)$$

Both reactions reach equilibrium so both reactions have acid dissociation constants. The K_a value for the first reaction is 4.3×10^{-7}, while the K_a value for the second reaction is 5.6×10^{-11}. Carbonic acid is a very weak acid, as indicated by the small K_a values for both reactions. Donating a second hydrogen ion is much more difficult than donating the first one as shown by the smaller K_a for the second reaction. For simple polyprotic acids, each successive loss of a hydrogen ion is 10^4 to 10^6 times more difficult than the previous loss. This means that the first dissociation of a polyprotic acid produces up to a million times more H_3O^+ ions than the second dissociation. Thus, the pH of a polyprotic acid solution depends primarily on the dissociation of the first hydrogen ion.

Section Review

12. Explain why dissociation constants apply only to weak acids and bases and not to strong acids and bases.

13. Define the pH of a solution.

14. How does the dissociation of water demonstrate the amphiprotic nature of its molecules?

15. One aqueous base has a pH of 8. Another has a pH of 11. Which solution has the larger concentration of OH^- ions? How many times larger? Which solution has the larger concentration of H_3O^+ ions? How many times larger?

16. An aqueous solution is found to have a pH of 3.1. Determine both $[H_3O^+]$ and $[OH^-]$ of this solution.

17. A 0.0160 M solution of a monoprotic acid has a pH value of 3.14. Calculate K_a for this acid.

18. Phosphoric acid is a triprotic acid that can go through three successive dissociation reactions.

$$H_3PO_4(aq) + H_2O(l) \rightleftharpoons H_3O^+(aq) + H_2PO_4^-(aq) \quad K_a = 7.1 \times 10^{-3}$$

$$H_2PO_4^-(aq) + H_2O(l) \rightleftharpoons H_3O^+(aq) + HPO_4^{2-}(aq) \quad K_a = 6.2 \times 10^{-8}$$

$$HPO_4^{2-}(aq) + H_2O(l) \rightleftharpoons H_3O^+(aq) + PO_4^{3-}(aq) \quad K_a = 4.5 \times 10^{-13}$$

Identify the conjugate acid-base pairs for each of the successive dissociation equations for phosphoric acid.

19. Which of the pairs in item **18** contains the strongest acid? Which contains the strongest base?

13-3

What is a titration?

Section Objectives

Write an equation for a neutralization reaction.

Describe how an acid-base titration is performed.

Determine the molarity of an acid or base solution using titration data.

Use Le Châtelier's principle to explain why indicators change color.

Distinguish between equivalence point and end point.

Neutralization

The acid shown in **Figure 13-13a** can dissolve metals; the base can unclog a drain. But if you mix these two solutions, you get an aqueous salt solution that cannot dissolve metals or unclog drains. To understand why this happens, look at the molecular equation for the reaction.

$$HCl(aq) + NaOH(aq) \longrightarrow NaCl(aq) + H_2O(l)$$

How would you classify this reaction? Notice that the products are a salt (NaCl) and water. This reaction is known as a neutralization reaction according to the Arrhenius concept of acids and bases. A **neutralization reaction** in aqueous solution is a reaction of an acid and a hydroxide base to produce a salt and water. Look at the ionic equations for this reaction.

neutralization reaction
a reaction between an acid and a hydroxide base in which H⁺ and OH⁻ react to form H₂O

Ionic equation

$$H_3O^+(aq) + Cl^-(aq) + Na^+(aq) + OH^-(aq) \longrightarrow Na^+(aq) + Cl^-(aq) + 2H_2O(l)$$

Net ionic equation

$$H_3O^+(aq) + OH^-(aq) \longrightarrow 2H_2O(l)$$

Figure 13-13a
The pH paper turns red because the solution in this beaker is acidic.

13-13b
The pH paper turns blue because the solution in this beaker is basic.

13-13c
The pH paper turns green because the solution in this beaker is neutral.

Figure 13-14
The juice from red cabbage leaves can be used as an indicator to measure the pH of household items. A set of color standards is made using the indicator in solutions of known pH from 1 through 14. When the household items are tested, they can be compared to the colors of the known standards to determine the pH of each.

You learned that a salt is defined as an ionic compound having a crystal lattice structure. You can now see that a **salt** can also be defined as a compound consisting of the anion of an aqueous acid and the cation of an aqueous hydroxide base. If you were to evaporate the solution formed from the neutralization reaction, you would obtain solid NaCl. Neutralization reactions are one way of preparing salts. What salt can be made by mixing H_2SO_4 and KOH?

Titration is used to find the concentration of an acid or base solution

In **Figure 13-13**, the concentrations of both the HCl and NaOH solutions were known when the solutions were mixed. But sometimes the concentration of either the acid or the base is not known. In that case, you can carry out a titration to determine the unknown concentration. A **titration** is a procedure in which a solution of known concentration is used to determine the concentration of a second unknown solution.

The solution of known concentration is the **titration standard** on which the analysis is based. For example, you could use a standard solution of NaOH to titrate an unknown concentration of HCl. The feature on page 512 shows how to carry out the titration. Notice that an indicator is added to the acid solution being titrated. Any substance in solution that changes its color as it reacts with either an acid or a base is called an **indicator**. Many dyes, as well as natural substances like the juice of red cabbage, can act as indicators as shown in **Figure 13-14**. Red cabbage juice turns red with vinegar but blue-green with baking soda. Some indicators produce a variety of colors depending on the pH of the solution.

Selecting the proper indicator is important because each indicator changes its color over a particular range of pH values. You can see this in **Table 13-5**. The pH range over which an indicator changes color is called its **transition interval**. The figure also shows that indicators are classified into three types based on the types of titrations and their transition intervals. What would be an appropriate indicator to use for titrating NaOH with HCl—a strong base and strong acid? Bromthymol blue would be a good choice. Notice in **Table 13-5** that bromthymol blue is yellow in an acidic solution, blue in a basic solution, and green in transition.

Control   Lemon, 2   Vinegar, 3   Soda water, 4

Ammonia, 11   Soap, 10   Baking soda, 8.5

Table 13-5
Color Ranges of Selected Indicators Used in Titrations

Titration type	Indicator	Acid color	Transition color	Base color

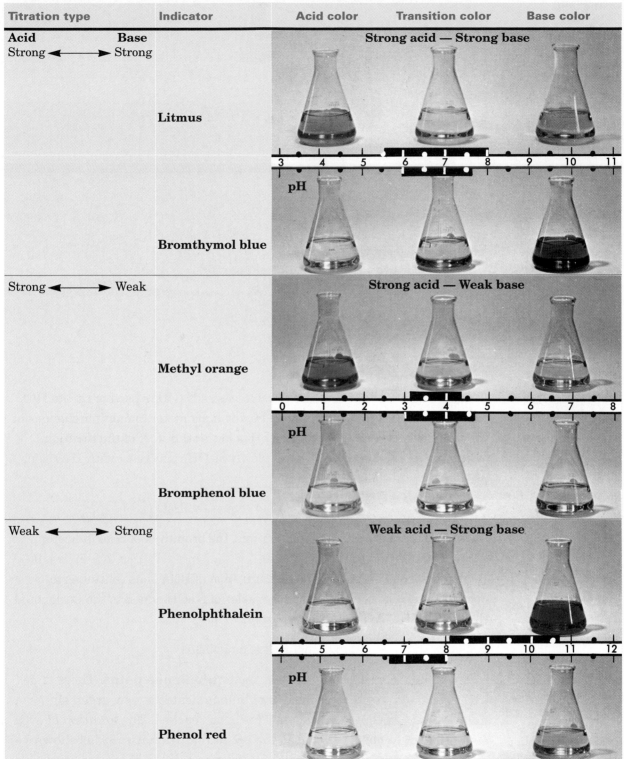

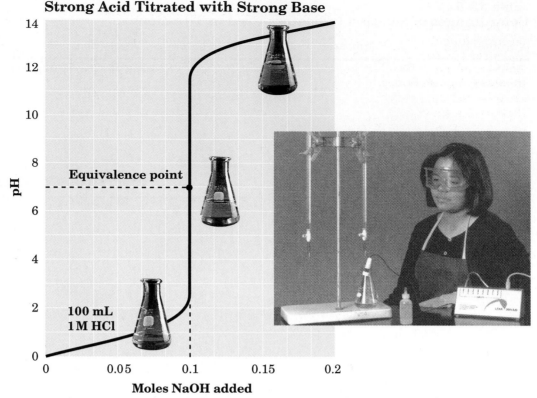

Figure 13-15
The titration curve for a strong acid and strong base reflects the set of pH data points collected using a pH probe. The rapid rise in pH at 0.1 moles NaOH added occurs with the addition of just a few drops of base. The curve has been smoothed to represent the best fit of the data.

Strong Acid Titrated with Strong Base

Equivalence point

100 mL
1 M HCl

pH

Moles NaOH added

Figure 13-15 shows how the pH changes as NaOH is used to titrate HCl. The data for this graph was obtained using a pH meter to monitor changes in the acid flask as base is added. The pH is low at the start of the titration. When NaOH is added, the pH rises slowly as OH^- ions react with H_3O^+ ions, as shown by the following equation.

$$OH^-(aq) + H_3O^+(aq) \longrightarrow 2H_2O(l)$$

As long as there is an excess of H_3O^+ ions, the bromthymol blue indicator stays yellow.

As more NaOH is added, the concentration of H_3O^+ ions continues to decrease until the point at which the moles of NaOH added to the flask equal the moles of HCl in the original solution.

$$\text{mol HCl} = \text{mol NaOH}$$

equivalence point
the point in a titration process where the moles of standard are stoichiometrically equivalent to the moles of substance titrated

This point in a titration is called the **equivalence point**. There is no excess acid or base. The bromthymol blue indicator is now green signalling that the equivalence point has been reached. The addition of even a small amount of NaOH causes the pH to rise dramatically, as shown in **Figure 13-15**. Notice that the equivalence point in this titration is reached when the pH is 7. The equivalence point for a titration of a strong acid with a strong base will be at pH 7. If more NaOH is added and the equivalence point is passed, the pH continues to rise very sharply for a bit and then more gradually as additional NaOH makes the solution increasingly basic.

Figure 13-16
The titration curve for a weak acid and strong base shows that the titration begins at a higher pH than that for the curve in **Figure 13-15**. The equivalence point occurs when the solution is basic at pH 8.7.

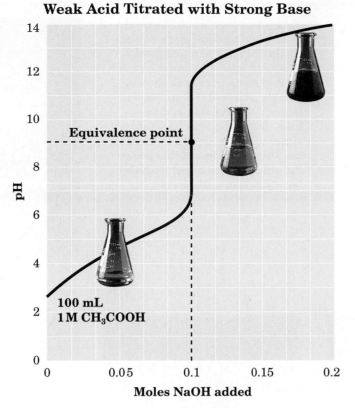

Weak Acid Titrated with Strong Base

Equivalence point

100 mL
1 M CH$_3$COOH

pH

Moles NaOH added

Titrating a weak acid with a strong base

The titration you just examined represents only one of three possible types of acid-base titrations, as shown in the following diagram.

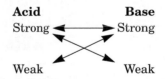

Acid **Base**
Strong   Strong

Weak   Weak

Suppose you want to determine the molarity of acetic acid, CH$_3$COOH, in vinegar by titrating it with a standard solution of NaOH. In this case, you would be titrating a weak acid with a strong base. To choose an appropriate indicator, you would check **Table 13-5**. Notice that phenolphthalein is an indicator that can be used in the titration of a weak acid by a strong base because the color range of the phenolphthalein falls within the pH range for the equivalence point.

Compare **Figure 13-16** with **Figure 13-15** to see how this titration differs from one between a strong acid and a strong base. The pH of the weak acid solution is higher than the strong acid solution at the same concentration. The addition of NaOH causes only a gradual change in the pH as H$_3$O$^+$ ions react with the added OH$^-$ ions. The equivalence point is reached when equal molar amounts of CH$_3$COOH and NaOH have combined. However, notice in **Figure 13-16** that the equivalence point in this titration occurs at a pH of 8.7. Why is it not at 7? Continued addition of NaOH past the equivalence point causes an immediate, rapid rise in pH and then a gradual increase as the solution becomes more basic, just as with a strong acid–strong base.

Carry out a titration

This procedure would be used to determine the unknown concentration of an acid using a standardized base solution. First, set up two clean burets as shown. Decide which of the burets will be used for the acid and the base. Rinse the acid buret three times with the acid to be used in the titration. Repeat this procedure in the base buret with the base solution to be used.

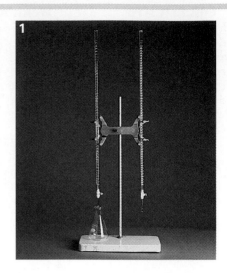

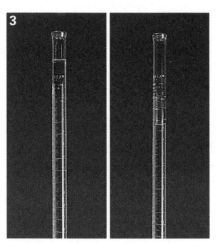

Fill the first to a point above the calibration mark with the acid of unknown concentration.

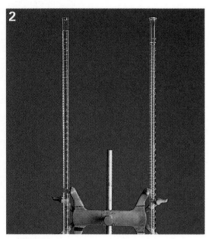

Release some acid from the buret to remove any air bubbles and to lower the volume to the calibrated portion of the buret.

Record the exact volume of the acid in the buret to the nearest 0.01 mL as your starting point.

Release a predetermined volume of the acid (determined by your teacher or lab procedure) into a clean, dry Erlenmeyer flask.

Record the exact volume of the acid released into the flask to the nearest 0.01 mL.

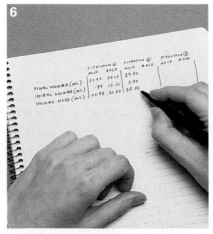

Add three drops of the appropriate indicator (in this case phenolphthalein) to the flask.

Fill the other buret with the standardized base solution to a point above the calibration mark. The concentration of the standardized base is known to a certain degree of precision because it was previously titrated with an exact mass of a solid acid.

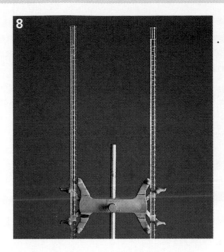

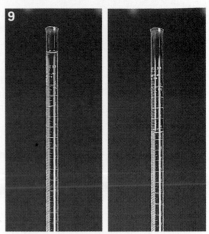

Release some base from the buret to remove any air bubbles and to lower the volume to the calibrated portion of the buret.

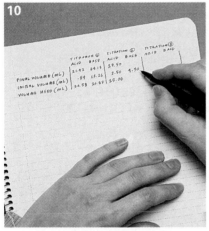

Record the exact volume of the base to the nearest 0.01 mL as your starting point.

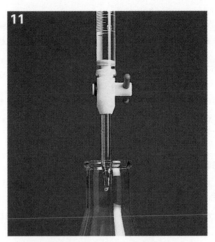

Place the Erlenmeyer flask under the base buret as shown. Notice that the tip of the buret extends into the mouth of the flask.

Slowly release base from the buret into the flask while *constantly* swirling the contents of the flask. The pink color of the indicator should fade with swirling.

The titration is nearing the endpoint when the pink color stays for longer periods of time. At this point, add base drop by drop.

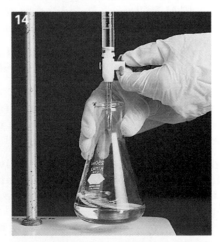

The equivalence point is reached when a very light pink color remains after 30 seconds of swirling.

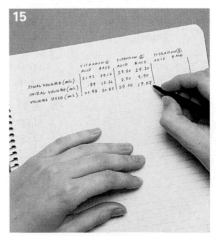

Record the volume to the nearest 0.01 mL. Repeat the titration until you have three results that agree within 0.05 mL.

Sample Problem 13H
Calculating concentration from titration data

Even though moles of acid and base are not specifically asked for in the problem statement, this problem is similar to other stoichiometry problems. You need moles.

Suppose that in the titration of 40. mL of vinegar, 20. mL of 0.50 M NaOH were needed to reach the equivalence point. What is the molarity of acetic acid in the vinegar? The molecular equation for the reaction is the following.

$$NaOH(aq) + CH_3COOH(aq) \rightleftharpoons NaCH_3COO(aq) + H_2O(l)$$

Sodium hydroxide   Acetic acid   Sodium acetate   Water

❶ List
- volume of NaOH = 20. mL
- concentration of NaOH = 0.50 M
- volume of vinegar = 40. mL
- mole ratio = 1 mol NaOH: 1 mol CH$_3$COOH
- moles of NaOH = **?**
- moles of CH$_3$COOH = **?**
- concentration of CH$_3$COOH = **?**

❷ Set up
- Both the volume and molarity of the base are known. From these values you can calculate the moles of NaOH used to titrate the acid.

$$20. \text{ mL NaOH} \times \frac{1 \text{ L NaOH}}{1000 \text{ mL NaOH}} \times \frac{0.50 \text{ mol NaOH}}{1 \text{ L NaOH}} = 0.010 \text{ mol NaOH}$$

- The balanced chemical equation shows that 1 mol of NaOH is needed for every 1 mol of CH$_3$COOH. Therefore, the amount of CH$_3$COOH in the vinegar is also 0.010 mol.

❸ Calculate and verify
- Use the volume of the vinegar to calculate its molarity. There are 0.010 mol CH$_3$COOH in 40. mL of vinegar.

$$\frac{0.010 \text{ mol CH}_3\text{COOH}}{40. \text{ mL CH}_3\text{COOH}} \times \frac{1000 \text{ mL CH}_3\text{COOH}}{1 \text{ L CH}_3\text{COOH}} = 0.25 \text{ M CH}_3\text{COOH}$$

The mole ratio for this reaction is 1:1. It makes sense that the CH$_3$COOH concentration would be half of the NaOH concentration, because there is twice as much vinegar used in the titration.

Practice 13H

1. In the titration of 35. mL of liquid drain cleaner containing NaOH, 50. mL of 0.40 M HCl must be added to reach the equivalence point. What is the molarity of the base in the cleaner?

2. Calculate how many milliliters of 0.25 M Ba(OH)$_2$ must be added to titrate 46. mL of 0.40 M HClO$_4$. (Hint: write the equation for the reaction and note the mole ratios.)

3. A 15.5 mL sample of 0.215 M KOH was titrated with an acetic acid solution. It took 21.2 mL of the acid to reach the equivalence point. What is the molarity of the acetic acid solution?

4. A 20.0 mL sample of an HCl solution is titrated with 27.4 mL of a standard solution of Ba(OH)$_2$. The concentration of the standard is 0.0154 M. What is the molarity of the HCl? The equation for the reaction is the following.

$$2HCl(aq) + Ba(OH)_2(aq) \rightleftharpoons BaCl_2(aq) + 2H_2O(l)$$

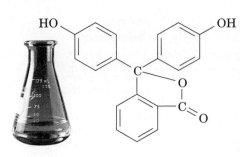

Le Châtelier's principle explains why indicators change color

What causes the color changes shown in **Table 13-5**? Indicators used in titrations are either weak acids or weak bases. Phenolphthalein is a weak acid that can be represented by the simplified formula HIn. Like all weak acids, phenolphthalein ionizes to a slight extent in aqueous solution and forms an equilibrium system. The addition of acid or base to the equilibrium system places a stress on the system. Le Châtelier's principle can be used to explain the color change for phenolphthalein.

$$HIn(aq) + H_2O(l) \Longleftrightarrow H_3O^+(aq) + In^-(aq)$$
$$\text{Clear} \qquad\qquad\qquad \text{Magenta}$$

HIn donates a hydrogen ion to the base H_2O. The In^- ion is the conjugate base of HIn. Undissociated HIn is clear in aqueous solution, while the In^- ion is magenta or deep pink in color.

In an acidic solution, H_3O^+ ions are present in excess. These react with the Brønsted base, In^-. As a result, the formation of HIn is favored, and the solution is clear. As a base is added in a titration in which phenolphthalein is the indicator, OH^- ions react with H_3O^+ ions to produce water molecules.

$$OH^-(aq) + H_3O^+(aq) \Longleftrightarrow 2H_2O(l)$$

As the H_3O^+ ions are used to form water, the equilibrium shifts to the right because H_3O^+ is being removed.

$$HIn(aq) + H_2O(l) \Longleftrightarrow H_3O^+(aq) + In^-(aq)$$

As this shift occurs, the magenta color of In^- ions appears. The indicator has reached its end point. The **end point** of an indicator is the pH at which the indicator changes color. To be useful in a titration, the end point of an indicator must be close to the equivalence point of the titration. Refer again to **Table 13-5**, and recall that bromthymol blue was used as the indicator in the titration of a strong acid with a strong base. Notice that the point at which bromthymol blue changes from yellow to blue is close to the pH of the equivalence point of a strong-acid–strong-base titration.

Figure 13-17
The molecular form of phenolphthalein is in equilibrium with the ionized form, which is magenta in color. Addition of acid favors the reverse reaction, and the colorless molecular form predominates.

end point
a point in a titration indicated by the color change of an indicator

Section Review

20. Write balanced equations for the neutralization of the following.
    a. HNO_3 and $Ca(OH)_2$ **b.** KOH and H_2SO_4
21. Refer to **Table 13-5** to identify an indicator for titrating a strong acid with a strong base and another for titrating a weak base with a strong acid.
22. If 20 mL of 0.010 M aqueous HCl are required to titrate 30 mL of an aqueous solution of NaOH, what is the molarity of the NaOH solution?
23. Explain how a color change of an indicator illustrates Le Châtelier's principle.
24. Explain the difference between end point and equivalence point. Why is it important that both occur at approximately the same pH in a titration?

What are the biochemical roles of some acids and bases?

Section Objectives

Explain how buffers keep pH relatively constant in the body.

Describe the behavior of amino acids in response to changes in pH.

List the structural components of nucleic acids.

Distinguish between saturated and unsaturated fatty acids.

Describe two functions of fatty acids in the body.

List sources of organic bases in the body.

Acids and bases in the body

Your body is a sea of acids and bases. The proteins in your hair, nails, cell membranes, and other parts of your body consist of amino acids. Enzymes that catalyze reactions in your body are composed of amino acids. Hydrochloric acid is secreted in your stomach to aid in the digestion of foods. Organic bases are major components of DNA and products of the digestion of proteins.

Enzymes that catalyze the many reactions in your body can function only within a limited pH range. Therefore, maintaining pH within the body is critical to life. You learned in other chapters that foods or drugs, such as aspirin, can change acidity levels in the body. Buffered aspirin, shown in **Figure 13-18**, was developed to keep the pH of the stomach at a more constant level and to prevent damage to the stomach lining. Your body contains a number of buffering systems like that in buffered aspirin to keep your internal pH where it should be. Without buffers, the thousands of reactions that take place in your body each day would not occur quickly enough to keep you alive.

Figure 13-18
Buffered products can maintain a relatively constant pH with small additions of acids or bases.

buffer
a system that is able to withstand small additions of acid or base without a significant change in pH; the system is composed of a conjugate acid-base pair

Some solutions can maintain their pH when small quantities of acid or base are added

A **buffer** is a system consisting of a conjugate acid-base pair that is capable of resisting changes in pH when small amounts of acid or base are added. A buffer solution contains similar concentrations of a weak acid and one of its soluble salts, or a weak base and one of its soluble salts. For example, a buffer can be made from acetic acid and one of its soluble salts, such as sodium acetate. Acetic acid will react with water to form the equilibrium system shown by the following equation.

$$CH_3COOH(aq) + H_2O(l) \rightleftharpoons CH_3COO^-(aq) + H_3O^+(aq)$$

The soluble sodium acetate salt will dissociate completely in water, as shown by the following equation.

$$NaCH_3COO(s) \xrightarrow{H_2O} CH_3COO^-(aq) + Na^+(aq)$$

When you put the acid solution and salt together in the same system, both reactions take place. There are two things you should notice about this system.

1. The system contains high concentrations of both the molecular and ion forms of the acid.
2. The acetate ion is a product of both reactions.

Let's look at how the acetic-acid–acetate-ion buffer system is able to absorb small amounts of acid or base without a significant change in pH. If OH^- ions (a base) are added, they will react with the molecular acid, as shown by the following equation.

$$CH_3COOH(aq) + OH^-(aq) \rightleftharpoons CH_3COO^-(aq) + H_2O(l)$$

If H_3O^+ ions (an acid) are added, they will react with the acetate ion in solution, as shown by the following equation.

$$CH_3COO^-(aq) + H_3O^+(aq) \rightleftharpoons CH_3COOH(aq) + H_2O(l)$$

A buffer is limited in the amount of acid or base that it can accept without changing pH. The pH range over which a buffer can respond effectively to the additions of an acid or base is called the *buffer capacity*. The buffer capacity of the acetic-acid–acetate-ion buffer system is in the pH range between 4.3 and 5.3.

Your body contains several buffer systems to handle the result of many acid–base reactions that occur as part of your metabolism. The pH of the blood rarely rises above 7.45 or drops below 7.35. One component of your blood that maintains this pH range is the buffer system consisting of a weak acid, carbonic acid, and its conjugate base, hydrogen carbonate ions, HCO_3^-. The hydrogen carbonate ions react with H_3O^+ ions from the acid, as shown by the following equilibrium equation.

$$HCO_3^-(aq) + H_3O^+(aq) \rightleftharpoons H_2CO_3(aq) + H_2O(l)$$

According to Le Châtelier's principle, the addition of an acid places stress on the equilibrium system. There is a net shift to the right as HCO_3^- neutralizes the added acid. If a base is added to the system, it reacts with carbonic acid molecules to form hydrogen carbonate ions, HCO_3^-.

$$H_2CO_3(aq) + OH^-(aq) \rightleftharpoons HCO_3^-(aq) + H_2O(l)$$

Excess OH^- ions are neutralized by forming water and the pH of your blood remains close to 7.4.

The phosphate buffer system in the cytoplasm of your cells works in much the same way.

$$H_2PO_4^-(aq) + H_2O(l) \rightleftharpoons H_3O^+(aq) + HPO_4^{2-}(aq)$$

The phosphate buffer system is effective in the pH range from 6.4 to 7.4.

Concept Review

Buffer action

25. The phosphate buffer system consists of the dihydrogen phosphate ion, $H_2PO_4^-$, and the hydrogen phosphate ion, HPO_4^{2-}. Describe how this system reacts to maintain a constant pH when OH^- ions are added.

amino acid
a carboxylic acid that is the structural subunit of a protein

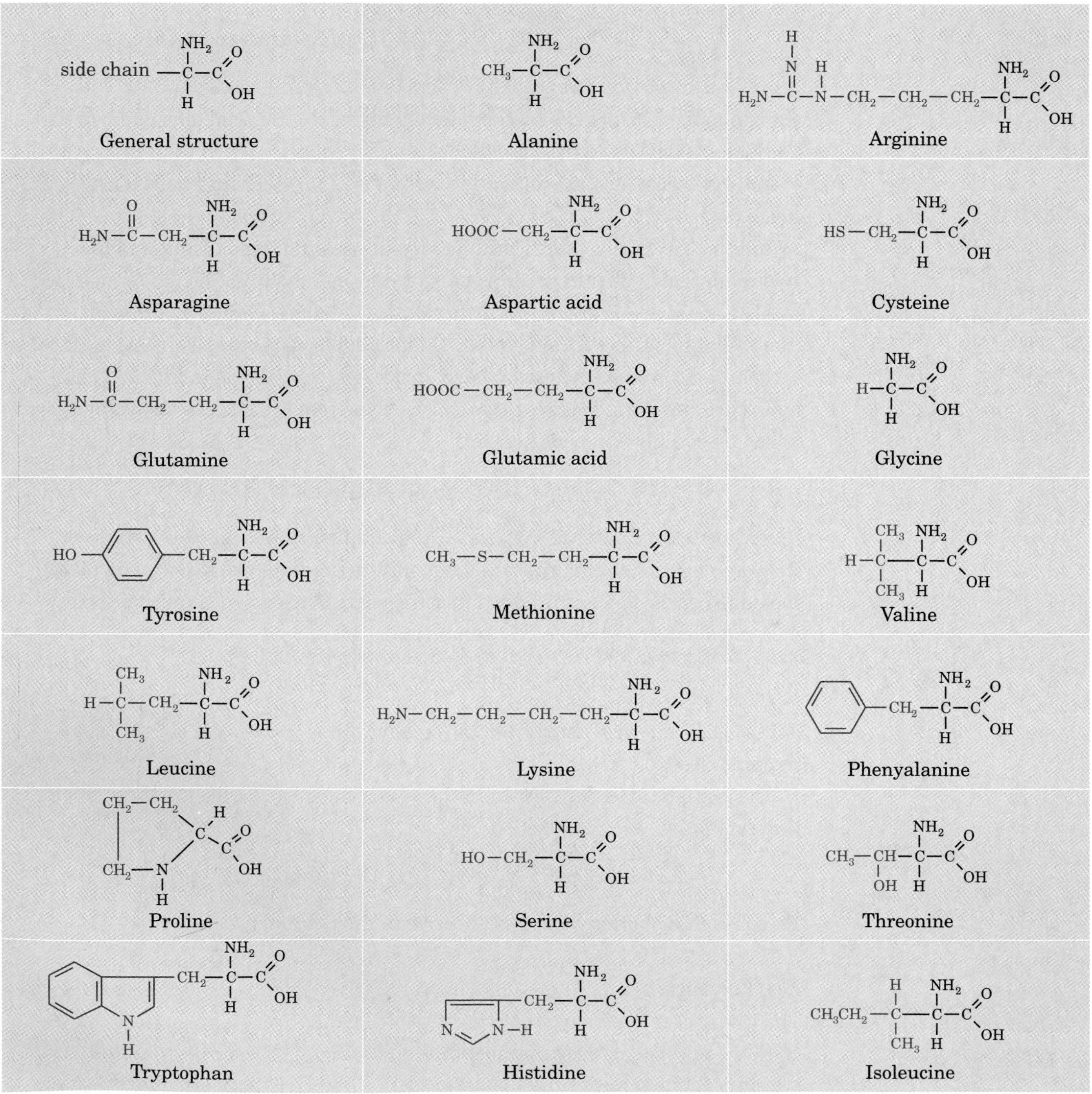

Figure 13-19
All amino acids fit the same general formula. The 20 essential amino acids are shown with all *R*-groups shown in pink.

Amino acids are weak organic acids that are the subunits of proteins

Amino acids are organic acids made mostly of carbon, hydrogen, oxygen, and nitrogen. All proteins in the body are built from a collection of 20 different amino acids arranged in different combinations. Amino acids have the general structure shown in the lavender box of **Figure 13-19**. Note that all amino acids have an amine group, —NH_2 or —NH, and the carboxyl group, —COOH, but differ in the nature of the *R*-group. You can see these groups by looking at the structural formulas of the 20 amino acids also shown in **Figure 13-19**.

General structure

Alanine

Arginine

Asparagine

Aspartic acid

Cysteine

Glutamine

Glutamic acid

Glycine

Tyrosine

Methionine

Valine

Leucine

Lysine

Phenylalanine

Proline

Serine

Threonine

Tryptophan

Histidine

Isoleucine

Figure 13-20
The zwitterion forms as a result of a hydrogen ion transfer from the carboxyl group to the amine group.

$$CH_3-\underset{\underset{H}{|}}{\overset{\overset{NH_2}{|}}{C}}-C\overset{O}{\underset{OH}{\diagup}}$$

Alanine

$$CH_3-\underset{\underset{H}{|}}{\overset{\overset{NH_3^+}{|}}{C}}-C\overset{O}{\underset{O^-}{\diagup}}$$

Alanine zwitterion

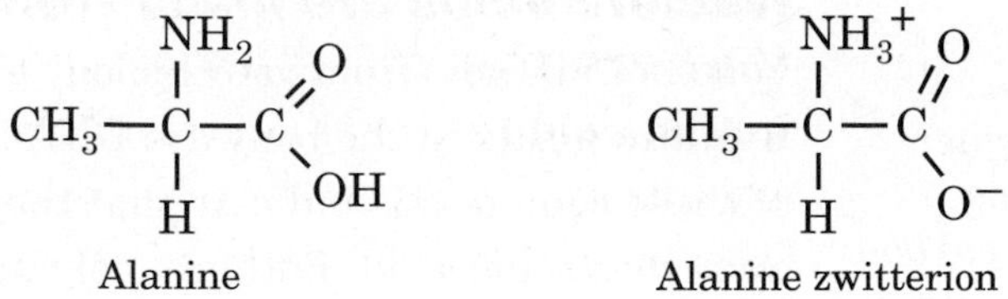

The acid properties of amino acids come from the carboxyl group, the functional group found in all organic acids. Their behavior is somewhat different than that of other acids of similar molecular mass and appears to be more like that of a salt than that of a neutral molecular compound. For example, even the smallest amino acids, glycine and alanine, have melting points close to 300°C. The solubilities of amino acids vary greatly depending on the *R*-groups. However, glycine is very soluble in water, but not in nonpolar solvents. To describe this behavior, chemists suggest that solid amino acids exist as dipolar ions that are formed from the transfer of a hydrogen ion from the carboxyl group to the amine group, as shown in **Figure 13-20**. This form of an amino acid is called a **zwitterion** and functions as a very polar molecule even though it has no net charge. The positive charge is centered on the nitrogen of $-NH_3$. The negative charge is centered between the oxygen atoms.

Zwitterions respond to changes in pH. In the presence of acids, the $-COO^-$ group accepts hydrogen ions. In the presence of bases, the $-NH_3^+$ group donates hydrogen ions. Because a zwitterion can act as an acid or base, as shown in **Figure 13-21**, it is amphiprotic. Amino acids donate hydrogen ions from the carboxyl group, but accept hydrogen ions from the amine group. As a result, amino acids demonstrate some slight buffering effects in the body. K_a values for amino acids range from 1.5×10^{-2} for histidine to 1.5×10^{-3} for tryptophan.

zwitterion

the reactive dipolar form of an amino acid

Figure 13-21
The zwitterion form of alanine is amphiprotic. In the presence of a base, it will shift to its anion form. In the presence of an acid, it will shift to its cation form.

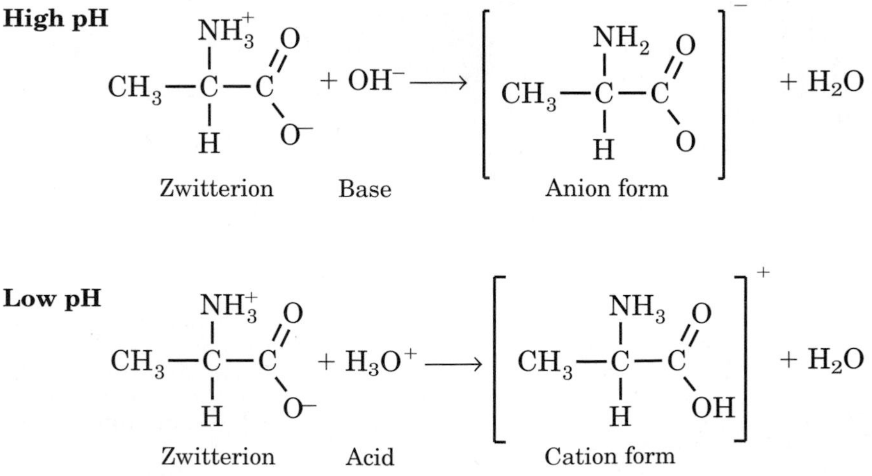

High pH

$$CH_3-\underset{\underset{H}{|}}{\overset{\overset{NH_3^+}{|}}{C}}-C\overset{O}{\underset{O^-}{\diagup}} + OH^- \longrightarrow \left[CH_3-\underset{\underset{H}{|}}{\overset{\overset{NH_2}{|}}{C}}-C\overset{O}{\underset{O}{\diagup}} \right]^- + H_2O$$

Zwitterion   Base   Anion form

Low pH

$$CH_3-\underset{\underset{H}{|}}{\overset{\overset{NH_3^+}{|}}{C}}-C\overset{O}{\underset{O^-}{\diagup}} + H_3O^+ \longrightarrow \left[CH_3-\underset{\underset{H}{|}}{\overset{\overset{NH_3}{|}}{C}}-C\overset{O}{\underset{OH}{\diagup}} \right]^+ + H_2O$$

Zwitterion   Acid   Cation form

Nucleic acids are made from acid and base components

nucleic acid
a biological polymer consisting of phosphoric acid, a 5-carbon sugar, and four nitrogen bases

You should know from your biology class that the two most important **nucleic acids** in the body are DNA and RNA. The actual names of both of these compounds indicate that they are acids—deoxyribonucleic acid and ribonucleic acid. Both are polymers consisting of the same structural subunits: phosphoric acid, a five-carbon sugar, and four organic nitrogen bases (amines), as shown in **Figure 13-22**. DNA and RNA differ from each other in the composition of their sugars and in one nitrogen base. DNA contains deoxyribose. RNA contains ribose. Three of the nitrogen bases are common to both DNA and RNA, but only DNA has thymine, and only RNA has uracil.

Figure 13-22
DNA and RNA have similar molecular components. DNA is the primary genetic compound in all living things. The linking of nitrogen bases between strands occurs through hydrogen bonding. RNA directs the synthesis of all proteins—the linking of amino acids.

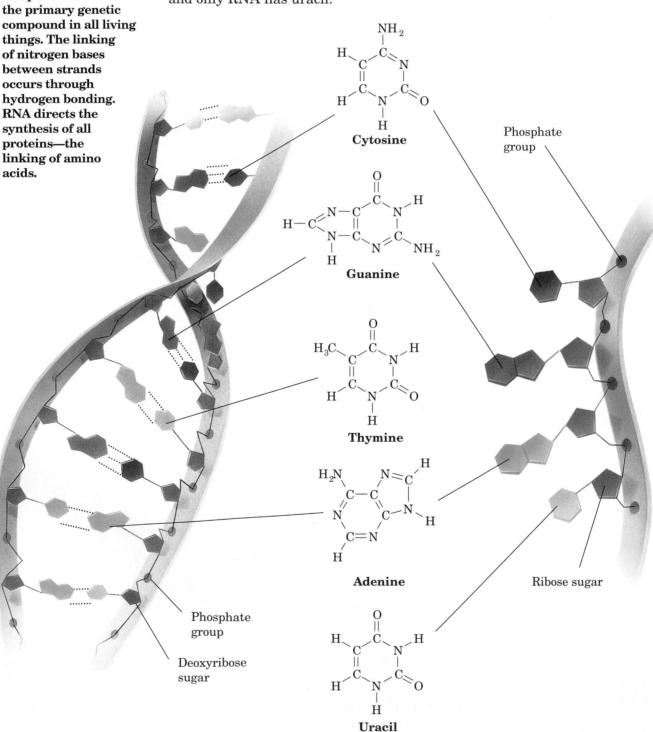

Cytosine

Guanine

Thymine

Adenine

Uracil

Phosphate group

Phosphate group

Deoxyribose sugar

Ribose sugar

$$CH_3 - CH_2 - CH_2 - CH_2 - CH_2 - CH_2 - CH_2 - CH_2 - CH_2 - OH$$

$$CH_3 - CH_2 - CH_2 - CH_2 - CH_2 - CH_2 - CH_2 - CH_2 - CH_2 - O^-$$

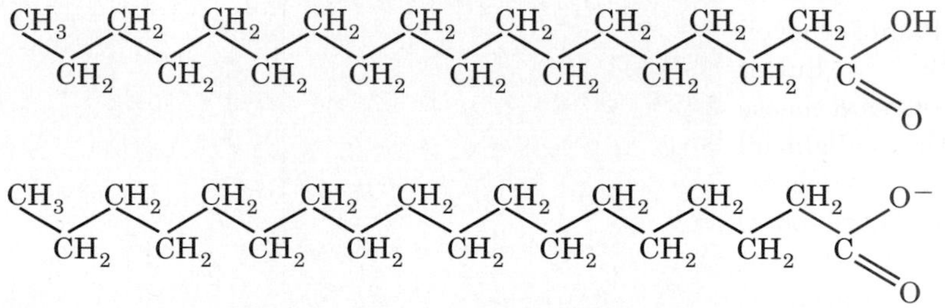

Fatty acids are the subunits of lipids

fatty acid
the long chain carboxylic acid subunit of a fat and oil

One of the structural components of animal fats and vegetable oils are compounds called **fatty acids.** Fatty acids consist of long chains of hydrocarbons with a carboxyl group, —COOH, at one end, as shown in **Figure 13-23**. The length of the chain determines the physical properties of the fatty acid. Short-chain fatty acids and unsaturated long-chain fatty acids are generally found in oils which are liquids (from four to seven carbon atoms long). Long-chain fatty acids (more than 12 carbon atoms long) are found in fats, which are generally solids at room temperature. Fatty acids are not very soluble in water even though the carboxyl group is very polar. Solubility of fatty acids decreases as the length of the fatty-acid chain increases.

saturated fatty acid
the long chain carboxylic acid subunit of a fat and oil with no double bonds

unsaturated fatty acid
a fatty acid with one or more carbon-carbon double bonds

The fats and oils in your diet contain varying amounts of two classes of fatty acids. These classes are saturated and unsaturated fatty acids, and they differ from each other by the relative numbers of hydrogen atoms bonded to the carbon chain. The structure of a **saturated fatty acid** is shown in **Figure 13-24**.

Compare its structure to an **unsaturated fatty acid** of similar length. A *polyunsaturated* fatty acid has more than one carbon-carbon double bond. The hydrogenation of oils involves addition of hydrogen atoms to the double bonds of an unsaturated fatty acid. This process causes the oil to be more solid. Margarines and shortenings are made from hydrogenated oils. Hydrogenated fats last longer before spoiling than unsaturated fats.

Figure 13-24
Saturated fatty acids have all carbons linked with single bonds. Unsaturated fatty acids will have one or more carbon–carbon double bonds in the chain.

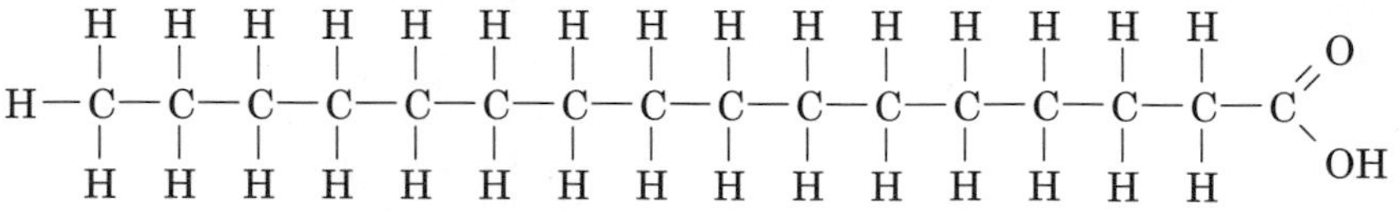

Palmitic acid, saturated

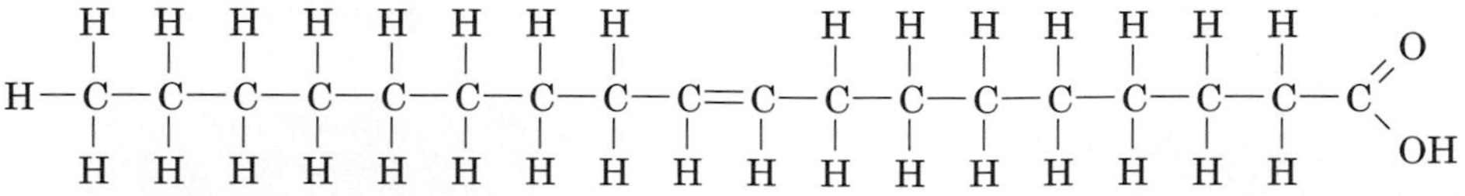

Oleic acid, unsaturated

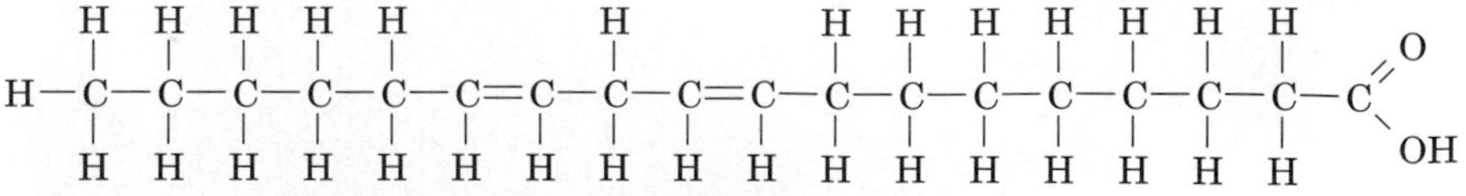

Linoleic acid, polyunsaturated

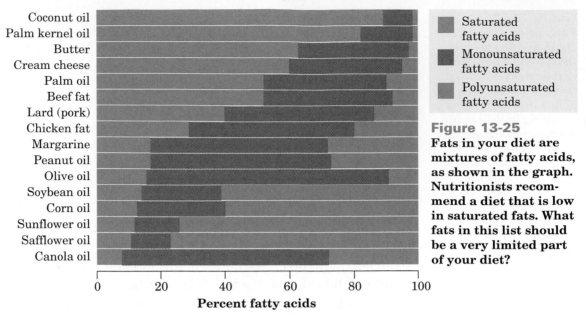

Coconut oil
Palm kernel oil
Butter
Cream cheese
Palm oil
Beef fat
Lard (pork)
Chicken fat
Margarine
Peanut oil
Olive oil
Soybean oil
Corn oil
Sunflower oil
Safflower oil
Canola oil

0   20   40   60   80   100
Percent fatty acids

■ Saturated fatty acids
■ Monounsaturated fatty acids
■ Polyunsaturated fatty acids

Figure 13-25
Fats in your diet are mixtures of fatty acids, as shown in the graph. Nutritionists recommend a diet that is low in saturated fats. What fats in this list should be a very limited part of your diet?

Most fatty acids in foods are in the form of triglycerides. You looked at a triglyceride structure when you studied soap-making in Chapter 11. Foods can also contain *monoglycerides* and *diglycerides*. When you see the fat content on a food label, the figure generally represents a mix of triglycerides. **Figure 13-25** shows the saturated fat composition of some familiar fats and oils found in a typical diet.

Fatty acids are also a component of the lipid bilayer that makes up the membrane of a cell. The fatty acid is the nonpolar end of a larger compound, as depicted by the model in **Figure 13-26**.

Figure 13-26a
This phospholipid molecule contains two fatty acid chains.

13-26b
This phospholipid is part of the lipid bilayer.

13-26c
The lipid bilayer is the framework of the cell membrane.

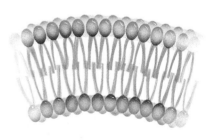

13-26d
The fatty acids are oriented toward the interior of the bilayer as they have a low attraction for water.

Consumer Focus

Antacids

You learned in Chapter 7 that antacids are used to neutralize excess stomach acid.

Although antacids contain a variety of ingredients, they all contain a base to counteract the stomach acid. The base is either sodium hydrogen carbonate, $NaHCO_3$, calcium carbonate, $CaCO_3$, aluminum hydroxide, $Al(OH)_3$, or magnesium hydroxide, $Mg(OH)_2$.

In any antacid, it is the carbonate or hydroxide ion that provides the alkalinity needed to offset excess stomach acid. However, the metal ion that is used in the antacid is also important. Antacids containing $NaHCO_3$ are the most potent and can seriously disrupt the acid-base balance in your blood. Consequently, some antacid manufacturers have substituted $CaCO_3$ for $NaHCO_3$. However, if taken in large amounts, calcium can promote kidney stones. Too much aluminum ingested from antacid products containing $Al(OH)_3$ can interfere with the body's absorption of important chemicals, including the phosphorus needed for healthy bones. Concern has also been raised about a possible connection between ingesting aluminum and Alzheimer's disease. Excess magnesium from antacids with $Mg(OH)_2$ may pose problems for people with kidney trouble.

You should know the active ingredient in any antacid product before you purchase it, and you should never use any antacid for a prolonged period of time. It's best to avoid the need for an antacid in the first place. You can minimize the production of excess stomach acid by eating a healthy diet, avoiding stress, and limiting your consumption of coffee, fatty foods, and chocolate.

Section Review

26. Describe how a lactic-acid–lactate-ion buffer reacts with both H_3O^+ and OH^- ions. (Hint: see the formula for lactic acid on page 504.)

27. Draw the structural formula for aspartic acid. Label the R group, the amine group, and the carboxyl group on your structure.

28. Draw the structural formula for the zwitterion form of aspartic acid and how it reacts in the presence of OH^- ions.

29. Label each of the following fatty acids as saturated or unsaturated.

    a. $CH_3CH_2CH_2CH_2CH_2CH_2CH_2CH_2CH_2CH_2CH_2COOH$

    b. $CH_3CH_2CH_2CH_2CH_2CH_2CH{=}CHCH_2CH_2CH_2CH_2CH_2CH_2CH_2COOH$

    c.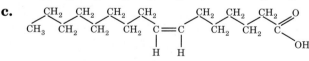

    d.

30. Draw the ionized form of the fatty acid from item **29a**.

31. What is it that is saturated in a saturated fatty acid?

32. What functional group is characteristic of organic bases?

 33. **Story Link**

What component of DNA makes it an acid?

Conclusion: Ancient Acids

You began your study of acids and bases by reading about a new field of science that has recently emerged—molecular archaeology. Scientists in this field are interested in the study of just one particular acid—DNA.

What makes DNA an acid? DNA consists of two giant strands of bases linked together in a helical formation. A chain of alternating ribose sugar molecules and phosphoric acid molecules, H_3PO_4, forms the backbone that holds the bases in place. Under ordinary pH levels in biological systems, DNA exists in the conjugate base form. The phosphoric acid molecules, having donated their hydrogen ions, form anions called phosphate groups. Thus, DNA contains thousands of sites where H^+ ion transfer can take place. Therefore DNA fits the definition of a Brønsted acid.

Is DNA a strong or weak acid? The K_a value for DNA is approximately 1×10^{-1} or 0.1. DNA is a weak acid, but it is stronger than phosphoric acid itself.

Why have some ancient DNA fragments been preserved better than others? Ancient DNA is retrieved in very small fragments from organisms that have been subjected to the forces of nature for thousands or even millions of years. The preservation of the organism is the result of the action of a compound known as tannic acid, commonly found in peat bogs. Unfortunately, tannic acid destroys DNA.

But even in a peat bog a body may be found that contains some ancient DNA if there are limestone rocks in the area. Limestone is a mineral containing calcium carbonate, $CaCO_3$. $CaCO_3$ neutralizes acids and tends to preserve the DNA fragments in the soft tissues from destruction by tannic acid.

Applying Concepts

1. Bases such as those shown on page 520 hold the two strands of DNA together by means of hydrogen bonds. Make a drawing that shows how these bonds are formed between thymine and adenine.

Research and Writing

1. Why do molecular archaeologists like Svante Pääbo think the idea of bringing extinct species back into existence is more a matter of science fiction than scientific research?
2. Molecular archaeologists are attempting to test the proposal that all living humans are descended from one woman, nicknamed Eve, who lived in Africa some 200 000 years ago. To do so, they are analyzing the DNA found in specialized structures called mitochondria that are found in the cytoplasm of cells. Report on the latest findings in this research.

Highlights

Key terms

acid anhydride	fatty acid
acid-dissociation constant	hydroxide ion
	indicator
amino acid	neutralization reaction
amphiprotic	
base anhydride	nucleic acid
base-dissociation constant	pH
	salt
buffer	saturated fatty acid
conjugate acid	titration
conjugate base	titration standard
dissociation constant for water	transition interval
	unsaturated fatty acid
end point	zwitterion
equivalence point	

Key ideas

What are acids and bases?

- Strong acids and bases dissociate completely in aqueous solution; weak ones dissociate only partially.
- A Brønsted acid is a hydrogen ion donor, and a Brønsted base is a hydrogen ion acceptor. Some compounds can function as both.
- A conjugate acid forms when a Brønsted base accepts a hydrogen ion. A conjugate base forms when a Brønsted acid releases a hydrogen ion.

- An acid anhydride reacts with water to form an acid. A base anhydride reacts with water to form a base.

How are weak acids and bases compared?

- Dissociation constants measure the relative strength of weak acids and bases. The smaller the numerical value of this equilibrium constant, the weaker the acid or base.
- The pH measures the hydronium ion concentration in a solution.
- Water, an amphiprotic substance, dissociates to form hydronium ions and hydroxide ions.

What is a titration?

- When combined, acids and bases neutralize each other to produce water and a salt.
- The concentration of a solution may be determined through a titration with a solution of known concentration.
- The equivalence point of a titration can be determined by the end point of an indicator.
- The end point of an indicator occurs when the indicator changes color. The equivalence point of a titration occurs when stoichiometric amounts of acid and base are present.

13-4 What are the biochemical roles of some acids and bases?

- Amino acids, nucleic acids, and fatty acids are biological molecules that function within the pH range of living systems.
- Buffers maintain pH in living systems.

Key problem-solving approach: Concentrations and pH conversions

When converting between concentrations and pH values, begin at the appropriate box, and follow calculation commands to the desired value.

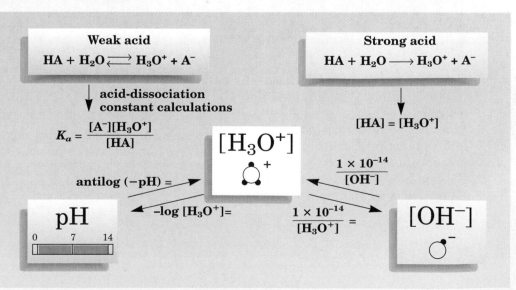

Review and Assess

Comparing acids and bases

R E V I E W

1. Compare the properties of an acid to those of a base.
2. Arrhenius was the first scientist to define the properties of acids and bases. Fill in the table below using Arrhenius's definitions.

	Ions released into solution by dissociation of acid or base	Acid or base
HCl		
Ba(OH)$_2$		

3. What is the acid anhydride in the following equation?

$$N_2O_5 + H_2O \longrightarrow 2HNO_3$$

4. Complete the table below by indicating the acid or base formed by the hydration of the oxides given.

Oxide	Substance formed when hydrated	Acid or base?
SO$_3$	H$_2$SO$_4$	acid
BaO		
P$_2$O$_5$		
SeO$_3$		
K$_2$O		
Li$_2$O		

5. How does Arrhenius's definition of a base fail to explain why sodium hydride, NaH, is a base?
6. What is the difference between a diprotic and a monoprotic acid? Is H$_2$CO$_3$ diprotic or monoprotic?
7. Explain how the hydrogen carbonate ion, HCO$_3^-$, acts as an amphiprotic ion.

A P P L Y

8. Write an equation for the reaction between hydrocyanic acid, HCN, and water. Label the acid, base, conjugate acid, and conjugate base.
9. Explain why sodium hydroxide, NaOH, is used in oil refining to remove acids.
10. Explain how the acetate ion formed as a product in the forward reaction can act as a base in the reverse reaction.

$$CH_3COOH(aq) + H_2O(l) \rightleftharpoons$$
$$CH_3COO^-(aq) + H_3O^+(aq)$$

Strengths of weak acids and weak bases

R E V I E W

11. What does the numerical value for K_a and K_b represent?
12. Using the table below, answer the following questions.
    a. Which is the strongest acid? Why?
    b. Which acid dissociates the least? Why?

Acid	Formula	Value of K$_a$
arsenic	H$_3$AsO$_4$	5.62×10^{-3}
acetic	CH$_3$COOH	1.76×10^{-5}
benzoic	C$_6$H$_5$COOH	6.5×10^{-5}
cyanic	HCNO	7.4×10^{-4}
phosphoric	H$_3$PO$_4$	7.5×10^{-3}
hydrofluoric	HF	6.8×10^{-4}
carbonic	H$_2$CO$_3$	4.3×10^{-7}

13. You add a substance to pure water, and the pH rises from 7 to 9. What has happened to the concentration of H$_3$O$^+$ ions? Is the substance added an acid or a base?

14. Classify the acids by placing a check in the columns that apply.

Acid	Formula	Triprotic	Diprotic	Monoprotic
arsenic	H_3AsO_4	✔		
acetic	CH_3COOH			
sulfurous	H_2SO_3			
phosphoric	H_3PO_4			
hydrofluoric	HF			

Acid	Binary	Ternary	Strong	Weak
arsenic		✔		✔
acetic				
sulfurous				
phosphoric				
hydrofluoric				

15. Explain the relationship between the dissociation of water and the pH of a neutral solution.

16. What is the relationship between the forward and reverse reactions and the strength of an acid or a base?

17. Why is the first dissociation constant for a polyprotic acid used to calculate the pH value for an aqueous solution of that acid?

A P P L Y

18. A solution of HCl has a pH of 1. You add NaOH to the solution, and the pH rises to 1.18. What has happened? What does this have to do with the relationship of acids to bases along the pH scale? Can you estimate what amounts of HCl and NaOH might have been used?

19. Use two arbitrary pH values and the mathematical method for determining pH to show how the concentration of H_3O^+ increases as pH decreases.

20. Write an equilibrium expression for the dissociation of benzoic acid C_6H_5COOH.

P R A C T I C E

Answers to items in a black square begin on page 841.

21 What is the pH of a 0.00256 M HCl solution? (Hint: see Sample Problem 13B.)

22. What is the pH of a solution with $[H_3O^+]$ of 6.35×10^{-10} M? (Hint: see Sample Problem 13B.)

23 What is the pH of a seawater solution that has a hydronium ion concentration of 1.35×10^{-8} M? (Hint: see Sample Problem 13B.)

24. What is the pH of lemon juice if $[H_3O^+] = 0.00363$ M? (Hint: see Sample Problem 13B.)

25 The average pH of precipitation in an area near a power plant is 3.45. What is $[H_3O^+]$? (Hint: see Sample Problem 13D.)

26. The pH of a glass of soda water is 4.3. What is $[H_3O^+]$? (Hint: see Sample Problem 13D.)

27 What is the pH of a 2.5×10^{-5} M KOH solution? (Hint: see Sample Problem 13E.)

28. What is the pH of an ammonia solution that has a hydroxide ion concentration of 10^{-3} M? (Hint: see Sample Problem 13E.)

29 A solution of 5% acetic acid has a concentration of 0.83 M and K_a of 1.8×10^{-5}. What is the pH of the solution? (Hint: see Sample Problem 13F.)

30. What is the concentration of all of the components of a benzoic acid solution if K_a is 6.5×10^{-5}, pH is 2.96, and C_6H_5COOH is 0.020 M? (Hint: see Sample Problem 13F.)

 **Titrations**

R E V I E W

31. Write the complete molecular and net ionic equations for the neutralization of sulfuric acid with potassium hydroxide.

32. Describe the role of an indicator in the titration of an unknown acid against a standardized base.

33. Why is the transition interval of an indicator critically important when performing different titrations?

34. How is the color change of an indicator related to pH?

35. Refer to the table below.
  a. Which indicator would be the best choice for a titration with an end point at a pH of 4.0?
  b. Which indicators would work best for a titration of a weak base with a strong acid?

Indicator	Acid color	Base color	pH range of color
thymol blue	red	yellow	1.2–2.8
bromphenol blue	yellow	blue	3.0–4.6
bromcresol green	yellow	blue	2.0–5.6
bromthymol blue	yellow	blue	6.0–7.6
phenol red	yellow	red	6.6–8.0
alizarin yellow	yellow	red	10.1–12.0

36. Why is a different indicator used for a strong acid/strong base titration than for a weak acid/strong base titration?

37. Why does an indicator need to be a weak acid or base?

38. How is the transition interval of an indicator related to the end point of a titration?

39. A 50 mL solution of CH_3COOH is titrated with a 1.000 M NaOH solution. Describe what species (molecules and ions) are present in the titration flask at the following points in the titration.
   a. pH 6   **b.** pH 9   **c.** pH 11

40. Using **Figure 13-16** as a guide, sketch a titration curve for 50 mL of 1 M solution of the weak base, NH_3, with 1.000 M HCl.

41. For the following titrations, select the best indicator from these choices: bromphenol blue, bromthymol blue, phenol red.
   a. formic acid, HCOOH, with NaOH
   b. perchloric acid with LiOH
   c. sulfuric acid with potassium hydroxide
   d. ethylamine, $C_2H_5NH_2$, with hydrochloric acid

P R A C T I C E

42 Formic acid is used in the production of leather. Residue from leather production is tested to determine the concentration of formic acid in excess. A 50.0 mL sample of formic acid, HCOOH, is neutralized by 35.0 mL of 0.250 M NaOH. What is the molarity of the formic acid solution? (Hint: see Sample problem 13H.)

43. You wish to determine the molarity of a lactic acid solution. A 150. mL sample of lactic acid, $CH_3CHOHCOOH$, is titrated with 125 mL of 0.75 M NaOH. What is the molarity of the acid sample? (Hint: see Sample Problem 13H.)

44 If 35.40 mL of 1.000 M HCl are neutralized by 67.3 mL of NaOH, what is the molarity of the NaOH solution? (Hint: see Sample Problem 13H.)

45. If 50.00 mL of 1.000 M H_2SO_4 are neutralized by 35.4 mL of KOH, what is the molarity of the KOH solution? (Hint: see Sample Problem 13H.)

46 If 18.5 mL of a 0.350 M H_2SO_4 solution neutralizes 12.5 mL of aqueous LiOH, how many grams of LiOH were used to make the LiOH solution?

47. A student is preparing a standardized NaOH solution for use in a titration. About 2 g of NaOH are dissolved in 500 mL of distilled water. This solution is titrated against an oxalic acid dihydrate solution, $H_2C_2O_4 \cdot 2H_2O$, which is made by dissolving 1.125 g of the solid acid in 40 mL of distilled water. The titration requires 174 mL of NaOH.
   a. Write the equation for the neutralization reaction.
   b. Calculate the molarity of the NaOH standard. (Hint: oxalic acid is a diprotic acid.)

A P P L Y

48. In the titration of a weak acid with a strong base, the pH of the equivalence point is not 7, but in the basic range. Use the concept of conjugate acids and bases to explain why the pH is in the basic range.

49. A student passes an end point in a titration. Is it possible to add an additional measured amount of the unknown and continue the titration? Explain how this process might work. How would the answer for the calculation of the molarity of the unknown differ from the answer the student would get if the titration had been run successfully?

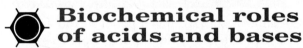

Biochemical roles of acids and bases

R E V I E W

50. Explain how weak acids in the body can help maintain the buffering capacity of a living system.

51. How would you test to see if a system is buffered?

52. The pH of your cells needs to be between 6.4 and 7.4 for the cells to function properly. How can this pH be kept constant even with DNA and RNA, two nucleic acids, inside the cell?

53. What structural feature of small fatty acids allows them to be more soluble in water than larger fatty acids?

A P P L Y

54. Enzymes and proteins are long chains of amino acids.
   a. How do the structures and functions of proteins and enzymes change with pH?
   b. Describe why an enzyme's activity changes with changes in pH.

55. Identify the fatty acids in the following fats as saturated, unsaturated, or polyunsaturated.

56. Classify the following compounds as organic acids or bases.

a.

b. $CH_3-S-CH_2-CH_2-\underset{\underset{H}{|}}{\overset{\overset{NH_2}{|}}{C}}-C\overset{\overset{O}{\diagup}}{\diagdown}_{OH}$

c. $H_3C-\underset{\underset{CH_3}{|}}{N}-CH_3$

d. $CH_3-\underset{\underset{OH}{|}}{\overset{\overset{H}{|}}{C}}-C\overset{\overset{O}{\diagup}}{\diagdown}_{OH}$

e.

f. $H-\underset{\underset{H}{|}}{\overset{\overset{H}{|}}{C}}-\underset{\underset{H}{|}}{\overset{\overset{H}{|}}{C}}-\overset{\overset{H}{|}}{C}=\overset{\overset{H}{|}}{C}-\underset{\underset{H}{|}}{\overset{\overset{H}{|}}{C}}-C\overset{\overset{O}{\diagup}}{\diagdown}_{OH}$

g.

h.

57. The structure of acetylsalicylic acid, $C_9H_8O_4$ is shown below. This chemical causes an increase in stomach acidity for some people. Aspirin manufacturers combat this problem by buffering their product. What substance could be used to buffer aspirin?

58. The amino acid tryptophan is pictured below.
   a. Draw the structure of this amino acid if it is in a solution with a pH of 3.
   b. Draw the structure of this amino acid if it is in a solution with a pH of 8.

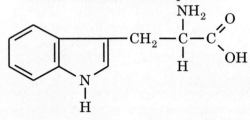

Linking chapters

1. *Applying scientific laws*
   How do nitrous acid, HNO_2, and nitric acid, HNO_3, demonstrate the law of multiple proportions?
2. **Theme:** *Systems and interactions*
   a. Identify the different systems that are involved in a titration.
   b. Explain how each system interacts with the other systems in a titration.
3. *Stoichiometry*
   An excess of zinc reacts with 250. mL of 6.00 M sulfuric acid.
   a. What mass of $ZnSO_4$ can be produced?
   b. How many liters of H_2 are produced at STP?
4. *Stoichiometry*
   A seashell (mostly $CaCO_3$) is placed in a solution of HCl. From the reaction, 1.50 L of CO_2 are produced at STP.
   a. How many grams of $CaCO_3$ were consumed in the reaction?
   b. If the HCl solution was 2.00 M, what volume was used in this reaction?

5. *Balancing equations*
   Write balanced equations for each of the following reactions between acids and metal oxides.
   a. $MgO(s) + H_2SO_4(aq) \longrightarrow$
   b. $CaO(s) + HCl(aq) \longrightarrow$
   c. $Al_2O_3(s) + HNO_3(aq) \longrightarrow$
   d. $ZnO(s) + H_3PO_4(aq) \longrightarrow$
6. *Balancing equations*
   Write balanced equations for each of the following reactions between acids and carbonates.
   a. $BaCO_3(s) + HCl(aq) \longrightarrow$
   b. $MgCO_3(s) + HNO_3(aq) \longrightarrow$
   c. $Na_2CO_3(s) + H_2SO_4(aq) \longrightarrow$
   d. $CaCO_3(s) + H_3PO_4(aq) \longrightarrow$
7. *Concentration*
   What is the molarity of an oxalic acid dihydrate standard, $H_2C_2O_4 \cdot 2H_2O$, made from dissolving 3.000 g of the solid acid to form 150 mL of solution?
8. *Stoichiometry*
   What would the molarity of a KOH solution be if 75.00 mL of base were used to neutralize the acid in item **7**? (Hint: oxalic acid is a diprotic acid.)

USING TECHNOLOGY

1. *Computer art*
   Draw the general structural formula of an amino acid. Now show that formula as a zwitterion. Show how the zwitterion reacts in both acidic and basic conditions.

2. *Calculator*
   Use your calculator to determine the following:
   a. log of 1×10^{-14}
   b. antilog of 4.6
   c. log of 5.738×10^{-6}
   d. antilog of 0

Alternative assessment

Performance assessment

1. Design an experiment to identify pH levels of four types of hair shampoo: baby shampoo, shampoo for extra body, shampoo for oily hair, and shampoo with conditioner. Chart any patterns you detect. Also compare and contrast two brands of "pH balanced" shampoo.

2. Your teacher will give you a solution to test for pH. Describe exactly how you would test the solution. If your teacher approves your plan, complete the test.

3. Design an experiment to test the neutralization effectiveness of various brands of antacid. Show your procedure, which includes all safety procedures and cautions, to your teacher for approval. Write an advertisement for the antacid you judge to be the most effective. Cite data from your experiments as part of your advertising claims.

Portfolio projects

1. **Chemistry and you**
   Hydrochloric acid, HCl, can be found in many cleaning products. Find three products in your home that contain acids. Determine if the acids are strong or weak. Does it seem that strength is a factor in whether these products are considered harmful? Use the product warning labels as a guide.

2. **Research and communication**
   A reaction between baking soda, $NaHCO_3$, and a baking batter that contains acidic ingredients produces carbon dioxide gas. The reaction results in a fluffier batter. Some recipes rely on baking powder instead of baking soda. Research the ingredients of regular baking powder and double-acting baking powder to discover how they differ from baking soda. Which is more likely to be used in creating a light, fluffy cake? How does the pH affect the final product?

3. **Chemistry and you**
   Collect data on the acidity of rain in your area over the last 10 years. Graph the data and make a prediction concerning acid-rain damage in your area for the year 2010. Use evidence to support your prediction.

4. **Cooperative activity**
   Research the Acid Rain Control Program. Debate the pros and cons of reducing oxide emission versus treating the effects of acid rain with base anhydrides. Discuss the environmental and economic impact of both plans.

DNA Fingerprinting
A New Solution or a New Problem?

The molecule common to all organic life has provided forensic scientists the basis for a new and complex technique to help solve crimes. This new technique, often used in identifying victims as well as criminals, is called DNA fingerprinting, or forensic DNA profiling.

Forensic science uses scientific methods to help solve crimes. Fingerprinting along with blood and semen typing are widely used in forensics to help prove guilt or innocence. But these tests can only suggest that a suspect might have committed a crime. For example, if a Type A blood sample is found at the crime scene and the suspect has Type A blood, this match only suggests the possibility of the suspect's involvement. Many people have Type A blood. Although suspects with Type O blood could be ruled out, there is no guarantee that a particular suspect with Type A blood actually committed the crime. Only recently could a more specific approach be used to identify a particular individual.

Discovered in 1984 by Alec Jeffreys at the University of Leicester in England, DNA fingerprinting is used to identify individuals from samples of body tissue left at the scene of a crime. These samples might include blood, hair, or semen. Also, DNA fingerprinting is now used to determine parentage. Previously, the use of blood types to establish parentage could prove only whether someone was definitely not the parent of a child. With the introduction of DNA fingerprinting, the unique genetic profiles of possible parents can now be examined and can positively determine a parent-child relationship. Because positive DNA matches can now be made, DNA fingerprinting has been used to identify children stolen from their parents and sold on the black market during Argentina's military regime of the 1970s and 1980s.

This technique is also being used to identify what are believed to be the remains of the Russian imperial family executed in 1918 during the Bolshevik revolution.

A DNA fingerprint being examined.

The current Duke of Edinburgh is related to the Russian imperial family. His grandmother was the sister of Alexandra, the murdered tsarina. A conclusive DNA match is being sought in comparing DNA from the Duke of Edinburgh with that taken from the skeletal remains of the imperial family.

Another case involves a series of rape murders, the first committed just one year before Alec Jeffreys invented his DNA-fingerprinting system. In December of 1986, police in Narborough, England, were convinced that two murders had been committed by the same suspect. A man they had in custody had confessed (falsely, it soon appeared) to the second murder.

Police decided to use Jeffreys' technique to solve the matter beyond question. Jeffreys compared the suspect's DNA with the sample taken in the second murder, and determined that it did not match. Comparison with the sample from the first murder proved conclusively that the suspect had not committed that crime either. DNA fingerprinting had exonerated an innocent man, but left the Narborough police with no suspect. DNA analysis of semen samples did prove however, that the two murders had been committed by the same unknown man. If they could find the suspect whose DNA matched the samples, both murders could be solved. The Narborough police then instituted an innovative mass collection and study of DNA data. Every man in Narborough and neighboring Enderby who was a suspect in the murders was required to give a blood sample for DNA analysis. Such a genetic "police lineup" was unprecedented and not likely to be duplicated, especially in the United States, where civil rights laws would prevent it. Although the killer—an aspiring cake decorator named Colin Pitchfork—attempted to conceal his guilt by paying someone to impersonate him during the testing, the truth of the substitution emerged, and Pitchfork was convicted of both murders.

What remains to be determined is the capacity of individual forensic researchers to be accurate, reliable, and responsible in their use of the information. In the application of DNA fingerprinting to forensics, several issues must be addressed. First, the integrity of the physical evidence itself must be ensured. In theory, two samples of DNA can be placed side by side and will either match or not match. In actual practice, however, a DNA sample can become contaminated or degraded before it is studied. Also, in the matching process, a phenomenon called

How the Duke of Edinburgh Is Related to Tsarina Alexandra

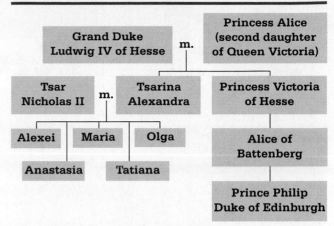

"band-shift" can occur spontaneously, causing differences in the pattern of DNA bands used for the comparison. In addition, the techniques used in DNA fingerprinting are the legal—and private—property of the companies holding the patents on the process, so they are not available for objective study by the scientific community at large. Thus, the body of information on this technique remains small and relatively limited. Until DNA fingerprinting information and techniques are made available for general study, the procedure cannot be used alone to prove guilt or determine family relationships. DNA fingerprinting is still subject to individual interpretation, inaccuracies, and potential abuse.

Researching the Issue

1. What standards could be set up to ensure that DNA fingerprinting is absolutely accurate?

2. How might DNA fingerprint data be misused in a courtroom? in a universal database? in employment practices?

3. Compare the advantages and disadvantages of a universal DNA database of the population.

4. Research a court case in which DNA fingerprinting was used as evidence in the United States. What role did this evidence have in determining the outcome of the case? Who did the testing, and who reported the results?

5. Find out what guidelines have been established for the use of DNA fingerprinting as evidence in the United States.

6. Find out how DNA fingerprinting is used to establish parentage.

Reaction Rates

Kinetics and Cooking Hamburgers

Alerted by Seattle area doctors on January 12, 1993,

the Center for Disease Control in Washington State traced the

source for the latest epidemic of food poisoning caused by

***E. coli* 0157:H7 bacteria to Jack in the Box restaurants.**

Samples of the hamburger meat sold to Jack in the Box were sent to the Washington State Department of Health and three independent labs for testing. *E. coli* 0157:H7 was present in 2 out of 10 hamburger patties. Acquired in the slaughterhouse through contact with the air or affected workers, the *E. coli* 0157:H7 bacteria were still present in the hamburgers served to customers because the meat had not been cooked long enough at a sufficiently high temperature to kill the bacteria.

The FDA internal temperature requirement of 140°F (60°C) must be maintained for at least 5 minutes to kill the bacteria: more than twice as long as the 2 minutes allowed by Jack in the Box. For these shorter cooking times to be effective, the internal cooking temperature must be much higher, says Michael Doyle, a food microbiology expert at the University of Georgia.

Experiments on the growth rate and survival of *E. coli* over a range of temperatures were performed by Dr. Doyle and others in the early 1980's after an *E. coli* 0157:H7 outbreak involving another fast food chain. These test results persuaded much of the fast food industry to raise their cooking temperature, because they indicate that during the short cooking times used by the fast food industry, temperatures between 150°F and 160°F are necessary to kill the *E. coli* bacteria.

Although the state of Washington had raised its requirement for the minimum internal cooking temperature to 155°F in May 1992, and the Jack in the Box equipment was designed to operate above the FDA minimum of 140°F, health department officials found internal temperatures of only 130°F when they tested patties cooked by the restaurant. In response to the outbreak of *E. coli* 0157:H7, Jack in the Box officially raised their minimum internal temperature standard from 140°F to 155°F, increased their cooking time to 2.5 minutes, and added an extra flipping of each burger.

Like the cooking process, the spoilage of meat is not immediate. It takes place over a period of time. That period of time can be lengthened by following accepted preservation techniques from the slaughterhouse to the table. The experiences of Jack in the Box and its meat supplier raise the following questions about the preparation and preservation of raw meat.

- *How does temperature affect the preparation of raw meat?*
- *What are some effective methods for preserving meat?*

Insights for answering these questions can be found in an exploration of reaction rates and the factors that affect them.

What is a reaction rate?

14-1

Rate is a ratio

How could you describe the following changes to someone who has not seen them? The gas gauge went down. The bread molded. The child's hair was cut. While these statements identify the changes taking place, they would be more informative if they were expressed in terms of numbers: the gas gauge fell from 3/4 to 1/2 full; mold patches 1 cm in diameter grew on the bread; the child's hair was shortened from waist length to shoulder length. It would also be more informative to have a series of pictures showing the changes as they progress. Look at the moldy bread in **Figure 14-1**. How could you describe the changes you see? If you knew the time elapsed between each picture, you could express mold growth as a function of time according to the following equation.

$$\text{mold growth} = \frac{\text{change in diameter of mold patch}}{\text{time elapsed}}$$

This expression would be called the rate of mold growth. Any measurable change in an activity expressed as a function of time is a rate. A heart beats at the rate of 75 beats per minute. A race car travels at 78.6 kilometers per hour. Half of a sample of uranium-238 decays to lead-206 in about 4.5 billion years. When the change under consideration is part of a chemical reaction, the expression is called a **reaction rate**. **Chemical kinetics** is the study of reaction rates and the factors that affect them.

reaction rate
the change in reactant concentration per unit of time as reaction proceeds

chemical kinetics
the branch of chemistry concerned with reaction rates and reaction mechanisms

Figure 14-1
Mold growth on a bread slice can be expressed as a function of time.

Reaction rate is an experimental quantity

A reaction rate describes how rapidly a chemical change takes place. It is an experimental quantity found by measuring the disappearance of a reactant or the appearance of a product over a period of time. Expressing a rate depends on the ability to report accurately a change in some physical property such as volume, temperature, color, mass, or acidity. Study **Figure 14-2**. Magnesium metal has been added to hydrochloric acid. The equation for this reaction is written as follows.

$$Mg(s) + 2HCl(aq) \longrightarrow MgCl_2(aq) + H_2(g)$$

What observations indicate that a reaction is taking place? Which of these could be measured and used to calculate the reaction rate?

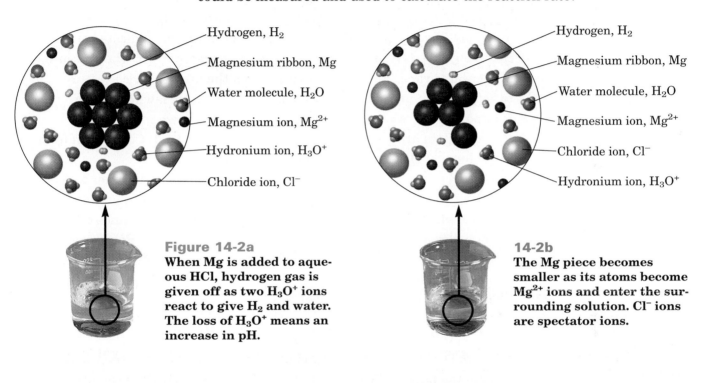

Hydrogen, H_2

Magnesium ribbon, Mg

Water molecule, H_2O

Magnesium ion, Mg^{2+}

Hydronium ion, H_3O^+

Chloride ion, Cl^-

Hydrogen, H_2

Magnesium ribbon, Mg

Water molecule, H_2O

Magnesium ion, Mg^{2+}

Chloride ion, Cl^-

Hydronium ion, H_3O^+

Figure 14-2a
When Mg is added to aqueous HCl, hydrogen gas is given off as two H_3O^+ ions react to give H_2 and water. The loss of H_3O^+ means an increase in pH.

14-2b
The Mg piece becomes smaller as its atoms become Mg^{2+} ions and enter the surrounding solution. Cl^- ions are spectator ions.

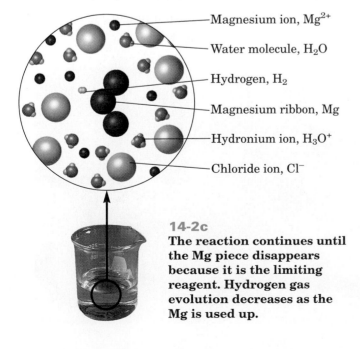

Magnesium ion, Mg^{2+}

Water molecule, H_2O

Hydrogen, H_2

Magnesium ribbon, Mg

Hydronium ion, H_3O^+

Chloride ion, Cl^-

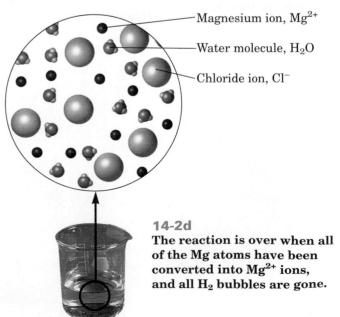

Magnesium ion, Mg^{2+}

Water molecule, H_2O

Chloride ion, Cl^-

14-2c
The reaction continues until the Mg piece disappears because it is the limiting reagent. Hydrogen gas evolution decreases as the Mg is used up.

14-2d
The reaction is over when all of the Mg atoms have been converted into Mg^{2+} ions, and all H_2 bubbles are gone.

Your list of observations should include three distinct, measurable properties: the reduction in mass of Mg, the volume or mass of the evolved gas, and the change in acidity of the solution. Changes in the mass of Mg can be determined by running the same reaction several times and stopping each one after a specified time period. The Mg must be quickly pulled out, rinsed, dried, and its mass determined. Dividing this experimentally determined mass of Mg by its atomic mass gives moles of Mg. The initial and final masses for Mg are recorded in columns 2 and 3 of **Table 14-1**. The negative number in column 4 is the difference between these two masses, and is equal to the total mass of Mg consumed during the reaction. The mass to mole conversion is given in column 5.

The setup in **Figure 14-3** suggests one way in which the reaction between Mg and aqueous HCl can be monitored through the collection of H_2 gas. The H_2 is collected over water, so the volume indicated on the collecting tube is a combination of H_2 gas and water vapor. The pressure of the water vapor must be subtracted from the atmospheric pressure to get the pressure of the H_2 gas alone. The ideal gas law relates the volume and pressure of H_2 to the moles of H_2 as shown in the figure. Reaction data are given in columns 1 to 4 of **Table 14-1**. Conversion from the volume of H_2 to the moles of H_2 is shown in column 5.

The pH of the solution can be monitored by adding a pH meter to the setup in **Figure 14-2**. Changes in the acidity, $[H_3O^+]$, can be calculated from the pH values measured. The change in $[H_3O^+]$ determines the number of moles of H_3O^+, or of HCl, consumed in the reaction. Remember HCl is a strong acid and, as such, is completely dissociated in water. Therefore, it is present only as its ions, H_3O^+ and Cl^-; no molecular HCl is present. The following equation represents the dissociation of HCl.

$$HCl(aq) + H_2O(l) \longrightarrow H_3O^+(aq) + Cl^-(aq)$$

The number of moles of H_3O^+ and of HCl are equal because their mole ratio in the balanced equation is 1:1. Calculation of $[H_3O^+]$ from pH is shown in **Figure 14-4** on the next page. Reaction data and the conversion to moles are summarized in columns 1 to 5 of **Table 14-1**.

Figure 14-3
Hydrogen gas evolved when Mg reacts with aqueous HCl can be collected over H_2O and the measurement used to calculate the reaction rate.

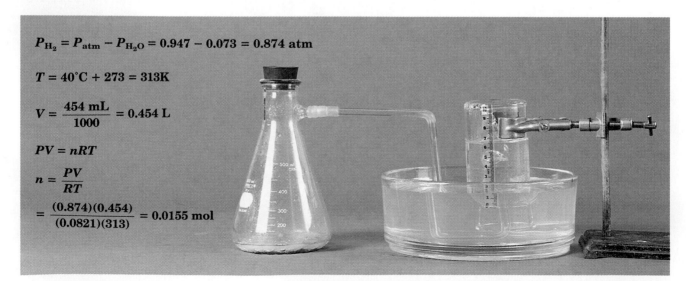

$P_{H_2} = P_{atm} - P_{H_2O} = 0.947 - 0.073 = 0.874$ atm

$T = 40°C + 273 = 313K$

$V = \dfrac{454 \text{ mL}}{1000} = 0.454$ L

$PV = nRT$

$n = \dfrac{PV}{RT}$

$= \dfrac{(0.874)(0.454)}{(0.0821)(313)} = 0.0155$ mol

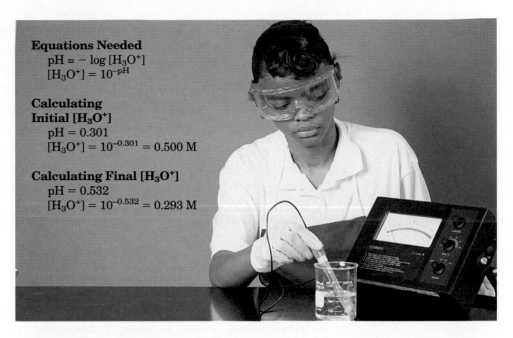

Figure 14-4
Changes in [H₃O⁺] are calculated from pH readings for the Mg in aqueous HCl reaction.

Equations Needed
$$pH = -\log[H_3O^+]$$
$$[H_3O^+] = 10^{-pH}$$

Calculating Initial [H₃O⁺]
$$pH = 0.301$$
$$[H_3O^+] = 10^{-0.301} = 0.500\ M$$

Calculating Final [H₃O⁺]
$$pH = 0.532$$
$$[H_3O^+] = 10^{-0.532} = 0.293\ M$$

These three observable properties permit you to express a change from initial to final conditions that occurs over a specified time interval. Dividing the change in the measured property by the time elapsed gives the **average rate** for the time interval as shown in column 7 of **Table 14-1**.

Consider the entries for Mg in **Table 14-1**. At the end of the reaction you have less Mg than at the beginning; consequently, subtracting its initial mass from its final mass gives a negative number. But the change is written as a positive number in the rate column. This is because, when discussing reaction rates, chemists are more interested in how fast substances are reacting rather than whether they are formed or consumed. Thus, multiplying the negative change by a −1 makes the rate a positive number. Any time the reaction rate is calculated from changes in reactants, multiply your result by −1 to make the number positive.

average rate
the change in the measured property divided by the time elapsed

Table 14-1
Reaction Rate Data and Calculations for Mg in Aqueous HCl Reaction

Col. (1) Property measured	(2) Initial quantity	(3) Final quantity	(4) Change in quantity	(5) Convert to moles so the rates will be comparable	(6) Time elapsed (s)	(7) Rate = $\dfrac{\text{Change in property (mol)}}{\text{elapsed time(s)}}$
Mass of Mg	0.376 g	0.0 g	−0.376 g	$\text{mol Mg} = \dfrac{-0.376\ g}{24.31\ g/mol}$	3.2	$\text{Rate} = \dfrac{0.0155\ \text{mol Mg}}{3.2\ s}$ $= 0.0048\ mol/s$
Volume of H₂ collected over H₂O at 40°C 0.947 atm	0.0 mL	454 mL	454 mL	$\text{mol H}_2 = \dfrac{(0.874)(0.454)}{(0.0821)(313)}$	3.2	$\text{Rate} = \dfrac{0.0155\ \text{mol H}_2}{3.2\ s}$ $= 0.0048\ mol/s$
[H₃O⁺] from pH of the 150 mL solution	0.500 M	0.293 M	0.207 M	mol HCl = mol H₃O⁺ mol H₃O⁺ = (0.207 M)(0.150 L)	3.2	$\text{Rate} = \dfrac{0.0310\ \text{mol HCl}}{3.2\ s}$ $= 0.0096\ mol/s$

Rate can be noted from the disappearance of a reactant or appearance of a product

Look at the numbers in the rate column of **Table 14-1**. How do they compare? The reaction rate calculated from the change in the mass of Mg is equal to that calculated from the collection of H_2 gas. The reaction rate calculated from the $[H_3O^+]$, however, is twice as large as that determined from either Mg or H_2. This suggests that $HCl(aq)$ is disappearing twice as fast as Mg is, and that $HCl(aq)$ is also disappearing twice as fast as H_2 is appearing. How can you account for this difference? Reconsider the balanced equation for the overall reaction.

$$Mg(s) + 2HCl(aq) \longrightarrow MgCl_2(aq) + H_2(g)$$

Look at the coefficients for Mg, HCl, and H_2. Both Mg and H_2 have a coefficient of 1. So H_2 is formed as quickly as Mg disappears. The mole ratio between $HCl(aq)$ and Mg, however, is 2:1. This means that 2 mol of $HCl(aq)$ must be used for every 1 mol of Mg atoms consumed which produces a rate that is twice as fast. The mole ratio between $HCl(aq)$ and H_2 is also 2:1. To compensate for this effect of stoichiometry on reaction rate, chemists divide the rate of change for each reactant or product by its coefficient in the balanced equation. Thus, for the reaction between Mg and aqueous HCl, rate is expressed as follows.

$$\text{rate} = \frac{1}{1}\frac{\Delta \text{ mol Mg}}{\Delta t} \text{ or } \frac{1}{2}\frac{\Delta \text{ mol HCl}}{\Delta t} \text{ or } \frac{1}{1}\frac{\Delta \text{ mol } H_2}{\Delta t}$$

The Greek letter Δ (a capital "delta") stands for "the change in." Therefore, Δ mol Mg is read as "the change in moles of magnesium." This change is equal to the number of moles of Mg at the stopping time minus the number of moles of Mg at the starting time.

The units for a reaction rate must always be expressed. The units for rate in this equation are moles per second. The most common units for a reaction rate are concentration per unit of time. When concentration units are moles of a substance per liter of solution (M), the general equation for rate is written as follows.

$$\text{rate} = \frac{-1}{a}\frac{\Delta [\text{reactant}]}{\Delta t} = \frac{1}{b}\frac{\Delta [\text{product}]}{\Delta t}$$

The minus sign makes the change in reactant concentration a positive number. The a is the coefficient for the reactant in the balanced chemical equation; b is the coefficient for the product. More specifically, when 0.1 M solutions of $BaCl_2$ and Na_2SO_4 are combined, $BaSO_4$ is precipitated according to the following equation.

$$BaCl_2(aq) + Na_2SO_4(aq) \longrightarrow BaSO_4(s) + 2NaCl(aq)$$

The rate can be expressed as follows.

$$\text{rate} = \frac{-1}{1}\frac{\Delta [BaCl_2]}{\Delta t} = \frac{-1}{1}\frac{\Delta [Na_2SO_4]}{\Delta t} = \frac{1}{1}\frac{\Delta [BaSO_4]}{\Delta t} = \frac{1}{2}\frac{\Delta [NaCl]}{\Delta t}$$

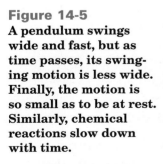

Concept Review

Defining rate

1. What characteristic of each of the following reactions could be used to qualitatively show the rate of reaction?
   a. $2H_2O_2(aq) \longrightarrow 2H_2O(l) + O_2(g)$
   b. $Cu(s) + 2Ag^+(aq) \longrightarrow Cu^{2+}(aq) + 2Ag(s)$
   c. $HC_2H_3O_2(aq) + NaHCO_3(s) \longrightarrow NaC_2H_3O_2(aq) + CO_2(g) + H_2O(l)$
   d. $CuCl_2(aq) + 2NaOH(aq) \longrightarrow Cu(OH)_2(s) + 2NaCl(aq)$
   e. $2C_2H_6(g) + 7O_2(g) \longrightarrow 4CO_2(g) + 6H_2O(g)$

2. For each reaction in item **1**, write one expression for the reaction rate that uses a reactant and one expression that uses a product.

3. The concentration of a substance in a reaction changes from 4.0 M to 2.0 M in 40 min. Is the substance a reactant or product? Explain how you know. Express the rate of this reaction in M/min.

4. Ammonia is formed from its elements according to the equation below.

$$N_2(g) + 3H_2(g) \rightleftharpoons 2NH_3(g)$$

   One mole of N_2 is mixed with one mole of H_2 in a one liter container. After 5 s the reaction is stopped, and the gases are remeasured. There are 0.9 mol of N_2, and 0.7 mol of H_2. Calculate the reaction rate in terms of each reactant.

5. Dinitrogen pentoxide decomposes into nitrogen dioxide and oxygen according to the following equation.

$$2N_2O_5(g) \longrightarrow 4NO_2(g) + O_2(g)$$

   If the change in O_2 concentration was found to be 2.5 M/s, what is the reaction rate in terms of $N_2O_5(g)$?

Answers for Concept Review items and Practice problems begin on page 841.

Reaction rates decrease with time

Few chemical reactions proceed at the same rate throughout the entire process. Most reactions are fast at the beginning when all of the reactant concentrations are high and slow down as the reactants are consumed, just as the amplitude of a pendulum slows over time, shown in **Figure 14-5**.

Figure 14-5
A pendulum swings wide and fast, but as time passes, its swinging motion is less wide. Finally, the motion is so small as to be at rest. Similarly, chemical reactions slow down with time.

Rates for equilibrium reactions become constant

In Chapter 12, on page 464, you studied a reaction in which NO_2 combines with a second NO_2 molecule to make N_2O_4 according to the following equation.

$$2NO_2(g) \rightleftharpoons N_2O_4(g)$$

NO_2 is a brown gas and N_2O_4 is colorless. The brown color of the NO_2 lightened as the colorless N_2O_4 was formed. The change in color continued until a steady uniform color was achieved. The casual observer might think that this reaction stopped when the color became constant, but from your study of equilibrium constants you know otherwise. The reaction has not stopped, because the rate at which the colorless N_2O_4 is decomposing into the brownish NO_2 equals the rate at which the NO_2 is combining to form the colorless N_2O_4. You see this equivalence as constant color. When the reaction appears to stop, it has reached equilibrium, and the rate is constant.

Rates for non-equilibrium reactions decrease to zero

Carefully study the progress of the reaction between Mg and aqueous HCl presented in **Figure 14-2**. The reaction's progress can be observed by noting the amount of bubbles produced. Only a glance at **Figure 14-2** is needed to see that fewer bubbles are produced as time passes. A more detailed examination of the reaction's progress reveals that the amount of Mg is getting smaller as the amount of bubbles becomes smaller and that the H_2 gas escapes to the atmosphere because there is no lid on the beaker. The last picture in this series shows no bubbles and no Mg. From what you have learned about equilibrium in Chapter 12, you would predict that the reaction would not come to equilibrium but would continue until the magnesium was consumed. As predicted, the reaction continues until the limiting reagent, Mg, is completely used up and then stops. The rate of the reaction decreases to zero as the reaction comes to a stop.

Reaction rates can be visualized through graphs of reaction data

Dinitrogen pentoxide, N_2O_5, decomposes very rapidly. To monitor this reaction for rate data, the N_2O_5 molecules are dissolved in carbon tetrachloride, CCl_4. The CCl_4 does not react with N_2O_5, so the only reaction that occurs is the decomposition of N_2O_5 in the CCl_4 solution at 45°C. It decomposes according to the following equation.

$$2N_2O_5(soln) \xrightarrow[45°C]{in\ CCl_4} 4NO_2(g) + O_2(g)$$

The plot in **Figure 14-6** on the next page shows how the concentration of N_2O_5 changes with time. The reaction rate can be calculated from the slope of the curve at any point because the following relationship has been determined.

$$slope = \frac{\Delta y}{\Delta x} = \frac{\Delta [N_2O_5]}{\Delta t}$$

Figure 14-6
Rate is equal to the slope of the curve, which decreases as time passes.

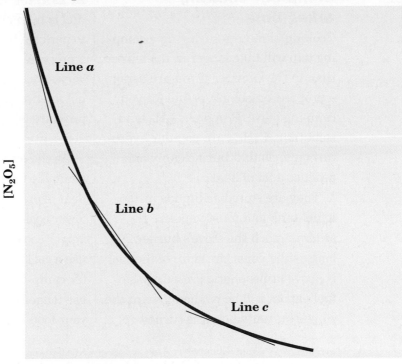

Concentration of N_2O_5 vs. Time for the Decomposition of N_2O_5 at 45°C in CCl_4 Solution

$[N_2O_5]$

Line *a*

Line *b*

Line *c*

Time (s)

However, the plot shows a curve, and the slope for a curve is not constant like it is for a straight line, so the section of the curve you examine affects the number you get for the reaction rate. To illustrate, look at lines *a*, *b*, and *c* in **Figure 14-6**. Compare the values for their slopes. Are they identical? The line that lies closest to the curve has a slope closest to that of the curve. Which line has a slope closest to that of the curve? Line *a* is almost parallel to the beginning of the curve, whereas line *b* intersects it, and line *c* touches it at only one point. Line *a* corresponds to the first few seconds of the reaction. Its slope is very near the initial reaction rate. The **initial rate** of a reaction is the fastest rate measured very close to the start of the reaction when reactant concentrations are highest. Line *b* corresponds to an *average rate* for the time interval bounded by its points of intersection with the curve.

initial rate
the highest rate measured very close to the start of the reaction where the curve is almost linear

Rates can be manipulated

For most chemical reactions, the reaction rate is fastest at the beginning when reactant concentrations are highest and slows down as reactant concentrations decrease and products are formed. The reaction rate either becomes constant, as for an equilibrium reaction, or stops altogether because the limiting reagent has been depleted. These observations lead to the conclusion that the reaction rate can be changed by manipulating the concentration. They also bring up the question, "Other than concentration, what affects the rate of a chemical reaction?" The next section identifies four of the five factors that affect reaction rates and explains why or how the rate is affected. The fifth factor will be discussed in Section 14-3.

Camp-out cooking takes time

Cooking hamburgers during a camping trip will take longer in the winter than in the summer if you are using a propane or isobutane fuel for your camping stove. Propane, C_3H_8, and isobutane, C_4H_{10}, are popular hydrocarbon fuels that burn cleanly and produce a lot of heat.

They are stored as liquids inside a fuel tank and must vaporize in order to reach the stove's burner. As long as the vapor pressure of the fuel is above atmospheric pressure, the fuel vapors will be pushed toward the stove's burner when it is turned on.

At 22°C the vapor pressure of either fuel is high enough for the stove to perform well. But at −12°C, a propane camping stove operates very slowly, and a butane stove may not operate at all because the vapor pressure of its fuel is no longer above atmospheric pressure.

As the amount of vapor that is available to burn decreases, less heat is produced. Less heat means lower cooking temperatures and longer cooking times. If you plan to use a cooking stove on a fall or winter camp-out, you should expect to use longer cooking times because your food heats up at a slower rate.

Section Review

6. Explain why the rate of a simple reaction is likely to be fastest at the beginning of the reaction.

7. The reaction between methanol and hydrochloric acid to form methyl chloride and water is written as follows.

$$CH_3OH(aq) + HCl(aq) \longrightarrow CH_3Cl\ (aq) + H_2O(l)$$

Time (min)	[H_3O^+]
0	1.83
79	1.67
158	1.52
316	1.30
632	1.00

The rate of disappearance of HCl is measured as a function of [H_3O^+]. The table shows the collected data. Plot the reaction data as a graph of concentration vs. time. Determine the average rate of the reaction for each time interval. Is the rate constant throughout the reaction? Explain your answer.

8. Express the reaction rate in terms of the rate of change of each reactant and each product in the following reactions.

   a. $4PH_3(g) \longrightarrow P_4(s) + 6H_2(g)$
   b. $S^{2-}(aq) + H_2O(l) \longrightarrow HS^-(aq) + OH^-(aq)$
   c. $C_2H_4(g) + Br_2(g) \longrightarrow C_2H_4Br_2(g)$

9. Ammonia, NH_3, reacts with O_2 to form NO and H_2O as follows.

$$4NH_3(g) + 5O_2(g) \longrightarrow 4NO(g) + 6H_2O(g)$$

   a. At the instant when NH_3 is reacting at a rate of 0.80 M/min, what is the rate at which O_2 is disappearing?
   b. At what rate is each product being formed?

14-2

How can reaction rates be explained?

Section Objectives

Discuss how collision theory explains reaction rates.

Relate an energy distribution graph to the effect of temperature on reaction rate.

List four major factors that affect the rate of a reaction and describe how changes in each factor affect the rate.

Modeling how reactions proceed

At one time a commercial for a powdered aspirin product claimed it worked better because it got to the headache faster than any competitor's tablet. This commercial was shown to a class of 30 chemistry students. Together, they surmised that to work faster the powder would have to dissolve more quickly than the tablet. The students were then asked to use what they knew about reaction rates to evaluate the commercial's claim. **Figure 14-7** shows the initial notebook entries and equipment setup of one student, George Cynric.

George Cynric investigates rate changes in aspirin systems

George's early results appeared to justify the commercial's claim because the powder did dissolve faster in water than the tablet. But aspirin dissolves in the stomach which is an acidic environment. Maybe the results would be different in an acid. The only acid available to him was vinegar. He repeated the experiment using vinegar even though the acidic component of vinegar, acetic acid, is a weaker acid than HCl, the acid present in the stomach. When the results had been recorded, he repeated the experiment but gently warmed the vinegar before adding the aspirin tablet or powder. This way he could simulate body temperature in case temperature had an effect on how the aspirin dissolved. He then recorded his results and the conclusions derived from them as shown in **Figure 14-7** on the next page. George Cynric looked back to the kinetic-molecular theory of gases for models to help explain his observations and conclusions.

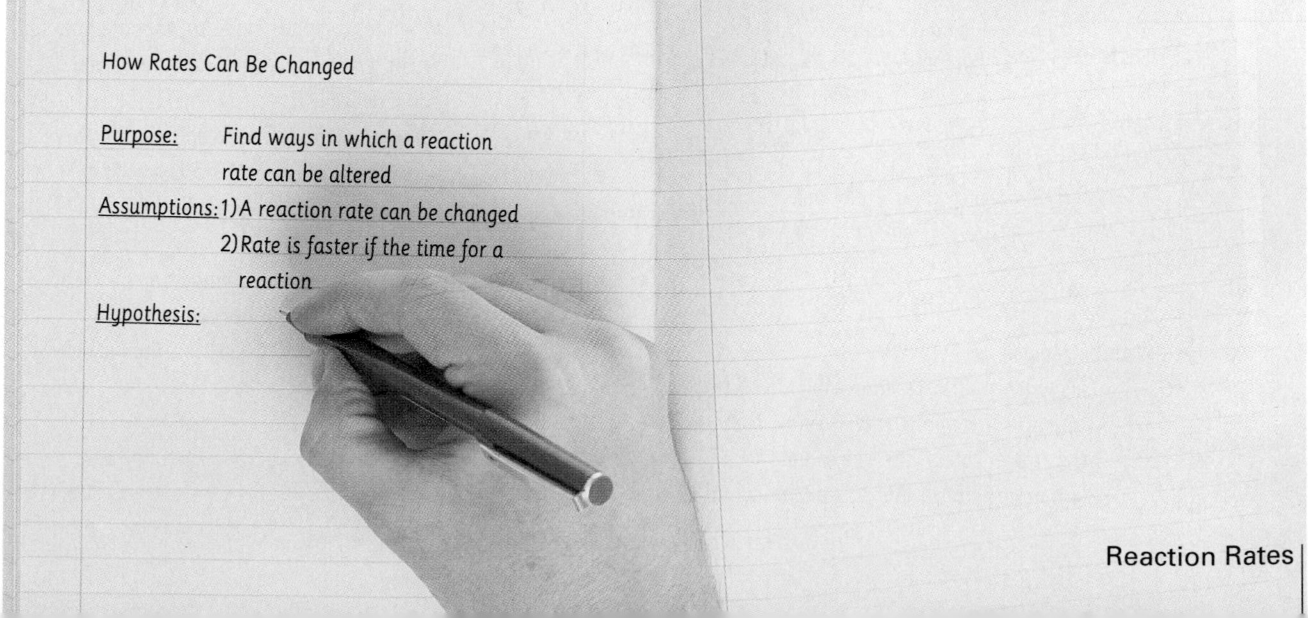

How Rates Can Be Changed
Purpose: Find ways in which a reaction rate can be altered
Assumptions: 1) A reaction rate can be changed
2) Rate is faster if the time for a reaction
Hypothesis:

How Rates Can Be Changed

Purpose: Find ways in which a reaction
            rate can be altered.

Assumptions: 1) A reaction rate can be changed.
              2) Rate is faster if the time for a
                 reaction decreases.

Hypothesis: Powdered aspirin will dissolve faster
             than tablet aspirin, so powdered
             aspirin works faster.

Equipment: 2 coffee cups (identical), drinking
             glass, colorless wooden chopsticks
             or other stirrer, waxed paper pieces,
             hammer or equivalent for crushing
             aspirin tablet, watch with
             second hand or stop watch

Chemicals: water (enough to fill cups—
             several times)
             aspirin tablets (several)
             vinegar (colorless type—
             small bottle)

Set up: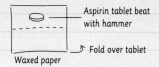

Tablet   Powder

Procedure: 1) Fill cups almost to the brim with
                water from tap
             2) Let it come to room temperature
                while crushing aspirin tablet

Setup — To crush tablet

Aspirin tablet beat
with hammer

Fold over tablet

Waxed paper

             3) Put tablet into cup. Wait. Stir if necessary.
             4) Record time when dissolved.
             5) Put powder into cup. Wait. Stir if necessary.
             6) Record time when dissolved.

Data table:

	Time
Tablet	98 min
Powder	90 min

Other things • Try again using vinegar in the cups instead
to do: of water (stomach is acidic).
              • Try again using 1/2 vinegar and 1/2 water
                 (probably stomach's not all acid).
              • Try again using all warm vinegar.
              • Try again using all warm water
                 (hottest from tap).
              • Try again using ice water
                 (Just for fun and comparison to hot water).

Data Table 2

	All vinegar	1/2 vinegar 1/2 water	Warm vinegar tap	Hot water	Ice water
Tablet	20	37	12	56	> 2 1/2 hrs.
Powder	16	28	7	45	~ 2 1/2 hrs.

Results and Conclusions:

        1) Powder goes faster than tablet in all trials.
           Particle size affects rate: if small, reaction
           goes faster than if the size is big.
        2) Changing from water to vinegar increases

           reaction rate. Probably because of some
           natural difference between water
           and vinegar.
        3) The hot water and warm vinegar have faster
           rates for both powder and tablet compared
           to the cooler room temperature trials.
           Also faster than ice water.
           When temperature goes up, the rate goes up.
           When temperature goes down, the rate goes
           down as well.
        4) Concentrated stuff makes rate go faster
           because the all-vinegar trial went faster
           than the half and half trial.

Summary: Rate speeds up when temperature increases,
           the amount of stuff present increases,
           or the size of stuff decreases. Rate is also
           changed by varying reactants.

a.

HI molecule

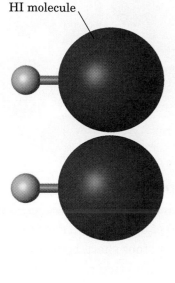

b.

HI molecules

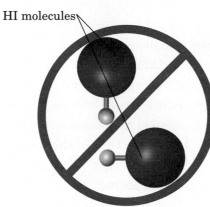

c.

HI molecules

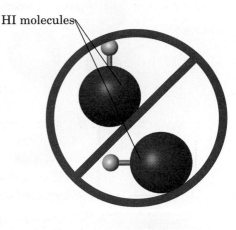

d.

HI molecules

e.

HI molecules

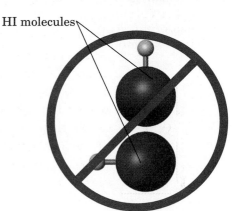

Figure 14-8
If HI molecules collide in any arrangement other that the one shown in a., the collision is ineffective, and no products are formed.

activated complex
a specific arrangement of high-energy reactant atoms or molecules, the decomposition of which leads to product or intermediate molecules; also called transition state

Colliding particles need the right orientation to react

A molecule moves about randomly, hitting one molecule and then another, while changing direction and speed in the process. This movement is similar to that of billiard balls on a crowded pool table. Rolling into a pool table pocket must be like forming a new molecule, George Cynric surmised. It happened sometimes but not all that often compared to the number of times the balls collided on the table top. Still, some pool players could put a particular ball into a pocket of their choosing. Success depended on having the right orientation among the cue ball, the specified playing ball, and the chosen pocket.

Molecules in motion are like the billiard balls. They must collide at just the right orientation in order to react. How specific the orientation must be depends on the type of bonding in the molecules as well as their spatial configuration. An effective collision between particles forms an activated complex. The **activated complex** is an unstable structure that represents the transition between the breaking of old bonds and the formation of new bonds. Therefore, the complexity of reacting particles, along with their geometry at the time of collision, plays a important role in collision effectiveness.

Figure 14-8 shows the orientation needed for two HI molecules to form an activated complex that can split apart to form H_2 and I_2. The chances of a collision being effective are increased when the colliding particles are less complex as in **Figure 14-9** on the next page.

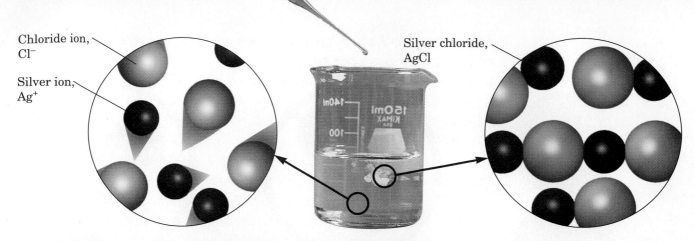

Chloride ion,
Cl⁻

Silver ion,
Ag⁺

Silver chloride,
AgCl

Figure 14-9
Both Ag^+ and Cl^- ions are spherically symmetrical. All orientations can produce an effective collision.

Colliding particles also need a minimum amount of energy in order to react

Even if the billiard balls and pocket were in the correct alignment, a specified ball does not always roll into the pocket. Sometimes it stops short, bounces off, or is followed into the pocket by the cue ball. It appears that a specified ball also needed a certain amount of energy as well as proper orientation. This is also true for molecules. They may collide with the proper orientation, but not have the energy needed to react, in which case the collision is not effective and no activated complex is formed.

Generalized energy diagrams for the decomposition of HI and the formation of AgCl are shown in **Figure 14-10**. Notice the shape and height of the curve in each graph. You learned in Chapter 7 that energy of activation, E_a, is the minimum amount of energy needed for colliding molecules to react. E_a is represented by the distance between the reactants' energy and the top of the energy hill. Therefore, when the curve is short, the value for E_a is small, and only a small amount of energy is required to get molecules over the hill. In **Figure 14-10b**, no energy is required to get oppositely charged ions together, so $E_a = 0$. Conversely, when the curve is tall, E_a is large, and a great deal of energy is required to get molecules over the hill.

Figure 14-10
The difference in energy between reactants and the peak of the potential energy curve is the energy of activation, E_a. The peak of the curve represents the energy of an activated complex.

Different Reactions Have Different Values for E_a

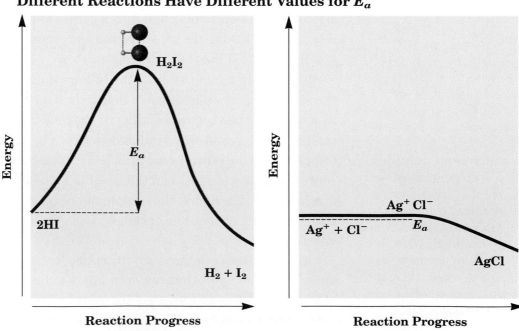

Effective collisions must have energies equal to or greater than E_a

If two properly oriented molecules collide with energy equal to or greater than E_a for the reaction, they form an activated complex. An activated complex is represented by H_2I_2 in the HI decomposition reaction. The activated complex can then rearrange to form products.

If the energy of the collision is less than E_a, the collision will not be effective; bonds will not be broken. So how can we increase the amount of energy in a reactant sample so that collisions will have sufficient energy to break bonds? Increasing temperature adds energy to the system by increasing the random kinetic energy of the particles. This increase in energy could be modeled by the breaking of racked billiard balls. A gentle hit, as shown in Figure 14-11 corresponds to a low temperature while the forceful hit corresponds to a higher temperature. The dashed line surrounding the outermost location of the balls after being hit by the cue ball looks somewhat like the Maxwell-Boltzman distribution curve shown in Chapter 7, where you learned that for a reaction to occur, molecules must collide with enough energy to exceed the activation energy of the reaction. But how can we tell how much kinetic energy reactants have at a given temperature?

Figure 14-11a
Low temperatures, modeled by the movement of gently hit billiard balls, provide less heat energy for activation of molecules than . . .

14-11b
. . . high temperatures, which are modeled by the movement of billiard balls that have been hit forcefully.

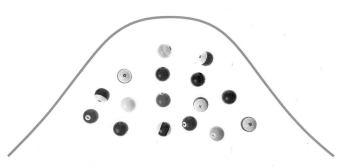

Low temperature, narrow energy distribution

High temperature, wide energy distribution

Temperature and reaction rates
Molecules at the same temperature have a range of energies

Think back to your study of gases in Chapter 10. In a sample of oxygen gas at 25°C, all the molecules have the same mass, but they do not all have the same velocity; therefore, they do not all have the same kinetic energy because of the following relationship.

$$KE = \frac{1}{2}mv^2$$

Figure 14-12 represents the kinetic energy distribution of particles in a sample of oxygen gas at 25°C. The values on this graph have been verified by experiments. What does this graph mean? The area under the curve represents the range of kinetic energies for all the particles in a sample. You see from the distribution that those molecules with the highest energies (on the right side of the graph) are few in number. The molecules with the lowest energies (on the left side of the graph) are also few in number. The majority of molecules have energies close to the peak of the graph. The average kinetic energy of the gas sample is the reading that represents the largest number of molecules. This value can be used to calculate the average velocity of the molecules in the sample.

Recall from the discussion of kinetic molecular theory in Chapter 10 that the distribution of molecular velocities is sensitive to temperature. Because kinetic energy is related to velocity, you would predict that the average kinetic energy of gas molecules and the distribution of molecular energies would also vary with temperature. So how would changing the temperature affect the energy distribution? How would the number of effective collisions be changed by increasing the temperature?

Figure 14-12
At low temperatures, most of the molecules have low KE, which accounts for the high peaked curve at the left end of the KE axis.

Energy Distribution of O₂ at 25°C

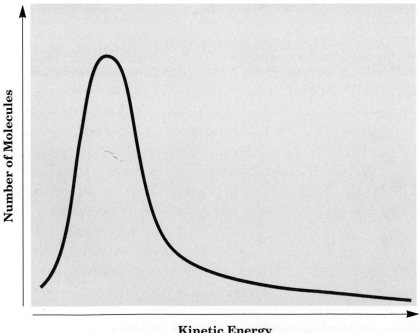

Number of Molecules

Kinetic Energy

Figure 14-13

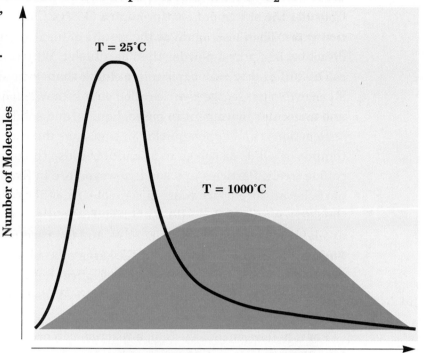

Effect of Temperature on KE of O₂

The number of effective collisions increases with increasing temperature

Figure 14-13 shows what happens to the sample of O_2 when it has been heated to 1000°C. The shape of the curve changes showing that the distribution changes. The curve is not as high and is more spread out. The molecules show a greater range of kinetic energies at the higher temperature, and the average kinetic energy of the sample is greater. An increase in temperature increases the average kinetic energy of an O_2 molecule; this can result in a greater number of effective collisions when O_2 is reacted with another substance. Cooling a reaction system has the opposite effect. Molecules move more slowly and collide with less energy, producing fewer effective collisions.

Rates of reaction increase (or decrease) as temperature increases (or decreases)

Look back at the results and conclusions George Cynric made concerning temperature and the reactions between vinegar and the aspirin. In both cases the time needed to dissolve decreased. Rates increased with temperature regardless of whether the aspirin was in tablet or powdered form. This observation indicates that temperature affects rate. When the reaction temperature was lowered by using an ice bath, both reactions slowed down, reinforcing the conclusion that temperature affects rate. Together these observations show that rate increases (or decreases) when temperature increases (or decreases) just as the kinetic theory suggests. For many common reactions, the reaction rate doubles for every 10°C rise in temperature.

Figure 14-14

The plates on the back of a stegosaurus may have gathered heat from the sunlight to warm the dinosaur's body. As the body heated up, the dinosaur could move less sluggishly.

Surface area and reaction rates

Consider the statement that prompted George Cynric to investigate reaction rates. Then look again at the results of his investigation. The aspirin dissolved faster as a powder than as a tablet. Why would water molecules collide differently with aspirin in a chunk than with aspirin in tiny pieces? To answer this George Cynric called on his knowledge of reaction processes and molecular movement in gases, liquids, and solids.

Reactions can happen quickly in a gaseous mixture or a liquid mixture (liquids or solids dissolved in a liquid) because the particles can mix and collide freely. Particles in a solid, however, are in fixed positions; only particles at the surface come in contact with other reactants. Therefore, if the surface area of the solid could be increased, the number of particles available for reaction would increase, and the reaction rate would increase. Figure 14-15 shows how the surface area of a solid can be increased by dividing the solid into smaller pieces. Notice that crushing a solid reactant increases the surface area of that reactant. It also increases the rate of any reaction in which the solid participates, as George Cynric observed.

For a heterogeneous system, a reaction can occur between a gas and a liquid, a gas and a solid, or a liquid and a solid. The rate of the reaction with a solid reactant depends on the exposed area of the solid reactant. The rate usually increases if the surface area is increased but still tends to be slower overall than a reaction between two liquids or two gases.

Figure 14-15a
Division of a solid . . .

14-15b
. . . makes the exposed surface of the solid larger.

14-15c
More divisions means more exposed surface, . . .

14-15d
. . . hence more spots are available for . . .

14-15e
. . . other reactant molecules to collide into.

Nature of reactants and also concentration affect reaction rates

Regardless of what products are formed, reactions involve the making and breaking of bonds. The rate at which bonds break and re-form depends on the type of bond and the nature of the molecules in which the bonds are found. Some processes, like the Mg in HCl reaction take place very rapidly, while others, like the oxidation of lead by oxygen dissolved in water takes place very slowly, if at all. The nature of a reactant cannot be adjusted to improve reaction rate.

Figure 14-16

Pieces of magnesium ribbon react more rapidly with HCl in the beaker on the right because it is more concentrated than the HCl in the beaker on the left.

Increasing concentration increases the number of effective collisions

George Cynric concluded that increasing the concentration of a reactant increases the reaction rate because his aspirin sample dissolved faster in pure vinegar than in the vinegar and water mixture. Likewise when Mg is added to an HCl solution that is more concentrated than the one in Section 14-1, the reaction rate noticeably increases as shown in **Figure 14-16**. Remember that reaction rate represents the number of effective collisions per unit of time. Therefore, if the number of effective collisions increases, the rate increases as well. The model in **Figure 14-17** shows how an increase in concentration can increase the number of effective collisions.

The mathematical relationship between reactant concentration and reaction rate is at times very simple and at other times very complicated. This is because most reactions occur in more than one step even though only one of these steps determines the rate. The molecules participating in this **rate-determining step** govern the form of the relationship between rate and concentration. What are the steps by which a reaction occurs? How is concentration related to reaction rate and the individual steps in a reaction?

rate-determining step

the slowest step in a reaction mechanism

Figure 14-17a
One possible collision can occur between two reactants, A and B.

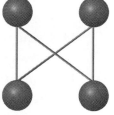

14-17b
Four possible collisions can occur in this system.

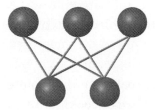

14-17c
Six possible collisions can occur in this system.

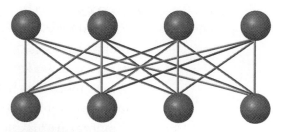

14-17d
Sixteen possible collisions can occur in this system.

10. Arrange the following three energy curves in order of increasing E_a values. If each curve is a separate reaction, which reaction would you predict to be the slowest?

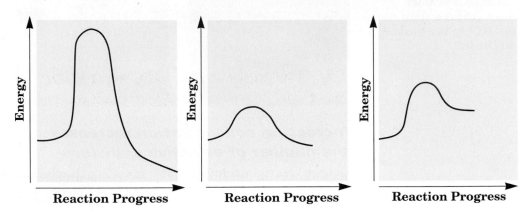

11. Look at the following two equations. Predict which would be slower and why.
    a. $Cu(s) + Cl_2(g) \longrightarrow CuCl_2(s)$
    b. $2KOH(aq) + Mg(NO_3)_2(aq) \longrightarrow Mg(OH)_2(s) + 2KNO_3(aq)$

12. For each of the following pairs, choose the substance or process you would expect to react more rapidly.
    a. 5 cm of thick platinum wire or 5 cm of thin platinum wire
    b. granulated sugar or powdered sugar
    c. zinc in HCl at 20°C or zinc in HCl at 35°C
    d. cooking hamburgers with moist heat or with dry heat.
    e. a spark igniting a gallon of gasoline an hour after it is spilled in a warehouse or in the trunk of a car.

13. A reaction occurs in 30 s as evidenced by a color change. The same color change occurs when the reaction is run at a lower temperature, but this time it takes 60 s. Is the rate of the second reaction faster or slower than the first?

14. Using what you know about the energy of molecules, explain why reaction rates vary with temperature.

15. Compare and contrast the terms *activation energy* and *activated complex*.

16. Compare the potential energies of the following components of a reaction, all at the same temperature: reactants, activated complex, and products.

17. When will a collision lead to chemical reaction?

18. Identify the factor that affects a reaction rate but cannot be adjusted itself.

 19. **Story Link**
    Explain why Jack in the Box added an extra flipping of the burger to their cooking process.

20. **Story Link**
    Which method is better for cooking a thick piece of food, cooking it for 10 minutes at a high temperature or cooking it for 20 minutes at a lower temperature? Explain your answer.

How can reaction rate be described?

Section Objectives

Derive a rate law from graphs relating concentration to time.

Given a rate law expression, determine the effects of changing concentrations on the rate.

Explain the relationship between the rate-determining step and the overall rate.

Explain the general effect of catalysts on a reaction mechanism and reaction rate.

The general rate law equation

Rate is directly proportional to reactant concentration, [A], raised to some power, n.

$$\text{rate} \propto [A]^n$$

This proportionality is made into an equality by the inclusion of k, an experimentally determined constant.

$$\text{rate} = k[A]^n$$

rate law
a mathematical expression for the rate of a reaction as a function of the concentration of one or more reactants: rate = k[A]^n[B]^m

order
the exponent for a specified reactant in a rate law expression

This equation is the general **rate law**. The exponent, n, on the reactant concentration indicates to what extent the rate for a given reaction depends on concentration. The exponent is called the **order** of reaction with respect to [A] and must be determined from experimental data. More specifically, if the concentration is doubled and the rate doubles as well, the exponent has a value of 1 and is read "first order." If the rate does not change when the concentration is doubled, the exponent has a value of 0 and is read "zero order." An exponent of 2, or second order, means the rate quadruples when the concentration is doubled. Determining the value of the exponent from graphs of experimental data for a specific reaction is part of deriving the rate law for that reaction.

Do not confuse the exponents in the rate law with those in an equilibrium equation. They are not obtained in the same way. Exponents in equilibrium equations are coefficients in the balanced chemical equation; *exponents in the rate law are derived from experimental data.* The equilibrium expression for the decomposition of N_2O_5 is derived from its balanced chemical equation on page 542 of Section 14-1.

$$K_{eq} = \frac{[NO_2]^4[O_2]}{[N_2O_5]^2}$$

N_2O_5 has an exponent of 2 because its coefficient in the balanced chemical equation is 2. However, the rate expression for this same reaction is the following.

$$\text{rate} = k[N_2O_5]^1$$

N_2O_5 has an exponent of 1. The reason the exponents differ lies within the differences between thermodynamics and kinetics, and is outside the scope of this text. The important point to remember is that exponents in rate equations must be determined experimentally.

From Section 14-1 you know that rate is a calculated quantity. It is a ratio found by monitoring the change in some property during a specified time interval and then dividing the change by the elapsed time. You also learned that the units for rate must always be expressed and that for chemical reactions these units are usually concentration per unit of time. Data taken from rate experiments, then, must be related to concentration and time. The conditions under which the experiment is run must also be recorded because rate is dependent on other variables, as discussed in Section 14-2. Once experimental data have been collected, they can be analyzed through graphs made from the collected data.

Rate laws can be derived from plots of concentration vs. time

Look again at the concentration vs. time plot for N_2O_5 in **Figure 14-6**. The reactant concentration decreases as time passes, so the slope of the curve decreases, changing ever so slightly from one point to the next. As mentioned in Section 14-1, rate is described by the slope of the curve, so the rate also decreases with time. This continuous change in slope is described mathematically through a process called integration. Integration is beyond the scope of this book, but its result, the *integrated rate equation*, tells chemists what they could plot to get a straight line from which the exponent in the rate law can be determined.

To illustrate, the general rate law has the following form when the exponent is 1.

$$rate = k[A]^1$$

After integration, you get the following equation.

$$\log [A]_t = k't + \log [A]_0$$

So when a plot of log [A] vs. time results in a straight line, the exponent on the concentration term of the general rate law is 1, or first order. Doubling the concentration of A doubles the rate because the order of reaction with respect to [A] is 1. Tripling the concentration of A triples the rate.

The $[N_2O_5]$ vs. time curve in **Figure 14-6** has been replotted as log $[N_2O_5]$ vs. time in **Figure 14-18**. The straight line tells you that the exponent on $[N_2O_5]$ in the general rate law is 1, so the reaction is first order in $[N_2O_5]$.

Figure 14-18
A first order relationship between concentration and reaction rate is verified when a log [A] vs. time plot gives a straight line.

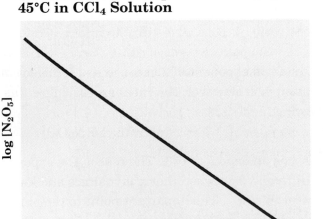

Log of the Concentration of N_2O_5 vs. Time for the Decomposition of N_2O_5 at 45°C in CCl₄ Solution

log $[N_2O_5]$

Time (s)

The Order for a Given Reactant is Determined by Graphing Some Form of Concentration Data

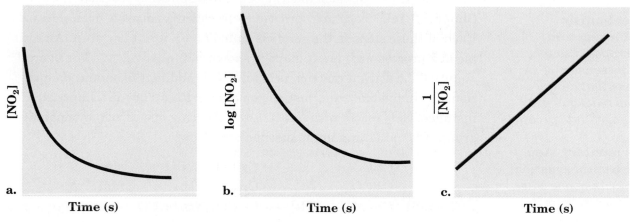

Figure 14-19
A second order relationship between reaction rate and concentration is verified when a graph of 1/[A] vs. time is a straight line.

The concentration vs. time graph for NO_2 decomposition in **Figure 14-19a** is also a curve with decreasing slope. Will the decomposition of NO_2 be first order like N_2O_5? The log $[NO_2]$ vs. time plot in **Figure 14-19b** is not a straight line. Therefore, the exponent for NO_2 in the rate equation is not 1. The experimenter must try something else. The integrated rate equation for an exponent of 2 suggests plotting 1/[A] vs. time. Such a plot for $[NO_2]$ results in a straight line, as shown in **Figure 14-19c**. The general rate law for this reaction is written as follows.

$$\text{rate} = k[NO_2]^2$$

The reaction is second order in NO_2. There is an x^2 relationship between concentration and rate; therefore, doubling the concentration of NO_2 quadruples (2^2) the rate. Tripling the concentration of NO_2 increases the rate by a factor of 9, or 3^2.

The rates calculated so far were for reactions involving only one reactant. But what about cases in which there are two or more reactants?

To handle situations in which more than one reactant is present, we revive the concept of a limiting reagent, first introduced in Chapter 8. When the limiting reagent is used up, the reaction stops. Analysis of the resulting mixture shows that in addition to the products, some of the excess reactant, is present. But if this excess reactant is grossly in excess, its concentration does not appear to change, so any change in the rate of reaction is due to the limiting reagent. This means then that for reactions in which two reactants, A and B, take part, two sets of data are recorded. In the first set, A is the limiting reagent, and B is in great excess. For the second set of data, B is the limiting reagent while A is in great excess. An appropriate concentration vs. time graph is plotted for each set of data. From them, the values for the exponents, n and m, are determined. The general rate law for the two reactants, A and B, is written as follows.

order of reaction
the sum of all the exponents on all concentration terms in a rate law expression

$$\text{rate} = k[A]^n[B]^m$$

[A] is the concentration of the first reactant, and n is its order. [B] is the concentration of the second reactant, and m is its order. The overall **order of reaction** is $m + n$.

Rate law and the reaction process

Most chemical reactions, like the cellular respiration reaction discussed in Chapter 9, take place in a series of steps called a pathway or **mechanism**. Each of these steps in the series is called an **elementary step**. An example of a process with many steps is shown in **Figure 14-20**. The overall equation for a given reaction is obtained by adding the balanced equations for individual steps just as you did for Hess's law in Chapter 9. For instance, NH_3 reacts with $Cr(CO)_6$ by replacing one carbon monoxide group (CO) according to the mechanism below.

Step 1:	$Cr(CO)_6$	$\longrightarrow Cr(CO)_5 + CO$	**slow**
Step 2:	$Cr(CO)_5 + NH_3 \longrightarrow Cr(CO)_5NH_3$		**fast**
Overall:	$Cr(CO)_6 + NH_3 \longrightarrow Cr(CO)_5NH_3 + CO$		

The slowest step determines the rate and defines the rate law

Although the elementary steps of a reaction occur in a particular order depending on the reacting substances, they do not all occur at the same rate. Some steps are slower than others. The slowest step determines the rate of the reaction and defines the rate law. If you know the reaction mechanism, you can write the rate law from the balanced equation for the slowest elementary step. The exponents for reactant concentrations are equal to their coefficients in the balanced equation for the slowest step. For the $Cr(CO)_6$ and NH_3 reaction, Step 1 is the slowest. It is rate determining. Because the rate law is defined by the slowest step, it can be written directly from the slowest step as follows.

$$rate = k[Cr(CO)_6]^1$$

Another example is the reaction between $CHCl_3$ and Cl_2. The following mechanism has been determined experimentally.

Step 1:	$Cl_2(g)$	$\rightleftharpoons 2Cl\cdot(g)$	**fast and reversible**
Step 2:	$Cl\cdot(g)$	$+ CHCl_3(g) \longrightarrow HCl(g) + \cdot CCl_3(g)$	**slow**
Step 3:	$\cdot CCl_3(g)$	$+ Cl\cdot(g) \longrightarrow CCl_4(g)$	**fast**
Overall:	$CHCl_3(g) + Cl_2(g)$	$\longrightarrow HCl(g) + CCl_4$	

Sidebar definitions

mechanism (of a reaction)

a proposed step-by-step sequence of reactions that describes how reactants are changed into products

elementary step

a chemical equation describing one stage of a reaction as it is theorized to occur

Figure 14-20
Some mechanisms are easier to figure out than others! But one step leads to the next just like a chemical reaction.

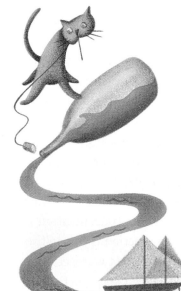

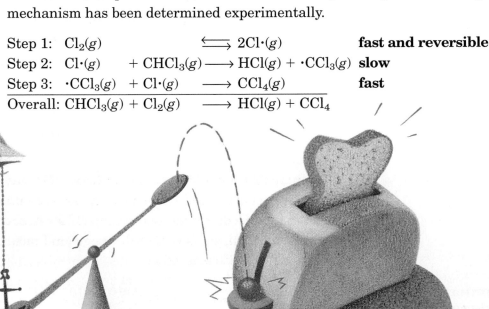

The rate law is written directly from Step 2 because it is the slowest step.

$$\text{rate} = k[\text{Cl·}][\text{CHCl}_3]$$

Rates are usually written in terms of the reactants that appear in the overall balanced equation for the reaction. Cl· is not such a reactant. It is a reaction **intermediate** formed in Step 1, which is an equilibrium reaction, so [Cl·] is proportional to $[\text{Cl}_2]^{1/2}$, and the rate law can be written using only the concentrations of original reactants according to these equations.

$$[\text{Cl·}] = (K_{eq})^{1/2}[\text{Cl}_2]^{1/2}$$

$$\text{rate} = k'[\text{Cl}_2]^{1/2}[\text{CHCl}_3]$$

intermediate
a structure formed in one elementary step, but consumed in a later step of a mechanism. It is neither an original reactant nor final product

From the rate law, the overall balanced equation, and experimental evidence for any reaction intermediates, we can propose pathways consistent with the data and design further experiments to test the proposals and reduce our choices. Still it is not always possible to identify just one mechanistic pathway for a reaction.

Concept Review

Reaction mechanism

21. Determine the overall balanced equation for a reaction having the following proposed mechanism.

Step 1: $\text{OCl}^- + \text{H}_2\text{O} \rightleftharpoons \text{HOCl} + \text{OH}^-$ **rapid**
Step 2: $\text{HOCl} + \text{I}^- \longrightarrow \text{HOI} + \text{Cl}^-$ **slow**
Step 3: $\text{HOI} + \text{OH}^- \rightleftharpoons \text{H}_2\text{O} + \text{OI}^-$ **fast**

22. How many elementary steps are in the proposed mechanism in item **21**?
23. Identify the slowest step for the mechanism in item **21**. Write the rate law for the reaction.
24. List the reaction intermediates found in item **21**.
25. When two I *atoms* collide to form an iodine molecule, I_2, in the presence of He, the He absorbs excess heat and stabilizes the I_2 molecule while the bond is being formed. Use the following mechanism to write the rate law in terms of the original reactants.

$$\text{I·} + \text{He} \longrightarrow \text{HeI·} \quad \textbf{fast}$$
$$\text{HeI·} + \text{I·} \longrightarrow \text{He} + \text{I}_2 \quad \textbf{slow}$$

Pathways are modified by catalysts

The energy diagram for a reaction indicates that if the height of the energy hill is increased, the rate slows down. If the height of the hill is reduced, the rate speeds up. Lowering the energy hill means changing the reaction mechanism and requires a catalyst. A catalyst lowers the energy barrier by forming an activated complex of lower energy than the one formed in the uncatalyzed reaction. In short, it provides the reactant molecules an energetically more favorable pathway to the products. The process by which a catalyst increases a reaction rate is **catalysis**.

catalysis
the process by which reaction rates are increased by the addition of a catalyst

Hydrogen peroxide, H_2O_2, decomposes slowly over time, as represented by the following reaction.

$$2H_2O_2(aq) \longrightarrow 2H_2O(l) + O_2(g)$$

A relatively pure 30% solution of H_2O_2 will decompose at a rate of 0.5% per year at room temperature. This rate corresponds to the uncatalyzed curve with an E_a of 75 kJ/mol in the energy diagram for the decomposition of H_2O_2 shown in **Figure 14-21**. E_a is lowered to 58 kJ/mol, if iodide ions, I^-, are added to the peroxide solution. The I^- ions form a reaction intermediate, HIO^-, when they react with H_2O_2 molecules. The HIO^- ions then react with other H_2O_2 molecules to regenerate iodide ions as products are formed. The I^- ions are a **catalyst** for the decomposition of H_2O_2 because they are added into the reaction to increase the reaction rate but are not actually used up in the reaction. Because catalysts are not consumed, they can be recycled almost indefinitely. Catalysts sometimes appear in equations written above the arrow.

$$2H_2O_2(aq) \xrightarrow{\text{KI}} 2H_2O(l) + O_2(g)$$

Catalase and manganese dioxide also catalyze the decomposition of H_2O_2 by lowering the E_a for the reaction to 4 kJ/mol or less. Note that although a catalyst changes the value for E_a of a reaction, the value of ΔH for the reaction is left unchanged. If a reaction is exothermic without a catalyst, it is exothermic to the same extent with a catalyst.

catalyst

a substance added to a chemical reaction to increase the rate and that can be recovered chemically unchanged after the reaction is complete

Figure 14-21
The activation energy for a reaction can be reduced by adding a catalyst. Some catalysts work better than others.

Comparison of Pathways for the Decomposition of H_2O_2 by Various Catalysts

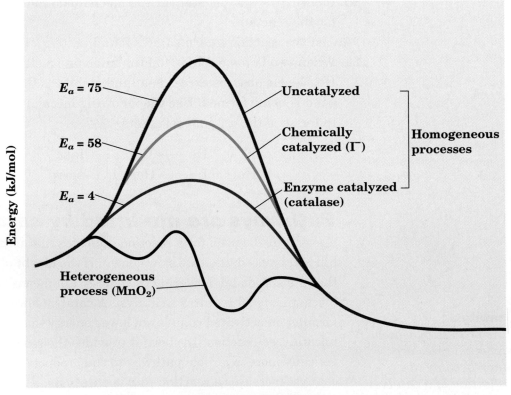

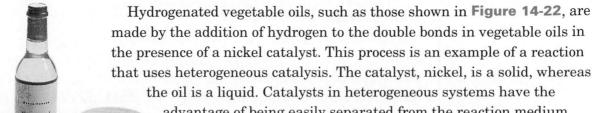

Hydrogenated vegetable oils, such as those shown in **Figure 14-22**, are made by the addition of hydrogen to the double bonds in vegetable oils in the presence of a nickel catalyst. This process is an example of a reaction that uses heterogeneous catalysis. The catalyst, nickel, is a solid, whereas the oil is a liquid. Catalysts in heterogeneous systems have the advantage of being easily separated from the reaction medium. A generalized comparison of E_a values for a homogeneously and heterogeneously catalyzed reaction appears in **Figure 14-21** on the previous page.

Figure 14-22
The naturally occurring liquid vegetable oils are converted to solid fats by catalytic addition of hydrogen.

enzyme
large protein molecule that catalyzes chemical reactions in living things

substrate
(biochemical) the molecule or molecules with which an enzyme interacts

Enzymes are nature's catalysts

Catalysts found in biological systems are called **enzymes**. Enzymes are large proteins. Like all catalysts, enzymes are not used up in a reaction, so only small amounts are needed. However, unlike most catalysts, enzymes are highly specific for a particular reaction or type of reaction. This high degree of specificity is possible because the enzyme molecule has a three-dimensional conformation. That is, the enzyme has a special location patterned to receive a particular type of reactant, much like the way that a lock is designed to receive a particular key. Look at the interaction between the enzyme and substrate shown in **Figure 14-23**. The **substrate** has to have the correct structure to bind to the enzyme and to be acted upon by the enzyme's active site. It is at the active site of the enzyme molecule that catalysis takes place. During the catalytic process, the enzyme's active site distorts the bonds in the substrate, forcing it to look more like the product. This distortion strains the substrate's bonds and weakens them. The reaction progresses more rapidly because the weaker bonds possess less energy, making the E_a value lower than that for the uncatalyzed reaction. When the substrate is most closely aligned with the active site, the activated complex at the top of the energy hill is formed. After this point, the enzyme will be restored, and the product will be formed. In some cases, there is an enzyme-product complex as an intermediate prior to the formation of the product. The overall ΔH for the reaction has not been changed, but the activation energy has been lowered.

Figure 14-23a
Energy of the system increases as the substrate nears the active site of the enzyme.

Figure 14-23c
Energy of the system decreases as products form and the enzyme is restored.

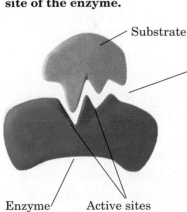

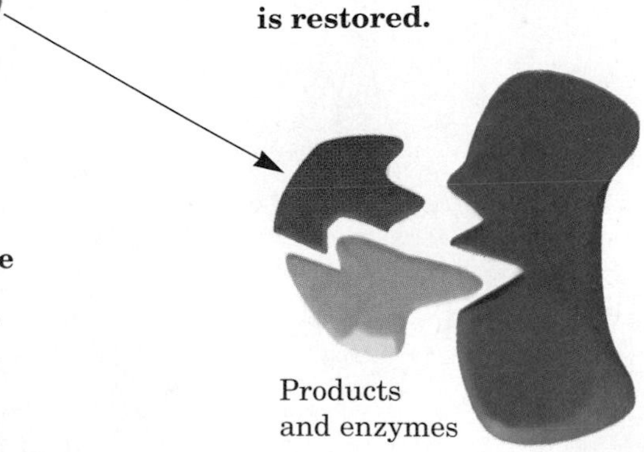

Substrate

Activated complex

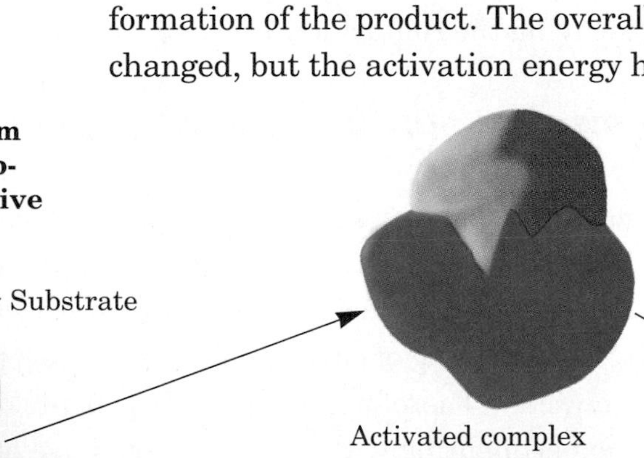

Figure 14-23b
The substrate-enzyme activated complex occurs at the peak of the reaction's energy curve.

Enzyme   Active sites

Products and enzymes

Enzymes in action

Enzymes in the body speed up the chemical processes that sustain life. Most reactions in the body are so complex that if they were not catalyzed, they would require extremely high temperatures to occur at rates fast enough for life to continue. Fortunately, enzymes alter reaction pathways so that the complex reactions of metabolism occur at 37°C (98.6°F) at a rate several billion times faster than they would without a catalyst. Life could not exist without the action of enzymes.

Enzyme supplements reduce the effects of lactose intolerance

Some people lose the ability to produce lactase, a digestive enzyme that cuts lactose, the sugar found in many dairy products. These people have what is known as lactose intolerance. Undigested lactose molecules collect in the intestine and attract water. As a result, a person with lactose intolerance can experience painful cramps or diarrhea after ingesting foods with lactose. Enzyme supplements are available that can be added to or taken with milk to hydrolyze the lactose and form its constituent sugars, glucose and galactose. The human body has hundreds of other highly specialized enzymes that control growth, reproduction, and other processes.

Enzymatic cleansers reduce protein buildup on lenses

Modern contact lenses are made of hydrophilic plastics that bind a great deal of water. Most lenses are gas permeable to enable sensitive corneas to receive enough oxygen. However, the protein matter in tears can clog the pores in contact lenses making both lenses and eyes susceptible to bacterial growth and possibly serious damage. Protein build-up is removed from the lenses by special enzymatic cleaners. Depending on the brand of cleaner, these enzymes are papain, pancreatin, or subtilisin. These enzymes are known as proteases because they cut proteins into small pieces that can be washed away, leaving the contact lenses clear and clean.

Figure 14-24
The white albedo in citrus fruits and the pectin in gelling agents can be effectively dissolved using pectinase, a safe-to-use, specific action enzyme.

Enzymes are now being used to peel fruit

Pectin, a long-chain polysaccharide found in many fruits, is the gelling agent in jams and jellies. Wine makers sometimes add an enzyme called pectinase to fruit juices to destroy the pectin and clarify the juices before fermentation. Pectinase can also digest the white inner lining of citrus fruits that makes peeling the fruit difficult. Therefore, a major citrus fruit company is experimenting with the commercial use of pectinase to peel large quantities of fruit quickly and effectively, as shown in **Figure 14-24**. The peels are scored, and the fruits are soaked in a warm solution of pectinase. After soaking, the fruit is rinsed, and the peels come off easily leaving the separate sections of fruit clean and ready to eat. If you live in southern California, you may already have eaten fruit peeled enzymatically.

An inhibitor slows down the rate of a reaction

inhibitor
a substance added to a chemical reaction to slow it down

Inhibitors are used extensively in the plastics industry to help control chain reactions from which polymers are made. Chain reactions occur in steps, so if one of the substances used to build the chain can be removed, the reaction slows down or stops. Inhibitors are added to react with substances that help build the chain.

Inhibitors and catalysts working together

If combustion in an automobile engine were 100% efficient, it would convert gasoline into carbon dioxide and water only. Unfortunately, significant amounts of carbon monoxide and unburned hydrocarbons are also produced and discharged into the air. Therefore, modern cars are equipped with a catalytic converter to reduce pollution. It converts some of the products from incomplete combustion to carbon dioxide and water. Some racing cars are supercharged by adding a nitrogen oxide compound to the fuel mixture. The reaction is complex, but the nitrogen oxide compound alters the mechanism of the combustion reaction and acts as an additional energy source. More energy is released more efficiently than with regular gasoline alone.

Gasoline is a mixture of short-chain hydrocarbons obtained from the fractional distillation of petroleum. Two components of gasoline are shown in **Figure 14-25**. Some of the hydrocarbon chains in the gasoline mixture are straight, and some are branched. The branched chains burn more smoothly and efficiently than the straight chains do. Therefore, the higher the percentage of branched chains in the gasoline mixture, the more efficiently it burns. Nevertheless, if it burns too quickly inside the cylinder, ignition occurs before the piston is in the proper position. Pressure from this early ignition pushes the piston in the opposite direction to that in which it was already traveling. This is a tremendous jolt to the crankshaft, and the subsequent shifting of the crankshaft, pistons, rods, and other parts is heard as knocking. To inhibit the fast combustion that causes knocking, tetraethyl lead was once added to gasoline. At the time, tetraethyl lead was an attractive choice because it mixed readily with gasoline, was inexpensive, and did its job well. However, scientists did not realize how much lead would be dumped into the atmosphere or how serious the effects of lead poisoning would be. Lead itself is a relatively inert metal, but its ions are toxic to most biological systems because they inhibit the actions of enzymes.

These ions also ruin the platinum catalyst in the catalytic converters of most modern cars by covering it with a layer of lead that renders the active sites useless. This is why cars with catalytic converters can use only unleaded fuels. Other antiknock agents such as ethanol and methyl-*t*-butyl ether are now used.

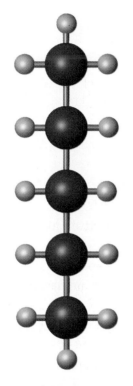

Figure 14-25a
Gasoline is a mixture of hydrocarbons. Some are straight like *n*-pentane, . . .

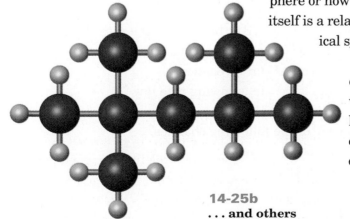

14-25b
. . . and others are branched like isooctane.

26. Lowering E_a for a reaction makes the reaction go faster but does not affect the overall ΔH of reaction. Consider the E_a values in the reaction diagramed below. Which, if any, would speed up the reaction if lowered? Support your answer.

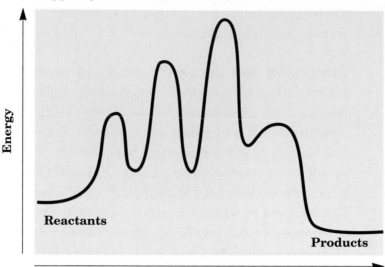

Reaction Progress

27. The observed rate law for the reaction of NO with Cl_2 is written as follows.

$$\text{rate} = k[NO]^2[Cl_2]$$

What is the order of reaction with respect to NO? with respect to Cl_2? How would the axes be labeled on a concentration versus time plot for each reactant in order to obtain a linear relationship?

28. How does a reactant with an exponent of zero in the rate law affect the reaction rate?

29. Nitric oxide can be reduced with hydrogen gas to give nitrogen and water vapor.

$$2NO(g) + 2H_2(g) \longrightarrow N_2(g) + 2H_2O(g)$$

A proposed mechanism for this reaction follows.

Step 1: $2NO \rightleftharpoons N_2O_2$ **fast**
Step 2: $N_2O_2 + H_2 \longrightarrow N_2O + H_2O$ **slow**
Step 3: $N_2O + H_2 \longrightarrow H_2O + N_2$ **fast**

Identify the rate-determining step. Write the rate law.

30. If the rate of a reaction is expressed by $k[B]^2$, how would the rate change if the initial concentration of B were increased by a factor of 1.5?

31. What effect does a catalyst have on ΔH for a reaction?

32. A particular reaction is found to have the following rate law.

$$\text{rate} = k[A][B]^2$$

How is the rate affected by each of the following changes?

a. the initial concentration of A is cut in half

b. the initial concentration of B is tripled

c. a catalyst is added

d. the temperature is increased

e. the concentration of A is doubled, but the concentration of B is cut in half

Conclusion: Kinetics and Cooking Hamburgers

At the beginning of this chapter you learned that *E. coli* 0157:H7 is responsible for meat spoilage and food poisoning. Destruction of this bacteria is related to the meat's internal cooking temperature. These points raised questions about the rate of bacterial growth and the factors that affect it. Look at these questions again.

How does temperature affect the preparation of raw meat? Chilling or freezing meat slows down decomposition reactions and bacterial growth. But warming the meat increases those reactions up to the bacteria's maximum reproduction temperature. At temperatures higher than this point, the bacteria die.

But most bacteria do not die immediately, so the meat must remain in contact with the higher temperatures long enough for its internal temperature to rise to the point that the bacteria are destroyed. Otherwise the warm center of the meat may still harbor live bacteria that multiply freely.

What are some effective methods for preserving meat? Preservation involves practices that retard bacterial growth. Bacteria are deposited on the surface of the meat through physical contact or exposure to the air. The relatively neutral pH of raw meat favors bacterial growth but lower pH values do not. In the slaughterhouse, the pH level of meat can be reduced by applying an acetic-acid-based antibacterial spray to the surface of the animal carcass after its hide is removed and before it is cut open.

The moisture in meat can be reduced by adding salt or by drying. These processes are effective preservation methods because bacteria seldom grow on foods with low water content.

Bacteria acquired during processing can be destroyed by bombarding packaged meat with gamma rays. The irradiation destroys the bacteria and the packaging prevents the surface from being recontaminated until the package is opened.

Applying Concepts

1. Water boils at a lower temperature on top of a mountain than at sea level. Explain the effect this has on the time needed to boil a hard egg.
2. Decomposition reactions involving O_2 or CO_2 present in the air cause meat to feel slimy and smell spoiled. Explain why meat spoils less rapidly when wrapped or left unsliced.

Research and Writing
Use the library to find out more about the following.
1. Write an editorial for your school or local newspaper that discusses the use of enzymes for destroying hazardous waste.
2. Why are expiration dates placed on foods and medications? Which government agencies require such dates?

Highlights

Key terms

activated complex
average rate
catalysis
catalyst
chemical kinetics
elementary step
enzyme
inhibitor
initial rate

intermediate
mechanism
order
order of reaction
rate-determining step
rate law
reaction rate
substrate

 ## What is a reaction rate?

- The average reaction rate is expressed as the ratio between a measured change in a physical property or concentration and the time interval during which the change took place.
- Rates generally decrease as time passes.

 ## How can reaction rates be explained?

- Factors affecting reaction rate include the nature of the reactants, concentration, temperature, and surface area. Increasing the concentration, temperature, or surface area increases the reaction rate because the number of collisions between reactants increases.
- Not all collisions result in a reaction. Particles must have the proper orientation and sufficient kinetic energy to break the chemical bonds in the reactants so that new bonds can form.

How can reaction rates be described?

- The reaction rate is proportional to the reactant concentration raised to some power. This exponent must be determined experimentally for each reaction.
- The mechanism of a reaction usually involves a step-by-step sequence. The slowest step determines the rate law and is called the rate-determining step.
- Catalysts increase the reaction rate by lowering the energy barrier for the reaction. Catalysts can be recovered unchanged after the reaction is complete. Inhibitors slow down the reaction.

Key problem-solving approach: Determining reaction order

Write and balance the chemical equation for the reaction; then follow the flowchart to determine the overall order of reaction.

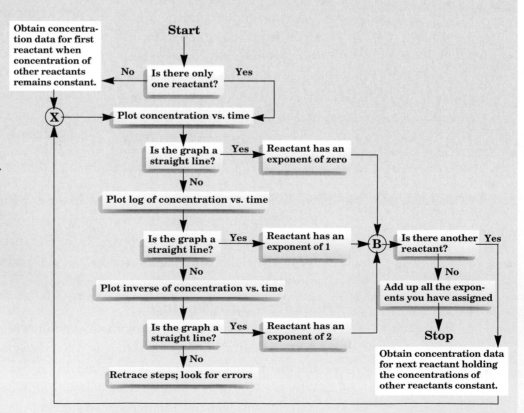

Review and Assess

Clocking chemical reactions

1. Describe the rate for each of the following, using appropriate units.
   a. water dripping from a leaky faucet
   b. walking speed on an exercise path
   c. a fan blade rotating
   d. water evaporating from a 1 L container
2. Write a rate expression for the decomposition of acetoacetic acid into acetone and carbon dioxide.

   $$CH_3C(O)CH_2COOH(l) \longrightarrow$$
   $$CH_3C(O)CH_3(l) + CO_2(g)$$

3. a. List four physical properties or observations that can be measured during the course of a reaction to determine reaction rate.
   b. For the four physical properties that you listed, what laboratory equipment would be necessary for making accurate measurements?
4. Why are some reaction rate expressions multiplied by a factor of -1?
5. Why not use a factor of -1 in the rate expression when the change in concentration of a product over time is being measured?
6. Why would measuring the rate of the following reaction be difficult?

   $$H_2(g) + CO_2(g) \longrightarrow H_2O(g) + CO(g)$$

7. Examine the following reactions. Complete the table as shown.
   Reactions:
   1. $CaCO_3(s) \longrightarrow CaO(s) + CO_2(g)$
   2. $Br_2(l) + C_6H_6(l) \longrightarrow HBr(g) + C_6H_5Br(l)$
   3. $N_2O_4(l) \longrightarrow 2NO_2(g)$
   4. $NaOH(aq) + HCl(aq) \longrightarrow$
      $$NaCl(aq) + H_2O(l)$$

Columns:
a. Indicate whether you would measure

   $$\frac{\Delta[\text{reactants}]}{\Delta t} \quad \text{or} \quad \frac{\Delta[\text{products}]}{\Delta t}$$

b. Indicate the substance measured.
c. Indicate how the change would be measured.

Reaction	Column A Change in reactant or product	Column B Substance measured	Column C Type of measurement
1	product	carbon dioxide	gas collection
2			
3			
4			

8. Many solutions to environmental problems involve changing a highly toxic substance into a harmless substance. If mercury(II) chloride, a highly toxic substance in aqueous solutions, is treated with sodium oxalate, mercury precipitates from solution as mercury(I) chloride, and carbon dioxide is released as a gas.

   $$2HgCl_2(aq) + Na_2C_2O_4(aq) \longrightarrow$$
   $$2NaCl(aq) + 2CO_2(g) + Hg_2Cl_2(s)$$

a. Write a rate expression using Hg_2Cl_2.
b. Why would it be easier to monitor the formation of Hg_2Cl_2 than the formation of the other two products?
c. Examine the data in the table. Would 30 min be sufficient time to treat 0.50 M $HgCl_2$ with 0.20 M $Na_2C_2O_4$?

Trial	Initial concentration (M)			Δt (min)	Final (M)
	HgCl₂	Na₂C₂O₄	NaCl		NaCl
1	0.50	0.10	0.00	30	0.010
2	0.50	0.20	0.00	30	0.042
3	0.50	0.30	0.00	30	0.168

9. A mixture of nitric acid and hydrochloric acid is called aqua regia. Aqua regia will dissolve gold and platinum due to the presence of nitrosyl chloride, NOCl, and chlorine. Nitrosyl chloride slowly decomposes into nitrogen monoxide and chlorine, causing the color of the aqua regia to change from reddish brown to light green.

$$2NOCl(soln) \longrightarrow 2NO(g) + Cl_2(g)$$

a. Use the following graph to determine the rate of decrease in NOCl concentration during the first 90 days and between days 360 and 450.

b. Propose a reason why the rates for days 1–90 and days 360–450 differ.

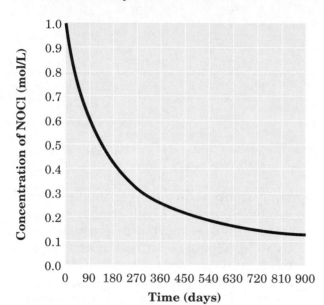

Time (days)

Causes for various reaction rates

REVIEW

10. Explain why many molecules must have a specific orientation to collide effectively to form a product, but simple ions such as Cl^- and Ba^{2+} are unaffected by orientation. Use the following models to illustrate your point.

Reacting ions

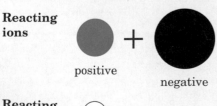

positive

negative

Reacting molecules

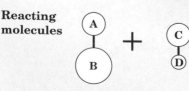

11. If we raise the energy states of reactants by increasing the temperature, are all of the reactant particles likely to have enough energy to form products? Why?

12. Why does grinding a solid cause an increase in reaction rate?

13. Iron nails will corrode slowly when placed in sulfuric acid. If iron filings are substituted, the reaction becomes instantaneous. Why?

14. Why is the basic chemical nature of a substance important when studying chemical kinetics?

15. Why does a change in concentration of reactants usually change the reaction rate?

16. Use graphs to illustrate the following situations.
   a. an exothermic reaction with a relatively large E_a value
   b. an exothermic reaction with a relatively small E_a value.

APPLY

17. At normal body temperature (37°C) the body can survive for only 5 min without oxygen. When the body temperature is lowered to a state of hypothermia (28–30°C), the body can survive almost 30 min without damage to tissues. Why?

18. The time for a reaction to come to completion is of considerable economic interest. Describe ways in which reaction rates could affect economic interests.

19. White phosphorus will ignite and burn spontaneously around 34°C.

$$4P(s) + 5O_2(g) \longrightarrow P_4O_{10}(s)$$

   a. Draw an energy diagram for this reaction.
   b. On the graph, label the following: x– and y– coordinates, reactants, products, activated complex, and E_a.
   c. Propose two ways that white phosphorus could be stored to prevent a reaction with oxygen.

20. Old newspapers that are stacked and stored will sometimes burst into flames spontaneously. Usually a high temperature is required to burn a stack of paper. How can you explain the spontaneous combustion of old newspapers when the temperature seems to be low?

21. Explosions are common in factories that grind wheat into flour. Would the heat released from the explosion of flour be greater than the heat released when whole grains of wheat burn? Why?

22. How can the order of reaction with respect to reactant concentration be determined from experimental data?

23. Why aren't the coefficients in a balanced equation used to write the rate law expression?

24. Reactant A participates in two different reactions. A plot of log[A] vs. time for the first reaction shows a straight-line relationship. For the second reaction, a straight-line plot occurs when 1/[A] vs. time is plotted. What is the order of each of these reactions with respect to [A]?

25. Determine the overall order of reaction for each of the following reaction rate expressions.
a. rate = $k[N_2O_5]$
b. rate = $k[CH_3OH]^2 [(C_6H_5)_3CCl]$
c. rate = $k[O_3] [NO]$

26. Does the position of the slow step in the reaction mechanism have an effect on the rate law expression? Why?

27. Compare an intermediate to an activated complex.

28. In the diagram below, the energy pathway for a reaction is represented by the curved line. Draw another line representing the possible energy pathway that would result if this reaction was enzyme mediated.

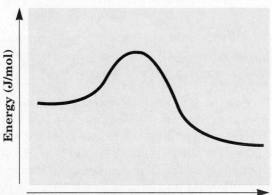

Time of Reaction

29. In terms of structure and function, compare and contrast enzymes and inorganic heterogeneous catalysts.

30. Briefly explain the process involved in the enzyme-catalyzed conversion of a substrate to a product.

31. Describe the effect of an inhibitor on the kinetics of a chemical reaction.

32. If the rate expression for a reaction is determined to be rate = $k[A]^2$, what happens to the rate if the concentration of A is tripled? What happens to the rate if the concentration of A is halved?

33. If the rate expression for a reaction is determined to be rate = $k[A][B]^2$, what happens to the rate if the concentration of A is doubled? What happens to the rate if the concentration of B is halved?

34. What are the units for k, for each rate law in item **25**?

35. Describe how you would carry out a typical experiment with two reactants that would determine a rate law expression.

36. If you were told that the rate law for the following reaction is second order with respect to H_2O because the coefficient is 2, how would you respond?

$$CaC_2(s) + 2H_2O(l) \longrightarrow$$
$$C_2H_2(g) + Ca(OH)_2(s)$$

37. At temperatures below 225°C the following reaction takes place.

$$NO_2(g) + CO(g) \longrightarrow CO_2(g) + NO(g)$$

Doubling the concentration of NO_2 quadruples the rate of CO_2 being formed if the CO concentration is held constant. However, doubling the concentration of CO has no effect on the rate of CO_2 being formed.
a. Write a rate law expression for this reaction.
b. Determine the order of the reaction with respect to NO_2 and with respect to CO.
c. If NO_3 is a reaction intermediate, suggest a possible mechanism for this reaction that accounts for the experimental results.

38. Carbon monoxide gas and oxygen gas bind to the hemoglobin molecule. The rate for the release of oxygen to the tissues is measured in seconds. The release of CO from hemoglobin takes from 5 to 8 h. Both reactions are first order with respect to oxygen or carbon monoxide. Compare the kinetics of these reactions, and explain why carbon monoxide poisoning occurs.

39. The nerve gas Soman is a cholinesterase inhibitor. Antidotes to poisoning by Soman are cholinesterase reactivators. What kind of substance is cholinesterase? Suggest what may happen to it when it is inhibited by Soman.

40. The following data were obtained in a bacterial growth experiment.

Time (min)	—	60.0	120	180	240	300
Concentration [(bacteria/L) × 10⁻³]	3.50	7.00	14.0	28.0	56.0	112

a. How many minutes must pass before the population of the colony doubles?

b. When the bacteria concentration has reached 22.4×10^{-2}/L, how much time has elapsed?

41. What is the overall order of reaction for each of the following reactions if their rate constants at 773 K are 6.1×10^{-4} s⁻¹ and 2.88×10^{-18} L mol⁻¹ s⁻¹, respectively?

a. △ ⟶ △

b. $Ar + O_2 \longrightarrow Ar + 2O$

42. a. Write the rate law for reaction **a** in item **41**, and determine the reaction rate if the concentration of cyclopropane is 2.0×10^{-3} M.

b. The rate constant for reaction **a** in item **41** is 5.70×10^{-4} M at 25°C. Write the rate law for this temperature.

c. Compare the rate law equations in parts **a** and **b**, and account for the difference in rate at the two temperatures.

43. The hydrolysis of thioacetamide is described by the following chemical equation.

$$CH_3CSNH_2 + H_2O \longrightarrow H_2S + CH_3CONH_2$$

The rate law for this hydrolysis is determined to be rate = $[H^+][CH_3CSNH_2]$. How does adding some solid NaOH to a solution that is 0.10 M in both hydrogen ion and thioacetamide affect the rate? the value of the rate constant?

44. Carbonic anhydrase is an enzyme that speeds the conversion of waste CO_2 to HCO_3^- in the body. The rate of the catalyzed reaction is 1×10^7 times faster than the uncatalyzed reaction. If 0.30 g of CO_2 can be converted in 1 min at 37°C using the appropriate amount of enzyme, how long would it take for the same amount of CO_2 (0.30 g) to be converted without the catalyst?

Linking chapters

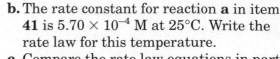

1. *Molarity*

Hydrogen peroxide solution is stored in dark bottles because light greatly increases the rate of decomposition.

$$H_2O_2(l) \longrightarrow H_2O(l) + O_2(g)$$

If a 500 mL bottle of 1.50 M H_2O_2 solution decomposes at a rate of 0.25 M/h in a clear bottle and 0.013 M/yr in a dark bottle, what is the difference in H_2O_2 concentration in the two bottles after 3 h?

2. *Molarity and Stoichiometry*

Iodate ion converts iodide ions to iodine in acidic solution, as represented by the following reaction.

$$IO_3^-(aq) + 5I^-(aq) + 6H^+(aq) \longrightarrow 3I_2(s) + 3H_2O(l)$$

This reaction is too fast to time with a stopwatch, so sodium hydrogen sulfite is added to slow down the formation of iodine by competing with the iodide ions.

$$IO_3^-(aq) + 3HSO_3^-(aq) \longrightarrow I^-(aq) + 3SO_4^{2-}(aq) + 3H^+$$

Because HSO_3^- is a strong competitor, no I_2 can form until all the HSO_3^- ions have reacted. Still, the formation of I_2 goes undetected to the human eye because the solution is colorless. However, starch can be added to complex I_2 the instant it forms which causes the solution to turn blue-black.

$$I_2 + starch \longrightarrow starch \cdot I_2 \text{ complex}$$

The rate law for the reaction between iodate ion and hydrogen sulfite ion is as follows.

$$rate = k[IO_3^-]^p[HSO_3^-]^q$$

To run the iodine clock reaction, a student prepares the initial solutions of KIO_3 and $NaHSO_3$ by adding 0.788 g of KIO_3 to 150 mL of water and 0.392 g of $NaHSO_3$ to 150 mL of water. The reactants are mixed in the following proportions.

Trial	KIO₃ solution (mL)	Starch and NaHSO₃ solution (mL)	Water (mL)	Molarity of IO₃⁻ after mixing	Time (s)
1	5	8	12		115
2	7	8	10		85
3	9	8	8		67
4	11	8	6		50

a. Calculate the IO_3^- concentration for each trial.

b. What role(s) does the HSO_3^- ion play in this series of reactions? Why does its concentration remain constant?

c. What role does the starch play in this set of reactions? Why is its concentration not a factor affecting the rate?

d. Why does the amount of water added decrease as the amount of KIO_3 added increases? How would the rate be affected if the amount of water were held constant and the amount of $NaHSO_3$ were varied?

e. Explain why the reaction time decreases as the amount of KIO_3 solution increases.

f. Why do you think this series of reactions is called the "iodine clock" reaction?

3. *Weak acid equilibrium and rate*
The pollutant sulfur dioxide forms HSO_3^- ion when it dissolves in water droplets. The bisulfite ion is then oxidized to sulfate ion by oxygen which is also dissolved in the water droplets. One mechanism for this oxidation reaction is the following sequence of reactions.

$$2HSO_3^-(aq) + O_2(aq) \longrightarrow \quad \textbf{fast}$$
$$S_2O_7^{2-}(aq) + H_2O(l)$$

$$S_2O_7^{2-}(aq) + H_2O(l) \longrightarrow \quad \textbf{slow}$$
$$2SO_4^{2-}(aq) + 2H^+(aq)$$

The following data were obtained in an experiment in which a 0.270 M aqueous solution of HSO_3^- ion was mixed with an aqueous solution of 0.0135 M O_2. The initial pH was 3.90.

Time (s)	[HSO₃⁻]	[O₂]	[S₂O₇²⁻]	[SO₄²⁻]
0.000	0.270	0.0135	0.000	0.000
0.010	0.243	0.000	13.5×10^{-3}	0.000
10.0	0.243	0.000	11.8×10^{-3}	3.40×10^{-3}
45.0	0.243	0.000	7.42×10^{-3}	12.2×10^{-3}
90.0	0.243	0.000	4.08×10^{-3}	18.8×10^{-3}

a. Explain why the HSO_3^- ion concentration is constant after 0.010 s.

b. How many moles of $S_2O_7^{2-}$ have been consumed after 45 s? how many moles of SO_4^{2-} have been formed? Explain why these numbers are not the same.

c. Write a balanced equation for the conversion of the bisulfite ion to sulfate ion.

d. Write a balanced chemical equation for the formation of H_2SO_4 from SO_2 dissolved in airborne water droplets. (Hint: remember that a weak acid is in equilibrium with its ions, and that a strong acid is present as its ions.)

4. *Characteristic properties*
Sodium and silver react with water at drastically different rates. A 5 g sample of sodium completely disappears within a minute of being placed in 100 mL of water. Conversely, a 5 g sample of silver can be left in 100 mL of water for years with little detectable change. What explains this large difference in reaction rates?

5. *Particle collisions*
2-methylpropanol decomposes into 2-methyl propene and water.

$$(CH_3)_3COH(l) \longrightarrow$$
$$(CH_3)_2C{=}CH_2(l) + H_2O(l)$$

For this decomposition to proceed at a perceptible rate, the temperature must be above 450°C. Use the particle collision theory to explain why 2-methylpropanol is stored at temperatures below 450°C.

6. Theme: *Equilibrium and change*
The following reaction has an equilibrium constant of 0.771 at 750°C.

$$H_2(g) + CO_2(g) \rightleftharpoons CO(g) + H_2O(g)$$

a. How do the rates of the forward and reverse reactions compare at equilibrium?

b. How do the concentrations of the products and reactants compare at equilibrium?

7. Theme: *Equilibrium and change*

a. Predict how the use of an enzyme would affect the reverse reaction of an equilibrium system.

b. What effect(s) does a catalyst have on the equilibrium constant for a given reaction? (Hint: how does a catalyst affect thermodynamic quantities such as ΔH?)

8. Theme: *Equilibrium and change*
Sketch a generalized concentration versus time graph for the formation of NO_2 as depicted in the following reaction.

$$N_2O_4 \rightleftharpoons 2NO_2$$

9. Theme: *Equilibrium and change*
The formation of nitrogen and water from nitrogen monoxide and hydrogen is believed to occur in three elementary steps. Each step is an equilibrium reaction as shown on the next page.

Step 1: $NO + NO \rightleftharpoons N_2O_2$

Step 2: $N_2O_2 + H_2 \rightleftharpoons N_2O + H_2O$

Step 3: $N_2O + H_2 \rightleftharpoons N_2 + H_2O$

When reactions are added, the K_{eq} of the overall reaction is equal to the product of the K_{eq} expressions for all the steps.

a. The K_{eq} expression for step 2 is as follows.

$$K_{eq} = \frac{[N_2O][H_2O]}{[N_2O_2][H_2]}$$

Explain the presence of water in the K_{eq} expression.

b. Write K_{eq} expressions for steps **1** and **3**, and determine the form of the K_{eq} expression for the overall reaction.

c. Write the balanced chemical equation for the overall reaction.

d. Why do concentration terms for the intermediates not appear in the K_{eq} expressions for the overall equation?

10. Theme: *Systems and interactions*
Iodine monochloride, ICl, a substance used to determine the iodine value of fats and oils, is a gas above 92°C. ICl reacts with hydrogen gas to form iodine gas and hydrogen chloride gas.

$$ICl(g) + H_2(g) \longrightarrow I_2(g) + 2HCl(g)$$

The rate law for this reaction is: rate = $k[ICl][H_2]$. At 230°C k has a value of 0.163 L/mol·s. Raising the temperature to 240°C increases the value of k to 0.348 L/mol·s.

a. If the initial concentration for both ICl and H_2 is 0.50 M, compare the rates at 230°C and 240°C.

b. Compare the rates at 230°C for reactant concentrations of 0.50 M and 0.25 M.

c. Which has a greater effect on the reaction rate, a 10°C increase in temperature or a doubling of the concentration?

USING TECHNOLOGY

1. *Graphics calculator*
Verify the decomposition of NO_2 is second order with respect to $[NO_2]$ by plotting the following reaction data.

Begin by clearing lists L1 through L4. Press STAT 4 2nd 1 ENTER. Repeat this key sequence three more times except press 2, 3, or 4 instead of 1. Now enter the data you will plot. L_1 will contain time data, L_2 concentration data, L_3 log concentration data, and L_4 the inverse concentration data. Press STAT 1.

Time (s)	[NO₂]
0	1.00×10^{-2}
60	0.683×10^{-2}
120	0.518×10^{-2}
180	0.418×10^{-2}
240	0.350×10^{-2}
300	0.301×10^{-2}
360	0.264×10^{-2}

Press 0, because this is the first number in the list of times, followed by ENTER. Continue this key sequence of number followed by ENTER until all data points are entered. Press ▶ and enter $[NO_2]$ data in L_2. Remember that "$\times 10^{-2}$" is entered as 2nd , (−) 2. Press ▶ to enter log $[NO_2]$ in L_3. Press LOG followed by a number in the $[NO_2]$ data list and ENTER. Press ▶ and enter data in L_4 by entering a number from the $[NO_2]$ data list followed by x⁻¹ and ENTER. Set the limits for the range and domain, and scaling for the axes. Press

WINDOW ▼ 0 ▼ 375 ▼ 10 ▼ 0 ▼ 0 . 0 1 ▼ 0 . 0 0 0 1. To plot concentration vs. time press 2nd Y= 1 ENTER ▼ ▶ ENTER ▼ ENTER ▼ ▶ ENTER GRAPH. Reset the range limits and y-axis scaling. Ymin = −3, Ymax = −2, and Yscl = 0.001. Plot log $[NO_2]$ vs time by pressing 2nd Y= 2 ENTER ▼ ▶ ENTER ▼ ENTER ▼ ▶ ▶ ENTER GRAPH. Reset range limits and y-axis scaling to plot $1/[NO_2]$ vs. time. Select plot 3 at the STAT PLOTS screen and set parameters. Press GRAPH.

2. *Graphics Calculator*
A reaction involving a single reactant, A, has the rate data shown to the right. Determine the order of the reaction by graphing the data. Use the instructions in item **1** as a guide.

Time (min)	[A]
5.0	0.100
5.63	0.090
6.16	0.080
7.00	0.070

3. *Graphics Calculator*
The decomposition of ethane, C_2H_6, is a first order reaction. Data for the reaction are to the right. From the plot of concentration versus time, estimate the rate at $t = 750$ s.

Time (s)	[C₂H₆]
0	0.01000
200	0.00916
400	0.00839
600	0.00768
800	0.00703

4. Graphics Calculator

Nitrogen(II) oxide reacts with hydrogen at 800°C to form nitrogen gas and water as in the following equation.

$$2NO(g) + 2H_2(g) \longrightarrow N_2(g) + 2H_2O(g)$$

Using the data in the table to the right, graphically determine the order of reaction with respect to both H_2 and NO, and write the rate law.

Trial	[NO]	[H₂]	Rate
1	0.0010	0.0040	0.12
2	0.0020	0.0040	0.48
3	0.0030	0.0040	1.08
4	0.0040	0.0010	0.48
5	0.0040	0.0020	0.96
6	0.0040	0.0030	1.44

5. Computer Program

a. Determine the rate for the reaction in item **4** if the initial concentration of NO is 0.0024 M and the concentration of H_2 is 0.0042 M. (Hint: the value of the rate constant is constant for a given temperature.)

b. Write a program that would allow you to determine the rate for any given set of concentrations.

Alternative assessment

Performance assessment

1. Boilers are used to heat large buildings. Deposits of $CaCO_3$, $MgCO_3$, and $FeCO_3$ can hinder the boiler operation, and aqueous solutions of HCl are commonly used to remove these deposits. The general equation for the reaction is written as follows.

$$XCO_3(s) + HCl(aq) \longrightarrow$$
$$XCl_2(aq) + H_2O(l) + CO_2(g)$$

X stands for Ca, Mg, or Fe. Design an experiment to determine the effect of various HCl concentrations on the rates of this reaction. Present your design to a panel group.

2. Fats and oils decompose into fatty acids and glycerin, which cause the spoilage of many foods. Antioxidants are added to fats and oils to inhibit decomposition.

To determine the extent of decomposition of a fat or oil, dissolve the sample in ethanol and titrate with an NaOH solution, using phenolphthalein as an indicator. The greater the volume of NaOH solution required for the solution to turn pink, the greater the concentration of free fatty acids, and the greater the extent of decomposition.

Design an experiment to study the effects of temperature and an inhibitor on the decomposition rates of samples of fat or vegetable oil. Present your design in the form of a proposal to your teacher.

Portfolio projects

1. Research and communication
Catalysts play a major role in many industrial processes. Research one particular catalyst and the industrial process that uses it. Try to determine how much of a difference the catalyst makes in the overall economics of the industrial process. Also research the environmental and occupational hazards associated with using the catalyst.

2. Cooperative activity
Have a class discussion about the use of inhibitors in food products. Each student should contribute important facts to the discussion by studying content labels and researching any substance listed as a preservative, spoilage inhibitor, or antioxidant. Health-related journals in the library are a good source of information on any substance found in a commercial food product. Focus the discussion on whether sufficient research was done on the substance before it received FDA approval. Also note any instances in which hazards associated with the use of a substance are not properly emphasized on the product label.

3. Research and communication
Biochemistry is a complex field of study. A high percentage of the chemical reactions that take place in living organisms are catalyzed by specific enzymes. Choose a biochemical process such as respiration, photosynthesis, vision, or muscular contraction. Prepare a diagram of this process, and detail all of the chemical reactions that take place and the enzymes associated with each reaction.

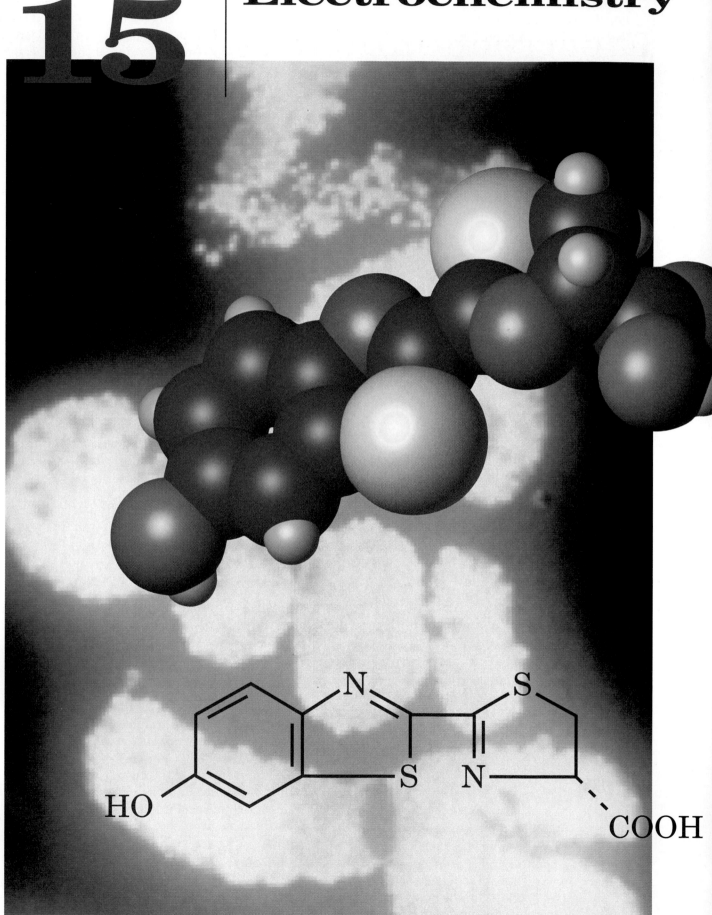

Fireflies and Electrochemical Cells

Drs. William Jacobs and Barry Bloom inject an antibiotic into a petri dish that contains glowing tuberculosis (TB) cells. They wait and watch, hoping the glow will dim and go out.

The glow is produced by the oxidation of firefly luciferin, the chemical compound responsible for light emission in the tails of fireflies. Jacobs and Bloom have placed the luciferin in a bacteria that will infect tuberculosis (TB) cells. Conditions inside active TB cells cause the luciferin to emit light or glow. The brightness of the glow is a measure of the bacteria's growth. If the glow brightens, the drug injected by Jacobs and Bloom does not kill this TB strain, and another drug must be tried. But, if the glow dims and goes out, the drug can be used to fight this TB strain.

Tuberculosis, a bacterial infection that usually affects the lungs, can be a life-threatening disease. Moreover, it is no longer easily treated because it has become more and more resistant to antibiotics. The spread of drug-resistant tuberculosis in major U.S. cities, where the death rate from this disease approaches 50%, has raised serious concerns.

One of the problems doctors face in the fight against TB is the time needed to determine if a person actually has it. Isolating and growing the bacteria responsible for tuberculosis can take from three to eight weeks. Once TB is diagnosed, another five or more weeks are needed to determine which antibiotic would be most effective. Knowing which drug is effective against a specific patient's TB strain is important to doctors because treating the disease with an ineffective drug can worsen the patient's condition. Screening possible antibiotics using this new luciferin test takes only a few days which substantially reduces the five-week waiting period before treatment can begin. In this way, the lights of fireflies, described by Smokey Mountain residents as breathtaking, may be described as breathgiving by persons with tuberculosis.

Emission of light by living organisms through the use of a chemical reaction is known as bioluminescence. Bioluminescence involves redox reactions. In this chapter, you will explore redox reactions as the basis for electrochemical cells. As a result, you will be able to answer the following questions.

- *How is the light generated by a firefly different from the light generated by a flashlight battery?*
- *How is the concentration of TB cells related to the brightness of the light emitted?*

Answering these questions requires some knowledge of how electricity is produced from chemical energy. Electrochemistry, the topic you will study in this chapter, is concerned with the interconversion of chemical and electric energy.

How does electric current flow?

Energy is released when electrons are transferred

Figure 15-1 shows a strip of zinc metal standing in an aqueous solution of copper(II) sulfate. What is the evidence that a chemical reaction has occurred? Copper metal has fallen out of solution into a pile on the bottom of the beaker. The solution has changed from a dark blue to a very light blue which suggests the loss of Cu^{2+} ions. Part of the zinc strip has been eaten away which suggests that the zinc atoms have become ions. These observations and analysis of the solution indicate a single displacement reaction with the following equation.

$$Zn(s) + CuSO_4(aq) \longrightarrow Cu(s) + ZnSO_4(aq)$$

This reaction involves the replacement of a Cu^{2+} ion by a Zn atom. If you check a periodic table, you will see that Zn has two valence electrons. For a Zn atom to replace a Cu^{2+} ion in solution, it must become an ion by transferring its two valence electrons to the Cu^{2+} ion which, in turn, becomes a solid. In this way, the system achieves stability.

Figure 15-1
A strip of Zn metal is suspended in an aqueous solution of CuSO₄. Heat energy given off when electrons are donated by Zn atoms to Cu²⁺ ions causes the solution temperature to rise.

Heat energy is released when redox reactions occur

Look at the solution temperature recorded in **Figure 15-1**. As electrons are exchanged between a Zn atom and a Cu^{2+} ion, energy is released in the form of heat causing the temperature to increase. As the reaction slows to a stop, less heat is produced, and the solution cools by transferring its heat to the surroundings. When the temperature of the solution equals that of the surroundings, no more heat flows. The temperature of the solution becomes constant. But what happens when the same two reactants are arranged without touching each other? Will heat still be produced?

Before

After

Zinc atom, Zn
Copper ion, Cu^{2+}
Sulfate ion, SO_4^{2-}
Water molecule, H_2O

Copper(II) sulfate, CuSO₄, solution   Zinc strip

Zinc atom, Zn
Copper ion, Cu^{2+}
Zinc ion, Zn^{2+}
Sulfate ion, SO_4^{2-}
Copper atom, Cu
Water molecule, H_2O

Separation of reactants produces electric energy instead of heat

porous barrier
any medium through which ions can slowly pass

electricity
energy associated with electrons that have moved from one place to another

In **Figure 15-2**, the **porous barrier** prevents Zn atoms and Cu^{2+} ions from mixing with one another, so a Zn atom cannot directly transfer its two valence electrons to a Cu^{2+} ion. However, electrons can be transferred from Zn atoms to Cu^{2+} ions through the external connecting wire. Electrons flowing through a wire generate energy in the form of **electricity**. The temperature increases only slightly as the reaction progressed, so little energy was produced as heat. When the reactants are arranged so they do not touch each other, energy is in the form of electricity rather than heat. How can you tell that electric current is being generated in **Figure 15-2**?

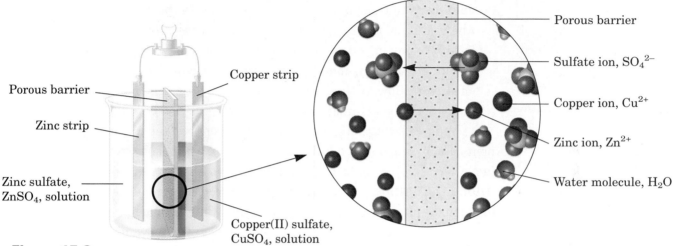

Figure 15-2
In electrochemical cells, the porous barrier keeps reagents separated. Ions flow through the barrier as the current inside the cell. Electrons flow in the external circuit.

Electricity is produced by electron transfer in voltaic cells

Electrons given up by Zn atoms pass along the wire, through the filament in the bulb, and cause it to light. The light indicates that chemical energy present in the reactants has been converted into electric energy. This conversion takes place in an *electrochemical cell*. An electrochemical cell is a container in which chemical reactions produce electricity or an electric current produces chemical change. When an electrochemical cell produces electricity, it is also known as a **voltaic cell**. The branch of chemistry concerned with the interconversion of chemical energy with electric energy is *electrochemistry*.

voltaic cell
an electrochemical cell in which a spontaneous redox reaction produces a flow of electrons through an external circuit

Separation of electrodes in a voltaic cell ensures that the major energy output is electrical. The Cu and Zn electrodes in **Figure 15-2** are immersed in sulfate solutions of their respective ions. These solutions are separated by a porous barrier that allows ions to pass through it, but prevents physical mixing of the solutions. Cu^{2+} ions gain two electrons at the surface of the Cu strip where they are deposited as Cu atoms. The removal of Cu^{2+} ions from solution reduces the positive ion concentration on the copper side of the barrier.

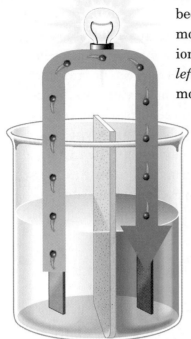

Figure 15-3
Electrons in an electrochemical cell flow from anode to cathode. Ion migration across the porous barrier closes the loop path, making a complete circuit.

Anode   **Cathode**

circuit
closed loop path for current to follow

half-cell
the part of a voltaic cell in which either oxidation or reduction occurs. It consists of a single electrode immersed in a solution of its ions

anode
the electrode at which oxidation occurs as electrons are lost by some substance

cathode
the electrode at which reduction occurs as electrons are gained by some substance

At the same time, atoms in the Zn strip are losing electrons to become Zn^{2+} ions that disperse into the surrounding solution. The motion of the ions in the solution is the internal current. The SO_4^{2-} ions migrate from *right* to *left*. The Zn^{2+} and Cu^{2+} ions migrate from *left* to *right*, in the solution, in the opposite direction. The SO_4^{2-} ions move through the barrier to meet the Zn^{2+} ions, which were produced at the anode. These SO_4^{2-} ions are not needed in the cathode compartment because Cu^{2+} ions are disappearing there.

Current flows in a complete circuit

In the wire of the external **circuit** the negative electrons go from left to right (anode to cathode). There must be a corresponding motion of charges in the solution to complete the circuit. This is the motion of the sulfate ions, from right to left, or by the flow of positive ions in the opposite direction. Electrons move in the external circuit, ions move in the internal circuit. You might think of current flow as the baton in **Figure 15-4** that is being transferred between runners in a relay race.

A voltaic cell, therefore, is actually made from two separate components. Each component, a **half-cell**, consists of a metal electrode in contact with a solution of its ions. Identify the two half-cells in **Figure 15-3**. **Anode** and **cathode** are the labels used to identify the half-cells that make up a voltaic cell. These labels describe what is happening at the electrodes. *An* comes from the term *anion* which you know means a negatively charged ion. Anode then suggests a source of electrons. Similarly, *cat* from the term *cation* implies a capacity to accept electrons.

Figure 15-4
The baton in this relay race is transferred from one runner to the next until it has gone completely around the track. Like the movement of the baton, current flows in a complete path. It is produced by electrons moving through the external wire and by ion movement within the cell.

Oxidation occurs when electrons are lost

You learned in Chapter 3 that individual atoms are neutral. In Chapter 5 you learned that ions have either a positive or a negative charge. Reexamine the anode for the electrochemical cell in Figure 15-5. The net reaction taking place is described by the following equation.

$$Zn(s) \longrightarrow Zn^{2+}(aq) + 2e^-$$

oxidation

loss of electrons by an atom or an algebraic increase in its oxidation state

Notice that Zn atoms have gone from a neutral, 0, charge in solid Zn to a 2+ charge as Zn^{2+} ion in the $ZnSO_4$ solution. Zinc has lost electrons. It is said to be *oxidized*. Any element that loses electrons is said to have undergone **oxidation**. Oxidation takes place at the anode. Zn atoms have been oxidized. But what happened to the Cu^{2+} ions?

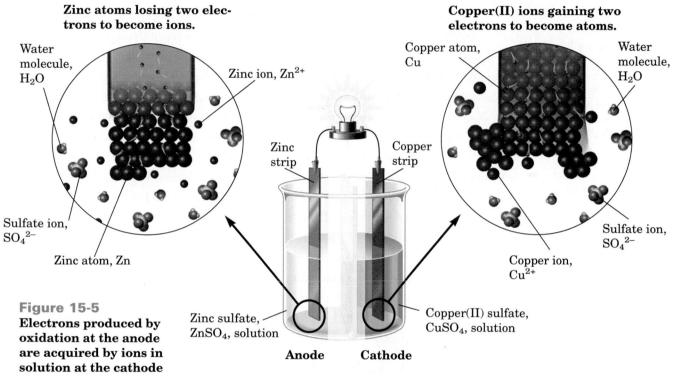

Zinc atoms losing two electrons to become ions.

Water molecule, H_2O

Zinc ion, Zn^{2+}

Sulfate ion, SO_4^{2-}

Zinc atom, Zn

Zinc strip

Copper strip

Copper(II) ions gaining two electrons to become atoms.

Copper atom, Cu

Water molecule, H_2O

Sulfate ion, SO_4^{2-}

Copper ion, Cu^{2+}

Zinc sulfate, $ZnSO_4$, solution

Copper(II) sulfate, $CuSO_4$, solution

Anode **Cathode**

Figure 15-5
Electrons produced by oxidation at the anode are acquired by ions in solution at the cathode (reduction). The anode and cathode are half-cells.

Reduction occurs when electrons are gained

The following equation describes the net reaction occurring at the cathode in Figure 15-5.

$$Cu^{2+}(aq) + 2e^- \longrightarrow Cu(s)$$

reduction

the gain of electrons by an atom or the algebraic decrease in its oxidation state

Cu^{2+} ions in the $CuSO_4$ solution surrounding the Cu electrode go from a 2+ charge to a 0 charge when they are deposited as copper metal, Cu. They have gained electrons; they have been *reduced*. Any element that experiences a gain in electrons has undergone **reduction**. Since electrons must be gained to achieve a decrease in charge, reduction is defined as the gain of one or more electrons by an element. Reduction takes place at the cathode.

Oxidation and reduction must occur together

Oxidation and reduction always occur simultaneously; you can't have one without the other. If one element is oxidized by losing electrons, then another element has to be reduced by taking on those electrons. Furthermore, the number of electrons lost must equal the number gained. Any reaction in which electrons are lost and gained in equal numbers is an oxidation-reduction reaction, or **redox reaction**. The net redox reaction for the electrochemical cell in **Figure 15-5** is described by the following equation.

$$Zn(s) + Cu^{2+}(aq) \longrightarrow Zn^{2+}(aq) + Cu(s)$$

Redox reactions in an electrochemical cell involve a continuous flow of electrons from anode to cathode. They are the basis of electrochemistry because their half-reactions make up voltaic cells. If voltaic cells are composed of two half-cells corresponding to the two half-reactions of a redox equation, what happens when you mix-and-match half-cells? How can you predict which direction current will flow?

Redox reactions cause the fruit in **Figure 15–6** to brown. Testing urine for sugar also involves a redox reaction. The test reagent is Benedict's solution which is an alkaline solution of copper(II) hydroxide. When glucose comes in contact with Cu^{2+} ions present in Benedict's reagent the aldehyde group of the sugar is oxidized to a carboxylic acid while the Cu^{2+} ion is reduced to Cu^{1+} ion. The Cu^{1+} ion precipitates as Cu_2O. Although Cu_2O is red, the color of the solution in which the reaction is taking place depends on the amount of sugar present. A high sugar concentration produces an orange-red solution. As the sugar concentration decreases, the color changes to yellow, to green, and, at very low sugar concentrations, to blue. Clinitest tablets that are used to test for glucose concentration in urine are a convenient, solid form of Benedict's reagent.

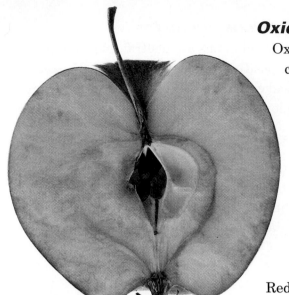

Figure 15-6
Fruit browns when it is cut open and left in contact with oxygen in the air. The discoloration is visual evidence of the redox reaction taking place.

redox reaction
a chemical reaction involving oxidation and reduction

Section Review

1. What is an electrochemical cell?
2. How does oxidation differ from reduction?
3. What is a redox reaction?
4. **a.** Outline the path taken by current in an electrochemical cell.
   b. When electrodes and their solutions are in two separate containers, an inverted, U-shaped tube extending between both solutions replaces the porous barrier. Known as a salt bridge, this tube contains a salt solution whose anions and cations migrate at the same rate. The ends are plugged with glass wool to prevent the solutions from mixing. Using **Figure 15-5** as a guide, draw and label a diagram for this type of voltaic cell.
5. Use **Figure 15-5** to answer the following questions.
   a. What happens to the Zn atoms during the cell reaction? Where do they go? What do they become?
   b. What happens to the mass of the cathode? the anode?

How do you get current to flow?

Section Objectives

Predict the outcome of redox reactions using reduction potentials.

Explain how the activity series and reduction potentials are linked to electronegativity and to each other.

Evaluate the ability of a metal atom to reduce hydrogen in quantitative terms.

Quantifying the activity series

You learned in Chapter 7 that the activity series is a list of metals with the most active one placed at the top. Activity decreases progressively down the list. Because reactions between atoms and ions of metals involve a transfer of electrons during a redox reaction, the activity series tells you, in effect, which metals generally give up electrons and which metal ions generally accept them.

Activity series is a model that allows you to make predictions

Compare the voltaic cells shown in **Figure 15-7** with the one in **Figure 15-3**. Although the parts are similar, the composition of the electrodes differs. The anode in **Figure 15-7a** consists of a strip of aluminum metal in aqueous $AlCl_3$ instead of Zn in aqueous $ZnSO_4$. The cathode is a strip of copper metal immersed in a solution of $CuCl_2$ instead of $CuSO_4$. The solution is blue, indicating the presence of Cu^{2+} ions. The porous barrier allows ions to move freely between the anode and the cathode while keeping the electrodes separated from each other. Using **Table 15-1** on page 585, predict what will happen in this electrochemical cell.

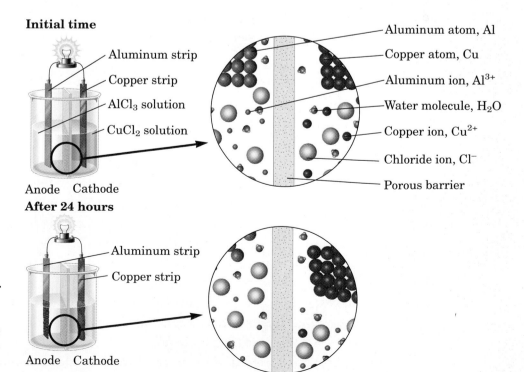

Initial time

Aluminum strip
Copper strip
$AlCl_3$ solution
$CuCl_2$ solution

Anode   Cathode

After 24 hours

Aluminum strip
Copper strip

Anode   Cathode

Aluminum atom, Al
Copper atom, Cu
Aluminum ion, Al^{3+}
Water molecule, H_2O
Copper ion, Cu^{2+}
Chloride ion, Cl^-
Porous barrier

Figure 15-7a
The activity series predicts electrons will flow from Al to Cu. A flow of electricity will light the bulb.

15-7b
As the reaction progresses, cell concentrations change and the reactions slow down. The light dims because less current is passing through it.

Figure 15-7b on page 581 shows the voltaic cell in Figure 15-7a after 24 hours. Examine it for evidence to support your prediction. Look closely at the anode. Part of the aluminum strip appears to have dissolved in the solution. If we knew the mass of the strip at the start of the reaction, we would now find that it shows a decrease in mass. Analysis of the cathode solution confirms the presence of Al^{3+} ions which were not found in this solution at the start of the reaction. Analysis of the anode solution shows an increase in Cl^- ion concentration compared to that at the start of the reaction. In spite of ion migration, Al^{3+} ions are still present in the anode solution. Thus, Al atoms have given up electrons to form Al^{3+} ions. Al atoms have been oxidized.

The strip of copper in Figure 15-7b has a dull, reddish brown solid deposited on it. Analysis of the electrode indicates it has increased in mass and that the solid is copper metal. The solution surrounding the copper strip is lighter blue, indicating that fewer Cu^{2+} ions are present. Thus, Cu^{2+} ions have formed Cu atoms by accepting the electrons given up by Al atoms. The Cu^{2+} ions have been reduced.

This redox reaction is exactly what should happen based on the activity series. The reaction occurred because aluminum is more reactive than copper. In other words, aluminum has a greater tendency than copper to give up its valence electrons. In fact, the entire activity series is made of such "electron-trade agreements," indicating the relative willingness of metals to give up their valence electrons. Is there a way to quantify this tendency? How much greater is the tendency for Al to give up its electrons than for Cu? or for Zn than Cu? Replacing the light bulb assembly in Figure 15-2 and Figure 15-7 with a voltmeter will allow the electric potential in these cells to be measured, as you can see in Figure 15-8. But how can this help predict the amount of electric potential in a voltaic cell made from Al and Zn? How much of the cell's electric potential is due to the anode? How much is due to the cathode?

Figure 15-8
Replacing the light bulb with a voltmeter quantifies the greater tendency of Zn and Al to give up their electrons relative to Cu. What would the voltmeter read if Zn were connected to Al?

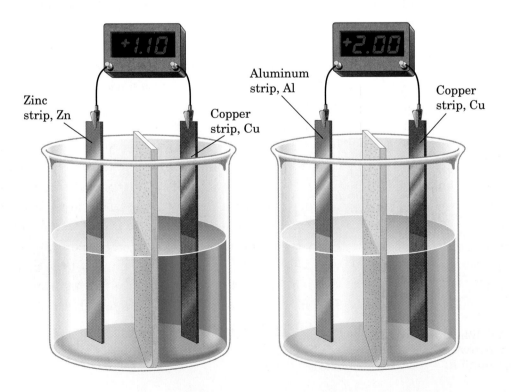

Metals are ranked according to their ability to reduce hydrogen

half-reaction
the oxidation or reduction portion of a redox reaction

reduction potential
a measure of the tendency of a given half-reaction to occur as a reduction in an electrochemical cell

Measuring the voltage generated in the separate half-cells requires the reaction that occurs at each electrode to be considered separately. The reaction occurring at an electrode is known as a **half-reaction**. Oxidation is the half-reaction occurring at the anode. Reduction is the half-reaction occurring at the cathode.

The amount of electric energy that each half-reaction can generate is determined by its **reduction potential**. Reduction potentials are measured in volts, V. The difference between the reduction potentials for the two half-reactions is the total voltage generated by the redox reaction.

As you saw in **Figure 15-8**, the voltage generated by a redox reaction is easily measurable. However, measuring the voltage generated by a half-reaction alone is impossible because there can be no transfer of electrons unless both an anode and cathode are connected to form a complete circuit. To complete the circuit, a standard half-cell is used. This standard half-cell consists of a platinum electrode that is immersed in a solution with an H^+ ion concentration of 1.00 M and surrounded by hydrogen gas at 1 atm pressure and 25°C. Metals are ranked according to their ability to reduce hydrogen under these conditions.

The anodic half-reaction occurring at the hydrogen electrode is shown by the following equation.

$$H_2(g) \longrightarrow 2H^+(aq) + 2e^-$$

standard reduction potential
by convention, the potential, E^0, of a half-cell connected to the standard hydrogen electrode when ion concentrations in the half-cells are 1 M, gases are at a pressure of 1 atm, and the temperature is 25°C

SHE
standard hydrogen electrode has the half-reaction $2H^+(aq) + 2e^- \longrightarrow H_2(g)$; the concentration of hydrogen ion is 1 M, the temperature is 25°C, and the pressure of the hydrogen gas is 101.3 kPa (1 atm)

The cathodic half-reaction is the reverse of this one. The voltage for both of these reactions is arbitrarily assigned a value of exactly 0 V. Consequently, any voltage measurement that is obtained can be attributed entirely to the half-cell that is connected to the hydrogen half-cell standard. Such a voltage measurement is the **standard reduction potential**, E^0. E^0 values represent the voltages generated by half-reactions.

Examine the voltaic cells in **Figure 15-9** on the next page. The standard hydrogen electrode or **SHE** is considered to be the anode in each cell. The metal electrode is the cathode. Compare the voltage readings. Some are positive values. Some are negative values. How can this observation be rationalized? Look back to **Figure 15-8**. The voltage readings are both positive values. These two cells produced electricity as drawn in the figure because you saw the lighted bulb. Positive E^0 values indicate a flow of electrons from anode to cathode as written. That is, hydrogen is more willing to give up its electrons than the metal is. A voltmeter cannot actually register a negative potential. Instead, it would show a reading of 0 V until the positions of the half-cells are reversed. Reversing the cells causes the voltage to register as a positive value, but the SHE is now the cathode instead of the anode, so electrons are flowing from the metal to the SHE. Therefore, negative E^0 values indicate that the metal is more willing to give up its electrons than hydrogen is.

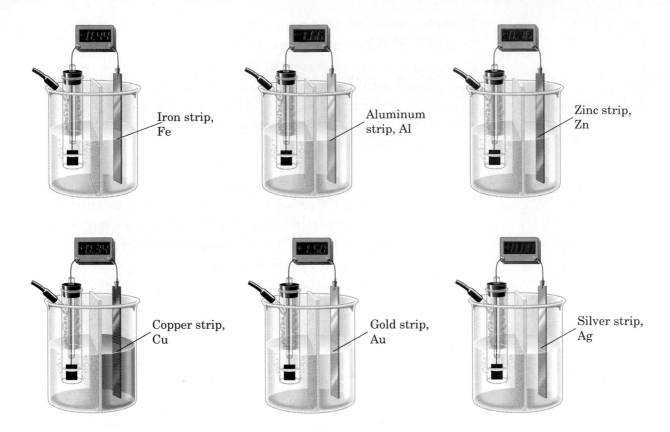

Figure 15-9
When connected to the SHE, the metal half-cell is considered the cathode. Because the SHE is arbitrarily assigned a voltage of exactly 0, the voltmeter gives the potential of the metal half-cell. Ordering the voltages produces a table of reduction potentials.

Iron strip, Fe

Aluminum strip, Al

Zinc strip, Zn

Copper strip, Cu

Gold strip, Au

Silver strip, Ag

Based on these constraints, an ordering of the voltage readings in **Figure 15-9** shows Zn is less willing to give up its electrons than is Al by 0.90 V, but is 1.10 V more willing to give up electrons than Cu. Locate Cu, Al, and Zn in the activity series portion of **Table 15-1**. Zn is less reactive than Al but more reactive than Cu. E^0 values are related to the activity of metals: the more reactive the metal, the greater the negative E^0 value associated with it.

The reduction potentials shown in **Table 15-1** are an ordering of reduction half-reactions by voltage. Compare this with the activity series in the far left column of **Table 15-1**. The table of reduction potentials extends the activity series by quantifying its relativeness. How can this agreement between the two tables be explained?

Activity and reduction potential result from electronegativity differences

In your study of the periodic table, you learned that certain properties exhibit trends as you move either across a period or down a group of elements. One such property is electronegativity. You learned that electronegativity is the measure of an atom's ability to acquire electrons. The more electronegative the atom, the more readily it acquires electrons.

If the metals in the activity series were listed in order of increasing electronegativity values, the list would have a general correspondence with the activity series as well as the table of reduction potentials. You can see this correspondence by comparing the color for a metal's entry in **Table 15-1** with its color in the table for electronegativity values on page 418.

Table 15-1
Activity Series and Reduction Potentials at 25°C

Element	Symbol	Electrode	Half-reaction	E^0(V)
lithium	Li	Li^+/Li	$Li^+ + e^- \longrightarrow Li$	−3.05
rubidium	Rb	Rb^+/Rb	$Rb^+ + e^- \longrightarrow Rb$	−2.98
potassium	K	K^+/K	$K^+ + e^- \longrightarrow K$	−2.93
barium	Ba	Ba^{2+}/Ba	$Ba^{2+} + 2e^- \longrightarrow Ba$	−2.90
calcium	Ca	Ca^{2+}/Ca	$Ca^{2+} + 2e^- \longrightarrow Ca$	−2.87
sodium	Na	Na^+/Na	$Na^+ + e^- \longrightarrow Na$	−2.71
magnesium	Mg	Mg^{2+}/Mg	$Mg^{2+} + 2e^- \longrightarrow Mg$	−2.37
aluminum	Al	Al^{3+}/Al	$Al^{3+} + 3e^- \longrightarrow Al$	−1.66
manganese	Mn	Mn^{2+}/Mn	$Mn^{2+} + 2e^- \longrightarrow Mn$	−1.19
		H_2O/H_2	$2H_2O + 2e^- \longrightarrow H_2 + 2OH^-$	−0.83
zinc	Zn	Zn^{2+}/Zn	$Zn^{2+} + 2e^- \longrightarrow Zn$	−0.76
chromium	Cr	Cr^{3+}/Cr	$Cr^{3+} + 3e^- \longrightarrow Cr$	−0.74
iron	Fe	Fe^{2+}/Fe	$Fe^{2+} + 2e^- \longrightarrow Fe$	−0.44
		$PbSO_4/Pb$	$PbSO_4 + 2e^- \longrightarrow Pb + SO_4^{2-}$	−0.36
nickel	Ni	Ni^{2+}/Ni	$Ni^{2+} + 2e^- \longrightarrow Ni$	−0.25
tin	Sn	Sn^{2+}/Sn	$Sn^{2+} + 2e^- \longrightarrow Sn$	−0.14
lead	Pb	Pb^{2+}/Pb	$Pb^{2+} + 2e^- \longrightarrow Pb$	−0.13
		Fe^{3+}/Fe	$Fe^{3+} + 3e^- \longrightarrow Fe$	−0.036
(hydrogen)	(H)	H^+/H_2	$2H^+ + 2e^- \longrightarrow H_2$	0.000
		$AgCl/Ag$	$AgCl + e^- \longrightarrow Ag + Cl^-$	+0.22
copper	Cu	Cu^{2+}/Cu	$Cu^{2+} + 2e^- \longrightarrow Cu$	+0.34
iodine	I	I_2/I^-	$I_2 + 2e^- \longrightarrow 2I^-$	+0.54
		Fe^{3+}/Fe^{2+}	$Fe^{3+} + e^- \longrightarrow Fe^{2+}$	+0.77
mercury	Hg	Hg_2^{2+}/Hg	$Hg_2^{2+} + 2e^- \longrightarrow 2Hg$	+0.79
silver	Ag	Ag^+/Ag	$Ag^+ + e^- \longrightarrow Ag$	+0.80
bromine	Br	Br_2/Br^-	$Br_2 + 2e^- \longrightarrow 2Br^-$	+1.07
platinum	Pt	Pt^{2+}/Pt	$Pt^{2+} + 2e^- \longrightarrow Pt$	+1.20
		O_2/H_2O	$O_2 + 4H^+ + 4e^- \longrightarrow 2H_2O$	+1.23
		MnO_2/Mn^{2+}	$MnO_2 + 4H^+ + 2e^- \longrightarrow Mn^{2+} + 2H_2O$	+1.28
		$Cr_2O_7^{2-}/Cr^{3+}$	$Cr_2O_7^{2-} + 14H^+ + 6e^- \longrightarrow 2Cr^{3+} + 7H_2O$	+1.33
chlorine	Cl	Cl_2/Cl^-	$Cl_2 + 2e^- \longrightarrow 2Cl^-$	+1.36
		PbO_2/Pb^{2+}	$PbO_2 + 4H^+ + 2e^- \longrightarrow Pb^{2+} + 2H_2O$	+1.46
gold	Au	Au^{3+}/Au	$Au^{3+} + 3e^- \longrightarrow Au$	+1.50
		MnO_4^-/Mn^{2+}	$MnO_4^- + 8H^+ + 5e^- \longrightarrow Mn^{2+} + 4H_2O$	+1.51
		$PbO_2/PbSO_4$	$PbO_2 + 4H^+ + SO_4^{2-} + 2e^- \longrightarrow PbSO_4 + 2H_2O$	+1.69
fluorine	F	F_2/F^-	$F_2 + 2e^- \longrightarrow 2F^-$	+2.87

Calculating E^0 values for electrochemical cells

Voltaic cells are made from spontaneous redox reactions. Spontaneity is represented by a positive value for E^0cell, which is calculated according to the following equation.

$$E^0 \text{ cell} = E^0 \text{ cathode} - E^0 \text{ anode}$$

When evaluating two half-reactions from which you expect to make a voltaic cell, the reaction with the lower value for E^0 in **Table 15-1** will be the anode.

Consider the zinc/copper cell discussed in Section 15-1. The two half-reactions involved and their E^0 values from the reduction potential table are as follows.

$$Zn^{2+}(aq) + 2e^- \longrightarrow Zn(s) \qquad E^0 = -0.76 \text{ V}$$

$$Cu^{2+}(aq) + 2e^- \longrightarrow Cu(s) \qquad E^0 = +0.34 \text{ V}$$

Reduction of Zn^{2+} ion has the lower value for E^0, so Zn is the anode. E^0 cell is +1.10 V, the difference between cathode and anode values for E^0. This agrees with the voltmeter reading in **Figure 15-8**.

Now consider a cell made from Al and Zn. The reduction half-reactions involved and their E^0 values from the table are as follows.

$$Zn^{2+}(aq) + 2e^- \longrightarrow Zn(s) \qquad E^0 = -0.76 \text{ V}$$

$$Al^{3+}(aq) + 3e^- \longrightarrow Al(s) \qquad E^0 = -1.66 \text{ V}$$

Al is the anode because its reaction has the lower reduction potential. E^0 cell for this reaction is + 0.90 V.

If the value calculated for E^0 cell is negative, the proposed redox reaction is not a voltaic cell because it is nonspontaneous. Voltaic cells are not limited to metal electrodes. The same approach is used for nonmetal electrodes.

Electrons move about an electrochemical cell in a circular path beginning at the anode. They are persuaded to move by differing tendencies to lose electrons at the anode and cathode. Reduction potentials assigned to half-reactions are used to predict the movement of electrons in the external circuit. But how many electrons are moving? Redox reactions require the number of electrons lost to equal the number of electrons gained. How can we be sure that electrons are conserved?

Section Review

6. What information concerning redox reactions does the activity series provide?
7. Why can the order of the metals in an activity series be considered a periodic trend?
8. Define the terms *half-cell* and *half-reaction*.
9. Explain what a standard reduction potential represents.
10. Two half-cells, one containing Fe^{3+} and Fe and the other containing Ag^+ and Ag, are connected to form a voltaic cell. Use **Table 15-1** to determine the direction of spontaneous reaction and the value for E^0 cell. Diagram the cell and label its parts. Give equations for the half-reactions.

How are electron transfers described?

Oxidation states

Redox equations are the basis of electrochemistry. As the name implies, they are made of two half-reactions, namely, reduction and oxidation. Oxidation involves the loss of electrons and takes place at the anode. Reduction involves the gain of electrons and takes place at the cathode. Reduction and oxidation must occur simultaneously, but they are balanced separately and then added together to give the overall balanced redox equation. Identifying the half-reactions and balancing redox equations requires a thorough knowledge of oxidation states.

oxidation state
a numerical representation of an atom's share of the bonding electrons. In ionic compounds, it is equal to the ionic charge. In covalent compounds, it is the average charge assigned to an atom according to electronegativities

Oxidation states represent an atom's share of the molecule's bonding electrons

Half-reactions, hence redox reactions, are characterized by the loss and gain of electrons. This trading of electrons brings about changes in the oxidation states of elements participating in the reaction. An **oxidation state**, also known as an *oxidation number*, is a value representing the apparent charge for each atom in a molecule based on the general distribution of bonding electrons among all the atoms in that molecule.

Keep in mind that an oxidation state, unlike an ionic charge, does not have an exact physical meaning. For example, an ionic charge of 1− means the gain of one electron whereas an oxidation state of −1 means a greater attraction for a bonding electron. That is, the oxidation state assigned to an atom in a molecule is related to the electronegativity value of that atom. Because electrons are negatively charged, negative numbers reflect stronger attraction for electrons than do positive numbers. The larger the negative value, the stronger the attraction. Conversely, the larger the positive value, the smaller the attraction.

The Lewis dot structures in the feature on the next page show how oxidation states are assigned to chlorine in Cl_2, NaCl, HCl, ClF_3, and ClO_4^-. As you know, NaCl is an ionic compound consisting of Na^+ and Cl^- ions. Their ionic charges are taken as a measure of their attraction for electrons. They are assigned oxidation states equal to their ionic charges.

Figure 15-10
Compounds of transition elements such as chromium produce colored solutions. The color is often an indicator of the element's oxidation state. Chromium is yellow or orange in its +6 state but green in its +3 state.

Step	Activity	Cl$_2$	NaCl
1	Identify the type of substance.	uncombined element	ionic compound
2	Draw the Lewis dot structure and determine bond polarity.	$:\ddot{C}l:\ddot{C}l:$	$\left[Na\right]^+ \left[:\ddot{C}l:\right]^-$
3	For each bond, assess which of the two atoms has a greater attraction for the bonding electrons.	Both Cl atoms contribute to the bond. Both atoms have the same electonegativity, so neither atom attracts the bonding electrons more than the other one. Their share in the bond is equal.	Both atoms contribute to the bond. The Cl atom is more strongly electronegative than Na and pulls the one electron from Na's valence shell to itself. The charge on the ion formed is the oxidation state for that atom.
4	Assign each atom an oxidation state (or charge) based on the results of step 3.	Cl = 0 Cl = 0	Na = +1 Cl = −1
5	Add all of the assigned oxidation states. They should equal zero or the total charge of the ion.	0 + 0 = 0	(+1) + (−1) = 0

Rules for assigning oxidation states

From these electronegativity-based assignments for oxidation states we can derive some general rules that will allow us to assign oxidation states to atoms quickly and easily.

1. The oxidation state of any free (uncombined) element is 0.
2. The oxidation state of a monatomic ion is equal to the charge on the ion.
3. The more electronegative element in a binary compound is assigned the number equal to the charge it would have if it were an ion.
4. The oxidation state of each hydrogen atom is +1 unless it is combined with a metal, then it has a state of −1.
5. The oxidation state of fluorine is always −1 because it is the most electronegative atom.

HCl	ClF$_3$	ClO$_4^-$
diatomic covalent compound	polyatomic covalent compound	polyatomic ion

H ⨯ Cl ⨯	(structure of ClF$_3$ Lewis dot)	(structure of ClO$_4^-$ Lewis dot, bracketed with − charge)

| Both atoms contribute to the bond. The Cl atom is more electronegative than H. It attracts its own bonding electron plus that from H, creating a permanent dipole. Cl has the greater share of the bonding electrons. | For each Cl—F bond, both atoms contribute to the bond. F is more electronegative than Cl, so it creates a polar bond by attracting its own electron plus the one donated from Cl. F has the greater share of the bonding electrons. Cl has the lesser share of three separate bonds, so its oxidation state is the accumulation from all three bonds. | The overall charge on this ion indicates one valence electron is from some element which formed the cation. It is shown here as ⬤ and given to one of the O atoms because O is more electronegative than Cl. The O for this Cl—O bond attracts both this electron from space and one bonding electron from Cl. The bonds between Cl and the remaining 3 O atoms are coordinate covalent bonds, i.e., both of the bonding electrons are donated by Cl toward O. Therefore, these 3 O atoms attract *both* electrons rather than one. |

| H = +1
Cl = −1 | Cl = (+1) + (+1) + (+1) = (+3)
F = −1
F = −1
F = −1 | Cl = (+1) + (+2) + (+2) + (+2) = +7
O = −2
O = −2
O = −2
O = −2 |

| (+1) + (−1) = 0 | (+3) + (−1) + (−1) + (−1) = 0 | (+7) + (−2) + (−2) + (−2) + (−2) = −1 |

6. The oxidation state of each oxygen atom in most of its compounds is −2. When combined with F, oxygen has a state of +2. In peroxides, such as H_2O_2, oxygen has an oxidation state of −1.

7. In compounds, the elements of Group 1 and Group 2, and aluminum have positive oxidation states of +1, +2, and +3, respectively.

8. The algebraic sum of the oxidation states for all the atoms in a compound is 0.

9. The algebraic sum of the oxidation states for all the atoms in a polyatomic ion is equal to the charge on that ion.

Rules 8 and 9 make it possible to assign oxidation states that are not known. The total of the known and the unknown oxidation numbers must satisfy rule 8 or rule 9, as illustrated in Sample Problems 15A and 15B.

Sample Problem 15A
Assigning oxidation states to atoms in covalent compounds

Assign oxidation numbers to all atoms in sulfurous acid.

❶ List
- the formula for sulfurous acid: H_2SO_3
- the charge on H using rule 4 from the list in the feature on page 588: $+1$
- the charge on O using rule 6 from the list in the feature on page 589: -2

❷ Set up
- You are trying to find the oxidation number for S in H_2SO_3. If more than one atom of an element is present in the formula, you must first calculate the total charge contributed by those atoms by multiplying the charge on the individual atom by its subscript in the formula.

  H: $(+1)\,2 = +2$

  O: $(-2)\,3 = -6$

  S: $(x)\,1 = x$

- Set up an equation using rule 8 from the feature on page 589: -2

  $(+2) + (x) + (-6) = 0$

❸ Calculate
- Solve for x.

  $(x) - 4 = 0$

  $x = +4$

- The oxidation state assigned to S in H_2SO_3 is $+4$; to H is $+1$; and to O is -2.

Sample Problem 15B
Assigning oxidation states to atoms in polyatomic ions

Assign oxidation numbers to all atoms in $S_2O_7^{2-}$.

❶ List
- the formula: $S_2O_7^{2-}$
- the charge on O using rule 6 from the list in the feature on page 589: -2

❷ Set up
- You are trying to find the oxidation number for S in $S_2O_7^{2-}$. If more than one atom of an element is present in the formula, you must first calculate the total charge contributed by those atoms by multiplying the charge on the individual atom by its subscript in the formula.

  O: $(-2)\,7 = -14$

  S: $(x)\,2 = 2x$

- Set up an equation using rule 9 from the feature on page 589.

  $2(x) + (-14) = -2$

❸ Calculate
- Solve for x

  $2(x) = +12$

  $x = +6$

- The oxidation state assigned to S in $S_2O_7^{2-}$ is $+6$ and to O is -2.

Practice 15A
1. Find the oxidation state assigned to P in H_3PO_4.

2. Find the oxidation state for each atom in BF_3.

15B
3. Find the oxidation state assigned to Mn in MnO_4^-.

4. Find the oxidation state assigned to each atom in NH_4^+.

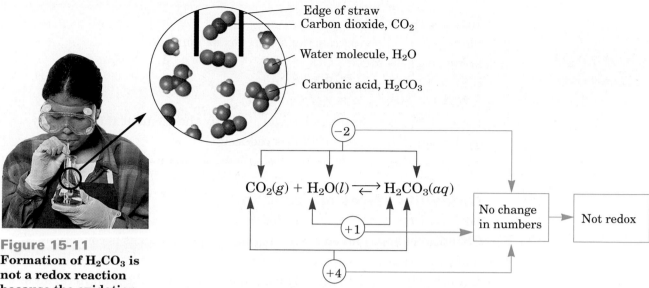

Edge of straw
Carbon dioxide, CO_2

Water molecule, H_2O

Carbonic acid, H_2CO_3

$$CO_2(g) + H_2O(l) \rightleftharpoons H_2CO_3(aq)$$

No change in numbers → Not redox

Figure 15-11
Formation of H_2CO_3 is not a redox reaction because the oxidation states for all three atoms remain the same.

Figure 15-12
Formation of sugar and H_2O during photosynthesis is a redox reaction because the oxidation state for C decreases from +4 to 0, and the oxidation state for some of the O increases from −2 to 0. Hydrogen's oxidation state does not change.

Changes in oxidation states indicate a redox reaction

Figure 15-11 shows how CO_2, an acid anhydride produced by your body, reacts with water. You learned in Chapter 13 that an acid anhydride is an oxide that reacts with water to form an acid. Is this a redox reaction? To decide, first assign oxidation states to all elements, as in **Figure 15-11**. Then compare the oxidation states of C, O, and H on the left side of the arrow with those on the right side of the arrow. The oxidation states for C, O, and H did not change, as evidenced by the values on the red arrows. Nothing has been oxidized or reduced, so this is not a redox reaction.

Now consider the reaction shown in **Figure 15-12**. Through photosynthesis, plants convert carbon dioxide and water into sugars and oxygen. The equation is not balanced as written, but oxidation states of the elements can still be assigned because they depend only on the relationship between atom and molecule.

The oxidation state for C has changed from +4 in CO_2 to 0 in $C_6H_{12}O_6$, as the arrow on the upper red line in **Figure 15-12** indicates. Carbon has been reduced because each C atom has gained four electrons. Arrows on the lower red line show that the oxidation state of O has gone from −2 in both CO_2 and H_2O to 0 in O_2. The oxidation state of O in $C_6H_{12}O_6$ is still −2; it did not change. Oxygen has been oxidized because each O atom that became part of an O_2 molecule has lost two electrons. There has been a change in oxidation states; this is a redox reaction. Any time a pure element appears as a reactant or product, the reaction is a redox reaction.

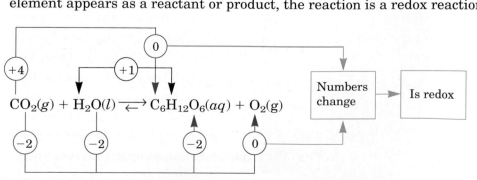

$$CO_2(g) + H_2O(l) \rightleftharpoons C_6H_{12}O_6(aq) + O_2(g)$$

Numbers change → Is redox

Redox reactions

11. Identify the following reactions as redox or nonredox.

    a. $MgCO_3 \longrightarrow MgO + CO_2$

    b. $Zn + CuSO_4 \longrightarrow ZnSO_4 + Cu$

    c. $NaCl + AgNO_3 \longrightarrow AgCl + NaNO_3$

12. For each redox reaction in item **11**, identify the element that is oxidized and the element that is reduced.

Answers for Concept Review items and Practice problems begin on page 841.

Oxidation states are used for balancing a redox equation

Chemical changes involve rearranging atoms and mass is conserved. You have seen that redox reactions are represented by chemical equations like any other chemical change. Thus, redox equations, like all others, must be balanced so that the law of conservation of mass is obeyed. In addition to mass, electrons are also transferred during redox reactions. Charge must be conserved; consequently, the sum of all the oxidation states on the left side of the equation must equal the sum of all the oxidation states on the right side of the equation. Every redox equation must be balanced in terms of mass and charge.

Figure 15-13
The alcohol in a person's breath is oxidized to acetic acid by dichromate ions in acidic solution. Dichromate ions are orange. The reduced Cr^{3+} ion is green. Appearance of a green color indicates an alcohol content greater than the legal limit.

Balancing redox equations by the half-reaction method

The person shown in **Figure 15-13** is suspected of driving while intoxicated. A Breathalyzer is an instrument for estimating blood alcohol levels outside a

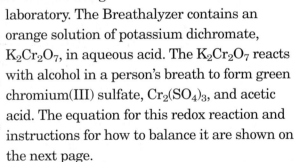

laboratory. The Breathalyzer contains an orange solution of potassium dichromate, $K_2Cr_2O_7$, in aqueous acid. The $K_2Cr_2O_7$ reacts with alcohol in a person's breath to form green chromium(III) sulfate, $Cr_2(SO_4)_3$, and acetic acid. The equation for this redox reaction and instructions for how to balance it are shown on the next page.

One approach to balancing a redox equation involves separating it into half-reactions, balancing them separately in terms of charge and mass, and recombining them. Since each half-reaction is balanced separately, this approach is called the *half-reaction method*. The oxidation states that change in the reaction are the only ones shown. Each Cr atom in $K_2Cr_2O_7$ went from a $+6$ oxidation state to a $+3$ oxidation state in $Cr_2(SO_4)_3$. Three electrons were gained, so Cr was reduced. Each carbon atom in the alcohol has gone from a -2 oxidation state to a 0 oxidation state in the acetic acid. Because two electrons were lost, each C atom was oxidized. The electrons that a C atom loses are gained, in turn, by a Cr atom. Oxidation and reduction occur simultaneously.

Balance equations by the half-reaction method

Balance the following redox reaction.

$$K_2Cr_2O_7(aq) + H_2SO_4(aq) + C_2H_5OH(sol) \longrightarrow$$

$$Cr_2(SO_4)_3(aq) + C_2H_4O_2(l) + H_2O(l) + K_2SO_4(aq)$$

1. Write the formula equation if it is not given in the problem. Then write the ionic equation.

$$2K^+(aq) + Cr_2O_7^{2-}(aq) + 2H^+(aq) + SO_4^{2-}(aq) + C_2H_5OH(sol) \longrightarrow$$

$$2Cr^{3+}(aq) + 3SO_4^{2-}(aq) + C_2H_4O_2(sol) + H_2O(l) + 2K^+(aq) + SO_4^{2-}(aq)$$

2. Assign oxidation numbers to each element and ion. Retain only those substances containing an element that changes oxidation state.

$$\overset{+6}{Cr_2}\overset{-2}{O_7^{2-}} + C_2H_5OH \longrightarrow 2\overset{+3}{Cr^{3+}} + \overset{0}{C_2H_4O_2}$$

3. Write the half-reaction for oxidation.

$$C_2H_5OH \longrightarrow C_2H_4O_2$$

When balancing redox equations, use the short-hand form of H_3O^+, which is H^+.

- **Balance the mass.** C atoms are balanced, but H and O atoms are not, so add 1 H_2O to the left side of the equation and 4 H^+ ions to the right. Because H_2O is the solvent and dissociates by itself into H^+ and OH^- ions, H^+ is used to balance H atoms and H_2O balances O atoms. The equation is now balanced for atoms but not for charge.

$$1H_2O + C_2H_5OH \longrightarrow C_2H_4O_2 + 4H^+$$

The left side has a net charge of 0. The right side has a net charge of +4.

- **Balance the charge.** Electrons are added to the side having the greater positive net charge. Add $4e^-$ to the right side to balance charge. C atoms on the left side of the equation lose $2e^-$ each.

$$1H_2O + C_2H_5OH \longrightarrow C_2H_4O_2 + 4H^+ + 4e^-$$

4. Write the half-reaction for reduction.

$$Cr_2O_7^{2-} \longrightarrow 2Cr^{3+}$$

The left side has a net charge of +12. The right side has a net charge of +6.

- **Balance the mass.** Cr atoms are balanced. Add $7H_2O$ to the right side to balance the O atoms. Then balance the H atoms by adding $14H^+$ to the left side of the equation.

$$Cr_2O_7^{2-} + 14H^+ \longrightarrow 2Cr^{3+} + 7H_2O$$

- **Balance the charge.** Electrons are added to the side having the greater positive net charge. Add $6e^-$ to the left side of the equation to make the charges equal. Cr atoms on the left side of the equation gain $3e^-$ each.

$$Cr_2O_7^{2-} + 14H^+ + 6e^- \longrightarrow 2Cr^{3+} + 7H_2O$$

How To continued on following page . . .

5. Conserve charge by adjusting the coefficients in front of the electrons so that the number lost in oxidation equals the number gained in reduction.

Set up a ratio of the electrons lost to the electrons gained. Reduce the ratio to its lowest terms.

The 4 comes from step 3.
The 6 comes from step 4.

$$\frac{4}{6} \text{ becomes } \frac{2}{3}$$

Multiply the oxidation half-reaction by the denominator, 3.

$$3H_2O + 3C_2H_5OH \longrightarrow 3C_2H_4O_2 + 12H^+ + 12e^-$$

Multiply the reduction half-reaction by the numerator, 2.

$$2Cr_2O_7{}^{2-} + 28H^+ + 12e^- \longrightarrow 4Cr^{3+} + 14H_2O$$

6. Combine the half-reactions, subtracting out the electrons from both sides of the equation.

$$3H_2O + 2Cr_2O_7{}^{2-} + 28H^+ + 3C_2H_5OH \longrightarrow$$
$$3C_2H_4O_2 + 12H^+ + 4Cr^{3+} + 14H_2O$$

You see that H_2O and H^+ ions are on both sides of the equation. Combine H^+ ions by subtracting the smaller quantity, $12H^+$, from both sides of the equation. Do the same for H_2O.

$$2Cr_2O_7{}^{2-} + 16H^+ + 3C_2H_5OH \longrightarrow 3C_2H_4O_2 + 4Cr^{3+} + 11H_2O$$

7. Combine ions to form the compounds shown in the formula equation and then add the remaining ions from the ionic equation.

Ions from K_2SO_4 were eliminated as spectators in the ionic equation.

To re-form reactant compounds, combine $Cr_2O_7{}^{2-}$ with $2K^+$ and $2H^+$ with $SO_4{}^{2-}$. To re-form products, combine $2Cr^{3+}$ with $3SO_4{}^{2-}$ ions and $2K^+$ ions with a $SO_4{}^{2-}$ ion.

$$2K_2Cr_2O_7 + 8H_2SO_4 + 3C_2H_5OH \longrightarrow$$
$$3C_2H_4O_2 + 2Cr_2(SO_4)_3 + 11H_2O + 2K_2SO_4$$

Section Review

13. Determine the oxidation numbers for each element in the following compounds: $Na_2S_2O_3$, H_2SeO_3, and H_2O_2.

14. Which of the following unbalanced equations represent redox reactions?
    a. $SO_3 + H_2O \longrightarrow H_2SO_4$
    b. $Pb(C_2H_3O_2)_2 + H_2S \longrightarrow PbS + HC_2H_3O_2$
    c. $I_2O_5 + CO \longrightarrow I_2 + CO_2$

15. Use the half-reaction method to balance the following equations.
    a. $Ag + NO_3{}^- \longrightarrow Ag^+ + NO$
    b. $H_2SO_4 + KI \longrightarrow K_2SO_4 + I_2 + SO_2 + H_2O$

How do batteries work?

Section Objectives

Identify criteria for selecting or designing a battery.

Describe the redox reactions that occur in dry-cell, alkaline, and mercury batteries.

Distinguish between an electrochemical cell and an electrolytic cell.

Describe the redox reactions that occur in rechargeable batteries.

Consumable batteries

All the batteries shown in **Figure 15-14** depend on redox reactions in which chemical energy is converted into electric energy. From what you have learned about electrochemistry, you can now examine various aspects of redox reactions that must be taken into account when designing a **battery**.

battery
single voltaic cell or group of voltaic cells that are connected together

1. Metals and their ions must be chosen so that a spontaneous redox reaction occurs.
2. The E^o values for the half-reactions should be such that when combined, the desired voltage is obtained.
3. The redox reactions should be easily reversible if a rechargeable battery is wanted. Metals chosen for the electrodes in rechargeable batteries should be close together in the activity series.
4. The effect of reaction products on the environment must be considered, especially if they are gases or toxic materials.

Figure 15-14
The size, voltage output, and longevity of a battery depends on the half-reactions that occur within it and the nature of the electrolyte.

Relative Longevity of Batteries

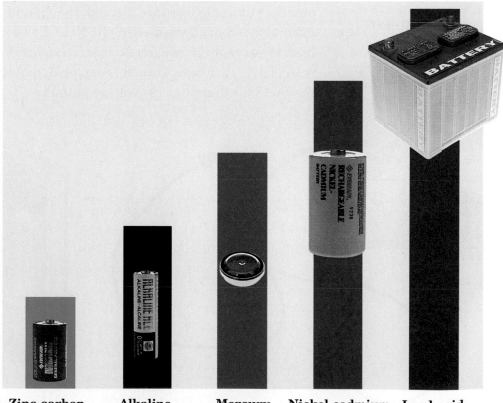

Zinc-carbon   Alkaline   Mercury   Nickel-cadmium   Lead-acid

The most common battery is a zinc-carbon cell bridged by an NH₄Cl paste

The most commonly used battery, known as a dry cell, depends on the energy generated by a redox reaction involving zinc and manganese dioxide. Each year, more than 5 billion such batteries are used throughout the world, requiring over 30 metric tons of zinc per day.

These batteries are really not dry at all. Rather, they consist of a zinc container that serves as the anode and is filled with a moist paste of MnO_2, graphite, and ammonium chloride, NH_4Cl, as you can see in **Figure 15-15**. Oxidation of the zinc metal occurs at the anode.

$$Zn(s) \longrightarrow Zn^{2+}(aq) + 2e^-$$

Electrons travel through the external circuit and re-enter the battery through the carbon rod. The carbon rod functions as the cathode where MnO_2 is reduced in the presence of H_2O.

$$2MnO_2(s) + H_2O(l) + 2e^- \longrightarrow Mn_2O_3(s) + 2OH^-(aq)$$

This reaction is followed by a secondary reaction between OH^- ions and NH_4Cl. Ammonia gas is produced in this secondary reaction. Dry-cell batteries should never be recharged because the buildup of product gases can cause the sealed dry cell to explode.

This redox reaction produces a voltage of 1.5 V, so if your flashlight needs 3 V to light the bulb, you must use two of these batteries connected in series.

Unfortunately, this type of battery has two disadvantages. First, if the current is drawn too rapidly from the battery, the gaseous products cannot be removed quickly enough causing the redox reactions to slow down and the voltage to decrease. Second, the Zn and NH_4Cl react to a slight extent even though the electrolytic NH_4Cl paste is surrounded by a paper liner to prevent the two from coming into direct contact. As the Zn reacts with NH_4Cl, its concentration is depleted, and the loss of Zn decreases the life. This decreases the voltage output.

Figure 15-15
Carbon supplies the surface for the manganese reduction reactions in a dry cell. The Zn container acts as the anode. The voltage for this battery is 1.5 V. It has a relatively short shelf life and cannot be recharged.

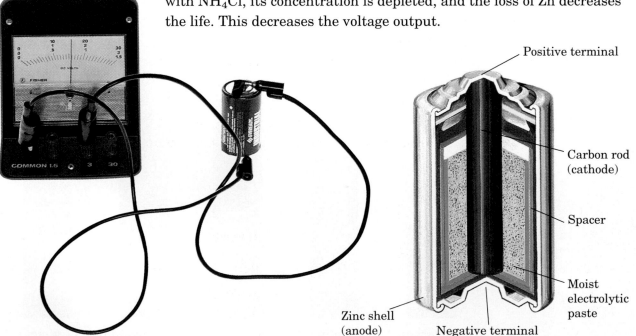

Positive terminal

Carbon rod (cathode)

Spacer

Moist electrolytic paste

Zinc shell (anode)

Negative terminal

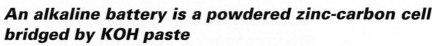

An alkaline battery is a powdered zinc-carbon cell bridged by KOH paste

As you can see in **Figure 15-16**, an alkaline battery differs from a dry cell in that it uses KOH instead of NH_4Cl. KOH is a base, so the electrolyte paste in this type of battery is alkaline. As with an ordinary dry cell, zinc is added, but this time as a powder in a gel-thickened mixture with KOH. Oxidation of Zn to either $[Zn(OH)_4]^{2-}$ or ZnO occurs at the anode while MnO_2 is reduced to $Mn(OH)_2$ at the cathode. It produces 1.5 V, the same as a dry cell battery. However, no gases are formed in an alkaline battery reaction, and no unwanted side reactions occur to reduce the voltage generated by the redox reaction. There is no acidic corrosion of the container as there is with a conventional dry cell. Elimination of the carbon post allows alkaline batteries to be made smaller than dry cells. Moreover, alkaline manganese batteries perform far better at temperatures significantly below freezing than conventional zinc-carbon batteries because their ions are more mobile.

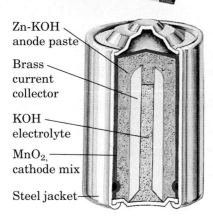

Zn-KOH anode paste

Brass current collector

KOH electrolyte

MnO_2, cathode mix

Steel jacket

Figure 15-16
The alkaline form of the dry cell performs better in a Walkman than does the acidic form in Figure 15-15. It is also easier to miniaturize because Zn is present as a powder, and there is no graphite rod.

A mercury battery is environmentally hazardous

The mercury battery shown in **Figure 15-17** is a close relative of the alkaline battery. Again, powdered zinc is oxidized by hydroxide ion at the anode, but solid mercury(II) oxide, HgO, is reduced to elemental mercury at the cathode. The equations for the electrochemical reactions are written as follows.

$$\text{Anode: } Zn + 2OH^- \longrightarrow ZnO + H_2O + 2e^-$$
$$\text{Cathode: } HgO + H_2O + 2e^- \longrightarrow Hg + 2OH^-$$
$$\text{Net redox: } Zn(s) + HgO(s) \longrightarrow ZnO(s) + Hg(l)$$

Because the electrolyte is not used up during the redox reaction, the cell potential changes very little as the alkali concentration changes. A steady output of 1.34 V makes this redox reaction especially valuable for use in communication equipment and scientific instruments for which power fluctuations would cause problems. However, the production of liquid mercury, a poisonous metal that can cause serious health and environmental problems, is a serious disadvantage for mercury batteries. Used mercury batteries must, therefore, be recycled to recover the elemental mercury.

Figure 15-17
The mercury cell, used to power the flash attachment in this camera, is an alkaline form of the dry cell. The cathode is HgO mixed with graphite, and the anode is Zn mixed with KOH.

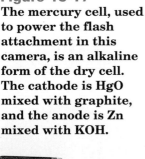

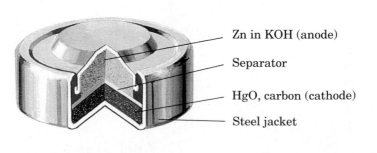

Zn in KOH (anode)

Separator

HgO, carbon (cathode)

Steel jacket

Rechargeable batteries
Electrochemical cells can be recharged

A voltage will be generated by a battery only if electrons continue to be removed from one substance and transferred to another. Once this process stops, voltage is no longer produced. This process stops when an equilibrium involving both half-cells is established, and the battery is "dead."

To regenerate a dead battery, it must be charged; that is, an external voltage source must be applied to the battery's electrodes so that all half-reactions are reversed and the electrodes are returned to their original state. Thus, while the battery is being used, it operates as a voltaic cell, converting chemical energy into electric energy. But, while the same battery is being charged, it operates as an electrolytic cell, converting electric energy into chemical energy.

The process in which electric energy is used to drive a redox reaction is **electrolysis**. The container in which electric energy drives a nonspontaneous redox reaction is an **electrolytic cell**.

A car battery is a combination electrochemical-electrolytic cell

A lead-acid battery like the type used in cars is shown in **Figure 15-18**. It produces 12 V from six cells that are connected to one another in a line. The anode in each cell is lead. The electrolytic solution is sulfuric acid, H_2SO_4.

The anode reaction is described by the following equation.

$$Pb(s) + SO_4{}^{2-}(aq) \longrightarrow PbSO_4(s) + 2e^-$$

The electrons move through the circuit to the cathode where PbO_2 is reduced.

$$PbO_2(s) + 4H^+(aq) + SO_4{}^{2-}(aq) + 2e^- \longrightarrow PbSO_4(s) + 2H_2O(l)$$

The following equation describes the net redox reaction.

$$Pb(s) + PbO_2(s) + 2H_2SO_4(aq) \longrightarrow 2PbSO_4(s) + 2H_2O(l)$$

Figure 15-18
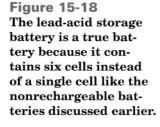
The lead-acid storage battery is a true battery because it contains six cells instead of a single cell like the nonrechargeable batteries discussed earlier.

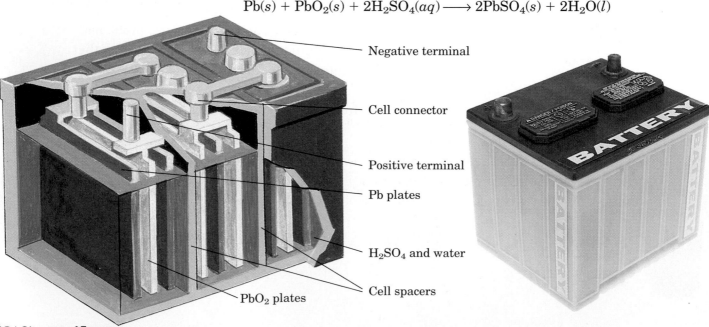

Negative terminal

Cell connector

Positive terminal

Pb plates

H_2SO_4 and water

Cell spacers

PbO_2 plates

A car's battery produces the 12 V needed to start its engine. H_2SO_4, present as its ions, is consumed and $PbSO_4$ accumulates as a white powder on the electrodes. Once the car is running, the alternator produces a voltage that reverses the battery's half-reactions and regenerates Pb, PbO_2, and H_2SO_4. A lead-acid battery can undergo many thousands of discharge-recharge cycles before it finally fails. At that point, too much $PbSO_4$ has flaked off the electrodes and is no longer available as a reactant for the reverse reactions. A battery can be recharged only when all reactants necessary for the electrolytic reaction are present, and all reactions are reversible.

A ni-cad battery is also rechargeable

Rechargeable and lightweight, nickel-cadmium batteries are becoming increasingly popular. They have two advantages over other rechargeable batteries: easily regenerated electrodes and production of a nearly constant 1.4 V.

Cadmium serves as the anode.

$$Cd(s) + 2OH^-(aq) \longrightarrow Cd(OH)_2(s) + 2e^-$$

NiO(OH) is reduced at the cathode.

$$2NiO(OH)(s) + 2H_2O(l) + 2e^- \longrightarrow 2Ni(OH)_2(s) + 2OH^-(aq)$$

The net reaction occurring in a Ni-Cad battery is written as follows.

$$Cd(s) + 2NiO(OH)(s) + 2H_2O(l) \longrightarrow Cd(OH)_2(s) + 2Ni(OH)_2(s)$$

Since the late 1970s cadmium as the element or in soluble compounds has been implicated in a number of very toxic effects on humans and wildlife. Therefore, some nations control the recycling and reprocessing of ni-cad storage batteries.

Figure 15-19
Current from a wall outlet provides the electric energy needed for recharging these nickel-cadmium batteries.

Section Review

16. Which of the following pairs of electrodes would make good batteries? Explain.
  a. $Cd \longrightarrow Cd^{2+} + 2e^-$; $Fe \longrightarrow Fe^{2+} + 2e^-$
  b. $Ag^+ + e^- \longrightarrow Ag$; $Cu^{2+} + 2e^- \longrightarrow Cu$

17. How is a 9 V battery made?

18. What advantages does an alkaline battery have over an ordinary dry cell?

19. What disadvantage does a mercury battery have that an alkaline battery does not have?

20. Describe an electrolytic cell.

21. Explain why a rechargeable battery can be considered a combination voltaic-electrolytic cell.

Breakthroughs in Properties of

1661
Robert Boyle introduces the concepts of element, molecule, compound, mixture, alkali, and acid. The following year he reports the inverse relation between pressure and volume for an ideal gas (Boyle's law).

1778
Joseph Priestley and **Karl Scheele** independently discover the element oxygen. **Antoine Lavoisier** recognizes it as the breathable component of air.

8
O
Oxygen
15.9994
[He]$2s^2 2p^4$

1782
Lavoisier observes that the total weights of reactants equal the total weights of products, thus establishing the law of conservation of matter.

1791
Jeremias Richter proposes the principle of stoichiometry, which states that chemicals always react in the same proportions.

$$2H_2(g) + O_2(g) \longrightarrow 2H_2O(g)$$

1864
Cato Guldberg and **Peter Waage**, in a series of experiments on equilibrium in incomplete reactions, establish the law of mass action, the first successful attempt to develop a theory of reaction rates. Their work anticipates Jacobus van't Hoff's more methodical version by six years.

$$Q = \frac{[C]^c[D]^d}{[A]^a[B]^b}$$

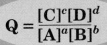

1869
Dmitri Mendeleev announces his periodic table of the elements. Gaps in the table successfully anticipate the discovery of unknown elements.

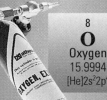

1898
Marie S. Curie, noting that the radioactivity from a uranium-bearing sample cannot come from the uranium alone, proposes that there are undiscovered radioactive elements. With her spouse Pierre Curie she discovers the elements polonium and radium.

1884
Svante Arrhenius proposes that electrolytes in solution dissociate into positive and negative ions, which carry current in the solution. Later, while relating temperature to reaction rates, he introduces the concept of activation energy.

1886
Charles Martin Hall and **Paul Héroult** independently prepare aluminum by electrolysis, a cheap process still used today.

Inorganic Substances

The following events significantly increased our understanding of chemistry through the identification of substances and their properties and the development of theoretical explanations of those properties.

1803

John Dalton, in the process of studying the behaviors of gases, forms the idea of atomic weights and, ultimately, the first systematic atomic theory.

1807

Humphry Davy isolates the alkali metals potassium and sodium through electrolysis. The following year he repeats the procedure, isolating the alkaline-earth metals barium, strontium, and calcium.

1811

Amedeo Avogadro, in a visionary paper, postulates the idea that equal volumes of gases contain equal numbers of particles and that some elements (such as oxygen) exist as diatomic molecules. Avogadro's ideas are ignored and forgotten until Stanislao Cannizzaro revives them in 1860.

$$6.022 \times 10^{23}$$

1833

Michael Faraday discovers that many nonconducting solids conduct electricity in a liquid state, leading to the first understanding of electrolytes. Later, Faraday notes that the amount a substance dissociates in electrolysis is proportional to the amount of current passing through the fluid.

1909

Danish chemist **S.P.L. Sørensen** proposes the concept of pH as a measure of the acidity or basicity of a solution.

1923

Thomas Lowry, J. N. Brønsted, and **Niels Bjerrum** suggest that acids donate hydrogen ions and bases accept them. By contrast, **Gilbert Lewis** suggests that bases donate electron pairs and acids accept them.

$$HB(aq) + H_2O(aq) \rightleftharpoons H_3O^+(aq) + B^-(aq)$$

1934

Arnold Beckman devises the first electronic instrument to directly measure the pH of a solution.

1962

Neil Bartlett demonstrates the first chemical reaction of a noble gas when he reacts xenon with platinum hexafluoride.

1967

Yuan Tseh Lee develops improved methods for observing chemical reactions. Using colliding beams of molecules he determines how energies are distributed in reactants to form products.

Conclusion: Fireflies and Electrochemical Cells

You have learned that luciferin is a chemical compound in the tail of a firefly. Under the proper conditions it can be made to produce light. This bioluminescence results from a series of redox reactions. You have also seen that light can be produced by redox reactions in electrochemical cells. Look again at the questions raised at the beginning of this chapter.

How is the light generated by a firefly different from the light generated by a flashlight battery? In a flashlight the electrons flow from the battery's anode to its cathode via the filament in a light bulb. Due to its resistance, the filament becomes hot and incandescent. It radiates all wavelengths in a continuous spectrum. On the other hand, special cells in the tail of a firefly oxidize luciferin, whose formula is $C_{11}H_8N_2O_3S_2$, to $C_{10}H_6N_2O_2S_2$. The electrons in the latter compound are in an excited state, and fall to the ground state, just as electrons do in excited atoms. They emit almost monochromatic light in the yellow region of the spectrum.

How is the concentration of TB cells related to the brightness of the light emitted? A firefly controls its light emission by controlling the amount of air supplied to the light-producing organs of its tail.

Adenosine triphosphate (ATP) is present in all living cells, including TB cells, and is required for the oxidation of luciferin. As long as TB cells are alive, they multiply. This makes ATP available for oxidizing luciferin so the glow continues. An antibiotic that kills the TB cells decreases the brightness of the glow by decreasing cell reproduction.

The voltage output of an electrochemical cell is related to the absolute concentration of the chemicals in the cell. Operation of the cell causes a decrease in reactants and voltage output. You see these changes as a dimmer light in a flashlight or as fainter volume in a tape player.

Applying Concepts

1. The range of a battery is estimated by adding the atomic masses of all the reactants, and dividing this sum by the number of electrons produced in the redox reaction. The answer is expressed in amu/electron. Calculate the range for both a lead-acid and a mercury battery.
2. If your gums and saliva act as a salt bridge, sketch the electrochemical cell that would produce a small jolt of pain when you bite down on an aluminum gum wrapper with a silver-filled tooth. Include half-reactions and E^O value for the cell.

Research and Writing

1. Determine how electroplating of metals is done, and cite examples of products made this way.
2. Investigate the use of cathodic protection in the construction industry.

15 Highlights

Key terms

anode

battery

cathode

circuit

electricity

electrolysis

electrolytic cell

half-cell

half-reaction

oxidation

oxidation state

porous barrier

redox reaction

reduction

reduction potential

SHE

standard reduction potential

voltaic cell

Key problem-solving approach:
Assigning oxidation numbers

When assigning oxidation numbers to molecules or polyatomic ions, first determine the oxidation numbers of the elements that are listed in the rules on pages 588–589. Then, solve for the unknown element so that the sum of the oxidation numbers equals zero or the ionic charge.

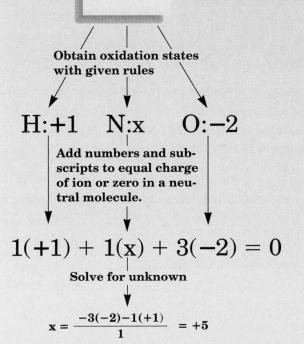

compound or ion

Ex: HNO_3

Obtain oxidation states with given rules

$$H:+1 \quad N:x \quad O:-2$$

Add numbers and subscripts to equal charge of ion or zero in a neutral molecule.

$$1(+1) + 1(x) + 3(-2) = 0$$

Solve for unknown

$$x = \frac{-3(-2)-1(+1)}{1} = +5$$

 ## How does electric current flow?

- A half-cell consists of a metal electrode immersed in a solution of its ions. Two half-cells combine to form an electrochemical cell. If electric energy is produced, the cell is voltaic.
- The flow of free electrons through a circuit produces electricity in a voltaic cell.
- An element loses electrons when it is oxidized and gains electrons when it is reduced.
- Reduction and oxidation are always paired in redox reactions.

 ## How do you get current to flow?

- Reduction potentials are linked directly to the activity series.
- The standard reduction potential, which is the voltage produced by a half-cell that is connected to the standard hydrogen electrode, can be used to predict the outcome of a redox reaction.
- Reduction potentials are assigned to the two half-reactions of an electrochemical cell. The cell potential is calculated by subtracting the lower reduction potential from the higher one.

 ## How are electron transfers described?

- An oxidation state represents the attraction of an atom for the bonding electrons in a molecule. The oxidation state of an atom varies depending on the other atoms present in a molecule or ion.
- Redox reactions involve changes in oxidation states.
- Redox equations may be balanced by separating the reaction into half-reactions, balancing the half-reactions in terms of mass and charge, and then recombining them.
- Both mass and charge are conserved in redox reactions.

 ## How do batteries work?

- Batteries run on redox reactions.
- A battery is "dead" when its component half-cells reach equilibrium with each other.
- Electrolytic cells are electrochemical cells in which electric energy is converted into chemical energy. They are the opposite of voltaic cells.
- Applied external current restores the half-cells of rechargeable batteries to their original, unreacted states.

The movement of electrons

REVIEW

1. a. What purpose does the porous barrier in an electrochemical cell serve?
   b. Would the cell produce electricity if the barrier were not there? Explain.
2. Why must oxidation and reduction always occur together in a reaction?
3. Can electricity be generated in a single half-cell? Explain.
4. a. Once electrons begin to flow, what happens to the cation concentration in the cathodic half-cell?
   b. How does the process in part **a** affect the cation concentration in the anodic half-cell?
   c. Would a light bulb shine if only water molecules could pass through the barrier? Explain.

APPLY

5. How is an electric circuit similar to a race track?
6. A friend tells you that only acids can dissolve metals. Is this true? Explain.
7. Identify the following half-reactions as oxidation or reduction.
   a. $Pb^{2+} \longrightarrow Pb^{4+} + 2e^-$
   b. $Pt^{2+} + 2e^- \longrightarrow Pt$
   c. $F_2 + 2e^- \longrightarrow 2F^-$
   d. $Ra \longrightarrow Ra^{2+} + 2e^-$
8. Use **Figure 15-2** to answer the following questions.
   a. Why does no reaction occur when zinc ions are in contact with the copper strip?
   b. Why do the copper ions not move towards the zinc strip?
9. Complete the following table.

	Oxidation/ reduction	Loss or gain of electrons	Change in charge
Cathode			
Anode			

10. Refer to the diagram below to answer the following questions.
   a. Why does heat production eventually stop in this reaction?
   b. What macroscopic observations suggest that a chemical reaction has taken place?
   c. What is happening at the microscopic level?

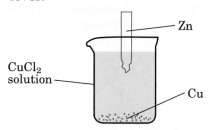

11. Draw diagrams of the following reactions at the particle level.
   a. oxidation
   b. reduction

Reduction potentials

REVIEW

12. Use **Table 15-1** to determine the E^o cell value for the spontaneous reaction of each pair of half-cells listed below.
   a. $Ag \longrightarrow Ag^+ + 1e^-$; $Fe^{2+} + 2e^- \longrightarrow Fe$
   b. $Mg \longrightarrow Mg^{2+} + 2e^-$; $Zn^{2+} + 2e^- \longrightarrow Zn$
   c. $Li \longrightarrow Li^+ + 1e^-$; $Mn^{2+} + 2e^- \longrightarrow Mn$
   d. $Cr \longrightarrow Cr^{3+} + 3e^-$; $Pt^{2+} + 2e^- \longrightarrow Pt$
   e. $Ni \longrightarrow Ni^{2+} + 2e^-$; $Cu^{2+} + 2e^- \longrightarrow Cu$
13. a. Why is a standard hydrogen electrode used to determine the number of volts produced by a half-cell?
   b. How is the reduction potential of the standard hydrogen electrode determined?
14. Why are some E^o values positive, while others are negative?
15. Compare the E^o value for a metal with the reactivity of that metal.

16. How does the ranking of metals in the activity series relate to the ranking of the following?
  a. electronegativities
  b. reduction potentials

17. Explain why the reduction potential for some half-reactions in **Table 15-1** are negative.

A P P L Y

18. How can the fact that iron dissolves in acid help predict how the iron will react in a voltaic cell?

19. Draw a diagram of what happens at each electrode at the particle level for each half-reaction in a voltaic cell. Compare your diagram to those from item **11**.

20. Label the cathode and the anode in the diagram below. Identify the half-reactions taking place in each half-cell.

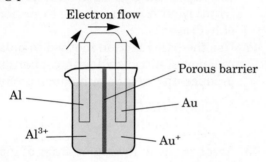

21. A friend has lost the labels for her experiment that identify the anode and cathode of the reaction below.
  a. List two observations that can determine the nature of the reaction.
  b. Label the anode and the cathode, and identify the half-reaction occurring in each of them.

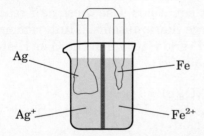

22. Evaluate a classmate's statement that because the E^0 value for H^+ is 0.00 V, hydrogen cannot be used in a voltaic cell.

23. Use **Table 15-1** to predict the voltage of the cells in the diagrams below.

a.

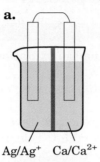

Ag/Ag⁺   Ca/Ca²⁺

b.

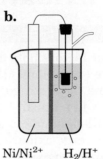

Ni/Ni²⁺   H₂/H⁺

c.

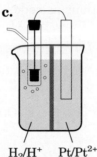

H₂/H⁺   Pt/Pt²⁺

24. Identify three nonmetal electrodes listed in **Table 15-1**.

25. Why does a negative E^0 cell indicate a non-spontaneous reaction?

26. One half-cell of a voltaic cell consists of a Zn strip dipped into a 1.00 M solution of $Zn(NO_3)_2$. In the other half-cell, solid indium adsorbed on graphite is in contact with a 1.00 M solution of $In(NO_3)_2$. Indium is observed to plate out as the cell operates. The initial voltage is measured to be + 0.425 V at 25°C.
  a. Write a balanced equation for the half-reaction at the anode and for the half-reaction at the cathode.
  b. Calculate the standard reduction potential for the In^{3+}/In half-cell. (Hint: consult **Table 15-1** for the reduction potential of the Zn^{2+}/Zn electrode, and use the equation on page 586.)

27. Iron or steel is often covered with a thin layer of a second metal to prevent rusting. Tin cans consist of steel covered with tin, and galvanized iron is made by coating iron with a layer of zinc. If the protective layer is broken, iron will rust more readily in a tin can than in galvanized iron. Explain this observation by comparing the half-cell potentials for iron, tin, and zinc.

Determining oxidation states

28. What factors help determine the oxidation state of an element?

29. Name the distinguishing characteristic of redox reactions.

30. Do all elements in a redox reaction have to undergo oxidation or reduction? Use an example to explain.

31. Identify the following reactions as redox or nonredox.

a. $2NH_4Cl(aq) + Ca(OH)_2(aq) \longrightarrow$
$2NH_3(aq) + 2H_2O(l) + CaCl_2(aq)$

b. $Ca(HCO_3)_2(aq) \xrightarrow{heat}$
$CaCO_3(aq) + CO_2(g) + H_2O(l)$

c. $2HNO_3(aq) + 3H_2S(g) \longrightarrow$
$2NO(g) + 4H_2O(l) + 3S(s)$

d. $[Be(H_2O)_4]^{2+}(aq) + H_2O(l) \longrightarrow$
$H_3O^+(aq) + [Be(H_2O)_3OH]^+(aq)$

e. $Mg(s) + ZnCl_2(aq) \longrightarrow$
$Zn(s) + MgCl_2(aq)$

32. Complete the table below.

	Electrons	Oxidation number	Charge
Oxidation			
Reduction			

Answers to items in a black square begin on page 841.

33. Assign oxidation numbers to the atoms in lead chloride, $PbCl_2$, an insoluble precipitate. (Hint: see Sample Problem 15A.)

34. Assign oxidation numbers to the atoms in magnesium hydroxide, $Mg(OH)_2$, an antacid. (Hint: see Sample Problem 15A.)

35. Assign oxidation numbers to the atoms in the following compounds. PbS, MnO_2, $LiAlH_4$, Na_2O_2, HgO, $NiO(OH)$, $PbSO_4$ (Hint: see Sample Problem 15A.)

36. Assign oxidation numbers to the atoms in the chlorate ion, ClO_3^-, used in explosives. (Hint: see Sample Problem 15B.)

37. Assign oxidation numbers to the atoms in a bicarbonate ion, HCO_3^-. (Hint: see Sample Problem 15B.)

38. Assign oxidation numbers to the atoms in the following ions. $AuCl_4^-$, $Zn(OH)_4^{2-}$, VO_2^+, $S_2O_3^{2-}$, SCN^-, $H_2BO_3^-$, BH_4^- (Hint: see Sample Problem 15B.)

39. Why is it important to balance the electrons in a redox reaction?

40. For the following reactions, identify the elements that are oxidized and reduced.

a. $H_2(g) + CuO(s) \longrightarrow Cu(s) + H_2O(l)$

b. $4Fe(s) + 3O_2(g) \longrightarrow 2Fe_2O_3(s)$

41. The owner's manual for a car includes a warning that overcharging a battery can produce explosive hydrogen gas. The hydrogen results from the electrolysis of water within the battery. At which electrode would you expect the hydrogen to be produced? (Hint: what happens to the oxidation state of hydrogen?)

42. Use the half-reaction method to balance the reaction of nitric acid with copper metal to produce nitric oxide, a noxious pollutant.

$Cu(s) + HNO_3(aq) \longrightarrow$
$Cu(NO_3)_2(aq) + H_2O(l) + NO(g)$

43. Arrange the following in order of increasing oxidation number of the xenon atom: $CsXeF_8$, Xe, XeF_2, $XeOF_2$, XeO_3, XeF

44. Arrange the following in order of decreasing oxidation number of the nitrogen atom: N_2, NH_3, N_2O_4, N_2O, N_2H_4, NO_3^-

45. Which of the sulfur containing species below cannot be reduced? SO_4^{2-}, $S_2O_3^{2-}$, S^{2-}, SO_3^{2-}

46. Identify the half-reactions in the following redox equations. Use these half-reactions to balance the equations. (Hint: remember to use H^+ and H_2O when the O or H atoms do not balance.)

a. $HNO_3(g) + H_2S(g) \longrightarrow$
$NO(g) + S(s) + H_2O(l)$

b. $Pb(s) + PbO_2(s) + 2SO_4^{2-}(aq) + 4H^+(aq)$
$\longrightarrow 2PbSO_4(s) + 2H_2O(l)$

c. $2Na + S \longrightarrow 2Na^+ + S^{2-}$

d. $H_2(g) + OF_2(g) \longrightarrow H_2O(g) + HF(g)$

e. $Br_2(l) + SO_2(g) \longrightarrow$
$Br^-(aq) + SO_4^{2-}(aq)$

 **Batteries**

47. What factors must battery manufacturers consider when designing batteries?

48. a. What determines the voltage of a battery?
b. How are alkaline batteries made so that they produce different voltages?

49. Compare and contrast voltaic cells and electrolytic cells.

50. How do the redox reactions for each of the following types of battery differ?
a. dry cell   **b.** alkaline   **c.** mercury

51. Explain the statement "All electrolytic cells are electrochemical cells, but not all electrochemical cells are electrolytic cells."

52. What dangers exist when recharging batteries that are not designed to be recharged?

53. Although the terms *cell* and *battery* are used interchangeably by many people, the term *battery* refers to a series of cells that are connected. Which of the batteries discussed in this section are cells and which is a true battery?

54. Why do batteries "run down?"

55. Why are dry cells referred to as dry?

56. Why is nickel not used with lithium to make a rechargeable battery?

57. Recently, battery companies have begun dating their batteries to inform the consumers of how long the battery will last in storage.
a. Why do batteries not last indefinitely in storage?
b. Why might batteries last longer if stored in a refrigerator?

58. The reduction potentials for the anodic and cathodic reactions in a lead-acid storage battery are, respectively, -0.356 V and $+1.685$ V. Calculate the cell voltage. What would be the voltage if six such cells are connected in series?

59. In the process called electroplating, the metal to be plated is connected to one terminal of an external source of electricity and is immersed in a bath of a salt of the coating metal. The other electrode is often made of the coating metal.
a. Should the metal to be plated be the anode or the cathode? Explain.
b. Computer floppy disks are made by plating the polymer Mylar with a metal oxide. Why must the Mylar be coated with graphite before being plated?

60. Is the statement "All chemical changes are electric in nature" true? Explain.

61. a. Use Le Châtelier's principle to explain why your tape player runs at a slower speed as the dry cell battery inside it goes dead.
b. The carbon rod in a dry cell allows for the dissipation of H_2 gas that builds up during usage. If the gas builds up while the cell is in use, the voltage output drops. But if the load is removed and the hydrogen is allowed to escape, the cell may again produce a voltage. Explain this in terms of Le Châtelier's principle.

62. Propose a reason why rechargeable batteries must have electrodes made of metals that are close to each other in the activity series.

63. On the dry cell below, label the areas where oxidation and reduction occur. Show the flow of electrons from anode to cathode.

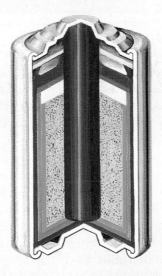

Linking chapters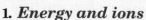

1. **Energy and ions**
   In Chapter 5, you learned that iron can form either of 2 ions, Fe^{3+} or Fe^{2+}. Use the half-reactions and E^0 values in **Table 15-1** to determine which oxidation state is preferred. Explain your reasoning.
2. **The activity series**
   Refer to **Table 15-1** to order the halogens by increasing E^0 values. Compare this ordering with their ordering in the activity series on page 259 in Chapter 7. Comment on your observations.
3. **Free energy**
   a. What would you expect the ΔG value to be for a voltaic cell?
   b. What happens to the ΔG value of the original redox reaction in an electrolytic cell?
   c. What is the ΔG value of a dead dry-cell?
   d. Electric energy is free energy, ΔG, and, in theory, it is all available for work. Calculate the amount of electrical work generated per gram of water produced in a fuel cell that operates at 60 % efficiency using the following overall equation.

   $$2H_2(g) + O_2(g) \longrightarrow 2H_2O(l)$$

(Hints: calculate ΔG for this reaction using **Table A-12** on page 799. This is the energy produced if the reaction is 100% efficient.)

4. **Limiting reactants**
   Both of the redox reactions shown below have reached completion. Identify the limiting reactant.

   a. 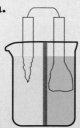   b.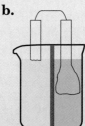

5. **Theme: *Classification and trends***
   When sulfur bonds with other elements, it displays oxidation states ranging from –2 to +6. Account for this in terms of sulfur's location on the periodic table, the definition of covalent bonding, and the rules for assigning oxidation numbers.
6. **Theme: *Conservation***
   What important factor is addressed when balancing redox reactions by the half-reaction method that might normally cause an error if the reaction were balanced conventionally?

USING TECHNOLOGY

1. **Graphics calculator**
   The reduction potential and electronegativity of an element are directly related. With the graphics calculator, you can estimate unknown reduction potentials. First, set the range by pressing [WINDOW] and entering the following values: Xmin = –4; Xmax = 4; Xscl = 1; Ymin = 0; Ymax = 5; Yscl = 1. Then press [STAT] [4] and clear all existing lists. Enter the list editor by pressing [STAT] [1]. Use **Table 15-1** and the electronegativity values from **Table 11-3** to enter two lists. Enter in L1, the reduction potentials of the elements in **Table 15-1**. Enter in L2, the electronegativity values of the same elements. Press [2nd] [STAT] [PLOT] and turn on Plot 1 by pressing [1] [ENTER] [▼] [ENTER] [▼] [ENTER] [▼] [►] [ENTER] [▼] [ENTER]. Press [STAT] [►] [5] [ENTER] to construct a line function. Enter that function into the calculator by pressing [Y=] [VARS] [5] [►] [►]

   [7]. Then press [GRAPH]. Use the [TRACE] feature to estimate the reduction potentials of the following elements listed by reading the x-value from the graph when the y-value is the electronegativity of that element.
   a. cadmium electronegativity = 1.7
   b. cobalt electronegativity = 1.8
   c. strontium electronegativity = 1.0
   Compare your estimated values with the accepted values, and comment on the accuracy of your estimate. If the percent error is greater than 10 percent, look for ways to improve the accuracy of your plot. Give reasons for your changes.
2. **Computer art**
   Use a computer to diagram a voltaic cell. Label the anode and the cathode and illustrate the movement of electrons through an external circuit. Then change the art to represent an electrolytic cell.
3. **Computer spreadsheet**
   Create a spreadsheet containing the reduction potentials of the substances listed in **Table 15-1**. Design the spreadsheet to calculate the E^0 of any cell made from the substances in the list.

Alternative assessment

Performance assessment

1. A voltaic cell produces electricity until the reactions driving it reach equilibrium or completion. Given what you know about the factors that affect chemical equilibrium, work with a partner to design an electrochemical cell that could produce electricity indefinitely. (Hint: consider Le Châtelier's principle.)

2. Your teacher will assign you a known metal with an unknown reduction potential. Devise a method to determine the E^O value of the metal from a list of metals with known E^O values. Present your method to your teacher in the form of a proposal.

3. Energy for electrically-driven cars comes from redox reactions that produce more energy per unit mass than a lead storage battery. Investigate the development and operation of the sodium-sulfur battery used for this purpose. Choose a stand for or against its use, and present your findings in a persuasive speech to your classmates.

4. *Computer program*
   The voltage output of a half-cell depends on the concentration of the substances present. The E^O values in **Table 15-1** are determined when the concentrations are 1.0 M. When the concentrations are not 1.0 M, the cell potential is calculated from a form of the equilibrium expression.

   Half-reactions for standard reduction potentials are represented by the following generalized equation.

   $$x \, \text{Ox} + n e^- \longrightarrow y \, \text{Red}$$

   "Ox" refers to the oxidized substance, and "Red" to the reduced substance. The half-cell potential is calculated from the following equation.

   $$E = E^O - \frac{0.0592}{n} \log \frac{[\text{Red}]^y}{[\text{Ox}]^x}$$

   Write a program to calculate the half-cell potentials for half-reactions involving a metal and its ion when the ion concentration varies from 1.0 M to 0.001 M.

Portfolio projects

1. *Chemistry and you*
   For one week, keep a record of how many times you use devices powered by batteries. Record what kind of device you used and the number and type of batteries it contained. Your teacher will provide you with various batteries and a balance. Record the mass of each type of battery you used during the week. Assuming that your battery usage is typical of everyone in the country, estimate the mass of waste material produced by battery usage in one year. Write a short response offering ways to reduce the amount of waste.

2. *Research and communication*
   Research the progress in the development of electric cars. Have a class debate about the advantages and disadvantages of replacing gasoline and diesel vehicles with electric vehicles.

3. *Cooperative activity*
   Break the class into several groups. Have each group research the environmental effects of different types of batteries. Analyze both the production and waste costs. Bring the groups together to share their research with each other.

4. *Chemistry and you*
   Consumer use of rechargeable batteries is growing. Many people either own devices using rechargeable batteries or have access to them. Nickel-cadmium batteries, a common rechargeable type of battery, are used in cellular phones, shavers, and portable video-game systems. Make a list of the items that you come in contact with that use nickel-cadmium batteries or other rechargeable batteries. Write a short essay about technology that was not and could not have been available before the development of the nickel-cadmium battery.

5. *Research and communication*
   Redox reactions are not limited solely to electrochemical cells and batteries. Research common occurrences of redox reactions, and identify the chemical that is oxidized and the chemical that is reduced.

Nuclear Chemistry

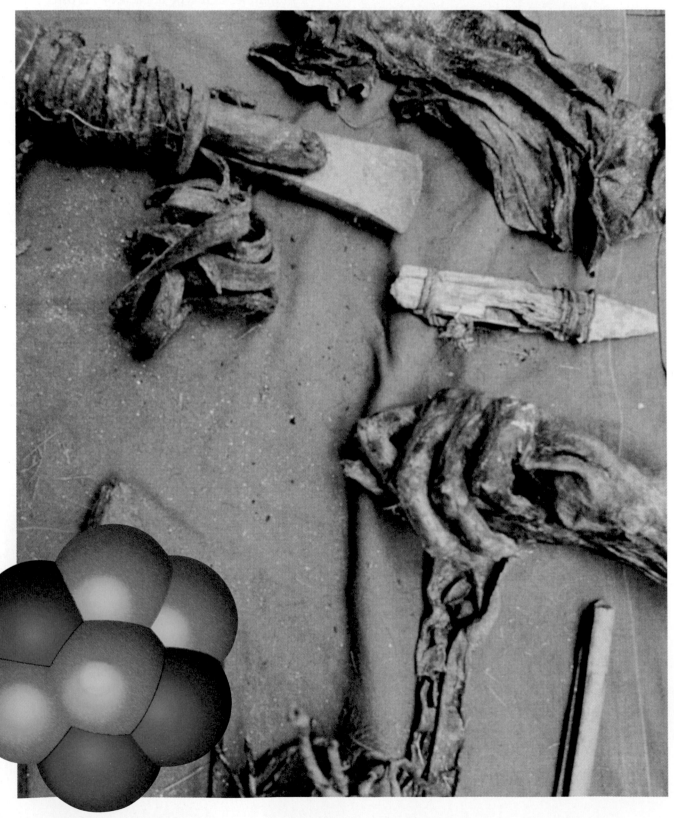

The Iceman Meets Nuclear Chemistry

While hiking through the Alps near the Austrian border on a September day in 1991, Helmut and Erika Simon noticed something protruding from the ice. At first, the Simons thought they were looking at a doll that had been discarded and covered with ice.

But on closer inspection, the Simons discovered they had stumbled across the frozen body of a man. What they saw sticking up out of the ice were the head and shoulders of a prehistoric man, now known throughout the world as the Iceman.

For four days following the Simons' discovery, workers struggled to free the Iceman's body. They hacked away the ice using axes and ski poles, unaware of the importance of what they were uncovering. In his haste, one worker broke the Iceman's left hip with a jackhammer. Others ripped and destroyed much of the Iceman's clothing while yanking and pulling on his body. But, finally, the figure was freed. The workers were astonished by what they saw.

The body was amazingly well preserved because it had been sealed in ice. In fact, the body was in such good condition that the Iceman's eyeballs were still intact. The Iceman stood five feet two inches tall. He had wavy, medium-length, dark hair and a beard. He appeared to be relatively young, somewhere between age 25 and 40. He wore clothes made of animal skins and boots stuffed with grass to keep his feet warm. His skin bore markings in various spots, including some stripes on his right ankle and a cross behind his left knee. Perhaps these were tattoos.

The Iceman had been carrying a stone knife, a wooden backpack, a small bag containing a flint lighter and some kindling, a bow and quiver containing 14 arrows, and a copper ax. Shortly after the Iceman's body had been freed from the ice, an archaeologist examined the ax. The ax indicated that the Iceman had lived about 4000 years ago.

If the Iceman were indeed that old, then his body would be the oldest ever retrieved from an Alpine glacier. At over 10 000 feet, the site where the Iceman had been found was the highest point where any prehistoric human had ever been found in Europe. Moreover, the Iceman was one of the best-preserved early humans ever found anywhere.

Scientists immediately arranged to have the body placed in a freezer where the temperature would be maintained at a constant $-6°C$ and the humidity would be constant at 98%. These conditions would replicate those of the ice in which the body had been preserved for so long. During the next few months, scientists closely examined the Iceman's body, with the following questions in mind.

- *Exactly when did the Iceman die?*
- *What did the Iceman look like when he was alive?*
- *How did the Iceman die?*

Answers to these questions have been obtained with the help of nuclear chemistry, the subject of this chapter.

Why are some atomic nuclei unstable?

Section Objectives

Describe how the strong nuclear force contributes to the stability of an atomic nucleus.

Predict the stability of an atomic nucleus based on its neutron to proton ratio.

Interpret the band of stability on a plot of neutrons versus protons.

Define and calculate the binding energy of a nucleus.

strong nuclear force
a short-range, attractive force that acts among nucleons

Figure 16-1
The girl in this photograph is touching a generator of static electric charge. As a result, the electric charges coat her hair and body. The negative electric charges on the strands of her hair repel one another, causing the effect you see in the photograph.

Nuclear stability

What is the explanation for the unusual "hairstyle" shown in **Figure 16-1**? The girl's hair has become charged because she is touching a generator of static electricity. Each strand of her hair is covered with negative charge. The mutual repulsion of these negative charges forces the strands of hair to repel one another and fly apart. You might think because of this example that the protons within an atomic nucleus should also fly apart due to mutual electrical repulsion between their like, positive charges. Yet protons cluster together tightly within the nucleus along with neutrons, which are uncharged. How is this possible?

The strong nuclear force holds nuclei together

Nuclear protons *do* repel one another through the electric force. However, another, stronger force present in the nucleus overwhelms the electrical repulsion among protons. This force, appropriately called the **strong nuclear force**, is exerted by protons and neutrons (collectively called *nucleons*) on each other. Through this force, all of the nucleons of an atom attract one another. The strong nuclear force is much stronger than either the electrical or the gravitational force, even though it acts only over short distances (10^{-15} m or so, the approximate distance between neighboring nucleons). The strong nuclear force is represented in **Figure 16-2**.

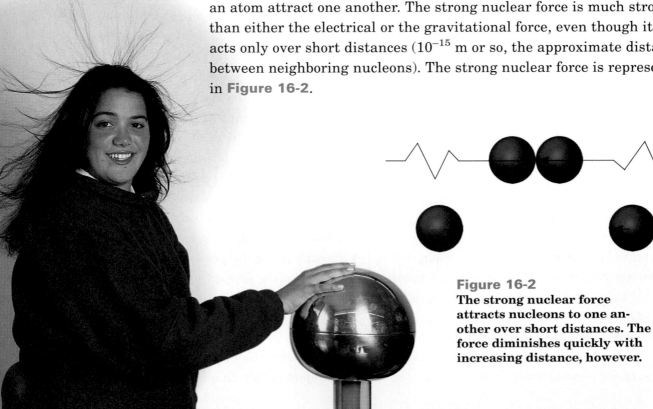

Figure 16-2
The strong nuclear force attracts nucleons to one another over short distances. The force diminishes quickly with increasing distance, however.

Most atoms on Earth are stable

stable nucleus
a nucleus that does not spontaneously decay to become the nucleus of a different element

unstable nucleus
a nucleus that spontaneously undergoes decay to become the nucleus of a different element

transmutation
a process by which a nucleus of one element is transformed into a nucleus of a different element

radioactivity
the ability of unstable nuclei to undergo spontaneous nuclear decay

Most of the atoms found on Earth have **stable nuclei**. All of the stable nuclear isotopes have atomic numbers from 1 (hydrogen) to 83 (bismuth). For example, the common isotopes of carbon, hydrogen, oxygen, and nitrogen that make up the bulk of your body mass are stable. Stable atoms give permanence to the matter in our environment.

However, a small fraction of the atoms on Earth have **unstable nuclei**, which undergo spontaneous change. Most unstable nuclei emit electromagnetic radiation or particles of various kinds and, at the same time, increasing or decreasing protons. By increasing or decreasing one or more protons, an unstable atom changes its atomic number to become an atom of a different element. Nuclear changes of this sort are called **transmutations**. For example, the unstable carbon isotope, carbon-14, is transformed into nitrogen-14 through nuclear transmutation, as shown in **Figure 16-3**. Nuclei that undergo transmutation are said to be **radioactive**. The transmutation of radioactive isotopes is commonly called *radioactive decay* or *nuclear decay*.

Many unstable nuclei are very short lived. Some last only fractions of a second before decaying into a different element. Other unstable nuclei may exist for long periods—even billions of years—without experiencing transmutation. In all cases, a nucleus decays because it loses energy in doing so. Radioactive nuclei undergo change to increase their stability by losing energy, just as chemicals in a reaction do.

Taking into account all isotopes of the 109 known elements, there are approximately 1500 different kinds. Only about 250 of these isotopes are stable. However, stable isotopes are generally much more abundant compared to unstable isotopes.

Stability depends on the ratio of neutrons to protons

Why are some nuclei stable and others unstable? And why are *all* isotopes of *all* elements with atomic number greater than 83 unstable? The key to nuclear stability is the ratio of neutrons to protons and the resulting contest between the strong nuclear force and electric force. For a nucleus to be stable, neutrons and protons must be present in just the right ratio.

Figure 16-3
Transmutation is the process through which a nucleus loses or gains protons to become the nucleus of another element. The unstable carbon-14 nucleus emits an electron, thereby changing a neutron into a proton, and becoming nitrogen-14.

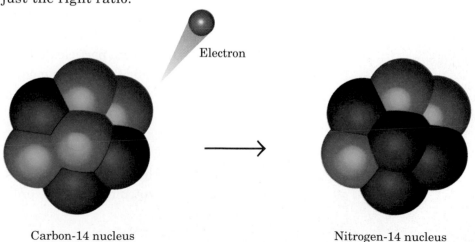

Electron

Carbon-14 nucleus

Nitrogen-14 nucleus

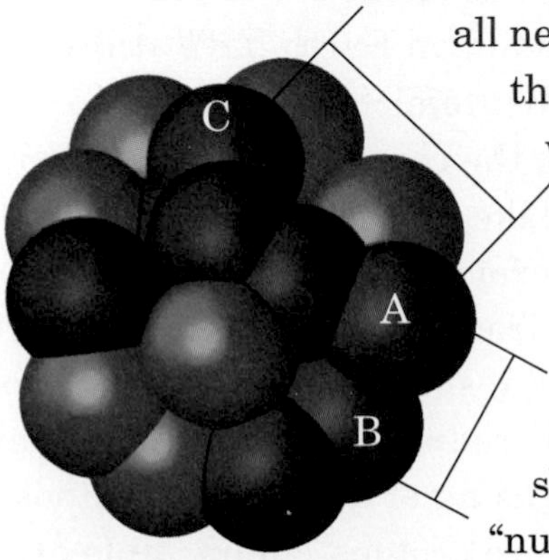

Figure 16-4
**Proton A attracts
proton B through
the strong nuclear
force but repels it
through the electric
force. Proton A
mainly repels proton
C through the electric
force. The strong
force applies only
over the short dis-
tance of a few nucleon
diameters.**

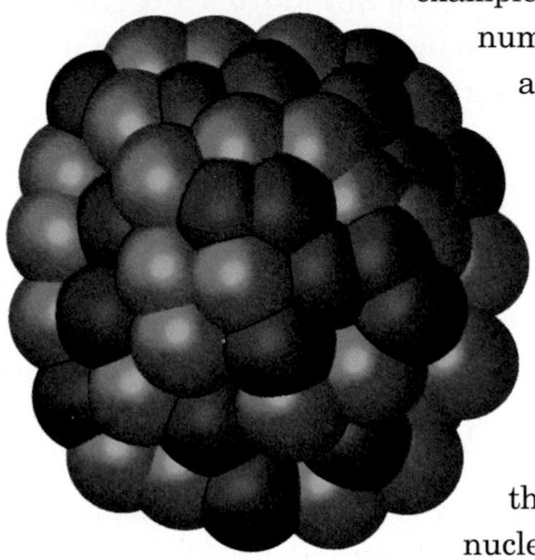

Figure 16-5
**Each of the 86 protons
in this radon nucleus
experiences electri-
cal repulsion from
85 other protons.
Neutrons in a
heavy nucleus are
separated by no
more than a few
nucleon diameters.
Electrical repul-
sion among protons
is a significant fac-
tor for large nuclei.**

Neutrons have no electric charge. Therefore they attract all nearby nucleons because they interact with them only through the strong nuclear force, which is always attractive between particles. Protons, however, repel one another through the electric force as well as attract one another through the strong nuclear force. For this reason, neutrons exert more of the force that keeps a nucleus together, as **Figure 16-4** shows. Can you see that neutrons behave as "nuclear glue"?

The more protons there are in a nucleus, the more electrical repulsion there is among them, and the more neutrons are needed to hold the nucleus together with the strong nuclear force. For example, each proton in a helium nucleus (atomic number 2) is repelled by one other proton. In a lithium nucleus (atomic number 3), each proton is pushed away by *two* other protons. But each proton in the relatively heavy gold nucleus (atomic number 79) feels the electrical repulsion of 78 other protons! This adds up to a lot of force pushing each proton out of the nucleus. Also, as **Figure 16-5** shows, in a large nucleus protons are so far apart that they fall out of the short range of the nuclear force, so they cannot attract one another through it. As you can see, the effects of electrical repulsion become an important factor for large nuclei.

Lighter elements require only about as many neutrons as protons for stability. Carbon has six neutrons and six protons, for example, and nitrogen has seven neutrons and seven protons. Heavier elements require more neutrons to hold the nucleus together. Mercury, with 80 protons and 122 neutrons for example, has about one-and-a-half times as many neutrons as protons.

There is a limit to the stabilizing capability of neutrons, however. If isolated, neutrons themselves are not stable. Unless a neutron is near a proton, the neutron emits a beta particle and turns into a proton. This process can be represented by the following equation in which the charge of each particle is represented as a subscript and mass number is shown as a superscript.

$$\,^{1}_{0}n \longrightarrow \,^{1}_{1}p + \,^{0}_{-1}e$$

Although neutrons in nuclei are usually stable, some radioactive nuclei change a neutron into a proton by the same process—emitting an electron.

As more and more neutrons and protons are added to heavier nuclei, the added protons repel all other protons. The repulsion increases steadily. However, added neutrons attract only nearby nucleons. Each added neutron gives about the same stability. Therefore, a stage is reached where additional neutrons cannot stabilize nuclei. All atoms above bismuth, atomic number 83, are unstable.

A plot of the number of neutrons versus the number of protons for stable nuclei is shown in **Figure 16-6**. Note that stable nuclei cluster together in a pattern called a *band of stability* which is highlighted in grey on the graph. As the plot shows, the ratio of neutrons to protons that leads to stability for light nuclei, such as sulfur($^{32}_{16}$S), is near 1.0. The ratio increases to about 1.5 for heavier nuclei, such as lead($^{207}_{82}$Pb). Nuclei not located on the band of stability are unstable. Unstable isotopes decay into isotopes that are located on the band of stability.

Figure 16-6
The plot shows the number of neutrons (*N*) versus the number of protons (*Z*) for the known stable nuclei. A plot of radioactive nuclei would show that they fall outside the band of stability. The maroon line shows where the data would lie for *N*/*Z* = 1. For stable lighter nuclei, the data falls near the maroon line. As nuclei become heavier, *N*/*Z* approaches 1.5 for stability and the data falls near the green line.

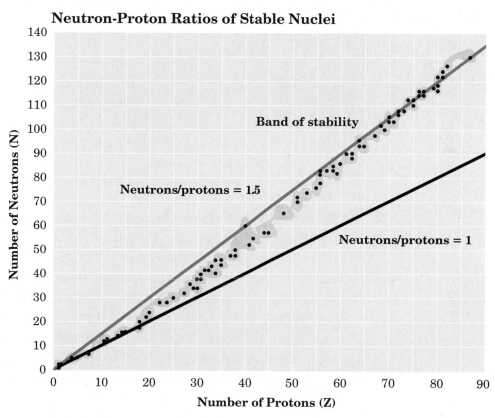

Neutron-Proton Ratios of Stable Nuclei

Band of stability

Neutrons/protons = 1.5

Neutrons/protons = 1

Number of Neutrons (*N*)

Number of Protons (*Z*)

Concept Review

Predicting nuclear stability

1. Which is generally more stable—a large nucleus or a small nucleus? Give the reason for your answer.
2. Which is expected to be more stable: $^{6}_{3}$Li or $^{9}_{3}$Li?
3. Use **Figure 16-6** to determine whether the following isotopes are stable or unstable: $^{12}_{6}$C, $^{3}_{1}$H, $^{206}_{82}$Pb, $^{32}_{15}$P, and $^{4}_{2}$He.

Answers for Concept Review items and Practice problems begin on page 841.

Binding energy

Binding energy indicates stability

Enormous energy, called the **binding energy**, is required to tear apart a nucleus by separating its nucleons. Also, when protons and neutrons come together to form a nucleus, a large amount of energy equivalent to the binding energy is released. Binding energy indicates the stability of a nucleus. The binding energies of various isotopes are plotted in **Figure 16-7**.

Figure 16-7
The plot of average binding energy per nucleon versus mass number indicates the relative stability of nuclei. Isotopes that have a high binding energy per nucleon are more stable. $^{56}_{26}$Fe is the most stable atom.

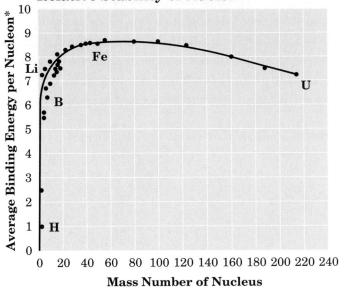

Relative Stability of Nuclei

* Energy is expressed in units of megaelectron-volts, an energy unit appropriate to the small scale of atomic events. One megaelectron-volt = 1.6×10^{-19} J.

Measurements reveal that the combined mass of protons and neutrons in a nucleus is always less than the sum of the masses of the same particles when they are isolated from one another. Some of the mass of the individual particles appears to be missing. Where does the excess mass of the protons and neutrons go when they combine to form a nucleus?

Recall from Chapter 2 that mass and energy are interconvertible, as shown by Einstein's equation, $E = mc^2$. If the mass that is lost by combining protons and neutrons is converted to energy, this "missing mass" is equal to the binding energy of the nucleus. Thus, the mass that neutrons and protons appear to lose when they combine is actually converted to energy that is given off as the nucleus forms. The mass of protons and neutrons that is converted to binding energy is called the **mass defect** of a nucleus and is represented by the symbol Δm.

Binding energy is easily calculated

Consider the stable oxygen isotope, oxygen-16, which contains the equivalent of 8 hydrogen atoms and 8 neutrons. The mass of each H atom is 1.007 825 amu. Each neutron has a mass of 1.008 665 amu. Therefore the overall mass of an oxygen-16 atom should be 16.131 920 amu. However, the measured mass of an oxygen-16 atom is 15.994 915 amu. From this information, mass defect can be easily determined as shown in Sample Problem 16A.

Sample Problem 16A
Calculating binding energy

Calculate the binding energy of a mole of oxygen-16 atoms.

❶ **List**
- mass of H atom (includes 1 proton and 1 electron): 1.007 825 amu
- mass of a neutron: 1.008 665 amu
- mass of particles making up oxygen-16 nucleus:
  8(1.007 825 amu) + 8(1.008 665 amu) = 16.131 920 amu
- mass of actual oxygen-16 atom: 15.994 915 amu
- $c = 3.00 \times 10^8$ m/s
- binding energy = **?** J
- The energy unit, the *joule*, is equivalent to kg·m²/s².

❷ **Set up**
- First determine the mass defect.
  Δm = (total mass of particles) − (measured mass of atom)

- Convert the mass defect to the binding energy with $E = mc^2$. The mass defect, Δm, is the mass, m, in the equation.

- This conversion will give the binding energy for one oxygen-16 atom. For one mole of oxygen-16 atoms, the mass defect will be in grams (not amu). Because the final answer will be in joules, it is necessary to convert grams to kilograms.

❸ **Calculate**

The mass defect can be converted directly to kg from amu by using the conversion factor 1.66054 × 10⁻²⁷ kg/amu.

- Δm = (total mass of nucleons) − (measured mass of nucleus)
  = 16.131 920 amu − 15.994 915 amu
  $= \dfrac{0.137\ 005\ \text{amu}}{\text{atom oxygen-16}}$
  $= \dfrac{0.137\ 005\ \text{g}}{\text{mol oxygen-16}}$

- $E = \Delta mc^2$
  $= 0.137\ 005\ \text{g} \times \dfrac{1\ \text{kg}}{1000\ \text{g}} \times \dfrac{(3.00 \times 10^8\ \text{m})^2}{\text{s}^2} = 1.23 \times 10^{13}\ \text{J}$

Practice 16A

Answers for Concept Review items and Practice problems begin on page 841.

1. Calculate the binding energy for one mole of deuterium atoms. Each deuterium nucleus is formed from one proton and one neutron. The measured mass of this atom is 2.0140 amu.

2. Calculate the binding energy of one lithium-6 atom, whose nucleus contains three protons and three neutrons. The measured atomic mass of lithium-6 is 6.0151 amu.

Section Review

4. Define the following terms: *radioactive*, *mass defect*, and *binding energy*.
5. Explain how nuclear stability relates to the neutron-proton ratio of a nucleus.
6. Name two properties of the strong nuclear force. What is the electric force? What role do each of these two forces play in the stability of the nucleus?
7. What is the "band of stability"? How do nuclei located on the band of stability differ from those that are not on it?

What kinds of nuclear change occur?

Section Objectives

Describe the particles and rays that make up radioactive emissions.

Distinguish among nuclear transmutation, fission, and fusion.

Explain how transuranium elements are synthesized.

Characterize chain reactions.

Give examples of fission and fusion reactions.

You began your study of nuclear chemistry with a look at the transmutations of unstable nuclei. Transmutation is one kind of *nuclear reaction*, or nuclear change. Other nuclear reactions are *fission* and *fusion*. Nuclear fission and fusion are of tremendous practical importance because they could fulfill society's energy needs or cause catastrophic harm, depending on how they are used. In this section, you will learn more about what happens in nuclear transmutation and in the fission and fusion processes.

Radioactive emissions
Nuclear transmutation results in radioactive emissions

While studying the properties of uranium compounds around the beginning of the twentieth century, French scientist Henri Becquerel noticed a surprising phenomenon. The uranium compounds he was studying exposed photographic film that was wrapped in black paper as if the film had been exposed to light. At Becquerel's suggestion, Marie and Pierre Curie also began to investigate the curious behavior of uranium compounds, particularly those found in an ore known as *pitchblende*.

While analyzing pitchblende, the Curies isolated and identified two new elements: *polonium* and *radium*. The Curies observed that these elements both exposed photographic film, just as the uranium compounds did. Also, polonium and radium killed bacteria and other tiny organisms that were placed near them.

The Curies also observed that the two new elements caused certain substances to glow brightly or become discolored. Furthermore, both polonium and radium raised the temperature of surrounding air by several degrees. The elements also turned air, which is normally a nonconductor, into a conductor of electricity.

Finally, Pierre Curie discovered that a sample of radium placed on his skin produced wounds that were very slow to heal.

Figure 16-8
Marie Curie theorized that pitchblende, a uranium-containing material, must contain tiny amounts of an unknown, highly radioactive element. By analyzing several tons of pitchblende, she discovered the element radium.

It was clear to the Curies that uranium, polonium, and radium were releasing significant amounts of energy in order to bring about all these effects. Marie Curie coined the term "radio-activity" to describe the process by which such elements release energy. In the early 1900s, only uranium, polonium, radium, and thorium were known to be radioactive. Today, scientists know that all isotopes of all elements after bismuth on the periodic table are radioactive. Furthermore, all radioactive nuclei undergo transmutation and produce emissions with the properties observed by the Curies. Also, it is now known that the mysterious, energetic emissions which Becquerel and the Curies first observed consist of *alpha particles*, *beta particles*, and *gamma rays*.

Some radioactive elements emit alpha particles

You have learned that one property of radioactive elements is that they can turn air into a conductor of electricity. This property has been put to practical use in the device shown in **Figure 16-9**. Smoke detectors use a small amount of a radioactive isotope such as americium-241. Americium-241 emits enough radiation to change the neutral molecules in air into ions. The ions can then conduct an electric current through the air inside the smoke detector. A small sensing device located inside the smoke detector monitors this current. However, when smoke particles interrupt this current, an alarm is set off, warning people of the presence of smoke and the possibility of a fire.

Recall from Chapter 4 that nuclear reactions can be represented by nuclear equations in which the element undergoing nuclear change is written on the left side of a reaction arrow and the decay products are shown on the right side. Atomic number appears as a subscript, and mass number is written as a superscript next to each isotope. The nuclear equation for the decay of americium-241 is written as follows.

$$^{241}_{95}\text{Am} \longrightarrow\ ^{237}_{93}\text{Np} +\ ^{4}_{2}\text{He}$$

Notice that this transmutation results in the production of a new element, neptunium, Np, and a helium nucleus, He. A helium nucleus that is emitted by a radioactive isotope is called an **alpha particle**. An alpha particle (as you may recall from studying Rutherford's experiments with the atom in Chapter 4) consists of two protons and two neutrons and has a 2+ charge. Very heavy nuclei whose neutron-proton ratio is too low for stability emit alpha particles. Emission of an alpha particle increases the neutron-proton ratio by a small amount.

With its relatively large mass and charge, an alpha particle does not travel very fast or very far. Consequently, a thin sheet of aluminum foil or even a sheet of paper can stop it. Americium-241 is therefore a good choice for a radioactive isotope in a smoke detector. The emitted alpha particles ionize air that flows through the detector, but they cannot pass through the plastic covering to pose a health hazard to people.

Figure 16-9
This smoke detector contains a radioactive isotope. The radioactive emissions of the smoke detector ionize air to conduct a current that is sensed by the detector. When smoke interrupts current flow to the detector, an alarm sounds.

alpha particle
a helium nucleus produced in nuclear decay

Radioactive emissions can be detected

Because of the radiation they emit, most radioactive elements can be easily detected. However, since you cannot see, hear, smell, taste, or feel radioactive emissions, you must use instruments such as the Geiger counter shown in **Figure 16-10** to detect them. The Geiger counter uses a gas-filled metal tube to detect radioactive emissions. The incoming radiation ionizes the gas in the tube, making it an electrical conductor. The current drives electronic counters or causes audible clicks from a built-in speaker. The frequency of these clicks indicates the intensity of radiation in the material or environment being tested.

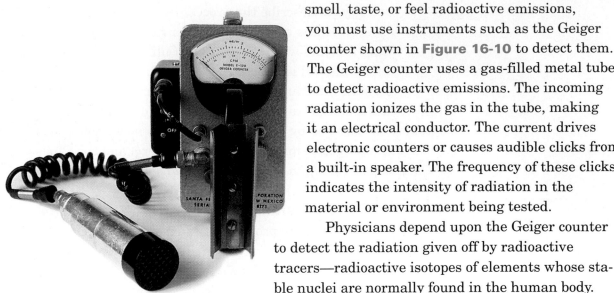

Physicians depend upon the Geiger counter to detect the radiation given off by radioactive tracers—radioactive isotopes of elements whose stable nuclei are normally found in the human body.

For example, your thyroid gland needs the element iodine to synthesize the hormone thyroxin. To check for a malfunctioning thyroid, a radioactive iodine tracer can be used. The patient is given a solution of NaI containing radioactive iodine-131. The radiation emitted by the radioactive iodine can be monitored with a Geiger counter so that the physician can check the rate at which the iodine accumulates in the thyroid to determine if the thyroid is functioning properly. Radiation can also be detected by a scintillation counter, which can be used to prepare a thyroid scan or picture of the thyroid showing areas that do not absorb the isotope.

Figure 16-10
The Geiger counter detects the presence of alpha, beta, gamma, and X radiation.

Radioactive elements can also emit beta particles

One kind of radiation emitted by iodine-131 consists of beta particles. A **beta particle** is a high-speed electron ejected by a radioactive nucleus. Emission of beta particles occurs in nuclei whose neutron-proton ratio is too high to be in the band of stability. Emission of a beta particle decreases the neutron-proton ratio.

The nuclear equation showing how iodine-131 emits a beta particle is written as follows.

$$^{131}_{53}I \longrightarrow {}^{131}_{54}Xe + {}^{0}_{-1}e$$

beta particle
an electron produced in nuclear decay

Notice that the element xenon, Xe, has been produced as a result of this transmutation. The beta particle, shown as ${}^{0}_{-1}e^{*}$, has practically no mass and half as much charge as an alpha particle. Consequently, beta particles travel much faster and have a penetrating ability about 100 times greater than that of alpha particles. They can be stopped only by several layers of aluminum foil or by thin pieces of wood, and they easily penetrate skin.

---

* Alternative representations for beta particles are β and ${}^{0}_{-1}β$.

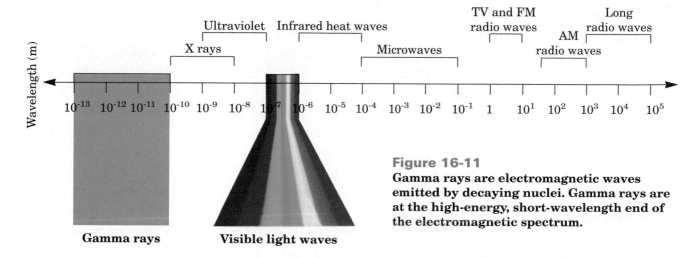

Figure 16-11
Gamma rays are electromagnetic waves emitted by decaying nuclei. Gamma rays are at the high-energy, short-wavelength end of the electromagnetic spectrum.

Gamma rays are a third type of radioactive emission

Radiation has long been used to treat cancer. For many years, the radiation given off by radium-226 was used. Today, cobalt-60, which is cheaper and emits even more radiation, is generally used for this purpose. The nuclear equations showing the radiation emitted by both of these elements are written as follows.

$$^{226}_{88}\text{Ra} \longrightarrow {}^{222}_{86}\text{Rn} + {}^{4}_{2}\text{He} + \gamma$$

$$^{60}_{27}\text{Co} \longrightarrow {}^{60}_{28}\text{Ni} + {}^{0}_{-1}e + \gamma$$

Compare these two nuclear equations. How do the emissions differ? What do both reactions have in common? The symbol γ is the Greek letter gamma. It represents the gamma rays emitted by a nuclear reaction. **Gamma rays** are high-energy electromagnetic waves. They are the same kind of radiation as visible light, but have much shorter wavelengths, as you can see in **Figure 16-11**.

Alpha and beta particles are never given off simultaneously from the same nucleus. Gamma rays are almost always emitted along with either alpha or beta particles. Gamma rays have no mass and no charge. Consequently, they are the most penetrating of radioactive emissions. Several feet of concrete are needed to stop gamma rays. **Table 16-1** summarizes the characteristics of the alpha, beta, and gamma emissions given off by nuclear reactions.

gamma ray
high-energy electro-magnetic radiation produced by decaying nuclei

Table 16-1
Characteristics of Alpha, Beta, and Gamma Emissions

Particle	Symbol	Composition	Charge	Penetrating power
Alpha	$^{4}_{2}\text{He}$	2 protons 2 neutrons	2+	short range, stopped by a sheet of paper
Beta	$^{0}_{-1}e$, β	1 electron	1−	intermediate range, stopped by a few centimeters of water
Gamma	γ	electromagnetic waves	0	long range, stopped by a few centimeters of lead

Irradiated foods

Gamma radiation is used to preserve food products because it can destroy the viruses, bacteria, fungi, parasites, and insects that infest and spoil food. Not only do such organisms cause food to spoil more quickly, but if consumed, they can also make people dangerously ill.

The Food and Drug Administration (FDA) regulates which foods can be irradiated and how much radiation each can receive. The first products were wheat and flour, which were approved for radiation in 1963 to destroy insects. Twenty years later, the FDA expanded the list to include spices imported from countries where health conditions and sanitary practices are not up to the standards of the United States. Meats, including both pork and poultry, fruits, and vegetables have recently been added to the list.

Nearly all food that is irradiated is exposed to the gamma rays emitted by cobalt-60. The length of exposure depends on the food. Strawberries are exposed for 8 minutes, while frozen poultry gets 20 minutes of radiation. On average, the radiation extends the shelf life of fresh fruits and vegetables from one to two weeks. Canned and frozen foods that are irradiated may have a shelf life of seven years.

While irradiated foods have been widely available for years in countries throughout the world, they are only now being introduced on a large scale in the United States food supply. Consumer reaction is mixed. Some are concerned about the chemical changes in the food that result from radiation. These changes, known as unique radiological products (URP), cannot exceed one part per million according to the FDA. Yet some suspect that even this level of exposure to URPs may be hazardous. In response to such concerns, research into the preservation of foods with gamma radiation continues. In the meantime, check your local supermarket to see if it carries irradiated food products. If so, and if you are concerned, you may want to do further research on the benefits and risks of irradiated foods.

Two other types of radioactive decay are possible

Unstable nuclei may decay by alpha, beta, or gamma emission or by two other processes. One of these is *positron emission*. A positron, generally represented as $_{+1}^{0}e$, is a particle identical to an electron except that it has a positive charge. For example, polonium-207 decays by positron emission to bismuth-207, as shown in the following equation.

$$^{207}_{84}\text{Po} \longrightarrow {}^{0}_{+1}e + {}^{207}_{83}\text{Bi}$$

Positron emission leads to a decrease in atomic number, as does another nuclear decay process called *electron capture,* EC. In electron capture, a nucleus captures an electron belonging to that atom. Beryllium-7 decays to lithium-7 via EC, as shown in the following equation.

$$^{7}_{4}\text{Be} \xrightarrow{\text{EC}} {}^{7}_{3}\text{Li}$$

Nuclear reactions may occur in series

radioactive series
a sequence of nuclei that arise from and are transformed by radioactive decay until a stable isotope is produced

Frequently, the emission of an alpha or beta particle results in the formation of an isotope that is radioactive. The new unstable isotope may therefore initiate a series of nuclear transmutations until a stable isotope is finally produced. A sequence of such reactions is called a **radioactive series**. A radioactive series, beginning with $^{238}_{92}U$ and ending with stable $^{206}_{82}Pb$, is shown in **Figure 16-12**.

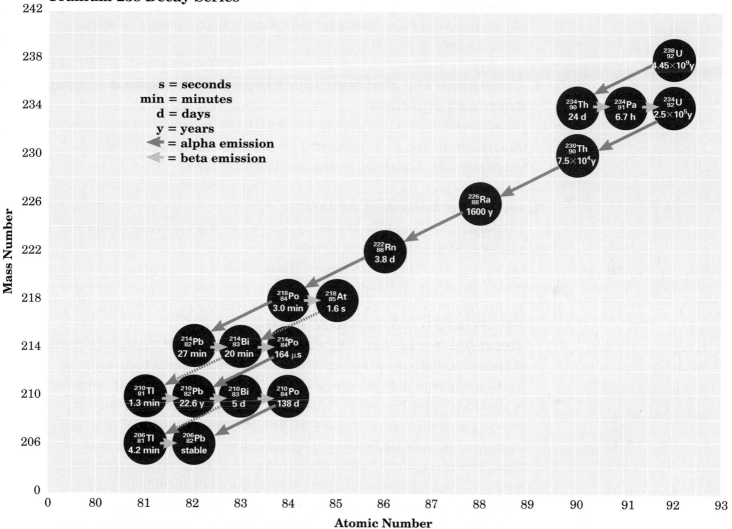

Uranium-238 Decay Series

Figure 16-12
Uranium-238 decays to lead-206 in a radioactive series consisting of many steps. In the first step, uranium-238 emits an alpha particle to give thorium-234. Thorium-234 emits a beta particle to give protactinium-234, which also emits a beta particle to continue the series. The half-life of each isotope is also listed.

Nuclear equations must be balanced

Now that you know how to represent the products of nuclear decay, you can write equations to represent transmutations—almost. There is one more thing to learn. In order to write nuclear equations, keep in mind that the equations must be balanced with respect to the number of nucleons and electric charge. If you know what kind of emission is produced in decay, you can write a balanced equation by following the process shown on the next page. Emission of an alpha particle increases the neutron-proton ratio slightly. It may take several alpha emissions to increase the ratio to a degree that causes beta emission. Emission of a beta particle causes a larger decrease in the neutron-proton ratio, so long chains of beta emission reactions do not occur.

1. Balance number of nucleons using mass number.

For example, consider the unstable $^{238}_{92}U$ nucleus that spontaneously decays by emitting an alpha particle. From the mass number of the uranium isotope, subtract the mass number of the alpha particle, which is 4. The mass number of the resulting atom is $238 - 4$, or 234.

2. Balance charge using atomic number.

The atomic number of uranium is 92. From this number, subtract the atomic number of the alpha particle, which is 2. This leaves an atomic number of 90.

3. Determine the decay product that will produce a balanced equation.

From the periodic table, you can see that the element with atomic number 90 is thorium. The mass number of the thorium isotope produced in this reaction is 234. The decay product is evidently $^{234}_{90}Th$.

4. Write the balanced equation.

Use an arrow to separate the decaying nucleus from decay products as if you were writing a chemical equation.

$$^{238}_{92}U \longrightarrow {}^{4}_{2}He + {}^{234}_{90}Th$$

Artificial transmutations
Unstable nuclei can be produced by nuclear bombardment

A transmutation, or conversion of an atom of one element to an atom of another element, may be caused by various processes of radioactive decay, as you have seen. However, a transmutation can also occur when high-energy particles, such as alpha particles, protons, or neutrons, bombard an atomic nucleus. Sometimes, transmutations occur naturally, such as when carbon-14 is produced from nitrogen-14 in the Earth's upper atmosphere. Today, transmutations are also produced artificially in giant machines called particle accelerators or in nuclear reactors.

In 1919, Ernest Rutherford brought about the first artificial transmutation. He bombarded nitrogen gas with alpha particles emitted by radium. The nuclear equation for this reaction is as follows.

$$^{14}_{7}N + {}^{4}_{2}He \longrightarrow [{}^{18}_{9}F] \longrightarrow {}^{17}_{8}O + {}^{1}_{1}H$$

Fluorine-18 produced in this reaction is extremely unstable and immediately decomposes. Note that a proton, which is also symbolized as $^{1}_{1}H$ in nuclear reactions, has been produced. In fact, this reaction provided the first physical evidence for the existence of the proton.

Figure 16-13
The cyclotron is used to accelerate particles to achieve the energy needed to bring about transmutations.

Elements with atomic numbers greater than that of uranium (92) are called transuranium elements. None of the transuranium elements are naturally occurring; they have been synthesized in particle accelerators or nuclear reactors. Each transuranium element is a product of artificial transmutations. Nuclear reactions that have been used to synthesize some of these elements are shown in **Table 16-2**.

Table 16-2
Reactions for the First Preparation of Transuranium Elements

Atomic number	Name	Symbol	Nuclear Reaction
94	plutonium	Pu	$^{238}_{92}\text{U} + {}^{2}_{1}\text{H} \longrightarrow {}^{238}_{93}\text{Np} + 2{}^{1}_{0}\text{n}$ $^{238}_{93}\text{Np} \longrightarrow {}^{238}_{94}\text{Pu} + {}^{0}_{-1}e$
95	americium	Am	$^{239}_{94}\text{Pu} + 2{}^{1}_{0}\text{n} \longrightarrow {}^{241}_{95}\text{Am} + {}^{0}_{-1}e$
96	curium	Cm	$^{239}_{94}\text{Pu} + {}^{4}_{2}\text{He} \longrightarrow {}^{242}_{96}\text{Cm} + {}^{1}_{0}\text{n}$
99	einsteinium	Es	$^{238}_{92}\text{U} + 15{}^{1}_{0}\text{n} \longrightarrow {}^{253}_{99}\text{Es} + 7{}^{0}_{-1}e$
101	mendelevium	Md	$^{253}_{99}\text{Es} + {}^{4}_{2}\text{He} \longrightarrow {}^{256}_{101}\text{Md} + {}^{1}_{0}\text{n}$
102	nobelium	No	$^{246}_{96}\text{Cm} + {}^{12}_{6}\text{C} \longrightarrow {}^{254}_{102}\text{No} + 4{}^{1}_{0}\text{n}$
103	lawrencium	Lr	$^{252}_{98}\text{Cf} + {}^{10}_{5}\text{B} \longrightarrow {}^{258}_{103}\text{Lr} + 4{}^{1}_{0}\text{n}$
104	unnilquadium (Russia)	Unq	$^{242}_{94}\text{Pu} + {}^{22}_{10}\text{Ne} \longrightarrow {}^{260}_{104}\text{Unq} + 4{}^{1}_{0}\text{n}$
104	unnilquadium (U.S.)	Unq	$^{249}_{98}\text{Cf} + {}^{12}_{6}\text{C} \longrightarrow {}^{257}_{104}\text{Unq} + 4{}^{1}_{0}\text{n}$
105	unnilpentium (U.S.)	Unp	$^{249}_{98}\text{Cf} + {}^{15}_{7}\text{N} \longrightarrow {}^{260}_{105}\text{Unp} + 4{}^{1}_{0}\text{n}$
106	unnilhexium (U.S.)	Unh	$^{249}_{98}\text{Cf} + {}^{18}_{8}\text{O} \longrightarrow {}^{263}_{106}\text{Unh} + 4{}^{1}_{0}\text{n}$
108	unniloctium (W. Germany)	Uno	$^{208}_{82}\text{Pb} + {}^{58}_{26}\text{Fe} \longrightarrow {}^{265}_{108}\text{Uno} + {}^{1}_{0}\text{n}$
109	unnilennium (W. Germany)	Une	$^{209}_{83}\text{Bi} + {}^{58}_{26}\text{Fe} \longrightarrow {}^{266}_{109}\text{Une} + {}^{1}_{0}\text{n}$

nuclear fission
the process by which a nucleus splits into two smaller fragments

Figure 16-14a
The single-celled paramecium is about to undergo fission, a process of reproduction. The term fission has nearly the same meaning in biology and chemistry.

Nuclear fission
Some unstable nuclei can split in two

Observe what is happening to the single-celled organism shown in **Figure 16-14**. This organism is dividing in two in a process called cell division or fission. Atomic nuclei can also divide or undergo fission. **Nuclear fission** refers to a nuclear reaction in which a very heavy nucleus splits into two smaller nuclei, each with higher nuclear binding energies, as in **Figure 16-7**. Whenever fission occurs, large amounts of energy are released. For example, the fission of 1 g of uranium-235 generates as much energy as the combustion of 2 700 kg of coal.

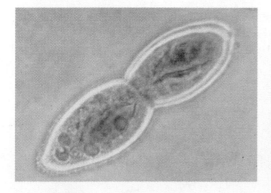

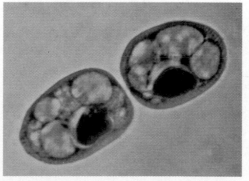

16-14b
The paramecium has fissioned, or divided, into two smaller organisms just as a nucleus divides into smaller nuclei during nuclear fission.

Fission is the source of energy generated by nuclear reactors. The main radioactive isotopes used by these reactors are uranium-235 and plutonium-239. **Figure 16-15** shows what happens to uranium-235 during fission. Notice that the nucleus of a uranium-235 atom must first be bombarded by a slow neutron. Once this is done, the nucleus splits in two, forming two new isotopes. What are these two isotopes?

In turn, each of these isotopes emits neutrons. As you can see in **Figure 16-15**, each of these neutrons when slowed down can cause the fission of another uranium-235 nucleus. Again neutrons are emitted. This process continues, forming a chain reaction. In a **chain reaction**, the material that starts the reaction is also one of the products.

The amount of material used in a chain reaction is important. Sufficient radioactive material is needed to absorb the number of neutrons required to sustain the chain reaction. The amount of radioactive material needed to sustain a chain reaction is known as the **critical mass**.

In a uranium-235 nuclear reactor, the fuel rods are surrounded by a moderator, a substance such as graphite or heavy water that slows down neutrons. The chain reaction is controlled with cadmium or boron rods. These rods absorb some of the neutrons that are produced by fission and thus control the number of neutrons that are available to bombard uranium-235 nuclei. If these control rods were not present, an uncontrolled chain reaction would occur. An uncontrolled reaction, in the worst case, could cause a nuclear meltdown. In a meltdown, dangerous radioactive material may be released. However, a nuclear meltdown does not involve a nuclear explosion, such as the one shown in **Figure 16-15**.

chain reaction
a self-sustaining nuclear or chemical reaction in which the product from each step acts as the reactant for the next step

critical mass
the minimum mass of fissionable material needed to produce a chain reaction

Figure 16-15
This chain reaction begins when a uranium-235 nucleus captures a stray neutron and splits into krypton and barium nuclei. Three neutrons are given off in the process. Each of these neutrons may collide with a uranium-235 nucleus, which then fissions. The fissioning uranium nuclei generate more neutrons which bombard more uranium-235 nuclei giving rise to more fission reactions. This chain reaction of uranium-235 is responsible for exploding atomic weapons.

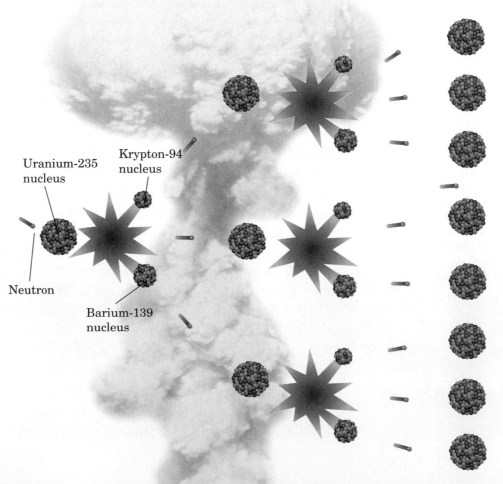

Uranium-235 nucleus

Krypton-94 nucleus

Neutron

Barium-139 nucleus

Nuclear fusion
Some unstable nuclei join to form heavier nuclei

nuclear fusion
the process by which two nuclei combine to form a heavier nucleus

In **Figure 16-16**, you see two examples of reactions involving nuclear fusion. **Nuclear fusion** is the process by which nuclei with low masses fuse to form heavier, more stable nuclei with higher binding energies as in **Figure 16-7**. In the process, tremendous amounts of energy are released.

In both the sun and in the explosion of a hydrogen bomb fusion reactions occur. In the case of the sun, a series of reactions cause four hydrogen nuclei to combine to form a single helium nucleus. The temperature of the Sun's core, where some of the fusion reactions occur, is about 1.5×10^7°C. High temperatures such as this are required to bring the nuclei together. When the hydrogen nuclei are fused to form a larger nucleus, some mass is lost and converted to energy. More energy is released per gram of reactant in fusion than in fission.

Currently, scientists are investigating ways to bring about fusion reactions at lower temperatures. Experiments using high-powered laser light to start the fusion process are being conducted. If fusion reactions are ever to become a practical source of energy, then the energy given off must be greater than the energy required to start them. At the moment, scientists have had limited success in this task.

Figure 16-16a
Nuclear fusion reactions occurring in the sun have supplied Earth with energy for billions of years.

16-16b
The hydrogen bomb uses nuclear fusion rather than fission. As a result, an exploding hydrogen bomb has even greater destructive power than a fission-based nuclear weapon.

Section Review

8. Write balanced nuclear equations for the following nuclear reactions.
    a. Uranium-233 undergoes alpha decay.
    b. Neptunium-239 undergoes beta decay.
    c. Copper-66 undergoes beta decay.
    d. Beryllium-9 and an alpha particle combine to form carbon-13. Carbon-13 then breaks apart to emit a neutron and carbon-12.
    e. Phosphorus-32 and a neutron combine to form phosphorus-33, which then decays to emit a beta particle.

9. Refer to **Figure 16-15**. Write the balanced nuclear equation for the fission reaction to show what happens to uranium-235 after it has been bombarded with a neutron.

10. One fusion reaction scientists are studying as a possible source of energy is that between a deuterium nucleus ($^2_1$H) and a tritium nucleus ($^3_1$H). One of the two products formed in this reaction is a helium nucleus. Write the balanced nuclear equation for this fusion reaction, being sure to include the other product that is formed.

How is nuclear chemistry used?

Section Objectives

Describe how the half-life of a radioactive isotope is used to calculate the ages of objects.

Describe how radioactive isotopes are used in the manufacture of consumer products.

Describe how the process of neutron activation is used to analyze objects.

Describe how nuclear imaging techniques are used as diagnostic tools in medicine.

Identify the possible health hazards of radiation exposure.

Half-life

At the beginning of this chapter, you read that the archaeologist who first examined the Iceman suspected that he had died some 4000 years ago. The investigator arrived at this conclusion based on his examination of the Iceman's ax. From the shape and composition of the blade, the archaeologist reasoned that the Iceman lived during the Early Bronze Age, which began around 2200 B.C.

However, the blade was found to be made of pure copper and not bronze. This indicated that the Iceman must have been older than the archaeologist first suspected because the Age of Copper began around 4000 B.C. and lasted until the advent of the Bronze Age. The Iceman could then have lived as long as 6000 years ago.

But rather than determining the Iceman's age on the basis of objects found with him, scientists have calculated his age by analyzing radioactive isotopes in the Iceman's body.

half-life
the time required for half of a sample of radioactive atoms to decay

Radioactive isotopes decay at a constant rate

The use of radioactive isotopes to determine the age of an object is called *radioactive dating*. Radioactive dating is based on the fact that the decay rates of radioactive nuclei are constant. The rate of nuclear decay is given in terms of half-lives. One **half-life** is the time that it takes for half of a sample of radioactive isotopes to decay, as you can see in **Figure 16-17**.

Figure 16-17
The radioactive isotope $^{131}_{53}\text{I}$ has a half-life of 8.07 days. In each successive 8.07-day period, half of the mass of $^{131}_{53}\text{I}$ in the original sample of $^{131}_{53}\text{I}$ decays to $^{131}_{54}\text{Xe}$.

Original sample of radioactive isotope $^{131}_{53}\text{I}$

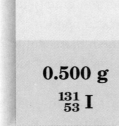

Amount of $^{131}_{53}\text{I}$ remaining after 1 half-life (8.07 days)

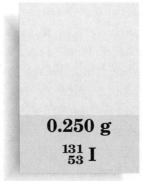

Amount of $^{131}_{53}\text{I}$ remaining after 2 half-lives (16.14 days)

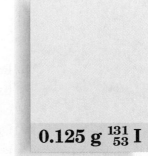

Amount of $^{131}_{53}\text{I}$ remaining after 3 half-lives (24.21 days)

Table 16-3
Half-Lives of Some Radioactive Isotopes

Isotope	Half-life	Radiation emitted
carbon-14	5.715×10^3 y	$_{-1}^{0}e$
potassium-40	1.3×10^9 y	$_{-1}^{0}e, \gamma$
radon-222	3.8 days	$_{2}^{4}He, \gamma$
radium-226	1.6×10^3 y	$_{2}^{4}He, \gamma$
thorium-230	7.5×10^4 y	$_{2}^{4}He, \gamma$
thorium-234	24 days	$_{-1}^{0}e, \gamma$
uranium-235	7.0×10^8 y	$_{2}^{4}He, \gamma$
uranium-238	4.5×10^9 y	$_{2}^{4}He, \gamma$

Every radioactive isotope has a characteristic half-life. Like binding energy, half-life indicates the stability of radioactive isotopes. The shorter the half-life, the quicker the isotope decays, and the more unstable it is. Highly unstable nuclei have very short half-lives. For example, silicon-26 has a half-life of two seconds. On the other hand, plutonium-242 is relatively stable. Nearly 4×10^5 years are required for half of a sample of plutonium-242 to decay. **Table 16-3** lists the half-lives for various radioactive isotopes.

Radioactive dating is used to find the ages of objects

The half-life of carbon-14 provides the key to the age of the Iceman. Most of the carbon that exists is the stable isotope carbon-12; less than one-millionth of one percent of the carbon in Earth's atmosphere is the radioactive isotope carbon-14. Because both these isotopes have the same electron configuration, they react chemically in almost an identical fashion. Both carbon-12 and carbon-14 join with oxygen to become carbon dioxide, which is taken in by plants. Therefore, all plants on Earth contain a small amount of carbon-14. All animals eat plants or plant-eating animals, so animals contain some carbon-14 too. Carbon-14 undergoes radioactive decay to become nitrogen-14 in the following reaction.

$$^{14}_{6}C \longrightarrow ^{14}_{7}N + ^{0}_{-1}e$$

Living plants continue to take in carbon dioxide while they are alive. In this way, they replenish the carbon-14 they lose due to decay, and the ratio of carbon-14 to carbon-12 remains constant. Plants use the carbon dioxide they consume from the atmosphere to make carbohydrates, such as glucose, which animals eat. Animals continually replenish the carbon-14 they lose through decay by consuming glucose and other carbon-containing compounds made by plants.

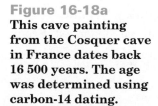

Figure 16-18a
This cave painting from the Cosquer cave in France dates back 16 500 years. The age was determined using carbon-14 dating.

16-18b
The origin of this Incan vessel was determined to be 1450 A.D. using dating techniques.

Nuclear Chemistry **629**

However, when a plant or animal dies, intake of carbon-containing substances ceases, so replenishment of carbon-14 comes to a halt. Then, the percentage of carbon-14 decreases—at a rate that is known and determined by its half-life. The half-life of carbon-14 is about 5715 years. So half of the carbon-14 atoms now present in a plant or animal will have decayed 5715 years after it dies; in another 5715 years half of the remaining carbon-14 atoms will have decayed; etc. The radioactive carbon-14 atoms, which can be detected with a Geiger counter, therefore continue to decrease at a steady rate after a plant or animal dies, as shown in **Figure 16-19**.

Once the relative amount of carbon-12 and carbon-14 in a fossil or other object of unknown age is measured, it is compared to the ratio of these isotopes in a sample of similar material whose age is known. For example, suppose the ratio of carbon-14 to carbon-12 in the tissues of the Iceman were found to be nearly one-half of that found in the tissues of a person who had recently died. Then, the Iceman must have lived about 5715 years ago. Using radioactive dating with carbon-14, scientists have concluded that the Iceman lived around 5000 years ago, between 3500 and 3000 B.C.

Radioactive dating is used to measure geologic time

After four half-lives, the amount of radioactive carbon-14 remaining in an object is too small to be of any use in radioactive dating. Consequently, carbon-14 is not useful for dating specimens that are more than 20 000 years old. Anything older than this must be dated with the use of a radioactive isotope that has a half-life longer than that of carbon-14.

Potassium-40 has a half-life of 1.3 billion years. Because of its long half-life, potassium-40 has been used to date ancient rocks and minerals. Potassium-40 produces two different isotopes in its radioactive decay. About 11% of the potassium-40 in a mineral decays to argon-40, which may be retained in the mineral sample. The remaining 89% of potassium-40 decays to calcium-40. The decay of potassium-40 to calcium-40 is not useful for radioactive dating because the calcium-40 cannot be distinguished from the original calcium in the rock. The argon-40, however, can be measured. From its amount, the minimum date of a rock can be determined.

Figure 16-19
Every 5715 years, the carbon-14 isotopes in the Iceman's body decrease by one-half.

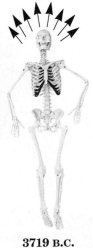 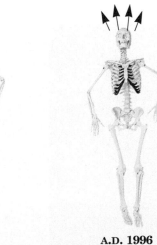 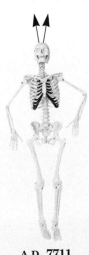

3719 B.C.   A.D. 1996   A.D. 7711

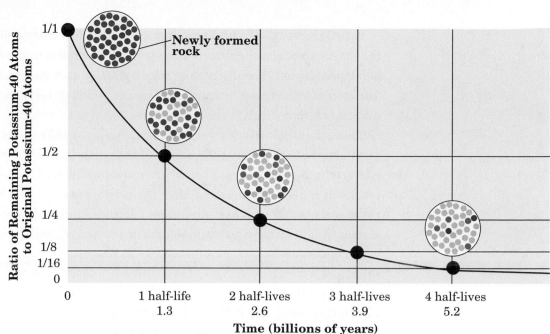

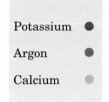

Potassium ●
Argon ●
Calcium ●

Ratio of Remaining Potassium-40 Atoms to Original Potassium-40 Atoms

Newly formed rock

1/1
1/2
1/4
1/8
1/16
0

| 0 | 1 half-life 1.3 | 2 half-lives 2.6 | 3 half-lives 3.9 | 4 half-lives 5.2 |

Time (billions of years)

In **Figure 16-20**, you can assume that there are 40 potassium-40 atoms at zero time. After one half-life, 20 atoms remain and 20 have decayed. Of those 20 that have decayed, 11% (approximately 2) are argon-40, and 89% (approximately 18) are calcium-40. After two half-lives, another 10 have decayed, for a total of 30. Of these 30, 11% are argon-40 (approximately 3), and 89% are calcium-40 (approximately 27). After four half-lives, a total of 37.5 have decayed. Of these, 11% are argon-40 (approximately 4), and 89% are calcium-40 (approximately 33). The decay of potassium-40 is widely used in geological investigations. For example, geologists use it to study motions of the sea floor.

Other isotopes with half-lives even longer than that of potassium-40 have been used to determine the age of the Earth. From these isotopes, the Earth has been revealed to be an impressive 4.5 billion years old!

Industrial applications
Radioactive isotopes are used to make consumer products

The products you see in **Figure 16-21** have all been manufactured with the help of radioactive isotopes. The manufacturing process for each of these products depends on producing the material at the proper thickness. If plastic wrap is too thin, it may tear easily and be useless for wrapping foods. If aluminum foil is too thick, manufacturing it may not be cost-effective. Radioactive isotopes can be used to determine and control the thickness during the manufacture of each of these products.

Figure 16-21
Radiation is used to measure the thickness of metal sheets, plastic wrap, and other products. The intensity of radiation transmitted through these products depends on thickness.

Nuclear Chemistry | **631**

Recall that beta particles or gamma rays can penetrate objects. However, the extent to which they can penetrate depends on the thickness of the object being penetrated. The thicker the object, the less radiation passes through. The decrease in the intensity of radiation depends directly on the quantity of matter through which it passes.

Thus, the thickness of a sheet of plastic wrap or aluminum foil can be measured by monitoring the amount of radiation that is able to pass through it. If too little radiation is detected, then the product is too thick. Conversely, if too much radiation is detected, then the product is too thin. During the manufacture of plastic wrap and aluminum foil, radiation intensity measurements are continuously fed into a computer. The computer then directs the machinery to make any necessary adjustments so that the product has the proper thickness.

Neutron activation analysis
Chemical composition can be determined without destroying a specimen

In order to perform a chemical analysis, part of an object being examined may have to be destroyed in the process. For example, a small sample of the specimen may have to be taken and subjected to various chemical reactions. This type of analysis may not pose any problem if the specimen is large or plentiful.

However, if the specimen is rare, valuable, or otherwise cannot be damaged, then a different approach such as *neutron activation analysis* must be used. First, the sample to be analyzed is exposed to a beam of neutrons emitted by a radioactive isotope in an artificial transmutation process. When the nuclei absorb these neutrons, some elements in the sample, in turn, become artificially produced radioactive isotopes. Each element can then be identified and its mass calculated based on the amount of radioactivity it emits.

Neutron activation analysis has been used to determine the composition of meteorites, as shown in **Figure 16-22**. Also, the identification of elements by neutron activation has been put to use in crime detection. Firing a gun leaves extremely small amounts of antimony, barium, and copper on a person's hand. A wax cast made of a suspect's hand picks up these elements. Subjecting the cast to neutron activation analysis will then reveal if these elements are present and thus show whether the suspect has recently fired a gun.

Figure 16-22
Neutron activation analysis is used to determine the chemical composition of objects such as this meteorite.

One of the most unusual applications of neutron analysis in crime detection involved the 12th president of the United States, Zachary Taylor. On July 4, 1850, President Taylor dedicated the cornerstone for the Washington Monument. Upon his return to the White House, he ate a bowl of cherries and drank a glass of milk. Soon after, he became seriously ill, suffering from diarrhea and severe vomiting. He died five days later.

Doctors attributed his death to natural causes. But some historians suspected for some time that Taylor may have been poisoned with arsenic. One hundred and fifty years after his death, Taylor's body was exhumed from his lead coffin to find out if he had been murdered. Scientists cut away some of his clothing to get samples of his hair. They also took small pieces of his nails and samples of body tissues. All of these samples were subjected to neutron activation analysis. The results revealed that arsenic was present, but only in levels that are normally present in the human body. The scientists concluded that President Taylor had not been poisoned.

Nuclear imaging
Electromagnetic and nuclear radiation are used to look inside the human body

X rays have been used since the late 1800s to look inside the human body to study such structures as bones and lungs. Most organs, however, do not show up well because they are soft and do not absorb the radiation given off by X rays. However, with nuclear imaging techniques, doctors can obtain a more detailed look inside a person's body.

One nuclear imaging technique is known as positron emission tomography (PET). A person is given a small dose of a radioactive isotope such as carbon-11, nitrogen-13, or oxygen-15. Each of these isotopes has a short half-life and emits a positron in the process of decay. Emitted positrons interact with electrons to produce gamma radiation, which is detected by a gamma-ray detector. A computer converts the measured gamma radiation to an image that reveals biological activity.

One nuclear imaging technique that does not depend on radioactivity is known as nuclear magnetic resonance (NMR). The application of NMR to produce images of human organs or tissues is called *magnetic resonance imaging* (MRI). This technique depends on how an atomic nucleus absorbs electromagnetic radiation, which, in turn, depends on the nucleus's chemical environment.

For example, H_2O, $C_6H_{12}O_6$ (a carbohydrate), $C_{57}H_{110}O_6$ (a fat), and $C_{254}H_{377}O_{75}N_{65}S_6$ (a protein) all contain hydrogen atoms. However, in each case, the hydrogen nuclei absorb electromagnetic radiation differently. Furthermore, the hydrogen nuclei in each of these compounds behave differently, depending on whether the organ containing them is normal or diseased. An MRI can check the functioning of an organ, such as the brain, by collecting data about how its hydrogen atoms absorb electromagnetic radiation. A computer converts this data into an image of the organ, such as the one shown in **Figure 16-23**.

Figure 16-23a
This image of a healthy brain was obtained with NMR imaging.

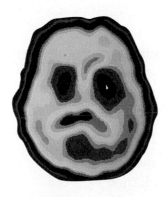

16-23b
This NMR image reveals a brain with Alzheimer's disease.

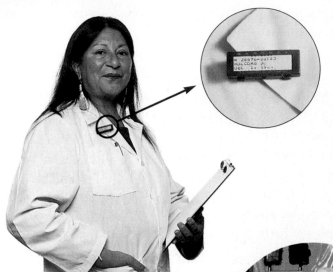

Health concerns
Exposure to radiation must be monitored

The effects of nuclear radiation on the body are cumulative. Repeated exposure to small doses over a long period of time is dangerous if the total amount of radiation received equals the amount of a single large dose. People working with radioactivity, whether in medicine or industry, must therefore monitor the amount of radiation to which they are exposed. The people in **Figure 16-24** wear a special device to monitor their exposure to radiation. One type of device, called a film badge, contains several layers of photographic film covered with black, light-proof paper. At frequent and predetermined intervals, the film is removed and developed. The strength and type of radiation that the worker was exposed to can be determined by examining how dark the film is. The film badge doesn't protect a person from radiation; it only tells them how much radiation exposure they have had.

The biological effect of exposure to nuclear radiation is expressed in a unit known as a *rem*. **Table 16-4** lists the effects of exposure to various doses of radiation. People working with radioactive isotopes are advised to limit their exposure to 5 rems per year. This exposure is 1000 times higher than the recommended exposure level for most people, including you.

Figure 16-24
These workers wear radiation detectors to monitor the level of nuclear radiation to which they are exposed.

Table 16-4
Effect of Whole-Body Exposure to a Single Dose of Radiation

Dose (rems)	Probable effect
0–25	no observable effect
25–50	slight decrease in white blood cell count
50–100	marked decrease in white blood cell count
100–200	nausea, loss of hair
200–500	ulcers, internal bleeding
>500	fatal

Section Review

11. Explain how carbon-14 is used to determine the age of an object.
12. How are radioactive isotopes used in the manufacture of certain consumer goods and in the preparation of certain food products?
13. What is neutron activation analysis?
14. Describe two nuclear imaging techniques used in medicine.
15. Airline crews are exposed to about 0.5–0.7 rems of radiation per year, which is higher than that of most people. Why are airline crews exposed to a higher level of radiation?

 Story Link

16. If the Iceman's body contains 0.50 times as much carbon-14 as it did when he died, how old is the Iceman? If the Iceman's body contains 0.55 times as much carbon-14 now as when he died, about how old is the Iceman?

Conclusion: The Iceman Meets Nuclear Chemistry

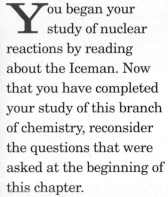

You began your study of nuclear reactions by reading about the Iceman. Now that you have completed your study of this branch of chemistry, reconsider the questions that were asked at the beginning of this chapter.

Exactly when did the Iceman die? Radioactive dating with carbon-14 has placed the Iceman's lifetime somewhere between 3500 and 3000 B.C., during the Age of Copper. The Age of Copper was a period of global climatic warming, allowing humans to climb high up into mountains, such as the Alps where the Iceman was found.

What did the Iceman look like when he was alive? To reconstruct the Iceman's face, scientists used nuclear imaging techniques to generate three-dimensional computer images. Based on these images, scientists built a model of the Iceman's skull. They then used clay to duplicate his muscles and soft urethane to reconstruct his skin. The completed model showed that the Iceman had distinctive features—a broad nose, a protruding lower lip, and prominent chin.

How did the Iceman die? Nuclear imaging techniques provided the key to this question. Scientists believe that the Iceman died from exhaustion, perhaps from having been exposed too long to adverse weather conditions. In this state of exhaustion, the Iceman lay down on his left side in a small depression on the mountain, where he froze to death. His body was gradually covered by snow, which eventually turned into the hard ice coffin in which the Iceman lay buried for the next 5000 years.

Applying Concepts

1. A fossil bone contains one-sixteenth as much carbon-14 as a living organism contains. How old is the fossil?
2. If a rock contained 1.2 mol of potassium-40 when it formed, how many grams remain after 3 billion years?

Research and Writing

Use the library to investigate the following topics.

1. Report on what procedures are proposed in the United States to bury radioactive waste. What are the problems and limitations of current disposal proposals?
2. Report on how nuclear weapons are currently tested in various countries.
3. Find out what foods the FDA has approved for irradiation. What requests are currently pending with the FDA? What pros and cons have been identified concerning the irradiation of foods? What scientific evidence supports or disproves these claims?

Breakthroughs in Developing Today's

1911

Based on studies of α-particle scattering from gold foil, **Ernest Rutherford** postulates the existence of the atomic nucleus. The small nucleus contains most of the mass of the atom and all of its positive charge.

1913

Danish physicist **Niels Bohr** (right) applies the new quantum theory to the atom and theorizes that the emission of light from atoms is due to electrons dropping in energy, each emitting a photon of light in the process.

H.G.J. Moseley, an English physicist, determines the atomic number (number of protons) of various elements by measuring the wavelength of X rays emitted by the pure elements. In the process, he discovers that the ordering of elements in the periodic table is based on atomic number, not atomic weight.

Atomic number

1
H
Hydrogen
1.007 94

Hungarian chemist **Georg de Hevesy** begins to study lead solubility, using radioactive lead as a tracer. Over the years he and others apply tracer techniques to a variety of chemical and biological systems, including plants, animals, and the human body. He is awarded the Nobel Prize in chemistry in 1943 for his work.

1942

Enrico Fermi, the head of a large group of distinguished physicists, initiates the first controlled nuclear fission chain reaction at the University of Chicago. The first nuclear reactor is called a pile because it is literally a pile of uranium blocks and graphite blocks.

1945

The Manhattan Project, a secret project sponsored by the United States government during World War II, culminates in the detonation of the first nuclear fission bomb near Alamogordo, New Mexico.

1952

The first **H-bomb** is detonated at Eniwetok, an atoll in the Pacific Ocean. This device uses a fission bomb to initiate the fusion of deuterium and tritium.

1956

The first commercial nuclear reactor begins operation at **Calder Hall, England**.

• Calder Hall

London •

Atomic Model

The following events significantly affected our understanding of the atomic and nuclear structure, and the uses and potentials of radioactive materials.

1931

Irène and Frédéric Joliot-Curie discover a new form of "radiation" when they bombard beryllium metal with α-particles. Working as a separate team, Walther Bothe and Wilhelm Becker make a similar discovery.

1932

Sir James Chadwick, an English physicist at the Cavendish Laboratory, shows that the "radiation" discovered in 1931 is really a neutral particle with a mass close to that of the proton. The new particle, called a neutron, had been predicted by Rutherford in 1920.

E. O. Lawrence's particle accelerator, dubbed the cyclotron, produces protons with an energy of 1 million electron volts, 1 MeV. Cyclotrons and similar accelerators become indispensable to physicists in the years to come.

1937

Technetium, the first artificial element, is discovered by **Emilio Segrè** in a sample of molybdenum that was bombarded with particles accelerated in Lawrence's cyclotron. Inconclusive evidence of this element had been found as early as 1925 by Walter and Ida Noddack in samples of uranium-containing ore.

43
Tc
Technetium
97.9072

1939

The German chemists **Otto Hahn and Fritz Strassmann** discover that an isotope of barium is produced when uranium is bombarded with neutrons. Shortly after Hahn's report, two Austrian physicists, **Lise Meitner and Otto Frisch,** correctly interpret Hahn's experimental observations and conclude that the uranium nucleus was being split into two smaller pieces. They name the process nuclear fission.

1963

The Limited Test Ban Treaty is signed by President Kennedy, and many nations agree to halt further atmospheric testing of nuclear weapons.

1964

Murray Gell-Mann postulates the existence of fundamental subatomic particles, which he names quarks. Protons and neutrons are theorized to consist of quarks.

1972

Fermi National Accelerator Laboratory, near Chicago, begins operation. Its main accelerator ring is a mile in diameter and produces protons with an energy of 200 GeV. In 1983, a second ring of superconducting magnets is installed, which increases the energy to 900 GeV.

1979

The Nobel Prize in physics is awarded to **Sheldon Glashow, Abdus Salam**, and **Steven Weinberg** for their theory that successfully unifies explanations of the electromagnetic and weak forces' effects on quarks, electrons, and other particles.

1994

The Superconducting Super Collider, a multibillion-dollar accelerator being built in Texas, is canceled by the United States government.

CHAPTER

Highlights 16

Key terms

alpha particle
beta particle
binding energy
chain reaction
critical mass
fission
fusion
gamma ray
half-life

mass defect
positron emission
radioactivity
radioactive tracer
stable nucleus
strong nuclear force
transmutation
unstable nucleus

Key problem-solving approach:
Calculating binding energy

To calculate the binding energy of one mole of a substance, follow the calculation pathway below.

atomic number × mass of hydrogen (in amu)	+	mass of neutrons (in amu)

=

mass of nucleons, (in amu)

−

actual atomic mass, (in amu)

=

mass defect, (in amu)

×

conversion factor for kg

$$\frac{1.660\ 540 \times 10^{-27}\ \text{kg}}{1\ \text{amu}}$$

×

constant c^2, $(3.00 \times 10^8\ \text{m/s})^2$

×

Avogadro's number, $6.022 \times 10^{23}/\text{mol}$

=

binding energy, (in J/mol)

Key ideas

 ### Why are some atomic nuclei unstable?

- In spite of repulsive forces between their like charges, protons cluster tightly together within the nucleus. The strong force in the nucleus overwhelms the repulsive forces of the protons and holds protons and neutrons together.
- A small percentage of atoms have nuclei that are unstable and subject to a nuclear change called transmutation, which results in the formation of a new element. Atoms that exhibit this behavior are called radioactive.
- The stability of the nucleus is dependent on the neutron-proton ratio. Stable atoms form a pattern called the band of stability.
- The amount of energy released when a nucleus is formed is called binding energy. Binding energy can be calculated by applying Einstein's equation, $E = mc^2$.

 ### What kinds of nuclear change occur?

- Radioactivity is composed of alpha and beta particles, gamma rays, and positron emission.
- Artificial transmutation occurs in laboratories in machines such as particle accelerators.
- Fission is a process in which a nucleus splits into two smaller nuclei, releasing large quantities of energy.
- Fusion is a process in which small nuclei combine into a larger nucleus, releasing large quantities of energy.

 ### How is nuclear chemistry used?

- Half-life is the time required for one half of the mass of a radioactive substance to decay.
- The half-life of the carbon-14 isotope can be used to date organic material that is up to 20 000 years old. Other radioactive isotopes are used to date more ancient rock and mineral formations.
- The effects of radiation may be measured in units called rems.

Review and Assess

Nuclear stability

REVIEW

1. Explain how the strong nuclear force overpowers the repulsive forces within the nucleus.
2. Explain why nuclear stability is a necessary condition for the stability of the environment.
3. Give at least three examples of how the instability of the nucleus affects the properties of radioactive atoms.
4. Through a nuclear reaction, an atom of a rubidium isotope becomes an atom of a krypton isotope. What has happened? Why?
5. a. What is the relationship among number of protons, number of neutrons, and the stability of the nucleus?
   b. Why is it increasingly hard to stabilize nuclei as the number of protons increases?

6. Refer to the graph at the bottom of the page to answer the following questions.
   a. Which point represents $^{102}_{45}$Rh? Is the rhodium nucleus stable? How do you know?
   b. Which point represents $^{209}_{83}$Bi? What can you predict about any isotopes heavier than this? Why?
   c. What can you say about the stability of a nucleus represented by point **d**? What about the stability of the nucleus at point **a**?
7. What is the relationship among protons, neutrons, and binding energy?
8. What is the relationship between mass defect and binding energy?

APPLY

9. Why do we compare binding energy per nuclear particle instead of the total binding energy per nucleus?

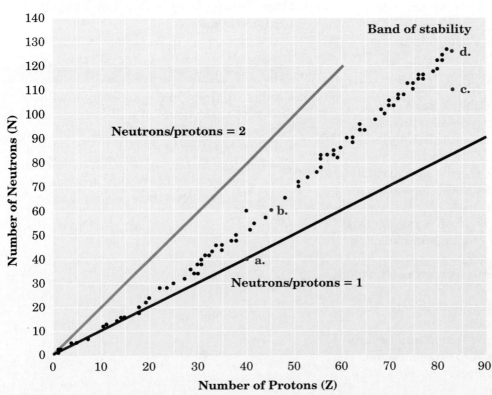

Neutron-Proton Ratios of Stable Nuclei

10 **a.** Compare the binding energies of the following two nuclei, and indicate which releases more energy when formed. You will need information from the periodic table and the text.
Nucleus #1: atomic mass 34.9880 amu, atomic number 19
Nucleus #2: atomic mass 22.9898 amu, atomic number 11

b. What is the binding energy per nucleon for each nucleus? Which nucleus is more stable?

11. Using Einstein's equation, $E = mc^2$, determine how much mass (in kilograms) is lost by the formation of a nucleus of $^{56}_{26}Fe$, if the binding energy released is 7.884×10^{-11} J.

Nuclear change

REVIEW

12. a. What is the relationship between an alpha particle and a helium nucleus?

b. The decay of uranium-238 results in the spontaneous ejection of an alpha particle. Write the nuclear equation that summarizes this process.

13. Compare and contrast the penetrating powers of alpha particles, beta particles, and gamma rays.

14. What type of radiation is emitted in the following equation?

$$^{43}_{19}K \longrightarrow {}^{43}_{20}Ca + \textbf{?}$$

15. Is the decay of an unstable isotope into a stable isotope always a one-step process?

16. How does artificial transmutation differ from natural radioactive decay?

17. Refer to **Table 16-2**. Describe how artificial transmutation resulted in the formation of unniloctium.

18. a. What role does the neutron serve in starting a nuclear chain reaction and keeping it going?

b. Why must neutrons in a chain reaction be controlled?

c. Describe the relationship between neutrons and critical mass.

19. a. Compare and contrast fusion and fission.

b. Explain the relationship among fusion, temperature, and energy.

20. Are the products of nuclear transmutation higher or lower in energy than the starting material? Why?

21. The plutonium isotope $^{239}_{94}Pu$ is sometimes used in nuclear reactors. What do transmutations and the relative abundance of uranium isotopes have to do with the use of the plutonium isotope in reactors?

Using nuclear reactions

REVIEW

22. Why is the constant rate of decay of radioactive nuclei so important in radioactive dating?

23. The Environmental Protection Agency and health officials nationwide are concerned about the levels of radon gas in homes. The half-life of one radon isotope is 3.8 days. If a sample of gas taken from a basement contains 4.38 μg of radon-222, how much radon will remain in the sample after 15.2 days?

24. A pathologist working in a police laboratory wants to analyze a small sample of blood from a crime scene. He cannot damage the blood sample because it will be used in court as evidence. What kind of radioactive analysis should he use? Why?

25. Many cancer patients lose hair during radiation therapy. How is this hair loss related to rem exposure?

APPLY

26. Use an example from your everyday life to illustrate the concept of half-life.

27. Why would someone working around radioactive waste in a landfill use a radiation monitor instead of a watch to determine when the workday is over? At what point would that person decide to stop working?

Linking chapters

1. **Structure of the nucleus**
   Compare and contrast the interaction, function, and stability of nuclear particles both inside and outside the nucleus.
2. **Theme: Classification and Trends**
   Explain the relationship among atomic number, size of the nucleus, and stability.
3. **Stoichiometry**
   Calculate the mass of 250 mol of plutonium-239.
4. **Density**
   Calculate the density in g/cm^3 of uranium-235 if 8.0 m^3 has a mass of 1.5×10^5 kg.
5. **Balancing equations**
   Balance the following.
   a. $^{1}_{0}n + ^{235}_{92}U \longrightarrow ^{89}_{37}Rb + ^{144}_{58}Ce + ^{0}_{-1}e + ^{1}_{0}n$
   b. $^{239}_{94}Pu + ^{1}_{0}n \longrightarrow ^{146}_{58}Ce + ^{90}_{38}Sr + ^{0}_{-1}e + ^{1}_{0}n$
   c. $Tl + O_2 + H_2O \longrightarrow Tl^+ + OH^-$
6. **Writing equations**
   The radioactive decay series that begins with uranium-235 and ends with lead-207, shows the following sequence of emissions for the series: alpha, beta, alpha, beta, alpha, alpha, alpha, alpha, beta, beta, and alpha. Write an equation for each reaction in the series.

USING TECHNOLOGY

1. **Computer art**
   Design a computer program that illustrates the path of particles through a magnetic field. Your program should show pathways representing movement and not simply stationary points. Use the path shown in the diagram as a model for the pathway that would be characteristic of a neutral particle.

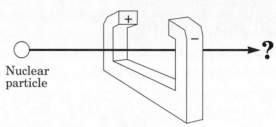

Nuclear particle

2. **Computer program**
   In order to calculate binding energy, you need to know the actual atomic masses of the elements. Design a computer program that stores atomic masses in your computer and allows you to access them with keyboard commands. Program a spreadsheet to calculate binding energy using the process shown on page 638.

Alternative assessment

Portfolio projects

1. **Chemistry and you**
   Your local grocery store may sell irradiated foods. Find out what stores in your area sell irradiated foods, and determine whether you have any of these foods at home. What are the shelf lives of these foods before and after irradiation? Report your findings to the class.
2. **Research and communication**
   Compare the physiological effects of the different kinds of radiation. Find out if any adults you know are exposed to radiation at work. Ask about the kind of radiation involved and what precautions they take to avoid the harmful effects of radiation. Report your findings to the class.

3. **Research and communication**
   a. Research some important historical findings that have been validated through radioactive dating. Report your findings to the class.
   b. You have made an important archaeological or geological find. Describe how you will use radioactive dating.
4. **Research and communication**
   Find out about the future of nuclear power in this country. How many plants are currently supplying power? How many are in the construction stage? How does the use of nuclear power in the United States compare with that of Europe?

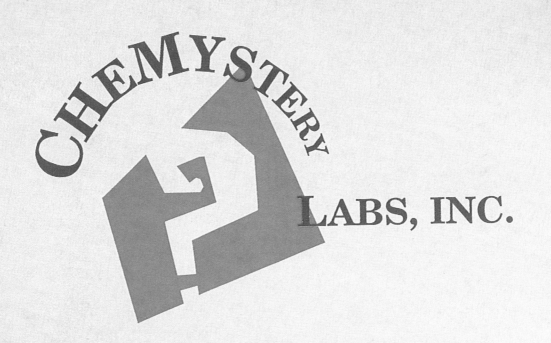

Explorations
Technique Builders

Investigations
Problem Solving

CHEMYSTERY LABS, INC.

Investigations
Analysis
Material Testing
Research and Development

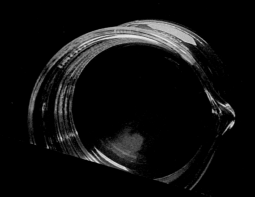

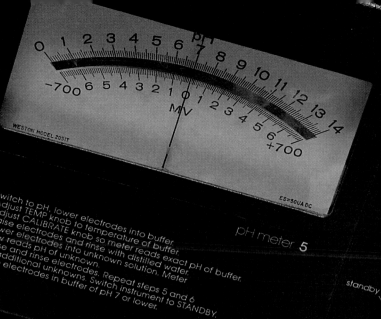

Working in the World of a Chemist

Meeting today's challenges

Even though you have already taken science classes with lab work, you will find the two types of laboratory experiments in this book organized differently from those you have done before. The first type of lab is called an *Exploration*, and it helps you gain skills in lab techniques that you will use to solve a real problem presented in the second type of lab, which is called an *Investigation*. The *Exploration* serves as a *Technique Builder*, and the *Investigation* is presented as an exercise in *Problem Solving*.

Both types of labs refer to you as an employee of a professional company, and your teacher has the role of supervisor. Lab situations are given for real-life circumstances to show how chemistry fits into the world outside of the classroom. This will give you valuable practice with real-world skills that you can use in chemistry and in other careers, such as creating a plan with available resources, developing and following a budget, and writing business letters.

As you work on these labs, you will better understand how the concepts you studied in the chapters are used by chemists to solve problems that affect life for everyone.

Explorations

The *Explorations* provide step-by-step procedures for you to follow, encouraging you to make careful observations and interpretations as you progress through the lab session. Each *Exploration* serves as a *Technique Builder* that gives you an opportunity to practice and perfect a specific lab technique or concept that will be needed later in an *Investigation*. The *Explorations* have the following sections.
- *Objectives:* what you will be expected to accomplish as you complete the Exploration.
- *Situation:* the setting in which the *Exploration* takes place
- *Background:* some of the chemistry information you will needed to work through the *Exploration*
- *Problem:* an overview of what you must do to meet the requirements of the *Situation*
- *Safety:* warnings and information on how to be safe during the *Exploration*
- *Materials:* items you will need to do the lab work
- *Preparation:* things to prepare before starting the procedure
- *Technique:* step-by-step explanations to follow for doing the lab work
- *Cleanup and Disposal:* specific guidelines for ending the lab session
- *Analysis and Interpretation:* items that will help you make sense of the data you collected and the observations you made
- *Conclusions:* items that will help you understand how your results relate to the key chemistry concepts involved in the procedure
- *Extensions:* challenging items that involve further calculations, research, or planning, many of which are good ideas for science fair projects

What you should do before an Exploration

Preparation will help you work safely and efficiently. The evening before a lab, be sure to do the following.

- **Read the lab procedure** to make sure you understand what you will do.
- **Read the safety information** that begins on page 651, as well as that provided in the lab procedure.
- **Write down any questions** you have in your lab notebook so that you can ask your teacher about them before the lab begins.
- **Prepare all necessary data tables** so that you will be able to concentrate on your work when you are in the lab.

What you should do after an Exploration

Most teachers require a lab report as a way of making sure that you understood what you were doing. Your teacher will give you specific details about how to organize the lab report, but most lab reports will include the following. A sample lab report you can use as a model is shown below.

- **title** for the lab
- **summary paragraph(s)** describing the purpose and procedure
- **data tables and observations** that are organized and comprehensive
- **worked-out calculations** with proper units
- **answers**, boxed, circled, or highlighted, for items in the *Analysis and Interpretation*, *Conclusions*, and *Extensions* sections

Tamara Kieklak
Fifth Period
March 31, 1994

Lab Report

<u>Title</u> Exploration 12A— Boiling Point Elevation and Molar Mass

<u>Summary</u> If a solute is dissolved in water, it will change the boiling point of water. First, I determined the boiling point of pure water, and then measured the boiling point with 10.0 g of each of the three solutes. The solutes used were NaCl, sucrose, and $MgSO_4$. Then I tested an unknown substance in the same manner. I compared the results to see what the unknown substance was.

<u>Data Table</u>

solution	Boiling Point
H_2O	100.0°C
NaCl	103.5°C
Sucrose	100.5°C
$MgSO_4$	101.8°C
Unknown	102.0°C

<u>Analysis and Interpretation</u>

1. Δt_b for NaCl = 103.5°C − 100.0°C = 3.5°C
   Δt_b for Sucrose = 100.3°C − 100.0°C = 0.3°C
   Δt_b $MgSO_4$ = 101.8°C − 100.0°C = 1.8°C
   Δt_b Unknown = 101.9°C − 100.0°C = 1.9°C

2. The data for unknown most closely matches that for $MgSO_4$.

3. $m = \dfrac{\Delta t_b}{K_b}$

Investigations

The *Investigations* may seem quite different because they do not provide step-by-step instructions. The *Investigations* require you to develop your own procedure to solve a problem presented to your company by a client. You must decide how much money to spend on the project and what equipment to use. Although this may seem very difficult, the *Investigations* contain a number of clues about what to do to be successful in *Problem Solving*.

Problem Solving

What you should do before an Investigation

Before you will be allowed to work on the lab, you must turn in a preliminary report. Usually, you must describe in detail the procedure you plan to use, provide complete data tables for the data and observations you will collect, and list exactly what equipment you will need and the costs. Only after your teacher, acting as your supervisor, approves your plans are you allowed to proceed. A sample preliminary report is shown below. Before you begin writing a preliminary report, follow these steps.

- **Read the *Investigation* thoroughly,** searching for clues.
- **Jot down notes** in your lab notebook as you find clues.

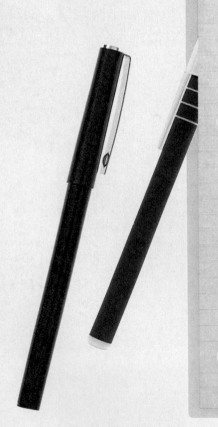

Stacy Rivera
Third Period
March 22, 1994

<u>Title</u> Boiling-Point Elevation — Contamination

<u>Summary</u> A sample of powdered sugar contaminated by another substance will be analyzed to determine the identity of the contaminant. Because the contaminant is either glucose, salt, or calcium chloride, the procedure can be a simple boiling-point elevation test. As a control for the procedure, the boiling point of pure water is determined by heating it with a Bunsen burner and measuring the temperature at boiling with a thermometer. Then the boiling point with 10.0 g of each of the possible contaminants is measured. Once the data is obtained, the same test for the boiling-point elevation of the unknown substance can be used to identify the contaminant.

<u>Data Table</u>

Solution	Boiling Point
H_2O	
Glucose	
Salt	
$CaCl_2$	
Unknown	

<u>Materials</u>

Lab space/fume hood/utilities	$15,000
Disposal fee for 40 g of solutes	$80,000
Beaker tongs	$1,000
$CaCl_2$, 10 g	$5,000
Glucose, 10 g	$5,000
NaCl, 10 g	$5,000
250 mL flask	$1,000
100 mL graduated cylinder	$1,000
Balance	$5,000

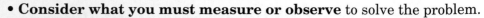

- **Consider what you must measure or observe** to solve the problem.
- **Think about *Explorations*** you have done that used a similar technique or reaction.
- **Imagine working through a procedure,** keeping track of each step and what equipment you will need.
- **Carefully consider** whether your approach is the best, most efficient one.

What you should do after an Investigation

After you finish, organize a report of your data as described in the *Memorandum*. This is usually in the form of a one- or two-page letter to the client. (Your teacher may have additional requirements for your report.) Carefully consider how to convey the information the client needs to know. In some cases, a graph or diagram can communicate information better than words can. As a part of your report, you must include an invoice for the client that explains how much they owe and how much you charged for each part of the procedure. Remember to include the cost of your work in the analysis. A sample that you can use as a model is shown below.

Kristeen McGonigal
Director of Operations
D & J Food Processing

Dear Ms. McGonigal,

The analysis has been completed on the contaminant that was accidentally included in your batch of powdered sugar. We are pleased to report that the contaminant is glucose, and you will still be able to use the processed batch.

The procedure we used tested the boiling-point elevation of 50.0 g of water with 10.0 g of each of the three possible contaminants added. In gathering our data, we found that glucose raised the boiling point of water 0.7°C, NaCl raised it 3.5°C, and $CaCl_2$ raised it 3.0°C. When we tested 10.0 g of the unknown contaminant you sent us, we found it to have a boiling point elevation of 0.6°C, indicating that the contaminant is glucose.

The following calculations were made for the molecular mass determination.

molality of particles, $m = \dfrac{\Delta t_b}{K_b}$

for glucose: $m = \dfrac{0.7°C}{0.51°C/m} = 1.4\ m$

for NaCl: $m = \dfrac{3.5°C}{0.51°C/m} = 6.9\ m$

for $CaCl_2$: $m = \dfrac{3.0°C}{0.51°C/m} = 5.9\ m$

for unknown: $m = \dfrac{0.6°C}{0.51°C/m} = 1.2\ m$

for glucose: molar mass $= \dfrac{10.0\ g}{50.0\ g\ H_2O} \times \dfrac{1000\ g}{1\ kg} \times \dfrac{1\ kg\ H_2O}{1.4\ mol} \times \dfrac{1}{1} = 140\ g/mol$

for NaCl: molar mass $= \dfrac{10.0\ g}{50.0\ g\ H_2O} \times \dfrac{1000\ g}{1\ kg} \times \dfrac{1\ kg\ H_2O}{6.9\ mol} \times \dfrac{2}{1} = 58\ g/mol$

for $CaCl_2$: molar mass $= \dfrac{10.0\ g}{50.0\ g\ H_2O} \times \dfrac{1000\ g}{1\ kg} \times \dfrac{1\ kg\ H_2O}{5.9\ mol} \times \dfrac{3}{1} = 100\ g/mol$

for unknown: molar mass $= \dfrac{10.0\ g}{50.0\ g\ H_2O} \times \dfrac{1000\ g}{1\ kg} \times \dfrac{1\ kg\ H_2O}{1.2\ mol} \times \dfrac{1}{1} = 170\ g/mol$

0.5M FeCl₃

Tips for success in the lab

Whether you are performing an *Exploration* or an *Investigation*, you can do the following to help ensure success.

- **Read each lab twice** before you prepare the data tables.
- **Make sure you understand** everything that will happen in the lab.
- **Read the safety precautions** in the lab and on page 651.
- **Prepare the data tables** before you enter the lab.
- **Record all data and observations immediately** in the tables in your lab notebook.
- **Use appropriate units** whenever recording data.
- **Keep your lab desk organized** and free of clutter.

If you need help with graphing or with using significant figures, refer to *Appendix B*. The following pages contain tips to help you in lab, from preparing and filling out data tables to understanding how your teacher will grade the lab reports.

Preparing data tables

Data tables need to be prepared *before* you start any lab work because the tables must be ready for recording your data and observations *as* you do your lab work. For one example of how, you might construct a data table, refer to the instructions below and to **Figure A**.

Preparation

I. Organizing Data

Prepare a data table in your lab notebook. It should have eight columns and five rows if you use the LEAP colormeter or a spectrophotometer, or four rows if this equipment will not be used. In the first row, label the boxes in the second through eighth columns *Test tube 0, Test tube 1, Test tube 2, Test tube 3, Test tube 4, Test tube 5,* and *Unknown*. In the first column, label the second box *mL 0.50 M FeCl₃*, the third box *mL H₂O*, and the fourth box *Estimates*. If you are using a colormeter or a spectrophotometer, label the fifth box in the first column *Measurements*. You will also need space for calculations.

Figure A

Col.1	Col.2 test tube 0	Col.3 test tube 1	Col.4 test tube 2	Col.5 test tube 3	Col.6 test tube 4	Col.7 test tube 5	Col.8 Unknown
mL 0.50 M FeCl₃ mL H₂O Estimates Measurements							

Completing data tables

An example of how you might fill in a data table is shown below in **Figure B**. Refer to the excerpt from an *Exploration* to understand how the procedure gives you the information you need to complete the data table.

Technique

2. Measure the mass of a clean, dry evaporating dish and watch glass to the nearest 0.01 g. Record this mass in your data table.

3. Add 2–3 g NaHCO₃ to your evaporating dish. Measure the mass, with the cover glass, to the nearest 0.01 g. Record this mass in your data table.

4. Slowly add 30 mL of the acetic acid solution to the NaHCO₃ in the evaporating dish. Add more acetic acid with a dropper or pipet until the bubbling stops.

5. If you are using a Bunsen burner, place the evaporating dish and its contents on a ceramic-centered wire gauze on an iron ring attached to the ring stand, as shown in the photograph below. Place the watch glass, concave side up, on top of the dish, making sure that there is a slight opening for steam to escape. If you are using a hot plate, place the watch glass the same way, but heat the evaporating dish directly on the hot plate.

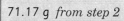

6. Gently heat the evaporating dish until only a dry solid remains. Make sure that no water droplets remain on the underside of the watch glass. ***Do not heat too rapidly, or the material will boil, and the product will spatter out of the evaporating dish.***

7. Turn off the gas burner or hot plate. Allow the apparatus to cool at least 15 min. Determine the mass of the cooled equipment to the nearest 0.01 g. Record the mass of the dish, residue, and watch glass in your data table.

8. If time permits, reheat the evaporating dish and contents for 2 min. Let it cool and measure its mass again. You can be certain the sample is dry when there are two successive measurements within 0.02 g of each other.

Figure B

Mass of empty evaporating dish and watch glass	71.17 g *from step 2*
Mass of evaporating dish, watch glass, NaHCO₃	73.27 g *from step 3*
Mass of evaporating dish, watch glass, NaC₂H₃O₂ – First heating	73.21 g *from step 7*
Mass of evaporating dish, watch glass, NaC₂H₃O₂ – Second heating	73.19 g *from step 8*

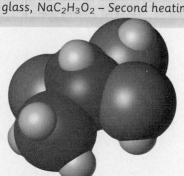

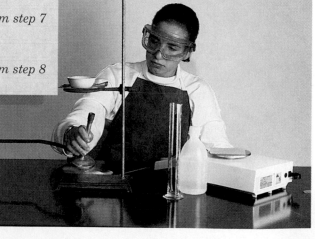

Lab report grades

Lab report requirements and grading criteria vary from teacher to teacher. A good lab report usually has the following characteristics.

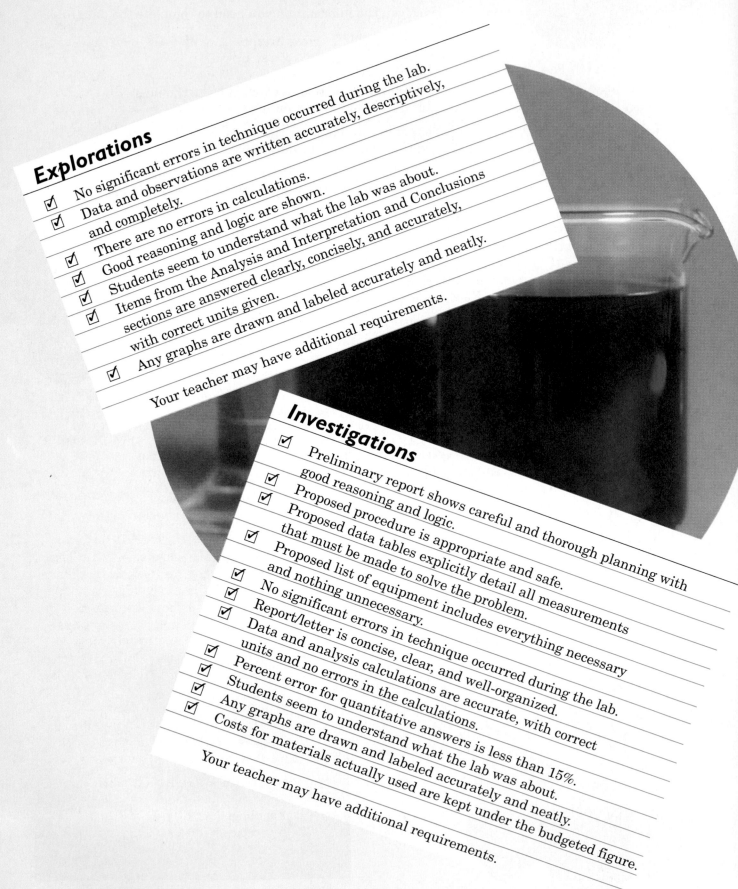

Explorations

☑ No significant errors in technique occurred during the lab.

☑ Data and observations are written accurately, descriptively, and completely.

☑ There are no errors in calculations.

☑ Good reasoning and logic are shown.

☑ Students seem to understand what the lab was about.

☑ Items from the Analysis and Interpretation and Conclusions sections are answered clearly, concisely, and accurately, with correct units given.

☑ Any graphs are drawn and labeled accurately and neatly.

Your teacher may have additional requirements.

Investigations

☑ Preliminary report shows careful and thorough planning with good reasoning and logic.

☑ Proposed procedure is appropriate and safe.

☑ Proposed data tables explicitly detail all measurements that must be made to solve the problem.

☑ Proposed list of equipment includes everything necessary and nothing unnecessary.

☑ No significant errors in technique occurred during the lab.

☑ Report/letter is concise, clear, and well-organized.

☑ Data and analysis calculations are accurate, with correct units and no errors in the calculations.

☑ Percent error for quantitative answers is less than 15%.

☑ Students seem to understand what the lab was about.

☑ Any graphs are drawn and labeled accurately and neatly.

☑ Costs for materials actually used are kept under the budgeted figure.

Your teacher may have additional requirements.

Safety in the Chemistry Laboratory

Chemicals are not toys

Any chemical can be dangerous if it is misused. Always follow the instructions for the experiment. Pay close attention to the safety notes. Do not do anything differently unless told to do so by your teacher.

Chemicals, even water, can cause harm. The challenge is to know how to use chemicals correctly so that they will not cause harm. If you follow the rules stated below, pay attention to your teacher's directions, follow cautions on chemical labels and the experiments, then you will be using chemicals correctly.

These safety rules always apply in the lab

1. **Always wear a lab apron and safety goggles.**
   Even if you aren't working on an experiment at the time, laboratories contain chemicals that can damage your clothing. Keep the apron strings tied. More importantly, some chemicals can cause eye damage, and even blindness. If your safety goggles are uncomfortable or get clouded up, you are not the first person to have these problems. Ask your teacher for help. Try lengthening the strap a bit, washing the goggles with soap and warm water, or using an anti-fog spray.

2. **No contact lenses in the lab.**
   Even while wearing safety goggles, chemicals could get between contact lenses and your eyes and cause irreparable eye damage. If your doctor requires that you wear contact lenses instead of glasses, then you should wear eye-cup safety goggles in the lab. Ask your doctor or your teacher how to use this very important and special eye protection.

3. **NEVER WORK ALONE IN THE LABORATORY.**
   You should do lab work *only* under the supervision of your teacher.

4. **Wear the right clothing for lab work.**
   Necklaces, neckties, dangling jewelry, long hair, and loose clothing can knock things over or catch on fire. Tuck in neckties or take them off. Do not wear a necklace or other dangling jewelry, including hanging earrings. You don't have to, but it might be a good idea to remove your wristwatch so that it is not damaged by a chemical splash.

   Pull back long hair, and tie it in place. Nylon and polyester fabrics burn and melt more readily than cotton, so wear cotton clothing if you can. It's best to wear fitted garments, but if your clothing is loose or baggy, tuck it in or tie it back so that it does not get in the way or catch on fire.

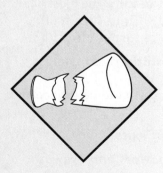

   Wear shoes that will protect your feet from chemical spills—no open-toed shoes or sandals, and no shoes with woven leather straps. Shoes made of solid leather or polymer are much better than shoes made of cloth. It is also important to wear pants, not shorts or skirts.

5. **Only books and notebooks needed for the experiment should be in the lab.**
   Do not bring textbooks, purses, bookbags, backpacks, or other items into the lab; keep these things in your desk or locker.

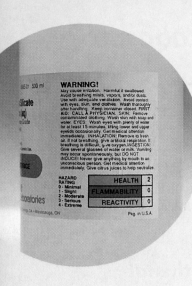

6. **Read the entire experiment before entering the lab.**
Memorize the safety precautions. Be familiar with the instructions for the experiment. Only materials and equipment authorized by your teacher should be used. When you do your lab work, follow the instructions and safety precautions described in the directions for the experiment.

7. **Read chemical labels.**
Follow the instructions and safety precautions stated on the labels.

8. **Walk with care in the lab.**
Sometimes you will have to carry chemicals from the supply station to your lab station. Avoid bumping into other students and spilling the chemicals. Stay at your lab station at other times.

9. **Food, beverages, chewing gum, cosmetics, and smoking are NEVER allowed in the lab.**
(You should already know this.)

10. **NEVER taste chemicals or touch them with your bare hands.**
Keep your hands away from your face and mouth while working, even if you are wearing gloves.

11. **Use a sparker to light a Bunsen burner.**
Do not use matches. Be sure that all gas valves are turned off and that all hot plates are turned off *and* unplugged when you leave the lab.

12. **Be careful with hot plates, Bunsen burners, and other heat sources.**
Keep your body and clothing away from flames. Do not touch a hot plate after it has just been turned off because it is probably hotter than you think. The same is true of glassware, crucibles, and other things after removing them from the flame of a Bunsen burner or from a drying oven.

13. **Do not use electrical equipment with frayed or twisted wires.**

14. **Be sure your hands are dry before using electrical equipment.**
Before plugging an electrical cord into a socket, be sure the electrical equipment is turned off. When you are finished with it, turn it off. Before you leave the lab, unplug it, but be sure to turn it off FIRST.

15. **Do not let electrical cords dangle from work stations; dangling cords can cause tripping or electrical shocks.**
The area under and around electrical equipment should be dry; cords should not lie in puddles of spilled liquid.

16. **Know fire drill procedures and the locations of exits.**

17. **Know the location and operation of safety showers and eyewash stations.**

18. **If your clothes catch on fire, walk to the safety shower, stand under it, and turn it on.**

19. **If you get a chemical in your eyes, walk immediately to the eyewash station, turn it on, and lower your head so your eyes are in the running water.**
Hold your eyelids open with your thumbs and fingers, and roll your eyeballs around. You have to flush your eyes continuously for at least 15 minutes. Call your teacher while you are doing this.

20. **If you have a spill on the floor or lab bench, call your teacher rather than trying to clean it up by yourself.**
Your teacher will tell you if it is OK for you to do the cleanup; if not, your teacher will know how the spill should be cleaned up safely.

21. **If you spill a chemical on your skin, wash it off using the sink faucet, and call your teacher.**
If you spill a solid chemical on your clothing, brush it off carefully without scattering it on somebody else, and call your teacher. If you get a liquid on your clothing, wash it off right away if you can get it under the sink faucet, and call your teacher. If the spill is on your pants or somewhere else that will not fit under the sink faucet, use the safety shower. Remove the pants or other affected clothing while under the shower, and call your teacher. (It may be temporarily embarrassing to remove pants or other clothing in front of your class, but failing to flush that chemical off your skin could cause permanent damage.)

22. **The best way to prevent an accident is to stop it before it happens.**
If you have a close call, tell your teacher so that you and your teacher can find a way to prevent it from happening again. Otherwise, the next time, it could be a harmful accident instead of just a close call.

23. **All accidents should be reported to your teacher, no matter how minor.**
Also, if you get a headache, feel sick to your stomach, or feel dizzy, tell your teacher immediately.

24. **For all chemicals, take only what you need.**
However, if you do happen to take too much and have some left over, DO NOT put it back in the bottle. If somebody accidentally puts a chemical into the wrong bottle, the next person to use it will have a contaminated sample. Ask your teacher what to do with any leftover chemicals.

25. **NEVER take any chemicals out of the lab.**
(This is another one that you should already know. You probably know the remaining rules also, but read them anyway.)

26. **Horseplay and fooling around in the lab are very dangerous.**
NEVER be a clown in the laboratory.

27. **Keep your work area clean and tidy.**
After your work is done, clean your work area and all equipment.

28. **Always wash your hands with soap and water before you leave the lab.**

29. **Whether or not the lab instructions remind you, all of these rules apply all of the time.**

Safety Symbols

To highlight specific types of precautions, the following symbols are used in the Explorations and Investigations. Remember that no matter what safety symbols are used in the lab instructions, all 29 of the safety rules previously described should be followed at all times.

- Wear laboratory aprons in the laboratory. Keep the apron strings tied so that they do not dangle.

- Wear safety goggles in the laboratory at all times. Know how to use the eyewash station. (Rules **1**, **17**, and **19** apply. Which rule says not to wear contact lenses? Do regular eyeglasses provide enough protection?)

- Never taste, eat, or swallow any chemicals in the laboratory. Do not eat or drink any food from laboratory containers. Beakers are not cups, and evaporating dishes are not bowls. (Rules **9** and **10** apply.)

- Never return unused chemicals to the original container. (Which rule applies?)

- Some chemicals are harmful to our environment. You can help protect the environment by following the instructions for proper disposal.

- It helps to label the beakers and test tubes containing chemicals. (This is not a new rule, just a good idea.)

- Never transfer substances by sucking on a pipet or straw; use a suction bulb. (This is a new rule.)

- Never place glassware, containers of chemicals, or anything else near the edges of a lab bench or table. (This is another new rule.)

Here is a question: Do any rules other than **9** and **10** apply in the lab when you see this safety symbol?

- If a chemical gets on your skin or clothing or in your eyes, rinse it immediately, and alert your teacher. (Rules **19** and **21** apply.)

- If a chemical is spilled on the floor or lab bench, tell your teacher, but do not clean it up yourself unless your teacher says it is OK to do so. (Rule **20** applies.)

Here is another question: What rules other than **19**, **20**, and **21** apply in the lab when you see this safety symbol?

- When heating a chemical in a test tube, always point the open end of the test tube away from yourself and other people. (This is another new rule.)

WARNING! From here to the end of this safety section, it is up to you to look at the list of rules and identify whether a specific rule applies, or if the rule presented is a new rule.

- Tie back long hair, and confine loose clothing. (Rule **?** applies.)

- Never reach across an open flame. (Rule **?** applies.)

- Use proper procedures when lighting Bunsen burners. Turn off hot plates, Bunsen burners, and other heat sources when not in use. (Rule **?** applies.)

- Heat flasks or beakers on a ringstand with wire gauze between the glass and the flame. (Rule **?** applies.)

- Use tongs when heating containers. Never hold or touch containers while heating them. Always allow heated materials to cool before handling them. (Rule **?** applies.)

- Turn off gas valves when not in use. (Rule **?** applies.)

- Use flammable liquids only in small amounts. (Rule **?** applies.)

- When working with flammable liquids, be sure that no one else is using a lit Bunsen burner or plans to use one. (Rule **?** applies.)

What other rules should you follow in the lab when you see this safety symbol?

- Check the condition of glassware before and after using it. Inform your teacher of any broken, chipped, or cracked glassware because it should not be used. (Rule **?** applies.)

- Do not pick up broken glass with your bare hands. Place broken glass in a specially designated disposal container. (Rule **?** applies.)

- Never force glass tubing into rubber tubing, rubber stoppers, or wooden corks. To protect your hands, wear heavy cloth gloves or wrap toweling around the glass and the tubing, stopper, or cork, and gently push in the glass. (Rule **?** applies.)

- Do not inhale fumes directly. When instructed to smell a substance, use your hand to wave the fumes toward your nose, and inhale gently. (Some people say "waft the fumes.")

- Keep your hands away from your face and mouth. (Rule **?** applies.)

- Always wash your hands before leaving the laboratory. (Rule **?** applies.)

Finally, if you are wondering how to answer the questions that asked what additional rules apply to the safety symbols, here is the correct answer.
Any time you see any of the safety symbols, you should remember that all 29 of the numbered laboratory rules always apply.

EXPLORATION 1A

Technique Builder

Laboratory Techniques

Demonstrate proficiency in using the Bunsen burner, the triple-beam balance, and the graduated cylinder.

Demonstrate proficiency in properly handling solid and liquid chemicals.

Develop proper safety techniques for all lab work.

Apply data-collecting techniques, and graph data.

Situation

You have applied to work at a company that does research, development, and analysis work. Although the company does not require employees to have extensive chemical experience, all applicants are tested for their ability to follow directions, heed safety precautions, perform simple laboratory procedures, clearly and concisely communicate results, and make logical inferences.

The company will use their opinion of your performance on the test in considering whether to hire you and in deciding your initial salary.

Background

Pay close attention to the procedures and safety precautions because you will continue to use them throughout your work if you are hired by this company. In addition, you will need to pay attention to what is happening around you, make careful observations, and keep a clear and legible record of these observations in your lab notebook.

Problem

This laboratory orientation session will teach you some of the following techniques.

- proper use of a Bunsen burner
- how to handle solids and liquids
- how to properly use a triple-beam balance
- basic safety techniques for all lab work

Safety

Always wear goggles and an apron to protect your eyes and clothing. If you get a chemical in your eyes, immediately flush it out at the eyewash station while calling to your teacher. Know the locations of the emergency lab shower and eyewash and how to use them.

Do not touch any chemicals. If you get a chemical on your skin or clothing, wash it off at the sink while calling to your teacher. Make sure you carefully read the labels and follow the directions on all containers of chemicals that you use. Do not taste any chemicals or items used in the laboratory. Never return leftovers to their original containers; take only small amounts to avoid wasting supplies.

When you use a Bunsen burner, do not heat glassware that is broken, chipped, or cracked. Use tongs whenever handling glassware or other equipment that has been heated because when it is hot, it does not look hot.

Always clean up the lab and all equipment after use, and dispose of substances according to proper disposal methods. Wash your hands thoroughly before you leave the lab after all lab work is finished.

Preparation

1. Organizing Data
Prepare spaces in your lab notebook for observations about the following.
- Bunsen burner flame when the ports on the burner's base are closed and open
- the mass of weighing paper with and without NaCl

Prepare a data table with two columns, each having spaces to record the following.
- the mass of an empty beaker
- the mass of the beaker and 50 mL of water
- the mass of 50 mL of water
- the mass of the beaker and 100 mL of water
- the mass of 100 mL of water
- the mass of the beaker and 150 mL of water
- the mass of 150 mL of water

2. Record in your lab notebook where the following items are located and how each item is used: emergency lab shower, eyewash station, and emergency telephone numbers.

3. Check to be certain that the gas valve at your lab station and at the next closest one are turned off. Notify your teacher immediately if a valve is on because the fumes must be cleared before any work continues.

Technique

4. Compare the diagram of the Bunsen burner to your burner. Construction may vary, but the air and methane gas, CH_4, always mix in the barrel, the vertical tube in the center of the burner.

Materials

- NaCl
- 250 mL beakers, 2
- 100 mL graduated cylinder
- Balance
- Bunsen burner and related equipment
- Copper wire
- Crucible tongs
- Evaporating dish
- Heat-resistant mat
- Spatula
- Test tube
- Wax paper or weighing paper

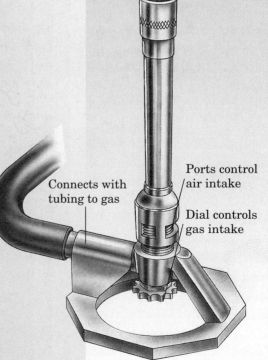

Ports control air intake

Dial controls gas intake

Connects with tubing to gas

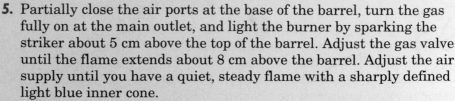

5. Partially close the air ports at the base of the barrel, turn the gas fully on at the main outlet, and light the burner by sparking the striker about 5 cm above the top of the barrel. Adjust the gas valve until the flame extends about 8 cm above the barrel. Adjust the air supply until you have a quiet, steady flame with a sharply defined light blue inner cone.
   If an internal flame develops, turn off the gas valve, and let the burner cool down. Otherwise the metal of the burner can get hot enough to set fire to anything nearby that is flammable. Before you relight the burner, partially close the air ports.

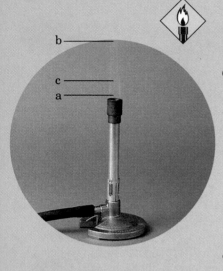

6. Using crucible tongs, hold a 10 cm piece of copper wire for 2–3 s in the part of the flame labeled *a* in the photograph on the left. Repeat for the parts of the flame labeled *b* and *c*. Record your observations. Which is the hottest part of the flame?

7. Experiment with the flame by completely closing the ports at the base of the burner. Observe the color of the flame and the sounds made by the burner. Using crucible tongs, hold an evaporating dish in the tip of the flame for about 3 min. Place the dish on a heat-resistant mat, and shut off the burner. After the dish cools, examine its underside, and record your observations.

8. Before using the balance, be certain it is leveled, and the pointer rests at zero. If all slider masses are set at zero, but the pointer is not at zero, adjust the calibration knob. Use the same balance for all measurements during a lab activity. *Never put chemicals directly on the balance pan.*

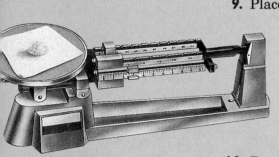

9. Place a piece of weighing paper on the balance pan. Determine its mass by adjusting the masses on the various sliding scales. Record this mass to the nearest 0.01 g. Then move the 10 g slide to the 10 g position, and move the 1 g slide to 3.00 g past the reading for the wax paper. Put a small quantity of NaCl on a separate piece of weighing paper, and place some of it on the weighing paper on the balance pan until you nearly balance the pointer. Slide the masses until the pointer is exactly balanced and record the exact mass to the nearest 0.01 g.

10. Remove the NaCl from the balance pan. Lay the test tube flat on the table, and transfer the NaCl into it by rolling the weighing paper and sliding it into the test tube. When you lift the test tube to a vertical position, tap the paper gently, and the solid will slip into the test tube.

11. Measure the mass of a dry 250 mL beaker, and record it in a data table. Add water up to the 50 mL mark. Determine the new mass, and record it in your lab notebook. Repeat the procedure by filling the beaker to the 100 mL mark and then to the 150 mL mark, recording the mass each time. Subtract the mass of the empty beaker from the other measurements to determine the mass of the water alone.

12. Repeat step **11** with a second dry 250 mL beaker, but use a graduated cylinder to measure the volumes of water to the nearest 0.1 mL. Read volumes from the bottom of the meniscus, the curve formed by the water's surface.

Cleanup and Disposal

13. Put the wire, NaCl, and weighing paper in the containers designated by your teacher. Pour the water from the beakers into the sink. Scrub the cooled evaporating dish with soap, water, and a scrub brush. Be certain that gas valves at your lab station and the next closest one are turned off. Be sure lab equipment is completely cool before storing it. Always wash your hands thoroughly after cleaning up.

Analysis and Interpretation

1. Organizing Ideas
Based on your observations, which type of flame is hotter: the flame formed when the air ports are open or closed? What is the hottest part of the flame? (Hint: the melting point of copper is 1083°C.)

2. Analyzing Information
Which of the following measurements could have been made by your balance: 3.42 g of glass, 5.666 72 g of aspirin, 0.000 017 g of paper?

3. Organizing Data
Make a graph of volume vs. mass for data from steps **11** and **12**. The mass of water (g) should be graphed along the *y*-axis as a dependent variable, and the volume of water (mL) should be graphed along the *x*-axis as an independent variable.

4. Organizing Ideas
For the following safety items, state the location of the item and how and when to use them: emergency lab shower, eyewash station and emergency telephone numbers.

Conclusions

5. Relating Ideas
When methane is burned, it usually produces carbon dioxide and water. If there is a shortage of oxygen, the flame is not as hot, and black carbon solid is formed. Which steps demonstrated these flames?

6. Inferring Conclusions
Which is the most accurate method for measuring volumes of liquids: a beaker or a graduated cylinder? Explain why.

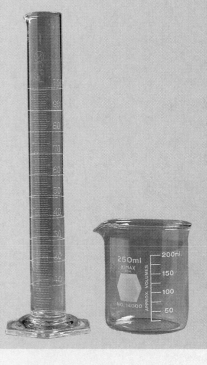

Extensions

1. Resolving Discrepancies
In Mandeville High School, Jarrold got only part way through step **7** of this experiment when he had to put everything away. Soon after Jarrold left, his lab drawer caught on fire. How did this happen?

2. Relating Ideas
The density of water is equal to its mass divided by its volume. Calculate the density of water using your data from step **11**. Then calculate the density of water using data from step **12**.

3. Designing Experiments
What steps would you take to make more accurate mass and volume measurements? If your teacher approves of your plan, try it. Are your new density values closer to the accepted value, 0.997 g/mL at 25°C?

INVESTIGATION 1A

Problem Solving

Percentage of Water in Popcorn

JULIETTE BRAND FOODS
Product Development Division · 2994 Effington Lane · Thornton, NE 68181

January 9, 1995

Director of Research
CheMystery Labs, Inc.
52 Fulton Street
Springfield, VA 22150

Dear Director of Research:

Juliette Brand Foods is preparing to enter the rapidly expanding home popcorn market with a new popcorn product. As you may know, the key to making popcorn pop is the amount of water contained within the kernel.

Thus far, the product development division has created three different production techniques for the popcorn, each of which creates popcorn with differing amounts of water. We need an independent lab such as yours to measure the percentage of water contained in each sample and to determine which technique produces the best-popping popcorn.

I've enclosed samples from each of the three techniques, labeled "technique beta," "technique gamma," and "technique delta." Please bill us when the work is complete.

Sincerely,

Mary Biedenbecker

Mary Biedenbecker
Director
Product Development Division

Required Precautions

 Lab aprons and goggles must be worn at all times. Confine loose clothing and long hair.

 Do not eat the popcorn; it is for testing purposes only.

 Remember, hot glass does not look hot. Be sure to use beaker tongs.

CheMystery Labs, Inc.
52 Fulton Street
Springfield, VA 22150

Memorandum

Date: January 11, 1995

To: Leon Fuller

From: Martha Li-Hsien

We have a budget of $250 000 for this project to take care of equipment, lab space, and labor costs. It is important that we use these funds conservatively and obtain quality results, ensuring a healthy profit and continued company growth.

Your team needs to design a procedure for determining the percentage of water in three samples of popcorn. Some of the popcorn was damaged in mailing, so each team will only have 80 kernels of popcorn per technique. Be sure to use your samples carefully!

Before you begin the lab work, I must approve your procedure. Give me the following items as soon as possible.
- detailed one-page plan for your procedure, with any necessary data tables
- detailed list of the equipment and materials you will need, with itemized and total costs for the accounting department (Remember, coming in under the $250 000 budget increases our profits, so don't order all the equipment available; order just what you need to get the job done right!)

When finished, prepare a report in the form of a two-page letter to Mary Biedenbecker that includes the following.
- paragraph summarizing how you analyzed the samples
- your findings about the percentage of water in each sample, including calculations and a discussion of the multiple trials
- detailed and organized data table
- graph comparing your findings to those of the other teams
- detailed invoice showing all costs, services, and employee hours spent working on this project
- suggestions for reducing costs and improving the analysis procedure

References

Popcorn "pops" because of the natural moisture inside each kernel. When the internal water is heated above 100°C, the kernel expands rapidly as the liquid water changes to a gas, which takes up much more room than the liquid.

The percentage of water in popcorn can be determined by the following equation.

$$\frac{mass_{before} - mass_{after}}{mass_{before}} \times 100$$

$$= \% \; H_2O \text{ in unpopped popcorn}$$

The popping process works best when the kernels have been coated with a small amount of vegetable oil. Be certain you account for the presence of this oil in measuring masses.

Spill Procedures/Waste Disposal Methods

- The popped popcorn should be disposed of in the designated waste container.
- Clean the area and all equipment after use.

Materials for
JULIETTE BRAND FOODS

Item	Cost	1	2	3
REQUIRED ITEMS (You must include all of these in your budget.)				
Lab space/fume hood/utilities	15 000 — /day			
Standard disposal fee	2 000 — /g of product			
Balance	5 000			
Beaker tongs	1 000			
Bunsen burner/related equipment	10 000			
REAGENTS and ADDITIONAL EQUIPMENT (Include in your budget only what you'll need.)				
Oil				
250 mL beaker	500 — /mL			
250 mL flask	1 000			
100 mL graduated cylinder	1 000			
Aluminum foil	1 000			
Glass funnel	1 000 — /cm²			
Glass stirring rod	1 000			
Paper clips	1 000			
pH paper	500 — /box			
Ring stand/ring/wire gauze	2 000 — /piece			
Six test tubes/holder/rack	2 000			
Wash bottle	2 000			
*No refunds on returned chemicals or unused equipment.	500			
FINES				
OSHA safety violation	2 000 — /incident			

Properties of Analgesics

Objectives

Measure, calculate, and *compare* the percentage of insoluble substances in aspirin, buffered aspirin, and aspirin substitutes.

Compare the pH of aspirin, buffered aspirin and aspirin substitute.

Graph the change in pH for the titration of the three analgesics.

Demonstrate proficiency in the following laboratory techniques: filtration, titration, and measuring pH.

Situation

You are a research chemist at a small pharmaceutical firm that intends to break into the lucrative market of analgesics. Although large companies dominate the market, your company is determined to create an improved product that will draw consumers away from the established brand names. Your first job is to analyze the competition.

Background

Acetylsalicylic acid

An analgesic is a compound that acts as a pain reliever. There are several types of analgesics on the market today, but they can be separated into two groups: ones that contain aspirin and ones that do not. The active painkiller in all brands of aspirin is acetylsalicylic acid. Besides relieving pain, acetylsalicylic acid reduces fever and acts as an anti-inflammatory drug by increasing the flow of blood and decreasing the amount of prostaglandins released. A different type of pain reliever is called acetaminophen. Acetaminophen is a pain reliever designed for people who are allergic to aspirin or who cannot tolerate aspirin. Like aspirin, acetaminophen reduces fever and relieves pain. However this medication does not have the anti-inflammatory properties of aspirin.

In addition to the active ingredients, analgesics contains fillers. The purpose of one type of filler is to keep the tablet from falling apart. Another type of filler keeps the tablet from breaking down due to moisture in the air. Buffered aspirin contains substances that help control the pH of the medication.

Acetaminophen

Problem

Your company has asked you to analyze aspirin, buffered aspirin, and an aspirin substitute to find out what percentage of these products is insoluble filler and what percentage is active ingredient. You will also add carefully measured amounts of base to these products to determine their pH and how easily they can be neutralized.

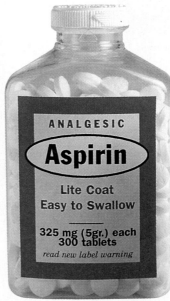

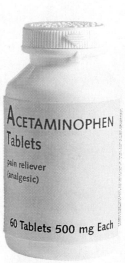

Safety

Always wear goggles and an apron to provide protection for your eyes and clothing. If you get a chemical in your eyes, immediately flush it out at the eyewash station while calling to your teacher. Know the locations of the emergency lab shower and eyewash and how to use them.

Do not touch any chemicals. If you get a chemical on your skin or clothing, wash it off at the sink while calling to your teacher. Make sure you carefully read the labels and follow the directions on all containers of chemicals that you use. Do not taste any chemicals or items used in the laboratory. Never return leftovers to their original containers; take only small amounts to avoid wasting supplies.

Never put broken glass or ceramics in a regular waste container. Broken glass or ceramics should be disposed of separately.

Call your teacher in the event of an acid or base spill. Acid or base spills should be cleaned up promptly, according to your teacher's instructions.

Always clean up the lab and all equipment after use, and dispose of substances according to proper disposal methods. Wash your hands thoroughly before you leave the lab after all lab work is finished.

Preparation

1. Organizing Data

Prepare two data tables in your lab notebook. The first should contain four columns and six rows. Fill in the first row with these labels for the columns: *Measurement, Aspirin, Buffered aspirin*, and *Aspirin substitute*. Fill in the first column with these labels for the second through sixth rows: *Mass of 5 tablets, Mass of first filter paper, Mass of second filter paper, Mass of beaker,* and *Mass of beaker with dried filter paper(s) and insoluble substance.*

Provide space below this table for recording your observations of the filtering processes.

The second data table should contain seven columns and four rows. The columns should be labeled *Analgesic, 0 mL, 1 mL, 2 mL, 3 mL, 4 mL,* and *5 mL.* Fill in the first column with these labels for the second through fourth rows: *Aspirin, Buffered aspirin,* and *Aspirin substitute.*

If you will be using a dropper bottle or micropipet, provide space below your table for the number of drops in a milliliter. If you will be using a buret, provide space below your table for six buret readings for each type of analgesic.

2. Label a 250 mL beaker, two 100 mL beakers, and a 50 mL beaker *Aspirin.* Label another similar set of beakers *Buffered aspirin,* and a third similar set of beakers *Aspirin substitute.* Label a 250 mL beaker *Waste.*

Materials

- 0.1 M NaOH solution, 50 mL
- Aspirin tablets, 6
- Aspirin substitute tablets, 6
- Buffered aspirin tablets, 6
- Distilled water
- 25 mL graduated cylinder
- 50 mL beakers, 4
- 100 mL beakers, 6
- 10 mL graduated cylinder
- 100 mL graduated cylinder
- 250 mL beakers, 4
- Balance
- Beaker tongs
- Ceramic spoon or rubber policeman
- Dropper bottle, micropipet, or buret with clamp
- Drying oven
- Filter paper
- Glass funnel or Büchner funnel and equipment
- Glass stirring rod
- Mortar and pestle
- pH paper, pH meter, or LEAP system with pH probe and test-tube clamp
- Ring and ring stand
- Wash bottle

Technique

Determining Mass of Insoluble Filler

3. Determine the masses of five aspirin tablets, five buffered-aspirin tablets, and five aspirin-substitute tablets. Record the three masses in your data table.

4. Using a 100 mL graduated cylinder, pour about 85 mL of distilled water into each of the three 250 mL beakers.

5. Using a mortar and pestle, grind the five aspirin tablets, one at a time, into a fine powder. First, gently pound a tablet to pulverize it and then grind it to a powder. When removing the powdered substance from the mortar, be sure to use a nonmetal tool such as a rubber policeman or ceramic spoon, as metal can scratch the finish of the ceramic mortar. Pour the powder into the 250 mL beaker labeled *Aspirin*. Carefully clean and dry the mortar and pestle, and repeat this procedure for the buffered aspirin and aspirin substitute, pouring each into the appropriately labeled 250 mL beaker.
Do not blow into the mortar to remove any remaining powder because dust may get into your eyes and nasal passages.

6. Stir the mixture in each of the beakers for approximately 3–5 min to dissolve as much of the substances as possible.

7. Measure the mass of a piece of filter paper. If you will be using vacuum filtration and a Büchner funnel, be sure that the filter paper is big enough to cover all of the holes in the Büchner funnel. Record the mass of this first piece of filter paper in the data table.

8. Filter the mixture. If you are using vacuum filtration and a Büchner funnel, follow the instructions given step **8a**. If you are using gravity filtration and a glass funnel, follow the instructions given in step **8b**.
(The vacuum filtration requires more complicated equipment, but it works faster than the gravity filtration.)

a. Vacuum Filtration with a Büchner Funnel
Screw an aspirator nozzle onto the faucet. Attach a piece of thick plastic tubing to the side arm of this nozzle. Attach the other end of the thick plastic tubing to the side arm of the filter flask. Place a one-holed rubber stopper on the stem of the funnel, and fit the stopper snugly in the neck of the filter flask as shown in the drawing to the left. Place the first filter paper on the bottom of the funnel so that it is flat and covers all of the holes in the funnel.

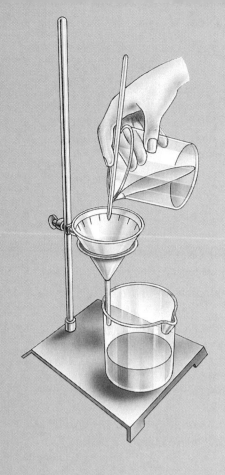

Turn on the water at the faucet. Stir the contents of the 250 mL beaker labeled *Aspirin* and pour the mixture against a glass stirring rod into the funnel. The drawing shows the proper technique for pouring. Continue pouring until the beaker is empty. Rinse the 250 mL beaker with a small amount of distilled water, and pour this into the funnel as well. When filtration is completed, pour the filtrate into one of the 100 mL beakers labeled *Aspirin*. Rinse the filter flask with a small amount of distilled water, and pour this into the 100 mL beaker as well.

b. Gravity Filtration with a Glass Funnel

Set up a glass funnel supported by a ring stand and ring as shown in the drawing to the left, with one of the 100 mL beakers labeled *Aspirin* beneath the stem of the funnel, so that it can catch the liquid filtrate after it passes through the funnel. To prepare the filter paper fold it in half along its diameter, and then fold it again to form a quadrant. Separate the folds of the filter paper so that three thicknesses are on one side and one thickness is on the other, as shown in the drawing below. Use your wash bottle to wet the funnel before the paper is placed in it. Fit the filter paper in the funnel, and wet it with a little water. Gently but firmly press the paper against the sides of the funnel so that no air can get between the funnel and the paper. The filter paper should not extend above the top of the funnel.

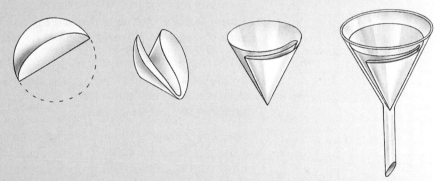

Pour the mixture from the 250 mL beaker along the side of glass stirring rod into the funnel. Be sure that you pour slowly enough so that the fluid level always remains at least 1.0 cm below the top of the filter paper. Do not fill the funnel to the top of the filter paper. Keep the funnel filled with fluid at this level so that a water column without air bubbles is established in the stem of the funnel. Rinse the 250 mL beaker with a small amount of distilled water, and pour this into the funnel as well.

9. When filtering is complete, look at the filtrate, the liquid that passed through the filter. Record your observations about the filtrate in your lab notebook. Be sure to note whether or not any undissolved particles are still visible.

10. Measure the mass of the empty 100 mL beaker labeled *Aspirin*, and record the mass in your data table.

11. Carefully remove the filter paper from the funnel, making sure you do not lose any of the insoluble substance that was left behind. Place it in the 100 mL beaker whose mass you just measured. If the filtrate in step **9** was clear, without particles, skip ahead to step **15**. If the filtrate still contained particles, consult with your teacher. If your teacher tells you to re-filter the mixture, continue with step **12**. If not, continue with step **15**.

12. Measure the mass of a second piece of filter paper and record this mass in your data table.

13. Filter the mixture once more, using either vacuum filtration or gravity filtration, as described earlier. For vacuum filtration, when you are finished, empty the filtrate into the now-empty 250 mL beaker labeled *Aspirin*. For gravity filtration, place this beaker underneath the stem of the glass funnel so that it can catch the filtrate.

14. Put the second filter paper into the appropriately labeled 100 mL beaker with the first filter paper.

15. Place the beaker with the filter paper in the drying oven, or leave it on the lab bench to dry overnight.
Remember to use beaker tongs to handle all glassware that may be hot, especially beakers that have been in a drying oven.

16. Repeat steps **5–15** for buffered aspirin and aspirin substitute, using new beakers and filter papers.

17. Dispose of the filtrate by pouring it down the drain with an excess of water.

18. When the insoluble substances are dry, measure the mass of each beaker containing the filter papers and the insoluble material, and record the masses in your data table.
To avoid damaging the balance, allow the beakers from the oven to cool before they are placed on the balance. Remember to use beaker tongs to handle the hot beakers.

Determining pH

19. Using a mortar and pestle, grind one aspirin tablet and transfer it to the 50 mL beaker labeled *Aspirin*. Add 20 mL of distilled water, and stir to dissolve the aspirin.

20. Measure the pH of the aspirin, and record your results in the data table in the box for *0 mL* of base added. Use the pH measurement procedure below that matches the equipment available in your lab.

a. pH paper
Dip a small piece of pH paper into the liquid. Remove the paper, and compare the color of the wet pH paper to the standard pH colors on a chart provided by your teacher.

b. pH meter
Turn on your pH meter. Put the pH electrodes into a buffer solution provided by your teacher. Calibrate the meter to the correct pH according to your teacher's directions. Then place the pH electrodes into the solution you are testing, and read the pH on the meter. Record your measurements in your data table.

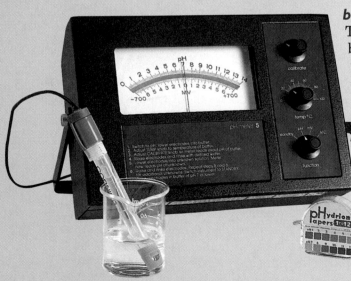

c. LEAP pH Probe

Your teacher should have the computer already set up for you. Make sure the probe is calibrated according to your teacher's directions. Hold the probe securely in the solution with a test-tube clamp attached to the ring stand. The probe should be submerged in the solution, but it should not touch the bottom of the beaker. On the computer, move the cursor to the green portion of the stoplight, and start the experiment. After the initial reading has been taken and the probe has stabilized, put the stoplight on stop, and record this initial data in your lab notebook. Then erase this initial data so that you are ready for the titration step.

Measuring pH Changes As Base Is Added

21. Using the titration method that matches your equipment, add 0.1 *M* NaOH solution to the beaker in 1.0 mL increments. After each addition is thoroughly mixed, measure the pH, recording it in your data table.

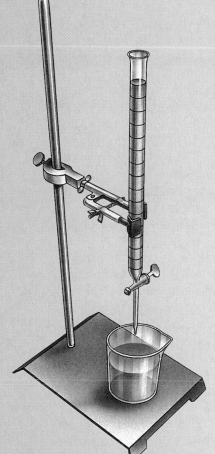

a. Dropper Bottle or Micropipet

Pour distilled water into a 10 mL graduated cylinder, until it is filled to the 5 mL mark. Remember to read the bottom of the meniscus when using a graduated cylinder. Fill your dropper or micropipet with distilled water. Count the number of drops that must be added from the dropper or micropipet before the level in the graduate cylinder reaches the 6 mL mark. Record this number in your data table. Then, add 1 mL worth of drops to the beaker labeled *Aspirin*. Swirl the beaker gently and wash down the sides with distilled water from a wash bottle. Measure and record the pH value in the data table in the box for *1 mL* of base added. Add the same number of drops again, and record the pH value in the data table in the box for *2 mL* of base added. Continue until a total of 5 mL of base have been added. Then, repeat the process for the buffered aspirin and the aspirin substitute.

b. Buret With pH Paper or pH Meter

Burets provide better precision because they are calibrated in intervals of 0.1 mL. Before using the buret, rinse the inside three times, using 5 mL of 0.1 M NaOH each time. Collect the NaOH used for rinsing in the *Waste* beaker.

Use a buret clamp to hold the buret in position on a ring stand as shown in the drawing to the left. Place the *Waste* beaker below the buret to catch any liquid that is drawn off. Into another 50 mL beaker, pour approximately 40 mL of 0.1 *M* NaOH solution from the reagent bottle. ***Carefully check the label of the reagent bottle before removing any liquid.***

Using the 50 mL beaker, fill the buret with NaOH, and then draw off enough liquid into the *Waste* beaker so that you can be sure the tip of the buret below the stopcock is filled. The level of the liquid should be on the scale. To measure the volume of the liquid, read the scale at the bottom of the meniscus.

After you have taken your first buret reading, practice using the buret and reading the volume several times. Open the stopcock and draw off approximately 1.0 mL. Read the volume of the liquid again. The exact amount drawn off is equal to the difference between your initial and final buret readings. When you can control the volume of base fairly well, record the latest buret reading in your data table.

Move the *Waste* beaker aside, and use the buret to add 1.0 mL of 0.1 M NaOH to the beaker containing the mixture of aspirin and distilled water. Record the exact buret reading in your data table. Swirl gently, measure the pH, and record it in your data table. Add the NaOH 1.0 mL at a time, recording the buret reading and the pH, until a total of 5.0 mL has been added. Then, repeat the process for the buffered aspirin and the aspirin substitute.

c. Buret with LEAP pH Probe

Burets provide better precision because they are calibrated in intervals of 0.1 mL. Use a buret clamp to hold the buret in position on a ring stand, as shown in the drawing on the left. Calibrate your buret

so that it will release 10 drops per second. To do this, fill your buret with water, and place the *Waste* beaker under the buret. Use a stopwatch to measure 10 second intervals. Open the stopcock just enough for the water to flow out at a rate of 10 drops per second. Practice this technique, so you know exactly how far to open the stopcock.

When you are ready to proceed, rinse the inside of the buret three times, using 5 mL of 0.1 M NaOH each time. Collect these rinses in the *Waste* beaker.

Into another 50 mL beaker pour approximately 40 mL of 0.1 *M* NaOH solution from the reagent bottle. *Carefully check the label of the reagent bottle before removing any liquid.*

Fill the buret with NaOH, and then draw off enough liquid to fill the tip of the buret below the stopcock. The level of the liquid should be on the scale. To measure the volume of the liquid read the scale at the bottom of the meniscus. Practice this procedure several times. Place the beaker labeled *Aspirin* under the buret. Use a test-tube clamp attached to the ring stand to keep the tip of the pH probe submerged in the solution near the bottom of the beaker as shown in the photograph on the left. Start the experiment and begin the titration. Continue titrating until approximately 950 readings have been taken. Then set the stoplight to red, and print your graph. *Only 1000 data points will be saved. If you continue taking data after this point, you will lose it.* Record the final volume on the buret.

22. Repeat steps **19–21** for the buffered aspirin and aspirin substitute.

Cleanup and Disposal

23. The insoluble part of the aspirin can be disposed of by placing it in the trash. Soluble portions can be washed down the sink. After all titrations are complete, dispose of the contents of each of the beakers in the containers designated by your teacher.

Analysis and Interpretation

1. Organizing Data

Calculate the mass of the insoluble portion of each analgesic. This mass can be found by subtracting the mass of the beaker and each filter paper from the mass of the beaker with both filter papers and the insoluble material.

2. Organizing Data

Calculate the change in pH for each substance by finding the difference between the initial pH value and the pH after adding 5.0 mL of NaOH solution.

3. Organizing Data

Make a graph of your pH data. Plot the number of drops or the milliliters of NaOH solution on the *x*-axis and pH on the *y*-axis. Graph data for all three analgesics on the same grid. Label each axis, and give your graph a title.

Conclusions

4. Inferring Conclusions

Which type of analgesic had the largest percentage of insoluble material? To calculate the percentage that is insoluble material, divide the mass of insoluble material by the total mass of the analgesic, and multiply by 100.

5. Inferring Conclusions

Review the graph of the pH values for the three types of analgesics. Which analgesic was most acidic (lowest pH)? Which was most affected by the addition of NaOH?

6. Inferring Conclusions

Using all the data you organized, write a paragraph summarizing your recommendation for the use of the three analgesics. Under what circumstances might one be better than another?

7. Relating Ideas

After analyzing several analgesic products now on the market, what improvements would you suggest for the new product your company wants to design?

Extensions

1. Research and Communication

Aspirin and aspirin substitutes are normally sold in a dosage of grains. Research what a grain is, and calculate the average dosage of the three analgesics in grains. Is the dosage the same for all three analgesics?

2. Designing Experiments

What possible sources of error can you identify with this procedure? If you can think of ways to eliminate them, ask your teacher to approve your plan, and run the procedure again.

3. Designing Experiments

When ingested, analgesics are dissolved in the acidic environment of the stomach. Design an experiment to determine the percent solubility of each analgesic in an environment similar to the stomach. If your teacher approves of your plan, try your procedure.

4. Designing Experiments

Obtain several different brands of regular and extra-strength aspirin products. Run the procedures again to determine if there are differences among brands and if regular and extra-strength products differ in terms of fillers and pH.

PROPERTIES OF ANALGESICS

Forensic Analysis

he knew of no ... on that the officer was ...ble.

...lieutenant who was ...ately responsible for ...ng the activities of ...'s Raiders, Martin, ...s the commander of ...nct in 1990, was pro-...his spring to head the ...ighway police patrol

...ty Inspector Peter J. ...r was transferred to ...9th Precinct on the ..., and he was recently ...ed to command the ...wide Bias Incident ...ting Unit.

...ract Younger ...ni, University ...s Modernize

...along Clubhouse Row ...town university clubs ...rying to knock their ...ess out.

...e Princeton Club asked ...graduates if dropping ...at-and-tie requirement ...Tiger Bar and Grill ...persuade them to go in. ...rvard Club formed a ...ee to find portraits of ...graduates after the ...lmingly male mem-...ealized that not one ...k oil paintings lining ...wood-paneled walls ...woman. And at the ...members can sign ...evening class that ...m to play the blues

...ges are earnest if ...teps in a fight ...ng memberships ...use at the tradi-...clubs many of ...v the blocks of ...streets between ...enue and the ...Americas. ...ing revenues

Harrington, 47, was listed in critical but stable condition at the Bellevue Hospital Center with cuts and bruises on the face and head so severe that responding police officers at first thought he had been shot in the face, said Lieutenant

...Holmes, a transit police spokesman.

Sergeant Wesley, who for many years served as president of the Transit Police Union said that there had been an increased number of

continued on page B8

was very cold, it

After busines the area first b plaining, in ea Millner commis odor study Resources Inc., a vania consulting helped the compa its permit for the s

David H. Sicler the study found lo smells. They annou caught the railroad of garbage from the Merco by surprise. and a nearby con Sabet, a spokeswo Martto, a garbage and from "the smel

Police, Vets Seek Clues in Canine Poisonings

1 Dog Dies, 2 Others Remain in Serious Condition

Veterinarians on the staff of the Animal Rescue Center are working feverishly to save the lives of two poisoned dogs. Another dog from the same neighborhood has already died from the unidentified toxin. Police are seeking clues to identify the poison.

Alma and David Brock, owners of the dog that died, discovered their pet, Shiloh, lying comatose near a bike path behind their home. Police were called to investigate after two more dogs were found unconscious in the same neighborhood. The two surviving dogs, whose owners have not been identified, are in serious condition at the Animal Rescue Center.

Police were led by David Brock to the spot where Shiloh was found. There they found the remains of some pills that could have been ingested by the dogs. Police spokesperson Deanna Jackson said that although police believe the poisoning was unintentional, they are looking for leads that will help identify the pills.

Dr. Enriqueta Sust-Newland, chief veterinarian at the clinic, suspects that they are analgesics. "Until we know what we are dealing with, we can't be certain that we are treating the affected dogs properly," she said. "Unfortunately, the clinic doesn't have the facilities or the personnel to analyze the pills."

Court Bloc Rent-Control Ev

The United S Supreme Court a lower court to its decisio

PAGE B4

company had no tasting coffee in t bor surrender its c export.

He added, "It' same sludge, and cials said they fresh perking smell." The plans to hand over also found "a sli noticed anyone else odor" across First Greene, a spokes from the rail yard a Cross Harbor Railr the moving the slu to railroad has bee steps to farther fr Avenue. Real with plaints.

Report Discovers Shortage of ATM's in Poor Areas

Bank branches in the outer boroughs are less likely to have automatic teller machines than downtown branches, and the disparity is much greater between middle-income and poor areas within each of the boroughs, a new study has found. The probla...

study released yesterday by the staff of Jerome Green, the city's Public Advocate.

And a simple, if limited, solution offered in the report is to put the machines inside or in front of police pre...houses. B...

Required Precautions

 Goggles and lab aprons must be worn at all times.

 Do not touch or taste any chemicals. Wash your hands thoroughly when finished.

 If you get acid or base on your skin or clothing, wash it off at the sink while calling to your teacher. If you get acid or base in your eyes, immediately flush it out at the eyewash while calling to your teacher.

CheMystery Labs, Inc.
52 Fulton Street
Springfield, VA 22150

Memorandum

Date: January 4, 1995

To: Michelle Dunnigan

From: Marissa Bellinghausen

I love dogs, and when I read this news clip, I called Dr. Sust-Newland and volunteered to analyze the pills. This will be a freebie, of course, because the Animal Rescue Center is operating on a shoestring and can't pay us a dime, but I think the company will get some much needed publicity that could generate new business. The center is a nonprofit organization, so all donated materials and time are tax-deductible. But any expenses will be taken out of the company's pocket, so remember to cut costs as much as possible without compromising the results. We were only given a small sample to work with.

Before you start in the lab, I need the following items.
- detailed procedure for identifying this unknown analgesic
- detailed chart for all data to be collected
- list of materials needed, along with individual and total costs
  (Be careful and keep accurate records so that we can deduct these expenses from our taxes!)

When your analysis is completed, I will call Dr. Sust-Newland with preliminary results. Please also submit a report in the form of a two-page letter. It must include the following.
- your conclusion about the identity of the analgesic
- explanation of the evidence you found
- description of the procedure(s) you used, and all data, organized in a table
- graphs comparing the pH curve for the unknown analgesic to those of analgesics we've already tested
- discussion of any discrepancies in your results

It is critical that we complete this job accurately and quickly. It would be a real feather in our cap if we were able to help save these dogs' lives.

References

Refer to page 15 for more information about different types of analgesics. You must refer to Exploration 1A to compare the test results for the different types of analgesics to the results for this unknown analgesic.

Spill Procedures/ Waste Disposal Methods

- In case of a spill, follow your teacher's instructions.
- Put excess chemicals and solutions in the containers designated by your teacher. Do not pour them down the sink or place them in the trash can.

Materials for FORENSIC ANALYSIS

Item	Cost	1	2	3
REQUIRED ITEMS				
(You must include all of these in your budget.)				
Lab space/fume hood/utilities	15 000 — /day			
Standard disposal fee	2 000 — /g of product			
Balance	5 000			
Beaker tongs	1 000			
Drying oven	5 000 — /day			
REAGENTS and ADDITIONAL EQUIPMENT				
(Include in your budget only what you'll need.)				
0.1 M NaOH	100/mL			
50 mL beaker	1 000			
250 mL beaker	1 000			
10 mL graduated cylinder	1 000			
100 mL graduated cylinder	1 000			
Büchner funnel	2 000			
Buret tube	5 000			
Filter flask with sink attachment	2 000			
Filter paper	500 — /piece			
Glass stirring rod and rubber policeman	1 000			
Glass funnel	1 000			
Mortar and pestle	2 000			
pH meter	3 000			
pH paper	2 000 — /piece			
pH probe—LEAP with test tube clamp	5 000			
Pipet or medicine dropper	1 000			
Ring stand with buret clamp	2 000			
Wash bottle	500			
* No refunds on returned chemicals or unused equipment.				
FINES				
OSHA safety violation	2 000 — /incident			

Accuracy and Precision

Objectives

Calculate values
from experimental
measurements.

Demonstrate profi-
ciency in measuring
masses and volumes.

Organize data
by compiling it in
tables.

Calculate an
average value from
class data.

Relate absolute
deviation, average
deviation, uncer-
tainty, and percent
error, and use them
as methods for
gauging accuracy
and precision.

Situation

As part of your orientation as a new employee at a chemical firm, you must participate in an assessment of your lab skills. This survey will help you evaluate the accuracy of your equipment and the precision of your lab technique.

Background

In Exploration 1A, you made measurements of volume and mass, but you did not evaluate these measurements. Measurements can be evaluated two different ways. *Accuracy* is how close to the actual value a measurement is; *precision* is how close each measurement is to others in the set.

The accuracy of a measurement can only be determined if you have some way of knowing what the measurement should be. For example, metal densities have been measured many times, so there is a consensus on the accepted value for each metal's density. One indicator of accuracy is the experimental error, which can be calculated using this equation.

$$\frac{\text{value}_{\text{accepted}} - \text{value}_{\text{measured}}}{\text{value}_{\text{accepted}}} \times 100 = \text{percent error}$$

Precision indicates whether the experimental data are consistent. Three common statistical tools used to check precision are *absolute deviation, average deviation,* and *uncertainty in measurement.*

For each experimental value, the absolute deviation is the difference between it and the average of all values. Average deviation is obtained by calculating the sum of the absolute deviations for an entire data set and dividing by the total number of measurements. To determine the uncertainty of a measurement, express one unit of the last significant digit as plus or minus to indicate that the last digit is an estimate, as in 24.65 ± 0.01 cm. The percent uncertainty is determined by dividing the uncertainty by the measurement and multiplying by 100, as shown here.

$$\frac{\pm 0.01 \text{ cm}}{24.65 \text{ cm}} \times 100 = \pm 0.04\%$$

Problem

You will use the measurement and analysis skills that you learn here to evaluate measurements of length, volume, mass, and temperature. You will also determine the identity of a metal sample by calculating its density and comparing the result to density values for various metals from chemical handbooks.

Safety

Always wear goggles and an apron to provide protection for your eyes and clothing. If you get a chemical in your eyes, immediately flush it out at the eyewash station while calling to your teacher. Know the locations of the emergency lab shower and eyewash and how to use them.

Do not touch any chemicals. If you get a chemical on your skin or clothing, wash it off at the sink while calling to your teacher. Make sure you carefully read the labels and follow the directions on all containers of chemicals that you use. Do not taste any chemicals or items used in the laboratory. Never return leftovers to their original containers; take only small amounts to avoid wasting supplies.

Never put broken glass or ceramics in a regular waste container. Broken glass or ceramics should be disposed of separately.

Always clean up the lab and all equipment after use, and dispose of substances according to proper disposal methods. Wash your hands thoroughly before you leave the lab after all lab work is finished.

Materials

- Distilled water
- Metal shot
- 250 mL beaker
- 25 mL graduated cylinder
- 100 mL graduated cylinder
- 15 cm plastic ruler
- Balance
- Chemical handbook or source of density values for water and metals
- Non-mercury thermometer or LEAP System with thermistor probe

Preparation

1. **Organizing Data**
   Prepare data tables in your lab notebook with spaces for the following.

   - smallest division on the ruler, the 100 mL and 25 mL graduated cylinders, and the balance

   - height of the 50 mL mark of the 100 mL graduated cylinder and its inside diameter

   - mass of the dry 25 mL graduated cylinder

   - temperature of water (several spaces)

   - handbook values for water density at these temperatures

   - volume of water added

   - mass of 25 mL graduated cylinder with water

   - volume of metal shot and water

   - mass of 25 mL graduated cylinder with water and metal

   Prepare another table with room for data from the rest of the class on the mass of the cylinder with water alone, the mass of the cylinder with water and metal, the volume of the water, and the volume of the water and metal.

2. Locate a handbook to use as a reference for comparing densities of metals and for determining the density of water at various temperatures.

Technique

3. Record the smallest division on your ruler and the 100 mL graduated cylinder in your data table.

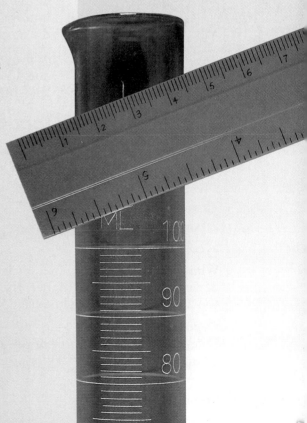

4. Measure the inside diameter of the 100 mL graduated cylinder with the ruler. Measure the height to the 50 mL mark. Record these measurements in your data table.

5. Examine the scale on the balance. What is the smallest division? Examine the 25 mL graduated cylinder. What is the smallest division? Record the results, with units, in your data table.

6. Using the balance, determine the mass of the dry 25 mL cylinder to the nearest 0.1 g. Record this mass in the data table.

7. Fill a beaker half full of water, and determine the temperature of the water to the nearest 0.1°C. Use step **7a** if you are using a thermometer and step **7b** if you are using the LEAP Thermistor probe. Record the temperature of the water in your lab notebook. In a handbook, look up the density of water at that temperature and record it in the data table.

a. Thermometer
Gently put the thermometer in the water, being careful not to break it. Wait 2 min before recording the temperature. After another 2 min, record the temperature again. Repeat this process every 2 min until two consecutive temperature measurements are the same.
Never use a thermometer to stir anything. It will break easily. The glass wall surrounding the bulb is very thin to provide quick and accurate temperature readings.

b. LEAP thermistor probe
Put the LEAP thermistor probe in the water as if it were a thermometer. It should be set for your use, and all you have to do is click on the green light on the computer screen to start and click on the red light to stop. Record the temperature of the water. Keep taking measurements until the temperature remains constant for 2 min. With the thermistor, you don't have to wait as long for the probe to reach the correct temperature as you do with a conventional thermometer.

8. Put between 10 mL and 15 mL of water from the beaker in the 25 mL graduated cylinder. Read the volume to the nearest 0.1 mL, and record it. Determine the mass of the water plus the cylinder to the nearest 0.1 g. Record this value in your data table. Keep the water in the cylinder for the next step.

9. Add enough of the sample of metal shot to the cylinder to increase the volume by at least 5 mL. Determine the volume and the mass of the water and shot together in the graduated cylinder; record your measurements.

Cleanup and Disposal

10. The water can be washed down the sink after the metal shot has been removed and placed in the container designated by your teacher. Always wash your hands thoroughly after cleaning up the lab area and equipment.

Analysis and Interpretation

1. **Organizing Data**
   What is the uncertainty in a measurement made by each of these devices: the ruler, the balance, the 100 mL graduated cylinder, and the 25 mL graduated cylinder?

2. **Organizing Data**
   Calculate the solid volume of the 100 mL graduated cylinder up to its 50 mL mark. (Hint: $V = \pi r^2 h$ for a cylinder.)

3. **Analyzing Data**
   Assuming the accepted value for the volume of a graduated cylinder at the 50 mL mark is 50.00 mL, calculate percent error in your calculations and measurements from item **2**.

4. **Organizing Data**
   Calculate the mass of water as determined by the balance and by its measured volume and known density. Using the mass obtained by the balance as the accepted value and the value calculated from the density as the experimental value, calculate percent error. Be sure to follow significant figure rules in your calculations.

5. **Organizing Data**
   Subtract the volume of the water from the combined volume of the metal and the water to calculate the volume of the metal alone. Subtract the mass of the water and cylinder from the mass of the metal, water, and cylinder to determine the mass of the metal; then calculate its density. Show all work.

6. **Evaluating Data**
   Record the metal density calculations made by the other teams, and calculate the average density of the unknown metal. Calculate the average deviation for the measurements.

Conclusions

7. **Inferring Conclusions**
   Compare your value and the class average of the unknown metal's density to the densities for metals given in handbooks. Determine the identity of the metal.

8. **Evaluating Methods**
   Calculate percent error by comparing your experimental value to the value you found in the handbook. Then, calculate percent error for the class average. Which is more accurate? The average or your value?

Extensions

1. **Evaluating Methods**
   Marie and Jason determined the density of a liquid three different times. They determined the values to be 2.84 g/mL, 2.85 g/mL, and 2.80 g/mL. The accepted value is 2.40 g/mL. Are the values determined by these two people precise? Are the values accurate? Explain your answers. Calculate the percent error and uncertainty of each measurement.

2. **Applying Ideas**
   When cutting the legs of a table to make them shorter, precision is more important than accuracy. Explain why.

3. **Applying Ideas**
   A store has a balance with a scale marked in gram units with one line halfway between each. A student working there after school measured a mass of a sample as 5.367 g using this balance. What is wrong with this measurement?

4. **Applying Ideas**
   There is a legend that the ancient Greek mathematician and scientist Archimedes used density to determine that a goldsmith had cheated when making a crown for the king. Explain what steps you would take to alter this procedure to check a metal's purity.

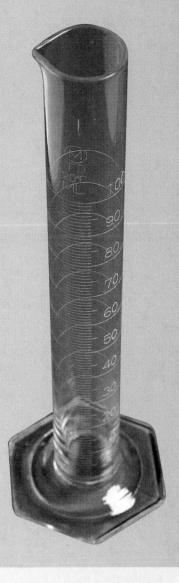

INVESTIGATION 2A

Problem Solving

Counterfeit Coins

SECRET SERVICE

MEMORANDUM

Secret Service Directive #1456

Date: January 12, 1995

To: CheMystery Labs, Inc.
Investigation Division
52 Fulton St.
Springfield, Va 22150

Subject: Counterfeit coinage

Over the years, we have eliminated most counterfeiting operations in the United States. The Secret Service has confiscated illegal equipment, and the paper currency was changed to make counterfeiting more difficult.

However, counterfeiting of coins has increased because coins are easy to reproduce but hard to trace. Counterfeit pennies made in the 1970s and 1980s were produced by substituting less expensive metals. Such substitutions can be detected by measuring densities. Samples are enclosed for you to analyze.

Your first task is to identify the year that the counterfeit coins entered the marketplace. Include a hypothesis of which metal was used in the coins. The next phase of our investigation will be to find companies that have the necessary equipment and that bought large quantities of the substituted metal.

Required Precautions

Lab aprons and goggles must be worn at all times. Confine loose clothing and long hair.

Memorandum

CheMystery Labs, Inc.
52 Fulton Street
Springfield, VA 22150

Date: January 13, 1995

To: Jorge Salizar

From: Marissa Bellinghausen,
Investigations Division

Re: Secret Service Contract

Before you begin, I need to review your plans. Please write up the following.
- detailed one-page summary of your plan
- all necessary data tables and graphs
- itemized expense sheet, including total expenditures
- explanation of what you think the greatest potential source of error might be in your data and analysis

When you complete your investigation, prepare a two-page report that includes the following for the director of the Secret Service.
- year the counterfeiting began
- mass of a penny in the year before, the year of, and the year following the counterfeiting
- density of a penny in the year before, the year of, and in the year following the counterfeiting
- your explanation of whether you believe the penny counterfeiting was either a gradual change or occurred all at once
- your hypothesis for which metal was used as the core of the counterfeited pennies, along with justification and a discussion of possible sources of error (be sure to indicate where you got this information)
- organized data and analysis section, with calculations and graphs

References

Refer to pages 60–63 for more information on accuracy and precision.

To determine penny volume and mass, use 10 pennies and divide to calculate average values. Remember to dry the pennies before measuring their mass.

Spill Procedures/ Waste Disposal Methods

- Return the dried pennies to the designated container.
- Water can be poured down the sink.
- Clean the area and all equipment.

Materials for SECRET SERVICE

Item	Cost		
REQUIRED ITEMS			
(You must include all of these in your budget.)			
Lab space/fume hood/utilities	15 000 — /day		
Standard disposal fee	2 000 — /g of product		
Balance	5 000		
Chemical handbook with metal densities	500		
REAGENTS and ADDITIONAL EQUIPMENT			
(Include in your budget only what you'll need.)			
250 mL beaker	1 000		
250 mL flask	1 000		
100 ml graduated cylinder	1 000		
Filter paper	500 — /piece		
Glass stirring rod	1 000		
pH paper	2 000 — /piece		
Test tube (large)	1 000		
Thermometer	2 000		
Wash bottle	500		
Weighing paper	500 — /piece		
No refunds on returned chemicals or unused equipment.			
FINES			
OSHA safety violation	2 000 — /incident		

EXPLORATION 2B

Technique Builder

Separation of Mixtures

Objectives

Recognize how the solubility of a salt varies with temperature.

Demonstrate proficiency in the following techniques: fractional crystallization, and vacuum filtration or gravity filtration.

Determine the percentage of two salts recovered by fractional crystallization.

Situation

Your company has been contacted by a fireworks factory. A mistake was made at the factory when a mislabeled container of sodium chloride, NaCl, was mixed with potassium nitrate, KNO_3, which is used as an oxidizer in fireworks. KNO_3 is used to be certain that the fireworks burn thoroughly. The fireworks company wants your company to investigate ways in which they could separate the two compounds. They have provided a water solution of the mixture for you to work with.

Background

The substances in a mixture can be separated by physical means. For example, if one substance dissolves in a liquid solvent but another does not, the mixture can be filtered. The one that dissolved will be carried through the filter by the solvent, but the other one will not. But both NaCl and KNO_3 dissolve in water, so this technique cannot be applied directly. However, there are differences in the way they dissolve. As you can see in the graph, about the same amount of sodium chloride will dissolve in water regardless of temperature. On the other hand, potassium nitrate is very soluble in warm water but much less soluble at 0°C.

Problem

You will make use of the differences in dissolving to separate the two salts. This technique is known as fractional crystallization. If the water solution of NaCl and KNO_3 is cooled from room temperature to a temperature near 0°C, not as much KNO_3 will be able to remain dissolved, as shown in the graph, and some of it will crystallize. This KNO_3 residue can then be separated from the NaCl solution by filtration. The NaCl can then be isolated by evaporating the water in the filtrate. To determine whether the method will work efficiently, you will measure the mass of each of the recovered substances, so that your client can decide whether this method is cost-effective.

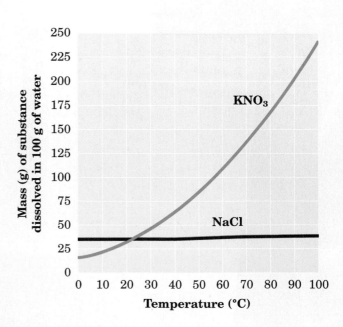

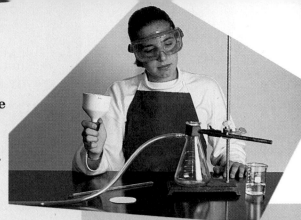

Safety

Always wear goggles and an apron to provide protection for your eyes and clothing. If you get a chemical in your eyes, immediately flush it out at the eyewash station while calling to your teacher. Know the locations of the emergency lab shower and eyewash and how to use them.

Do not touch any chemicals. If you get a chemical on your skin or clothing, wash it off at the sink while calling to your teacher. Make sure you carefully read the labels and follow the directions on all containers of chemicals that you use. Do not taste any chemicals or items used in the laboratory. Never return leftovers to their original containers; take only small amounts to avoid wasting supplies.

Confine long hair and loose clothing. Do not heat glassware that is broken, chipped, or cracked. Use tongs or a hot mitt to handle heated glassware and other equipment, because it does not always look hot when it is hot. If your clothing catches on fire, WALK to the emergency lab shower and use it to put out the fire.

Always clean up the lab and all equipment after use, and dispose of substances according to proper disposal methods. Wash your hands thoroughly before you leave the lab after all lab work is finished.

Materials

- Ice
- NaCl-KNO$_3$ solution, 50 mL
- Rock salt
- 100 mL graduated cylinder
- 150 mL beakers, 4
- Balance
- Büchner funnel, one-hole rubber stopper, vacuum filtration setup with filter flask, and tubing; or glass funnel
- Bunsen burner and related equipment or hot plate
- Filter paper
- Glass stirring rod
- Nonmercury thermometer
- Ring and wire gauze
- Ring stand
- Rubber policeman
- Spatula
- Tray, tub, or pneumatic trough

Optional equipment
- LEAP System with thermistor probe

Preparation

1. **Organizing Data**
   Prepare a data table in your lab notebook. It should contain spaces for *Volume of salt solution added to beaker 1, Mass of beaker 1, Mass of the filter paper, Mass of beaker 1 with filter paper and KNO$_3$, Mass of beaker 4,* and *Mass of the beaker 4, with NaCl.* You will also need room to record the temperature of the mixture before and after cooling.

2. Obtain four clean, dry 150 mL beakers, and label them *1, 2, 3,* and *4.*

Technique

3. Measure the mass of beaker *1* to the nearest 0.01 g and record its mass in your data table.

4. Measure about 50 mL of the NaCl-KNO$_3$ solution into a graduated cylinder. Record the exact volume in your data table. Pour this mixture into beaker *1.*

5. Using a thermometer or the LEAP system with a thermistor probe, measure the temperature of the mixture. Record this temperature in your data table.

6. Measure the mass of a piece of filter paper to the nearest 0.01 g, and record the mass in your data table.

7. Set up your filtering apparatus. If you are using a Büchner funnel for vacuum filtration, follow step **7a**. If you are using a glass funnel for gravity filtration, follow step **7b**.

a. Vacuum filtration

Screw an aspirator nozzle onto the faucet. Attach a piece of plastic tubing to the sidearm of this nozzle. Attach the other end of the thick plastic tubing to the sidearm of the filter flask. Place a one-hole rubber stopper on the stem of the funnel and fit the stopper snugly in the neck of the filter flask as shown in the photograph. Place the filter paper from step **6** on the bottom of the funnel so that it is flat and covers all of the holes in the funnel. When finished, continue with step **8**.

b. Gravity filtration

Set up a ring stand with a ring. Gently rest the glass funnel inside the ring. Be sure that there is enough room between the lab bench surface and the bottom of the funnel's stem so that a 150 mL beaker can be moved under the funnel without breaking the stem. Fold the filter paper from step **6** in half along its diameter, and then fold it again to form a quadrant. Separate the folds of the filter paper so that three thicknesses are on one side and one thickness is on the other, as shown in the illustration at left. Fit the filter paper in the funnel and wet it with a little water, so that it will adhere to the sides of the funnel. Gently but firmly press the paper against the sides of the funnel so that no air is between the funnel and the filter paper. Be certain that the filter paper does not extend above the side of the funnel.

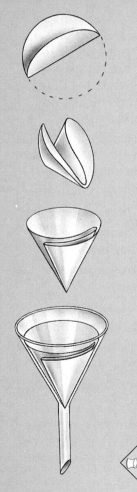

8. Make an ice bath by filling a tray, tub, or trough half full with ice. Add a handful of rock salt. The salt lowers the freezing point of water so that the ice bath can cool to a lower temperature. Fill the ice bath with water until it is three-quarters full.

9. Using a fresh supply of ice and distilled water, fill beaker *2* half full with ice and add water. Do not add rock salt to this ice-water mixture. You will use this water to wash your purified salt.

10. Put beaker *1* with your NaCl-KNO$_3$ solution into the ice bath. Place a thermometer or a LEAP thermistor probe in the solution to monitor the temperature. Stir the solution with a stirring rod while it cools. The lower the temperature of the mixture, the more KNO$_3$ will crystallize out of solution. When the temperature nears 4°C, follow step **10a** if you are using the Büchner funnel, or step **10b** if you are using a glass funnel.
Never stir a solution with a thermometer, as the bulb is very fragile.

a. Vacuum filtration

Turn on the water at the faucet that has the aspirator nozzle attached. This creates a vacuum, which helps the filtering step go much faster. If the suction is working properly, the filter paper should be pulled against the bottom of the funnel, covering all of the holes. If the filter paper appears to have bubbles of air under it, or is not centered well, turn the water off, reposition the filter paper, and begin again. Prepare the filtering apparatus by pouring approximately 50 mL of ice-cold distilled water from beaker 2 through the filter paper. After the water has gone through the funnel, empty the filter flask into the sink. Reconnect the filter flask, and pour the salt-water mixture into the funnel. Use the rubber policeman to transfer all of the cooled mixture into the funnel, especially any crystals that are visible. It may be helpful to add small amounts of ice-cold water from beaker 2 to beaker 1 to wash any crystals onto the filter paper. After all of the solution has passed through the funnel, wash the KNO_3 residue by pouring a very small amount of ice-cold water from beaker 2 over it. When this water has passed through the filter paper, turn off the faucet, and carefully remove the tubing from the aspirator. Empty the filtrate, which has passed through the filter paper and is now in the filter flask, into beaker 3. When finished, continue with step **11**.

b. Gravity filtration

Place beaker 3 at the bottom of the glass funnel. Prepare the filtering apparatus by pouring approximately 50 mL of ice-cold water from beaker 2 through the filter paper. The water will pass through the filter paper and drip into beaker 3. When dripping stops, empty beaker 3 into the sink. Place beaker 3 back at the bottom of the glass funnel, so that it will collect the filtrate from the funnel. Pour the salt-water mixture into the funnel. Use the rubber policeman to transfer all of the cooled mixture into the funnel, especially any crystals that are visible. It may be helpful to add small amounts of ice-cold water from beaker 2 to beaker 1 to wash any crystals onto the filter paper. After all of the solution has passed through the funnel, wash the KNO_3 by pouring a very small amount of ice-cold water from beaker 2 over it.

11. After you have finished filtering, use either a hot plate or a ring stand, ring, and wire gauze to heat beaker 3. When the liquid in beaker 3 begins boiling, continue heating gently until enough water has vaporized to decrease the volume to approximately 25–30 mL. ***Be sure to use beaker tongs. Remember that hot glassware does not always look hot.***

12. Allow the solution in beaker 3 to cool, and then set it in the ice-bath, stirring until the temperature is approximately 4°C.

13. Measure the mass of beaker 4. Record the mass of this beaker in your data table.

14. Repeat step **10a** or step **10b**, pouring the solution from beaker 3 onto the filter paper, and using beaker 4 to collect the filtrate that passes through the filter.

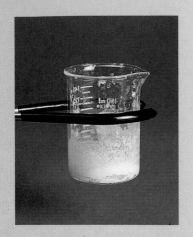

15. Wash and dry beaker *1*. Carefully remove the filter paper with the KNO_3 from the funnel and put it into the beaker. Be certain to avoid spilling the crystals. Place the beaker in a drying oven overnight.

16. Heat beaker *4* with a hot plate or Bunsen burner until it begins to boil. Keep heating gently, until all of the water has vaporized and the salt appears dry. Turn off the hot plate or burner and allow the beaker to cool. Use beaker tongs to move the beaker, even if you believe it is cool. Measure the mass of beaker *4* with the NaCl to the nearest 0.01 g and record this mass in your data table.

17. The next day, use beaker tongs to remove beaker *1* with the filter paper and KNO_3 from the drying oven. Allow the beaker to cool. Measure the mass, using the same balance you used when you measured the mass of the empty beaker. Record the new mass in your data table. ***Be sure to use beaker tongs. Remember that hot glassware does not always look hot.***

Cleanup and Disposal

18. Once the mass of the NaCl has been determined, add water to dissolve the NaCl and rinse the solution down the drain. Do not wash KNO_3 down the drain. Dispose of the KNO_3 in the waste container designated by your teacher.

Analysis and Interpretation

1. **Organizing Data**
   Calculate the mass of NaCl in your 50 mL sample by subtracting the mass of beaker *4* from the mass of beaker *4* with NaCl.

2. **Organizing Data**
   Calculate the mass of KNO_3 in your 50 mL sample by subtracting the mass of beaker *1* and the mass of the filter paper from the mass of beaker *1* with the filter paper and KNO_3.

3. **Organizing Data**
   Calculate the total mass of the two salts.

4. **Analyzing Information**
   How many grams of KNO_3 and NaCl would be found in a 1.0 L sample of the solution? (Hint: for each substance, make a conversion factor using the mass of the compound and the volume of the solution.)

5. **Interpreting Graphics**
   Use the graph at the beginning of this exploration to determine how much of each compound would dissolve in 100 g of water at room temperature and at the temperature of your ice-water bath.

Conclusions

6. **Inferring Conclusions**
   Calculate the percentage by mass of NaCl and KNO_3 in the salt mixture.

7. **Applying Conclusions**
   The fireworks company has another 55 L of the salt mixture dissolved in water just like the sample you worked with. How many kilograms of each compound can the company expect to recover from this sample? (Hint: use your answer from item **4** to help you answer this question.)

8. Evaluating Methods

Use the graph shown at the beginning of this Exploration to estimate how much KNO_3 could still be contaminating the NaCl you recovered.

9. Relating Ideas

Use the graph shown at the beginning of this Exploration to explain why it is impossible to separate the two compounds completely using fractional crystallization.

10. Evaluating Methods

Why was it important that you use ice-cold water to wash the KNO_3 after filtration?

11. Evaluating Methods

If it was important to use very cold water to wash the KNO_3, why wasn't the salt and ice water mixture from the bath used? After all, it had a lower temperature than the ice and distilled water from beaker 2. (Hint: consider what is contained in rock salt.)

12. Evaluating Methods

Why was it important to keep the amount of cold water used to wash the KNO_3 as small as possible?

13. Relating Ideas

Your lab partner tries to dissolve 95 g of KNO_3 in 100 g of water, but no matter how well he stirs the mixture, some KNO_3 remains undissolved. Using the graph, explain what your lab partner must do to make the KNO_3 dissolve in this amount of water.

Extensions

1. Interpreting Graphics

Use the graph shown at the beginning of this Exploration to determine the minimum mass of water necessary to dissolve the amounts of each compound from items **1** and **2** of the Analysis and Interpretation section at room temperature and at 4°C. What volumes of water would be necessary? (Hint: the density of water is about 1.0 g/mL.)

2. Designing Experiments

Describe how you could use the properties of the compounds to test the purity of your recovered samples. If your teacher approves your plan, use it to check your separation of the mixtures. (Hint: check a chemical handbook for more information about the properties of NaCl and KNO_3.)

3. Designing Experiments

How could you improve the yield or the purity of the compounds you recovered? If you can think of ways to modify the procedure, ask your teacher to approve your plan, and run the procedure again.

4. Research and Communication

Petroleum products are separated from crude oil through the process of fractional distillation. Contact the American Petroleum Institute, 1220 L Street, NW, Washington, D.C. 20005, for information on petroleum refining. Write a short paper on fractional distillation and note ways in which this process is similar to fractional crystallization.

5. Designing Experiments

For each of the following mixtures, write a paragraph outlining the steps you would take to separate each of them.
a. water and alcohol   **b.** water and food coloring   **c.** sand and salt

GOLDSTAKE MINING CORPORATION

January 20, 1995

George Taylor
Director of Analytical Services
CheMystery Labs, Inc.
52 Fulton Street
Springfield, VA 22150

Dear George:

I thought of you—and your new company—when a problem came up here at Goldstake. I think I have a job for you. While performing exploratory drilling for natural gas near Afton in western Wyoming, our engineers encountered a new subterranean geothermal aquifer. We estimate the size of the aquifer to be 1×10^{12} liters.

On the advice of our contact with the Bureau of Land Management, we alerted the Environmental Protection Agency. Preliminary qualitative tests of the water identified two dissolved salts: potassium nitrate and copper nitrate.

The EPA is concerned that a full-scale mining operation may harm the environment if the salts are present in large enough quantities. They're requiring us to halt all operations while we obtain more information for an environmental impact statement. We need your firm to separate, purify, and make a determination of the amounts of the two salts in the Afton Aquifer.

Lynn L. Brown

Lynn L. Brown
Director of Operations
Goldstake Mining Corporation

Required Precautions

Goggles and lab aprons must be worn at all times.

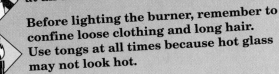

Before lighting the burner, remember to confine loose clothing and long hair.
Use tongs at all times because hot glass may not look hot.

Do not touch or taste any chemicals.
Wash your hands thoroughly when finished.

CheMystery Labs, Inc.
52 Fulton Street
Springfield, VA 22150

Memorandum

Date: January 23, 1995

To: Andre Kalawiescz

From: George Taylor

We received this contract because the D.O. at Goldstake is an old friend of mine. She knows we're a new company and hungry for work. It's important that we get her an answer quickly and accurately. We can't afford to fail.

Because this is our first mining-industry contract, we need to plan carefully to get good results at minimum cost. Each research team will receive a 50.0 mL sample of the aquifer water, but that's all.

I'd like the following information from each analytical team before the work begins.
- detailed one-page plan for the procedure that you will use to accomplish the analysis, including all necessary data tables
- list of the materials and supplies you will need and the individual and total costs (Remember, with all the costs associated with starting the company, we don't have much money—you've got to keep your costs under $200 000!)

Goldstake would like the following information presented in a two-page report soon after the completion of lab work.
- mass of potassium nitrate, KNO_3, and copper nitrate, $Cu(NO_3)_2$, in the 50. mL sample
- extrapolated mass of KNO_3 and $Cu(NO_3)_2$ in the Afton Aquifer
- summary paragraph describing the procedure used
- detailed and organized data and analysis section showing your calculations and explanations of any possible sources of error
- detailed invoice for the services rendered and the expenses incurred

Doing this job well could mean a long term contract with Goldstake.

References

Refer to pages 52–54 for a discussion of techniques for separating mixtures. The procedure is similar to one your team recently completed involving the separation of sodium chloride, NaCl, and potassium nitrate, KNO_3.

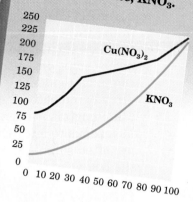

Spill Procedures/ Waste Disposal Methods

- Do not try to rinse the $Cu(NO_3)_2$ and KNO_3 down the drain. Dispose of them in separate designated waste containers, so that they can be reused.

Materials for GOLDSTAKE MINING CORPORATION

Item	Cost	1	2	3
REQUIRED ITEMS (You must include all of these in your budget.)				
Lab space/fume hood/utilities	15 000 — /day			
Standard disposal fee	2 000 — /g of product			
Balance	5 000			
Beaker tongs	1 000			
Drying oven	5 000			
Ring stand/ring/wire gauze	2 000			
REAGENTS and ADDITIONAL EQUIPMENT (Include in your budget only what you'll need.)				
Ice				
Rock salt	500			
250 mL beaker	2 000			
100 mL graduated cylinder	1 000			
Büchner funnel	1 000			
Bunsen burner/related equipment	2 000			
Filter flask with sink attachment	10 000			
Filter paper	2 000			
Glass funnel	500 — /piece			
Glass stirring rod	1 000			
Hot plate	1 000			
Plastic bags	8 000			
Rubber policeman	500 — /each			
Spatula	500			
Thermistor probe—LEAP	500			
Thermometer	2 000			
Wash bottle	2 000			
* No refunds on returned chemicals or unused equipment.	500			
FINES				
OSHA safety violation	2 000 — /incident			

EXPLORATION 3A
Technique Builder

Flame Tests

Objectives
Identify a set of flame test color standards for selected metal ions.

Relate colors of a flame test to the behavior of excited electrons in a metal atom.

Identify an unknown metal ion by a flame test.

Demonstrate proficiency in the following techniques: performing a flame test and using a spectroscope.

Situation
Your company has been contacted by Julius and Annette Benetti. They are worried about some abandoned, rusted barrels of chemicals that their daughter found while playing in the vacant lot behind their home. The barrels have begun to leak a colored liquid that flows through their property before emptying into a local sewer. The Benettis want your company to identify the compound in the liquid. Earlier work already indicates that it is a dissolved metal compound. Many metals, such as lead, have been determined as hazardous to our health. Many compounds of these metals are often soluble in water and therefore easily absorbed into the body.

Background
After electrons of an atom absorb energy to move from their ground state to an excited state, they will eventually fall back to their ground state. When they do this, the energy they absorbed will be re-emitted in the form of light. Because each atom has a unique structure and arrangement of electrons, each atom emits a unique type of light. This is how the chemical test known as a flame test works. The atoms are excited by being placed within a flame. As they re-emit the energy in the form of light, the color of the flame changes. For most metals, these changes are easily visible. However, even a tiny speck of another substance can interfere with identification of the true color for a test, so be sure to keep the equipment very clean, and perform multiple trials to check your work.

Problem
To determine what metal is contained in the barrels behind the Benettis' house, you must first perform flame tests with a variety of standard solutions of different metal compounds. Then, you will perform a flame test with the sample from the site to see if it matches any of the solutions you've used as standards.

Safety

Always wear goggles and an apron to provide protection for your eyes and clothing. If you get a chemical in your eyes, immediately flush it out at the eyewash station while calling to your teacher. Know the locations of the emergency lab shower and eyewash and how to use them.

Do not touch any chemicals. If you get a chemical on your skin or clothing, wash it off at the sink while calling to your teacher. Make sure you carefully read the labels and follow the directions on all containers of chemicals that you use. Do not taste any chemicals or items used in the laboratory. Never return leftovers to their original containers; take only small amounts to avoid wasting supplies.

Confine long hair and loose clothing. Do not heat glassware that is broken, chipped, or cracked. Use tongs or a hot mitt to handle heated glassware and other equipment because it does not always look hot. If your clothing catches on fire, WALK to the emergency lab shower, and use it to put out the fire.

Call your teacher in the event of an acid spill. Acid spills should be cleaned up promptly, according to your teacher's instructions.

Always clean up the lab and all equipment after use, and dispose of substances according to proper disposal methods. Wash your hands thoroughly before you leave the lab after all lab work is finished.

Materials

- 1.0 M HCl solution
- $CaCl_2$ solution
- K_2SO_4 solution
- Li_2SO_4 solution
- Na_2SO_4 solution
- NaCl crystals
- NaCl solution
- $SrCl_2$ solution
- Unknown solution
- 250 mL beaker
- Bunsen burner and related equipment
- Cobalt glass plates
- Crucible tongs
- Flame test wire
- Glass test plate

Optional Equipment
- Spectroscope

Preparation

1. **Organizing Data**

   Prepare a data table in your lab notebook. The table should contain a row for each of the solutions of metal compounds listed in the materials list, as well as an additional row for the unknown solution. The table should have three wide columns for the three trials you will perform with each substance. Each column should have room to record colors and wavelengths of light. In addition, be sure that you have plenty of room for observations about each test.

2. Label a beaker *Waste*. Thoroughly clean and dry a glass plate. Put five drops of 1.0 M HCl on the plate. Clean the test wire by first dipping it in the HCl and then holding it in the colorless flame of the Bunsen burner. Repeat this procedure until there is no color from the wire in the flame. When the wire is ready, rinse the plate with distilled water, and collect the rinse water in the *Waste* beaker.

3. Put two drops of each metal ion solution except NaCl in a row on one side of the plate. Put a row of 1.0 M HCl drops on the plate across from the metal ion solutions, as shown in the illustration on the right. The wire will need to be cleaned thoroughly between each test solution, to avoid contamination from the previous test.

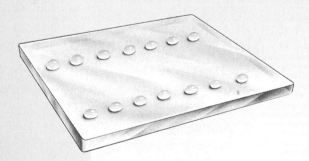

Technique

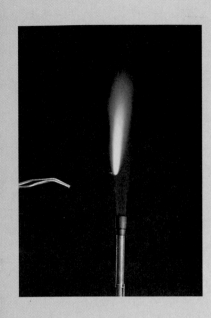

4. Dip the wire into the $CaCl_2$ solution, and then hold it in the Bunsen burner flame. Observe the color of the flame, and record it in the data table. Repeat the procedure again, but look through the spectroscope to view the results. Record the wavelengths you see from the flame. Perform each test three times. Clean the wire with the HCl as in step **2**.

5. Repeat step **4** with the K_2SO_4 and each of the remaining solutions on the plate. Record the color of each flame, and the wavelength observed with the spectroscope for each solution that you test. Clean the wire thoroughly, and rinse the plate with distilled water into the *Waste* beaker after the solutions are tested.

6. Test another drop of Na_2SO_4, but view the flame through two pieces of cobalt glass. Clean the wire and plate, rinsing the plate with distilled water into the *Waste* beaker. Repeat the test using the K_2SO_4 flame with the cobalt glass. Record the colors and wavelengths of the flames as they appear when viewed through the cobalt glass in your data table. Clean the wire and plate, rinsing the plate with distilled water into the *Waste* beaker.

7. Put a drop of K_2SO_4 on a clean part of the plate. Add a drop of Na_2SO_4. Flame-test the mixture. Observe the color of the mixture in the flame when viewed without the cobalt glass. Repeat the test again observing the flame through the cobalt glass. Record the colors and wavelengths of the flames in the data table. Clean the wire and plate, rinsing the plate with distilled water into the *Waste* beaker.

8. Test a drop of the NaCl solution in the flame and then while viewed through the spectroscope. (Do not use the cobalt glass.) Record your observations. Clean the wire and plate, rinsing the plate with distilled water into the *Waste* beaker. Place a few crystals of NaCl on the plate, then dip the wire in the crystals and do the flame test once more. Record the color of the flame test. Clean the wire and plate with distilled water, rinsing the plate with distilled water into the *Waste* beaker.

9. Obtain a sample of the unknown metal solution. Do flame tests for it, both with and without the cobalt glass. Record your observations. Clean the wire and plate, rinsing the plate with distilled water into the *Waste* beaker.

Cleanup and Disposal

10. Dispose of the contents of the waste beaker in the container designated by your teacher. Always wash your hands thoroughly after cleaning up the area and equipment.

Analysis and Interpretation

1. **Organizing Data**
   Examine your table of data, and create a summary of the flame test for each metal.

2. **Analyzing Data**
   Account for any differences in the individual trials for the flame tests for the metals.

3. **Organizing Ideas**

   Explain how using cobalt glass can make it easier to analyze the ions being tested.

4. **Relating Ideas**

   Explain how the lines seen in the spectroscope relate to the positions of electrons in the metal atom.

5. **Relating Ideas**

   For three of the metals tested, explain how the color seen by your eyes relates to the lines of color seen when you looked through the spectroscope.

Conclusions

6. **Inferring Conclusions**

   What metal(s) are in the unknown solution from the barrels on the vacant lot?

7. **Evaluating Methods**

   How would you characterize the flame test with respect to its sensitivity? What difficulties could there be identifying ions with the flame test?

8. **Evaluating Methods**

   Explain how you can use a spectroscope to identify the components of solutions containing several different metals.

Extensions

1. **Inferring Conclusions**

   A student performed flame tests on several unknowns and observed that they were all shades of red. What should she do to correctly identify these substances? Explain your answer.

2. **Applying Ideas**

   During a flood, the labels from three bottles of chemicals were lost. The unlabeled bottles of white solids were known to contain the following: strontium nitrate, ammonium carbonate, and potassium sulfate. Explain how you could easily test the substances and relabel these three bottles. (Hint: ammonium ion does not provide a distinctive color when flame-tested.)

3. **Applying Ideas**

   Some stores sell jars of "fireplace crystals." When sprinkled on a log, they turn the flames colors, such as blue, red, green, and violet. Explain how these crystals can change the flame color. What ingredients do you expect them to contain?

4. **Designing Experiments**

   Identify substances that contain metal ions. If your teacher approves of your selections, bring them to the lab, dissolve them, and perform flame tests with them to identify the metals they contain.

5. **Research and Communications**

   Research how instruments that work like spectroscopes can identify substances that are far away. Report to the class on a specific use of such equipment in astronomy.

SPECTROSCOPY AND FLAME TESTS

Identifying Materials

ETA EXPERIMENTAL TESTING AGENCY

January 27, 1995

Director of Investigations
CheMystery Labs, Inc.
52 Fulton Street
Springfield, VA 22150

Dear Director:

As you may have seen in news reports, one of our freelance pilots, Davin Matthews, was killed in a crash of an experimental airplane that was struck by lightning.

What the reports did not mention was that Matthews's airplane was a recently perfected new design that he'd been developing for us. The notes he left behind indicate that the coating on the nose cone was the key to its speed and maneuverability. Unfortunately, he did not reveal what substances he used, and we were able to recover only flakes of material from the nose cone after the accident.

We have sent you samples of these flakes dissolved in a solution. Please identify the material Matthews used so that we can duplicate his prototype. We will pay $200,000 for this work, provided that you can identify the material within three days.

Sincerely,

Jared MacLaren

Jared MacLaren
Experimental Testing Agency

Required Precautions

 Lab aprons and goggles must be worn at all times.

 Do not touch or taste any chemicals. Wash your hands thoroughly before you leave the lab.

 Confine loose hair and clothing.

 If you get acid or base on your skin or clothing, wash it off at the sink while calling to your teacher. If you get acid or base in your eyes, immediately flush it out at the eyewash while calling to your teacher.

Memorandum

CheMystery Labs, Inc.
52 Fulton Street
Springfield, VA 22150

Date: January 28, 1995

To: Edwin Thien

From: Marissa Bellinghausen

We have narrowed down the possibilities of the material used to four. It is a compound of either lithium, potassium, strontium, or calcium. Using flame tests and the wavelengths of spectroscopic analysis, you should be able to identify which of these is in the sample.

Because our contract depends on timeliness, give me a preliminary report that includes the following as soon as possible.
- detailed one-page summary of your plan for the procedure
- itemized list of equipment, with total costs (Remember that the less you spend, the more profit for the company—provided you can get accurate results!)

After you complete your analysis, prepare a report in the form of a two-page letter to MacLaren. It must include the following.
- identity of the metal in the sample
- summary of your procedure
- detailed and organized analysis and data sections, showing tests and results
- detailed invoice for all expenses and services

References

Refer to page 89 for information about spectroscopic analysis. The procedure is similar to one your team recently completed to identify an unknown metal in a solution. As before, use small amounts and clean equipment carefully to avoid contamination. Perform multiple trials for each sample.

The following information is the bright-line emission data (in nm) for the four possible metals.

- **Lithium:** 670, 612, 498, 462
- **Potassium:** 700, 695, 408, 405
- **Strontium:** 710, 685, 665, 500, 490, 485, 460, 420, 405
- **Calcium:** 650, 645, 610, 485, 460, 445, 420

Materials for
EXPERIMENTAL TESTING AGENCY

Item	Cost		
REQUIRED ITEMS			
(You must include all of these in your budget.)			
Lab space/fume hood/utilities	15 000 — /day		
Standard disposal fee	2 000 — /g of product		
Bunsen burner/related equipment	10 000		
Crucible tongs	2 000		
Flame-test wire	2 000		
REAGENTS and ADDITIONAL EQUIPMENT			
(Include in your budget only what you'll need.)			
1 M HCl	500 — /mL		
250 mL beaker	1 000		
100 mL graduated cylinder	1 000		
Aluminum foil	1 000 — /cm²		
Balance	5 000		
Cobalt glass plate	2 000		
Filter paper	500 — /piece		
Glass funnel	1 000		
Glass plate	1 000		
Glass stirring rod	1 000		
Litmus paper	1 000 — /piece		
Six test tubes/holder/rack	2 000		
Spectroscope	15 000		
Wash bottle	500		
* No refunds on returned chemicals or unused equipment.			
FINES			
OSHA safety violation	2 000 — /incident		

Spill Procedures/
Waste Disposal Methods

- In case of spills, follow your teacher's instructions.
- Place all remaining solutions in separate disposal containers as indicated by your teacher.
- Clean the area and all equipment after use.

EXPLORATION 5A
Technique Builder

Percent Composition of Hydrates

Objectives

Demonstrate proficiency in using the balance and the Bunsen burner.

Measure the mass of a substance before and after its water of crystallization has been removed.

Relate results to the law of conservation of mass and the law of multiple proportions.

Perform calculations using the molar mass.

Determine the empirical formula and percentage by mass of water in the hydrate.

Situation

You are a research chemist working for a company that is developing a new chemical moisture absorber and indicator. The company plans to seal the moisture absorber into a transparent porous pouch attached to a cellophane window on the inside of packages for compact disc players. This way, moisture within the packages will be absorbed, and any package that has too much moisture can be quickly detected and dried out. Your company's efforts have focused on copper(II) sulfate, $CuSO_4$, which can absorb water to become a hydrate that shows a distinctive color change.

Background

As discussed in Chapter 5, when many ionic compounds are crystallized from a water solution, they include individual water molecules as part of their crystalline structure. If the substances are heated, this water of crystallization may be driven off, leaving behind the pure anhydrous form of the compound. Because the law of multiple proportions also applies to crystalline hydrates, the number of moles of water driven off per mole of the anhydrous compound should be a simple whole number ratio. You can use this information to help you determine the formula of the hydrate.

Problem

To help your company decide whether $CuSO_4$ is the right substance for the moisture absorber and indicator, you will need to examine the hydrated and anhydrous forms of the compound and determine the following.

- the empirical formula of the hydrate, including its water of crystallization
- whether the change from hydrated to anhydrous form is obvious enough for the compound to be useful as an indicator
- the mass of water that can be absorbed by the 25 g of the anhydrous compound that the company proposes to use

Even if you can guess what the formula for the hydrate should be, carefully perform the procedure so that you know how well your company's supply of $CuSO_4$ absorbs moisture.

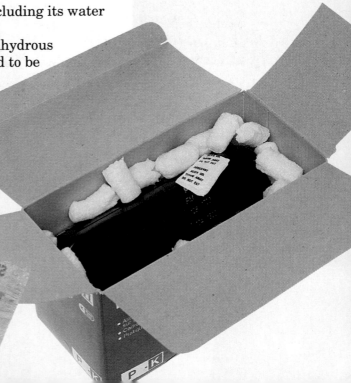

Safety

Always wear goggles and an apron to provide protection for your eyes and clothing. If you get a chemical in your eyes, immediately flush it out at the eyewash station while calling to your teacher. Know the locations of the emergency lab shower and eyewash and how to use them.

Do not touch any chemicals. If you get a chemical on your skin or clothing, wash it off at the sink while calling to your teacher. Make sure you carefully read the labels and follow the directions on all containers of chemicals that you use. Do not taste any chemicals or items used in the laboratory. Never return leftovers to their original containers; take only small amounts to avoid wasting supplies.

Open flames are dangerous, and you should tie back loose clothing and hair for safety reasons. Use proper methods to hold equipment being heated. The crucible and cover are very hot after each heating. Remember to handle the crucible and cover only with tongs designed to hold a crucible.

Never put broken glass or ceramics in a regular waste container. Broken glass or ceramics should be disposed of separately.

Always clean up the lab and all equipment after use, and dispose of substances according to proper disposal methods. Wash your hands thoroughly before you leave the lab after all lab work is finished.

Materials

- $CuSO_4$, hydrated crystals
- Distilled water
- Balance
- Bunsen burner
- Crucible and cover
- Crucible tongs
- Desiccator
- Dropper or micropipet
- Glass stirring rod
- Ring and pipe-stem triangle
- Ring stand
- Spatula
- Weighing paper

Preparation

1. **Organizing Data**

   Prepare a data table in your lab notebook with spaces for the mass of the empty crucible with cover and for the initial mass of the sample, crucible, and cover; and several spaces for the mass of the sample, crucible, and cover after heating. Leave room for observations about the procedure.

2. Make sure that your equipment and tongs are very clean for this work so that you will get the best possible results. Remember that you will need to cool the heated crucible in the desiccator before measuring its mass. *Never put a hot crucible on a balance; it will damage the balance.*

Technique

3. To prepare the crucible and cover, place the crucible and cover on the triangle with the lid slightly tipped. The small opening will allow gases to escape. Heat the crucible and cover until the crucible glows slightly red. Using the tongs, transfer the crucible and cover to the desiccator, and allow them to cool for 5 min. Determine the mass of the crucible and cover to the nearest 0.01 g, and record it in your data table.

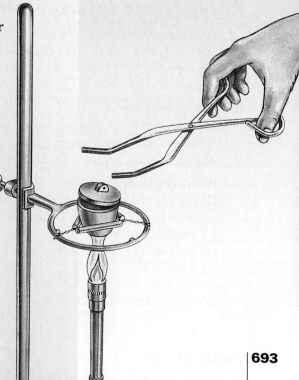

4. Using a spatula, add approximately 5 g of copper sulfate hydrate crystals to the crucible. Break the crystal up before placing it in the crucible. Put on the crucible's cover, determine the mass of the covered crucible and crystals to the nearest 0.01 g, and record it in your data table.

5. Place the crucible with the copper sulfate hydrate on the triangle, and again position the cover so there is only a small opening. If the opening is too large, the crystals may spatter as they are heated. Heat the crucible very gently on a low flame to avoid spattering. Increase the temperature gradually for 2 or 3 min, and then heat until the crucible glows red for at least 5 min. Be very careful not to raise the temperature of the crucible and its contents too suddenly. You will observe a color change, which is normal, but if the substance remains yellow after cooling, it was overheated and has begun to decompose. Allow the crucible, cover, and contents to cool for 5 min in the desiccator, and then measure its mass. Enter the mass in your data table.

6. Heat the covered crucible and contents to redness again for 5 min. Allow the crucible, cover, and contents to cool in the desiccator, and then determine their mass, recording it in the data table. If the two mass measurements differ by no more than 0.01 g, you may assume that all of the water has been driven off. Otherwise, repeat the process until the mass no longer changes, indicating that all of the water has evaporated. Record this constant mass in your data table.

7. After recording the constant mass, set a part of your sample aside on a piece of weighing paper. Using the dropper or pipet, put a few drops of water onto this part to rehydrate the crystals. Record your observations in your data table.

Cleanup and Disposal

8. Clean all apparatus and your lab station. Make sure to completely shut off the gas valve before leaving the laboratory. Remember to wash your hands. Place the rehydrated and anhydrous chemicals in the disposal containers designated by your teacher.

Analysis and Interpretation

1. Analyzing Methods
Why do you need to heat the clean crucible before using it in this lab? Why do the tongs used throughout this lab need to be especially clean?

2. Organizing Data
Why do you need to use a cover for the crucible? Could you leave the cover off each time you measure the mass of the crucible and its contents and still get accurate results? Explain your answer.

3. Analyzing Information
Calculate the mass of anhydrous copper sulfate (the residue that remains after heating to constant mass) by subtracting the mass of the empty crucible and cover from the mass of the crucible, cover, and heated $CuSO_4$. Use the molar mass for $CuSO_4$, determined from the periodic table, to calculate the number of moles present.

4. Resolving Discrepancies
Explain why the mass of the sample got smaller after it was heated, despite the law of conservation of mass.

5. Analyzing Information
Calculate the mass and moles of water originally present in the hydrate using the molar mass determined from the periodic table.

Conclusions

6. Analyzing Information
Using your answers from items **3** and **5**, determine the empirical formula for the copper sulfate hydrate.

7. Organizing Data
What is the percentage by mass of water in the original hydrated compound?

8. Organizing Conclusions
How much water could 25 g of anhydrous $CuSO_4$ absorb?

9. Evaluating Conclusions
When you rehydrated the small amount of anhydrous copper sulfate, what were your observations? Explain whether this substance would make a good indicator of moisture.

Extensions

1. Evaluating Methods
What possible sources of error can you identify in your procedure? If you can think of ways to eliminate them, ask your teacher to approve your suggestions, and run the procedure again.

2. Applying Conclusions
Some cracker tins include a glass vial of drying material in the lid. This is often a mixture of magnesium sulfate and cobalt chloride. As the mixture absorbs moisture to form hydrated compounds, the cobalt chloride changes from blue-violet $CoCl_2 \cdot 2H_2O$ to pink $CoCl_2 \cdot 6H_2O$. When this hydrated mixture becomes totally pink, it can be restored to the dihydrate form by heating it in the oven. Write equations for the reactions that occur when this mixture is heated.

3. Applying Ideas
Three pairs of students obtained the following results when they heated a solid. In each case, the students observed that when they began to heat the solid, drops of a liquid formed on the sides of the test tube.

Sample number	Mass before heating (g)	Constant mass after heating (g)
1	1.92	1.26
2	2.14	1.40
3	2.68	1.78

a. Could the solid be a hydrate? Explain how you could find out.

b. If the solid has a molar mass of 208 g/mol after heating and a formula of XY, how many formula units of water are there in one formula unit of the unheated compound?

LOST ART GYPSUM MINE

February 9, 1995

Director of Research
CheMystery Labs, Inc.
52 Fulton Street
Springfield, VA 22150

Dear Sir:

Lost Art Gypsum Mine previously sold its raw gypsum to a manufacturing company that used it to make anhydrous calcium sulfate, $CaSO_4$ (a desiccant), and plaster of Paris. That firm has now gone out of business, and we are currently negotiating the purchase of their equipment to process our own gypsum into anhydrous calcium sulfate and plaster of Paris.

Your company has been recommended to plan the large-scale industrial process for our new plant. We will need a detailed report on the development of the process and formulas for these products. This report will be presented to the bank handling our loan for the new plant. As we discussed on the telephone today, we are willing to pay you $250,000 for the work, with the contract papers arriving under separate cover today.

Sincerely,

Alex Farros
Vice President
Lost Art Gypsum Mine

Required Precautions

Goggles and lab aprons must be worn at all times in the laboratory.

Confine loose clothing and hair.

Do not touch or taste any chemicals. Always wash your hands thoroughly when finished.

Memorandum

CheMystery Labs, Inc.
52 Fulton Street
Springfield, VA 22150

Date: February 10, 1995

To: Kenesha Smith

From: Martha Li-Hsien

This job involves many different tasks. Your team needs to develop a procedure to experimentally determine the correct empirical formulas for both hydrates of this anhydrous compound. You will use gypsum samples from the mine and samples of the plaster of Paris product, but both are available at a cost.

Once this work is complete, our chemical engineering division will examine the most efficient way to implement the necessary procedures for manufacturing. Of the $250,000 fee we're getting from Lost Art, your end of the job must cost less than $125,000 so that the chemical engineering division has enough money to do its job.

As soon as possible, I need a preliminary report from you that includes the following.
- detailed one-page summary of your plan for the procedure, with all necessary data tables
- itemized list of equipment, with total costs for the accounting department (Remember to keep your costs under $125,000.)

After you complete the analysis, prepare a two-page report for the chemical engineering division that includes the following information.
- formulas for anhydrous calcium sulfate, plaster of Paris, and gypsum
- summary of your procedure
- detailed and organized data and analysis sections that show calculations, along with estimates and explanations of any possible sources of error
- detailed invoice of all expenses and services

This report will become Chapter 2 of our final report to Mr. Farros.

References

Refer to pages 179–180 for information about hydrates and water of crystallization. The procedure and reaction is similar to one your team recently completed involving hydrated copper(II) sulfate. Gypsum and plaster of Paris are hydrated forms of $CaSO_4$. One of the largest gypsum mines in the world is located outside of Paris, France. Plaster of Paris has less water of crystallization than gypsum. Plaster of Paris is commonly used in plaster walls and art sculptures.

Spill Procedures/ Waste Disposal Methods
- Solids must go in the designated waste containers.
- Clean the lab area and all equipment after use.

Materials for LOST ART GYPSUM MINE

Item	Cost		
REQUIRED ITEMS (You must include all of these in your budget.)			
Lab space/fume hood/utilities	15 000 — /day		
Standard disposal fee	2 000 — /g of product		
Balance	5 000		
Bunsen burner/related equipment	10 000		
Crucible tongs	2 000		
Ring stand/ring/pipe-stem triangle	2 000		
REAGENTS and ADDITIONAL EQUIPMENT (Include in your budget only what you'll need.)			
Gypsum sample	500 — /g		
Plaster of Paris sample	500 — /g		
250 mL beaker	1 000		
100 mL graduated cylinder	1 000		
Aluminum foil	1 000 — /cm²		
Crucible and cover	5 000		
Desiccator	3 000		
Filter paper	500 — /piece		
Glass funnel	1 000		
Glass stirring rod	1 000		
Litmus paper	1 000 — /piece		
Mortar and pestle	2 000		
Six test tubes/holder/rack	2 000		
Spatula	500		
Wash bottle	500		
Weighing paper	500 — /piece		
* No refunds on returned chemicals or unused equipment.			
FINES			
OSHA safety violation	2 000 — /incident		

Polymers and Toy Balls

Objectives

Synthesize two different polymers.

Prepare a small toy ball from each polymer.

Observe the similarities and differences of the two balls.

Measure the density of each polymer.

Compare the bounce height of the two balls.

Situation

Your company has been contacted by a toy company. They have always specialized in toy balls made from vulcanized rubber. Recent environmental legislation has increased the cost of disposing of the sulfur and other chemical byproducts of the manufacturing process for this type of rubber. The toy company wants you to research some other materials.

Background

Isoprene monomer

Rubber is a polymer of covalently bonded atoms. The simplest formula unit for the rubber monomer is called *isoprene* and is shown on the left. Three monomers bonded together are also shown. The *n* indicates a very large number, usually about 3000. The zigzag chain created when monomers bond together accounts for rubber's strength and elasticity.

When rubber is vulcanized, it is heated with sulfur, and the sulfur atoms form bonds between adjacent molecules of rubber, increasing its strength and making it more elastic.

Three isoprene monomers

Latex rubber is a colloidal suspension that can be made synthetically or found naturally in plants such as the para rubber tree (*Hevea brasiliensis*), in which it dries to form a waterproof layer for protection. Latex is composed of approximately 60% water, 35% hydrocarbon monomers, 2% proteins, and some sugars and inorganic salts. Commercially, latex is preserved with ammonia so that it remains a liquid until it can be molded or stretched into its final form. It is used in paints and disposable gloves.

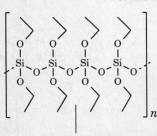

Another polymer with covalent bonds can be formed from ethanol, C_2H_5OH, and a solution of sodium silicate, mostly in the form of $Na_2Si_3O_7$, which is known as water glass because it dissolves in water. When the polymer is formed, water is also a product. The polymer has the structural formula shown at left.

Four ethanol-silicate monomers

Problem

Latex and the ethanol-silicate polymer are the two materials you will investigate. You need to do the following.

- synthesize each polymer
- make a ball 2–3 cm in diameter from each polymer
- make observations about physical properties of each polymer
- measure how well each ball bounces

Safety

Always wear goggles and an apron to provide protection for your eyes and clothing. If you get a chemical in your eyes, immediately flush it out at the eyewash station while calling to your teacher. Know the locations of the emergency lab shower and eyewash and how to use them.

Do not touch any chemicals. If you get a chemical on your skin or clothing, wash it off at the sink while calling to your teacher. Make sure you carefully read the labels and follow the directions on all containers of chemicals that you use. Do not taste any chemicals or items used in the laboratory. Never return leftovers to their original containers; take only small amounts to avoid wasting supplies.

Wear disposable plastic gloves; the sodium silicate solution and the alcohol-silicate polymer are irritating to your skin.

Ethanol is flammable. Make sure there are no flames anywhere in the laboratory when you are using it. Also, keep it away from other sources of heat.

Always clean up the lab and all equipment after use, and dispose of substances according to proper disposal methods. Wash your hands thoroughly before you leave the lab when all lab work is finished.

Materials

- 5% acetic acid solution (vinegar), 10 mL
- 50% ethanol solution, 3 mL
- Distilled water
- Liquid latex, 10 mL
- Sodium silicate solution, 12 mL
- 2 L beaker or plastic bucket or tub
- 10 mL graduated cylinder
- 25 mL graduated cylinder
- Paper cup, 5 oz., 2
- Paper towels
- Wooden stick

Preparation

1. Organizing Data
Prepare two data tables in your lab notebook, one for each polymer. Each table must have spaces for three trials of the bounce height in centimeters, the mass of each ball, and the diameter of each ball. Leave space to record observations about the balls.

Technique

2. Fill the 2 L beaker or the bucket or tub about half-full of distilled water.

3. Using a clean 25 mL graduated cylinder, measure 10 mL of liquid latex, and pour it into one of the paper cups.

4. Thoroughly clean the 25 mL graduated cylinder with soap and water. Then, rinse with distilled water.

5. Measure 10 mL of distilled water. Pour it into the paper cup with the latex.

6. Measure 10 mL of the 5% acetic acid solution, and pour it into the paper cup with the latex and water.

7. Stir the mixture with the wooden stick immediately.

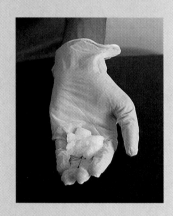

8. As you continue stirring, a polymer "lump" will form around the wooden stick. Pull the stick with the polymer lump from the paper cup and immerse it in the 2 L beaker or bucket or tub.

9. While wearing gloves, gently pull the lump from the wooden stick, keeping it immersed under the water.

10. Keeping the latex rubber under water, use your gloved hands to squeeze the lump into a ball, as shown in the figure on the left, and then squeeze several more times to remove any unused chemicals. You may remove the latex rubber from the water as you roll it in your hands to smooth the ball.

11. Set aside the latex-rubber ball to dry. While it is drying, you should begin to make a ball from the ethanol and sodium silicate solutions.

12. In a clean 25 mL graduated cylinder, measure 12 mL of sodium silicate solution, and pour it into the other paper cup.

13. In a clean 10 mL graduated cylinder, measure 3 mL of 50% ethanol. Pour the ethanol into the paper cup with the sodium silicate, and mix with the wooden stick until a solid substance is formed.

14. While wearing gloves, remove the polymer that forms, and place it in the palm of one hand. Gently press it with the palms of both your hands until a ball that does not crumble is formed. This takes a little time and patience. The liquid that comes out of the ball is a combination of ethanol and water. Occasionally moisten the ball by letting a small amount of water from a faucet run over it. When the ball no longer crumbles, you are ready to go on to the following steps.

15. Observe as many physical properties of the balls as possible, and record your observations in your lab notebook.

16. Drop each ball several times, and record your observations.

17. Drop each ball from a height of 1 m, and measure its bounce. Repeat for three trials for each ball.

18. Measure the diameter and the mass of each ball.

Cleanup and Disposal

19. Dispose of any extra solutions in the containers indicated by your teacher. Clean up your lab area. Remember to wash your hands thoroughly when your lab work is finished.

Analysis and Interpretation

1. **Analyzing Information**
   Give the chemical formula for the latex (isoprene) monomer and the ethanol-silicate polymer.

2. **Analyzing Information**
   List at least three observations you made of the properties of the two different balls.

3. **Applying Models**
   Explain how your observations in item **2** indicate that the polymers in each ball are not ionically bonded.

4. **Organizing Data**
   Calculate the average height of the bounce for each type of ball.

5. Organizing Data
Calculate the volume for each ball. Even though they may not be perfectly spherical, assume that they are. (Hint: the volume of a sphere is equal to $\frac{4}{3} \times \pi \times r^3$, where r is the radius, which is one-half of the diameter.)

6. Organizing Data
Calculate the density of each ball using your measurements for the mass and the volume from item **5**.

Conclusions

7. Inferring Conclusions
Which polymer do you recommend for the toy company's new toy balls? Explain your reasoning.

8. Evaluating Viewpoints
Using the table shown to the right, find the unit cost, the amount of money it costs to make a single ball. (Hint: remember to check how much of each reagent is needed to make a single ball.)

Reagent	Price (dollars per liter)
Acetic acid solution	1.50
Ethanol solution	9.00
Latex solution	20.00
Sodium silicate solution	10.00

8. Evaluating Viewpoints
What are some other possible practical applications for each of the polymers you made?

Extensions

1. Research and Communication
Polymers are used daily in our lives. Describe or list the polymers you come into contact with during a one-day period in your life.

2. Designing Experiments
Design a mold for a polymer ball that will make it symmetrical and smooth. If your teacher approves of your design, try the procedure again with the mold.

3. Designing Experiments
What possible sources of error can you identify in this procedure? If you can think of ways to eliminate them, ask your teacher to approve your plan, and run the procedure again.

4. Predicting Outcomes
When a ball bounces up, kinetic energy of motion is converted into potential energy. With this in mind, explain which will bounce higher: a perfectly symmetrical, round sphere or an oblong shape that vibrates after it bounces.

5. Predicting Outcomes
Explain why you didn't measure the volume of the balls by submerging them in water.

INVESTIGATION 6A

Problem Solving

FUNLAND TOYS®

February 10, 1995

Reginald Brown
Director of Materials Testing
CheMystery Labs, Inc.
52 Fulton Street
Springfield, VA 22150

Dear Mr. Brown:

We are pursuing research and development work relating to new polymers that will be used as part of a new inflatable toy trampoline.

We need a material that has plenty of "bounce," but it must be able to withstand strong forces without tearing.

We want your firm to investigate the properties of different shapes and thicknesses of latex rubber. As we discussed on the phone, we are drafting a contract to pay you $250,000 for the research resulting in a report that explains the possible pros and cons of each material and your test results.

Sincerely,

Kohl Logan

Kohl Logan
President
Funland Toys

Required Precautions

 Goggles and lab aprons must be worn at all times.

 Do not touch or taste any chemicals. Wash your hands thoroughly when finished.

 Disposable plastic gloves should be worn during lab work because the latex solutions can be irritating to the skin.

 Keep the bottles of reagents within a working fume hood.

CheMystery Labs, Inc.
52 Fulton Street
Springfield, VA 22150

Memorandum

Date: February 11, 1995

To: Sophia Carlucci

From: Reginald Brown

I thought of your team as soon as this research and development opportunity came in because I know you have been working on the possibility of using the same polymers in toy balls.

There are several important differences about this job. Instead of making spheres, I suggest we work on disks of the material because that will be more like a trampoline surface. You'll need to measure bounce height, and how well the material deals with strong forces. I suggest we make measurements of the size of the polymer before and after stretching, and the amount of force a sample can take before breaking. I haven't figured out exactly how we will model the repeated stress of bouncing. I'll let you figure that out. If you decide you need equipment other than what's listed below for your tests, let me know as soon as possible.

Before you get started, I need the following information.
- detailed one-page plan for the procedure and all necessary data charts, including a description of the tests you will do
- detailed list of all of the equipment and materials you will need, along with the individual and total costs (The lower you keep the costs, the more profit we can make!)

When your tests are complete, send a report to Logan in the form of a two-page letter that includes the following.
- discussion concerning the material you recommend and the reasons why you recommend it
- description of your tests and the data you collected (if at all possible, use a graph to present your data.)
- detailed invoice itemizing services rendered and expenses incurred

References

Refer to page 210 for more information on polymers. The procedure and reaction are the same as in an Exploration your team recently performed. Use toothpicks to stir the polymer mixture. Instead of taking the material out of the paper cup to form a ball, leave it in the cup. After it has polymerized and you remove any excess material, remove the solid disk, or cut away the cup.

Spill Procedures/ Waste Disposal Methods

- In case of spills, follow your teacher's instructions.
- Leftover solutions may be poured down the drain.

Materials for
FUNLAND TOYS

Item	Cost	
REQUIRED ITEMS		
(You must include all of these in your budget.)		
Lab space/fume hood/utilities	15 000 —	/day
Standard disposal fee	2 000 —	/g of product
REAGENTS and ADDITIONAL EQUIPMENT		
(Include in your budget only what you'll need.)		
5% acetic acid solution (vinegar)		
Liquid latex	500 —	/mL
2 L beaker or bucket (and water)	1 000 —	/mL
250 mL beaker	1 000	
400 mL beaker	1 000	
10 mL graduated cylinder	2 000	
25 mL graduated cylinder	1 000	
Aluminum foil	1 000	
Can with reclosable lid	1 000 —	/cm²
Glass stirring rod	500	
Marbles	1 000	
Paper clips	500 —	/dozen
Paper cup (assorted sizes available)	500 —	/box
Ring stand/ring	1 000	
Rubber bands	2 000	
String	500 —	/dozen
Tape	500 —	/10 cm
Toothpicks	500 —	/10 cm
Wash bottle	500 —	/dozen
*No refunds on returned chemicals or unused equipment.	500	
FINES		
OSHA safety violation	2 000 —	/incident

AMALGAMATED CHEMICAL

February 1, 1995

Director of Research
CheMystery Labs, Inc.
52 Fulton Street
Springfield, VA 22150

Dear Director:

Amalgamated Chemical is the manufacturer of a variety of chemical products. As a result of processing, our plant generates wastewater containing dissolved compounds of copper, tin, and zinc.

These metals could be recycled back into production if we had a method of reclaiming them from the waste solution. This would save money and reduce the amount we expel as waste, which could help protect the environment.

Several firms have been asked to submit reports on the development of a reclamatory process. We will reimburse each firm for reasonable costs. Based on the quality of the reports and cost of the research, we will offer the most efficient firm a contract to provide hazardous waste recycling services. We look forward to evaluating your report soon.

Sincerely,

Lloyd Chan
Director, Hazardous Waste Division
Amalgamated Chemical

Required Precautions

Wear goggles and lab aprons. Confine loose clothing and long hair.

Don't get the toxic solutions used in this lab on your hands. Keep your hands away from your face and mouth. Wash your hands thoroughly when finished.

CheMystery Labs, Inc.
52 Fulton Street
Springfield, VA 22150

Memorandum

Date: February 3, 1995

To: Sarah Muller

From: Martha Li-Hsien

This is our first chance to break into the chemical manufacturing market! We won't be able to afford any computerized analytical equipment, but I have a plan. We can add reactive metals that will undergo single-displacement reactions, causing the copper, tin, and zinc to precipitate from the solution. Then they can be separated from the wastewater. These metals are available: Mg, Ca, Cu, Fe, Sn, and Zn. We also have stock solutions of compounds of each metal.

First, predict which should work based on the activity series. Then, test each possible combination to confirm your predictions. Be sure to note whether or not the reaction occurs quickly enough to be useful. After you rank the metals by reactivity, recommend a recycling procedure. (Remember to include a suitable method for purifying the metal once it has re-formed.)

Before you begin, I will need the following items.
- detailed one-page plan for the procedure and all necessary data tables
- detailed list of all equipment and materials that you plan to use, including individual and total costs
- your prediction of which metal(s) will work best

When you've found an answer, send Mr. Chan a two-page letter that includes the following.
- detailed suggestions on how the plant could recover the tin, zinc, and copper (Remember, we don't need to perform the entire procedure at this time. We just need to show what would work.)
- metals listed in order of decreasing activity
- detailed and organized observation section
- detailed invoice for services rendered and costs incurred

References
Refer to page 258 for information on single-displacement reactions.
Refer to pages 259–260 for information on the activity series.

Spill Procedures/ Waste Disposal Methods

- If any acid is spilled, use water to dilute it, and inform the teacher immediately.

- Do not rinse any solutions into the sink. Dispose of them in the designated waste containers so that they may be reused.

- Do not throw any metal in the trash can. The pieces of metal may be reused if unreacted. Rinse them with distilled water, and place them in the designated containers for recycling. Pieces of metal formed in reactions should be placed in the designated waste container.

Materials for AMALGAMATED CHEMICAL

Item	Cost	1	2	3
REQUIRED ITEMS				
(You must include all of these in your budget.)				
Lab space/fume hood/utilities	15 000 —	/day		
Standard disposal fee	2 000 —	/g of product		
Balance	5 000			
Six test tubes/holder/rack	2 000			
REAGENTS and ADDITIONAL EQUIPMENT				
(Include in your budget only what you'll need.)				
0.2 M Ca(NO₃)₂				
0.2 M Cu(NO₃)₂	500 —	/mL		
0.2 M Fe(NO₃)₃	500 —	/mL		
0.2 M Mg(NO₃)₂	500 —	/mL		
0.2 M SnCl₂	500 —	/mL		
0.2 M Zn(NO₃)₂	500 —	/mL		
Small pieces of metal: Ca, Cu, Fe, Mg, Zn, Sn	500 —	/mL		
250 mL beaker	1 000 —	/piece		
Evaporating dish	1 000			
Filter paper	1 000			
Glass stirring rod	500 —	/piece		
Mortar and pestle	1 000			
Ring stand with buret clamp	2 000			
Rubber policeman	2 000			
Test tube (small)	500			
Wash bottle	500			
Watch glass	500			
* No refunds on returned chemicals or unused equipment.	1 000			
FINES				
OSHA safety violation	2 000 —	/incident		

EXPLORATION 8A

Technique Builder

Stoichiometry and Gravimetric Analysis

Objectives

Observe the double-displacement reaction between solutions of strontium chloride and sodium carbonate.

Demonstrate proficiency with gravimetric methods.

Measure the mass of insoluble precipitate formed.

Relate the mass of precipitate formed to the mass of reactants before the reaction.

Calculate the mass of sodium carbonate in a solution of unknown concentration.

Situation

You are working for a manufacturing company that makes water-softening agents for homes with hard water. Recently, there was a mix-up on the factory floor, and the sodium carbonate solution in a vat was mistakenly mixed with an unknown quantity of distilled water. You must determine the amount of Na_2CO_3 in the vat in order to properly predict the percent yield of the water-softening product. You have been given a small sample from the 575 L of new solution.

Background

When faced with problems that require them to determine the quantities of a substance by mass, chemists often turn to a technique called gravimetric analysis. In this technique, a small sample of the material undergoes a reaction with an excess of another reactant. The chosen reaction is one which almost always provides a yield near 100%. In other words, all of the reactant of unknown amount will be converted into product. If the mass of the product is carefully measured, you can use stoichiometry calculations such as those in Chapter 8 to determine how much of the reactant of unknown amount was involved in the reaction. Then, by comparing the size of the analysis sample with the size of the original material, you can determine exactly how much of the substance is present.

Professional chemists have expensive instruments available to directly measure amounts of a substance, but techniques such as gravimetric analysis are still useful when cost or equipment availability is an important consideration.

This procedure involves a double-displacement reaction between strontium chloride, $SrCl_2$, and sodium carbonate, Na_2CO_3. In general, this reaction can be used to determine the amount of any carbonate compound in a solution.

Problem

Remember that accurate results depend on precise mass measurements, so keep all glassware very clean, and do not lose any reactants or products during your lab work. You will react an unknown amount of sodium carbonate with an excess of strontium chloride. After purifying the product, you will determine the following.
• how much product is present
• how much Na_2CO_3 must have been present to produce that amount of product
• how much Na_2CO_3 is contained in the 575 L of solution

Safety

Always wear goggles and an apron to protect your eyes and clothing. If you get a chemical in your eyes, immediately flush it out at the eyewash station while calling to your teacher. Know the locations of the emergency lab shower and eyewash and how to use them.

Do not touch any chemicals. If you get a chemical on your skin or clothing, wash it off at the sink while calling to your teacher. Carefully read the labels and follow the directions on all containers of chemicals that you use. Do not taste any chemicals or items used in the laboratory. Never return leftovers to their original containers; take only small amounts to avoid wasting supplies.

Use tongs whenever handling glassware or other equipment that has been heated because when it is hot, it does not look hot.

Always clean up the lab and all equipment after use, and dispose of substances according to proper disposal methods. Wash your hands thoroughly before you leave the lab after all lab work is finished.

Materials

- 0.30 M $SrCl_2$ solution, 45 mL
- Na_2CO_3 solution of unknown concentration, 15 mL
- 100 mL graduated cylinder
- 250 mL beakers, 3
- Balance
- Beaker tongs
- Glass funnel or Büchner funnel with related equipment
- Distilled water
- Drying oven
- Filter paper
- Glass stirring rod
- Paper towels
- Ring and ring stand
- Rubber policeman
- Spatula
- Water bottle

Preparation

1. **Organizing Data**
   Prepare a data table in your lab notebook. It should include spaces for the following.
   - volume of Na_2CO_3 solution added
   - volume of $SrCl_2$ solution added
   - mass of dry filter paper
   - mass of beaker with paper towel
   - mass of beaker with paper towel, filter paper, and precipitate

2. Clean all of the necessary lab equipment with soap and water. Rinse each piece of equipment with distilled water.

3. Measure the mass of a piece of filter paper to the nearest 0.01 g, and record this value in your data table.

4. Set up a filtering apparatus, either a Büchner funnel or a gravity filtration, depending on what equipment is available. Instructions are given in Exploration 1B.

5. Label a paper towel with your name, your class, and the date. Place the towel in a clean, dry 250 mL beaker, and measure and record the mass of the towel and beaker to the nearest 0.01 g.

Technique

6. Measure about 15 mL of the Na_2CO_3 solution into the graduated cylinder. Record this volume to the nearest 0.5 mL in your data table. Pour the Na_2CO_3 solution into a clean, empty 250 mL beaker. Carefully wash the graduated cylinder and rinse it with distilled water.

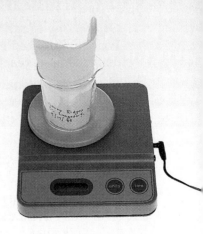

7. Measure about 25 mL of the 0.30 M $SrCl_2$ solution into the graduated cylinder. Record this volume to the nearest 0.5 mL in your data table. Pour the $SrCl_2$ solution into the beaker with the Na_2CO_3 solution. Gently stir the solution and precipitate with a glass stirring rod.

8. Carefully measure another 10 mL of $SrCl_2$ into the graduated cylinder. Record the volume to the nearest 0.5 mL in your data table. Slowly add it to the beaker. Repeat this step until no more precipitate forms.

9. While the precipitate settles, place the filter paper in the funnel, and wet it with a small amount of distilled water so that it will adhere to the sides of the funnel. Then, once the precipitate has settled, slowly pour the mixture into the funnel. Be careful not to overfill the funnel, as that will cause some of the precipitate to be lost between the filter paper and the funnel. Use the rubber spatula to transfer as much of the precipitate into the funnel as possible.

10. Rinse the rubber spatula into the beaker with a small amount of distilled water, and pour this solution into the funnel. Rinse the beaker several more times with small amounts of distilled water, pouring it into the funnel each time.

11. After all of the solution and rinses have drained through the funnel, slowly rinse the precipitate on the filter paper in the funnel with distilled water to remove any soluble impurities.

12. Carefully remove the filter paper from the funnel, and place it on the paper towel that you have labeled with your name. Unfold the filter paper, and place the paper towel, filter paper, and precipitate in the rinsed beaker. Then place the beaker in the drying oven. For best results, allow the precipitate to dry overnight.

Cleanup and Disposal

13. Using beaker tongs, remove your sample from the drying oven, and allow it to cool. Measure and record the mass of the beaker with paper towel, filter paper, and precipitate to the nearest 0.01 g.

14. Dispose of the precipitate in a designated waste container. Pour the filtrate in the other 250 mL beaker into the designated waste container. Clean up your equipment and lab station. Thoroughly wash your hands after completing the lab session and cleanup.

Analysis and Interpretation

1. **Organizing Ideas**
   Write a balanced equation for the reaction. (Hint: it was a double-displacement reaction.)

2. **Organizing Ideas**
   What is the precipitate? Write its empirical formula.

3. **Applying Ideas**
   Calculate the number of moles of precipitate produced in the reaction. (Hint: use the results from item **2**.)

4. **Applying Ideas**
   How many moles of Na_2CO_3 were present in the 15 mL sample? (Hint: use the mole ratio from the equation in item **1**.)

5. Evaluating Methods

There were 0.30 mol of $SrCl_2$ in every liter of solution. Calculate how many moles of $SrCl_2$ were added. Identify whether $SrCl_2$ or Na_2CO_3 was the limiting reactant. Would this lab have worked if the other reactant was chosen as the limiting reactant? Explain why or why not.

6. Evaluating Methods

Why was the precipitate rinsed in Step **11**? What soluble impurities could have been on the filter paper along with the precipitate?

Conclusions

7. Inferring Conclusions

How many grams of Na_2CO_3 were present in the 15 mL sample?

8. Applying Conclusions

How many grams of Na_2CO_3 are present in the 575 L? (Hint: create a conversion factor to convert from the sample with a volume of 15 mL to the entire solution with a volume of 575 L.)

9. Applying Conclusions

For every jar of water-softening product produced at the factory, 155 g of Na_2CO_3 are necessary. How many jars of water-softening product can you make from the 575 L of solution? Would the company be able to fill an order for 40 jars of water-softening product, or would they have to order more Na_2CO_3?

10. Evaluating Methods

How would the calculated results vary if the precipitate wasn't completely dry? Explain your answer.

Extensions

1. Evaluating Methods

Find out from your supervisor what the correct mass of Na_2CO_3 in the sample was, and calculate your percent error.

2. Designing Experiments

What possible sources of error can you identify with your procedure? If you can think of ways to eliminate them, ask your teacher to approve your plan, and run the procedure again.

3. Designing Experiments

In this Exploration, a chemical property of Na_2CO_3 was used to measure how much of it was dissolved in a solution. Design a technique that determines amount using other properties, such as density of solution, pH of solution, electrical resistivity, etc. Describe how to calibrate your method with solutions of known concentration. If your teacher approves your plan, carry it out, and then analyze the unknown using your new technique. Calculate percent error for your measurement.

4. Research and Communications

Research some methods other than gravimetric analysis that are used to measure amounts of substances. How do they work? List advantages and disadvantages of each method. Report back to the class about the method you would select to analyze the amount of Na_2CO_3 in the solution.

GRAVIMETRIC ANALYSIS

Hard Water Testing

EDWARD F. QUIMBY, MAYOR
DANA RUBIO, CITY MANAGER

March 3, 1995

George Taylor, Director of Analysis
CheMystery Labs, Inc.
52 Fulton Street
Springfield, VA 22150

Dear Mr. Taylor:

The city's Public Works Department is investigating new sources of water. One proposal involves drilling new wells into a nearby aquifer that is protected from brackish water by a unique geological formation. Unfortunately, this formation is made of calcium minerals. If the concentration of calcium ions in the water is too high, the water will be "hard," and treating it to meet local water standards would be too expensive for us.

Water containing more than 120 mg of calcium per liter is considered hard. Enclosed is a sample that has been distilled from 1.0 L to its present volume. Please determine whether or not it is of suitable quality.

We are seeking a firm to be our consultant for the entire testing process. Interested firms will be evaluated based on this analysis. We look forward to receiving your report.

Sincerely,

Dana Rubio
City Manager

Required Precautions

 Goggles and lab aprons must be worn at all times.

 Do not touch or taste any chemicals. Wash your hands thoroughly when finished.

 Use beaker tongs to remove glassware from the drying oven.

CheMystery Labs, Inc.

52 Fulton Street
Springfield, VA 22150

Memorandum

Date: March 4, 1995

To: Shane Thompson

From: George Taylor

We must do a very accurate and efficient job on this analysis because
this contract would be valuable for us in terms of both income and
prestige. On the other hand, losing the contract to some out-of-town
analysis firm would be awful!

We still don't have any capital expenditure funds for elaborate
equipment purchases, but we can solve this problem with some careful
gravimetric analysis because calcium salts and carbonate compounds
undergo double-displacement reactions to give insoluble calcium
carbonate as a precipitate.

Before you begin your work, I will need the following information
from you so that I can put together our bid.
- detailed one-page summary of your plan for the procedure along
  with all necessary data tables
- description of necessary calculations
- itemized list of equipment, with total costs (Our financial
  planner tells me that even though we will bill the city for this
  work, we can afford to spend only $200 000 on this project.)

After you complete the analysis, prepare a two-
page report for Dana Rubio. Remember that this
report will be seen by a variety of city officials, so be certain it projects the image we
want to present. Make sure the following items
are included.
- calculation of calcium concentration, in
  mg/L, for the aquifer water
- explanation of how you determined the amount
  of calcium in the sample, including measurements and calculations
- balanced chemical equation for the reaction
- explanations and estimations for any possible sources of error
- detailed invoice for services rendered and
  expenses incurred

References

Refer to pages 276–278 for
information about mass-mass
stoichiometry. The gravimetric
analysis techniques are similar
to those used in an Exploration
you and your team recently
completed. At that time, you
used strontium chloride, $SrCl_2$,
as a reagent to identify the
amount of sodium carbonate,
Na_2CO_3, present in a sample.
In this investigation, you will
use a similar double-displacement reaction, but Na_2CO_3 will
be used as a reagent to identify
how much calcium is present
in a sample. Like strontium
and other Group 2 metals,
calcium salts react with
carbonate-containing salts to
give an insoluble precipitate.

Spill Procedures/
Waste Disposal Methods

- Solids must go in the trash
  can. Do not wash them down
  the sink.
- Liquids may be washed down
  the sink with an excess of
  water.
- Clean the area and all equipment after use.

Materials for
CITY OF SPRINGFIELD

Item	Cost		
REQUIRED ITEMS			
(You must include all of these in your budget.)			
Lab space/fume hood/utilities	15 000 —	/day	
Standard disposal fee	2 000 —	/g of product	
Balance	5 000		
Beaker tongs	1 000		
Drying oven	5 000 —	/day	
REAGENTS and ADDITIONAL EQUIPMENT			
(Include in your budget only what you'll need.)			
0.5 M Na_2CO_3 solution			
250 mL beaker	1 000 —	/mL	
400 mL beaker	1 000		
250 mL flask	2 000		
100 mL graduated cylinder	1 000		
Büchner funnel	1 000		
Filter flask with sink attachment	2 000		
Filter paper	2 000		
Glass funnel	500 —	/piece	
Glass stirring rod	1 000		
Paper clips	1 000		
Ring stand/ring/pipe stem triangle	500 —	/box	
Six test tubes/holder/rack	2 000		
Spatula	2 000		
Wash bottle	500		
Weighing paper	500		
* No refunds on returned chemicals or unused equipment.	500 —	/piece	
Fines			
OSHA safety violation	2 000 —	/incident	

Stoichiometry of Reactions

Objectives

Demonstrate proficiency in measuring masses.

Determine the number of moles of reactants and products in a reaction experimentally.

Use the mass and mole relationships of a chemical reaction in calculations.

Perform calculations that involve density and stoichiometry.

Situation

Your company has a contract to determine the reaction requirements for a large-scale baking operation. The bakery purchases large quantities of ingredients and needs to know the correct proportions to avoid waste or inferior quality. They have determined that they need to produce 425 mL of carbon dioxide, CO_2, for every cake during the rising step that takes place just before baking. The bakery needs you to determine exactly what amount of ingredients are necessary to provide this amount of CO_2.

Background

Some recipes use baking soda, $NaHCO_3$, to make cakes rise. When you add a weak acid such as vinegar, which contains acetic acid, $HC_2H_3O_2$, or buttermilk, which contains lactic acid, $HC_3H_5O_3$, to baking soda, bubbles of carbon dioxide gas are produced. The word equation for the reaction with vinegar is as follows: acetic acid and sodium hydrogen carbonate yields sodium acetate, water, and carbon dioxide. But you can't merely add an excess of baking soda to be sure enough CO_2 is formed because too much baking soda can make the cakes crumbly and bitter tasting. Similarly, too much acid can cause a cake to taste sour. The amount of each reactant must be perfectly matched to produce the correct amount of CO_2, which has a density of 1.25 g/L at baking temperature.

Problem

To figure out the needs of the bakery, you will need to do the following.

- react a carefully measured mass of the reactant, $NaHCO_3$
- measure the mass of the product, $NaC_2H_3O_2$
- determine the mass and mole relationships for the other reactants and products
- calculate the number of moles and mass of each reactant required to produce 425 mL of CO_2

CO_2

$HC_2H_3O_2$

$HC_3H_5O_3$

Safety

Always wear goggles and an apron to provide protection for your eyes and clothing. If you get a chemical in your eyes, immediately flush it out at the eyewash station while calling to your teacher. Know the locations of the emergency lab shower and eyewash and how to use them.

Do not touch any chemicals. If you get a chemical on your skin or clothing, wash it off at the sink while calling to your teacher. Make sure you carefully read the labels and follow the directions on all containers of chemicals that you use. Do not taste any chemicals or items used in the laboratory. Never return leftovers to their original containers; take only small amounts to avoid wasting supplies.

Confine long hair and loose clothing. Do not heat glassware that is broken, chipped, or cracked. Use tongs or a hot mitt to handle heated glassware and other equipment because it does not always look hot. If your clothing catches fire, WALK to the emergency lab shower, and use it to put out the fire.

Never put broken glass or ceramics in a regular waste container. Broken glass or ceramics should be disposed of in a separate container designated by your teacher.

Call your teacher in the event of an acid or base spill. Acid or base spills should be cleaned up promptly, according to your teacher's instructions.

Always clean up the lab and all equipment after use, and dispose of substances according to proper disposal methods. Wash your hands thoroughly before you leave the lab after all lab work is finished.

Materials

- 1.0 M acetic acid
- 2–3 g NaHCO$_3$
- 100 mL graduated cylinder
- Balance
- Beaker tongs
- Bunsen burner and related equipment or hot plate
- Dropper or pipet
- Evaporating dish
- Ring stand and ring (for use with Bunsen burner)
- Spatula
- Watch glass
- Wire gauze with ceramic center (for use with Bunsen burner)

Preparation

1. **Organizing Data**

   Prepare a data table in your lab notebook. It should contain space to record the mass of the empty evaporating dish and watch glass, the mass of the evaporating dish with the watch glass and NaHCO$_3$, and several spaces for recording the mass of the evaporating dish with the watch glass and NaC$_2$H$_3$O$_2$ after heating.

Technique

2. Measure the mass of a clean, dry evaporating dish and watch glass to the nearest 0.01 g. Record this mass in your data table.

3. Add 2–3 g NaHCO$_3$ to your evaporating dish. Measure the mass, with the cover glass, to the nearest 0.01 g. Record this mass in your data table.

4. Slowly add 30 mL of the acetic acid solution to the NaHCO$_3$ in the evaporating dish. Add more acetic acid with a dropper or pipet until the bubbling stops.

5. If you are using a Bunsen burner, place the evaporating dish and its contents on a ceramic-centered wire gauze on an iron ring attached to the ring stand, as shown in the photograph on the left. Place the watch glass, concave side up, on top of the dish, making sure that there is a slight opening for steam to escape. If you are using a hot plate, place the watch glass the same way, but heat the evaporating dish directly on the hot plate.

6. Gently heat the evaporating dish until only a dry solid remains. Make sure that no water droplets remain on the underside of the watch glass. ***Do not heat too rapidly, or the material will boil, and the product will spatter out of the evaporating dish.***

7. Turn off the gas burner or hot plate. Allow the apparatus to cool at least 15 min. Determine the mass of the cooled equipment to the nearest 0.01 g. Record the mass of the dish, residue, and watch glass in your data table.

8. If time permits, reheat the evaporating dish and contents for 2 min. Let it cool and measure its mass again. You can be certain the sample is dry when there are two successive measurements within 0.02 g of each other.

Cleanup and Disposal

9. Dispose of any unused chemicals in the containers designated by your teacher. Wash your hands thoroughly after cleaning up the area and equipment. Make sure to turn off all gas valves.

Analysis and Interpretation

1. **Analyzing Results**
   Write a balanced equation for the reaction of baking soda and acetic acid. Be sure to include states of matter for all of the reactants and products.

2. **Organizing Data**
   Use a periodic table to calculate the molar mass for each of the reactants and products.

3. **Analyzing Results**
   Explain what caused the bubbling when the reaction took place.

4. **Analyzing Methods**
   How do you know that all of the residue is actually sodium acetate rather than a mixture of sodium bicarbonate and sodium acetate?

5. **Organizing Data**
   Calculate the mass of $NaHCO_3$, the number of moles of $NaHCO_3$, the mass of $NaC_2H_3O_2$, and the number of moles of $NaC_2H_3O_2$.

6. **Evaluating Data**
   Using the balanced equation and the amount of $NaHCO_3$, determine the theoretical yield of $NaC_2H_3O_2$ in moles and grams. (Hint: see Chapter 8 for a discussion of theoretical yield, and assume the acetic acid was present in excess.)

Conclusions

7. Analyzing Conclusions

What is the percent yield for your reaction? (Hint: see Chapter 8 for a discussion of percent yield.)

8. Inferring Conclusions

What is the theoretical yield for CO_2? Using the density value given, 1.25 g/L, calculate what volume of CO_2 would be produced by this reaction in an oven. Show your calculations.

9. Applying Conclusions

How many moles of $NaHCO_3$ and $HC_2H_3O_2$ are necessary to produce 425 mL of CO_2 at baking temperature? Show your calculations. (Hint: be sure to include your percent yield for this reaction in your calculations.)

Extensions

1. Inferring Conclusions

Baking soda, $NaHCO_3$, is also known as sodium bicarbonate. Baking *powder* is a mixture of baking soda and another substance, such as cream of tartar. If you add water to baking soda, it dissolves, but water added to baking powder produces CO_2, as shown by the bubbling action. Is cream of tartar acidic or basic?

2. Designing Experiments

If your percent yield is less than 100%, explain why. If you can think of ways to eliminate any problems, ask your teacher to approve your plan, and run the procedure again.

3. Research and Communications

Many recipes for breads use yeast, instead of baking soda, as a source of CO_2. Research the use of yeast and explain what ingredients are necessary for the yeast to produce carbon dioxide. What is the balanced chemical equation for the reaction that yeast use to produce CO_2?

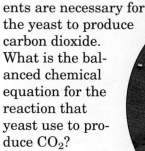

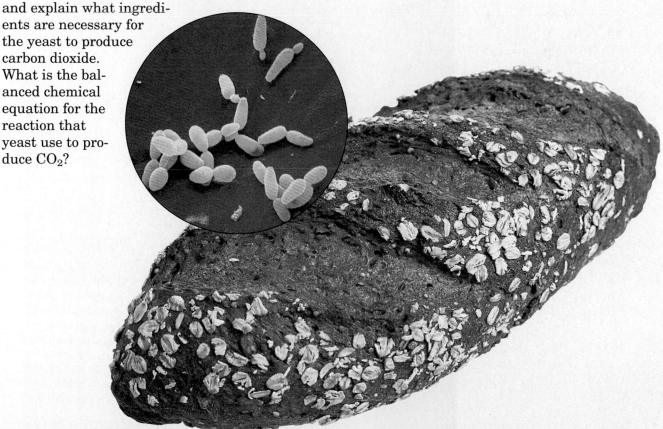

INVESTIGATION 8B

Problem Solving

CDC

Centers for Disease Control

March 7, 1995

Ms. Sandra Fernandez
Director of Development
CheMystery Labs, Inc.
52 Fulton Street
Springfield, VA 22150

Dear Ms. Fernandez:

The CDC has been monitoring reports of a cluster of illnesses near the town of Grover's Corner, New Jersey. Toxicology reports indicate that the disease is spread like viral meningitis, only more quickly. We estimate that irreparable harm to the nervous system occurs approximately 12 hours after initial exposure to the virus. It is imperative that we procure a treatment soon.

Preliminary research indicates that zinc chloride acts as an inhibitor to the reproduction of this unidentified virus. Several companies have been contacted to produce a large quantity of zinc chloride quickly and economically.

Sincerely,

Rhonda Baclig, M.D.
Centers for Disease Control
Special Pathogens Branch

Required Precautions

Lab aprons and goggles must be worn at all times.

Do not touch or taste any chemicals. Always wash your hands thoroughly when finished.

If you get acid or base on your skin or clothing, wash it off at the sink while calling to your teacher. If you get acid or base in your eyes, immediately flush it out at the eyewash while calling to your teacher.

CheMystery Labs, Inc.
52 Fulton Street
Springfield, VA 22150

Memorandum

Date: March 8, 1995

To: Michael Belan

From: Sandra Fernandez

A rush job! If the disease spreads past this town and towards larger cities, an uncontrollable situation will develop very soon. Dr. Baclig has asked several companies to develop procedures for making small amounts of ZnCl₂ for $200 000. Based on the CDC's evaluation, a primary subcontractor will be chosen to prepare the inhibitor in bulk. She needs a preliminary report tomorrow that includes the following.

- detailed one-page summary of your plan for the procedure including a suggested synthesis reaction
- itemized list of equipment, with total costs

After you receive her approval, go ahead. When the work is complete, prepare a two-page letter and a minimum sample of 1.5 grams of the inhibitor to go to Dr. Baclig. She will present them at a joint Center for Disease Control/New Jersey Health Department meeting. Your letter must include the following.

- balanced chemical equation of the reaction you chose for producing the antidote
- molar masses and moles of the reactants and products
- theoretical and actual yield of the product
- percent yield for your antidote, along with a discussion of what you did to keep the yield as high as possible and cost as low as possible
- description of a procedure and cost for producing 37.50 kg of ZnCl₂
- detailed analysis and data sections, showing calculations, along with estimates and explanations of any possible sources of error
- detailed invoice for all expenses and services

References

Refer to page 276 for information on stoichiometric calculations. Pages 287–291 have information on theoretical yield, actual yield, and percent yield. The methods used in this procedure are very dependent upon using clean and dry equipment. Remember that 1.0 M HCl contains 1.0 mol of HCl formula units in every liter.

Spill Procedures/ Waste Disposal Methods

- In case of spills, follow your teacher's instructions.
- All solid and liquid wastes must be disposed of in the containers designated by your teacher.
- Clean the area and all equipment after use.
- Wash your hands when you are finished working in the lab.

Materials for CENTERS FOR DISEASE CONTROL

Item	Cost
REQUIRED ITEMS	
(You must include all of these in your budget.)	
Lab space/fume hood/utilities	15 000 — /day
Standard disposal fee	2 000 — /g of product
Balance	5 000
Bunsen burner/related equipment	10 000
Beaker tongs	1 000
Drying oven	5 000 — /day
REAGENTS and ADDITIONAL EQUIPMENT	
(Include only what you'll need in your budget)	
1.0 M HCl	100 — /mL
1.0 M CaCl₂	1 000 — /mL
MgCl₂	500 — /g
Mossy zinc, Zn	2 000 — /g
NaCl	500 — /g
Zn(NO₃)₂	500 — /g
250 mL beaker	1 000
400 mL beaker	2 000
250 mL flask	1 000
100 mL graduated cylinder	1 000
Evaporating dish	1 000
Filter paper	500 — /piece
Glass funnel	1 000
Glass stirring rod	1 000
Hot plate	8 000
Ring stand/ring/wire gauze	2 000 — /day
Wash bottle	500
Watch glass	1 000
* No refunds on returned chemicals or unused equipment.	
FINES	
OSHA safety violation	2 000/incident

EXPLORATION 9A

Technique Builder

Calorimetry and Hess's Law

Objectives

Demonstrate proficiency in the use of calorimeters and related equipment.

Relate temperature changes to enthalpy changes.

Determine heats of reaction for several reactions.

Demonstrate that heats of reaction can be additive.

Situation

The company you work for has been hired as an expert witness in a lawsuit. A man working for a cleaning firm was told by his employer to pour some old cleaning supplies into a glass container for disposal. Some of the supplies included muriatic or hydrochloric acid, $HCl(aq)$, and a drain cleaner containing lye, $NaOH(s)$. When the substances were mixed, the container shattered, spilling the contents onto the worker's arms and legs. The worker claims that the hot spill caused burns, and he is therefore suing his employer. The employer claims that the worker is lying because the solutions were at room temperature before they were mixed. The employer says that a chemical burn is unlikely because tests after the accident revealed that the mixture had a neutral pH, indicating that the HCl and NaOH were neutralized. The court has asked you to evaluate whether the worker's story is supported by scientific evidence.

Background

Chemicals can be dangerous because of their special storage needs. Acids cannot be stored in metal containers, and organic solvents cannot be kept in plastic ones. Chemicals that are mixed and react are even more dangerous because many reactions release large amounts of heat. Glass, although relatively nonreactive with solutions of pure substances, is heat sensitive and can shatter if there is a sudden change in temperature due to a reaction. Some glassware, such as Pyrex, is heat conditioned but can still fracture under extreme heat conditions, especially if it has been scratched.

Problem

You will carefully measure the amount of heat released by mixing the chemicals. To be sure your results are accurate, you will measure the heat of reaction in two ways. First, you will break the reaction into steps and measure the heat change of each step. Then you will measure the heat change of the reaction when it takes place all at once. When you are finished, you will be able to use the calorimetry equation from Chapter 9 to determine the following.

- the amount of heat evolved during the overall reaction
- the amount of heat for each step
- the amount of heat for the reaction in kilojoules per mole
- whether this heat could have raised the temperature of the water in the solution high enough to cause a burn

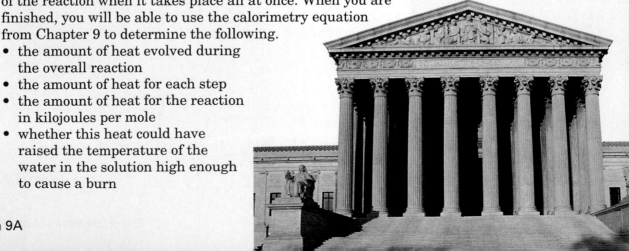

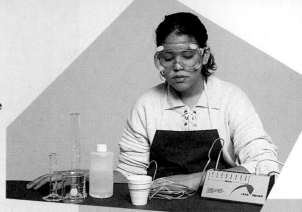

Safety

Always wear goggles and an apron to provide protection for your eyes and clothing. If you get a chemical in your eyes, immediately flush it out at the eyewash station while calling to your teacher. Know the locations of the emergency lab shower and eyewash and how to use them.

Do not touch any chemicals. If you get a chemical on your skin or clothing, wash it off at the sink while calling to your teacher. Make sure you carefully read the labels and follow the directions on all containers of chemicals that you use. Do not taste any chemicals or items used in the laboratory. Never return leftovers to their original containers; take only small amounts to avoid wasting supplies.

Never put broken glass in a regular waste container. Broken glass should be disposed of separately in the container designated by your teacher.

Call your teacher in the event of an acid or base spill. Acid or base spills should be cleaned up promptly, according to your teacher's instructions.

Always clean up the lab and all equipment after use, and dispose of substances according to proper disposal methods. Wash your hands thoroughly before you leave the lab after all lab work is finished.

Materials

- **Distilled water**
- **0.50 M HCl solution, 100 mL**
- **1.0 M HCl solution, 50 mL**
- **1.0 M NaOH solution, 50 mL**
- **NaOH pellets, 4 g**
- **100 mL graduated cylinder**
- **Balance**
- **Glass stirring rod**
- **Plastic foam cups (or calorimeters)**
- **Spatula**
- **Thermometer or LEAP System with thermistor probe**
- **Watch glass**

Preparation

1. **Organizing Data**
   Prepare a data table in your notebook with four columns and four rows. In the first row, label the second through fourth columns *Reaction 1*, *Reaction 2*, and *Reaction 3*. In the first column, label the second through fourth rows: *Volumes of fluid*, *Initial temperature*, and *Highest temperature*. Reactions 1 and 3 will each require two additional spaces to record the mass of the empty watch glass and the mass of the watch glass with NaOH.

2. If you are not using a plastic foam cup as a calorimeter, ask your lab supervisor for instructions on using the calorimeter. At various points in steps **3** through **13**, you will need to measure the temperature of the solution within the calorimeter. If you are using a thermometer, measure the temperature using the instructions given in step **2a**. If you are using a LEAP System with a thermistor probe, measure the temperature according to the instructions given in step **2a**.

   a. Thermometer
   Measure the temperature by gently inserting the thermometer into the hole in the calorimeter lid. The thermometer takes time to reach the same temperature as the solution inside the calorimeter, so wait to be sure you have an accurate reading.
   Thermometers break easily, so be careful with them, and do not use them to stir a solution.

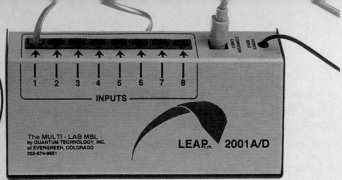

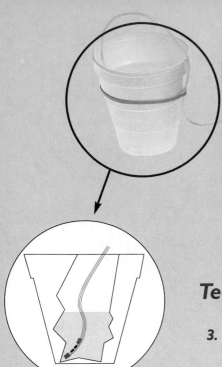

b. LEAP System with thermistor probe

Arrange the thermistor probe as shown. Lay it in the bottom of the calorimeter, and use a rubber band on the outside of the calorimeter to hold the wire for the thermistor probe in place. Then, plug the probe into the LEAP System box attached to the computer.

Technique

Reaction 1

3. Pour about 100 mL of distilled water into a graduated cylinder. Measure and record the volume of the water to the nearest 0.1 mL. Pour the water into your calorimeter. Record the water temperature to the nearest 0.1°C.

4. Determine and record the mass of a clean and dry watch glass to the nearest 0.01 g. Remove the watch glass from the balance. Obtain about 2 g of NaOH pellets, and put them on the watch glass. Measure and record the mass of the watch glass and the pellets to the nearest 0.01 g.

It is important that this step be done quickly because NaOH is "hygroscopic." It absorbs moisture from the air, increasing its mass as long as it remains exposed to the air.

5. Immediately place the NaOH pellets in the calorimeter cup, and gently stir the solution with a stirring rod.
Do not stir with a thermometer.

Place the lid on the calorimeter. Record the highest temperature in the data table. When finished with this reaction, pour the solution into the container designated by your teacher for disposal of basic solutions.

6. Be sure to clean all equipment and rinse it with distilled water before continuing with the next procedure.

Reaction 2

7. Pour about 50 mL of 1.0 M HCl into a graduated cylinder. Measure and record the volume of the HCl solution to the nearest 0.1 mL. Pour the HCl solution into your calorimeter. Record the temperature of the HCl solution to the nearest 0.1°C.

8. Pour about 50 mL of 1.0 M NaOH into a graduated cylinder. Measure and record the volume of the NaOH solution to the nearest 0.1 mL. *For this step only, rinse the thermometer or LEAP thermistor probe in distilled water, and measure the temperature of the NaOH solution in the graduated cylinder to the nearest 0.1°C. Record the temperature in your data table and then replace the thermometer or LEAP thermistor probe in the calorimeter.*

9. Pour the NaOH solution into the calorimeter cup, and stir gently. Place the lid on the calorimeter. Record the highest temperature in the data table. When finished with this reaction, pour the solution into the container designated by your teacher for disposal of mostly neutral solutions.

10. Clean and rinse all equipment before continuing with the next procedure.

Reaction 3

11. Pour about 100 mL of 0.50 M HCl into a graduated cylinder. Measure and record the volume to the nearest 0.1 mL. Pour the HCl solution into your calorimeter. Record the temperature of the HCl solution to the nearest 0.1°C.

12. Measure the mass of a clean and dry watch glass, and record it in your data table. Obtain approximately 2 g of NaOH. Place them on the watch glass, and record the total mass to the nearest 0.01 g. *It is important that this step be done quickly because NaOH is "hygroscopic." It absorbs moisture from the air, increasing its mass as long as it remains exposed to the air.*

13. Immediately place the NaOH pellets in the calorimeter, and gently stir the solution. Place the lid on the calorimeter. Record the highest temperature in the data table. When finished with this reaction, pour the solution into the container designated by your teacher for disposal of mostly neutral solutions.

Cleanup and Disposal

14. Check with your teacher for the proper disposal procedures. Any excess NaOH pellets should be disposed of in the designated container. Always wash your hands thoroughly after cleaning up the lab area and equipment.

Analysis and Interpretation

1. **Organizing Ideas**
   Write a balanced chemical equation for each of the three reactions that you performed. (Hint: be sure to include states of matter for all substances in each equation.)

2. **Organizing Ideas**
   Find a way to get the equation for the total reaction by adding two of the equations from item **1** and then canceling out substances that appear in the same form on both sides of the new equation, as was demonstrated in Chapter 9. (Hint: start with the equation that has a product which is a reactant in a second equation. Add those two equations together.)

3. **Analyzing Methods**
   Explain why a plastic foam cup makes a better calorimeter than a paper cup does.

4. **Organizing Data**
   Calculate the change in temperature (Δt) for each of the reactions.

5. **Organizing Data**
   Assuming that the density of the water and the solutions is 1.00 g/mL, calculate the mass, m, of liquid present for each of the reactions.

6. **Analyzing Results**
   Using the calorimeter equation, calculate the heat released by each reaction. (Hint: use the specific heat capacity of water in your calculations; $c_{p,H_2O} = 4.180$ J/g•°C.)

   Heat $= m \times \Delta t \times c_{p,H_2O}$

7. Organizing Data

Calculate the moles of NaOH used in each of the reactions. (Hint: to find the number of moles in a solution, multiply the volume in liters by the molar concentration.)

8. Analyzing Results

Calculate the ΔH value in terms of kilojoules per mole of NaOH for each of the three reactions.

9. Organizing Ideas

Using your answer to item **2** and your knowledge of Hess's law from Chapter 9, explain how the enthalpies for the three reactions should be mathematically related.

10. Organizing Ideas

Which of the following types of heats of reaction apply to the enthalpies calculated in item **8**: heat of combustion, heat of solution, heat of reaction, heat of fusion, heat of vaporization, and heat of formation?

Conclusions

11. Evaluating Methods

Use your answers from items **8** and **9** to determine the ΔH value for the reaction of solid NaOH with HCl solution by direct measurement and by indirect calculation.

12. Inferring Conclusions

Third-degree burns can occur if skin comes into contact for more than 4 s with water that is hotter than 60°C (140°F). Investigators believe that there were about 55 g of NaOH in the drain cleaner and 450. mL of muriatic acid solution containing a total of 1.35 mol of HCl (a 3.0 M HCl solution). If the initial temperature of the solutions was 25°C, could a mixture that is hot enough to cause burns have resulted?

13. Applying Conclusions

Which chemical is the limiting reactant, given the amounts in item **12**? How many moles of the other reactant remained unreacted?

14. Applying Conclusions

What molar amounts of each reactant would be necessary for a reaction that heats 450. mL of water from 25°C to 40°C, a much safer temperature?

Extensions

1. Designing Experiments

What possible sources of error can you identify with this procedure? If you can think of ways to eliminate them, ask your teacher to approve your plan, and run the procedure again.

2. Designing Experiments

When you work with a calorimeter, the assumptions are made that the heat energy from the reaction is used entirely to heat the water and that no heat energy escapes the calorimeter. With this in mind, design a better calorimeter. If your teacher approves your plan, build an improved calorimeter, and run the procedure again.

3. **Applying Ideas**

   How could you determine the maximum temperature that laboratory glassware can withstand? Explain your answers.

4. **Applying Ideas**

   When chemists make solutions from NaOH pellets, they often keep the solution in an ice bath. Explain why.

5. **Applying Ideas**

   When a strongly acidic or basic solution is spilled on a person, the first step is to dilute it by washing the area of the spill with a lot of water. Explain why adding an acid or base to neutralize the solution immediately is not a good idea.

6. **Evaluating Methods**

   You have worked with heats of solution for exothermic reactions. Could the same type of procedure be used to determine the temperature changes for endothermic reactions? How would the procedure stay the same? What would change about the procedure and the data?

7. **Applying Ideas**

   Thinking that two cleaners should be better than one, someone mixes a drain cleaner containing NaOH with a toilet-bowl cleaner containing HCl. Will this make a better cleanser than either of the substances alone? Explain your answer.

8. **Applying Ideas**

   A chemical supply company is going to ship NaOH pellets to a very humid place, and they've asked for your advice on packaging. Design a package for the NaOH pellets. Explain the advantages of your package's design and materials. (Hint: remember that the reaction in which NaOH absorbs moisture from the air is an exothermic one, and NaOH reacts exothermically with other compounds as well.)

9. **Inferring Conclusions**

   Which is more stable: solid NaOH or NaOH solution? Explain your answer.

10. **Designing Experiments**

    In this experiment, the calorimeter was used to measure the temperature change when two dilute solutions react. Because the solutions were dilute, it was assumed that the mixture had the same specific heat capacity as pure water. Design an experiment to determine the specific heat capacity of the solution after the reaction. If your teacher approves of your plan, test it. Using the new specific heat capacity value, recalculate the ΔH values for Reactions 2 and 3, and check to see if the adjusted results are better than your original ones.

CALORIMETRY Biological Incubator

BPS◆

Bio-Pharmaceutical Supplies

March 13, 1995

Sandra Fernandez
Director of Development
CheMystery Labs, Inc.
52 Fulton Street
Springfield, VA 22150

Dear Ms. Fernandez:

Recently, customers have written to us concerning problems they have had with a bacteria-screening test we developed. The test requires that a bacteria culture be taken and kept at body temperature for a short time while the reagents react.

Physicians and nurses trying to use our bacteria-screening test have found it difficult to keep the bacteria warm enough for the length of time needed for the test. We want to offer them a portable chemical heater that can be contained in a sealed package underneath the culture. The heater must keep the culture between 35°C and 40°C for at least five minutes.

We are soliciting bids from different firms for the development of such a product. Please send an estimate of your costs to investigate the problem. We will select a firm to develop the product based on costs required for your initial investigation.

Sharon Palmer, Ph.D.
Director of Research
Bio-Pharmaceutical Supplies

Required Precautions

 Goggles and lab aprons must be worn at all times in the laboratory.

 Do not touch or taste any chemicals. Always wash your hands thoroughly before you leave the lab after all lab work is finished.

 When you get acid or base on your skin or clothing, wash it off at the sink while calling to your teacher. If you get acid or base in your eyes, immediately flush it out at the eyewash while calling to your teacher.

CheMystery Labs, Inc.
52 Fulton Street
Springfield, VA 22150

Memorandum

Date: March 14, 1995

To: Edward Untermeyer

From: Sandra Fernandez

We are competing for this contract, so we must work quickly. The more common and easily accessible the ingredients are, the better. For this reason, I suggest that you explore the possibilities of using the reaction of solid sodium hydroxide, NaOH(s), and one molar hydrochloric acid solution, HCl(aq). Use a 50 mL beaker with 20 mL of distilled water to model the culture. Use a 250 mL beaker as the heating system. You may need to show some creativity in figuring a way to keep the temperature at the right level for five minutes.

Before you begin your work, I need the following items from you.
- detailed one-page summary of your plans for making the heater and for a testing procedure to make sure it works
- list of supplies, with itemized and total costs

When you complete the project, prepare a two-page report that includes the following information for the client.
- results of a five-minute temperature test of the reaction
- moles and masses of each reactant used and discussion of the time periods for the completion of each trial
- balanced chemical equation for the reaction, including the enthalpy change for one mole of HCl and one mole of NaOH
- detailed and organized data and analysis sections, showing calculations
- detailed invoice of all expenses and services

References
Refer to pages 316–318 for more information about measuring heats of reaction and specific heat capacity. The reaction is similar to one your team recently completed, and your conclusions about the heat of reaction for the neutralization may prove useful now. Remember that the number of moles of a compound dissolved in a solution can be determined by multiplying the volume in liters by the molar concentration.

Spill Procedures/ Waste Disposal Methods
- In case of spills, follow your teacher's instructions.
- Place the neutralized solutions and any leftover acid or base solutions or NaOH pellets in the separate disposal containers designated by the teacher. Do not wash these solutions down the drain. Do not place NaOH pellets in the trash.

Materials
BIO-PHARMACEUTICAL SUPPLIES

Item	Cost	1	2	3
REQUIRED ITEMS				
(You must include all of these in your budget.)				
Lab space/fume hood/utilities	15 000 — /day			
Standard disposal fee	2 000 — /g of product			
Balance	5 000			
REAGENTS and ADDITIONAL EQUIPMENT				
(Include in your budget only what you'll need.)				
1.0 M HCl				
NaOH pellets	500 — /mL			
50 mL beaker	5 000 — /g			
250 mL beaker	1 000			
250 mL flask	1 000			
100 mL graduated cylinder	1 000			
Crucible and cover	1 000			
Filter paper	5 000			
Glass funnel	500 — /piece			
Glass stirring rod	1 000			
Plastic foam cup/calorimeter	1 000			
Ring stand/ring/wire gauze	1 000			
Six test tubes/holder/rack	2 000			
Spatula	2 000			
Thermistor—LEAP	500			
Thermometer	2 000			
Wash bottle	2 000			
Watch glass	500			
Zipper-sealed plastic bag	1 000			
* No refunds on returned chemicals or unused equipment.	1 000			

FINES
OSHA safety violation	2 000 — /incident

EXPLORATION 9B

Technique Builder

Energy Requirements and Food Testing

Situation

You work for a chemical analysis firm that has been hired by a group of dietitians to analyze food in order to plan the meals of the U.S. Olympic Team. The athlete's meals must contain plenty of sources of energy, as well as the protein they need for healthy muscles. Foods that are very fatty or oily are not recommended.

Background

As discussed in Chapter 9, food contains nutrients, most of which are naturally formed organic polymers, sometimes called *macromolecules.* The three primary types of macromolecules are *carbohydrates, lipids,* and *proteins.*

Carbohydrates are broken down by organisms to provide energy. The empirical formula for a carbohydrate is CH_2O, as indicated by the two parts of the name, *carbo-* and *-hydrate.* Sugars are relatively small carbohydrates that usually have several alcohol functional groups and an aldehyde or ketone group as well.

Many sugar molecules are able to link together to form polymer chains. One polymer of glucose is a molecule called *starch,* which plants use as a form of stored energy.

Lipids provide long-term energy storage for organisms. Lipids exist in several types, but all dissolve poorly in water. Fatty acids are the structural subunits for lipids in the diet. They consist of long hydrocarbon chains with a carboxylic acid functional group on one end.

Proteins are another type of polymer. In proteins, the monomers are amino acids, molecules containing both the amine and carboxylic acid functional groups. These molecules are used by the body to make enzymes, hormones, and substances that make up the body's structure. Proteins are not usually used as a primary energy source.

In addition to carbohydrates, lipids, and proteins, people need another type of nutrient—*vitamins*, which are molecules that play a very specific role in metabolic reactions.

Glucose

Problem

To help the dietitians analyze the foods, you will need to do the following.
- check samples of known composition so that you will know what positive tests look like
- perform the tests on the food samples
- based on the results, make recommendations on whether to include these foods in the athletes' meals

Safety

Always wear goggles and an apron to provide protection for your eyes and clothing. If you get a chemical in your eyes, immediately flush it out at the eyewash station while calling to your teacher. Know the locations of the emergency lab shower and eyewash and how to use them.

Do not touch any chemicals. If you get a chemical on your skin or clothing, wash it off at the sink while calling to your teacher. Make sure you carefully read the labels and follow the directions on all containers of chemicals that you use. Do not taste any chemicals or items used in the laboratory. Never return leftovers to their original containers; take only small amounts to avoid wasting supplies.

Use tongs whenever handling glassware or other equipment that has been heated because when it is hot, it does not look hot. Keep the brown paper away from the hot plate.

Because the isopropanol is flammable, no Bunsen burners or other open flames should be in use during this lab. Hot plates can also be a source of ignition; carry out all work with isopropanol and Lugol's solution in a hood as far away from any hot plates as possible.

Always clean up the lab and all equipment after use, and dispose of substances according to proper disposal methods. Wash your hands thoroughly before you leave the lab after all lab work is finished.

Materials

- 1% starch solution
- Benedict's solution
- Biuret reagent
- Distilled water
- Food samples
- Gelatin, dissolved
- Glucose solution
- Isopropanol
- Lugol's iodine solution in dropper bottle
- Shortening
- Vitamin C solution
- 10 mL graduated cylinder
- 250 mL beaker
- Beaker tongs
- Brown wrapping paper
- Hot plate
- Pipet or medicine dropper
- Test tubes, 6
- Test tube holder
- Test tube rack

Preparation

1. Organizing Data

Prepare a data table in your lab notebook with six rows. Be sure there is plenty of room within the boxes to describe the results of the reactions. The boxes in the first row should be labeled *Nutrient, Reagent, Positive test,* and *Negative test (H₂O)*. Then, make enough additional columns so that there is one for each sample of food you will test. In the first column, label the second through six rows *Sugar, Starch, Protein, Vitamin C* and *Lipid*.

2. Label two test tubes *Positive test* and *Negative test (H₂O),* and then label an additional test tube with the name of each food you will test.

Technique

Sugar Test

3. Using a graduated cylinder, measure about 5 mL of distilled water, and pour it into the test tube labeled *Negative test.*

4. Using a graduated cylinder, measure about 5 mL of the glucose solution, and pour it into the test tube labeled *Positive test.*

5. For each of the samples of food to be tested, add about 5 mL of the food to the appropriately labeled test tube.

6. To test for sugar, add 5 mL of Benedict's solution to each of the test tubes.

7. Fill a 250 mL beaker about two-thirds full with water. Place the test tubes in the beaker using the test-tube holder.

8. Place the beaker with the test tubes on a hot plate, and heat for approximately 5 min. Use beaker tongs to remove the beaker.

9. Record any color changes in the test tubes after the heating is completed.

10. Pick up the test tubes with a test-tube holder. After they have cooled, empty the test tubes into the disposal containers designated by your teacher for sugar and protein tests. Clean all of the test tubes and the graduated cylinder thoroughly, but keep the labels on the test tubes.

Starch Test

11. Using a graduated cylinder, measure about 5 mL of distilled water into the test tube labeled *Negative test*. Measure about 5 mL of the starch solution, and pour it into the test tube labeled *Positive test*.

12. For each of the samples of food to be tested, add about 5mL of the food to the appropriately labeled test tube.

13. To test for starch, add about 1 mL of Lugol's iodine solution to each of the test tubes, and record any color changes in the test tubes.

14. Empty the test tubes into the disposal containers designated by your teacher for starch and vitamin C tests. Clean all of the test tubes and the graduated cylinder thoroughly, but keep the labels on the test tubes.

Protein Test

15. Using a graduated cylinder, measure about 5 mL of distilled water into the test tube labeled *Negative test*. Measure about 5 mL of the dissolved gelatin, which contains protein, and pour it into the test tube labeled *Positive test*.

16. For each of the samples of food to be tested, add about 5 mL of the food to the appropriately labeled test tube.

17. To test for proteins, add about 1 mL of biuret reagent, and record any color changes in the test tubes.

18. Empty the test tubes into the disposal containers designated by your teacher for sugar and protein tests. Clean all of the test tubes and the graduated cylinder thoroughly, but keep the labels on the test tubes.

Vitamin C Test

19. Place 5 drops of distilled water in the test tube labeled *Negative test*, and 5 drops of vitamin C solution in the test tube labeled *Positive test*.

20. For each of the samples of food to be tested, add about 5 drops of the liquid part of the food to the appropriately labeled test tube.

21. Put one drop of the 1% starch solution into each of the test tubes to be tested. For each test tube, add and count drops of iodine solution, one by one, until the solution in the test tube turns blue-purple and remains that color for at least 15 s. Record the number of drops in your data table in the *Vitamin C* column.

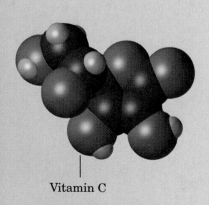

Vitamin C

22. Empty the test tubes into the disposal containers designated by your teacher for starch and vitamin C tests. Clean all of the test tubes and the graduated cylinder thoroughly, but keep the labels on the test tubes.

Lipid Test

23. Measure about 2 mL of distilled water into the test tube labeled *Negative test*. Measure about 2 mL of shortening into the test tube labeled *Positive test*.

24. For each of the food samples, place about 2 mL of the food in the appropriate test tubes.

25. To test for lipids, add 5 mL of isopropanol to each sample. Mix the samples, and allow them to sit for about 10 minutes.

26. For each test tube, pour about 2–3 mL of the liquid from each test tube onto a clean part of the brown paper. Record your observations in the data table.

Cleanup and Disposal

27. The used brown paper from the lipid test may be put in the trash can. Liquids from the lipid test should be poured into their own designated disposal container. Leftover test solutions can be placed in the disposal containers designated by your teacher. Benedict's solution and biuret reagent can be disposed of together along with solutions from sugar and protein test. Starch and iodine solutions can be disposed of together along with solutions from starch and vitamin C tests.

Analysis and Interpretation

1. Evaluating Methods

Which tests were quantitative tests, ones that measured how much of a substance there was in a sample? Which were qualitative, ones that only measured whether a substance was present?

Conclusion

2. Applying Conclusions

Write a paragraph summarizing your recommendations. Which tested foods should be given to athletes? Why?

Extensions

1. Applying Ideas

Nutritional tables are available in many sources, including the *CRC Handbook of Chemistry and Physics*. Look up the foods you tested, and determine the amounts of sugar, starch, protein, and lipids in them. Using the equations given in Chapter 9, calculate the number of kilojoules of energy that would be provided by a 175 g serving of each of the foods you tested.

2. Applying Ideas

Keep a written record of the quantities of foods you consume in a single day. Look up the nutrient composition of each food and classify the foods depending on whether they contain primarily carbohydrates, proteins, or lipids.

FOOD TESTING

Baby-Food Label Fraud

Center for Food Safety and Applied Nutrition

FOOD AND DRUG ADMINISTRATION

6500 Fishers Lane · Rockville, MD 20857

Memorandum

Date: March 14, 1995

To: Analytical Chemist Contractors

From: R. T. Gutierrez, Infant Foods Division

Re: False advertising in "natural" baby foods

Recently, the Food and Drug Administration (FDA) has received a number of complaints about false advertising in some brands of baby foods. Spot checks by FDA's investigators have turned up a number of infractions of food labeling laws.

For example, some foods labeled as containing no starch or sugar actually contained these substances. Others advertised as "high in protein" contained no protein. It is important that these fraudulent companies are identified and prosecuted quickly.

The FDA has received authorization to request bids from private contractors to perform testing of three different brands of baby food on the market for sugar, lipids, starch, vitamin C, and protein.

Required Precautions

Goggles and lab aprons must be worn at all times.

Do not touch or taste any chemicals. Wash your hands thoroughly when finished.

Use tongs to handle equipment that has been heated.

Isopropanol is flammable. No open flames should be used during this lab. Keep isopropanol in the hood, away from hot plates.

Memorandum

CheMystery Labs, Inc.
52 Fulton Street
Springfield, VA 22150

Date: March 15, 1995

To: Frederica Sanchez

From: George Taylor

You know as well as I do that getting on the FDA's list of contractors would help us put the company on top. I'm counting on you to do a good job on this one.

Send Gutierrez a two-page letter containing our bid as soon as possible. She will need details on the following items.
- plan for our measurement procedure and any necessary data tables
- detailed list of the equipment and materials needed, along with the costs (Don't forget to include labor costs as a part of the bid!)

Once you get approval, begin work immediately. We want to impress the FDA with our quickness and efficiency! When you are finished, immediately send a two-page letter that includes the following.
- your recommendations of companies to be prosecuted, with explanations
- description of the tests performed, including discussion of positive and negative test standards
- complete report of your data
- detailed invoice showing all costs, services, and time for work

References
Refer to page 319 for more information on fats, carbohydrates, and proteins. The tests for the different nutrients and additives are the same as ones your team recently completed. Be very careful in observing results because the color of the food may interfere with proper reading of the indicator. It may help to dilute some of the food with water so that the results can be seen more easily.

Spill Procedures/ Waste Disposal Methods
- In case of a spill, follow your teacher's instructions.
- Put excess chemicals and solutions in the containers designated by your teacher. Do not pour them down the sink or place them in the trash can unless specifically instructed to do so by your teacher.
- Pieces of brown paper may be thrown into the garbage can.

Materials for FDA

Item	Cost	1	2	3
REQUIRED ITEMS (You must include all of these in your budget.)				
Lab space/fume hood/utilities	15 000 — /day			
Beaker tongs	1 000			
Standard disposal fee	2 000 — /g of product			
Hot plate	8 000			
REAGENTS and ADDITIONAL EQUIPMENT (Include in your budget only what you'll need.)				
1% starch solution	500 — /drop			
Benedict's solution	2 000 — /mL			
Biuret reagent	2 000 — /mL			
Brown paper	500 — /sheet			
Isopropanol	1 000 — /mL			
Lugol's iodine	2 000 — /mL			
250 mL beaker	1 000			
250 mL flask	1 000			
10 mL graduated cylinder	1 000			
Glass funnel	1 000			
Glass stirring rod	1 000			
Litmus paper	1 000 — /piece			
Paper clips	500 — /box			
Ring stand/ring/pipe stem triangle	2 000			
Ruler	500			
Six test tubes/holder/rack	2 000			
Spatula	500			
Weighing paper	500 — /piece			
* No refunds on returned chemicals or unused equipment.				
Fines				
OSHA safety violation	2 000 — /incident			

GAS DIFFUSION

Industrial Spill

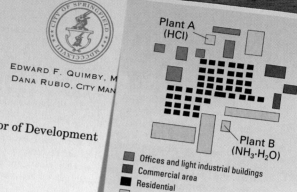

Plant A (HCl)

Plant B (NH₃·H₂O)

Offices and light industrial buildings
Commercial area
Residential
Manufacturing

1 km

March 17, 1995

Sandra Fernandez, Director of Development
CheMystery Labs, Inc.
52 Fulton Street
Springfield, VA 22150

EDWARD F. QUIMBY, M
DANA RUBIO, CITY MAN

Dear Ms. Fernandez:

Your company has been commissioned by the city's Hazardous Waste and Emergency Response Commission (H.W.E.R.C.) to model a chemical disaster. Recently, two new chemical plants have been built on the perimeter of our city in compliance with our new zoning laws. One plant manufactures hydrochloric acid, and the other manufactures ammonia water (NH₃•H₂O, or NH₄OH).

Residents are concerned about a dangerous release of chemicals from the factories. We know about the dangers of a spill at each one. Recently, however, city officials were made aware that a cloud of toxic material could form if fumes from both plants combined.

Attached is a map showing the chemical plants. Determine the likeliest location for a toxic combination, and calculate the necessary response time for local agencies. H.W.E.R.C. will evaluate reports and bids to select a company to serve as the chemical response team in the event of a local emergency.

Sincerely,

Dana Rubio
City Manager

Required Precautions

Goggles and lab aprons must be worn at all times.

Do not touch or taste any chemicals. Wash your hands thoroughly when finished.

Avoid breathing fumes from these chemicals.

If you get acid or base on your skin or clothing, wash it off at the sink while calling to your teacher. If you get acid or base in your eyes, immediately flush it out at the eyewash station while calling to your teacher.

Memorandum

CheMystery Labs, Inc.
52 Fulton Street
Springfield, VA 22150

Date: March 18, 1995

To: Greg Buntz

From: Sandra Fernandez

The previous work we did with the city has paid off. But this contract means more than just money for us. We are in competition with several companies from nearby towns to be the local response team, and many of our employees live in Springfield. My idea for modeling the spill is to take a piece of plastic tubing, such as a piece from an extra long micropipet, and insert two cotton swabs in either end. Each swab will be soaked in solutions of one of the chemicals. Then, we can observe the fumes without making the lab into a disaster area.

I need a preliminary plan from you that includes the following.
- detailed one-page summary of the procedure, including your plans for measurements, that will enable you to calculate the necessary response time and the likeliest location of the toxic product
- balanced chemical equation for the reaction
- theoretical calculations of molecular velocity ratios for the two compounds
- itemized list of materials, with costs

When you've finished, prepare a two-page letter to Dana Rubio that includes the following.
- approximate time elapsed and location of the toxic interaction
- summary of the model and a discussion of its limitations
- theoretical and experimental molecular velocity ratios
- detailed analysis, including a balanced chemical equation, with calculations for Graham's law and experimental errors
- detailed and organized data tables
- detailed invoice for materials and services

Spill Procedures/ Waste Disposal Methods

- In case of spills, follow your teacher's instructions.

- Do not pour any solutions down the drain. Do not place any material in the trash can.

- Dispose of the swabs in the designated waste container.

- To clean the deposit from the middle of the pipet tube, rinse with 10 mL of 1.0 M NaOH, and pour the rinse into the disposal container designated by your teacher.

- Clean the area and all equipment.

Materials for CITY OF SPRINGFIELD

Item	Cost		
REQUIRED ITEMS (You must include all of these in your budget.)			
Lab space/fume hood/utilities			
Standard disposal fee	15 000 — /day		
	2 000 — /g of product		
REAGENTS and ADDITIONAL EQUIPMENT (Include in your budget only what you'll need.)			
1.0 M HCl			
1.0 M NaOH	500 — /mL		
1.0 M NH₃·H₂O	500 — /mL		
250 mL beaker	500 — /mL		
100 mL graduated cylinder	1 000		
Aluminum foil	1 000		
Balance	1 000 — /cm²		
Cotton swab	5 000		
Glass stirring rod	500		
Grease pencil	1 000		
Litmus paper	500		
Plastic pipet, extra long	1 000 — /piece		
Ring stand with buret clamp	1 000		
Ruler	2 000		
Scissors	500		
Six test tubes/holder/rack	500		
Spatula	2 000		
Stopwatch	500		
Wash bottle	5 000		
* No refunds on returned chemicals or unused equipment.	500		
FINES			
OSHA safety violation	2 000 — /incident		

GAS STOICHIOMETRY
Fire Suppression System

Lyon + Abel

March 20, 1995

Director of Development
CheMystery Labs, Inc.
52 Fulton Street
Springfield, VA 22150

Dear Director:

Our small printing company needs to update our fire extinguisher system immediately to avoid losing our insurance. With our high-tech equipment and computers, a standard water sprinkler system is inappropriate. We understand that buildings with electronic equipment usually have fire suppression systems that use a nonreactive gas.

Because we are planning to move soon to a new location, we would like your firm to develop a short-term fix for our current extinguishing needs. Consider using carbon dioxide, CO_2, produced by a reaction between 1.0 M HCl solution and $NaHCO_3$ powder. The reaction vessel may be located inside or outside the building. Design requirements are enclosed.

Sincerely,

Greg Lyon

Greg Lyon
Vice-President
Lyon and Abel Printing Incorporated

Required Precautions

 Goggles and lab aprons must be worn at all times in the laboratory.

 If you get acid or base on your skin or clothing, wash it off at the sink while calling to your teacher. If you get acid or base in your eyes, immediately flush it out at the eyewash while calling to your teacher.

 Do not touch or taste any chemicals. Always wash your hands thoroughly when finished.

Memorandum

CheMystery Labs, Inc.
52 Fulton Street
Springfield, VA 22150

Date: March 21, 1995

To: Brad Bishop

From: Sandra Fernandez

We have been contacted about a $250 000 job. As part of the job, we will need to build a cardboard 1:100 scale model of the facility. The model should be 30 cm long, 15 cm wide, and 10 cm high, according to the plan of the facility shown at right. Tea candles will be used to represent simultaneous fires in each room. You can save money if you have the box, glue, tape, and candles that you can bring from home.

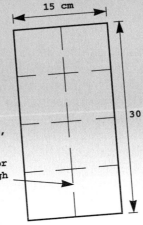

model's interior walls 10 cm high →

I need your design for an extinguishing system soon, along with the following.
- detailed one-page summary of your plans, including sketches if necessary
- itemized list of materials, with total costs
- stoichiometric calculations of the amount of reactants required to produce enough gas to extinguish the fires Remember that some gas may be lost prior to its use as a fire extinguisher.

After you finish testing your design model, prepare a two-page report for Mr. Lyon that includes the following.
- description of the delivery system, including sketches if necessary
- balanced chemical equation for the CO_2-producing reaction
- results of the candle-extinguishing tests
- detailed and organized data and analysis sections
- calculations of amounts necessary for the full-scale system
- detailed invoice with costs for equipment, materials, and services

References

Refer to pages 384–386 for more information on stoichiometric calculations involving gases. Remember, 1.0 M HCl solution contains 1.0 mol/liter. Build your model at home first. Cut notches in the box for the walls and then glue or tape the walls into place. Be creative with your delivery system design, but plan it out on paper first. Get others' opinions on your system before trying it out. If you (and anyone else observing) wear goggles and lab aprons, you can try your system out at home first with $NaHCO_3$ (baking soda) and CH_3COOH (in vinegar) as your reactants for producing CO_2 gas. Base your costs for disposal on the amount of NaCl produced.

Materials for LYON and ABEL PRINTING

Item	Cost	2	3
REQUIRED ITEMS (You must include all of these in your budget.)			
Lab space/fume hood/utilities	15 000 — /day		
Standard disposal fee	2 000 — /g of product		
Balance	5 000		
REAGENTS and ADDITIONAL EQUIPMENT (Include in your budget only what you'll need.)			
1.0 M HCl	500 — /mL		
$NaHCO_3$	500 — /g		
250 mL beaker	1 000		
2 L plastic bottle	2 000		
250 mL flask	1 000		
100 mL graduated cylinder	1 000		
Cardboard box	500		
Duct tape	500 — /cm		
Glass funnel	1 000		
Glue	500		
Plastic straw, bendable	500		
Rubber tubing	500 — /10 cm		
Ring stand/ring/buret clamp	2 000		
Rubber stopper, one hole	1 000 — /cm		
Scissors	500		
Spatula	500		
Tea candle	500		
Wash bottle	500		
Weighing paper	500 — /piece		
* No refunds on returned chemicals or unused equipment.			

FINES
OSHA safety violation	2 000/incident

Colorimetry and Molarity

Objectives

Demonstrate **proficiency in preparing a solution and performing colorimetric measurements or observations.**

Relate **colorimetric measurements or observations to concentration.**

Determine **the molarity of a solution of unknown concentration.**

Situation

You are working in the quality control department of a pharmaceutical company. One of the company's products is a test solution for phenylketonuria. The test solution should contain iron(III) chloride, $FeCl_3$, at a concentration of 0.30 M. Lately there have been some problems in the production line in the factory. It is important that you analyze the solution to make sure it is of the proper concentration. If it is too dilute, the color change might not be noticeable enough. If it is too strong, the production process is wasting money by putting too much $FeCl_3$ in the solution.

Background

Doctors can use the $FeCl_3$ test solution to detect phenylketonuria in infants. People who have this disease are unable to break down the amino acid phenylalanine. If they eat foods containing too much phenylalanine, the toxic byproducts made when it is not completely broken down can make them sick. In the screening test, a few drops of the solution are sprinkled on a baby's wet diaper. If the solution turns a deep bluish green color, phenylpyruvic acid, a product of incomplete phenylketonuria metabolism, is present. Then a special diet with very small amounts of phenylalanine is prescribed for the child.

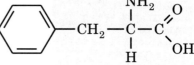

Phenylalanine

Problem

Phenyl-alanine

Like many solutions, $FeCl_3$ is colored, and in general, the more concentrated the solution, the darker its color will be. This is the basis for colorimetry, in which the color of a solution is used as a measure of its concentration. According to a relationship known as Beer's law, the amount of light of a specific wavelength that the solution absorbs, its absorbance, is proportional to its concentration. In some cases, there are slight deviations from Beer's law, so the graph of the relationship is a curve instead of a straight line. To determine the concentration of the sample pulled from the factory's production line, you must do the following.

- make several standard solutions of known concentration
- if special equipment such as a LEAP colormeter or a spectrophotometer are available, make a graph of absorbance vs. concentration
- compare the solutions of known concentration to the unknown to determine the concentration of the unknown
- compare this extrapolation to the expected value, 0.30 M

Safety

Always wear goggles and an apron to provide protection for your eyes and clothing. If you get a chemical in your eyes, immediately flush it out at the eyewash station while calling to your teacher. Know the locations of the emergency lab shower and eyewash and how to use them.

Do not touch any chemicals. If you get a chemical on your skin or clothing, wash it off at the sink while calling to your teacher. Make sure you carefully read the labels and follow the directions on all containers of chemicals that you use. Do not taste any chemicals or items used in the laboratory. Never return leftovers to their original containers; take only small amounts to avoid wasting supplies.

Always clean up the lab and all equipment after use, and dispose of substances according to proper disposal methods. Wash your hands thoroughly before you leave the lab after all lab work is finished.

Preparation

1. Organizing Data

Prepare a data table in your lab notebook. It should have eight columns and five rows if you use the LEAP colormeter or a spectrophotometer, and four rows if this equipment will not be used. In the first row, label the boxes in the second through eighth columns *Test tube 0*, *Test tube 1*, *Test tube 2*, *Test tube 3*, *Test tube 4*, *Test tube 5*, and *Unknown*. In the first column, label the second box *mL 0.50 M FeCl₃*, the third box *mL H₂O*, and the fourth box *Estimates*. If you are using a colormeter or a spectrophotometer, label the fifth box in the first column *Measurements*. You will also need space for calculations.

2. Label seven test tubes *0, 1, 2, 3, 4, 5,* and *Unknown*. Label the beaker *Waste*.

3. If you will be using a spectrophotometer, turn it on now, because it must warm up for approximately 10 min.

4. Using a periodic table, determine the molar mass of $FeCl_3 \cdot 6H_2O$. Record it in your lab notebook.

5. Perform the necessary calculations to determine how many grams of $FeCl_3 \cdot 6H_2O$ would be needed to make 250 mL of a 0.50 M solution. Record this amount in your lab notebook.

Technique

Solution Preparation

6. Using the appropriate technique described in Chapter 11 and the amount calculated in step **5**, prepare 250 mL of a 0.50 M standard solution using $FeCl_3 \cdot 6H_2O$. Dilute the solution to 250 mL with 25 mL of 1.0 M HCl and more distilled water. Be sure to measure to the nearest 0.01 g. Record the amount used in your lab notebook.

Materials

- **Distilled water**
- **1.0 M HCl**
- **$FeCl_3 \cdot 6H_2O$ crystals**
- **10 mL graduated cylinder**
- **250 mL beaker**
- **250 mL volumetric flask**
- **Glass stirring rod**
- **Test tubes, 7**
- **Test tube rack**
- **Unknown solution**

Optional equipment

- **LEAP System with colormeter**
- **Spectrophotometer**
- **Cuvettes**
- **Lint-free wipes for cuvettes**

7. Place the test tubes in a test tube rack. Measure 10.0 mL of distilled water into the graduated cylinder. Pour it into test tube *0*.

8. Pour 2.0 mL of the 0.50 M $FeCl_3$ standard solution into a 10 mL graduated cylinder, and dilute it with distilled water to a total volume of 10.0 mL. Mix the solution with a glass stirring rod. Pour this solution into test tube *1*. Rinse the graduated cylinder and stirring rod with distilled water, and discard the rinse in the *Waste* beaker. Record the amounts of the solution and H_2O in your data table.

9. Pour 4.0 mL of the 0.50 M $FeCl_3$ standard solution into a 10 mL graduated cylinder, and dilute it with distilled water to a total volume of 10.0 mL. Mix the solution with a glass stirring rod. Pour this solution into test tube *2*. Rinse the graduated cylinder and stirring rod with distilled water, and discard the rinse in the *Waste* beaker. Record the amounts of the solution and H_2O in your data table.

10. Pour 6.0 mL of the 0.50 M $FeCl_3$ standard solution into a 10 mL graduated cylinder, and dilute it with distilled water to a total volume of 10.0 mL. Mix the solution with a glass stirring rod. Pour this solution into test tube *3*. Rinse the graduated cylinder and stirring rod with distilled water, and discard the rinse in the *Waste* beaker. Record the amounts of the solution and H_2O in your data table.

11. Pour 8.0 mL of the 0.50 M $FeCl_3$ standard solution into a 10 mL graduated cylinder, and dilute it with distilled water to a total volume of 10.0 mL. Mix the solution with a glass stirring rod. Pour this solution into test tube *4*. Rinse the graduated cylinder and stirring rod with distilled water, and discard the rinse in the *Waste* beaker. Record the amounts of the solution and H_2O in your data table.

12. Pour 10.0 mL of undiluted 0.50 M $FeCl_3$ standard solution into test tube *5*.

13. Obtain a 10.0 mL sample of the solution of unknown concentration, and pour it into the test tube labeled *Unknown*.

Colorimetric Estimation and Measurement

14. Estimate the intensity of the color of your solutions on a scale from 0 (distilled water from test tube *0*) to 1.00 (solution from test tube *5*). To make comparisons easier, hold a piece of white paper behind the test tubes you are comparing. Record these values in your data table as *Estimates*. Based on how the unknown compares to the known solutions, estimate its concentration. If you will be using neither the LEAP colormeter nor a spectrophotometer, continue with step **19**.

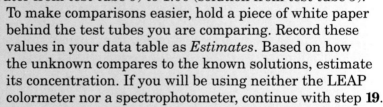

15. Check with your teacher about whether you should evaluate your sample using measures of absorbancy or percent transmittance. If you are using a LEAP colormeter and measuring absorbance, set it up and calibrate it as discussed in step **15a**. If you will be using the LEAP colormeter to measure transmittance, follow the instructions in step **15b**. If you are using a spectrophotometer, set it up and calibrate it as discussed in step **15c**.

a. LEAP Colormeter—Absorbance

Your teacher will have the experiment on the screen. Plug the color-meter into the input cable of your station. Set the wavelength to 590 nm, which corresponds to a yellowish green light.

Never wipe cuvettes with paper towels or scrub them with a test-tube brush. Use only lint-free tissues which will not scratch the cuvette's surface. The outside of the cuvette must be completely dry before it is placed inside an instrument, or you will get an invalid reading.

Pour some of the solution from test tube 5 into the cuvette. Be sure the outside of the cuvette is dry by wiping it clean with a lint-free tissue. Then, place the cuvette into the meter and place the cover over the sample. Adjust the ZERO ADJ knob until the reading on the LEAP graph is 1. Allow the meter a few seconds to stabilize, and readjust the ZERO ADJ knob if necessary. When the reading remains at 1, put the system on WAIT, and proceed with step **16**.

b. LEAP Colormeter—Percent Transmittance

Your teacher will have the experiment on the screen. Plug the color-meter into the input cable of your station. Set the wavelength to 590 nm, which corresponds to a yellowish green light.

Never wipe cuvettes with paper towels or scrub them with a test-tube brush. Use only lint-free tissues which will not scratch the cuvette's surface. The outside of the cuvette must be completely dry before it is placed inside an instrument, or you will get an invalid reading.

Fill the cuvette three-quarters full with distilled water from test tube *0*. Be sure the outside of the cuvette is dry by wiping it clean with a lint-free tissue. Because this should provide a reading of no absorbance or 100% transmittance, it is called a blank. Place this cuvette into the meter, and place the cover over the sample. Start the data collection by clicking on the green light of the traffic light on the computer screen. Adjust the ZERO ADJ on the LEAP graph on the computer screen so that the sample reads 100%. Allow the meter a few seconds to stabilize, and readjust the ZERO ADJ knob if necessary. When the reading remains at 100%, put the system on WAIT, and proceed with step **16**.

c. Spectrophotometer—Percent Transmittance or Absorbance

Check to be certain that the spectrophotometer has warmed up for about 10 min. Then, with the sample compartment empty and the lid closed, adjust the %T dial to 0%. Turn the right knob clockwise until you meet resistance. Insert a clean and dry cuvette. Turn the wave length knob to 625 nm (yellow light), and then turn the right front knob until the %T dial reads 100%.

Never wipe cuvettes with paper towels, or scrub them with a test-tube brush. Use only lint-free tissues which will not scratch the cuvette's surface. The outside of the cuvette must be completely dry before it is placed inside an instrument, or you will get an invalid reading.

Check with your teacher about whether you should evaluate your sample recording measures of absorbance or percent transmittance. Proceed with step **16**.

16. Remove the cuvette, and rinse it several times with distilled water, discarding rinses in the *Waste* beaker. Fill the cuvette approximately three-quarters full with the solution from test tube *1*. Be sure the outside of the cuvette is dry by wiping it clean with a lint-free tissue. Place the cuvette in the sample compartment, and place the cover over the cuvette. If you are using the LEAP colormeter, take the system off WAIT. Allow the meter to stabilize at this reading for a few seconds, and record the percent transmittance or absorbance reading for sample *1* in your data table.

17. Remove the cuvette, and pour sample *1* back into the test tube. Rinse the cuvette several times with distilled water, discarding rinses in the *Waste* beaker. Repeat the procedure for samples from test tubes *2–5*. Be sure to dry the outside of the cuvette with a lint-free tissue after each transfer. Between samples *3* and *4* check the calibration of the meter as follows. If you are measuring percent transmittance, retest the distilled water to be certain the reading is 100%. If you are measuring absorbance, retest the solution from test tube *5* to be sure the reading is 1. If the calibration test does not give the appropriate reading, start over with step **15**. Otherwise, continue with step **18**.

18. Test the sample of unknown concentration, and record the results in your lab notebook.

Cleanup and Disposal

19. Dispose of the solutions in the container designated by your teacher. Rinse the cuvettes several times with distilled water before putting them away.

Analysis and Interpretation

1. **Analyzing Ideas**
   What are the concentrations of $FeCl_3$ in test tubes *0, 1, 2, 3, 4,* and *5*?

2. **Analyzing Results**
   What is your estimate for the concentration of the unknown? Explain your answer.

3. **Analyzing Methods**
   Would you get better results if, during the dilution steps, you had used a volumetric pipette that measures exactly 2.00 mL instead of using the graduated cylinder? Explain your answer.

4. **Organizing Data**
   If you used a colormeter or spectrophotometer and measured percent transmittance instead of absorbance, convert to absorbance using the following equation. If not, go on to item **5**.

$$\text{absorbance} = \log \left(\frac{100}{\text{percent transmittance}} \right)$$

5. **Analyzing Data**
   Make a graph of your data with concentration of $FeCl_3$ on the *x*-axis and absorbance on the *y*-axis. (If you did not use equipment to make your measurements, use your values from the *Estimate* part of your data table as absorbance values.)

6. Analyzing Data

If your graph was a straight line, give the equation for the line in the form $y = mx + b$. If it was not a straight line, explain why, and draw the straight line that comes closest to including all of your data points. Give the equation of this line. (Hint: if you have a graphics calculator, use the STAT mode to enter your data and make a linear regression equation using the LinReg function from the STAT menu.)

7. Interpreting Graphics

Using the graph from item **5** or the equation from item **6**, determine what the concentration of the unknown must have been for it to have given the measured absorbance value.

Conclusions

8. Applying Conclusions

Which of the following could be a likely source of the pharmaceutical plant's problems: too much $FeCl_3$ added to the solution, too little $FeCl_3$ added to the solution, too much water added to the solution, or too little water added to the solution?

Extensions

1. Evaluating Methods

What are some advantages or disadvantages of colorimetry when compared to other methods, such as gravimetric analysis?

2. Relating Ideas

Absorbance describes how much light is blocked by a sample. Transmittance describes how much light passes through a sample. As absorbance values go up, how do transmittance values change?

3. Designing Experiments

What possible sources of error can you identify with this procedure? If you can think of ways to eliminate them, ask your teacher to approve your plan, and run the procedure again.

4. Predicting Outcomes

How would your absorbance or percent transmittance values for the unknown solution change if someone added an additional yellow-colored compound along with the $FeCl_3$?

5. Applying Ideas

Run the procedure again using one of the following wavelength settings: 950 nm or 640 nm. Can you explain why 590 nm was chosen for the lab procedure?

6. Evaluating Methods

If you used a LEAP colormeter or a spectrophotometer, calculate the percent error for each of your estimates of absorbance, compared to the values given by the equipment. (Hint: divide each absorbance measurement by the largest measurement, so they will be on a scale from 0 to 1.00, just like your estimates.)

COLORIMETRY **Reservoir Contaminant**

ennis pro
t 14
AGE B4

has got a new idol
PAGE B6

police cuts
PAGE B8

moves replace lawyers
PAGE B14

March 24, 1995

TRO DIGEST

**AL IS FAULTED IN
ENT'S SLAYING**

side hospital failed the safety of an patient who was summer in his pri-m according to a rt released yester-report found, among ngs, that the eighth the unit where the was killed, had no security alarms or that would allow the staff to better moni-corridors. B4.

REGION

**TTERY OFFICIAL
INDICTED**

rmer national sales r for the Fink ation, the world's rgest vendor of gov-sponsored lottery tems, was indicted es of generating by paying inflated fees to compan-olled by two men authorities named rators. B6.

**UNCILMAN
S TO THEFT**

stfall, a former lman, pleaded ling $ 250,000 ds by putting loyees on his l and cashing for himself, ed the names uerto Rico, a cky and the

Contamination Closes Reservoir Indefinitely

Backup Available for Only 2 days; Firms Asked to Help

Pumps feeding water from the city's James Knox Polk Reservoir to a treatment plant were shut down suddenly last night when a water depart-ment crew discovered leaking and rusty barrels of chemicals on the reservoir's south shore.

The barrels, which were dumped illegally, appeared to be leaking directly into the reservoir. Daniel Baden, director of the Department of Health Services, ordered an immediate switch to the city's reserve water supply. Although service continued without interruption, the water department's supervi-sor, Jose Vaculez, warns that the city has only enough water in reserves to last for two days.

"Until we find out what chemical we're dealing with and how much is there, it's difficult to know whether the wisest course would be to try to purify the water or to find a long-term alternative," Baden told the city council, which met in emergency session this morning.

The council unanimous-ly passed a resolution spon-sored by Councilmember Joanna Wooldridge to pro-vide a $250 000 reward to the first analytical firm that can provide an answer to the water department by 4 p.m. tomorrow.

"Our options for alterna-tive sources are so expensive that we will be saving our taxpayers' money if we can fix what's wrong with the reservoir now," Wooldridge said. "I'm certain that the expertise to reach an answer promptly is available."

Police are still seeking leads on who dumped the bar-rels. "We have determined that they must have been put there since last Thursday," said Jordan Freeman, a police department spokesman. "The area was clearly marked with 'No Dumping' signs, and we intend to fine the responsible parties to the maximum amount allowable by law. We are also studying other penal-ties associated with creating a public health hazard."

Fine in Shutdov

The Nuclear Reg Commission fined Public Service Elect Gas Company $5 today, saying that six tions had led to an al partial shutdown at or nuclear power plants East Coast in Spring

The executive dir the commission, Go Blythe, announced

Dividend Bill Ain State Is Withdr

The Chairman o House Banki Committee has w rawn proposed le tion that would compelled the ci give to other states dreds of millions o lars in unclaimed dividends and inte

SPECIAL REPORT

PAGE B4

in a letter to compan cials that accused the of bumbling and of ing lax security con the plant.

The problems be April 7, 1994, the c sion said, whe

Few Details Provided in Whitfield Proposal

The Whitfield administra-tion unveiled its long awaited school voucher program today, an experiment that would subsidize Bay

a highly emotional one," Mr. DelVecchio wrote in the pro-posal presented to the of Ed

Required Precautions

 Goggles and lab aprons must be worn at all times. Confine loose clothing and long hair.

 Do not touch or taste any chemi-cals. Wash your hands thoroughly when finished.

CheMystery Labs, Inc.
52 Fulton Street
Springfield, VA 22150

Memorandum

Date: March 24, 1995

To: Antonio Gallini

From: George Taylor

One of our analysis teams got a head start on this project early this morning. They managed to identify the contaminant as $CuCl_2$, so now I need your team to finish the job by determining the concentration of $CuCl_2$ in a sample of the reservoir water. I recommend that you use colorimetric analysis techniques. We have pure crystals of $CuCl_2$ available so that you can make standard solutions.

We can't afford to waste time on mistakes, so I want to look over your plan before you start. Include the following.
- one-page procedure and necessary data tables
- detailed list of equipment and materials you will need, along with individual and total costs (I'll rush this information to the supply and accounting departments.)

As soon as you complete your work, write up a two-page report to fax to the water department. All of the following items must be covered in the report.
- chemical name and formula of the spilled compound
- concentration of the spilled compound in molarity and ppm by mass
- mass of chemical spilled (Note: the reservoir has a volume of 2.5×10^9 L.)
- summary of your procedure, including the wavelength chosen for colorimetric analysis
- detailed and organized data and analysis section that includes all data tables and calculations, as well as the graph of your standard curve for colorimetry analysis

In addition, prepare a list of your final costs for the accounting department.

Spill Procedures/ Waste Disposal Methods

- In case of a spill, follow your teacher's instructions.
- Put all liquids and solids into the container designated by your teacher. Do not pour them down the sink or place them in the trash can.

References

For a discussion of concentration units and solution preparation, see pages 411–413. The colorimetric analysis necessary to determine the concentration is similar to one that your team recently completed. Make a stock solution of 0.050 M concentration. Use 640 nm as the wavelength to analyze the $CuCl_2$ concentration if you are using a LEAP colormeter probe or a spectrophotometer. Remember to determine the compound's molar mass from the periodic table in order to calculate amounts necessary to make standard solutions for comparison in your colorimetric analysis.

Materials for RESERVOIR CONTAMINANT

Item	Cost	
REQUIRED ITEMS (You must include all of these in your budget.)		
Lab space	15 000 —	/day
Standard disposal fee	2 000 —	/g of product
Balance	5 000	
REAGENTS and ADDITIONAL EQUIPMENT (Include in your budget only what you'll need.)		
$CuCl_2 \cdot 2H_2O$		
250 mL beaker	500 —	/g
250 mL Erlenmeyer flask	1 000	
250 mL volumetric flask	1 000	
10 mL graduated cylinder	5 000	
100 mL graduated cylinder	1 000	
Colormeter—LEAP and cuvettes	1 000	
Filter paper	8 000	
Glass funnel	500 —	/piece
Glass stirring rod	1 000	
Lint-free wipes	1 000	
Litmus paper	500 —	/box
Ring stand/ring/pipe stem triangle	1 000 —	/piece
Six test tubes/holder/rack	2 000	
Spatula	2 000	
Spectrophotometer and cuvettes	500	
Wash bottle	8 000	
Weighing paper	500	
* No refunds on returned chemicals or unused equipment.	500 —	/piece
FINES		
OSHA safety violation	2 000 —	/incident

INVESTIGATION 11B

Problem Solving

Sparkle-Clean

Sparkle-Clean Industries

March 23, 1995

Reginald Brown, Director of Materials Testing
CheMystery Labs
52 Fulton Street
Springfield, VA 22150

Dear Mr. Brown:

Our company sells soaps and detergents to grocery stores throughout the country. Due to a recent merger our firm has an overabundance of available products in the soap and detergent industries.

We need to determine which of these products are the best so that we can concentrate on marketing only those. We need your firm to run some independent tests to help us learn as much as possible about the products so that we can plan an effective marketing campaign. Along with cleaning ability, please check pH, density, effect on surface tension of water, amount of suds produced, and ability to clean in hard water. Make observations about other properties such as color, perfume, texture, etc.

We have enclosed separate samples of hand soap (brands F, H, and J), dishwashing liquid (brands Q, R, and U), and laundry detergent (brands M, N, and P). We are organizing our fall sales drive, and we need your results as soon as possible.

Sincerely,

Martin Green

Martin Green
Vice President
Sparkle-Clean Industries

Required Precautions

Lab aprons and goggles must be worn at all times.

Do not touch or taste any chemicals. Wash your hands thoroughly when finished.

CheMystery Labs, Inc.
52 Fulton Street
Springfield, VA 22150

Memorandum

Date: March 24, 1995

To: Sabrina Moore

From: Reginald Brown

There are many tests involved with this work, and we have only $350,000 to spend, but I have some ideas. One of our references suggests that a soap's effect on surface tension can be tested by filling a petri dish about half-full with water, sprinkling pepper on it, and adding a drop of soap solution to the center. The reference didn't explain why this test works, so make careful observations.

To test sudsing ability, put similar amounts of soap detergent in test tubes with water. Stopper the tubes and shake. We can simulate the effects of hard water by performing this test with $MgCl_2$ and $CaCl_2$ solutions instead of water.

You're on your own in figuring out ways to test cleaning ability, pH, and density. Be creative, but come up with tests that are quantifiable. I recommend that you bring in some items from your home to test cleaning ability. Then rate soaps on a scale of 1 to 10.

Before you start, I will need to review the following items
- detailed one-page summary of your plan for the procedure
- itemized list of materials, with total costs
- data tables for recording the results of your tests

After you complete the analysis, prepare a two-page report for Mr. Green that includes the following.
- your recommendation and an explanation of the reasons for your choice of the best product in each category
- summary of your procedure
- analysis, including the properties, advantages, and disadvantages of each soap or detergent
- detailed data sections, showing results of each test and observations you made
- detailed invoice for all expenses and services

Spill Procedures/ Waste Disposal Methods

- Pour any leftover soap into the disposal containers designated by your teacher.
- Clean the area and all equipment after use.

References

Refer to pages 429–431 for information about soaps and detergents. It is very important to thoroughly wash and rinse glassware with distilled water between tests so that you can be sure your test results are accurate and that there is no contamination of your samples. Base your disposal costs on the amounts of $CaCl_2$ and $MgCl_2$ solution used.

Materials for SPARKLE-CLEAN INDUSTRIES

Item	Cost	1	2	3
REQUIRED ITEMS (You must include all of these in your budget.)				
Lab space/fume hood/utilities	15 000 — /day			
Standard disposal fee	2 000 — /g of product			
REAGENTS and ADDITIONAL EQUIPMENT (Include in your budget only what you'll need.)				
$CaCl_2$ solution	500 — /mL			
$MgCl_2$ solution	500 — /mL			
Pepper	2 000 — /g			
250 mL beaker	1 000			
10 mL graduated cylinder	1 000			
100 mL graduated cylinder	1 000			
Balance	5 000			
Filter paper	500 — /piece			
Glass funnel	1 000			
Glass stirring rod	1 000			
Paper clips	500 — /box			
Petri dish	1 000			
pH meter	3 000			
pH paper	2 000 — /piece			
pH probe—LEAP	5 000			
Pipet or medicine dropper	1 000			
Rubber stopper	1 000			
Six test tubes/holder/rack	2 000			
Spatula	500			
Wash bottle	500			
*No refunds on returned chemicals or unused equipment.				
FINES				
OSHA safety violation	2 000 — /incident			

EXPLORATION

12A
Technique Builder

Boiling-Point Elevation and Molar Mass

Objectives
Demonstrate proficiency in measuring masses, temperatures, and boiling points.

Relate the concentration of a solution to boiling-point elevation data.

Determine the molar mass of a solute from experimental data.

Situation
Your company needs to determine the identity of a white powder. A young boy swallowed it, and doctors need to know its identity to treat him. The substance must be one of the following: sodium chloride, NaCl; sugar (sucrose), $C_{12}H_{22}O_{11}$; or hydrated magnesium sulfate (Epsom salts), $MgSO_4 \cdot 7H_2O$. Along with the unknown, you have pure samples of the three substances.

Background
The boiling point of a solution is always higher than that of a pure liquid. The reason is that the attraction of the solute for individual water molecules hinders their ability to move into the gaseous state. Properties of solutes that affect solutions such as this are known as *colligative properties*. When dealing with colligative properties, the concentration units of *molality* (m) are used instead of *molarity* (M). Molality is defined as the number of moles of solute per kilogram of the solvent.

$$m = \frac{\text{moles solute}}{\text{kilograms solvent}}$$

Experiments have determined that the boiling-point elevation of a 1.00 m solution for any molecular solute in water is 0.51°C. This value is known as the molal boiling-point constant, K_b. The constant has the units °C/m, and it can be used to predict the boiling point of any concentration of solute. For example, if 2.00 mol of sugar are dissolved in 1.00 kg of water, the boiling point will be 101.02°C (100°C + (2.00 m × 0.51°C/m).)

These properties depend upon the number of particles in solution. For example, when one mole of NaCl is dissolved in a kilogram of water, two moles of particles are formed: one mole of Na^+ ions and one mole of Cl^- ions. Thus, a 1.00 m NaCl solution will have a particle concentration of 2.00 m, and will have a boiling point like that of the 2.00 m sugar solution.

Problem
To identify the unknown, you must do the following.
- make solutions using the same solute mass for each of the standards and the unknown
- compare the boiling points of the resulting solutions to determine which matches that of the unknown

As a check on your work, you can calculate the molality of each solution based on the value of the boiling point. Then you can use the amount of solute you added and the number of moles (from the molality) to determine the molar mass.

$$\text{molar mass of solute} = \frac{\text{g of solute}}{\text{kg of solvent} \times \text{molal conc.}}$$

Safety

Always wear goggles and an apron to provide protection for your eyes and clothing. If you get a chemical in your eyes, immediately flush it out at the eyewash station while calling to your teacher. Know the locations of the emergency lab shower and eyewash and how to use them.

Do not touch any chemicals. If you get a chemical on your skin or clothing, wash it off at the sink while calling to your teacher. Make sure you carefully read the labels and follow the directions on all containers of chemicals that you use. Do not taste any chemicals or items used in the laboratory. Never return leftovers to their original containers; take only small amounts to avoid wasting supplies.

When you use a Bunsen burner, confine any long hair and loose clothing. Do not heat glassware that is broken, chipped, or cracked. Use tongs or a hot mitt to handle heated glassware and other equipment because hot glassware does not look hot. If your clothing catches on fire, WALK to the emergency lab shower, and use it to put out the fire.

Always clean up the lab and all equipment after use, and dispose of substances according to proper disposal methods. Wash your hands thoroughly before you leave the lab after all lab work is finished.

Preparation

I. Organizing Data

Prepare a data table in your lab notebook. The data table should have four columns and six rows. The first row should contain the following headings in the first through fourth columns: *Solution, Mass of solute (g), Mass of flask + water (g),* and *Boiling point.* In the second through sixth rows of the first column, add the following labels: *Water, NaCl, Sucrose, MgSO$_4$·7H$_2$O,* and *Unknown.* Be certain there is space in your lab notebook to record the mass of the Erlenmeyer flask and perform some calculations.

2. Measure the mass of the Erlenmeyer flask. Record this mass in your lab notebook.

Technique

3. Add distilled water to the Erlenmeyer flask until the total mass is as close as possible to 50.0 g more than the amount recorded in your lab notebook for the mass of the flask. Record this mass in your data table.

4. Place the flask of water on the wire gauze on the ring stand. Using the thermometer clamp, suspend the thermistor or thermometer in the water so that it does not touch the sides or bottom of the flask. Do not use a one-hole stopper to hold the thermometer, because the solution will be boiled.

Materials

- **Distilled water**
- **MgSO$_4$·7H$_2$O, 10.0 g**
- **NaCl, 10.0 g**
- **Sucrose, 10.0 g**
- **Unknown sample, 10.0 g**
- **Balance**
- **Beaker tongs**
- **Bunsen burner/ related equipment or hot plate**
- **125 mL Erlenmeyer flask**
- **Ring stand and ring**
- **Thermometer (nonmercury with 0.1°C markings) or LEAP System with thermistor probe**
- **Thermometer clamp**
- **Wire gauze with ceramic center**

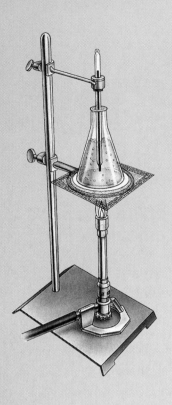

5. Heat the water until it boils vigorously and the temperature remains constant. This temperature is the boiling point. Record it in your data table. (Note: leave the box in your data table for *Mass of solute* (g) blank for this trial involving only water.)

6. Pour the contents of the flask into the sink. Then add distilled water to the flask until the total mass is as close as possible to 50.0 g more than the mass of the flask. Record this mass in your data table. Add 10.0 g of NaCl to this water, and swirl the flask gently until the salt dissolves completely. Record the mass of solute in your data table. *Do not allow the water to splash out of the flask, as it will cause inaccuracy in your results.*

7. Place your flask on the wire gauze, and suspend the thermistor or thermometer in the water as before. Heat the solution to boiling, and record the boiling point in your data table.

8. Pour the contents of the flask into the sink. Rinse it three times with distilled water. Repeat steps **6** and **7** for sucrose, $MgSO_4 \cdot 7H_2O$, and the unknown sample.

Cleanup and Disposal

9. Solutions may be rinsed down the sink. Check with your teacher for the proper disposal of other chemicals. Wash your hands thoroughly after cleaning up the area and equipment. Be certain all gas valves are turned off.

Analysis and Interpretation

1. **Organizing Data**
   For the trials with solutes including the unknown, calculate the solution's change in boiling point, Δt_b. (Hint: use the boiling point you measured for the pure water as the solvent's boiling point.)

2. **Analyzing Information**
   Given that similar masses of each substance were used, does the data for the unknown most closely match NaCl, sucrose, or $MgSO_4 \cdot 7H_2O$?

3. **Analyzing Data**
   Calculate the approximate molalities of dissolved particles for the known and unknown solutes using the following equation and your answers to item **1**. (Hint: $K_b = 0.51°C/m$)

   $$m = \frac{\Delta t_b}{K_b}$$

4. **Organizing Data**
   For each trial, calculate the mass of water in the flask in kilograms.

5. **Analyzing Data**
   Using your answers from items **3** and **4** and your data, calculate an experimental value for the molar mass of each solute. (Hint: see the Problem section of the introduction, but remember that a calculation indicating 2.00 *m* of Na^+ and Cl^- particles means a solution that is 1.00 *m* in NaCl. The water molecules that are a part of the $MgSO_4 \cdot 7H_2O$ crystal do not raise the boiling point.)

Conclusions

6. Evaluating Conclusions

How close is the estimated molar mass for the unknown solute to the estimated molar mass of the solute chosen in item **2**? Calculate percent error, using the unknown solute's molar mass estimate as the experimental value.

7. Evaluating Methods

Determine the molar mass of NaCl, sucrose, and $MgSO_4 \cdot 7H_2O$ from a periodic table. Calculate percent error for your experimental molar mass values.

8. Evaluating Methods

How accurate do you think it is to identify the unknown substance using this procedure? Can you explain any deviations that occur?

9. Applying Ideas

Explain in your own words why adding a solute raises the temperature at which a substance boils. (Hint: consider what you know about bonding, phase changes, and kinetic molecular theory.)

10. Analyzing Methods

Why do you need to determine the boiling point of water without a solute dissolved in it? Explain your answer.

Extensions

1. Designing Experiments

What possible sources of error can you identify with this procedure? If you can think of ways to eliminate them, ask your teacher to approve your plan, and run the procedure again.

2. Research and Communications

Consult chemical handbooks and other reference works to determine the possible health hazards of these solutes. For each one, what should be done if someone swallows it?

3. Applying Ideas

Find out how much and what type of salt a large northern city such as New York or Chicago uses on icy roads in the winter. What problems result from use of this salt? What salt substitutes can melt ice and snow? Which would be safest for our environment?

4. Designing Experiments

Obtain a water-soluble unknown from your teacher, and determine whether it is NaCl, sucrose, or $MgSO_4 \cdot 7H_2O$ using the freezing-point depression method. (As determined by experimentation, the freezing-point depression of a $1.00\ m$ solution of any molecular solute in water is $-1.86\,°C$.)

5. Research and Communications

Find out about the different types and ratios of ingredients in antifreeze solutions and coolants for automobile radiators, and give a report that explains how they make use of colligative properties.

6. Research and Communications

What are some of the primary uses of $MgSO_4 \cdot 7H_2O$, and how is it produced for commercial use?

INVESTIGATION 12A

Problem Solving

D&J

D & J FOOD PROCESSING

April 10, 1995

Ms. Martha Li-Hsien
Director of Research
CheMystery Labs
52 Fulton Street
Springfield, VA 22150

Dear Ms. Li-Hsien:

Each year, our company processes several thousand metric tons of sugars, seasonings, and other household products. Recently, an unknown ingredient was accidentally included in several tons of powdered sugar before we discovered the mistake. Our quality control department analyzed a sample and was able to isolate the contaminant. I am sending you a small amount of this contaminant. Please identify it as soon as possible.

Based on the production schedule, it is most likely that the contaminant is either glucose, NaCl, or CaCl₂. If the contaminant is glucose, we can still sell the product; otherwise, the entire batch will be a loss.

As discussed in our telephone conversation, we are prepared to pay $200 000 if this work is performed to our satisfaction. An official contract will arrive soon under separate cover.

Sincerely,

Kristeen McGonigal

Kristeen McGonigal
Director of Operations
D & J Food Processing

Required Precautions

Goggles and lab aprons must be worn at all times.

Tie back loose hair and clothing. Use tongs to handle equipment.

Do not touch or taste any chemicals. Wash your hands thoroughly when finished.

Memorandum

CheMystery Labs, Inc.
52 Fulton Street
Springfield, VA 22150

Date: **April 11, 1995**

To: **Patricia Edgerton**

From: **Martha Li-Hsien**

Recently, our management team has been reviewing the accuracy of the work we did in the first quarter of this year. Their reviews indicate that there is room for improvement in our cost-efficiency and accuracy. We should start with this job. To make certain that your plan is as efficient as possible, I need to review your plans before you start. Please include the following.
- detailed one-page summary of your plan for the procedure (I suggest we compare boiling-point elevations for the unknown and some standard samples.)
- any necessary data tables
- itemized list of equipment and materials, with individual and total costs

After you complete the analysis, prepare a two-page letter to McGonigal at D & J Food Processing. Make sure your letter covers the following points.
- identity of the contaminant
- brief summary of the procedure you used to identify the contaminant
- detailed analysis and data sections, showing calculations
- estimates and explanations for possible sources of error
- detailed invoice for all expenses and services

References

Refer to pages 459–460 for information about colligative properties. The procedure is similar to one your team recently completed to differentiate between NaCl, sucrose, and $MgSO_4 \cdot 7H_2O$. Remember that one mole of particles dissolved in one kilogram of water will raise the boiling point of the solution by 0.51°C. This value is called the molal boiling-point constant of water, represented by K_b. Base your disposal costs on the amounts of solute used.

Spill Procedures/ Waste Disposal Methods

- Any solid materials must go in designated waste containers.
- Solutions can be washed down the drain with 20 times as much water as waste volume.
- Clean the area and all equipment after use.

Materials for D & J FOOD PROCESSING

Item	Cost	1	2	3
REQUIRED ITEMS				
(You must include all of these in your budget.)				
Lab space/fume hood/utilities	15 000 — /day			
Standard disposal fee	2 000 — /g of product			
Beaker tongs	1 000			
REAGENTS and ADDITIONAL EQUIPMENT				
(Include in your budget only what you'll need.)				
$CaCl_2$	500 — /g			
Glucose	500 — /g			
NaCl	500 — /g			
250 mL beaker	1 000			
400 mL beaker	2 000			
250 mL flask	1 000			
100 mL graduated cylinder	1 000			
Balance	5 000			
Bunsen burner/related equipment	10 000			
Drying oven	5 000 — /day			
Glass stirring rod	1 000			
Hot plate	8 000			
Ring stand/ring/wire gauze	2 000			
Spatula	500			
Thermistor probe—LEAP	2 000			
Thermometer	2 000			
Thermometer clamp	1 000			
Wash bottle	500			
Weighing paper	500 — /piece			
No refunds on returned chemicals or unused equipment.				
Fines				
OSHA safety violation	2 000 — /incident			

Equilibrium Expressions

Objectives

Demonstrate proficiency in preparing serial dilutions from a standard solution and comparing solutions by eye, by spectrophotometer, or with a LEAP colormeter probe.

Relate spectrophotometric determinations to solution concentration.

Determine experimentally the equilibrium expression of a chemical reaction.

Situation

You work for a company that makes home tests for chemicals. Some homes have iron pipes, which can slowly leach iron(III) ions into the water, causing a brownish tint. Although not a health hazard, at high concentrations it can cause rust stains on laundry and dishes. Your company plans to use KSCN as a reagent to detect the iron, but an exploration of the reaction is necessary in order to calibrate the test for determining concentration. This test involves a reaction that reaches an equilibrium point, so you must determine the equilibrium constant to calibrate the test.

Background

Colorimetry can be used to measure the intensity of the red color of the $FeSCN^{2+}$ ions. Because this reaction is not always complete, it is not possible to set up a standard curve using known concentrations as in other colorimetry experiments. Consider the net ionic equation for this reaction.

$$Fe^{3+}(aq) + SCN^-(aq) \rightleftharpoons FeSCN^{2+}(aq)$$
Yellow   Colorless   Red

At equilibrium, $FeSCN^{2+}$ is being produced at a rate equal to the rate at which $FeSCN^{2+}$ is breaking up into Fe^{3+} and SCN^-. If the concentration of Fe^{3+} ions is increased, the equilibrium will be disturbed, and a new equilibrium will be reached to accommodate these new conditions.

As discussed in Chapter 12, the molar concentrations of substances at equilibrium can be arranged in a mathematical expression, the *equilibrium expression*, that has a constant value, the *equilibrium constant*, K_{eq}. Because this value should stay the same, you can use this method to check your determinations of $FeSCN^{2+}$ concentration.

Problem

The following must be done to adapt the test for measuring the iron(III) concentration of an unknown solution.
- prepare several solutions with different Fe^{3+} concentrations, and add similar amounts of the testing solution to each
- compare the amount of red color produced by the solutions
- relate the intensity of the red color to the concentrations of $FeSCN^{2+}$ at equilibrium
- determine the concentrations of Fe^{3+}, SCN^-, and $FeSCN^{2+}$ at equilibrium
- calculate the equilibrium constant for each trial, and evaluate your determinations of $FeSCN^{2+}$ concentration

Safety

Always wear goggles and an apron to protect your eyes and clothing. If you get a chemical in your eyes, immediately flush it out at the eyewash station while calling to your teacher. Know the locations of the emergency lab shower and eyewash and how to use them.

Do not touch any chemicals. If you get a chemical on your skin or clothing, wash it off at the sink while calling to your teacher. Carefully read the labels and follow the directions on all containers of chemicals that you use. Do not taste any chemicals or items used in the laboratory. Never return leftovers to their original containers; take only small amounts to avoid wasting supplies.

Always clean up the lab and all equipment after use, and dispose of substances according to proper disposal methods. Wash your hands thoroughly before you leave the lab after all lab work is finished.

Materials

- 0.200 M $Fe(NO_3)_3$, 10 mL
- 0.6 M HNO_3, 25 mL
- 0.002 00 M KSCN, 25 mL
- 10 mL graduated cylinder
- Glass stirring rod
- Test tube rack
- Test tubes, 6

Optional equipment
- LEAP system with colormeter probe
- Spectrophotometer
- Cuvettes
- Lint-free wipes for cuvettes

Preparation

1. **Organizing Data**
   Prepare a data table in your lab notebook. The table should contain five columns and seven rows. Label the columns of the first row: *Test tube no.*, *Fe^{3+} conc.*, *mL of Fe^{3+}*, *mL of KSCN*, and *Absorbance value*. Fill in the following test tube numbers in the second through seventh rows of the first column: *1, 2, 3, 4, 5,* and *6*. Be sure there is also room for observations.

2. If you will be using a spectrophotometer, turn it on now, as it must warm up for approximately 10 min.

3. Label six test tubes as *1, 2, 3, 4, 5,* and *6*.

Technique

4. Carefully measure 5.0 mL of 0.200 M $Fe(NO_3)_3$ into a 10 mL graduated cylinder. Pour this into test tube *1*. Record this volume and concentration in the data table.

5. Carefully measure another 5.0 mL of 0.200 M $Fe(NO_3)_3$ into the 10 mL graduated cylinder. Add 5.0 mL of 0.6 M HNO_3. Mix well with a glass stirring rod. Pour 5.0 mL of this mixture into test tube *2*. Record this volume and Fe^{3+} concentration in the data table. (Hint: the concentration of Fe^{3+} is half of what it was for test tube *1* because it has been diluted by an equal volume of HNO_3.)

6. Add 5.0 mL of 0.6 M HNO_3 to the remaining 5.0 mL of the mixture in the graduated cylinder. Mix well with a glass stirring rod. Pour 5.0 mL of this mixture into test tube *3*. Record this volume and concentration in the data table.

7. Repeat step **6** until you have filled all six test tubes.

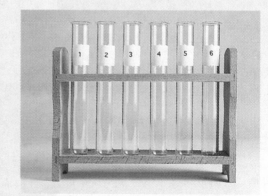

8. Discard the contents of test tube *2*, pouring it into the waste container designated by your teacher. (This dilution is not great enough to provide a measurable difference in light absorption.)

9. Add 5.0 mL of 0.002 00 M KSCN to test tubes *1*, *3*, *4*, *5*, and *6*. Mix each solution thoroughly with a stirring rod.

10. Compare the solutions holding a piece of white paper behind the test tubes. If you are not using a spectrophotometer or LEAP colormeter, estimate the intensity of the red color on a scale from 0 (clear) to 1.00 (test tube *1*), and enter your estimate in the *Absorbance value* column of the data table.

11. If you are using a LEAP colormeter, set it up and calibrate it as discussed in step **11a**. If you are using a spectrophotometer, set it up and calibrate it as discussed in step **11b**. *For both instruments, note that you should be measuring absorbance*, NOT percent transmittance. If you are using neither, go on to step **14**.

a. LEAP Colormeter

Your teacher will have the experiment on the screen. Plug the colormeter probe into the input cable of your station. Set the wavelength to 590 nm, which corresponds to a yellowish green light. Record the wavelength in your data table.

Never wipe cuvettes with paper towels or scrub them with a test tube brush. Use only lint-free tissues that will not scratch the cuvette's surface. The outside of the cuvette must be completely dry before it is placed inside an instrument, or else you will get an invalid reading.

Calibrate the colormeter by pouring some solution from test tube *1* into a cuvette and inserting the cuvette in the sample compartment. Turn the ZERO ADJ knob until the absorbance value is as close to 1.00 as possible. When the reading remains at 1.00, put the system on WAIT and proceed to step **12**.

b. Spectrophotometer

If the spectrophotometer has warmed up for about 10 minutes, set the wavelength to 590 nm. Calibrate it by turning the left front knob to 0% transmittance, while using an empty sample compartment with the lid closed. Then, pour some solution from test tube *1* into the cuvette, and adjust the absorbance value with the right front knob to read as close to 1.00 as possible.

Never wipe cuvettes with paper towels or scrub them with a test tube brush. Use only lint-free tissues that will not scratch the cuvette's surface. The outside of the cuvette must be completely dry before it is placed inside an instrument, or else you will get an invalid reading.

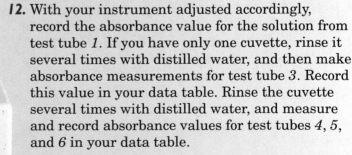

12. With your instrument adjusted accordingly, record the absorbance value for the solution from test tube *1*. If you have only one cuvette, rinse it several times with distilled water, and then make absorbance measurements for test tube *3*. Record this value in your data table. Rinse the cuvette several times with distilled water, and measure and record absorbance values for test tubes *4*, *5*, and *6* in your data table.

13. As a check on your measurements, retest the solution from test tube *1* at the end of the measurements. Its absorbance value should still be the same, close to 1.00. If not, repeat the procedure for all solutions.

Cleanup and Disposal

14. Dispose of all solutions in the container designated by your teacher. Wash your hands thoroughly after cleaning up the area and equipment.

Analysis and Interpretation

1. Analyzing Data
Determine how each of the absorbance values relates to that for test tube *1* by dividing each by the value obtained for test tube *1*. (Hint: after this calculation, the new value for test tube *1* should be 1.00, and the values for the other test tubes should be less than 1.00, as they were less concentrated than test tube *1*. If you were using estimates instead of colorimetry measurements, this step can be skipped.)

2. Analyzing Data
Calculate the initial concentrations of SCN^- for test tubes *1, 3, 4, 5,* and *6*. Remember that each 5.0 mL of 0.002 00 M KSCN was mixed with 5.0 mL of $Fe(NO_3)_3$ solution to give a total volume of 10.0 mL. (Hint: the value will be the same for all the test tubes.)

3. Analyzing Data
Calculate the actual initial concentration of Fe^{3+} in the test tubes in a similar way. (Hint: the values recorded in the data table show the concentrations of Fe^{3+} before being diluted by 0.002 00 M KSCN.)

4. Applying Ideas
Determine the equilibrium concentrations for test tube *1*. Because the initial concentration of Fe^{3+} was 0.100 M, much larger than the initial concentration of SCN^-, 0.001 M, assume that practically all of the SCN^- ions are consumed in the reaction. (Even though this is not necessarily true, the deviation from the true SCN^- concentration will be so much smaller than the other factors in this equation that it can be disregarded temporarily.)

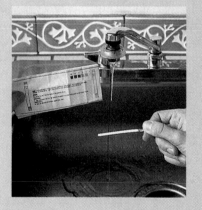

5. Analyzing Data
Calculate the $FeSCN^{2+}$ equilibrium concentration for test tubes *3–6*, based on the equilibrium concentration for test tube *1* determined in item **4** and the absorbance data. (Hint: multiply the concentration for test tube *1* by the factors calculated in item **1**.)

6. Analyzing Data
Calculate the SCN^- concentration for test tubes *3–6* at equilibrium. (Hint: you know the initial SCN^- concentration from item **2**, and you know the amount of SCN^- that has formed $FeSCN^{2+}$ from item **5**.)

7. Analyzing Data
For test tubes *3–6*, calculate the Fe^{3+} concentration at equilibrium. (Hint: you know the initial Fe^{3+} concentration from item **3**, and you know the amount of Fe^{3+} that has formed $FeSCN^{2+}$ from item **5**.)

8. Analyzing Data
Graph the adjusted absorbance values from item **1** against the initial concentration values for $[Fe^{3+}]$.

Conclusions

9. Evaluating Data

For test tubes *3–6*, determine the value of the equilibrium constant, K_{eq}, for this reaction by using the equation given below. (Hint: use the equilibrium concentrations determined in items **5**, **6**, and **7**.)

$$K = \frac{[FeSCN^{2+}]}{[Fe^{3+}][SCN^-]}$$

10. Evaluating Data

Calculate the average value for the equilibrium constant from item **9**. Calculate each value's absolute deviation from this average. Then calculate the average deviation of all of the values. (Hint: instructions on calculating absolute and average deviation can be found in Exploration 2A.)

11. Evaluating Data

Based on your answers from item **10**, do you think the procedure was precise? Can you tell whether or not it was accurate? Explain your answers. (Hint: K_{eq} values that are within the same order of magnitude can be considered reasonably precise.)

12. Evaluating Methods

Although the values for K_{eq} should be equal, explain several conditions that could cause these values to differ.

13. Interpreting Graphics

What general statement can you make about the absorbance values compared to the concentration of Fe^{3+} and $FeSCN^{2+}$?

Extensions

1. Applying Conclusions

The company developing the Fe^{3+} ion test kit needs instructions and a color key for customers that relates the different shades of red seen after adding KSCN to different concentrations of Fe^{3+} ions. Using art supplies or a computer with a color printer, create a small pamphlet or brochure that contains simplified instructions on how to perform the procedure, a color key on a strip of paper, and notations about concentration.

2. Designing Experiments

How would you revise this procedure to determine the value of the equilibrium constant at different temperatures? Would you be able to maintain accurate data analysis for high or low temperature ranges? Explain your answers.

3. Designing Experiments

What possible sources of error can you identify with this procedure? If you can think of ways to eliminate them, ask your teacher to approve your plan, and run the procedure again.

4. Applying Conclusions

In item **4** of the Analysis and Interpretation section, the assumption was made that absolutely all of the SCN^- reacted. Now you can make a better estimate of the actual equilibrium concentrations for the ions in test tube *1* by following these directions.

- Assign x to be the concentration of $FeSCN^{2+}$. Then the equilibrium concentrations of the other ions will be their initial concentrations subtracted by x.
- Use the equilibrium expression given in item **9**. Fill in the average value of K_{eq} calculated in item **10**. Then fill in the equilibrium concentrations of the ions from the previous step.
- Simplify the equation, and use algebra to subtract from one or both sides of the equation until there is only a zero on one side of the equation.
- Apply the quadratic formula to the equation from the previous step to determine the value of x. For any equation with the form given below, x has the values shown.

$$ax^2 + bx + c = 0$$

$$x = \frac{-b \pm \sqrt{b^2 - 4ac}}{2a}$$

- Using the value you calculate for x, determine the equilibrium concentrations of each ion.
- Assume that this newly calculated value of $FeSCN^{2+}$ concentration at equilibrium is the actual value, and calculate the percent error from assuming that the reaction went to completion and had an equilibrium $FeSCN^{2+}$ concentration of 1×10^{-3} M.

5. *Applying Ideas*

Hundreds of different equilibrium reactions are taking place constantly in your body. One very important equilibrium reaction involves oxygen, O_2, and hemoglobin, a complex protein abbreviated as Hb, to form oxyhemoglobin (HbO_2).

$$O_2(g) + Hb(aq) \rightleftharpoons HbO_2(aq)$$

In your lungs, where oxygen is in abundance, the equilibrium shifts to the right. The oxyhemoglobin then travels in your bloodstream to your oxygen-starved cells. At the cells, the equilibrium shifts to the left, releasing the oxygen. In this way, the equilibrium constant is maintained as you continue to live and breathe. Write the equilibrium expression for oxygen, hemoglobin, and oxyhemoglobin.

6. *Predicting Outcomes*

At the elevation of Mexico City, 2300 m (7500 ft), the concentration of oxygen is 75% of that at sea level. Yet, the same amount of oxygen needs to be delivered to the muscle cells. To compensate, does the body produce more or less hemoglobin? Explain your answer.

EQUILIBRIUM EXPRESSIONS

Iron Content of Tea

Far East
TRADING COMPANY

April 12, 1995

Reginald Brown
Director, Materials Testing Department
CheMystery Labs, Inc.
52 Fulton Street
Springfield, VA 22150

Dear Mr. Brown:

At the Far East Trading Company, we seek to dispel the myth that spinach is the best source of iron in a healthy diet. We believe that regular servings of our jasmine tea can provide just as much iron to the consumer as spinach.

Our products have never been marketed on their nutritional value, so we need to have hard data to back up these facts. Our researchers developed a procedure for extracting iron from food, and now we need an outside laboratory to perform an independent analysis of the iron content. Extracts of iron from our jasmine tea and from spinach are being sent to you.

Although we can extract the iron in our quality control lab, we do not have the analytical equipment to perform the iron content analysis. We hope your tests will verify our bold statement. We propose a $300 000 contract for your services.

Sincerely,

Richelle Pomeroy

Richelle Pomeroy
Director of Sales and Marketing
Far East Trading Company

Required Precautions

Lab aprons and goggles must be worn at all times.

Do not touch or taste any chemicals. Wash your hands thoroughly when finished.

If you get acid or base on your skin or clothing, wash it off at the sink while calling to your teacher. If you get acid or base in your eyes, immediately flush it out at the eyewash while calling to your teacher.

Memorandum

CheMystery Labs, Inc.
52 Fulton Street
Springfield, VA 22150

Date: April 13, 1995

To: Alvin Horton

From: Reginald Brown

Because the solutions of iron are in the form of Fe^{3+} solutions, I believe we should use colorimetric methods to determine their concentration. However, these solutions will be somewhat dilute, so we may need to make use of the Fe^{3+}-$FeSCN^{2+}$ equilibrium to measure concentration.

We need to be efficient and very accurate because by the terms of the contract, we are liable for any false advertising claims filed against Far East Trading Company over the iron content of the tea. To help ensure accuracy, give me a preliminary report that includes the following before you begin.
- detailed one-page summary of your plan for the procedure
- all necessary data tables
- itemized list of equipment, with individual and total costs

After you complete the analysis, prepare a two-page report for Richelle Pomeroy at the Far East Trading Company. Be sure to include the following information.
- molar concentration of iron in each solution
- number of moles and grams of iron in 100.0 mL of each solution
- explanation of this analysis and its use of the concept of chemical equilibrium
- estimates and explanations of any possible sources of error
- value of the equilibrium constant
- equilibrium concentrations for each solution
- analysis and data sections, showing calculations
- detailed invoice for all expenses and services

References

Refer to pages 469–471 for information about equilibrium expressions. This analysis is similar to one you recently performed to determine the average value of the equilibrium expression for the Fe^{3+}-$FeSCN^{2+}$ equilibrium at the temperature in your lab. You can measure $FeSCN^{2+}$ concentration using the calibration data from your previous analysis. Then you can use the average value of the equilibrium expression from the previous analysis to determine the equilibrium and initial concentrations of Fe^{3+}. Or else, you can repeat the steps to be certain you have the correct values for K_{eq}.

Spill Procedures/ Waste Disposal Methods

- In case of spills, follow your teacher's instructions.
- Each type of solution and solid precipitate must go in a designated waste container.
- Clean the area and all equipment after use.
- Wash your hands before leaving the lab.

Materials for
FAR EAST TRADING COMPANY

Item	Cost	1	2	3
REQUIRED ITEMS				
(You must include all of these in your budget.)				
Lab space/fume hood/utilities	15 000 — /day			
Standard disposal fee	2 000 — /g of product			
REAGENTS and ADDITIONAL EQUIPMENT				
(Include in your budget only what you'll need.)				
0.200 M Fe(NO₃)₃				
0.6 M HNO₃	1 000 — /mL			
0.00200 M KSCN	1 000 — /mL			
250 mL beaker	1 000 — /mL			
250 mL flask	1 000			
10 mL graduated cylinder	1 000			
Balance	1 000			
Colorimeter—LEAP and cuvettes	5 000			
Filter paper	8 000			
Glass funnel	500 — /piece			
Glass stirring rod	1 000			
Lint-free wipes	1 000			
Paper clips	500 — /box			
Ring stand/ring/wire gauze	500 — /box			
Six test tubes/holder/rack	2 000 —			
Spatula	2 000			
Spectrophotometer and cuvettes	500			
Toothpicks	8 000			
Wash bottle	500 — /dozen			
No refunds on returned chemicals or unused equipment.	500			
FINES				
OSHA safety violation	2 000 — /incident			

EXPLORATION 13A
Technique Builder

Acid-Base Titration of an Eggshell

Objectives
Determine the amount of calcium carbonate present in an eggshell.

Relate experimental titration measurements to a balanced chemical equation.

Infer a conclusion from experimental data.

Apply reaction-stoichiometry concepts.

Situation

You are a research scientist working with the Department of Agriculture. A farmer from a nearby ranch has brought a problem to you. In the past ten years, his hens' eggs have become more and more fragile. So many of them have been breaking that he is beginning to lose money on the operation. The farmer believes his problems are linked to a landfill upstream, which is being investigated for illegal dumping of PCBs and other hazardous chemicals.

Background

Birds have evolved a chemical process which allows them to rapidly produce the calcium carbonate, $CaCO_3$, that is required for eggshell formation. The shell provides a strong protective covering for the developing embryo. Research has shown that some chemicals, like DDT and PCBs, can decrease the amount of calcium carbonate in the eggshell, resulting in shells that are thin and fragile.

PCB

Problem

To determine if the farmer's troubles are related to such weakened eggshells, you need to determine how much calcium carbonate is in sample eggshells from chickens that were not exposed to PCBs. The farmer's eggshells contain about 78% calcium carbonate. The calcium carbonate content of eggshells can easily be determined by means of an acid/base back-titration. In this back-titration, a carefully measured excess of a strong acid will react with the calcium carbonate. Since the acid is in excess, there will be some left over at the end of the reaction. The resulting solution will be titrated with a strong base to determine how much acid remained unreacted. Phenolphthalein will be used as an indicator to signal the endpoint of the titration. From this measurement, you can determine the following:

- the amount of excess acid that reacted with the eggshell
- the amount of calcium carbonate that was present to react with this acid

PCB

Safety

Materials

- 1.00 M HCl
- 1.00 M NaOH
- Distilled water
- Eggshell
- Phenolphthalein solution
- 100 mL beaker
- 50 mL bottle or small Erlenmeyer flask
- 10 mL graduated cylinder
- Balance
- Desiccator (optional)
- Drying oven
- Forceps
- Mortar and pestle
- Three medicine droppers or thin-stemmed pipets
- Weighing paper
- White paper or white background

Preparation

1. Remove the white and the yolk from the egg and dispose of them according to your teacher's directions. Wash the shell with distilled water and carefully peel all the membranes from the inside of the shell. Discard the membranes. Place ALL of the shell in a premassed beaker and dry the shell in the drying oven at 110°C for about 15 min. Continue with steps **2–5** while the eggshell is drying.

2. *Organizing Data*
   Prepare two data tables in your lab notebook. The first should contain four columns, for initial and final volumes from the acid pipet and initial and final volumes from the base pipet. This table will require space for three trials. Also leave space to record the mass of the entire eggshell, the mass of the ground eggshell sample, the number of drops of HCl added, and the number of drops of NaOH added.

3. Put exactly 5.0 mL of water in the 10.0 mL graduated cylinder. Record this volume in the data table in your lab notebook. Fill the first dropper or pipet with water. This dropper should be labeled *Acid*. ***Do not use this dropper for the base solution***. Holding the dropper vertical, add 20 drops of water to the cylinder. ***For the best results, keep the sizes of the drops as even as possible throughout this investigation.*** Record the new volume of water in the first data table as Trial 1.

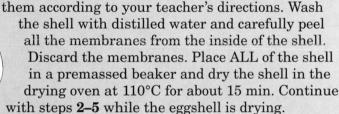

4. Without emptying the graduated cylinder, add an additional 20 drops from the dropper as before, and record the new volume as the final volume for Trial 2. Repeat this procedure once more for Trial 3.

5. Repeat Steps **3** and **4** for the second thin-stemmed dropper. Label this dropper *Base*. ***Do not use this dropper for the acid solution.***

6. Make sure that the three trials produce data that are similar to each other. If one is greatly different from the others, perform steps **3–5** over again. If you're still waiting for the eggshell in the drying oven, calculate and record in the first data table the total volume of the drops and the average volume per drop.

7. Remove the eggshell and beaker from the oven. Cool them in a desiccator. Record the mass of the entire eggshell in the second data table. Place half of the shell into a clean mortar and grind to a very fine powder. This will save time when dissolving the eggshell. (If time permits, dry again and cool in the desiccator.)

Technique

8. Measure the mass of a piece of weighing paper. Transfer about 0.1 g of ground eggshell to a piece of weighing paper, and measure the eggshell's mass as accurately as possible. Record the mass in the second data table. Place this eggshell sample in a clean 50 mL bottle or Erlenmeyer flask.

9. Fill the acid dropper with the 1.00 M HCl acid solution, and then empty the dropper into an extra 100 mL beaker. Label the beaker *Waste*. Fill the base dropper with the 1.00 M NaOH base solution, and then empty the dropper into the 100 mL beaker.

10. Fill the acid dropper once more with 1.00 M HCl. Using the acid dropper, add exactly 150 drops of 1.00 M HCl to the bottle (or flask) with the eggshell. Swirl gently for 3 to 4 min. Wash down the sides of the flask with about 10 mL of distilled water. Using a third dropper, add 2 drops of phenolphthalein solution. Record the number of drops of HCl used in the second data table.

11. Fill the base dropper with the 1.00 M NaOH. Slowly add NaOH from the base dropper into the bottle or flask with the eggshell mixture until a faint pink color persists, even after it is swirled gently. It may help to use a white piece of paper as a background, so you will be able to see the color as soon as possible. ***Be sure to add the base drop by drop, and be certain the drops end up in the reaction mixture and not on the sides of the bottle or flask. Keep careful count of the number of drops used.*** Record the number of drops of base used in the second data table.

Cleanup and Disposal

12. Dispose of any unused solutions, as well as the neutralized solutions, in the containers designated by your teacher. Remember to wash your hands thoroughly before leaving the laboratory.

Analysis and Interpretation

1. Organizing Ideas

The calcium carbonate in the eggshell sample undergoes a double-replacement reaction with the hydrochloric acid in step **9**. Then, the carbonic acid that was formed decomposes. Write a balanced chemical equation for these reactions. (Hint: the gas observed was carbon dioxide.)

2. Organizing Ideas

Write the balanced chemical equation for the acid/base neutralization of the excess unreacted HCl with the NaOH.

3. Organizing Data

Make the necessary calculations from the first data table to find the number of milliliters in each drop. Using this mL/drop ratio, convert the number of drops of each solution in the second data table to volumes in milliliters.

4. Organizing Data

Calculate what volume of the HCl solution was neutralized by the NaOH. (Hint: this relationship was discussed in Section 13-3.) Then subtract this amount from the initial volume of HCl to determine how much HCl reacted with $CaCO_3$.

Conclusions

5. Organizing Data

Calculate the number of moles of $CaCO_3$ that reacted with the HCl. Determine the mass of $CaCO_3$. Then calculate the percentage of $CaCO_3$ in the eggshell sample.

6. Inferring Conclusions

Compare your results to those of the farmer, given in the Problem section of this lab. Explain whether or not you think the farmer's eggs show signs of PCB-induced weaknesses. (Hint: consider how much of a difference in values is enough to indicate a link to PCBs.)

7. Evaluating Methods

Other workers in a lab in another city have also tested eggs, and found that a normal eggshell is about 97% $CaCO_3$. Calculate the percent error for your measurement.

Extensions

1. Inferring Conclusions

Calculate an estimate of the mass of $CaCO_3$ present in the entire eggshell, based on your results. (Hint: apply the percent composition of your sample to the mass of the entire eggshell.)

2. Designing Experiments

What possible sources of error can you identify with this procedure? If you can think of ways to eliminate them, ask your teacher to approve your plan, and run the procedure again.

3. Applying Ideas

Find out how much calcium carbonate is in another type of shell (clam, oyster, snail, etc.).

4. Research and Communications

Investigate the procedures and costs for cleaning up a PCB-tainted site. Debate about who should pay for the cleanup operations.

B

Vacaville Bleachex Production Facility

3617 Industrial Parkway · Vacaville, CA 90627

DELIVER BY OVERNIGHT COURIER

Date: April 21, 1995
To: EPA National Headquarters
From: Anthony Wong, Plant Supervisor
Re: Vacaville Bleachex Corp. Plant Spill

As a result of last night's earthquake, the Bleachex plant in the industrial park south of Vacaville was severely damaged. The safety control measures failed because of the magnitude of the earthquake.

Bleachex manufactures a variety of products using concentrated acids and bases. Plant officials noticed a large quantity of liquid, believed to be sodium hydroxide or hydrochloric acid solution, flowing through the loading bay doors. An Emergency Toxic Spill Response Team attempted to determine the source and identity of the unknown liquid. A series of explosions and the presence of chlorine gas forced the team to abandon their efforts. The unknown liquid continues to flow into the nearly full containment ponds.

We are sending a sample of the liquid to you by overnight courier and hope that you can quickly and accurately identify the liquid and notify us of the proper method for cleanup and disposal. We need your answer as soon as possible.

Anthony Wong

Anthony Wong

Required Precautions

Goggles and lab aprons must be worn at all times.

Do not touch or taste any chemicals. Always wash your hands thoroughly when finished.

If you get acid or base on your skin or clothing, wash it off at the sink while calling to your teacher. If you get acid or base in your eyes, immediately flush it out at the eye-wash while calling to your teacher.

CheMystery Labs, Inc.

Memorandum

52 Fulton Street
Springfield, VA 22150

Date: April 21, 1995

To: Cicely Jackson

From: Marissa Bellinghausen

This is a rush job from the EPA. We have been promised $300 000, three times their normal fee of $100 000, so give this project top priority!

First, we must determine the pH of the unknown so that we know whether it is an acid or a base. Then titrate the unknown using a standard solution to determine its concentration so that we can advise Bleachex on the amount of neutralizing agents they will need for the three 1.75×10^7 L containment ponds.

Because we have only a limited sample, I need to approve your plans before you begin your lab work. Therefore, I need the following items.
- detailed one-page plan for your procedure with all necessary data tables (include multiple trials)
- detailed list of the equipment and materials you will need, with itemized and total costs

When finished, prepare a report in the form of a two-page letter that we can fax to Anthony Wong. The letter must include the following.
- identity of the unknown and its concentration
- pH of the unknown and how you determined it
- paragraph summarizing how you titrated the sample to determine its concentration
- detailed and organized data table
- detailed analysis section with calculations, a discussion of the multiple trials, and a statistical analysis of your precision
- your proposed method for cleanup and disposal, including amount of neutralizing agents necessary
- detailed invoice showing all costs, services, and time for this work

Spill Procedures/ Waste Disposal Methods

- In case of a spill, follow your teacher's instructions.
- Put excess chemicals and solutions in the containers designated by your teacher. Do not pour them down the sink or place them in the trash can.

Materials for BLEACHEX

Item	Cost	1	2	3
REQUIRED ITEMS (You must include all of these in your budget.)				
Lab space/fume hood/utilities	15 000 — /day			
Standard disposal fee	2 000 — /g of product			
REAGENTS AND ADDITIONAL EQUIPMENT (Include in your budget only what you'll need.)				
0.5 M HCl for titration	500 — /mL			
0.5 M NaOH for titration	500 — /mL			
Phenolphthalein	2 000			
250 mL beaker	1 000			
250 mL flask	1 000			
400 mL beaker	2 000			
Aluminum foil	1 000 — /cm²			
Balance	5 000			
Buret	5 000			
Filter paper	500 — /piece			
Glass funnel	1 000			
Glass stirring rod	1 000			
Index card (3 in × 5 in)	1 000			
Magnetic stirrer	5 000			
pH meter	3 000			
pH paper	2 000 — /piece			
pH probe—LEAP	5 000			
Ring stand with buret clamp	2 000			
Six test tubes/holder/rack	2 000			
Stopwatch	5 000			
Wash bottle	500			
* No refunds on returned chemicals or unused equipment.				
FINES				
OSHA safety violation	2 000/incident			

Buffering Capacity

Objectives

Demonstrate proficiency in measuring pH and performing a titration.

Relate the ability of a solution to absorb acid or base and still maintain its pH to its buffering capacity.

Determine which ratio of acetic acid to sodium acetate provides the most efficient buffer for this system.

Graph the curve for the titration of the acetic acid and acetate buffer system.

Interpret the shape and size of the buffer titration curve.

Calculate the buffering capacity for the ratio you determined.

Situation

You work in the research and development department of a company that wants to create a new hair conditioner product. Experiments have determined that the hair conditioner performs best at a pH of about 5.0. You need to determine which proportions of acetic acid and sodium acetate will work best to maintain a pH of 5.0.

Background

Acetic acid is a weak acid. When it is dissolved in water, only a small proportion of the molecules ionize. Similarly, sodium acetate is a weak base. When dissolved in water, a few acetate ions are able to bond to hydrogen to form acetic acid.

Hydronium ion, H_3O^+

As a result, a mixture of these two compounds dissolved in water can serve as a buffer. When hydronium ions are added, they react with the acetate anions to form acetic acid, which exists mainly as non-ionized acetic acid molecules. In other words, acid is added, but the pH doesn't change.

$$C_2H_3O_2^-(aq) + H_3O^+(aq) \rightleftharpoons HC_2H_3O_2(aq) + H_2O(l)$$

On the other hand, if hydroxide ions are added to this buffer solution, they react with any hydronium ions present to form non-ionized water molecules. But then, the acetic acid molecules ionize, restoring equilibrium to the buffer system. Once more, base is added, but the pH doesn't change.

$$OH^-(aq) + H_3O^+(aq) \rightleftharpoons 2H_2O(l)$$

$$HC_2H_3O_2(aq) + H_2O(l) \rightleftharpoons H_3O^+(aq) + C_2H_3O_2^-(aq)$$

The effectiveness of any buffer system depends on the ratio of weak acid to weak base in the solution. For every ratio, there is a limit to how many hydronium ions or hydroxide ions any buffer system can absorb. Eventually, the pH rises or drops substantially because the limit has been exceeded. The amount of hydronium ions or hydroxide ions that can be added to a buffer before the pH changes is called the *buffering capacity* of the system.

Problem

To determine whether the company can use the acetic acid and sodium acetate buffer in the new hair conditioner product, you will need to do the following.

• determine the ratio of acetic acid to sodium acetate that provides the best buffer
• titrate a solution with this ratio, and determine its buffering capacity

Safety

Always wear goggles and an apron to provide protection for your eyes and clothing. If you get a chemical in your eyes, immediately flush it out at the eyewash station while calling to your teacher. Know the locations of the emergency lab shower and eyewash and how to use them.

Do not touch any chemicals. If you get a chemical on your skin or clothing, wash it off at the sink while calling to your teacher. Make sure you carefully read the labels and follow the directions on all containers of chemicals that you use. Do not taste any chemicals or items used in the laboratory. Never return leftovers to their original containers; take only small amounts to avoid wasting supplies.

Never put broken glass or ceramics in a regular waste container. They should be disposed of separately. Put the glass and ceramic pieces in the container designated by your teacher.

Acids and bases are corrosive. If any gets on you, wash the area immediately with running water. Call your teacher in the event of an acid or base spill. Acid or base spills should be cleaned up promptly.

Always clean up the lab and all equipment after use, and dispose of substances according to proper disposal methods. Wash your hands thoroughly before you leave the lab after all lab work is finished.

Preparation

1. **Organizing Data**

   Prepare two data tables in your lab notebook.
   - The first data table should have fifteen rows and seven columns.
   - Put these labels in the columns of the first row: *Solution, Original pH, pH after 1 drop, pH after 2 drops, pH after 3 drops, pH after 4 drops,* and *pH after 5 drops.*
   - Put the following labels in the first column of the second through fifteenth rows: *Solution 1/HCl, Solution 1/NaOH, Solution 2/HCl, Solution 2/NaOH, Solution 3/HCl, Solution 3/NaOH, Solution 4/HCl, Solution 4/NaOH, Solution 5/HCl, Solution 5/NaOH, Solution 6/HCl, Solution 6/NaOH, Solution 7/HCl,* and *Solution 7/NaOH.*
   - The second data table is not necessary if you are working with a LEAP System with a pH probe. It should have 3 rows and 22 columns. If space is a problem, break the table, making two with 11 columns instead of one with 22.
   - Put the following labels in the first row: *Solution, Original pH, pH after 1 drop, pH after 2 drops,* and so on, up to *pH after 20 drops.*
   - In the first box of the second row, insert the label *HCl.* In the first box of the third row, insert the label *NaOH.*

Materials

- **Distilled water**
- **0.10 M $HC_2H_3O_2$**
- **0.10 M $NaC_2H_3O_2$**
- **1.0 M HCl in dropper bottle**
- **1.0 M NaOH in dropper bottle**
- **50 mL beakers, 2**
- **400 mL beaker**
- **10 mL graduated cylinder**
- **pH meter or pH paper**

Procedure with LEAP System and pH probe

- **0.10 M NaOH in buret**
- **0.10 M HCl in buret**
- **LEAP System with pH probe**
- **Ring stand with buret clamp**
- **Stopwatch**

2. Calibrate the pH meter or LEAP System with pH probe using a standard buffer of known pH. This step is not necessary if you are using pH paper.

3. Label the two 50 mL beakers *Solution* and *Solution + HCl*. Label the 400 mL beaker *Waste*.

Technique

Determining best ratio for buffer

4. Measure 10.0 mL of sodium acetate in a 10 mL graduated cylinder, and pour it into the 50 mL beaker labeled *Solution*. Measure 10.0 mL of distilled water, and add it to the beaker, swirling the mixture gently to mix thoroughly. This is *Solution 1*.

5. Measure the initial pH of *Solution 1*, and record it in the first data table under *Original pH*.

6. Pour about half of *Solution 1* into the beaker labeled *Solution + HCl*. Add one drop of 1.0 M HCl, and swirl the beaker gently. Measure and record the pH in the first data table.

7. Continue adding HCl drop by drop. After each drop, record the pH. Stop when 5 drops have been added.

8. Repeat steps **4–7** with the remainder of *Solution 1* that was left in the beaker labeled *Solution*, but this time add drops of 1.0 M NaOH. Measure and record the pH in the first data table.

9. Empty both 50 mL beakers into the *Waste* beaker. Clean both beakers and the graduated cylinder. Rinse them several times with distilled water.

10. Repeat steps **5–9** for *Solutions 2–7*. For best results, prepare solutions one at a time.
    - *Solution 2* should contain 8.0 mL $NaC_2H_3O_2$, 2.0 mL $HC_2H_3O_2$, and 10.0 mL of distilled water.
    - *Solution 3* should contain 6.0 mL $NaC_2H_3O_2$, 4.0 mL $HC_2H_3O_2$, and 10.0 mL of distilled water.
    - *Solution 4* should contain 5.0 mL $NaC_2H_3O_2$, 5.0 mL $HC_2H_3O_2$, and 10.0 mL of distilled water.
    - *Solution 5* should contain 4.0 mL $NaC_2H_3O_2$, 6.0 mL $HC_2H_3O_2$, and 10.0 mL of distilled water.
    - *Solution 6* should contain 2.0 mL $NaC_2H_3O_2$, 8.0 mL $HC_2H_3O_2$, and 10.0 mL of distilled water.
    - *Solution 7* should contain 10.0 mL $HC_2H_3O_2$ and 10.0 mL of distilled water.

11. Clean the two beakers and the graduated cylinder, and rinse them several times with distilled water.

Determining buffering capacity

12. Examine the pH measurements in your first data table. Calculate the difference between the pH values obtained after adding 5 drops of HCl and the pH obtained after adding 5 drops of NaOH to each solution. Which ratio of weak acid to weak base shows the smallest change in pH whether acid or base is added?

13. In the beaker labeled *Solution + HCl*, prepare another batch of the solution you identified in step **12** as the best buffer. If you are working with a pH meter or pH paper, follow step **13a**. If you are using the LEAP System with a pH probe, follow step **13b**.

a. pH meter or pH paper
Add 1.0 M HCl one drop at a time. Measure and record the pH after each drop. Stop adding HCl when the pH drops suddenly, which indicates that the solution has lost its buffering capacity. Empty the solution into the *Waste* beaker, and continue with step **14**.

b. LEAP system with pH probe
Calibrate your buret to release liquid from the tip at the rate of 10 drops per second. To do this, put the *Waste* beaker under the buret, and fill the buret with water. Use a stopwatch to measure drops per second, and practice positioning the stopcock so that you have a rate of 10 drops per second.

When you are ready to proceed, empty the buret, and fill it with 0.10 M HCl. Make sure your probe is calibrated and the cap is removed. Put the probe into the solution you are testing. On the computer, move the cursor to the green portion of the stoplight and start the experiment. After you have taken the initial reading and the probe has stabilized, set the stoplight to red, and erase the data collected during calibration.

Start the experiment again, and begin the titration. Add HCl until approximately 950 readings have been taken or until the buffer solution's pH is no longer constant. (Only 1000 data points will be saved. If you continue taking data after this point, you will lose earlier data.) When finished, set the stoplight to red, and print your graph. Empty the solution into the *Waste* beaker.

14. In the beaker labeled *Solution*, prepare another batch of the solution you identified in step **12** as the best buffer. If you are working with a pH probe or pH paper, follow step **14a**. If you are using the LEAP System with a pH probe, follow step **14b**.

a. pH probe or pH paper
Add 1.0 M NaOH one drop at a time. Measure and record the pH after each drop. Stop adding NaOH when the pH rises suddenly, indicating that the solution has lost its buffering capacity. Empty the solution into the *Waste* beaker, and continue with step **15**.

b. LEAP system with pH probe

Calibrate your buret to release liquid from the tip at the rate of 10 drops per second as before. When you are ready to proceed, empty the buret, and fill it with 0.10 M NaOH. Make sure your probe is calibrated and the cap is removed. Put the probe into the solution you are testing. On the computer, move the cursor to the green portion of the stoplight, and start the experiment. After the probe has stabilized, set the stoplight to red, and erase the data collected during calibration Start the experiment again, and begin the titration. Add NaOH until approximately 950 readings have been taken or until the buffer solution's pH is no longer constant. Then set the stoplight to red and print your graph. Empty the solution into the *Waste* beaker.

Cleanup and Disposal

15. Pour the solution in the *Waste* beaker into the container designated by your teacher. Place any leftover acid solutions in a designated container. Leftover basic solutions should be placed in a different designated container. Thoroughly clean the area.

Analysis and Interpretation

1. Organizing Data

Determine the seven $NaC_2H_3O_2$-$HC_2H_3O_2$ mole ratios for the seven buffer solutions you prepared in steps **4–10**.

2. Applying Ideas

If you needed a solution that had to maintain the same pH with additions of acid only, which solution would you pick? If you needed a solution that had to maintain the same pH with additions of base only, which solution would you pick?

3. Analyzing Data

Using your data, explain why neither of the solutions you chose in item **2** was the buffer you chose in step **12**.

4. Organizing Data

Plot the pH data from the two titrations on one graph. Label the y-axis with the pH of the solution. Position a vertical line at the midpoint of the x-axis. To the left of this vertical line, plot the increasing numbers of drops of HCl. To the right of the line, plot the increasing numbers of drops of NaOH.

Conclusions

5. Inferring Conclusions

Which ratio of acetic acid to sodium acetate provides the best buffering system? Use your data to support your choice.

6. Interpreting Graphics

Examine the way that the slope of your titration curve changes. In what pH range does the slope change the least? In what pH range would the acetic acid and sodium acetate buffer be most suitable? Could you use this buffer system to run a reaction that requires a pH of approximately 5?

7. Applying Ideas

For the buffer you chose, how many drops of acid or base was it able to absorb before the pH changed by more than 1.0 unit?

8. Analyzing Methods

When water is left out in air, the equilibrium reactions shown below can take place. With this knowledge, explain why it might be important to make pH measurements with solutions prepared one at a time, so that they are not left out in the air for long periods of time.

$$CO_2(g) + H_2O(l) \rightleftharpoons H_2CO_3(aq)$$

$$H_2CO_3(aq) + H_2O(l) \rightleftharpoons H_3O^+(aq) + HCO_3^-(aq)$$

Extensions

1. Designing Experiments

What possible sources of error can you identify with this procedure? If you can think of ways to eliminate them, ask your teacher to approve your plan, and run the procedure again.

2. Applying Ideas

Write the balanced equilibrium equation for the dissociation of acetic acid. Also write the equilibrium expression. Determine the numerical value for the acid-dissociation constant, K_a, by consulting a chemical handbook. Substitute the numerical values for K_a and the initial concentrations of $HC_2H_3O_2$ and $C_2H_3O_2^-$ into the equilibrium expression. Solve the equation for the $[H_3O^+]$, and convert your answer to pH. Does this result support your answer for item **6** in the Conclusions section?

3. Applying Ideas

Using the value of the acid-dissociation constant, K_a, explain why the assumption was made that the equilibrium concentrations were the same as the initial concentrations for $HC_2H_3O_2$ and $C_2H_3O_2^-$.

4. Designing Experiments

Buffers are found in a variety of over-the-counter medicines such as antacids and analgesics. Give a detailed procedure for determining the buffering capacity of a medication and preparing a titration curve. If your teacher approves your plan, carry out the experiment.

5. Designing Experiments

Many organisms and biological systems need a narrow pH range to live. Give a detailed procedure for determining the buffering capacity of some living materials such as a potato, egg white, or milk. If your teacher approves your plan, carry out the experiment.

6. Applying Conclusions

Chemists officially define buffering capacity as the number of moles of H_3O^+ or OH^- needed to cause 1.00 L of the buffered solution to undergo a 1.00-unit change in pH. Calculate the buffering capacity for your solution. (Hint: in order to figure out the number of moles of H_3O^+ or OH^-, you will need to determine the volume of a drop. This can be done by measuring the volume of 50 drops and dividing to determine the volume of an individual drop.)

7. Research and Communication

Find out some ways that buffering is important in chemistry and physiology. Prepare a report on your findings.

BUFFERING CAPACITY

Viral Growth Medium

ViroTech, Inc.
CAMBRIDGE, MA

April 25, 1995

Ms. Sandra Fernandez
Director of Development
CheMystery Labs, Inc.
52 Fulton Street
Springfield, VA 22150

Dear Ms. Fernandez:

We are researching a virus that may hold the key to a vaccine for common viral infections. This virus is weaker than most disease viruses, so to develop an effective vaccine, we need to find a way to keep the virus alive in storage for long periods of time. The key to keeping the virus alive is to maintain a pH range of 8.5–9.5 in its environment.

Please develop a simple buffer system that will meet our needs. You can understand how important it would be to develop a vaccine for preventing the common cold and flu.

We are willing to pay up to $400 000 for a satisfactory solution to this problem. We look forward to hearing from you very soon.

Sincerely yours,

Christina M. Williams

Christina M. Williams, Ph.D.
President

Required Precautions

Goggles and lab aprons must be worn at all times.

If you get acid or base on your skin or clothing, wash it off at the sink while calling to your teacher. If you get it in your eyes, immediately flush it out at the eyewash station while calling to your teacher.

Do not touch or taste any chemicals. Wash your hands thoroughly when finished.

CheMystery Labs, Inc.
52 Fulton Street
Springfield, VA 22150

Memorandum

Date: April 26, 1995

To: Regina Walter

From: Sandra Fernandez

Virotech is an up-and-coming biotechnology and genetic-engineering firm. This is an excellent opportunity for our company to break into this rapidly expanding market for our services, so make sure your work is extremely efficient and accurate!

I suggest that we examine either a buffer system with ammonia and ammonium chloride or one with acetic acid and sodium acetate. Decide which buffer system you want to investigate. Determine the ratio of ingredients that provides the most efficient buffer at the pH specified in the letter. Before you begin your work, let me review the following items.
- buffer system you chose and why
- detailed one-page summary of your plan for the procedure
- any necessary data tables
- itemized list of equipment, with individual and total costs

After you complete the project, prepare a three-page report for Williams. It should include the following.
- proportions for the buffer system that works best, along with a brief description of how to prepare it
- discussion of the buffering capacity of the buffer system
- summary of your procedure
- detailed analysis and data sections showing all necessary calculations and the titration curve for the buffer
- itemized bill for materials used and services rendered

References

Refer to page 516–517 for information about buffered solutions. The procedure for determining the best proportion for a buffer and measuring buffering capacity are similar to one your team recently completed with the sodium acetate–acetic acid buffering system. Note that a different pH level is required in this Investigation.

Spill Procedures/ Waste Disposal Methods

- In case of a spill, follow your teacher's instructions
- Place buffer solutions, leftover acid, and leftover base in separate disposal containers designated by your teacher.
- Clean the area and all equipment after use, and wash your hands before leaving the lab.

Materials for VIROTECH, INC.

Item	Cost	
REQUIRED ITEMS		
(You must include all of these in your budget.)		
Lab space/fume hood/utilities	15 000 —	/day
Standard disposal fee	2 000 —	/g of product
REAGENTS and ADDITIONAL EQUIPMENT		
(Include in your budget only what you'll need.)		
0.10 M $HC_2H_3O_2$	1 000 —	/mL
1.0 M HCl, in a dropper bottle or buret	8 000	
0.10 M $NaC_2H_3O_2$	1 000 —	/mL
0.10 M $NH_3 \cdot H_2O$	1 000 —	/mL
0.10 M NH_4Cl	1 000 —	/mL
1.0 M $NaOH$, in a dropper bottle or buret	8 000	
50 mL beaker	1 000	
400 mL beaker	2 000	
10 mL graduated cylinder	1 000	
Filter paper	500 —	/piece
Glass funnel	1 000	
Glass stirring rod	1 000	
pH meter	3 000	
pH paper	2 000 —	/piece
pH probe—LEAP	5 000	
Ring stand with buret clamp	2 000	
Stopwatch	5 000	
Wash bottle	500	
Weighing paper	500 —	/piece
*No refunds on returned chemicals or unused equipment.		
FINES		
OSHA safety violation	2 000 —	/incident

EXPLORATION

14A

Technique Builder

Reaction Rates

Objectives

Prepare and observe several different reaction mixtures.

Demonstrate proficiency in measuring reaction rates.

Relate experimental results to a rate law that can predict the results of various combinations of reactants.

Situation

Your company has been contacted by a toy company. They want technical assistance in designing a new executive desk gadget. The idea they want to investigate incorporates a reaction that turns a distinctive color in a specific amount of time. Although it will not be easy to determine the precise combination of chemicals that will work, the profit they stand to make would make it all worthwhile in the end. Executive "playtoys" are a big business, with corporate prices to match the corporate market.

Background

The reaction investigated here is a special kind of electron-transfer reaction called a *reduction-oxidation*, or *redox*, reaction. Reactions of this type will be studied further in Chapter 15. The net equation for the reaction in the gadget is written as follows.

$$3Na_2S_2O_5(aq) + 2KIO_3(aq) + 3H_2O(l) \xrightarrow{H^+}$$

$$2KI(aq) + 6NaHSO_4(aq)$$

You will measure the progress of this reaction using a starch-indicator solution. When the $Na_2S_2O_5$ solution is used up, the buildup of I_2, an intermediate in the reaction, will cause the indicator to change to a blue-black color. In the investigation, the concentrations of reactants are discussed in terms of drops of Solution A and Solution B. Solution A actually contains $Na_2S_2O_5$, the starch-indicator solution, and dilute sulfuric acid to supply the hydrogen ions needed to catalyze the reaction. Solution B contains KIO_3.

Problem

To determine the best conditions and concentrations for the reaction, you must do the following.

- prepare and observe reactions of several different concentrations of the reactants
- measure the time elapsed for each reaction
- determine the rate law for the reaction that will allow you to predict the results with other combinations
- use tools of statistical analysis to compare your data to that of the rest of the class

Safety

Always wear goggles and an apron to provide protection for your eyes and clothing. If you get a chemical in your eyes, immediately flush it out at the eyewash station while calling to your teacher. Know the locations of the emergency lab shower and eyewash and how to use them.

Do not touch any chemicals. If you get a chemical on your skin or clothing, wash it off at the sink while calling to your teacher. Make sure you carefully read the labels and follow the directions on all containers of chemicals that you use. Do not taste any chemicals or items used in the laboratory. Never return leftovers to their original containers; take only small amounts to avoid wasting supplies.

Call your teacher in the event of an acid or base spill. Acid or base spills should be cleaned up promptly according to your teacher's instructions.

Always clean up the lab and all equipment after use, and dispose of substances according to proper disposal methods. Wash your hands thoroughly before you leave the lab after all lab work is finished.

Materials

- Distilled or deionized water
- Solution A
- Solution B
- Eight-well microscale reaction strips, 2
- Fine-tipped dropper bulbs or small micro-tip pipets, 3
- Stopwatch or clock with second hand

Preparation

1. **Organizing Data**
   Prepare a data table in your lab notebook. The table should have six rows and six columns. Label the boxes in the first row of the second through sixth columns *Well 1*, *Well 2*, *Well 3*, *Well 4*, and *Well 5*. In the first column, label the boxes in the second through sixth rows *Time reaction began*, *Time reaction stopped*, *Drops of A*, *Drops of B*, and *Drops of H₂O*.

2. Obtain three dropper bulbs or small micro-tip pipets, and label them *A*, *B*, and *H₂O*.

3. Fill the bulb or pipet *A* with solution A, the bulb or pipet *B* with solution B, and the bulb or pipet *H₂O* with distilled water.

Technique

4. Using the first eight-well strip, place five drops of solution A into each of the first five wells. (Disregard the remaining three wells.) For best results, try to make all drops about the same size. Record the number of drops in the appropriate places in your data table. ***For best results, try to make all of the drops about the same size.***

5. In the second eight-well reaction strip, place one drop of solution B in the first well, two drops in the second well, three drops in the third well, four drops in the fourth well, and five drops in the fifth well. Record the number of drops in the appropriate places in your data table.

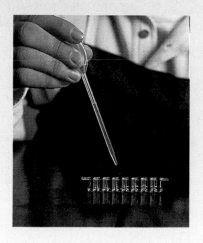

6. In the second eight-well strip, which contains drops of solution B, add four drops of water to the first well, three drops to the second well, two drops to the third well, and one drop to the fourth well. Do not add any water to the fifth well.

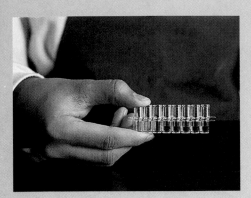

7. Carefully invert the second strip. The surface tension should keep the solutions from falling out of the wells. Place the second strip well-to-well on top of the first strip as shown in the photograph on the left.

8. Holding the strips tightly together, record the exact time, or set the stopwatch, as you shake the solutions once, using a vigorous motion. This procedure should effectively mix the upper solutions with each of the corresponding lower ones.

9. Observe the lower wells. Note the sequence in which the solutions react, and record the number of seconds it takes for each solution to turn a deep blue color.

Cleanup and Disposal

10. Dispose of the solutions in the container designated by your teacher. Wash your hands thoroughly after cleaning up the area and equipment.

Analysis and Interpretation

1. **Organizing Data**
   Calculate the time elapsed for the complete reaction of each of the combinations of solution A and B.

2. **Organizing Data**
   Make a graph of your results. Label the x-axis *Number of drops of solution B*. Label the y-axis *Time elapsed*. Make a similar graph for drops of solution B against rate (1/time elapsed).

3. **Analyzing Information**
   Which mixture showed the fastest reaction? Which mixture showed the slowest reaction?

4. **Evaluating Methods**
   Why was it important to add the drops of water to the wells that contained fewer than five drops of Solution B? (Hint: figure out the total number of drops in each of the reaction wells.)

Conclusions

5. **Analyzing Methods**
   How can you be sure each of the chemical reactions for the gadget began at about the same time? Why is this important?

6. **Evaluating Conclusions**
   Which of the following variables that can affect rate is tested in this experiment: temperature, catalyst, concentration, surface area, or nature of reactants? Explain your answer.

7. **Applying Ideas**
   Use your data and graphs to determine the relationship between the concentration of solution B and the rate of the reaction. Describe this relationship in terms of a rate law.

Extensions

1. **Evaluating Data**
   Share your data with other lab groups, and calculate a class average for the rate of the reaction for each concentration of B. Compare results from other groups to your results. Calculate the average deviation and the standard deviation. Explain why there are differences in the results. (Hint: instructions for these calculations are given in Exploration 2A.)

2. **Analyzing Methods**
   What are some possible sources of error in this procedure? If you can think of ways to eliminate them, ask your teacher to approve your plan, and run your procedure again.

3. **Predicting Outcomes**
   What combination of drops of solutions A and B would you use if you wanted the reaction to last exactly 2.5 min? Design an experiment to test your answer. If your teacher approves your plan, perform the experiment, and record these results. Make another graph including both the old and new data.

4. **Predicting Outcomes**
   What would your data be if the experiment was repeated, but solution A was diluted, with one part solution A for every seven parts distilled water? Design an experiment to test your answer. If your teacher approves your plan, perform the experiment. (Calculate percent error.)

5. **Designing Experiments**
   How would you determine what would be the smallest interval of time you could distinguish with the clock reaction? Design an experiment to find out. If your teacher approves your plan, perform the experiment.

6. **Designing Experiments**
   How would the results of this experiment be affected if the reaction took place in a cold environment? Design an experiment to test your answer, using materials available. If your teacher approves your plan, perform your experiment, and record the results. Make another graph, and compare it to your old data.

7. **Designing Experiments**
   How could you determine the effect of solution A on the rate law? If your teacher approves your plan, perform your experiment, and determine the rate law for this reaction.

8. **Relating Ideas**
   If solution B contains 0.02 M KIO_3, calculate the value for the constant, k, in the expression below. (Hint: remember that solution B is diluted when it is added to solution A.)
   $Rate = k[KIO_3]$

Effervescent Tablet Evaluation

Kravitz Morrow & Jones

May 1, 1995

Martha Li-Hsien
Director of Research
CheMystery Labs, Inc.
52 Fulton Street
Springfield, VA 22150

Dear Mr. Brown:

We are currently developing an advertising campaign for a new effervescent tablet that will relieve indigestion. Our marketing strategy will be to compare the leading brands of effervescent tablets with the new brand, now referred to as brand X. We want independent testing to be sure that our claims are valid.

We would like you to investigate how the reaction rate of brand X compares with that of two other leading brands. Enclosed are samples of these tablets, which are labeled brand A and brand B. Provide as much quantitative data as possible. Please also provide data on other factors that affect rates. This information will be used to make certain that the labeling includes instructions to help consumers make the most effective use of the product.

We have asked several analytical firms to perform this evaluation and will choose a long-term product consultant based on the reports we receive. Your bid should include the cost of completing this analysis and 10 similar analyses over the next year.

Sincerely,

Chris Strong
Director of Product Research
Kravitz, Morrow, and Jones

Required Precautions

 Goggles and lab aprons must be worn.

 Do not taste any of the chemicals, including the tablets. If you get any on your skin or clothing, wash it off at the sink. If it is in your eyes, immediately flush it out at the eyewash station while calling to your teacher. Wash your hands thoroughly when finished.

 Confine long hair and loose clothing. Do not heat cracked glassware. If your clothing catches fire, WALK to the lab shower and put it out.

CheMystery Labs, Inc.
52 Fulton Street
Springfield, VA 22150

Memorandum

Date: May 2, 1995

To: Tom de los Santos

From: Martha Li-Hsien

Becoming the consultant for a large marketing firm could mean big profits. But we have to be certain that we provide quality work at a reasonable price. Before you begin this analysis, I'd like to review the following items.

- detailed one-page plan for the procedure and all necessary data tables
- detailed list of the equipment and materials you plan to use, along with individual and total costs
- final cost figure for our bid that reflects 10 future analyses, taking into consideration the actual costs incurred during the analysis as well as a profit margin

After you have completed your analysis prepare a report in the form of a two-page letter to Ms. Strong at Kravitz, Morrow, and Jones. The report should include the following.

- suggestions for wording to be used in advertising and on the instruction panel of the label
- rankings of the rate of reaction for each brand of tablet in a simulated stomach acid solution, as well as criteria for the rankings and examples of specific data that support the rankings
- detailed and organized data and analysis section showing any calculations you used to reach your conclusions, and graphs that show visual proof of your conclusions (Considering that this work is being done for a marketing firm, we need clean, easy-to-understand graphs to display your results.)
- detailed invoice for the services rendered and the expenses incurred for this investigation
- revised bid for the other 10 proposed analyses

References

Refer to pages 550–553 for more information on reaction rates and the reaction conditions that can affect reaction rate. Remember that the rate of a reaction is not the same as the time it takes for a reaction to occur, but is rather a measure of the amount of reactant converted to product in a certain amount of time. Be sure to consider how you will judge when the reaction is over. Stomach contents for someone with acid indigestion are typically at a pH of about 1.0, corresponding to a concentration of 0.10 M HCl solution. Normal internal body temperature is 37°C. Base your disposal cost on the masses of the tablets and the HCl solution.

Spill Procedures/ Waste Disposal Methods

- All tablets and their solutions may be washed down the sink after they have been diluted with 20 times as much water.

- Any leftover acid should be disposed of in the container designated by your teacher.

Materials for KRAVITZ, MORROW, and JONES

Item	Cost		
REQUIRED ITEMS *(You must include all of these in your budget.)*			
Lab space/fume hood/utilities	15 000 — /day		
Standard disposal fee	2 000 — /g of product		
Beaker tongs	1 000		
REAGENTS and ADDITIONAL EQUIPMENT *(Include only what you'll need in your budget.)*			
0.10 M HCl	100 — /mL		
Ice	500		
250 mL beaker	1 000		
250 mL flask	1 000		
100 mL graduated cylinder	1 000		
Balance	5 000		
Bunsen burner	10 000		
Glass stirring rod	1 000		
Hot plate	8 000		
Mortar and pestle	2 000		
Ring stand/ring/wire gauze	2 000		
Rubber policeman	500		
Six test tubes (large)/holder/rack	2 000		
Stopwatch	5 000		
Test tube (small)	500		
Thermistor—LEAP	2 000		
Thermometer	2 000		
Wash bottle	500		
Weighing paper	500		
* No refunds on returned chemicals or unused equipment.			
Fines			
OSHA safety violation	2 000 — /incident		

Redox Titration

Objectives
Demonstrate proficiency in performing redox titrations and recognizing endpoints of a redox reaction.

Write a balanced oxidation-reduction equation for a redox reaction.

Determine the concentration of a solution using stoichiometry and volume data from a titration.

Situation

You are a chemist working for a chemical analysis firm. A large pharmaceutical company has hired you to help salvage some of their products after a small fire broke out in their warehouse. Although there was only minimal smoke and fire damage to the warehouse and products, the sprinkler system ruined the labeling on many of the pharmaceuticals. The firm's best-selling products are iron tonics, used to treat low-level anemia. The tonics are produced from hydrated iron(II) sulfate, $FeSO_4 \cdot 7H_2O$. The different types of tonics contain different concentrations of $FeSO_4$. You need to help them figure out what labels to put on the bottles of tonic.

Background

Hydrated iron(II) sulfate, $FeSO_4 \cdot 7H_2O$, is a useful compound of iron in the +2 oxidation state, that is used as a reducing agent and in medicines. Because this substance is a reducing agent, it can undergo a redox reaction with an oxidizing agent. Redox reactions involve the processes of oxidation (the loss of electrons by a reactant, Fe^{2+}) and reduction (the gain of electrons by a reactant, in this case MnO_4^-).

You have already studied acid-base titrations in Chapter 13, in which an unknown amount of acid is titrated with a carefully measured amount of base. In this procedure, a similar approach called a *redox titration* is used. In a redox titration, the reducing agent, Fe^{2+}, is oxidized to Fe^{3+} by the oxidizing agent, MnO_4^-. When this process occurs, the Mn in MnO_4^- changes from a +7 to a +2 oxidation state and has a noticeably different color. You can use this color change in the same way that you used the color change of phenolphthalein in acid-base titrations—to signify a redox reaction "endpoint." When the reaction is complete, the addition of excess MnO_4^- will give the solution a pink or purple color.

Problem

To determine how to label the bottles, you need to determine the concentration of iron(II) ions in the sample from an unlabeled bottle from the warehouse.

- titrate the Fe^{2+} sample with a $KMnO_4$ solution of known concentration
- use mole ratios from the balanced redox reaction and the volume data obtained from the titration to determine the concentration of the sample
- identify which tonic the sample is, given information about the concentration of each tonic

Safety

Always wear goggles and an apron to provide protection for your eyes and clothing. If you get a chemical in your eyes, immediately flush it out at the eyewash station while calling to your teacher. Know the locations of the emergency lab shower and eyewash and how to use them.

Do not touch any chemicals. If you get a chemical on your skin or clothing, wash it off at the sink while calling to your teacher. Make sure you carefully read the labels and follow the directions on all containers of chemicals that you use. Do not taste any chemicals or items used in the laboratory. Never return leftovers to their original containers; take only small amounts to avoid wasting supplies.

Never put broken glass in a regular waste container. Broken glass should be disposed of separately according to your teacher's instructions.

Call your teacher in the event of an acid, base, or potassium permanganate spill. Such spills should be cleaned up promptly. Acids and bases are corrosive; avoid breathing fumes. $KMnO_4$ is a strong oxidizer. If any of the oxidizer should spill on you, immediately flush the area with water and notify your teacher.

Always clean up the lab and all equipment after use, and dispose of substances according to proper disposal methods. Wash your hands thoroughly before you leave the lab after all lab work is finished.

Materials

- 0.0200 M $KMnO_4$
- 1.0 M H_2SO_4
- Distilled water
- $FeSO_4$ solution
- 250 mL beaker, 2
- 400 mL beaker
- 125 mL Erlenmeyer flask, 4
- 100 mL graduated cylinder
- Burets, 2
- Double buret clamp
- Ring stand
- Wash bottle

Preparation

1. Prepare a data table in your lab notebook. The table should have four rows and five columns. Label the boxes in the top row *Trial, Initial KMnO₄ volume, Final KMnO₄ volume, Initial FeSO₄ volume,* and *Final FeSO₄ volume.* In the first column, number the second through fourth rows *1, 2,* and *3.*

2. Clean two 50 mL burets with a buret brush and distilled water. Rinse each buret at least three times with distilled water to remove any contaminants.

3. Label two 250 mL beakers *0.0200 M KMnO₄,* and *FeSO₄ solution.* Label three of the flasks *1, 2,* and *3.* Label the 400 mL beaker *Waste.* Label one buret *KMnO₄* and the other *FeSO₄.*

4. Measure approximately 75 mL of 0.0200 M $KMnO_4$ and pour it into the appropriately labeled beaker. Obtain approximately 75 mL of $FeSO_4$ solution and pour it into the appropriately labeled beaker.

5. Rinse one buret three times with a few milliliters of 0.0200 M $KMnO_4$ from the appropriately labeled beaker. Collect these rinses in the *Waste* beaker. Rinse the other buret three times with small amounts of $FeSO_4$ solution from the appropriately labeled beaker. Collect these rinses in the *Waste* beaker.

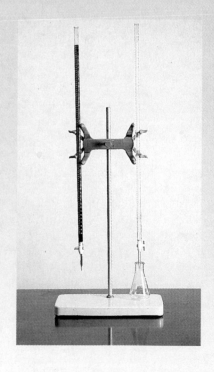

6. Set up the burets as shown in the photograph on page 781. Fill one buret with approximately 50 mL of the 0.0200 M KMnO₄ from the beaker and the other buret with approximately 50 mL of the FeSO₄ solution from the other beaker.

7. With the *Waste* beaker underneath its tip, open the KMnO₄ buret long enough to be sure the buret tip is filled. Repeat for the FeSO₄ buret.

8. Add 50 mL of distilled water to one of the 125 mL Erlenmeyer flasks, and add one drop of 0.0200 M KMnO₄ to the flask. Set this aside to use as a color standard, to compare to the titration and determine the endpoint.

Technique

9. Record the initial buret readings for both solutions in your data table. Add 10.0 mL of the hydrated iron(II) sulfate, FeSO₄•7H₂O, solution to flask *1*. Add 5 mL of 1.0 M H₂SO₄ to the FeSO₄ solution in this flask. The acid helps keep the Fe²⁺ ions in the reduced state to allow you time to titrate.

10. Slowly add KMnO₄ from the buret to the FeSO₄ in the flask, while swirling the flask. When the color of the solution matches the color standard you prepared in step **7**, record the final readings of the burets in your data table.

11. Empty the titration flask into the *Waste* beaker. Repeat the titration procedure in steps **9** and **10** with flasks *2* and *3*.

Cleanup and Disposal

12. Dispose of the contents of the *Waste* beaker in the container designated by your teacher. Also pour the color-standard flask into this container. Always wash your hands thoroughly after cleaning up the area and equipment.

Analysis and Interpretation

1. **Organizing Ideas**
   Write the balanced equation for the redox reaction of FeSO₄ and KMnO₄.

2. **Evaluating Data**
   Calculate the number of moles of MnO₄⁻ reduced in each trial.

3. **Analyzing Information**
   Calculate the number of moles of Fe²⁺ oxidized in each trial.

4. **Applying Conclusions**
   Calculate the average concentration (molarity) of the iron tonic.

5. **Analyzing Methods**
   Explain why it was important to rinse the burets with KMnO₄ or FeSO₄ before adding the solutions. (Hint: consider what would happen to the concentration of each solution if it was added to a buret that had been rinsed only with distilled water.)

Conclusions

6. **Inferring Conclusions**
   The company makes three different types of iron tonics: *Feravide A* with a concentration of 0.145 M FeSO₄, *Feravide Extra-Strength* with 0.225 M FeSO₄, and *Feravide Jr.* with 0.120 M FeSO₄. Which tonic is your sample?

Extensions

1. **Evaluating Methods**

   Calculate the absolute and average deviation for your measurements of the concentration of the $FeSO_4$. What reasons can you give for any differences in the values? (Hint: see Exploration 2A for information on absolute and average deviations.)

2. **Designing Experiments**

   What possible sources of error can you identify with this procedure? If you can think of ways to eliminate them, ask your teacher to approve your plan, and run the procedure again.

3. **Applying Ideas**

   Hydrogen peroxide, H_2O_2, was once widely used as an antiseptic. It decomposes by the oxidation and reduction of its oxygen atoms. The products are water and molecular oxygen. Write the balanced redox equation for this reaction.

4. **Applying Ideas**

   When gaseous hydrogen sulfide burns in air to form sulfur dioxide and water, the oxidation number of hydrogen does not change, but that of sulfur changes from a -2 state to a $+4$ state, and that of oxygen changes from a zero state to a -2 state. Which substances are oxidized, and which are reduced? Write the balanced chemical equation for the combustion reaction.

5. **Research and Communication**

   Blueprints are based on a photochemical reaction. The paper is treated with a solution of iron(III) ammonium citrate and potassium hexacyanoferrate(III) and dried in the dark. When a tracing-paper drawing is placed on the blueprint paper and exposed to light, Fe^{3+} ions are reduced to Fe^{2+} ions, which react with hexacyanoferrate(III) ions in the moist paper to form the blue color on the paper. The lines of the drawing block the light and prevent the reduction of Fe^{3+} ions, resulting in white lines. Find out how sepia prints are made, and report on this information.

6. **Relating Ideas**

   Electrochemical cells are based on the process of electron flow in a system with varying potential differences. Batteries are composed of such systems and contain different chemicals for different purposes and price ranges. You can make simple experimental batteries using metal wires and items such as lemons, apples, and potatoes. What are some other "homemade" battery sources, and what is the role of these food items in producing electrical energy that can be measured as battery power? Explain your answers.

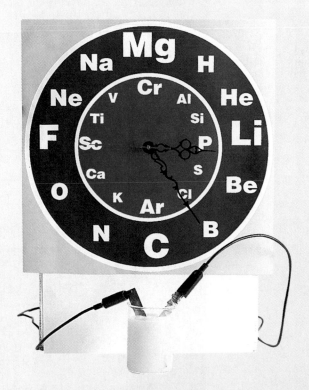

REDOX TITRATION

Mining Feasibility Study

GOLDSTAKE MINING CORPORATION

May 11, 1995

George Taylor
Director of Analytical Services
CheMystery Labs, Inc.
52 Fulton Street
Springfield, VA 22150

Dear George:

Because of the high quality of your firm's work in the past, Goldstake is again asking that you submit a bid for a mining feasibility study. A study site in New Mexico has yielded some promising iron ore deposits, and we are evaluating the potential yield.

Your bid should include the costs of evaluating the sample we're sending with this letter and the fees for 20 additional analyses to be completed over the next year. The sample is a slurry extracted from the mine using a special process that converts the iron ore into $FeSO_4$ dissolved in water. The mine could produce up to 1.0×10^5 L of this slurry daily, but we need to know how much iron is in that amount of slurry before we proceed.

The contract for the other analyses will be awarded based on the accuracy of this analysis and the quality of the accompanying report. Your report will be used for two purposes: to evaluate the site for quantity of iron and to determine who our analytical consultant will be if the site is developed into a mining operation. I look forward to reviewing your bid proposal.

Sincerely,

Lynn L. Brown

Lynn L. Brown
Director of Operations
Goldstake Mining Corporation

Required Precautions

Goggles and lab aprons must be worn at all times.

If you get acid, base, or permanganate on your skin or clothing, wash it off at the sink while calling to your teacher. If you get acid, base, or permanganate in your eyes, immediately flush it out at the eyewash station while calling to your teacher.

Do not touch or taste any chemicals.
Wash your hands thoroughly when finished.

CheMystery Labs, Inc.
52 Fulton Street
Springfield, VA 22150

Memorandum

Date: May 12, 1995

To: Crystal Sievers

From: George Taylor

Good news! It looks as though the quality of our work has earned us a repeat customer, Goldstake Mining Corporation. We've done work for them in the past, and they pay their bills on time. This analysis could turn into a long-term arrangement, so when bonus time arrives, I'll be looking favorably on lab teams that produce accurate, high-quality reports for this job. Perform the analysis more than once so that we can be confident of our accuracy.

Before you begin, send Ms. Brown the following items.
- detailed one-page plan for the procedure and all necessary data tables
- detailed bid sheet that lists all of the equipment and materials you plan to use, including individual and total costs

As soon as you have completed the laboratory work please prepare a report in the form of a two-page letter to Ms. Brown, containing the following information.
- moles and grams of $FeSO_4$ in 10 mL of sample
- moles, grams, and percentage of iron(II) in 10 mL of the sample
- kilograms of iron that the company could extract from the mine each year, assuming that 1.0×10^5 L of slurry could be mined per day, year-round
- balanced equation for the redox equation
- detailed and organized data and analysis section showing calculations of how you determined the moles, grams, and percentage of iron(II) in the sample (include calculations of the mean (average) of the multiple trials)
- detailed invoice for this analysis that includes our equipment and labor costs (and a small amount of profit)
- bid for 20 additional analyses based on the costs incurred for this one

References

See pages 591–592 for more information on redox reactions. The reaction and procedure used here is the same as one your team recently completed in an Exploration, so use your notes from that procedure to help you with this one. Remember to add a small amount of H_2SO_4 so the iron will stay in the Fe^{2+} form. Calculate your disposal costs based on the mass of $KMnO_4$ and $FeSO_4$ in your solutions, plus the mass of the H_2SO_4 solution.

Spill Procedures/ Waste Disposal Methods

- In case of spills, follow your teacher's instructions.
- Dispose of solutions from the waste beaker and other leftover reagents in the disposal container designated by your teacher.

Materials for GOLDSTAKE MINING CORPORATION

Item	Cost		
REQUIRED ITEMS *(You must include all of these in your budget.)*			
Lab space/fume hood/utilities	15 000 — /day		
Standard disposal fee	2 000 — /g of product		
REAGENTS and ADDITIONAL EQUIPMENT *(Include only what you'll need in your budget.)*			
0.020M $KMnO_4$			
1.0 M H_2SO_4	1 000 — /mL		
Phenolphthalein	1 000 — /mL		
250 mL beaker	2 000		
250 mL flask	1 000		
400 mL beaker	1 000		
100 mL graduated cylinder	2 000		
Buret	1 000		
Filter paper	5 000		
Glass funnel	500 — /piece		
Glass stirring rod	1 000		
pH paper	1 000		
Ring stand with buret clamp	2 000 — /piece		
Spatula	2 000		
Stopwatch	500		
Wash bottle	5 000		
Watch glass	500		
Weighing paper	1 000		
* No refunds on returned chemicals or unused equipment.	500 — /piece		
Fines			
OSHA safety violation	2000 — /incident		

Detecting Radioactivity

Objectives

Objectives

Build a radon detector, and use it to detect radon emissions.

Observe the tracks of alpha particles microscopically and count them.

Calculate the activity of radon.

Evaluate radon activity over a large area using class data, and draw a map of its activity.

Situation

Local officials have received calls from concerned citizens regarding the possibility of radon in their homes. Radon is a major source of natural background radiation. Ordinarily, it does not pose a health problem because radon is a gaseous element and normal air circulation prevents the accumulation of the gas in buildings. However, in some air-tight, energy-efficient homes, there could be cause for concern. The local health commissioner has asked your company to survey the area to determine the level of radon emissions.

Background

The element radon is the product of the radioactive decay of uranium. The $^{222}_{86}$Rn nucleus is unstable and has a half-life of about 4 days. Radon decays by giving off alpha particles (helium nuclei) and beta particles (electrons) according to the equations below with $^{4}_{2}$He indicating an alpha particle, and $^{0}_{-1}\beta$ indicating a beta particle. Chemically, radon is a noble gas. Other noble gases can be inhaled without causing damage to the lungs because of the gases' nonreactive nature. When radon is inhaled, however, it can rapidly decay into polonium, lead, and bismuth, all of which are solids that can react and lodge in body tissues. The lead isotope shown at the end of the chain of reactions, $^{210}_{82}$Pb, has a half life of 22.6 years, and it will eventually undergo even more decay before creating the final stable product, $^{206}_{82}$Pb.

$$^{222}_{86}\text{Rn}$$
$$\searrow$$
$$^{218}_{84}\text{Po} + {}^{4}_{2}\text{He}$$
$$\searrow$$
$$^{214}_{82}\text{Pb} + {}^{4}_{2}\text{He}$$
$$\searrow$$
$$^{214}_{83}\text{Bi} + {}^{0}_{-1}\beta$$
$$\searrow$$
$$^{214}_{84}\text{Po} + {}^{0}_{-1}\beta$$
$$\searrow$$
$$^{210}_{82}\text{Pb} + {}^{4}_{2}\text{He}$$

Problem

First, you must construct an inexpensive detector using a plastic (CR-39) that is sensitive to alpha particles. Then you will place the detectors in your home or somewhere in your community for a three-week period. In the lab the plastic will be etched with sodium hydroxide to make the tracks of the alpha particles visible with a microscope, so you can determine the activity of radon at each location. Finally, you will pool all data to make a map of radioactivity throughout your community.

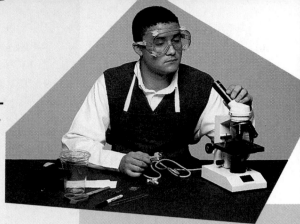

Safety

Although you will not use any chemicals in this investigation, there are hazardous chemicals in the lab where you will work, so wear goggles and an apron to provide protection for your eyes and clothing. You may remove your goggles only while you are using the microscope. Wash your hands thoroughly before you leave the lab after all lab work is finished.

Always clean up the lab and all equipment after use, and dispose of substances according to proper disposal methods. Wash your hands thoroughly before you leave the lab.

Scissors and push pins are sharp; use with care to avoid cutting yourself or others.

Preparation

I. Organizing Data

Read each section of the laboratory guidelines and prepare tables for data. Your first data table should provide space to record the date and the time of day that the detector was put in place, the location of the detector in your home, the floor level of the location, and the date and the time of day the detector was removed. Your second data table should provide space for recording the number of tracks that you count in each of 10 fields, as well as the diameter of the microscope's field of view. You will also need room for other observations.

Technique

Detector Construction

2. Cut a rectangle, 2 cm × 4 cm, from the 3 in × 5 in index card.

3. Locate the side of the CR-39 plastic that has the felt-marker lines on it. Peel off the polyethylene film, and use the push pin to inscribe an ID number or other identification near the edge of the piece. With a short piece of transparent tape, form a loop with the sticky side out. Place the tape on the back of the piece of CR-39 plastic (the side that is still covered with polyethylene), and firmly attach it to the index card rectangle.

4. With a permanent marker, write the ID number or other identification on the outside of the plastic cup. Place the paper rectangle, with the CR-39 plastic on top, in the cup.

5. Cut a hole in the center of the plastic lid. Place a small piece of tissue over the top of the cup to serve as a dust filter. Then snap the lid onto the cup.

6. Place the completed detector in the location of your choice. (Check with your instructor first.) The detector must remain undisturbed at that location for at least three weeks.

7. At the end of the three weeks, return the entire detector to school for the chemical-etching process and the counting of the radiation tracks.

Materials

- CR-39 plastic (with polyethylene film covering on both sides)
- 3 in × 5 in index card
- Clear plastic metric ruler or stage micrometer
- Etch clamp
- Microscope
- Paper clip
- Push pin
- Scissors
- Small plastic cup with lid
- Tape
- Toilet paper or other tissue

Etching

8. Remove the CR-39 plastic from the detector and the index card, and peel the polyethylene film from the back. Slip the ring of an etch clamp over the top of the CR-39 plastic, and hook it onto a large paper clip that has been reshaped to have "hooks" at each end, as shown in the diagram.

9. When you have completed this work, give it to your teacher for the etching step. During this step, NaOH solution will be used to remove the outer layer of the plastic so that the tracks of the alpha particles become visible.

Counting the Tracks

10. Examine the illustration below. Notice the various shapes of the tracks left as alpha particles entered the CR-39 plastic. The circular-shaped tracks are due to alpha particles that entered straight on, and the teardrop shaped tracks are due to alpha particles that entered at an angle.

11. Use a clear plastic metric ruler or a stage micrometer to measure the diameter of the microscope's field of view. Make this measurement for low power (10×). Record this diameter in the data table in your lab notebook.

12. The tracks are on the top surface of the CR-39 plastic. Make certain that you focus on that surface and that the tracks look like those in the illustration. These tracks were produced by placing the CR-39 plastic within a radium-coated clay urn. Your radon detector should not have nearly as many tracks. If there are too many tracks, switch to a high power (40×) objective, after recording the diameter of the field of view. Place your piece of CR-39 plastic on a microscope slide. Count and record the number of tracks in 10 different fields. Record these numbers in the data table.

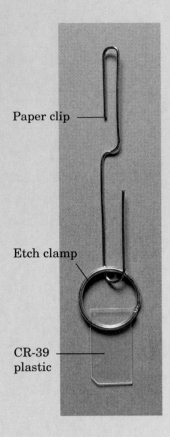

Paper clip

Etch clamp

CR-39 plastic

Analysis and Interpretation

1. **Organizing Data**
   In order to increase the accuracy of your data, you counted tracks in 10 different areas. Find the average number of tracks in a single area for your piece of CR-39 plastic.

2. **Evaluating Data**
   Find the absolute deviation and average deviation for each of the 10 measurements. This calculation was described in Exploration 2A.

3. **Organizing Data**
   You counted the number of tracks within the field of view of your microscope. In order to calculate the number of tracks per cm^2, you need to know the area of the field. Use the diameter of the field to calculate the area. (Hint: the field is circular; $d = 2r$; $A = \pi r^2$.)

4. **Organizing Data**
   Using your answers to items **1** and **3**, calculate the average number of tracks per cm^2.

5. **Organizing Data**
   In item **4** you calculated the number of tracks that accumulated per cm^2 over the total period the detector was in place. Divide this number by the number of days the detector was in place to calculate tracks/cm^2/day.

Alpha particle tracks

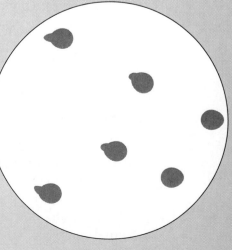

Conclusions

6. Organizing Data

Several pieces of CR-39 plastic were sent to a facility that had a radon chamber in which the activity of the radon was known to be 13.69 Bq/L (becquerels per liter of air), as measured by a different technique. A becquerel is the name for the SI unit of activity for a radioactive substance and is equal to 1 decay/s. The exposed pieces of CR-39 plastic were etched, counted, and found to have an activity of 2370 tracks/cm^2/day. Calculate the radon activity measured by your detector in becquerels/liter. (Hint: use the proportion 13.69 Bq/L : 2370 tracks/cm^2/day as a conversion factor to convert your data.)

7. Relating Ideas

The Environmental Protection Agency and other government agencies use non-SI units of picocuries per liter (pCi/L) to measure radiation. One curie is 3.7×10^{10} Bq, and one picocurie is 10^{-12} curies. Convert your data into units of pCi/L.

8. Organizing Data

Combine your data with that of other teams in your class, and jointly construct a map of your region that shows the levels of radon activity in both Bq/L and pCi/L at various locations throughout your community.

Extensions

I. Applying Ideas

The half-life of $^{222}_{86}$Rn is 3.823 days. After what time will only one-fourth of a given amount of radon remain?

2. Designing Experiments

Factors other than geographic location can have an effect on radon emissions. For example, readings taken in basements are likely to be higher than those in attics. Design an experiment to test different aspects of the three highest and three lowest regions of radiation on the map to examine the influence of these other factors. If your teacher approves your suggestion, try it.

3. Designing Experiments

CR-39 plastic could be used for further investigations of naturally occurring radiation. Design an experiment to explore one of the following areas. If your teacher approves your plan, carry out the experiment.
- the range of alpha particles
- the radon activity in soil
- radioactivity of common items such as lantern mantles (green Coleman label), glow-in-the-dark clock faces, and pieces of Fiestaware

4. Research and Communication

Investigate the ways in which people are exposed to nuclear radiation. Is there an acceptable level of radiation? Is there a place where you can go to avoid all radiation? What can you do to avoid excessive radiation? Present your findings in the form of a chart or a poster to share with your class.

DETECTING RADIOACTIVITY

Shielding From Alpha Particles

SOUTH WEST VIRGINIA
STATE UNIVERSITY

May 19, 1995

Mr. Reginald Brown
Director of Materials Testing
CheMystery Labs, Inc.
52 Fulton Street
Springfield, VA 22150

Dear Mr. Brown:

Recently, Professor Madeline Hoffmann joined our physics department faculty. She is eager to begin work on alpha-radiation, but we have told her this work cannot continue until we create a lab site that will not endanger anyone with radiation.

Professor Hoffmann assures me that alpha particles are relatively easy to block, but for legal reasons, I must make sure that we have independent confirmation for this claim.

Please test a variety of materials for their ability to block alpha radiation, so we can work with our maintenance and engineering services team to create a lab that will be safe yet inexpensive.

The university's president has authorized me to offer you $200 000 for this work, as outlined in the contract you will receive from the university's general counsel.

Sincerely,

John C. Hill

John C. Hill
South West Virginia State University

Required Precautions

 Goggles and lab aprons must be worn at all times in the laboratory.

 Wear disposable polyethylene gloves when you handle point source radioactive material. When finished, remove the gloves by turning them inside out as they are taken off. Keep them turned inside out, and dispose of them in the trash.

 Do not touch or taste any chemicals. Wash your hands thoroughly when finished.

Memorandum

Date: May 22, 1995

To: Martin Reed

From: Reginald Brown

This is the final project before the end of the fiscal year. When the board of directors meets next month, decisions concerning company size will be made. I'll be making a request for new equipment. If this project goes well, my argument will be much stronger.

The board is setting their agenda for next month's meeting and want me to provide some detail about recent projects. I need something substantial, so I'd like you to submit to me the following information for this project.

- detailed one-page plan of your procedure and all necessary data tables
- detailed list of all of the equipment and materials you need, along with the individual and total costs (Note: we will be using a subcontractor to etch the detector plastic for us.)
- list of materials you propose to test for shielding ability

On completion of the work, prepare a report in the form of a two-page letter to the client. The report should include the following.

- your recommendation of shielding materials for alpha radiation
- any research/information your team collected for this project.
- detailed and organized data section including a table listing all of the shielding materials your research team tested, costs per square centimeter and per square meter, average number of tracks for each trial, tracks per square centimeter, and tracks per centimeter per day
- radon activity in Bq/L and pCi/L
- detailed and organized analysis section showing calculations and explanations of any possible sources of error
- detailed invoice for services rendered and expenses incurred

References

Refer to page 615 for more information about unstable nuclei and alpha particle radiation. The decay of radon-222 was discussed in relation to a procedure your team recently completed, in which you used radiation detectors to create a map of the radon emissions in your community.

Spill Procedures/ Waste Disposal Methods

- Be sure to return the alpha particle source to the designated location.

Materials for:
SOUTH WEST VIRGINIA STATE UNIVERSITY

Item	Cost	1	2	3
REQUIRED ITEMS				
(You must include all of these in your budget.)				
Lab space/fume hood/utilities	15 000 — /day			
Standard disposal fee	2 000 — /g of product			
Microscope	10 000			
Alpha particle point source	10 000			
REAGENTS and ADDITIONAL EQUIPMENT				
(Include in your budget only what you'll need.)				
CR-39 radiation-detecting plastic	25 000 — /piece			
Analysis fee for etching CR-39 plastic	5 000 — /piece			
400 mL beaker	1 000			
Buret clamp	1 000			
Etch clamp	500			
Glass stirring rod	1 000			
Index card (3 in. × 5 in.)	1 000			
Paper clips	500 — /box			
Plastic cup and lid	2 000			
Plastic ruler	500			
Push pin	500			
Scissors	500			
Tape	500 — /10 cm			
Test tube (large)	1 000			
Tissue	500			
Wash bottle	500			
* No refunds on returned chemicals or unused equipment.				
FINES				
OSHA safety violation	2 000 — /incident			

Appendix A

SI Measurement

Most measurements in this book are expressed in SI units. Scientists throughout the world use SI and the metric system, and you will always use these units when you make measurements in the laboratory. The official name of the measurement system is the Système International d'Unités, or International System of Units.

SI is a decimal system—that is, all relationships between units of measurement are based on powers of 10. Most units have a prefix that indicates the relationship of that unit to the seven base units presented in Chapter 2.

Metric Prefixes

Prefix	Symbol	Factor of Base Unit
giga	G	1 000 000 000
mega	M	1 000 000
kilo	k	1000
hecto	h	100
deka	da	10
deci	d	0.1
centi	c	0.01
milli	m	0.001
micro	μ	0.000 001
nano	n	0.000 000 001
pico	p	0.000 000 000 001

Mass

1 kilogram (kg)	= SI base unit of mass
1 gram (g)	= 0.001 kg
1 milligram (mg)	= 0.000 001 kg
1 microgram (μg)	= 0.000 000 001 kg

Length

1 kilometer (km)	= 1 000 m
1 meter (m)	= SI base unit of length
1 centimeter (cm)	= 0.01 m
1 millimeter (mm)	= 0.001 m
1 micrometer (μm)	= 0.000 001 m
1 nanometer (nm)	= 0.000 000 001 m
1 picometer (pm)	= 0.000 000 000 001 m

Area

1 square kilometer (km^2)	= 100 hectares (ha)
1 hectare (ha)	= 10 000 square meters (m^2)
1 square meter (m^2)	= 10 000 square centimeters (cm^2)
1 square centimeter (cm^2)	= 100 square millimeters (mm^2)

Volume

1 liter (L)	= common unit for liquid volume (not SI)
1 cubic meter (m^3)	= 1000 L
1 kiloliter (kL)	= 1000 L
1 milliliter (mL)	= 0.001 L
1 milliliter (mL)	= 1 cubic centimeter (cm^3)

Table A-2
Symbols and Abbreviations

Symbol		Meaning
α	=	helium nucleus (also $_2^4\text{He}$) emission from radioactive materials
β	=	electron (also $_{-1}^0e$) emission from radioactive materials
γ	=	high-energy photon emission from radioactive materials
Δ	=	change in a given quantity (e.g., ΔH for change in enthalpy)
c	=	speed of light in vacuum
c_p	=	specific heat capacity (at constant pressure)
D	=	density
E_a	=	activation energy
E^0	=	standard electrode potential
$E^0\text{cell}$	=	standard potential of an electrochemical cell
G	=	Gibbs free energy
ΔG^0	=	standard free energy of reaction
ΔG^0_f	=	standard molar free energy of formation
H	=	enthalpy
ΔH^0	=	standard enthalpy of reaction

Symbol		Meaning
ΔH^0_f	=	standard molar enthalpy of formation
K_a	=	dissociation constant (acid)
K_b	=	dissociation constant (base)
K_{eq}	=	equilibrium constant
K_{sp}	=	solubility-product constant
KE	=	kinetic energy
m	=	mass
N_A	=	Avogadro's number
n	=	number of moles
P	=	pressure
pH	=	measure of acidity ($-\log[\text{H}_3\text{O}^+]$)
R	=	ideal gas law constant
S	=	entropy
S^0	=	standard molar entropy
T	=	temperature (thermodynamic, in kelvins)
t	=	temperature ($\pm$ degrees Celsius)
V	=	volume
v	=	velocity

Abbreviations

amu	=	atomic mass unit (mass)
atm	=	atmosphere (pressure, non-SI)
Bq	=	becquerel (nuclear activity)
°C	=	degree Celsius (temperature)
J	=	joule (energy)
K	=	kelvin (temperature, thermodynamic)

Abbreviations

mol	=	mole (quantity)
M	=	molarity (concentration)
N	=	newton (force)
Pa	=	pascal (pressure)
s	=	second (time)
V	=	volt (electric potential difference)

Table A-3
Vapor Pressure of Water at Selected Temperatures

Temperature °C	Pressure (kPa)	Temperature °C	Pressure (kPa)	Temperature °C	Pressure (kPa)	Temperature °C	Pressure (kPa)
0	0.61	18	2.06	23	2.81	35	5.63
5	0.87	18.5	2.13	23.5	2.90	40	7.38
10	1.23	19	2.19	24	2.98	50	12.34
12.5	1.45	19.5	2.27	24.5	3.10	60	19.93
15	1.71	20	2.34	25	3.17	70	31.18
15.5	1.76	20.5	2.41	26	3.36	80	47.37
16	1.82	21	2.49	27	3.57	90	70.12
16.5	1.88	21.5	2.57	28	3.78	95	84.53
17	1.94	22	2.64	29	4.01	100	101.32
17.5	2.00	22.5	2.72	30	4.25		

Table A-4
Physical Constants

Quantity	Symbol	Value
Atomic mass unit	amu	$1.660\ 5402 \times 10^{-27}$ kg
Avogadro's number	N_A	$6.022\ 137 \times 10^{23}$/mol
Electron rest mass	m_e	$9.109\ 3897 \times 10^{-31}$ kg
Ideal gas law constant	R	8.314 L·kPa/mol·K = 0.0821 L·atm/mol·K
Molar volume of ideal gas at STP	V_M	22.414 L/mol
Neutron rest mass	m_n	$1.674\ 9286 \times 10^{-27}$ kg
Normal boiling point of water	T_b	373.15 K = 100.00°C
Normal freezing point of water	T_f	273.15 K = 0.00°C
Proton rest mass	m_p	$1.672\ 6231 \times 10^{-27}$ kg
Speed of light in a vacuum	c	$2.997\ 924\ 58 \times 10^{8}$ m/s
Temperature of triple point of water		273.16 K = 0.01°C

Table A-5
Common Ions

Cation name	Symbol	Anion name	Symbol
aluminum	Al^{3+}	acetate	CH_3COO^-
ammonium	NH_4^+	bromide	Br^-
arsenic(III)	As^{3+}	carbonate	CO_3^{2-}
barium	Ba^{2+}	chlorate	ClO_3^-
calcium	Ca^{2+}	chloride	Cl^-
chromium(II)	Cr^{2+}	chlorite	ClO_2^-
chromium(III)	Cr^{3+}	chromate	CrO_4^{2-}
cobalt(II)	Co^{2+}	cyanide	CN^-
cobalt(III)	Co^{3+}	dichromate	$Cr_2O_7^{2-}$
copper(I)	Cu^+	fluoride	F^-
copper(II)	Cu^{2+}	hexacyanoferrate(II)	$Fe(CN)_6^{4-}$
hydronium	H_3O^+	hexacyanoferrate(III)	$Fe(CN)_6^{3-}$
iron(II)	Fe^{2+}	hydride	H^-
iron(III)	Fe^{3+}	hydrogen carbonate	HCO_3^-
lead(II)	Pb^{2+}	hydrogen sulfate	HSO_4^-
magnesium	Mg^{2+}	hydroxide	OH^-
mercury(I)	Hg_2^{2+}	hypochlorite	ClO^-
mercury(II)	Hg^{2+}	iodide	I^-
nickel(II)	Ni^{2+}	nitrate	NO_3^-
potassium	K^+	nitrite	NO_2^-
silver	Ag^+	oxide	O^{2-}
sodium	Na^+	perchlorate	ClO_4^-
strontium	Sr^{2+}	permanganate	MnO_4^-
tin(II)	Sn^{2+}	peroxide	O_2^{2-}
tin(IV)	Sn^{4+}	phosphate	PO_4^{3-}
titanium(III)	Ti^{3+}	sulfate	SO_4^{2-}
titanium(IV)	Ti^{4+}	sulfide	S^{2-}
zinc	Zn^{2+}	sulfite	SO_3^{2-}

Table A-6
The Elements—Symbols, Atomic Numbers, and Atomic Masses

Name of element	Symbol	Atomic number	Atomic mass
actinium	Ac	89	[227.0278]
aluminum	Al	13	26.981539
americium	Am	95	[243.0614]
antimony	Sb	51	121.757
argon	Ar	18	39.948
arsenic	As	33	74.92159
astatine	At	85	[209.9871]
barium	Ba	56	137.327
berkelium	Bk	97	[247.0703]
beryllium	Be	4	9.012182
bismuth	Bi	83	208.98037
boron	B	5	10.811
bromine	Br	35	79.904
cadmium	Cd	48	112.411
calcium	Ca	20	40.078
californium	Cf	98	[251.0796]
carbon	C	6	12.011
cerium	Ce	58	140.115
cesium	Cs	55	132.90543
chlorine	Cl	17	35.4527
chromium	Cr	24	51.9961
cobalt	Co	27	58.93320
copper	Cu	29	63.546
curium	Cm	96	[247.0703]
dysprosium	Dy	66	162.50
einsteinium	Es	99	[252.083]
erbium	Er	68	167.26
europium	Eu	63	151.965
fermium	Fm	100	[257.0951]
fluorine	F	9	18.9984032
francium	Fr	87	[223.0197]
gadolinium	Gd	64	157.25
gallium	Ga	31	69.723
germanium	Ge	32	72.61
gold	Au	79	196.96654
hafnium	Hf	72	178.49
helium	He	2	4.002602
holmium	Ho	67	164.93032
hydrogen	H	1	1.00794
indium	In	49	114.818
iodine	I	53	126.90447
iridium	Ir	77	192.22
iron	Fe	26	55.847
krypton	Kr	36	83.80
lanthanum	La	57	138.9055
lawrencium	Lr	103	[262.11]
lead	Pb	82	207.2
lithium	Li	3	6.941
lutetium	Lu	71	174.967
magnesium	Mg	12	24.3050
manganese	Mn	25	54.93805
mendelevium	Md	101	[258.10]
mercury	Hg	80	200.59
molybdenum	Mo	42	95.94
neodymium	Nd	60	144.24

Name of element	Symbol	Atomic number	Atomic mass
neon	Ne	10	20.1797
neptunium	Np	93	[237.0482]
nickel	Ni	28	58.6934
niobium	Nb	41	92.90638
nitrogen	N	7	14.00674
nobelium	No	102	[259.1009]
osmium	Os	76	190.23
oxygen	O	8	15.9994
palladium	Pd	46	106.42
phosphorus	P	15	30.973762
platinum	Pt	78	195.08
plutonium	Pu	94	[244.0642]
polonium	Po	84	[208.9824]
potassium	K	19	39.0983
praseodymium	Pr	59	140.90765
promethium	Pm	61	[144.9127]
protactinium	Pa	91	231.03588
radium	Ra	88	[226.0254]
radon	Rn	86	[222.0176]
rhenium	Re	75	186.207
rhodium	Rh	45	102.90550
rubidium	Rb	37	85.4678
ruthenium	Ru	44	101.07
samarium	Sm	62	150.36
scandium	Sc	21	44.955910
selenium	Se	34	78.96
silicon	Si	14	28.0855
silver	Ag	47	107.8682
sodium	Na	11	22.989768
strontium	Sr	38	87.62
sulfur	S	16	32.066
tantalum	Ta	73	180.9479
technetium	Tc	43	[97.9072]
tellurium	Te	52	127.60
terbium	Tb	65	158.92534
thallium	Tl	81	204.3833
thorium	Th	90	232.0381
thulium	Tm	69	168.93421
tin	Sn	50	118.710
titanium	Ti	22	47.88
tungsten	W	74	183.84
unnilennium	Une	109	[266]
unnilhexium	Unh	106	[263.118]
unniloctium	Uno	108	[265]
unnilpentium	Unp	105	[262.114]
unnilquadium	Unq	104	[261.11]
unnilseptium	Uns	107	[262.12]
uranium	U	92	238.0289
vanadium	V	23	50.9415
xenon	Xe	54	131.29
ytterbium	Yb	70	173.04
yttrium	Y	39	88.90585
zinc	Zn	30	65.39
zirconium	Zr	40	91.224

Table A-7
Properties of Common Elements

Name	Form/color at room temperature	Density† (g/cm³)	Melting point (°C)	Boiling point (°C)	Common oxidation states
aluminum	silver metal	2.702	660.37	2467	3+
antimony	blue-white metalloid	6.684[25]	630.5	1750	3+, 5+
argon	colorless gas	1.784*	−189.2	−185.7	0
arsenic	gray metalloid	5.727[14]	817 (28 atm)	613 (*sublimes*)	3−, 3+, 5+
barium	bluish-white metal	3.51	725	1640	2+
beryllium	gray metal	1.85	1278 ± 5	2970 (0.0066 atm)	2+
bismuth	white metal	9.80	271.3	1560 ± 5	3+
boron	black metalloid	2.34	2300	2550	3+
bromine	red-brown liquid	3.119	−7.2	58.78	1−, 1+, 5+
calcium	silver metal	1.54	839 ± 2	1484	2+
carbon	diamond	3.51	3500 (63.5 atm)	3930	2+, 4+
	graphite	2.25	3652 (*sublimes*)	—	
chlorine	green-yellow gas	3.214*	−100.98	−34.6	1−, 1+, 5+, 7+
chromium	gray metal	7.20[28]	1857 ± 20	2672	2+, 3+, 6+
cobalt	gray metal	8.9	1495	2870	2+, 3+
copper	red metal	8.92	1083.4 ± 0.2	2567	1+, 2+
fluorine	yellow gas	1.69‡	−219.62	−188.14	1−
germanium	gray metalloid	5.323[25]	937.4	2830	4+
gold	yellow metal	19.31	1064.43	2808 ± 2	1+, 3+
helium	colorless gas	0.1785*	−272.2 (26 atm)	−268.9	0
hydrogen	colorless gas	0.0899*	−259.34	−252.8	1−, 1+
iodine	blue-black solid	4.93	113.5	184.35	1−, 1+, 5+, 7+
iron	silver metal	7.86	1535	2750	2+, 3+
lead	bluish-white metal	11.3437[16]	327.502	1740	2+, 4+
lithium	silver metal	0.534	180.54	1342	1+
magnesium	silver metal	1.74[5]	648.8	1107	2+
manganese	gray-white metal	7.20	1244 ± 3	1962	2+, 3+, 4+, 7+
mercury	silver liquid metal	13.5462	−38.87	356.58	1+, 2+
neon	colorless gas	0.9002*	−248.67	−245.9	0
nickel	silver metal	8.90	1455	2730	2+, 3+
nitrogen	colorless gas	1.2506*	−209.86	−195.8	3−, 3+, 5+
oxygen	colorless gas	1.429*	−218.4	−182.962	2−
phosphorus	yellow solid	1.82	44.1	280	3−, 3+, 5+
platinum	silver metal	21.45	1772	3827 ± 100	2+, 4+
plutonium	silver metal	19.84	641	3232	3+, 4+, 5+, 6+
potassium	silver metal	0.86	63.25	760	1+
radium	white metal	5(?)	700	< 1140	2+
radon	colorless gas	9.73*	−71	−61.8	0
silicon	gray metalloid	2.33 ± 0.01	1410	2355	2+, 4+
silver	white metal	10.5	961.93	2212	1+
sodium	silver metal	0.97	97.8	882.9	1+
strontium	silver metal	2.6	769	1384	2+
sulfur	yellow solid	1.96	119.0	444.674	2−, 4+, 6+
tin	white metal	7.28	231.88	2260	2+, 4+
titanium	white metal	4.5	1660 ± 10	3287	3+, 4+
tungsten	gray metal	19.35	3410 ± 20	5660	6+
uranium	silver metal	19.05 ± 0.02[25]	1132.3 ± 0.8	3818	3+, 4+, 6+
xenon	colorless gas	5.887 ± 0.009*	−111.9	−107 ± 3	0
zinc	blue-white metal	7.14	419.58	907	2+

† Densities obtained at 20°C unless noted (superscripted).   *Densities of gases are given in g/L at STP.
‡ Density of fluorine is given in g/L at 1 atm and 15°C.

Table A-8
Densities of Gases at STP

Gas	Density (g/L)
air, dry	1.293
ammonia	0.771
carbon dioxide	1.997
carbon monoxide	1.250
chlorine	3.214
dinitrogen monoxide	1.977
ethyne (acetylene)	1.165
helium	0.1785
hydrogen	0.0899
hydrogen chloride	1.639
hydrogen sulfide	1.539
methane	0.7168
nitrogen	1.2506
nitrogen monoxide (at 10°C)	1.340
oxygen	1.429
sulfur dioxide	2.927

Table A-9
Density of Water

Temperature (°C)	Density (g/cm^3)
0	0.999 84
2	0.999 94
3.98 (maximum)	0.999 973
4	0.999 97
6	0.999 94
8	0.999 85
10	0.999 70
14	0.999 24
16	0.998 94
20	0.998 20
25	0.997 05
30	0.995 65
40	0.992 22
50	0.988 04
60	0.983 20
70	0.977 77
80	0.971 79
90	0.965 31
100	0.958 36

Table A-10
Solubilities of Gases in Water
Volume of gas (in liters) at STP that can be dissolved in 1 L of water at the temperature (°C) indicated.

Gas	0°C	10°C	20°C	60°C
air	0.029 18	0.022 84	0.018 68	0.012 16
ammonia	1130	870	680	200
carbon dioxide	1.713	1.194	0.878	0.359
carbon monoxide	0.035 37	0.028 16	0.023 19	0.014 88
chlorine	—	3.148	2.299	1.023
hydrogen	0.021 48	0.019 55	0.018 19	0.016 00
hydrogen chloride	512	475	442	339
hydrogen sulfide	4.670	3.399	2.582	1.190
methane	0.055 63	0.041 77	0.033 08	0.019 54
nitrogen*	0.023 54	0.018 61	0.015 45	0.010 23
nitrogen monoxide	0.073 81	0.057 09	0.047 06	0.029 54
oxygen	0.048 89	0.038 02	0.031 02	0.019 46
sulfur dioxide	79.789	56.647	39.374	—

*Atmospheric nitrogen—98.815% N_2, 1.185% inert gases

Table A–11
Solubilities of Compounds
Solubilities are given in grams of solute that can be dissolved in 100 g of water at the temperature (°C) indicated.

Compound	Formula	0°C	20°C	60°C	100°C
aluminum sulfate	$Al_2(SO_4)_3$	31.2	36.4	59.2	89.0
ammonium chloride	NH_4Cl	29.4	37.2	55.3	77.3
ammonium nitrate	NH_4NO_3	118	192	421	871
ammonium sulfate	$(NH_4)_2SO_4$	70.6	75.4	88	103
barium carbonate	$BaCO_3$	—	$0.0022^{18°}$	—	0.0065
barium chloride dihydrate	$BaCl_2 \cdot 2H_2O$	31.2	35.8	46.2	59.4
barium hydroxide	$Ba(OH)_2$	1.67	3.89	20.94	$101.40^{80°}$
barium nitrate	$Ba(NO_3)_2$	4.95	9.02	20.4	34.4
barium sulfate	$BaSO_4$	—	$0.000\ 246^{25°}$	—	0.000 413
cadmium sulfate	$CdSO_4$	75.4	76.6	81.8	60.8
calcium acetate dihydrate	$Ca(C_2H_3O_2)_2 \cdot 2H_2O$	37.4	34.7	32.7	29.7
calcium carbonate	$CaCO_3$	—	$0.0014^{25°}$	—	$0.0018^{75°}$
calcium fluoride	CaF_2	$0.0016^{18°}$	$0.0017^{26°}$	—	—
calcium hydrogen carbonate	$Ca(HCO_3)_2$	16.15	16.60	17.50	18.40
calcium hydroxide	$Ca(OH)_2$	0.189	0.173	0.121	0.076
calcium sulfate	$CaSO_4$	—	$0.209^{30°}$	—	0.1619
cerium(III) sulfate nonahydrate	$Ce_2(SO_4)_3 \cdot 9H_2O$	21.4	9.84	3.87	—
cesium nitrate	$CsNO_3$	9.33	23.0	83.8	197
copper(II) chloride	$CuCl_2$	68.6	73.0	96.5	120
copper(II) sulfate pentahydrate	$CuSO_4 \cdot 5H_2O$	23.1	32.0	61.8	114
lead(II) chloride	$PbCl_2$	0.67	1.00	1.94	3.20
lead(II) nitrate	$Pb(NO_3)_2$	37.5	54.3	91.6	133
lithium chloride	$LiCl$	69.2	83.5	98.4	128
lithium sulfate	Li_2SO_4	36.1	34.8	32.6	$30.9^{90°}$
magnesium hydroxide	$Mg(OH)_2$	—	$0.0009^{18°}$	—	0.004
mercury(I) chloride	Hg_2Cl_2	—	$0.000\ 20^{25°}$	$0.001^{43°}$	—
mercury(II) chloride	$HgCl_2$	3.63	6.57	16.3	61.3
potassium aluminum sulfate	$KAl(SO_4)_2$	3.00	5.90	24.8	$109^{90°}$
potassium bromide	KBr	53.6	65.3	85.5	104
potassium chlorate	$KClO_3$	3.3	7.3	23.8	56.3
potassium chloride	KCl	28.0	34.2	45.8	56.3
potassium chromate	K_2CrO_4	56.3	63.7	70.1	$74.5^{90°}$
potassium iodide	KI	128	144	176	206
potassium nitrate	KNO_3	13.9	31.6	106	245
potassium permanganate	$KMnO_4$	2.83	6.34	22.1	—
potassium sulfate	K_2SO_4	7.4	11.1	18.2	24.1
silver acetate	$AgC_2H_3O_2$	0.73	1.05	1.93	$2.59^{80°}$
silver chloride	$AgCl$	$0.000\ 089^{10°}$	—	—	0.0021
silver nitrate	$AgNO_3$	122	216	440	733
sodium acetate	$NaC_2H_3O_2$	36.2	46.4	139	170
sodium chlorate	$NaClO_3$	79.6	95.9	137	204
sodium chloride	$NaCl$	35.7	35.9	37.1	39.2
sodium nitrate	$NaNO_3$	73.0	87.6	122	180
sucrose	$C_{12}H_{22}O_{11}$	179.2	203.9	287.3	487.2
ytterbium(III) sulfate	$Yb_2(SO_4)_3$	44.2	$22.2^{30°}$	10.4	4.7

Dashes indicate values not available.

Table A-12
Standard Thermodynamic Properties (P = 100 kPa = 0.987 atm; T = 298.15 K = 25°C)

Substance	Standard enthalpy of formation ΔH^{o}_{f} (kJ/mol)	Standard entropy S^{o} (J/mol·K)	Substance	Standard enthalpy of formation ΔH^{o}_{f} (kJ/mol)	Standard entropy S^{o} (J/mol·K)
Aluminum			**Lead**		
Al(s)	0.0	28.3	Pb(s)	0.0	64.8
AlCl$_3$(s)	−705.6	110.7	PbCl$_2$(s)	−359.4	136.2
Al$_2$O$_3$(s, corundum)	−1676.0	51.0	PbO(s)	−219.4	66.3
Bromine			**Lithium**		
Br$_2$(l)	0.0	152.2	Li(s)	0.0	29.1
Br$_2$(g)	30.9	245.5	LiOH(s)	−484.9	42.8
HBr(g)	−36.4	198.6	LiCl(s)	−408.8	59.3
Calcium			**Magnesium**		
Ca(s)	0.0	41.6	Mg(s)	0.0	32.7
CaCO$_3$(s, calcite)	−1206.9	92.9	MgCl$_2$(s)	−641.6	89.6
CaCl$_2$(s)	−795.8	104.6	**Mercury**		
CaO(s)	−634.9	38.2	Hg(l)	0.0	76.0
Ca(OH)$_2$(s)	−986.1	83.4	Hg$_2$Cl$_2$(s)	−265.2	192.5
Carbon			HgO(s)	−90.8	70.3
C(s, graphite)	0.0	5.7	**Nitrogen**		
C(s, diamond)	1.9	2.4	N$_2$(g)	0.0	191.6
CCl$_4$(l)	−135.4	216.2	NH$_3$(g)	−45.9	192.8
CCl$_4$(g)	−95.8	309.9	NH$_4$Cl(s)	−314.5	94.6
CH$_4$(g)	−74.9	186.3	NO(g)	90.3	210.8
CH$_3$OH(l)	−239.1	127.2	NO$_2$(g)	33.1	240.0
C$_2$H$_2$(g)	226.7	201.0	N$_2$O(g)	82.4	220.0
C$_2$H$_4$(g)	52.5	219.3	N$_2$O$_4$(g)	9.1	304.4
C$_2$H$_6$(g)	−83.8	229.1	HNO$_3$(g)	−134.3	266.4
C$_2$H$_5$OH(l)	−277.7	161.0	**Oxygen**		
C$_3$H$_8$(g)	−104.7	270.2	O$_2$(g)	0.0	205.1
C$_4$H$_{10}$(g, n–butane)	−125.6	310.1	O$_3$(g)	142.7	238.9
C$_4$H$_{10}$(g, isobutane)	−134.2	294.6	**Potassium**		
C$_6$H$_6$(l)	49.0	173.4	K(s)	0.0	64.7
C$_6$H$_{12}$O$_6$(s)	−1273.3	212.1	KCl(s)	−436.7	82.6
C$_6$H$_{14}$(g, n–hexane)	−167.1	388.4	KNO$_3$(s)	−494.6	133.1
C$_7$H$_{16}$(g, n–heptane)	−187.7	427.9	KOH(s)	−424.7	78.9
C$_8$H$_{18}$(g, n–octane)	−208.6	466.7	**Silicon**		
C$_8$H$_{18}$(g, isooctane)	−224.0	423.2	Si(s)	0.0	18.8
CO(g)	−110.5	197.6	SiCl$_4$(g)	−657.0	330.9
CO$_2$(g)	−393.5	213.8	SiO$_2$(s, quartz)	−910.9	41.5
CS$_2$(g)	117.1	237.8	**Silver**		
HCOOH(l)	−425.1	129.0	Ag(s)	0.0	42.7
Chlorine			AgCl(s)	−127.1	96.2
Cl$_2$(g)	0.0	223.1	AgNO$_3$(s)	−124.4	140.9
HCl(g)	−92.3	186.8	**Sodium**		
Copper			Na(s)	0.0	51.5
Cu(s)	0.0	33.2	NaCl(s)	−411.2	72.1
CuCl$_2$(s)	−220.1	108.1	NaOH(s)	−425.9	64.4
CuSO$_4$(s)	−770.0	109.3	**Sulfur**		
Fluorine			S(s)	0.0	32.1
F$_2$(g)	0.0	202.8	SO$_2$(g)	−296.8	248.1
HF(g)	−272.5	173.8	SO$_3$(g)	−395.8	256.8
Hydrogen			H$_2$S(g)	−20.5	205.7
H$_2$(g)	0.0	130.7	H$_2$SO$_4$(l)	−814.0	156.9
H$_2$O(l)	−285.8	70.0	**Tin**		
H$_2$O(g)	−241.8	188.7	Sn(s, white)	0.0	51.6
H$_2$O$_2$(l)	−187.8	109.6	Sn(s, gray)	−2.1	44.1
HCN(g)	135.1	201.7	SnCl$_4$(l)	−511.3	258.6
Iron			**Zinc**		
Fe(s)	0.0	27.3	Zn(s)	0.0	41.6
FeCl$_3$(s)	−399.4	142.3	ZnCl$_2$(s)	−415.1	111.5
Fe$_2$O$_3$(s, hematite)	−825.5	87.4	ZnO(s)	−348.3	43.6
Fe$_3$O$_4$(s, magnetite)	−1120.9	145.3			

Appendix B

Graph scientific data

Graphs are a useful tool for displaying scientific data because they show relationships among variables in a compact, visual form. You probably know how to make and interpret several types of graphs such as pie charts and bar graphs (or *histograms*). You may have also used *x-y* graphs (or *Cartesian* graphs) in your math classes. However, you may not know how to use *x-y* graphs to display experimental data in chemistry laboratory work. The following guidelines will help.

1. Determine the independent variable

- Determine which of the quantities that you will be graphing is the *independent variable* and which is the *dependent variable*. The independent variable, denoted as x, is the variable whose values are chosen by the experimenter. The independent variable is plotted on the horizontal axis. The dependent variable, denoted y, is plotted on the vertical axis. Values of the dependent variable are determined by the independent variable.

- For example, the data shown in the table to the left was gathered in an experiment in which the temperature of a gas was increased and the resulting volume increase was measured. In this case, temperature was the independent variable and volume was the dependent variable. In the graph for this experiment, temperature is plotted on the horizontal axis and volume is plotted on the vertical axis.

Temperature (K)*	Volume (L)*
120	1
240	2
360	3
480	4

*Values specified at standard pressure.

2. Scale the axes

- Each axis must have a scale with equal divisions.
- Allow as much room as possible between divisions.
- Each division must represent a whole number of units of the variable being plotted, such as 1, 2, 5, 10 or some multiple of these. To decide which multiple to use for the horizontal axis, divide the maximum value of the independent variable by the number of major divisions on your graph paper. For example, Graph A, on the next page, shows 10 divisions along the grid on the horizontal axis. The data used to plot the curve for Graph A is shown to the left. The maximum value of T is 480 K. Divide the number of divisions into the maximum value of the variable to get 480 K/10 divisions or 48 K per division. To simplify, round up to allow 50 K per division on the horizontal axis.
- To scale the vertical axis follow the same procedure. The maximum value of the dependent variable, V, is 4 L. The grid allows for 6 divisions in the vertical direction. Divide 4 L/6 divisions to obtain 0.66 L per division. Round up to allow 1.0 L per division. Then there will be 2 divisions left over on the top of the vertical axis. Check Graph A to see how this looks.

- Label each axis with the quantity to be plotted and the units used to express each measurement. For example, the axes of **Graph A** are *Volume* (L) and *Temperature* (K).

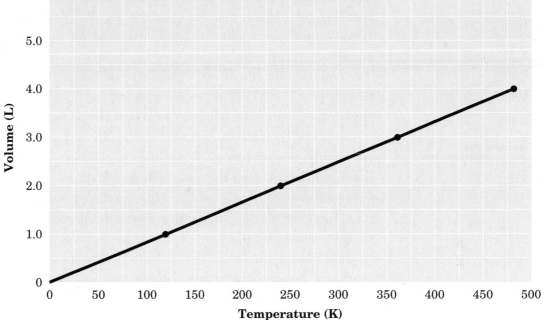

Graph A
Volume Versus Temperature Change in a Gas

3. Plot the data

- Plot each data point by locating the proper coordinates for the ordered pair on the graph grid. If the data points look like they fall roughly on a straight line, use a transparent ruler to find the line of best fit for the data points. Draw the best-fit line through or between the points.
- If the data points clearly do not fall along a straight line, but appear to fit another smooth curve, lightly sketch in the smooth curve that connects the points.
- Once you have sketched a smooth curve, draw over it in ink.

4. Title your graph

- Title your graph to indicate the *x* and *y* variables. If you can also tell how the variables relate to one another without making the title too long, include this information. For example, "Volume Versus Temperature Change in a Gas" is a suitable title for **Graph A**. Write the title at the top of the graph.

How To continued on following page . . .

Pressure (atm)*	Volume (L)*
0.100	224
0.200	112
0.400	56.0
0.600	37.3
0.800	28.0
1.00	22.4

*Values specified at constant temperature.

5. Interpret your graph

- If your data points lie roughly along a straight line, the x and y variables have a **linear relationship** or are **directly proportional**. This means that as one variable increases, the other does too, in a constant proportion—as x doubles, y doubles; as x triples, y triples; etc. Directly proportional quantities, x and y, relate to one another through mathematical equations of the form $y = mx + b$, where m is a constant and b is zero. The equation for the directly proportional linear relationship shown in **Graph A** is $V = kT$. Here, $m = k$ and $b = 0$.

- If your data points lie along a curve that drops from left to right as shown in **Graph B**, then the quantities have an **inverse relationship** or are **inversely proportional**. In an inverse relationship, one quantity increases as the other decreases. **Graph B** shows that gas pressure and volume have an inverse relationship; as the pressure of a gas increases, its volume decreases. The mathematical relationship that expresses an inverse relationship is $y = 1/x$. The expression relating gas pressure and volume follows the form $PV = k$. Note that inverse relationships are nonlinear because the increase of one variable is not accompanied by a constant rate of decrease in the other variable.

Graph B

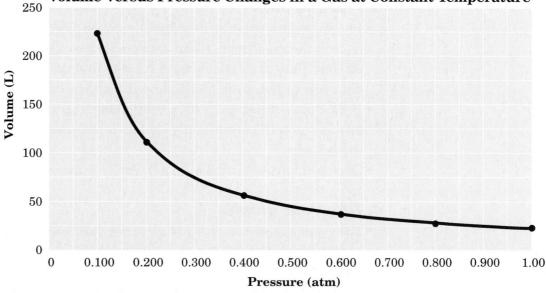

Volume Versus Pressure Changes in a Gas at Constant Temperature

Pressure (atm)*	1/P (1/atm)	Volume (L)*
0.100	10.0	224
0.200	5.00	112
0.400	2.50	56.0
0.600	1.67	37.3
0.800	1.25	28.0
1.00	1.00	22.4

*Values specified at constant temperature.

6. Use your graph

- Straight-line graphs are the easiest graphs to analyze and to express as equations. More complex graphs illustrate inversely proportional, exponential, or logarithmic relationships. It is often useful to replot a nonlinear graph to obtain a straight-line graph.

Graph C shows the inverse relationship $PV = k$ replotted as a straight line. To obtain this graph, both sides of the equation $PV = k$ were divided by P.

$$\left[\frac{PV}{P} = \frac{k}{P} \right] = \left[V = k \times \frac{1}{P} \right]$$

The resulting equation, $V = k \times 1/P$, has the same form as $y = mx$, which if plotted would produce a straight line that passes through the origin. To plot the actual data, the pressure values in the table must be converted to $1/P$ values. The first pressure conversion is as follows.

$$\frac{1}{0.100} = 10.0$$

V is plotted on the y axis and $1/P$ is plotted on the x axis.

Graph C
Volume Versus the Reciprocal of Pressure for a Gas at Constant Temperature

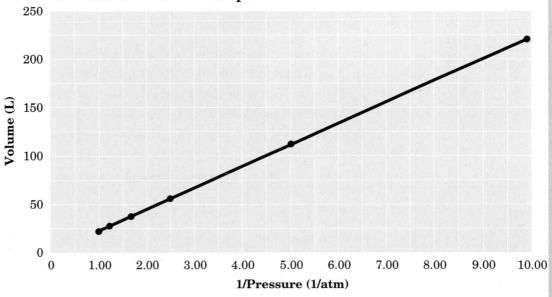

Graphing

1. Draw a horizontal axis on graph paper that is suitable for plotting the following mass measurements: 20.5 g, 39.7 g, 61.0 g, 92.8 g, and 116.9 g.

2. Prepare a graph representing the solubilities of potassium nitrate, KNO_3, in water at the following temperatures. From your graph, estimate the solubility of KNO_3 at 65°C and at 105° C.

Temperature (°C)	Solubility (g solute/100 g water)
0	13.9
20	31.6
40	61.3
60	106
80	167
100	245

3. The pressure of 1 mol of ammonia gas was varied and the following volume measurements were made. Temperature was kept constant at 25° C.

Pressure (atm)	Volume (L)
0.100	245
0.200	122
0.400	61.0
0.800	30.4
2.00	12.2
4.00	5.98
8.00	2.92

   a. Graph the data recorded in the table above.
   b. Do you have an inverse or direct relationship?
   c. Write the equation that expresses the mathematical relationship between P and V.
   d. Replot the data to obtain a straight-line graph. Write the equation that represents the linear relationship shown by your graph.

Answers for Concept Review items and Practice problems begin on page 841.

How To

Use significant figures and scientific notation

Scientists use significant figures to report information about the certainty of measurements and calculations. With this method, a measurement of 2.25 m means that while the 2 in the ones place and the 2 in the tenths place are certain, the 5 in the hundredths place is an estimate. If this measurement is combined with several other measurements in a formula, there must be some way of tracking the amount of uncertainty in each measurement and in the final result. For example, using a calculator to find the volume of a cube that measures 2.25 m on a side, you get 11.390625 m^3. This answer indicates far greater precision in the volume measurement than is realistic. Remember that the 5 in 2.25 is an estimated digit.

The rules and examples that follow will show you how to work with the uncertainty in measurements to express your results with an appropriate level of precision.

1. Determining the number of significant figures

The first set of rules shows you how to look at a measurement to determine the number of significant figures. A measurement expressed to the appropriate number of significant figures includes all digits that are certain and one digit in the measurement that is uncertain.

Rules for Determining the Number of Significant Figures

Rule	Example
The following are always significant	
• All nonzero digits	673 has three, 2.8 has two
• All zeros between nonzero digits	506 has three, 1.009 has four
• Zeros to the right of a non-zero digit and left of a *written* decimal point	34 800. mL has five, 200. cm has three
• Zeros to the right of a non-zero digit and right of a *written* decimal point	4.0 kg has two, 57.50 K has four, 2.90×10^3 has three
The following are never significant	
• Zeros to the left of the decimal point in numbers less than one	0.984 kg has three, 0.6 has one
• Zeros to the right of a decimal point, but to the left of the first non-zero digit	0.067 has two, 0.004 has one
Exceptions to the rules	
• Exact conversion factors are understood to have an unlimited number of significant figures	By definition there are exactly 100 cm in 1 m so the conversion factor 100 cm/1 m is understood to have an unlimited number of significant figures.
• Counting numbers are understood to have an unlimited number of significant figures	There are exactly 30 days in June, not 30.1 or 29.005, so an unlimited number of significant figures is understood in the expression "30 days".

2. Calculating with significant figures

When measurements are used in calculations, you must apply the rules regarding significant figures so that your results reflect the number of significant figures of the measurements.

How To continued on following page . . .

Rules for Making Calculations with Significant Figures

Rule	Example
Addition and subtraction The answer must be rounded so that it contains the same number of digits to the right of the decimal point as there are in the measurement with the smallest number of digits to the right of the decimal point.	2.89 m + 0.00043 m = 2.89043 m = 2.89 m
Multiplication The product or quotient should be rounded off to the same number of significant figures as in the measurement with the fewest significant figures.	3.5293 mol × 34.2 g/mol = 120.70206 g = 121 g

3. Rounding answers to get the correct number of significant figures

To obtain the correct number of significant figures in a measurement or calculation, numbers must often be rounded. To round numbers correctly, observe the following rules.

Rules for Rounding

Rule	Example
If the digit immediately to the right of the last significant figure you want to retain is	
• Greater than 5, increase the last digit by 1.	56.87 g ⟶ 56.9 g
• Less than 5, do not change the last digit.	12.02 L ⟶ 12.0 L
• 5, followed by nonzero digit(s), increase the last digit by 1.	3.7851 ⟶ 3.79
• 5, not followed by a nonzero digit and preceded by odd digit(s), increase the last digit by 1.	2.835 s ⟶ 2.84 s
• 5, not followed by nonzero digit(s), and the preceding significant digit is even, do not change the last digit.	2.65 mL ⟶ 2.6 mL

4. Expressing numbers in scientific notation

Measurements made in chemistry often involve very large or small numbers. To express these numbers conveniently, *scientific notation* is used. In scientific notation, numbers are expressed in terms of their order of magnitude. For example, 54 000 can be expressed as 5.4×10^4 in scientific notation, and the number 0.000 008 765 can be expressed as 8.765×10^{-6}.

As the preceding examples show, each value expressed in scientific notation has two parts. The first factor is always between 1 and 10, but it may have any number of digits. To write the first factor of the number, move the decimal point to the right or left so that there is only one nonzero digit to the left of it. The second factor of the number is written raised to an exponent of 10 that is determined by counting the number of places the decimal point must be moved. If the decimal point is moved to the left, the exponent is positive. If the decimal point is moved to the right, the exponent is negative.

For calculations involving scientific notation, the rules are the same as for exponents in algebra.

Rules for Calculations with Numbers in Scientific Notation

Rule	Example
Addition and Subtraction All values must have the same exponent before they can be added or subtracted. The result is the sum or difference of the first factors all with the same exponent of 10.	$4.5 \times 10^6 - 2.3 \times 10^5 =$ $45 \times 10^5 - 2.3 \times 10^5$ $= 42.7 \times 10^5$ $= 4.3 \times 10^6$
Multiplication The first factors of the numbers are multiplied and the exponents of 10 are added.	$(3.1 \times 10^3)(5.01 \times 10^4) =$ $(3.1 \times 5.01) \times 10^{4 + 3}$ $= 16 \times 10^7 = 1.6 \times 10^8$
Division The first factors of the number are divided, and the exponent of 10 in the denominator is subtracted from the exponent of 10 in the numerator.	$\dfrac{7.63 \times 10^3}{8.6203 \times 10^4} = \dfrac{7.63 \times 10^{3-4}}{8.6203}$ $= 0.885 \times 10^{-1}$ $= 8.85 \times 10^{-2}$

5. Expressing significant figures using scientific notation

Using scientific notation along with significant figures is especially useful for measurements such as 200 L, 2560 m, or 10 000 kg, because it is unclear which zeros are significant. In such cases follow the procedure described below.

Rules for Expressing Scientific Notation with Significant Figures

Rule	Example
Use scientific notation to eliminate all placeholding zeros. Convert the number to scientific notation and eliminate zeros before an unwritten decimal point that are not significant figures.	$2400 \longrightarrow 2.4 \times 10^4$ (if both zeros are not significant) $600 \longrightarrow 6.0 \times 10^2$ (if only one zero is significant) $750\,000 \longrightarrow 7.5000 \times 10^5$ (if all zeros are significant)

Concept Review

Significant figures and scientific notation

1. How many significant figures are there in these expressions?
   a. 470. km   **b.** 0.0980 m   **c.** 30.8900 g
   d. 0.09709 kg   **e.** 1000 g/1 kg   **f.** 4.870×10^5 s

2. Perform the following calculations and express the answers in significant figures.
   a. 32.89 g + 14.21 g   **b.** 34.09 L − 1.230 L   **c.** 100 m + 0.7 m
   d. 1.8940 cm × 0.0651 cm   **e.** 24.897 mi / 0.8700 h   **f.** 111.0 in × 1.020 in

3. Perform the following calculations.
   a. $\dfrac{8.369 \times 10^3 + 4.58 \times 10^2 - 6.30 \times 10^3}{4.156 \times 10^7}$

   b. $(6.499 \times 10^2)(5.915 \times 10^4 + 3.4733 \times 10^5)$

   c. $(7.23780 \times 10^{-3} - 3.65 \times 10^{-5})(3.6792 \times 10^2 + 2.67)$

   d. $\dfrac{(2.1267 \times 10^{-5})(3.3456 \times 10^{-2} - 0.012)}{(2.6 \times 10^{-2} - 3.23 \times 10^{-2})}$

Appendix C

A concept map presents key ideas, meanings, and relationships for the major concepts being studied. A concept map for a chapter can be thought of as a visual road map for learning the material in the chapter. Using concept maps, this learning happens efficiently because you work with only the key ideas and how they fit together.

The concept map shown as **Map A** was made from most of the vocabulary terms in Chapter 2. Vocabulary terms are generally labels for concepts, and concepts are generally nouns. Concepts are linked using linking words to form propositions. A proposition is a phrase that gives meaning to the concept. For example, in the map shown "matter is changed by energy" is a proposition.

Studies show that people are better able to remember materials presented visually. The concept map is better than an outline because you can see relationships among many ideas. Because outlines are linear there is no way of linking the ideas from various sections of the outline. Read through the map, to become familiar with the information presented. Look at the map and in relation to all of the text pages in Chapter 2, which would be more useful to study before an exam?

Map A

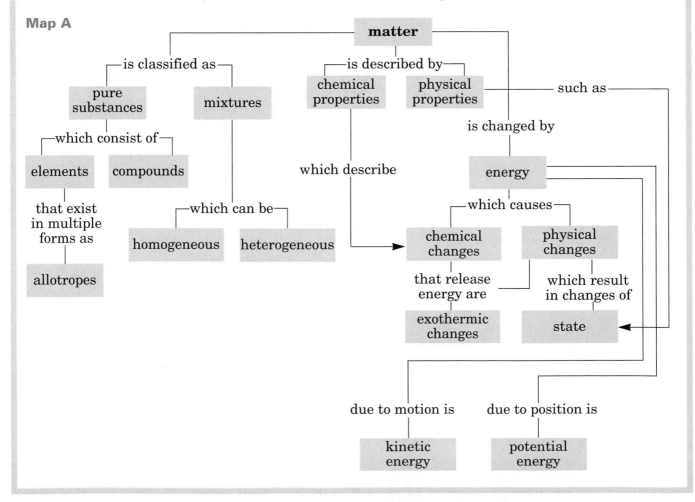

1. Start by taking a text section and listing all the important concepts.

We'll use the boldface terms in Section 2–3.

pure substance
mixture
homogeneous mixture
heterogeneous mixture
phase
element
compound
allotrope

- From this list, group similar concepts together. For example, one way to group these concepts would be into two groups—one that is related to mixtures, and the other that is related to pure substances.

mixture	*pure substance*
homogeneous mixture	element
heterogeneous mixture	compound
phase	allotrope

2. Select a main concept for the map.

We'll use matter as the main concept for this map.

3. Start building the map by placing the concepts according to their importance under the main concept, matter.

One way of arranging the concepts is shown in **Map B**.

Map B

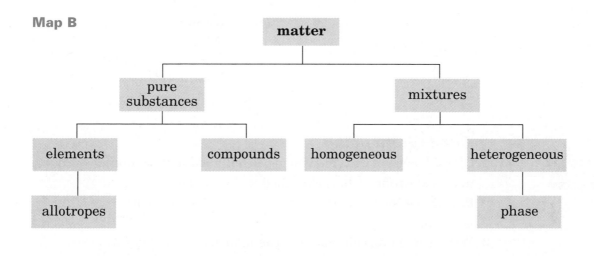

4. Now add the linking words that give meaning to the arrangement of concepts.

When adding the links, be sure that each proposition makes sense. To distinguish concepts from links, place your concepts in circles, ovals, or rectangles—like the ones in the map shown. Now look for cross links. Cross links are made of linking words and lines that connect information from various parts of the map. Cross links can be shown as links made with an arrow head. Map C is the finished map covering the main ideas of Section 2-3.

At first, making maps might seem difficult. However, the process of making maps forces you to think about the meanings and relationships among the concepts. Therefore, if you don't understand those relationships, you can get help.

One strategy to try when practicing mapping is to make concept maps about topics you know. For example, if you know a lot about a particular sport (such as basketball) or you have a particular hobby (such as music), you can use those topics to make practice maps. You'll perfect your skills with information that you know very well and you'll then feel more confident about your skills when you make maps from the information in a chapter.

Remember, the time you devote to mapping will pay off when it is time to review for an exam.

Map C

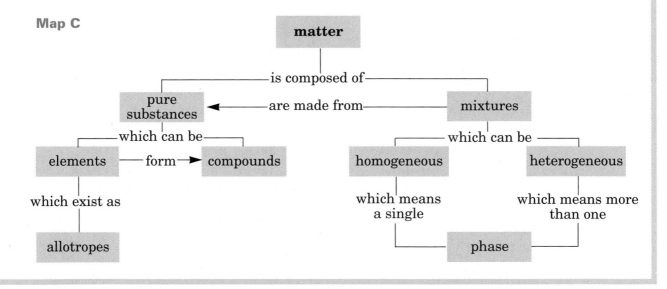

Concept Review

Concept mapping

1. Classify each of the following as either a concept or linking word(s).
   - **a.** classification
   - **b.** is classified as
   - **c.** forms
   - **d.** is described by
   - **e.** reaction
   - **f.** reacts with
   - **g.** metal
   - **h.** defines
2. Write three propositions from the information in **Map A**.
3. List two cross links shown on **Map A**.

Answers for Concept Review items and Practice problems begin on page 841.

Glossary

absolute temperature scale: a temperature measurement made relative to absolute zero—the lowest possible temperature (369)

accuracy: the extent to which a measurement approaches the true value of a quantity (60)

acid: a class of compounds whose water solutions taste sour, turn blue litmus to red, and react with bases to form salts (5)

acid anhydride: an oxide that forms an acid when reacted with water (491)

acid-dissociation constant: a quantity derived from the ratio of the concentrations of the products and reactants at equilibrium for a weak acid equilibrium system (498)

actinides: metallic elements with atomic numbers 90 through 103 that fill the 5*f* orbitals (117)

activated complex: a specific arrangement of high-energy reactant atoms or molecules, the decomposition of which leads to product or intermediate molecules; also called transition state (547)

activation energy: the minimum amount of energy that must be supplied to a system to start a chemical change (326)

activity series: arrangement of elements in the order of their tendency to react with water and acids (259)

actual yield: measured amount of product actually produced from a given amount of reactant (287)

alkali metals: highly reactive metallic elements which form alkaline solutions in water, burn in air, and belong to Group 1 of the periodic table (113)

alkaline-earth metals: reactive, metallic elements which belong to Group 2 of the periodic table (114)

allotropes: different molecular forms of an element in the same physical state (49)

alloy: a solid or liquid mixture of two or more metals (406)

alpha particle: a helium nucleus produced in nuclear decay (619)

amino acid: a carboxylic acid that is the structural subunit of a protein (518)

amphiprotic: having the property of behaving as an acid and base (496)

anion: ion with a negative charge (156)

anode: the electrode at which oxidation occurs as electrons are lost by some substance (578)

atom: the basic unit of matter (35)

atomic mass: the mass of an atom in atomic mass units (133)

atomic mass unit: one-twelfth the mass of the carbon-12 isotope (133)

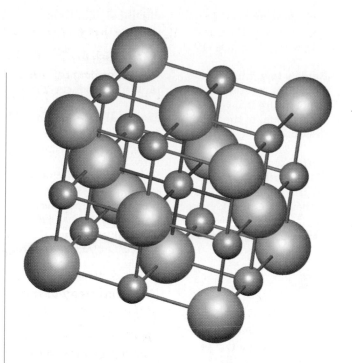

atomic number: the number of protons in the nucleus of an atom (93)

atomic radius: one-half of the distance from center to center of two like atoms (121)

average rate: the change in the measured property divided by the time elapsed (539)

Avogadro's number: 6.022×10^{23}, the number of particles in a mole (134)

Avogadro's principle: equal volumes of different gases under the same conditions have the same number of molecules (366)

basal metabolic rate: one's resting energy expenditure measured in the morning, at least 12 hours after the last meal (344)

base: a class of compounds that taste bitter, feel slippery in water solution, turn red litmus to blue, and react with acids to form salts (5)

base anhydride: an oxide that forms a base when reacted with water (493)

base-dissociation constant: a quantity derived from the ratio of the concentrations of the products and reactants at equilibrium for a weak base equilibrium system (499)

battery: single voltaic cell or group of voltaic cells that are connected together (595)

beta particle: an electron produced in nuclear decay (620)

binary compound: compound composed of two elements (166)

binding energy: the energy needed to separate nucleons within a nucleus or, equivalently, the energy released by nucleons combining to form a nucleus (616)

bond energy: the energy required to change the atoms in one mole of bonds from a bonded state to an unbonded state (153)

bond length: average distance between the nuclei of two bonded atoms (193)

Boyle's law: the volume of a gas at constant temperature is inversely proportional to the pressure (372)

buffer: a system that is able to withstand small additions of acid or base without significant change in pH; the system is composed of a conjugate acid-base pair (516)

cathode: the electrode at which reduction occurs as electrons are gained by some substance (578)

cation: ion with a positive charge (156)

catalyst: a substance added to a chemical reaction to increase the rate and that can be recovered chemically unchanged after the reaction is complete (560)

chain reaction: a self-sustaining nuclear or chemical reaction in which the product from each step acts as the reactant for the next step (626)

Charles's law: the volume of a gas at constant pressure is directly proportional to the absolute temperature (370)

chemical: any substance formed by or used in a chemical reaction (4)

chemical change: a change that produces one or more new substances (45)

chemical equation: symbols that describe a chemical reaction and indicate identities and relative amounts of reactants and products (238)

chemical kinetics: the branch of chemistry concerned with reaction rates and reaction mechanisms (536)

chemical properties: properties that can be observed only when substances interact with one another (38)

chlorofluorocarbons: a family of organic compounds in which the hydrogen atoms have been replaced by fluorine and chlorine (359)

circuit: closed loop path for current to follow (578)

coefficient: numeral used in a chemical equation to indicate relative amounts of reactants or products (239)

colligative property: a physical property that is dependent on the number of particles present rather than on the size, mass, or characteristics of those particles (459)

combustion: exothermic reaction that usually involves oxygen to form the oxides of the elements in a reactant (252)

common ion: an ion that comes from two or more substances making up a chemical solution (477)

common ion effect: a process in which an ionic compound becomes less soluble upon the addition of one of its ions by adding another compound (478)

complex ions: an ion having a structure in which a central atom or ion is bonded by coordinate bonds to other ions or molecules (called ligands) (466)

compounds: pure substances composed of two or more different elements (50)

concentration: ratio of solute to solvent or solution (411)

conductance: the measurement of a solution's ability to conduct electrical energy (452)

conjugate acid: the particle formed when a base has accepted a H^+ ion (497)

conjugate base: the particle formed when an acid has donated a H^+ ion (497)

covalent bond: bond formed when atoms share pairs of electrons (191)

critical mass: the minimum mass of fissionable material needed to produce a chain reaction (626)

crystal lattice: three-dimensional arrangement of atoms or ions in a crystal (158)

Dalton's law of partial pressures: the total pressure in a gas mixture is the sum of the partial pressures of the individual components (375)

decomposition: chemical reaction in which a single compound is broken down to produce two or more simpler substances (257)

diffusion: the process by which particles disperse from regions of higher concentration to regions of lower concentration (378)

dissociation: a process using energy to separate a compound into ions in water (456)

dissociation constant for water: the ion product constant for water that is equal to 1.00×10^{-14} (505)

double bond: covalent bond formed by the sharing of two pairs of electrons between two atoms (201)

double-displacement: chemical reaction in which two elements in different compounds exchange places (261)

effusion: the motion of a gas through an opening into an evacuated chamber (379)

electricity: energy associated with electrons that have moved from one place to another (577)

electrolysis: a process in which electric energy is used to bring about a chemical change (598)

electrolyte: any substance that, when it is dissolved in a solution, will conduct an electric current by means of movement of ions (452)

electrolytic cell: an electrochemical cell in which electric energy from an external source causes a nonspontaneous redox reaction to occur (598)

electromagnetic spectrum: the total range of electromagnetic radiation, ranging from the longest radio waves to the shortest gamma waves (90)

electron affinity: the energy change that accompanies the addition of an electron to an atom in the gas phase (124)

electronegativity: the tendency for an atom to attract electrons to itself when it is combined with another atom (125)

elementary step: a chemical equation describing one stage of a reaction as it is theorized to occur (558)

elements: the 109 simplest substances from which more complex materials are made (48)

empirical formula: simplest whole-number ratio of atoms that matches the relative ratio found in a chemical compound (169)

emulsifying agent: stabilizes an emulsion that would otherwise separate into different phases (428)

emulsion: colloidal-sized droplets (about 100 nm wide) of one liquid suspended in another liquid (427)

end point: a point in a titration indicated by the color change of an indicator (515)

endothermic change: a physical or chemical change in which a system absorbs energy from its surroundings (44)

energy: the capacity to do work (40)

energy level: a specific energy or group of energies that may be possessed by an electron in an atom (87)

enthalpy: total energy content of a system (324)

enthalpy change: heat energy released or absorbed when a physical or chemical change occurs at constant pressure (324)

entropy: a measure of the randomness or disorder of a system (333)

enzyme: large protein molecule that catalyzes chemical reactions in living things (561)

equilibrium: a reversible reaction in which the rates of the forward and reverse reactions are equal (22)

equilibrium constant (K_{eq}): for a reversible reaction, a number expressing the relationship between the mathematical product of the molar concentrations of the products divided by the mathematical product of the molar concentrations of the reactants, each raised to the power of its coefficient in the balanced equation (470)

equilibrium vapor pressure: a measure of the tendency of the particles of a liquid substance to enter the gas phase at a given temperature (389)

equivalence point: the point in a titration process where the moles of standard are stoichiometrically equivalent to the moles of substance titrated (510)

excess reactant: reactant that will not be used up in a reaction that goes to completion (285)

excited state: the condition of an atom in a state higher than the ground state (89)

exothermic change: a physical or chemical change in which energy is released by a system to its surroundings (44)

fatty acid: the long chain carboxylic acid subunit of a fat and oil (521)

formula unit: simplest collection of atoms from which a compound's formula can be established (169)

free energy: a quantity of energy related to the capacity of a system to do work, which can be used to predict spontaneity (339)

functional group: group of atoms that determines an organic molecule's chemical properties (219)

gamma ray: high-energy electromagnetic radiation produced by decaying nuclei (621)

Graham's law of effusion: the rates of effusion for two gases are inversely proportional to the square roots of their molar masses at the same temperature and pressure (379)

greenhouse effect: an increase in the warming effects of infrared radiation absorption brought about by an increase in levels of carbon dioxide and other greenhouse gases in the atmosphere (357)

ground state: the lowest energy state of a quantized system (89)

group: a series of elements that form a column in the periodic table (75)

half-cell: the part of a voltaic cell in which either oxidation or reduction occurs. It consists of a single electrode immersed in a solution of its ions (578)

half-life: the time required for half of a sample of radioactive atoms to decay (628)

half-reaction: the oxidation or reduction portion of a redox reaction (583)

halogens: elements that combine with most metals to form salts and that belong to Group 17 of the periodic table (119)

heat: the total of kinetic energy of random motion of molecules, atoms, or ions in a substance (315)

heat of reaction: the amount of heat energy absorbed or released during a chemical change (320)

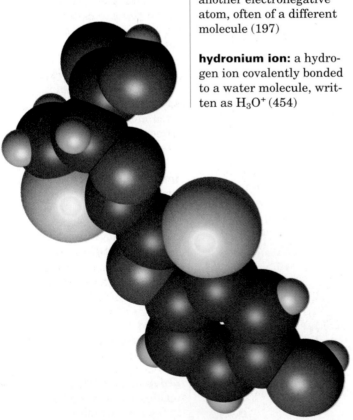

Hess's law: the total enthalpy change for a chemical or physical change is the same whether it takes place in one or several steps (329)

heterogeneous mixture: a mixture containing substances that are not evenly distributed (47)

homogeneous mixture: a mixture containing substances that are uniformly distributed (47)

Hund's rule: the most stable arrangement of electrons is that with the maximum number of unpaired electrons, all with the same spin direction (97)

hydration: the process by which water molecules surround each ion as it moves into solution (456)

hydrogen bond: attraction occurring when a hydrogen atom bonded to a strongly electronegative atom is also attracted to another electronegative atom, often of a different molecule (197)

hydronium ion: a hydrogen ion covalently bonded to a water molecule, written as H_3O^+ (454)

hydroxide ion: the OH^- anion (490)

hypothesis: a proposition based on certain assumptions that can be evaluated scientifically (18)

ideal gas: a model that effectively describes the behavior of real gases at conditions close to standard temperature and pressure; a gas for which the product of the pressure and volume is proportional to the absolute temperature (360)

ideal gas law: the equation of state for an ideal gas in which the product of the pressure and volume is proportional to the product of the absolute temperature and the amount of gas expressed in moles (382)

immiscible: indicates liquids or gases that will not dissolve in each other (405)

indicator: (as applied to acid-base chemistry) a particle that reversibly changes color depending on the pH (508)

inhibitor: a substance added to a chemical reaction to slow it down (563)

initial rate: the highest rate measured very close to the start of the reaction where the curve is almost linear (543)

inorganic compound: all compounds outside the organic family of compounds (5)

insoluble: does not dissolve appreciably in a particular solvent (406)

intermediate: a structure formed in one elementary step, but consumed in a later step of a mechanism. It is neither an original reactant nor final product (559)

intermolecular forces: attraction resulting from forces between molecules (196)

ion: an atom or group of atoms that has gained or lost one or more electrons to acquire a net electric charge (123)

ionic bond: bond formed by the attraction of oppositely charged ions (157)

ionic compound: chemical compound composed of cations and anions combined so that the total positive and negative charges are equal (157)

ionization energy: the amount of energy needed to remove an electron from a specific atom or ion in its ground state in the gas phase (123)

isotope: one of two or more atoms having the same number protons but different numbers of neutrons (93)

kinetic energy: energy that moving objects possess by virtue of their motion (40)

kinetic molecular theory: the theory that explains the behavior of gases at the molecular level (360)

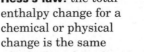

lanthanides: shiny, metallic elements with atomic numbers 58 through 71 that fill the *4f* orbitals (117)

lattice energy: energy released when a crystal containing one mole of an ionic compound is formed from gaseous ions (162)

law of conservation of energy: the observed fact that in any chemical or physical process, energy is neither created nor destroyed (43)

Le Châtelier's principle: a principle stating that if a system at equilibrium is disturbed by applying stress, the system will adjust in such a way as to counter the stress (464)

Lewis structure: diagram showing the arrangement of valence electrons among the atoms in a molecule (199)

ligand: a functional group, atom, or molecule that is attached to the central atom of a complex ion (467)

limiting reactant: reactant that is consumed first in a reaction that goes to completion (285)

main-block elements: elements that represent the entire range of chemical properties and belong to Groups 1, 2, and 13 through 18 in the periodic table (118)

mass: the quantity of matter in an object (34)

mass defect: the difference between the mass of an atom and the sum of the masses of its individual components (616)

mass number: the total number of protons and neutrons in the nucleus of an atom (94)

matter: anything that has mass and volume (34)

mechanism (of a reaction): a proposed step-by-step sequence of reactions that describes how reactants are changed into products (558)

metal: any of a class of elements that generally are solid at room temperature, have a grayish color and shiny surface, and conduct electricity (78)

metalloid: an element having properties of metals as well as nonmetals (79)

miscible: indicates liquids or gases that will dissolve in each other (405)

mixture: a collection of two or more pure substances physically mixed together (46)

molar mass: sum of the molar masses of all atoms represented by 1 mol of formula units (176)

molar volume: the volume of one mole of a substance at STP (366)

molarity: concentration unit, expressed as moles of solute per liter of solution (411)

mole: the fundamental SI unit used to measure the amount of a substance (134)

mole fraction: the number of moles of an individual substance compared with the total number of moles in the mixture expressed as a ratio (377)

molecular compound: substance consisting of atoms that are covalently bonded (191)

molecular formula: gives type and actual number of atoms in a chemical compound (209)

molecule: a neutral group of atoms held together by chemical bonds (35)

monatomic ion: cation or anion formed from a single atom (164)

mutagen: any substance or agent that causes a noticeable increase in the frequency of mutations (358)

neutralization reaction: a reaction between an acid and a hydroxide base in which H^+ and OH^- react to form H_2O (507)

noble gas: an element that exists in the gaseous state at normal temperatures and is nonreactive with other elements (79)

nonelectrolyte: a substance that, when dissolved in an aqueous solution, will not conduct an electric current (453)

nonmetal: any chemical element that is neither a metal, metalloid, or a noble gas (78)

nonpolar covalent bond: covalent bond in which the bonding electrons are shared equally between the two bonding atoms (196)

normal boiling point: the temperature at which a substance boils at 1.0000 atm of pressure (391)

normal freezing/melting point: the temperature at which a substance melts and freezes at 1.0000 atm of pressure (392)

nuclear fission: the process by which a nucleus splits into two smaller fragments (625)

nuclear fusion: the process by which two nuclei combine to form a heavier nucleus (627)

nuclear reaction: a reaction that involves a change in the nucleus of an atom, as opposed to a chemical reaction which involves changes to the arrangement of electrons that surround the nucleus (128)

nucleic acid: a biological polymer consisting of phosphoric acid, a 5-carbon sugar, and four nitrogen bases (520)

nucleus: the central region of an atom made up of protons and neutrons (86)

octet rule: main-block elements form bonds by rearranging electrons so that each atom has a stable octet in its outermost energy level (151)

orbital: a region of an atom in which there is a high probability of finding electrons (91)

order: the exponent for a specified reactant in a rate law expression (555)

order of reaction: the sum of all the exponents on all concentration terms in a rate law expression (557)

organic compound: any covalently bonded compound containing carbon (except carbonates and oxides) (5)

oxidation: loss of electrons by an atom or an algebraic increase in its oxidation state (579)

oxidation number: apparent charge assigned to an atom based on the assumption of complete transfer of electrons (205)

oxidation state: a numerical representation of an atom's share of the bonding electrons. In ionic compounds, it is equal to the ionic charge. In covalent compounds, it is the average charge assigned to an atom according to electronegativities (587)

partial pressures: the pressure of an individual gas in a gas mixture that contributes to the total pressure of the mixture (375)

pascal: a unit of pressure equal to the force of 1 N/m^2 (365)

percent yield: ratio of actual yield to theoretical yield, multiplied by 100 (289)

period: a series of elements that form a horizontal row in the periodic table (77)

periodic law: properties of elements tend to change with increasing atomic number in a periodic way (109)

pH: the negative logarithm of the hydronium ion concentration of an aqueous solution; used to express acidity (499)

phase: any part of a system that has uniform composition and properties (47)

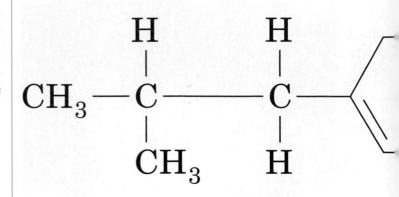

phase diagram: a graphic representation of the relationships between the physical state of a substance and its pressure and temperature (391)

physical change: a change that affects only physical properties (44)

physical properties: properties that can be observed or measure without changing the composition of matter (37)

polar covalent bond: covalent bond in which the bonding electrons are more strongly attracted by one of the bonding atoms (196)

polyatomic ion: ion made of two or more atoms bonded together that function as a single ion (170)

polymer: large molecule made of many repeated small subunits, each of which is a small molecule or group of atoms (210)

polymerization: chemical reaction in which many simple molecules combine in chains to form a very large molecule (256)

porous barrier: any medium through which ions can slowly pass (577)

potential energy: energy an object possesses because of its position (41)

pressure: the force exerted per unit area (363)

precision: the degree of exactness or refinement of a measurement (60)

principal energy level: a specific energy or group of energies that may be possessed by an electron in an atom (87)

pure substance: matter composed of only one kind of atom or molecule (46)

quantum theory: the field of physics based on the idea that energy is quantized and that this has significant effects on the atomic level (91)

radioactivity: the ability of unstable nuclei to undergo spontaneous nuclear decay (613)

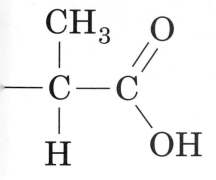

radioactive series: a sequence of nuclei that arise from and are transformed by radioactive decay until a stable isotope is produced (623)

rate law: a mathematical expression for the rate of a reaction as a function of the concentration of one or more reactants: rate = $k[A]^n [B]^m$ (555)

rate-determining step: the slowest step in a reaction mechanism (553)

reaction rate: the change in reactant concentration per unit of time as reaction proceeds (536)

reagent: a chemical used to convert one substance into another substance in a chemical reaction (7)

redox reaction: a chemical reaction involving oxidation and reduction (580)

reduction: the gain of electrons by an atom or the algebraic decrease in its oxidation state (579)

reduction potential: a measure of the tendency of a given half-reaction to occur as a reduction in an electrochemical cell (583)

resting metabolic rate: energy expended by a person at rest in a thermally neutral environment (344)

salt: a compound with an ionic lattice that is formed from an acid when H^+ is replaced by a metal ion or cation (157, 508)

saturated: containing the standard amount of solute specified by the solubility at a given temperature (408)

saturated fatty acid: the long chain carboxylic acid subunit of a fat and oil with no double bonds (521)

SHE: standard hydrogen electrode has the half-reaction $2H^+(aq) + 2e^- \rightarrow H_2(g)$. The concentration of hydrogen ion is 1 M, the temperature is 25°C, and the pressure of the hydrogen gas is 101.3 kPa (1 atm) (583)

shielding effect: the reduction of the attractive force between a nucleus and its outer electrons due to the blocking effect of inner electrons (122)

single bond: sharing of one pair of electrons between two atoms (199)

single-displacement: chemical reaction in which one element replaces another element in a compound (258)

solubility: the maximum amount of a chemical that will dissolve in a given amount of a solvent at a specified temperature while the solution is in contact with some undissolved solute (407)

solubility-product constant (K_{sp}): the equilibrium constant for a solid in equilibrium with its ions in a saturated solution; used for substances that are described as "insoluble" because they are only very slightly soluble (475)

soluble: can be dissolved in a particular solvent (406)

solute: the material dissolved in a solution (405)

solvent: the material dissolving the solute to make the solution (405)

specific heat capacity: the amount of heat energy required to increase the temperature by one gram of a substance by one degree Celsius (315)

spontaneous change: a change that will occur because of the nature of the system, once it is initiated (323)

stable nucleus: a nucleus that does not spontaneously decay to become the nucleus of a different element (613)

standard reduction potential: by convention, the potential, E^0, of a half-cell connected to the standard hydrogen electrode when ion concentrations in the half-cells are 1 M, gases are at a pressure of 1 atm, and the temperature is 25°C (583)

standard temperature and pressure (STP): standard conditions for a gas of 0°C and 1.0000 atm (365)

state: the condition of being a gas, liquid, solid, plasma, or neutron star (37)

stoichiometry: mass and quantity relationships among reactants and products in a chemical reaction (272)

strong electrolyte: a substance that is completely or largely dissociated in an aqueous solution (453)

strong nuclear force: a short-range, attractive force that acts among nucleons (612)

structural formula: indicates the spatial arrangement of atoms and bonds within a molecule (211)

sublevel: one orbital or a group of orbitals within an energy level which have the same value of ℓ (95)

sublimation: a change of state in which a solid is transformed directly to a gas without going through the liquid state (392)

substrate: (biochemical) the molecule or molecules with which an enzyme interacts (561)

supersaturated: containing more than the standard amount of solute specified by the solubility at a given temperature (408)

surface tension: the measure of a liquid's tendency to decrease its surface area to a minimum (393)

surfactant: a compound that stabilizes an emulsion by acting at the surface between two immiscible substances (431)

suspension: mixture that appears uniform while being stirred, but separates into different phases when agitation ceases (405)

synthesis: the process of building compounds from elementary substances through one or more chemical reactions (6)

system: all the parts that form a unified whole (22)

technology: the application of scientific knowledge for practical purposes (15)

temperature: a measure of the average kinetic energy of random motion of the particles in a sample of matter (315)

theoretical yield: calculated maximum amount of product possible from a given amount of reactant (287)

theory: an explanation of an observation that is based on experimentation and reasoning (19)

theory of ionization: the explanation of the process by which electrolytes break apart in solution in the form of freely moving ions that can conduct an electrical current (456)

titration: an analytical procedure used to determine the concentration of a sample by reacting it with a standard solution (508)

titration standard: a solution of precisely known concentration; also called a titrant (508)

transition elements: metallic elements that have varying properties and belong to Groups 3 through 12 of the periodic table (116)

transition interval: the pH range over which an indicator exhibits different colors for its acidic and alkaline forms (508)

transmutation: a process by which a nucleus of one element is transformed into a nucleus of a different element (613)

triple bond: covalent bond formed by the sharing of three pairs of electrons between two atoms (201)

triple point: the temperature and pressure at which all three states of a substance exist in equilibrium (392)

unit cell: the simplest portion of a crystal lattice that portrays the three-dimensional structure of the entire lattice (159)

unsaturated: containing less than the standard amount of solute specified by the solubility at a given temperature (408)

unsaturated fatty acid: a fatty acid with one or more carbon-carbon double bonds (521)

unshared pair: pair of electrons that is not involved in covalent bonding, but instead belongs exclusively to one atom (198)

unstable nucleus: a nucleus that spontaneously undergoes decay to become the nucleus of a different element (613)

Valence Shell Electron Pair Repulsion (VSEPR): system for predicting molecular shape based on the idea that pairs of electrons orient themselves as far apart as possible (213)

valence electron: electron present in the outermost energy level of an atom (198)

volatile: a term used to describe a substance that is readily vaporized at low temperature (390)

voltaic cell: an electrochemical cell in which a spontaneous redox reaction produces a flow of electrons through an external circuit (577)

volume: the amount of space an object occupies (34)

weak electrolyte: a compound that experiences only a small degree of dissociation in an aqueous solution (453)

zwitterion: the reactive dipolar form of an amino acid (519)

Index

arabic gum, t 429

archeologist. *See also*
radioactive dating
molecular, 487, 524

area, 59

argon
in air, t 357
electron orbital notation
for, 151, t 151

aroma, 53, 272, 378, 390

aromatic compound(s), **7**

Arrhenius, Svante, 490,
490

Arrhenius acid(s), 490,
495, t 495

Arrhenius base(s), 490,
495, t 495

arsenate ion, t 171

arsenic
properties of, **79**
suspected poisoning of
Zachary Taylor, 629
uses of, **79**

arsenic acid, t 498

artificial transmutation,
620–621, **620**

ascorbic acid. *See*
vitamin C

asparagine, t 499

aspirin, **220**
action in body, 26
buffered, 5, 26, 516, **516**
history of, 3, 6, 26
production of, 6–8, **6–7**
product warning label, 14
properties of, 5
rate changes in aspirin
systems, 545, **545–546**
synthesis of, **6–7**, 252,
252, 290
taste of, 488

"-ate" ending, 172

atmosphere, 357.
See also air; ozone
gases in, 357, t 357

greenhouse effect,
357–358, **357**
partial pressure of oxygen
in, 377
regions of, **358**

atmosphere (pressure
unit), 365, t 365

atmospheric pressure,
363–365, **363**

atom(s), 35
bond formation by,
150–153
conservation in chemical
reaction, 238
counting or measuring of,
132–140
excited state of, 89, **91**
ground state of, 89, **91**
location of electrons in,
94–99
mass of, 139–140
sublevels of, 95–97, t 96
visualization in scanning
tunneling microscope,
92, **92**

atomic bomb, 81, **81**, 93,
622

atomic emission, 100

atomic mass, 109, 132–133
average, 133
relative, 132–133

atomic mass unit, 132–133

atomic number, 93–94, **93**,
109

atomic radius, 121–122,
121–122, t 121, 125, t 126

atomic structure, 74–77,
81–92
Bohr model of, 87–88, **88**
modern view of, 89–92
plum pudding model of,
85, **85**
quantum mechanical
model of, 91

atomic theory, 19, **19**
Dalton's, 83
evidence for, 82–83
five principles in, 83

ATP, 602

automobile
air bags, 294–296,
294–295
battery of, 598–599, **598**
battery-powered, 311
catalytic converter, 563
electric, 114
exhaust gases, 300–302,
t 300
hydrogen-powered, 311,
347
low-emission, 311, 347
solar-powered, 311

average atomic mass, 133

average rate, 539

Avogadro, Amedeo, 134,
134, 366

Avogadro's law, 382

Avogadro's number,
134–135, **134–135**

Avogadro's principle, 366,
366

baking soda
pH of, **501**
reaction with vinegar, **45**

balance
analytical, 34, **34**
measurement of mass
with, 34, **34–35**
triple beam, 34, **35**

balanced equation, **23**,
t 248–249, 249, 274

balancing an equation,
239–244, t 242
by inspection, 241

balloon
atmospheric studies, 355,
394
helium, 49, **49**, 384
weather, **79**, 112

band of stability, of stable
nuclei, 611, **611**

bar (pressure unit), t 365

barium
properties of, 114, **114**
reduction potential of,
t 585

barium hydroxide, t 489

barium nitrate, 176

barium oxide, 166

barium sulfate
solubility of, 475–476,
t 475
X-ray contrast medium,
477–478, **477–478**

barometer, **78**, 363, **363**

basal metabolic rate
(BMR), 344

base(s)
Arrhenius, 490, 495, t 495
Brønsted, 495–496, **495**
conduction of electricity
by, 489
conjugate, 496–497
in human body, 516–522
pH of, 503
properties of, 5, t 5, 23,
489, **489**
reaction with acid,
507–515
strength of, 498–499
strong, 489, t 489
weak, 489, t 489, 498–506

base anhydride(s),
491–493
counteracting acid rain,
493

base-dissociation constant
(K_b), 499, t 499

battery, 595–599, **595**
consumable, 595–597
"dead," 598
flashlight, 42
lithium-based, 114
rechargeable, 598–599
recharging of, 462
recycling of, 597, 599

battery-powered automo-
bile, 311

batting average, 289, **289**

Becquerel, Henri, 614

"the bends," 435

benzene, **6–7**, 7, t 10, 220,
220

benzoic acid, **488**

beryllium, 88, 114, **114**,
129

beta particle(s), 620,
t 621

beverage stain, 433

bias, 60

bicarbonate ion, t 171
in blood, 496

Big Bang, 127–128

binary acid(s), 494, **494**

binary compound(s), 166,
166

binding energy, 612–613,
612
calculation of, 612–613

biochemical equilibrium
system, 472–473, **472**

biodegradable product(s),
189, 223

bioluminescence, 575, 602

bitter taste, 489

blimp, **118**

blueprint, **20**

BMR. *See* basal metabolic
rate

body fluid(s), 451, 455, 479

body temperature, **409**

Bohr, Niels, 87

Bohr model, 87–88, **88**

boiling, 44, 312–315, 390,
390

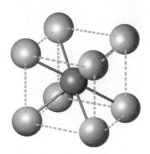

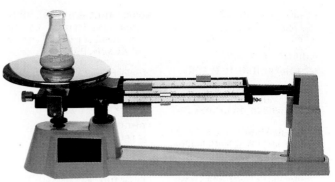

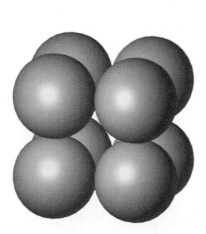

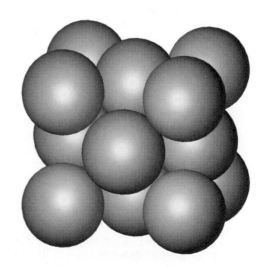

Credits

List of Abbreviations
All safety symbols were designed by Michael Helfenbein/Evolution Design.

Special thanks to the students, faculty, and staff of Poly Prep Country Day School, Brooklyn, NY for the use of their chemistry laboratory and other facilities. Many of the student models in this book are students at the school.

Archive; **619** (detector) Sergio Purtell/Foca, (smoke) © Comstock Inc./Georg Gerster; **620** (tl) Sergio Purtell/Foca; **621** (t) Foca; **622** (all) Sergio Purtell/Foca; **623** (c) Foca; **624** (bl) © Fermilab Visual Media Services; **625** (all) © A.M.Siegelman/Visuals Unlimited; **626** (b) Dept. of Defense/FPG International Corp.; **627** (l) Roger Ressmeyer/© 1994 Corbis, (c) © The Bettmann Archive; **628** (b) Foca; **629** (bl) © Gaillarde Raphael/Gamma Liaison, (br) © American Museum of Natural History/Courtesy Department Library Services/K4676; **630** (all) Sergio Purtell/Foca; **631** (bl) Sergio Purtell/Foca; **632** (b) © American Museum of Natural History/P. Hollembeak/Courtesy Department of Library Services/3316; **633** (t) SPL/Custom Medical Stock Photo, (b) © 1990 Science Photo Library/Custom Medical Stock Photo; **634** (tl) Sergio Purtell/Foca, (badge) © Southern Illinois University/Photo Researchers, (bunny suit) © Nuclear Energy Institute; **635** (l) © SNS/Sipa Press, (iceman head and skull) © Kenneth Garrett/National Geographic Imaging Collection; **636** (Bohr/Einstein) © AIP Emilio Segrè Visual Archives, (Fermi) © The Bettman Archive, (H-bomb) © Los Alamos National Laboratory, (Hevesy) © UPI/Bettmann, (hydrogen block, map) Foca, (Manhattan Project) © Los Alamos National Laboratory/Mark Marten/Photo Researchers, (Moseley) Public Domain/Sergio Purtell/Foca, (Rutherford) © Stock Montage; **636–637** (green ribbons) Greg LaFever/Scott Hull Associates; **637** (cyclotrons, technetium block, neutron) Foca, (Chadwick) © Nobel Foundation/Courtesy AIP Emilio Segre Visual Archives, (Curies) © The Bettman Archive, (Fermi accelerator) © Fermilab Visual Media Services, (Gell-Mann) © Archive Photos/Express Newspapers, (Glashow,Salam, Weinberg) © UPI/Bettman, (Hahn) © 1967 Archive Photos/DPA, (Kennedy) © UPI/Bettmann, (Lawrence) © Lawrence Berkeley Laboratory, University of California, (Meit-

ner) © UPI/Bettmann, (Super Collider) © Bruno Torres/UPI/Bettmann; **641** (r) Foca; **642–643** (spread) Sergio Purtell/Foca; **644** (tl) Sergio Purtell/Foca; **645** (all) Sergio Purtell/Foca; **646** (all) Sergio Purtell/Foca; **647** (all) Sergio Purtell/Foca; **648** (all) Sergio Purtell/Foca; **649** (tl, bl, cr) Foca; **649** (tr, l, bl, r) Sergio Purtell/Foca; **650** (bkgrd) Sergio Purtell/Foca; **656** (br) Sergio Purtell/Foca; **657** (tr) Sergio Purtell/Foca, (br) Greg LaFever/Scott Hull Associates; **658** (tl) Sergio Purtell/Foca, (br) Sergio Purtell/Foca, (c) Greg LaFever/Scott Hull Associates; **659** (r) Sergio Purtell/Foca; **662** (cl, bl) Foca, (br) Sergio Purtell/Foca; **663** (tr) Sergio Purtell/Foca; **664** (tl, tc, tr) Sergio Purtell/Foca, (bl) Greg LaFever/Scott Hull Associates; **665** (all) Greg LaFever/Scott Hull Associates; **666** (bl) Sergio Purtell/Foca; **667** (all) Greg LaFever/Scott Hull Associates; **668** (l) Sergio Purtell/Foca; **669** (br) © Comstock Inc./ Russ Kine; **672** (br) Sergio Purtell/Foca; **673** (all) Sergio Purtell/Foca; **675** (tr) Sergio Purtell/Foca; **678** (tl) © Telegraph Colour Library/FPG International Corp.; **679** (tr) Sergio Purtell/ Foca; **680** (tl) Sergio Purtell/Foca, (bl) Greg LaFever/Scott Hull Associates; **681** (l) Sergio Purtell/ Foca; **682** (tl) Sergio Purtell/Foca; **683** (br) David Bartruff/ FPG International Corp.; **686** (l) Foca, (br) © Gary Milburn/Tom Stack & Associates; **687** (tr) Sergio Purtell/Foca, (br) Greg LaFever/Scott Hull Associates; **688** (tl) Sergio Purtell/Foca; **689** (br) © R. Carlton/Photo Researchers; **692** (all) Sergio Purtell/Foca; **693** (tr) Sergio Purtell/Foca, (br) Greg LaFever/Scott Hull Associates; **694** (br) Sergio Purtell/Foca; **695** (r) Sergio Purtell/Foca; **698** (br) Josef Beck/FPG International Corp., (others) Foca; **699** (all) Sergio Purtell/Foca; **700** (all) Sergio Purtell/Foca; **701** (br) © 1991 Eugen Gebhardt/FPG International Corp.; **706** (all) Sergio Purtell/Foca; **707** (all) Sergio Purtell/Foca; **708** (tl) Sergio Purtell/Foca; **709** (br) Sergio Purtell/Foca; **712** (br) © Tom Tracy/FPG International Corp.,

(all others) Foca; **713** (all) Sergio Purtell/Foca; **714** (tl) Sergio Purtell/Foca; **715** (br, bread) Sergio Purtell/Foca, (inset) © Science Photo Library/Photo Researchers; **718** (br) © Harvey Lloyd/Peter Arnold, Inc.; **719** (all) Sergio Purtell/Foca; **720** (t) Sergio Purtell/Foca; **721** (tl) Sergio Purtell/Foca; **722** (r) Sergio Purtell/Foca; **723** (tr) Sergio Purtell/Foca; **726** (br) © Benelux Press/Photo Researchers, (c) Foca; **727** (tr) Sergio Purtell/Foca; **728** (tl) Sergio Purtell/Foca, (bl) Foca; **729** (br) Sergio Purtell/Foca; **736** (bl, r) Foca, (br) Sergio Purtell/Foca/Provided courtesy Mead Johnson Nutritional Group, **737** (all) Sergio Purtell/Foca; **739** (all) Sergio Purtell/Foca; **741** (tr) Sergio Purtell/Foca/Reprinted by Permission of Texas Instruments.; **746** (br) Sergio Purtell/Foca; **747** (tr) Sergio Purtell/Foca; **748** (tl) Greg LaFever/Scott Hull Associates, (all others) Sergio Purtell/Foca; **749** (br) Ron Rovtar/FPG International Corp.; **752** (br) Sergio Purtell/Foca; **753** (tr) Sergio Purtell/Foca, (br) Sergio Purtell/Foca; **754** (tl) Sergio Purtell/Foca, (bl) Sergio Purtell/Foca; **756** (br) Sergio Purtell/Foca; **757** (br) © AP/Wide World Photos; **760** (br) © M. Bertinetti/Photo Researchers, (others) Foca; **761** (tr, br) Sergio Purtell/Foca, (c) Greg LaFever/Scott Hull Associates; **762** (c) Greg LaFever/Scott Hull Associates; **763** (br) Sergio Purtell/Foca; **766** (c) Foca, (br) Sergio Purtell/Foca; **767** (tr) Sergio Purtell/Foca; **768** (all) Sergio Purtell/Foca; **769** (l) Sergio Purtell/Foca; **771** (br) Sergio Purtell/Foca; **774** (br) Sergio Purtell/Foca; **775** (tr) Sergio Purtell/Foca, (br) Sergio Purtell/Foca; **776** (tr) Sergio Purtell/Foca; **777** (br) Sergio Purtell/Foca; **780** (br) © Ewing Galloway; **781** (all) Sergio Purtell/Foca; **782** (tl) Sergio Purtell/Foca; **783** (br) Sergio Purtell/Foca; **786** (br) ©Comstock Inc./ Van Garmon; **787** (all) Sergio Purtell/Foca; **788** (tl) Sergio Purtell/Foca, (br) Foca; **789** (br) Sergio Purtell/Foca; **811** (tr) Foca; **813** (c) Sergio Purtell/Foca; **814** (bl) Foca; **815** (tl)

Sergio Purtell/Foca; **816–817** (t) Foca; **818** (b) Foca; **820** (tl) Sergio Purtell/Foca; **824** (bl) Sergio Purtell/Foca; **825** (tr) Foca; **828** (tl, cl) Sergio Purtell/Foca; **831** (br) Sergio Purtell/Foca; **834** (bl) Sergio Purtell/Foca; **835** (tr) Sergio Purtell/Foca; **836** (all) Foca.

Answers to Selected Problems

Chapter 2
Concept Review
page 43

6. The skier has both kinetic and potential energy. The potential energy arises from the skier's elevation. The kinetic energy comes from the skier's motion.

7. 40 J

8. Answers may vary but should include chemical energy (or internal energy) transformed to thermal energy transformed to electrical energy.

Concept Review
page 48

12. c, d, e, h, i

13. a. true
b. false
c. true
d. true

14. a. Pictures should show NO particles only within the field of view. Spaces between particles should reflect those of the model for a gas.
b. Pictures should show diatomic oxygen and diatomic nitrogen molecules within the field of view. Spaces between particles should reflect those of the model for a gas. The picture should show an even mixing of the gas molecules.

Concept Review
page 62

24. a. 4.42
b. 0.684
c. 2.2×10^{-3}
d. 4.4
e. 24.78
f. 3.5

25. 2.0×10^4 kg$\cdot$m^2/s^2

26. $V = (5 \text{ cm})^3 = 125 \text{ cm}^3$
$D = 8.56 \times 10^{-2}$ g/cm^3

Chapter 3
Concept Review
page 77

1. a. Li
b. Ba
c. Cr
d. P
e. Pu
f. S

2. a. hydrogen
b. chlorine
c. iron
d. californium

Chapter 4
Practice
page 133

1. 28.09 amu
2. 15.99 amu

(Note: Due to rounding of isotope masses, this value varies slightly from that stated in the periodic table.)

Practice
page 137

1. 2.2×10^{24} atoms Na
2. 9.33×10^{25} atoms As
3. 9.40×10^2 mol Xe
4. 4.796×10^{-9} mol Ag

Practice
page 139

1. 690 g Br
2. 212 g Si
3. 3.2 mol C
4. 2 mol H

Practice
page 140

1. 1.68×10^{-24} g/atom H
2. 2.52×10^{-22} g/atom Eu

Chapter Review and Assess
pages 145, 146

40. 6.94 amu
47. 3.01×10^{22} O atoms
49. 2.49×10^{-7} mol Au
51. 0.908 g Ne
53. 1.52×10^{-3} mol Na
55. 4.37×10^{-22} g/atom

Chapter 5
Concept Review
page 165

18. O^{2-}
19. P^{3-}
20. Sn^{2+}, tin(II) ion, and Sn^{4+}, tin(IV) ion
21. a. 5+
b. 4+, 7+
c. 3+
d. 1+
e. 2+
(from **Figure 5-12**)

Practice
page 167
1. a. $CaCl_2$
b. FeO
c. MgO

Practice
page 173
1. a. $Al_2(SO_4)_3$
b. $Mg(OH)_2$
c. $Cu(C_2H_3O_2)_2$
d. H_2O_2
e. Fe_2S_3
f. $Pb_3(PO_4)_2$

Practice
page 176
1. a. 122.55 g/mol
b. 234.06 g/mol
c. 132.17 g/mol
d. $NaHCO_3$; 84.01 g/mol
e. $K_2Cr_2O_7$; 294.20 g/mol
f. $Mg(ClO_4)_2$; 223.21 g/mol

Practice
page 177
1. 34.6% Cu, 30.4% Fe, 34.9% S
2. pure chalcocite because the percentage of copper is greater

Practice
page 178
1. Mn_2O_3
2. $Cd(OH)_2$

Practice
page 180
1. 233 g hydrate
2. 34.4 g $CaCl_2$

Chapter Review and Assess
pages 185, 186
31. a. AlF_3
b. MgO
c. CaS
d. $SrBr_2$
33. a. K_2HPO_4
b. $Sr(NO_3)_2$
c. Li_2SO_4
d. $Mg(H_2PO_4)_2$
45. 197.34 g/mol
47. 119.99 g
49. 40.04% Ca, 12.00% C, 47.96% O
51. 1.87 mol N, 7.43 mol H, 1.87 mol Cl

$$\frac{7.43}{1.87} = 3.97$$

$$\frac{1.87}{1.87} = 1.00$$

1.00 mol N: 3.97 mol H: 1.00 mol Cl

NH_4Cl

53. First compound:
1.00 mol P: 1.50 mol O
2.00 mol P: 3.00 mol O
P_2O_3
Second compound:
1.00 mol P: 2.50 mol O
2.00 mol P: 5.00 mol O
P_2O_5
55. 54.73% $Cr_2(SO_4)_3$

Chapter 6
Practice
page 202

1. a. **b.**

c. **d.**

2.

3.

Concept Review
page 204
7.

8.

9.

Practice
page 208
1. $K_2Cr_2O_7$; moles 0.6793 K, 0.6810 Cr, 2.377 O; mole ratio 1:1:3.5; whole-number ratio 2:2:7

2. P_2O_5; moles 0.1431 P, 0.3573 O; mole ratio 1:2.5; whole-number ratio 2:5

3. Na_2SO_4; moles 1.409 Na, 0.7063 S, 2.812 O; mole ratio 2:1:4

Practice
page 210
1. C_6H_6
2. $C_{18}H_{34}O_2$

Chapter Review and Assess
pages 228, 229, 230
15. a.   **b.**   **c.**

$$H:\overset{..}{\underset{..}{C}}:H$$

17. a. $:\overset{..}{O}=\overset{..}{O}:$

b. $:\overset{..}{S}=C=\overset{..}{S}:$

c.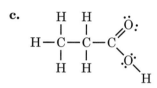

31. $C_6H_8O_7$
33. The molecular formula is $4 \times CH_2O$, or $C_4H_8O_4$.
39. a.

Cl
C 109.5°
Cl—C—Cl
Cl

b. Cl—Be—Cl   180°

c.

48.

Chapter 7
Practice
page 244
1. a. $3CaSi_2 + 2SbCl_3 \longrightarrow 6Si + 2Sb + 3CaCl_2$
  b. $2C_2H_2 + 5O_2 \longrightarrow 4CO_2 + 2H_2O$
  c. $2Al + 6CH_3OH \longrightarrow 2Al(CH_3O)_3 + 3H_2$
2. $Ca + 2H_2O \longrightarrow Ca(OH)_2 + H_2$
  $Ca(OH)_2 \overset{\Delta}{\longrightarrow} CaO + H_2O$

Concept Review
page 253
19. $C_3H_8 + 5O_2 \overset{\Delta}{\longrightarrow} 3CO_2 + 4H_2O$

Practice
page 255
1. $4C + S_8 \longrightarrow 4CS_2$
2. $4Fe + 3O_2 \longrightarrow 2Fe_2O_3$

Concept Review
page 260
20. a. $Ba(s) + 2H_2O(l) \longrightarrow Ba(OH)_2(s) + H_2(g)$
  b. $2Rb(s) + 2H_2O(l) \longrightarrow 2RbOH(s) + H_2(g)$
  c. $Zn(s) + 2H_2O(l) \longrightarrow Zn(OH)_2(s) + H_2(g)$
21. a. $4Au(s) + 3O_2(g) \longrightarrow 2Au_2O_3(s)$
  b. $2Mn(s) + O_2(g) \longrightarrow 2MnO(s)$
    (Other reactions are possible.)
  c. $2Pb(s) + O_2(g) \longrightarrow 2PbO(s)$
    (Other reactions are possible.)

Practice
page 261
Reactions are listed from most to least likely.
  2. $Mg(s) + Pb(NO_3)_2(aq) \longrightarrow Pb(s) + Mg(NO_3)_2(aq)$
  1. $Zn(s) + CuCl_2(aq) \longrightarrow Cu(s) + ZnCl_2(aq)$
  4. $Cu(s) + 2AgNO_3(aq) \longrightarrow 2Ag(s) + Cu(NO_3)_2(aq)$
  3. $Ni(s) + Al_2(SO_4)_3(aq) \longrightarrow$ no reaction

Chapter Review and Assess
pages 267, 268
12. formula equation: $CH_4 + Cl_2 \longrightarrow CCl_4 + HCl$
  balanced equation: $CH_4 + 4Cl_2 \longrightarrow CCl_4 + 4HCl$
30. $2Mg(s) + O_2(g) \longrightarrow 2MgO(s)$
32. Zinc is higher than lead on the activity series, so zinc will displace lead from compounds.
  $Zn(s) + PbCl_2(aq) \longrightarrow ZnCl_2(aq) + Pb(s)$

Chapter 8
Practice
page 279
1. 215 g SnF_2
2. 37.72 kg $C_{20}H_{12}O_5$

Practice
page 280
1. 0.453 g CO_2
2. 0.186 g H_2O

Practice
page 281
1. 3.57 L CO_2
2. 648 g $NH_2C_6H_4CO_2H$

Practice
page 286
1. 0.933 mol HCl
  0.154 mol $Al(OH)_3$
  0.311 mol $Al(OH)_3$ needed
  0.154 mol $Al(OH)_3$ less than 0.311 mol
  $Al(OH)_3$; there is not enough $Al(OH)_3$

2. $N_2 + 3H_2 \longrightarrow 2NH_3$
   1.32×10^5 mol H_2 present
   9.93×10^3 mol H_2 required
   9.93×10^3 mol $H_2 < 1.32 \times 10^5$ mol H_2; therefore
   N_2 is the limiting reactant.

Practice
page 291
1. 37.2%
2. Because the formula mass and mole ratios are the same as in item **1**, the theoretical yield for *o*-nitrotoluene is also 819 g.
   57.1%

Practice
page 296
1. $2NaN_3 \longrightarrow 2Na + 3N_2$
   $6Na + Fe_2O_3 \longrightarrow 3Na_2O + 2Fe$
   37.7 g Fe_2O_3
2. $6Na + Fe_2O_3 \longrightarrow 3Na_2O + 2Fe$
   $Na_2O + 2CO_2 + H_2O \longrightarrow 2NaHCO_3$
   119 g $NaHCO_3$
3. 54.1 mL $NaHCO_3$
4. 128 g CH_3COOH, 179 g $NaHCO_3$
5. 175 g CH_3COONa, 38.4g H_2O

Practice
page 299
1. **a**. yes, 35 000 L >26 110 L
   b. no, 2.00×10^5 L $< 2.15 \times 10^5$ L
   c. no, 400. L $<$ 499 L
2. **a**. Note that this is a mixture and two equations are needed.
   $2C_8H_{18}(g) + 25O_2(g) \longrightarrow 16CO_2(g) + 18H_2O(g)$
   $2C_7H_{14}(g) + 21O_2(g) \longrightarrow 14CO_2(g) + 14H_2O(g)$
   b. 7824 L + 850. L = 8674 L of air

Chapter Review and Assess
pages 305, 306, 307, 308
6. $H_2CO_3 \longrightarrow H_2O + CO_2$
   0.177 g CO_2
8. 1.53 mol O_2
10. 112 L O_2
17. $Cu(s) + 2AgNO_3(aq) \longrightarrow 2Ag(s) + Cu(NO_3)_2(aq)$
    Because there is less $AgNO_3$ than is needed to react with the Cu, $AgNO_3$ is the limiting reactant.
    63.5 g Ag
23. 72.46% yield
25. 710. g CH_4
31. 10.7 g baking powder
33. 3130 L H_2O
35. 12.5 mol *p–tert*-butylphenol

Chapter 9
Practice
page 316
1. –23.4 kJ
2. 66.7 kJ

Practice
page 320
1. heat gained by H_2O = heat lost by oatmeal
   $\Delta H = 22\ 990$ J = 23 kJ
2. 26.8°C

Practice
page 322
1. mass of C_8H_{18} = 420 g
   mass of O_2 = 1500 g
2. 1750 kJ

Concept Review
page 326
9. No; the amount of heat in the initial and final states has not changed, so ΔH_{rxn} has not changed.
10. E_a for the reverse reaction is greater than that for the forward reaction, so more heat is required for the reverse reaction. The reactants are at a higher enthalpy than the products, so they are less thermodynamically stable.

Practice
page 331
1. 1.9 kJ/mol
2. –592.7 kJ

Practice
page 337
1. $-$ 3.3 J/K; no
2. $+$ 5.3 J/K

Practice
page 340
1. 638.3°C
2. $-$ 394.4 kJ/mol
   It is spontaneous.
3. raise the temperature
4. $-$869 kJ/mol

Chapter Review and Assess
pages 349, 350, 351, 352
7. -1.9×10^7 J
9. 50. kJ
   12 Cal
11. 49.4 g $C_6H_{12}O_6$
23. $-$114 kJ
31. $-$550 J/K
42. 155 kJ
    The reaction is not spontaneous.

Chapter 10

Practice
page 371
1. 9.0×10^2 K
2. 0.67 L

Practice
page 373
1. 5.0×10^2 kPa
2. $0.50 \ m^3$

Practice
page 374
1. 7.4 L
2. 2 L
   The balloon compresses to a 2 L volume.
3. 38.8 kPa
4. 200. mL
5. 10. L

Practice
page 377
1. 82.66 kPa
2. 98.51 kPa

Practice
page 380
1. 236 m/s
2. $v_1 = 450$ m/s
   $v_2 = 213$ m/s
   $v_3 = 255$ m/s
   Hydrogen sulfide will be smelled first, followed by benzaldehyde, and then methyl salicylate.

Practice
page 383
1. 29.0 L of CO_2
2. 22.4 L
3. 0.17 mol
4. 3.9×10^3 kPa
5. 5.2×10^4 K

Practice
page 384
1. $4.0 \ m^3$
2. 6.02×10^3 kPa
3. 165 K
4. $81 \ m^3$

Practice
page 386
1. Assume that the pressure and temperature for each gas is the same.
   6.0 L
2. a. 19 L O_2
   b. 5.25 mol H_2O
   c. 14 g
3. 8.1×10^3 g

pages 397, 398
14. 2.18 L
16. 10.0 L
18. 4.00×10^8 L
30. Partial pressure of water at 20.0°C = 2.34 kPa, so P_{oxygen} = 98.0 kPa − 2.34 kPa = 95.7 kPa
32. 1.32×10^3 m/s
34. 70.8 g/mol
40. 248 kPa
42. 482 mL
44. 10.4 L H_2
46. 0.484 g Mg

Chapter 11

Concept Review
page 407
1. 98 g
2. RbCl at 0°C, $NaNO_3$ at 70°C
3. $NaNO_3$

Practice
page 416
1. 0.840 M
2. 486 mL
3. 1.70 L
4. 4.68 g $CuSO_4 \cdot 5H_2O$
5. 1.38 kg $C_{12}H_{22}O_{11}$
6. 676 g H_2O, 4390 g $Ca(H_2PO_4)_2$
7. 9.45×10^{-5} M

Practice
page 425
1. BCl_3 is a nonpolar molecule with polar bonds.
2. SO_2 is a polar molecule with polar bonds. It can dissolve in water.

Concept Review
page 435
23. Because CO_2 is only moderately soluble in water at normal air pressure, higher CO_2 pressures are necessary for more CO_2 to dissolve in the water.
24. Keep the soda covered tightly, and keep it cold. Less CO_2 remains in solution as the temperature increases, and the uncapped bottle allows more CO_2 to escape.

Chapter Review and Assess
pages 443, 444, 445
19. a. 3.5 M $NaNO_3$ b. 2.5 M KOH
    c. 0.80 M Na_2S
21. a. 4.0 mol $AgNO_3$ b. 1.25 mol HCl
    c. 0.100 mol HNO_3
23. a. 0.250 M NaOH   b. 0.953 M NH_4Br
    c. 1.61 M $CuCl_2$
25. a. 87.7 g NaCl   b. 315 g NaOH
    c. 327 g K_2SO_4
27. 698 g $Ca_3(PO_4)_2$, 243 g H_2O
36. C_4H_{10} (2.5 − 2.1 = 0.4); will dissolve in CS_2 (2.5 − 2.5 = 0) because both are nonpolar substances.
50. 2.8×10^{-5} M $C_6H_8O_6$

Chapter 12

1. a. $CaCl_2(s) \xrightleftharpoons{H_2O} Ca^{2+}(aq) + 2Cl^-(aq)$

   b. $Al_2(SO_4)_3(s) \xrightleftharpoons{H_2O} 2Al^{3+}(aq) + 3SO_4^{2-}(aq)$

2. Because more energy is usually released in the hydration of ions that are smaller in size or higher in charge, smaller $AlCl_3$, with a cation charge of $3+$, should release more energy during hydration than $MgCl_2$ with a cation charge of $2+$.

3. a. $HCl(aq) + H_2O(l) \rightleftharpoons H_3O^+(aq) + Cl^-(aq)$

   b. $H_2CO_3(aq) + H_2O(l) \rightleftharpoons$
   $$H_3O^+(aq) + HCO_3^-(aq)$$

   c. $Na_2CrO_4(s) \xrightleftharpoons{H_2O} 2Na^+(aq) + CrO_4^{2-}(aq)$

   d. $NH_4NO_3(aq) + H_2O(l) \rightleftharpoons$
   $$NH_3(aq) + H_3O^+(aq) + NO_3^-(aq)$$

Concept Review
page 471

15. a. $K_{eq} = \dfrac{[ClO^-][H^+]}{[HClO]}$

    b. $K_{eq} = \dfrac{[[Cu(NH_3)_4]^{2+}]}{[[Cu(H_2O)_4]^{2+}][NH_3]^4}$

16. a. $K_{eq} = \dfrac{[NO_2]^2}{[N_2O_4]}$

    b. $K_{eq} = \dfrac{[CO][H_2O]}{[CO_2][H_2]}$

    c. $K_{eq} = \dfrac{[NO]^2}{[N_2][O_2]}$

    d. $K_{eq} = \dfrac{[CH_3COO^-][H_3O^+]}{[CH_3COOH]}$

    e. $K_{eq} = \dfrac{[H_2][I_2]}{[HI]^2}$

Practice
page 474

1. 0.720
2. 3.6×10^{-1}
3. 0.046 mol/L
4. 1.1 mol/L

Practice
page 476

1. 2.06×10^{-35}
2. 3.62×10^{-5} M
3. 1.69×10^{-3} M

Chapter Review and Assess
pages 482, 483

28. 1.74×10^{-5}
30. 1.12×10^{-2} M
32. 7.91×10^{-9} M

Chapter 13

Concept Review
page 494

1. $Na_2O + H_2O \longrightarrow 2NaOH$
   $Cl_2O_7 + H_2O \longrightarrow 2HClO_4$

2. chloric acid, nitric acid, perchloric acid, periodic acid, permanganic acid, tetrafluoroboric acid, acetic acid, hydrocyanic acid, hypochlorous acid, nitrous acid

3. CsO, base
   TeO, acid
   I_2O_5, acid
   SrO, base

Concept Review
page 496

4. a. base, CH_3NH_2; acid, H_2O
   b. acid, HSO_4^-; base, H_2O

5. a. base
   b. acid

Practice
page 503

1. a. 5
   b. 2
2. a. 5.60
   b. 3.058
3. a. 1.0×10^{-13}
   b. 1.0×10^{-11}
4. a. 4.0×10^{-8}
   b. 3.2×10^{-4}
5. a. 10.7
   b. 10.4

Practice
page 505

1. a. 1×10^{-11}
   b. 5.0×10^{-8}
   c. 1.5×10^{-4}
   d. 6.3×10^{-4}
   e. 3.2×10^{-11}
   f. 2.0×10^{-12}

Practice
page 514

1. $HCl + NaOH \longrightarrow NaCl + H_2O$
   0.57 M NaOH
2. $2HClO_4 + Ca(OH)_2 \longrightarrow 2H_2O + Ca(ClO_4)_2$
   37 mL
3. $CH_3COOH + KOH \longrightarrow H_2O + CH_3COOK$
   0.157 M CH_3COOH
4. $2HCl + Ba(OH)_2 \longrightarrow 2H_2O + BaCl_2$
   0.0422 M HCl

Concept Review
page 517

25. $H_2PO_4^- + OH^- \longrightarrow HPO_4^{2-} + H_2O$
    Added OH^- accepts a proton from $H_2PO_4^-$ to form H_2O.

pages 527, 528
21. 2.59
23. 7.87
25. antilog $(-3.45) = 3.55 \times 10^{-4}$
27. pH = 9.4
29. pH = 2.4
42. 0.175 M HCOOH
44. 0.526 M NaOH
46. 0.310 g LiOH

Chapter 14
Concept Review
page 541
1. **a.** evolution of a gas
   b. change in solution's color; appearance or disappearance of metals
   c. evolution of a gas
   d. precipitation of $Cu(OH)_2$
   e. pressure changes; condensing the water out of reaction gases

2. **a.** $\dfrac{1}{2} \times \dfrac{-\Delta H_2O_2}{\Delta t} = \dfrac{\Delta O_2}{\Delta t}$

   b. $\dfrac{1}{2} \times \dfrac{-\Delta Ag^+}{\Delta t} = \dfrac{\Delta Cu^{2+}}{\Delta t}$

   c. $\dfrac{-\Delta HC_2H_3O_2}{\Delta t} = \dfrac{\Delta CO_2}{\Delta t}$

   d. $\dfrac{-\Delta CuCl_2}{\Delta t} = \dfrac{\Delta Cu(OH)_2}{\Delta t}$

   e. $\dfrac{1}{2} \times \dfrac{-\Delta C_2H_6}{\Delta t} = \dfrac{1}{4} \times \dfrac{\Delta CO_2}{\Delta t}$

3. Reactant; concentration *decreases* with time; 0.050M/min
4. N_2: 0.02 M/s
   H_2: 0.02 M/s
5. 5.0 M/s

Concept Review
page 559
21. $I^- + OCl^- + H_2O \rightleftharpoons Cl^- + OI^- + H_2O$
22. three
23. step 2; rate = $k[HOCl][I^-]$
24. HOCl, OH^-, HOI
25. rate = $k[HeI\cdot][I\cdot] = k[He][I\cdot]^2$

Chapter 15
Practice
page 590
1. +5
2. F = −1; B = +3
3. +7
4. H = +1; N = −3

Concept Review
page 592
11. **a.** not redox
    b. redox
    c. not redox
12. Zn is oxidized, and Cu is reduced.

Chapter Review and Assess
page 606
33. Pb = +2; Cl = −1
    $(+2) + 2(-1) = 0$
35. Pb = +2, S = −2; Mn = +4, O = −2; Li = +1, Al = +3, H = −1 (rules 4, 7, and 8 on pages 588–589); Na = +1, O = −1 (rules 5, 7, and 8 on pages 588–589); Hg = +2, O = −2; Ni = +3, O = −2, H = +1; Pb = +2, S = +6, O = −2.
37. H = +1; C = +4 ; O = −2
    $(+1) + (+4) + 3(-2) = -1$

Chapter 16
Concept Review
page 615
1. A small nucleus is generally more stable because all of the nuclear particles are affected by each other's strong nuclear force. The repulsion between two protons is counteracted by their nuclear attraction.
2. ^6_3Li (For elements with an atomic number lower than 30, stability usually occurs with equal numbers of protons and neutrons, in this case three of each.)
3. $^{12}_6C$ is stable.
   ^3_1H is unstable.
   $^{206}_{82}Pb$ is stable.
   (The chart and the rule of thumb aren't entirely reliable in this case. $^{205}_{82}Pb$ is not stable but should be, according to both the rule and chart.)
   $^{32}_{15}P$ is unstable.
   (Again, the rule of thumb and chart are not entirely helpful. $^{30}_{15}P$ is extremely unstable, yet this is an isotope with a neutron-to-proton ratio of 1. $^{31}_{15}P$ is the stable isotope of phosphorus.)
   ^4_2He is stable

Practice
page 617
1. 2.25×10^{11} J for 1 mol of deuterium
2. 5.14×10^{-12} J for each lithium-6 nucleus

Chapter Review and Assess
page 640
10. **a.** Nucleus #1: 2.69×10^{13} J/mol
    Nucleus #2: 1.80×10^{13} J/mol
    Nucleus #1 releases more binding energy than nucleus #2.

b. Binding energy per nucleon in nucleus #1 =

$$\frac{4.47 \times 10^{-11} \text{ J}}{35 \text{ nucleons}} = 1.28 \times 10^{-12} \text{ J/nucleon}$$

Binding energy per nucleon in nucleus #2 =

$$\frac{2.99 \times 10^{-11} \text{ J}}{23 \text{ nucleons}} = 1.30 \times 10^{-12} \text{ J/nucleon}$$

Nucleus #2 has a greater binding energy per nucleon. Because the sodium-23 nucleus has fewer nucleons than the potassium-35 nucleus, fewer nucleons lie beyond the range of the strong force. Therefore it is easier for the repulsion between protons to be overcome.

Appendix B
Concept Review
page 804
  1. The axis should extend from 0 to 120 grams. Check that the scale is consistent between divisions. Students should not scale their axes by the points listed.
  2. The *x*-axis should extend from 0°C to about 110°C as the minimum. The *y*-axis should extend from 0 g to about 250 g as the minimum. Check that both axes are correctly labeled using the labels given in the data table. The solubility of KNO_3 at 65°C is about 120 g. The solubility of KNO_3 at 105°C is about 265 g.
  3. **a.** The *x*-axis should extend from 0 atm to about 10 atm as the minimum. The *y*-axis should extend from 0 L to about 250 L as the minimum. Check that both axes are correctly labeled using the labels given in the data table.
     b. inverse relationship
     c. $PV = k$
     d. $V = k \times \frac{1}{P}$

Concept Review
page 807
  1. **a.** 3
     b. 3
     c. 6
     d. 4
     e. unlimited number
     f. 4
  2. **a.** 47.10 g
     b. 32.86 L
     c. 101 m
     d. 0.123 cm^2
     e. 28.62 mi/h
     f. 113.2 in^2
  3. **a.** 6.08×10^{-5}
     b. 2.642×10^8
     c. 2.67
     d. -7.2×10^{-5}

Appendix C
Concept Review
page 810
  1. **a.** concept
     b. linking words
     c. linking word
     d. linking words
     e. concept
     f. linking words
     g. concept
     h. linking word
  2. Answers will vary. Check against Map A. Some possible responses are the following.
     matter is described by chemical properties, matter is classified as mixtures, chemical changes that release energy are exothermic changes, physical properties such as state, and so on.
  3. Cross links are denoted by the arrowhead. The two cross links in Map A are: *chemical properties which describe chemical changes, physical properties such as state.*